Praise for MAEVE BINCHY and . . .

. . . *The Lilac Bus*

"Each story is seamless, rich and true, as Binchy uses her easygoing style not merely to entertain but also to create real people, touch real emotions."
—*Chicago Tribune*

"A heartwarming collection that is greatly understated yet deeply poignant."
—*Milwaukee Sentinel*

. . . *Firefly Summer*

"Sparkles with emotion . . . one of those juicy, old-fashioned novels full of lovable characters, humor and tears. . . . The characters seem real and the insight into human nature . . . is on target." —*Milwaukee Journal*

"Emotional power . . . vibrant characters . . . in the time it takes you to read *Firefly Summer,* you've become a resident of Mountfern, and cannot bear to see it irrevocably changed." —*Los Angeles Times*

. . . *Silver Wedding*

"Binchy exhibits her gift for astute and loving characterization as she examines the way relationships and families work." —*Publishers Weekly*

"Her trademark combination of elegance, sly observation, and gossipy intimacy (leaves you feeling as if) you had a wickedly long lunch with a dear friend who always has the best stories in town." —*L.A. Life*

MAEVE BINCHY

THREE COMPLETE BOOKS

MAEVE BINCHY

THREE COMPLETE BOOKS

The Lilac Bus

Firefly Summer

Silver Wedding

WINGS BOOKS

New York • Avenel, New Jersey

This 1995 edition is published by Wings Books,
distributed by Random House Value Publishing, Inc.,
40 Engelhard Avenue, Avenel, New Jersey 07001,
by arrangement with Dell Publishing,
a division of Bantam Doubleday Dell Publishing Group, Inc.

Random House
New York • Toronto • London • Sydney • Auckland

Printed and bound in the United States of America

Library of Congress Cataloging-in-Publication Data

Binchy, Maeve.
[Novels. Selections]
Three complete novels.
p.   cm.
Contents: The Lilac bus—Firefly summer—Silver wedding.
ISBN 0-517-14864-1
1. Ireland—Social life and customs—Fiction. I. Binchy, Maeve. Lilac bus. II. Binchy, Maeve. Firefly summer. III. Binchy, Maeve. Silver wedding. IV. Title. V. Title: Lilac bus. VI. Title: Firefly summer. VII. Title: Silver wedding.
PR6052.I7728A6   1995
823'.914—dc20 95-10831

CIP

8   7   6   5   4   3   2   1

❧ Contents ❧

The Lilac Bus

For my dear Gordon,
with all my love

❧ Contents ❧

The Lilac Bus

Dublin Four

Nancy

Nancy was early, but then she always was, and she didn't like being seen there too soon. It looked as if you had nothing else to do if you arrived far too early for the bus home. The others all arrived rushing and panting and afraid they'd miss it, because if they missed it then they really did. Tom turned the key in the ignition at 6:45 and swung the Lilac Bus out into the road. That way he had them all home before ten o'clock and that was his promise. No point in going home for a weekend if you aren't in the pub by ten, that was his philosophy. It wasn't Nancy's, but she was compulsively early for everything. It was just her way. She went into a shop that sold magazines and cards. She knew a lot of the cards by heart from studying them on a Friday. There was the big one with tears falling down it: "Sorry I missed your birthday." They had the country papers in this shop, too, but Nancy never bought one. There'd be a paper at home and she could catch up on everything then.

She examined her new perm in the big round mirror that was not meant so much as a mirror as a deterrent to shoplifting. It was set high on the wall and at a funny angle, or she hoped it was. Otherwise the perm looked very odd indeed. She stared up at her reflection anxiously. Surely she didn't look like some small worried animal with fuzzy hair and huge terrified eyes. That's what she saw in the mirror, but of course that's not what people down at her own level would see? After all, everyone looked silly from this point of view. She patted her head and had another pang about the perm. It looked to her dangerously like those old-fashioned perms that people like her mother got in Rathdoon. The summer perm and the Christmas perm. Frizz, fuzz . . . tight curls growing out into what looked like flashes of lightning or electric shocks as the weeks went by. The girls in the salon assured her that she was mad to think this. She had got a modern perm, one of the newest on the market. Think what she'd have paid if she had to pay for it! Nancy had smiled grimly. Paid for it! At that price! Nancy Morris wouldn't have paid half that price or a quarter of that price for a perm. Nancy Morris had crossed Dublin to go to a salon where she heard they needed people to practice on. *Models* was the expression, but Nancy was more realistic. They needed heads with hair and smart people like Nancy found out which were the big salons with lots of trainees and on what nights their classes and demonstrations were. She had only paid for two visits to a hairdresser since she came to Dublin six years ago. That wasn't bad going, she smiled proudly. Still, it was done now, this perm, no point in peering up at herself and worrying. Better go across and get on the bus. Surely some of the others would be there by now, and it was well after half-past six.

Tom was sitting there reading an evening paper. He looked up and smiled. "Evening, Miss Mouse," he said pleasantly, and lifted her big suitcase up onto the roof rack with one easy movement. She got in crossly. She *hated* him calling her Miss Mouse, but it was her own fault. When she had rung to ask for a place in his minibus she had given her name as Miss Morris. Well, she was used to being formal on the phone—that was what her job was about, for heaven's sake. How was she to know that she should have said her first name and that he genuinely misheard the Morris bit. But it was very galling that he still refused to call her Nancy, even though he always called old Mrs. Hickey Judy and she could have been his mother.

"It's light for such a big case," he said pleasantly. Nancy just nodded. She didn't feel like telling him it was her only suitcase and she had no intention of going out and spending over a fiver on some kind of nylon holdall like the others had. And anyway she needed a big case: there were always things to take back to Dublin, like potatoes and whatever vegetables there were, and anything else that turned up. There was the time that her mother's friend, Mrs. Casey, was getting rid of her curtains: Nancy brought them back and they were lovely in the flat.

She sat down in one of the middle seats, straightened her skirt under her so that it wouldn't crease and took out her glucose sweets. They had jars of them in the hospital, and they always told her to help herself. She didn't eat them normally but it was nice on a bus journey to have something; the others often bought barley sugar or toffees, but what was the point of spending money on sweets when they were there for the asking? She unfolded a newspaper that one of the patients had left behind in the waiting room. She got a lot of her reading material this way—people waiting for the specialists were inclined to be forgetful about papers and magazines, and there was rarely an evening she didn't have something to read. And it was nice to have a variety, she told herself. It was like a surprise. Mairead didn't understand. Nancy's brow darkened when she thought of Mairead. All that had to be sorted out. It had been so unexpected and so unfair.

She held up the newspaper so that Tom would think she was reading and she went over it all again. Mairead coming in on Wednesday and walking around restlessly picking things up and putting them down. You didn't have to be a genius to know there was something on her mind. Nancy thought she was going to ask about the television again. They had a perfectly good black and white set, which was a bit snowstormish now and then but usually got a terrific reception. What on earth was the point of paying out a fortune renting a color set? And even a video: Mairead had once mentioned this as if they were some kind of millionaires. She had looked up from the telly, which was admittedly having one of its bad nights and you had to guess a lot from the soundtrack; but Mairead had wanted to talk about something much bigger.

"I've been thinking all week at work how to say this, Nancy, and I can't think of any proper way, so I'll just say it straight out. I want to share the flat with someone else, and I am going to have to ask you to leave. In your own time, of course, I'm not throwing you out on the road . . ." She had given a little nervous laugh, but Nancy had been too astounded to join in. "You see," Mairead had gone on, "it was never permanent. It was just to see what we thought. . . . That was the arrangement. That was what we said. . . ." Her voice had trailed away guiltily.

"But we've been sharing for three years," Nancy said.

"I know," Mairead said miserably.

"So why? Don't I pay the rent in time always and the electricity? And I contribute to the food from home and I got curtains for the hall windows and—"

"Of course, Nancy, nobody's saying you didn't."

"So why?"

"It's just . . . no, there's no reason, can't we do it nice and easily now, without quarrels and questions? Can't you just find another place and we'll still meet now and then, go to the pictures, you come over here one evening, me go to your place? Come on, Nancy, that's the grown-up way to do things."

Nancy had burned with rage. Mairead, who worked in a flower shop, telling her what was the grown-up way to do things. Mairead, who hadn't got one honor in her Leaving Certificate, ordering Nancy out of her flat. *Her* flat. True, she had found it, and when she needed someone to share the rent her aunt, Mrs. Casey, the friend of Nancy's mother, had suggested Nancy. Where had Mairead got these notions and more important, why? Who did she want to share with?

The worst thing was that Mairead didn't seem to know or care, she just said she would like a change. At this point Nancy had turned off the flickering telly and had settled in for what she thought was going to be a heart-to-heart where Mairead would tell her all about some star-crossed love. But no. Mairead was busy looking at the calendar. Would we say just over a month, like the middle of October? That would surely give her time to find somewhere.

"But who will I share with?" Nancy had wailed.

Mairead had shrugged. She didn't know, maybe Nancy could get a bed-sit on her own. She didn't do much cooking or entertaining, a bed-sit might be just as good. But they cost a *fortune*! Mairead had shrugged again as if it didn't concern her.

The following morning Nancy was having her tea in the kitchen—she never bothered with a breakfast since there was always food in the hospital, and what was the point of being a receptionist for all these doctors unless you got some perks like a canteen and glucose sweets? Mairead rushed in late as usual and Nancy asked her had she forgiven her.

"Forgive you, Nancy? What for? What in heaven's name for?"

"Well, I must have done something, otherwise you wouldn't be asking me to leave our flat."

"It's *my* flat and don't be such a clown. We're not married to each other,

Nancy. You came in here to share my rent, now that bit's over. Right? Yes. That's all there is to it." She was gulping down a bowl of cornflakes and trying to pull on her boots at the same time. Mairead loved these boots; they horrified Nancy—they had cost a week's salary. For a pair of boots.

"What'll I tell them in Rathdoon?" Nancy asked solemnly. Mairead was startled.

"About what?" she had asked, bewildered.

"About us breaking up?"

"Who would want to know? Who even knows we share a flat?"

"Everyone: your mother, my mother, your aunt—Mrs. Casey—everyone."

"Well, what do you mean what will you tell them?" Mairead was genuinely surprised.

"But your mother, what will she think? What will I tell her?"

Mairead had lost her temper suddenly. Nancy still felt a shock just thinking about it.

"My mother is a normal woman; she's like everyone else's mother, including your mother. She doesn't think anything. She wants to know that I'm not pregnant and I'm not on drugs and I'm still going to Mass. That's all any mother wants to know in the name of God, those same three things. In India mothers want to know that or Russia or wherever, and it may not be Mass for them but it's something. People's mothers don't give two flying damns about their daughters sharing flats with people and whether they get on well or whether, as in our case, they drive each other up the wall. They just want to be told the essentials."

"We don't drive each other up the wall," Nancy had said quietly.

"No, well, irritate each other. What's the difference? Why bother your head explaining and telling and reporting back? People aren't bloody interested."

"Do I irritate you?"

"Yes."

"How?"

"Oh Nancy, *please*." Mairead was stricken. "We agreed last night to be grown up and not to have pointless rows and recriminations. We agreed. Now look what you're starting. Of course people irritate each other. I probably drive you mad. Listen, I must go."

Nancy had a terrible day: she had looked at the prices of flats and bed-sitters and they were sky-high. The further out you went they came down a bit, of course, but she had to be within cycling distance of the hospital. There was no way she was going to spend her hard-earned money on bus fares. She had thought, too, about what Mairead had said. She couldn't think why she was irritating. She didn't smoke, she never invited rowdy people in like Mairead often did, people who brought a bottle of wine each and then went out for chicken and chips. She didn't play records loud—she didn't have any records. She did everything to help. Often she cut special offers out of the paper and collected vouchers for foods or detergents. She suggested often to Mairead that it would be cheaper to come home every weekend to Rathdoon, because people spend a fortune at weekends in Dublin and you could live free at home. How had she been so irritating?

Even this very morning she had asked Mairead if it was definite, and Mairead had nodded wordlessly. Nancy had offered to let Mairead have the weekend to consider her decision, but in a low, soft voice, unlike her harangue of the previous morning, Mairead had said there would be no considering and she realized that Nancy would be cooperative and start looking for another place straightaway.

She looked up at the sound of voices. Dee Burke had arrived; she wore her college scarf even though she had left UCD two years previously, and she carried a canvas grip, which she threw up on the roof herself. Tom was laughing at her.

"You'll be a discus champion yet," he said.

"No, it's to show you that women are genuinely liberated, that's all—besides, there's nothing in it except a couple of pairs of knickers and some law books I'm meant to be studying."

Nancy was amazed that Dee, who was Dr. Burke's daughter and lived in a big house covered with creeper, could talk about knickers to Tom Fitzgerald in such a relaxed way. It didn't even sound rude the way she said it. Dee was a law unto herself, though, and always had been. You'd think she'd have her own car, but she said that she wasn't earning much as a solicitor's apprentice. Still, Nancy would have thought that this minibus would have been beneath the Burkes. They were people of such standing in Rathdoon, they must find it strange that their daughter traveled with anyone and everyone. Dee never seemed to notice. She was friendly with everyone; with that tinker of a fellow, Kev Kennedy, that you'd try to cross the road to avoid; with desperate Mikey Burns and his dirty jokes. Dee was specially nice to Nancy; she came and sat beside her and asked, as she often did, about Nancy's work.

It was quite extraordinary the way Dee remembered the names of the doctors she worked for, and knew that one was an eye specialist, one an orthopedic surgeon and one an ear, nose, and throat man. She knew there was Mr. Barry and Mr. White and Mr. Charles. Even Nancy's mother wouldn't know that, and as for Mairead, she could hardly remember the names of her own bosses, let alone Nancy's.

But then Dee was nice and she had great breeding. People like that were courteous, Nancy always thought, and they had the manners to be interested in other people.

Rupert Green arrived next. He was wearing a very smart jacket.

"Merciful God, Rupert, is that Italian? Is that the real thing?" Dee asked, feeling the sleeve as Rupert got in.

"Yes, it is actually." Rupert's pale face flushed with pleasure. "How did you know?"

"Aren't I worn out looking at them in magazines? It's gorgeous."

"Yes, it's a second, or a discontinued line or something, but a friend got it for me anyway." Rupert was very pleased that it had caused such a stir.

"Well, they'd need to be a second or something, otherwise your father would have to sell his practice to buy it," Dee laughed. Rupert's father was the solicitor, and it was through Mr. Green she had got her apprenticeship in Dublin. Nancy looked at them enviously. It must be great to have such an easy way of going on. It was like a kind of shorthand in professional families, she noticed, they could all talk to each other at the drop of a hat. She felt a twinge of annoyance that her father, long dead, had been a postman and not a lawyer. The annoyance was followed by a stronger twinge of guilt. Her father had worked long and hard and had been pleased to see them all do well at their books and get secretarial or clerical jobs.

Rupert went to the backseat and almost on cue Mrs. Hickey arrived. Suntanned even in winter, she looked healthy and strong and as if she might be any age. Nancy knew she must be in her late fifties, but that was only by questioning people and piecing it all together. Judy Hickey worked in some kind of mad place that sold herbal cures and grain and nuts, and she even grew some of the things herself, which was why she came home every weekend to harvest them and bring them back to this shop in Dublin. Nancy had never been to the shop; Dee told her it was marvelous, that everyone should go and see it just for the experience of it, but Nancy took her position as receptionist to three of Dublin's leading consultants very seriously. It wouldn't do for her to be seen going in and out of some quack's shop, would it?

Judy went to sit beside Rupert in the back and Mikey Burns had begun to squeeze himself into the front seat. Laughing and rubbing his hands, he told them a joke about hairy tennis balls. Everyone smiled and Mikey seemed to be able to settle down now that he had told at least one dirty story. He looked out eagerly.

"Will I be lucky and get the beautiful Celia beside me or do I get Mr. Kennedy? Oh dear, just your luck Mikey, here comes Mr. Kennedy."

Kev sneaked into the bus looking over his shoulder as if he expected a guard to lay a hand on him and say "Just a minute," like they do in films. Nancy thought she had never seen anyone who looked so furtive. If you spoke to Kev Kennedy he jumped a foot in the air, and he never said much in reply, so he wasn't spoken to much.

Lastly, Celia came. Big and sort of handsome in a way, though Nancy didn't admire that kind of looks. She often wore tight belts; as she wore them when she was nursing, she had probably got used to them. They made her figure very obvious. Not sexy, but it certainly divided it for all to see: a jutting-out top half in front and a big jutting-out bottom half at the back. Nancy would have thought she might have been wiser to wear something more floppy.

Celia sat in beside Tom: the last person always sat beside the driver. It was only twenty to seven and they set off with five minutes in hand.

"I have you very well trained," Tom laughed as he nosed the minibus out into the Friday evening traffic.

"Indeed you have. No wee-wees until we're across the Shannon," said Mikey, looking around for approval, and since he didn't hear any he said it again. This time a few people smiled back at him.

Nancy told Dee all about Mr. Charles and Mr. White and Mr. Barry and how they saw their private patients on certain days of the week and how she kept their appointment books and shuffled people around and how patients were often very grateful to her and gave her little presents at Christmas. Dee wanted to know were they well thought of, the doctors, and whether people praised them. Nancy tried to dredge examples but couldn't. She was more on the administrative side, she kept insisting. Dee wanted to know whether she met them socially, and Nancy had laughed to think such a thing was possible. That was the joy of being a doctor's daughter, you didn't think class distinctions existed anymore. No, of course she didn't get involved in their home lives. Mr. Barry had a Canadian wife and two children, Mr. White's wife was a teacher and they had four children, and Mr. Charles and his wife had no children. Yes, she sometimes spoke to their wives on the phone; they all seemed very nice, they all remembered her name. "Hallo Miss Morris," they would say.

Dee fell asleep when Nancy was explaining about the hospital switchboard, which was very awkward, and how they had been looking for a separate switchboard for the consultants for ages, but maybe things would get better with the new set-up in the phone headquarters. Nancy was a bit embarrassed at that. Maybe she had been rabbiting on, possibly she did irritate people by talking too much about little things; sometimes her own mother got up and went to bed in the middle of one of their conversations. Mairead might be right. But no, that couldn't be, Dee had been positively pressing her for details of her working life, she had asked question after question. No, Nancy couldn't blame herself for being boring. Not this time. She sighed and looked at the fields flying by.

Soon she nodded off too. Behind her Judy Hickey and Rupert Green were talking about someone they knew who had gone to an ashram in India and everyone had to wear yellow or saffron. In front of her Kev Kennedy was half-listening as Mikey Burns explained a card trick with a glass of water. Mikey said that it was better if you saw it done but you could still grasp the point if you concentrated.

In front of them Tom was saying something to Celia; she was nodding and agreeing with it, whatever it was. It was very comfortable and warm, and even if she did lean over a bit in sleep and slump on top of Dee, well, it didn't matter. She wouldn't have let herself doze if she were beside one of the men. Or indeed beside Judy Hickey: there was something very odd about her.

Nancy was asleep.

Her mother was still at the kitchen table when she got in. She was writing a letter to her daughter in America.

"There you are," she said.

"All in one piece," said Nancy.

It wasn't much of a greeting between mother and daughter, when the whole country had been crossed. But they had never been a demonstrative family. No hugging and kissing, no linking arms.

"How was the journey?" her mother asked.

"Oh, the same. I had a bit of a sleep, so I have a crick in my neck." Nancy rubbed it thoughtfully.

"It's great to be able to sleep on that road, with maniacs screeching past you in all directions."

"Oh, it's not that bad." Nancy looked around. "Well, what's been happening?"

Her mother was poor at handing out news. Nancy would have liked her to get up, wet a pot of tea and come back full of detail and information. She wanted to hear the week's events and who had been home, who had been heard from, who had revealed what. But somehow it was never like that.

"Whatever happens? Nothing's been happening—weren't you here until Sunday night?" Her mother went back to the letter, sighing, "Do you never write to Deirdre at all? Wouldn't it be a Christian thing to write to your own sister in America and tell her what's going on? She loves to hear little things, you know."

"So do I, but you can never remember anything to tell me!" Nancy cried in complaint.

"Ah, will you stop that nonsense? Aren't you here the whole time? You only go up to Dublin for a couple of days in the week. Poor Deirdre's on the other side of the Atlantic Ocean."

"Poor Deirdre has a husband and three children and a freezer and an icebox and a sprinkler in her garden. Poor Deirdre indeed."

"Couldn't you have all that yourself if you wanted to? Stop grudging things to your sister. Have some bit of niceness in you."

"I've plenty of niceness." Nancy felt her lip tremble.

"Well, stop giving out about Deirdre then, and go on, take a sheet of paper and put it in with mine. It'll save you getting a stamp and everything."

Her mother shoved a writing pad across the table. Nancy hadn't even sat down yet. The big suitcase with the hard corners was in the middle of the floor. She felt this was a shabby welcome home, but she was also a practical person. If she scribbled off a page to Deirdre now, well, it would save her having to do it some other time, and it would please her mother, who might go and bring out some soda bread and apple tart if she was in a good humor. Nancy wrote a few lines hoping that Deirdre and Sean and Shane and April and Erin were all well, and saying she'd love to come over and see them all but the fares were desperate and it was much easier for them to come over this way because of the pound and the dollar. She told Deirdre about Mr. White's new car, and Mr. Charles going to Russia on his holidays and Mr. Barry's wife having a new handbag that was made from the skin of a baby crocodile and had cost what you wouldn't believe. She added that it was nice to get back to Rathdoon at weekends because . . . She paused at this point. It was nice to get back to Rathdoon because . . . She looked at her mother sitting at the table, frowning over the letter writing. No, that wasn't why she came home. Her mother was only mildly pleased, and if she weren't here there was the television or Mrs. Casey or the bingo or half a dozen other things. Sometimes on the long summer evenings, Nancy had come home and found the house empty and her mother out at ten o'clock. She didn't come home for the dance like Celia did, or Kev or Mikey on the bus. She had not got what you'd call friends in Rathdoon.

She finished the letter, "It's nice to get back at the weekends because the Lilac Bus is really very good value and you'd spend a small fortune in Dublin over the weekend without even noticing it."

Her mother was packing up for bed. No tea, no apple tart.

"I think I'll just make myself a sandwich," Nancy said.

"Did you have no tea? Aren't you very disorganized for a high-up receptionist?" said her mother, who went to bed without a word of good night.

It was a bright sunny September Saturday. The tourists were mainly gone, but there were always a few golfers around. Nancy wandered up the street with no plan. She could have bought a newspaper and gone to the hotel to have coffee, but apart from the money altogether she wouldn't do that. It was being uppity going in there sitting as if you were the type. No. She saw Celia's mother washing the step of the pub. She looked older, her face was lined like that Gypsy-looking Judy Hickey's. She called out a greeting, but Celia's mother didn't hear, she kept scrubbing. Nancy wondered was Celia still in bed or was she helping to clean up inside. Celia worked weekends in the pub, that's why she came home. Her mother must have made it worth her while, because it was a hard job to stand on your feet all weekend there after having stood on your feet as a nurse all week. But you'd never know the time of day with Celia, she was so tight with information or anything at all. It was odd to see her talking away to Tom on the bus last night; usually she looked out the window with a moon face. Not like Dee, who was so full of life and so interested in everything. Nancy often wished that things were different, and that she could call on Dee at the weekend, or go off somewhere with her. But she wouldn't dream of going up to the Burkes. Not in a million years would she call on the house. The surgery was a different matter, that was the way things were.

She passed Judy Hickey's cottage and saw signs of great activity out in the back. Big packing boxes were laid all around, and Judy was wearing old trousers and had her hair tied up in a scarf. The house itself was shabby and needed a coat of paint but the garden was immaculate. It was odd that so many people watered and weeded and kept the birds off for Mrs. Hickey, Nancy thought; she wasn't the kind of woman that you'd think people would like at all. She only went to Mass one Sunday in four, if that. She never spoke of her husband and children. They had gone away years ago when the young lad was only a baby; Nancy could hardly remember the time there were children in that house. Anyway, up and away with the father and the two children and not a word out of the mother. She never got the court to give them back to her; people had said there must be some fine secrets there that they didn't want to come out, otherwise she would surely have gone to law. And for years her working in this shop, which sold things gurus used out in the East and things that must be disapproved of, ginseng and all that. Still, Judy Hickey seemed to have more friends than a few. Even now there were two of Kev Kennedy's brothers helping her, and last week Mikey Burns was there with his shovel. Young Rupert would probably have been in the team, but his father was very sick and that's why he had been coming home every weekend.

Nancy sighed and passed on. A half-thought that she might help, too, had come in one side of her mind but flashed quickly out the other. Why should she dig and get dirty in Judy Hickey's garden for nothing? She had better things to do. When she got back home and there was a note on the kitchen table, she wondered what better things she meant. Her mother had scribbled that Mrs. Casey had called to take her for a spin. Mrs. Casey had learned to drive late in life and had a dangerous-looking old car, which was the joy of her heart. It had brightened life for many people, including Nancy's mother; indeed there was talk of a few of them coming the whole way to Dublin in it. The plan had been that Mrs. Casey and Mrs. Morris would stay at the flat. After all, Mrs. Casey was Mairead's aunt. Now there would be no flat and no Mairead. Nancy's heart lurched at the memory of it all.

And nothing for the lunch and no mention of when the spin would be over, and nothing much in the press or in the little fridge, nothing you could eat. Nancy put on two potatoes to boil and went across to Kennedy's shop.

"Can I have two small rashers, please?"

"Two pounds is it?" Kev Kennedy's father didn't listen much to people: he was always listening to the radio in the shop.

"No, just two single ones."

"Huh," he said, picking two out and weighing them.

"You see, my mother hasn't done the shopping yet, so I don't know what she wants."

"You can't go far wrong on two slices of bacon," Mr. Kennedy agreed, morosely wrapping them in greaseproof paper and putting them in a bag. "She'll never accuse you of getting the family into debt over that."

She heard a laugh and to her annoyance noticed that Tom Fitzgerald was in the shop. For some reason she didn't like him hearing her being made fun of like that.

"Oh, Miss Mouse is a great one to live dangerously," he said.

Nancy managed a smile and went out.

The afternoon seemed long. There was nothing on the radio, and nothing to read. She washed her two blouses and put them out on the line. She remembered with great annoyance that nobody, not even her mother, had remarked on her perm. What was the point of getting one if people didn't notice? Paying good money for one of the newest perms. Well, paying money if she had had to: fortunately she hadn't. At six she heard the banging of car doors and voices.

"Oh, there you are, Nancy." Her mother always seemed surprised to see her. "Mrs. Casey and I've been for a great drive altogether."

"Hallo, Mrs. Casey. That's nice," Nancy said grumpily.

"Did you get us any supper?" Her mother looked expectant.

"No. Well, you didn't say. There wasn't anything there." Nancy was confused.

"Oh, come on, Maura, she's only joking. Surely you've something made for your mother, Nancy?"

Nancy hated Mrs. Casey's arch voice treating her as if she were a slow-minded five-year-old.

"No, why should I have? There was no food there. I presumed my mam was getting something."

There was a silence.

"And there was nothing for lunch either," she said in an aggrieved tone. "I had to go over to Kennedy's to get rashers."

"Well, we'll have rashers for our supper." Mrs. Morris brightened up.

"I've eaten them," Nancy said.

"All of them?" Mrs. Casey was disbelieving.

"I only got two," she said.

There was another silence.

"Right," Mrs. Casey said, "that settles it. I wanted your mother to come back with me but she said no, that you'd probably have the tea made for us all and she didn't want to disappoint you. I said it was far from likely, judging from what I'd heard. But she had to come back, nothing would do her." She was halfway back to the door. "Come on, Maura, leave the young people be. . . . They have better things to do than getting tea for the likes of us." Nancy looked at her mother, whose face was set in a hard line of disappointment and shame.

"Enjoy your evening then, Nance," she said. And they were gone. The car was starting with a series of jumps and leaps.

What could Mrs. Casey have heard? What did she mean? The only person she could have heard anything from was Mairead, or Mairead's mother. What could they have been saying—that Nancy was irritating? Was that it?

* * *

She didn't want to be in when they came back, but where could she go? She had arranged no lift to the dance: she would as soon be hanged as to go out on the straight road and hitch all the way to the night entertainment—which she wouldn't enjoy anyway. She supposed she could always go to Ryan's pub. She'd be bound to know people and it was her own hometown and she was twenty-five years of age so she could do what she liked. She put on one of her freshly cleaned blouses, which she ironed with great care. She decided the perm was an undoubted success and gave herself a spray of the perfume she had bought her mother last Christmas and set out.

It wasn't bad in Ryan's; some of the golfing people were buying big rounds, shouting at each other from the counter: What did you want with the vodka, Brian; Did you want water with the Power's, Derek? Celia was behind the counter helping her mother.

"You don't usually come in here," Celia said.

"It's a free country and I'm over twenty-one," Nancy said snappishly.

"Oh Jesus, take it easy," Celia had said. "It's too early for the fights."

There was a phone in a booth and she saw Dee Burke making a call; their phone must be out of order at home. Nancy waved but Dee didn't see her. Biddy Brady, who had been two classes below Nancy at school, had got engaged and she was celebrating with a group of the girls. The ring was being passed around and admired. She waved Nancy over to the group, and rather than sit on her own she went.

"We're putting a sum into the kitty each and then the drinks keep coming and we pay for it until the money runs out," said one girl helpfully.

"Oh, I don't think I'll be here all that long," Nancy said hastily, and noticed a few odd looks being exchanged.

She waved at Mikey Burns, who was carrying two drinks over to a corner.

"Have you any pub jokes?" Nancy asked, hoping he might stop and entertain them for a moment.

"Not tonight, Nancy," he said, and didn't even pause. Mikey! Who would do anything for an audience! He was heading for the corner; a woman with her head down sat there; it looked like Billy Burns's wife.

Billy was Mikey's brother, the one that got the looks and the brains and the luck, people said.

There was a bit of commotion behind the bar and Celia's mother seemed to be shouting at her. It was hushed up, but Celia looked very anxious. One of the Kennedy brothers had stepped in behind the bar to help wash glasses.

Nancy felt a bit dizzy. She had drunk two gins and orange, which she had bought for herself, and two as part of Biddy Brady's celebration. She had had nothing to eat since lunchtime. She decided to get some fresh air and some chips in that order. She could always come back. She sat on the wall near the chip shop and ate them slowly. You could see the whole town from here: the Burkes' house with all that lovely creeper cut away from the windows so neatly. She thought she saw Dee leaning out a window smoking, but it was darkish, she couldn't be certain. Then there was the Fitzgeralds' drapery, Tom's family's business. His two brothers and their wives worked there, as well as his father. They had a craft shop now attached to it, and they made up Irish tweeds into skirts for the visitors. Mrs. Casey lived about a mile out, so she couldn't glare at her windows and imagine her mother eating lamb chops and looking at television, counting the days with Mrs. Casey until the *Late Late Show* came back from its summer break. When they had been planning the Dublin trip they had wanted Mairead and Nancy to get them tickets for the show, and Mairead had actually written and found out what the chances were. Nancy had thought it was madness of the first order.

It was chilly and the last chip was gone. She walked back to Ryan's and thought she would go in the side entrance and visit the Ladies' on the way. She nearly fell over Mrs. Ryan, who was sitting on the step.

"Oh, it's *Miss* Morris," the woman said with a very snide little laugh.

"Good night, Mrs. Ryan," said Nancy a bit nervously.

"Oh, Miss Morris, Miss Mean Morris. Mean as all get-out, they say about you."

She didn't sound drunk. Her voice was steady and cold.

"Who says that about me?" Nancy was equally cold.

"Everyone. Every single person who ever speaks your name. Poor Biddy Brady's crowd of girls, just to mention a few. You sat down and took a couple of spirits off them and walked off. That's class, Miss Morris, strong men have wanted to be able to do that and they're not."

"Why do you call me Miss Morris?"

"Because that's what you call yourself, that's what you think you are. And by God that's the way you're going to stay. No man would take you on, Miss Morris, a mean woman is worse than a nag and a slut put together. . . ."

"I'll be off, I think, Mrs. Ryan."

"Oh, I would, Miss Morris; those little girls in there have had a few drinks now and if you haven't come back to put a couple of fivers into their kitty, I think you'd be far better to be off."

"Put *what* into their kitty?" Nancy was stunned.

"Oh, be off, Miss Morris, I beg of you."

But her blood was up now. She pushed past the woman and went into the smoke and heat.

"Sorry, Biddy," she said loudly, "I went home for change. I hadn't my money with me. Can I put this into the kitty and I'm having a gin and orange when the round comes."

They looked at her in disbelief and with some guilt. Those who had been loudest against her were abashed.

"A large gin and orange for Nancy," they called; and Celia, who was working alone with only Bart Kennedy to help her, raised her eyebrows. Nancy Morris ordering large ones.

"They cost a fair whack nowadays, Nancy," she said.

"Oh, for Christ's sake, will you give me a drink, not a sermon," Nancy said, and the others all laughed.

They were singing "By the River of Babylon, Where I Sat Down," but Nancy was only mouthing the words.

Mean, Mean, Mean. That was what Mairead thought, what she told her mother and her aunt, why she wanted her out of the flat; that's what Mrs. Casey thought, that's what her mother had felt tonight, that's what the Kennedys' father had been jeering at in the shop. That's what Celia meant now, talking about the price of a drink. That is what Mrs. Ryan, who must have gone stone mad tonight, meant, sitting on the floor of her own public house in the side entrance.

Mean.

But she wasn't mean: she was careful, she was sensible, she was not going to throw away her money. She was going to spend it on what she wanted. Which was . . . which was . . . Well, she didn't know yet. It certainly wasn't clothes, or a holiday, or a car. And it wasn't on dear things to furnish rented accommodation, and it wasn't on going to dances or discos or to hotels with fancy prices. And it wasn't on smart hairdressers or Italian shoes or fillet steaks or a stereo radio with headphones.

They had linked arms now and they were singing "Sailing" and swaying from side to side. Mrs. Ryan had come back and was singing with the best; in fact, she was standing up in the middle of the circle and playing the Rod Stewart role with somebody's golf club as a microphone.

Celia was pulling pints still; she looked at her mother with neither embarrassment nor pride—it was just as if she were another customer. Tom Fitzgerald was talking to her over the bar. They were very thick, those two. Tears came down Nancy's face at Mrs. Ryan's words. A mean woman. She wasn't at all mean. But if people *thought* she was, then she must be. Mustn't she?

Deirdre had once said she was a bit tight with money, but she had thought that was Deirdre being all-American and accusing people face to face of things. Her brother in Cork had once said that she must own massive property up in Dublin now, what with her earning a good salary and paying hardly a penny out a week except her rent and the Lilac Bus. She had said nonsense, that it cost a packet to live in Dublin. He had pointed out that she had a bicycle and she got a three-course meal in the hospital at midday, and what else did she spend it on? The conversation had ended fairly unsatisfactorily, she had thought. Now she realized that he was saying she was mean. Mean.

Suppose people *really* thought she was mean? Should she explain that it wasn't meanness, and she was only making sure she didn't throw money away? No, somehow it was one of those things that you couldn't explain. It was either there, the belief, or it wasn't there. And so, unfair as it was, she was now going to have to go overboard the other way.

Tomorrow she would suggest to her mother that she take them both to a nice Sunday lunch in the hotel as a treat. It was too late to do anything about Mairead, there was no promising to be more generous or to spend more or whatever it was people wanted. And maybe she could get some posters of Ireland and send them to Deirdre's children. Happy birthday Shane or April or Erin from your auntie Nancy in the Emerald Isle. And to the silent brother in Cork, some book about fishing and a pressing invitation to visit her when next he came up for the Spring Show.

It must work: look at Biddy Brady's party, they were delighted with her. But why shouldn't they be, she had put ten whole pounds into their bowl on the table. But it seemed to please them a lot and they were raising their glasses a bit crookedly and saying Nancy Whiskey and things to her that they'd never have said otherwise.

There was no sign of Mrs. Ryan; she had gone out again after her party piece. Nancy would like to have thanked her. Because now she had a lot of problems licked. And the great thing, the really great thing was this: It needn't cost a lot of money. In fact, if she was very careful, it need cost hardly anything.

She could take a lot of those glucose sweets and put them in a box, say, that could be a present for her mother one week. And she could give as presents those paperweights that she got from the drug companies—sometimes you could hardly see the name of the medicine they were advertising. And wasn't it just as well she had told nobody about the rise in her wages. She had negotiated it herself quietly, so no one need ever know about that at all.

Dee

They often had a drink on a Friday night in the pub beside the office. Dee would only stay for half an hour. The Lilac Bus wouldn't wait, she knew that. She knew, too, that a lot of people in the practice were surprised that she went home every weekend. It was so far, and there was so much to do in Dublin. Wasn't she very dutiful? Oh no, she had denied, no. It was selfishness: she went home because it was peaceful, there were no distractions, she could study at home. But the law books that crossed Ireland in her canvas bag came back again unopened as often as not. Dee Burke spent much of her weekends sitting at her bedroom window and staring out at Rathdoon. Until it was time to go back to Dublin again on Sunday evening.

And of course, her parents were pleased. She could get off the bus at the corner and walk up to the golf club, waving cheerily as the Lilac Bus went on into town. For every Friday night in human memory Dr. and Mrs. Burke were at the golf club, and if there was a birth or a death or something untoward in between, people knew to phone the club and the doctor would take the call.

They had been surprised at the beginning of the summer when she began to come home so regularly. Surprised but glad. It was great to have company around the house, and Dee was always the liveliest of the family. They would jump up with pleasure when she put her face around the door on a Friday night to join them and whoever else in the club bar. Her father would get her a toasted sandwich and put his arm around her shoulder if she stood beside him at the bar counter. Her mother would smile over from the table. They were so delighted to have Dee home again. Sometimes her stomach rose and fell at their innocence and their kind welcome. What did people do when they didn't have the Burkes to go back to, Dee wondered. Went mad maybe? Went to discos?

Got sense? Pulled themselves together? Oh, who knew what other people did? Who cared?

Tom Fitzgerald was quite handsome; she had never thought of it until tonight when he was laughing at her for flinging her own bag up on the roof rack. He had a lovely grin. He was an odd fellow—you could never get a straight answer out of him on anything. She knew nothing about him, nothing at all, and she had grown up fifty yards from him and his brothers. She didn't even know what he did for a living. She had asked her mother once.

"Don't you travel across the country sitting beside him? Why don't you ask him yourself?" her mother had said, not unreasonably.

"Oh, he's not the kind you could ask," Dee had said.

"Well then, you'll have to remain ignorant." Her mother had laughed. "At this stage of my life I'm not going to go into the drapery and ask personal questions to the Fitzgeralds about what occupation their son follows."

Nancy Morris was sitting in the bus, first as usual. She looked different somehow. Was it a new blouse or her hair? Dee wasn't sure—she wouldn't ask in case Nancy would start bewailing the cost of everything, as she usually did. Yet, she was getting a fine big salary, so Sam had told her. Far more than any of the receptionists or clerks were getting in the solicitors' office. Maybe I won't sit beside her tonight, Dee resolved, but she knew she would. Who else knew Sam, who else could tell her about Sam Barry and his daily life except Nancy? Imagine being able to travel home with Sam's receptionist every weekend. It was like having a bit of Sam with her. It took a lot of the loneliness away just to be able to talk about him. Even very indirectly, even if it meant talking about Mr. Boring White and Mr. Boring Charles as well. Because Nancy must never, never know that it was only Mr. Sam Barry that she was interested in.

Nancy would talk forever: she explained the routine and the kind of problems the consultants had, not being able to get beds quickly enough in the hospital, and all the complications of the Voluntary Health Insurance and the forms and people not understanding them. But she knew nothing about their lives outside the hospital. Nothing except what they told her and what the nurses told her, and that was little.

"Do their wives ever ring them at work?" Dee asked. It was like probing a sore tooth; she knew she shouldn't ask.

"Oh yes, sometimes they do." Nancy was maddening.

"And what do they say?"

"They're all very nice, they call me by my name."

That surprised Dee: Nancy was so unforthcoming and businesslike, you couldn't imagine anyone chatting to her.

"Oh yes, 'Hallo Miss Morris,' they say. All of them: Mrs. White, Mrs. Charles, Mrs. Barry."

So that's what she meant by calling her by her name!

"And has Mrs. Barry much of a Canadian accent?"

"Gosh, Dee, you do have a great memory for them all. No wonder you're so brainy and going to be a solicitor. Imagine you remembering she was a Canadian. No, not much of an accent, but you'd know she was from over there. American sounding."

Imagine my remembering she was Canadian? Imagine my being able to forget it! *She doesn't know many people here; she's far from home; it's not as if she grew up here and has her own circle of friends; she needs time to make a life for herself; we have to wait until things settle down.*

Dee could never understand the logic of that. If they were going to wait until Candy Barry settled into Irish life, they were building up more and more trouble for themselves. Why didn't they settle her back into Canadian life, she wanted to know. Before she had become isolated from her roots there. Why? Because of the children of course, the two little Barrys, small clones of their father, five and seven. He wasn't going to let those go four and a half thousand miles away and see them once a year on a visit.

But what about the children that he and Dee would have together? That would be different. Wonderful but different. You didn't parcel away your two lovely sons because you were going to have a new family with somebody else. No indeed. Dee was immature to suggest it.

Sam used that word as a great insult. He said it had nothing to do with age. People younger than Dee could be mature and people much older than both of them would never achieve it. She didn't like the word, it seemed to mean whatever he wanted it to mean. Like when you're playing poker and the two is wild, the two can be any card you want it to be.

She didn't know why she asked Nancy about his work. She never learned anything new, but it was like seeing a photograph of some scene that you knew well; it was always interesting to see it again from another angle. The only bit she shouldn't have asked was about their wives ringing up. That had made her uneasy now.

Sam said that Candy never called him at work and yet Nancy Morris said she did. Nancy probably wanted to show off about how well she knew them all. Boasting. She was in the middle of some complicated diatribe about the telephone system now. Dee felt her eyes closing. She slept and dreamed that she was getting her parchment from the Chief Justice and Sam was there congratulating her, and a photographer from the *Evening Press* had the three of them lined up and was writing their names down in his notebook.

Dee often dreamed that Sam was part of her life: she felt that this must signify that she was not guilty about him and that everything they had together was aboveboard and out in the open. Not too much out in the open, of course, but not hole-in-the-corner either. For example, her flatmate Aideen knew all about Sam, and met him when he called. And Sam's friend Tom knew too: he used to go out to meals with them sometimes. So it wasn't as furtive as you might think. Sam had wanted to know why her parents didn't cop on, but Dee had said it would never cross their minds, and anyway she was softening them up for the future by insisting she had no romantic interests yet but would certainly fall for somebody highly unsuitable when the time came. Dee had pealed with laughter over this, and Sam had looked sad. She had stopped laughing suddenly and he had been very quiet.

"The future mightn't be perfect," he said. "Not for us. You shouldn't hope too much, you know."

"The future's not going to be perfect for most people," she had said cheerfully. "But they have to keep hoping, otherwise what's the point of anything?"

That had seemed to cheer him a little, but he had been quieter than usual.

Dee wasn't sure why she came home so often now. Aideen couldn't understand it either.

"Sure, if you're down there, he'll never see you. Can't he ring you here, if he has a free minute?"

True. But he was having less and less free minutes. Candy's parents were over from Toronto. They had to be shown around. One of the little blond boys had fallen off a bicycle and opened his forehead; he had to be visited in hospital, and looked after when he got home.

There was the family holiday on the Shannon, on the cruiser, and the hurried phone calls from coin boxes when he was meant to be buying drinks or going to the Gents'.

Recently, there were times that weren't explained at all, but they were times that seemed to have no minutes in them all the same. It was easier in Rathdoon, he *couldn't* ring her there, even if he wanted to. Her father would recognize his name, the phone was in the hall, it would be hopeless. Perhaps that's why she went, because anything was better than sitting in a place where he could ring and didn't.

Aideen said she should fight harder for him, force him to leave that Candy. He had been so keen on Dee at the start that he would have done anything for her; now she had let him believe that he could have it both ways. But Dee thought she might want it both ways too. She didn't want a huge scandal, and having to leave her apprenticeship and end up half-qualified, half-married, half-home-wrecker and half-disgraced. Aideen said that was nonsense and that Dee's parents had been able to accept that her brother was living with a girl, so why couldn't they accept what she planned to do? Dee thought there was a lot of difference between Fergal living with his girlfriend when everyone knew that they would get married soon anyway, and her making off with a well-known Dublin consultant and forcing him to abandon his wife and two little boys. It was a matter of degree. Aideen had said that was nonsense, it was all Sin and it was all Not Respectable. So why not do it?

Why not? It wasn't really up to her anymore: Sam was not nearly so ardent. In fact, once or twice he had made excuses that seemed just like the things he had said to Candy on the phone a year ago. "Sorry, love, I tried, but it's useless, there's this meeting, it's the only time they can get all the people together. I pulled out last time. I can't be seen to do it again." Very familiar. Frighteningly familiar. But was he making excuses to his young mistress so that he could be with his middle-aged Canadian wife? Or was there another young mistress? Someone even younger than twenty-three? Someone who didn't sigh and groan when he canceled an arrangement? Someone who never suggested that Candy be sent back to Toronto?

Dee was remarkably calm about the possibility of a rival. She couldn't take it seriously. He really *was* a busy man, by anyone's standards; he worked long hours and there were still more people straining to see him. He had barely time for one relationship, not to mention two. To think of three would be ridiculous. Nobody could juggle that many romances and promises and endearments in the air. Nobody.

She was glad when they stopped, just for the chance to stretch her legs. Tom gave them ten minutes and not a minute more in the pub beside the garage where he filled up the Lilac Bus. The men usually had a half-pint each and sometimes Dee bought Nancy a gin and orange and Celia a bottle of Guinness. She would have a little brandy herself if her stomach felt cold and nervous. But tonight she felt all right. Sam was away on his conference.

He had rung her from the airport to say good-bye. He had said he loved her and that he'd see her on Monday night, late, when he got back from London. He'd tell Candy the conference went on until Tuesday. That was fine, it was ages since he had been able to stay a full night, she would make sure that there'd be no confrontation and scenes. Just like it had been in the beginning.

They were settling back in the bus. Poor Mikey Burns, the bank porter, who was so nice apart from all his lavatory jokes, said that he felt much better now that he'd shaken hands with the wife's best friend. He said it twice in case people hadn't got it. Kev Kennedy still hadn't.

"You're not married, Mikey," he had said.

Mikey looked defeated.

Dee said she mustn't sleep too much on the bus, it gave her a cramp in her shoulders, and Nancy said there was a great way of getting rid of tension in the neck: you had to hang your head down as if it were a great weight and then roll it around. Judy Hickey joined in the conversation unexpectedly and said that this was one of the principles of yoga and seemed greatly in agreement. Dee thought Nancy was put out by this, as if she didn't want to join up with yoga over anything.

He would be in London now, staying in that big posh hotel near the American Embassy where she had once spent a weekend with him as Mrs. Barry. It had been so racy, and she kept thinking she'd meet someone from home, as if anyone from Rathdoon would ever go inside a place like that. He had said there would be a reception at 8:30 and they would all wear name badges. It would have begun now. She felt an urge to talk about him again. This would be her last chance since she wouldn't be able to mention him at home.

"I expect they go away a lot on conferences, professional sorts of things," she said to Nancy.

"Sometimes." Nancy was vague. "Not often. Of course, they've all had their holidays in August, and you've no idea how hard it is to fix appointments; people don't understand that doctors, specialists, have to have holidays like anyone else. More than anyone else," she added righteously.

Dee wasn't going to go down that martyr road; she wanted to hear about Mr. Barry being invited to this very prestigious gathering in London. She wanted to hear what he said when he got the invitation, and she wanted to hear Nancy say that he was coming back on Tuesday, so she could hug that to herself like a little secret.

"Yes, but didn't you say one of them was off to a conference this weekend?" she said.

"No." Nancy was puzzled. "No, definitely not."

"Maybe they'd go and not tell you?" Dee's heart had started to move in a very unacceptable rhythm.

"I don't think so." Nancy was lofty. "But anyway, it wouldn't be this weekend, because I know where they're all going, as it happens. It's a big do. Mr. and Mrs. Barry—she's a Canadian, you know—well, they're having their tenth wedding anniversary party tomorrow, and it's going to be a big barbecue. Mr. Barry asked me to pray especially that it wouldn't rain."

She didn't hear anything else for the rest of the journey home. But she must have managed to nod or smile or something because she certainly didn't notice Nancy looking at her puzzled or anything. She felt as if somebody had opened her throat just under the gold horseshoe he had bought her as a pendant that time in London, and poured in a jug of iced water. The water was freezing up again. Why? That was all she wanted to know. Why the elaborate lies? Filled with such detail, about the name badges, the names of Americans and French and Germans that he was going to meet? Did these people exist at all, or had he picked names out of a phone book or out of literature? Why? If he and his wife had such a good marriage that they were gloating publicly with a big, babyish barbecue over the whole thing . . . then why did he need Dee as well?

She went over it all, from the very start, when they had met at a party on the day of a Rugby International. It had been a big lunch where people had been invited to prematch snacks, and most people had such a good time they had stayed on and watched the match on telly instead. Dee had felt guilty about their tickets and all the young disappointed hopefuls who could have used them and Sam had gathered up half a dozen and run out on the road and given them to the first crowd of passersby he saw. They had looked through the window and laughed at the waving kids and the eager way they had run toward Lansdowne Road. She and Sam had laughed a lot that afternoon, Candy was at the other end of the room talking about recipes. When they were leaving, Sam had said, "I must see you again," and she had laughed a peal of delight, and told him it was pure Hollywood.

"I am pure Hollywood," Sam had said, and somehow it had sounded endearing and nice. She had given him work and home numbers and he had called the next day. He had pursued her, yes, that wasn't too strong a word for it. *Pursued*. She had said she didn't want to get involved with a married man, and he said that he knew it was more pure Hollywood and pure corn and pure things-that-married-men-said, but actually his marriage was empty and a great mistake and something he should never have done, but he had been in Canada and lonely and far from home; and that, apart from Dee altogether, he and Candy would undoubtedly drift their separate ways when the children were old enough to understand, and that he would be very gentle and careful, and that he would love her always. Now, why would someone do that? If you loved one person and thought they were smashing and lovely and fresh, why would you then have big parties and hand-holding and a lot of bullshit with another person? What was the point? Or suppose you loved the other person and enjoyed being married to her for ten years and adored the two little boys and everything, then why would you tell lies about being fresh and lovely and tell tall tales about conferences in London with name badges to someone else? It was beyond understanding, and Dee felt that something in her head was about to break with the effort of understanding. She bent forward a little. Tom's eyes in the mirror caught the movement.

"Are you okay, Dee?" he called.

"Sure," she muttered.

"Right, coming to your corner in five minutes," he said. He must have thought she was carsick.

"We're never home already?" She was genuinely shocked. She thought they were seventy miles from Rathdoon. "You should try driving Concorde," she said, managing a sort of joke for him.

"Sure, that would be child's play after the Lilac Bus." Tom grinned back at her.

She wondered should she go straight home and not get off at the golf club.

But that would be worse, back to an empty house on her own. No, better join in and be with people who would talk and laugh and be pleased to see her.

She opened her bag and got out a mirror before she went in. Unbelievably she was not too bad, her face tanned from all those weekends at home, her hair straight and shoulder length—Sam said it was like an advertisement for shampoo, which was high praise. Her eyes normal looking, not wild. No, she wouldn't frighten her parents and their friends. In she would go, and when they asked her what she'd have, she'd say she had a stomach upset and could she have a brandy and port. Someone told her once that this was a great drink and it cured every ill. Or most ills anyway.

They were delighted to see her as always, but they were bursting with news. They couldn't wait for the drink to be in her hand so that they could drink a toast. They had had a phone call from Fergal—what do you think, he and Kate had bought the ring, they were getting married just before Christmas, wasn't it marvelous? And Kate's parents had been on the phone, too, and they had all said wasn't it wonderful the way things turned out, and maybe young people nowadays were much wiser than their parents and didn't rush into things. Dee Burke raised her glass of port and brandy and drank the health of her brother Fergal and her new sister-in-law-to-be, Kate, and she wondered with her mother what they both would wear to the wedding. And the drink went down through that channel where there had been iced water before, and it sort of burned it with a fiery anesthetic, and she began to think that whoever said it cured all ills might have had a point.

But it didn't bring sleep. And she had to move gently if she moved at all. The big old house was full of creaks and bumps. If you went to the lavatory during the night, you woke the whole house. It was considered courteous to arrange your functions so that you didn't have to. Her parents talked on long downstairs. They had been married for thirty years, she realized. They never made much of anniversaries and when her mother was fifty last year it had been very politely ignored. No showy barbecues for them, no public displays.

But that didn't matter. What was she going to do? Was she going to pretend that she knew nothing, let him lie on about London? No, that would be living out a total dishonesty. But then wasn't he prepared to do that with her? Some of the time. And with Candy some of the time. He didn't have this high regard for total honesty. How had he not known that Nancy would prattle about it? She had told him that she traveled home on the same minibus every weekend as his receptionist. But Sam didn't know that she talked to Nancy about the consultants, and Sam would never believe for one moment that Nancy would mention something as trivial as his party to someone who was not meant to know him. Would she ring him at home and confront him? What earthly good would that do? None.

She would try to be calm and wait until daylight. What was that thing you were meant to do to your neck and shoulders? She tried what she remembered of the instructions but it just made her feel worse.

An hour later she understood what insomnia was about. She had never understood why people didn't just turn on the light and read if they couldn't go to sleep.

Another hour later she laughed mirthlessly to herself about her lack of sleeping pills. There she was, a doctor's daughter, and another doctor's lover and she hadn't one little Mogadon to call her own. A bit after that she started to cry and she cried until she fell asleep at twenty to eight just as her mother was creaking down the stairs to put on the coffee.

She woke after one o'clock: her mother was standing by the bed.

"Is your tummy better?"

Dee had forgotten the so-called gastric attack to excuse the ports and brandy.

"I think so," she said, bewildered.

"If you're well enough, can you do me a favor? We've had another phone call from Fergal." Her mother paused expectantly.

"The wedding's off?" Dee said, rubbing her eyes.

"No, stupid, but they're coming this evening, about six o'clock. Can you run me into town, I'll want to get things." "Into town" meant the big town seventeen miles away. "Downtown" meant Rathdoon itself.

"What do we want to go into town for?"

"You can't get anything nice here, anything different."

"Mummy, in the name of God, isn't it only Fergal? Why do we want anything *nice,* anything *different* for Fergal?"

"But it's Kate as well."

"But hasn't he been living with Kate for a year? Are you losing your marbles or something, what would she want anything nice and different for? Can't we go to Kennedy's and get some ham or lamb or whatever we'd be having anyway?"

"Well, if you don't want to drive me, you need only say so. I'm sure your father won't mind giving me a quick spin into town." Her mother was huffy now and annoyed.

"It's not a quick spin, you know it, it's seventeen miles. It's a bad road, it's jam packed with shoppers on a Saturday in there, we'll never get a parking place, the whole thing will take three hours."

"Well, don't *you* worry about it, madam: you're so busy you can sleep on into the broad daylight—I see what a demanding life *you* have. No, your father may be able to give up his one game of golf a week to take me."

Dee got out of bed, and picked up a dressing gown.

"I'll have a bath and I'll take you now, but I want you to know that there's a grave danger you're going mad. Next week you'll be going into town to get something nice and unusual for me."

"If you were bringing home a fiancé I'd be glad to," her mother said. "And by the way, do you never wear pajamas or a nightdress or anything? Isn't it very peculiar to wear nothing at all in bed?"

"It's very peculiar, Mummy—I'd say I'd be locked up if anyone knew."

"Oh, there's nothing like a smart aleck, nothing as lovely as your own daughter turning into a smart aleck," said her mother, and went downstairs happily to make a list.

Mrs. Burke bought a new tablecloth and six napkins to match. Dee cast her eyes to heaven so often her mother asked her not to come into the next shop to be making a show of her. She was moved on three times by guards, hot harassed men who could never have dreamed that this is what it would be like when they joined the force. She saw a woman slap her three-year-old hard on the legs until he roared in fright and his father thought she had gone too far and gave the woman a hard shove. Marriage! Dee thought. Family life. If a Martian were looking at us, he would think we must be insane to run toward it like a crowd of lemmings. And it's all we want, everywhere: romantic books, *Dallas* on the telly, everyone we know. Nobody seems to learn any lessons on the way.

Her mother came out weighed down with parcels just as a guard was coming at her again; she dragged the parcels and her mother into the car with one movement.

"You're becoming very rough, Dee, very ill-mannered," her mother said, annoyed and flustered.

"It's all this naked sleeping," Dee said, smiling up at the guard. "That's the cause of it, I'm certain."

Halfway home Dee realized what had happened. That stupid Nancy had got the weekend wrong. That was it. Hadn't Sam said he'd be tied up with the family *next* weekend. Imagine believing the daylight from Nancy Morris. She really was going mad, it wasn't just a joke she made to her mother, of course that was it. Nancy was fussing and filling in her appointment book and complaining about the cost of living and she hadn't heard.

The relief was immense: it was the joy of getting an exam, it was like going to confession, not that there had been much of that lately—it was like passing your driving test.

She laughed happily and her mother looked at her in alarm.

"Mummy, I was just thinking of the day I passed my driving test," she began.

"Well, I don't know whether you'd pass it if you had it to do again," her mother said. "You've been hitting those potholes at a great rate; your father wouldn't like his car to be belted about like that."

"No, I was just thinking of the lovely feeling when the man said I passed. Would you like me to teach you to drive, Mummy, seriously?"

"I would not," her mother said. "And what's more I don't think I'll ever sit in a car with you again. Will you look at the *road*, Dee!"

"It's an open invitation. One lesson on a Saturday, one on a Sunday—you could drive us all to Fergal's wedding."

She felt light-headed and happy. If she had seen stupid Miss Mouse, as Tom called her, she would have mown her down.

When Fergal and Kate arrived, Dee thought they both looked slightly touched. They were a revolting mixture of overtalkativeness and utter wordlessness. They explained at tedious length how they had become mature in the last few months and both of them had developed this sense of their immaturity and lack of responsibility at exactly the same time. They wanted to make their commitment now in front of everyone, rather than shilly-shallying any longer. Dr. Burke, who looked as if he wouldn't have minded if they never married, nodded and grunted appreciatively. Kate's mother gasped and pounced on every word, and reminded them of every detail of John's wedding five years before—every detail, that is, except the one that his bride was four months pregnant. Dee switched off for a little and thought of Sam in London. He had said there would be papers all of Saturday afternoon, but that he was going to skip the official dinner. Together they had looked at an English newspaper and circled plays or shows he might see. She wondered was it a nice warm night in

London as it was here. Then it hit her like a tennis ball coming suddenly into her stomach. He had asked Nancy Morris to pray for a fine weekend for the barbecue. *This* weekend.

She wasn't able to eat the meringues that her mother had filled so carefully with a coffee-flavored cream to impress Fergal and Kate. She asked to be excused for a few minutes because she had remembered there was something she had to give Celia Ryan down in the pub.

"Won't it do later?" her mother had asked.

"No, she wants it now." Dee was standing up.

"Will I come down with you and have a pint?" She shooed Fergal away. "What a thought, after all this lovely meal Mummy's got for you. No, I'll be back in a few minutes."

"What does Celia want at this time of night?" her father asked mildly. "Won't she be pulling pints and trying to help that poor mother of hers to cope?"

"See you," Dee called.

She ran up to her room for her handbag and swung down the road.

"Can you give me a pound of change for the phone, Celia?" she asked.

"God, you're a great customer; if we had more like you we could open a singing lounge and have a cabaret on the profits," Celia laughed.

"Piss off, Celia. I'll have a brandy in a minute, I just want to make a call to Dublin."

Celia's level glance never changed, she never inquired whether the Burke phone was out of order, she just gave her the money.

"Could I get a call back in that box?" Dee wanted to know.

"Yes. I'll give you the number, but I don't put it up—I don't want other people to know."

"You're a pal," Dee said.

"Barry residence," said the Canadian voice she hadn't heard since the one and only time she met its owner at that rugby party, which was only a year and a half ago but felt like a lifetime.

"May I speak to Mr. Sam Barry, please."

"Well, it's a little awkward just at this very minute. Who is this, please?"

"It's Miss Morris, his receptionist."

"Oh, Miss Morris, I didn't recognize your voice. I am sorry. Sam is just getting the barbecue going, it's a very delicate moment." There was a little laugh. "Once the thing has taken we can all relax. Can I ask him to call you, Miss Morris? I assume it's urgent?"

"I'm afraid it is, Mrs. Barry." She sounded apologetic. "It's just a short message, but I should speak to him. It won't take a moment."

"Well, listen, I know he says that you are a rock of stability in a changing world. I'll have him call you."

"In the next half hour, if he could." Dee gave the number that Celia had written down.

"Rathdoon, what a pretty name!" Mrs. Barry was determined to be charming to the rock of stability. Or else she was so happy about the anniversary barbecue, she was at peace with the world. Dee didn't wait to find out.

"Very pretty. 'Bye, Mrs. Barry." She hung up; she was shaking. She sat on a stool at the bar. Celia made it a large brandy but charged only for a small one. Dee made a move to protest.

"Nonsense, you're always buying me drinks."

"Thanks." She held the glass with both hands. Celia must have noticed the shake.

"They tell me your Fergal's engaged," Celia said.

"Lord, that didn't take long." Dee grinned.

"Oh, it's stale news, I heard last night when I came off the bus."

"So did I. The parents are over the moon."

"Well, they don't have to pay for the wedding." Celia laughed.

"Celia, stop that, you sound like Nancy Morris."

The phone rang. Celia refilled her glass wordlessly and Dee slipped into the booth.

"Hallo," she said.

"A call for you," exchange said.

"Miss Morris?" Sam asked.

"No, Miss Burke," Dee said.

"What?"

"Miss Burke speaking, can I help you?"

He wasn't sure. "I'm sorry, I was asked to ring a Miss Morris at this number . . ."

"No, you weren't, you were asked to come in from the barbecue and talk to your mistress, Miss Dee Burke. That was the message I gave your wife."

"Dee. Dee." He was horrified. There was actual fear in his voice.

"Oh, she was very nice about it, she got a pencil from her purse and wrote down the number. She said Rathdoon sounded a pretty place."

"Dee, what are you doing?" His voice was a whisper.

"I'm at home for the weekend, like I told you I would be. The question is, what are *you* doing? Did they cancel the conference? Let's see, you were leaving the airport about four thirty—gosh, did they tell you at London airport or did you have to get into town?"

"Dee, I can explain exactly what happened, but not here and now; what did you really say to Candy?"

"Oh, just that, and she really did say that Rathdoon sounded pretty—ask her."

"You didn't . . . but why?"

"Because I felt it was all so confusing, all this business of lies and saying one thing and everyone knowing it wasn't true. Everyone. I thought it would be easier not having to pretend so much."

"But—"

"I mean she knows, Candy does, that you'll be spending Monday night with me, and so now you don't have to lie to her about that, and I know that you and Candy are having a marvelous tenth anniversary barbecue and that Mr. Charles is there and Mr. White and all your friends and they were all watching you start up the fire. She told me all that, so there's no more pretending: it will be much easier from now on."

"You didn't, Dee. You didn't really say those things to Candy."

Her voice was very hard now. Very hard. "You'll have to find out now, won't you?"

"But she said it was Miss Morris on the phone."

"Oh, I told her to say that." Dee sounded as if she were explaining things to a child. "Much simpler for your guests; I mean, I don't know what you want to tell other people, but we'll talk about it all on Monday, won't we?"

"Dee, please don't go, you've got to explain."

"I have explained."

"I'll ring you back."

"Ring all you like, this is a pub."

"Where are you going now?"

"I see the real Miss Morris over here in a corner. I think I'll buy her a gin and orange and tell her all about us. That will make it easier for me to ring you at work; you see, I couldn't before because she knew me, but now with all this new honesty . . ."

"What new honesty?"

"What Candy and I have been talking about."

"You're a bitch, you told Candy nothing; this is a game, some vicious little game."

"Hush hush, don't let them hear you."

"Where will you be tomorrow?"

"I'll see you on Monday night, as arranged: come anytime, straight from work if you like, now that there's no need to hide things anymore."

"I beg *you,* tell me what you told Candy."

"No, *you* must ask Candy that."

"But if you told her nothing, then . . ."

"That's right, you'll have walked yourself into it."

"Dee."

"Monday."

"I'm not going to be blackmailed into coming around to you on Monday."

"Suit yourself. I'll be at home then, if I don't get called away or anything." She hung up.

"If he rings again, Celia, will you say you never heard of me and I haven't been in all night?"

"Sure," said Celia.

She went back to the house. Fergal was explaining that there came a time in your life when you couldn't play anymore—you had to face up to things.

"Jesus, Mary and Joseph, Fergal, you should have been a philosopher!" Dee said admiringly.

"Did you have a drink with Celia Ryan?"

"I had two large brandies, Mother dear," Dee said.

"How much was that?" Fergal, the man saving for a mortgage, was interested now in the cost of fun.

"I don't know; I only paid for one small one, when I come to think of it." There were sudden tears in her eyes.

"Dee, why don't you and I go for a walk for a bit and let the wedding talk go on to a crescendo here?" Dr. Burke had his blackthorn stick in his hand.

They walked in silence. Down past the chip shop and over the bridge and on to the fork in the road.

It was only coming back that there was any chat.

"I'll be all right, Dad," she said.

"Sure, I know you will—aren't you a great big girl and won't you be a solicitor one day, a fierce terror making them all shake in the district court?"

"Maybe."

"Of course you will, and all this other stuff will sort itself out."

"Do you know about him?" She was genuinely surprised.

"This is Ireland, child. I'm a doctor, he's a doctor—well, a sort of one; when they get to that level it's hard to know."

"How did you hear?"

"Somebody saw you and thought I should know, I think, a long time ago."

"It's over now."

"It may be, for a while—"

"Oh no, it is, tonight."

"Why so suddenly?"

"He's a liar and nothing else; he lied to her and to me. Why do people do that?"

"Because they see themselves as having lost out and they want some of everything, and society doesn't let us have that, so we have to tell lies. And in a funny way the secrecy keeps it all going and makes it more exciting at the start."

"You know what it's like all right; I don't know how you could."

"Oh, the same way as your fellow does."

"*Daddy.* No, not you. I don't believe it."

"Oh, years and years ago. You were only a toddler."

"Did Mummy know?"

"I don't think so. I hope not. But she never said, anyway."

"And what happened to the girl?"

"Oh she's fine; she hated me for a bit, that was the worst part—if she had been just a little bit understanding. Just a small bit."

"But why should she?" Dee was indignant.

"Why, because she was young and lovely like you are, and she had the world before her; and I had made my way and it was nice but a bit—you know . . . a bit samey."

"She should have shook your hand like a chap and said, 'No hard feelings, Johnny Burke, you'll be a treasured memory.' " Dee was scathing.

"Something like that." Her father laughed.

"Maybe she should have." Dee linked arms with her father companionably. "Because you're a much nicer man than Sam Barry will ever be. I think he deserves a bit of roasting, actually."

"Ah well, roast away," her father said good-naturedly. "You've never listened to me up to now—there's no reason why you should now."

Dee sat in her room and looked down at the town. She thought she saw Nancy Morris sitting on the wall near the chip shop, but decided that it couldn't be. Nancy . . . pay for a whole portion of chips . . . ridiculous.

Mikey

*M*ikey always said that you couldn't come across a nicer crowd of girls than the ones who worked in the bank. The men were grand fellows, too, but they were often busy with their careers and they wouldn't have all that time to talk. And one of the men, a young buck who'd be some kind of a high manager before he was thirty, had taken it upon himself to say to Mikey that it would be appreciated if he watched his sense of humor, since the bank ladies had found it rather coarse on occasions. Mikey had been very embarrassed and had said nothing all day. So silent was he that the nice Anna Kelly, who was pure gold, asked him if he felt all right. He had told her what the young buck said, and Anna Kelly had said that banks were stuffy old places and maybe the buck had a point: jokes were fine with friends, but God, the bank—it wouldn't know how to laugh if you were tickling its funny bone for a year.

So he understood now and he never uttered a pleasantry within the bank walls again. If he met them on the street that was different; he could pass a remark or make a joke like anyone then, because they were all on neutral ground. And he used to tell the girls about his family in Rathdoon—well, about the family that Billy and Mary had, really. The twins with the red hair and the freckles, and then Gretta with the pigtails and the baby, a big roll of butter with a laugh you could hear half a mile away. He told Anna Kelly that sometimes on the summer evenings when it would be very bright the twins wouldn't have gone to bed, and they'd be sitting at their window waiting till the Lilac Bus turned into the street and Uncle Mikey would get off. They collected stamps and badges, any kind of badges; and he had them all on the lookout for anything of that order so as he never went home empty-handed.

He was the only one of the bank porters who came from the country. The rest were all Dubliners: they used to laugh at him and say there'd have to be an official inquiry as to how he got the job. But they were a very good-natured lot, and there was great chat all day as they manned the doors, or wheeled the big boxes on trolleys where and when more money was needed or had to be put away. They delivered letters and documents up and down the street. They knew

a lot of the customers by name and they got great Christmas presents altogether.

The Lilac Bus had started just when Mikey had needed it. His father was
getting senile now, and it was hard on poor Billy and Mary to have the whole
business of looking after him. But it would have been a long way to come back
without Tom Fitzgerald and the little minibus that dropped you at the door.
Imagine having to get yourself to the town by a crowded train, packed on a
Friday night and maybe not a seat, and then after that try to organize the
seventeen miles home. It would take all day and all night and you'd be exhausted.

His old father was pleased to see him sometimes, but other times the old
man didn't seem to know who he was. Mikey would take his turn spooning the
food, and combing the matted hair. He would play the Sousa marches his father
liked on the record player, and put the dirty clothes in the big buckets of Dettol
and water out in the back. Mary, who was Billy's wife and a sort of a saint, said
that there was no problem to it if you thought of it all as children's nappies. Into
a bucket of disinfectant for a while, throw that out, into a bucket of water
awhile and throw that out and then wash them. Weren't they lucky to have
space out the back and a tap and a drain and all. It would be desperate altogether for people who lived in a flat, say.

And the nurse came twice a week and she was very good too. She even said
once to Mikey that he needn't come back *every* weekend, it was above the call of
duty. But Mikey had said he couldn't leave it all to Billy and Mary, it wasn't fair.
But they'd be getting the house: what would Mikey be getting? the nurse had
pointed out. Mikey said that sort of thing didn't come into it. And anyway,
wasn't it a grand thing to come back to your own place.

The twins told Mikey that there was never any fighting when he came
home, and Mikey was surprised.

"Why would there be fighting in this house?" he asked.

The twins shrugged. Phil and Paddy were afraid of being disloyal.

"Sure, you couldn't be fighting with your poor old grandfather, he would
never harm the hair of your heads," Mikey said.

The twins agreed and the matter was dropped.

They loved Mikey around the house and he had a fund of jokes for them.
Not risqué ones, of course, but ones they could tell anyone. Gretta even wrote
them down sometimes so that she'd remember them to tell them in class. Mikey
never told the same one twice; they told him he should be on the television
telling them one after another with a studio audience. Mikey loved the notion
of it. He had once hoped that he might be asked to do a turn for the bank's
revue, but nobody had suggested it, and when he had whispered it to that nice
Anna Kelly, she said she had heard that you had to be a member of the union to
be invited, that only members of the IBOA were allowed to perform. He had
been pleased to know that, because otherwise he would have felt they were
passing him over.

He had his doubts about the Lilac Bus when he arrived the very first Friday.
Tom Fitzgerald had asked them to be sure not to wave any money at him,

because the legalities of the whole thing were what you might call a gray area. He did have the proper insurance and everything, and the Lilac Bus had a passenger service vehicle license, but there was no point in courting disaster. Let them all give him the money when they were home in Rathdoon, where it would be nice and calm. None of them had understood the ins and outs of it, but they all agreed. Mikey wondered if people like Dr. Burke's daughter and Mr. Green's son, Rupert, would fancy sharing a journey home with Mikey Burns, the bank porter and the son of poor Joey Burns, who before he lost his wits had been a great man for standing waiting till Ryan's pub opened and nothing much else. But Dee and Rupert were the salt of the earth, it turned out. There wasn't an ounce of snobbery between the pair of them. And Mrs. Hickey, she was a lady, too, but she always seemed pleased to see him. Nancy Morris was the same as she always had been since she was a schoolgirl, awkward and self-conscious. Nothing would get her out of that, she'd be an old maid yet. Celia Ryan was another fish altogether: it was a mystery she hadn't married someone by now. She always looked as if her mind was far away, yet she was thought to be a powerful nurse. He knew a man who'd been in Celia's ward, and he couldn't speak highly enough of her. He said she was like a legend in the hospital.

Nowadays he enjoyed the journey home, after he had got over his shyness of the first few runs. He would tell them a joke or two; they weren't a great audience, not like Gretta and Phil and Paddy, but they did smile and laugh a little, and didn't it cheer them up?

Sometimes he sat beside Celia and he would tell her tales of the world of banking. He told her of all the new machines, and the days of bank inspections, and how the tourists would drive you mad, and how in the summer you'd have a line half a mile long of Spanish and French students all wanting to change about £1 each of their foreign money. Celia didn't tell many tales of the hospital, but she often gave him helpful advice about his own father, all in a low voice so that the others didn't hear her talking about incontinence pads and Velcro fastenings for clothes.

But tonight it was the young Kennedy fellow sitting beside him. There was something seriously wrong with that boy. His brothers Bart and Eddie were the nicest fellows you could meet in a day's walk, but whatever had happened to young Kev he looked as if he had seen the Day of Judgment. You only had to address a civil word to him to have him leap out of his skin. Try to tell him a good story and he'd miss the point altogether. Mikey thought he'd teach him a few tricks that might be of use to him, to be able to do a trick in a pub. But the young fellow looked at him with the two eyes staring out of his head and didn't take in a word of it. In the end Mikey let him be, staring out the window as if the goblins were going to leap out of the hedges and climb into the bus after him.

Mikey nodded off. It was easy to sleep in the bus. The two girls behind him were already asleep, dreaming of fellows probably. Mikey dreamed that his father was well and strong again and had opened some kind of import and export agency in Rathdoon and that he, Mikey, was the manager and that he was able to give grand summer jobs to Phil and Paddy and Gretta, delivering letters to people up and down the street. He often dreamed of the children. But he never saw a wife for himself in the dream. Mikey Burns had missed the boat as far as wives were concerned. Too nervous and eejity at the time he should have been looking for one, and now at forty-five he wasn't the kind of forty-five-year-old that would be in the race at all. Better not make a fool of yourself going to dances or picking up fast-knowing women in pubs and being made to look thick altogether.

When they crossed the river and were really in the West they paused for the ten-minute comfort stop, and the half-pint to open the throat a bit. Celia came up to him quietly and put an envelope into his hand.

"That's for the bedsores: it's all written on it, keep him moving as much as you can."

"Aw, Celia, you're terribly good. Can I pay for this?"

"Are you mad, Mikey? Do you think I paid for it? Dublin Health Authority would like you to have it as a little gift." They laughed. She was very nice.

What a pity he hadn't found a grand girl like Celia when he was young and promising looking. After all, he had a grand well-paid job now, he'd be able to make a home for anyone. The reason he didn't really have one wasn't money, it was lack of interest. He couldn't be buying a place and furnishing it and getting tables and chairs in it all for himself. The room he rented was grand and comfortable and he denied himself nothing. He had a grand big telly and he had bought himself a mirror to fix to the front of the wardrobe—that way he'd go out properly dressed. Beside the bed he had a lovely radio, which was a lamp and a clock and an alarm all in one. When he went out to people's houses, and the Dublin fellows often invited him up to their places, he was always able to bring a big box of chocolates, a fancy one with a ribbon on it. He was able to give a good account of himself.

But when he'd been a young lad, who were they, except the sons of poor Joey Burns and his mother had taken in washing and cleaned people's floors? It hadn't held Billy back: Billy strutted around Rathdoon as if he owned it, as if he were as good as any other citizen of the place. And wasn't he right? Look where he was now, he had all kinds of business interests, he employed five people in Rathdoon. He had the take-away shop; nobody believed there was a need for it until it appeared. Half the families in the place ate Billy's chicken and chips on a Saturday night, and they had fried fish, too, and hamburgers. They sold cans of lemonade, and stayed open late to get the crowds going home from Ryan's, and Billy had put up two huge mesh litter bins at his own expense and everyone was delighted with him.

And he had an insurance business as well. Not a big one, but anyone who wanted cover went through him—it could all be filled in quickly, in the house. And he had some kind of a connection with a fellow who came to do tarmacadaming. If you wanted the front of a place all smartened up, then Billy would get other people with their places facing the same way to agree and the man with the machine and the tar would come and it was cheaper for everyone, and the place looked a king to what it looked before. A whole section of the main street looked really smart now, and Billy had got a tree planted in a tub and it was like something you'd see in a film. Billy had the brains and Billy never ran away the way Mikey ran off up to Dublin after his mother had died. Billy had stayed to marry Mary Moran, who was way beyond anyone they'd ever have thought about. Or that Mikey would have thought about.

He was looking forward to being home tonight. He had a computer game for the twins' birthday. It was several cuts above the Space Invaders they had tried out once, and it could be plugged into any kind of television; he had been playing it on his own television all week, but the shop assistant said it would work as well on a smaller set. The twins had their birthday on Monday and he was going to give them the game on Sunday afternoon. He would set up the room with the curtains pulled and pretend they were going to watch something on the television, and then would come the surprise. He had got a smart red girl's handbag for Gretta, even though it wasn't her birthday, because he didn't want her to be left out, and a yellow rabbit for the baby in case it might have feelings of discontent in its pram.

Mary would never let him near his father on the Friday night; she'd have a supper warm for him, or if it had been a busy day she'd run across the road to the family take-away and get him fish and chips as soon as she saw the Lilac Bus pull up. She used to thank him so much for coming back to help with his father, and she'd tell him funny things about the children and what they had done during the week. They were back at school now, so there would be tales of what devilment Phil had got up to and the threatening messages that came home about him from the Brothers.

Mikey was the second to get out. They would leave Dr. Burke's daughter up at the golf club entrance; her parents were always there of a Friday night and she'd go and join them. Then when it came to the end of the street, the first drop was Mikey. He would take down Nancy Morris's huge suitcase, which weighed as light as a feather, and leave it inside the bus because she and Kev Kennedy would be next out, and Kev had nothing with him ever except a parcel that he kept under his seat.

Mikey advised them all to be good and if they couldn't they should be clever and if they couldn't be clever then they should buy a pram. He laughed happily and closed the door behind him.

There was no light in the kitchen and no meal on the table. There was no sign of Mary and no note either. He didn't mind not seeing Billy—his brother was usually up at the take-away or in Ryan's doing some deal with someone. But Mary?

He looked in the other rooms. His father was asleep, mouth open, wheelchair near the bed; on the chair was a large chamber pot, optimistic since the old man was never able to time things so accurately.

There was a smell of disinfectant mixed with better smells. Mary had big bunches of flowers around the room. She always said that she thought it cheered the old man up, and sometimes she had seen him stretch out and touch the flowers gently. He snored lightly. There was a night-light, and a Sacred Heart lamp as well.

Then Mikey went up the stairs quietly. The twins had bunk beds; their toys and clothes and books were all around. Phil slept in a ball with his fists clenched; Paddy was more peaceful, lying on his side. Gretta looked funny with her long straight hair brushed out. He remembered her with plaits for as long as she had been old enough to force her hair into them. She had a smile as if she were dreaming. She was a thin little thing, gawky and plain-looking, but she had a smile that would tear the heart out of you. Even when she was asleep.

The door of Billy and Mary's bedroom was open: they weren't there. The baby, round and soft like a cream bun, lay in its cot near the bed. There was a lovely white lacy bedspread, and on the wall there was a picture of Our Lady in a field of flowers. It had a blue lamp lighting under it. It was called "Queen of the

May." Mary told Mikey once that the day she and Billy got engaged he had won a competition at a carnival where you had to throw rings over things and he had chosen that picture for her because she liked it so much.

Mikey put his small bag in his own room, which was neat as anything. She always had a bright clean pillowslip on the top, as if he was the highest quality coming for the weekend. Sometimes Mikey's mind went back to what the house had looked like in his mother's day, when they hadn't any such style or time for it.

It was puzzling, but maybe she had gone to get him fish and chips. He waited downstairs and listened to the news on the television. Eventually he began to get worried. They never left the children all alone in the house, even though they were perfectly safe, but it was just the way they were. His anxiety increased. He walked across to the take-away and to his surprise there was Mary serving. There were four people waiting for their order and only one of the young girls who worked there was behind the counter. They were working flat out.

"Mikey! Lord, is it that time already?" She was pleased but flustered to see him.

"Will I get behind there and give you a hand?" He knew the way—he had done it with them a few Saturday nights during the summer when they had been very busy. And the prices were on the wall.

"Oh, Mikey, would you?" She was very grateful.

He hung up his jacket and took an apron from a drawer. In a few moments they had the crowd thinned, and Mary was able to draw breath again. She spoke first to the girl who worked there.

"Treasa, would you take off your apron like a good child and run up to Ryan's. Tell them that we're short-staffed tonight and we'll be closing early. Tell them if they want anything, to come down in the next half hour for it otherwise they'll be disappointed."

"Who will I tell, ma'am?" The child seemed worried.

"That's a point—not much use telling poor Mrs. Ryan these days. Let me see, if there's anyone behind the bar helping, like Bart Kennedy, anyone like that, someone who looks in charge."

"Celia's home: she was on the bus, she'll probably have got behind the counter by now," Mikey said.

"That's it, tell Celia."

Treasa skipped off up the road, pleased to be out of the heat.

"Where's everyone?" Mikey looked around.

"Oh, there's been a lot happening, I'll tell you all when we get back. Keep a brave face on it for half an hour more and then it will be done." A trickle of people came in, and Mikey served them, and just as Mary had guessed would happen, a great influx came from Ryan's pub. They were full of good-natured abuse about it being against the law of the land to close the chipper before the pub. Mary had laughed good-naturedly and said wasn't she going above and beyond the call of duty to let them know now, rather than have them going home with stomachs full of beer and nothing to soak it up.

She didn't want a portion for herself, so Mikey wrapped up his own choice, and when they had drained the fat, scrubbed the tops and swept up anything that could be swept up into black plastic bags, which were tied with little wires at the top, they crossed the street and went home.

Mary heated a plate under the hot-water tap, got out the tomato sauce and some bread and butter.

"Will I wet you tea or would you like a drop of anything?"

They got a bottle of Guinness each and sat down.

"Billy's gone. Gone for good."

He stared at her, fork halfway to his mouth.

"He went this day before lunch, he'll not be back. Ever."

"Ah, no, Mary. That's not possible."

She took a sip of her drink and made a face.

"I never like the first sip, but it tastes grand after that." She smiled a weak little smile.

Mikey swallowed and said, "It was just a bit of a row, that's all. People have rows, they get patched up."

"No, there was no row, there was no difference of opinion even."

Mikey remembered the way the twins had said there was no fighting when he was around the place.

"But just a bit of a barney now and then, these things sort themselves out, really they do." He was pleading now.

"No, I'll tell you it from start to finish—there was no row. Back there early on in the summer we did have rows all right: he was very touchy, I thought, bite the head off you as soon as look at you, but he said that's the way I was too. The children even noticed us."

"So what happened?"

"Well, I don't know, honestly. But anyway we had a great summer; as you know, business was booming. He used to be tired, but he was never cross anymore, and what with the baby getting to be so grand—you know they're like devils for the first few weeks—anyway we hadn't a worry under the sun." She stopped and looked away beyond him.

Mikey was silent.

"Eat up your fish and chips, Mikey. You can eat and listen."

"I can't."

She lifted the plate from him and put it into the oven very low down. "You'll eat it later then. Today was when it all happened, and if I hadn't come back I wouldn't have known: I wouldn't have known at this moment. I wouldn't have known until the end of next week. The whole of Rathdoon would have known before me."

"Known what, for God's sake?"

"He's gone off with Eileen Walsh, you know the one we said was too good to be working in a chipper. Well, she was far too good, she was only biding her time to go off with the owner of the chipper. That was the little plan. Could you beat it?" The voice was steady but the eyes were overbright.

"But it's only a fancy, isn't it? It's a bit of madness. I mean, where would they go, and what would they do? And how could he leave you and the baby and the whole family?"

"He's in love with her. That's the word: *in love*. Isn't it marvelous? He was never *in* love with me; he loved me, of course, but that was different apparently."

Mikey stood up, but he didn't know what to do so he sat down again. Mary went on with the story.

"I was meant to be going into the town. There's always a lift in on Fridays and I had a list of things we needed for the take-away, not things we get from the suppliers, but stupid things, big ashtrays for example and a couple of tins of bright red paint—we were going to paint the windows to match the geraniums, can you believe? But to go on with what happened: You know old Mrs. Casey, who's only just learned to drive. Well, she was giving me the lift and as soon as we were out on the road beyond the golf club, didn't the engine splutter and make these desperate sounds.

"Ah, well, I said to myself, there's my day in town gone for its tea. But she's such a nice woman, Mrs. Casey, you couldn't offend her. I told her it was a blessing in disguise and I could get the things next week and maybe I'd go home and make an apple tart since Mikey'd be coming back on the bus tonight."

A big lump came up in Mikey's throat.

"And I said to her to sit tight, I'd walk back and tell the Brennans in the garage to go out for her."

Mary took another sip.

"It was a gorgeous day, and I picked wildflowers from the hedges, and when I came in, there was Billy at the table with a whole load of papers all around him. I was delighted because he was meant to have been gone for the day. So I said wasn't this grand and we'd have a bit of lunch the two of us— something we hadn't done in years—and I saw that there was 'Dear Mary' on one piece of paper and on another and only two or three lines on each. And I *still* didn't know anything was wrong, so I said, 'Are you writing me love letters at my age?' as a kind of joke. You see, I thought he was just back unexpectedly and was writing me a note to explain that he'd been in."

"Oh, Mary, isn't this terrible," said Mikey, believing it for the first time since the saga had started.

"This is the awful bit: he started to cry, he started to cry like a child. Well, I nearly dropped dead—Billy Burns crying. I ran to him to try to put my arms around him and he pushed me away. And he was sobbing like a baby that's getting teeth, so I said to him to hush it down or his father would hear. I'd left the baby next door, but your father would have been having a doze and it would have frightened the daylight out of him like it was doing to me." She paused for a moment.

"Then he said about Eileen, and her expecting and all."

There was a silence and the clock ticked and the soft snoring sound of the old man could be heard from the back room.

"He said he couldn't face me, and he was leaving a letter. And I said that he didn't have to go now, not at once, that surely he could stay and we could talk about what was to be done. But he said there'd been too much talking and that was it, now he was going." Mikey put out his big hand and patted Mary's arm hopelessly.

"There was a lot of this and that—but funny, no fight, no shouts or me saying he was a bastard or him saying he couldn't bear me anymore, that I was an old nag or anything."

"Well, no one could think that," Mikey cried loyally.

"No, he said I'd been the best wife and mother in the world, and that he couldn't tell me how sorry he was, he was just heartbroken, he said. All the papers were to show me that the chip shop is in my name, and the thousand pounds in the building society is for me, and the name of a solicitor who'd be able to find him, who'd pass letters on."

"And where does he think he's going?"

"To England. Where else?"

"How will he earn a living for himself and this floozy?"

"She's not a floozy—Eileen a floozy? Billy would earn a living on the planet Mars, don't worry about that."

Mikey was struck dumb.

"But the thing that upset him most was his father, your father."

"Billy never gives much time to poor old Dad."

"No, but he thought it wasn't just for me to be left with him—to have to look after an old man who isn't my own father. I said that Da was the least of the problems, what I wanted to know was how he could leave me, his wife, his friend for years and years, for fourteen years married, and a year before that mad about each other. That's when he explained all this *in love* business."

"What did you do?"

"What could I do? His mind was made up, he was leaving. He had a list of things he wanted me to do. There was a special sum of money left in one envelope that was for me to have driving lessons. I was to find out who taught Mrs. Casey: whoever taught her could teach the devil himself. He was leaving the van. I was to ask Bart Kennedy to give me a hand and pay him a proper wage. I was to decide whether he should write to the children or not and what I should tell them, if anything. He thought I should say he had gone away for a bit and then they'd grow used to it."

Mary stood up to get another bottle of stout.

"He had been packing his things, too, it nearly broke my heart to see his good shirts stuffed in all creased, and he had forgotten all his shoes. I asked him to say good-bye to your father—he's been very clear the past couple of days, knows all of us—but no, he wouldn't. I said he might never see him again and he said that he'd never see any of us again. That's when I got a bit frightened about it all. I knew there's never any changing his mind. So I decided I'd let him go, without screaming and roaring and begging."

"You let him walk out—"

"No, I said I'd go out and let him finish at his ease. I said he needn't bother about the letter now, he'd said it all, that I'd go out and get more flowers and things and keep out of his way for an hour or two until he left. That he could leave all the insurance papers where they could be found, and the solicitor who would pass on the messages to him if there was anything we hadn't thought of. He was *so* relieved: you should have seen his face—you see, he was afraid there'd be this big scene. He said that maybe I'd be glad of the change, too, and I said, oh no, I wouldn't, I would miss him every day of the year and so would his children, and on the days when his father was clear his father would miss him too. I wasn't going to give him the nice comfortable feeling that he was doing us any favors. And out I went. I crept along the back way and he finished his packing and his leaving things out on the table, and your one came along in her car and he put the boxes and cases in and she kissed him just standing at our door and they drove off.

"When I came in it was all in neat piles on the table and a piece of paper saying 'Thank you very much, Mary. All the best, Billy.' So now you know everything, everything that's to be known."

"Isn't he a callous bastard, isn't he the biggest, most selfish—"

"That won't bring him back."

"I'll bring him back, I'll get him back. He's not going to desert you, there's ways of bringing him back."

"Not if he doesn't want to come back! Will you have your fish and chips now? They'll go all hard otherwise."

He hardly slept all night; it was only when the dawn came that he fell off, and it wasn't long after that that the twins were in the room followed by Gretta carrying a cup of tea. That was always their excuse to wake him: it was called bringing him his tea in bed. Most of it was in the saucer and some of it was on the stairs, but it was still an excuse. They were full of plans for the day. They'd come down and wait while he was feeding Grandpa and changing him. They accepted that routine as part of life, like sunsets or having to wash your hands before meals. They wanted to show him a new game that had arrived in Brophy's shop. It was a huge thing like a Space Invaders but it cost twenty pence a time and they could only have three goes altogether, unless of course Uncle Mikey wanted an extra game. And Mammy had said they could go on a picnic in the afternoon because since Daddy was gone to Dublin for a bit there'd be no work to be done around the house and no one coming in about insurance who had to have tea. And hadn't he better get up now in case all the good went out of the day.

Mikey felt the day was very heavy on his hands, that things kept happening as if he were outside looking in at all the things that were happening instead of being part of them. He saw himself feeding his father slowly with a spoon, he saw himself cutting crusts off the sandwiches for the picnic, and climbing for the blackberries. It was like playing a part in a play.

He was glad when it was evening and the children went to bed; they went easily because he had promised them the most monstrous surprise of their lives tomorrow. Something that he absolutely guaranteed they would never expect. He assured Gretta that it was something she could share, too, and that there was a small non-birthday present for her as well.

"I don't know what I'd have done without you, and that's the truth," Mary said. "The day just flew by for me." He was glad it had. He had arranged for two girls to help Treasa in the chip shop.

"Will Eileen not be in again?" Treasa complained. Her tone was guileless, she didn't know.

"No, she won't, she's gone off somewhere; we'll get you these two young ones you've had in there before on bank holidays and high summer," he said firmly. "Mrs. Billy and I are going to be down in Ryan's for a bit, so you'll know to send one of them down there if there's any problem, but a big bright girl like you, Treasa, you'll manage it. Don't you know it all like the back of your hand?"

Treasa was delighted with him.

"Oh, go on, Mr. Mikey, you and your Dublin chat," she said.

"Are we going off down to Ryan's?" he asked her.

He was going to make a joke and say something about stepping out together or hitting the high spots, but he felt it would have been the wrong thing to do. She looked up at him, pleased and surprised that he seemed so eager.

"I'm not much company for you."

"I think we should go out though, don't you? From the start like. No hiding away in corners, no crawling out when people think you've got two heads. Be out there from the word 'go.' After all, *you* haven't done anything."

"I've failed to hold on to my husband, that's a great crime around these parts."

"Oh, I don't think so; aren't they all stuck into television every night here? I think you'd have to do far more than that to be a disgrace."

"I hate you to be involved in it, Mikey, you've been nothing but kindness itself, every weekend as nice as anything and look what happens to you: caught up in all the scandal, all the gossip."

"There won't *be* scandal and gossip, and that's up to you to make sure of." He heard his own voice in his ears. He thought it sounded very confident, very sure. Mary must have thought so too.

"You're a great help to me making all these decisions, I'm like one of those things in films that just walk about not knowing what they're at."

"Zombies," he said.

"Imagine you knowing that," Mary said.

"I see a lot of films," Mikey said. "What else have I to do?"

Ryan's was crowded. He put Mary in a corner and went up to the counter. Celia was going full strength and Bart Kennedy was giving her a hand. Mikey remembered his brother's instructions about paying Bart a proper wage and bile against Billy rose in his throat. To be able to calculate like that, to plan for her desertion, to deceive her so long.

"It's not like you to be short of a word, Mikey Burns." Celia was standing in front of him. She must have asked him his order and he hadn't heard.

"I'm sorry." He had to force his sense of outrage down before he could speak.

"Are you all right?" Celia's voice was concerned.

Mikey shook himself. *He* was full of brave words to his sister-in-law about how *she* was to behave, now he must do the same for himself. He could speak again, but he hadn't the heart for jokes.

He gave his order and carried the pint and the glass of Snowball across to Mary. As he was passing young Biddy Brady's engagement party, Nancy Morris of all people put her hand out as if to stop him. Wanted him to come and tell them some funny stories. He always thought she was such a superior-acting kind of a one, always looking in on herself and never having time for other people. Well, well.

"Not now, Nancy," he had said, and he saw her face turning away embarrassed. He hadn't meant to be so short with her, but honestly, *now* of all times.

"Here we are," he said.

She had her head down looking at the floor.

"Look up, Mary Burns, look up and smile."

She looked up and gave a watery smile.

"That's marvelous but it isn't a patch on your daughter's." She gave one of Gretta's sudden grins, the kind of grin that split a face in half; they both laughed.

"That's better," said Mikey. "Now, let's see what we'll do."

* * *

They got out a writing pad and made out a list of things she had to do this week. Ring suppliers—their names were all on some kinds of bits of paper on various spikes around the office. Billy Burns hadn't kept any books that would gladden the heart of a taxman, but at least there was some method in his ways. They wrote out a kind of notice that she could give to anyone who called about insurance: "Mr. Burns' policies are all being dealt with by the following office . . ." followed by the name of the solicitor. She would give these to anyone with a laughing explanation that unfortunately as a mere woman she was never kept informed of the Master's doings. It seemed fairly sure that he hadn't absconded with other people's money, so his Book had been passed on or sold to some other agent by now. The solicitors would know. They listed the people they could call on to work in the take-away, and how much they should be paid. He went for two further pints and two further Snowballs, and by that time they had covered every eventuality and worn themselves out.

"I'll sleep tonight, I'm that exhausted," Mary said, letting out that she hadn't slept the previous night.

"I'll sleep too: I'm less frightened," Mikey said.

She looked at him gratefully. "You're very very good to me, but there's one thing you haven't mentioned at all."

"What's that?"

"What about you? Will you still be coming home on the bus at weekends?"

"I'll get off the Lilac Bus before ten every Friday, with the help of God," he said.

"You're very different tonight, you're not always cracking jokes and making games out of things people say. I find it much easier to talk to you, but hard to believe it *is* you, do you know what I mean?"

"I think so," he said.

"Like I want to ask you do you want to come home to Rathdoon even more than at weekends, but I don't know how to put it. If I say, will you come back altogether, it looks as if I want you to come back and look after us all and take it all on, and that's *not* it. And then, if I don't ask you, you might get the notion you're not welcome."

"I've thought all that out too," Mikey Burns said.

"And what did you arrive at?" She leaned over the glass with its rim of froth. She couldn't wait to hear.

"You're still hoping in your heart he'll come back. That it's only a bit of summer madness. That it'll be all forgotten by the end of the month."

"I'd like it, but I don't think it's going to happen," she said simply.

"So, suppose I came home and settled myself in and Billy Boy came over the hill one fine day, where would that leave us all?"

"As we were, wouldn't it?" She looked at him inquiringly.

"No. I'd have to run away again, there wouldn't be room for us all in the one nest."

"So are you not coming back to us. I always thought you had a great soft spot for us altogether." She sounded sad.

"I'll come back for good if he isn't back for Christmas. That's the best way. That's the way to do it." He looked proud of his deductions.

"It's your home," she said gently. "You were always as welcome in it as the sun coming in the windows."

"You say that because you're like that. My brother Billy didn't say it, did he, when he was leaving. He told you to get Bart Kennedy and pay him a proper wage."

"He did say it but I didn't repeat it. I didn't want to be making you think you had to do anything." She looked troubled now.

"What did he say?"

"He said . . . ah, it doesn't matter what he said. He made it clear he thought of the place as your house too."

"I want to hear it."

"Why? What does it matter? We know he hardly knows what he's doing: he's half mad these days, he couldn't string words together."

"Well, I'd like to know anyway, please," he said simply but firmly. This wasn't the giggling, jokey man of last weekend.

"He said something like: 'Mikey's not likely to settle down anywhere with anyone at his age, and he's very good to the old man, and the children love him. Maybe if he could find something for himself around here, he'd be in the place. Sure, the house is half his anyway, he has a right to it.' It was something along those lines."

She didn't look at him, and he looked hard at the beer mat, which had a puzzle on it.

"Full of charm, my little brother, isn't he?"

"That's what he is: your little brother, don't ever forget that."

"Would it suit you, Mary, if I were to be about the place?"

"Would it suit me? Wouldn't I love it, isn't it what I always wanted? There's always been a living for us all in that take-away alone, you've seen the takings, and if we were working in it together . . ."

"Well then, I'll come back at Christmas, that's the best. I might even get myself made redundant up at the bank, and have a lump sum. Those fellows up in the bank, the porters, are fierce organized, you'd never know what kind of a deal they'd get for me."

"Wouldn't it be dull for you, after Dublin?"

"No, don't I come home for nearly half the week as it is?"

"And maybe finding yourself a girl?" She was hesitant.

"I think brother Billy was right on that one, the time is past." He smiled an ordinary smile, not a screwed-up one.

Rupert Green passed the table. "Did you see Judy Hickey at all?" he asked.

"No, I'm afraid we were talking, I didn't notice," Mary said.

"She could be around the corner behind the pillar there." Mikey pointed. Biddy Brady's party had linked arms and were singing "Sailing," and Celia's mother was arriving with a golf club as if she were about to brain them, but as they all watched horrified it turned out that she had no such intention: she was about to join in the singing, and was in fact calling for one voice only, her own.

"I've met everyone from the Lilac Bus except the one I set out to meet," grumbled Rupert. "Dee Burke was just flying out the door, Miss Morris looks as if she's had a skinful, Kev is cowering in a corner, and the rest of the cast is at the counter canoodling."

"If she comes in, what'll I tell her?"

"Oh, I'll find her, I have to tell her something extraordinary."

Mary and Mikey looked politely interested.

He was gone.

"It's probably about some toadstool or mushroom; they're always talking about herbs and elderflowers and things," Mikey said. Mary laughed and tucked her bag under her arm.

"Won't you want another man?" he said suddenly. "I mean, you're still young. Won't living with a brother-in-law cramp your style?"

"No," she said. "No, I won't. I mean, even if I could have one and I can't. But I think I'm through with all that sort of thing. I think I just want a bit of peace and for the children to be able to grow up happily enough and for me to have a place here, you know, just like you said, not running away. That will do me."

He remembered the dream that he had on the bus: the dream where there had been no wife but he was in charge of the children, sending them on little messages up and down the street. He realized now there had been no Billy in the dream either. Some of the details were different, of course, but the central part was the same. He would be safe at home with them all. And there would be no demands made on him as a man. He could be just himself, and he'd be as welcome as the sun that came in the windows.

Judy

There had been four customers in the shop that afternoon. Judy had been taking note recently and writing it down in a little book. After lunch two students came in and spent almost half an hour reading books on herbalism and the art of homemade wines. An elderly man bought a copper bracelet for his arthritis and said that when the savages who came into his house and robbed him blind were leaving, they pulled his copper armband off in case it had been valuable. A woman with a tight, hard face bought some Evening Primrose oil and asked could you dilute it with ordinary vegetable oil or baby lotion to make it go further.

It was a matter of weeks now before they had to close. Judy's heart was heavy as she walked toward the Lilac Bus. She was tired, too, and not in form for a long drive to the West. She had been tempted to opt out. To go back to her little flat and have a long, long bath listening to some nice music on the radio. Then to put on her caftan and her soft little slippers and lie there until the aches in her limbs and the buildup of a headache behind her eyes was gone. Fine advertisement I am for a health shop. . . . She smiled to herself as she strode on toward the bus. Aching and creaking and bankrupt. No wonder people live such unhealthy lives if they see what good living leads to!

She hoped that Mikey Burns wouldn't be too loud tonight with his school-boy jokes. He was a decent poor fellow but he was hard to take at any length. The trouble was that if you made no response to him he thought you hadn't heard and said it all again, and if you did manage a laugh he got encouraged and told you a few more.

She arrived just at the same time as Rupert: that was good, they could sit together in the backseat. It looked a bit standoffish if you were to keep a seat for anyone, but she really couldn't bear to be nudged by Mikey the whole way to Rathdoon, or even worse, to hear that solemn tedious little Nancy Morris telling her how to get free soap by buying toothpaste on a Wednesday or some such harebrained scheme.

He was a good boy, Rupert. Yes, that was exactly how she would describe him if anyone asked her. Good. He was an only child of parents who were middle-aged when he was a toddler and who were old now that he was a man of twenty-five. His mother was sixty-seven and his father was seventy this year. But Rupert said there were no celebrations; his father was bedridden now and was failing by the week. Rupert said it was harder and harder each time he came home because he had this vision of his father as a hardy man with views of his own on everything, and then when he got into the big bedroom on a Friday night it was the same shock, the same readjustment—a paper-thin man with a head like a skull, with nothing alive except the big restless eyes.

Judy had known Rupert since he was a baby and yet she had only got to know him since the bus. He had always been a polite child. "Good morning, Mrs. Hickey. Do you have anything for my pressed-flower collection?" Protestants were like that, she had always thought in her good-natured generalizations: pressed flowers, politeness, neat haircuts, remembering people's names. Mrs. Green was so proud of her Rupert, she used to find excuses to walk him down the town. The Greens had been married for twenty years when Rupert was born. Celia Ryan's mother in the pub had whispered that she gave Mrs. Green a novena to St. Anne that had never been known to fail, but because of her religion she had delayed using it. The moment she had said it, Catholic or no Catholic, St. Anne had intervened and there you were, there was Rupert.

Judy told him that one night on the Lilac Bus and he laughed till the tears came down his face. "You'd better tell me about St. Anne and what class of a saint she is. I suppose I should be thanking her that I'm here, or speaking sharply to her when times are bad."

Judy often smiled at Rupert's quaint ways. He was wonderful company and the same age as her own son, Andrew, miles away in the sun of California. But she could never talk to Andrew like she talked to Rupert—in fact, she could never talk to Andrew at all over the years. That was the legal agreement.

Judy wondered, would you recognize your own child?

Suppose she went to San Francisco now and walked through Union Square, would she immediately know Andrew and Jessica? Suppose they passed her by? They would be grown man and woman—imagine, twenty-five and twenty-three. But if she didn't know them and they didn't know her, what was all the point of giving birth and holding a child inside you for all that time? And suppose they did recognize her, that something like an instinct made them stop and look at this fifty-year-old woman standing in the sunshine. . . . What would they do? Would they cry "Momma, Momma" and run to her arms like a Hollywood film? Or would they be embarrassed and wish she hadn't turned up? They might have their own idea of a momma back in Ireland. A momma who was just not suitable. That's what Jack said he would tell them. Their mother hadn't been able to look after them—no other details. And when they were old enough to hear details and understand them, they would be given Judy's address to write to and she could send them an explanation if she felt able to. She never felt able to because they never wrote. For years and years she had been rehearsing it and trying out new phrases, like practicing for a job interview or a school essay.

Little by little she realized they were eighteen, nineteen, twenty. Well old enough to ask about an unsuitable mother. Well old enough to be told. But no request ever came.

She didn't even write to Jack's brother after a while. Jack's kind big brother, who had given them all a home on the West Coast of America, but who had always tried to patch up the split. He had told her nothing in his letters except to assure her that the children were settling in to their school and that all was for the best.

This evening she wondered about them both, Andrew and Jessica—golden Californians now. Were they married? Very probably. Californians married younger, divorced sooner. Was she a grandmother? Very possibly. His name might be Hank or Bud or Junior. Or were those all old names? Why did she think it was a grandson, it might be a girl, a little girl in a sunhat like Jessica had been the day they took her away. She had a Californian clock in her mind always, ever since they left twenty years ago. She never paused and said, "I wonder what time it is out there," she always knew. It was coming up to a quarter to eleven in the morning for them. It was always that when she came around the corner to the Lilac Bus. And she didn't know if they were married or single, working in universities or as domestics. She didn't know if they were happy or wretched, she didn't even know if they were alive or dead.

She slipped neatly in beside Rupert on the backseat, passing young Dee Burke, who had been looking so troubled for the last Lord knows when, it was amazing she hadn't cracked up. Past the odd young Nancy Morris. What a cuckoo in the nest that little one was—her mother was a grand little woman altogether, and Deirdre who had gone to the States was very nice, whenever she came back, full of chat. The brother in Cork was a nice lively fellow too. What had come over Nancy to make her so prissy or whatever it was she had become?

Rupert was wearing a new jacket that obviously thrilled him to the core. It just looked like an ordinary teddy-boy jacket to Judy, but then she was the first to admit she knew nothing about smart clothes. Dee Burke had gone into ecstasies over it and Rupert had flushed with pleasure.

"It's a birthday present," he whispered as the bus started. "I'll tell you all about it later."

She didn't want to hear all about it on the bus, not while her hip was aching and her head was throbbing, and that young Morris girl might well pretend not to be listening but was only two feet away from them. She felt old tonight. She was years older than everyone on the bus except Mikey Burns, and she was a good few years beyond him too. She was twenty years older than the young couple who had set up the health shop and who would be dismantling it within six weeks unless there was a miracle and they discovered the Elixir of Youth and bottled it in expensive but appealing packaging. Surely she was past all this rattling backwards and forwards across the country. Surely she should have some peace and settle down, in one place or the other.

She rooted in her big bag and gave Rupert a small parcel. "It's green tea," she said. "Just a little, to see if you like it."

His eyes lit up. "This is what you make the mint tea, the proper mint tea with?" he said.

"Yes, a handful of fresh mint, a little sugar in a glass, and you make the tea separately in a silver pot, if you have one, and then pour it on the mint leaves."

Rupert was very pleased. "I'd been making it with tea bags since we came back from Morocco, and it tasted really terrible, but out there it was like heaven. Oh, I *am* grateful to you, Judy."

"It's only a little," she said warningly.

"Look on it as a sample. If we like it we'll come in and buy kilos of the stuff and make your shop do a roaring trade."

"It would need it." She told him about the kind of trade they were doing. He was reassuring, it was the same everywhere.

He worked in an estate agency. Things were very slow. Houses that would have leaped off the books weren't moving at all. And there were shops closing down all over the place. But these things went in phases, he said. Things had to get better soon, the kind of people who knew about these things were confident, that's what you had to remember. Judy said wryly that the kind of people who knew about such things could probably still afford to be confident, they had so many irons in the fire. It was the rest of the world that was the problem.

They felt like old friends, the way they talked. She asked him to come and advise for a bit at the cutting of the elderflower, and to help choose some of the dried rosemary and lemon balm for the little herb pillows she was making. Rupert said that for the Christmas trade she should make dozens of those and sell them herself to big shops in Grafton Street—they would make great Christmas gifts. Fine, Judy said, but what about her own shop, the shop she worked in? That's the one she wanted to help, not big stores, which would make money anyway.

He told her about a politician's wife who had come into the auctioneer's and inquired politely about the location of her husband's new flat. Somehow they all knew that this flat was not a joint undertaking and that the wife was trying to find out. Everyone in the place had copped on and they all became vaguer and more unhelpful by the minute. Eventually the woman had stormed out in a rage. They had drafted an immensely tactful letter to the politician pointing out that his nest had not been revealed but was in danger of coming under siege.

"Poor, stupid woman," said Judy. "She should have let him install a harem in there if it kept him happy."

"You wouldn't have let him do that, you'd have too much spirit," Rupert said admiringly.

"I don't know. I let a man walk away with my two babies twenty years ago. That wasn't showing much spirit, was it?" Judy said.

Rupert gasped. Never had Judy Hickey mentioned the amazing happening that the whole town knew about in garbled versions. He had asked his mother, who had said that nobody knew the whole ins and outs of it, and that Rupert's father, who had been the local solicitor then also, had been very annoyed because nobody consulted him, and he was the obvious person to have been brought in on it. But there had been something about a Garda charge and a lot of conversation and a solicitor from Dublin coming down for Jack Hickey and then documents being drawn up and Jack and the two children going to America and never coming back.

"But people must know *why*," Rupert had insisted.

His mother said there were more explanations than there were days in the year.

She had been only six years married and twenty now without her man and her children, but she always kept the name Hickey. It was in case the children ever came back, people said. There was a while when she used to go into the town seventeen miles away and ask at the tourist office if you could get the lists of American tourists, or just those with children. There was a while she would go up to the bus tours that sometimes came through Rathdoon and scan the seats for nine-year-old boys with seven-year-old sisters. But all that was long in the past. If it was so long in the past, why had she mentioned them now?

"Are they on your mind then?" Rupert asked gently. She replied as naturally as if she was in the habit of talking about them. She spoke with no more intensity than she had talked of the mint tea.

"They are and they aren't. We'd probably have nothing to say to each other at this stage."

"What kind of work does he do now? He's not retired, is he?"

"Who? Andrew? He's only your age. I *hope* he hasn't retired yet." She looked amused.

"No, I meant your husband. I didn't know whether your children were boys or girls." Rupert felt he had put his foot in it.

"Boy and girl, Andrew and Jessica. Andrew and Jessica."

"Nice names," he said foolishly.

"Yes, they are nice names, aren't they? We spent ages choosing them. No, I've absolutely no idea whether Jack Hickey is working or whether he is lying in a gutter being moved on by big American cops with sticks. And I don't know if he ever worked in California or whether he lived off his brother. I never cared. Honestly, I never gave him a thought. It sounds like someone protesting, I know it does, but it's funny: I have great trouble remembering what he looked like then and I never until this moment wondered how he's aged. Possibly got fatter. His elder brother, Charlie, was a lovely man; he was fat, and there was a family picture I remember, and the parents were fat."

Rupert was silent for a moment. Such obvious indifference was chilling. You could understand hate or bitterness even. You could forgive a slow fire of rage and resentment. But she talked about him just as you would about some minor celebrity who had been in the news one time. Is he dead or alive? Who knows, who remembers? On to another topic.

"And do the children, well . . . do Andrew and Jessica keep in touch even a little bit?"

"No. That was the agreement."

If he was ever to know, it would be now. He inclined his head slightly to see if anyone else was listening. But no, Dee was fast asleep with her head at an awkward angle, and that awful Morris girl was asleep too. The others were too far ahead to hear.

"That was a harsh sort of agreement," he said tentatively.

"Oh, they thought they were justified. People used to think it was quite justifiable to hang a sheep stealer, don't forget."

"Is that what you did?" he asked, smiling. "Steal a sheep?"

"Would that it had been so simple. No, no, I thought you knew, I thought your father might have told you. No, I was a dope peddler. That's even worse than anything, isn't it?"

She looked like a mischievous girl the way she said it. He felt she couldn't be serious.

"No, what was it about really?" He laughed.

"I told you. I was the local drugs person." She spoke without pride or shame. Just as if she was saying what her name was before she was married. Rupert had never been so startled. "You do surprise me," he said, hoping he was managing to keep the shock out of his voice. "But that was *years* ago."

"It was the sixties. I suppose it is years ago, but your lot aren't the first to know about drugs, you know—the sixties had their own scene."

"But wasn't that only in America and England? Not like now."

"Of course it was here, too, not in huge housing estates, and not kids and not heroin. But with brightish, youngish things, at dances, and people who just left college who had been abroad, and it was all very silly, and to this day I think perfectly harmless."

"Hash, was it?"

"Oh yes, marijuana, pot, a few amphetamines, a bit of LSD."

"You had acid? *You* had acid?" He was half-admiring, half-shocked.

"Rupert, what I had was everything that was going, that wasn't the point. The point was that I was supplying it, and I got caught."

"Why on earth were you doing that?"

"Out of boredom in a way, I suppose. And the money was nice, not huge but nice. And there was a lot of fun too; you met great people—not deadwood people like Jack Hickey. I was very stupid really. I deserved all that happened. I often think that." She had paused to muse. Rupert mused with her for a bit. Then he spoke again:

"Were you doing it for long? Before you were caught?"

"About eighteen months. I was at a party and we all smoked something, Lord knows what it was called. I thought it was great, Jack had said nothing at the time, but when we got home he roared and shouted, and said that if this ever happened again, and what he'd do and what he wouldn't do."

"Had he refused it, then?"

"Ah, you didn't know our Jack, not at all, he had passed the poor little cigarette with the best, but he had kept his mouth closed and only pretended to inhale. He was sober and furious. Oh, there was a barney that went on all week, then the ultimatum: if I ever touched it again—curtains, he'd take the children off to America, I'd never see them again, no court in the land. . . . You could write it out yourself as a script and it would be right, it would be what he said." Rupert listened, fascinated. Judy's soft voice went on.

"Well, Jack was dealing with the livestock. It wasn't like a farm, you know, the house then, it was like a ranch: there were only livestock—no milking, no hens, no crops, just beasts in the field—buy them, graze them, sell them. We had poor old Nanny, she had been my nanny in the days of old decency and she minded Andrew and Jessica. I used to go here and there, gathering material for a book on the wildflowers of the West. Gathering bad company more likely. Anyway, because I had my little car and because I went here and there, what could be more natural than I go to Dublin or to London—as I did twice to get some stuff for people. Others suggested it; I took it up like a flash."

"It's like a story out of a book," Rupert breathed admiringly.

"A horror story then. I remember it as if it were yesterday: acting on information received, warrant, deeply embarrassed, Mr. Hickey, a person of such importance as yourself, absolutely sure there's nothing in it, but have to apply the same laws to the high as to the low, and if we could get it all over as quickly as possible wouldn't that be for the best? Dear, dear, heavens above, what have we here, in *Mrs.* Hickey's car, and *Mrs.* Hickey's briefcase in the bedroom. And hidden away behind *Mrs.* Hickey's books. Well, he was at a loss for words, and perhaps Mr. Hickey could come up with some explanation?"

She was like an actress, Rupert thought suddenly. He could see the sergeant or the superintendent or whoever it was. She could do a one-woman show, the way she was telling the story; and it was without gesture or emphasis, since it was being told in a low voice not to wake the others as the minibus sped through the evening.

"It took forever. And there were people down from Dublin and there was a TD, someone I didn't even know Jack knew. And Jack said that the whole place was becoming too much for him anyway and he had been thinking about selling it for a while, but if there was this scandal then people would know he was doing it under a cloud and the price of the place would drop right down. They were all businessmen, even the guards, they could understand that.

"Then the documents. Jack was going to take the children to his brother unless I signed a sworn statement that I agreed I was an unfit person to act as their mother any longer. The sergeant could charge me, as soon as Jack had the place sold, his plans made and was off to California with the babies. He begged me to think of the children."

"He did that and yet took them away from you?" Rupert was confused.

"Yes, you see, his point was that I was a drugs criminal, that wasn't a good start for any child: they'd be better without me. A deal had been done; kind, wise people had seen extenuating circumstances; it was up to me to make the most of them."

She looked out the window for a while.

"I didn't think it would be forever. I was frightened, I was sure it would all die down. I said yes. He sold the place—well, he sold it to that gangster, remember, who conned everyone and went off with a packet. Then the Liquidator or whatever sold it to the nuns and they made it into the conference center. So now you know the story of the Big House and all the bad people who lived there until the present day." He hadn't realized that she was once mistress of the big Doon House where she now lived in the gate lodge. Today the house had priests, nuns, and laypeople coming to do retreats, have discussions. And sometimes there were ordinary conferences that weren't religious at all: that's how the community made the costs of the place. But it was usually a very quiet type of conference where the delegates weren't expecting much of a night life. Rathdoon could offer Ryan's Pub and Billy Burns's chicken and chips; people usually expected more if they came a long way to a conference.

"I had to leave Doon House within a month. But he tricked me in one way. Even with the slightest hint of a drugs offense in those days you couldn't get into the States. They wouldn't give me a visa. And in order to make the distance as great as possible between poor Andrew and Jessica over there and their mad mother over here, Jack arranged that I be charged with a minor offense: possession. It was a nothing, even here, and compared to what I could have been charged with, which was dealing, it was ludicrously light. But then the deal had been done, don't forget. And even being charged with possession kept me out of the States."

There was another silence.

"Wasn't that a bad trick to play on you?" Rupert said.

"Yes. Yes. I suppose he thought like the people who burned people in the Inquisition . . . that they were doing the right thing. You know, rooting out evil."

"It was very drastic, even for the sixties, wasn't it?"

"Will you stop saying the sixties as if it was the stone age. *You* were born in the sixties, don't forget."

"I don't remember much about them." Rupert grinned.

"No. Well, I suppose you'd call it drastic; Jack would have called it effective. He was a great man for getting the job done." She spoke with scorn. "That's all he cared about. 'That's done,' he'd say proudly. It was the same coping with me. But Rupert, did you not know all this before? I mean, I don't want to make out that the whole town talks of me morning, noon, and night, but I would have thought that you must have heard some drift of it?"

"No, never. I knew that the children had gone away with their father and I think I asked why but I was never told."

"That's because you're so nicely brought up! They're too well bred in your house, they'd never talk of other people's business."

"I think my mother'd be glad to if she knew about it. And it's not only us. I once asked Celia why you didn't have your children, and she said there was some desperate row years ago when judges were even worse than they are today. That's all, nobody knows about the . . . er . . . the smoke and things."

"I don't know whether to be pleased or disappointed." Judy laughed. "I always thought people believed I was up to no good with all the herbal remedies, bordering on the witch doctor nearly."

"I'm afraid people think that's very worthy, we'll have to make your image more villainous for you," Rupert said.

"Oh, for ages the unfortunate guards used to come and inspect my herb garden. I had a map of it for them in the end, and told them they must come in whenever they liked and that I would explain anything that looked a bit amiss. Then by the time I went to Dublin, they'd more or less written me off as a dangerous drugs pusher."

"You mean you're in the clear at last, after twenty years?"

"I don't know: sometimes I see the imprint of heavy boots around the camomile beds. Eternal vigilance."

"Do you hate Jack Hickey for it?"

"No, I said to you I never think of him. But you'd probably find that hard to believe, especially when I think of the children a lot, and to all intents and purposes I don't know them at all. They're strangers to me."

"Yes." Rupert obviously did find it hard to understand.

"It's the same with your mother, you know. Even though she doesn't let on, she thinks of you every day up in Dublin, she is aware of you in a way that it's hard to explain."

"Oh, I don't think so."

"I know it, I asked her once, just to know whether I was odd. She said that when you were away at school it was the same and at university and then when you went into the company. She says that often in her day she pauses and wonders what Rupert's doing now."

"Heavens," he said.

"Not for long, just for a second, you know, not brooding. But I expect you don't pause and wonder what she's doing."

"No, well I think of them a lot, of course, and since Father's been so badly and everything. I *do* think of them, of course," he said somewhat defensively.

"Stop getting upset, I was only using you as an example. Even if Andrew and Jessica had lived with me until they were grown up, they might still be away and not thinking about me anymore. It's the way things happen."

"You're dead easy to talk to, I wish I could talk to my mother like I talk to you. She's much older, of course," he added tactfully.

"She is indeed, she could nearly be *my* mother, too, but that's not the point. . . . You can never talk to your own mother, it's a law of nature."

She smiled and looked out the window, and when that Nancy Morris started talking sense for once about how to relax neck muscles, she joined in. She was afraid that young Rupert Green had too much of the Meaning of Life and the Wronged Woman's viewpoint. She decided to let him snuggle back into his expensive Italian jacket and dream whatever his dreams were.

She always got on better with young people. Someone once said she should have been a teacher, but she said no, that would have been putting herself on the other side of the desk from them. But she had many more young friends than people her own age. Bart Kennedy, for example. She could talk to Bart till the cows came home, and she only exchanged the time of day with his father. Kev Kennedy up there in the front of the bus, he was another story: it was very hard going having a chat with Kev. He'd remind you of a young lad who'd been posted at a doorway to give a warning when the master was approaching. And she liked Celia and Dee, she thought, looking around the bus. And young Tom Fitzgerald, he was a great lad. You couldn't like Nancy Morris, but she wasn't young anyway. Despite her years she was an old woman and always had been.

The young people of Rathdoon had always been a great help to her with the things she grew in the small bit of land that Jack Hickey had given her twenty long years ago. She was *different* from other people, they told her: she didn't pass judgment on them all, she didn't tell them they should be married, or settled down, or more provident or less drinky. And even though they may have thought she was half cracked they came and helped her dig and pick and dry and pack.

She never found the house lonely, no more than the flat in Dublin. Not after all this time. She liked her own company, she ate meals at odd times, she would listen to music at midnight if she liked. In the flat she wore padded earphones and thought she must look like some aging raver if anyone could see her, but it was a house with many bed-sits and flats and you couldn't wake civil servants and people who worked in big office blocks by playing your music through their walls. She did not feel the need of headphones in the lonely little lodge that was all Jack Hickey gave her from the big house. There was nobody near enough to hear, and the birds seemed to like hearing concertos and symphonies. They came and sat on the fence to listen more carefully.

The first time Tom had dropped her there he said he'd wait till she turned on the light. She had been pleased. He had enough nature in him to make sure that she got in safely. But then he was like all the youngsters she knew nowadays, far more natural and a lot more decency in them than the bombasts of her time. Like young Chris and Karen, who ran the health shop. They cared so much about it, they never wanted to be rich, to find a good line in anything that would be a snazzy seller and move quickly. They knew none of the jargon of the middle-aged businessman, and because they *were* idealistic and simple about things they were going to go to the wall. Her heart was heavy thinking about them. Maybe over in California somewhere Jessica and her husband, if she had one, were starting a health shop. Suppose they were in difficulties, wouldn't it be great if some kind older person were to help?

Judy only had a life interest in her gate lodge, she couldn't sell it even if she wanted to. She only rented her bed-sitter in Dublin, she had no savings. Once she had saved the fare to America and kept the post office book thumbed and touched so often, it was almost illegible. She had it always in her handbag and would finger it as if it were the ticket to the States. But not now. And she would love so dearly to be able to contribute to Chris and Karen and their dream. Because it was her dream, that shop too. They could make her a director or some such nonsense. If only she had a small lump sum and a regular little subsidy for them instead of taking a small wage from their very sparse little till.

She told Rupert not to waste his weekend coming up to help her in the garden. He had come home to be with his parents and he might as well stay in Dublin if he didn't spend his time with his dying father and give his mother some lift by being in the house all weekend. She was very firm about this, even when he said he'd like the work and the exercise. There'd be plenty of time for all that later. Let him not waste the last months or weeks of his father's life digging and hoeing in a stranger's garden.

"You're not a stranger, Judy, you're a friend," Rupert had said. She had been pleased at that too.

It was a bright, sunny September Saturday. The place seemed to be full of activity. You got weekends when that happened, when Rathdoon seemed to hum with excitement, and you got other weekends when not even a tornado coming down Patrick Street would shake them up. She saw Nancy Morris prowling up and down as if she were looking for lost treasure, Kev Kennedy was in and out of his father's shop with a face on him that made it clear the Mafia had put out a contract on him that morning. Every time you stepped out on the road there was someone driving into town that would nearly mow you down. Mrs. Casey's ramshackle car with Nancy Morris's mother in it, Mikey Burns going around the place with a set face on him, either doing messages or taking his brother Billy's children blackberrying. He was preoccupied to a degree she had never known. She saw Celia, too, during the day, driving a car with the intent look of someone in a rally. Tom Fitzgerald came in for a couple of hours to help in the garden, saying that since he hadn't had one single cross word from any member of his family or their spouses he felt things were too good to be true and he wouldn't risk staying in their company one more minute in case the whole thing would fall apart. She saw Dee Burke driving her mother to town, her face empty and sad, her mother talking away without seeing any emptiness at all beside her. Imagine anyone thinking the country was quiet. Some weekend she must ask Karen and Chris to come and stay—some bank holiday, if they were still in business.

Red Kennedy come in to help his brother Bart.

"Would these make a lot in Dublin?" he asked, looking at the little boxes of seeds.

Judy reflected. "Not a lot. In a way, we're just the wrong size. If it were a one-woman operation selling them at the side of the road, yes, there's a living; otherwise it should really be huge nurseries and big chain stores and all that. Still, we struggle on."

But it underlined to her the fruitlessness of it all, and the waste of effort not just from her but from decent young fellows like Bart and Red, like Mikey last week and Tom Fitzgerald's nephews when they were home from school. Was it really fair asking them to help in such a doomed business venture? They never did it for money, there wasn't any, but even in terms of their enthusiasm was it wrong to take so much of that as well? She thought of Chris and Karen in Dublin, anxious and also anxious on *her* behalf. They felt they owed her a place and a living because she had been so solidly supportive of them. How she wished that there had been a letter from a firm of American solicitors saying that the late James Jonathan Hickey of San Francisco, California, had left her a legacy and that her two children were going to fly over and deliver it personally. She often had fantasies about the children arriving, but this was the first time she had thought about the money. Yes, she'd even take a legacy from Jack, even if the children didn't deliver it. Anything to help Chris and Karen.

Soon she called a halt to the work. Judy's great success was that she stopped her helpers before they got tired.

There were huge glasses of her elderflower wine, which some said was better and reached you more powerfully than anything that was pulled as a pint down in Ryan's. They sat on a wall in the sun and drank it, and the Kennedys went home.

It was dark in the small house and she felt well when she had washed the earth off. She lay out on her window seat with her hands behind her head.

"You look like a cat," Rupert said as he came in. The door was never closed in summer, never locked in winter.

"That's good. Cats are very relaxed," Judy said.

"Are you relaxed?" he wanted to know.

"Not in my head. My head is worrying about inessential things like money. I never worried about money before."

"I suppose it was always easy to get it before."

"Yes, well, in the old days I told you how I got it, but since then I haven't needed it much. Now I'd like to keep the shop open, that's all."

Rupert sat down on a rocking chair that squeaked. He got up immediately and went for the oil.

She thanked him, but said his mother had a rocking chair, he should be sitting on that.

"There's nothing to say; I had to escape for a little bit," he pleaded.

"Only a little," Judy said.

"It's just that he tried to talk. He asks are there many houses on the market and things." Rupert had a face full of pain.

"But isn't that good? He's well enough, alert enough to know. Kind enough to care."

"Mother says that he really likes having me home. But it's nothing. Nothing at all."

"Only if you make it nothing for them." Judy lost her sympathy. She stood up and stretched. "Listen to me, Rupert Green, not one more minute of your father's time am I taking. I'm going for a walk in Jack Hickey's woods." He looked hurt.

"Please, boy, please. Think of all those years when you'll say, if only I could have just sat there and talked about any old thing. And for your mother, please. I'll meet you and you can buy me a pint of that synthetic stuff they call chilled wine down in Ryan's." He brightened up.

"Will you? That would be nice."

"When he's asleep, when he's had some return from you."

"I'm not *that* bad."

"No, but he was nearly fifty years of age when you arrived in his life and he had to be woken up with your teething and your screaming and then you didn't come into his office: he couldn't put Green and Son. It's Green and MacMahon. Go on, sit with him, talk about anything. It doesn't matter if it seems formal and meaningless, you're there, you're trying . . . that's all that matters."

"And what time will we go to Ryan's?" He was eager.

"*Rupert!* Will you give over! This is not a date. Ryan's is not a cocktail lounge, it's the only bar in Rathdoon. I'll be down there when I feel like it and you come when your father's well asleep and you've had a bit of time with your mother."

"Around nine or so?" he said, desperate to be specific.

"Around nine or so," she said resignedly.

She put on her boots. It was a long time since she had walked the woods. The three nuns who ran the ecumenical conferences and the diocesan seminars in the big house knew vaguely that Mrs. Hickey in the gate lodge had once lived in the big house. They were always polite to her and encouraged her to wander around if she ever felt like it. They were possibly relieved that the wildish looking woman in the Gypsy-style headscarves didn't take them up too often on their offer. She never went anywhere near the house, but she had told them it was nice to be able to feel free to walk under those old trees and pick flowers. Sometimes she would leave a great bunch of bluebells at their door, wrapped up in damp leaves. She never rang or asked to be entertained in the parlor. It was an ideal relationship.

Today she walked more purposefully. She didn't just stroll, following a whim or a line of young saplings. No, today she knew where she was heading.

It was still there in among the ivy-covered trees. Wild now, but hidden from the most determined searchers because of that old fallen tree. It looked as if there was nothing beyond. She eased herself over the tree and stood once more in her own little marijuana grove. She saw the cannabis plants that she had begun twenty-two years ago, many dead, many seeded and wasted. Some living though, some needing only a little attention.

It wouldn't take her long to find a proper outlet in Dublin. It must be done well away from the shop; Chris and Karen must never know.

She felt as strongly about this as her husband had felt that Andrew and Jessica must never know.

She felt the old quickening under her heart. It would be exciting to be back in the business again after all these years.

Kev

*K*ev thought he'd never get away from the Pelican. The Pelican was in one of those good moods, very rarely seen of late, where he'd ramble on about people known only to himself. There was a cast of thousands in the Pelican's stories and the same people never appeared twice. Kev listened attentively because if you missed the bit where your man came in one day and your other man was already in there and your old fellow came out the other door then you lost the whole grasp of it, and the Pelican might easily snap some kind of a question at you to make sure you were on the ball.

Kev was only afraid of the Pelican; he was *terrified* of some of the others. But even though the Pelican was not the highest in the terror stakes, Kev would have let the Lilac Bus go to Rathdoon without him rather than risk insulting this man whose big hooked nose was the cause of his name. You didn't mess with the Pelican. Kev didn't know much, but he knew that much.

Fortunately, the Pelican was hailed by someone more interesting and Kev was released; he sprinted around the corner. The bus was almost full. But he wasn't the last. Mikey Burns was rubbing his hands: oh please, may he not have any quiz games tonight. Mikey was perfectly nice when he quietened down, but all this "I say I say I say" like one of those comics on a music hall show on telly. He was no *good* at it, that was what was so hopeless; he always laughed in the wrong place. It would have been nice to sit beside Celia; that's what he liked best: she'd address about five civil sentences to him and then she'd leave him to his own thoughts, as she looked out the window. Or Rupert, he was a quiet fellow, too, and not toffee-nosed or anything. Kev's brothers, Bart and Red, were always surprised that he didn't seem to know Mrs. Hickey better. They were mad about her. In fact, his da was always saying that they'd go over to her place and dig her witch's brews in the garden and her lavender and her forget-me-nots, and they wouldn't dig their own potatoes, like men. Mrs. Hickey was nice enough, but she had a disconcerting way of looking right through you when she was talking, as if she didn't want any small talk. Neither did Kev, of course, want any small talk, but he didn't want that dark intense face with those X-ray eyes looking at him either. He always got the feeling that she saw just a little bit too much.

Kev worked in security—well, not real security, with helmets and coshes and alsatians and vans with no hand signals. More like being a porter really or a commissionaire, but it was called security. When anyone phoned down to the front desk to ask if a letter had been delivered by hand or if a visitor had arrived Kev answered the phone with the words, "Hallo. Security?"

Once he had got a phone call from his father asking him to bring down boxes of some new potato chips that had been advertised on the television and the place was going mad looking for it. Kev's father had been so entertained by Kev calling himself security that he had threatened to telephone every day just for the sheer pleasure of it. Kev had told him anxiously that they had been told to keep personal calls down to the minimum. But he shouldn't have worried; his father wasn't going to waste good money on hearing the same joke over and over.

Bart and Red didn't know what he came home for every weekend. It wasn't that they didn't want to see him, they were just as happy that he was back as not. But why *every* weekend? That was what would fox you. He didn't even go to the dance on a Saturday night. And he didn't have a crowd to drink with in Ryan's; he'd go in and out for a couple, but he wouldn't have a session there. The Kennedys had little or no conversation with their da, who had a cigarette in his mouth and the radio on full blast from morning to night. It was unlikely to be for company.

Kev knew that he was a bit of a mystery to them. And to Tom Fitzgerald, who had explained that the bus only made a profit if he could be sure of his seven passengers on a Friday. That's why he could do it so cheaply. You agreed to come on the bus every Friday for ten weeks, or if you couldn't you'd send someone in your place—not to Rathdoon, of course, but part of the way, or as far as the big town seventeen miles from home. Or if you could find nobody you still paid for your seat. That way it was half the cost of any other bus going that route, and what's more, it brought you to the door. Kev was getting out of the bus before ten o'clock and saying good night to Nancy Morris, who only lived across the street. He was home in Rathdoon safe. He would take a big breath of air and let it all out in a long sigh of relief. Tom often looked at him puzzled, and his father would nod welcomingly over the radio and tell him it was just coming up to the news. A mug of tea might be handed to him and a slice of shop cake cut. They had never known any other kind of cake, Kev and his brothers. Their mother had died long ago and even Bart, who could remember her, never knew her when she was well enough to make bread or cakes. When the news was over his father might ask had it been a hard week and were there any savages with crowbars in. He said there were more cases of violence in Dublin than there were in Chicago and he would never set his foot in the city again without an armed guard. Kev had tried to argue with him in the beginning, but now, he didn't bother. Anyway, nowadays he was beginning to think his father was right.

* * *

Nobody at work knew where Kev went at weekends: they all thought that he was some kind of lay monk or something and that he went to do good works but part of the goodness was that you didn't talk about it. The kind old Mr. Daly, one of the nicest people Kev had ever met, would shake his head in its uniform cap, full of admiration.

"I don't know why they give out about the younger generation," old Mr. Daly would say, "I really don't. There's that young Kev who works with us in the front hall, and he's off giving soup to winos and praying in front of the Blessed Sacrament, and teaching illiterates to read. Gone out of here like a bow from an arrow at six o'clock and we never hear hair nor hide of him until Monday morning."

Kev had never told one word of this fabrication to Mr. Daly or to anyone else. But having heard it, and seen that it was accepted, he let it pass. After all, if anyone came nosing around and asking questions, wasn't it better that old Mr. Daly and John and the others thought he was with the Simon Community or the Legion of Mary rather than knowing he caught a lilac-colored minibus as regularly as clockwork and sped out of Dublin and all its danger every Friday night.

Just suppose for one sickening minute that Daff or Crutch Casey or the Pelican came around, upset over something—well, there was nothing they could be told. Nobody knew where Kev went at weekends.

He had always had this secrecy, even when he was a young fellow. He remembered Bart telling a total stranger in the shop that their mother was dead, that she had died in the hospital after two months and a week. Kev would never have given that information to a woman who had come in to buy bars of chocolate and ice cream for the children in the car. No matter how nice she had been, no matter how much she had praised the three young lads serving in the shop because their father was out getting the shed at the back built to hold the gas cylinders and the briquettes. Kev would have told her nothing and put his arm in his mouth, which was a great way to stop having a conversation. But Bart and Red would tell anyone anything. . . . Bart even told about the time when Kev was seventeen and he had tried to get Deirdre Morris, who was the much nicer sister of Nancy, to come into a field with him and swore it was to show her a nest of small birds.

Deirdre Morris had thrown back her head laughing, pushed him over so that he fell in the mud and had gone home laughing. "A nest of small birds—is that what they call it nowadays?" Kev was shocked. To admit to such a lustful thing, and even worse, to admit to such a defeat. But no, Bart thought it was a scream; and that time that Deirdre had come back from America, married, with a baby called Shane, Bart was still able to laugh over it with her. And Red was the same, a demon dancer and he'd tell half the country their business, and about how they should have got an agency for tarmacadaming the place but his da hadn't moved quick enough and Billy Burns had got it first. Kev told nothing. But then Kev had much more to hide.

Celia arrived just after him and the doors were closed. They were off. Around the corner and through the open door of the pub he could see the Pelican holding a pint in one hand and a rolled-up newspaper in the other. A rolled paper was a great thing for making a point, for emphasizing something. That was the Pelican's style. Emphasizing things.

Mikey was unfortunately in top form tonight: tricks with matches and a glass, have them rolling in the aisles in a pub. Didn't poor Mikey realize that it was only drunks that suddenly started doing match tricks in a pub, or lonely people, or madmen. Not ordinary people, unless they were all in a group of friends, and if you had a group of friends, why would you need to do tricks anyway? He was explaining how to weight the matchbox; Kev looked out the window and saw the housing estates outside Dublin flashing by. Old Mr. Daly said to him that any day now Kev would find himself a young woman and they'd save for a house in a place like that and there'd be no knowing him ever after. People like Mr. Daly and Mikey knew nothing about the real world. There was Mikey going on about how you weighted the matchbox deliberately with a twopenny piece in it and it always fell over on the side you'd put the coin in, so you could bet someone that it would always fall on the side you said. Kev had looked at him vacantly.

"I bet you Bart or Red Eddie would love a trick like that," Mikey muttered. Kev knew they would. They had the time and the peace of mind to enjoy it.

Kev never told Mikey that he was a porter, too, in a way. Well, security really, but it was the same field. He never told any of them where he worked, except that it was in the big new block. You could be doing anything there, literally anything. They had civil servants and they had travel agencies, and airlines and small companies with only two people in them; they had a board in the hall with a list a mile long of the organizations who were tenants of the building. Kev just said he worked there; when anyone asked him what he did, he said this and that. It was safer. One morning he was standing there in his uniform and he saw Dee Burke coming. She was going with some papers to a solicitor on the fifth floor. Mr. Daly phoned up and announced her, and Kev had sorted furiously on the floor for something so she didn't see him. Later he wondered why. It couldn't matter whether Dee Burke knew that he worked at the front desk of the big new office block. She hardly thought when she went to buy her cigarettes at the Kennedy shop that their youngest son was the chairman of some company up in Dublin. He didn't even want her to think he was in a clerical job. Why hide then? Wiser. Like not walking on cracks in the road. No reason, but it just *seemed* the right thing to do.

Of course, in a way it was all this secrecy that had him where he was. If he had been a different type he'd never have got into this mess at all.

It began on his birthday, he was twenty-one. It was an ordinary working day. His father had sent him a ten-pound note in a card with a pink cat on it. Bart and Red Eddie had said that there would be great drink in Ryan's next Friday on account of it. Nobody else knew. He hadn't told Mr. Daly in case the old man might get a cake and embarrass him; he didn't tell anyone back up in the house where he had a room. They kept to themselves a lot and if they heard him saying he was twenty-one they'd feel they had to do something for him. He didn't tell anyone up at the pigeons either. In the lofts they didn't have time for birthdays and such things. So that day nobody in Dublin knew that Kevin, youngest son of Mr. Michael Kennedy, shop proprietor, and the late Mrs. Mary Rose Kennedy of Rathdoon had now reached twenty-one. He thought of it a lot all morning and somehow it began to seem overimportant to him. Other people had records played for them on radio programs, other people who were twenty-one had cards, lots of them, not just one. Dee Burke had a party in a hotel—he remembered hearing about it just a couple of months back; Bart and Red had been invited and Bart said he couldn't get into a monkey suit, but Red the demon dancer had hired one and had a great time. And even his own brothers had bits of celebration. Bart and all his pals had a barbecue down by the river; those were before every Tom, Dick, and Harry were having barbecues. They roasted a bit of beef and ate it between doorsteps of bread and it was gorgeous, and there'd been great singing and goings-on. And when Red was twenty-one two years back, there had been a crowd of them who had all come to the house for a few drinks and a cake, then they'd got into a truck and driven off to the dance. But nothing at all for Kev.

It got on his mind. He made an excuse to Mr. Daly and said that he wanted to go out the back for half an hour. He didn't feel well. Mr. Daly was so concerned that he immediately felt ashamed. Those were the days before he had been a regular disappearer at weekends, before Mr. Daly had assumed that he was an unsung and uncanonized saint.

He sat out in the loading area, as it was called, a place where vans could come with deliveries of paper, or messengers on those big motor bikes with speaking handlebars could leave their machines. He took out a cigarette and thought about other fellows his age and wondered why he had been so anxious to get away and why he had ever thought it would be any better. Four men were loading a van efficiently. A fifth was standing leaning on a crutch and staring around him idly. Into the van were going sanitary fittings, hand basins, lavatories, small water heaters. Without haste but with commendable speed they loaded.

Kev dragged his cigarette. They must be getting new fitments somewhere upstairs, that looked like a big contract. Wait. He hadn't seen any of them come through security, and everyone had to come to the front desk. Even if they went straight out the door again and were sent around to the loading bay. The rules said desk first.

His eyes took on the merest flicker of interest, but it was enough to alert the man with the bent leg leaning so casually on the crutch.

"Not wearing a cap, didn't notice him," he said out of the corner of his mouth.

A big man with a beak-shaped nose paused momentarily and then slid from the human chain that was stacking the fitments. He strolled over to Kevin, whose stomach knotted in fright. He realized like a shower of cold rain coming down his gullet that this was a Job, these were five men taking fitments *out* of the new building, fitments that would turn up again in houses all over the city. He swallowed hard.

The Pelican walked slowly: he didn't look a bit furtive, nor did he look worried.

"Can I have a smoke?" he asked casually. Behind him the loading continued regular as clockwork, innocent as anything.

"Yes, um." Kev handed him the packet.

"What are you doing with yourself here?" The Pelican's eyes narrowed.

The question was perfectly polite. It could have been a gentle inquiry of any fellow lounger on a summer morning. He might even have added something like "on this fine day." But he hadn't. The Pelican and all of them were waiting to know what Kevin would say and Kevin knew that what he said now was probably going to be the most important question he ever answered in his life.

"It's my twenty-first birthday," he said. "And I got annoyed sitting inside there in security and nobody knowing, so I thought I'd come out here and have a bit of a smoke, anyway, to celebrate."

There was absolutely no doubt that what he said was true. You didn't need a lie detector or the experience of years with truth drugs to know that Kev Kennedy had given a perfectly accurate account of why he was there, and something about him made the Pelican believe that there was going to be no trouble here.

"Well, when we're finished here maybe we'll buy a drink at your lunch hour. A fellow shouldn't be twenty-one and have nobody know."

"That's what I think," Kev said eagerly, averting his eyes from the biggest and most barefaced theft from the building where he was meant to be part of security. It seemed to be winding up now, the convoy were closing the doors and getting into the van.

"So, what is it? One o'clock?" The Pelican's nose was like a scythe, so large and menacing did it appear, and his eyes were like two slits.

"It's a bit difficult at lunchtime, you see, I only get forty-five minutes and I suppose you'll be moving on out of the area." Kev's face was innocent.

"But where would you like your birthday drink then, and when?" There was no area for argument in the proposal, only a small margin of latitude for the time and place.

"Well, wherever you like, of course, and at about six. Is that all right?"

Kev was eager. The Pelican nodded. He named a city-center pub.

"We'll give you a drink each, and as you no doubt saw there's five of us, so that's five drinks."

"Oh, God, that would be great altogether," Kev said. "Are there five of you? I didn't notice."

The Pelican nodded approvingly. He swung his way back to the van and in beside the driver, who looked like a champion wrestler.

"Six o'clock," he called cheerfully out the window.

It wasn't discovered until four-thirty. A lot of offices on the sixth floor weren't occupied yet. Some people just assumed that the bathrooms were being refitted, and sighing, had gone to other floors. It was only when one of the secretaries said she was getting dropped arches and told Mr. Daly that it was an extraordinary thing to think that brand-new cloakrooms should be redone within three months, that any kind of alarm was raised. The broad-daylightness of it all staggered them. The guards were called, the confusion was enormous. Kev had difficulty in getting away by six. He was ninety percent sure that they wouldn't be there. They could be walking into a trap for all they knew. How were they to know that they were dealing with Kev Kennedy who never told anybody anything? They might have assumed he would have plainclothes guards drinking pints of shandy all around the pub. But just in case. And just in case they came back and dealt with him. After all, they knew where he worked, he knew nothing about them.

They were all there.

"There was a bit of commotion at work, I got delayed," he said.

"Ah, you would all right," said the Pelican generously. He was introduced to Daff and John, and Ned and Crutch Casey.

"What's your real name?" he asked the man with the twisted leg.

"Crutch," the man said, surprised to be asked.

They each bought him a pint and they raised their glasses solemnly and said Happy Birthday at each round. By the fourth round he was feeling very wretched. He had never drunk more than three pints in Ryan's and never more than two anywhere else. Ryan's led you to be daring because even if you fell down you got home on all fours without too much difficulty.

Daff was the man like a wrestler. Kev wondered why he was called that, but he decided it might not be wise. Daff bought the last drink and handed Kev an envelope.

"We were sorry to see a culchie all on his own with no one to wish him a happy birthday, so that's a small present from Pelican, Crutch, John, Ned and me." He smiled as if he were a foolish, generous uncle dying for the nephew to open the electric train set and begin to call out with excitement.

Kev politely opened the envelope and saw a bundle of blue twenty-pound notes. The room went backwards and forwards and began to move slowly around to the left. He steadied himself on the bar stool.

"I couldn't take this, sure you don't know me at all."

"And you don't know us." Daff beamed.

"Which is as it should be," the Pelican said approvingly.

"But I'd not know you, without . . . without this, you know."

He looked at the envelope as if it contained explosives. There were at least six notes, maybe more. He didn't want to count them.

"Ah, but this is better, this *marks* the day for all of us. Why don't we meet here every week around this time, and if you've that invested properly then you could buy us a drink, and slowly we could sort of *get* to know each other."

Kev's mouth felt full of lemon juice.

"Well, I'd love to . . . sort of keep in touch with you all . . . but honestly, this is too much. Like, I mean, I'd feel bad."

"Not at all, you wouldn't." The Pelican smiled and they were gone.

Every Tuesday since he had met them; sometimes it was just a drink. Sometimes it was more. Once it had been a driving job. He would never forget it to his dying day. They went into a new block of flats and carefully unrolled the brand-new stair carpet. They had heard that the fitting men were coming that afternoon, so they had anticipated the visit by removing every scrap of it. The timing had been of the essence on that one. The expensive wool carpet had arrived that morning; there was only a four-hour period when it could be removed, and that meant watching the flats very carefully in case any untoward inquiries were made. It was all completely successful, of course, like all their enterprises seemed to be. Kev had taken a day off work for the carpet heist, but the carpet heist had taken years off his life. He felt as if he had been put down on the street and the whole crowd coming out of Moran Park had walked over him. He couldn't understand how they remained so untouched. Crutch Casey told of horses that had fallen at the last fence. Ned and John were more dog people, they talked of evil-minded and corrupt greyhounds who *knew* how to slow down, through some instinct. The Pelican told long tales full of people that nobody knew, and Daff seemed to say nothing much, but he was as relaxed as a man coming out after a swim about to light his pipe on the beach on a sunny day.

They never told him he *had* to join in, and they didn't ask him so much that he felt he should run away to America to escape them. Often he didn't have to do anything except what they called "re-sorting." That might mean wrapping a whole load of Waterford glass, which arrived from a hotel before it got time to get out of its boxes, into different kind of containers. Each glass to be held carefully and sorted according to type, wrapped in purple tissue paper in gift boxes of six. He became quite an authority on the various designs, or suites as they were called, and decided that the Colleen Suite was his favorite; and that when he got married he would have two dozen Colleen brandy glasses and use them around the house as ordinary everyday glasses, or in the bathroom for his toothbrush. Then he remembered what he was doing and the fantasy would disappear. He would look around the garage and keep parceling in the nice anonymous gift boxes. He never knew where they went, and what happened to them. He never asked. Not once. That's why they liked him, that's why they trusted him utterly. From that very first day in the loading area they thought he was one of their own, and it was too late now to tell them that he wasn't. The longer it went on, the more ludicrous it would be trying to get out.

On calmer days Kev asked himself what was so terrible. They never took from individuals, they didn't do people's houses and flats. It was companies who had to replace miles of red wool carpet, boxes of prestigious glassware, rooms full of sanitary fittings. They never did over old women, young couples; they never carried a weapon, not even a cosh. In many ways they weren't bad fellows at all. Of course, they never actually went out to work in a normal way, and they did lie to people, with their clipboards and their air of being perfectly legitimate. And people did get into trouble after they'd visited places, like poor old Mr. Daly, who'd been hauled in by everyone and though it was never said, the thought had been in the air that he might be getting too old for the job. And they stole. They stole things almost every week and by no standards could that be a thing that Kev Kennedy from Rathdoon wanted to be in. Or worse, caught in. It was unthinkable. They still talked about that young fellow who was a cousin of the Fitzgeralds and worked in their shop for a bit; he was given three years for doing a post office in Cork. The whole of Rathdoon had buzzed with it for months and Mrs. Fitzgerald, Tom's mother, had said she hoped everyone realized that he wasn't a first cousin, he was a very far out one, and they had tried to give him a start and look at the thanks they got. Could you imagine what old Da would have to go through? And all Red's hopes of getting some gorgeous wife would go for their tea, and poor Bart was so decent and helpful, wouldn't it be a shame on him forever?

But how did you get out? He couldn't live in a city that contained the Pelican and Daff and Crutch Casey if they thought he had ratted on them. There was no point trying to pretend that he had left town or anything. They knew everything: it was their business to know things, to know when deliveries were expected, when watchmen went for their coffee, when regular porters were on holidays, when managers were young and nervous, when shops were too busy to notice their furniture being loaded into private vans. They knew where Kev lived and worked; he wouldn't dream of lying to them.

But he got out of weekend work. That's when they did some of their bigger jobs, and he wanted to be well away from it. He told them vaguely that he had to go out of town. He had been going home that very first weekend after they met him and so it had seemed a natural continuation, not a new pattern of behavior. He didn't say it was Rathdoon, he didn't say it was home, but they knew he wasn't lying when he was saying that he went out of town for weekends. Crutch Casey had said good night to him one Sunday night outside the house where he had a room, and Kev knew that it was just a routine inspection. He had been cleared now; even the Pelican, whom he had met by accident just on the corner, knew that he was leaving Dublin for the weekend—he didn't even bother to check.

But how could he get out of working for them midweek? Some of the jobs were getting bigger and Kev was getting tenser. Once or twice Daff had asked him not to be so jumpy—that he was like some actor playing a nervous crook in an old black-and-white B movie. It was fine for Daff, who didn't have a nerve in his body. Simply fine for him. Others didn't find it so easy. The very sight of a guard was enough to weaken Kev's legs, even the shadow of anyone fairly big was enough to make him jump. Oddly enough it hadn't made him feel guilty about religion. He went to Mass, and at Christmas and Easter to communion; he knew that God knew that there wasn't much sin involved. No grievous bodily harm or anything. But he had never been much of a one for talking to God individually like you were meant to: he didn't feel like putting the question personally. And there was nobody else, really, *but* God, when all was said and done, because everyone else would have a very strong view one way or the other, and mainly the other. Like get out of that gang at a rate of knots, Kev Kennedy, and stop acting the eejit.

Mikey's poor, kind face was there a few inches from him. Mikey Burns, who'd be the kind of bank porter that would get shot in a raid—certainly not like Kev, the kind of security man who had become best buddies with the gang that had ripped off all the fittings from the place where he worked. Mikey Burns, sleeping with a little smile, dreaming about something—jokes with glasses of water and coins maybe—and there was he, Kev, who had driven getaway vans and done watch duty and helped to reparcel stolen goods. Kev felt alien as he looked out at the darkening countryside. Lonely and guilty as hell.

His father told him after the news that Red had notions about a farmer's daughter and was going to bring her to tea during the weekend no less, and they were all to keep their shoes on, talk nicely and put butter on a plate and the milk in a jug. He said that he thought Bart might as well join the Franciscans and put on sandals and carry a begging bowl for all the good he was ever going to do with his life and his share of the business. When he wasn't digging up Mrs. Hickey's foxgloves and hemlocks, or whatever it was she grew, he was helping Mrs. Ryan in the pub to stand on her own two shaky legs and serving the customers from behind the bar and not a penny piece was he getting from either of them. He was surprised that Bart hadn't gone into Fitzgerald's shop and said that if they'd like someone to stand there and serve for a few days a week without wages he'd be happy to do it. Kev didn't know what to say to this. He nibbled a slice of cake and thought about the difference between people. There was Daff, who had a nice big open face like Bart, organizing the transfer of twenty microwave ovens from one warehouse to another by a deceptively simple scheme that involved Ned, who was the most forgettable of them all, going up with a sheaf of papers, an air of bewilderment, and an instruction that they were apparently to go back to have something checked. And there was Bart Kennedy, who had a big open face like Daff, digging Judy Hickey's garden for her and helping Celia's mother to stay upright in Ryan's. God, what different worlds he moved in; Kev thought with a shudder at the danger of it all. "Are you not going down to the pub?" his father asked.

"No, I'm tired after the week and the long journey. I'll just go up and lie on my bed," he said.

His father shook his head: "I really wish I knew what brings you home, you do so little when you arrive, and you've lost your interest in football entirely. You could have been a good footballer if you'd put your mind to it."

"No, I was never any good. You only say that because you wanted a son a county footballer. I'm no good."

"Well, what *does* bring you back here? What are you running from . . . ?" He hadn't finished, but Kev's cup was in pieces on the floor and his face was snow-white.

"Running, what do you mean?"

"I mean, is it the violence up there or the dirt, or those blackguards roaming in tribes or what? Haven't you good wages, and you're always very generous giving me the few quid here . . . but a young man of your age, you should be up to all kinds of devilment and diversions, shouldn't you?"

"I don't know, Da, I don't think I was ever much good at anything, football, devilment, anything." He sounded very glum.

"Haven't you got a fine job up in one of the finest buildings in the land, and you earn your own living, which is more than those two boyos there—oh, they're a great pair I have on my hands. One a sort of Martin de Porres, going around the place giving half his cloak to everyone he meets; one a dandy who has the bright red hair nearly combed off his scalp and the mirrors nearly cracked in bits staring into them. You're the best of them, Kev, don't be running yourself down."

Kev Kennedy went up to bed without a word, and he lay there as the sounds of Rathdoon, which were not very loud, went past his window, a small window over the shop, which looked out on the main street.

Red's girl was coming the very next day it turned out, so they all had to do a spring clean on the back room. There were to be cups instead of mugs, a clean cloth was spread and bread was cut on a tray and then put onto a plate to avoid all the crumbs. They took ham and tomatoes and a bottle of salad cream from the shop, and Red hard-boiled three eggs.

"This is a feast—she'll marry you immediately," Bart said when he saw Red looking speculatively at some of the frozen cakes in the cold-food section.

"Quit laughing and keep looking around the room to see what it would look like to a new eye." Red had it bad this time. Her name was Majella and she was an only child. She was used to much greater style than the three Kennedy brothers and their father could provide, even if they had been trying seriously. But none of them except Red was making much of an effort: their father wanted to be in his shop, Bart wanted to get over to Judy Hickey, and Kev wanted to go off down by the river, where he felt nice and quiet and miles from all that was happening at this very moment to microwave ovens in a warehouse in Dublin.

Majella was arriving at five o'clock. Her father would give her a lift, but he wouldn't call in; it was much too early for that yet. They did a deal, the brothers. Bart and Kev agreed to wear proper ties and jackets and have polished shoes. Red agreed to go over to Judy Hickey's and put in two hours because she needed it this weekend particularly and because it would keep him calm. There would be no bad language, eating with fingers, and picking of teeth, but in return Red would not embarrass them by giving moon-faced sick-calf impersonations, nor would he ask them to delight Majella with stories of their exotic lives. When the bell rang to say that somebody had come into the shop, they would go in order of seniority. Da first, then Bart, then Kev, then Da and so on. Red was not to abandon them to talk to Majella on their own.

She was a lovely big girl with no nonsense in her, and by the time they had sat her down she was like part of the family. She said they must be great fellows altogether to have the butter on the plate and the milk not in a bottle but in a jug. Whenever she went over to her cousin's place they were all putting their dirty knives into the butter at once; they needed a woman to civilize them. Red began to look like a sick calf when she talked of the civilizing influence of a woman, and he had to be kicked until he dropped it again. Majella said she was going to do the washing up and they could all dry, and seeing out of the corner of her eye that the dishcloths were not all they might be she called to Red to bring a new packet out of the shop.

"Isn't it paradise to be here!" she said with a big smile at them all. "Who could want anything better than a shop right off your own living room?"

They had dried up in no time; the big room looked better somehow than it had done for years. Majella said that maybe she and Red might go for a bit of a tour around Rathdoon now and get out of everyone's way. By half past six she had a blushing, delighted Red firmly by the arm and was linking him on her own little lap of honor around the community she had decided to join.

"Oh, there's no escape there, that knot will be tied, poor Red." Bart laughed good-naturedly about the fate that could well be happening to his brother.

"Will you stop that nonsense: poor Red, my hat! Wouldn't a girl have to be half mad or have the courage of a lion to marry any one of the three of you." His father sounded very pessimistic indeed.

"Would you say she *is* mad?" Kev asked interestedly. "She was a very nice class of a girl, I thought."

"Of course she's nice, she's far too good for him. The thing is, will she realize it in time?" Bart and Kev exchanged glances. Their father seemed to be torn between the delight of having the lovely, laughing Majella around the place and the strictly honest course of action, which was to warn the girl that his son was a bad bargain.

"Let her work it out for herself maybe?" Bart suggested and his father looked relieved.

Bart had a lot of sense, Kev realized, suddenly. He wasn't just a do-gooder and a big innocent. But he was the other side of the tracks now, he wasn't in the Underworld like Kev was, there could be no talking to him about the problem.

"Would you fancy an early pint down in Ryan's before the mob gets in there?" Bart said to him. Kev was pleased.

"That'd be the way to do it," he said sagely. Their father had gone back to the shop and was twiddling the dial for the news.

They walked down the road. It was quiet—most people were in at their tea; the sound of the half-past six news that their father was listening to back in the shop came from several windows. Down they walked, past Billy Burns's chip shop. Billy wasn't there today, just Mikey and that bright little Treasa who worked there. No sign of the new girl Eileen—well, she had always looked too good to spend her day lifting pieces of cod or wings of chicken out of a deep fryer in Rathdoon. They came to the bridge. Bart leaned over and looked at the river. They used to race sticks under the bridge here when they were kids, and there were always so many arguments about whose stick had won, Bart invented a system of tying different colored threads onto each one. It seemed very long ago.

"What's eating you?" Bart asked.

"I don't know what you mean."

"I'm not the world's brainiest man, but I'm not blind either. Tell me, Kev, can't you? It can't be any worse when you've told me. It might even be a bit better. Like, I'm not going to be saying, aren't you an eejit, or blame you or anything, but there's something terribly wrong up in Dublin, isn't there?"

"Yes," Kev said.

"Before Red fell so much in love that he can't think of anything else, he and I were going to go up there one day on the excursion and try and sort it out, whatever it was."

Kev gulped with gratitude at the thought of his two brothers taking on a heavy gang like Daff, the Pelican, Crutch Casey, and their team.

"What did *you* think the problems might be?" he asked nervously, fishing to see had Bart any notion of how bad things were or was he still in a world like the playground of the infants' school.

"I thought it might be a girl you got into trouble, but it's going on too long for that. I thought it might be a debt—you know, poker or the horses— but you don't seem to have any interest in either."

Bart's big innocent face looked puzzled. Kev drew a long breath. Well, it seemed that Bart could take on that much anyway. What about the next step? Could Bart listen to the story that had begun on his twenty-first birthday a year and a half ago, or would he run for the guards? Kev didn't know. Bart was shaping a stick and tying a bit of string around it.

"Here," he said to Kev, "let this be yours: I'll beat you any day with my one." They threw the sticks over the side and rushed across to see them coming through. Kev's stick was in front.

"Would you beat that?" Bart seemed surprised. "I've been up here practicing and I thought I had the shape of stick that ran best with the flow."

Kev began to tell him; in fact, once started it tumbled out of him: a mixture of names and commodities, Crutch Caseys and microwaves, Daffs and cut glass, Pelicans and Axminster carpet. Kev had no starring role the way he told it, his only stroke of genius had been to go home every weekend on the Lilac Bus to avoid even more major crime in the city at weekends. He was in now and there was no getting out. Bart must know that; they'd all seen the films, they knew the plot. If Kev said to Daff that he'd had enough, thank you, he couldn't answer for the consequences but he knew it'd be awful. He didn't think they'd beat him up: they never used violence, he said almost pleadingly to Bart. But they would punish him. They'd send the guards around to his house or to work, or they'd send a note to Mr. Daly accusing Kev of giving the tip-off about the cloakroom fittings that time. It was a nightmare: he was in it forever.

He hardly dared to look at Bart during some of the confession, and once or twice he gave the odd glance and got the feeling that Bart was half smiling.

Maybe he didn't understand the hugeness of it all. Once he was almost certain he got a smile and Bart had hastily put his hand over his face.

"So now, you see, I'm caught entirely," he ended.

"I don't think so," Bart said slowly.

"But it's not *like* here, Bart. You don't know, they're different from us. They're not our type of people."

"But they must have thought you were their kind of person, otherwise they wouldn't have pulled you in," Bart said.

"But I *told* you how that happened. I'm not a thief by nature, I'm fairly happy to work for my wages. Not very, but fairly. I'm not any good as a criminal."

"No, I don't mean their type as a thief; you're secretive like they are. That's what they liked about you—you're not a blabber about who you know, what you do. That'll make them think you won't blab about them."

"Well, I don't—haven't until now, that is."

"So that's how you get out if you want to. Tell them you're in with another lot now. No hard feelings, handshakes, pints all around, and that's it."

"Bart, you haven't any idea—"

"But you see, you keep up this hard-man image with them, except once or twice when you've had a fit of the shivers. You never try to talk them out of it, or discuss what they do with the stuff. They probably think you're a silent pro and someone has made you a better offer."

"They wouldn't have such a high regard for me as that."

"They must have a very high regard for you if they let you in on all their jobs. No, leave them as you joined them, with no chat, no explanations except the one they are owed. That you've got a new scene."

Bart talking about scenes, Bart saying that these gangsters are owed an explanation—it was like the end of the world.

"I don't think I'd be able to go through with it."

"You were able to join them; that was harder."

"And should I give them back the money?"

"Give them *what*?"

"My share, I mean, if I'm not staying on, like?"

"Your share . . . you have it still?"

"Of course I do, I didn't spend any of it, in case . . . you know . . . the guards and everything and a court case and I'd have to give it all back."

"Where is it?"

"It's upstairs in the room."

"In Dublin?"

"No, here, back at the house. Under the bed."

"You're not serious."

"But what else would I do with it, Bart? I carry it with me home and back each weekend in a parcel with my clothes."

"How much is it all? Your share?"

"I'm afraid it's about four thousand, two hundred pounds," Kev said with his eyes cast down.

Eventually he raised his glance and Bart was smiling at him with pride.

"Isn't that the direct intervention of God?" Bart said to him. Kev would never have seen it like that; however confused his relationship with God was and however nonpersonal it had become, he couldn't imagine that the Almighty was delighted with such a sum of stolen money arriving under a bed in Rathdoon.

"This solves all our problems," Bart said. "When Romeo back there went courting Majella, the only fly in the ointment was would we have enough to build on a bit at the back. We were afraid it would get a bit crowded with us all on top of each other, and we saw the very thing we wanted, a kind of ready-made extension that they dig foundations for and then sort of plant on top of. Do you follow?"

Kev nodded nervously.

"But Red and I were afraid you were in some kind of financial trouble and we'd better not get ourselves too far into a loan. But here you are, a millionaire. Now we can go ahead, and if you'd like to contribute a bit . . ."

"Yes, well, of course I would, but don't you think if I'm getting out of their gang I should *offer* them the share back?"

"What kind of criminal are you at all?" roared Bart. "Won't they know immediately you're a ninny if you start a caper like that. You've got to consider that your wages, your share of the deal. Now you're meant to be going on to a bigger one, you eejit; you're not meant to be giving them conscience money."

"No."

"And there's no way you can give it to the carpet people or the lavatory makers or the microwave people—"

"I wasn't in on the microwave—that's this weekend."

"See?" Bart felt this proved some point. "So what are you going to do with it—wouldn't building up the family home be as good as anything?"

Kev was astonished. No blame, no lecture, no accusation. Sheer hard practical advice, as if he knew the kind of people that Daff and the Pelican were. Because when you thought of it, that was *exactly* the way to go about it. And then he need never see them again.

"I'll give it all to you tonight, Bart," he said eagerly. "Where will we say we got it? Like if anyone asks?"

"You'll keep some of it, put it in the post office, but we'll say nothing to anyone, like you've been doing all your life. We'll get in touch with those people about the extension on Monday. What could be more natural than that country eejits like us would have money in a paper bag under the bed, they'll only be delighted—no VAT, nothing."

Kev was stunned. Saint Bart, in the black economy.

"Thanks to your very generous donation, we'll be able to get the bigger extension, and there'll be plenty of room if Majella produces a brood of Kennedys."

A stone fell off the bridge and into the water and Kev Kennedy didn't jump at all, and his eyes didn't widen with anxiety.

Rupert

He bought a packet of mints because Judy Hickey had told him last week that he reeked of garlic, and much as she loved all good herby smells she didn't want to sit cooped up beside a porous sponge of garlic for three hours on a small minibus. Funny, Judy: if he had met her in Dublin, he would never have suspected that she came from home. She wasn't a Rathdoon sort of person. He had told her that once and she had retorted that neither was he—a thin, pale, artistic young Protestant: what could be more unlikely?

But she was wrong. There were handfuls of Protestants in every town in the West; they were as much part of the place as the mountains and the phone boxes and the small beautiful churches with hardly any attendance standing dwarfed by the newer Catholic churches, which were bursting at the seams. No use explaining that to Judy, trying to tell her that she was much more unusual, dark and Gypsylike, living in a small gate lodge at the end of the drive from Doon House, growing herbs and working all week in a health-food shop in Dublin. In another time she'd have been burned as a witch without any discussion, he had once told her. Judy had said gloomily that the way the country was going it could happen yet, so he shouldn't joke about it.

He smelled of garlic because he had eaten a very good lunch. He always did on a Friday; that was because he wouldn't be back again until late on Sunday night when it was the wrong time to have a meal. So Friday lunchtime was the only opportunity they could get to have anything approaching a relaxed weekend meal before he went back to Rathdoon for the weekend. Of course there *was* the rest of the week, but it wasn't quite the same, as there was work next day, and anyway there was something about a weekend that gave you more time —more anticipation. He hated not having his weekends in Dublin. He hated going home on the Lilac Bus.

Rupert had never had an argument with his father in his whole life. And he could remember only three differences of opinion with his mother. Those went back to the time he was away at school and she had written three times to the headmaster to receive assurances that the beds were aired. He knew nobody else in the world who had such a relationship with their parents. Everyone else fought and forgave and loved or hated and stormed and railed or became fiercely protective. Nobody had this polite, courteous distance based entirely on gratitude and duty. Nobody else who felt such irritation couldn't express it.

They didn't really need him, that was his whole point, and he wished them well, but he didn't need them either. So why should the pretense be kept up? It made it so much harder on all of them. Not only on Rupert—but maybe it was a little harder on him, he felt—after all, their lives were ending. His hadn't really begun and couldn't begin as things were.

There hadn't even been a row when Rupert had decided to give up his law studies. He had been apprenticed to a firm in Dublin, begun his lectures with the Incorporated Law Society and at the same time read for a degree in Trinity. It wasn't a superhuman load—a lot of people did it easily—but Rupert never took to it. Not any of it. The bit he liked best, oddly, was the office. He was quite happy doing the clerical work, the part that Dee Burke, who worked there now, said she hated. Rupert had made few friends in Trinity, which surprised him; he thought it would be like school, which had been fine. But it was very different and he felt totally outside it all.

He had come home the weekend he knew he had failed his First Law with a heavy heart. He hadn't tried to excuse himself, he just apologized as if to a kind stranger, and his father accepted the apology as if it had been given by a kind stranger. They had sat one on either side of the table while his mother looked left and right at whoever was speaking.

Rupert said it was a great waste of his father's money and a disgrace to him in his profession. His father had brushed these things aside: heavens no, people often failed their first examination, there was no cause for alarm, some of the greatest lawyers claimed that they had never been showy scholars. No need for any regrets, it should all be written off as part of sowing wild oats, part of getting your freedom. Next year it would be more serious, head in book, down to it, wasn't that right?

On into the night Rupert had talked, saying that he wasn't cut out for it. It wasn't what he wanted. He didn't believe he would love it when he was in his father's office: he didn't love the office he was apprenticed to in Dublin, he only liked the more mechanical parts. He couldn't get interested in the theory of the law or the way it was administered. He was so sorry it had turned out like this, but wasn't it better that they should know now rather than discover later. They agreed logically that it was. They asked him what *did* he want. He didn't know; he had been so sure that he would like Trinity, and like studying law, he had never given it much thought before. He liked thinking about the way people lived and their houses and all that. But wasn't it going to be very hard to try to get accepted to study architecture? his father wondered. He didn't mean study it; he didn't know, Rupert said desperately. He would get a job, that's what he'd do. His parents didn't understand this: they thought you had to have a degree to get a job, the kind of job Rupert would want. When he found the position as a junior in the estate agent's, they said they were pleased if that's what he wanted. They didn't sound displeased, they sounded remote as they always had been.

His father was remote when he told Rupert that the time had come to get someone else into the office and that if Rupert was absolutely sure that he didn't intend to come into the profession he was going to offer a position to

David MacMahon's son. Rupert assured him it would be fine, and got only a minor start when he realized that young MacMahon would have to be offered a partnership and the name of the office would be repainted to read Green and MacMahon. Once or twice they had asked him whether he had thought of coming back to Rathdoon and setting up his own little auctioneering business. There must be plenty of sites being sold and garages and people liked to keep things local. "It might be no harm to get in before Billy Burns sets one up, he's started everything else in the town," his mother had said, but firmly and politely he had assured them that this was not going to happen. He left them in no doubt that his plans involved staying in Dublin. This had happened on the day his mother had said that she wondered whether they should put a new roof on the house or not. Sometimes she felt that the one she had would do for their time and wasn't that all it would be needed for . . . ? Rupert had answered her levelly as if she had been asking no deeper question or making no last desperate plea. He talked of roofs and the value they added to houses and gave the pros and cons as he knew them, bringing himself no more into their plans than if he had been asked by a passing tourist.

His mother asked a bit coyly once or twice if he met any nice girls in Dublin. She didn't ask that anymore. He must have given her some fairly firm answers, because he was only twenty-five, an age when you might be assumed to be still meeting girls. If people didn't know that you never met girls, you only met Jimmy.

Rupert's throat tightened just thinking of Jimmy. They had met for lunch this Friday; it had now become a bit of a ritual. Jimmy had no classes on a Friday afternoon: they had found the boys didn't study too well and had given them games or art or music. So Jimmy could jump into his little car and drive off to meet him. Rupert had noticed with an alarm mixed with pleasure that Dublin was becoming very slap-happy on Friday afternoons anyway, and not just in schools. At the office they did very little business and people seemed to be leaving for home—even if it was just the suburbs—earlier and earlier. If the noise in a nearby pub was anything to go by, those particular workers of the world weren't going to do much to change it when they got back to their desks —if they got back. Still, it was nice for Rupert. He could take a long lunch hour with no questions asked. They had found a restaurant that both of them liked (not easy, as they had such arguments about food), and it was a very happy couple of hours.

Jimmy insisted that he go home every weekend; it was even Jimmy who found the Lilac Bus for him. Jimmy said it was a pity that they couldn't have weekends, but it wouldn't be forever, and since the old man had always been so undemanding, wouldn't it only be right to go back to him now in his last few months? And it must be desperate on his mother waiting all week for him: of course he had to go. Jimmy wouldn't even let him pretend he had flu, not even for one weekend. He was very definite about it.

Jimmy was definite about everything; it was part of his charm. He never wondered about anything or deliberated or weighed things up. And if as it turned out sometimes he was utterly wrong, then he was equally definite about that.

"I was all wrong about the man who invented those cats' eyes for the road at night. I was thinking about somebody totally different. I couldn't have been more wrong." Then he would go ahead with the new view. But he had never changed his view about Rupert going home at weekends; that was an absolute.

Jimmy didn't have any home to go off to on a Friday. Jimmy's home was right there in Dublin. He was the youngest of six, and his two sisters and three brothers had gone exactly the way their father wanted, which was into the newspaper vendor business. Some had pitches on good corners, others had roofs over their heads and sold ice creams and birthday cards as well. But Jimmy's father was in the habit of saying gloomily, "There's always one arty-farty cuckoo in the nest, one who won't listen to reason." Jimmy had been a bit of a pet when he was a youngster: they all encouraged him at his books, and then to university and into teaching in a very posh school. They made jokes about him being gay, but it was never said straight out whether they believed he was or not. Anyone overeducated, as they regarded him, would have had the same abuse, the accusations of being limp-wristed, the mockery of his clothes, the vain search for an earring and the camp clichés from the television: "Ooh Jimmy, you are awful."

But he went there every Wednesday evening. They all called in on the small crowded house; they talked about rivals and which magazine would be seized by the censor as soon as somebody in authority had a look at it. They talked of how the dailies were doing and how there was no point in taking this magazine because it wouldn't survive to a second issue. They told each other how they had long, narrow sticks and beat the hands off any kid stealing a comic. Jimmy would join in by asking questions. He always brought a cake, a big creamy one from the nice delicatessen where they often went. His family would have a communal coronary arrest if they knew how much the cake cost. His mother used to say it was a nice piece of cake even though the smallest bit soggy just in the middle. Jimmy would scoop up the bit where the Cointreau or Calvados had concentrated and eat it with a spoon. His brothers said it was a very fair cake, and reminded them of children's trifle.

It would be so easy to have a family like Jimmy's. They asked so little of him; they were so complete in themselves. If Jimmy were to disappear from their lives forever, he would be spoken of affectionately, but if Rupert were to forgo just one weekend going home on the Lilac Bus it would be a national crisis for the Green family. Sometimes he thought that this was very unfair, but Jimmy would have none of it.

"You're a difficult, sensitive plant, Roopo," he'd say. "Even if you had my family, you'd feel threatened and anguished—it's the way things are."

Rupert would laugh. "Don't call me Roopo, it sounds like some exotic bird in the zoo."

"That's what you *are:* like a dark, brooding exotic bird that finds almost every climate too difficult for it!"

He had met Jimmy one great lucky day in the office. There was a picture of what they called a "charming unconverted cottage" in the window. It was a bit far out, too, not in the more fashionable direction and it could not be described as trendy, even by the most optimistic of those who wrote the descriptions.

Jimmy came in, a slight figure in an anorak, wearing tinted glasses. He had blond hair that fell over his forehead and he looked a bit vulnerable. Rupert didn't know why he moved over at once to him even though Miss Kennedy was nearer. He didn't feel any attraction to him at that stage—he just wanted to see that he got a fair deal. He had been studying the picture of the cottage, and had an eager smile on his face.

Rupert had told him the good and the bad: the bad being the roof and the distance and awful boulders of rocks in what had been loosely called the garden. He told him the good, which was that it was fairly cheap, that it was nice and private, and that if you had any money now or later there was another building attached to it that was a sort of an outhouse but that could easily be made into another small dwelling. Jimmy listened with growing interest and asked to see it as soon as possible. Rupert drove him out there, and without anything being said they knew they were planning their future as they stood in the wild overgrown rocky ground around the little house and climbed the walls of the outhouse to find that the roof there was perfect.

"It's not handy for where you work," Rupert pointed out, as Jimmy had said where he taught.

"I don't want to live handy to where I work, I want to live miles away. I want to have my own life, away from the eyes of the school."

Rupert felt an unreasonable sense of exclusion.

"And will you share it, do you think? That is, if you take it," he had asked.

"I might," Jimmy had said levelly. "I have no plans yet."

He bought the house. He had been saving with a building society for four years and he was considered reliable. The estate agency was pleased with Rupert: they had had the cottage on their books for rather too long. When all the negotiations were over, Rupert felt very lonely. This small, smiling Jimmy was going to be off now, living his own life in the windswept place. He would build that wall that they had discussed as a shelter, he would do up the second part of the house, paint it white, paint a door bright red maybe, grow some geraniums and get a suitable tenant. It would pay his mortgage. And Rupert would hear no more of it. Or of him.

He phoned on the Friday.

"Rupert, will you help me? I've lost all the fire for the place. I can't *see* it anymore; what it's like; what's going to be so great about it. Will you come out and remind me?"

"Yes," Rupert said slowly. "Yes, that's what I'd love to do."

He sat in a kind of trance all that Friday; if people spoke to him he only heard them vaguely. It was all so clear now: the confusions, the guilt, the hope that it would all settle down and sort itself out and that one day a woman would come along who would make him forget all this short-term stuff—which frightened him rather than making him satisfied. But all the time knowing there would be no woman, and not really wanting a woman. But had he read the signs right? Suppose Jimmy was just a charming fellow with nothing on his mind but a good cheery chat with that nice fellow from the estate agent's? Suppose Jimmy said he had a fiancée or some married lady that he wanted to meet in secret. He drove out, noting that it would take him half an hour from door to door should he ever need to go that way again. Jimmy was standing at the gate. Waiting.

He knew it was going to be all right.

And it had been more than all right for three years now. They had done the two little houses up with such love that now they really *did* merit a glowing description on an auctioneer's books. But they would never be for sale. They were separate enough to pretend that they were two dwellings if it were ever needed. But it never was. When Jimmy invited his family out to see the place, they all thanked him and said they must get around to it, but they never arrived. Rupert didn't press his elderly parents to come to Dublin, and just showed them pictures of his part of the house and of the garden. They made it all into a giant rockery and knew as much about alpines and rock plants as anyone for miles around. They had a big kitchen with a sink and work area on each side so that they could both cook if they wanted to. Every penny they had went into their little place. They had friends soon, people who came to dinner and admired or offered advice but mainly admired. It was so ideal and they were so happy.

That's why he hated leaving it at weekends. It was on Saturdays that they used to be most peaceful there, often shopping and cooking a meal—not only for Martin and Geoff or other gay friends but for the nice young married couple who lived nearby and who kept an eye on their garden that time they went to Morocco. These were people to relax with. These and one or two people in the estate agency didn't have to have any pretenses arranged for them. It was only in Jimmy's school and Rupert's hometown that the acting was essential.

Jimmy said it was so ludicrous in the 1980s not to be able to say that he was gay. And he would have at once if it were remotely possible. But no, apparently the boys' parents would think he had designs on them: they would think he was looking at them speculatively.

"I don't want any of those horrible ink-covered filthy ignorant kids," Jimmy would wail. "I want you, Rupert, my beautiful dark Rupert that I love."

And Rupert would fill up with pleasure and pride that Jimmy could be so natural and open and say all that to him. He tried to say spontaneous things, too, but they came out with greater difficulty. He was a bit buttoned up, as Judy Hickey had once said to him. He wondered often if Judy knew that he was gay. Probably. But it had never been the right time to tell her or to invite her out to see the rock plants and alpines that she would love.

Of course, he could tell Judy Hickey: after all, she was a scandal herself in some way, wasn't she? There had been some really murky business years ago. She would be pleased to know there was another Great Secret in Rathdoon. But he could never tell Judy that one of the real reasons he hated so much leaving every Friday for these empty weekends was that he was so afraid Jimmy would find someone else. Or maybe even had found someone else.

At lunch this very Friday he had asked Jimmy what he would do all day Saturday, and there had been no satisfactory answer. Martin and Geoff were having people in for drinks—he would go to that in the evening. He'd mark exercise books, he'd try to fix up the hi-fi, which had never been satisfactory. It was all very vague. Suppose, suppose, Jimmy had begun to like somebody else? His heart was cold inside, like the unexpected bit you find when you take a loaf out of the freezer and it hasn't properly thawed. He could never tell anyone that fear. Not anyone in the whole world.

It was easy to talk to Judy. She told him about her little herb pillows; he told her all the fuss over the politician with the love nest. They both laughed at that and for some reason that he couldn't quite see, it brought her into talking about her own past. He was astounded at her story, a young wife and mother dealing in drugs all those years ago. And the husband doing deals with the law as if he were part of the Wild West. Imagine her not seeing the children, but imagine even more her getting supplies of LSD for the huntin', shootin', fishin' set! And hash! Jimmy would go wild when he heard. He could have listened forever, but suddenly she decided she was boring him and launched into chat with that half-mad Nancy Morris. She had also said that his mother thought about him every day. That couldn't be so. Mother thought about Father, and the house, and the vegetable garden and the hens, but mainly Father and how she was afraid that young Mr. MacMahon didn't have the respect due to the senior partner and founder of the firm. Mother hardly showed any interest in Rupert's life in Dublin, which was, of course, a relief, but it did mean that it was most unlikely that Mother would think about him every day. Surely Judy was being fanciful? She probably hoped no matter what she said her lost children thought of her every day. That was it.

Their house was small and white with clematis growing up over the porch. Jimmy thought that a Protestant solicitor's family would live in a manor house, heavy with creeper and inspiring awe among the peasantry. Rupert had said that only two houses had proper creeper. One was Dr. Burke's, which was beautifully kept, and one was the old vicarage, which was so neglected it now looked like a huge stone covered with ivy. They had a service each Sunday in Rathdoon in the beautiful church, but had no vicar, no rector; he came out from the big town seventeen miles away and had Matins in Rathdoon, and another, later Matins another fifteen miles down the road. Jimmy was fascinated, but Rupert had never asked Jimmy home to meet the family. Jimmy had asked him to his house many a time. Rupert had gone once and felt awkward, even though nobody else had, and they had all buttonholed him about the price of property.

His mother was waiting just inside the door. That always annoyed him, too, and he got annoyed with himself over the very annoyance. Why shouldn't she wait to stop him ringing or knocking and disturbing his father's sleep? But it always made him think she had been standing waiting for his shadow to fall through the glass panels. He said good night with a much lighter tone than he felt, and braced himself. The soft leather of the magnificent jacket touched the back of his neck. It was Jimmy's birthday present to him. A few days early, but Jimmy said it would cheer him up for the weekend. Dee Burke had been right, they did cost a fortune. Again the niggling worry: how had Jimmy been able to spend that much money, even if it was a second? Put these doubts away, Rupert, he told himself firmly. Jimmy is good and true. Why pour vinegar onto it all with your stupid suspicions. Jimmy is at home tonight marking books and looking at television; Jimmy is not in a bar in town cruising someone. Why destroy *everything*?

"He's very well, very clear," his mother whispered delightedly.

"What?"

"Your father. He's very clear. He's awake; he asked several times what time would the Lilac Bus be in. Every time he heard anything change gear on the corner, he said, 'Is that the bus?' "

Rupert put his carrier bag down on the hall floor. "That's great, Mother, that's really great," he said with heavy heart, and went up the little stairs slowly to see the man with the head like a skull and the skin like plastic wrap. The man he had never been able to talk to in his life.

It was a sunny Saturday, but his father's room was darkened and the dim light hurt his eyes. His mother was bottling fruit downstairs. Jimmy said Catholics never bottled fruit or preserved eggs—it was something their religion didn't go along with. Jimmy had told him more lies about Roman Catholicism than he ever believed anyone could invent. He had always been brought up carefully to respect it at a distance by his parents, and even though they thought it definitely held the people back, they were impressed by the piety and the crowds going to Mass. His parents had gone to Galway to see the Pope. Jimmy said that his parents had made a small fortune the weekend the Pope arrived, since the whole of Dublin wanted to buy every newspaper twice in case they missed anything.

Back at home in the cottage, Jimmy would be drinking freshly brewed coffee and reading the *Irish Times*. Then he might go out to the garden and do some transplanting. September was the month to move the evergreens if you wanted to change the plan a bit. But no, Jimmy would wait for him to come back for that. Maybe he would be puzzling over the hi-fi. Please may he not be driving into town just because he's bored; please may he meet nobody at lunch over a drink and smoked salmon sandwich.

"You're very good to come down every weekend," his mother said suddenly, as if she could read the homesickness for his real place written all over his eyes. "Your father really does like talking to you. Do you notice that? Can you see it?"

Jimmy had begged him not to cross the whole of Ireland and then have a row. How could Jimmy understand that there were *never* rows, and there never would be. Well, a coldness then, Jimmy would say. If you are going to go to all that trouble, it's silly to mess up your weekend: if you're making the gesture, make it properly.

"I think he *does* seem to like talking," Rupert said. "It doesn't tire him too much, does it?"

"No, he plans all week what he's going to say to you. Sometimes he asks me to write it down, or just headings. I want to talk to Rupert about this, he'll say, and I write it down. Often he forgets what it was he was going to say about it, but it's there at the time."

Rupert nodded glumly.

"Like he was going to ask you about those flats you sell in blocks; he was very interested in how they work out the leasehold. He said that there was never any of that in the conveyancing he had to do. But all he asked me to write down was 'Block of Flats,' you see, and then he couldn't remember last week what it was he wanted to say about them."

"I see," Rupert said, trying to sound more sympathetic than he was afraid he might appear.

"But this week, he seems very much brighter and more aware, doesn't he?" She was pleading.

"Yes, much more. Oh, indeed. He was talking about this house here and what we would say if we had it on an auctioneer's books. I was giving him funny descriptions and he smiled a bit at it."

Rupert's mother was pleased. "Good, he hasn't smiled a lot. That's nice."

"Why don't you have a bit of time off, Mother, when I'm here. Why can't you go into town, maybe, you'd like that. I can keep an eye on Father and be here if he wants anything."

"No no, I want you to enjoy yourself," she said.

"But really, Mother, I mean, I'm not doing anything anyway." He shrugged. "I might as well look after Father and let you have a few hours to yourself." He meant it generously, but he knew it had come out all wrong.

"But you're home for the weekend," she cried. "I wouldn't want to miss that by going off to the town. I can do that any day: Mrs. Morris or young Mary Burns, Billy's wife, would sit with him. No, I want to get value out of your being here."

"Sure. Of course," he said, appalled at his own insensitivity. Jimmy would never in a million years have said anything like that. Jimmy would have brought life and laughter into the house the moment he got back. Jimmy. Oh Jimmy.

They had lunch, the kind of lunch that only his mother could serve: endless preparation and toasting of bread and cutting of crusts and spreading of cheese and slicing of tomatoes. And yet it was nothing—it managed to be both stodgy and insubstantial. If only she would let him cook. But then, he had never asked her. Perhaps it might be giving something away to say that he could have made them a light and delicious lunch in a quarter the time. It was his own fault, like everything.

His father struggled all afternoon. And Rupert struggled back.

Sometimes his mother was there, sewing. She was always making little things for her sister, who was married to a vicar and who always needed things for parish sales. His father would struggle and concentrate. His efforts to please meant that he could even be rerouted back to his own old days as a solicitor coming first to the town, when things were different and better. There was a time when his father had been happy to ramble through the times gone by. But not now: it was as if he was determined to show a guest in his eyes that he *was* interested in whatever kind of strange thing the guest did for a living. All afternoon Rupert's soul was crying out, "It's all *right*, Father. Look, can't you rest? I have an okay life and I wish you and Mother well, but why do we go through all this meaningless chat. There is nothing to say anymore."

The sun was almost going down when he could bear it no more; he said he had promised Judy Hickey he would do something for her and he had better dash over to her.

"A brave woman, Judy Hickey—she held her head high in this place for two decades," his father said in a surprisingly strong voice.

"Yes, well, why not?" Rupert was defensive. "She got a harsh punishment."

"She took it, and she didn't run away and hide. She stepped down from being lady of the manor and lived in the gate lodge."

"And lost her children," Rupert's mother added. "That was the worst bit."

"Yes, well, I won't be long." He felt he could breathe again when he was out in the air; he left the square and went off toward the gate lodge of the big Doon House.

Judy was lying curled up like a cat. She wasn't pleased to see him—in fact, she nearly sent him back straightaway. She was like Jimmy really, but without the persuasive charm: Jimmy made it seem reasonable; Judy made it seem like a duty.

But she meant it: she got up and stretched and said she was going to go out and walk in her husband's wood. Jack Hickey's wood she called it. She said he should talk about anything, anything to show his father that he was trying too.

But what could he say? He couldn't tell him that his heart was tearing with the barbed wire of jealousy in case his male lover might have been unfaithful. Then, *nobody* could tell a father that about a lover of any sex. But Rupert was worse off: he couldn't talk about his life, about the beautiful gentians that he and Jimmy had planted and how the willow gentian had burst into a whole pool of dark-blue flowers last July and they had taken photographs of each other admiring it. He found it hard to talk about the garden without mentioning Jimmy because the two were twined together, like the house, like cooking, like holidays and reading and laughing and the things people did, for heaven's sake.

Annoyed with Judy for being short with him, he walked home. He passed the Kennedys' shop and saw a big handsome girl being ushered in. The red-headed Kennedy boy, Eddie, was looking at her with a foolish grin: they must be courting. She was very attractive; how simple life would have been if only he had been born to court a big handsome girl who would bring life and laughter into his quiet house.

Suddenly he thought of Jimmy in the house. Jimmy pausing at the door to touch the clematis and cup it in his hands with admiration. Jimmy saying to Rupert's mother that she should sit down and put her feet up and let her big ugly son and himself make the meal for a change. Jimmy telling Rupert's father tales of the boys' school where he taught, and the fees and the extras and the awful school concerts. Jimmy walking casually down the road with him to Ryan's for a drink before dinner while the carbonade was in the oven. Jimmy would lighten their house better than any strapping girl from a well-to-do farm outside town.

"I was just thinking," he said to his mother when she let him in the door again as if she had been hovering. "Could I bring a friend home next week-end?"

After that it was easy. His mother said she was glad that she had got good notice, because she would clear out the guest room. It had been something she had meant to do for a long time, but never had the heart somehow. His father said that it would be very interesting to meet someone who taught in that school, because he had known a lot of people in his time who had been there and they were all united in never having a good word to say for it but having done extremely well as a result of being there.

Then a sudden shock. Suppose Jimmy didn't want to come?

"I hope he'll be able to make it; I didn't think of asking him," he stammered.

"Why don't you ring him?" his mother suggested. His mother, who made trunk calls as one might try to get in touch with another planet—cautiously and without much hope of success.

"God, isn't that lovely to hear you," Jimmy said.

"I'm ringing from home," said Rupert.

"Well, I hope so. I did think sometimes you went off to exotic places without me, but I decided to trust you." Jimmy's laugh was warm. Rupert swallowed.

"It's lovely here this weekend and I was wondering . . . I was wondering . . ."

"Yes?"

"I was wondering if you'd like to come down next week and stay, you know?"

"I'd love to."

There was a pause.

"You would? You would, Jimmy?"

"Sure, I thought you'd never ask," Jimmy said.

Celia

$\mathcal{H}$er friend Emer used to call it the Dancing Bus. All over Dublin people got on buses on Friday night to go home to great dances in the country. It had been a revolution, they said—hicks choosing to go home because it was more fun there than in Dublin. And they had the advantages of a bit of freedom in the city during the week and not losing touch with the home place either.

Celia laughed at the thought of her bus being a Sweetheart Special. She told Emer when they had cups of tea in the day room about the cast that turned up at a quarter to seven every week. Emer had sighed in envy. It sounded great, a nice spin across to the West, a weekend with no washing and housecleaning and trying to tell the three teenagers that there wasn't enough money for anything and trying to tell her husband who had been out of work for three years that there was plenty of money for everything. Emer had a sister married in the town that was seventeen miles from Rathdoon. Wouldn't it be lovely to go off there once in a while? Oh Lord, she'd love it.

And so that's what happened. Celia had to work one in every four weekends. So she gave her place on the bus to Emer. It had suited them all, and Emer said her family in Dublin were so grateful to see her back on a Sunday night that they never complained about anything, they just made her a coffee and said they'd missed her. Of course, Celia did go to the dances at one time, and they were great altogether: you got a first-rate band to come to a place where the people drove in for miles and there would always be a big crowd. She used to dance with Kev Kennedy's brother, Red, sometimes, but she much preferred Bart, the eldest of that family. He was so solid and reliable. You never quite knew what he was thinking, but he was always there. In fact, you never had to *ask* him to help, he seemed to know when it was necessary and turn up. Emer said he sounded a very suitable sort of man indeed, but Celia thought not. She said he wasn't interested in settling down and she wasn't going to set her sights on another one who was a permanent bachelor. She'd had enough trouble getting over the first. Emer had sighed supportively and wondered why as a married woman she was trying to encourage others to join the club. It certainly wasn't what it was cracked up to be, and in many ways it wasn't much good at all.

But Celia only laughed at her. Emer was thirty-eight and sounded tough and cynical, but deep down she would die for that handsome, whining husband of hers and those tall, rangy kids, who got bigger and needed more clothes every time you looked at them. Celia wasn't going to be put off love and marriage by any of Emer's protests; it was what she wanted. Not urgently, not immediately, not at any price, but she wanted it sometime. Despite what she had seen of it in her own family.

She could hardly remember a day at home when there hadn't been some kind of a row. A lot of them were in public, too, because if the whole of Rathdoon was coming into the pub from eleven o'clock in the morning on, then they would have to be aware of the shouts and the disagreements and the sight of Mr. or Mrs. Ryan coming flushed with anger from the back room into the bar and serving a pint, only to disappear again and fight the point further. Celia had often heard that children grew anxious and withdrawn when their parents fought in the home. But that's not what happened to the Ryans. They grew up and went away, that was all. As soon as they were able to get out, out they got. Her eldest sister had joined a band of Australian nuns who had come to Ireland looking for vocations. Looking for very young vocations, since Celia's sister had only been sixteen. But the offer of further education had been attractive as well. She wrote home from time to time, incomprehensible letters of places and things that were never explained. Then the boys had gone too. Harry to Detroit and Dan to Cowley in England. They wrote rarely, hard sorts of letters with a kind of graspingness they never had as youngsters—how a bar in Ireland must be a gold mine now. Harry had read in Detroit that Ireland was booming since the Common Market, and Dan had been told in Cowley that having a publican's license in the west of Ireland was like having a license to print money. These letters hurt Celia: there was much more than a hint, there was a direct statement that Celia and her mother were doing very nicely out of the family business, thank you. When she saw how things really were she felt she should laugh, but before she laughed she should weep.

Five years ago when her father died, people said that at least one blessing was that Kate Ryan had always been more or less running the business single-handed and so there'd be no doubt at all that she'd be able to carry on. It wasn't like some establishments where the wife had always been in the back-ground. No, poor Kate had been managing on her own while the husband drank down at one end of the bar with his own little circle.

And poor Kate had carried on for a good bit. In the summer she'd hire a young fellow to wash glasses, and there was always Bart Kennedy to give a hand if things got very busy. No, she was fine. There was no shortage of customers, and mercifully drink wasn't the kind of thing that came and went in fashions—people always loved drink. Apart from the first week of Lent, the custom was always steady and at weekends it was roaring. There was no opposition, and you'd never get another license for a place as small as this. Rathdoon was unusual in that it had only one pub; other places might have had three. There had been talk once that Billy Burns was thinking of applying for a license; he had been interested in buying a place about twenty miles away and asking to transfer that license to Rathdoon, but nothing had come of it.

Celia had been thinking about Billy Burns during the day for some reason. She had woken with that silly tune on her mind, "Where have you been all the day, Billy Boy, Billy Boy?" and she thought it fitted Mikey's brother down to the ground. Mikey was such an innocent old eejit, and there was something a bit too smart about Billy. Nothing to do with his setting up another pub or not. In fact, if he did, that might be a solution to a lot of their problems. If her mother's pub went downhill due to legitimate competition, that would be an honorable way out. If her mother drank Ryan's into the ground, that was a less honorable way altogether.

But you couldn't say anything even vaguely like this to Celia's mother. Other people were hitting it a bit hard these days, other people were making fools of themselves and running up debts: there were men in Rathdoon who had big pores in their noses and red and blue veins in their cheeks from drink; there were women in Rathdoon who went into the big town seventeen miles away to do the shopping, but Kate Ryan could tell you that it was little shopping they did except half a dozen half-bottles hidden under the tea towels or whatever they bought as an excuse. Half bottles were easier to hide and they were easier to dispose of. Kate Ryan could tell you of those who came in at night for "Just one drink, Mrs. Ryan," and she had seen them topping it up from their handbags. They didn't want to be seen ordering more than the one. But Celia's mother would have no tales of a woman who didn't even have to hide it because she had it there on her own shelves, and she was surrounded by it as her way of earning a living for twelve hours a day.

It had been such a shock the first time she saw her mother drunk. Mam had been the one who didn't and Da had been the one who did. It was like left and right and black and white. To hear those slurred words, to have to cope with an inarticulate argument—Celia had been quite flustered and not at all the calm Nurse Ryan that could cope with anything on her corridor. The next day her mother had made great excuses, frightening excuses. It was food poisoning: she had eaten some of that chicken paste out of a jar; she was going to write to the manufacturers and enclose the label. Not only had it made her sick several times during the night, but it had also affected her mind in some way. She couldn't remember clearly, she couldn't piece everything together. When Celia said agreeably enough that the chicken paste might well have been bad but it was probably the drink that made her forget the night before, she flew into a rage, one of those real rows like there used to be when Da was alive. It was *not* drink. Could Celia kindly tell her what drink she was referring to? Had Celia seen her mother sitting down to have a drink even once last night? Celia shrugged. She thought it might have been just this one time. Let it pass.

Three weeks later she came home for the weekend, and her mother was mixing up the gin and the vodka, forgetting to take the money from people and letting the pints overflow while she went to deal with someone else. It was then that Celia decided she had better book herself onto the Lilac Bus and come home every weekend that she could. This had been going on for a year now and her mother was getting worse and worse. And the really bad thing was that she wouldn't admit it, not for one moment. Not even to herself.

* * *

In the hospital Celia had seen dozens—more than dozens, probably hundreds—of people who were trying to help people who wouldn't help themselves. There had been endless conversations about old men who wouldn't go into sheltered accommodation and had set fire to their kitchens three times and old women who had broken their hips over and over because they wouldn't ask anyone to help them across a street. There were shriveled anorexics who wouldn't eat, there were ashen-faced coronary patients who had insisted on doing overtime in stress-filled jobs and eating huge meals filled with cholesterol. There were women worn out with the fourteenth pregnancy, there were the mothers of the schoolchildren who had overdosed, there were the wives of the men whose livers had packed up despite a hundred arguments that alcohol was poisoning them slowly to certain death. Always she had sounded sympathetic, always she had appeared to understand. But inside there was a bit of her that said that they couldn't have tried hard enough. If Celia had a daughter who was desperately unhappy at school and who had lost four stone in weight, she wouldn't hang around—she'd try to cope with it. If she had a father who couldn't cope, she'd have him to live with her. Only now was she beginning to realize that it was not to be so simple. People had minds of their own. And her mother's mind was like a hermetically sealed box in the vault of a bank.

Emer had been in high good humor: she had won a hundred pounds on the hospital draw. Each week they all had to buy a ticket for the building fund. It cost fifty pence, and they *had* to buy it—there wasn't any choice. Three hundred fifty pences added up to £150 and every second week the prize was £50 and every other one it was £100. It kept people interested and that small weekly contribution to the building fund was assured. Even if you were going to be on holidays you had to give someone else your sub. The winning ticket was announced on a Friday afternoon by number and you went to Wages to collect the prize. Emer was going to say nothing about it at home. Not one word. They would never hear. They would want jeans, they'd want a holiday, they'd think you could go on a holiday for a hundred quid. They'd want to go to McDonald's every night for a month, they'd want a video. Her husband would say it should go into the building society, it should be saved in case he never worked again. No, much better to keep it for herself. She and Celia would have a night out next week. Celia had laughed at her affectionately. "Sure," she had said. "People do what they want in the end, isn't that what you always say?"

She knew that what Emer would want despite all the protestations of independence and keeping the money to herself was totally different. She would want to arrive home this Friday night bursting with the news. She would want to send out for chicken and chips and plan endless treats which would indeed include jeans and a bit saved to please her anxious husband and a promise to look into the economics of a down payment on a video. That's what Emer would want and that's what she would do in the end. They both knew it.

And if Celia had a husband and kids she hoped that's what she would want too. Otherwise what was the point of the whole thing?

She was tired. It had been a long day. In other hospitals they worked twelve-hour shifts: eight in the morning till eight at night. Celia thought she'd be ready to strangle some of the patients, most of the visitors, and all of the staff if they had to have that routine. It had been quite enough to have eight hours today. A young woman had become desperately upset because at visiting time her brother, a priest, had said that he was saying a special Mass for her in their house. He had thought she would be pleased; she had thought that this meant it was the end. Then her husband told the priest that he had a neck to come in and upset the wife and there was a row of such proportions that everyone in the ward stopped talking to their own visitors and began to listen. Celia had been called. She pulled the curtains around the bed, she organized some light sedation, she explained in a crisp, cool voice that the woman's diagnosis had been entirely optimistic, that nothing was being hidden from her or from anyone. She said that since priests had the power to say the Mass, what could be more natural than he would say one in the family home as a thanksgiving for her recovery so far and a hope that it would continue?

She also said with a particularly pointed look at the priest that it was a pity some people couldn't explain things sensibly without using voices laden with doom and ritual, and have some sensitivity about people's association of having Masses said with being very ill indeed. Then with a reprimanding glance at the husband she said that the whole point of a visiting hour was for the patient to be made more comfortable and happy and not to be plunged into the middle of a huge family row, with accusations being hurled for the whole ward to hear. They were all younger than her except the priest, and he was probably under thirty. They took it very well and nodded their apologies to her and to each other. She drew the curtains open again and busied herself around the ward until she was sure they were all properly calm again. When the priest and the husband had gone she sat with the woman and held her hand and told her not to be an eejit: priests would want to say a Mass in a house at the drop of a hat. And after all, it was their life. If they didn't believe it was important, who did? It was only the rest of the world, Celia explained, who thought that Masses and God were only brought in when all else had failed. For priests they were there all the time. She hit the right note exactly and the woman was laughing by the time she left the ward.

Would that it were going to be so easy at home.

Last weekend Bart Kennedy had let slip that he had been there several nights during the week as well as the weekends. She was alarmed. She and Bart never spoke of the reason for his being there. He never said that her mother was drunk, he would say she needed a bit of a hand. He never said that her mother had insulted one of the customers, he would say there had been a bit of a barney but it was probably all sorted out now. She had asked him to take wages for himself, and he had laughed and said not at all. He was only helping out and how could he go and sign on if he was getting a regular salary? He assured her that he took the odd pint for himself and offered one to a friend occasionally, but it was peanuts and couldn't go on. Emer wondered had he perhaps any hopes of marrying into the establishment, but Celia said that was nonsense— Bart wasn't the type. Nothing funny about him, mind you, but just one that would never marry. Don't forget, Celia knew all about those: she had served her time for five years on a hopeless cause. She could spot them a mile off now.

But enough: she wasn't going to think of that fellow anymore. That was all behind her and at least the humiliations weren't known in Rathdoon. It was to another town that she had followed him hopefully at weekends, thinking that there was much more to it than there was, being there, being available; eventually, because it seemed the one thing he was sure he wanted, she had slept with

him. That was what he had called it but there was no sleeping involved: it was guilt for fear of discovery, and not very much pleasure for either of them. She hadn't lost him because she had been too easy to get; she hadn't lost him at all, because he was never hers to lose; he had no intention of disturbing the very even pattern of his life by a wife and house and children. No, no, no, he would stay on with his parents while they lived and maybe with a sister later. There would always be girls—girls now and later women—who would believe that they had the secret and the key to unlock his independence. No, Celia could write a book on the Irish bachelor if she wanted to, but she hadn't time: she *had* to sort it out this weekend, otherwise she'd better leave the hospital and come home. It wasn't fair on everyone else in Rathdoon.

She was glad that Kev Kennedy was a little bit ahead of her. That meant that he would sit beside Mikey. Tonight she was not in the mood for Mikey's jokes; some evenings she could take a few and then turn to her own thoughts, but there was too much on her mind, and Mikey was so easily hurt. It was good not to have this battle between offending him or going mad herself. She slipped easily in beside Tom, the driver. He leaned over her and slammed the door shut.

"It's only twenty to seven. I have you all very well trained," he said, and they all laughed with him as the bus went out into the traffic and headed for home.

Tom was a fine companion. He always answered agreeably and gave long answers if he was in the mood to chat and short ones if he wasn't. The silences were companionable. He never talked to the people behind because it distracted him, and he liked the person sitting beside him to tell him if it was all clear on the left as they nosed onto main roads from side roads. Much nicer than the rest of the Fitzgeralds up in the craft shop, but then it was silly to expect families to be the same. Look at Billy Burns: he'd buy and sell Mikey a dozen times before breakfast. Nancy Morris—there was something wrong with her, Celia thought. She had a very fixed look, a look that really was fixed on nothing. Celia had seen it in hospital sometimes. Nancy was as different from that laughing Deirdre, her sister in America, as she was different from a Martian. And there was poor Kev, Bart's young brother behind her there in the bus. And possibly she was different from her own brothers and sister. At the thought of her own family, her brow darkened. Why would none of them do a thing to help? How had it happened? She *could* write them a round robin: "Dear Maire and Harry and Dan, Sorry to have to tell you, but Mam is hitting the bottle worse than ever Dad did. What will we do? Looking forward to hearing by return from New South Wales; Cowley, Oxfordshire; and Detroit, Michigan, Your loving sister, Celia, Dublin." That was the point: Dublin. It was only up the road as far as they were concerned, and she wasn't married, that was even more the point, wasn't it? If she had been a wife then none of them would have expected her to abandon that and look after her mother, no matter how near she was. But being a nurse, an angel of mercy, helping the sick and earning her living . . . that would be written off.

What's more, they wouldn't understand, any of them. Maire would write from Woolowogga or wherever she had gone on a course—she was always going to ludicrous places on courses—and she would say it was blessed to give and blessed to help. Great. Harry would write from Detroit and say she must do what she thought was best, as she was the one on the ground. He would add something about it being a nice tidy living for her, and probably put in a really sensitive bit about not wanting his share out of the family business yet. Dan would write, he might even ring from England: he'd encourage her like mad to go home, he'd say that nursing wasn't a *real* career or anything, and that it was all for the best. His bit of tact might be to hope that now she was known as the landlady of a pub in all but name, perhaps Celia might get a few offers of marriage. She was only twenty-six, why had they written her off in three countries? She was their baby sister; she remembered them as big and strong and great fun, but in their letters and their rare appearances they were selfish and they were strangers. And they thought of her as an old maid.

"Do your family drive you mad?" she asked Tom as they had just overtaken a huge dangerous-looking lorry that seemed about to shed everything it had on everything that was near it.

"Oh, yes, of course they do," Tom said. "I mean, that *is* what drives people mad actually, families. It's not strangers in the street or the bomb or the economy, it's always their relations."

"Or love, I suppose, or lack of it?" Celia was impersonal, interested in talking about ideas. So was Tom. That's why they found their chats easy and never found their long silences threatening.

"Yes, love, but love usually involves some idea of family: you love someone, you want her to be your wife; she won't, you go mad. That's family. You hate your wife, you don't love her anymore, you wish she'd fly off on the next space shuttle. That's family."

Celia laughed. "God, you'd be great in one of those family counseling places with psychiatrists and all."

"I'm always surprised they never asked me in on one," said Tom, and they didn't speak for another fifty miles.

She was glad to get out and stretch. She had heard of other buses where they got stuck into a pub like this one for a real session and maybe it would be an hour and a half before people got back on the road. But Tom Fitzgerald ruled his Lilac Bus very firmly, it was time to visit the Ladies' and a very quick drink. There really wasn't even time for a coffee, because they always took such ages to make it in pubs, and indeed in Ryan's of Rathdoon they wouldn't make it at all.

"What'll you have, Celia?" Dee had a knack of getting to the counter quickest and an even better knack of getting served. Celia had a bottle of Guinness and a few words. Dee had never changed, not since she was a schoolgirl bursting with pride at her new uniform and coming into the bar to show it off to the Ryans. She had been everywhere to show it off, and everyone had given her a lemonade, or a bar of chocolate or even half a crown. Nobody had anything but good wishes for the doctor's daughter off to her posh convent boarding school. Dr. Burke was part of every life and death in Rathdoon; nobody would have a jealous thought about his children and what they had. Who would deserve it more?

She slipped Mikey some ointment that they used up in the hospital to ease bedsores. She didn't want to let Dee see her in case it was thought that she might be trying to improve on the doctor, but Dee would probably never think that in a million years. She was a grand girl with a very infectious laugh, and, of course, she had the patience of Job that she could talk to Nancy Morris so animatedly about Nancy's boring job and her endless tales of Mr. This the consultant and Mr. That the consultant. How did Dee put up with it and even look interested and remember their bloody names? The ten minutes were up and they were back in the dark comfort again.

She saw that Tom had tapes in the van; she had never noticed them before.

"Is that a player as well as a wireless?" she asked with interest when they were on the road again.

"Yes, do you wonder I have to guard this vehicle with my life? All I own is tied up in her." He laughed.

"You don't play any, while we're driving?"

"No. I thought about it: everyone would have a different taste and I wouldn't want to inflict my choice on all of you."

"Oh, it would have to be yours, would it?" Celia threw back her head of thick brown hair, laughing at him. "Where's the democratic bit then? Why couldn't everybody choose their own, even bring one each week?"

"Because if I had to hear any more of the Nashville sound than I already hear by accident in my life, I think I'd drive off the road and into the deepest bog that would close over us," he said.

"Let's have no music then," Celia said agreeably, and they drove on, thinking their own thoughts. Celia was wondering what time she would catch her mother at the most receptive. There must be *some* moments in the day when the unfortunate woman was not suffering from a hangover or withdrawal or had got stuck into it again. There must be a time—late morning maybe—when she could ask Bart to man the place. Not that anyone came in much on a Saturday until it was well into lunchtime. She could always put *closed* on the door—. Father Reilly put *closed* on the presbytery, for heaven's sake, when he simply had to have an hour to himself, or maybe it was for some poor devil that couldn't be disturbed. That was it, no more drawing on poor Bart. Anyway, he liked to work with Judy Hickey during the daytime when she was home for the weekend. She could put *closed* on the door for an hour or two, but apart from chaining her mother by both wrists and ankles, how was she going to get her to stay and listen to the very unwelcome view that she was now incapable of managing her own pub and must get herself into an alcoholic unit before it was too late? It was gone beyond false promises now, and assurances and little games. Celia had been present when a surgeon told a forty-two-year-old man last month that he had terminal cancer and had less than two months to live. This is what it felt like again. That sense of dread and half hoping the world would end before you had to say it. Of course, it had turned out very oddly in the hospital; they had thought the shock might be intense and that was why Celia was there as part of a backup. But he had been very quiet, the man, and said, "Is that a fact?" They had stood dumbfounded, Celia, the great surgeon, and the anesthetist. Then the man had said, "And I never went to America. Imagine, in my whole life I never saw America. Isn't it ridiculous in this day and age." He had said that several times before he died; it seemed to disturb him more than death itself and leaving his wife and three young children.

Suppose her mother were to say something equally unexpected—like that she had been wondering was this what was wrong with her, and she would like to go at once as a voluntary patient to some kind of place that would dry her out. Stop thinking like Alice in Wonderland, Celia told herself sternly. You're a grown-up, it's no use shutting your eyes, wishing things would happen.

"There's a lot of rags tied to a bush coming up now. I think it's a holy well or a wishing tree or something," Tom said suddenly. "Maybe we should all get out and tie our shirts to it," Celia said. They passed it, and indeed there were ribbons and what looked like holy pictures pinned onto it.

"I never saw that before, and all the times we must have driven past it," Celia said, looking back over her shoulder. She thought she saw Dee Burke crying, her face was working in that sort of way a child's does to keep off the sobs. But Nancy Morris was yammering on as usual, so there couldn't be anything really wrong.

"I never saw it before. Maybe it's a new saint; you know the way they get crossed off, like St. Philomena, maybe one got put on."

"Why *did* St. Philomena get crossed off, I wonder?" asked Celia.

"I don't know, maybe they found her out." Tom grinned. "I know my sister Phil was very annoyed indeed at the time, she felt it was an attack of some sort."

"Oh yes, Phil, that would be her name. How is Phil, by the way? I haven't seen her for a while."

"She's fine," Tom said shortly.

Celia went back to the tree for conversation. "Are they pagan or are they religious, I wonder?" she said.

"A mixture, I think." He was still short.

Celia thought about the tree. Wouldn't it be great to go there and pray to some saint who had a special interest in drunken mothers, leave an offering or whatever they left and then go home and discover that it had worked. Bart Kennedy would be serving behind the bar and her mother would be sitting with a packed suitcase and face full of optimism.

"See you during the weekend," Tom said with a friendly smile.

She nodded. He had been a bit moody tonight, she thought. She didn't mind their stops and starts normally, in fact she liked it. But tonight she had wanted to talk. Actually, what she had really wanted was Emer. You could say anything to Emer and you knew she would think about it, but she wouldn't bring it out again on every occasion and ask you how you felt about it. Emer would give you advice but not be annoyed if you didn't take it. "Everyone does what they want to in the end," she would say. She wasn't as specific when it came to knowing how to convince someone else to do the right thing—or the best thing. Celia had long discussions with her over this. Did you wire the jaws of fat kids who were compulsive eaters? Did you have medical cards for smokers and only those who were certified as having good, strong lungs and no trace of emphysema would be allowed to buy a packet—they'd have to show the card first. That would save life, wouldn't it? Celia might suggest. Emer would shrug. Temporarily only: the child with the wired jaw would wait eagerly until the contraption was removed; the smoker would get the cigarettes somehow or smoke butts. But then why were drugs banned? Why not just sell heroin by the kilo in Quinnsworth and be done with it? Those who wanted to kill themselves would and there would be no drugs racket and pushers and people having to turn to prostitution or theft for it.

Emer said that drugs were different: they were poison, they killed. You wouldn't sell arsenic or strychnine, would you?

What about alcohol? That killed, they had seen enough rotted livers to know that; they could see the slow death around them. Emer said that if Celia felt as strongly as that she shouldn't own a pub, and she should have a temperance banner. Then they would both have a bottle of Guinness and talk about something else. But she was such a comfort; no wonder that her handsome husband and her three giant children were always waiting so eagerly for her to come home from work. And she wasn't a superwoman either. There were bad times and low times in Emer's life as well as in everyone else's. That's why she was so good to talk to.

"Good night." She nodded, and added, "Thanks for getting us here." She didn't want to be curt with Tom just because he hadn't been like Emer! That would be unfair.

"Best to the West, as Mikey would say," Tom laughed.

"Don't encourage him—he has enough catchphrases already." She went in the door and knew from the loud greeting that her mother called across the bar that it was going to be a long, hard hour and a half. She put her bag in the kitchen, she hung up her jacket and came out quietly to stand beside Bart Kennedy, who patted her on the arm as she wordlessly began to pull the pints.

Her mother shouted for two hours when the pub eventually closed. She sat at one of the tables and hurled abuse as Celia methodically emptied the ashtrays and wiped the surfaces. She would *not* be patronized in her own pub, she cried; she would not have Celia coming off the bus and taking over as if she owned the place. Celia did *not* own the place, and in fact, the place would never be hers. She hoped that Celia knew this. She had made a will with that nice young Mr. MacMahon in Mr. Green's office, and she had said that after her death the pub should be sold and the money divided equally in four and shared out between Maire and Harry and Dan and Celia. So now. Celia said nothing. She washed the glasses under hot water first, then under cold, then turned them upside down to drain on a plastic grid: that way the air got at them from all angles and dried them without smears.

Her mother had a brandy bottle on the table beside her. Celia made no attempt to touch it. She just moved past her and locked the door. The place was now ready for the next day. She gulped a bit at the thought of the conversation she was going to have in the morning, when the closed sign would appear on Ryan's door for the first time since her father's funeral.

"Aren't you going to have the common manners to say good night, Miss High and Mighty?" her mother called.

"Good night, Mam," said Celia as she wearily went up the narrow stairs to the small white bedroom with the iron bed. She lay awake for a while. Long enough to hear her mother stumbling up the stairs and hitting off the chest of drawers on the landing. She must have known it was there: it had been there for thirty-eight years, all her married life.

It was very sunny, too sunny. Celia woke with a jump. The curtains had been pulled back, and there was her mother, with a cup of tea.

"I thought you might like this, after your week's work, and you must have stayed up late last night doing the glasses." The voice was steady enough and the hand wasn't shaking as it passed the teacup and saucer.

Celia sat up and rubbed her eyes. "You were with me when I washed the glasses," she said.

"I know, I know, of course." Her mother was flustered, she hadn't remembered. "Yes, well, naturally, but thanks for . . . um . . . organizing it all the same."

There was no smell of drink, but Celia realized that she must have had a cure, maybe a vodka. That's why she was able to cope. She had smartened herself up, too, combed her hair and worn a dress with a white collar. Apart from her eyes, which looked terrible, Mrs. Ryan didn't cut too bad a figure at all.

This might be the time. Celia swung her legs out of the bed, and took a great swig of the tea.

"Thanks, Mam. Listen, I wanted to say something to you. I've been trying to get a good time—"

"I have a kettle on downstairs; I'll come back up to you when I have a minute."

She was gone. There was no kettle on. Celia got up and dressed quickly. She decided against jeans and put on a skirt and blouse and a big wide belt. It made her look more authoritative, more nurselike in a way. There was no sign of her mother in the kitchen. Where could she have gone? There was a sound of scrubbing out the side entrance, and there was Mrs. Ryan on hands and knees with bucket and scrubbing brush, working away.

"I was noticing this last night: it's in a very bad way, we mustn't let the place go to rack and ruin around us." She was sweating and puffing. Celia let her at it. She went back into the kitchen and made more tea. Eventually her mother had to come back in.

"There, that's much better," she said.

"Good," said Celia.

"I saw that Nancy Morris, a proper little madam, that one. 'Hallo, Mrs. Ryan' if it suits her, and wouldn't give you the time of day if it didn't. I pretended I didn't hear her. She has her mother scalded, coming home every weekend."

"I'm sure," Celia said. Mrs. Ryan's jaw dropped.

"Oh, not like you. I mean, it's grand that you come home, and you're such a help."

"I'm glad you think so this morning. It was a different tune last night," Celia said.

"Oh, you wouldn't need to mind me on a Friday night, the place gets so crowded and they're coming at you from all sides. I probably sounded a bit impatient, but didn't I thank you for doing the glasses, didn't I bring you a cup of tea in bed?" She was pleading now, almost like a child.

Celia took the bucket and the brush away from her gently and closed the door behind her. She lulled her to the table with soft talk. She didn't want the woman to bolt from the room.

"Of course you brought me a cup of tea in bed, and I *know* that deep down somewhere you are grateful to me for coming back and helping out, but that's not the point, Mam, not the point at all. You don't remember anything about last night, not from about nine o'clock on, that's what I'd say."

"What are you talking about?"

"You were well gone when I arrived—that was before ten. You fought with a man and said he'd only given you a fiver, not a ten. You told young Biddy Brady that you didn't want a whole crowd of her girlfriends cluttering up the pub tomorrow—fortunately, Bart got us out of that one. You spilled a whole bottle of lime juice and you wouldn't let anyone wipe it up, so the counter was sticky all night. You couldn't find the tin of potato crisps and you told a group who had come here for the golfing that you didn't give a damn whether you found them or not, because they smelled to you like a child's fart. Yes, Mam, that's what you said."

Her mother looked up at her across the table. She showed no signs of getting up to run away. She looked at Celia quite calmly.

"I don't know why you are saying all this," she said.

"Because it happened, Mam." Celia begged her. "Believe me, it all happened, and more and much more other nights."

"Why would you make this up?"

"I didn't. It was like that; it will be like that again tonight, Mam, you're not able to cope. You've had a drink already today, I can see. I'm only telling you for your own good."

"Don't be ridiculous, Celia." She was about to stand up. Celia reached out and held her there. Hard by the wrist.

"I haven't written to the others yet: I didn't want to alarm them, I thought it might pass. I thought it was only weekends, when you were under a bit of pressure. Mam, you have to accept it and *do* something about it."

"Others?"

"Maura, Harry, Dan."

"You're going to write all over the world with these tales?"

"Not if you can help yourself first. Mam, you're drinking far too much, you can't control it. What you're going to have to do is—"

"I'm going to have to do nothing, thank you very much indeed. I may have had one too many sometimes, and all right, I'll watch that. Now, will that satisfy you? Is the interrogation over? Can we get on with the day?"

"*Please*, Mam, listen. Anyone will tell you—will I get Bart in here to tell you what it's been like? Mrs. Casey was saying, Billy Burns was saying, they were all saying . . . it's getting too much for you here. . . ."

"You were always prudish about drink, Celia, even when your father was alive. You didn't realize that in a bar you have to be sociable and drink with the customers and be pleasant. You're not cut out for a pub, the way we were, the way I am. You're too solemn, too sticky for people. That's always been your mistake."

There was no point in putting *Closed* on the door; she wouldn't talk. The most she would admit was a drop too much on some occasions. She denied all the scenes, she remembered none of the conversations.

People started drifting in around lunchtime. Celia watched her mother accept a small whiskey from Dr. Burke, who had come in to get some drink to celebrate his son's engagement. Celia wished that Dee's father would lean over the counter to her mother and say "Mrs. Ryan, your eyes are all bloodshot and there are big lines under them; for your health's sake you must give up drink." She wished that Father O'Reilly would come down from the presbytery on a home visit and tell her that for the good of her soul she must go and have some treatment and then take the pledge. But doctors and priests didn't interfere enough these days maybe.

The phone box was way at the end of the bar, quiet and discreet. No wonder half of Rathdoon made their calls from there rather than beside the eager ears of the post office people.

Emer was just getting the lunch. They had all been to the pictures last night on her winnings and tonight they might go again. Videos had gone through the roof: even the kids realized that a video was out of the question.

"What will I do with her?" Celia asked.

"She doesn't admit it to herself?"

"No. I gave her chapter and verse—what she said, what she spilled and broke, who she insulted. Not a word does she believe."

"And you can't get support troops in."

"Not really. Bart will be too polite and anyone else would be embarrassed."

"I suppose you'll have to wait."

"I can't wait anymore, and neither can she. It's terrible. There *must* be some way. How do people come to see things? Is there no way of hurrying it up?"

"Well, I did hear of a man who signed himself in for treatment the moment he saw himself on a video of his daughter's wedding. He had no idea that he was so bad until—"

"That's it. Thanks, Emer."

"*What?* You're going to turn a video on your mother in Rathdoon? Have sense."

"I'll tell you about it on Monday." Celia was gone.

Mrs. Fitzgerald invited her in. Yes, Tom was here. They were having a pot of coffee—would Celia join them? She felt they had been having a chat, that she shouldn't interrupt. She said she'd only be a minute. Yes, he did have a small cassette recorder, and yes, a blank tape . . . or a tape that she could record over. What was it—something from the radio? No, okay, it didn't matter. Look, it was easy to work. No, he didn't mind being without it until they were on the bus again. He was puzzled, but he didn't ask any more. She took it back to the pub.

There was so much clutter under the pub counter that the small tape recorder passed unnoticed.

Celia used it judiciously, half an hour on one side and half an hour on the other.

She even moved it out in her hand to be closer to her mother when the solo singing began and Mrs. Ryan was screaming a tuneless, racy version of a song that she hardly knew. She let it play for the insults to Bart Kennedy and for the bad language.

At one stage Tom Fitzgerald came into the bar; he saw his recorder and said, "Is that fair?"

"You have your standards, I'll have mine," she snapped, and then much more wearily: "She doesn't know, you see, she really doesn't know."

"She's not going to like it," he said.

"No."

"When will you . . . ?"

"Tomorrow morning, I'd say."

"I'll come in around lunch and pick up the pieces." He smiled. He had a very, very nice smile.

Her mother sat stonily through the first few minutes. She railed with anger at the arguments and the bad language. Then she decided it was a fake, and when she heard her maudlin conversation about what a great man her husband had been, tears of shame came into her eyes.

She folded her hands on her lap and sat like some timid employee waiting to be fired.

Out of the little tape recorder came the voice of Mrs. Ryan as it called on Biddy Brady's engagement party to shut up and let *her* sing. Tears fell from her closed eyes as the voice came out in its drunken, tuneless wail. Celia started to turn it off.

"Leave it," her mother said.

There was a long silence.

"Yes," said Mrs. Ryan, "I see."

"If you wanted to, we could say you had pneumonia or that you were off to see Dan in Cowley. That would sort of cover it up."

"There'd be no point in covering it up. I mean, it's only more lies, isn't it? Might as well say what it is." Her face was bleak.

"Sure, you're halfway there, Mam, if that's the way you think—you're nearly better," said Celia, leaning across the small, dark tape recorder to hold her mother's hand.

Tom

$\mathcal{H}$e remembered the day he painted the Lilac Bus. It had been a sort of dirty beige before, and there was an exhilaration about pointing the spray can at it and seeing it change before his eyes. His mother had been appalled. It looked so vulgar and called attention to itself. That was about the worst crime in her book—attracting attention. The good went by unnoticed and understated; the bad were flashy and loud and painted their vans this silly mauve color. Tom's father just shrugged. What could you expect? he asked his wife in a tone that meant the one thing he really didn't expect was an answer. Tom's father hardly ever spoke *to* Tom anymore: he spoke about him, in his hearing.

"I suppose that boy believes that money grows on trees . . . that boy thinks we should have the itinerants living in our garden . . . that boy feels that work is beneath him." Sometimes Tom answered; sometimes he let it pass. It didn't really matter which he did. His father's mind was fixed anyway: that boy was a waster, a left-wing long-haired layabout. A purple minibus was only what you'd expect.

It wasn't what Tom expected. He just decided one day on a whim, one day when the washing didn't seem to be making the van look any better. And he *loved* it now that it was lilac-colored: it had much more personality and more life. That was when he decided to go into the transport business. It wasn't *exactly* legal, of course, but suppose they did have an accident: an insurance company would have a hard time proving that he wasn't driving seven friends home for the weekend. No money was ever seen to change hands in Dublin. He didn't stand at the door selling tickets as the bigger bus people did. They were the same people all the time, give or take one or two a month. It wasn't a moneyspinner or anything; he paid for his petrol and cigarettes out of it, that was all. But it did mean he could smoke as much as he liked and he could come home every weekend to Rathdoon, which was what he wanted to do. The Lilac Bus had made all this possible.

Tom knew all about his passengers' lives in Rathdoon, but very little about what they did in Dublin. He had thought of finding out where they all lived and dropping them home rather than leaving them in the city center at ten o'clock on a Sunday night, but something told him that they might prefer the anonymity of the city to be kept absolute; they mightn't want the others to see their digs or their rooming houses or their set-up. More than once Tom had noticed a small, fair-haired fellow in tinted glasses in a car parked near where the bus began and ended its weekend run. He would wave eagerly to Rupert Green. Now, Rupert very clearly might not want that known. It was only because Tom had X-ray eyes that he had noticed the car. And his eyes had sometimes caught Dee Burke slipping into a big car and the arms of an older man. The older man had never been mentioned by Dee or by anyone in Rathdoon, so it was safe to assume that he was a secret older man, not a legit one. No amount of watching or guessing could tell him what young Kev Kennedy was so afraid of. It hadn't always been that way: he used to be a very nice young fellow, and the only one of that family to get up from the kitchen table and leave their father and their slices of bread and ham and the radio on from Good morning to Close down. But for the past year or so he was in bits.

Celia lived in a nurses' house. Six of them shared a place, which was apparently highly successful. They had two television sets, a washing machine, and an ironing board always in position in the back room. Celia had said there was never a cross word exchanged in that house—it was an ideal way to live until they married and had homes of their own. Nancy Morris shared a flat with that nice, bouncy Mairead Hely; how Mairead stuck it was a mystery. He had met her one night at a party and she told him that Nancy's newest trick was to watch out for food tastings in supermarkets and rush in before they closed and have paper cups of soup or bits of cheese on toothpicks and then to come home triumphantly to the flat and say "I've had my supper." That night, and it was about three months back, Mairead had said that she was gathering up her courage to ask Nancy to leave, but she couldn't have gathered it yet. Poor Mikey was so nice, Tom would have driven him home willingly, but he just laughed and walked to a bus stop with the never-failing sense of good humor that was so hard to take. Judy Hickey took a bus the same direction and Tom often saw them talking together as he turned the Lilac Bus and drove off home.

None of them knew where his home was, that was certain. Long ago he had developed a gift for not answering direct questions so skillfully that people thought they had been given some kind of answer but didn't ask again. When Nancy Morris had asked him how much he paid a week for his flat, he said it was hard to work out, and that was that from Miss Morris. Rupert once asked him on which side of the city did he live, and Tom had said that he was sure Rupert must know the trends in what people wanted. He often thought that it was interesting looking at people in cinema queues, for example, and wondering where they lived; he supposed that if he were working in an auctioneer's like Rupert, he'd think it even more interesting. Rupert agreed and had talked cheerfully about the unexpected ambitions of a lot of the people who came into his office. He never again asked Tom where he lived, and he didn't sound as if he had been rebuffed.

Dee Burke had told him that her brother was living in sin and wasn't it monstrous that boys could get away with it and girls still couldn't really. She had asked him suddenly, "Maybe you live in sin too. Do you?"

"I don't know," he had said. "I'm very confused about sin; they never explained it properly at our school. What about yours?" Dee had said gloomily that they never stopped explaining it at her school and they were all so sick of it by the time they left, they had hardly the energy to commit any, which might have been the aim all along. But she still didn't find out what his life-style was. And down in Rathdoon he was spoken of as the one Fitzgerald boy that didn't join the family firm, the only one who didn't want to build an empire. He did something arty up in Dublin. But in any gathering of three, if his name came up, there would be three different theories on what he did. It gave the lie to the obsession with gossip that small towns were meant to have automatically, Tom thought. There was Dee with her older chap, Rupert with his boyfriend, Kev with his gambling debts or whatever it was, and no one back home knew a thing about any of them—or about Tom. In Rathdoon only one person knew how Tom lived and why: his mother.

Nobody would guess that in a million years. His mother tutted with the best, sighed over his clothes and bus—genuine sighs. She really would have preferred a nice inconspicuous bus and more conservative clothes: nice neutral colors, stone-colored trousers and brown jackets like her other sons wore. Suits, white shirts, restrained ties for Mass on Sunday. When his father railed about the young generation in general and That Boy in particular, Tom's mother was gentle in her reproach. Anyone looking on might have thought she agreed with her husband. Who could have known that Tom was her lifeline?

She was a handsome woman, Peg Fitzgerald. Fifty-two, very well groomed; you never saw a hair out of place on Mrs. Fitzgerald. She wore knitted suits, in lilacs or dark green, and a good brooch to tone in with whatever color it was. In summer she wore lighter linen suits, but they were the same colors and she had looked the same for years. She had three perms a year in the big town, and she had a shampoo and set every Friday morning of her life with little Sheila O'Reilly, the niece of the parish priest. Sheila didn't do much business in Rathdoon, but she never seemed to mind. She was always cheerful and if there were no heads of hair to deal with she did knitting instead and made a little out of that as a sideline. She wished there were more regular customers like Mrs.

Fitzgerald, who wanted their hair done the same way at the same time every week.

Mrs. Fitzgerald was in the shop every day. The craft shop side of it had been her idea and was very successful. Anytime a tour bus stopped there was a heavy electronic buzzing of tills in the Fitzgerald Craft Center. There were shawls, lengths of tweed, pottery—a very wide range to suit all tastes. It was also the place where the whole of Rathdoon bought birthday presents for each other. Peg had difficulty persuading the family that it was a good idea, but now they looked at her with a new respect. She was a firm believer, too, that things should be kept in the family. When the boys married it was understood that their wives would work there. In fact, one potential daughter-in-law broke off the engagement because she said all she would get from the marriage contract was to be an unpaid shopworker instead of the bank official that she was. Tom had thought that showed some spirit, but the rest of the family—including the jilted brother —all combined in thinking they had a lucky escape if that was going to be her attitude.

From the outset Tom had said he wouldn't work in the shop; there had been no fight about it, only scorn. He had said reasonably that he thought it was better for his three brothers and two sisters if they *knew* from the word go that he would not be joining them. Then they could make their own plans without any question marks hanging over him. He decided this as long ago as his school days. But they had thought it was like being an engine driver and took no notice. What he would like to do was go to Dublin and live. Just live, not necessarily *do* anything, until he found something he'd like to do, and then maybe America or Paris or Greece. If you didn't have high living standards and want a comfortable house and a lot of possessions and rich food, you could live very cheaply. They had thought it was a phase.

He had got a lot of honors in his Leaving, much more than the brothers who were well on their way to being merchant princes: expanding to other towns, opening new branches, developing their mother's much-mocked idea of a craft shop in other centers all over the West. Tom was pronounced brighter than any of them by the masters who had taught all the Fitzgeralds, but he was adamant and very firm for an eighteen-year-old. He had all these bits of paper to prove he was educated, now could he get on with his own life? He thanked his father as warmly as he could for the grudging offer of university fees, but still it was no. All he wanted was to be left alone. He wouldn't go to the bad, he would come home regularly if they liked so that they could see him and satisfy themselves that he was still normal. He would hitch. He would sign on for the dole each week, and *no,* that would not be an almighty disgrace in Dublin. Who would see him or know him, for God's sake, and *no,* it was not unfair, that's what people did nowadays: the rich paid taxes and there was at least bread and a roof for those who weren't rich. We didn't let them die in the streets today, stepping over them saying wasn't it a pity they didn't have the get up and go to find a good job and earn their living. *No,* he did not intend to stay on national assistance forever. And *yes,* he was very grateful for the offer of a place in the family firm, but we only had one life and that was not how he was going to spend his.

And wasn't it lucky that this is what he had decided to do? What on earth would have happened if he hadn't been around?

It had been very easy to live cheaply in Dublin. For a while he lived with a young couple who gave him a bed and some food; they didn't have all that much themselves. He taught their children every evening, two nice bright little boys. He went over everything they had done at school and helped them with their homework. But he didn't really like it because he felt they should be out playing instead of doing more and yet more. They knew enough, he kept telling their worried young parents, they're fine: don't pack their heads with facts and more and more. The parents didn't understand. Surely the best thing was to get a good start, to be in there with a better chance than the others? But they were only ten and nine, it was *years* before they would need to be in there fighting the others for places and points and positions. No, the pale mother and father hadn't got on in their lives because they had nobody to guide them; they weren't going to let the same thing happen to the children. He left them amicably. He worked as a gardener for an old lady and slept in her garden shed for a year without her knowing. She never knew in the end, and he had moved his camp bed and primus stove long before the funeral, so nobody ever knew.

He worked in a nightclub as a sort of bouncer. He was slim and not the typical bouncer material, but he had a look in his eye that was as important as muscle. His boss, who was one of the sharpest men in Dublin, was anxious to keep him on, promote him even, but it wasn't the life Tom wanted. He left again amicably, and before he left he asked the sharp boss what was good about him. He'd like to know just for his own record. The boss said he owed him no explanation if he was leaving, but okay, Tom had a look in his eye that said he would go the distance. People didn't mess with him. Tom liked this reference just as he had liked the old lady saying he was a loving sort of gardener, and the nine-year-old boy saying that he made Latin so much more interesting than they did at school, because there was none of this treating it as a language—more as a puzzle really. But these were not written references. Each new job had to be found on charm or effort; each time he had to go in cold.

He had a summer in Greece driving a minibus, not unlike the Lilac Bus, over mountainy roads, taking holidaymakers to and from airport and hotels. He had a summer in America working at a children's camp with seventy discontented youngsters who would all rather have been at home. He had a winter in Amsterdam working in a souvenir shop. He had a funny three months in London working in market surveys—going up to people on the street with a clipboard and asking them questions. He had a different kind of three months in London working as a hospital orderly; he found it harrowing, and his respect for nurses went way, way up. He had been on the point of telling Celia about those months several times, but he never told stories about what he had done—it led to questions and questions often needed answers.

He didn't think of himself as a drifter, and yet for nine years, since he had left school, he had done nothing with any purpose or any permanence. Still, he wouldn't have missed any of it, not even those strange days in the hospital, pushing frightened elderly people on trolleys through crowds, all speaking different languages, all the nationalities under the sun working in the hospital and coming in as patients. And now it meant that he could look after Phil, for he had no job to give up, no real life-style to interrupt.

Phil was the nicest in his family, there was no doubt about it. They all agreed on that, just as they all agreed that Tom was the oddest and the most difficult. Phil was the nearest to him in age: she was almost a year to the day older than he was. All the six Fitzgeralds arrived within seven years, and then the young Peg stopped producing a new baby every season. There were pictures of them all when they were toddlers, and Tom always thought it looked like a nursery school rather than one family. But his mother had always said it was great to get it all over at once. You had a period when they all seemed to be unmanageable and then suddenly they had all grown up. Anyway, Phil had always been his special friend, and in the great sixteen- and seventeen-year-old arguments about Tom not joining the firm, Phil had been very supportive. She had been in the big town seventeen miles from Rathdoon learning shorthand and typing at the time, it had been agreed that she should work in the office rather than the shop. But she used to come home at weekends during her commercial course and encourage Tom to live his own life. She had a big round face, Phil had, and she was always laughing. Years ago he remembered her dancing with Red Kennedy and getting a lecture that the Kennedys were perfectly nice, not a thing wrong with them, but she should set her sights a little higher. Phil had said indignantly that she wasn't setting her sights at Red Kennedy or at anyone, she was just dancing with him, but there had still been a lot of head shaking.

Phil was what they called a fine girl in Rathdoon; Mrs. Fitzgerald used to say that she'd slim down when the time came. Hadn't Anna, the eldest of the family, had a lot of puppy fat too? But Mrs. Fitzgerald always thought that there was some kind of law which said that a girl needed to be nice and slim and attractive when she was thinking of choosing a husband and settling down. It was just the way things were. But Phil didn't notice some magical trick of nature: she remained plump and round-faced and never developed the hollow cheeks and small waist which were generally agreed to have been important when her sister Anna attracted and married the very suitable Dominic, whose family made tweeds.

Tom had never thought she was too fat; he had told her that several times when he came home for the weekend. He said she must be losing her marbles to think she was a fatty, and cracked to think that she had no friends because of this.

"Who are my friends then? List them," she had cried.

Tom couldn't, but he said he couldn't list any friends of his family, for God's sake, he was away, he didn't live here. She *must* have friends. No, she claimed, she didn't. That was when meaning to be helpful he had suggested this singles type of holiday. Everyone went on their own, there were no loving couples to start out with but hopefully plenty of them on the way back. Phil had read the brochure eagerly and decided that she should go on it.

"Don't tell anyone it's a singles special," her mother had advised. "It looks a little pathetic. Say it's an ordinary holiday in Spain."

Tom never knew quite what happened, but it wasn't a success. Phil said that Spain was all right, and the weather had been fair, but nothing else. Later, much later, he heard that all the girls except Phil had been topless on the beaches, that almost everyone on the group charter had enjoyed a close physical relationship with one or more other people on the same group charter—again, everyone except Phil—and that there was no question of meeting people and dancing with them and talking to them and getting to know them. This was apparently a much more swinging type of holiday than some singles outings, and swinging meant going to bed with people, people who were total strangers.

But Tom didn't know all this at the time. Phil had come back quiet and noncommunicative. He noticed shortly after this that she seemed to have lost weight, but he didn't say anything, because he had been the one to tell her that weight wasn't important. If he admired her now, she would believe that he had only been kind before. Phil didn't go to the dance anymore and she didn't go out to the sea with a crowd of girls like she used to. But to be honest, he didn't notice these things at the time; it was only afterward he remembered it all.

Phil had come to Dublin on one of the day excursions by train from the town. It was a bit of a killer: the train left at 9 A.M., you were in Dublin at noon, and then the train back was at 6 P.M. So it was some concentrated shopping before they all fell back with sore feet and bulging parcels to go home again that night. Phil always rang Tom if she went on one of these marathons, and he came to meet her at the station in his minibus, which was a dirty beige in those days.

She looked very pale, and said that she had been having really terrible pains like a knife on the train, so bad that the people in her carriage said she should go to a hospital or a doctor, since she had been crying out with the sharpness of them. Tom looked concerned and just at that moment she bent over again, doubled up with pain and letting out a long, low scream, so his mind was made up. He drove her to the out-patients of a hospital. He was quiet and firm. He got her seen before anyone by saying it was an emergency. As her brother, he signed the permission to operate for a burst appendix and he was there when she woke up to tell her that it had all been fine, and it was over and all she had to do now was to rest. Her troubled face smiled at him sadly. Their mother came up the next day with a suitcase of things that Phil would need, a lot of reassurance, sighs of how good God was to let it all happen when Tom was there to take charge, and messages of love, boxes of chocolates, bottles of lavender water from the rest of the family.

She was recovering quite well, Tom thought. Well, her strength was coming back quickly and he was very startled when one of the nurses said she would like to talk to him about his sister. Privately. She had made a report to the people who should know already, like the matron and the surgeon who had operated, but this was now something that must be taken further, through Miss Fitzgerald's own doctor perhaps.

He was alarmed. The nurse spoke reprovingly, as if poor Phil had been caught stealing in the wards. What was it? Well, the nurse had noticed she spent a long time at the lavatory, and she had asked her about constipation or diarrhea. Apparently neither, but she was still in there for a considerable time, so the nurse had listened at the door. Tom felt his heart beating: what horror was he going to be told?

It was what the nurse had suspected. Vomiting, retching. Two or three times a day.

"What's causing it?" Tom cried. He had no idea what the tone of shock was all about. Why wasn't he being told this by a doctor?

"She's doing it herself," the nurse said. "Eating chocolates, biscuits, banana, slices of bread and butter. You should have seen the papers and the empty boxes. And then vomiting it all up."

"But why on earth would she do that?"

"It's called bulimia; it's like anorexia nervosa—you know, where people starve themselves to death if they can. It's a form of it. They binge and gorge and then they make themselves sick to get rid of the food they've eaten."

"Phil does this?"

"Yes, she's been doing it for some time."

"And did this cause her appendix to burst?"

"Oh, no, not at all, that was something totally unconnected. But maybe lucky in a way. Because at least now you know and the family will know and help her try to fight it."

"Can't you just tell her to stop? Can't we all tell her it's . . . it's revolting —it's so senseless."

"Oh, no, that's not the way, that's not what they'll say at all when she goes in."

"Goes in where?"

"To a psychiatric hospital. It's a mental condition, you know, it's got nothing to do with us."

The nurse wasn't quite correct. It did have a little to do with them because Phil was admitted to the psychiatric wing of that same hospital and there was a medical side to her treatment as well as all the therapy and group discussions on the psychiatric side. She had been very relieved at the beginning to know that other people did the same thing. She thought she was the only person in the world who had ever done it, and she felt a great burden of guilt taken off her shoulders. She never felt guilty about the self-induced vomiting: she said it was the easiest thing in the world. If you just put your finger in the right place down your throat it happened automatically. But she did feel guilty about stuffing herself with the food. Especially eating in a lavatory—that was the thing she felt shameful about. She wasn't ready at all to talk about why she did it. Tom was told that she would undoubtedly do it again and again before she was cured. Before she came back to reality and accepted that she was perfectly fine as she was. The help and support of a family at a time like this was crucial. If Phil was to see that she was a person of high esteem in her own family, that would go a very long way toward helping her have a good image of herself again. The family, yes. But Lord God, the Fitzgerald family. At this time.

Poor Phil couldn't have picked a worse time to call on them, Tom thought grimly. It was the very period that the newspapers were full of the case about the armed raid on the post office in Cork and the subsequent conviction and sentencing of Teddy Fitzgerald, their cousin, who had worked in the business with the family. That had been a heavy cross. Then there was the infidelity of Dominic, the highly suitable husband of Anna, the eldest. There had been many a tale of a relationship and finally the birth of a child that Dominic grudgingly acknowledged as his, even though it was born not to his wife but to one of the most unsuitable women in the west of Ireland, tinkers who had settled down— and according to Mrs. Peg Fitzgerald the only thing worse than a tinker on the road was a tinker who had settled down. So there was that disgrace. There had been a few other things, too, none of them as shocking but all of them adding up to a general family anxiety. It was the wrong time to hear that a member of the family was now entering on to a long period of psychiatric treatment and would need their support.

Mrs. Fitzgerald made her point of view absolutely clear. There would be no talk about Phil whatsoever. This was final. Phil had recovered from her burst appendix, she had been convalescing, she had been visiting friends, she would come back shortly. Meanwhile they would get a temporary girl for the office. Mrs. Fitzgerald would go to Dublin once a month to give this support that the hospital said it needed, Tom would go to see her as often as he could, and that was it. It would not be discussed; they had quite enough problems already without adding this one. And what would it do to Phil's chances of getting a husband if it was widely known she had been in a mental institution? No more arguments.

Tom was sure that this was not what the doctors meant by family support: hushing it all up, making it into a greater shame than Phil already felt it was. He was certain that his mother's monthly visits—full of assurances that nobody knew, no one suspected, people had been fooled and hoodwinked, cover stories had been invented—were all the worst thing for his sister, who would listen with stricken face and apologize for all the trouble she had caused. Sometimes his mother would reach out awkwardly and take Phil's hand.

"We love you . . . um . . . very much. You are much loved, Phil." Then she would draw her hand back, embarrassed. She had been told by the psychiatrist that this was a good line to emphasize, but she recited it as if it were learned by heart. They were not a demonstrative family, they had never hugged or kissed each other. It was hard for his mother to reach out and say that to Phil—and bewildering for Phil to hear it, just before her mother gathered her gloves and handbag and started to leave.

He went to see Phil every day, every single day, and he telephoned her on each Saturday and Sunday. His mother said that she would telephone except that there was nothing to say, but Tom found things. After all, he knew her much better: they had been meeting each other constantly, and he was able to pick from a variety of things to say. He never felt as if he were talking to someone who wasn't well. He didn't talk down to her, he would never apologize profusely if he hadn't been able to ring or visit, just briefly. He wouldn't let on that he thought his presence was essential to her. He treated her as if she were as sane as he was.

They talked about childhood a lot. Tom remembered his as happy enough, too much talk about the business, a bit too much of covering over and not letting the neighbors know this or that, and keeping our business to ourselves. Phil remembered it quite differently. She remembered that they were always laughing, and that they had all been sitting around the table together talking to each other, though Tom said they couldn't have been. There would have to have been either their mother or their father in the shop. Phil remembered them going on great outings to the sea and picnics; Tom said he honestly could only remember one. Phil said they used to play games like I Spy and the Minister's Cat, and Sardines, where one person had to hide and when you found them you squeezed in like a sardine beside them. Tom said that was only at parties. But they didn't fight over the memories; they talked them over like an old film that you'd seen years ago and everyone could remember bits of, but nobody could remember all of.

They talked about boyfriends and girlfriends and sex. Tom wasn't surprised to hear that she was a virgin, and she wasn't surprised to hear that he was not. They talked easily and without guilt, sometimes for hours in the day room or in the garden, sometimes just for short times because Phil was silent and withdrawn, or because Tom had to work. He was working in an auction showroom these days, helping to carry furniture in and out, put lot numbers on things and write them up in a catalogue. He had been thinking of moving on, but the hours suited him and it was near the hospital, so he could come and go easily.

One of the other patients asked if Tom was her boyfriend. She had laughed uneasily and said she never had a boyfriend. The other girl had shrugged and said she was probably as well off: they were a barrelful of trouble, that's all they were. She hadn't assumed for a moment that Phil *couldn't* have a boyfriend. It made Phil feel a lot more cheerful. She asked Tom what kind of girls he liked, and he said unusual ones, not people who talked about houses and engagement rings and the future. He had a very nice girlfriend once, but unfortunately she met a really dull guy and he offered her all this other business—security, respectability—and she came and told Tom straight out she was going to take it. Phil had been very sympathetic.

"You never told us any of this," she said.

"True, but you never told us that you half fancied Billy Burns, even though he was a married man," he said, laughing.

"You dragged that out of me." She laughed too. He thought it was all too slow, she *must* be better now.

He said this more than once to the psychiatrist, and was depressed to hear that Phil was still not happy, still not at ease with herself and sure of her place in the world. They all thanked Tom for coming and said he was invaluable. Not only in his own visits but in the lifeline he offered back to Rathdoon. She never minded his going back home at weekends. In fact, she liked it because it brought her closer to the family and because he always brought back news of them all and, better still, a cheerful letter from her mother.

Every Saturday morning he forced his mother to write her a letter. He literally sat there while she wrote. He wouldn't accept that she had nothing to write about, and he refused to let her wriggle out of it.

"Do you think I'd be doing this, do you think I'd sit here every Saturday morning unless it was important?" he had shouted. "She is desperate to know that we are fond of her, and that her place is here; she won't be *able* to come back unless she knows this."

"But of course it's here; naturally we want her back. For heaven's sake, Tom, you're making a big drama out of it all."

"It is a big drama. Phil is in a psychiatric hospital and mainly because we can't let her know that she is important here."

"Your father and I think that's all mumbo jumbo. She was never made to feel anything but important; we treated her with great respect; people loved having her in the office. She was always so cheerful, and she knew everyone's names: wasn't she the life and soul of that place?"

"Write it. Write it down on paper," he would order.

"I'd feel stupid saying that to Phil. It's silly, it's treating her as if she's not all there. She'll know I'm only acting."

"But you said you meant it, a minute ago."

"Yes, of course I mean it, but it's not something you say, not something you write down."

"Since you're not there to say it, you have to write it. Since you won't let her come home and be treated in the town where you'd only be seventeen miles away, where you could see her every day, then you're going to have to write it. Otherwise how is she to know, how in God's earth can she *know* that she's important here?"

"It's not that I won't let her come back here. It's for her own good, to keep things quiet, to keep our business to ourselves." He had heard it so often, maybe he would hear it forever. Perhaps Phil would never get better.

He was in the middle of yet another Saturday confrontation when Celia Ryan came in. He was surprised to see her, and in a way relieved. His mother had been very hard to pin down today. She had escaped him in the morning by saying she was needed in the shop, and it was only when he brought her a cup of coffee and a writing pad that he could get her to listen. She had been going through one of her Phil-must-pull-herself-together phases. Tom felt a mad urge to ask Celia to sit down and explain to his mother her own firsthand knowledge of anorexia and bulimia, mentioning casually that Phil was in a psychiatric ward with the latter. His mother would probably fall senseless to the ground if he were to tell the family disgrace to Mrs. Ryan's daughter. The temptation had only been a flicker.

Celia wanted a loan of his tape recorder, of all things, and a blank cassette. She wanted to record something. She seemed flustered. She didn't tell him what she wanted it for, but then he rarely told people anything, whether they asked him or not, so he couldn't fault her there. She said she'd give it to him on the bus.

"Terrible time she has with that mother of hers," Mrs. Fitzgerald said.

Tom nodded. He thought he didn't have a great time with his own mother, but it was not in him to say it; he just wanted the letter to give to Phil on Monday.

"She'll probably marry Bart Kennedy, and they can keep an eye on the place that way," Tom said.

"Bart Kennedy? Not at all. Sure, nobody will marry Bart Kennedy, he's not the type that marries." Mrs. Fitzgerald was positive.

"Bart, a fairy? Go on out of that."

"No, I don't mean that or anything like it. He's just not the kind of man who marries, you must see that. Maybe men don't notice these things: women do. Red Kennedy, now, he'll be married within the year, I'd say; I hear he's courting. But Bart—not at all."

"I thought that's what she came home for," Tom said.

"She comes home to stop that place going down the drain, that's all."

"Really?" Tom felt pleased. He didn't know why, but he felt a sense of relief.

He went into the pub that night and discovered why she had wanted the tape recorder. It seemed a bit sneaky somehow. Like taking advantage of the poor woman who was slobbering and messing around behind her own bar. Even more humiliating was the thought that Mrs. Ryan's daughter was recording the tuneless singing.

"She doesn't know, she really doesn't know," Celia said as an explanation when he had asked her was it fair. He imagined Celia trying to tell her mother about the excesses of the night before and Mrs. Ryan brushing it away with that businesslike, cheerful manner she had when sober. It wasn't the kind of thing anyone else would say to her, so she would be bound to believe that Celia was making it up at worst or at the very least exaggerating it.

"I'll come around tomorrow and pick up the pieces," he said. She smiled back at him, a warm grateful smile. He looked at Bart Kennedy. Bart was pulling pints and laughing with the lads—he and Celia didn't have eyes for each other at all. Tom must have been mad to have thought it in the first place.

There were no pieces to pick up next day. Celia's mother had taken it very well. She was sitting in the back room while Celia and Bart dealt with the Sunday lunchtime trade.

"She's coming to Dublin. I thought it would be easier. I'd be able to get to see her."

"When?"

"Tomorrow. I won't come back on the bus tonight. I'll wait and go with her. I've a great friend, a nurse in Dublin—she'll work for me tomorrow even though it's meant to be her day off."

"Does she live in your harem of nurses?"

"Emer? Not at all: she's a respectable married woman with a family."

"Would you work if you were married?"

"Bloody sure, I would. Catch me giving up a job to cook meals and clean a house for a man. Anyway, everyone has to nowadays. How would you have any life at all if you didn't? And nursing's fine, I'd hate to lose it."

"How long will it be . . . ?" He nodded toward the back room, where Mrs. Ryan sat waiting in a chair.

"I don't know. It depends on her—you know, if she wants to."

"Doesn't it depend on her family, too, and support?"

"Well, there's only me; she can't have the beauties in Australia and Detroit and England, so she'll have to make do with me."

"My sister Phil isn't well, she's got the same problem," he said suddenly.

"I never knew Phil had a drink problem." She said it without censure or shock.

"No, not that, I meant she has the same problem: she only has me in Dublin. She's got an anorexic thing, you know, but she does eat and makes herself vomit."

"She's a better chance with that; so many of the anorexics die, it's desperate to see them, little wizened monkeys, and they think that this is the best way to be. But bulimia is very stressful, poor Phil. Isn't that very bad luck."

He looked at her gratefully. "Will they be any help, the ones who've gone away?"

"I shouldn't think so. Will yours?"

"No. I'm beginning to realize it now. I kept thinking I could change them, but it's all head in the sand, pretend it isn't happening, don't tell anyone."

"In time, in their time maybe. Not yours." She was very gentle.

"Well, they'll have to make do with us then," he said, "your half-mad ma and my half-mad sister."

"Aren't they lucky they've got us," said Celia Ryan, and laughed like a peal of bells.

"I'll miss you going back on the bus tonight," he said.

"Well, maybe you might come and console me when I've got my mother in. And if it would be any help, I could come and see Phil with you—if you'd like it, that is?"

"I'd like it a lot," said Tom Fitzgerald.

Dublin Four

Dinner in Donnybrook

She drew the dinner table six times and it always came out the same. If you put the host at one end and the hostess at the other it didn't work out. She would sit with her back to the window and have a man on either side of her. Fine so far. Dermot would sit opposite her with a woman on either side of him. Fine again, but what about the two places in between? Whatever way you did it you would have to have man sitting beside man, and woman beside woman.

She shook her head, puzzled. It was like those problems they had always done at school; if you have three missionaries and three cannibals on an island and the boat can only hold two . . . Not that it mattered, of course, and anybody who knew how much time she had spent working it out would say she should spend a week in St. Patrick's, but still it was very irritating. There must be a way.

"There is," said her daughter, Anna. She had telephoned Anna to talk about something else but brought the conversation around to the perplexing dinner table. "At a party for eight, host and hostess can't sit opposite each other. You sit opposite the most important lady . . . and put Dad on that lady's left." Anna had gone on talking about other things, not realizing that her mother was now drawing the dinner table again, with Dermot sitting facing the sideboard and the most important lady sitting at the other end of the table facing herself.

"Are you all right, Mother?" Anna asked. Anna used to call her "Mum," but now she said "Mother." She said it in a slightly joky tone as if she had been saying Your Ladyship, it was as if the word Mother were equally unsuitable.

"I'm fine, dear," said Carmel. It irritated her when people asked was she all right. She never asked anyone else were they all right, even when they sounded most odd or distrait. Everyone felt they could patronize her, and pat her on the head. Even her own daughter.

"Oh, good, you sounded a bit vague as if you'd gone off somewhere. Anyway, as I said, we're off to the cottage at the weekend so you'll have to tell me how the great entertaining went. I'm glad you and Dad are having people around. It's good to see you stirring yourself to do something."

Carmel wondered again why Dermot could still be "Dad" and not "Father," and why it was good to be stirring herself. Why should things be stirred? Particularly, why should people be stirred? They should be left to simmer or cool down or even grow a crust on top of them if they wanted to. She said none of this to her eldest daughter.

"Oh, no, dear, the dinner party isn't this weekend. It's in a month's time. . . . I was just thinking ahead."

Anna burst out laughing. "Mother, you *are* full of surprises. A month ahead! Not even James would insist on that much planning. Anyway, we'll have plenty of time to talk about it before then." She made it sound like basketwork in an occupational therapy ward. Carmel hid her annoyance and hoped they would have a nice weekend. The weather forecast was good, and especially in the southwest.

She thought that Anna and James were quite insane to drive two hundred and nine miles on a Friday afternoon and the same distance again on Sunday. She could see no point in having a house and garden out in Sandycove and never getting to spend a weekend there. The cottage in Kerry had been an albatross around their necks as far as Carmel could see. She never believed that they could enjoy the five-hour drive. "Four hours thirty-five minutes, Grandmama, if you know the shortcuts . . ." James always made her feel even more foolish with his Grandmama; she felt like a grand duchess. But still Anna never complained, she spoke of it eagerly: "Oh, Mother, it's so great, we get there around nine-thirty and light a fire, take out the steaks, open the wine, kiddies half asleep already, pop them into bed . . . it's so free . . . the country . . . our own place . . . you can't believe it."

Anna had heard the weather forecast too. "Yes, I am glad, because we're having a huge lunch there on Sunday and it will be so much nicer if we can have them all out-of-doors."

A huge lunch, down at that cottage, in the wilds of Kerry, miles from her kitchen, her deep freeze, her dishwasher. No wonder Anna must think her pathetic, worrying about seating people at a dinner party a whole month away. But, of course, Anna didn't have the same kind of worries. Anna would never let herself get into a situation where she would have those kind of worries.

Carmel drew the table plan again. She wrote in the names of the guests carefully. At one end of the table with her back to the window she wrote Carmel, and at the opposite end she wrote out Ruth O'Donnell, Most Important Lady. She filled in the other names and wrote things under them too. Dermot, Loving Husband. Sheila, Wise Friend. Ethel, Upper Class Friend. Martin, Kind Husband of Wise Friend. David, Pompous Husband of Upper Class Friend. And then on the right-hand side of Ruth O'Donnell she wrote, slowly and carefully, Joe, Life-Saver. She sat and looked at the plan for a long time. It stopped being a drawing of a rectangle with little squares around it holding names and descriptions. It became a table with glasses and flowers and good china and shining silver. She could almost smell the food and hear the conversation. She learned it off by heart, the order they sat in, just like she had learned the Great Lakes or the towns of Cavan when she was a child, by rote with her eyes tightly closed, relating not to things as they were but as they were written down.

Then she took all the bits of paper and put them into the firegrate. There were still some warm embers and some bits of red from last night's fire, but she didn't trust them to burn. She took out half a firelighter and set a match to it. And there in the room where she would give the party in a month's time, she sat and watched the flames burn the lists and the table plans. They burned away until there were only powdery ashes left on top of yesterday's.

"I think Carmel Murray is losing her marbles," said Ethel at breakfast.

David grunted. He was reading his own letters and he did not want to be distracted by Ethel's chat.

"No seriously, listen to this . . ." Ethel went back to the start of the letter.

"In a moment, Ethel . . ."

"No, you'll just leap up and go off, I want you to hear."

He looked at her and knew he might as well give in. Ethel got her way in everything, and it made for an easy life to accept this.

"Carmel has lost her marbles? Go on from there."

"Well, she must have. She's written to us. Written to ask us to dinner . . . next *month* . . . can you believe it?"

"Well, that's nice of her," said David vaguely. "I suppose we can get out of it. What's the fuss, what's so mad about that? People do ask each other to dinner. They do it all the time."

He knew he was courting trouble to try to be smart-alecky with Ethel. He was right; it had been a mistake.

"I know people do it all the time, dear," she said. "But Carmel Murray has never done it before. Poor Carmel that we have to be nice to because Dermot's a good sort . . . that's why it's unusual. And did you ever hear of anything so strange? A letter when she only lives five minutes away, when she may have heard of the telephone."

"Yes, yes. It is odd. I do agree. You must do what you wish, say we're away, say it's a pity . . . some other time. What?"

"She'll know we're not away. That's what's so odd, it's on the day of Ruth O'Donnell's exhibition, she'll know that we won't be out of town for that."

"How do you know it's that day?"

"Because she says so in the letter . . . she says that she's asked Ruth as well. Now do you see why I think she's losing her marbles?"

Ethel looked flushed and triumphant, having proved her point. She sat imperiously at the breakfast table wearing her silk breakfast kimono and waited for the apology from her husband. It came.

"She's inviting Ruth. . . . Oh, my God. Now I see what you mean."

Sheila hated being disturbed at school. It made the nuns so edgy and uneasy to call someone to the telephone. They hadn't moved into the modern age in terms of communications; their telephone was still in a cold and drafty little booth in the main entrance hall, inconvenient for everyone. She was alarmed when she heard that her husband wanted her.

"Martin, what is it, what's happened?" she said.

"Nothing. Nothing, relax."

"What do you mean, nothing? What is it?"

"Stop fussing, Sheila, it's nothing."

"You brought me the whole way down here from third years for nothing? Sister Delia is looking after them as a great favor. What *is* it, Martin? Are the children—?"

"Look, I thought you ought to know, we've had a very odd letter from Carmel."

"A what . . . from Carmel?"

"A letter. Yes, I know it's sort of out of character, I thought maybe something might be wrong and you'd need to know—"

"Yes, well, what did she say? What's the matter with her?"

"Nothing, that's the problem. She's inviting us to dinner."

"To dinner?"

"Yes, it's sort of funny, isn't it? As if she wasn't well or something. I thought you should know in case she got in touch with you."

"Did you really drag me all the way down here, the third form is at the top of the school you know, I thought it had burned down! God, wait till I come home to you. I'll murder you."

"The dinner's in a month's time, and she says she's invited Ruth O'Donnell."

"Oh, Jesus Christ."

Henry shouted out to Joe, "Hey, that letter's come from Ireland. She must have fixed the date, poor old bat."

Joe came in and opened it.

"Yeah, in a month's time. She says it's all going according to plan. She sent the ticket and the money."

"She's all right, isn't she?" Henry sounded approving.

"Oh, she's really fine, and I owe her, I owe her in a big way. I'll make it work."

"Well, if you can't, I don't know who could," Henry said admiringly, and Joe smiled back as he fetched the coffee percolator.

"I think Mother's coming out of herself a bit more, darling," Anna said to James as they negotiated the early evening traffic.

"Good. It's no wonder this country's going to the dogs. Look at the buildup of traffic here and it's not even four o'clock. I mean, half of them must be taking the whole afternoon off. Never mind, we'll lose them in a few minutes. What were you saying about Grandmama?"

"She's talking of having a dinner party, you know, with a proper dining table, and a seating plan. It all sounds good."

"I've always said that she's not nearly so sleepy and dozy as you and Bernadette make out. I find plenty of things to talk to her about."

"No, you don't, you just talk at her. She sits enthralled because you're so interesting, but it's not a real conversation."

James didn't agree. "You're wrong, she tells me things. No, I can't remember anything immediately. That's silly, looking for examples. But I do get on well with her . . . she just needs a bit of flattery, a few cheerful things. 'You look very dishy, Grandmama,' and she blossoms. She doesn't like people telling her she's silly."

Anna thought for a while.

"I suppose people do tell her she's silly. Yes, you're right. I always say 'Don't be silly, Mother,' but I don't mean it. It's just that she fusses so much, and I think that if I say she's not to be silly, then it's sort of reassuring to her. I'll be very supportive about her poor old dinner party. I'll give her a tactful hand here and there."

James patted her knee.

"You're marvelous, sweetheart. And talking about parties, tell me what you've arranged for Sunday."

Anna settled back happily in her seat and told him about all the good things that were foil wrapped, vacuum packed and airtight in the huge cardboard box which they had loaded carefully into the boot of the car.

Bernadette said, "That's great, Mummy. Great. I'm sure it will be marvelous."

"I just thought you'd like to know," Carmel said.

"Well, of course I'm thrilled, Mummy. Is it tonight, or when?"

"Oh, no, dear, it's a dinner party. It's not for a month."

"A *month*! Mummy, are you all right?"

"Yes, dear, perfectly."

"Oh. Well. I mean, is there anything . . . do you want me to come and help you plan it, or anything?"

"No, no, it's all planned."

"Or serve it? You know, keep you calm and stop you fussing on the night?"

"No, no, dear, thank you, but I won't fuss at all."

"Well, that's great, Mummy, and is Daddy pleased that you're sort of getting into entertaining and everything?"

"It's not exactly getting into entertaining . . . it's just one dinner party."

"You know what I mean. Is Daddy thrilled?"

"I haven't told him yet."

"Mummy, are you sure you're all right, you're not getting upset or anything like . . ."

"Like what, dear?"

"Like that time when you *did* get upset."

"Oh no, dear, of course I'm not. That was when I had the trouble with my sleep patterns, they got out of kilter. . . . No, that's all totally cured, thank God, now. You know that, Bernadette dear. I sleep like a log these nights. No, no, that's not come back at all, thank heavens."

Bernadette sounded troubled.

"No, well, good. You have to look after yourself, Mummy. You know the way you fuss about silly things, I don't want you fussing about this party—"

"You don't understand, child, I'm looking forward to it."

"Good, oh, and we'll come and see you soon, it's been ages."

"Whenever you can, dear. Ring first though, I'll be out a lot in the next few weeks."

"Will you, Mummy? Where?"

"Here and there, dear. Anyway, it will be great to see you. How's Frank?"

"He's fine, Mummy. Take care of yourself, won't you?"

"Yes, Bernadette. Thank you, dear."

Dermot thought that Carmel was a hundred miles away that morning. Twice he had said that he might be late and not to worry if he dropped into the golf club on the way home. He had to have a few chats and that was the best place to have them. Twice she had nodded amiably and distantly as if she hadn't really heard or understood.

"Will you be all right? What are you going to do today?" he had asked, uncharacteristically.

She had smiled. "Funny you should ask that. I was just thinking that I hadn't anything to do all day so I was going to stroll downtown and look at the shops. I was thinking that it was almost a sinful thing to do . . . just idling away the day."

Dermot had smiled back. "You're entitled to be that sinful, enjoy yourself. And as I said, if I'm late I won't want anything to eat. We might go and have a steak . . . you know. Don't fuss, don't go to any trouble."

"No, that's fine," she had said.

As he sat in the traffic on Morehampton Road listening to the fool on Radio Eireann telling him exactly what he knew, that Morehampton Road was blocked solid, Dermot had a vague sense of unease about Carmel. But he shook himself and decided to put it out of his mind.

"I'm becoming quite neurotic," he told himself. "If she does hound me about my movements and tell me detail by detail the trivia of her day I become annoyed. Now I'm uneasy because she doesn't. Impossible to please me." He decided that everyone was being too bright on the radio and turned to the BBC where they were more solemn and in keeping with a man's thoughts in the morning as he drove in to his office.

Ruth O'Donnell hadn't got her invitation because she was away. She had gone to a farmhouse in Wales for a complete rest. She could have gone to an Irish farmhouse, but she wanted to be sure that she didn't meet anyone she knew. It wouldn't be a complete rest if she met people. She wanted to be absolutely on her own.

Carmel waited until the end of the *Gay Byrne* show. During *The Living Word* she put on her coat and took out her shopping basket on wheels. She never liked to miss Gay; once she had been able to give him a small cooker for a one-parent family. She hadn't spoken to him himself but the girl on the show had been very nice, and they had sent a nice girl to collect it, or else she was from the organization that had asked for it. It had never been made quite clear. Carmel had sent in one or two entries for the mystery voice competition, too, but she had never been called on to guess it. She didn't like to leave the house before *The Living Word*. It seemed rude to God, to walk out just when the few short minutes of religion were on.

She knew she should really listen to programs like *Day by Day,* which followed it, they would make her informed, but somehow she always felt her mind wandering and she never quite understood why people got so hot under the collar about things. Once she had said to Sheila that it would be nice to have someone sitting beside you to tell you what was going on in life, and Sheila told her to shut up, otherwise everyone would say they had learned nothing after all those years with the Loreto nuns. She thought that Sheila had been upset that day but she couldn't be sure.

It was bright and sunny out, a nice autumn day. She pushed her tartan shopping bag on wheels in front of her, remembering when it had been a pram that she pushed. She used to know many more people in those days. She was always stopping and talking to people, wasn't she? Or was that memory playing tricks, like thinking that the summers were always hot when she was young and that they had spent their whole time on Killiney beach? That wasn't true, her younger brother Charlie said that they only went twice or three times a summer; perhaps the other memory wasn't true either. Perhaps she didn't stop at the bottom of Eglinton Road when she pointed out to the girls where the buses went to sleep in the bus home, perhaps there had been nobody much around then either.

She looked at the prices of wine in the off-license and wrote down the names of some of them so that she could make her list and selection later on. She then spent a happy hour looking at books in the big bookshop. She copied down recipe after recipe in her little jotter. From time to time she got a look from one of the assistants, but she looked respectable and was causing no trouble so nobody said anything. Seared in her mind was a remark that Ethel had once made about a house where she had dined. "The woman has no imagination. I can't understand why you ask people around for prawn cocktail and roast beef. . . . I mean, why not tell them to eat at home and come around later for drinks?" Carmel loved prawn cocktail, and had little glass dishes which it would look very well in. They used to have trifle in them when she was young. She had kept them after things had been divided up between herself and Charlie, but she had never used them. They stood gathering dust, eight of them, at the back of the cupboard in the scullery. She would make another kind of starter, not prawn cocktail, and she would use those selfsame glasses for it, whatever it was. She rejected grapefruit segments and worked it out methodically. You couldn't have pâté, that would have to be on a plate, or soup, that couldn't be in a glass, or any kind of fish, of course. . . . No, it had to be something cold you ate with a spoon.

She would find it eventually, she had all day, she had twenty-nine more days —there was no rush. She must not get fussed. She found it. Orange Vinaigrette. Ethel couldn't say that that was unimaginative. You cut up oranges and black olives and onions and fresh mint . . . sounded terrific, you poured a vinaigrette sauce over it . . . it would be perfect. Carmel smiled happily. She knew that she was doing the right thing. All she had to do was go at it slowly.

She would go home now and rest; tomorrow she would come out and find a main course, and then a dessert. She had work to do at home too. Joe had said that if he was going to come and help her he would need cooperation. She mustn't have turned into a dowdy, middle-aged old frump, she must look smart and glamorous and well turned-out. She had thirty afternoons to organize that.

Sheila dropped in on her way home from school. She seemed relieved to find Carmel there, and there was a look of worry on her face.

"I was a little alarmed. Martin told me you had sent us a letter."

"It was only an invitation." Carmel smiled. "Come on in and we'll have a coffee. I was in the middle of tidying out some cupboards. I've a lot of clothes that should go to the Vincent de Paul . . . but you know what always happens, you're ashamed to give them the way they are, so you get them cleaned first. Then when they come back from the cleaners they're better than anything else you have in the press so you never give them at all." Carmel laughed happily as they went into the kitchen, and she put on the kettle.

"It just seemed so funny to write, when I talk to you nearly every day."

"Did it? Oh, I don't know, I'm such a bad hostess I thought you have to write things down as invitations or people didn't believe you. I suppose that's why I wrote. I'd have told you anyway."

"But you didn't tell me yesterday."

"No, I must have forgotten."

"There's nothing wrong, is there, Carmel? You *are* all right?"

Carmel had her back to Sheila. She deliberately relaxed her shoulders and refused to clench her fists. Nobody was going to see just how annoyed she became when people asked her in that concerned tone whether she was all right.

"Sure I am, why wouldn't I be, a lady of leisure? It's you who must be exhausted coping with all that noise and those demons all day. I think you should be canonized."

"Tell me about the dinner party," Sheila said.

"Oh, it's not for a month yet," Carmel laughed.

"I know." Sheila's patience seemed strained. "I know it's not for a month, but you actually put pen to paper and wrote, so I thought it was a big thing."

"No, no, just eight of us. I said it in the letter."

"Yes, Martin told me. I wasn't at home when it arrived."

"He rang you? Oh, isn't he good? There was no need to. I mean, you could have told me anytime."

"Yes, and you could have told *me* anytime." Sheila looked worried.

"Yes, of course. Heavens, we are both making a production of it! When you think how many parties Ethel goes to, and indeed gives—"

"Yes, well, Ethel is Ethel."

"And you, I mean you and Martin often have people around, don't you? I often hear you say you had people in."

"Yes, but that's very casual."

"Oh, this will be too. Mainly people we all know well."

"But Ruth—Ruth O'Donnell—we don't know her all that well, and honestly, do you know, I think that's the night that her exhibition opens—in fact I'm sure of it."

"Yes, I know it is, I said that in the letter. Didn't Martin tell you? So I know we'll all be going to it. But it's at four o'clock . . . it will be well over by six, and even if people go to have a drink afterward . . . well, they're not invited here until eight, for half past."

"Yes, but don't you think on the night of her own exhibition she might want to go out with her own friends?"

"But we're her friends, in a way."

"Not really, are we? I mean, are you? She doesn't normally come here?"

"No, I don't think she's ever been here. I thought it would be nice for her . . . and she doesn't live far away, in that new block of flats, so she won't have far to go to change."

Sheila put down her mug of coffee.

"I don't think it's a good idea. We don't know her. Why ask someone we don't know very well to a dinner? Let's just have the six of us . . . it would be more friendly."

"No, I've asked her anyway, and I can't think what you say that for. You're the one who tells me to go out and meet more people."

"I didn't tell you to go out and invite well-known artists to dinner," muttered Sheila.

"Don't lecture me," Carmel said with a laugh, and Sheila had to admit to herself that Carmel did look more cheerful and like herself than she had in the last while. She looked a bit more like the Carmel of the old days.

"All right, I won't. Let me see your cupboard cleaning. Maybe you could give something to me instead of the Vincent de Paul. I could do with it. A teacher doesn't get paid much, God help us, when you consider how we put our lives at risk."

"How's Martin feeling?"

"Oh, he's fine. He's great, you know, he never complains. I'm sure he's fed up but he never complains." Martin had been made redundant two years ago when two firms had merged. He had got a golden handshake. He was still only fifty-two and he expected to get another job, then he expected to write a book. Everybody else thought he was writing a book, but Sheila never lied to Carmel. To Carmel she admitted that Martin was doing the vacuuming and the shopping. They pretended that Sheila loved being back in the classroom. Not many people knew how much she hated it. Her children didn't know, not even Martin really knew. Carmel sometimes suspected, but Carmel was a longtime friend. It didn't matter what she knew. It was just a bit worrying sometimes the things she did. Like inviting that woman to dinner. Was there a possibility that Carmel's nerves were bad again? She sounded so well, and she looked fine. But it *was* the act of a madwoman.

"Hey, you are doing a thorough job. You've taken everything out. Which is the good pile and which is the bad pile?"

"I don't know, they all seem the same. They're like mouse clothes, aren't they? Do you remember when we went to pantomimes years and years ago? People were dressed in mouse outfits and rat outfits . . . that's what these are like!"

"Carmel, you are preposterous! Of course your clothes aren't like that, they're smashing. Have you two of these blue cardigans?"

"I think I've three of them. Whenever I go to a shop I can never think of anything to buy except gray skirts and blue cardigans. Have one of each."

"I mean it. Quite, quite preposterous."

Carmel smiled happily. Other people said "Don't be silly"; Sheila said she was preposterous. It was much, much nicer.

"Well?" Martin wanted to know.

"I *think* she's all right. It's hard to know."

"You mean it was a joke about the invitation?"

"No, she means it. She's having the party, she just doesn't want to talk about it."

"Then she's not all right."

"I know, but she *seems* normal. She gave me a skirt and a cardigan."

"That makes her normal?"

"No, you know what I mean. She was talking about ordinary things. She hadn't gone off on any flight of fancy or anything."

"So did you talk her out of it?" Martin wanted to know.

"I couldn't; she wouldn't talk about it at all. I *told* you."

"Oh, great," he sighed. "That's all we need. You're her friend, for Christ's sake."

"Martin, I've had a bad day. Not just a bit of a bad day—every single bit of it was bad. I don't want to talk about it anymore. I did my best to talk to Carmel. She wouldn't talk back, that's all. Can't you leave me alone!"

"Yes, I know I should have had a drink ready and the fire lighting and tried to soothe away your cares . . . like a proper housewife. I'm sorry I'm bad at it. You don't have to tell me."

"Jesus, Martin, if this is the night you've picked to do a wretched 'I'm not a good provider' act, then you've picked the wrong night. Will you shut up and sit down. I love you, I don't want you to fart around pandering to me just because *my* outfit didn't close down . . . do you hear me?"

He was contrite.

"I'm sorry. I really am. I'm just worried, that's all."

"So am I."

"Do you think she knows about Ruth? Do you think she heard anything?"

"How could she have heard anything? Who does she meet? Where does she go? Unless it was on the *Gay Byrne Hour* or in the *Evening Press Diary,* she'd not have heard."

"What are we going to do?"

"I haven't a clue."

"I'm sorry I'm late," called David. "The traffic was bloody terrible. There's no point in taking a car in these days, I've said it over and over."

"So have I. The number ten would take you to your door."

"I can't travel on the number ten. It never comes, or it's full when it does."

"Anyway, why buy a big car and not show it off?"

"What?" David sounded bad-tempered in the hall.

"Nothing. You said you're sorry you're late, get a move on then, if you want to change or wash or anything."

"For what?" David sounded even crosser. "Oh, God, I'd forgotten. Do we have to? Can't we—?"

"We *do* have to and we *can't* ring and say we're tied up. We accepted two weeks ago."

"It's all very well for you." David was pounding up the stairs crossly. "You have nothing to do all day but get yourself ready . . . titivate . . . titivate."

"Thank you," Ethel said icily.

She sat at the dressing table in their bedroom. The door to the bathroom was open and he could see the thick colored towels piled up on the chest of drawers. He knew he would feel much better when he had a bath, he knew it was unfair to blame her.

"I'm sorry," he said.

He kissed her at the dressing table. She smelled whiskey.

"Do they serve cocktails in traffic jams?" she asked.

He laughed. "You've caught me out. I dropped into the club." He looked contrite.

"Which is, of course, on the route home." She was still cold.

"No, of course it wasn't, but I took the lower road. Oh, hell, I only had two, but do you know who was there? You'll never guess what happened."

She was interested. He rarely told tales of interest from the outer world; she had to prod and pry and ferret to find out anything that might be happening. She followed him into the bathroom. He flung off his coat and struggled with his shirt.

"I met Dermot, Dermot Murray."

"Oh, yes?" She was as sharp as a hawk now, pique forgotten. "What did he say?"

"Well, it's amazing, it's quite amazing."

"Yes? Yes?"

"He was sitting talking to some fellows, I don't know who they were. I've seen one of them, perfectly respectable, in the property business, I think, out the Northside. Anyway, he was in that corner place with them."

"Yes . . . what did he say?"

"Wait, wait, I'm telling you." David had run the bath as he was speaking. The water gushed with powerful pressure from each tap, the room had steamed up in under a minute.

"I said to him, 'How are you, Dermot?' "

David stood in his underpants, tantalizing his wife by the meticulous way he was repeating the trivia of the conversation. She decided not to be drawn.

"I'll sit on the loo here and when you feel like telling me, do."

He pulled the shower curtains around him when he got into the bath. This was a modesty that had grown somewhere around the same time as his paunch. When they had been younger they had often bathed together, and had always bathed in front of each other.

"No, it's really strange," came the voice from inside the curtain. "I said, 'Thanks very much for that invitation,' and he said, 'What invitation?' and I got such a shock I started to play the fool. You know. I said, 'Come on now. You can't welch on us now, an invite's an invite.' "

"What did he say then?"

"He said, 'You have me on the wrong foot, David. I don't actually know what you mean.' He said it so straight, I felt a bit foolish. I just got out of it. I said that I had probably made a mistake, or that you hadn't looked at the letter properly."

"Thank you very much again," said Ethel.

"I had to say something. Anyway he said, 'Letter, what letter?' I was right into it then. I said, 'Oh, it's some mistake. I thought we'd got a letter from you and Carmel inviting us to dinner. I must have got it wrong.' He said it wasn't very likely that she'd have invited people without telling him. Maybe it was a surprise party."

"Boy, some surprise if it is!" said Ethel.

"That's what I thought, so I said the date. I said it's on the eighth. He said, 'Well, I never. Maybe it's all a birthday treat and I'm not meant to know.' But he looked worried. He said 'the eighth' again, as if it were familiar. Then he said, 'Not the eighth?' And I said, nervously you know, 'I'm sure I got it wrong.' "

"He doesn't know. She's doing it without telling him. She's asking us all around there for some kind of terrible drama. That's what it's all about."

Ethel's face looked stricken rather than excited. It should be an exciting thing
. . . a public row, a scandal. But not with Carmel Murray. Poor Carmel, she
was too vulnerable.

David got out of the bath and dried himself vigorously in one of the big
yellow towels.

"He really doesn't know she's giving the party, the poor devil. Isn't that a
dreadful thing? Thank God I said something, even though I felt I had walked
into it. At least it will give him a bit of time to know what action to take."

"But she can't know about Ruth, she can't possibly know." Ethel was
thoughtful.

"Somebody may have sent her a poison pen letter—you know, 'I think you
ought to know . . .' " David was still toweling himself dry.

"You'll rub the skin off your back. Come on, get dressed. She can't know.
If she knew would she in a million years ask her to dinner?"

Joe and Henry were cooking for a party. They often did home catering; it
was very easy money. They made the canapés while they watched television, and
put everything in the freezer. They got lots of free perks like plastic wrap and
foil from the hotel where Henry worked, and the use of a car from the tourist
guide service where Joe worked.

"Why won't the old bat let you do the cooking for her if she's so nervous?
You could run up a dinner in two hours."

"No, that's part of it. She has to be able to do it all herself."

"What does she look like? All sad and mopey, is she?"

"I don't know," said Joe. "I haven't seen her for twenty years. She may
have changed a lot since then."

"Hallo, Carmel, is that you?"

"Of course it is, love, who else would it be?"

"Carmel, I'm at the club. I told you, I've had to have a few chats, I told
you."

"I know you told me."

"So I won't be home, or I wasn't coming home. Have you had your
supper?"

"Supper?"

"Carmel, it's eight o'clock. I'm ringing you from the club to ask you a
simple question: Have you or have you not had your supper?"

"I had some soup, Dermot, but there's steak here, and cauliflower. . . . I
can cook whatever you like."

"Did you write to David?"

"*What?* It's very hard to hear you. There's a lot of noise behind you."

"Forget it. I'll come home."

"Oh, good. Would you like me to—?"

He had hung up.

All the way home he said to himself it was impossible. She couldn't have
decided to hold a dinner party without telling him, and if she had, if by some
mind-blowing horror she had decided to invite all their friends around to
witness a scene of marital bliss . . . how could she have chosen the eighth of
October?

It was Ruth's birthday, her thirtieth birthday. He had persuaded her to hold her exhibition that day, to show everyone that she had arrived. Ruth had said that she wanted no public exhibitions, no showing the world anything, unless he could stand beside her. She didn't want to go on hiding and pretending. When the reporters were sent to interview her she didn't want to have to laugh anymore and parry questions about why she had never married. She felt foolish telling people that her art was her life. It sounded so hollow, so second best and so phony. She wanted to tell them that she loved and was loved. It was this that gave her strength to paint.

She had agreed reluctantly. The gallery had been found with no trouble. People were anxious to hang the work of Ruth O'Donnell. The work was ready. She was drained. She said she wanted time away, far away, from him. She would not spend the days planning how to walk out of his life, she assured him of that, and he believed her. She just wanted to be free, to rest, and not to hide. He believed that too. He promised he wouldn't telephone her, nor write. That would be the same as being with him, she said. There was no point in a separation if you spent hours writing a letter and waiting for the post.

She was coming back on the first, a full week before it opened, in time to see everything hung. She had only left yesterday. It wasn't possible that coincidence should be so cruel as to mar this night for him by having a weeping Carmel on his hands. Because, by God, if she had arranged a dinner party for the eighth she was going to unarrange it fast. That was why he had left those two auctioneers sitting like eejits in the club. This had to be sorted out immediately.

"I think Mummy's a bit lonely," Bernadette said to Frank.

"We're all lonely. It's the lot of men and women to go through life alone, thinking they are with friends, but only brushing off people."

"I mean it," Bernadette said. "She's very good to us, Frank. She pretends she doesn't mind about us living together but she does, underneath."

"Nonsense. Just so long as we don't do anything too public in front of all those friends of hers, she's as right as rain."

"All what friends of hers? There are no friends."

"There must be. Posh house there in the heart of society . . . of course she has friends. Didn't you tell me tonight that she's organizing dinner parties months in advance?"

"That's what I don't like."

"God, there's no pleasing you! You're like a gnat; say out what you want and I'll debate whether we'll do it or not. Do you want us to kidnap her and keep her in the bathroom here tied by a dressing-gown cord for the rest of her life?"

"No," she laughed.

"What do you want, Ber?"

"I wondered if we might drop in tonight, on our way to the party. Please."

"Aw, God," he said.

"Just for a little bit," she begged.

"We'll be there all night," he said.

"We won't. We'll just get off the bus, run in and have a few words, and then run off again."

"That's worse than not going at all."

"No, it would ease my mind."

"Ten minutes then, right?"

"Half an hour, right?"

"Twenty minutes."

"Done."

"Don't say anything to the O'Briens about it, will you?" Ethel said when they were in the car.

"What would I say? I'm not a one for gossip, I never talk about people. You're the one who likes to tell and be told."

David had his eyes on the road but he knew his wife's profile was stern. "No, I'll say nothing to anyone. God, do you think we should do something or say something? We can't sit back and let it all happen."

"What can we do that would help, heavens above? You sound like Superman or the archangel Gabriel stepping in. What can we do?"

"I suppose we could say to Carmel that it's not a good idea, that she might like to think again."

"It's amazing how you manage to hold down a job, let alone run your own business," said Ethel acerbically.

"It's all due to the loyal little woman behind me. She had faith in me when no one else had," he said in a mock country-and-western accent.

"Well, if ever I meet the woman behind you I can tell you one thing, I'll not invite her to dinner with all our friends," said Ethel, and they drove on to the O'Briens in silence.

Frank and Bernadette were just leaving when Dermot's car drew up.

"Maybe he'd give us a lift," said Frank optimistically.

"I think that's a bit too sunny a view. I wouldn't ask him," said Bernadette. "How are you, Dad?"

"I see it's the annual visit," Dermot said.

"Hi, Mr. Murray," said Frank.

"Hallo, er . . ." said Dermot desperately, stumbling over his name.

Bernadette's fist clenched in her pocket. "We were just in having a chat with Mummy. We're off to a party."

"Don't let me delay you," Dermot said.

"Oh, Daddy, you can be very rude," Bernadette said. "Why can't you be nice and easygoing, and—"

"I don't know," Dermot said. "It must be something to do with having to go out and earn a living and take on responsibilities."

"We work too, Daddy."

"Huh," said Dermot.

"Nice to have talked with you, Mr. Murray," said Frank in an affected American accent.

"Sorry," Dermot said. "I'm in a bad mood. You do work, both of you. I'm just worried about something. Come back into the house and I'll give you a drink."

"That's mighty white of you, sir," said Frank.

"No, Dad, we've got to be off. We just looked in to see was Mummy all right."

"And she is, isn't she?" Dermot sounded alarmed.

"Oh, yes," Bernadette said, a little too quickly. "She's fine."

"I heard your voices. Did you meet them in the drive?" Carmel asked.

It had always irritated Dermot that she called the small distance to the gate a "drive": it was eleven steps from the hall door to the gate if you took giant steps, and the most you could make out of it was twenty little ones.

"Yes. What did they want?"

"Oh, Dermot, they just called in, it was nice of them."

"They said they came to see were you all right. Why did they do that?"

"That's what people do, dear, when they call to see other people."

She looked cheerful and calm. There was no resigned martyred air about her. She wasn't making little jokes that were not funny. She had no hint of tears.

"Will we have a proper meal at the table or would you like a snack by the television?" she asked. "The phone was so crackly and with the sound of people behind I couldn't hear whether you had a meal or you hadn't. You kept asking me had I . . ."

"Sit down, love," he said.

"Yes, I will in a minute, but what would you—"

"Sit down now, Carmel. I want to talk to you, not to your back drifting out the door."

"All right, Dermot, all right. Now, will this do?"

"Have you or have you not invited a whole lot of people here on the eighth of October?"

"Certainly not."

"You haven't?" The relief was overwhelming. It spilled all over his face. "I'm sorry, love. There was a silly misunderstanding."

"No. I just asked our friends and decided we'd have a nice evening and cook a nice dinner. You know you often said—"

"What do you mean—?"

"You've often said that we should have people around more, and somehow I didn't used to feel able for it, but I decided you were right, so I just asked a few people . . . for dinner."

"When? When?"

"Oh, ages away. The eighth as you said, the eighth of October. Just a simple dinner."

"Who have you asked?"

"Just friends. Sheila and Martin, and David and Ethel, and—"

"You've invited them all here on the eighth?"

"Yes. And I've asked that nice Ruth O'Donnell, you know, the artist."

"Carmel. What are you—?"

"You remember her, we met her lots of times, and you told me how good she was. We haven't seen her for ages, but I did say when I wrote to her that there would be lots of people she'd know. I mean, David even knows her professionally. His company gave her a grant once, I read . . ."

"Yes . . ."

"And she'll know Sheila, because I think she came to her school to give a lecture."

"Why didn't you ask me—tell me?"

"But, Dermot, you're always telling me to do things on my own, use my own initiative. I did for once. I sent out all the invitations . . . and now that doesn't please you either."

"But I think you've picked the wrong night. I think that's the night she's having her opening. I thought I told you—"

"Yes, you did, I remember. You said she was only thirty and how well she'd done. I remember the date."

"God."

"So I thought it would be nice for her to have somewhere to go after it. I read in the papers that she isn't married and she doesn't even have a 'situation' like our Bernadette, so I thought what would be nicer than for her to have somewhere to go on the night."

"Yes."

"So that's what I said in my letter to her, that it would be a nice rounding off for the evening."

"How did you know where she lives?" His voice was a gasp.

"I looked it up in the telephone directory, silly!"

"You might have sent it to the wrong person—"

"But she told us she lived in the new flats. Remember? I'm not such a featherbrain after all, am I?"

"Sheila, can I have a quick word with you before you go into the school?"

"God, you frightened the life out of me, Dermot Murray. I thought you were a guard."

"Look, have you a minute? Can we get back into your car?"

"Half the sixth form already think you're propositioning me! What is it, Dermot? Tell me here."

"No, it's nothing to tell. I want to ask you, ask you something."

Sheila's heart was leaden.

"Ask on, but make it quick. That bell rings and I'm like a bolt from the blue in the door."

"Does Carmel know about Ruth?"

"I beg your pardon?"

"You heard me."

"I didn't. I did *not* hear you. Begin again."

"Does Carmel know about Ruth and me?"

"Ruth? Ruth O'Donnell?"

"Sheila, stop playing around. I know you know, you know I know you know. All I want to know is does Carmel know?"

"You're assuming a great many things. What is there to know? What should I have known? Stop standing there like a guessing game."

"Sheila, please, it's important."

"It must be. Why else are you up here in a convent? I haven't an idea what you're talking about."

"Think, think quickly. I know you're being a good friend and an old school chum. But think what's for the best. I don't just mean the best for me, I mean the best for everyone."

"What am I to think about?"

"Look, I've known you for years, Sheila, I'm not a shit, now, am I? I'm a reasonable human being. Would I be up here at this hour of the morning if I were a real bum?"

Every day that Sheila had paused at her car for one moment to search for an exercise book, to write a shopping list, to listen to the last bars of some song on the radio . . . the bell had shrilled across her consciousness. Why did it not do it today?

"I can't help you, Dermot," she said. "I don't know anything, I really don't. I don't talk about anything, I don't listen to anything. I'm no help."

He believed her. Not that she didn't know about Ruth. He knew she knew about Ruth. But he believed her when she said she couldn't help him. She didn't know whether Carmel knew or not. She was as much in the dark as he was.

"What am I going to do?" he asked her.

And then the bell shrilled.

"I just telephoned to ask you more about this party you're giving," Ethel said.

"I explained it all in the letter," said Carmel. "You will be able to come? You see, I know how busy you all are so I trapped you by choosing the night of Ruth's exhibition."

"Yes, of course we'll come. You don't have to trap us. Looking forward to it . . . I was wondering whether it was a surprise—a birthday surprise for Dermot or anything. David met him in the club, and I hope he didn't let anything slip."

"No, it's not Dermot's birthday. It may well be Ruth's—I think hers is in October—but no, it doesn't matter at all. I did tell Dermot I was thinking of having a party, but you know what men are, they never listen. Their minds are elsewhere. Probably just as well that we don't know where they are half the time, don't you think?"

Ethel had the uneasy feeling that Carmel was laughing at her. Nonsense, of course, but there was that kind of a feel about the way she spoke.

"Oh, Dermot, I can't tell you where she is. She said the whole point was that you and she were having a separation, wasn't it?"

"Look, I'll go down on my knees to you."

Dermot had never liked Ruth's younger sister. A know-all, a moralizer, and worst of all a contemporary of his daughter Anna's when they were at UCD.

"No, I swore I would reveal nothing. Ruth only told me just in case there was any real crisis, about the gallery, you know."

"There's a very big crisis. I can't tell you how big."

"Honestly, Dermot, be fair. Play it by the rules. Just leave her alone, can't you? It's only a couple of weeks."

"Listen here, smarty pants." Dermot had lost any veneer of manners by now. "Go into Ruth's flat, where there will be a letter with a Dublin 4 postmark addressed to her. Open it and read it. If you think then that it's serious enough perhaps you could ring your sister and ask her to ring me. That's all." He stood up to leave the travel agency where she worked.

"Wait. It's not some awful sordid thing . . . some scandal, is it?" The girl's lip wrinkled with disgust.

"It's only a dinner invitation, but she might want to ring me about it."

He nearly took the door off the hinges as he left.

* * *

Dermot telephoned his office.

"Oh, there you are, Mr. Murray," the girl on the switch said with relief. "It's not like you to be late. I didn't know what to do with your calls. We've had—"

"I'm not feeling well today, Margaret. Please ask Miss O'Neill to put someone else on the Foreign Exchange and move her own things to my desk."

"But Mr. Murray—"

"I'll call back later, Margaret. The important thing is that Miss O'Neill sits at my desk. Put any calls for me through to her, she will know how to deal with them."

"When will you—?"

"As I said, I'll call back later, Margaret. The bank is not going to grind to a halt just because for once the manager isn't well."

He hung up and regretted it immediately. The child on the switch didn't care whether the bank ground to a halt or not. Probably hoped it would, if the truth was known. Why had he been so snappy? She was bound to gossip about it too. If only he had just taken thirty more seconds to be soothing and reassuring then it would have passed unnoticed in the minutiae of the day . . . poor Mr. Murray's not well, must have that bug, oh well, Miss O'Neill's looking after his work . . . and that would be that. Now the girl on the switch would be full of indignation . . . bit my nose off, snapped at me over nothing, all I was doing was asking, what do I bloody care where he is, what he does, he can take a running jump at himself.

Why couldn't he have had the patience to exchange just two more conventional remarks? He had been so patient, so very patient about everything so far. Why couldn't he have kept his temper this morning? He frowned at his reflection in the car mirror when he got back into the driving seat. He didn't like the middle-aged tense man that looked back at him. In his mind's eye he didn't see himself that way; in his mind's eye he saw himself as Ruth's man, her strong support, the one she ran to when she was exhausted with her work, when she was full of doubts. To the little girl on the switch back at the bank, he was probably middle-aged Mr. Murray, and if she knew about Ruth (which she might well in this village that they called a city), then she would think he was pathetic with his bit on the side, or a louse cheating on his wife.

Dermot didn't feel like driving anywhere. He got out of the car again and walked until he reached the canal. It was a nice crisp morning. Other people were still in their cars choking with fumes. These must be big executives, the top men, if they could come in to work as late as ten to ten, or was that right? If they were top men maybe they should have been at their desks since seven-thirty? Maybe they were the kind of men who had inherited a family business and who didn't have to work hard because they were the bosses' sons. Funny how you saw different sides of society when you stepped off your own little treadmill for a bit.

Two women passed him on the canal path, bright laughing women in headscarfs. One was carrying a huge plastic bag and the other a large stuffed pillowcase; they were on their way to the launderette. They were the kind of women that Carmel would describe as nice poor things. Yet they weren't nearly as poor as poor Carmel. They were carting their families' washing off without a look of resentment about them. Carmel might be bending over the controls of a washing machine in her own kitchen but more likely she would just sit and stare out into the back garden. He had looked at her in off-guard moments over the last few months and this was how she was when in repose. Her face was empty as if she had left it and gone somewhere else.

He had hoped she would find interests, but he realized more and more that this was a vain hope. She had no interests. She had nothing whatsoever that would lift her out of that sad pose. When Anna and James had had the first baby, Dermot thought that this would absorb Carmel's time, a grandchild out in Sandycove. He was certain she would be out there every second day, or encouraging Anna to leave the child in Donnybrook while she went about her business. But Dermot hadn't understood about modern young mothers like Anna. Cilian first, and then Orla, had just become part of her own life as if they were adults. They were constantly being strapped and unstrapped into car seats. They moved with a battery of educational toys, they were quite self-sufficient wherever they went. Doting grandmothers did not come into the picture at all.

And then, of course, that strap Bernadette shacked up with that Frank; "my flatmate," no less, she called him. She hadn't been much help or support for her mother, had she? Dermot muttered to himself about her. A lot of use it had been paying for her at the College of Art, quite happy to help friends out, to step in and sell things for someone who was stuck.

And friends? Carmel was a great one for talking about the Girls. Where were the girls now when they were needed? That Sheila, the schoolmistress, rushing into the convent this morning as if her life depended on it. Great friend she'd be if anyone needed one: "I don't talk, I don't listen, I don't know things . . ." marvelous! And who else was there? There was Ethel . . . she and Carmel had got on quite well at one stage. But there as well as anywhere else Carmel hadn't been able to cope. She had talked and talked about not returning David and Ethel's hospitality, and not accepting any more of it. Why hadn't she just said "Come around to supper," the way Ruth did, the way anyone did . . . anyone except Carmel.

It was fooling himself really to think she would be happier without him, fooling himself to say she wouldn't really notice if he left. She would not be able to cope. She couldn't even muster the politics of solidarity and hate, like that woman they had heard of in Ballsbridge, the wife of the man in the public relations agency. She had been so outraged when he left that she had aligned dozens of women on her side. You could hardly mention the man's name now without hearing a sibilant hiss, so blackened had it become. No, Carmel would do nothing like that.

Dermot stopped suddenly. Carmel would do nothing. And that was why he could never leave her. She would do nothing at all. For the rest of his life he would come home, tell lies, make up excuses, invent conferences, be telephoned by mythical clients who had to be seen after hours. And Ruth would do nothing. Ruth would not make a scene, demand that he choose between them, Ruth would confront nobody, insist on no showdowns. This had been the way things were for two whole years . . . everyone secure in the knowledge that nobody else would do anything; Ruth knowing she would never have to make her mind up about him fully, Carmel knowing that she would never lose him utterly and he knowing that he need never be forced to say "I'll take this one" or "I'll take that."

He laughed wryly to himself. It was most people's idea of a married man's dream: an unquestioning wife and an unquestioning mistress. But it was a bad dream, he could write a book on what a bad dream it was. You were happy in neither place, you were guilty in both places. The very fact that nobody was making any move made it all the more insoluble. If Carmel had threatened and pleaded, perhaps, if Ruth had issued ultimatums, perhaps. *Perhaps* it might have been better. But nothing ever happened. Until now. Until Ruth had been invited to dinner.

Carmel *must* know, he said to himself for the five hundredth time. She *must* know. And yet the memory of last night had been like a vivid movie running through over and over.

"Tell me, why have you decided to ask Ruth O'Donnell, whom we hardly know, whom you only met twice, to dinner? Carmel, what are you playing at?"

"I'm not playing at anything except being a better homemaker. She's nice. Everyone says so."

"But why? Tell me, what made you think of a dinner? Why a month away?"

"To give me time to prepare, to get ready. I'm not like all these marvelous women you admire so much, who can have the entire golf game around for a six-course meal with no notice. I like to take my time."

She had looked at him with a round innocent face. She had prattled on about Sheila having called in, about Anna and James driving off to the cottage, about how she wished she could get the Christmas presents months ahead in September when the shops were nice and empty.

Four times he asked her in a roundabout way, four times she had answered him with a level look. She just liked the idea of having people to dinner; why was he finding fault with it? And he never answered that question, not even with a lie.

They went to Mass at eleven o'clock in Donnybrook church and bought the papers outside.

"Do you need anything from the shops?" Dermot asked. "Ice cream? A pudding?"

"No, I'm on a diet, but you get some if you like," she said pleasantly. He had looked at her face as she prayed; he had watched her come back from Communion with her head down. She never asked him why he didn't go to Communion; she never asked him anything.

Anna and James were happy. It had been a glorious day and they had had their lunch out in the open. Twelve of them had sat and looked out over the bay and said that this was the life and they must all be mad to live in Dublin. Anna had arranged that a local woman make fresh soda bread and they had had this with their pâté. Everyone had raved about it. Cilian and Orla played at a distance with the three visiting children. Some of their friends had been staying at a hotel, others had rented a cottage. They all looked with open envy at the ease and comfort which James and Anna had built for themselves. This was balm to Anna and James. They stood and waved in the evening as the last guests drove off, they had cups of tea to get rid of the sleepiness the white wine had spread, and they looked at the clock. James had an iron rule: on the road back at seven. This meant an hour to wash up and tidy and pack the children and themselves— plenty of time.

They moved around the cottage gathering the bagful of educational toys.

They plunged their twelve plates, twelve glasses, twelve forks and twelve knives into the hot soapy water. A rubbish sack was carefully tied up, and put in the boot as well. There was no collection in this part of heaven, they laughed to each other. Cilian and Orla, sleepy from the day in the sun, were strapped in, the cassette of James Last was at the ready and they faced the road across the country.

They spent much of it congratulating each other on the cottage. Although they would never have admitted it, even to each other, there were times when they thought it was becoming a bit much for them. But on a day like today when they could see the admiration and the jealousy of the people who sat around in the sunshine, then it was all worth it a hundred times over. They forgot the weekends they had arrived to find pipes burst, roof leaking, ants walking the kitchen floor in their thousands, mice making nests in the window boxes . . . all that was as nothing. The strings of the Last orchestra thudded and swept in the background.

James said, "Do you know that your father's having an affair with Ruth O'Donnell, the artist?"

"Dad? Don't be ridiculous."

"He is, though, I heard it before. I heard it from someone who met them in London, of all places. Wouldn't you think you'd be safe having it away in London, ten million people, but no, spotted *in flagrante*."

Anna looked around almost automatically to see if the children were asleep. If their grandfather's adultery was going to be discussed it would not be *devant* these *enfants,* she thought.

"I don't believe a word of it."

"Honestly, sweetheart, Frances and Tim were talking about it this afternoon. They didn't like to mention it in front of you."

"So that's what you were wittering on about. I thought it was business."

"No, they tell me they see him often coming out of Ruth's apartment block, you know."

"The new one . . . yes . . . heavens above."

"Are you upset? Are you upset that I told you?"

"I don't believe it, not *Dad*. I mean, he fancies her maybe and goes in and has the odd little drink. But not an affair, not sleeping with her, not Dad."

"Um."

"Well, don't you agree?"

"I don't know, I only tell you what I hear."

"You think it's possible that Dad would have a real affair?"

"That's what is said."

"But why would she? I mean, she's young and well known and got her own life . . . she could have anyone or no one if she wanted. What on earth would she want with Dad?"

"Who knows? People want extraordinary people."

"Yes."

"You are upset. I shouldn't have told you like that, straight out. It's just . . . well, it was on my mind."

"I'm not upset. I don't know why. I suppose when I was young, like everyone I was always terrified if they had a row that they were going to part. But they didn't, nobody ever did. Things just go along drifting. That's what happened to marriages in those days."

"And in *these* days, it would appear."

"What do you mean?"

"Well, they say that your papa and Ms. O'Donnell have been constant companions for two to three years."

"Never!"

"Apparently."

"Imagine at Christmas, and the year before and the year before . . . all the family parties . . . and all the time. . . . I don't believe it."

"Do you think Grandmama knows?"

"I'm certain she doesn't. Poor Mother. How odd, I don't know why I'm not crying and thinking it's the end of everything. I suppose I just haven't accepted it."

"I don't know why I told you." James looked worried. "It's only making you sad, but it seemed a big secret to keep from you. . . . We don't have secrets."

"No."

"And you're so practical, I thought you'd want to know about it in case there's anything you wanted to do."

"Like what, frighten her off? Please leave my daddy alone?"

"No, but you do know her sister, don't you? Deirdre?"

"Yes, Deirdre O'Donnell, she was in college with me. God."

"So there we are."

"There we are all right. Are you shocked?"

"I'm a bit stunned, like you. I can't see my father-in-law in the role, but I think I'm mainly sorry for poor Grandmama. I thought that's what you'd feel most."

"No. Mother will survive. She's very rarely living in the real world anyway. She seems a bit stoned to me a lot of the time. I wouldn't be surprised if that doctor has her on Valium most of the time. That's why he's such a success with all that generation, he just prescribes it by the ton. Takes the edge off life, that's his motto."

"Yes, well, it looks as if your mother's going to need her supply."

"Yes, but in a way, why should she? I mean, if it's been going on for years, nothing's going to change."

"I suppose not. Check the mileage, will you, I'm turning in here for petrol."

Anna got out the little leather-covered book and wrote in *11878* under mileage, *Tralee* under place, and then sat with her pencil poised until she could fill in the remaining two columns, gallons and price.

"I'm not going to spend a month going in and out playing cat and mouse with them. I'm not going to do it," Sheila said on Sunday evening. She had the dining-room table covered with books that she was marking for tomorrow's class.

"I suppose you could just be there, you know, if she needed you, that would be a help," said Martin. He was doing the crossword while Sheila corrected her exercises.

"That's not the point. It's unforgivable being drawn into other people's rows and scenes and disasters. I'll never forgive him for accosting me like that and forcing me to take sides and attitudes. People shouldn't drag you into their unhappinesses, it's not fair." She looked very cross and bit on the end of her pencil in annoyance. "No, stop being tolerant and forgiving, Martin. It's a fact. We never drag people into our marriage, now do we?"

"No," said Martin thoughtfully. "But then we're very lucky we don't have any problems in our marriage."

"No," said Sheila sharply, going back to the exercise books. She had resolved long ago that if she was going to be the breadwinner, she wasn't going to complain and ruin it all by being a martyr. The only thing that made the whole bloody business worthwhile was that Martin had no idea how tired she was and how much she hated going into that school each day. She thought of Carmel for a moment, and a great wave of impatience flooded over her. Carmel could get up at any time she liked, she had nothing more pressing in her day than to decide which clothes she should send to the St. Vincent de Paul. Carmel's children were married. Well, Bernadette was as good as married. They weren't pounding home with huge appetites for meals which had to be prepared and shopped for. Sheila tried to give the appearance of being in charge of the kitchen so that Martin's sons should not think him a sissy. They still said "thanks, Mum" when they found their clean clothes in their bedrooms, though as often as not it was their father who had done them.

In a way Carmel had only herself to blame if she was miserable and wretched over all this business about Ruth O'Donnell. Carmel was a lady of leisure with too much time to think about the too little she had to do. Then with a jolt Sheila remembered that it was she and Martin and Dermot who were wretched. Carmel had been very cheerful, and was in fact busy organizing a dinner party and smartening up her wardrobe. Not at all what this wronged wife would have been expected to do.

Ethel and David had people in to bridge on Sunday night. They always had what they called a curfew on Sunday nights, and everyone had to have played the last card by eleven-thirty.

When the cars had driven off and they were emptying the ashtrays, opening the windows, and taking out the dirty glasses to the dishwasher, Ethel said, "I have the most awful feeling, like doom, as if something dreadful is going to happen. Do you know that feeling?"

"Every day going into work, and it's always accurate," said David.

"Don't be trivial, you love your work, and why wouldn't you? People fussing over you, fuss fuss fuss all day. No, I have a sense of foreboding and I can't think what's causing it."

"Maybe you feel guilty about something," David said.

"It's that kind of feeling, that sort of heavy feeling in the chest, but I've nothing to be guilty about."

"I think it's the bank manager's bit of skirt. I honestly think that's what's making us all so uneasy. I feel a bit edgy myself."

"But we've known about it for ages."

"Yes, but the poor sad wife must have only just found out."

Ethel stood looking at a plate of peanuts thoughtfully. Eventually she tipped them into the pedal bin. "I'd only eat them," she said as an explanation, "and they're more fattening than large g's and t's. I suppose that is what's making us nervous. It's such a mad thing to do. Such a very men-in-white-coats mad thing to do. Ask the woman to dinner and have a public scene."

"She won't go, of course," said David.

"No, but the fact that poor Carmel actually asked her is so mad. That's what's upsetting. Who knows what she'll do next, walk down Grafton Street in her knickers?"

Deirdre O'Donnell had no trouble in getting the porter to give her a key to her sister's flat. She said that Ruth wanted her to post on some things.

She wandered around, luxuriating in being alone among someone else's possessions. Now you could look and stare and ponder to your heart's content. Everyone else in the block had their sitting rooms carefully draped and framed. They looked like the rooms in a doll's house from outside. But Ruth's sitting room was bare, it was in fact her studio, and what other people regarded as the master bedroom and decked with fitted cupboards and thick carpets, Ruth used as a secondary studio and office. The small spare bedroom was her bed-sitting-room; a sofa that turned into a bed sat neatly in its sofa role, and in the kitchen the saucepans sat shining in a row.

For an artist her sister was very neat, Deirdre thought. Spinsterish, she had once believed—that was before she knew about the regular visits of Anna Murray's father. *Father*. A bank manager. Maybe she should go to him to authorize an overdraft. Seriously, that's not a bad idea at all.

On the mat there were a dozen envelopes. Some were obviously brochures or advertisements. Then she saw the letter in the neat round handwriting. She eased it out carefully. It might be full of terrible, intimate things . . . things that Ruth would not want her to have read. She must steam the envelope; she could stick it all back with glue if it really was too yucky and Ruth would get into a temper.

Dear Ruth,

I don't know whether you remember me or not, but we met a couple of times with David and Ethel O'Connor and you also know my friend Sheila Healy, who says you gave a wonderful lecture at her school. Anyway, we are great admirers of yours and so looking forward to your exhibition on October 8th.

I'm going to try to steal you for that night to come to dinner with us. This is why I'm writing to you so far in advance; I am sure you will get many invitations nearer the time, but I want to be first in with mine. We will have the O'Connors and the Healys as well, so you will be among friends.

Please let me know soon if you can come. I'm one of these middle-aged fussy sort of women who spend ages getting things organized, not like you and your friends. I'm sure you can combine about three lives successfully, but I'll be setting and resetting the table for days before you come, and then I'll pretend it all happened of its own accord. It will give us all a great deal of pleasure if you say yes, and I know Dermot, my husband, would be thrilled. He has bought three of your paintings for our home. I hope you will like the way we have had them hung. So looking forward to seeing you.

Yours cordially,
Carmel Murray

Poor old cow, thought Deirdre, probably something wrong with her glands. She must know about Ruthie, half the country does. I don't think there's anything for old Dermot to get his knickers in a twist about, but I'd better ring her just in case.

Because Deirdre O'Donnell was essentially a frugal person she saw no reason why she shouldn't make the call from Ruth's own telephone. After all, it was Ruth's romance. It was Ruth's fellow's wife who had gone off her head . . . why not let Ruth pay for the call?

The farmer's wife knocked on her door and said there was a telephone call from Dublin.

"Your sister said you mustn't get alarmed. She says there is no problem."

Ruth got up. She had been lying on the bed over the covers, reading. It was very luxurious somehow to do that, like going to the pictures in the afternoon.

"Ruthie?"

"What's happened?"

"Nothing, I told the old dame that. Nothing. Listen, Romeo asked me to contact you . . ."

"I told you I didn't want any messages. *Any.*"

"I told him that. He said that his wife has gone off her head, and she's written to you."

"Oh, no."

"It's all right, she hasn't called you the whore of Babylon. She's inviting you to dinner actually, the night your exhibition opens."

"She's *what?*"

"Do you want me to read it to you? 'Dear Ruth, I don't know whether you remember me or not . . .' "

"Stop, stop. Is this serious?"

"Yes, but there's no abuse in it. Honestly, it's all full of admiration."

"Oh, Lord. What does Dermot say?"

"He wants to get in touch with you about it. I told him to leave you alone, but he said—"

"Did he say that she knows?"

"Ruthie . . . of course she knows. What are you talking about? She must know."

"Dermot always said she didn't, or that if it came into her head she put it out again."

"You must be mad. Do you think you're invisible or something, Ruthie? The two of you go everywhere together."

"But if she knows, what's she inviting me to dinner for?"

"Well, that's the point, that's what lover boy was so much in a tizz about."

"What does he think?"

"I don't know. I suppose he thinks that she's gone over the top, poor old thing. Do you want me to read it to you?"

"Yes, I suppose you'd better. If I've got to ring Dermot about it I'd better know what she says."

"Right. 'I don't know whether you remember me—' "

"Hey, Deirdre. This must be costing you a fortune."

"No, it's costing you a fortune . . . the wages of sin, you know."

"Oh, go on, read it."

* * *

Carmel planned her week carefully. It was nice to have so many things to do, it reminded her of being young again, when every day was so full and there seemed to be no waiting about. She would have to choose the main course and the dessert too. That would take two mornings in the bookshop reading the recipes. She was going to have a facial twice a week . . . oh, over on the north side of the city where she wouldn't be known . . . she would take the bus. She was going to spend two mornings shopping for her shoes. She had the dress already; the very good black dress which she had bought when Anna was twenty-one, five years ago. She had worn it that evening . . . the first time . . . that first time when she had discovered about Dermot and the other girl . . . the time she had got so upset. She had never worn it again. But this time she would wear it and it would look magnificent. She would be much thinner . . . she was going to lose a stone this month. Her hair would be much more attractive . . . that man in Grafton Street who had done Ethel's hair was going to put highlights in for her a week before the party. She had telephoned and asked him what would be the best time. She had even told him she was a middle-aged lady, not a dollybird. "I like coiffing mature ladies," he had said.

Coiffing. It had sounded vaguely suggestive.

And there were so many other things to do. Window cleaners to come in. That firm which came and shampooed your carpet in the house. And her notebook to fill in.

She had written down anything anyone said about successful entertaining, like that thing Ethel had mentioned about the prawn cocktails and the roast beef.

She remembered Anna once talking about a house she had visited. "They had fresh flowers in the bathroom, Mother, in the bathroom!" That had been included in the notebook. She had read an interview with a famous hostess who had said that the whole secret of successful entertaining was to have plenty of highly polished glass and thick damask napkins on the table. That was noted, beside the advice about having a lot of salts, peppers, and butter dishes so that people didn't have to keep passing them from one end of the table to the other.

Happier than she had been for a long time and armed with a list of the better cookery books, she started off for Donnybrook. At the hall door she met Anna.

"Oh dear! Why didn't you let me know you were coming, dear? I'm just off," she said, regretfully but firmly pulling the door behind her.

"Hey, that's very welcoming," Anna said, surprised. "I bring your only grandchildren to visit you and that's what we get shown . . . the door."

"Hallo, Cilian . . . hallo, Orla." She waved at them through the window.

Cilian struggled with his harness. "Grandmama, Grandmama," he called.

"Ah, look, he wants to come to you," Anna said.

"I'm sorry, darling, Granny's got to go out. Hallo, Orla, blow Granny a kiss."

"You might just ask us in for a cup of coffee." Anna sounded huffed. "We drove all the way in from Sandycove to see you."

"Oh, I am sorry." Carmel was on her way to the gate.

"But where are you going to, Mother?"

"I'm going out, dear, I have things to do. Will you still be in town this afternoon? Bring them in then and we'll have afternoon tea. Wouldn't that be nice?"

"Yes, but Mother, I wanted to have a little chat . . ."

"Grand. We'll have a little chat this afternoon."

She was gone. Walking purposefully off toward the main road and the good brisk invigorating stretch toward the shops.

Anna looked after her, bewildered. Normally Mother was almost pathetically grateful for a visit, and fussed and ran about like an overgrown puppy. Here she was, striding off with no explanation. She looked after her, and Mother, as if she felt her eyes, turned and waved before she went around the corner. It was funny how people looked much younger when they moved quickly. Mother didn't look bad at all in her navy jacket and her check skirt. She didn't look fifty or fifty-one or whatever she was. Sometimes when she sat in that chair looking out into the back garden she looked seventy. Poor Mother, wasn't Dad awful to be fooling around with a young girl? Ruth O'Donnell, too . . . but James was wrong, it couldn't be sex . . . it was just the thrill of the thing, the illicit excitement. Dad in bed with a girl? It was hard enough to imagine Dad being in bed with Mother years ago, but now . . . these days . . . Dad was so old he wouldn't even be interested in it, would he? And suppose he was, who in their right mind would go to bed with Dad?

Anna shrugged and got back into the car.

"Wasted journey," she said to the children, who set up a simultaneous squawk of disappointment.

"Private call, Mr. Murray, will you take it here or—?"

"That's all right, put me through."

He knew it was Ruth from the way she spoke. She had a way of saying "private call" that was almost lascivious.

"Dermot, can you talk?"

"Go ahead."

"In other words, you can't."

"Not yet."

"I got a call from Deirdre."

"So she told you the situation."

"She read me the letter. It sounded as if she doesn't have a clue."

"Yes, well, that's what I've always been saying."

Dermot Murray's secretary felt she had tortured him enough. "Excuse me," she murmured, and left the room.

"So what will I do?"

"Listen, darling love, when are you coming back?"

"In ten days, two weeks."

"I love you."

"You're alone now, presumably."

"No, I'm in the board room, and the board all agree. They love you too." She giggled. "Dermot, what will I do, will I write and say I'm tied up?"

"It means a lot to her, it means a great, great deal. She's so lively and happy since she thought of the party, you have no idea, it stops that deadness. When I see her like this I can really imagine her living a life, a normal life of her own."

"So, what do you want?"

"Could you accept?"

"Say I'd love to, and then sort of opt out at the last moment?"

Dermot paused. "Yes . . . and, well, maybe in the end, if you could come, could go to the dinner. Could you?"

"*What?*"

"Well, it wouldn't mean all that much to you . . . to us. We have so much, and there you are, a brilliant young girl with your life before you and all that."

"You can't seriously expect me to come into your house as a guest, and say how nice, how delicious, you must give me the recipe for that boiled cabbage."

"Ruth, please."

"No, no please about it, you're sick, that's what you are. I couldn't possibly do it. I wouldn't dream of doing it to another woman, go in triumphantly and sit down with a lot of people who are in the secret. It's monstrous!"

"You don't understand—"

"I don't like what I do understand. Why are you going along with it?"

Her voice was upset; the pips went.

"We can't talk on the phone, let me come to see you."

"*No.* I wanted to be alone. You set all this up as a trick, didn't you? Admit it."

"I swear to God I didn't, I swear I only heard about it on Friday. I might never have heard if I hadn't met David in the club. I don't think she was going to tell me."

"You mean you were going to come home and find everyone there?"

"I don't know. I don't know."

"But she must have known that I would have told you. She must have known that."

"She doesn't *know* about you and me! I keep telling you!"

"Deirdre says that's lunacy . . . half of Dublin knows."

"Deirdre doesn't know anything—anyway, Carmel never meets half of Dublin."

"Oh, God, I knew you couldn't let me have this time without spoiling it. I knew you'd have to do something to mess it up for me."

"That is so unfair. I don't even know where you are. I won't talk to you again until you come back. I just wanted you to know what happened. If I hadn't told you, you'd have said I was being devious, wouldn't you? Well, wouldn't you?"

She softened. "I know."

"So if you could do one thing for me, just one. Write a note and say that you are away in the country, that the letter was forwarded to you, and that you'd love to come. Can you do that?"

"No, Dermot, I am not a puppet, I will not be manipulated into awful, sordid, cruel scenes like that. I will not do it."

"Just say you'll come, accept, people are always accepting things they don't go to in the end. Accept, and when you come back you and I will talk, and then you'll do whatever you like."

"And you won't steamroll me into doing what I don't want to do?"

"No, Ruth my love, I will not."

"And if I write this hypocritical note saying yes, you really think this is for the best . . . ?"

"I do."

"For all of us, for her and for me, as well as for you?"

He paused. "Yes. Seriously I do. For her, because she can go on planning her party and it will make her, well, busy and active again, and that's what we want. We want her to have a life of her own."

"And how will it help *me*, to accept?"

"Well, you can stop worrying about it. Once you've written a letter saying yes, then a decision is made. You can unmake it anytime, but you don't have to dither."

"And how will it help you?"

"Then I can see her absorbed in something, and that's a hell of a lot more positive than seeing her sitting staring out the window and wondering what the future has in store."

"What does the future have in store?"

"It has you coming home to me soon. It has your exhibition and all *that* means."

"I wish I didn't love you."

"I'm very glad you do."

"A ridiculous married bank manager, hundreds of years older than me, knowing nothing about painting—"

"I know, I know." He sounded soothing. He was happy now; once Ruth got on to the groove of how unsuitable he was, he felt safe.

"I must be quite mad."

"You are, you are. Very," he said.

"I'll write the letter, but I won't go."

"Good girl," he said.

Dear Mrs. Murray,

What a nice surprise to get your letter.

I didn't even think you'd remember that we had met. It's very nice of you to say such flattering things about my work and I am most grateful for your dinner invitation on the night of the exhibition.

I am writing this from Wales, where I am spending a quiet holiday. (My post is forwarded to me, so that's how I got your letter.) I should be very happy to accept. I look forward to renewing my friendship with you, your husband, and your other friends.

Sincerely,
Ruth O'Donnell

Carmel held the letter tightly in her hand after she'd read it. Relief flooded her face. She had been almost certain that Ruth O'Donnell would accept, but there had been the slight fear that she might ruin the whole plan. Now everything was all right. Everything was on target.

That night Dermot told her that she was looking very well, very healthy-looking. Carmel smiled, pleased. "I've been walking a lot lately, I find it does me good." That was true, she did walk and it did make her feel as if it were doing good. But she didn't tell him about the facial she had had—the second this week. The beautician had been giving her a rejuvenating mask. And she didn't tell him that she had now settled on veal with Marsala for the main course, and pears baked in wine for the dessert.

She didn't tell him that she had got a letter that day from Ruth O'Donnell.

* * *

Bernadette and Anna had lunch together. Anna had a salad and a coffee; Bernadette had a huge lump of French bread and cheese, and drank a pint of Guinness.

"Only point in having lunch in a pub, really, having a pint," she said.

Anna swallowed her disapproval. They had met to discuss what they should do about Mother and Dad, if anything. There was no point in beginning by criticizing each other.

"Are you sure . . . it's not just gossip?"

"No, a lot of people know, apparently we're the last to know."

"Well, that stands to reason," Bernadette said logically, "people aren't going to discuss our father's little peccadillos in company where we are sitting there listening."

"Now, should we say anything?"

"What could we say? Do you mean ask Dad, Is it true?"

Anna thought. "Yes, we could do that, I suppose, and sort of say that we think it's dreadful and that it must come to an end."

Bernadette pealed with laughter.

"Anna, you are marvelous, you're just like a dowager duchess. 'I think, Father, this is quite dreadful. It must come to an end. Back to Mother. Quick quick. As you were.' " She rocked with amusement at the thought of it. Anna did not rock at all.

"Why is that funny? What do *you* suggest?"

"I'm sorry, I shouldn't laugh. What *do* I suggest? I don't know. I suppose we could ask him does he intend to go off with Ruth and leave Mother, because that's the only thing we have a *right* to know really. I mean, if he does, she'll crack up."

"Yes," Anna agreed. "That's the point. He must be made to see that he can't do that to her."

"He may want to do it, but he must realize that's what's going to happen, and I suppose he should be given the facts about how much he can rely on you and on me . . . to pick up the bits."

"Well, he can't expect us to look after—"

"No, he probably doesn't expect anything. . . . I think he should be put in the picture, that's all."

Anna was surprised to see her younger sister being so firm. She always thought of Bernadette as a bit eejity, but she was being very crisp today.

"Well, Frank and I are thinking of going to Australia in the New Year."

"To Australia, like Uncle Charlie? *He* didn't make a fortune."

"That's not the point. There's a crafts cooperative we are interested in. It's not definite yet, but I don't want Mummy to be one of my reasons for going or staying. I mean, I'll write home every week and all . . . but I don't want to go not knowing whether she'll end up in a mental ward or whether she'll be all right."

"Yes . . . yes." Anna felt left behind.

"And *you're* not really going to move in and look after her, are you, Anna? You've got your own life . . . Dad should be told this . . . just so that he knows the options."

"Yes. But isn't it all a bit harsh . . . a bit final? Mightn't we be sort of taking too much for granted."

"Yes, that's the point. It was you who said we must meet and discuss what to do. I think that's the only thing to do if we do anything, let him know just how far he can rely on us so that there's no misunderstanding."

"Yes, well, I don't know, maybe we should say nothing. . . . Mother's probably better able to look after herself than we realize."

"And you were saying that she actually seems more lively these days."

"Yes, and she looks better, her skin looks less sort of muddy . . . and she's lost a bit of weight, I think."

"She always seems very cheerful when I call in or ring."

"Yes. When you think how awful it was that time her nerves did get bad."

"Oh, years ago, when I was still at college?"

"Yes, it was awful, she used to go and see this psychiatrist and cry all the time."

"What did they do with her, how did they cure her?"

"Oh, Bernadette, you know psychiatrists, they don't do anything or cure anyone . . . they just listen and say yes, yes—or so I hear."

"Why do people go on going to them then?"

"Who knows? I suppose the world's a bit short on people who will listen and say yes, yes."

"But she did get better, she stopped crying and everything."

"I told you, it works, all this yes-yessing."

"And we'll say nothing for the moment."

"I think not, don't you?"

Joe arrived a week before the party. He telephoned one morning and said he was in town.

"Did I send you enough money?" Carmel sounded anxious.

"Darling, you sent me too much money. How are you, Carmel, am I going to come and see you?"

"No, I'll come and see you. I don't want you coming here until the night."

"Where will we go?"

"Let me see . . . I'll go into the hotel. . . . We can have tea or coffee sent up, can't we?"

"Yeah, it's costing a fortune, the hotel. I wonder, Are you putting too much money out on all this, Carmel? There might have been another way."

"I have the money . . . I've always had money, that was never a problem. I'm so grateful to you for coming over, Joe, I'll never be able to thank you. I wish your friend had come too."

"No, a job's a job. Henry understands. . . . It would have messed things up if he'd come here. He says you're as mad as a coot but he wishes you luck."

She laughed happily. "Oh, good, he's on our side. I'll come down to the hotel this afternoon. What room are you? I'll just slip along and get into the lift."

"Oh, Mrs. M., you sound as if you're accustomed to this kind of racy life," Joe laughed. He was pleased that Carmel was so cheerful, he had been afraid that it might be a very glum Carmel. A sort of doom-laden Lady Macbeth. This sounded a lot more jolly. He sat back in his bed and lit a cigarette. It was really the most extraordinary business.

"How nice of you to call, Ethel. No, I'm fine . . . and you? Good. And David? Great. Oh, what a pity, no, I'm just off out as a matter of fact. Yes, it is a long time, isn't it? But never mind, we'll see you next week, won't we? The eighth. Oh good, good. No, not a thing, thank you, no, no, it's all under control. But very nice of you to think of it, Ethel. . . . What? Oh yes, every-one's coming . . . but it's only a small gathering, heavens, compared to all the ones you go to. Yes, that nice Ruth O'Donnell—I had such a sweet letter from her, Wales is where she was. She's looking forward to seeing you all again, she said. Was there anything else, Ethel? I'm in a bit of a rush. Right, see you both then, love to David. Bye."

"Yes, Aunt Sheila, I'm on my own. I've plenty of time to talk. She seems in great form to me, very perky. And looking very well, I think she looks better now than I've seen her looking for a long time . . . good, yes, I thought I wasn't imagining it. No, of course I don't mind you talking frankly. I mean, I know you're her oldest friend, for heaven's sake. No, honestly Aunt Sheila, I'm telling you the truth, I haven't noticed anything odd about Mother recently. . . . She's in very good form. . . . Yes, well she doesn't have much time for me, either. No, I'm not actually sure what she *is* doing, but whatever little things they are seem to keep her occupied. The way I look at it, isn't she far better this way, all cheerful and mysterious, than she was the time she got upset and her nerves were bad? Do you remember she sat there all day and we all found it a terrible drag to talk to her? She had no interest in anyone."

Anna said to James, "You know that friend of Mother's, the one we call Aunt Sheila, who went back to teaching, remember? She was on the phone whinging and whining and says that she thinks Mother's behaving oddly. How oddly, I ask, and she can't explain. Apparently Mother is too cheerful. Did you ever?"

"Poor Grandmama," said James. "It's bad if she's gloomy, it's bad if she's cheerful. She can't win."

"You look a million dollars. . . . You're *not* an old hag . . . you're smashing." Joe was full of admiration.

"I had a makeup lesson. You know the kind of thing the women's maga-zines advise you to do if your husband's unfaithful. 'Is your makeup old-fash-ioned?' they ask, and recommend you try out the new shades."

They both laughed, and she looked at him carefully and nodded with approval.

"You look well, Joe, really well. I'm different, I'm just painted up a bit, that's why I appear to be okay, but you're really great. . . . You look like a boy."

"An old boy," Joe laughed. "Oh, a very old boy . . . I'll be forty-five soon. That's not a boy these days!"

"You look still in your thirties and you look terrific."

Joe was pleased that her admiration was genuine. "Do you know what I did for us, I went out to that supermarket up in Baggot Street. . . . Lord, has the place all changed . . . and I got us a bottle of fizz, on me. I decided that if we're going to do this mad thing we'll celebrate it in style."

"Do you think we should wait until it's done?" Carmel was unwilling to celebrate yet.

"Hell no, if we say we'll do it, then it will be done." He opened the bottle with a practiced hand and poured into the tooth mugs. "Of course, I still think you're as daft as a brush."

"Why? To get what I want? To try to get what I want?"

"No." He raised his glass to her. "Cheers, good luck. No, that's not daft. To want it is daft."

"Cheers," she said, raising her glass. "Ninety calories for four fluid ounces . . . how many in this glass?"

"I think we could say bang goes one hundred eighty calories there."

They laughed like old times.

"We've done nothing but fight since you came back. It's the last thing on God's earth that I want to do."

"We haven't been fighting," Ruth said wearily. "I keep asking one question and you keep asking it back. I keep saying why do I have to go to this dinner and you keep saying why not. It's not so much a fight, it's a cul-de-sac."

Dermot sighed. "I keep telling you that we're buying time, that's all it is . . . buying peace of mind and opportunities. . . . All of these things we want, and we can get them if you just come to the house and behave nice and naturally and let everybody tell you how wonderful you are for one evening. I know, I know, you don't want to, but it doesn't seem too hard a thing to me."

She got up and walked around her kitchen. "And it seems amazing to me that you don't see how hard it is to do. To go and talk to her, and to smile . . . and eat the food she's been slaving over, and go to the lavatory in your bathroom, and leave my coat on your bed, your marriage bed . . . really, Dermot."

"If I've told you once there are single beds I've told you twenty times. This time you'll be able to see for yourself."

"It's almost as if you felt like a big man, having us both there—"

"Christ, God, if you knew how that is not true. I'll feel nervous and uneasy and anxious . . . and I'll feel a cheat and a deceiver. Do you think I want to draw all that on myself?"

"Please, Dermot—"

"Please, Ruth, please . . . I never asked you anything like this before and I swear I'll never ask you again."

"Oh, for all I know it could become a weekly affair, maybe I'll be invited to move in . . . put a third bed in the room."

"Don't be coarse."

"Isn't it bad enough to deceive her without rubbing her nose in it?"

"Ruth, I love you, don't you know?"

"I think you do, but it's like believing in God—sometimes it's very difficult to remember why you ever did."

"Aren't you having even numbers, Mother? I thought you were asking me once about how to seat eight at a table."

It was the day before the party. Anna had dropped in to check up on Mother. Bernadette was right, Mother had never looked better, slimmer and with color in her cheeks, or could that possibly be a blusher? And what smart shoes! Mother said she had bought them for tomorrow and she was running them in. They were super, they cost about twice as much as Anna would have paid for a pair of shoes and ten times what she thought Mother would have paid.

"No, just seven . . . I suppose I did think of getting an extra man, but people say that it's very old-fashioned nowadays making up the numbers. Ethel says that more dinners have been ruined by people struggling to make the sexes equal."

"Oh yes . . . I quite agree, really dreary men being dragged in, there are more really dreary men than dreary women around, I always think."

"So do I, but maybe we're prejudiced!" Mother laughed, and Anna laughed too. Mother was fine, what was all the fuss about? In order to let Mother think she was interested in the famous dinner, she asked brightly, "Who's coming then, Mother? Aunt Sheila and Uncle Martin, I suppose . . ."

"Yes, and Ethel and David . . . and Ruth O'Donnell, that nice young artist."

Anna dropped her handbag.

"Who?"

"Oh, you must know her, the painting in the hall, and this one. And the one on the stairs. Ruth O'Donnell . . . her exhibition opens tomorrow, and we're all going to it and then coming back here for dinner."

Bernadette wasn't in, but Anna told the whole thing to Frank and had a glass of parsnip wine to restore her.

"Are there bits of parsnip in it?" she asked suspiciously.

"No, it's all fermented, it's all we have," Frank said ungraciously.

Anna told the whole story, interspersed with explanations of how her heart had nearly stopped and she hadn't known what to say, to think, to do. Frank listened blankly.

"Isn't she a fifteen-carat bitch," Anna said in the end.

"Your mother?" Frank asked, puzzled.

"No, the woman. Ruth O'Donnell. Isn't she a smug, self-satisfied little bitch? It's not enough for her to have her own exhibition, which half the country seems to be going to; it's not enough for her to have poor Dad like a little lap poodle running after her . . . she has to get him to get Mother to ask her to a dinner party and make a public humiliation of her in front of all Mother's friends."

Frank looked unmoved.

"Well, isn't it appalling?" she snapped.

He shrugged. "To me there are two ways of looking at it, and both of them are from your ma's point of view. Either she knows, in which case she knows what she's doing, or she doesn't know, in which case nobody's about to announce it to her over the soup, so either way *she's* all right."

Anna didn't like the way Frank had emphasized the word *she*. If he meant that Mother was all right, who wasn't? Could it be Anna, sharp and shrill and getting into a tizz? She drained her parsnip wine and left.

"For God's sake, stay out of it," James said. "Don't ring all those fearful old women up. Let it go its own way. You'll hear soon enough if something disastrous happens."

"But they're my own mother and father, James. It's not as if they were just neighbors. You have to care about your own mother and father."

"Your own daughter and son seem to be yelling for you in the kitchen," he said.

She flounced out. James came out after her and gave her a kiss. She smiled and felt better. "That's soppy," said Cilian, and they all laughed.

Radio Eireann rang and asked if Ruth would go on the *Day by Day* program. She said she would call them back.

"Should I?" she asked Dermot.

"Definitely," he said. "Absolutely. Go straight out."

Thank God, he thought, at least that will take her mind off Carmel and the dinner. This time tomorrow it would all be over, he told himself. This time tomorrow he would sit down and take stock of his life. He had all the information that anyone could ever gather about early retirement plans . . . or he could ask for a transfer.

Ruth had often said she would like to live out of Dublin, but of course in a small place it wouldn't be acceptable. Anyway, no point in thinking about all that now; the main thing was that Carmel was quite capable of living a life of her own now . . . might even get herself a job like her friend Sheila. That was something that could be suggested—not by him, of course. Oh God, if she only knew how he wanted her to be happy, he didn't want to hurt her, or betray her, he just wanted her to have her own life.

"Your wife on the line, Mr. Murray."

He jumped physically. "What? What?"

"Shall I put her through?"

"Of course."

Carmel never rang him at the bank; what could have happened?

"Hallo, Dermot, I'm awfully sorry for bothering you, were you in the middle of someone's bank account?"

"No, of course not. What is it, Carmel?"

"Do you remember Joe Daly?"

"What? Who?"

"I was asking you did you remember Joe Daly, he used to write for the paper here, then he went off to London. Remember?"

"Vaguely, I think. Why?"

"Well, I met him quite by chance today, and he's been doing interviews with Ruth O'Donnell, he knows her quite well it turns out. Anyway, I thought I'd ask him tonight, isn't that a good idea?"

"Joe who?"

"Daly, do you remember, a mousy little man . . . we knew him ages ago before we were married."

"Oh, he's our age . . . right, whatever you say. If you think he's nice, then do. Whatever you like, dear. Will he fit in with everyone else?"

"Yes, I think so, but I wanted to check."

"Sure, sure, ask him, ask him."

Thank God, he thought, thank God, a mousy little failed journalist to talk about things that none of them were tied up in. There was a God in heaven, the night might not be so dreadful after all. He was about to dial Ruth when he realized she was probably on her way to the studio.

"Can you record *Day by Day,* please, on the machine over there," he said to Miss O'Neill. "There's going to be an item on banking I'd like to hear later."

He watched as she put on the cassette, checked her watch and set the radio tape recorder to begin at eleven.

Joe rang her at noon.

"Can I come up now?" he asked.

"Be very careful, look like a tradesman," she said.

"That's not hard," he said.

She looked around the house. It was perfect. There were flowers in the bathroom, lovely dahlias and chrysanthemums, all in dark reds, they looked great with the pink soaps and pink towels. The bedroom where they were going to leave their coats was magnificent, with the two thick Kilkenny Design bedspreads freshly cleaned. The kitchen had flowers in it, too, orange dahlias and rust chrysanthemums; she had bought tea towels just in that color. Really, it was such fun showing off. She didn't know why she hadn't done it ages ago.

He came in very quickly. She looked left and right, but the houses weren't near enough for anyone to see.

"Come in and tell me everything," she said.

"It's worked . . . so far."

She poured a coffee for him.

"Won't it spoil the beautiful kitchen?" he teased.

"I have five hours to tidy it up," she laughed.

"So, I'll tell you from the start. I arrived at her flat, your man was in there, I could hear his voice. They were arguing."

"What about?" Carmel was interested.

"I couldn't hear. Anyway, I waited, I went down to the courtyard place. I sat on the wall and waited, he left in an hour. I pressed her bell. I told her who I was, that I had an interest in a gallery in London, that I didn't want to set up huge business meetings and press her in the week of her exhibition but I was very interested in seeing whether it was the kind of thing we could bring to London."

"Did she ask why you were at the door?"

"Yes. I said I'd looked her up in the phone book . . . she thought that was very enterprising."

"It is," laughed Carmel. "Nobody ever thinks of it."

"Anyway, I told her I was staying at the hotel, but that if she liked we could talk now. She laughed and said why not now, and let me in."

"And . . . ?"

"And it's very nice, all done up as a studio, not a love nest at all . . . hardly any comfort, nothing like this." He looked around the smart kitchen and through the open door into the dining room with its dark polished wood. "So we had a long talk, all about her work. She showed me what she was doing, showing, we went through the catalogue. I explained what I could do. . . . Jesus, if you'd heard the way I dropped the names of galleries and people in London—I even impressed myself. I promised nothing. I said I'd act as a middleman. I even sent myself up a bit and said I saw myself as a Mister Fixit. . . . She liked that and she laughed a lot—"

"Yes," said Carmel before he could say it. "I know, I know, I've heard. She's very nice. Go on."

"Yes, well. I think I played it well. I must have. When I was leaving I said that we must keep in touch, that I could be here for a week and perhaps she would like to have a lunch one day. She said that would be nice, and I said the next day and we picked the place you said. . . . I said I'd heard it was good."

"Was it?" asked Carmel with interest.

"It was and so it should be, it cost you an arm and a leg. I kept the receipt for you."

"Joe, I don't need receipts."

"I know, but it is *astronomical*."

"Was it the right place?"

"Yes, we sat on and on. She doesn't drink much but they kept bringing pots of coffee. . . . Nobody rushed us . . . it was very relaxed and we broadened the conversation. . . . She told me about how she began and how this nun at the school she went to had great faith in her even when her parents didn't really believe she had talent."

Joe paused. "I kept leaning heavily on the notion that I was just passing through, not a permanent fixture. She was quite anxious to talk, actually, I don't need much congratulation."

"So she did tell you . . ."

"Yes, I sort of squeezed it out of her bit by bit—not with crude questions like, 'Why isn't a girl like you married?' More about Dublin being full of gossip and disapproval. . . . I told her I'd never be able to live here nowadays because of my own life. She said no, it wasn't too bad . . . things had changed, but people did let others go their own way. I argued that with her, and then she had to get down to specifics. She had a false start, then she said she didn't want to be unburdening her whole life story to a total stranger.

"I said that total strangers were the only people you could possibly unburden things to. They passed like ships in the night. Sometimes it happened that you got a bit of advice from a passing ship but even if you didn't, what the hell, the ship had passed on . . . it wasn't hanging around embarrassing you every time you saw it."

"And?"

"And she told me . . . she told me about her married man."

"Was it anything like the truth? I mean, did she describe things the way things are?"

"Very like the way you told me. She met him when she was doing a job for the bank. He had taken her out to lunch, she had been lonely, he had understood. . . . her father had died recently. Her mother was dead years ago. The married man was very sympathetic."

"I'm sure," said Carmel.

"They met a lot and he was so interested in her work and so encouraging—and he believed in her—and the reason she liked him so much . . ."

"Yes . . . ?" Carmel leaned forward.

"He didn't want to hurt people or do people down. He never wanted her to score over other people. He wanted her to be content in herself and with her work. . . . She liked that most about him."

Joe paused. "So I put it to her that he must have a bit of the louse in him to maintain two ménages, he must be a bit of a crud to have it both ways . . . you know, not disturbing his own life-style . . ."

"What did she say?"

"She thought not, she thought he was a victim of circumstances. His wife hadn't been well, she had been—sorry, Carmel—the phrase she used was 'suffering from her nerves.' "

"Fine, fine," said Carmel.

"Then I talked about Henry a bit, I didn't want her to think that she was confiding too much, you know . . . people turn against people when they tell them too much."

"Yes, I know," Carmel agreed.

"So anyway, it went on from there . . . could she guide me around Dublin a bit? We had lunch at the National Gallery . . . we went in and out of the place that's giving her the exhibition, we went—oh, God knows where. . . . I kept her occupied during the days, and I faded out a bit at night because I knew she'd be meeting your man after work. On Wednesday she asked me would I like to meet him. I said no."

"Wednesday," Carmel said softly to herself.

"Yes. I said no way did I want to get involved in people's private lives. That was the night she told me that she had been invited here and she was worried sick, she couldn't think why—she said she didn't want to come and hurt you."

"No. No, indeed," said Carmel.

"So she said she didn't know how to get out of it, the Man wouldn't hear of her refusing. I said the married man wanted to get a kick out of seeing you both together. She went quite white over it all. 'He wouldn't want that,' she said. 'I don't know, it gives some fellows a real charge,' I said, 'seeing the two women there and knowing they've screwed both of them.' "

"Really?" Carmel said.

Joe laughed. "That's what she said too. Anyway, it upset her. And she said he wasn't like that. Well then, he shouldn't force you to come to the dinner, I said. It's being a real voyeur, isn't it, having the both of you there?"

Joe paused for a gulp of his coffee.

"Then I said, 'I wouldn't be surprised if he forced the wife to ask you to dinner, after all. Why would the wife ask you? If she doesn't know about you and him it's an odd thing she should suddenly decide to pick you of all the people in Dublin and if she *does* know it's even odder.' She said that's what she'd been thinking herself. She's just an ordinary woman you know, Carmel, just an ordinary female with a slow brain ticking through and working things out. . . . She's no Mata Hari."

"I know," said Carmel.

"So I said then, and the others are his friends really, maybe they're all in on it, they know about you and him, don't they?" Joe leaned over. "So that was part one over, she really believed he was setting her up, she was so convinced. I don't know what kind of an evening they had that night, but it didn't last long. He was out of there in an hour."

"Yes, he was home very bad-tempered and very early on Wednesday," Carmel said, smiling.

"So Thursday I ring her and say come on, I'll buy you lunch and no gloomy chat, because isn't it a small world, I've just run into my old friends the Murrays and ha ha isn't Dublin a village? I now know who the mystery bank manager is, it's Dermot Murray. I didn't know he knew you. . . . She's amazed.

" 'Oho,' I say, 'can't keep a secret in this town. No, really, isn't it a scream, I knew brother Charlie years ago, long before he went to Australia or anything, and I remember Carmel, and Carmel was walking out with Dermot Murray, a lowly bank clerk then . . .' Oh, she's all upset, she can't believe it, it's too much. I say stop all that fussing and fretting, I'll buy you a big lunch. I keep saying it's a scream."

Carmel smiled.

"I arrive and collect her. She's been crying, she's so ashamed, she wouldn't have dreamed of telling me all those intimate things if there was a chance I'd have known anyone . . . but I was a stranger in town and outside, someone who went away years ago. I kept laughing, the odds against it must be millions to one, forget it, anyway, wasn't it all for the best? Because now that I knew that it was Carmel and Dermot I could say definitely that they weren't the kind of people who would be involved in anything sordid. Everyone had spoken very well of Dermot, and poor Carmel had always been very nice."

"Poor Carmel," Carmel said, smiling still.

"You asked me to play it for all I could," Joe said.

"I know. Go on."

"It took a lot of coaxing to get her back where she was. I reminded her of all the indiscretions I had told her, about being gay, about Henry. I told her that nobody in Ireland knew that about me, that we each knew secrets about the other. We shook hands over lunch. I felt a real shit."

"Joe, go on."

"She left more cheerful. I rang her yesterday morning and asked could I come by for coffee. I told her that I had heard at the hotel a man talking to a friend. I described David perfectly . . . he's not hard to describe from what you told me."

"There's only one David," said Carmel.

"Yes, well she identified him, and oh, I wove a long tale. It could have been something else entirely, but it did sound as if it could have been Dermot he was talking about. . . . I kept pretending that it might have been imagination, but she saw it wasn't. She knew that if I had heard him talking like that it must be Dermot, and Dermot must indeed have told David that she was coming to the party and wasn't it all very risqué."

Joe looked at Carmel. "She cried a lot, she cried and cried. I felt very sorry for her."

"I cried a lot. I cried for four months the first time, the time he went off with that Sophie."

"But she has nobody to comfort her."

"I had nobody to comfort me."

"You had a psychiatrist."

"Great help."

"He cured you, didn't he?"

"No, he didn't, he asked me to ask myself was my marriage with Dermot so important that I should save it at all costs. What the hell does he know about marriage and importance, and all costs? What else is there for me but to be married to Dermot? There *is* nothing else. It's not a choice between this and something else, it's this or nothing."

"You're fine, you could live on your own. You don't need him. I can't see what you want him around for. He hasn't been any good to you for years, he hasn't been kind or a friend. You haven't wanted any of the things he wanted. Why didn't you let him go then, or indeed now?"

"You don't understand. It's different for . . . er . . . gays, it's not the same."

"Hell, it's not the same, of course it's not the same. I love Henry, Henry loves me. One day one of us will stop loving the other. Hopefully we'll split and go our own ways . . . but the worst is to stay together bitching."

"But your world, it's so different . . . so totally different . . . I couldn't do that."

"Well, you didn't. And you've won."

"I have, haven't I?"

"Yes . . . it's all fixed up. I told her this morning that I'd be here for moral support if she wanted to come. She said no, she didn't want to make a fool of herself in front of everyone. She'll tell you tonight at the exhibition that she can't come after all. She says she'll do it gently, she knows you are just as much a pawn as she is."

"Good, good."

"And she's not going to tell him at all. She's going to leave him stew, let him think what he likes."

"Suppose he runs after her, suppose he won't let her go?"

"I think she'll make it clear to him. Anyway, she's already set up some other friends to go out with. She says she's sorry for you because you're a timid sort of person and you'd been planning this for a month. . . . She's afraid that the whole thing will be a damp squib."

"That's very nice of her."

"It is, actually, Carmel, she's a very nice person."

"So you keep saying, but I'm a very nice person. I'm an extremely nice person, and very few people ever realize that."

"I realize it. I've always realized it," Joe said.

"Yes," Carmel said.

"I'd have done this for no money, you were always good to me."

"I sent you money because I have it, you don't. It seemed only fair that your week should be subsidized."

"You were always a brick, Carmel. Always. I'd have had no life if it weren't for you."

There was a silence. In the gleaming kitchen they sat and remembered the other kitchen, the kitchen where Carmel's brother Charlie and Joe had stood scarlet-faced in front of Carmel's father. Words that had never been used in that house were used that evening. Threats of ruin were made. Joe would be prosecuted, he would spend years and years in jail, the whole world would know about his unnatural habits, his vile seduction of innocent schoolboys . . . an act so shameful not even the animal kingdom would tolerate it, and Charlie might grow up warped as a result. Joe's father, who worked as the gardener, would be sacked, and the man would never work again. He would be informed this night of his son's activities.

It was then that Carmel had found her voice. She was five years older than Charlie; she was twenty-two. She had been a quiet girl, her father had not even noticed her in the kitchen so great had been his rage.

"It was Charlie's fault, Dad," she had said in a level voice. "Charlie's been queer for two years. He's had relationships with a lot of boys, I can tell you their names." There had been a silence which seemed to last for an hour. "I don't like unfairness. Joe Daly has done nothing that Charlie didn't encourage. Why should his father be sacked, why should he be disgraced, why should Charlie get away with it, Dad, because Mr. Daly is a gardener and you're a company director?"

It was unanswerable.

Charlie went to Australia shortly afterward. Mr. Daly was never told, and Joe Daly got a little assistance from Charlie's father indirectly, so that he could go to a technical school and do English and commerce and bookkeeping. During that time he wrote the odd article for evening papers, and Carmel had seen him casually around Dublin. He had sent her a wedding present when she married Dermot two years after the distressing events in the kitchen. It was a beautiful cut glass vase, nicer than anything she had got from any of her father's friends, or any of Dermot's side. It would be on the dining table tonight, with late summer roses in it.

"So will I leave you to rest and think over it all?" Joe said.

"I *wish* you thought I'd done the right thing," she said.

"You know what I think. I think you should have given him away. I really do. There are other lives."

"Not for fifty-year-old women there aren't."

"I know what you mean, but there are. Anyway, there you go."

"Why are you so fed up with me?"

"Carmel, I'm not fed up with you. I owed you, I'd do anything for you anytime, I told you that and I meant it. You asked me one favor. You've paid me handsomely for it. I've done it, but I don't have to approve of it."

"Oh, Joe, I thought you'd understand."

"You see, it's the total reverse of all that happened, years ago. Then you did something brave just—well—just so that the right thing should be done."

"But this is the right thing! She's young, she'll find somebody else, a proper person, not a married man . . . not somebody else's husband."

"No, you see, this time you've arranged it so that the truth is hidden, lost. She thinks that Dermot is setting her up, she thinks he's having a laugh at her, that he wanted her to come to the party as some kind of macho thing. Dermot thinks that she's let him down, promised to go through with it and then thrown him over unexpectedly. Neither believes that the other is actually honest."

Carmel stood up. "I know it's complicated. That psychiatrist said to me, you know, the first time, that there's no such thing as absolute right and absolute wrong. He also said that we can't control other people's lives, we must only take responsibility for our own. I decided what I wanted to do with mine, and I did it. That's the way I see it. I don't see it as meddling or playing God or anything."

Joe stood up too. "No, whatever else it is, I don't think it's playing God," he said.

He slipped quietly out of the house, making sure that he wasn't observed, because he wasn't meant to be a great friend of Carmel's—he was only a casual friend whom they had met luckily again, and his last job was to make sure that the dinner party was great fun.

Flat in Ringsend

They said you should get the evening papers at lunchtime and as soon as you got a smell of a flat that would suit you were to rush out and sit on the step at the head of the queue. You shouldn't take any notice of the words "After six o'clock." If you got there at six o'clock and the ad had sounded any way reasonable, then you'd find a line trailing down the road. Finding a good flat in Dublin at a price you could afford was like finding gold in the gold rush.

The other way was by personal contact; if you knew someone who knew someone who was leaving a place—that often worked. But if you had only just arrived in Dublin there was no chance of any personal contact, nobody to tell you that their bed-sit would be vacant at the end of the month. No, it was a matter of staying in a hostel and searching.

Jo had been to Dublin a dozen times when she was a child; she had been up for a match, or for a school outing, or the time that Da was in the Chest Hospital and everyone had been crying in case he wouldn't get better. Most of her friends had been up to Dublin much more often; they talked about places they had gone to in a familiar way, and assumed that she knew what they were talking about.

"You *must* know the Dandelion Market. Let me see, you come out of the Zhivago and you go in a straight line to your right, keep going and you pass O'Donoghue's and the whole of Stephen's Green, and you don't turn right down Grafton Street. Now do you know where it is?"

After so much effort explaining things to her, Jo said she did. Jo was always anxious to please other people, and she felt that she only annoyed them by not knowing what they were talking about. But Dublin was a very big blank spot. She really felt she was stepping into the unknown when she got on the train to go and work there. She didn't ask herself why she was going in the first place. It had been assumed by everyone that she would go. Who would stay in a one-horse town, the back of beyonds, the end of the world, the sticks, this dead-and-alive place? That's all she had heard for years. At school they were all going to get out, escape, see some life, get some living in, have a real kind of existence, and some of the others in her class had gone as far as Ennis or Limerick, often to stay with cousins. A few had gone to England, where an elder sister or an aunt would see them settled in. But out of Jo's year none of them were going to Dublin. Jo's family must have been the only one in the place who didn't have relations in Glasnevin or Dundrum. She was heading off on her own.

There had been a lot of jokes about her going to work in the post office. There'd be no trouble in getting a stamp to write a letter home; what's more, there'd be no excuse if she didn't. She could sneak the odd phone call, too, which would be fine, but they didn't have a phone at home. Maybe she could send a ten-page telegram if she needed to say anything in a hurry. They assumed that she would know the whole business of the high and the mighty in Dublin the way Miss Hayes knew everyone's business from the post office at home. People said that she'd find it very easy to get to know people, there was nowhere like a post office for making friends, it was the center of everything.

She knew she wouldn't be working in the GPO, but whenever she thought of herself in Dublin it was in the middle of the General Post Office chatting up all the people as they came in, knowing every single person who came to buy stamps or collect the children's allowances. She imagined herself living somewhere nearby, maybe over Clery's or on the corner of O'Connell Bridge so that she could look at the Liffey from her bedroom.

She had never expected the miles and miles of streets where nobody knew anyone, the endless bus journeys, the having to get up two hours before she was meant to be at work in case she got lost or the bus was canceled. "Not much time for a social life," she wrote home. "I'm so exhausted when I get back to the hostel I just go to bed and fall asleep."

Jo's mother thought that it would be great altogether if she stayed permanently in the hostel. It was run by nuns, and she could come to no harm. Her father said that he hoped they kept the place warm; nuns were notorious for freezing everyone else to death just because they wore thermal underwear. Jo's sisters who worked in the hotel as waitresses said she must be off her head to have stayed a whole week in a hostel; her brother who worked in the creamery said he was sorry she didn't have a flat, it would be somewhere to stay whenever he went to Dublin; her brother who worked in the garage said that Jo would have been better off to stay where she was—what would she get in Dublin— only discontented—and she'd end up like that O'Hara girl, neither one thing nor the other, happy neither in Dublin nor at home. It had to be said that he had fancied the O'Hara girl for a long time, and it was a great irritation to him that she wouldn't settle down and be like a normal woman.

But Jo didn't know that they were all thinking about her and discussing her, as she answered the advertisement for the flat in Ringsend. It said OWN ROOM, OWN TELEVISION, SHARE KITCHEN, BATHROOM. It was very near her post office and seemed too good to be true. Please, St. Jude, please. May it be nice, may they like me, may it not be too dear.

There wasn't a queue for this one because it wasn't so much FLAT TO LET, more THIRD GIRL WANTED. The fact that it had said "own television" made Jo wonder whether it might be in too high a class for her, but the house did not look any way overpowering. An ordinary red-bricked terraced house with a basement. Her father had warned her against basements; they were full of damp, he said, but then her father had a bad chest and saw damp everywhere. But the flat was not in the basement, it was upstairs. And a cheerful-looking girl with a college scarf, obviously a failed applicant, was coming down the stairs.

"Desperate place," she said to Jo. "They're both awful. Common as dirt."

"Oh," said Jo and went on climbing.

"Hallo," said the girl with "Nessa" printed on her T-shirt.

"God, did you see that toffee-nosed bitch going out? I can't stand that kind, I can't stand them."

"What did she do?" asked Jo.

"Do? She didn't have to *do* anything. She just poked around and wrinkled her lip and sort of giggled and then said 'Is this it?' in a real Foxrock accent. 'Oh dear, oh dear.' Stupid old cow, we wouldn't have had her in here if we were starving and needed her to buy us a crust, would we, Pauline?"

Pauline had a psychedelic shirt on; it almost hurt the eyes, but was only marginally brighter than her hair. Pauline was a punk, Jo noted with amazement. She had seen some of them on O'Connell Street, but hadn't met one close up to talk to.

"No, stupid old bore. She was such a bore. She'd have bored us to death. Years later our bodies would have been found here and the verdict would have been death by boredom."

Jo laughed. It was such a wild thought to think of all that pink hair lying on the floor dead because it hadn't been able to stand the tones of the flatmate. "I'm Jo, I work in the post office and I rang." Nessa said they were just about to have a mug of tea. She produced three mugs; one had NESSA and one had PAULINE and the other one had OTHER written on it. "We'll get your name put on if you come to stay," she said generously.

Nessa worked for the bus company, and Pauline worked in a big firm nearby. They had got the flat three months ago and Nessa's sister had had the third room, but now she was getting married very quickly, very quickly indeed, and so the room was empty. They explained the cost, they showed her the geyser for having a bath and they showed her the cupboard in the kitchen, each shelf with a name on it, Nessa, Pauline, and Maura.

"Maura's name will go, and we'll paint in yours if you come to stay," Nessa said again reassuringly.

"You've no sitting room," Jo said.

"No, we did it in three bed-sits," said Nessa.

"Makes much more sense," said Pauline.

"What's the point of a sitting room?" asked Nessa.

"I mean, who'd sit in it?" asked Pauline.

"And we've got two chairs in our own rooms," Nessa said proudly.

"And each of us has our own telly," said Pauline happily.

That was the point that Jo wanted to discuss.

"Yes, you didn't say how much that costs. Is there a rental?"

Nessa's big happy face spread into a grin. "No, that's the real perk. You see, Maura's Steve, well, my brother-in-law as he now is, I hope, my brother-in-law Steve worked in the business and he was able to get us tellys for a song."

"So you bought them outright, did you?" Jo was enthralled.

"Bought in a manner of speaking," Pauline said. "Accepted them outright."

"Yeah, it was his way of saying thank you, his way of paying the rent . . . in a manner of speaking," Nessa said.

"But did he stay here too?"

"He was Maura's boyfriend. He stayed most of the time."

"Oh," said Jo. There was a silence.

"Well?" Nessa said accusingly. "If you've anything to say, you should say it now."

"I suppose I was wondering, did he not get in everyone's way? I mean, if a fourth person was staying in the flat, was it fair on the others?"

"Why do you think we organized it all into bed-sits?" Pauline asked. "Means we can all do what we like when we like, not trampling on other people. Right?"

"Right," Nessa said.

"Right," Jo said, doubtfully.

"So, what do you think?" Nessa asked Pauline. "I think Jo would be okay if she wants to come, do you?"

"Yeah, sure, I think she'd be fine, if she'd like it here," said Pauline.

"Thank you," said Jo, blushing a bit.

"Is there anything else you'd like to ask? I think we've covered everything. There's a phone with a coin box in the hall downstairs. There's three nurses in the flat below, but they don't take any messages for us so we don't take any for them. The rent on the first of the month, plus five quid each and I get a few basics."

"Will you come, then?" asked Nessa.

"Please. I'd like to very much, can I come on Sunday night?"

They gave her a key, took her rent money, poured another cup of tea and said that it was great to have fixed it all up so quickly. Nessa said that Jo was such a short name it would be dead easy to paint it onto the shelf in the kitchen, the shelf in the bathroom, and her mug.

"She wanted to paint the names on the doors, too, but I wouldn't let her," said Pauline.

"Pauline thought it looked too much like a nursery," said Nessa regretfully.

"Yes, and also I wanted to leave a bit of variety in life. If our names are on the doors then we'll never get any surprise visitors during the night—I always like a bit of the unexpected!"

Jo laughed too. She hoped they were joking.

She assured her mother in the letter that the flat was very near Haddington Road, she told her father how far it was from the damp basement, and she put in the bits about the television in each bedroom to make her sisters jealous. They had said she was an eejit to go to Dublin; the best Dublin people all came to County Clare on their holidays. She should stay at home and meet them there rather than going up and trying to find them in their own place.

They were having tea in the hostel on Sunday when Jo said good-bye. She struggled with her two cases to the bus stop.

"Your friends aren't going to arrange to collect you?" Sister said.

"They haven't a car, Sister."

"I see. Often, though, young people come to help a friend. I hope they are kind people, your friends."

"Very, Sister."

"That's good. Well, God bless you, child, and remember that this is a very wicked city, a lot of very wicked people in it."

"Yes, Sister, I'll keep my eye out for them."

It took her a long time to get to the flat.

She had to change buses twice, and was nearly exhausted when she got there. She had to come down again for the second case, and dragged the two into the room that had been pointed out as hers. It was smaller than it had looked on Friday, yet it could hardly have shrunk. The bedclothes were folded there, two blankets, two pillows and a quilt. Lord, she forgot about sheets; she'd assumed they were included. And God, she supposed there'd be no towel either, wasn't she an eejit not to have asked.

She hoped they wouldn't notice, and she'd be able to buy some tomorrow —or she hoped she would, as she only had an hour for lunch. She'd ask one of the girls in the post office, and she had her savings for just this kind of emergency.

She hung up her clothes in the poky little wardrobe, and put out her ornaments on the windowsill and her shoes in a neat line on the floor. She put her cases under the bed and sat down feeling very flat.

Back home they'd be going to the pictures or to a dance at eight o'clock on a Sunday night. In the hostel some of the girls would watch television in the lounge, others would have gone to the pictures together and go for chips on the way home, throwing the papers into the litter bin on the corner of the street where the hostel was, since Sister didn't like the smell of chips coming into the building.

Nobody was sitting alone on a bed with nothing to do. She could go out and take the bus into town and go to the pictures alone, but didn't that seem ridiculous when she had her own television. Her very own. She could change the channel whenever she wanted to; she wouldn't have to ask anyone.

She was about to go out to the sitting room to see was there a Sunday paper, when she remembered there was no sitting room. She didn't want to open the doors of their rooms in case they might come in and think she was prying. She wondered where they were. Was Nessa out with a boyfriend? She hadn't mentioned one, but then, girls in Dublin didn't tell you immediately if they had a fellow or not. Perhaps Pauline was at a punk disco. She couldn't believe that anyone would actually employ Pauline with that hair and let her meet the public, but maybe she was kept hidden away. Perhaps they'd come home about eleven o'clock (well, they had to get up for work in the morning); perhaps they all had cocoa or drinking chocolate in the sitting room—well, in the kitchen, to end the day. She'd tell them how well she'd settled in. In the meantime she would sit back and watch her own television set.

Jo fell asleep after half an hour. She had been very tired. She dreamed that Nessa and Pauline had come in. Pauline had decided to wash the pink out of her hair and share a room with Nessa. They were going to turn Pauline's room into a sitting room, where they would sit and talk and plan. She woke suddenly when she heard giggling. It was Pauline and a man's voice, and they had gone into the kitchen.

Jo shook herself. She must have been asleep for three hours; she had a crick in her neck and the television was flickering. She stood up and turned it off, combed her hair and was about to go out and welcome the homecomers when she hesitated. If Pauline had invited a boy home, presumably she was going to take him to bed with her. Perhaps the last thing she might need now was her new flatmate coming out looking for company. They were laughing in the kitchen, she could hear them, then she heard the electric kettle hiss and whistle.

Well, she could always pretend that she had been going to make herself a cup of tea.

Nervously, she opened the door and went into the kitchen. Pauline was with a young man who wore a heavy leather jacket with a lot of studs on it.

"Hallo, Pauline, I was just going to get myself a cup of tea," Jo said apologetically.

"Sure," Pauline said. She was not unfriendly, she didn't look annoyed, but she made no effort to introduce her friend.

The kettle was still hot, so Jo found a mug with VISITOR on it and put in a tea bag. "Nessa's going to paint my name on a mug," she said to the man in the jacket, just for something to say. "Oh, good," he said. He shrugged and asked Pauline, "Who's Nessa?"

"Lives over there," Pauline said, indicating the direction of Nessa's room.

"I'm the third girl," Jo said desperately. "Third in what?" he said, genuinely bewildered. Pauline had fixed the tray of tea and biscuits and was moving toward the door.

"Night," she said, companionably enough.

"Good night, Pauline, good night . . . er . . ." Jo said.

She took the cup of tea into her own room. She turned up the television slightly in case she heard the sound of anything next door. She hoped she hadn't annoyed Pauline. She couldn't see what she had done that might annoy her, and anyway she had seemed cheerful enough when she was taking this boy off to—well, to her room. Jo sighed and got into bed.

Next morning she was coming out of the bathroom when she met Nessa.

"It's just *J* and *O*, two letters, isn't it?" Nessa asked.

"Oh yes, that's right, thank you very much, Nessa."

"Right. I didn't want to do it and then find you had an *E* on it."

"No, no, it's short for Josephine."

"Right on." Nessa was off.

"What time are you coming home tonight?" Jo asked.

"Oh, I don't think I'll have them done tonight," Nessa said.

"I didn't mean that, I just wondered what you were doing for your tea . . . supper. You know?"

"No idea," said Nessa cheerfully.

"Oh," said Jo. "Sorry."

Jacinta, who worked beside her, asked her how the flat was.

"It's great altogether," Jo said.

"Dead right to get out of that hostel, you'd have no life in a hostel," Jacinta said wisely.

"No, no indeed."

"God, I wish I didn't live at home," Jacinta said. "It's not natural for people to live in their own homes, there should be a law about it. They have laws over stupid things like not importing live fowl, as if anyone would want to, but they have no laws about the things that people really need."

"Yes," said Jo dutifully.

"Anyway, you'll have the high life from now on. You country ones have all the luck."

"I suppose we do," Jo agreed doubtfully.

* * *

If she had stayed in the hostel they might have been playing twenty-five in the lounge now, or someone might have bought a new record. They would look at the evening paper, sigh over the price of flats, wonder whether to go to the pictures and complain about the food. There would be talk and endless tea or bottles of cola from the machine. There would not be four walls as there were now.

She had bought a hamburger on the way home and eaten it. She washed her tights, she put the new sheets on the bed and hung her new towel up in the bathroom on the third hook. The other hooks had *N* and *P* on them. She took out her writing pad but remembered that she had written home on Friday just after she had found the flat. There was nothing new to tell. The evening yawned ahead of her. And then there would be Tuesday and Wednesday and Thursday. . . . Tears came into her eyes and fell down onto her lap as she sat on the end of her bed. She must be absolutely awful to have no friends and nowhere to go and nothing to do. Other people of eighteen had great times. She used to have great times when she was seventeen, at school and planning to be eighteen. Look at her now, sitting alone. Even her flatmates didn't want to have anything to do with her. She cried and cried. Then she got a headache so she took two aspirins and climbed into bed. It's bloody fantastic being grown up, she thought, as she switched off the light at nine o'clock.

There was a *J* on her towel rack, her name was on the bathroom shelf that belonged to her, and her empty kitchen shelf had a "Jo" on it also. She examined the other two shelves. Nessa had cornflakes and a packet of sugar and a lot of tins of soup on her shelf. Pauline had a biscuit tin and about a dozen tins of grapefruit segments on hers.

The kitchen was nice and tidy. Nessa had said the first day that they never left any washing up to be done and that if you used the frying pan you had to scrub it then, not let it steep until the morning. It had all seemed great fun when she was talking about it then, because Jo had envisaged midnight feasts, and all three of them laughing and having parties. That's what people *did*, for heaven's sake. She must have just got in with two recluses, that was her problem.

Pauline came into the kitchen yawning, and opened a tin of grapefruit segments. "I think I'd never wake up if I didn't have these," she said. "I have half a tin and two biscuits for my breakfast every day, and then I'm ready for anything."

Jo was pleased to be spoken to.

"Is your friend here?" she said, trying to be modern and racy.

"Which friend?" Pauline yawned and began to spoon the grapefruit out of the tin into a bowl.

"You know, your friend—the other night?"

"Nessa?" Pauline looked at her blankly. "Do you mean Nessa?"

"No, the fellow, the fellow with the jacket with the studs. I met him here in the kitchen."

"Oh, yes. Shane."

"Shane. That was his name."

"Yeah, what about him, what were you saying?"

"I was asking was he here?"

"Here? Now? Why should he be here?" Pauline pushed her pink hair out of her eyes and looked at her watch. "Jesus Christ, it's only twenty to eight in the morning. Why would he be here?" She looked wildly around the kitchen as if the man with the studded leather jacket were going to appear from behind the gas cooker. Jo felt the conversation was going wrong.

"I just asked sociably if he was still here, that was all."

"But why on earth would he be still here? I went out with him on Sunday night. *Sunday.* It's Tuesday morning now, isn't it? Why would he be here?" Pauline looked confused and worried, and Jo wished she had never spoken.

"I just thought he was your boyfriend—"

"No, he's not, but if he was, I tell you I wouldn't have him here at twenty to eight in the morning talking! I don't know how anyone can talk in the mornings. It beats me."

Jo drank her tea silently.

"See you," said Pauline eventually, when she had finished her biscuits and grapefruit and crashed into the bathroom.

Jo thanked Nessa for putting up the names. Nessa was pleased. "I like doing that, it gives me a sense of order in the world. It defines things; that makes me feel better."

"Sure," said Jo. She was just about to ask Nessa what she was doing that evening when she remembered yesterday's rebuff. She decided to phrase it differently this time.

"Are you off out with your friends this evening?" she said timidly.

"I might be, I might not, it's always hard to know in the morning, isn't it?"

"Yes, it is," said Jo untruthfully. It was becoming increasingly easy to know in the morning, she thought. The answer was coming up loud and clear when she asked herself what she was going to do in the evening. The answer was Nothing.

"Well, I'm off now. Good-bye," she said to Nessa.

Nessa looked up and smiled. "Bye bye," she said vaguely, as if Jo had been the postman or the man delivering milk on the street.

On Thursday night Jo went downstairs to answer the phone. It was for one of the nurses on the ground floor, as it always was. Hesitantly she knocked on their door. The big blond nurse thanked her, and as Jo was going up the stairs again she heard the girl say, "No, it was one of the people in the flats upstairs. There's three flats upstairs and we all share the same phone."

That was it! That was what she hadn't realized. She wasn't in a flat with two other girls, she was in a flat by herself. Why hadn't that dawned on her? She was in a proper bed-sitter all of her own, she just shared kitchen and bathroom facilities, as they would put it in an ad. That's what had been wrong. She had thought that she was meant to be part of a jolly all-girls-together. That's why she had been so depressed. She went over the whole conversation with Nessa the first day; she remembered what they had said about doing it up as bed-sitters but not telling the landlord anything, it never did to tell landlords anything, just keep paying the rent and keep out of his way.

There was quite a bounce in her step now. I'm on my own in Dublin, she thought. I have my own place, I'm going out to find a life for myself now. She didn't have to worry about Pauline's morals anymore now. If Pauline wanted to bring home a rough-looking person with studs on his jacket, that was Pauline's business. She just lived in the flat next door. That's what Pauline had meant when she had said Nessa lived next door. And that's why Nessa went in for all this labeling and naming things. No wonder they had been slightly surprised when she kept asking them what they were doing in the evening; they must have thought she was mad.

Happy for the first time since Sunday, Jo did herself up. She put on eyeshadow and mascara, she put some color in her cheeks and wore her big earrings. She didn't know where she was going, but she decided that she would go out cheerfully now. She looked around her room and liked it much better. She would get some posters for the walls, she would even ask her mother if she could take some of the ornaments from home. The kitchen shelves at home were chock-a-block with ornaments; her mother would be glad to give some of them a new home. Humming happily, she set off.

She felt terrific as she swung along with her shoulderbag. She pitied her sisters, who were only finishing the late shift now at the hotel. She pitied the girls who still had to stay in a hostel, who hadn't been able to go out and find a place of their own. She felt sorry for Jacinta, who had to stay at home and whose mother and father interrogated her about where she went and what she did. She pitied people who had to share television sets. What if you wanted to look at one thing and they wanted to look at something else? How did you decide? She was so full of good spirits that she nearly walked past the pub where the notice said: "Tonight—the Great Gaels."

Imagine, the Great Gaels were there in person. In a pub. Cover charge £1. If she paid a pound she would see them close up. Up to now she had only seen them on television.

They had been at the Fleadh in Ennis once about four years ago, before they were famous. She had seen an advertisement, all right, saying that they would be in this pub, and now here she was outside it. Jo's heart beat fast. Was it a thing you could do on your own, go into a concert in a pub? Probably it was a thing people went to in groups; she might look odd. Maybe there'd be noplace for just one person to sit. Maybe it would only be tables for groups.

But a great surge of courage came flooding over her. She was a young woman who lived in a flat on her own in Dublin, she had her own place and by the Lord, if she could do that, she could certainly go into a pub and hear the Great Gaels on her own. She pushed the door.

A man sat at the desk inside and gave her a cloakroom ticket and took her pound.

"Where do I go?" she almost whispered.

"For what?" he asked.

"You know, where exactly do I go?" she asked. It seemed like an ordinary pub to her, no stage, maybe the Great Gaels were upstairs.

The man assumed she was looking for the Ladies'. "I think it's over there near the other door, yes, there it is beside the Gents'." He pointed across the room.

Flushing a dark red she thanked him. In case he was still looking at her she thought she had better go to the Ladies'. In the cloakroom she looked at her face. It had looked fine at home, back in her flat. In here it looked a bit dull, no character, no color. She put on much more makeup in the dim light and came out to find out where the concert would be held.

She saw two women sitting together. They looked safe enough to ask. They told her with an air of surprise that it would be in the pub, but not for about an hour.

"What do we do until then?" she asked.

They laughed. "I suppose you could consider having a drink—it is a pub after all," said one of them. They went back to their conversation. She felt very silly. She didn't want to leave and come back in case there was no readmittance. She wished she had brought a paper or a book. Everyone else seemed to be talking.

She sat for what seemed like a very long time. Twice the waiter asked her would she be having another drink as he cleaned around her glass of orange, which she was eking out. She didn't want to waste too much money; a pound already coming in was enough to spend.

Then people arrived and started to fix up microphones, and the crowd was bigger suddenly and she was squeezed toward the end of the seat, and she saw the Great Gaels having pints up at the bar just as if they were ordinary customers. Wasn't Dublin fantastic? You could go into a pub and sit and have a drink in the same place as the Great Gaels. They'd never believe her at home.

The lead singer of the Great Gaels was tapping the microphone and testing it by saying, *"a haon, a dhó, a thrí."* Everyone laughed and settled down with full drinks.

"Come on, now, attention please, we don't want anyone with an empty glass now getting up and disturbing us," he said.

"Divil a fear of that," someone shouted.

"All right, look around you. If you see anyone who might be fidgety, fill up their glass for them."

Two men beside Jo looked at her glass disapprovingly. "What have you in there, miss?" one said.

"Orange, but it's fine, I won't get up and disturb them," she said, hating to be the center of attention.

"Large gin and orange for the lady," one man said.

"Oh, no," called Jo. "It's not gin—"

"Sorry. Large vodka and orange for the lady," he corrected.

"Right," said the waiter, eyeing her disapprovingly, Jo felt.

When it came she had her purse out.

"Nonsense, I bought you a drink," said the man.

"Oh, but you can't do that," she said.

He paid what seemed like a fortune for it; Jo looked into the glass nervously.

"It was very expensive, wasn't it?" she said.

"Well, that's the luck of the draw, you might have been a beer drinker." He smiled at her. He was very old, over thirty, and his friend was about the same.

Jo wished they hadn't bought the drink. She wasn't used to accepting drinks. Should she offer to buy the next round? Would they accept, or would they, worse still, buy her another? Perhaps she should just accept this one and move a bit away from them. But wasn't that awfully rude? Anyway, now with the Great Gaels about to begin, she wouldn't have to talk to them.

"Thank you very much indeed," she said, putting the orange into the large vodka. "That's very nice of you, and most generous."

"Not at all," said the man with the open-neck shirt.

"It'sh a pleashure," said the other man.

Then she realized that they were both very drunk.

The Great Gaels had started, but Jo couldn't enjoy them. She felt this should have been a great night, only twenty feet away from Ireland's most popular singers, in a nice, warm pub, and a free drink in her hand, what more could a girl want? But to her great embarrassment the man with the open-neck shirt had settled himself so that his arm was along the back of the seat behind her, and from time to time it would drop around her shoulder. His friend was beating his feet to the music with such energy that a lot of his pint had already spilled on the floor.

Jo hoped fervently that they wouldn't make a scene, and that if they did nobody would think that they were with her. She had a horror of drunks ever since the time that her Uncle Jim had taken up the leg of lamb and thrown it into the fire because somebody crossed him when they had all been invited to a meal. The evening had broken up in a shambles and as they went home her father had spoken about drink being a good servant but a cruel master. Her father had said that Uncle Jim was two people, one drunk and one sober, and they were as unlike as you could find. Her father said that it was a mercy that Uncle Jim's weakness hadn't been noticeable in any of the rest of the family, and her mother had been very upset and said they had all thought Jim was cured.

Sometimes her sisters told her terrible things people had done in the hotel when they were drunk. Drunkenness was something frightening and unknown. And now she had managed to land herself in a corner with a drunk's arm around her.

The Great Gaels played encore after encore, and they only stopped at closing time. Jo had now received another large vodka and orange from the friend of the open-shirted man, and when she had tried to refuse, he had said, "You took one from Gerry—what's wrong with my drink?"

She had been so alarmed by his attitude, she had rushed to drink it.

The Great Gaels were selling copies of their latest record, and autographing it as well. She would have loved to have bought it in some ways, to remind herself that she had been right beside them, but then it would have reminded her of Gerry and Christy, and the huge vodkas which were making her legs feel funny, and the awful fact that the evening was not over yet.

"I tried to buy you a drink to say thank you for all you bought me, but the bar man told me it's after closing time," she said nervously.

"It is now?" said Gerry. "Isn't that a bit of bad news."

"Imagine, the girl didn't get a chance to buy us a drink," said Christy.

"That's unfortunate," said Gerry.

"Most unfortunate," said Christy.

"Maybe I could meet you another night and buy you one?" She looked anxiously from one to another. "Would that be all right?"

"That would be quite all right, it would be excellent," said Gerry.

"But what would be more excellent," said Christy, "would be if you invited us home for a cup of coffee."

"Maybe the girl lives with her mam and dad," said Gerry.

"No, I live on my own," said Jo proudly, and then could have bitten off her tongue.

"Well, now." Gerry brightened. "That would be a nice way to round off the evening."

"I don't have any more drink, though, I wouldn't have any beer—"

"That's all right, we have a little something to put in the coffee." Gerry was struggling into his coat.

"Are you far from here?" Christy was asking.

"Only about ten minutes' walk." Her voice was hardly above a whisper. Now that she had let them know that the coast was clear, she could think of not one way of stopping them. "It's a longish ten minutes, though," she said.

"That'll clear our heads, a nice walk," said Christy.

"Just what we need," said Gerry.

Would they rape her? she wondered. Would they assume that this was why she was inviting them back—so that she could have sexual intercourse with both of them? Probably. And then if she resisted they would say she was only leading them on and insist on having their way with her. Was she stark staring mad? She cleared her throat.

"It's only coffee, mind, that's all," she said in a schoolmistressy way.

"Sure, that's fine, that's what you said," Christy said. "I have a naggin of whiskey in my pocket. I told you."

They walked down the road. Jo was miserable. How had she got herself into this? She knew that she *could* turn to them in the brightly lit street and say, "I'm sorry, I've changed my mind, I have to be up early tomorrow morning." She *could* say, "Oh, heavens, I forgot, my mother is coming tonight, I totally forgot, she wouldn't like me bringing people in when she's asleep." She *could* say that the landlord didn't let them have visitors. But she felt that it needed greater courage to say any of them than to plod on to whatever was going to happen.

Gerry and Christy were happy, they did little dance steps to some of the songs they sang, and made her join in a chorus of the last song the Great Gaels had sung. People looked at them on the street and smiled. Jo had never felt so wretched in her whole life.

At the door she asked them to hush. And they did in an exaggerated way, putting their fingers on their lips and saying "shush" to each other. She let them in and they went upstairs. Please, please God, may Nessa and Pauline not be in the kitchen. They never are any other night, let them not be there tonight.

They were both there. Nessa in a dressing gown, Pauline in a great black waterproof cape; she was coloring her hair apparently, and didn't want bits of the gold to fall on her clothes.

Jo smiled a stiff "good evening" and tried to manipulate the two men past the door.

"More lovely girls, more lovely girls," said Gerry delightedly. "You said you lived by yourself."

"I do," snapped Jo. "These are the girls from next door, we share a kitchen."

"I see," Pauline said in a huffed tone. "Downgraded."

Jo wasn't going to explain. If only she could get the two drunks into her own bed-sitter.

"What are you doing, is that a fancy-dress?" Christy asked Pauline.

"No, it's not a fancy-dress, wise guy, it's my nightdress—I always go to bed in a black sou'wester," Pauline said and everyone except Jo screeched with laughter.

"I was just going to make us some coffee," said Jo sharply, taking down three mugs with VISITOR painted on them. Gerry thought the mugs were the funniest thing he had ever seen.

"Why do you put visitor on them?" he asked Jo.

"I have no idea," Jo said. "Ask Nessa."

"So that you'll remember you're visitors and won't move in," Nessa said. They all found this very funny too.

"If you'd like to go into my bedroom—my flat, I mean—I'll follow with the coffees," Jo said.

"It's great fun here," said Christy, and produced his small bottle from his hip pocket.

Nessa and Pauline got their mugs immediately. In no time they were all friends. Christy took out a bit of paper and wrote Christy and Gerry and they stuck the names to their mugs—so that they would feel part of the gang, he said. Jo felt the vodka and the heat and the stress had been too much for her. Unsteadily she got to her feet and staggered to the bathroom. She felt so weak afterward that she couldn't face the kitchen again. She went to the misery of her bed, and oblivion.

She felt terrible in the morning. She couldn't understand why people like Uncle Jim had wanted to drink. Drinking made other people ridiculous and made you feel sick, how could anyone like it? She remembered slowly, like a slow-motion film, the events of the night before and her cheeks reddened with shame. They would probably ask her to leave. Imagine coming home with two drunks, and then abandoning them in the kitchen while she had gone away to be sick. God knows who they were, those two men, Gerry and Christy. They might have been burglars even. . . . Jo sat up in bed. Or suppose when she had disappeared . . . suppose they had attacked Nessa and Pauline?

She leaped out of bed, uncaring about her headache and her stomach cramps, and burst out of her door. The kitchen was its usual tidy self: all the mugs washed and hanging back on their hooks. Trembling, she opened the doors of their bedrooms. Pauline's room was the same as ever—huge posters on the wall and a big long clothes rail, like you'd see in a shop that sold dresses, where Pauline hung all her gear. Nessa's room was neat as a pin, candlewick bedspread, chest of drawers, with photographs neatly arranged; little hanging bookshelf with about twenty paperbacks on it. No sign of rape or struggle in either room.

Jo looked at her watch; she was going to be late for work, the others had obviously gone ages ago. But why had they left her no note? No explanation? Or a note asking her for an explanation?

Jo staggered to work, to the wrath that met her as she was forty minutes late. Jacinta said to her at one stage that she looked pretty ropy.

"Pretty ropy is exactly how I feel. I think I'm having my first hangover."

"Well for you," said Jacinta jealously. "I never get a chance to do anything that might give me even a small hangover."

She was dreading going home. Over and over she rehearsed her apologies. She would put it down to the drink. Or would that be worse? Would they find her even more awful if they thought she was so drunk last night she didn't know what she was doing? Would she say she had been introduced to them by a friend, so she thought they were respectable and when she found out they weren't it was too late? What would she say? Just that she was sorry.

Neither of them was there. She waited for ages but they didn't come in. She wrote out a note and left it on the kitchen table. "I'm very very sorry about last night. Please wake me when you come in and I will try to give you an explanation. Jo."

But nobody woke her, and when she did wake it was Saturday morning. Her note was still on the table. They hadn't bothered to wake her. She was so despicable they didn't even want to discuss it.

She made her morning cup of tea and stole back to bed. It was lunchtime before she realized that neither of them was in the flat. They mustn't have come home.

Jo had never felt so uneasy in her life. There must be a perfectly reasonable explanation. After all, there had been no arrangement to tell any of the others their movements. She had realized this on Thursday night. They all lived separate lives. But what could have happened that they had disappeared? Jo told herself that she was being ridiculous. Nessa lived in Waterford, or her family did, so she had probably gone home for the weekend. Pauline was from the country, too, somewhere. Well, she had to be, otherwise she wouldn't be in a flat. She'd probably gone home too.

It was just a coincidence that they had gone the same weekend. And just a coincidence that they had gone after the visit of the two drunks.

Jo stood up and sat down again. Of course they had to be at home with their families. What else was she imagining? Go on, spell it out, what do you fear, she said to herself, that those two innocent-looking eejits who had a bit too much to drink kidnapped two big strong girls like Pauline and Nessa? Come on! Yes, it was ridiculous, it was ludicrous. What did they do, hold them at gunpoint while they tidied up the flat and then pack them into a van and bear them off?

Jo had often been told she had a vivid imagination. This was an occasion when she could have done without it. But it wouldn't go away. She couldn't pull a curtain over the worries, the pictures that kept coming up of Christy hitting Nessa and of Gerry strangling Pauline, and all through her mind went the refrain, There must be something wrong, otherwise they would have left me a note.

It was her fourth Saturday in Dublin. The first one she had spent unpacking her case and getting used to the hostel; the second one had been spent looking at flats which were too expensive and too far from work, and which had already been taken by other people; the third Saturday she had spent congratulating herself on having found Nessa and Pauline; and now on this, the fourth Saturday, Nessa and Pauline had most likely been brutally murdered and ravaged by two drunks that she had brought back to the flat. How could she explain it to anyone? "Well, you see, it was like this, sergeant. I had two double vodkas in the pub bought by these men, and then when we came home—oh yes, sergeant, I brought them home with me, why not? Well, when we came home they poured whisky into our coffees and before I knew where I was I had passed out in a stupor and when I woke up my flatmates were gone, and they never came back. They were never seen again."

Jo cried and cried. They *must* have gone home for the weekend. People did. She had read a big article in the paper not long ago about these fellows making a fortune driving people home in a minibus; apparently lots of country girls missed the fun at home at weekends. They must have gone off in a minibus. Please, please, St. Jude, may they have gone in a minibus. If they went in a minibus, St. Jude, I'll never do anything bad for the rest of my life. More than that. More. If they're definitely safe and they went off yesterday in a minibus, St. Jude, I'll tell everyone about you. I'll put a notice in the two evening papers —and the three daily papers, too, if it weren't too dear. She would bring St. Jude's name into casual conversation with people and say that he was a great man in a crisis. She wouldn't actually describe the whole crisis in detail, of course. Oh, dear Lord, speak, speak, should she go to the guards? Should she report it or was she making the most ludicrous fuss over nothing? Would Pauline and Nessa be furious if the guards contacted their homes? God, suppose they'd gone off with fellows or something? Imagine, if the guards were calling on their families? She'd have the whole country alerted for nothing.

But if she didn't get the guards, suppose something had happened because of those drunk men she'd invited into the house, yes, she, Josephine Margaret Assumpta O'Brien had invited two drunk men into a house, not a week after that nun in the hostel had said that Dublin was a very wicked city, and now her two flatmates, innocent girls who had done nothing to entice these men in, were missing, with no trace of them whatsoever.

She had nothing to eat for the day. She walked around hugging herself, stopping when she heard the slightest sound in case it might be a key in the lock. When it was getting dark she remembered how they had written their names on bits of paper: they could have taken them away with them, but they might be in the rubbish bin. Yes, there they were, Christy and Gerry, scrawled on paper with bits of tape attached to it. Jo took them out with a fork in case they might still have fingerprints on them. She put them on the kitchen table and said a decade of the rosary beside them.

Outside, people passed in the street going about the business of a Saturday night. Was it only last Saturday that she had gone to the pictures with Josie and Helen, those two nice girls in the hostel? Why hadn't she stayed there? It had been awful since she left, it had been frightening and worrying and getting worse every day until . . . until *this*.

There was nobody she could talk to. Suppose she phoned her sister in the hotel, Dymphna would be furious with her; the immediate reaction would be, come-home-at-once, what-are-you-doing-by-yourself-up-in-Dublin, everyone-knew-you-couldn't-cope. And it was a temptation to run away. What time was the evening train to Limerick? Or tomorrow morning? But she didn't want to go home, and she didn't want to talk to Dymphna and she couldn't explain the whole thing on the phone downstairs in the hall in case the people in the flat below heard—the people in the flat below! *That* was it!

She was halfway down the stairs when she paused. Suppose everything were all right, and suppose St. Jude had got them on a minibus, wouldn't Nessa and Pauline be furious if she had gone in and alarmed the three nurses downstairs? They had said that they kept themselves very much to themselves; the nurses were all right but it didn't do to get too involved with them. Yes, well, going in and telling them that you suspected Nessa and Pauline had been abducted and maltreated was certainly getting involved.

She went back up the stairs. Was there anything that the nurses could do to help that she couldn't do? Answer: No.

Just at that moment the big blond nurse that she had spoken to came out. "Hey, I was just going to go up to you lot above."

"Oh, really, what's wrong?" Jo said.

"Nothing's wrong, nothing at all. We're having a party tonight, though, and we just wanted to say if any of you lot wanted to come, it starts at—well, when the pubs close."

"That's very nice of you. I don't think—"

"Well, all we wanted to say is, there may be a bit of noise, but you're very welcome. If you could bring a bottle it would be a help."

"A bottle?" asked Jo.

"Well, you don't have to, but a drop of wine would be a help." The nurse was about to walk past her up the stairs.

"Where are you going?" Jo asked, alarmed.

"I've just told you, to ask the others, the ones in the other flats, if they'd like to come."

"They're not there, they're not at home, they're gone away."

"Oh, well, all for the best, I suppose." The girl shrugged. "I've got my meat and my manners now, can't say they weren't asked."

"Listen," Jo said urgently, "what's your name?"

"Phyllis," she said.

"Phyllis, listen to me, do the girls up here go away a lot?"

"What?"

"I mean, I'm new here, do they go home for the weekends or anything?"

"Search me. I hardly know them at all. I think the punk one's a bit odd, a half-wit, between ourselves."

"But do they go away at weekends, or what? Please, it's important."

"Honestly, I'd never notice, I'm on nights a lot of the time, I don't know where I am or whether people are coming or going. Sorry."

"Would the others know, in your flat?"

"I don't think so, why? Is anything wrong?"

"No, I expect not. It's just, well, I wasn't expecting them to go off and they, sort of, have. I was just wondering whether . . . you know, if everything's all right."

"Why wouldn't it be?"

"It's just that they were with some rather, well, unreliable people on Thursday, and—"

"They're lucky they were only with unreliable people on Thursday, I'm with unreliable people all the time! Maureen was meant to have hired the glasses and she didn't, so we had to buy paper cups, which cost a fortune."

Jo started to go back upstairs.

"See you later then. What's your name?"

"Jo O'Brien."

"Okay, come on down when you hear the sounds."

"Thank you."

At twelve o'clock she was wider awake than she had ever been in the middle of the day; she thought she might as well go down as stay where she was. The noise was almost in the room with her. There was no question of sleep. She put on her black dress and her big earrings, then she took them off. Suppose her flatmates were in danger or dead? What was she doing dressing up and going to a party? It somehow wasn't so bad going to a party without dressing up. She put on her gray skirt and her dark gray sweater, and went downstairs.

She arrived at the same time as four others who had been beating on the hall door. Jo opened it and let them in.

"Which are you?" said one of the men.

"I'm from upstairs, really," Jo said.

"Right," said the man, "let's you and I go back upstairs. See you later," he laughed to the others.

"No, no, you can't do that, stop it," Jo shouted.

"It was a joke, silly," he said.

"She thought you meant it!" The others fell about laughing. Then the door of the downstairs flat opened and a blast of heat and noise came out. There were about forty people crammed into the rooms. Jo took one look and was about to scamper upstairs again, but it was too late and the door had banged behind her. Someone handed her a glass of warm wine. She saw Phyllis in the middle of it all, her blond hair tied in a topknot and wearing a very dazzling dress with bootlace straps. Jo felt foolish and shabby: she was jammed into a group of bright-faced, laughing people and she felt as gray as her jumper and skirt.

"Are you a nurse too?" a boy asked her.

"No, I work in the post office."

"Well, can you do anything about the telephones? Do you know there isn't a telephone between here and—"

"I don't give a damn about telephones," she said, and pushed away from him. Nessa and Pauline were dead, battered by drunks, and here she was talking about telephones to some fool.

"I was only making conversation—piss off," he shouted at her, hurt.

Nobody heard him in the din.

"Which are your flatmates?" Jo asked Phyllis.

"The one in the kitchen, Maureen, and the one dancing with the man in the aran sweater, that's Mary."

"Thanks," said Jo. She went into the kitchen.

"Maureen," she said. The girl at the cooker looked up with an agonized face. "I wanted to ask you—"

"Burned to a crisp, both of them. Both of them burned to a bloody crisp."

"What?" said Jo.

"Two trays of sausages. 'Just put them in the oven, stop fussing,' Mary says. I put them in the oven. And now look, burned black. Jesus, do you know how much sausages are a pound, and there were five pounds altogether. I told her we should have fried them. Stink the place out, frying them, she said. Well, what will this do, I ask you?"

"Do you know the girls upstairs?" Jo persisted.

"No, but Phyllis said she asked them, they're not making trouble, are they? That's all we need."

"No, I'm one of them, that's not the problem."

"Thank God. What will I do with this?"

"Throw it out dish and all, I'd say, you'll never clean it."

"Yes, you're right. God, what a fiasco. What a mess."

"Listen, do you know the girls, the other ones, Nessa and Pauline?"

"Just to see. Why?"

"Do you know where they are?"

"What? Of course I don't. If they're here they're in the other room, I suppose, waiting to be fed, thinking there's some hot food. I'll *kill* Mary, I'll literally *kill* her, you know."

"Do they normally go away for the weekend?"

"God, love, I don't know whether they go up to the moon and back for the weekend. How would I know? There's one of them with a head like a lighthouse and another who goes around with that dynatape thing putting names on anything that stands still . . . . bells and doors and things. I think they're all right. We never have many dealings with them. That's the best way in a house of flats, I always say."

Jo left it there. It seemed unlikely that Mary would know any more, and she decided to leave her happily with the man in the aran sweater until she was given the bad news about the sausages.

A hand caught her and suddenly she was dancing herself. The man was tall and had a nice smile.

"Where are you from, Limerick?"

"Not far out," she said, laughing. Then dread seized her again. What was she doing dancing with this stranger and chatting him up like she might have done at a dance at home? "I'm sorry," she said to him, "I'm sorry, I have to go. I've got something awful on my mind, I can't stay."

At that moment the window in the kitchen was broken by a big stone, and glass shattered everywhere. There were screams from the garden and shouts.

"I'm getting the guards, this looks like a bad fight," said the tall boy, and like a flash he was out in the hall. Jo heard him speaking on the phone. In the kitchen people were shouting to each other to move carefully. A huge lump of glass lay precariously on top of a cupboard: it could fall any moment.

"Is anybody hurt? Stop screaming, is anybody cut?" Jo recognized Phyllis and felt a small amount of relief flood back into her. At least they were nurses; maybe a lot of them were. They'd be able to cope better than ordinary people. People had run out the front door and an almighty row was going on in the garden. Two men with cut heads were shouting that they only threw the stone in self-defense, people had started firing things at them from the window first; one of them was bleeding over his eye. They only picked up the stone to stop the barrage coming at them.

The guards were there very quickly, four of them. Suddenly everything was different; what had looked like a party began to look like something shameful. The room that had been full of smoke and drink and music and people dancing and people talking about nothing was now a room full of broken glass and upturned chairs and people shouting trying to explain what had happened, and people trying to comfort others, or get their coats and leave. Neighbors had come to protest and to stare: it was all different.

It didn't take long to work it out: the two men in the garden were crashers. They had tried to come in the front door and been refused admittance; they had then gone around to see if there was a back entrance. That was when the first one had been attacked with a hot weapon which had both burned and cut his face. Investigating the attack, the other one had been wounded in exactly the same way. (The weapons were, of course, Mary's burnt sausages.) They thought that everybody in the party was firing things at them so they threw one stone before leaving.

Notebooks were being put away. Phyllis said that one of the men needed a stitch, and she would go to the hospital with him, taking Mary as well, since Mary's arm had been cut by flying glass. The party was over. The guards said that too much noise was being made for a built-up area and, since two of the hostesses were disappearing to the hospital, there didn't seem to be any point in guests staying on in a flat which was now full of icy winds because of the window. Some of the men helped to pick the last bit of broken glass out, and a sheet of tin was found in the boot of somebody's car. It was a sorry end. The guards were leaving; one of them saw Jo sitting on the stairs.

"Are you all right for a lift home?" he asked.

Jo shook her head. "I don't need one. I live upstairs."

"You look a bit shook, are you all right?"

She nodded wordlessly.

"What a night, not much of a Saturday night in Dublin for a little country girl, is it?"

He was trying to cheer her up. It didn't work.

"Well, I'll be off, you go off, too, and get some sleep, you need it by the look of you."

She nodded again.

"You are all right, you're not in shock or anything? It's all over, it was only a broken window," he said soothingly. "There'll be worse than that before the night's over."

"Oh, God," she said.

"Hey, Sean," he called, "this one's going to faint, I think, give me a hand."

She came to as they were getting her in the door of the flat. She had had the key in her hand and it had fallen when she fell.

"Which is her room?" Sean said.

"How would I know?" said the one who was carrying her. "Here's the kitchen, get her in there."

She saw the names on the table.

"Don't touch those, they're evidence," she said. "Please don't touch them."

They decided they'd better all have a cup of tea.

"It's television, that's what it is," Mickey said.

"It's that and eating too much rich food late at night," said Sean.

"But how can you be sure they're all right?" Jo wasn't convinced.

"Because we're normal human beings," said Sean.

Jo flushed. "So am I. I'm normal, too, that's why I'm worried. I'm just concerned and worried about them. Stop making horrible jokes about my eating rich food and having nightmares. I haven't eaten anything, I'm so worried, and that is exactly why I didn't come to the Garda station, because I knew that's the kind of reception I'd get."

She burst into tears and put her head down on the table.

"Mind the evidence," Sean giggled.

Mickey frowned at him. "Leave her alone, she *is* worried. Listen here, those two will be back tomorrow night right as rain. Nobody abducts people like that, honestly. Nobody says please wash up all the mugs and tidy up your rooms and come on up the Dublin mountains to be abducted, now do they?" He smiled at her encouragingly.

"I suppose they wouldn't."

"And you are kind to be concerned, and we'll say no more about it tonight now because you're exhausted. Go to sleep and have a lie-in tomorrow. Those two rossies will be home tomorrow night and you'll think you were mad, crying your heart out over them. Do you hear me?"

"But I'm so stupid, I'm so hopeless. I can't cope with Dublin, I really can't. I thought I'd have a great time when I got a flat, but it's all so different, and so lonely, so terribly lonely, and when it isn't lonely it's like a nightmare—"

"Now, stop that," Mickey said firmly. "Stop it at once. You never talk about anyone but yourself, I this, I that. You're constantly wondering what people are thinking about you. They're not thinking about you at all."

"But I—"

"There you go again. I, I, I. You think that there's some kind of gallery of people watching you, sitting there as if they were at the pictures, watching you leave the house each day, all your movements, saying, is she having a good time, is she being a success in Dublin? Nobody gives one damn. Why don't you start thinking about other people?"

"But I *am* thinking about other people, I'm thinking about Nessa and Pauline—"

"Oh, no, you're not, you're only thinking about what *you* did to them, whether *you're* responsible for their kidnapping and disappearance, or whether they'll think *you're* silly."

Jo looked at him.

"So, lecture over. Go to sleep." He stood up. So did Sean.

"You're probably right," she said.

"He's always right, known for it," said Sean.

"Thank you very much indeed, it is a bit lonely at first, you get self-centered."

"I know, I felt a bit the same last year."

"Sligo?"

"Galway."

"Thank you very much again."

"Good-bye, Jo."

"Good-bye, Guard, thank you."

"Mickey," he said.

"Mickey," she said.

"And Sean," Sean said.

"And Sean," Jo said.

"And maybe some night you might come out with me," said Mickey.

"Or me, indeed?" said Sean.

"I saw her first, didn't I?" said Mickey.

"You did," said Jo. "Indeed you did."

"I'll wait a bit until the two lassies are back and installed, but I've a night off on Monday."

"You're sure they'll come back?"

"Maybe if I called for you about eight on Monday? How's that?"

"That's grand," said Jo. "That's grand altogether."

Decision in Belfield

She had been reading the Problem Pages for years. One or two of them always said things about having done grievous wrong in the eyes of God and now the only thing to do was to Make Restitution. Most of them said that your parents would be very understanding—you must go straightaway and tell them. You will be surprised, the Problem Pages said, at how much tolerance and understanding there will be, and how much support there is to be found at home.

Not in Pat's home. There would be no support there, no understanding. Pat's mother wasn't going to smile like people did in movies and say maybe it was all for the best and it would be nice to have another baby around the place, that she had missed the patter of tiny bootees. And Pat's father wasn't going to put his arm around her shoulder and take her for a long, supportive walk on Dun Laoghaire pier. Pat knew all this very well, even though the Problem Pages told her she was wrong. But she knew it from personal experience. She knew that Mum and Dad would not be a bundle of support and two big rocks of strength. Because they hadn't been any of that five years ago when her elder sister Cathy had been pregnant. There was no reason why their attitude should have changed as time went by.

Cathy had actually finished college when her little drama broke on the family. She had been twenty-two years old, earning her own living and in most ways living her own life. Cathy had believed the Problem Pages, she thought that Mum wouldn't go through the roof. Cathy had thought that there were ways you could talk to Mum and Dad like ordinary people. She had been wrong. Pat remembered as if it were yesterday the weekend of the announcement. It seemed to have gone on all weekend, Cathy saying she didn't want to marry Ian and Dad saying Ian must be brought around to the house this minute; Mum saying this was the result of trusting people to behave like adults and like responsible people; Cathy looking frightened and bewildered. She had said over and over that she thought people would be pleased.

Pat had been sixteen, and she had been shocked to the core. She had never heard words used like the words that were used that weekend. Dad had even apologized for some of the things he had called Cathy, and Mum had never stopped crying. Cathy had come and sat on her bed on the Sunday evening. "It's not the end of the world," she had said.

"Oh, but it is," Pat had said, almost afraid to look at Cathy in case she saw under her waist the whole dreadful shame that was going to cause such trouble.

"It's just that I can't see myself spending the rest of my life with Ian," Cathy had said. "We'd be ridiculous together, we wouldn't last a year. It's such a terrible way to start a marriage with anyone."

"But don't you love him?" Pat had asked. The only possible reason you could do the things that Cathy must have done with Ian to get herself to this stage must have been love.

"Oh, yes, in a way, I love him, but I'll love other people and so will he."

Pat had not understood, she had been no help. She had said useless things like maybe it wasn't really positive, the test, and maybe Ian might like to get married if Cathy explained it properly. Cathy had taken the whole thing very badly; she had refused to accept that Mum and Dad might have any right on their side. "They're so liberal, they *say* they're so liberal," she had scoffed. "They keep saying they're in favor of getting divorce introduced and they want contraceptives, and they want censorship abolished, but they refuse to face facts. They want me to marry a man, knowing it will ruin my life and ruin his life, and probably wreck the baby's life as well. What kind of liberal view is that?"

"I think they believe that it would be the best start for the . . . er . . . the child," Pat had said uncertainly.

"Great start . . . forcing two people who should love the child most into a marriage they're not prepared for in a country which doesn't see fit to set up any system to help when the marriage breaks down."

"But you can't have people going into marriages knowing they can get out of them." Pat was very familiar with the argument from fourth-year debating clubs at school.

"Well, you certainly can't go into a marriage, a doubtful marriage, knowing you can't get out of it," Cathy had said.

She had gone to London five days later. Everyone else had been told that she was doing this wonderful new postgraduate course. It was a special qualification in EEC law; it was obviously the absolutely necessary qualification of the future. Mum had said that with all the changes that were going to come about from Brussels and Strasbourg and everything, Cathy was doing the right thing. Pat had known that Cathy would not come back. She knew that the family had broken up, and broken much more permanently than when Ethna had gone to be a nun. Ethna hadn't really left at all, even though she was in Australia: Cathy was only an hour away but she had gone forever.

Ethna had never been told why Cathy had gone to England. At Christmas the long letter with the small, slanted writing had wanted to know all about the course that Cathy was doing and what her address was and what holidays she would get for the Christmas festivities. Nobody wrote and told Ethna that Cathy hadn't come home for Christmas. Perhaps Cathy had written, but it was certainly never mentioned in the weekly letters which came and went—every week a green Irish air letter on the hall table begun by Mum, where Dad and Pat added bits; and every week, but slightly out of synch, a blue air letter from Australia with details of Sister this who had done that and Sister that who had done this. And all of the time nothing from Cathy.

At about the time that Cathy's baby should be born Pat had asked Mum for the address. "I wanted to write and see if there was anything we could do."

"Oh, there's nothing any of *us* could do," Mum had said bitterly. "If there had been anything then we would have been glad to do it, but no, we knew nothing, your sister knew everything. So she knew best and went off on her own. No, I don't think there's anything *we* could do. I don't think it would be welcomed."

"But, Mum, it's your grandchild. Your own grandchild." Pat had been almost seventeen and full of outrage.

"Yes, and Ian's mother, Mrs. Kennedy, it's her first grandchild too. But are either of us being allowed the privilege of having a grandchild, and a baby we all want, and a christening, and a fuss, and the birthright of any child? No, no, a lot of claptrap about not wanting to settle down and not wanting to be tied down. I wonder does Miss Cathy ever ask herself where she would be if I had felt that way?" Mum had got very pink in the face about it.

"I'm sure she's very grateful to you, Mum."

"Oh, I'm sure she is, very sure. Yes, she must be. Fine life *she'd* have had if she had been given away to an adoption society the moment she saw the light of day, because I couldn't be tied down."

"But you were married already, Mum, and you did have Ethna."

"That's not the *point*," Mum had roared.

And suddenly Pat had realized what had been said.

"Is Cathy giving the baby away, she can't be giving the baby away, can she?"

"I'm not permitted to know what she's doing. We're not in her confidence, your father and I, but I *assume* that's what she's doing. If she can't be 'tied down' to a perfectly reasonable, nice boy like Ian Kennedy, then it's very unlikely that she can be tied down to an illegitimate baby which she would have to rear on her own."

Pat had gone to the firm of solicitors where Ian Kennedy worked with his father. He was a nice, red-haired boy, about the friendliest of all Cathy's boyfriends; it was a pity she hadn't married him.

"I came to talk to you about Cathy," she had said.

"Yeah, great, how is she?" he had asked.

"I think she's fine." Pat had been nonplussed.

"Good, give her my love when you write, will you?"

"I don't have her address, and Mum is being difficult. You know, not being able to lay her hands on it."

"Oh, I don't know where she is now," Ian had said.

"Doesn't she keep in touch?" Pat had been shocked again.

"No, she said she didn't want to. Said she wanted to be free."

"But . . . ?"

"But what?"

"Doesn't she keep you informed . . . let you know . . . ?"

"Know what?"

Pat had paused. Now, it had been definitely said, definitely, about six months ago, that Ian had been told of her decision to go to England on account of the pregnancy. Yes, Ian had even been in the house. He had said to Dad that he was very happy indeed to acknowledge that he was responsible for the child, and to marry Cathy if she would have him. Pat knew that he had said he wanted to support the child, and to see it when it was born; he couldn't have forgotten about all that, could he?

"I'm sorry for being silly," Pat had said. "I'm the baby of the family and nobody tells me anything."

"Yes?" Ian had smiled kindly.

"But I thought she'd be having the, er, baby, now and I wanted to know how she was. . . . That's why I'm here."

"But didn't she tell you? She must have told you?" Ian's face was lined with concern.

"What? Told me what?"

"It was a false alarm—she wasn't pregnant at all."

"I don't believe you."

"Of course! Hey, you must know this. She wrote and told everyone just after she went to London."

"It's not true—"

"Of course it's true. She wrote and told us all. It was a very early test she had here, not a proper one."

"So why didn't she come back?"

"What?"

"If it was a false alarm why didn't she come back to her job and home and to you and everything?"

"Oh, Pat, you *know* all this . . . she was a bit peeved with your mum and dad. She thought there'd be more solidarity, I think. And she was very pissed off with me."

"Why was she pissed off with you? You said you'd marry her."

"But that's not what she wanted, she wanted . . . oh, I don't know . . . anyway, it wasn't necessary."

"So why isn't she back?"

"As I said, we all let her down. She was annoyed. She wrote, when she told me about the false alarm bit, and said she didn't feel like coming back. She must have written to your family too. Of course she did."

"She didn't," Pat had said definitely.

"But whyever not? Why didn't she put them out of their agony?"

"*Their* agony?"

"You know what I mean. It's an expression."

"She never wrote."

"Oh, Pat, nonsense, of course she did. Maybe they didn't tell you. You said yourself they kept things from you."

"They don't know it was a false alarm, I know that much."

She had said good-bye to Ian, and had promised she wouldn't make a lot of trouble for everyone, she'd be a good little girl.

"You're a real *enfant terrible*, you know. You're much too grown-up and pretty to be playing that Saint Trinian's kind of thing."

She had put out her tongue at him, and they had both laughed.

Mum had said she didn't want to discuss Cathy. Cathy had found nothing to discuss with her, why should she spend time talking about Cathy?

"But Ian says he heard from her as soon as she went. It was all a false alarm, she never had a baby, she was never pregnant at all. Aren't you pleased now, isn't that good news, Mum?" Pat had pleaded with her.

"That's as may be," Mum had said.

Just as she was dropping off to sleep that night, Pat had thought of something that made her sit up again, wide awake.

Now she knew why Mum hadn't been pleased. Cathy must have had an abortion. That's why there was no baby, that's why Cathy had not come back. But why hadn't she told Ian? Or Mum? And mainly why hadn't she come back?

"Do you think the other nuns read Ethna's letters?" Pat had asked a few days later when the green aerogram was being sealed up and sent off.

"Very unlikely," Dad had said.

"It's not the dark ages. They don't censor their correspondence," Mum had said.

"Anyway, she can be fairly critical of some of the other nuns; she gives that Sister Kevin a hard time," Dad had said. "I don't expect she'd do that if they read her outgoing letters anyway."

Pat thought that it was nice that Dad read Ethna's letters so carefully that he knew which Sister was which.

Pat had written to Ethna; first of all a probing letter. "I'm getting older and a bit, though not much, wiser. One of the things that upsets me is the cloak of silence that hangs over Cathy, and where she is in England and what she's doing and what the situation is. Could you tell me what the situation is as far as you know it and then I'll take it from there . . ."

She had a letter from Ethna, not on an aerogram but in an envelope. On the outside of the envelope it said "The Stamps You Wanted." That satisfied any curiosity Mum and Dad might have had. Inside, it was very short.

"I really think you are making a mystery about nothing. Poor Cathy has been punished quite enough, she thought that she was indeed going to have a child. And since she was not at all willing or ready to marry the father, then it is merciful that this was not so. She is happy in London, where she is doing social work. She has hardened her heart to Mother and Father, which is a great pity, but in time I am sure she will feel ready to open up doors of friendship again. She doesn't write to me, apart from that one letter which told me all these things; since nobody has ever mentioned anything to me about it in letters from home, I have never mentioned anything either. I pray for her, and I pray for all of you. Life is so short, it seems sad that any of it should be spent in feeling a grievance and a hurt when a hand held out would brush all the unhappiness away."

Great help, Pat had thought at the time; punished enough, hardened her heart, brush all the unhappiness away; nun's phrases, and not a word of blame about Mum and Dad, who were always writing letters to the paper protesting about letting South African rugby teams into the country. They were always talking about itinerants, and they had raised money for refugees. Why were they so hardhearted about Cathy?

Pat had decided that she was not going to allow Cathy to disappear without trace as if some terrible crime or shame had settled on the family and people hoped that by ignoring it things would return to normal. She had tackled them at supper the night she had got Ethna's letter.

"This family is becoming a bit like nine green bottles," she had said.

"What on earth do you mean?" Dad had smiled.

"First Ethna goes off to the other side of the world, and then we are four. Then six months ago Cathy disappears without trace and now we are three. Will I go off somewhere too?"

Dad had kept smiling, but he looked puzzled. He stood up to fetch the coffee percolator. He looked tired and a bit beaten. Not the cheerful doctor, always in a smart suit, always optimistic, always seeing the best for patients and neighbors alike. He wore his cardigan at home, and Mum wore an old jumper that was torn under the arms. They looked shabby and a bit disheveled as they sat in the big dining room with its good furniture and its expensive cut-glass decanters. Pat felt that somehow they didn't make any effort when it was only just her. She was sure they had been far more elegant and lively when Ethna was at home and when Cathy was there.

"Are you just waiting for me to go off and that will be the hat trick?"

"What is this, Pat, what silly game are you playing?" Mum had not been very amused.

"No, I mean it, Mum. It's not much of a family, is it?"

"Don't speak to your mother like that." Dad had been surprised and hurt. He had thought that talking about green bottles was going to be a joke; now it had turned into a row.

"It's not normal. People marry and have children, they don't have them just to export them off as fast as possible."

Mum had been very annoyed indeed. "Ethna was twenty-one when she left. She had wanted to join this order for two years. Do you think we wanted Ethna to go to that outlandish place? Or to be a nun at all? Don't be so ridiculous, and have some thought for other people before you start your hurtful accusations."

"No, I know that's Ethna, but then Cathy's gone. This house used to be full of people, now it's just us. And soon I suppose you'll want me to go. Would you prefer if I tried to get into UCC or Galway or maybe England rather than Belfield, then you wouldn't have to have me around the place and you could be all on your own?" She stood up, tears in her eyes.

"Apologize this minute to your mother, this minute, do you hear me!"

"Why to Mum? I'm saying it to both of you."

She was about to leave the room when Mum had said wearily, "Come back, Pat. Come back and I'll talk to you about Cathy."

"You owe her no explanation, Peggy, none, not after the way she's spoken to you." Dad's face had been red with disappointment.

"Sit down, Pat. Please." Grudgingly and shrugging, Pat had sat down.

"I'm not going to fight with you. I'm going to agree with you. It's not much of a family, it certainly isn't. When your father and I got married this is not what we had in mind at all."

"Now, Peg; now, Peg," Dad had said warningly.

"No, the girl is right to question what's happened. We question it ourselves, for God's sake. Not at all what we had in mind. I suppose we had in mind the practice getting bigger and going well. It has. That's all fine, that side of it. And we had in mind our friends and all the people we like being around, and that's gone well. And our health has been fine. But mainly what we had in mind was the three of you. That's what people do have in mind actually, Pat, that's what they have in mind most of the day and night when they have children. From the time that Ethna was here we've had you three in mind more than anything else."

Pat had given a very slight shrug. It was a disclaimer. It was meant to say, you don't have to tell me all this. I know you tried. As a shrug it worked. Mum had known what she meant.

"I know you think I'm just saying this to be nice to you, or maybe perhaps that we started out with good intentions and lost them on the way. But it wasn't like that. I think some of my best times, and yours, Hugh, were when Ethna was about six or seven, and Cathy was five, and you, Pat, were a baby. Three little girls totally dependent on us, all lighting up with enthusiasm—"

"Sure, Mum. Yes. Sure."

"No, give me a very short minute for the sentimental sugary bit, because it didn't last long. Then, you were all so bright. This was another joy, some of our friends had problems. Well, we didn't call them problems but so-and-so's child couldn't read until he was seven, or someone couldn't settle at school, or another wouldn't manage to get on with the teachers, or failed the third Honors in her leaving. Not you three, from Ethna on we knew, top of the class, exams no real problem. Do you remember Ethna's conferring?"

"Yes . . . I got the day off school."

"And she looked so bright . . . that's a funny word, but she did, you know, clear eyes and alert face, compared to a lot of the others. I thought, ours is very bright, there's so much before her when she gets this ridiculous nunnish thing out of her system—"

"But I thought you approved?"

"We had to approve in the end." Dad had spoken for the first time. "Of course we didn't approve. Use your head, Pat, suppose you had brought up a lovely girl like Ethna, as bright as a button as Mum says, who has just got a first class honors degree in history and who wants to go with a crowd of half-educated women to a school in the outback of somewhere because she read a book about the damn place and she met a recruiting team!"

"But you never said. I don't remember—"

"You don't remember. How old were you—twelve, thirteen? What discussions could we have had with you about it that would have helped anything except add to the argument?"

Mum had interrupted. "We didn't even discuss it with Cathy because we didn't want gangs forming and pressure being put on Ethna. We just talked to her."

"And what did you want her to do?" Pat had wanted to know.

"I'd have liked her to do an M.A. and then a doctorate. She was very, very good. I spoke to some of the people in there, they said she had the makings of a scholar, and I'd have liked her to have had a good, lively life here, instead of putting up with Sister Kevin's tantrums in a jungle." Dad had sounded very defeated when he said that, as if remembering the whole battle and how it was lost.

"Yes, that's what I'd have liked too. I'd have liked her to go on living here, it was so near and handy, and got a small car and had friends and gone off to the West for weekends. And then married someone in her own field, some professor, and got a house nearby and I could have seen the whole thing over again with her children, growing up and learning to walk . . ."

"It's a fairly normal, reasonable wish, isn't it?" Dad had asked defensively. "Rather than see a whole life, a whole education, and talent, thrown away."

"She's happy though, she says she is," Mum had said.

"I suppose her letters to us are about as near the truth as ours are to her," Dad had said. And there was a silence as they thought about the implications of that.

"So Cathy . . . ?" Pat had spoken softly, hoping that the mood hadn't been broken, that she could still get her mother to talk.

"Cathy," Mum had said.

"Cathy was no trouble either. Everyone else told us of all their sleepless nights over their terrible teenage children. We never had any." Dad smiled at Pat as if he was thanking her. She felt a twinge of guilt.

"And Cathy did have her friends around much more than Ethna, and they used to laugh, and they were full of life. Do you remember the summer they did the whole garden, Hugh?"

Dad had laughed. "All I had to do was provide one of those big cans of beer at the end of the day. They dug and they weeded and they cut hedges and grass."

"It never looked back since," Mum had said. "It used to be a wilderness and they tamed it."

"All for a few cans of beer," Dad had said. They stopped talking for a moment. Pat said nothing.

"So Cathy was going to be the one who might be with us, when Ethna went. It wasn't a transfer of love. I suppose it was changing the plans or hopes. And she was so enthusiastic, about everything."

"We felt we were qualifying with her, she was so entertaining about it all— the lectures, the course, the solicitors' exams down in the Four Courts, the apprenticeship—it was all so alive," Dad had said.

"And she seemed to get on so well with Ian. I kept thinking, she's only twenty-two, she's far too young to settle down, but then of course I told myself I was only twenty-two when I married. Then on the other hand, I didn't have a career to decide about. Then I went back to the first hand and said, since Ian and Cathy were both solicitors and Ian's father had a firm, well then, surely if they did have a couple of children and she wanted to work part-time it couldn't be too hard to arrange."

Dad had interrupted. "This is what your mother meant about you children always being in our minds. We had Cathy married to Ian in our minds long before they even kissed each other."

"But why couldn't you accept Cathy's decision like you did for Ethna? You didn't want Ethna to go off and be a nun but when she did you sort of acknowledged it."

"Yes," Mum had said. "Yes, it made her so happy and it was her life. Much as I wanted to I couldn't control it anymore . . . she had to do what she wanted."

"So why couldn't Cathy do what she wanted?"

"That was different."

"But why, Mum, why? It's not as if you and Dad were prudes or anything, it's not as if your friends would cut you off, or as if you'd be ashamed to lift your heads. Why can't Cathy bring her baby home?"

"It's different," Dad had said.

"I can't think why, I really can't. Nobody minds. Ian doesn't mind. I talked to him. He's very casual about Cathy—'send her my love' he said. Ethna won't mind. I wrote to her about it, but, but—"

"You wrote to Ethna?" Mum had said, surprised.

"Yes, to try to clear things up."

"And did it?"

"No, not at all."

"What did you want cleared up?" Dad had asked.

"Whether Cathy is having a baby or is not. Something very basic and simple like that, which most normal families would know."

Dad had looked at Mum, and she had said, "Tell her."

"The answer is . . . that we don't know."

"You don't *know*?"

"No. That's the truth." Mum had continued, "We were very shocked by Cathy's attitude. She was very harshly critical of us, and the way we lived, and thought that our attitudes were hypocritical, you know, to preach some kind of broad-mindedness and then not to follow it.

"But we didn't see it like that. You see, it was nothing to do with acceptance or reputations, we thought Cathy was being silly and making extravagant gestures, turning herself into a Protest just for the sake of it. 'Look at me, I'm too modern to do like anyone else, give my child a name and a home and a background, no, I'm far too sophisticated for that!' We didn't like it, Pat, it was too studenty.

"There's no need to go over all that was said, you probably heard most of it, but to cut a long story short we have only heard from Cathy once since she went to London. I always imply—well, let's be honest, I always tell people lies and say that we've heard from her, but she wrote only once two weeks after she left."

"Did she say . . . ?"

"She said that it had been a false alarm, that her dates had been wrong, that she was only a shorter time overdue than she thought and that everything was fine."

There was a silence.

"And did you believe her, Mum?"

"No."

"Did you, Dad?"

"No. I didn't."

"It was too far for there to be a mistake?"

"Well, she said she had left a specimen in Holles Street and they had said it was positive. They don't make mistakes."

"But she says they did."

"No, she's forgotten she told us that bit, I think."

"Oh."

"So we know no more than you do," Mum had said, spreading out her hands helplessly.

"But why do you say everything's all right . . . ?"

"Because it will be one way or another, sometime, and we don't want Cathy to have to walk back into a whole lot of complications. Keep it simple, is our motto."

"So what do you believe if you don't believe what Cathy said?"

"Well, what do you think?"

"No, what do you think?"

"Pat, either she had a termination or she is in fact having the child, and as you so rightly pointed out to me, if she is having the baby it's due this month."

"And we don't know?"

"We don't know."

"We don't even know where she is?"

"No."

Then Mum had started to cry, and she cried with her arms down on the table and her head on top of them. Right into the dishes and the food. And Dad had stood up and come over and patted her awkwardly on one side and Pat had patted her awkwardly on the other.

"It's all right, Peg," Dad had said, over and over.

"It's all right, Mum," Pat had said, over and over.

It had been a hard thing to sit your Leaving Certificate not knowing where your sister was, whether she was alive or dead, and not knowing if you were an aunt or not. But Pat had gone on and done it; she had got all her Honors and plenty of points. Peggy and Hugh's third daughter was on her way to University College, Dublin, registering as a student in Belfield.

Cathy wrote home that year just before Christmas. She said she had seen enough of other people's miseries in her caseload in London to make her realize that most of life's troubles were caused by families. She would like to say very sincerely that she had been entirely to blame for any little fracas they had had. She asked forgiveness and if they liked she would love to come home for Christmas, but since she had been so difficult and stayed out of touch for so long, over a year, she could well understand if they said no. She gave her address for them to reply. It was in Hackney. Mum and Dad had sent a telegram five minutes after the letter arrived. The telegram had read, "Welcome home, darling Cathy, to the silliest parents and the happiest Christmas ever."

Cathy had also written to Pat.

"You may well wonder what the Prodigal thinks she's up to, and I don't want to put your nose out of joint. I'll tell you everything you want to know, if you want to know anything, when I see you, and if you have no time for me I'll understand that too. It was utterly selfish of me to go away and leave you as a teenager, in your last year at school, to cope with all the trauma and drama. But when there's a crisis people only think of themselves, or I did anyway. I hope the reunion won't be a damp squib. I haven't kept in touch with most of my friends, so can I ask you to fill the house a bit with people so that we don't become too hothouse and raise our family expectations too high? I'll stop asking and taking soon and start giving, I promise."

Pat had thought this was very sensible. She asked her college friends in on the evening that Cathy came back. Mum had gone to the airport to meet her and by the time Pat had come home conversation was quite normal. In fact, so normal it was almost frightening. It was as if Cathy had never gone away, as if no mystery hung over the events of the past year. Cathy had said that Pat looked smashing, and that students must be dressing better than in her day, and there wasn't time for much more conversation because they had to get the mulled wine ready, which involved a lot of conversation about what you did to mull it, and how to ensure you didn't boil the alcohol out of it. Pat had been startled to see that they were all laughing quite naturally in the kitchen when Dad had said he should test each batch they made, just in case the flavoring needed adjusting. "You haven't changed, Dad," Cathy had laughed, and nobody made any flicker of an eyelid as the moment passed and Cathy's long absence had now sunk into the collective memory. It could be mentioned without being questioned.

It had been like that all that Christmas, and nothing seemed more natural at the end of the holiday than for Cathy to say that she would be coming back for good as soon as she had found a replacement for herself. She was going to work in Ian's office; they had a vacancy in a couple of months. Pat had been puzzled when she saw Cathy and Ian Kennedy strolling around the wintry wilderness of garden, plucking at bushes and pointing out what should be done with hard, frozen-looking flower beds. What was going on inside that red head of Ian Kennedy's? Did he not wonder whether Cathy had given birth to his child in London all by herself in a hospital with no friends to come and visit her? Did he not worry about his child, their child, being given to an adoption society and never knowing what it should have known?

Did Ian Kennedy wonder whether Cathy had gone long, long ago to a doctor in England in order to organize a termination of pregnancy and then overnight in one of those nursing homes everyone knew about, where simple minor surgery under anesthetic would ensure that Cathy and Ian's child didn't ever come into being? Surely he wasn't so foolish as to think that a girl could be pregnant, disappear for over a year, and have some vague belief that the pregnancy was all a false alarm.

People were really behaving more and more peculiarly, Pat decided. The older they got the vaguer they became. Ethna's letters now had nice bland welcoming bits about Cathy in them. Had she forgotten all that earlier stuff about punishment, and hardening her heart, and praying for her? Once people got any way settled they seemed to lose touch with reality and built themselves a comfortable little world, like a Wendy House, entirely of their own creation.

She had told this to Rory a few times, and he had tried to understand it. But Rory thought that her whole life was a fraud, and that anyone who owned any kind of private house was already out of touch with society. Rory was in her economics tutorial, by far the most brilliant student of his year, a great thorn in a lot of university flesh. Rory had economic arguments for revolution which could not be faulted. Rory agreed with Pat that the whole Cathy business was very unreal. Rory said he loved Pat, and Pat was very sure that she loved Rory.

"It's a mistake to get too involved with anyone your first year in college," Cathy had said. "It ties you down, you should have the freedom to roam around and see who you like and who you don't. You should get to know a lot of people, not just sticking together two by two as if you were the animals going into the ark." Pat didn't like this remark. It was too reminiscent of Cathy saying she couldn't be tied down to marry Ian. It also implied a criticism of Rory. And that was not allowed.

There was nothing that Mum and Dad could find fault with in Rory; they wanted to, but they couldn't actually put a finger on anything. He certainly didn't distract her from her work; in fact he insisted that she work harder than she was prepared to. He said her essays weren't sufficiently researched; he lent her books, he came with her to the library and sat opposite her. It was easier to do the damn stuff than to find excuses. He didn't keep her out at all-night parties. He had explained to Mum and Dad that he didn't drink much so there wouldn't be any danger of drunken driving late at night in his little beat-up car. When they went away to conferences or student festivals in Cork or Galway, Rory always managed to drop the one phrase which would reassure Mum and Dad about the set-up. "I'll leave Pat at the girls' house first and then she can settle in and I'll go off and find where they're putting the lads up." Some trivial little remark which would prevent Mum and Dad from wondering what exactly the score was.

The score was exactly as Rory described it for a long time.

"I suppose you think it's silly not to," Pat had said.

"Silly, no. Wasteful, yes," Rory had said. "It's up to you entirely what you would like to do. I don't ever believe in putting on the pressure. Too much of what's wrong is wrong because people felt forced to do things for approval. But I think you're wrong. It would give us both so much pleasure and it would hurt exactly nobody. We aren't betraying anyone, we can be sure that we aren't irresponsibly conceiving a child we don't want. So wasteful is all I think I'd say it was."

She adored Rory, his intensity and his boyish enthusiasms. She went to the family planning clinic. She knew the doctor who was on duty that day. It was a friend of her father's. "Glad to see you, that's a good sensible girl," the friend of Dad's had said. No explanations asked for, no curiosity, no condemnation. It was all so simple. Why hadn't Cathy done this? They had clinics, even in her time.

Cathy was still a mystery. There she was, living at home so calmly. If anyone ever asked about the Common Market legal course she was meant to have done, she would shake her head and say that she hadn't done it after all, she had worked for the council in East London. Mum had been right in her way to have kept things simple, to have rocked no boats. Cathy came back and stepped in more or less where she had got out. It was just that time, all those months that remained as inexplicable. What had she been doing, what had she been thinking? She was so placid now, sometimes going out to the theater with Ian, sometimes with other people. Holidaying with two girls in the Greek islands, sitting with Mum and Dad sometimes in the evenings looking at television.

Pat had insisted on Rory discussing it. "Is it natural for them not to mention it? Is it normal? I mean, there she is at home, and nobody ever once refers to the fact that she left home pregnant and stayed away from home for fourteen months and came back and everything is as you were."

"Um." Rory was reading.

"But why, why do they say nothing? It's like not noticing someone is naked or not referring to someone being in a car crash or in jail. It's not real."

"Um. I know," he said.

"But they don't seem to want to know, it's only me, it's only me that wants to know."

"Well, why don't you ask her then?" Rory said.

* * *

"Cathy, did you have any problems with the Pill, you know, have you had to change brands or anything?"

Cathy looked up from the papers she was studying. She was sitting at the big desk in her bedroom, which she had converted into a kind of study.

"No, I was never on the Pill, so it didn't occur."

"Never on the Pill, at all?"

"No."

"How amazing."

"Pat, you are twenty, going on twenty-one. You aren't actually a wise old sociologist commenting on the funny things society does." Cathy laughed good-naturedly as she spoke.

"Yes, but . . . not ever?"

"Not ever. If I *had* been, that little incident which you may remember would never have happened."

"Yes, well, after the little incident . . . ?"

Pat felt she was treading on a minefield. She had to remain lighthearted and casual.

"Oh, after the little incident, I didn't—how shall I put it—well, I didn't actually need the services of a contraceptive."

"Not ever?"

"No, not ever." Cathy smiled, relaxed and calm as if they had been talking about the replanting of the herbaceous border.

"Oh."

"So I'm not much help. But you could go to the family planning clinic, tell them if it doesn't suit you. They'll change it."

"Yes, good idea. Cathy?"

"Yes?"

"Remember that time . . . the little incident. . . . What happened?"

"How do you mean, what happened?"

"I mean, did you go through with it? Did you have the baby?"

"Did I what?"

"Did you have the baby? In London?"

"Hey, what is this? A joke?"

"No, seriously. I wish you'd tell me. I hate us all pretending, it's so artificial."

"Tell you what?"

"When you went off to London, did you actually have the baby?"

"No, of course I didn't, are you feeling all right? What an extraordinary question to ask. Have a baby? Where is it, then, if I had it, was I meant to have left it in a telephone box?"

"Well, what did you do? Did you have an abortion?"

"Seriously, is this some kind of game? Of course I didn't. What on earth are you saying?"

"But you *were* pregnant."

"No, I thought I was. I wasn't."

"You were, Dad knows, he said so when you were gone."

"Oh no, he can't have, I wrote telling them it was a false alarm."

"He didn't believe you."

"Listen, don't start stirring up a lot of trouble over nothing. It was nothing. Why all this interrogation?"

"Is that what put you off the whole thing, fellows and making love?" Pat asked. "They say people can get very depressed."

"I *didn't* have an abortion, and I wasn't very heavily into fellows and making love, and I haven't gone off fellows."

"That's all you'll say."

"Jesus Lord, what is this, Pat, one of Rory's revolutionary tribunals? You've asked me about ten questions. I've answered all of them honestly—which is rather good of me since *none* of them are any of your business."

"I'm sorry."

"No, you're not, you want some awful group where everyone sits and tells the most god-awful, self-centered, boring details of what they did and what they thought and what they felt and what they did then, and what they thought then and what they felt then. . . . Honestly, I can't stand that kind of thing. Even Woody Allen laughs at it, for heaven's sake. It's not going to solve the world's problems."

"What is?"

"I don't know, but a lot of people's are solved by playing down dramas rather than creating them."

"And is that what you're doing?"

"I'm refusing to invent them, refusing to make myself into a tragedy queen."

"I'm sorry I spoke."

"I'm not, but I'm glad you've stopped." Cathy grinned.

Pat gave a watery grin back.

"So you see, she's *got* to be lying. Somewhere along the line she told a lie." Pat frowned as she ticked the items off on her fingers.

"There are times you can be very boring, Pat," said Rory.

She was hurt and upset. "You're often analyzing what people say and why society forces us to tell lies and role-play. Why is it boring when I do it?"

"Because it's repetitive and it's slapdash."

"How do you mean?"

"Well, you haven't even included all the possibilities, have you?"

"I *have*. Either she was not pregnant, or she was and she had either a baby or an abortion."

"She could have had a miscarriage, you clown."

All that had been a year ago. Pat remembered the conversation word for word. They had been all at the turning points of things somehow. The very next day, the day following the interrogation, Cathy said that she and Ian were going to get married. The news coincided with a letter from Ethna. She was leaving the order. And everyone might remember that she had spoken quite a lot of Father Fergus. Well, Fergus was in Rome at the moment and the laicization process was well under way. She and Fergus would be married in Rome during the summer. Then they would come home, possibly try to get a teaching job. It shouldn't be hard. Both of them had a lot of qualifications and a lot of experience.

"It's all working out as you want, isn't it, Mum?" Pat had said.

"It's what all you girls want that's important, you know that," Mum had said; she was laughing at herself a little, and she tried to take the triumphant look off her face.

That time had been a turning point for Pat too. Rory had told her about the South American woman, Cellina. Pat had liked Cellina; she had helped her to organize a solidarity campaign for fellow students back home, and she had introduced her to Rory. She had been pleased when Rory had liked Cellina. She had never seen exactly how much he had liked Cellina until he told her.

She had stopped taking the Pill. To use Cathy's marvelous, old-fashioned phrase, she felt she didn't need the services of a contraceptive. She did a lot of work on her thesis, and she did a great deal of work at home too. A family wedding for Cathy, with the Kennedys screaming their delight as loudly as Mum and Dad. Then there was the trip to Rome. Why not? If Ethna was doing something as huge as this they must all be there, and they were. Mother had Ethna back, and she had Cathy back.

But she was about to lose Pat. Temporarily perhaps, who could tell? Rory had come back from Bonn where he and Cellina had been living. He had come home alone. They had met a lot during the two weeks he was back. It seemed silly and wasteful not to go to bed with him. They were giving each other a lot of pleasure and they weren't hurting anyone, since Cellina would never know. And were they betraying anyone? The word betrayal is such a subjective one.

But now Rory had gone back to Bonn, and Holles Street, which is never wrong over such things, had said Positive. And Pat had learned enough over the years not to believe the Problem Pages. It would be best if she went to London, on her own. Connected with work. And the possibility of getting into the London School of Economics—yes, that would be a good one. She had often spoken of the LSE. Mum and Dad would be interested in that as a project.

And as long as she wrote regularly and seemed happy, that was the main thing.

Murmurs in Montrose

Seven people woke up that morning and remembered that this was the day Gerry Moore came out of the nursing home. He wouldn't be cured, of course. You were never cured if you were an alcoholic. Four of them shrugged and thought that perhaps he wasn't really an alcoholic—these things were so exaggerated nowadays. There was a time when a man took a drop too much, but now it was all endogynous, and in the glands, and in the bloodstream, and there were allergies and addictions that had never existed before. Two people knew very well that he was an alcoholic, and the remaining one, waking up that morning, looking forward to his release, had never believed for one moment that there was anything the matter with Gerry. He had gone into that home for a good rest, and that's all there was to it.

Gerry's mother was seventy-three, and there had never been any scandal in her life before and there wasn't going to be any. She had reared five boys on her own. Three of them were abroad now, all of them making a good living; only two were in Ireland, and of those Gerry was easily her favorite. A big innocent bear of a man without a screed of harm in him. He worked too hard, that was the problem; and in his job, Gerry had told her often, the best place to meet clients was in pubs. A grown man couldn't sit like a baby in a pub, drinking a pint of orange juice! Naturally a man had to drink with the people he talked to. They wouldn't trust him otherwise. His health had broken down from all the antisocial hours, that's what he had told her. He had to go into the nursing home for six weeks for a total rest. No one was to come to see him. He would be out in the first week of May, he had said. Now it was the beginning of May and he'd be home, as right as rain. That's if anyone could be as right as rain in the house his precious Emma ran for him. Stop. She mustn't say a word against Emma, everyone thought Emma was the greatest thing since sliced bread. Keep your own counsel about Emma. Even her son Jack had said that Emma was a walking saint. Jack! Who never noticed anyone . . .

Jack Moore woke up that morning with a leaden feeling in his chest. He couldn't identify it for a while. He went through the things that might cause it. No, he had no row going on with Mr. Power in the showrooms; no, he had no great bag of washing to take down to the launderette. No, there had been no bill from the garage for his car—and then he remembered. Gerry came home today. Insisted on taking a bus home in his own time, no, he didn't want anyone to collect him, didn't want to look like a wheelchair case. Anyway, he had to start taking control of his own life again. Jack knew that the visit to the nursing home was going to be a big talking point, a drama, a bit of glamour, just like losing his driving license had been. Gerry had held them spellbound with his story of the young guard asking him to blow into the bag. The jokes that Gerry had made had cracked a smile even in the Gardai. It hadn't done any good in the end, of course, he had been put off the roads for a year. Emma had taken twenty-five driving lessons in ten days: she had passed her test. She drove the car, remembering to take the keys out of it when she was going to leave both the car and Gerry at home. Emma was a saint, a pure saint. He hoped her children appreciated her.

Paul and Helen Moore woke up and remembered that this was the day that Daddy came home. They were a lot more silent at breakfast than usual. Their mother had to remind them of the good news. When they got back from school their dad would be sitting at home as cured from his disease as he could hope to be. Their faces were solemn. But they should be cheerful, their mother told them, everything was going to be fine now. Dad had gone of his own choice into a place where they gave him tests and rest and therapy. Now he knew that drinking alcohol for him was like drinking poison, and he wouldn't do it. Paul Moore was fourteen. He had been going to go and play in his friend Andy's house after school, but that wouldn't be a good idea now. Not if a cured father was coming back. He never asked his friends to play in their house. Well. It was only one day. Helen Moore was twelve; she wished that her mother didn't go *on* about things so much, with that kind of false, bright smile. It was better really to be like Father Vincent, who said that the Lord arranged things the way the Lord knew best. Father Vincent believed that the Lord thought it was best for Dad to be drunk most of the time. Or that's what it seemed that Father Vincent thought. He was never too definite about anything.

Father Vincent woke wishing that Gerry Moore had a face that was easier to read. He had been to see him six times during his cure. Gerry had ended up the most cheerful patient in the nursing home; he had nurses, nuns, and other patients agog with his stories of the people he had photographed; the adventures, the mistakes corrected just in time, the disasters miraculously averted. Alone with the priest, he had put on a serious face the way other people put on a raincoat, temporarily, not regarding it as anything to be worn in real life. Yes, Gerry had understood the nature of his illness, and wasn't it bad luck—a hell of a lot of other fellows could drink what he drank and get off scot-free. But he would have to give it up. Heigh-ho. But then the priest had heard him tell stories about photographing film stars on location, and meeting famous people face-to-face. Nowhere did he seem to remember that he hadn't done a book for four years, nor a proper commission for two. He had spent most of his time drinking with that friend of his from the TV station, the fellow who was apparently able to get his work finished by twelve noon and spend the rest of the day in Madigan's. A hard man, poor Gerry used to call him. Des the hard man. Father Vincent hoped that Des-the-hard-man would be some help when Gerry got out of all this. But he doubted it. Des didn't look like a pillar for anyone to lean on.

Des Kelly woke up at five o'clock as he always did. He slipped out of the bed so as not to wake Clare; he had become quite an expert at it over the years. He kept his clothes in a cupboard on the stairs so that he could dress in the bathroom without disturbing her. In half an hour he was washed, dressed, and had eaten his cornflakes; he took his coffee into his study and lit the first cigarette of the day. God, it was great that Gerry was being let out of that place at last, the poor divil would be glad to be out. He'd been up once to see him and he'd known half the crowd in the sitting room, or half-known them. Gerry wasn't well that day, so he'd scribbled a note to say he'd called. He'd felt so helpless, since his automatic response had been to leave a bottle of whiskey. Still, it was all over now, and no harm done. Pumped all the poison out of him they had, told him to lay off it for a bit longer, then go easy on it. Or that's what Des supposed they told him, that made sense anyway. If you got as reached by the stuff as poor old Gerry had been getting there over the last few months, it was wiser to call a halt for a bit. What he couldn't stand was all this sanctimonious claptrap about it being an illness. There was no fitter man in Dublin than Gerry Moore. He had been a bit unfortunate. But now he had time to take stock and get his career together, well, he'd be back on top in no time. That's if know-all Emma, you-name-it-I'm-a-specialist-in-it Emma, didn't take control of him and crush any bit of life that was left in him right out of him. Gerry would need to watch it: With a friend like that creeping Jesus Father Vincent, with a coffin-face of a brother like Jack and with know-all Emma for a wife, poor Gerry needed a couple of real friends. One of the few things he and Clare ever saw eye to eye about these days was what a mystery it was that a grand fellow like Gerry Moore had married that Emma. Des sighed at the puzzle of it all and opened his file; he always got his best work done at this time of the morning.

Emma woke up late. She had hardly slept during the night but had fallen into one of those heavy sleeps at dawn. She was sorry now that she hadn't got up at six o'clock when she was so restless; the extra three hours weren't worth it. She tumbled out of bed and went to the hand basin. She gave herself what her mother had called a lick and a promise. She smiled at the way she had accepted the phrase for so long and never questioned it until today. Today of all days she was up late and examining her face in the mirror, musing over what old childhood sayings might mean. She pulled on her pale blue sweater and jeans and ran downstairs. Paul and Helen looked at her as reproachfully as if she had handed them over to Dr. Barnardo's.

"We had to get our own breakfast," said Helen.

"You'll be late for work," said Paul.

"The place looks awful for Daddy coming home," said Helen.

With her lip well bitten in to stop her shouting at them, Emma managed a sort of smile. They had managed to spill water, cold and hot, all over the kitchen. God almighty, it's not that hard to fill an electric kettle and then to pour hot water into cups of instant coffee, is it? She didn't say it, she didn't ask the rhetorical question which would result in shrugging and counter-accusation. They had trailed coffee powder, buttered the sink as well as their bread, there was a line of crumbs from the toaster . . . calm, calm.

"Right, if you've had your breakfast, you head off, and we'll have a celebration supper tonight. Isn't it marvelous?" She looked brightly from one to another.

"Why didn't you get up in time, Mummy, if it's such a marvelous day?" Helen asked. Emma felt that she would like to slap her hard.

"I was awake most of the night and I fell into one of those heavy sleeps just a short time ago. Come on now, hoosh, you should be gone."

"Will the celebration supper last long? Can I go over to Andy's afterward?"

"Yes!" snapped Emma. "When supper's over you can do what you like."

"Is Father Vincent coming to supper?" Helen asked.

"Heavens, no. I mean, who would have asked him, why do you think he might be here?" Emma sounded alarmed.

"Because he's often here when there's a crisis, isn't he?"

"But this isn't a crisis. This is the end of the crisis, Daddy is cured, I tell you, cured. All the awful things about his disease are gone, there's no need for Father Vincent to come and be helpful."

"You don't like Father Vincent much, do you?" said Helen.

"Of course I do, I like him very much, I don't know where you got that idea. It's just that he's not needed tonight." Emma was wiping and cleaning and scooping things into the sink as she spoke.

"Would you say you like Father Vincent less or more than you like Dad's friend Mr. Kelly?"

Emma put her hands on her hips. "Right, is there anything else you'd like to do before you go to school? Play I Spy? Maybe we could have a few games of charades as well or get out the Monopoly? Will you get yourselves—"

They laughed and ran off. She ate the crusts of their toast, rinsed the cups and plates and ran from the kitchen into the sitting room. The children had been right, it was a mess. She took a deep breath and made a big decision. One hour would make all the difference. Please God, may she get someone who was understanding and nice, someone who realized that she wasn't a shirker.

"Hallo? Can you put me through to—" No, suddenly she hung up. It was bad enough having one in the family who let people down: she had never missed a day since she had got the secretarial job in Montrose, she was damned if she was going to miss even an hour today. She swept up the worst of the untidiness, shoving newspapers and magazines into the cupboard, gathering any remaining cups or glasses from last night. Gerry wasn't one to notice what a place looked like.

She threw out the worst of the flowers and changed the water in the vase; then she took out her Welcome Home card and wrote "from all of us with love." She propped it up beside the flowers, ran out pulling the door, leaped on her bicycle and headed for Montrose. Because she was a little later than usual there was more traffic, but she didn't mind, she thought of it as a contest. She would fight the cars and the traffic lights and the bits that were uphill. She would think about nice things, like how she had lost a stone and a half in two months, how she could fit into jeans again, how someone had really and truly thought she was a young woman, not the forty-year-old mother of teenagers. She thought of the great suntan she would get in the summer; she thought that she might get highlights in her hair if it weren't too dear. She thought of everything in the world except her husband Gerry Moore.

Gerry Moore was going to be a great loss in the nursing home. The nurses all told him that and so did the patients. The doctor had his last chat with him that morning and said that in many ways he had been one of the most successful patients who had ever done the program because he had refused to let it depress him.

"You've been in such good form all the time, Gerry, you've actually helped other people. I must admit at the start I was less than convinced. I thought you were just marking time to get out and get at the stuff again."

"Wouldn't I have to be half mad to do that?" Gerry said. The doctor said nothing.

"I know, I know, a lot of the lads you get in here are half mad. But not me. Honestly, I know what I'm doing now. I just have to change my life-style, that's all. It can be done. I once had a life-style, a grand life-style, without drink. I'll have one again."

"You'll be in here lecturing to us yet," the doctor laughed.

Gerry had a dozen people to say good-bye to; he promised he'd come back to see them. "They all say that," people said, yet people believed that Gerry Moore would, he had that sort of way with him.

Nurse Dillon said she was surprised that a man like Mr. Moore with so many friends of his own didn't want anyone to come and collect him. Gerry had put his arm around her shoulder as she walked him to the door.

"Listen here to me, I'm thinner, I'm much more handsome, I'm a sane man, not a madman. I'm a great fellow now compared to the way I was when I walked in—so don't you think I should go home my own route and let the world have a look at me?"

She waved at him all the way to the end of the avenue. He was a gorgeous man, Mr. Moore, and actually he was right, he did look fabulous now. You'd never think he was an old man of forty-five.

"Mind yourself as you go your own route," she called.

His own route. Now, where would that have taken him in the old days? Stop remembering, stop glorifying . . . a taste was only a taste, it wasn't anything special. He knew that. Stop glamourizing it all. These pubs, the ones he might have dropped into, they weren't welcoming corners where friends called him to join their circles; some of them were sordid and depressing. If ever he had got talking to anyone it had been a sour, depressed man who might have looked at him with suspicion. It was only when he got back nearer home that he would find people he knew in pubs. Friends. Stop glorifying it. It had *not* been a constant chorus of "There's Gerry, the very man, come on over here, Gerry, what'll you have?" No, it hadn't been like that. People had avoided him, for God's sake, in the last months. He knew that, he had faced it. People he had known for years. Boy, was it going to come as a shock to them when they saw him with his big glass of slimline tonic and a dash of angostura bitters, the nondrinkers' cocktail. Ho, they'd be surprised, never thought old Gerry Moore had it in him to change his life.

Gerry walked to the bus stop. He had a small overnight case. He hadn't needed much in the hospital, just his dressing gown and pajamas and a wash bag, really, a couple of books and that was it. Why had his suitcases always been so heavy in the old days? Oh, of course, booze in case he would ever be caught short, and gear for work. No more attention to booze *ever* again, but a lot of attention to work. He was looking forward to spending a good month sorting himself out and seeing where he was, then another month sending out mail shots offering specialized work. By midsummer he should be back where he had been, only better. A bus came and he got into it. Happily, he reached into his pocket and got out the money Emma had brought him. He hadn't wanted money but of course he had been admitted to that nursing home penniless; she had given him money for tipping and taxis or whatever he needed. He hated taking her money, he hated that more than anything.

He got off the bus in the city center. Other people were walking about normally, it seemed to him; they had no problems and big decisions. They looked vacantly into windows of shops, or screwed their eyes up against the sunlight to see whether the traffic lights were green or red. A few early tourists strolled, everyone else seemed to bustle a bit. He looked at them wonderingly; most of them would have no problems handling a few glasses of spirits, a few pints, a bottle of wine with their meal, yet a lot of them wouldn't even bother to. He saw with annoyance a couple of Pioneer Pins pass by; that total abstinence in order to make reparation to the Sacred Heart always annoyed him deeply. Nine tenths of these fellows didn't know what they were giving up. It was as if he said that he'd give up mangoes or passion fruit, something he'd never tasted. The Lord couldn't be all that pleased with such a sacrifice; the Lord, if he was there at all, must know that these Pioneers were a crowd of hypocritical show-offs. Easy, easy. Stop thinking about drink as some wonderful happiness creator. Don't imagine that a drink suddenly turns the world into an attractive technicolor. The world's fine now, isn't it? He didn't want a drink this moment, did he? No. Well then, what was the problem?

He caught the number ten with agility just as it was about to pull out. There right in front of him was Clare Kelly. "The lovely Clare . . . well, aren't I steeped?" he said with a mock gallant manner that played to the rest of the bus.

Clare was embarrassed and irritated to have run into him. Gerry could see that. She was a distant, cold sort of woman, he had always thought. Full of sarcasm and the witty answer. Gave poor Des a bloody awful time at home. Des had nothing to say to her these days, he had often told that to Gerry. He had said that he and Clare didn't actually talk, have real conversations; there was always a state of war, where one or the other was winning. Nobody could remember when the war had been declared but it was there, in private as well as in public, putting each other down. Not that there was much in public these days. Clare didn't have much time for her husband's friends. Des preferred it that way. Let her have her meetings and her own life, let her laugh and sneer with her own friends, mock and make little of people. That suited him fine. Gerry had been very sorry for Des, the best of fellows. No matter what things went wrong in his own life at least Emma didn't mock him.

Clare had moved over to make room for him. "You're looking marvelous," she said.

"Why wouldn't I, with all it cost?" he said, laughing. "Can I get your ticket? Two to—are you going home or are you off to reform the world somewhere?" He paused as the conductor waited.

"Home," she laughed at him. "You haven't changed Gerry, they didn't knock the spirit out of you."

"No, only the spirits," he laughed happily, and handed her her ticket like you would give it to a child. "Here, take this in case we have a fight before we get home and you and I separate."

"Are you on your way home now from—you know?"

"Yes, just released. They gave me back my own clothes, a few quid to keep me going and the names and addresses of people who might take on an ex-con." He laughed, but stopped when he noticed that Clare wasn't laughing at all.

"Wouldn't you think Emma . . . ? It's awful to have you coming out on your own, like this."

"I wanted to. Emma said she'd come in the car after work, your Des said he'd come for me in a taxi, Brother Jack, the ray of sunshine, said he'd arrive and escort me home after work, Father Vincent said he would come with a pair of wings and a halo and spirit me home, but I wanted to come home on my own. You could understand that, couldn't you?"

"Oh, yes," said Clare, managing to get some lofty superiority into the two words.

"Well, how's everything been, out in the real world?"

"Quiet, a bit quieter without you." She didn't smile as she said it. She said it as though he were a dangerous influence, someone who had been upsetting people. There was ill-concealed regret that he was back in circulation. He smiled at her pleasantly as if he hadn't understood her tone. He had to be very calm, no point in becoming touchy, no seeing insults, fancying slights, imagining hostilities; no running away to hide because people were embarrassed about his treatment; no rushing out to console himself because the world didn't understand. Nice and easy.

"Ah, if that's the case we'll have to liven it up a bit. A quiet world is no use to God, man, or the devil, as they say." He left the subject and drew her attention to some demolition work they could see from the bus. "Hey, that reminds me," he said cheerfully, "did you hear the one about the Irish brickie who came in to this site looking for a job . . ."

Clare Kelly looked at him as he told the story. He looked slimmer and his eyes were clear. He was quite a handsome man in a way. Of course it had been years since she had seen him sober, so that made a difference. She wondered, as she had wondered many times, what people saw in him; he had no brain whatsoever. In between his ears he had sawdust.

She smiled politely at the end of the story, but it didn't matter to Gerry because the bus conductor and three people nearby had laughed loudly. And he was really telling the joke to them as much as to Clare.

He was pleased to see the flowers. That was very nice of Emma. He put his little case down in the sitting room and moved automatically to the cupboard under the music center to pour himself a drink. He had his hand on the door when he remembered. God, how strong the old habits were. How ridiculous that in all those weeks in the hospital he never found himself automatically reaching for some alcohol, but now here at home. . . . He remembered that nice young Nurse Dillon saying to him that he would find it hard to make the normal movements at home because he would be so accustomed to connecting them with drink. She had said that some people invented totally new things to do, like drinking Bovril when they came in to the house. Bovril? He had wrinkled his nose. Or Marmite, or any unfamiliar beverage, like hot chocolate. She had been very nice, that Nurse Dillon, regarded the whole thing as a bit of bad luck like getting measles; she had even given him a small Bovril last night and said that he might laugh, but it could well come in handy. He had said that he was such a strong character he would go to the drinks cupboard and pour the bottles down the sink. Nurse Dillon said that he might find his wife had already done that for him.

Gerry opened the doors. Inside there were six large bottles of red lemonade, six of slimline tonic, six of Coca-Cola. There was a bottle of lime cordial and a dozen cans of tomato juice. He blinked at them. It was a little highhanded of Emma to have poured away all his alcohol without so much as a byyour-leave. He felt a flush of annoyance creep up his neck. In fact it was bloody high-handed of her. What did all this business about trusting him, and relying on him, and not pressuring him, mean if she had poured his drink away? There had been the remains of a case of wine, and two bottles of whiskey there. Money to buy things didn't grow on trees.

Very, very upset he went out to the kitchen and put his hands on the sink deliberately to relax himself. He looked at the plug hole. Without a word of consultation she had poured about twenty pounds' worth of drink down there.

Then his eye fell on a box in the corner of the kitchen, with a piece of writing paper taped to it. "Gerry. I took these out of the sitting room cupboard to make room for the other lot. Tell me where you want them put. E." His eyes filled with tears. He wiped his face with the back of his hand and sniffed as he struck the match to light the gas to boil the kettle to make his cup of Bovril.

Mrs. Moore had rung once or twice during the day, but there had been no reply. That Emma and her precious job. What was she, except a glorified typist? Just because she was in Montrose, just because she had sat at the same table as Gay Byrne in the coffee shop, and walked down a corridor with Mike Murphy, just because she had given Valerie McGovern a lift and had a long chat with Jim O'Neill from Radio Two, did that make her special? Oh, no, it didn't, just a clerk is all she was. And a clerk with a heart of stone. The girl had no feeling in her. Wouldn't any normal person have taken the day off to welcome her husband back from six weeks in hospital? But not Emma. The poor lad had to come back to an empty house.

"Ah, there you are, Gerry, how are you, are you feeling all right now, did you have a good rest?"

"Like a fighting cock, Mother, grand, grand altogether."

"And did they give you medicines, injections, did they look after you properly? I can't think why you didn't go to Vincent's. Isn't it beside you? And you have the Voluntary Health."

"Oh, I know, Mother, but they don't have the course there. I had the whole course, you know, and thank God it seems to have worked. But of course, you never know. You're never really sure."

"What do you mean you're not sure, you're all right! Didn't they have you in there for six weeks? Gerry? Do you hear me? If you don't feel all right, you should see someone else. Someone we know."

"No, Mother, I'm fine, really fine."

"So what did they tell you to do, rest more?"

"No, the contrary in fact, keep busy, keep active, tire myself out even."

"But wasn't that what had you in there, because you were tired out?"

"Don't you know as well as I do what had me in there? It was the drink." His mother was silent.

"But it's all right now, I know what I was doing to myself and it's all over."

"A lot of nonsense they talk. Don't let them get you involved in their courses, Gerry. You're fine, there's nothing the matter with you, you can have a drink as well as the next man."

"You're not helping me, Mother, I know you mean well, but those are not the facts."

"Facts, facts . . . don't bother with *your* facts, with *their* facts up in that place. The fact is that your father drank as much as he liked every evening of his life and he lived to be seventy, Lord have mercy on him. He would have lived to be far more if he hadn't had that stroke."

"I know, Mother, I know, and you're very good to be so concerned, but believe me, I know best. I've been listening to them for six weeks. I can't touch drink anymore. It's labeled poison as far as I'm concerned. It's sad, but there it is."

"Oh, we'll see, we'll see. A lot of modern rubbish. Emma was explaining it to me. A lot of nonsense. People had more to do with their time when I was young than to be reading and writing these pamphlets about not eating butter and not smoking and not drinking. Wasn't life fine in the old days before all these new worries came to plague us, tell me, wasn't it?"

"It was, Mother, it was," said Gerry wearily.

It *had* been fine for a while. When Gerry and Emma got married he had a good career. There was a lot of money to be made from advertising in the sixties: one day it had been a bottle and an elegant glass, another it had been a consultation about photographing new banks, the sites, and personnel, the buildings. He had known all the agencies, there was no shortage of work. Emma had been so enthusiastic about his work—she had said it was much more vibrant and alive than her own. She had taught bookkeeping and accountancy for beginners in a technical school. She never called it a career; she had been delighted to leave it when Paul was expected, and she had never seemed to want to go back when Helen was off to school and out of the way, and that was a good seven years ago. Now that the bottom had fallen out of the market in advertising and there were no good photographic jobs left, Emma wasn't able to get back into teaching either. They didn't want people who had opted out for fifteen years, why should they? That's why she was up in the television station doing typing, and thinking herself lucky to get the job.

They had said in the nursing home it wasn't very helpful to look back too much on the past; it made you feel sorry for yourself, or wistful. Or else you began to realize what had happened was inevitable, and that wasn't a good idea either. You started to think you had no responsibility for your actions. So let's not think of the past, the old days when life was fine. He made the Bovril and took it, sniffing it suspiciously, into the sitting room. Hard not to think of the old days. A picture of their wedding in the silver frame, laughing and slim, both of them. His own father and both Emma's parents, now dead, smiled out more formally. His mother had looked confident, as if she knew she would be a long-liver.

Then the pictures of Paul and Helen, the series he had done; they looked magnificent, people said, on an alcove wall, a record of the seventies children growing up, turning into people before your eyes. But they had stopped turning into people photographically about five years ago. The children seemed stuck in a time warp of his making.

He looked back at the wedding picture and again he felt the prickling in his nose and eyes that he had felt when he read Emma's note in the kitchen. Poor girl, she was only a girl, she was only thirty-nine years old and she had been keeping four people for two years on a typist's salary. That's really what it boiled down to. Of course, there had been the odd check coming in for him, the royalties from some of those coffee-table books; a little here for a print he'd taken from stock for someone's calendar, a little there for a permission to reprint. But he had cashed those checks and spent them himself. Emma had kept the family. God, he would make it up to her, he really would. He would make up every penny and every hour of worry and anxiety. He wiped his eyes again, he must be big and strong. Gerry Moore was home again, he was going to take over his family once more.

Emma hadn't liked to make a phone call while the office was quiet. It was too important a call, she couldn't suddenly hang up if she felt that people were listening to her. Anxiously she watched the clock, knowing that he must be home by now, wishing that she had done more to make the place welcoming, mentally ticking off the shopping she had done at lunchtime; she was going to make them a celebratory meal. She hoped he wasn't regretting his decision to come home alone; going back to an empty house, to a changed life-style after six weeks in a hospital, it wasn't such a good idea. To her great delight the office filled up with people and she was able to turn her back and call home.

"Hallo?" His voice sounded a little tentative and even snuffly, as if he had a cold.

"You're very welcome home, love," she said.

"You're great, Emma," he said.

"No, I'm not, but I'll be home in an hour and a half and I can't wait to see you. It's grand you're back."

"The place is great. Thank you for the flowers and the card."

"Wait till you see what we're going to have tonight—you'll think you're in a first-class hotel."

"I'm cured, you know that."

"Of course I do. You're very strong and you've got a terrific life ahead of you, we all have."

His voice definitely sounded as if he had a cold, but maybe he was crying— she wouldn't mention it in case it was crying and it upset him that she noticed.

"The kids will be in any minute, you'll have plenty of company."

"I'm fine, I'm fine. You're very good to ring. I thought you couldn't make calls there." She had told him that the organization expressly forbade private calls in or out. She had said this to stop him ringing when he was drunk.

"Oh, I sneaked one because today is special," she said.

"I'll soon have you out of that place, never fear," he said.

She remembered suddenly how much he hated her being the breadwinner.

"That's great," she said. "See you very soon." She hung up. He sounded grand. Please, please God may it be all right. There was a man at work who hadn't touched a drop in twenty years, he told her. A lovely man, great fun, very successful, and yet he said he was a desperate tearaway when he was a young fellow. Maybe Gerry would be like him. She must believe. She must have faith in him. Otherwise the cure wouldn't work.

Paul came home first. He shuffled a bit when he saw his father sitting reading the *Evening Press* in the big armchair. It wasn't just six weeks since he had seen such a scene, it was much longer; Dad hadn't been around much for ages.

He put down his books on the table.

"You're back, isn't that great?" he said.

Gerry stood up and went and put both hands on his son's shoulders. "Paul, will you forgive me?" he asked, looking straight into the boy's eyes.

Paul squirmed, and flushed. He had never been so embarrassed. What was Dad saying these awful corny lines for? It was worse than some awful old film on the television. Would he forgive him? It was yucky.

"Sure, Dad," he said, wriggling away from the hands. "Did you get the bus home?"

"No, seriously, I have been very anxious to say this to you for a few weeks, and I'm glad to have a chance before there's anyone else here."

"Dad, it doesn't matter. Aren't you fine now, isn't that all that counts?"

"No, of course it isn't. There's no point in having a son unless you can talk to him. I just want to say that for too long this house hasn't been my responsibility. I was like someone who ran away, but I'm back, and it will all be like it was when you were a baby and don't remember . . . but this time you're grown up."

"Yes," said Paul, bewildered.

"And if I make rules and regulations about homework and helping in the house, I'm not going to expect you to take them meekly. You can say to me, what kind of sod are you to be ordering us about, where were you when I needed you? I'll listen to you, Paul, and I'll answer. Together we'll make this a proper family."

"I wouldn't say things like that. I'm glad you're home, Dad, and that it's cured, the illness bit, honestly."

"Good boy." His father took out a handkerchief and blew his nose. "You're a very good boy. Thank you."

Paul's heart sank. Poor old Dad wasn't in good shape at all, maybe his mind had gone in that place, talking all this sentimental crap, and tears in his eyes. Oh, shit, now he couldn't ask to go over to Andy's house. It would cause a major upheaval and maybe his father would burst into tears. God, wasn't it depressing.

Helen went into the presbytery on her way home in order to speak to Father Vincent.

"Is anything wrong?" The priest immediately assumed the worst.

"No, Mummy keeps saying there's no crisis, so it must all be fine, but I came to ask if you'd call in tonight on some excuse. If you could make up some reason why you had to call—"

"No, child, your father's coming home tonight, I don't want to intrude on the family, you'll all want to be together. Not tonight, I'll call in again sometime, maybe in a day or two."

"I think it would be better if you came in now, at the beginning, honestly."

The priest was anxious to do the best thing but didn't know what it was. "Tell me, Helen, what would I say, what would I do? Why would I be a help? If you could explain that to me then I would, of course."

Helen was thoughtful for a moment. "It's hard to say, Father Vincent, but I'm thinking of other times. Things were never so bad when you were there, they used to put on a bit of manners in front of you, you know, Mummy and Daddy, they wouldn't be fighting and saying awful things to each other."

"Yes, but I don't think—"

"It mightn't have looked great to you, but if you weren't there, Daddy would be drinking much more and saying awful things and Mummy would be shouting at him not to upset us."

The child looked very upset; Father Vincent spoke quickly. "I know, I know, and a lot of homes that sort of thing happens in. Don't think yours is the only one where a voice is raised, let me assure you. But you're forgetting one thing, Helen, your father is cured. Thank God he took this cure himself. It was very hard and the hardest bit was having to admit that he couldn't handle drink. He now has admitted this and he's fine, he's really fine. I've been to see him, you know, up in the home. I know he didn't want you children going there, but he's a new man, in fact he's the old man, his old self, and there won't be a thing to worry about."

"But he's still Daddy."

"Yes, but he's Daddy without drink. He's in grand form, you'll be delighted with him. No, I won't come in tonight, Helen, but I'll give a ring over the weekend and maybe call around for a few minutes."

Helen looked mutinous. "I thought priests were meant to help the community. That's what you always say when you come up to the school to talk to us."

"I am helping, by not poking my nose in. Believe me, I'm older than you are."

"That's the thing people say when they've no other argument," Helen said.

Emma cycled down the road and saw Helen moodily kicking a stone.

"Are you only coming home now?" she asked, annoyed that Helen hadn't been back to welcome Gerry earlier.

"I called in to see Father Vincent on the way," said Helen.

"What about?" Emma was alarmed.

"Private business, you're not to ask people what goes on between them and their confessor, it's the secrecy of the confessional."

"Sorry," said Emma. "He's not coming around here tonight by any awful chance, is he?"

Helen looked at her mother with a puzzled look. "No, he's not actually."

"Good, I want us to be on our own today. You run ahead and say hello to your father, I'll be in in a moment."

Unwillingly Helen walked on; as she turned in the gate she saw her mother take out a comb and mirror and pat her hair. How silly Mummy could be at times. What was she combing her hair for now? There was nobody at home to see her. You'd think she'd have combed it when she was at work where she might meet people who'd be looking at her.

Gerry gave Helen a hug that nearly squeezed the breath out of her.

"You're very grown up, you know, a real teenager," he said.

"Oh, Dad, it isn't that long since you've seen me, it's only a few weeks. You sound like an old sailor coming back from months abroad."

"That's what I feel like, that's exactly the way I feel—how clever of you to spot it," he said.

Helen and Paul exchanged fairly alarmed glances. Then they heard Mum's bicycle clanking against the garage wall and everyone looked at the back door. She burst in through the scullery and into the kitchen. She looked flushed from riding the bicycle; she had a huge bag of groceries which she had taken from the basket. In her jeans and shirt she looked very young, Gerry thought.

They hugged each other in the kitchen, rocking backward and forward as if the children were not there, as if Gerry weren't holding a second mug of Bovril in his hand and as if Emma weren't holding the shopping in hers.

"Thank God, thank God," Gerry kept saying.

"You're back, you're back again," Emma said over and over.

Solemn-eyed, their children looked at them from the door into the hall. Their faces seemed to say that this was almost as bad as what they had been through before.

* * *

The telephone rang as they were having supper. Emma, her mouth full of prawns, said she'd get it.

"It's probably your mother, she said she'd ring."

"She has," said Gerry.

It was Jack. He had been kept late at the shop. Mr. Power had decided at the last moment that all the furniture in the showrooms should be shifted around so that the cleaners could get at the place from a different angle. Emma spent two and a half minutes listening to a diatribe against Mr. Power; she grunted and murmured soothingly. Then the tone of Jack's voice changed, it became conspiratorial.

"Is he home?" he whispered.

"Yes, thank God, he came home this afternoon. Looks as fit as a fiddle. We'll all have to go up there and be pampered, I tell you." She laughed and sounded lighthearted, hoping Jack would catch her mood.

"And is there—is there any sign of—?"

"Oh yes, very cheerful, and he sends you his good wishes—we're just having a welcome-home supper for him actually." Would Jack take this heavy hint, was there the remotest chance that he might realize he had rung at a mealtime?

"Is he listening to you, there in the room?"

"Yes, that's right."

"Well, I obviously can't talk now. I'll ring later, when he's asleep maybe."

"Why don't you ring in the morning, Jack, say, late morning. Saturday's a good day, we'll all be around then, and you could have a word with Gerry himself. Right?"

"I'm not sure if I'll be able to ring in the late morning."

"Well, sometime tomorrow." She looked back at Gerry and affectionately they both raised their eyes to the ceiling. "If only you'd get a phone, we could ring you. I hate you having to find the coins always for calls."

"There's no point in paying the rental for a telephone, and they charge you any figure that comes into their heads, I tell you, for the number of calls. No, I'm better to use the coin box, it's not far away. It's just that there's often a lot of kids around on a Saturday."

"Well, whenever you can, Jack."

"You're marvelous with him, marvelous. Not many women would be able to cope like you."

"That's right," she laughed. He was such a lonely figure she didn't like to choke him off too quickly. "And how are you keeping yourself?" she asked.

Jack told her at length: he told her that he had a bad neck which resulted from a draft that came through a door which Mr. Power insisted on being open. He told her that people weren't buying as much furniture as they used to, and that this craze for going to auctions and stripping things down was ruining the trade. She motioned to Paul, who was nearest to her, to pass her plate. She was annoyed with Jack's timing and his insensitivity, but if she hung up she would feel guilty and she wanted to be able to relax tonight of all nights without another problem crowding her mind.

She looked over at the table as she let Jack ramble on; they all seemed to be getting on all right. Gerry looked great, he had lost weight too. The two of them were much more like their wedding photograph than they had ever been.

His jaw was leaner, his eyes were bright, he was being endlessly patient with the kids, too, which was a lot more difficult than it sounded. Helen in particular was as prickly as a hedgehog, and Paul was restless. Jack seemed to be coming to an end. He would ring tomorrow and talk to Gerry, he hoped Gerry appreciated all that she did for him, going out and earning a living, keeping the family together. If only he had had sense long ago and not put so much at risk. "But it's all fine now," Emma said wearily. Jack agreed doubtfully and hung up.

"Was he repenting of my wicked life?" asked Gerry.

"A bit," Emma laughed. Gerry laughed, and after a moment the children laughed too. It was the nearest to normal living they had known for about four years.

Gerry spent Saturday in his study. It was a four-bedroom house and when they had bought it they had decided at once that the master bedroom should be his study. Other men rented offices, so it made sense that the big bedroom with the good light should be where Gerry worked. The little bathroom attached to the bedroom was turned into a darkroom. Once it had been a miracle of organization: a huge old-fashioned chest of drawers, a lovely piece of furniture, held all his up-to-date filing system. As efficient as any steel filing cabinet, only a hundred times more attractive. The lighting was good, the walls were hung with pictures; some of a single object, like his famous picture of a diamond; some were pictures that told a success story. Gerry receiving an award here, Gerry sharing a joke there. Then there was the huge, bulging desk, full recently of bills or handouts, or refusals or rubbish, making a mockery of the filing.

He had sighed when he saw it, but Emma had been beside him.

"Tell me what you want except a couple of black plastic sacks to get rid of the rubbish," she had said.

"And a bottle of Paddy to get rid of the pain of looking at it," he had said.

"You poor old divil, it's not that bad, is it?" she said lightly.

"No," he said, "I'm only being dramatic. I'll need a dozen plastic bags."

"Don't throw everything out," she said, alarmed.

"I'll throw a lot out, love. I have to start again from scratch, you know that."

"You did it once, you'll do it again," she said, and went downstairs.

Gerry made himself four big, sweeping categories: Real Rubbish; Browsing Through Later Rubbish; For the Filing Cabinet; and Contacts for the New Life.

Almost everything seemed to fit into those; he was pleased with himself and even hummed as the marathon sorting work went on.

Emma heard him as she made the beds and she paused and remembered. Remembered what it used to be like; a cheerful, confident Gerry, whistling and humming in his study, then running lightly down the stairs and into his car, off to another job. In those days there was a big pad beside the phone where she put down the time the person called, their name, their business. She had always sounded so efficient and helpful; clients had often asked was she Mr. Moore's partner and she would laugh and say "a very permanent partner"—they had found that entertaining. For months, years, the phone had hardly rung for Gerry, except a call from Des Kelly or a complaint from his brother Jack, or a list of complaints about something from his mother. Should she dare to believe that things were ever going to be normal again? Was it tempting fate to believe that he might really stay off the drink and build his business up? She didn't know. She had nobody to ask, really. She couldn't go to Al-Anon and discuss it with other wives and families, because that somehow wasn't fair. It would be different if Gerry had joined Alcoholics Anonymous; then she would be able to join something that went hand in hand with it, but no. Gerry didn't want to go to some room every week and hear a lot of bores standing up and saying, "I'm Tadgh, I'm an alcoholic." No, the course was the modern way of dealing with things and he had done that and been cured.

She sighed; why was she blaming him? He had done it his way and he had done it. For six weeks in that home he had become stronger and more determined. For two days now at home he was managing. She must stop fearing and suspecting and dreading, dreading things like the first phone call from Des Kelly, the first row, the first disappointment. Would he have the strength to go on being sunny after all these?

Gerry had tucked three bags of Real Rubbish into the garage, all neatly tied at the neck. He insisted that Emma come up and admire what he had done. The room still looked very much of a shambles to her, but he seemed to see some order in it, so she enthused. He had found three checks as well—out of date, but they could be redated. They totaled over £200. He was very pleased with himself for finding them and said that it called for a dinner out.

"Are you sure they weren't reissued already? One's three years old." Emma wished she hadn't said it. It sounded grudging. She spoke on quickly. "If they have been, so what? You're quite right, where will we go?"

He suggested a restaurant which was also a pub. She kept the smile on her face unchanged. There was going to be a lot of this kind of thing, she'd better learn to get used to it. Just because Gerry Moore had to cut alcohol out of his life, it seemed a vain hope that the rest of Ireland would decide to stop selling it, serving it, and advertising it.

"I'd love that," she said enthusiastically. "I'll wash my hair in honor of it."

Des Kelly rang a bit later.

"How are you, old son?" he asked.

"Ready for the Olympics," Gerry said proudly.

"Do they include a few jars of orange juice, or is that more than flesh and blood could stand?"

"Oh, this flesh and blood can stand anything, but not tonight—I'm taking Emma out to a slap-up meal to say thank you."

"Thank you?"

"For holding the fort and all while I was above in the place."

"Oh, yes, of course, of course."

"But tomorrow, Des, as usual. Twelve-thirty?"

"Great stuff. Are you sure you won't—"

"I'm sure, I'm sure. Tell me about yourself—what have you been doing?"

Des told him about a script which he had sweated blood on which was refused by a jumped-up person who knew nothing, and he told him about one that had gone well and got a few nice write-ups in the paper.

"Oh, yeah, I remember that, that was before I went in," Gerry said.

"Was it? Maybe it was. The time gets confused. Well, what else? The same as usual. I've missed you, old son, I really have. There's not much of a laugh around. I tried leaving Madigan's and I went to McCloskey's and I went down to the Baggot Street area for a bit, Waterloo House, Searson's, Mooney's, but there was no one to talk to. I'm glad you're out."

"So am I."

"Were they desperate to you in there?"

"Not at all, they were fine, it was up to me. If I didn't want to go along with any of it I didn't have to."

"Well, that's good."

"And you can relax, I'm not going to be producing leaflets at you and telling you that you should cut it down a bit." Gerry laughed as he said it. Des laughed, too, with some relief.

"Thanks be to God. See you tomorrow, old son, and enjoy the second-honeymoon night out."

Gerry wished that he had found checks for two thousand, not two hundred, then he would have taken Emma on a second honeymoon. Maybe when he got himself set up again he'd be able to do that. He'd think about it. It would be great to be out with a villa hired for two weeks in one of these places like Lanzarotte. There was a fellow in the nursing home who had bought a house there with a whole group of other Irish people, like a little complex of them out there. They made their own fun, they brought out a ton of duty-free—well, forget that side of it, but there were marvelous beaches and great weather even in winter. He went back to his sorting. It was the section on contacts that was giving him most trouble. A lot of agencies seemed to have changed, merged with others, or gone out of business. A lot of new names. A lot of bad blood with some of the old names—work promised and not done, work done but not accepted. Jesus, it might be easier starting afresh in another country. Australia? This place was a village, what one knew at lunchtime everyone else knew at teatime. Still, nobody had said it was going to be easy.

Gerry was in very low form by the time it came to dress up for going out. The children were out of the house: Paul was with Andy as usual and Helen had gone to a tennis lesson. She had asked that morning at breakfast if the household budget would cover tennis lessons. She didn't really mind if it didn't, and she wasn't going to be a strain on people, but if the money was there she would like to join the group. Gerry had insisted she join, and said that he would get her a new racquet if she showed any promise. She had departed in high spirits and would stay and have tea with one of her friends who lived near the courts.

Emma was fixing her newly washed hair; she sat in a slip at the dressing table and watched Gerry come in. At first she had thought he might want them to go to bed. They hadn't made love last night, just lay side by side holding hands until he drifted off to sleep. This seemed like a good time. But no, that was the last thing on his mind, so she was glad he hadn't really attended to her slightly flirtatious remarks. It didn't seem so much of a rejection if he hadn't heard what she had said. His brow looked dark.

"It will be nice to go out, I'm really looking forward to it."

"Don't rub it in. I *know* you haven't been out for a long time," he said.

She bit back the aggrieved retort. "What will you have, do you think?" she said, searching desperately for some uncontroversial side to it all.

"How the hell do I know until I see the menu? I don't have radar eyes. I'm not inspired by the Holy Ghost to know what's going to be served."

She laughed. She felt like throwing the brush and every single thing on the dressing table at him. She felt like telling him what to do with his dinner invitation—an invitation she would have to pay for anyway until those out-of-date checks were cleared—if they ever were. She felt like saying the house had been a peaceful and better place while he was in the nursing home. But she managed to say, "I know. Deep down I'm just a glutton, I expect. Don't mind me."

He was shaving at the small hand basin in their bedroom. His eyes caught hers and he smiled. "You're too good for me."

"No, I'm not, I'm what you deserve," she said lightly.

In the car he took her hand.

"Sorry," he said.

"Don't mind about it," she said.

"The night just seemed hard ahead of us, no wine with the dinner and all."

"I know," she said sympathetically.

"But you're to have wine, you must, otherwise the whole thing's a non-sense."

"You know I don't mind one way or the other. You know I can easily have a Perrier water."

"Part of the fact of being cured is not to mind other people. It was just that I got a bit low there, inside, in the house, I don't know. I'm fine now."

"Of course you are, and I'll certainly have a glass or two if it doesn't annoy you." She put the key into the ignition and drove off.

Technically he was allowed to drive again now, but he hadn't reapplied, or whatever you were meant to do. And in the last few months he wouldn't have been able to drive. She had offered him the keys as they came to the car and he had shaken his head.

In the bar, as they looked at their menus, they met a couple they hadn't seen for a while. Emma saw the wife nudge her husband and point over at them. After what looked a careful scrutiny he came over.

"Gerry Moore, I haven't seen you looking so respectable for years. And Emma . . ." They greeted him with little jokes and little laughs; both of them patted their flatter stomachs while the man said they must have been at a health farm, they looked so well. Emma said she owed hers to her bicycle and Gerry said that, alas, he owed his to laying off the booze. It was like the first hurdle in an obstacle race. Emma knew from the whispers between the couple that there would be many more. The news would get around, people would come to inspect, to see if it was true. Gerry Moore, that poor old soak, back to his former self, you never saw anything like it, doesn't touch a drop now, made a fortune last year, back on top as a photographer, you never saw anything like him and the wife. Please. Please, God. Please let it happen.

Father Vincent called around on Saturday night and knocked for a long time at the door. The car was gone, Emma's bicycle was there, and there was no reply. He assumed they must all be out at some family gathering. But that child had seemed so white and worried, he hoped that Gerry hadn't broken out immediately and been taken back into the home. He debated with himself for a long time about whether to leave a note or not. In the end he decided against it. Suppose poor Gerry had broken out and been taken back in, it would be a sick sort of thing to leave a welcome home card. Father Vincent wished, as he often did, that he had second sight.

Paul came home from Andy's and turned on the television. Helen came in shortly afterward; they sat with peanut-butter sandwiches and glasses of milk and watched happily. They heard voices, and a key turn in the lock.

"Oh, Lord," said Paul, "I'd forgotten *he* was back, pick up the glass, Helen, give me those plates. We're meant to be running a tidy ship here!" Helen laughed at the imitation of her father's voice, but she looked out into the hall anxiously to make sure that Daddy wasn't drunk.

It was very expensive having Gerry home. Emma realized this, but couldn't quite think why. She realized that he wasn't spending any money on drink; apart from that one Saturday night out they didn't entertain people. Gerry bought no clothes or household things. Why then was her money not stretching as far as it used to? A lot of it might be on stationery and stamps. Gerry was as good as his word about writing to people with ideas—just bright, cheery letters which said, without having to spell it out, I'm back, I'm cured, and I'm still a great photographer. Then he liked to cook new things, things that he wouldn't associate with alcohol. Together they had spent a great deal of money on curry ingredients, but then he had tired of it, and said it wasn't worth all the trouble—they could slip out and buy a good curry if they needed one. She didn't grudge it, but she had been so used to accounting for every penny carefully, putting this little bit there toward the electricity, this toward the gas, and that toward the phone. She didn't know what she was going to do when the next bills came in. And talking of bills, what the phone bill was going to be like made her feel weak around the legs.

Gerry had been talking to somebody in Limerick for nearly fifteen minutes one night, and he mentioned calls to Manchester and London. She had said nothing; she just prayed that the rewards and results of all these phone calls might be felt by the time the telephone bill came in.

Gerry's mother thought that he wasn't himself at all since he came out of that place. He had gone up to see her and the visit was not a success. She had bought a naggin of whiskey for him specially. It was in the glass-fronted cupboard there beside the china dogs. Ah, go on, surely one wouldn't do him any harm.

"No, Mother. That's the whole point. I've got something wrong with my insides, it turns to poison in me. I told you this. Emma explained—"

"Huh, Emma. High-brow talk. Allergy addiction. I'm sick of it."

"Yes, Mother, so am I"—Gerry's patience was ebbing—"but it happens to be true."

"Look, have just the one and we'll quit fighting," his mother had said.

"It would be easy for me to say Thank you, Mother, to hold it here in my fist and when you weren't looking to throw it away. But I can't do that. I can't bloody do it. Can you have the wit of a half-wit and understand that?"

"There's no need to shout at me, I've quite enough to put up with," his mother had said, and then she had started to cry.

"Listen, Mother, give me the bottle you so kindly bought for me. I'll give it to Father Vincent for his sale of work, he can use it on the tombola or something. Then it won't be wasted."

"I will not. If I bought whiskey it will be there to offer to someone who has the manners to take it."

No other subject managed to bring them onto the same plane. Gerry left, and hoped that nobody who lived on earth had such a poor relationship with a parent as he had. That was the day that he went home and found Paul fighting with Emma in the kitchen. They hadn't heard him come in.

"But *why,* if you could tell me *why* I might do it. He's not an invalid, he's not soft in the head, so why does he want to play happy families sitting down to supper together every night? If I go over to Andy's after supper it's too late, then the evening's spoiled."

"Ask Andy here."

"No fear."

Gerry came in and looked at them, first one and then another.

"Please spend the evening with your friend tonight, Paul. Emma, can I have a word with you in my study when you're ready?"

He walked on upstairs. He heard Helen, giggling nervously.

"That's just the voice that Reverend Mother uses when she's going to expel someone," she said, stifling her laughs.

"The boy is right. I am not soft in the head. I get weary of all these family meals, if you must know."

"I thought with my being out all day and you getting back into a routine—"

"You thought, you thought, you thought—what else is it in this house except what you think?"

She looked at him in disbelief.

"I mean it, Emma, morning, noon, and night . . ."

Two large tears fell down her face and two more were on the way down like raindrops on a window. She didn't even brush them aside; she didn't try to deny it, to reason with him, or to agree with him. She just looked beaten.

"Well, say something, Emma. If you don't agree with me say something."

"What is there to say?" she sobbed. "I love you so much and everything I do seems to hurt you. God almighty, how can I do what will please you? I'm obviously doing all the wrong things."

He put his arms around her and stroked her hair. "Stop, stop," he said. She cried into his chest.

"You're very good. I'm really a shit, a terrible shit." She made a muffled denial into his shirt.

"And I love you, too, and need you . . ."

She looked up at him with a tear-stained face. "Do you?"

"Of course," he said.

Downstairs, Helen said, "They've gone into the bedroom, isn't that odd?"

Paul said, "He can't be going to expel her then."

Helen said, "What do you think they're doing?"

Paul laughed knowingly. "I'll give you one guess," he said.

Helen was horrified. "They can't be. They're much too old."

Paul said, "Why else have they closed the door?"

"God, that's awful, that's all we need."

Father Vincent called just then. Helen was so embarrassed when she recognized his shape through the door that she ran back for Paul.

"I can't tell him what we think," she said. "You couldn't tell a priest something like that."

Paul let him in. "Mum and Dad are upstairs at the moment, having a bit of a lie-down. If you don't mind, Father, I won't disturb them."

"Of course, of course." Father Vincent looked confused. "But can I get you a cup of tea, coffee?" The priest said he didn't want to be any trouble.

"A drink?"

"No, no, heavens, no."

"We have drink. Dad insists it be kept there for visitors."

Father Vincent stayed for about ten minutes with no drink and hardly any conversation. When he was at the porch again, he looked timidly at the stairs. "If your father has taken a turn for the worse and your mother wants any help, she only has to call on me." Paul said that he didn't think Mother wanted any help just now, and when the door was safely closed he and Helen rolled around the sitting room floor laughing at the idea of leading Father Vincent upstairs, knocking on the bedroom door and calling out that Father Vincent wanted to know if Mother wanted any help or could manage on her own.

Gerry and Emma lay in their big bed and Gerry said, "It's been so long, I was afraid to, I was afraid, in case. . . ." Emma said, "You were lovely, as you were always lovely." She lay counting the days since her last period; she was safe, she had to be safe. The very notion of becoming pregnant, now, was too much to contemplate. She had stopped taking the Pill two years ago. It was said to have some side effects and women were warned not to stay on it forever. And what on earth had been the point of taking the Pill when there was simply no risk of becoming pregnant?

Jack was sorry that Gerry was back. It sort of put a stop to his Monday visits. He used to visit Gerry at the nursing home on a Sunday, and then took the bus to their house on a Monday night after work to report on what he saw, what he said, what was said back to him, and what he thought. The first couple of times they had been eager to know what he reported, because they still hadn't got used to life without Gerry. Then, after that, it had become a little ritual. Emma used to cook a nice meal, and then they would all wash up. Jack would sit down in the comfort of a nice big sitting room, not his own cramped little bed-sitter. They used to watch television, while Emma sometimes did mending; the television set was turned low so as not to disturb the two children, who did homework. All through April and May Jack had been involved in their life. There was no excuse for him to come anymore.

He had liked those evenings sitting there with Emma; she had been so nice and interested in everything he had been doing at work. It was so cozy. Gerry must have been a madman, stark staring mad to throw away all his money and his good living and spend time drinking with a crowd of eejits. You wouldn't mind a man who had nothing at home, but a man who had Emma. It was past understanding.

It seemed a very long summer for everyone. Father Vincent spent a lot of time wondering what he had done to offend the Moores; every time he went there those two young children, who had seemed nice and normal at one stage, were exceedingly silly with giggles. Gerry wanted to hear no inspiring tales of how others triumphed, he had said curtly, and Emma was too busy to say more than the time of day. She had taken some home typing and had rung him once to inquire whether there was any parish work to be done on a professional basis.

He had said they would always be glad of some voluntary help, but she had said sorry, that she was not yet in a position to be able to offer that.

Mrs. Moore thought that Gerry had become short-tempered and intolerant. Her grandchildren never came near her, and that Emma seemed to be too busy even to talk to her on the telephone.

Paul fell in love with Andy's sister, but Andy's whole family, sister and all, went to Greece for a month. If Paul had two hundred pounds he could have gone out to visit them. His dad had said he could bloody earn it if he wanted it, and his mum had said he must be a selfish little rat to think that money like that was available for a holiday for him.

Helen was very bored and very worried. She had become very ugly suddenly, she thought, after years of looking quite reasonable; now, when it was important, she had become revolting-looking. In books people's mothers helped them when this kind of thing happened, lent them makeup and bought them dresses. In real life her Mum told her to stop sniveling, there would be time enough for that later.

Des felt the summer was long too. He had nothing but admiration for Gerry—he sat there with the best of them, bought his round like any man, but it wasn't the same. Des could never relax like he had, he couldn't get it out of his head that he was waiting for Gerry to start, to catch up on the rest of them. It was restless drinking with him. God damn it, Gerry was very extreme; when he was going on that batter he was a fierce drinker, got them barred from several places, but now that he'd had a fright, instead of taking it nice and easy like any normal person and just watching it, here he was like a bloody Pioneer, sitting there with a glass of lime and soda or whatever he drank nowadays.

Gerry found the summer slow. He found the replies to his letters even slower, and the offers of any work were the slowest of all. How could the whole photography world have collapsed without his noticing it? There must be people getting work; he saw their pictures in the advertisements, on the television, in the magazines. "Maybe," Emma had said, "maybe you should show them what you can do *now,* rather than old portfolios, maybe you should get a collection for another book together?" But did Emma have a clue of any sort how long it took to put a book together? You didn't go out with a camera and snap one hundred fifty things and mark them pages one to one hundred and fifty. There was a theme, there was an interest, there was a commission: a lot of the pictures had been done and paid for already in somebody else's time. Oh, it was all so slow getting back, and it had seemed so very fast, the fall down the ladder. Or was he just being melodramatic?

Emma realized one day during that endless summer that she had no friend. Not no friends but not even one friend. There was nobody she could talk to about Gerry. There never had been. Her mother had thought he was a little too flash for her and her father had wondered about security. But no matter who had asked her to marry them her mother would have seen flashness and her father suspected insecurity all around him. She never talked to her sister about anything except her sister's five children, all of whom seemed to be doing spectacularly well in exams at any given season of the year. She couldn't talk to her mother-in-law, she certainly couldn't talk to that Des Kelly, who always looked at her as if she were a particularly dangerous kind of snake. Poor Jack was so kind and anxious to help, but really the man was so limited, he couldn't have a serious conversation about Gerry's future to save his life. She had formed an unreasonable dislike of Father Vincent, who used to be quite a friend of theirs ten years ago. He had always been quick with liberal attitudes and a broad spectrum but that was not what she needed now. She needed specific advice. It was now four months since Gerry had come home from that nursing home; he had not earned one penny from his trade of photography. To complain about that seemed untimely and ungracious because after all, the man had not touched one drop of alcohol either. There was no point in going to the nursing home and asking the doctors. They had asked her to be cooperative and not to boss him around. She thought that she was doing that part of it. But Lord God, how long would it go on? Already the small debts were building up—paradoxically more frightening than when he had been drinking and the bill from the off-license would arrive. Those drink bills had a terrifying unreality about them. Today's bills, high telephone charges, photography equipment, printing costs, expensive cuts of meat, they had a ring of permanency. And what Emma wanted to know was how long to go on. How long did the ego have to be flattered, the image of self restored? How soon, in other words, could she tell him that there was a job going in a photography studio in town, a very down-market photography job for the great Gerry Moore, but she knew the man who ran it needed an assistant? Did she dare yet tell Gerry, suggest it to him, say that it would be a good idea for a year or two and he could build up his contacts after work? No, it must be too soon, otherwise why would she feel sick at the stomach even thinking about it?

That September they went to a wedding. They didn't know the people well and in fact they were rather surprised at the invitation. When they got there and discovered that they were among four hundred people it became clear that the net had been spread fairly wide. It was a lavish do and there was no effort spared to see that the guests had a good time.

"Isn't it marvelous to give two kids a send-off like this—they'll remember it all their life," Gerry had said. Something about the way he spoke made Emma look up sharply from her plate of smoked salmon. She stared at his glass. He was drinking champagne. She felt the blood go out of her face.

"It's only a little champagne for a wedding," he said. "Please. Please, Emma, don't give me a lecture, don't start to tell me it's the beginning of the end."

"Gerry," she gasped at him.

"Look, it's a wedding. I don't know people, I'm not relaxed, I'm not able to talk to them. Just three or four glasses and that's it. It's all *right*, tomorrow it's back to the everyday business of drying out."

"I beg you—" she said. He had held his glass out to a passing waiter.

"What do you beg me?" His voice had turned hard and the edge of it, the cutting edge, had a sneer as well. "What could you possibly beg from me, you who have everything?"

His voice was loud now and people were beginning to look at them. Emma felt the kind of dread and panic that she used to know as a child when she was at the carnival. She hated the carnival each year—the bumpers, the chairoplane, and the ghost train. Most of all she hated the helter-skelter, and this is what it felt like now. Fast and furious and not knowing what lay ahead.

"Could we go home, do you think?" she asked faintly.

"It's only beginning," he said.

"Please, Gerry, I'll give you anything."

"Will you give me champagne, and fun and a bit of a laugh? No, you'll give me a lecture and a flood of tears and then if I'm very good a piece of shepherd's pie."

"No."

"What, no shepherd's pie? Oh, that settles it, I'll have to stay here."

She whispered, "But the whole life, the plans . . . the plans. Gerry, you've been so good, God almighty, five months and not a drop. If you were going to have a drink, why here, why at this place, why not with friends?"

"I haven't any friends," he said.

"Neither have I," she said seriously. "I was thinking that not long ago."

"So." He kissed her on the cheek. "I'll go and find us some."

He was sick three times during the night, retching and heaving into the hand basin in their room. Next morning she brought him a pot of tea and a packet of aspirins, half a grapefruit and the *Irish Times*. He took them all weakly. There was a picture of the wedding they had been at, of the young couple. They looked smiling and happy. Emma sat down on the bed and began to pour tea.

"Hey, it's after nine, aren't you going to work?" he asked.

"Not today. I'm taking the day off."

"Won't they fire you? Recession and all that?"

"I don't think so. Not for one day."

"That's the problem hiring married women, isn't it, they have to stay at home and look after their babies?"

"Gerry."

"You told them you'd no babies, but still here you are staying at home looking after one."

"Stop it, have your tea."

His shoulders were shaking. His head was in his hands. "Oh, God, I'm sorry, poor poor Emma, I'm sorry. I'm so ashamed."

"Stop now, drink your tea."

"What did I do?"

"We won't talk about it now while you feel so rotten. Come on."

"I must know."

"No worse than before, you know."

"What?"

"Oh, it's hard to describe, general carry-on, a bit of singing. A bit of telling them that you had had the cure and you could cope with drink now; a servant, not a master—"

"Jesus."

They were silent, both of them.

"Go to work, Emma, please."

"No. It's all right, I tell you."

"Why are you staying at home?"

"To look after you," she said simply.

"To do sentry duty," he said sadly.

"No, of course not. It's your decision, you know that well. I can't be a jailer. I don't want to be."

He took her hand. "I'm very, very sorry."

"It doesn't matter."

"It does. I just want you to get inside my head. Everything was so drab and hard and relentless. Same old thing. Dear Johnny, I don't know whether you remember my work. Dear Freddie. Dear Everybody."

"Shush, stop."

"No, thanks, I'll have a Perrier water, no, thanks, I don't drink, no, seriously, I'd prefer a soft drink, nothing anywhere, nothing, nothing. Do you blame me for trying to color it up a bit, just once, with somebody else's champagne? Do you? Do you?"

"No, I don't. I didn't realize it was so gray for you. Is it all the time?"

"All the bloody time, all day, every day."

She went downstairs then and sat in the kitchen. She sat at the kitchen table and decided that she would leave him. Not now, of course, not today, not even this year. She would wait until Helen's fourteenth birthday perhaps, in June. Paul would be sixteen, nearly seventeen then. They would be well able to decide for themselves what to do. She made herself a cup of instant coffee and stirred it thoughtfully. The trouble about most people leaving home is that they do it on impulse. She wouldn't do that. She'd give herself plenty of time and do it right. She would find a job first, a good job. It was a pity about RTE, but it was too close, too near, in every sense. She could rise there and get on if she had only herself to think of. But no, of course not, she had to get away. Maybe London, or some other part of Dublin anyway, not on her own doorstep. It would cause too much excitement.

She heard him upstairs brushing his teeth. She knew that he would go out for a drink this morning. There was no way she could play sentry. Suppose he said he wanted to go out and buy something; she could offer to get it for him, but he would think up a job that he could only do himself.

There were maybe another thirty-five or forty years to go. She couldn't spend them with her heart all tied up in a ball like a clenched fist. She could not spend those years half-waking, half-sleeping in an armchair, wondering how they would bring him in. And even more frightening was sitting watching and waiting in case he broke out, the watching and waiting of the last five months. She would be blamed, of course—selfish, heartless, no sense of her duty. Could you believe that anyone would do it? Emma believed that quite a lot of people could do it, and would if the occasion presented itself, or if the situation was as bad at home as hers was.

She heard Gerry come downstairs.

"I brought down the tray," he said like a child expecting to be praised.

"Oh, that's grand, thanks." She took it from him. He hadn't touched the grapefruit, nor the tea.

"Look, I'm fine. Why don't you go into work? Seriously, Emma, you'd only be half an hour late."

"Well, I might, if you're sure—"

"No, I'm in great shape now," he said.

"What are you going to do this morning, follow up some of those letters?"

"Yes, yes." He was impatient.

"I might go in." She stood up. His face was pure relief.

"Do. You'd feel better. I know you and your funny ways."

"Listen before I go. There's a job going in Paddy's business, only an assistant at the moment, but if you were interested he said that he'd be delighted for you to come in, for a year or two, say, until you got yourself straight." She looked at him hopefully.

He looked back restlessly. He didn't know that so much of his future and hers rested on the reply he gave.

"An assistant? A dogsbody to Paddy, Paddy of all people. Jesus, he must be mad to suggest it. He only suggested it so that he could crow. I wouldn't touch it with a barge pole."

"Right. I just thought you should know."

"Oh, I'm not saying a word against you, it's that eejit Paddy."

"Well, take it easy."

"You're very good to me, not giving out, not telling me what an utter fool I made of myself, of both of us."

"There's no point."

"I'll make it up to you. Listen, I have to go into town for a couple of things this morning, is there anything you—?"

She shook her head wordlessly and went to the garage to take out her bicycle. She wheeled it to the gate and looked back and waved. It didn't matter that people would blame her. They blamed her already. A man doesn't drink like that unless there's something very wrong with his marriage. In a way her leaving would give Gerry more dignity. People would say that the poor divil must have had a lot to put up with over the years.

Firefly Summer

I want to thank all my friends for their support and encouragement, particularly Rosie Cheetham and Chris Green.

And to Gordon Snell, who has made my life so good and so happy, I would like to dedicate *Firefly Summer* with all my gratitude and all my love.

LONDON AND DUBLIN, SUMMER 1987

Part One

One

The sun came in at a slant and hit all the rings and marks on the bar counter. Kate Ryan managed to take a cloth to them at the same time as she was kicking off her house shoes and pulling on her wellington boots. She tucked her handbag under the counter and in almost the same movement opened the kitchen door to make sure that Eddie and Declan weren't torturing the new girl. The new girl had red eyes and a sad face and was missing her farm home. She might run back to it if Eddie and Declan were at their worst. But mercifully the appeal of the tortoise was still very strong even after three weeks. They lay on their stomachs and fed it stalks of cabbage, screaming with delight when it accepted them.

"John," she shouted, "will you come down to the bar, I have to go across the river and see what's keeping the twins. They have to be polished and smartened up for the concert and there isn't a sign of them."

John Ryan groaned. His train of thought was gone again. He had thought he would manage an hour or two on his own, struggling with his poetry. "Give me a minute," he called, hoping to catch the idea before it was gone.

"No, they'll be late as it is. Listen, bring your paper and pencil down, there's likely to be no one in, but there has to be someone behind the counter."

The door banged behind her and John Ryan saw, through the bedroom window, his wife run across the small footbridge opposite the pub. She climbed over the gate like a girl instead of a woman in her thirties. She looked altogether like a girl in her summer dress and her boots as she ran lightly across to the ruined house, Fernscourt, to find the twins.

He sighed and went down to the pub. He knew there were poet publicans, he knew there were men who wrote the poetry of angels in the middle of the stinking trenches of war. But he wasn't like that.

John Ryan moved slowly, a big man with a beer belly that had grown on him sneakily during the years standing behind a bar, jowls that had become flabby at the same trade. His wedding picture showed a different person, a thinner more eager-looking figure, yet the boyish looks hadn't completely gone. He had a head of sandy brown hair only flecked with grey and big eyebrows that never managed to look ferocious even when he willed them to, like at closing time or when he was trying to deal with some outrage that the children were reported to have committed.

Kate had hardly changed at all since their wedding day, he often said, which pleased her, but she said it was just a bit of old softsoaping to get out of having to stand at the bar. It was true, though; he looked at the girl with the long, curly dark hair tied back in a cream ribbon that matched her cream dress and coat. She looked very smart on that wet day in Dublin, he could hardly believe she was going to come and live with him in Mountfern. Kate hadn't developed a pot belly from serving drinks to others, as she often told him sharply. She said that there was no law saying you must have a drink with everyone who offered you one or pull a half pint for yourself to correspond with every half-dozen pints you pulled for others.

But then it was different for women.

John was the youngest of the seven Ryan children and the indulged pet of a mother who had been amazed and delighted at his arrival when she had been sure that her family was complete. He had been overfed and given fizzy drinks with sweet cake as long as he could remember. As a lad the running and leaping and cycling miles to a dance had kept him trimmer. Now, between sessions of writing his poetry and serving in his bar, it was a sedentary life.

He didn't know if he wanted it for his sons; he had such hopes for them— that they might see the world a bit, study maybe and go on for the university. That had been beyond the dreams of his parents' generation. Their main concern had been to see their children well settled into emigration; the church had helped of course, educating two nuns and two priests out of the Ryan family. John didn't see any vocation among his own offspring. Michael was dreamy and thoughtful: maybe a hermit? Or Dara a resourceful Reverend Mother somewhere? Eddie was a practical child, possibly a missionary brother teaching pagan tribes to build huts and dig canals. Declan the baby. Maybe they could make a curate out of him near home where they could keep an eye on him.

This was all nonsense, of course. None of them would end up within an ass's roar of a religious life. Still, John Ryan never saw the future standing surrounded by three sons and possibly his daughter all in the trade.

There would never be enough business, for one thing. Like many Irish towns Mountfern had the appearance of having far too many pubs already. If you went down the main street, Bridge Street, there were no less than three public houses. Foley's at the top of the town, but that was hardly a pub at all these days, just a counter really and a few friends of old Matt Foley drinking at night, they'd hardly know how to serve a real customer. Then there was Conway's which was more a grocery but it had the bar at the back. Conway's had a clientele of secret drinkers, people who didn't admit to any kind of drinking, who were always going out for a packet of cornflakes or a pound of flour and would toss back a brandy for their health. Often too, it had a funeral business since old Barry Conway was the undertaker as well. It seemed only right to come back to his place to drink when someone had been buried up on the hill. And Dunne's was always on the verge of closing. Paddy Dunne never knew whether to reorder supplies; he always said that it would hardly be worth it since any day now he'd be going to join his brother who ran a pub in Liverpool. But then either there would be a downturn in the fortunes of the Liverpool pub or an upswing in the drinking patterns of Mountfern. There was an unsettled air about his place and constant speculation about how much he would get if he were to sell his license.

John Ryan's pub had its rivals then, three of them in a small place like Mountfern. Yet he had all the business that came from the River Road side of the place. He had the farmers on this side of the town. It was a bigger and better bar than any of the other three, it had not only more space but it had more stock. And there were many who liked the walk out along the river bank.

John Ryan knew that he was a man who had been given a great deal by fate. Nobody had gathered *him* up to swoop him off to a religious order when he was a young impressionable boy. Neither had he been sponsored out to a life of hard graft in America like two of his elder brothers. By all their standards he had a life of ease and peace where he should well have been able to run his business and write his poetry.

But he was a man who did one thing at a time, almost overmethodically, too predictable sometimes for his wife who felt that people should be able to fire on several cylinders at the same time.

John wanted time to write or time to serve drink, he couldn't switch from one mode to another like lightning. Like Kate. He couldn't switch toward the children like she could as well. Either they were good or they weren't. He wasn't able to see the swift changes of mood like Kate was. He would not be cross and then smile minutes later. If he was cross he was very cross indeed. It was rare but it was all-embracing when it happened. One of Daddy's great angers was remembered long, whereas Mammy had a dozen quick and easily forgotten angers in a week.

John sighed again at his wife's swiftness and the annoyance at having to leave his work, his real work, just at that time. He knew that in this pub fate had handed him something that many a man in Ireland would envy mightily. It didn't bring in enough money for them to employ another pair of hands, but it wasn't so slack that a man could sit at the counter and write undisturbed. John Ryan hadn't brought his paper and pencils with him, any more than his thoughts. If customers saw you with paper and pencil they thought you were doing the accounts and making a small fortune. Anyway, what would have been the point? There was Jack Coyne from the garage who had just sold a heap of rusty metal to some unsuspecting farmer and they were in to seal the bargain with a pint.

Jack Coyne had a face like a ferret and two sharp eyes looking around him for a bargain or a business deal. He was a small wiry man equally at home underneath a car, covered in grease and shouting out about the extent of the repairs, or in a suit showing off his newly acquired vehicles which was what he called his second-hand stock. Everything about him seemed to be moving, he never stood still; even now at the bar he was shifting, moving from foot to foot.

"Great day, John," said Jack Coyne.

"It's been a great day all the time," said John, preparing to pull the pints.

"Bad for the crops," the farmer said.

"When were you lot ever pleased with the weather?" Jack Coyne laughed, the happy sound of a man who could sell second-hand cars no matter what the weather did.

The children of Mountfern had a place to play like no other children in the land. It was Fernscourt, the ruined house on the bank of the River Fern. It had been burned down one day forty years ago in 1922 during the Troubles. The Fern family had not been there on the day of the fire, they had been gone for many months before.

The children often asked their grandfathers about the fire but found a strange lapse of memory. The passions that had run so high in those years had settled down as time went by. The Ferns and all they symbolized had been forgotten. Their house stood as a beautiful ruin, where once it had stood as a beautiful big empty shell anyway. Now as a place to spend the long summer days it was quite simply perfect.

The orchards that the Ferns had asked their gardeners to plant all those years ago still grew wild and plentiful. The apple trees didn't know that the Ferns had gone. Their old gnarled branches bent to the ground, sometimes making even more places for the children to play.

There was thick trailing ivy everywhere over the walls that remained of the house. The outhouses which had once been the stable-yard had survived better than the main house. Here there were still rooms with roofs to run through, here there were limestone arches and well-made stone walls. In the days when Fernscourt had been built people saw the stables as being very important; guests would expect them to be of the same high standard as the rest of the house.

As Kate Ryan marched through the laurels that grew wild now on each side of the path up from the river she could hear the cries and the laughter. She thought back on her own childhood in a small silent house in Dublin, her mother always an invalid. She had not had brothers and sisters to play with; friends were frowned on and kept well away from the home.

These children had a wild, free life by comparison.

Fernscourt belonged to the group that were here today. Those who were the right age for it. It had always been like that. You were too young if you were Eddie and Declan's age, you were hunted away and sent about your business, which was anywhere but here. Then the older boys and girls went to the bridge and showed off to each other. Where boys dived from the ledge to oohs and ahhs, where girls were sometimes pushed in horseplay and had to climb up the bank with wet dresses clinging.

But if you were in Fernscourt, no other world existed. It had been a fine summer and as soon as any work that had to be done in the various homes in Mountfern was finished they gathered, coming in dribs and drabs across the fields, up the River Road and across the footbridge in front of Ryan's, or some of them braving the brambles and briars on the towpath at the other side of the river, a disused way that saw no traffic these days.

Fernscourt belonged to all the children but it was Dara and Michael's special home. The twins had their own place, a pretend-house. They played there even when none of the others came up to join them. They had an old table and two broken stools from the bar. There was cutlery too, a twisted fork and a rusty knife, and some chipped plates. These were for private feasts. Ever since they had been old enough to go across to Fernscourt alone the twins had said that this is where they would live when they were grown up.

It would be nice and near home, they said reassuringly, but it would be theirs. They would buy the whole place and have a boat and go everywhere by river instead of by road.

It would be their palace, their castle, their home.

It was because they lived so close to the place, because they could see it from their windows over the pub, and they could go there every day winter and summer, that they felt it was their own.

But of course they didn't want to own it exclusively. Fernscourt was also for everyone, particularly during the long summer holidays when no day was long enough for the games they all played there.

There was no form to the games, but the huge mossy stones, the crumbling walls, the great fronts of ivy hanging down like curtains, and the window and doorway gaps in half-standing walls meant there were plenty of places to climb, to perch, to jump, to sit and giggle.

The girls had made a makeshift home in the old clock tower which still stood in the stableyard, though the clock and dome were long gone. The boys would use the long shallow steps that were now almost indistinguishable as steps, so overgrown with weeds and moss had they become, and arrange a jumping competition that was a cross between a longjump and a chicken run. They would all gather to see who could jump down the greatest number of steps; it was the sissy who would opt out of the jump that seemed likely to break a limb.

Yet they had ways out of being a softy. It was always time to go home or to milk the cows or to go for a swim. The boys of Mountfern had no death wish as they played in their own magnificent ruined house.

Kate saw that some of the children were already heading for home where they would be ill-received because of the need to smarten up for the concert. She saw Tommy Leonard racing down to the towpath—it would be a bit quicker that way for him. Leonard's paper shop was near the big bridge, he would do the distance faster than by crossing over to the River Road where there was a proper surface to walk on. At Tommy's age children didn't mind having half their clothes and even bits of their arms torn and scratched by the thorny branches, Kate thought in wonder. Little Maggie Daly, who was Dara's great friend, was heading toward the laurels and Kate.

"Just running, Mrs. Ryan," Maggie said, knowing well that the twins' mother was not coming to pay a social call. "I think Dara and Michael are just finishing up now."

"I'm sure they are." Kate was grim. Maggie Daly had big anxious eyes; she always looked startled by the most ordinary things. She was terrified of Leopold, the pub's big harmless dog. When poor Leopold stretched his misshapen body in the sun, little Maggie Daly would look at him fearfully as if he were about to go for her throat.

And Maggie's older sister Kitty, who was nearly grown up enough for the crowd on the bridge, was sauntering down the laurel path too. Kitty was too mature to scuttle; she was being bored this summer, bored by Fernscourt and the games they played, bored by having to go home and dress up for the concert. Bored by being neither one thing nor the other. Neither a real person of fifteen who could have a smart red bathing costume and be able to sit on the raft having a crowd laughing and admiring; too old to find fun every day climbing up to an old room in a ruined clock tower, or squeezing through the chinks in the mossy walls. Kitty Daly sighed heavily as she passed Kate Ryan.

"I suppose you're coming to beat their heads in," she said as if this was the usual practice of elderly parents when they arrived in Fernscourt.

"Not at all," Kate said brightly, "I came to wonder was there anything they'd like, afternoon tea on a tray maybe, I'd be delighted to . . . my beloved twins . . ."

Kitty moved on hastily.

Dara and Michael had taken after their mother. No sandy brows like John Ryan—those only seemed to come out in Eddie. They were thin and wiry too, but of course their father had been as a boy. But Kate realized that in their strong dark good looks they didn't have the Ryan laugh lines either, the face that always seemed to smile even when nobody was watching. All the Ryans looked like that—even the disapproving old mother-in-law who hadn't thought Kate a suitable wife for her favorite son, she had had a face that seemed to smile. Dara and Michael often looked solemn, their eyes big, dark, and too concentrated. Like her own. Whenever Kate saw a photograph of herself she would scream and say she looked like the hag of Bearra or an avenging angel. She always seemed to be burning with intensity rather than smiling at the camera.

Nobody else noticed it at all.

And everyone always said the twins were a handsome pair, particularly in the summertime when, tanned and eager in their shorts and colored shirts, they roamed the countryside far and wide and explored every corner of Mountfern and its environs.

Kate wondered briskly how they would accept the blame today. They should have been home a good half hour ago to get smartened up for the school concert. She was annoyed but she would try not to show it, otherwise they would be mutinous about the washing and brushing and maybe less sure in their party pieces. Dara had a poem in Irish to recite and Michael with the boys from the brothers would be singing Moore's melodies.

Young Miss Lynch up at the school had been so enthusiastic and given so much of her free time to organizing it that everyone in Mountfern had been drawn into the whole thing unwillingly. Normally the convent and the brothers had few joint undertakings but old Canon Moran thought it seemed a much better notion to have one concert rather than two, and everyone agreed with them, so Nora Lynch had won the day; it was being held in the church hall and all participants had to be there in their finery at five o'clock. The concert began at six o'clock sharp and promised to be finished by eight.

Kate was nearly at the house now. In the old days it must have been an impressive place: three stories tall but with high, high ceilings, big rooms, and tall windows. The Fern family who had lived here, different generations of them for over a century, surely loved this home. Kate wondered if any of them had ever paused in their gracious way of life to imagine that one day it would be a ruin played in by all the children of the village who would never have gotten inside the walls except to carry scuttles of coal or great jugs of water in the old days.

The children had all scattered. Only her own two were inside. What could they be doing that made them stay when all the others had gone? A wave of annoyance came over Kate at their disregard for any kind of order in life. She pushed through the hanging wall of ivy and saw them: sitting on a great fallen pillar and looking ahead of them through the gaps in the wall.

They looked at something in the distance with a caution that was more like fear than anything else.

Below them two men with instruments mounted on tripods peered and wrote notes in their pads. Then they would replace the tripods and start again.

Kate came up behind the twins.

"What are they?" Michael asked in a whisper.

"They're called theodolites," Kate said. "I know that word, it's always very useful in crosswords."

"What do they do?" Dara wanted to know.

"It's a sort of survey, you know, getting levels. I'm not totally sure, to be honest."

"They shouldn't be here, the theodalists," Michael said, face red with upset. "Tell them it's private land. Go on Mam, tell them to go away."

"No, the things are called theodolites, not the people. The men are surveyors, I suppose. Anyway it isn't private land. If it was we couldn't be here."

"Could you ask them . . . like will they be coming back again or is it only today that they're doing their photographing or whatever? You could ask them, Mam," Dara pleaded. "You're good at asking people awkward things. Please."

"I have one awkward thing to ask at the moment and it's this: Why, when I gave you my good alarm clock and the strictest instructions to be back home at four o'clock, why is it half-past four and we're all here? That's the awkward question I'm asking today, and I want an answer to it."

The twins seemed not to hear the rising impatience in her tone; they barely heeded her.

"We didn't really play at all, we've been wondering what . . ." Dara said.

"And hoping that they'd go away . . ." Michael finished for her. They often finished each other's sentences.

"And not understanding it one bit . . ."

"And not liking it one bit . . ."

Kate took them by the shoulders and marched them back for the alarm clock and their uneaten lunches, then headed for the footbridge. There seemed to be a commotion on the other side. Eddie and Declan were lying on the edge of the water trying to reach something that was floating downstream on a piece of plywood.

Carrie, the new maid, was standing twisting her hands helplessly as the boys screamed, and Kate realized that Maurice the tortoise was heading off into the unknown.

"Get the garden rake, and the big broom," she shouted. Michael and Dara raced across to find them, delighted to be released from the pinching grip and abuse. Eddie, who was eight, was scarlet with the knowledge that he would get the blame; Declan was only six and the baby—he got off with everything.

Kate maneuvered the tortoise ashore and with a face like thunder brought it back to its original home in the mudroom. Watched by the four children and the terrified Carrie, she dried the animal with a clean towel and put it in a bed of hay. With a voice that was going to take no argument, she said that she would very much like to see Carrie at the kitchen sink washing the faces and hands of Eddie and Declan. She would like to see Michael and Dara in the bathroom and emerging in five minutes with necks, ears and knees all shining. She mentioned knees, ears and necks only because *particular* attention would be paid to those parts, but the rest was to be spotless too. A great deal of heavy scrubbing took place, and after inspection Dara and Michael were allowed to head off toward the hall. An unusually silent Eddie and Declan sat waiting sentence from their mother. They didn't know whether they were going to be barred from the concert . . . which mightn't be a bad thing. Or if there might be a slapping of the legs administered. The slapping wasn't too likely; if it was coming at all it would have been done at the time.

They were unprepared for the severity of it.

"That is no longer your tortoise, Edward and Declan. That is now my tortoise. Do you understand?"

Things were bad when Eddie was called Edward.

"But do you mean . . ."

"Yes, he's mine now. And I can do what I like with him. I can bring him back to the pet shop where I so stupidly bought him, thinking you were the kind of children who could love a pet. Or I could eat him. I could ask Carrie to serve him for lunch tomorrow."

They were aghast.

"Well, why not?" she continued airily. "You tried to drown Maurice, why don't I try to roast him? It's a hard old life being a tortoise."

Eddie's eyes filled with tears. "Ma, we weren't trying to drown him. It was to see if he could swim, and when he didn't seem to be managing it too well we got him a raft, then it floated off."

"Thank you, Edward. You are telling me it was just a careless accident, is that it?"

"Well, yes?" Eddie thought salvation lay this way but he wasn't totally sure.

"Right, well now that he's mine other careless accidents could happen. I could let him fall into the oven or something. Still, that is none of your business now. You are forbidden to go near him in the mudroom or near the stove or wherever else he happens to be."

Declan let out a roar. "Mammy, you wouldn't burn Maurice. Please don't burn my tortoise."

"It's mine," Kate said.

"You're not allowed to kill things," Eddie raged. "I'll tell the guards. I'll tell Sergeant Sheehan."

"Certainly do, and I'll tell him about the drowning."

There was a silence.

"Don't be stupid," Kate said. "I'm not going to hurt Maurice, but he *is* mine, you know, so you can't play with him anymore. And no ice creams in Daly's tonight after the concert."

It was bad but it was better than what might have been. They accepted it.

"Come on, Carrie," Kate said, suddenly pitying the seventeen-year-old spending her first Saturday night away from home. "Tidy up your hair a bit and we're off."

"Am I to come with you?" Carrie's face lit up.

"Of course you are. Did you think we'd leave you here on your own?" Kate had only just thought of it, looking at the stricken face of the girl as she had listened to the possible future of the tortoise.

"You're a real gentleman, Mam," said Carrie, and ran to put on a clean blouse and fix two new barrettes in her hair.

Canon Moran was small and fussy, a kind man with pale blue eyes that didn't see very far or very much. He believed that basically most people were very good. This made him a nice change from many other parish priests in the country who believed that most people were intrinsically evil. The word went around for young curates that Mountfern would be a great posting altogether. And the young priest Father Hogan knew he was indeed a lucky man. Once Canon Moran had a nice big chair for the concert and a little footstool because he sometimes got a cramp, then he would be happy. He would clap every item enthusiastically, he would praise all the brothers and the nuns by name, he would know that old Mr. Slattery the solicitor had made a contribution so that they could have proper curtains instead of the desperate old screens they used to make do with before. The canon would thank him briefly because that was all the Slatterys would need, but he would dwell longer on the generosity of Daly's Dairy in providing the cakes for the tea at eight o'clock, and the excellence of the programs printed free thanks to Leonard's the stationers. The canon began confessions on a Saturday at five, and he would make sure that they were all well completed in time for the concert. Father Hogan knew that Canon Moran believed a kind word of encouragement and a pious hope that things would be better soon helped a lot of his parishioners. And they felt sure, because of his pale dreamy blue eyes, that he was also somehow deaf and wouldn't recognize the voices that whispered their sins.

Father Hogan thought Mountfern was a warm, kind place to live, and though it didn't perhaps offer as much of a challenge as he had dreamed about in the seminary, he followed his canon's belief that there were souls to be saved everywhere, and that running a concert for the people of this place might have equal value in the great scheme of things to working in the missions or running a boys' club for delinquents in a tough city parish.

Miss Lynch was more or less walking out with young Mr. Slattery so he had to come to the concert as moral support. He sat beside Kate Ryan and the two chastened small boys, and the girl with reddened eyes called Carrie.

"And how does the master of your house escape this great cultural event?" Fergus Slattery asked with envy.

"Someone has to run the bar. I know it looks as if half the county is here, but you'd be surprised how many men find the excuse for a drink when their children are up here on the stage," Kate said.

"Well for him, then." Fergus was genuinely admiring. "I can't say that I have to work on a Saturday evening, they don't think solicitors work at all, but my office is too near. I'd actually have to be in the window in my shirt sleeves before they'd believe me."

Fergus grinned boyishly. He was very like a tall gangly boy, Kate thought, though he must be in his mid or late twenties now. She had always thought of him as a kind of irrepressible student home for the holidays. Even though he ran his father's office almost entirely on his own now, it was hard for her to think of him as a grown-up. Maybe it was because he looked untidy; his hair was sort of jutting out at an angle no matter whether he had been to the barber or not. His shirts were perfectly and lovingly ironed by the Slatterys' faithful housekeeper, Miss Purcell, yet the collars sometimes stood at an angle away from his neck.

Kate wouldn't be at all surprised if he bought the wrong size or had the button in the wrong place. He had dark eyes and if he had held himself differently and worn long smooth dark coats he might have been thought very handsome and elegant indeed.

But part of his charm was that he would never be elegant; he was totally unaware of his tall, dark and almost handsome looks, and that he had caused many a flutter and several specific hopes around Mountfern.

"You mean you wouldn't want to come—what with that Nora Lynch killing herself to impress you?" Kate was disbelieving.

"Impress *me*!"

"Of course. Why else would that young girl kill herself and show herself to be part of a small backwater like this unless it was to prove to you that she could fit in and be part of it?"

"But why would she prove that to me?"

"Aren't you and she going out?" Kate wondered about men a lot. They couldn't all be as dim as they often seemed.

"Yes, sure, we go out to the pictures and we go to a dance, but there's nothing in it." Fergus looked baffled and honest.

"What do you mean there's nothing in it, aren't you a right beast to be leading her on and then tell me there's nothing in it? You know, the older I get the more I believe the nuns were right; men are basically wild animals at heart."

"But there *is* nothing in it," Fergus pleaded. "I mean we don't love each other or anything, or have the same plans or the same hopes. Nothing's been said or agreed. Truly."

"I believe you." Kate was cynical. "O Lord, protect me or mine from ever falling for a lawyer. You'll have yourself covered from every angle."

"But she doesn't think . . ." Fergus began, but at that moment Nora Lynch, resplendent in a new hair do from the Rosemarie salon, in a new yellow dress short enough to be fashionable but not so short as to cause adverse comment from the canon, the nuns and the brothers, appeared on stage. She said she hoped everyone would enjoy this show, the first combined effort; she thanked the canon, the brothers, the convent and the sponsors, the children and the parents, and knew that everyone would have a wonderful evening. She said that as an outsider she felt very privileged to be allowed to get involved in something as much a part of the community as this was. But then in many ways she felt that she had always been part of this place and always would.

"How old are you, Fergus Slattery?" Kate whispered suddenly.

"I'm twenty-seven," he replied, confused.

"Twenty-seven years in the world and you try to tell me that young woman has no hopes of you. May God forgive you, I mean it, Fergus, may he forgive you and send you some kind of sense."

"Thanks, Kate," said Fergus, not knowing whether he was being attacked or pitied, and not liking it whichever it was.

Dara Ryan felt as if she had swallowed an ice cream whole; her stomach was cold and heavy and she wondered if she might be sick.

"I'll never be able to say it," she told Maggie Daly.

Maggie believed Dara could do anything. "You're great, Dara, you never minded saying it at school in front of everyone there."

"That's different." Dara hopped around on one leg and looked through the door that they were meant to keep firmly closed, to see how big the audience was.

"Lord, it's full of people," she said theatrically.

"They'll love it." Maggie was loyal.

Dara would have fought with her shadow at this stage. "No, they'll hate it, it's in Irish, they won't understand a word of it."

"But it will *sound* terrific."

"Why don't I just go and make sounds then, nice sounds, or better still take up a gong and just bang it for three minutes and bow to the applause?"

Maggie giggled. Things were all right once Dara started making up outlandish things.

Maggie was not doing any solo piece. She was in the girls' choir which would sing Gounod's "Ave Maria," and later on come back and sing "I think that I shall never see, a poem lovely as a tree." But Dara would stand in front of the whole of Mountfern and recite "Cill Cais" which Miss Lynch had told them was a lament for an old house, a ruin like Fernscourt, except that it had been a different kind of household who had lived there, an Old Catholic family who used to have mass said in the stately home and everyone would come from far and near to attend it.

"Dara, you're on."

Crossing her fingers and giving Dara a squeeze for luck, Maggie Daly stood and watched her friend walk up on the stage.

Miss Lynch, knowing very well that hardly anyone would get even the vaguest glimmer of what the poem was about without some kind of translation, said that of course everyone knew the story of "Cill Cais," and told it without appearing to. The audience, flattered to be thought of as people who would know this, nodded at each other sagely and waited for the young Ryan girl to tell it to them again in Irish. Dara's voice sounded confident and she fixed her eyes on the back of the hall as Miss Lynch had told her to do. There was a storm of clapping and people told each other that she made a very good fist of it, then she was off and it was time for the choir from the brothers.

Brother Keane had chosen three of Moore's finest Irish melodies. He announced that the boys would sing them in the same magnificent spirit that Thomas Moore had brought to bear when he was writing them. Brother Keane had calculated without the enormously humorous content that the songs seemed to hold for his choir of twelve-year-olds, depleted as it was by six whose voices chose the time of the concert to break.

"Silent, O Moyle, be the roar of thy water,
Break not, ye breezes, your chain of repose."

Brother Keane loved this above all other of Moore's melodies. He could see none of the allusions to breaking wind, pulling chains and passing water that the entire group in front of him seemed to see written in letters of fire on their song sheets. He glared at them ferociously as with the most enormous difficulty the forty boys tried to stifle their mirth, and led them into the next song called, unhappily, "The Meeting of the Waters." The entire choir seemed to choke with the daring double entendre of the name and Brother Keane resolved to deal with them very sternly in a less public place.

The admission price had included tea, sandwiches and cakes. The sandwiches had been supervised by Mrs. Whelan who ran the Post Office and was generally accepted to be the nicest person in Mountfern. A small wiry woman with a skin that seemed to have been tanned by whatever sun shone intermittently in the Irish midlands or beaten by the winds that blew more regularly from one coast across to the other, Sheila Whelan had three cameo brooches she had bought from a tinker: a pink one, a green one and a beige. She wore them at the neck of her white blouses and had done for as long as anyone could remember. She owned about three skirts which she must have worn forever and a series of soft knitted cardigans which she must have made herself. Usually she was knitting for someone else, for the new babies that were arriving with great regularity around Mountfern, or shawls for the old, even school jumpers for the children who might need them. She always managed to have an extra bit of wool which she said it would be a pity to waste. She had a kind, dreamy face and far-away pale blue eyes that were never known to concentrate inquisitively on anything that might not bear too much scrutiny.

She seemed to have no interest in the private lives of the rest of the parish: she never appeared to notice, let alone comment on the emigrants' remittances that came home or didn't come home; nor did she seem to notice the disability pensions for people who were perfectly well, or the dole for those who were obviously working. She was able to discuss the most direct questioning about the whereabouts of Mr. Whelan with calm and even with interest, but without ever revealing that he had left her for a married woman in Dublin, and that the two of them now had four children. If anyone asked whether he was coming back, Mrs. Whelan was always able to get into the same interrogative mood and say it was very hard to know, wasn't it? She found that some things were almost impossible to work out, weren't they? And somehow the questioner found himself or herself enmeshed in the Meaning of Life instead of the specific whereabouts of Mrs. Whelan's husband.

She was the kind of woman you'd go to if you had committed a murder, Fergus Slattery had always said. And oddly, there was one killing near Mountfern. A farmer's son had attacked his father in a drunken fight and killed him. It was to the post office, not the presbytery or the Garda station that he had come, carrying the murder weapon, a pitchfork.

Mrs. Whelan had involved the presbytery and the Garda station, but gently and in her own time. Nobody had thought it even remotely unusual that the demented man had come to Mrs. Whelan nor had she made anything of the incident; she said she supposed he was on his way to the canon and her light had been on.

Nobody knew, either, that it was Mrs. Whelan who had encouraged the sandwich makers to cut the crusts off and to do just one plate each. That way she was sure of getting what everyone had promised, though it meant much more work for her. Fergus knew, because Miss Purcell had been fussing about whether to have chicken salad or egg and mayonnaise in her offering and this had meant at least three calls to Mrs. Whelan for discussion.

"You are the only sensible woman in this town, Mrs. Whelan," he began.

"What can I do for you, Fergus?" she asked simply.

"You mean I wouldn't say it unless I wanted something?"

"Not at all." But she waited.

"Is my name up with Nora Lynch?" he asked.

"Why do you ask?" she said.

"Because Kate Ryan, a woman I like and respect, told me it was, and as true as the day is long I didn't mean it to be."

"Well if there's any misunderstanding I'm sure you'll sort it out."

"But *is* there any misunderstanding, Mrs. Whelan? That's what I'm asking you. I don't want to go sorting things out if there's nothing to sort out."

"Ah, nobody tells me anything, Fergus."

"But I'm only asking you about *me*, not about other people."

"As I said, I've not got an idea in the wide world, but I know if you think that there's some confusion you'd be the man to clear it up. One way or another."

"By saying something out straight, you mean? Like 'I don't want to marry you'?"

Mrs. Whelan's eyes were shuttered. Open but closed at the same time. They told him he had gone too far in his revelations. That she expected a solicitor to be even more discreet than a postmistress.

"Other people go to you with their business, Fergus, you're as much in demand now as your father, and that's your job after all. If there's a need for the right words you'll find them."

"You'd have been great as a prisoner of war, Mrs. Whelan," said Fergus. "The secrets would have been safe with you all right."

Fergus and Nora went for a drive after the concert. The last thank yous and congratulations had been said; people walked home in the sunny early summer evening. The older children had gone to sit on the bridge. The cinema had a special late start, so many of them headed to the pictures. Fergus had the car out ready and waiting. Nora Lynch came running over to join him.

Small and slightly plump, she had the perfect skin and apple cheeks of a picture poster. Her fair hair was curled carefully, and she wore a little lipstick but not enough to do any damage.

"I thought we might go up on the hill," he said as Nora put on her white jacket with the little yellow trim which matched her dress so well.

"The hill?" She was surprised.

"It's a nice quiet place to talk, and I have something I want to say to you."

Nora's eyes lit up with pleasure and her face was pink. "I'd love that," she said in a sort of husky way, not in her usual voice at all.

With a sickening lurch of his stomach Fergus realized that this pleasant, empty-headed, chirruping little teacher whom he had kissed a dozen times thought that he was about to propose marriage to her.

Slowly he started the car and headed for the hills.

Two

*R*yan's Licensed Premises, like any other pub in Ireland in 1962, had a steady clientele that would never desert it. There never seemed to be any need to do renovations to attract new trade. The trade was there, like it had been in John's father's time; the people who lived on that side of Mountfern found it handy to call in rather than walk all the way down to the center. Ryan's had the great advantage, some thought, of being on the outskirts. The whole place didn't see you going in and coming out as they would if you visited Foley's, Conway's or Dunne's.

When John's father was alive the place still sold groceries but though the big old chest of tea drawers still stood there they held no stock now. There was a little huckster's shop run by Loretto Quinn, whose husband had been killed in a terrible accident. It wouldn't have been right for the Ryans to take the bread from her mouth even if they wanted to get back into the grocery business. And anyway most people liked going into Mountfern proper and walking along Bridge Street to see what was going on. Ryan's was a bit out of the way in terms of doing your weekly shopping.

John Ryan was glad that Kate agreed with him on this. For a Dublin woman she had adapted extraordinarily well to Mountfern; she knew better than he did all that went on, who was speaking and who not. It was Kate who helped the children with their homework, found and trained the girls from the country who would leave for brighter lights and noisier towns once they knew the way to run a house. Kate served behind the bar as if she had been born to do it. She knew when to join in the conversation and when to stay far from it.

She polished glasses and cleaned the big ashtrays with Gold Flake printed around the rim. She loved the words Whiskey Bonder on the sign over the door, even though it wasn't true anymore. John's father, like many a publican, used to buy whiskey in a cask from the distiller, lodge it in a bonded warehouse and pay the excise duty when he took it from the warehouse for bottling and sale. In those days the name James Ryan was on the bottle, but nowadays distillers discouraged such fancy and old-fashioned notions. They preferred to sell whiskey already bottled. But Kate would still polish the sign lovingly, getting up on a ladder early in the morning with a soapy cloth, a wet cloth and a dry cloth.

She was the same behind the bar, she shined the bar decorations as if they were precious ornaments. A lot of pubs had the mock Staffordshire figures of a hurler and a footballer standing on a plinth, dressed in the colors of the particular county. Underneath it said, "On all grounds, Players Please." Kate had explained the puns to the twins as John had marveled. He had looked at the thing a thousand times and never even noticed the words and what they meant. Fine that for a man who thought himself a poet.

And Kate had been great about that too. She never came up with any talk about what did a fat, country pub owner think he was doing rambling away in verse. Far from it, she would sit at his knee and ask him to read what he had written. Sometimes her head rested on his lap, and she would sigh in appreciation or else she might question it and ask what image was in his mind. She had long dark curly hair and very dark brown eyes, almost black. She never grudged the time he spent up in their bedroom trying to write—and trying it often was. She minded the bar happily, only suggesting that John should be there at set times like for the lunchtime trade and for the time when they had the half-past-six news on Radio Eireann, and the customers would expect the man of the house to be present to serve their pints and comment on the day's events.

John Ryan was not a great man for formal prayers. Mass time was spent as near the back of the church as possible; in summertime right out in the open air and in thoughts not connected with the actual liturgy taking place. But he did offer prayers of thanks to somewhere, that he had met Kate. He could so easily have not met her. Suppose Jack Coyne's had not been closed that time when she came in with the puncture, suppose the puncture had happened eleven miles on down the road—they'd have gone to the big town instead. Suppose she had been traveling with a girl who could mend a puncture instead of that giggling friend of hers, who could hardly ride a bike.

All these things were too much to think about. Like the really black bit after John had seized his chance and arranged to meet Kate again and again, and his mother had said that he was to bring no flighty Dublin girl into this pub, the business belonged to the whole family. John had nearly upped and off at that stage, but Kate had begged him to be understanding. What did the poor old mother mean except that she was afraid of losing him like she had lost her husband and all the rest of her family, two sons priests and far away, two daughters nuns and even farther away in Australia, and the other two sons in America without a notion of coming back.

Kate said he should be patient, sit it out. Old Mrs. Ryan would come around in time: in the meantime Kate would learn the bar trade in Dublin. And learn it she did, dropping her good salary as a secretary in a firm of solicitors and becoming a maid of all work in a small hotel so that she could become accustomed to working the bar.

By the time Mrs. Ryan had mellowed, Kate knew all she would need to know about serving a ball of malt, a half one, a black and tan, and a half. She knew when a customer had too much and when to cash a check or start a tab. They had been married quietly. It was 1948, there wasn't much money about and not many relations either. John's mother was there, face sour, clothes black, but at least she was there.

Kate had no family at all. Her mother had died after a life of martyrdom and self-pity. Her father had married again and believed that his new wife had been slighted by everyone, so went nowhere. No amount of persuasion would make them come to her wedding, so Kate O'Connell stood with four friends including Lucy, the girl who couldn't mend punctures either, and married John Francis Ryan, sandy-haired, plump poet who had to run his family pub to please his mother and then to continue running it after his mother's time to keep his wife and four children.

Kate told him that she thanked God for him too. Yes, seriously, when she prayed at night as she always did on her knees for three or four minutes no matter how great his need and desire for her.

"You can say your prayers afterwards," he used to beg.

"Not at all, I'll fall asleep in your arms afterwards," she would reply.

But she assured him she thanked God for his honesty and his kindness and the marvelous way he had of looking at things, and for the four marvelous children. She, who had nobody for so long, had everybody who mattered now. Outsiders said they were well matched but they had no idea how well.

Nobody watching the quick Kate and the slower John as they smiled at each other across their busy public house would know how much they needed each other and relied one on the other for the qualities that they each lacked. Probably the men might have thought that the youngest of old Ryan's sons did well for himself getting this handsome city girl to liven up his business. Possibly the women in Mountfern might have said that Kate O'Connell, who came in one day on a bicycle and seemed to have no people to speak of, fell on her feet marrying into Ryan's pub. But this was to miss the point.

Kate, uncertain of herself in so many ways, unsure that she had a place anywhere, was more aware than anyone would suspect of how she had found a home and a base and an anchor in the reliable John Ryan. She knew he would never change and cease to love her, as her father had. She knew she didn't have to act out a role to please and entertain him as she had done to everyone else in the world since she was fourteen. She had got by through being brisk—and sometimes she knew that she was too brisk, she left the children bewildered and bothered, and only John could make the world seem sensible to them again.

Kate marveled at the time and patience John had with their children, how he could sit for what seemed like forever on the bank of the river with them, making them as still as he was himself to lure the fish out of the water. Only the other day he had them all—even Declan, who never stopped moving around—transfixed over the workings of the old clock which he had taken to bits and put back together. He told them stories of the Fern family who lived over the river, tales of long ago, since John Ryan never knew the house when it stood. The twins would listen forever to how the provisions might come up the river by boat.

"How would they get them up to the house?" Dara had asked and her father had led the children out to the footbridge and they had all stood speculating what way the great boxes would have been carried up to the mansion. All this when he should have been seeing to the barrels and getting the pub ready for opening.

But Kate loved him for it, and sometimes she wanted to go over and put her arms around his neck and kiss him full on the lips to tell him how much she loved him and how good he was. Not only to his children and to her, but to the old farmer who would tell the same story twice a day. John could nod and polish a glass and hear it again and again. Kate sometimes got a lump in her throat as she watched his patience and his respect for people, for all kinds of people.

She felt a tenderness and love for him that was just as strong as any love you saw in the pictures where she sometimes went on a little outing with Sheila Whelan as a treat. But she didn't show that love too openly. Mountfern wasn't a place where endearments were used openly. There were no darlings or loves or dears used in Ryan's pub. They accused each other good-humoredly of all kinds of failings. . . .

"My wife would spend the takings of the year if you didn't watch her . . . all women are exactly the same."

"John, would you ask Mrs. Connolly there would she like a drop more lemonade in her port? A man wouldn't notice your drink, Mrs. Connolly. If it wasn't a pint or a glass of whiskey he wouldn't know how to handle it."

But together, alone together, they knew they had something that a lot of people didn't have. That their own parents certainly didn't come anywhere near having. And they determined on the day that the twins were born that no child of this new family would grow up in a house of uncertainty and loneliness like the young John and the young Kate in the dark days. Money was not important to either of them but recently they had realized that four children did not live off the air and neither were shoes, schoolbags, dentists' bills, notebooks, winter coats, more shoes, text books, to be found growing in the rushes along the river bank.

One of the reasons they had gotten the young country girl to come in was because Kate was going to get a job. She had discussed it with Fergus Slattery last night after the concert and he had said there was no reason she couldn't start right away. With office experience in Dublin, with day-to-day experience of balancing the books in a business, she would be perfectly qualified to help in the solicitor's office. Kate Ryan was known not to be a teller of other people's business. This was most important of all.

She was looking forward to the whole business of going out to work. The children did not share her enthusiasm.

"Does this mean we're poor?" Dara wanted to know.

"Of course, we're not poor," Kate snapped. It was hard enough to find something that would look smart for going out to an office from all her shabby clothes in the bedroom cupboard without having to answer questions like this.

"Well why are you going out to work for a living then?"

"In order to keep you and your brothers in leather shoes which you will kick to bits, to buy nice schoolbags that you'll lose and a few things like that." Kate looked without any pleasure at what she had always thought of as a smart green two-piece and which now turned out to be a crumpled, faded rag.

"Will we have to sell the pub?" Michael was behind her, always the more anxious of the two. His eyes seemed troubled.

"Lord, not at all, what has the pair of you so worried?" Kate softened her tone.

"You look very upset, you keep frowning," Michael said.

"Oh that's only because my clothes look like a lot of jumble."

The other two children had come to join in. It wasn't usual to find a council of war upstairs on a summer evening; Eddie and Declan had come to investigate.

"Are you afraid of looking like Miss Barry?" Eddie asked. Kate looked at him. Miss Barry was the elderly alcoholic who lived in the presbytery and passed by the dignified title of Priest's Housekeeper. In fact she was there because of the goodness of the canon, who couldn't bear to turn her out on the roads. For long periods of time Miss Barry didn't touch a drop and was a sober if rather erratic worker, cooking and cleaning for the two priests. When she did go on a tear it was an almighty one. At no stage did she ever look like anyone Kate would wish to be compared to.

"Thank you, Edward," she said.

"What have I said?" Eddie wailed.

The twins felt the conversation was degenerating, as it usually did when Eddie came into it.

"We'll be off now." Dara was lofty.

"We'll leave Eddie with you, Mam," Michael said. He could see an awful clinging look in Eddie's face that meant he wanted to come with them.

"The last thing I want is any of you with me." Kate rummaged deeper. She had to have something that looked like what a person wore in an office.

"It's a free country," Eddie said, his face red with fury. "I can go anywhere I like in Mountfern, anywhere. You can't stop me."

"It shouldn't be a free country," Dara said, "not if it means Eddie's free to go wherever he likes."

"Go away from me," Kate cried. "And Declan, if you set one foot outside this door you are not going to like what happens to you."

"Why isn't it a free country for me?" Declan asked. Not very hopefully.

"Because you're the baby," Dara said.

"Not that so much. It's because you're six. Six-year-olds, in places with rivers in them, stay at home at night." Kate smiled at his round cross face.

"Will we have another baby?" he suggested.

"We will not, thank you," Kate said firmly.

Dara and Michael giggled at this, and Eddie was put out because he felt there was something else he was being kept out of.

"What am I going to do? It's ages before it gets dark," Declan complained.

Kate was going to give in over the tortoise and let him have visiting rights to the mudroom where the tortoise was going to live under her sole control. But it was too soon, they wouldn't realize the seriousness of the near drowning if she weakened so quickly.

"Why don't you go and teach Leopold some tricks?" she suggested, not very hopefully. You couldn't teach Leopold any tricks. He had joined the household when he was found with a broken leg and a poor bark by Jack Coyne in the back of a truck, and when nobody had claimed him, the Ryans saved him from being put in a sack by Jack Coyne and meeting a watery death.

Leopold's bark had never improved significantly, he did have a plaintive yowl, but Jaffa, the huge orange cat who had a purr like thunder, would have been a greater source of alarm to any burglar than the lame and silent Leopold. But there weren't burglaries or crimes like that in Mountfern. Sergeant Sheehan was always proud to say that people in his place didn't have to lock their doors at night.

Leopold was more of an indulgence than a watchdog.

"Teach him some tricks?" Declan was astounded.

"You couldn't even teach Leopold to walk straight, Mam." This was undeniable.

"You could exercise Jaffa in the garden," she offered.

"We don't have a garden."

"We do. I call it a garden, you call it a yard. Go on, Jaffa would love a bit of exercise."

"Will I make her do handstands?" Declan was interested now. Kate realized this had been a wrong road to travel down. She would never find anything to wear, she would spend the rest of the evening wondering if the big orange cat's back would be broken.

"Sit in the garden until it's dark . . . tell Jaffa to come toward you and then go to the other end of the garden and ask her to come back," she told Declan.

"That's a very dull thing to do. There's no point in spending the evening doing that," Declan complained.

"You'll find as you grow older there's a lot of things you'll spend morning, noon and night doing that there's no point in," Kate said, holding a blue houndstooth skirt up to the light. It looked so respectable there must be a reason why it was not to the fore in her meager selection.

"When I'm old I'll have a great time," Declan said wistfully. "I'll have bags of potato chips for every meal and I'll stay out all night until even eleven o'clock if I feel like it."

His small round face looked sadly out the window at Dara and Michael racing off down River Road, and at Eddie, hands in pockets, striding across the footbridge.

Kate Ryan had discovered the fatal flaw, a broken zipper and a triangular rip where she had caught it on a door handle.

"Maybe half-past eleven," Declan said, looking at her sideways to show that he was a person of no half measures when it came to long-term plans for the future.

It was a bright warm evening. Eddie looked at the men with the clipboards and instruments.

"What are you doing?" he asked them.

"A survey."

"What's that?"

"Making a measurement of the land."

"Why haven't you got a ruler, then?"

They looked at each other. Eddie was small and sandy and tousled-looking. He was like a caricature of a Troublesome Boy.

"We managed without one," one of the men said.

"Is it a game, like guessing the weight of a cake?"

"A bit more scientific I hope."

"Who wants to know how wide it is?"

"The fellow who's going to buy it."

"There's someone going to live in there?" Eddie looked up at the ruined Fernscourt in amazement.

"That would appear to be what it's about all right."

"God, isn't he lucky," Eddie said with feeling. "I'd love to live in a place like that with no roof, and no floors and no wiping your feet."

* * *

Dara and Michael went first to Loretto Quinn's for sweets. Mam had always said to give Loretto the turn, toffees were the same price there as everywhere, but Loretto would appreciate it.

The twins thought they must be her only customers for Scots Clan. The jar showed no signs of any other takers. She weighed out the two ounces and gave them an apple each free.

"We couldn't," Dara said. A polite and meaningless protest since Michael had already sunk his teeth in his.

"Ah go on, don't I get them for nothing," Loretto said.

This was not strictly true; she got them from an old man, Papers Flynn, a tramp of sorts who had encircled Mountfern all his life. He lived by picking fruit from low-hanging boughs or feeling gently into the soft nesting places that contrary hens used to find for themselves far from their rightful quarters. Sometimes he offered these as gifts to shopkeepers, who gave him a cheese sandwich or a mug of tea in return.

"Fierce activity across the river: fellows with cameras on long stilts," Loretto said conversationally.

She liked the twins, full of chat without being cheeky. Their young brother Eddie was a different kettle of fish.

"They're theologists," Dara said confidently.

"Or something a bit like that." Michael was a stickler for getting things right.

"Maybe they're going to make a film." Loretto was hopeful. "Like *Quiet Man* all over again, wouldn't it be great?"

Dara didn't smile. "I think it's something to do with changing it all over there, someone buying it and making it different."

"We'll let you know if we find out anything," Michael said.

Loretto stood at the doorway of her shabby little shop and watched the twins as they headed for the bridge and the heart of Mountfern.

People used to say that if you bent your head to light a cigarette on the main road you'd miss the two signs to Mountfern and that even if you did see one of the signs and drive off the road through the semi-circle that led down Bridge Street to the River Fern and then back up River Road to the main road again you would wonder what kind of a place it was that you had been through.

One street, Bridge Street, more or less petered out at the bridge where the church was. The road got narrow across the bridge, and went off meandering to the various townlands and small farms. Bridge Street looked well when the sun shone on the different pastel colors of the houses and shops that fronted right onto the road. Some of them were whitewashed still like Judy Byrne's house and Conway's, the place that was both undertaker and pub. Others were pink like Leonard's the stationers and paper shop, like Meagher's the small jewelry shop where watches and clocks were mended and gifts were displayed in boxes with cellophane fronts. Daly's Dairy was a very bright lime green. Mrs. Daly had been very pleased with the color, and was flattered when Fergus Slattery said they would all have to wear sunglasses now to cope with the sudden brightness that radiated from its walls.

There were some houses that didn't have coats of paint on them. Like old Mr. Slattery's tall house with the steps going up to it, which was covered with ivy. And the Garda barracks was just stone, as was the presbytery. The Classic Cinema had once been a smart beige color but it had gotten very shabby-looking, with paint peeling off. Mr. Williams, who was the rector-in-charge of the small Protestant church, had a cottage that was all covered with climbing roses—his wife spent from dawn to dusk gardening. To the outsider Mountfern looked a slow sleepy place, badly planned, straggling toward a river, but not having any real purpose.

It had been an estate village, of course, a collection of small holdings which all depended on the big house. The days of a community depending on one family seat for livelihood and living quarters were long gone. But Mountfern had not died with the house.

The farmers would always need somewhere to send their children to school, and shops where their wives could sell vegetables, eggs and poultry, where they could buy the essentials without having to travel to the big town, sixteen miles down the main road.

The visitor might have thought Mountfern a backwater but there were few visitors to have such thoughts. It hadn't anything to offer to the sightseer; you had to have some reason to come to Mountfern, otherwise you would think it was a place where nothing happened at all.

Dara and Michael Ryan never thought of Mountfern like that. It was the center of their world and always had been. They hardly ever left it except to go to the town maybe four times a year. They had been to Dublin of course, with the school on educational tours, and once with Dad and Mam when they were very young and there had been an excursion to see Santa Claus in the various Dublin shops. Eddie always resented hearing about this excursion and wanted to know why it hadn't been repeated for the rest of the family.

"Because Santa Claus would vomit if he saw you," Dara had explained.

This evening, however, they had forgotten what a thorn in the flesh their younger brother Eddie was. They were setting out with a purpose. To find out what was happening to Fernscourt. They had seen the men with the measuring instruments but had not wanted to ask them straight out—it was almost too direct. They felt without actually saying it to each other that they would find out what was the collective view first. Then armed with this knowledge they would face the people that Loretto thought were making a version of *The Quiet Man* (a tamer version, the scenery in this part of the Irish midlands wasn't spectacular and there were very few Maureen O'Haras around the place).

They passed Coyne's Motor Works before they got to the bridge. Jack was working as he always seemed to be, day and night, a cigarette hanging out of his mouth.

The twins had heard their father say that it was the mercy of God that Jack Coyne hadn't set himself alight with all the petrol and oil around the place, and that one day he could well blow the whole of Mountfern sky high with his dangerous practices. Dara and Michael didn't like Mr. Coyne much, he always looked as if he were about to have a fight with someone. He was old of course, nearly as old as Mam and Dad, small and pointed looking. He wasn't married, and he always said that a man who voluntarily took on a wife to nag the life out of him, and spend all he earned, was a man on whom no sympathy should be wasted. Dara had once said to him that if everyone had felt the way he did, the world would have come to an end long ago. Jack Coyne said that everyone might have been better off if it had, and let Dara remember that when she grew up and her head got full of nonsense about love and the like.

"Good evening Mr. Coyne." It didn't matter that he might be an old grouch, they still had to be polite and salute him.

"Out gallivanting," he said disapprovingly. "Still I hear that they've big plans for Fernscourt. That'll put a halt to your gallop, the lot of you."

"What plans?" The twins ignored the gratuitous offense; they had never done anything to irritate Jack Coyne.

To his own immense annoyance Jack Coyne didn't know what plans were afoot. Those fellows doing a survey had been far from forthcoming. But he had his own views.

"A big religious house I hear, so that's the end of all the trick-playing by the children of this parish, I'm glad to say. You'll have to start to do a day's work for a change and be like we were at your age."

"Is it brothers or nuns would you say?"

"That would be telling," said Jack Coyne, who didn't know.

"Isn't he a pig?" Dara said cheerfully when they had left him. "A small dark offensive-looking pig."

"Imagine him young," Michael said, as they passed the bag of toffees between them. It was a feat of imagination too difficult for either of them.

"An offensive piglet," Michael said, and they were in a fit of giggles by the time they reached the bridge and turned left up the main street.

There would be no place for Dara and Michael on the bridge, even Kitty Daly was a bit too young for the small group that met there in the evenings. They saw fellows sitting up on the stone parapet clowning, and a group of girls laughing. There was Teresa Meagher whose mother and father were always fighting. If you went past Meagher's any night when the shop was closed you always heard voices raised. Teresa was going to get a job in Dublin it was always being said, but then her parents would cry and cling on to her so she had to relent and stay. Nobody on the bridge was courting. If you were courting you were down the river bank, or in Coyne's wood, or at the pictures.

Devotions were over and Father Hogan was closing up the church. He waved at Michael.

"Any hope you'd be able to sing *Panis Angelicus*?" he said without much confidence.

"No Father, sorry Father, I haven't a note in my head," Michael said.

"Come on out of that, you were in the choir at the concert. Why don't you . . ."

"No Father, I can't sing, and anyway you'd never know what might happen to my voice." Michael had been dying for his voice to break like Tommy Leonard's had. Every morning he tried it out and was disappointed that it still sounded the same.

Dara was no help. "You should hear him singing from the bathroom, Father, he'd have the tears in your eyes."

"I'll kill you," Michael said.

"Well I'm certainly not going to beg and cajole you." Father Hogan was huffy now. "I didn't think a Catholic boy would have to be flattered and pleaded with to sing in the House of God."

Dara realized she had gone too far.

"I was only saying that to tease him, Father. Really and truly he'd be no good, he'd embarrass you, it's like an old tin can. I know he would sing if he could, but he's just in the choir to make up the numbers for Brother Keane, to sort of fill the stage up a bit."

Father Hogan said that was all right then.

"Now." Dara was triumphant. "Didn't I rescue you?"

"You needn't have gone on so much." Michael hadn't enjoyed being described as an old tin can that would embarrass you. There were times when Dara felt the need to give far too many explanations. They had reached Tommy Leonard's house. The stationery shop was closed for business so the twins knocked at the door beside the shop. Tommy was there to greet them, his finger on his lips. Behind him a voice called.

"Where are you going, Thomas?"

"Just out for a bit of a walk."

"All right, but be back at nine o'clock, and no giggling and playing with all that crowd of hooligans."

"Right oh." Tommy was good-natured. It was easier not to bring the whole thing down around your ears with a catechism of questions. That was Tommy Leonard's view. Just say yes and no, don't get involved in long explanations. Michael thought he was dead right; if he had desperate parents like Tommy's he would be exactly the same. Dara thought that this was entirely the wrong way to handle things, and if she were Tommy she would make it all clear from the word go, instead of giving in to all the cracked notions. That only made them come up with more cracked notions still.

Maggie Daly said they were to wait until she showed Dara the gorgeous yellow dress that had arrived in the parcel from America. There were often parcels from America for all of them. Not as many as years back, when Mountfern was poorer maybe, and American uncles and aunts more generous, or postage cheaper. An American parcel was a rarity nowadays. Mrs. Daly probably would say nothing about it and its contents, but Maggie was so excited by the yellow net that she couldn't wait to show it off.

The bad thing was that Kitty was in the bedroom.

Kitty yawned when Dara came in. "Going to try on the yellow are you?"

"Well look at it anyway," Dara said. Kitty was a pain.

"Not at all, you're coming to try it on. Half of Mountfern will pass through here trying it on, I can see that. The room will be full of people in vests and knickers bursting into the yellow dress."

"Are you going to wear it?" Dara asked Maggie, deliberately ignoring the elder girl.

"I don't think so." Maggie was pleased to be consulted.

"You see it's a bit low-necked, and it's a bit big, I'm kind of lost in it. And it's so gorgeous it would be a pity to cut it down for me. Wasting so much material, you see." Her face showed her longing for the yellow satin with an overskirt of yellow net, and with yellow embroidery and sequins on the bodice. It was like something you'd see in the pictures; it was far too old for them in one way, and yet it was a girlish-looking dress with big puff sleeves. Dara was dying to put it on but she wouldn't give Kitty the satisfaction of watching her.

"You wouldn't have to get much taken out of it, Maggie, wouldn't Miss Hayes do a great job on it?" Miss Hayes did some dressmaking in Mountfern but had never been let loose on exotic fabric like this, to their knowledge.

Kitty was lying on her bed reading the life story of Helen Shapiro who had managed to escape from childhood by having a voice that took her into the hit parade. She'd never have escaped if she had been born in Mountfern, Kitty Daly thought darkly.

"It would look ridiculous on Maggie, no matter what Miss Hayes did to it. That's a dress that needs a chest. Maggie hasn't got a chest to put into it."

"None of us has a chest to put into it yet," Dara cried with spirit. "While we're waiting we could put a rolled-up pair of socks. Like you often do, Kitty Daly."

"You told her!" Kitty's face was dark red with rage, and she looked menacingly at Maggie.

"I didn't know!" Maggie was transparently honest and terrified.

"Come on, Maggie, let's leave Kitty the room to herself, we're only in the way." Dara felt it was time to escape. They hung up the yellow dress carefully and pulled back the transparent plastic cover that came with it. It was the most beautiful thing they had ever seen. They envied the cousin of the Dalys somewhere in America who had worn it to her Junior Prom. Whatever a Junior Prom might be.

They were going to the Protestant graveyard at the top of the town. Nobody would disturb them there. Mr. Williams the vicar had realized that the children didn't tear around playing hide and seek among the headstones, there was no disrespect to the graves of the various members of the Fern family and the rest of the small Protestant community hereabouts.

It was a peaceful place for the children to come and talk. Mr. and Mrs. Williams had no children of their own, they were indulgent with the children of others.

Up Bridge Street the little band walked slowly. They looked wistfully at the Classic which was showing *The Glass Mountain*. Imagine having the money and freedom just to drop in to the pictures whenever you wanted to.

"We'll be able to do that when we're old," Dara said.

Tommy Leonard didn't think so; he thought being old was going to be more of the same.

They looked into Conway's grocery and pub. At the back, hidden away, they saw the feet of three drinkers in the discreet bar area. They often had a game guessing whose feet they were.

They never tried to play this game in any other pub since anyone who drank in Foley's or Dunne's, or indeed in Ryan's itself, did so openly. It was only in Conway's that they pretended not to be there.

Beyond Conway's was Dr. White's and they called there for Liam and Jacinta. That was it for tonight; some of the other children they played with lived out in the countryside, and others weren't allowed out to wander in the evenings. There were some boys who were up at the brothers' in the football field and there were some girls who had to help in their houses, or who had been bad and therefore denied the night's outing.

The six went to the graveyard and sat on a tombstone which they particularly liked.

It was the memorial for a William James Fern who had died in 1881 at Majuba Hill in the Transvaal, aged eighteen. It was during the Boer War they knew that, and he had been fighting for the British against the Dutch in South Africa.

"It was a long way to go," Maggie Daly often said.

"I suppose he wanted to get away." Tommy Leonard could understand it only too well.

Dara had never understood it.

"What did he want to go off and fight in other people's wars for? If he was a Mountfern man then, why wasn't he here having a great time? And if he was eighteen he could have done what he liked. Think of it, he could have gone to the Classic every night." She looked at their faces. "That is if the Classic was there in the 1880s, which I don't think it was."

But tonight they didn't talk long about the dead William James who fell at Majuba Hill. Tonight they talked about what was going to happen to William James's old home. What was happening in Fernscourt.

They were not alone, this little group, in their speculations. If they could have seen into every house down Bridge Street and along River Road they would have come across conversations on the same theme.

Over in Foley's Bar at the top of the town old Matt Foley and his friends said that there was oil sighted there. Some fellow had pulled a pike from the fern and his gills were full of oil. So the drilling would start any day now.

Next door to Foley's, in her neat little house, Judy Byrne the physiotherapist sat with Marian Johnson whose family owned the Grange, a country house which took guests of a superior type and even arranged hunting for them. They were women of around the same age, one side or the other of forty, not married and not likely to find any husbands at this stage of their lives in this part of the country. Neither ever admitted that to the other.

They had heard that Fernscourt was going to be an agricultural college, which would be very good news indeed as it would mean lectures and all kinds of talent not seen in these parts before. While saying that the people would probably be quite unspeakable they were having a small sherry to celebrate.

Seamus Sheehan in the Garda barracks was taking a lot of abuse from his wife. Why had he heard nothing about Fernscourt? Everyone else in the place had some view on what was happening. There was no point in being married to the sergeant if he was the one man in the whole country who seemed to be too remote as to inquire what was going on in his own back yard.

Next to the barracks Jimbo Doyle lived with his mother. Jimbo's mother had heard that the new place had been bought by an order of contemplative nuns. They would have a grille on the window and pull it back so that one nun, the Reverend Mother, would be able to address the outside world. When it was necessary, which would not be often.

Jimbo's mother told him that they would need a reliable man around the place, and that he should get in quick before someone else did.

Jimbo, whose idea of opportunities in life did not include being a reliable handyman to an order of contemplative nuns, asked what his mother expected him to do. Write to the pope, or just the bishop saying he was the man? His mother said he should be glad that someone in the family was looking to the practical side of things instead of singing raucous songs and laughing loud laughs.

In Paddy Dunne's pub all talk of emigration to Liverpool to the brother's pub had stopped. This was now the hub of the universe. Paddy Dunne had it from one of the traveling salesmen who came in trying to get him to take biscuits. Biscuits in a pub! Anyway this man knew all about Fernscourt: it was an agricultural research place. Foreigners were going to come and test soil and plants and the place was going to be a boom town as a result of it. The smart man would expand now or expand a little and then sell when prices were going up. It provided hours of speculation.

Sheila Whelan sat in the comfortable sitting room behind the post office and listened to a concert on Radio Eireann. She loved all that Strauss music and it didn't sweep her into a world of people waltzing in Vienna; instead it reminded her for some reason of the first time she had come to Mountfern with Joe Whelan. He had taken her to Coyne's wood which was full of bluebells. Literally carpeted with them. They had picked armfuls of them and Joe had told her that he loved music and that he would take her to concerts. He told her lots of things. Sheila lay back in her chair, tired. She knew a bit more about Fernscourt than the others because the telegrams all came through her post office. But she didn't know it all. She sighed and wondered what the changes would mean.

Across the road in the Whites', the doctor was telling his wife all the theories he had heard. It was mainly nuns, he reported, but there was a considerable weight of opinion behind a college, and a strong vocal minority thought it was going to be a development of twelve luxury bungalows each with a quarter acre of garden and a river view.

"What would be the best?" Mrs. White wondered.

"It depends where you stand." Dr. White was philosophical. "If Jacinta were going to join the Poor Clares or whatever, it would be nice to have her down the road; on the other hand if she were to land a millionaire let's hope she might buy one of the new bungalows."

"It's going to make everyone look out for themselves," said Mrs. White suddenly, as if the thought had just hit her.

Close to Dr. White's house, in Conway's, Miss Barry was having a small port for her stomach. She sat fearfully on a high stool. The Conways wished she would buy a bottle of port and take it home with her, she made everyone uneasy by looking around nervously and protesting that she had a cramp which meant that her body was crying out to be warmed.

Miss Barry had heard that there was definitely oil in the ground, that a research organization was going to come and test it, but they were going to install an order of silent enclosed nuns there as a disguise to keep people away—three theories rolled comfortably into one. She found a ready and unexpected audience in Conway's. They looked at her as if there might be some truth in it; they had all heard elements of this story and this explanation would at last tie it all together.

In the Classic Cinema twenty-three people sat and watched the romantic tale of *The Glass Mountain* unfold itself on the screen, while Declan Morrissey who ran the place sat in the projection room and read an article he had cut out of a Sunday newspaper. Are the days of the cinema numbered? He wondered should he get out now or wait and see if these daft rumors about half the civil service being transplanted from Dublin to the midlands were true. Wouldn't it be a very stupid thing to sell the Classic just as the horde of possible cinema viewers were about to arrive?

In Meagher's, the watch-menders and small jewelers, Teresa's parents fought on bitterly. Mrs. Meagher said it didn't matter if the Prince of Wales had left and that Mrs. Simpson was coming to live in Mountfern and give parties, life still wouldn't be any way good for her. It had been a vale of tears since she had married Mr. Meagher.

Mr. Meagher tired suddenly of the arguments; he had a pain in his chest and down his arm. He said he would call a halt to the fight and go to bed. He might feel better in the morning. He said that his wife was probably right. Life was a vale of tears and perhaps he had contributed to it. In the morning he would try to consider what could be done about it.

Next morning Teresa Meagher was sent running for Dr. White but it was too late. Mr. Meagher had not recovered from his heart attack. Dr. White knew that he was dead but still arranged for him to be taken to the hospital in the town. It would be less distressing for the family. That's what a lot of his work was about. Minimizing the distress. There was little he could have done to prevent Frank Meagher's heart attack. The man ate like a fat man in a circus, smoked four packets of cigarettes a day and existed on a level of tension that should have finished him off years ago. Dr. White left Mrs. Meagher weeping to the canon, whose faded blue eyes clouded further with the memory of the happy family life the two Meaghers had led, and before long Mrs. Meagher began to believe it herself.

The news of Frank Meagher's death did not take long to travel around Mountfern. In Leonard's stationers, Tommy's mother and father discreetly moved the Deepest Sympathy cards to the front of the stand. They hunted in the drawers for the black-edged Mass cards and flowery Spiritual Bouquet cards as well. People would want to pay their respects.

In Conway's they realized that a coffin would be needed. Discreetly they set about getting one ready. Frank Meagher was a big man. It would be a big coffin. His wife would be as guilty as hell about the life she had led him, it could be an expensive one. But they probably didn't have much insurance, maybe standard was the right thing to suggest.

At seven o'clock mass that morning he was prayed for. The religious bent their heads. Miss Purcell, Miss Hayes and Jimbo Doyle's mother exchanged glances. They could have said a lot about the Meaghers, but they would say no more now, not after a bereavement like this.

Miss Purcell looked after the Slattery household with an unsmiling face and unstinting effort. Old Mr. Slattery's clothes were clean, ironed and mended, his shoes were polished and his newspaper laid in front of his well-served breakfast at eight-thirty every morning. Miss Purcell would already have been to seven o'clock mass, she was a daily communicant; she would have collected fresh milk at Daly's and the newspaper at Leonard's. His son Fergus was equally well looked after. His shirts were ironed for him, and left hanging on the big heavy wardrobe in his room. Miss Slattery always took the one he was going to wear next day to give it a little warm in the hot press. She had a horror of the damp.

Fergus had a series of sleeveless vee-necked knitted pullovers, almost all of them in a grey to blue shade. In the long evenings when others went out looking for diversion Miss Purcell knitted fresh supplies and darned the existing force. Though old-fashioned and obviously home-made, they gave him an even more boyish charm than he had already. Many a girl's heart turned over to see him sitting at his desk in his shirt sleeves with the light on of an evening, reading through papers with hair tousled and glasses often pushed back into his thick dark hair.

If someone had offered Fergus a thousand pounds to strike attitudes or adopt a pose he wouldn't have been able to do it. Like his father he was a pleasure to work for, Miss Purcell told her few cronies, a courteous and considerate man, always opening doors, carrying buckets of coal for her, and saying how much he liked whatever she put on the table. It would be hard to find his equal in three counties or more. Miss Purcell never understood any of his jokes but Fergus seemed to be very witty and make clients laugh. Often when they were leaving she heard them say that he was too human to be a lawyer. She had been worried about this and made two novenas that he should become less human in case he endangered the practice. Sometimes Fergus cleaned his own shoes—he didn't think it was right to let a woman polish the black laced shoes that had been on his feet all day—but Miss Purcell didn't like any changes in routine. She sniffed disapprovingly at his efforts and said she would prefer if he wouldn't disgrace her in the town by going about with such ill-kept feet.

It was said that Canon Moran had often looked with envy at the Slatterys and wished they would give him their housekeeper. The purse-faced Miss Purcell who kept such a good house would be indeed a delight compared to poor Miss Barry, but she had been there so long and had no other home to go to, so in Christian kindness Canon Moran couldn't, and made no efforts to replace her.

Miss Purcell was tall, thin and had a small face with two deceptively cheery-looking spots of red on her cheeks. These were not jolly ruddy cheeks, they were in fact two spots of color whose redness increased according to how disapproving she was. At breakfast that morning they were very red indeed: a sure sign that something was about to blow up. Father and son avoided recognizing this for as long as they could.

"Do you want a bit of the *Independent?*" Fergus's father offered him the middle pages.

"I wish we'd get the *Times,* it's a better paper altogether," Fergus said. They were both avoiding the eye of Miss Purcell who stood ready to sound off.

"Well it is and it isn't, but nobody dies in the *Irish Times.* You don't get the list of deaths in it like the *Independent.* A country solicitor needs to know who has died."

"Couldn't we go into Leonard's and sort of race down the deaths without buying the paper at all?" Fergus suggested.

"Fine thing that would be to do in a small town, depriving the Leonards of their income. Couldn't the whole town do that? Couldn't they come in here and look at our law books? Where's the sense in that?" Mr. Slattery rattled his half of the paper in annoyance.

Miss Purcell cleared her throat.

"Miss Ryan is here. A bit early I said to her but she seemed to think that you expected her before nine."

"Is that Marian Ryan come to make her will again?" Old Mr. Slattery looked over his glasses.

"No, it's Kate, Kate Ryan from the pub up the River Road," said Fergus. "Isn't it, Miss Purcell?"

"Oh yes, Mr. Fergus, that's the Mrs. Ryan it is, all right. And if I might say . . ."

"Yes, Miss Purcell?" Fergus decided to take it manfully, whatever it was.

"Mrs. Ryan arrived five minutes ago with the information that she is going to be working here."

"That's right," Fergus said cheerfully. "She's going to start this morning. Well she's nice and punctual, that makes a change from the rest of Mountfern."

"I can't recall any occasion anything was late in this house . . ." Miss Purcell began to bristle.

"Oh not you, Miss Purcell, for heaven's sake, everyone else."

"And what work will Kate Ryan from the pub be doing here, and why wasn't I consulted?" The spots on the cheeks were dangerously red now. Even old Mr. Slattery had put down his paper and was looking anxiously like an old bird from one to the other.

"Well, lots of things, I hope." Fergus was still bewildered by this storm, and the sudden dropping of the Mrs. Ryan, and changing it to Kate from the pub.

"In nineteen years working in this house I have never had such treatment." Miss Purcell looked ten feet tall; she had drawn herself up into a long thin stick quivering with rage. "If my work was not to your satisfaction, the very least I would have expected was to be told. Instead of allowing me to be humiliated by seeing that Kate Ryan from the pub, come along with her apron and things in a basket prepared to do my work for me."

The eyes were very bright. Old Mr. Slattery's glasses had fallen off his nose with shock.

Fergus was on his feet. "Miss Purcell, Miss Purcell! What an idea, what a thought that we would dream of improving on your housework! Don't you keep the best house in the town? Aren't we the envy of the whole of Mountfern, including I might say the canon himself? You can't have thought for a moment that we'd as much as contemplate getting anyone else, let alone doing it without telling you. . . ."

"But Kate from the pub out there with her basket?"

"I don't know what she has in the basket but Mrs. Ryan is going to work in the office. She was trained in a solicitor's office in Dublin, you know. She'll be doing the files and typing letters."

"Oh," Miss Purcell had to spend a moment doing some social adjustment.

"So you see you were quite wrong to think we have anything except the highest regard for you, isn't that right, Dad?"

"Heavens yes. Oh Miss Purcell, the house would fall down without you," said Mr. Slattery anxiously.

"But that would mean Kate . . . that Mrs. Ryan and her family would know all your business, confidential business of the town." Miss Purcell wasn't going to give in.

"We wouldn't take her on if we didn't know she could be trusted. It's not easy to find the kind of discretion and loyalty that you have, Miss Purcell. You are, as my father has said, the mainstay of this house, but we think we have found someone who will be able to keep our business private, as you do. It's very good of you to be worried about it."

There was no more to be said. Miss Purcell had to go back to the hall where she had left Kate standing, and usher her into the office, asking the while whether she took sugar in her tea and if she would like a plain biscuit, a sweet biscuit or a slice of home-made currant bread. Kate wisely chose the home-made bread and disclosed four pints of raspberries which she had brought as a gift because she had heard it said that Miss Purcell made the best jam in the county. The pink spots began to lose their ferocity and the "Mrs. Ryan" was pronounced without the sarcastic overtones. Kate was in, she was starting a new career. There was hardly any trade in the pub in the mornings, and John was in agreement with her that the few pounds the Slatterys paid would be helpful. Young Declan was off at school, so they were all out of the house, and Carrie knew how to put a lunch on the table at the stroke of one. It would be nice to be behind a typewriter again for a change rather than behind a bar. Mr. Slattery was such a gentleman, a real old-fashioned man who was spending more and more time fishing; and Fergus was the best company in the world, self-mocking and droll, full of compassion for some of the people who came to see him, slow to send a bill where it would be a hardship to pay it, but also quick with his tongue to abuse anyone who wanted to work a fiddle or hide an income.

Fergus had told her that it wasn't a big practice and that normally he was well able to deal with the clerical side. He could type like the wind with two fingers and he had a fairly reasonable filing system but he wanted his father to take more time off; now people really did trust him with their affairs rather than thinking of him as a boy in short trousers. So Kate would be a godsend. And indeed she was. It took her about three days to see that his reasonable filing system was hopeless, and to set up a better one.

"Come here till I show you what we do with these papers now," she ordered him.

"No, no, that's your work, that's what we pay you inordinate sums of money for, so that I don't have to look at things like that."

"Wrong," Kate cried. "You have to understand it, otherwise it's useless to any of us. You won't know where to put back a letter, find a counsel's brief, where the deeds are, anything. Suppose I get flu or you sack me, or you're working late at night. Come on now, it will only take ten minutes a day."

"Do you run the pub like this too?" Fergus asked.

"Of course not, but I do the accounts, and I've insisted that John does them with me otherwise he'd have to leave them till the wife gets back and it would just double the work."

"I'm surprised the place isn't a gold mine with your organizational skills."

"Come out our way one evening and have a pint in it and you'll see what a gold mine it is. Would I be in here setting up filing systems for beautiful idle professional men too lazy to look at them if it was a gold mine? Now suppose you had this query from the town agent's clerk about the fee in that workman's compensation case which was appealed, where would you look first?"

"In the bad old days I'd look on the table at the window."

"But in the good days that have now come?"

"I've forgotten, young Mrs. Ryan, show me, show me."

"Oh thank God I'm happily married. You'd break my heart."

"You're sure you're happily married?"

"Very sure. And isn't it time you had a romance yourself? Now that Nora Lynch has gone off to fresh fields and better chances we hear nothing about your activities."

"Listen to me, after that business with Nora I'm afraid to lay my hand or eye on anyone. There's no activities to hear about. It was all a terrible misunderstanding."

"You lost us a fine schoolteacher over it all. My Dara loved her. She hates

the new woman, about a hundred she says, and a habit of hitting them accidentally on the knuckles with a ruler."

"Poor Dara, maybe I should have given Miss Lynch an engagement ring to
keep her in the town, and keep all the little girls like Dara happy."

"I don't think anything's going to make my Dara happy for a long time,
but no stories about children. This workman was called Burke, Fergus, in the
name of God where are you going to look for this file?"

"Under the Bs, Miss?"

"We have a child prodigy," said Kate Ryan and went back to her typewriter.

"What are you doing, Daddy?" John jumped guiltily at Dara's voice.

What he should have been doing was writing. This was the time that Kate
stood minding the bar, tired already from her morning in the office. But there
was just so long you could look at blank paper without it beginning to drive you
mad. John Ryan had nothing to say and no way of saying it. He had come out
to what Kate called the garden and everyone else called the yard to do a little
experiment. Ryan's licensed premises was flush on the road. Its front door
opened straight onto River Road. It would have been unheard of to have a pub
with a garden in front. The supplies came to the back yard and the barrels took
up most of it . . . a place of half-used outhouses and sheds. That was where
the back door of the house was, that was the only way the children were ever
allowed to enter their home. But beside the house there was what they called
the side yard. Here the hens wandered, and Jaffa sat like a buddha in calm
control, purring and lazily washing her big orange face. Leopold didn't sit
much in the yard, there wasn't an audience sufficiently sympathetic to his
whimperings and cringings. He liked to cower in the pub. Maurice was still in
the mudroom after the ugly river-bank incident. John had devised a marvelous
way to avoid working on his poems: he was going to build a large hen coop, a
wired-off area for the hens to live in, so that they could scratch and wander but
be away from the few pathetic attempts that Kate had started in the line of
making a real garden. Once the hens were corraled life would be easier. But
John Ryan had wanted to do it quietly and undisturbed by his family. He didn't
want to admit, even to himself, that he was shirking his writing work, and
playing hooky. Dara stood with a mutinous look on her face. Her eyes were
dark and cross under her fringe of black hair . . . her hands thrust into the
pockets of her shorts.

"Are you changing things, is that it?" she said in the tones of someone
looking for a fight and determined to find one.

"I have a bit of a plan. I was working it out, that's all," her father said,
looking guilty and shifty.

"I bet it's something new and desperate," Dara said.

"It was just a plan to gather the hens all together in a run, that's all it was,"
John said mildly.

"They're perfectly all right the way they are, they don't want to be gathered, they don't want to be changed, they love things just as they are." Her eyes
were suspiciously bright as if she could start to cry any minute. Dara had never
expressed any view about the hens up to this. The hens were like the river bank
and the crates in the yard, they were just part of the background.

John Ryan sat back on his haunches and put an arm around his daughter's
knees. "Come here and give your old father a hug."

"There's no point in hugs," Dara said.

"Right." He stood up. "I know exactly. It's the same with me. I don't feel like writing now so I came down to play with the chickens."

Dara couldn't help laughing at the thought of her father playing with chickens. She managed a snort but John Ryan wisely didn't build on it. He knew she was upset and it would all come out. He supposed it was a row with Kate. But he was wrong.

"Daddy, are we poor?"

"No we're not poor. You know that."

"But we're not rich are we?"

"You don't have to be one or the other, you can be in between, like most of us are around here."

"Will we ever be rich?"

"We'll be all right. What's this worry about money?"

"We're going to need it to buy our house." Her face was very determined.

"But we have our house, silly old thing, this is our house," he indicated the pub and the whitewashed walls of the house with a wave of his hand.

"Not here, our house across in Fernscourt. You know where they have the bulldozers. They're clearing it for someone to live there, some American, he'll live there unless we can buy it."

"Now, now, Dara," John began soothingly.

But she was on her feet full of anger and wouldn't be soothed.

"It's our house, Michael's and mine, and everyone's."

John sighed.

"Will you come for a bit of a walk with me?"

"I don't feel like a walk."

"I don't feel like a walk with such a disagreeable weasel as you, but it might help."

"Where will we go?"

"We could go to Fernscourt."

"All right then."

Kate Ryan was in the bar talking to Jimbo Doyle and Jack Coyne, who were not her idea of the best of company, when she saw through the window the two figures crossing the footbridge. Her husband who was meant to be working on his poetry and her daughter who had been like a bag of hedgehogs all week. Her knuckles ached to rap on the window, but she wouldn't give that sharp-faced Jack Coyne the satisfaction of seeing her act the bossy wife.

Kate had always spoken impetuously, and not long ago in confession had told Canon Moran that she was quick-tempered. Canon Moran had suggested that she think of Our Lord's Blessed Mother whenever she was tempted to say something sharp. She should think what Our Lady might have said. She needn't actually say what Our Lady would have said, but thinking it might delay the caustic response or the hurtful crack.

Looking at the man and girl hand in hand walking across the footbridge Kate Ryan thought that the Mother of God might have blessed them and wished them well and happiness and thanked God for her good fortune. Right, Kate Ryan would think similar noble thoughts. She turned around and faced Jack Coyne and Jimbo Doyle with what she thought was a saintly smile.

"Jesus, Kate, have you a toothache?" asked Jimbo Doyle in alarm.

* * *

"And Michael and I planned to live here when we grew up. Everyone knew that we'd get a proper roof made over this bit, and probably build windows and a door." Dara was pointing out the extent of the house.

"But it was only a dream." John was gentle.

"No it wasn't."

"Yes, of course it was . . . and is. Like going to see the man in the moon. Do you remember when you were very young we used to take you out to have a look at the man in the moon before you went to bed? Now you don't think it's a man up there, you're quite happy to look at the moon for itself, as something beautiful lighting up the sky over Mountfern."

"Yes but . . ."

"And when you were very young altogether you and Michael used to be staring up the chimney in the kitchen, didn't you, at Christmas time, the way Declan did last Christmas? You thought that if the chimney was too old and too awkward you wouldn't get any presents. But they came all the same, didn't they, and you don't mind now where they come from?"

"That's not the same . . ."

"I know it's not the same . . . but I was just saying that the way we look at things changes as life goes on, it couldn't always stay the same, otherwise we'd all be still living in caves with clubs or if we didn't grow up in some kind of way wouldn't we all be in nappies waddling around the place in playpens . . ."

"You don't understand . . ." she wailed.

"I don't understand completely, but I understand a bit. Don't I?" She looked up at him, her face softening.

"I know, Dara, it'll always be here in some way for you, not the same way, remember the man in the moon. The moon didn't go, and it still looks beautiful, doesn't it, when you can see all the cattle over on the hills, and the spire of the church and the woods and . . . and Fernscourt . . ."

"Will it be the same when this awful man comes, him with all his American money?"

"He's not going to be awful. He has children, we hear, you'll love them as sure as anything."

"I won't, I won't."

"Well you'll meet them anyway, and you *might* like them. Would that be reasonable?"

"And we'd never be able to afford to buy it ourselves."

"No, that isn't a thing you should think about, that's not a possible thing, that's like imagining a square circle, or imagining that Jaffa grew a long neck like a giraffe in the picture books. Cats don't grow long necks, this isn't a *real* home for you and Michael, it was a home for last summer and before that."

"And now?" Her lip had stopped trembling.

"It's still special but it isn't anything you start getting all het up about and start saving your pocket money to buy. That's like the days when you used to want to know if the man in the moon had to wash his neck."

"Will you explain that to Michael, Daddy? I'm not great at explaining."

"I'm not great at it either."

"Well, you're better than me," Dara said in the matter-of-fact voice which meant that he had sorted this one out anyway.

John Ryan hadn't written a poem or built a hen run, but he had convinced his angry little daughter that the world wasn't going to come to an end. Now all he had to do was to get into the house without his wife knowing he had played hooky from his poetry writing.

It was a busy night in the bar, they had hardly time for a word of any kind let alone the attack that John feared was brewing. Kate moved so quickly around the place, she had glasses swept up, and washed or refilled quicker than he would have decided whether to move the glass in the first place. Yet she didn't give the customers the impression that they were being rushed, only that there was an urgency in getting their pint in front of them.

Kate had decided to say nothing until everyone was gone, then she was going to force her voice to stay low, not to get high and excited, and she would not allow herself to speak too quickly until it became a gabble. She was going to point out—in tones that no one could find offense in—that she got up every morning and saw the children off to school, then she went and did what amounted to a day's work in an office, and not that she was complaining but she spent the afternoon listening to almighty bores rambling out of them instead of getting on with her own work of which she had plenty, but she had stood in the bar to let her husband work . . . She would keep her voice very calm as she told him how she would like to take a cleaver to him and split him in two.

Her humor was not helped by the behavior of Eddie and Declan who had come into the pub, despite all the strictures against this, to know could they take possession of the tortoise again. They had burst into the pub, mouths stained with the jam which Carrie had been making a very poor fist of setting. They looked like the children of tinkers both of them in the most torn clothes that they could have found. In front of the drinking population of Mountfern— who probably had looked at her askance because she was an outsider from the first day and had now committed the crime of going outside the family home to work—she had been guilty of the worst sin of all . . . neglecting her children. And had John supported her, had he removed them with an authoritative wave and a thunderous warning? He had *like hell*!

John Ryan had put an arm around the shoulder of each small furious son and he chose with a slow deliberation for each of them a chocolate biscuit from the shelf behind the bar and he had walked them out as if they had been honored guests instead of his own children who had broken his own most strict rule of coming into the family pub.

But Kate would not let her tone betray her rage, otherwise he would just walk away from it saying that the last thing on earth he wanted was a fight. It was infuriating. The only way she could convince him of how badly he was behaving was to speak in a reasonable tone as if she were the most contented woman on earth.

For a wild moment she wondered how the Mother of God would have coped, and then realized that Mary wouldn't have had nearly as many problems in Nazareth. There was never any mention of her running Joseph's carpentry business almost single-handedly and doing another job for a local lawyer as well. Kate's resentment knew no bounds.

The last straggler finally went home. The glasses were washed, the windows opened to air the place, two clean dishcloths lay out to dry on the counter. Kate felt sweaty and weary, not in the mood to list her wrongs.

Her husband smiled at her across the counter. "May I pour you a port wine?" he asked.

"Oh Jesus, Mary and Joseph isn't that all I'd need tomorrow, a roaring port hangover."

"Just one glass each, we'll bring it out to the side garden and I'll tell you my plans for it."

She bit her lip. He was like a big child.

"Well?" He had the glass and the port bottle ready.

She was too tired.

"Hold on till I rinse this blouse out," she said, and took off the blue and white cotton blouse that was sticking to her back. Standing in her slip top and dark blue skirt, she looked flushed and very beautiful, John thought. He touched her neck where the long dark curly hair was loosely tied with a narrow blue ribbon.

"That's lovely for them to see that kind of carry on if they pass the window," she said shaking his hand away.

"Well you're the one who's half-dressed, I'm quite respectable," he laughed.

The blouse was left to hang on the back of a chair, it would be dry in the morning. Kate gave herself a quick sluice with the water in the sink that was meant to wash only glasses.

"If we're going to go to the side garden, let's go then," she said more ungraciously than she felt; she was glad at any rate that he was calling it a garden rather than a yard. That was an advance.

The moonlight made it look a great deal better than it seemed by day. Jaffa sat still as a statue on the wall. Leopold was dreaming of beatings and his hard life. He gave a gentle whimper now and then in his sleep. From the hen house there was a soft cluck.

John folded a sack and left it on an upturned barrel. "I was to ask you about the tortoise."

"No, no." Her eyes flashed with rage. "It's not fair, John, really it isn't. You're always the lovey dovey one, ask poor old Daddy, he's so soft, he'd melt as soon as he looks at you. Mammy's the nagging old shrew . . . It's not fair to let them grow up thinking that."

"They do not think that."

"They do, and they will more if you say they can have the tortoise back. Do you think I want the smelly old thing in the mudroom looking at me like something out of one of those horror pictures they have in the picture house? I've wished a hundred times it would die one day and we could have a funeral and it would all be over, and all the fighting."

"They live for years, you know, you're on a loser there," he grinned.

She wouldn't give in. "No, they can't have it back, they broke all the rules coming into the pub like pictures of children you'd see when they're collecting for charity. They're worse than Leopold, they pretend they never got a meal or a bath in their lives."

Kate Ryan was very aggrieved.

"Did I ever try to countermand any of your decisions?" John asked.

"No, but you try to get around me. We've got to be consistent, John, otherwise how do they know where they are?"

"I couldn't agree more."

"But?"

"But nothing. I couldn't agree more."

"So what about the bloody tortoise? What were you going to suggest?"

"Come here, I want to show you something . . ." He took her by the hand and pointed out where they should build a long hen run, with netting over it. The hens would have freedom, but within frontiers. The rest was going to be a garden. He showed where they could have a rockery. And how they would build a raised flower bed maybe and she could grow the flowers she had always said she would like.

"You should have been writing your poetry."

"It's not like making things in a factory, Kate, you can't sit down in front of a conveyor belt and turn out bits of writing and in the end a poem emerges." He spoke quietly and with dignity.

"I know, I know." She was contrite.

"So when it didn't seem to come, I thought I'd do something for you and plan you a garden."

"That's lovely."

"I'll have a word with Jimbo Doyle and he could do a couple of days and build up a few beds. Now wouldn't that be nice?"

"It would." She was touched, she couldn't deliver her attack now. It would be ingratitude, flying in the face of God, to attack a husband who was so kind.

"I was over in Fernscourt today, there's heaps of stones lying around the place. We could get some nice big rocks, Jimbo could wheel them across the footbridge."

"I don't suppose they belong to anyone." Kate didn't want her voice to sound grudging . . . "That would be grand," she added.

"And this thing about the tortoise, I wouldn't countermand your orders. God, what would be the point? What I was wondering was now that the hens have a place of their own someone will have to feed them properly you know, mix up the scraps with the bran . . ."

"Yes."

"So suppose we made those two scallywaggers do that? They'd be well able for it, and they'd give the hens a feed twice a day . . . and to encourage them maybe they could have some kind of access to that tortoise, maybe take him out of your way in the mudroom, not have him looking up at you like a prehistoric monster. What do you think?"

Kate tried to hide her smile. Unsuccessfully.

"What do I think?" she said, laughing in spite of herself. "I think I might be persuaded . . . but . . ."

"But it would have to come from you. If you think it would be a good idea, then you should suggest it." He was adamant about this.

"I suppose you sorted Dara out too," Kate said gently and with admiration. "They should have you up on the platform in Geneva sorting things out for everyone."

"Ah, the poor child was very upset, it's giving up a bit of fairyland. None of us like doing that."

"People like you didn't have to, it's still all there in your heads," Kate said, but she said it with a hint of envy in her voice, and she kissed his lips softly so that he tasted the port wine.

Three

That night Michael sat on the landing window seat and looked across at Fernscourt in the moonlight.

The curtains of ivy waved over the hummocks of moss. It was easier than ever to see the ruins since some of the big straggly trees and bushes had been cut down.

Eddie and Declan were long asleep in their bunk beds. Michael had been reading with a torch, but his mind had strayed from the knight who had rescued the Lady Araminta with the golden tresses. He wanted to look at real life, which was Fernscourt. For a long time he looked at the shadows over the moon and the patterns they made on the soft green banks up from the river toward the house.

Then he saw a figure moving in the moonlight. Nobody *ever* walked there at night. Michael knelt up and opened the window to have a better view. It was a man, an old man even older than Daddy. He was wandering around with his hands in his pockets looking up at the walls. Sometimes he touched the moss, sometimes he pushed aside the ivy. Michael was kneeling on the window seat now, peering and straining to see as the figure disappeared and emerged again behind the ruined walls. He felt a hand on his shoulder, and there was his father in his pajamas.

"Dad, I think he's come. I think he's here."

"Who?"

"The American. I think that's him in our house." The boy's face was white even on the shadowy landing with moonlight coming in irregular darts through the window.

John Ryan looked out and saw a figure walking around touching walls and almost patting the bits of building that still stood. John felt he was spying somehow. The man was as if naked over there, in that he didn't know he was being observed.

Michael was wriggling off the seat. "I'll have to wake Dara," he said, his face working anxiously.

"Wait, Michael."

"But it's our house, he's here, he came after all. People said he might not be going to live here. But look at him, he *is* going to live in it, isn't he? Isn't he?"

John sat down on the window seat, and lifted his feet a little off the cold linoleum floor covering. "Michael, don't wake the child up."

"She's not a child, she's twenty minutes older than I am."

"That's true. She's not a child any more than you are."

Michael's face was troubled. "She'll need to know, Dad."

"Nobody needs to know."

"It's partly her house."

"It's *his* house Michael." John indicated the man across the river.

"I know, I know." The boy's thin shoulders were raised, tense. He was troubled and unsure what to do.

"Give me something to put my feet on so they're not like two big blocks of ice when I get back into the bed with your mother."

Michael rooted around under the comics and books that were on the window seat and found a raggedy cushion.

"Will this do?"

"That's fine, thank you son."

Some of the quivering tension had left the boy. He sat down, still looking out of the window, but prepared to talk rather than wake his sister and the whole house in his grief.

"Do you know, when I was a lad your age we used to go over there and play too. Your Uncle Barry, now, he was a great climber, there was nothing he couldn't get right up on, and there were more bits of wall then than now."

Michael was interested.

"And then your Aunt Nuala; my heavens wouldn't those little Australian boys and girls be surprised to know that their Mother Superior used to climb trees like a boy? She used to tie her skirts up around her waist and climb with Barry."

"What did you do, Daddy?"

"Sure I was only like poor Eddie, looking at them," John sighed. "They usually wanted me to go away, if I remember rightly."

Michael took this as a criticism of the twins' own attitude to their younger brother.

"I'm sure you were fine when you were young, Dad. But God, you couldn't have Eddie hanging around with you, I mean really and truly."

"Oh I know that, I'm not disputing it, Eddie would have your heart scalded. But I was only talking about the old days across there . . . and the kind of things we used to do . . ."

He talked on gently, his voice low enough that it wouldn't wake Kate and have her storming out onto the landing. Yet raised enough for Michael to think it was a normal conversation and that these were normal times.

John dug deep into his memory of games played, and accidents averted, of guards on bicycles, of two young bullocks that ran wild, away from someone's secure field up the hill. He talked until he saw the lids begin to droop on his son's thin white face, and knew that sleep was going to come at last, that Michael wouldn't wake Dara and sit all night watching in helpless despair as this stranger walked through what they still wanted to think their home.

* * *

That night old Mr. Slattery couldn't sleep and he came down to get himself some warm milk. He dozed off at the kitchen table as the milk boiled and didn't smell the burning until Fergus appeared, wild-eyed with shock.

"Don't put me away, don't put me in the county home," wept the old man. "I'll take milk to bed in a flask. I'll never try to boil it again. Please."

Fergus had been filling the blackened saucepan with water and opening the windows.

"Are you going mad altogether, Father? Would I put you in the county home? Would I?"

"If I were mad altogether you'd have to," Mr. Slattery said reasonably.

"Yes, but you're not, and even if you were I don't think I would."

"Why not? It would be the right thing to do, we've often advised clients ourselves."

"You're not a client. You're my father."

"You've got to get on with your own life."

"But I *do* get on with my own life, for God's sake. I was out getting on with it this evening and I'd only just gotten to bed. That's why it was my nose that caught the milk, not Miss Purcell's."

"I'm a burden, I don't do much work in the office."

"You're not a burden, we don't *have* much work in the office."

"I've let the place run down, why else didn't we get the business for Fernscourt?"

"Oh is *that* what's worrying you? I'll tell you why. Your man O'Neill is in business in a big way over there, really big, owns at least half a dozen restaurants or bars or whatever they are. He has other business too, he pays accountants and lawyers big fees. Now he's opening here, the big lawyers look up a map . . . Ireland they say, Ireland, where's that? Then they find it. What's the capital they say, what's the capital? Then someone tells them and they get Dublin solicitors. That's all."

"You make it sound so simple. I suppose it will be good when he arrives, this American. He's given work in the place already."

"Here's some fresh milk." Fergus had boiled another saucepan. "We'll tell Miss Purcell that I was drunk and burned the arse out of the saucepan. The American? It has to be good for the place. I suppose the poor devil will be full of nonsense and trying to hunt and shoot and fish. We'll have great sport with him. Imagine worrying about the American! It'll be the best sport we ever had. I can't wait for him to arrive."

That night Sergeant Sheehan found somebody lying in a very awkward position, legs splayed, head lolling, and stretched right across the footbridge at the end of the town. Sergeant Sheehan was a thickset man who used to be a great hurler in his day, a man with ferocious eyebrows which made him look very frightening when he had to. But he was running to fat now, with slow and undemanding life in a country town. He felt his uniform was constantly tight around his neck, and rolls of fat gathered when he buttoned his top collar.

He loosened the collar now by opening several buttons, and looked at the sleeping woman. It was Miss Barry, the canon's housekeeper. A fine place for her to have passed out and to be snoring at 1 A.M. Sergeant Sheehan went back to the station to think the matter over, having tidied her legs into a more respectable position. He wasn't quite sure what his next move would be. To wake the canon with such bad news would be unwise. To allow Miss Barry to be found by someone else, asleep and obviously the worse for wear, would hardly be wise either. To wake Miss Barry might be the least wise course of all. What a pity Mrs. Whelan wasn't around. He walked up Bridge Street. There was still a light on.

He tapped gently. She came to the door fully dressed.

"Do you ever sleep, Sheila?" he asked, full of relief to see her.

"Not so much these days. Telegrams come in at funny times too. They don't know what time we wake or sleep," she said.

He told her; she pondered. She decided it was best left; even another three or four hours would mean she had slept the worst off. Had she anything to support her head? No, but the sergeant would arrange it.

"I get up early," Mrs. Whelan said. "I could throw some water over her at around six, and then we could pretend she had been out early to pick mushrooms for His Reverence's breakfast and fallen into the river."

This way face was saved. He couldn't thank her enough. Mrs. Whelan said they would speak no more of it; she was flattered to be asked for her advice. She would sleep now for a couple of hours.

It was years since Patrick O'Neill had stayed up all night. He tried to think back. In the 1930s during the Depression often, very often, hardly a week went by when nights were not spent hauling boxes and crates, doing favors here, moving goods that had to be out of warehouses there. Counting, taking note, proving himself reliable. Telling Italians and fellows with long Polish names that they could always rely on Patrick O'Neill. He used to say his own name with pride to these men, roll it around as if it were an incantation. He spoke of himself in the third person to these business associates in the early days: "Patrick O'Neill won't let you down. You can always rely on Patrick O'Neill."

They could rely on him and his truck at first, and then on his fleet of truck drivers who didn't ask questions but just shifted what had to be shifted.

And then Patrick O'Neill's name was over neighborhood bars. He was one of the first to welcome the end of Prohibition, just as he had enjoyed the income and lifestyle which Prohibition had created for him, and those Italians and Poles who had given him early jobs were not forgotten. When life became less risky Patrick O'Neill invited them and their wives to his bar-restaurants and treated them with respect. Flowers for the wives, discreet smiles when they brought girlfriends instead. They appreciated it; they sent him custom. But it had meant a lot of staying up all night. There had been the night when he had gone through the books over and over again. It was dawn when he had to admit that it was a fellow Irishman who had been cheating him. He called to Tom Brady's house at seven, shirt open and eyes red.

Tom Brady realized what had happened and tried to run.

"Mrs. Brady," Patrick O'Neill had said quietly, "take the children out, maybe for the day. To family perhaps? Don't let them come back before nightfall. Oh and move any really good ornaments and pieces from your front parlor."

"This isn't a movie, Patrick," Tom started to bluster.

"Sure it isn't, otherwise you'd be dead on your floor for what you've done to me."

Tom Brady's wife gasped.

"Take the children," Tom had said, "and do what he says. He's not going to kill me."

Patrick beat him with a violence he didn't even know he possessed. With every blow he grunted and spat out more rage. *This* was for the false smiles and the drinks after a day spent cheating. *This* was for letting Patrick fire an innocent Italian two months back. *This* was for the sleazy shabby way the goods were stolen, taking them out in trash cans and coming back later to root among the garbage and remove the good bottles of liquor. *This* was for taking a bonus last Christmas, and *this,* the hardest blow of all, had been for being an Irishman and doing it all to another Irishman. He had been up all that night all right. And on the night he had met Kathleen.

He had never intended to marry, or fall in love. There wouldn't be time. Work was scarce first and then it was too plentiful, and then came responsibility and long hours. There wouldn't be time for a wife and family. But Kathleen had looked so lovely and she was so lively then, eyes dancing, long fair hair swept up into a top knot of some sort. She had been so excited about his bars and restaurants, and so enthusiastic. She said over and over that America was so alive and so full of hope she pitied anyone who lived anywhere else.

"Except Ireland, of course," Patrick had said.

"Particularly Ireland." She had tossed her curls.

It was the one thing they differed on. Huge in ways, and yet it never mattered all that much, because he knew that when he was ready to go back— "to go back" was how he put it, though he himself had never seen Ireland— Kathleen would come too. He wasn't to know that as her health deteriorated she would become less and less interested in any scheme, be it in New York or in Ireland. Kathleen, who used to sit on the tables in a new bar holding swaths of material up to the light at the window to see which would make the classiest curtains, lost her involvement in anything except the big white house in New Jersey, and in the latter years even that couldn't hold her frail attention.

He hadn't spent any night awake over Kathleen's illness; there was not one night when he knew she wouldn't get better. He was never given any bad diagnosis, or expectation or time when her illness would run its course. Possibly, the last time he had stayed up all night without going to bed or lying down was the night Kerry was born. In 1947. The child had been born at home and the doctors told Patrick it was going to be long and hard, even though Kathleen was still young and strong in those days. He had spent all night pacing, trying to read, doing anything to distract himself from the cries upstairs. It had been a clear bright dawn when he held his son in his arms and rocked him. Kerry's tiny, scrunched-up face was so touching, Patrick had swallowed hard and swore that no harm would come to this boy, and that he would go back and walk in his rightful place in Ireland with head held high.

As he clutched the little bundle to him he felt tears in his eyes and wondered how his own father, Michael O'Neill—amiable, drunken, good-for-nothing Michael O'Neill—felt when he had held Patrick in his arms. Did he not wish too that he could take his son back to Mountfern? No, Patrick's father must have felt no such thing. At the age of twenty Michael O'Neill, his parents, brothers and sisters, had left Mountfern because there was no work and his father had been thrown out on the road. He never went back, nor had he ever thought it possible. He had sung songs about Ireland, and told tales, and filled young Patrick with a hatred of this Fern family whom he had never met.

Patrick was eight when he heard that the Ferns' house had been burned down. The news came by letter. It was too late to be any good to any of the O'Neills then. There was no O'Neill around to watch the flames lick through the windows of this house, the house which had held the family and brought them down.

Patrick O'Neill touched the moss-covered stones almost religiously; he leaned against the ivy-covered walls and walked by the moonlight into a room which still had its walls. To his surprise there were orange boxes as furniture, and toy tea-sets. Some local children had obviously been playing there. He smiled at the jam jars full of wild flowers. He wondered who the children were. Certainly they wouldn't have been allowed in the door during the Ferns' time. He would love to see their faces when they heard his plans for the old ruin.

Mrs. Whelan was the first to see him. She had just delivered a dripping Miss Barry back to the presbytery while Father Hogan and Canon Moran clucked sympathetically at the mishap that caused their housekeeper to fall into the river. Mrs. Whelan had even provided some mushrooms as a kind of proof that the bewildered woman had been on an errand for her employers. Just as she was walking back to her post office, she saw a man in a crumpled suit, tie loosened, walk up Bridge Street toward a hired car. It could be no one else.

Patrick O'Neill stood handsome and pale in his unaccustomed dark suit. Big and broad-shouldered with a head of dark brown curly hair, he was a man who normally wore tan or beige jackets. Few people in the States ever remembered seeing him in dark colors. Even if there had been a formal occasion he had worn a green tuxedo in deference to his national origins.

His enemies in business had often said that he had the thickset looks of an Irish paddy who should still be shoveling dirt. This pleased Patrick rather than otherwise; he said he was glad to wear the signs of his forefathers so openly, and to be living proof that they had to work hard and that they survived. But he didn't have the pugilistic face of a man who would like to have a fight, he had no boxer's scowl, nor the low forehead of a man who found it hard to cope with whatever life dealt him. His face was broad and open, his eyes blue and twinkling. From his eyes lines came out like a star, meaning that they often looked as if he was smiling even when he was far from it.

He was more attractive and younger than Sheila had expected. But then, what should she have expected, just seeing telegrams and telex messages pile up for him? He looked as if he could do with a welcome.

She crossed the street. "And you're very welcome to these parts, Mr. O'Neill," she said warmly.

Patrick looked at her gratefully. "How did you know it was me, did you know my people?"

"Who else would it be, Mr. O'Neill? And I have a foot of telegrams and messages for you up at the post office. Would you like a cup of tea and I'll give them to you?"

"Now that's what I call efficiency." He threw back his head and laughed.

Mrs. Whelan led him through the post office to her room behind. She put him sitting down beside a pile of communications and put on the kettle. She said no more till she placed a cup of tea beside each of them, and some buttered soda bread. Yes, a very handsome man, she thought, he was going to cause a bit of a stir. Mrs. Whelan smiled to herself, thinking of all the excitement there would be.

Patrick read the telegrams from Gerry Power, the man who had replaced Tom Brady as his second in command all those years ago. He read the telegrams from Rachel too quickly, and put them into a different pocket. He felt the heat coming back into his body with the strong tea and the thick buttered bread. She was a gracious woman, this Mrs. Whelan. No curiosity about him, no need to talk and chatter like so many women, telling you their business and wanting to know yours. If they were all going to be like this in Mountfern, he had made the best move in his life.

Despite the hard, silent disapproving face of Gerry Power.

Despite the hurt, bewildered eyes of Rachel Fine.

Despite the confused chirrupings of little Grace.

And the stern scornful look of Kerry, the tall golden-haired son. The boy he had promised to take back home. The boy who said so little to him these days that Patrick had no idea what he was thinking about, at all.

Fergus wondered what it would be like to be a solicitor in a big place where you had no idea what the day would bring. In other places he supposed he could stand on his own doorstep and stretch without four passers-by asking him had he a bad back like his father, and sending messages in to Miss Purcell or advising him on the rather glum-looking window boxes. Still he wouldn't change it. And he could escape and get on with his life a bit, as he had told his father last night, if he went twenty-five miles to a dance organized by a rugby club. There were grand girls there who wouldn't expect to be taken to Meagher's jewelry shop next morning if a kiss and a cuddle had been part of the night's entertainment.

He saw Kate Ryan walking up River Road and turning into Bridge Street. She waved.

"Are you out with your stopwatch in case I'm a second late?"

"Just waiting for the bells to ring for mass. If there had been one peal you'd have been fired. No, I was having a good stretch actually."

"Don't you look like a young Greek god. Did you have a good time in Ballykane last night?"

His arms dropped to his sides mid-stretch. "How did you know where I was . . . ?"

"I was there myself dancing away beside you. You never saw me?"

"No you weren't, don't be ridiculous, who said it to you?"

"Jack Coyne. Some fellow couldn't start his car and rang Jack at all hours in the morning to go and pick him up."

"God, you can't do much in this place, can you? And there was I thinking it wasn't such a bad place. No surprises."

"It isn't a bad place. Do you want surprises?"

They were walking companionably in to start the day's work as the church bells began to peal at ten to nine to let the devout know it was time to put on the hats and pick up the missals for daily mass. The early devout would already have attended seven o'clock mass, said this morning by a perplexed Father Hogan, whose mind was as much on the dripping and drunken housekeeper as it was on the liturgy.

"No I don't want surprises," Fergus said. "In the last few hours I've found my father nearly burning the house down, and now you tell me Jack Coyne has the entire details of my little escapade last night."

Kate was at her desk opening mail. It was a job they did together since the invention of the filing system. Kate wanted to check that the young master knew not only where to find everything but where to file it as well. She had arranged a bowl of flowers, a blotter and pens on his famous table by the window where every document used to end up in the old days.

"I think I'll lay off surprises for a while," Fergus said, throwing a heap of papers on the floor beside him out of habit, and picking them up sheepishly to place them in the pending tray on the desk.

"You know they say they come in threes," said Kate absently, as she began to read a letter which had been delivered by hand. It was a request from Patrick J. O'Neill that Slattery and Slattery should act for him in his application to build a hotel and apply for a pub license as well. He thought that since he was going to live in the area he would very much like the local man to act on his behalf.

"God Almighty, he's going to build a hotel," Kate said, standing up.

Fergus had come to read the letter over her shoulder. "I won't act for him —he can find his own attorney and counsellors and whatever they call them over there," he said after a long silence.

She looked at him blankly. "Why won't you act for him?"

"Because if his application is granted and he gets his license, then he'll open a pub . . ."

"You have to take his business . . ." Kate was pale.

"I do not have to take his business, thank you. I can accept or refuse any work I like. I am not going to accept anything which is going to take the bread and butter out of your mouth." He looked angry and upset as he stood beside her and she found herself weeping on his shoulder. "Do you want to go home, and tell John?"

"No, not yet." Kate shook her head and sat down purposefully at her desk. "Not for a while. If our bread and butter's going to disappear in the pub I'd better make sure I don't lose the job in the office as well." She gave a smile to show that the emotional bit was over.

"You'd never lose a job here," Fergus said gently. "I just wish it paid better. Maybe you should tell John now, before someone else does."

"Nobody else will. It's silly but last night he was saying, when we were sitting out in the side garden bit . . . he was saying that nothing bad was ever going to happen to us. Maybe this isn't very bad. I want to have a think before I tell him. That's all." There were no words to say. It was about as bad as it could be. Fergus didn't say anything. He took off his glasses and polished them. He saw Kate looking at him gratefully.

"All right. All right, I know I have a weak face without them, I'm putting them back on. Let's open more mail, shall we? Who knows what other little surprises may be lurking in these nice brown envelopes?"

Patrick O'Neill drove to the Grange, some three miles from Mountfern. It was a big, gracious house that had always been in the Johnson family. It had known good days and bad, and just now was going through a fairly prosperous phase. Marian Johnson had discovered that there was a business in offering riding holidays. City people and English visitors liked to come and stay in the vaguely country house atmosphere. The Johnsons always left a decanter of sherry out instead of charging people by the glass, it gave them the feeling that they were guests on a country weekend. Last summer Marian had quite a few Americans, who usually came in groups. This big, handsome O'Neill man was different.

He said he would like to ride, but since he had not sat on a horse's back for years he wondered if it was foolish to begin again at the age of forty-eight.

Marian Johnson aged thirty-nine looked into his blue eyes with the crinkly laugh lines coming away from them at the sides. No, she thought that was the perfect age to start again. She would take him riding herself.

Marian was fair-haired, but no one would ever have called her a blonde; her hair was wispy and flyaway, and no style ever seemed to tame it. She had a big soft bosom and often wore twinsets, mauves or pale green light jumpers with a matching cardigan. She looked her best when her hair was tidied into a net and under a bowler hat, and her soft drooping bosom gathered into the mannish coat of the hunt. The Johnsons were people who considered themselves of importance in the neighborhood; normally Marian would never have shown the slightest interest in any American visitor. A man passing through, a man with no family, no background or stake in the area. Marian would have little time to waste. Yet there was something about Patrick O'Neill that attracted her.

"Does your wife like the idea of riding?" Marian asked.

"My wife passed away this year," Patrick said.

"Oh, I am most awfully sorry."

"She had been in poor health for a long time," murmured Patrick.

Marian said no more; she arranged for the horses and assured Patrick that there would be no broken bones.

Companionably they walked the horses over to a stile where she advised Patrick to mount his animal.

"Go on," she laughed. "It's more dignified than all this getting a leg up by putting your foot in someone's hand. It's like stepping on."

"It's too easy," Patrick complained. "I don't mind the undignified way."

Astride their horses, they rode down the quiet lane with the fuchsia-filled hedges. Marian pointed out landmarks, towers on small hills and when they came to the corner she said, "And that's Fernscourt . . . they say it's going to be . . ."

"I bought it. It's mine," he said quickly.

"Of *course,* they said you'd be here soon. How stupid of me not to recognize it must have been you, I thought you were another tourist. Well, well, what a beautiful place you've got for yourself, Mr. O'Neill, and will you be making a home of it, or what?"

"I'm going to be the opposition, Miss Johnson," he said simply. "I'm going to build a hotel. I don't know whether we will be exactly in competition or not; I feel sure that we will be going for different markets. But what I was hoping was that we might be able to cooperate . . . If you wanted to expand your riding school say, and incorporate some of the guests from Fernscourt . . . ?" He looked at her openly and eagerly.

It was very honest of him to come right out and say it straight, she thought. Another man might have sniffed around her hotel to steal a few ideas before declaring his hand.

"Do you know anything about the hotel business?" she asked.

"I have one small motel in New Jersey. I bought it really for tax purposes, so I'm not what you'd call experienced. But I have bars and restaurants, so I guess you could say I know something about what the public wants. Only the New York public mind you, but New York is pretty cosmopolitan, and it might be a good sample of what all kinds of people want." He wasn't only after the American package-tour business, he explained, he wanted local people to feel involved. It was to be their place too. Too long the walls of Fernscourt had kept them out. For nearly a hundred and fifty years the real Irish people of the parish had been refused access to places that rightly belonged to them. That wouldn't be the way anymore.

"I don't think people were refused access," Marian said. "It's been a ruin for years. It belonged to the Land Commission, didn't it? We used to go there on picnics when I was a girl."

"No, I mean before that, when the Ferns were there, barring everyone from their door."

Marian was cheerfully vague about that side of things. "Did they? How stupid of them. They were gone long before my time, of course, but I think my father remembers them. He used to play bridge with someone called Fern. But it mightn't have been them, the people from the house. It could have been a cousin or something."

Patrick was slightly irritated by this affectionate view. He thought that perhaps Marian had been overprotected and didn't really know the story of the big house. After all, the Johnsons were Catholics, Patrick had seen the Infant of Prague in the hall and there was a picture of Our Lady of Perpetual Succor in the bedroom where he had laid his case. Suddenly the tiredness of last night began to reach him. His eyes felt heavy.

"Do you think it's a possibility . . . our getting together over some aspects of the tourist trade?" he asked Marian.

"I see unlimited possibilities," said Marian, running her tongue lightly across her lower lip and thinking that life was looking up.

Four

*N*ow that he was here they all claimed to have been the first to meet him and the one who knew him best. Those who had been telling stories only hours ago about the certainty of the nuns or the agricultural research institute were now eager to tell how they had known all along that it was going to be a hotel. The possibilities of a big tourist undertaking were legion. Patrick O'Neill was said to have told people that this was going to be his home, and his home would be open three hundred and sixty-five days a year, no closing down in the winter leaving the boys and girls to find some other jobs for the long harsh wet months from September to Easter.

Judy Byrne was peeved to note that he had been spotted riding horses with Marian Johnson in the morning light. That was fast moving of a spectacular nature. Kate Ryan had heard that he was seen in Conway's and Dunne's, and she was sure he must have been in Foley's too. Rita Walsh, who ran the Rosemarie hair salon, had seen what she thought must have been him in the moonlight over at the ruin. Hard to see at that distance but he had looked a fine cut of a man.

Tommy Leonard's mother said that Tommy was under no circumstances to be seen running wild with that gang of young criminals he called his friends. This was a chance sent from heaven for him to better himself. Maybe his whole future could be assured if he were seen by the new owner of Fernscourt to be a sensible boy. Tommy wondered how could it sort out his future if he turned his back on his friends? But Mrs. Leonard said there were a million ways if Tommy would put his mind to it. That hotel was going to need a shop on the very premises to sell things to its visitors who mightn't want to walk the whole way to Mountfern. What was more sensible than to offer the concession to the local existing stationers and booksellers? Tommy must be ready to seize the chance.

"But I'm only twelve," Tommy wailed. "How could I seize a shop in a hotel?" He saw his whole youth and adolescence trickling away standing behind counters of one sort or another.

"By the time that hotel is up and ready to have a shop you'll be well old enough to work in it," his mother said firmly.

Maggie Daly's mother couldn't understand how it was that they hadn't seen him. He was meant to have been in Sheila Whelan's, and in all three pubs on Bridge Street; he had been seen standing looking at the Stations of the Cross in the church, but Canon Moran hadn't focused on him properly and didn't want to interrupt a man at prayer, so he was no use as an informant.

Then he had been observed driving up past Coyne's wood. Could he have been going to the convent maybe? The whole thing might still have something to do with an order of cloistered nuns. The only people who knew for sure were Sheila Whelan, because he had been in the post office for an age, but of course it was hopeless trying to get anything out of Sheila. And Marian Johnson, she didn't talk to everyone easily in Mountfern, so there would be no news from that quarter.

Jack Coyne was very anxious for a description of the American who had bought Fernscourt and was going to turn it into a hotel. Very anxious indeed. Yesterday he had gotten a call from the railway station in the big town: an American wanting to hire a car. Jack had driven in to him.

"Why did a well-heeled person like yourself not hire a car from Avis or Hertz?" Jack inquired.

"Always believe in supporting the local industry," the Yank had said.

"Here for the fishing?"

"Yup," the man said.

Jack Coyne had too much on his mind to make conversation with a taciturn foreign visitor whom he would never see again. He charged the American two and a half times the normal price and gave him a poor rate for his dollar. Jack was ashen-faced trying to get a proper account of the Patrick O'Neill who had bought Fernscourt. He had an uneasy feeling that he might have cheated the man who was going to live across the river from him. The man who could have brought him the kind of wealth he never dreamed of.

Miss Barry was quite unaware that she had met Mr. O'Neill. She had been struggling under the weight of two heavy shopping bags when a man stopped to give her a lift. She had climbed clumsily into the car, opening the window with that native cunning she had when she smelled of drink. Fresh air was an ally, closed spaces were a giveaway. She told this man about the saintly Canon Moran, the angelic young Father Hogan and even sang a few bars of a song.

"Tell me does your poor wife take a drink?" she asked him suddenly. She got the reply that the late Mrs. O'Neill had not in fact been partial to liquor.

"Best way to be," Miss Barry said approvingly. "She'll live to be a hundred, God spare her."

She rattled her plastic bags which contained bottles and smiled at him beatifically.

But none of this remained in any part of her consciousness.

Patrick had indeed gone to the convent when he had been sighted driving toward Coyne's wood. He left the car at Coyne's garage and walked up the shabby ill-kept avenue to the school. Sister Laura greeted him, a small shrew-like woman, eyes dark and bright in her round face, like two currants in a bun. She saw within minutes why he was there. He was trying to work out whether this country school would in any way approach his hopes and plans for his only daughter's education.

Sister Laura was a sensible woman. She knew that it would be counterproductive to encourage this American to believe that hers was the finest educational establishment in Ireland. She spoke praisingly of the Sacred Heart Convent, the Loretto nuns, the Holy Child Order, the FCJ (Faithful Companions of Jesus), all of them excellent sisters running very highly thought of boarding schools for girls. But that was just the point. They would be boarding schools. And if Mr. O'Neill wanted his child with him, then this was the only game in town.

She didn't put it as racily as that, but Patrick realized that if she had known the phrase she would have.

She listed the disadvantages. Grace would be much more sophisticated than the simple girls who came from smallholdings over the fields to this school each day. Grace would have to learn Irish: it was compulsory in schools, and they wouldn't have any facility for her to study something else at the time Irish-language lessons were taking place. It would be fairly rough and ready; sports would not be as she had known them in the United States, the girls played camogie, a form of hockey. Sister Laura said it was the female equivalent of hurling for boys.

But on the plus side Grace would grow up with the children among whom her father intended her to live. She would be at his side, she would make friends of all kinds, which was essential if a family were to live in a small community. She would avoid the princess-in-the-castle role. Patrick had looked with dismay at the shabby building, and particularly what Sister Laura described with pride as the new extension: classrooms thrown together, without thought or design. The finish was shoddy, obviously a local builder doing it for half nothing and knowing that the nuns weren't going to complain. The library where the small nun lingered so lovingly was a big barren room lined with jerry-built shelves. Soon to contain a couple of hundred books, most of them the lives of the saints. But the nun was right, he could see all this. He knew that he would send his child to the convent. What Grace Mary O'Neill might lose on polish and a broader approach to education, she would surely gain in a sense of belonging. And that was what this journey was all about.

Sister Laura had pursed her lips over the thought of Mr. O'Neill's son being educated in Mountfern. Of course the brothers were the best in the world. But . . .

And of course one had to take into consideration that a boy, a young man would have to be prepared to make his way in the world. Especially a young man who would inherit a huge property. So, she didn't actually say that he should forget the brothers, nor was there a mention of any inadequacies. But there was a veiled hint that only a madman might entrust the son and heir to Brother Keane and his colleagues in the big red-brick school behind the church. Mention was made of Jesuits, of Benedictines and of Holy Ghost Fathers. All known to Mr. O'Neill, certainly, in the United States, she was sure, and all running exceptionally good boys' boarding schools in Ireland, for the sons of gentlemen and people who were going to get on in life. After all, with a boy it was much more important. And with a boy there wouldn't be the same sense of loss seeing the child go to boarding school.

For courtesy and diplomacy Patrick O'Neill called on Brother Keane too. He went with no sense of apology. Instead he asked the man for advice. He had to send his son as a boarder. He would be most grateful if Brother Keane could mark his card. Would he favor the Jesuits in County Kildare, the Benedictines in Limerick, the Holy Ghost or Vincentians in Dublin?

Brother Keane had never been so flattered in his life. He gave great care to his deliberations and between them the two men came up with the ideal school for Kerry O'Neill.

Patrick O'Neill felt that slowly things were placing themselves together.

He was back in Mountfern, the sale of the land was going through. He had been assured there would be no problems with the licenses. The grants toward building a hotel would be even greater than he had thought. The people were friendly from what he could judge; usual sprinkling of rogues and drunks but basically a solid place. The place his people had come from. He let his mind rest lightly on the images of his children. Grace with the beautiful curls and dimples, Grace almost twelve now, the prettiest girl in her year, the apple of his eye. And Kerry. Handsome distant Kerry. Fifteen and as tall as Patrick. No paddy features in Kerry, his face was chiseled and had classic good looks. Even as a small child.

What would his two striking children make of Mountfern? They had never really believed that he would change their lives so totally. Part of them thought it was a huge adventure, another—perhaps the greater—part would find it a wrench to leave their surroundings, their friends, the memory of the way things had always been when their mother was alive. Patrick squared his shoulders. There was to be no wallowing in the past. This had been his dream, to take his family back to the place they had come from.

This town would be their home now. It had its shortcomings. He was not so blinded with the yearning to return that he couldn't see that. The untidiness of it irritated him. An Irish village, his Irish village shouldn't have yards full of rusting, broken machinery, there should be bright paint on all the doors. There should be a fountain or something at the end of Bridge Street instead of just letting it peter out and wind away.

He had called into the local public houses, each one in turn. None of them would be any opposition to him, of course, but even more importantly he didn't think his hotel would be a threat to any of them. Dunne's looked as if it were about to do a moonlight flit, Conway's had three serious drinkers sitting on high stools behind its grocery. You'd need radar to find out that there was a bar there at all. And in Foley's he had the distinct impression he had wandered into a private house. Matt Foley had eyed him beadily but the chat died down while he was there. No, there was only that place with the nice old sign, Ryan's, which was right opposite his new estate. He would need to handle them with tact. If anyone was going to lose by his plans for Fernscourt it would be this little place. While still incognito he had inquired about the family. He heard that the mother went out to work, a rare thing in Irish country towns, and that the business was steady. The rest of the brothers and sisters who had owned the place had all emigrated, so John Ryan had only his own family to support out of it.

Patrick had looked at it often when he had been visiting the site. He had even looked at it by moonlight last night when he was walking around his land. It had been very still with everyone asleep, and nobody knowing that he watched it from across the river.

He walked from the brothers past the church and along in front of the bridge, and looked up Bridge Street. It could be a fine town. He would make so many changes here, give people a bit of pride in their surroundings again. He would walk to Fernscourt now. This was not New York, home of the automobile, this was his place, to walk around, to stop and talk, or just to watch the river if he wanted to. Past Jack Coyne's, past a shabby little store with the name Quinn in faded lettering, then across a rickety footbridge. He would walk his land before going to introduce himself to the Ryans in that attractive little shebeen.

He heard the sound of children's voices as he walked through the laurel bushes on the path from the footbridge to the house.

Then he saw them.

A boy and girl obviously twins, dark-eyed, dark-haired and moving in exactly the same way, gestures and smiles utterly identical.

Patrick looked at them fondly.

"Hey, is it moving day?" he asked good-naturedly.

They hadn't seen him arrive. They looked at him, startled. There was no doubt in their eyes. They knew who he was, the man who had come to take away their place for playing in.

He knew he would have to walk warily. His smile was broad but it got nothing in response.

"You're packing up. Is that right?"

The dark-eyed twins talked to him alternately, one beginning a sentence and the other finishing it, as if they had always done this.

"People always come here . . ." the girl said defensively.

"Always as far as *anyone* can remember," supported the boy.

"So it's not as if it was trespassing . . ."

"Or being on private property . . ."

Patrick gave a big infectious laugh.

"But I know that, I *know*. I saw your home last night, it was mighty impressive. I came up to see the place by moonlight. Have you lot ever been here in the moonlight?" They shook their heads.

"It's very strange. It has a life of its own, all the shadows seem to mean something. You'd really like it." He spoke as if he were their own age, suggesting they do something as out of their world as going off on midnight treks across the river. Mammy and Daddy would kill them.

"Come some evening with me, I'll square it with your folks, and I'll go off for a walk by myself and leave you in your . . . in your house?" He sought for the right word to describe the dismantled room.

"It's not going to be knocked down, is it?"

He answered the girl indirectly. "Changed a bit," he said. "You know, roofs and good firm walls."

"You mean it *is* to be knocked down."

He decided not to talk baby talk to the girl with the big dark eyes under her bangs of black hair.

"That's it, knocked down to be rebuilt. They tell me a lot of these old walls are dangerous, you could tip them over with your little finger. Not the things to build on, unfortunately."

She nodded silently. The boy nodded too. It was as though they had both accepted what he said in exactly the same way and were thinking about it.

"Still, it won't be for a while. No need to move all your things." He indicated with his head their box of possessions.

"If it's coming down anyway . . ." Michael began.

"There's really not any point . . ." Dara took up.

"In leaving things here . . ."

"That'll have to come out anyway."

"Sure, everyone's got to do what they've got to do. All I'm saying is that there's no great rush. It will be weeks before anyone gets as far as this room. What do you call it, by the way?" He smiled at them, looking from one to the other. They were not to be won over.

"What do you call what?" the girl asked.

"This . . . this room . . . do you have a special name for it or anything?"

"No. No special name," she said.

"It used to be the morning room," the boy said. The first offer.

"Not by us. We didn't call it the morning room. Or any name." The dark girl was giving nothing away.

"I guess it was the morning room because it got the morning sun. It faces east, southeast. That's right, would you say?"

But the boy felt he had been too friendly, and his sister was suggesting they leave.

"We've really got to go now."

"Come back again, anytime; you're welcome here always," he said. Somehow he knew it was the wrong thing to have said.

"Well, like you always were. When a place is special you don't need anyone to welcome you to it. That's right, isn't it?"

They nodded at him, shoulders slightly less tense, their stance not so hostile.

"So we have to be off," the boy said, picking up one side of the box that contained their life in this room.

"So goodbye," said the girl, picking up the other side. They walked away from him, two little figures probably the same age as his Grace. Reasonably well cared for, grubby knees and dirty hands from playing . . . or indeed packing all their house things—they must have been covered in clay and dust. He watched them through the open walls of the house. They headed not for the town and the big bridge across into Bridge Street itself, but they went the other way toward River Road. Going to cross that little footbridge . . . maybe they belonged to that crook Jack Coyne?

Patrick was glad he hadn't asked them if they were twins. It was obvious they were and yet people always had a habit of asking the obvious. He found it very irritating even when it was well meant, like when people said to him "You're an American!" with an air of discovery. They were fine kids, a little prickly, especially the girl. He'd catch up with them again, give them some job maybe, make them a few pounds. Or maybe they might resent that. He'd see. And when Grace came over, she'd charm them to bits anyway.

Now to see the Ryans in the poky little pub and then back to the dark room with the heavy mahogany furniture which had been in the Johnson family for generations, and the picture of Our Lady of Perpetual Succor which had helped them through some of the bad times. And a long, long sleep.

Kate had come back early. Fergus was right. She couldn't really concentrate and John would have to be told before anyone else came with the news.

The angelus was ringing as she walked down River Road. She looked across the banks and tried to imagine what it would be like with a huge hotel, a car park, with signs for a pub, with music maybe . . . Americans did things in style. She called into Loretto Quinn's little shop for a bag of sugar and a dozen candles. She always tried to give Loretto the turn; the small white face behind the counter moved Kate to pity. Loretto and Barney Quinn had saved and saved for a business, any business. They had done any work to get the deposit on the tumbledown place. They could be seen night and day working to make it right. They knew they were no competition to the shops on Bridge Street, so Barney Quinn had bought a van in which to do deliveries.

A week after the van was delivered, Barney threw it into reverse and went into the river. It happened so quickly that Loretto never even knew. She was still out in the back filling bags of potatoes when the alarm was raised and she realized half the town was outside her front door with ropes and pulleys trying to get her husband, dead now in his van, out of the River Fern. There had never been any color or much life in her face after that. The child she had been expecting was stillborn, and she kept the shabby little shop as a memory of her young husband and in honor of the way things might have been.

Jack Coyne had been helpful about the unpaid-for van and the insurance and everything. People had been kind at the time. Not everyone continued to be helpful like Mrs. Ryan. Loretto knew it would be very easy for her to get things cheaper in Bridge Street where she went to work, or to get them delivered, but nearly every day she called in for something. Today she was early.

"You're not taken sick coming home early?" she asked, concerned.

"Ah, not at all Loretto, nothing would make me feel badly, thank God. No, it's light there this morning and I thought I'd come on back to John to give him a hand. Not that there's likely to be any custom much for another hour."

"Will the place across make any difference to you? Jack Coyne was in earlier. He wondered would it take any of your custom. I said it would be a different class of person entirely . . ."

"Thanks, Loretto." Kate should have left earlier. John Ryan must know by now that his livelihood was threatened and that the days of Ryan's, Whiskey Bonder, were numbered.

John was sitting on a high stool reading the paper. He put down the newspaper automatically as the door opened.

"That's never the time!" he said, amazed, looking up at the old clock and back at his watch trying to work it out.

"No. I came home a bit early." Kate put down her parcels and sat up as if she were a customer.

"Couldn't wait for a ball of malt?" he teased her.

"John."

"What is it?" His face showed that he knew something was wrong. "Are you all right, do you feel all right?"

"I'm fine." Suddenly she was weary; she knew it would be an uphill struggle trying to make him realize how serious things were going to be.

"What *is* it then?"

"Did you hear what's happening to Fernscourt? They're going to make it into a hotel, have a bar. Americans are going to stay there, and there'll be a bar the size of a football field. He's put in for planning permission."

"I heard that it was going to be a hotel all right. Tommy was round with the mineral water deliveries. Oh, he left the invoice there on the shelf, by the way, it's behind the—"

"Will you stop bleating on about invoices? It's mighty few of those we'll be seeing in the future. Did you hear what I said?"

"I heard you, Kate. There's no need to shout like a fishwife."

"Like a what?"

"A fishwife, look at you; you have your hands on your hips even. Stop being so impatient, and let's discuss this thing properly."

"I'm the one who ran the whole way back from Fergus as soon as I heard about it. Don't you think I want to discuss it properly?"

"Yes, Kate. But not in public. Not in the middle of the bar."

Kate looked around at the empty room.

"God Almighty, have you lost your mind? Who's here except Leopold, are you afraid the dog's going to start gossiping about us and our business around town?"

"Don't let's start something that we'll have to cut off as soon as someone comes in that door."

"All right, all right." She made a gesture with her hands as if calming things down. "Very well, but in the meantime do you mind if we talk about what's going to become of us, or would you rather read me Curly Wee out of the paper, or have a discussion about the weather?"

"We can't know what to think, until we know what's going to happen. How many times do I tell you not to go off at half cock about every single thing? We'll hear in good time what he's going to do. It might be the making of us for all we know. A whole lot of new people coming to the place, a lot of business we never had before. How many times have we wished that we were a tourist area where the people came on holidays? Now we will be, if what Tommy said is true."

"The making of us; the making of us. How could it be anything except the end of us? For as many times as we said we'd like tourists, haven't we been thanking the stars that they're all so dozy in there in Foley's and Conway's and half packed to leave in Dunne's? We never had any competition, and even then we barely make a living. How can you be so blind?"

A flash of annoyance crossed John's big, good-natured face.

"Listen to me, I know you work hard, I know you put in all the hours that God gives you making a life for us, but answer me this, why am I being blind? What should I have done? Should I have bought the place myself? Or killed the fellow who did? Come on now, tell me. I'm standing here minding what I agree is at the moment a very slow business, some would say non-existent . . . and hoping that there's going to be some kind of good spin-off instead of doom and disaster for us, and you come rushing in the door shouting at me like a tinker's woman and saying I'm blind. That's a lot of help, Kate, thank you very much."

Before she could reply the door opened and in came Marian Johnson, face flushed and wispy hair blowing all directions. Rita Walsh of the Rosemarie hair salon said that she had often known people with two crowns in their head of hair, but Marian Johnson had three. The woman couldn't be blamed for looking like a refined haystack. Marian was anxious to know if John Ryan could oblige her with a bottle of Jack Daniels.

John Ryan couldn't. He had Scotch all right, but nothing else except Irish whiskey. They might have it in the town, he supposed.

"Very fancy tastes you're getting above at the Grange," he said companionably. He couldn't have said anything more welcome. Marian was dying to release the news. It was for the American, the man who was going to buy Fernscourt, or who had bought it in fact, but was going to open a hotel there. She went on and on, words falling over each other in excitement. There were going to be fishermen, not people like from here, not just the visitors from England who stayed in guest houses, but rich Americans with their own rods going to come and fish the Fern for pike and rudd, for bream and perch. And there were going to be Americans who would want to ride horses, they would even come in winter so they could hunt. They'd be here the whole year round. She was unaware of the silence that she spoke to. But eventually even Marian ran out of wind.

"Isn't it great?" she said, looking from one to the other.

"I'd have thought you'd be very put out. Isn't that all your kind of business that he's going to be taking?" Kate said, avoiding the look of caution that her husband was trying to beam at her.

Marian tossed her head. "Heavens no, isn't it all to the good, isn't it going to build the whole thing up for all of us? They're going to want horses. Apparently I'll be expanding all that side of our business. It's going to change the whole place." Marian hugged herself almost girlishly at the thought of it.

"That's what I'm afraid of," Kate said. "That it's going to change the whole place."

"Oh, Kate Ryan, you're as young as I am," tinkled Marian, who was most definitely the older of the two. "Don't be an old stick-in-the-mud. It's going to transform your lives. Think of all the people that'll come tripping across that footbridge there to have a drink in your place. It will be just what you need."

John seized her words as if they were a lifeline. "That's just what I was saying to Kate when you came in the door. It could be the making of us. It could be the bit of luck we were always hoping for." His face was bright with enthusiasm.

Kate watched, wordless, as her husband and Marian Johnson made plans for the future. They never talked about all the people who would like to go and have a drink in the big hotel, who would trip across the footbridge in the other direction. She looked at John and tried to work out whether he really believed this optimistic line of chat, or if he was only trying to buoy up the Ryan family. She decided that he really believed it; he wanted so much for things to turn out well that he refused to look at any other possibility. She felt a mixture of annoyance that he should be so naïve, and a protective, almost maternal anxiety because she had this cold fear that things were indeed going to change, and that something very bad was about to happen.

The twins crept in through the back door. They were filthy and carrying a big battered box between them. They looked like small dark criminals. They both put their fingers on their lips, warning Carrie not to cry out.

"Oh God, you'll get killed," Carrie said, half pleased and half worried on their behalf. They'd been up to no good whatever they'd been doing.

"We'll be clean by the time Mammy gets back," Michael said to reassure her.

"She's back already," Carrie cried triumphantly. "She'll take you apart so she will."

Carrie, who greatly feared Mrs. Ryan's hurricane-like visits to the kitchen, and her great ability to see things that were not done right, was always guiltily pleased when the wrath fell elsewhere. Carrie had long straight hair that fell into her frightened eyes—except when she saw Mrs. Ryan looking, then she took a barrette from her apron pocket. She was a mousy little thing who could look very nice when she tidied herself up. Mrs. Ryan was always finding a blouse or a brooch or some little thing for her. Carrie only wore this finery on her day off when she walked four miles back to the farm from which she had been glad to escape.

She was fine unless she was fussed, and this was fussing her, the twins having skipped school and dragging this big box guiltily upstairs. Nobody ever came to Carrie's kitchen during the mornings except young Declan. And now here were Dara and Michael home, way in advance. And the mistress was home early too. Really it was very troublesome. Carrie always arranged to have the kitchen looking well when Mrs. Ryan came back at one o'clock; the pots were washed and put away. Now it looked a mess, and she was bound to be criticized. She sighed heavily and started to clear up the things that were most likely to offend.

Gently Michael and Dara eased themselves into the bathroom to shake out their crumpled school clothes and wipe off most of the grime. *What* was Mammy doing home so early, on this of all days? They had banked on at least an hour to get themselves to rights. This was the very first time they had ever played hooky from school. Dara had told Sister Laura that she had a pain in her tummy, and Michael had told Brother Kevin that he had eaten too many potato chips. Sister Laura had been understanding in case it might be Dara's first period, Brother Kevin had been dismissive and said what could you expect of a boy brought up in a pub but to eat like a pig all the rubbish in packets that was put in front of him? But it was too dangerous for them to go to school that day. If the man had been wandering around Fernscourt in the middle of the night they had to go and take their things away. Somehow they both knew that at the same time and realized it had to be done. They never dreamed they'd meet the man himself.

The Ryans never ate lunch together as a family since John was always in the bar. And the first rule of the house was that the children never appeared in the bar at all. John said that most of his customers came there to escape from households of screaming children racing around the place, and they mustn't be allowed to see a hint of the same thing in Ryan's. So Dara and Michael would have had no idea who was in the bar as they sat down to lunch.

Eddie and Declan had come in at the normal time.

"You were quick," Eddie said to Michael. Normally they all raced together from the brothers, beyond the bridge down River Road. Dara's convent was up the other way, past the Rosemarie hair salon and Jack Coyne's. Nobody could tell whether or not she had come home. It was only Michael who might have been missed.

"Yes, we got out a bit early." Michael looked from under his lashes to see if Mammy had made anything of this exchange, but her mind seemed to be miles away. She hadn't even noticed how crushed their clothes were from being bundled in a bag.

The twins hadn't decided what to do for the afternoon. They would have to walk toward school of course, and then they could meet somewhere else. Eddie and Declan had no afternoon school so there would be no need for Michael to go all the way to the brothers. There were a host of possibilities. But before any were settled, the door of the pub opened and Daddy came through.

"Kate, Kate, come out and meet Mr. O'Neill who's bought Fernscourt. He's called to pay his respects. And bring the children too, he says he'd like to meet them."

Leopold, who was the most antisocial dog in the world, decided for once that he was included in the invitation too. Looking exactly like an advertisement from a Cruelty to Animals brochure, he walked ahead of them, sidling and cringing as if expecting a blow at every turn.

Kate smoothed her skirt and shepherded the children in front of her. There was time only to wipe the excess of food from Declan's mouth; to pause and titivate them would have been a weakness with the door open and the great O'Neill waiting for them. Declan and Eddie hung back and had to be pushed forward. Dara and Michael were equally unwilling. In fact they both looked as if they had been caught out in some crime. Kate supposed they felt awkward meeting the man whose arrival they had hated so much. She didn't realize how deadly accurate her first thought was. They had been caught out. He was going to say he had met them this very morning. They would be discovered.

Kate was surprised at his looks. Like a handsome Irishman on a fair day with a drove of young bullocks to sell. Not like an American tycoon. He had a tweed jacket in a pepper and salt color. It was very well cut. It would suit John, she thought, hide some of his stomach. This man was big, with bright blue eyes and a million laugh lines. His big hand was stretched to her.

"Mrs. Kathleen Ryan. My own wife, the Lord have mercy on her, was Kathleen too. I'm glad to know you."

He *seemed* glad to know her.

She had never gotten such a shock in her life.

All morning she had been thinking of him as the enemy, and here he was standing in their own pub, all smiles. No man could do that if he was going to take all your business. Even in America, where you had to be shrewd and tough to get on, they wouldn't do that. There were half a dozen customers all eager and interested to see the introductions. They, too, would be introduced, they knew. But first the children.

"These are the twins, Dara and Michael, and here's Eddie. Take your arm from over your face, Eddie and Declan. Declan, come out from behind me."

He repeated their names slowly. *That's* why Americans were so good at remembering people. They didn't just say how do you do, or hello. They actually repeated the name.

"Dara . . . there's a name. Is it short for something?"

"It means oak tree. You know Kildare. That's Cill Dara, the churchyard of the oak tree."

"Oak tree . . . Isn't that something? And Michael. That's the archangel, I guess?"

"And my grandfather," Michael said more prosaically.

"And you'll come back and spend more mornings in Fernscourt, I hope," he said.

The twins were glum. Here it was. The discovery.

"They will on their holidays, if they aren't in the way," Kate said, filling the silence. "But these days it's all schoolwork, I'm afraid. No idle mornings playing in Fernscourt until they get their holidays."

Dara closed her eyes.

Michael looked at him in desperation.

"Sure," said Patrick O'Neill. "Sure, I know that, but after school or at weekends or any time. The place is always there and I'm sure you must love it, what with living so near and everything." He wasn't going to say anything.

They looked at him in amazement.

John and Kate Ryan also exchanged glances of relief. Whatever else was going to happen, at least this big man understood somehow that the place was important to the twins. What a relief that they would not be getting into trouble over trespass or being a nuisance. The man in full view of the whole bar had literally invited the children to continue playing in the house.

"That's very kind of Mr. O'Neill; thank him, children," Kate said.

"Thank you," said Dara.

"Very much," finished Michael.

It was time for them to go back to school. They were hurried out back through the house again. The children had never been known to go out on to River Road through the pub entrance. Kate went silent behind the bar and helped to serve. Nobody would move until the introductions had been properly made. Jimbo Doyle, the man who did a bit of everything in Mountfern, was particularly pleased. If he could be present as a friend of the establishment it might mean work on the new place across the river. He was a big fair man with hair like straw and a healthy red face. He often wore a check shirt and looked about to break into a square dance at any moment.

Charlie, who worked in Daly's, would be sure to be a frequent visitor there anyway, with milk and cream. Unless, of course, the man was going to have his own cow, his own dairy. Maybe Charlie could ask him now.

Patrick O'Neill was open with all of them. He wasn't at all sure if they would have their own cows. Someday possibly. But not for a good bit. He'd be needing all the milk, butter and cream that Daly's Dairy would provide. Charlie felt very important to be the bearer of this news and specially so when Mr. O'Neill remembered his name.

"See you again then, Charlie," and a cheerful wave as he was leaving to ride down River Road and back to Bridge Street to Mrs. Daly with the good tidings.

Jimbo Doyle's red face was positively scarlet after the encounter. Mr. O'Neill said that the work on the site was all in the hands of an overseer, a Brian Doyle who came from the big town sixteen miles away. Possibly Jimbo and Brian were related? It could be, couldn't it? Jimbo shook his head ruefully. Ah no, there were lots of Doyles and if this man was a building contractor and in a big way over in the town then it wasn't likely that he would be any family to Jimbo. But still, maybe it was an omen. If the man's name was Doyle, he might find it hard to refuse another Doyle.

"He won't refuse you, Jim," Patrick O'Neill said. "I'll tell him I met you and that your work has been highly spoken of."

Kate polished glasses with a snow-white cloth and watched the big, handsome American speaking easily with them all. One by one they left, secure in the knowledge that they would be remembered, and somehow warmed by his interest. Kate felt admiring and then a little fearful. It wasn't that she feared he would forget these men in their working clothes, with their humble hopes. No, she was afraid more that he *would* remember them. And this all meant that he was very determined to come back to some kind of roots. Roots which he was finding it increasingly hard to establish, as he'd just told them in the bar. Nobody, not even the older men, could remember any O'Neills around the place, not living on the demesne in Fernscourt anyway. There were O'Neills up the other side of the town, the far end of Bridge Street. But Patrick's kith nobody could recall. "It was all a long time ago," they said, as if to forgive themselves and each other.

Yet the man who had come back to build here remembered it all. As if he had been present.

Kate made the glasses shine as she puzzled over it. A man like that must have another wife in mind, someone in America, an Irish-American widow perhaps. Would she be coming over too? He must be worth a fortune. Look at what he must have paid out already for site investigation, and that was before he started work on the house. He must be very determined to make this a success. And if he did, what would happen to them?

They were alone in the bar now, the three of them. Patrick had let them buy him a drink to welcome him to these parts; now they let him buy one for them. Kate's small port felt as if it were choking her, but she drank it and smiled at the handsome man with the open face, the open shirt and the well-cut tweed jacket.

"To the dream." He raised his glass. "John, Kate . . . I want you to be part of the dream as well. I want us all to share in it."

"Well sure, we'll be glad to share anything there is to share," John said, a bit at a loss.

"I'll drink to the dream," Kate said. "And to your happiness and success across the river. You won't find it too tame for you after New York?"

"All my life I wanted to come back here," he said simply. "In the middle of big deals and buying more neighborhood bars I always said to myself . . . Patrick, this is one step nearer coming home."

"Imagine that, and you weren't born and brought up here at all." John shook his head in wonderment.

Kate hoped her voice didn't sound tinny. "And what exactly do you plan, or have you worked it out yet?"

She tried to listen to the words as they came out, and wondered, did they betray her anxiety. If they had, the big man didn't seem to notice. He leaned over the bar eagerly, and like a boy told his plans. The house was going to rise again, like it had been before. There were old pictures and drawings, and he had people working on those country homes built all over the land in the 1780s; it would all be in keeping and in the right period. It was going to be a hotel for the kind of Irish-American who wanted to feel welcome, and as if he had come home. Limo services would be arranged to take them to their own part of the country so that they could find their own roots. There would be fishing and horse riding, and in the correct seasons there would be shooting and hunting. Very few of the Irish who had emigrated to America had any of the gentlemanly sports like these in their background. They had gone to the States because other gentlemen, gentlemen of a different race and religion, had ousted them from their homes. It would be a real homecoming in every sense of the word for any American of Irish stock.

And there would be names on the rooms instead of numbers. Like the O'Brien room, or the Lynch room, or the Kennedy room, or whatever. Kate listened to the list and gave her little oohs and aahs to coincide with the genuine ones of her husband. Her lower lip was almost flattened with the effort of staying calm until he came to the bit about the bar.

Oh, there would be a cocktail lounge certainly, for pre-dinner drinks where orders could be taken before guests went into the dining room. And then there would be the Thatch Bar. A thatched cottage on the grounds in what Patrick thought must be the exact spot his own ancestors lived before they were thrown out on the road. There was a lot of talk about ancestors being forced to work-houses before Kate could get him silkily back to the Thatch Bar. A real traditional Irish Bar, with fiddlers playing and every night some little entertainment, like Irish dancing or a singer, or some old storyteller telling a tale.

And there would be ordinary prices in it too, not fancy ones. Patrick O'Neill wanted his own to come to his bar, not just the gentry. The pint would cost the same in the Thatch Bar as it would anywhere else. It would attract the local people in and the visitors would really and genuinely get to know them.

Kate looked at the boyish face in astonishment. What kind of a mind did you need to get on in America if this was the proof of it sitting opposite her? What did he *mean,* he didn't want just the gentry? What gentry would go to a flash place like this anyway? Could he see the Walters, or the Harrises, or the Johnsons from the Grange even, spending an evening in the Thatch Bar? The man must be mad. But what was he thinking about, telling them these plans? He must know that he would ruin their trade if this all came to pass. He must know they would try to oppose his license on the ground that the area was well covered with licensed premises already. What was he talking about, telling them that he wanted to share a dream with them?

Kate looked at John for some support, and found that she couldn't read his face. It was just as it had been when he was talking to Marian Johnson earlier on, smiling and thoughtful. Was he really taken in by all this patter, or had his heart missed a beat when he heard of the Thatch Bar and all the dangers it looked like bringing on top of them? She could find no words to speak; everything she wanted to say would sound harsh and hysterical. She wanted to take this O'Neill man by the lapels and look straight into his smiling blue eyes. Burrow into them until she could see the truth. She would like to beg him not to ruin their business. She wanted to tell him that, as he had so much money, and so many chances, could he not just have Fernscourt as a home, to entertain his American friends. Surely he didn't *need* a bar business there. Then that mood vanished, and she wanted to tell him there would be no further pretense at amicable conversation. She and her husband would oppose his getting a license, and they would raise everyone in the neighborhood to support them in their case.

But Kate Ryan knew with heavy heart that she could do nothing of the sort. Had she not seen the gratified delight already on everyone's face? There would be a very slender army to raise against Patrick O'Neill.

John was asking all kinds of questions, idiotic questions, Kate thought, as if he were delighted to see such opposition arriving on his doorstep.

Would the guests go around in buses? What part of America would they come from mainly?

Kate could have killed him for his eager interest in the unimportant side of things. What did it matter if these visitors traveled by bus or by wheelbarrow? Who could care less if they came from one part of America or another? They didn't know *any* parts of America, for God's sake. And yet little by little John was learning more about the whole undertaking across the river than anyone else would have learned from this clever American. There could be a purpose to his questions. She looked hard at John, fighting the lump in her throat which made her want to burst into tears. He looked so good and patient; he had worked for so many years at a job that he would never have chosen. It would be cruel to see it swept away by this successful man who could have had power and riches anywhere else on the earth.

Kate knew she should join in the conversation. She had been conspicuously silent. In fact she saw John glance at her, his face still cheerful and his smile all-embracing.

"Well I can't tell you, Patrick, what an excitement all this will be." He looked at his wife as if he were leaving the way open for her to add her words of delight and welcome. Kate was still too full to trust herself to conversation.

"The excitement is mainly mine," Patrick said. "If you knew how many times I dreamed of this, and often I had to say it aloud to myself, you know like a chant or a prayer. It will happen; it will happen." He looked at them both with an engaging smile.

"Now I almost have to tell myself it *has* happened, it *has* happened." He looked so boyish and delighted it was hard not to like him.

Kate decided to speak. "And how would we come into all this? How can we . . . um . . . help you in it all?" she asked. Her voice was definitely faltering and she wasn't far from tears.

"But that's what good neighbors will always do," he cried triumphantly. "I'll get my guests to come to you, send them over to you before lunch or in the early afternoon . . . when maybe you could do with an injection." He looked around the empty bar and left a short significant pause. "I guess this would be a good time to send a group over for an Irish coffee or something. And you can tell your regulars when there's entertainment on in the Thatch that they might like to come and see. Or better, any of them who are talented, if they want to come and perform. Play for people. It's their place now." He smiled from one to another.

"I guess you know that it's a principle of business that one successful establishment leads to another. Business grows out of custom to an area. Mark my words, there's going to be new places starting up out on River Road before we know it. By the end of the sixties they'll be asking where Bridge Street is . . . they'll all think that River Road is the center of the universe, and the Ryans and O'Neills will have been here from the outset."

John was smiling back at him. Was John Ryan under the net? Had the web of companionship and complicity caught him? Kate realized that there were going to be very few people who would not be caught in that net. Even her own Dara and Michael, who had vowed never to speak to the new owner of Fernscourt, were flashing him grateful smiles and friendly glances when he said that they could continue playing there.

So far only Fergus Slattery had managed to remain aloof, and he hadn't met the American yet; perhaps he would be bowled over like the others had been. Kate smiled on, though she felt there was a distant ache in her face. If John could smile so could she. Anyway there was nothing to be gained by showing her hand now. She must remember that if she came straight out with all her worries and hostilities, it would do nothing but harm. Living all these years with the solid John Ryan had taught her that much anyway.

So she accepted with a dimpling smile when the laughing American begged to be allowed to buy them one more drink so that they could toast the success of River Road and especially those who were in at the very start.

Fergus Slattery heard that the American was doing the rounds. He didn't want to be in. His father had gone fishing; he put a closed sign on the door and headed out.

"Where will I say you've gone?" Miss Purcell asked, not because she thought anyone would call, but because she wanted to know what was taking him away from his business in the middle of the afternoon.

"Go out on the doorstep every hour and say to the crowds that Sergeant Sheehan and I have raised a posse of men and we've gone out to see if we can bring in any poachers. Dead or alive. That should satisfy them," he said.

"You have a very strange way of going on, Master Fergus. It's not every woman that could stay in this house and put up with it."

"Haven't we always said you are a woman in a million, a woman different to all others?" Fergus said, and he was gone before she could put another question to him.

He took the car not because he had any idea where he was going, but at least in the car he wouldn't have to answer half a dozen questions about where he was going in the middle of the afternoon. He waved and nodded as he drove up Bridge Street to the main road. He saw the signpost to Dublin and parked for a while. Suppose he was in Dublin, he wouldn't be even slightly affected by a licensing application. He would do it; there was no chance that he would know the people it would hurt, there was no way in Dublin that he might already feel slighted by this applicant. Without meeting Patrick O'Neill, Fergus was somehow prejudiced against him. He had heard about the way he had bought the fishing rights and it was perfectly legal, the way he had organized the searches on the land, and dealt with the Land Commission, was all above board. If in the future he was seen to have had drinks with this politician and with that local councillor, nobody was going to cast an aspersion. This was how things were done. The planning permissions and the license would go through and he would build his monstrosity. After a few years it might be a white elephant and it could be written off as a tax loss. Patrick O'Neill was of the breed who would start again. Somewhere else, different scheme.

Fergus was old-fashioned, he wanted things to remain the same. The same kind of quiet practice, the same kind of food. He didn't like moving on, cutting losses. He didn't at all like the notion of a stage-Irish bar across the Fern, and taking all the trade from Kate Ryan. It took a lot to upset that woman, and today she had left early, saying truthfully that she couldn't concentrate. Perhaps he would call in and see had they any news. A half of Guinness would go down very well on a warm summer afternoon.

He decided to leave the car parked where it was near the main road to the big town in one direction and Dublin in the other. He could walk down that lane which came out through Jack Coyne's wood, right onto River Road, not far from Ryan's. He whistled as he walked. Partly from the sheer freedom of being out among the trees, and partly because he wanted to cheer himself up over this Yank business. The rhododendrons were out in a great purple show, and darker red ones too. In other countries, Fergus thought, this place would be a public park with manicured grass and seats and litter bins. As he was debating to himself whether this would be good or bad he came across four frightened dark eyes.

Kate Ryan's twins Dara and Michael who were quite obviously meant to be at school, and had no business, any more than himself, wandering the woods on a working afternoon.

"You see, Mr. Slattery . . ."

"We didn't exactly say at home . . ."

"Just we weren't going back to school . . ."

"If you see what I mean . . ."

Fergus pretended neither to hear nor see them. He began to talk to himself.

"Ho hum, what a lovely thing it is to walk in a wood, and see nobody at all. That's what I like best: a walk where you don't see another human being. That's the kind of thing that does me good when I'm on my way to Ryan's Bar to have a drink. A walk where I don't meet another sinner."

He began whistling.

Dara and Michael looked at each other in amazement.

"Grown-ups are extraordinary," said Michael.

"They seem to be improving all the time."

That was twice in one day they had been rescued. Dara wondered if it would be possible to leave school entirely. There seemed to be a great conspiracy working for them at the moment.

Patrick O'Neill declined the invitation of Marian Johnson to dine with her that night. He pleaded great fatigue, and said he would be no company. A glass of milk and a sandwich and bed in the elegant room were what he wanted. He noticed the disappointment on Marian's face and the fact that she had had her hair fixed since they had been out riding; maybe she had gone to a beauty parlor specially.

"You look very nice," he said tiredly.

Marian's face lit up. That was compliment enough.

He said that if she were free he would love another ride on that nice mild-mannered horse tomorrow. That brought on further smiles. He could go to bed now without being thought boorish.

He wished there were phones in the bedrooms. He wanted to call Grace back home. It would be great to dial direct and hear the reassurance of Bella and Andy that Grace was at home. It was eight-thirty here in Mountfern: it would be three-thirty in New Jersey, just the time that Andy was driving Grace up the avenue. Patrick's sister, a fussy woman called Philomena, was in residence as chaperon. Kerry was away at school. Rachel was in her apartment. He really should call her. But not from the hall of the Grange. Not with Marian Johnson listening to every word. There were obviously some calls which were going to be made through that pleasant woman who ran the post office, who had made tea for him this morning. Was it only *this* morning? Lord, why had he stayed up all night in Fernscourt? His bones ached with tiredness.

He took a hot bath and felt much better. Better still after the milk and sandwiches. He lay on his bed and looked out at the green fields leading off to clumps of trees. Behind those trees was the winding River Fern, and his own place. It had been some day. Still he had done almost everything he set out to do. The lawyer chap hadn't been in, which was rather lackadaisical. Even in a sleepy hollow like this, someone should have been looking after the shop. And Kate Ryan hadn't been convinced. She was the only real opposition—not that she had said it, of course. That made her smart. A handsome woman too, probably the brains of that business. The dreamy pleasant husband was not a man with much drive. Bright smart children too. Lucky he had been able to get them on his side by shielding them. Little rascals, skipping school.

Canon Moran had been so helpful about looking up records, and the young curate had promised to inquire about burial grounds and possible tombstones. Strangely, that old wino bag lady he had picked up in the car was their house-keeper. She looked extremely ropy today, as if she had just had another night on the tiles.

And the Dalys had been magnificent, and the Leonards, and Jack Coyne—knowing now too late that he had blown it by overcharging Patrick for the car—said that he hoped they would be able to talk man to man about business one day. Patrick had smiled and said of course, but he and Jack Coyne knew that not one cent's worth of business was ever going to cross the River Fern from Fernscourt to Coyne's Garage. He talked to Sergeant Sheehan casually, to Dr. White who happened to be in Daly's, to assorted others whose names would come back to him when he was less tired. He had an excellent memory and never had to write down the names of the people he met through work. To some people today might seem like a leisure day, wandering around talking to folk. But to Patrick O'Neill it was work. His life's work. And really and truly it had gone very well today. It wouldn't take long to convince that fine tall Kate Ryan that he didn't mean her and hers any harm. It was true he did not. And it was always a bit easier convincing people if the thing was actually true.

* * *

Rachel Fine applied her throat cream exactly as the label had advised with short upward strokes. She then applied her eye cream in the recommended manner with a feather-light fingertip so as not to damage the delicate tissue around the eye. She sat in her cotton nightdress looking without pleasure at the reflection that stared from the mirror. She looked like any sad Jewish mamma left on her own this night. There must be a thousand of them in this area alone. But she hadn't even the satisfaction of being a mamma. And her husband, Herbert had been in California for eight years. She and he had ended their relationship long before hers with Patrick had begun. Herbert had given her the apartment and a car. The divorce had been genuinely amicable. They sent each other postcards even; they remained casual friends, bewildered that they had ever thought they knew each other well enough to marry and to remain married for so long.

But however lonely, Rachel would not telephone Herbert for company. And she had very few friends left. When you devote your life to a man, his business, and his limited free time as Rachel had done, it didn't leave much time for friends. She still had work to do for O'Neill Enterprises even while he was in Ireland, but she did it in a mechanical way. When there was no Patrick to discuss her ideas with the fire went out of them.

Sure she was a designer. Sure, sure, everyone realized that she was worth her salary, her ideas had been praised in the newspapers and magazines, and her style had lifted the O'Neill chain way out of the commonplace. Rachel had never wanted to see her own name over the smart corner-bistro-type restaurants, it was quite satisfying enough to know that her choosing of colors and fabrics, her layout and her selection of decor, waitresses' uniforms and lighting techniques contributed to the O'Neill empire. When Patrick had eight pub-restaurants and the motel in New Jersey he said he had enough. He bought no more until this huge bottomless pit that was Fernscourt, bleeding away his profits in a way that nobody would believe.

Gerry Power, Patrick's second in command, knew this. He was tight-lipped and disapproving, but not even to Rachel, whose position he knew very well, would he hint that he took anything less than delight in all of Patrick's schemes.

Rachel looked again at the telephone. It was ten P.M. here. It was three o'clock tomorrow morning in that godforsaken place. Perhaps he would call tomorrow. Perhaps he might even call at his lunchtime, which would be getting up time here. Yes, surely that's what he would do.

Rachel laid a towel over her pillowcase. The only advantage of not having your man living with you all the time was that you could do your beauty routines adequately. On the nights when Patrick stayed, there was a satin nightgown, not a cheap cotton one, there was no throat cream or eye cream. There were certainly no exercises.

But what was Patrick's great phrase? "It's always either a feast or a famine." Rachel Fine sighed deeply. It had been a famine for her for a very long time, and the worst bit was that she could see long lean years of famine still ahead.

Mrs. Whelan understood without being told and without the need for comment that Patrick would need to make calls in privacy. She settled him next day in her own sitting room, two closed doors away from anyone who might be standing in the post office with their ears flapping.

She gave him a table for his papers and said she would add up the charges each time and he could pay at the end. Another cup of strong tea, a cushion to cure his saddle sores.

"You're a wonderful woman. Did the late Mr. Whelan appreciate you?"

"He's not late, he just went off," she said simply.

Patrick knew how hard it was for a woman in a small community to admit something like this, she would say it to him once because her common sense would tell her that he would hear it elsewhere, then it would never be mentioned again. He too would acknowledge it once and then forget it.

"A foolish man. Did he find the happiness he thought he was going to find? Most people who run away don't."

She thought about it.

"At first he did, I'd say. But times aren't great now, I hear. When I do hear, which isn't often." That meant the subject was closed. "I'd better leave you and start to get through to the operator for you."

Patrick hadn't been thinking of phoning Kerry in his big school. But why not? They would certainly get him to the phone. As he settled himself into the chair and cushions provided by Sheila Whelan, Patrick realized that in ways she was a little like Rachel. She knew how to make a man feel welcome and comfortable and important. How strange that Rachel was sitting alone in Brooklyn just as Sheila lived alone in Mountfern. Did it prove that it was a bad thing to make a man comfortable?

Patrick had never been able to understand people who could use the telephone for long chatty conversations. For too many years now he had used it for work to be able to think of it as a way of talking unselfconsciously. Grace could talk for hours on the telephone to friends whom she had just left at school. People told Patrick that it was the same with their daughters, and indeed their wives.

He put the first call through to Gerry Power. At least Gerry felt the same way about telephones. A necessary but unappealing part of business life. He wouldn't complain that Patrick was not being sufficiently warm or forthcoming over three thousand miles on a piece of machinery.

Gerry Power wasted no time congratulating him or expressing any surprise. If Mr. O'Neill had said he was going to go and throw away his fortune on this heap of old stones, then this is what he was going to do. He listened to instructions, and nodded and grunted. At the end of the catalogue he read them back. Patrick smiled; he could almost see Gerry Power in his shirt sleeves, writing with a stubby pencil.

"And that's three air tickets you want. Three not four?"

"You're very numerate Gerry, three. One each for Kerry, Grace and me."

"Just checking." Gerry Power was in no way put out. He hated grey areas and wanted to make sure that his boss hadn't expected him to book a seat for Mrs. Fine, without asking him directly to do so.

Grace was always excited to hear from him. When was he arriving? Good, good. And how long was he staying home? Only a few days, but that was awful! He had been gone so long. He was *what?* Was this true? He was really and truly going to take Kerry and Grace with him to Ireland? And she could go to school there? Grace's voice disappeared into squeaks of excitement.

Patrick spoke to his sister Philomena. She shared neither Grace's excitement nor Patrick's enthusiasm. She listened to the facts in a disapproving silence. Yes she would have clothes organized; and she would explain to the nuns here that Grace would not return in the fall.

"Well, what do you think of my getting back to the old country in the end?" Patrick hated having to ask her, despised himself for fishing for the praise and congratulation that he felt were his due.

He was getting none of them from Philomena anyway.

"You've always done whatever you wanted to do, Patrick, and to be fair, the rest of us have done well out of your endeavors. But it is quite beyond us to know why you want to go and undo the work of the very people who got us here. Our grandfather as sure as hell didn't come over here on the deck of a ship so that his grandson and his great-grandchildren should end up going back to the godforsaken bog that he left behind him. But it was never any use talking to you and it won't be any use now."

They got Kerry out of class to talk to him. It was the first time he had ever called his son at school; he could not credit the time it took to find the boy. Kerry could not believe that his father had called just for a conversation. Especially as he learned, he would see his father within a few days.

"I wanted to share the good news with you." Patrick felt a trace of tears come into his voice, and fought it desperately. Kerry hated emotion. More than once he had accused his father of being what he called Italian. In flatter tones than he intended, he told his son that the dream was now a reality. He said that the land had been bought, the plans were underway. And that he had heard of a good school where Kerry would start in the fall. There was a silence at the other end of the telephone which chilled him.

In business Patrick had never pleaded on the telephone, and he knew it was pathetic to ask if someone was still there when there was a silence. Sitting in Sheila Whelan's floral armchair, he steeled himself and waited. But Kerry waited longer.

Eventually Patrick spoke. "So we'll talk about all that when I see you. Right?"

"What do we talk about?"

"About how great it will all be. So many people have something that they always want to do, all their lives they talk about it and so often it never happens. Your mother and I talked about this for so long . . ."

This time Kerry spoke. "Mother never talked about it to me," he said.

"But you know it was what she wanted?"

"Maybe."

With difficulty Patrick controlled himself. His hands were shaking when he put down the telephone. He had one more call to make, and he needed something stronger than tea to steady him for this one.

Sheila Whelan wouldn't hear of his going to buy a brandy. She would slip into Conway's for it. No point in his getting a reputation in the first couple of days. She was back in minutes and the half bottle of brandy, glass and jug of water were beside his elbow on a round tray advertising Craven A cigarettes. Patrick O'Neill took a long swallow and made a person to person call to Mrs. Rachel Fine.

Afterwards he walked out into Bridge Street; he looked down to the river as his grandfather must have done, and up the town. It would all have changed so much since those days. There would have been no calling the States. And no calling home once he had arrived on the other side of the world. Patrick crossed the street, nodding at Mr. Conway, the man who unbelievably ran twin trades of publican and mortician without anyone thinking it was slightly odd. He waved at the two young White children going into their house and he gave a glance to see what ancient movie the Classic was offering tonight.

His grandfather would have had no contact at all with the family. Going to America was like going to the next world. No wonder the Irish held American wakes for the man who was leaving for America and would be out of touch with his kith and kin from now on. Maybe it might have been sensible, Patrick thought gloomily. His sister, his son, his manager and Rachel Fine had hardly been overjoyed to hear from him.

"He's only staying a few more days," John said. "He was in here earlier with some plans, showing me an artist's impression. You never saw the like of it."

"No permission or no license granted yet," Kate remarked coolly.

"A formality," Fergus Slattery said. Fergus had called again. It was a restful place, Ryan's. You could read your paper, or you could join in the chat. It made a nice stretch to his legs after his supper. And anyway he felt an overwhelming loyalty to the shabby little place.

"You shouldn't have refused good money," John Ryan said in a low voice so that the others wouldn't hear. "Kate told me you won't handle his business in case it might be in conflict with us . . . No, no . . . let me finish. Fergus, you're a decent man as your father before you is, but there's no conflict. There's nothing but cooperation with that man. The best man you could meet; he'll put new life in the place."

"I did meet him," Fergus said.

"Well. Didn't you like him?"

"Of course I liked him," Fergus growled. "You couldn't not like him. I told him that I'd feel it more sensible not to get involved in his application just in case there was the unlikely event of one of my fellow parishioners wanting to get involved on the other side."

"And what did he say?" John and Kate were both eager. This was new; this had happened this afternoon.

"Oh he was charm itself. Said he quite understood, said it was very ethical of me, showed I was a man with a community spirit, hoped he'd be able to prove that he felt the same community spirit himself."

"That's just it."

"I know, John. I'm not disputing it. I'm just saying that he's a mixture, we're always one thing or the other here; he's more than one thing."

"How do you mean?"

"Well at the same time he was telling me how much he wanted to feel part of the place and a member of the local community, he also made sure I realized that he had extinguished a license. Ahearne's pub, way beyond. Now that's sharp legal talk for an innocent Yank who's building his own place. He not only knows that you have to buy up and extinguish one pub license before you get another, but he's done it. That's a bit quick for me."

John Ryan smiled as he polished the bar counter. "Well by God you're a very impatient young fellow, Fergus, for all your great education and studies at the universities."

"Stop making fun of me. Wouldn't I need to be impatient with all that's going on around here?"

"No," said John slowly. "That's the last thing you'd need to be. There's all the time in the world. Look at all that could happen before any of this comes into being."

"What do you mean?"

"Your father would understand better than you. He has a feeling for the river, and how things go on and on. That river was there just the way it is now when your man's grandfather left Mountfern, and it will be here forever."

"John, you sound like some old soothsayer, will you stop it?" Kate laughed at him good-naturedly.

"No, I mean it. Patrick O'Neill has great plans like fireworks but they may never materialize."

"He's hardly bought Ahearne's license just for fun," Fergus said.

"No, but look at what could happen. I remember that place that was going to be built about ten miles out on the Galway road. *That* never materialized, did it?"

"They ran out of money," Fergus said.

"Exactly," said John.

"But that fellow O'Neill has a fortune."

"So had the other crowd. Or maybe he'd lose interest, or something else would distract him, or it wouldn't turn out right for him."

"But aren't you only helping him to install himself instead of praying that it will turn out wrong for him?" Kate was mystified.

"None of us would pray that things would turn out wrong for people, Kate, that would be only asking for trouble to come on ourselves. All I mean is that there's no point in getting hot and bothered until things do happen."

"That's not the American way," Fergus said, doing a poor imitation of Patrick's accent. "That's not your up-and-attem-boy."

"That's not my way," John said quietly.

"We're two of a kind then, John. Give me another pint, if you will. I can't see myself practicing law for ten minutes in New York without having a very bad nervous breakdown."

Kate smiled at them affectionately as they toasted each other on the notion of savoring life, rather than racing through it. She would prefer to race a bit faster herself, but not as fast nor in the same direction as the smiling American, who had seemed to read her mistrust of him and smile yet more warmly on the two occasions in two days that she had met him. She was glad he was going back soon.

A few nights later Dara crept from her room to the window just at the very moment Michael left his bed. They were never surprised that their timing was so exact, they took it for granted that they would turn up at the same time. In Fernscourt they could see him walking, touching this wall and that.

"If he loves it so much why is he tearing it down?" Dara asked yet again.

"Well he keeps saying he tried to think of ways of keeping the old ruin like it was," Michael said, always his defender.

"He didn't try very hard. He's so rich, all he has to do is to say let it stay and it stays," Dara grumbled. "Look, he's leaving now. I wonder where did he park his car?"

"He leaves it up a bit when he comes at night, so as not to wake people when he leaves. Look, look he's coming over the bridge."

They watched as Patrick O'Neill paused on the little footbridge opposite their pub and stared across at Fernscourt in the same way that they had done so often, a hand on each railing of the narrow bridge.

"He's saying goodbye before he goes home," Michael breathed.

"Will you ever realize that to him this is his home?" said Dara.

The moonlight wasn't bright enough for them to see the tears on Patrick's face as he said goodbye to Fernscourt.

Five

It took a little time to get things organized, but compared to the speed that most people would have moved at, Patrick was a human tornado. The finances had been organized already. The big white house in New Jersey, the symbol of his success, would be put on the market. Not at once, because that way he would have to take any price from any bidder. But it would be rented for a year first.

Bella and Andy, the couple who had looked after him, had to be paid off, thanked, found new positions. Aunts and cousins had to be placated and reassured that it wasn't the act of a madman. He saw to passports, visas for the children, had endless discussions with numerous priests and nuns in the two schools, all of whom were sorry to see Mr. O'Neill, the number one benefactor, disappear off to Ireland with his two handsome children.

There were never quite enough hours in the day for all the form-filling, document-signing, telephoning, crating, packing, sorting, and deciding what had to be done.

But in a far swifter time than anyone would have believed possible, Patrick had everything done. He was ready to come home to Ireland.

Patrick was so proud of his children when they stepped from the plane at Shannon Airport that he wanted to cry aloud to anyone who would listen that these two shining golden people belonged to him. Even after the night flight when others were blinking sleepily into the dawn, Kerry and Grace O'Neill looked untouched and stared around them with interest at the land that was going to be their home.

Patrick had noticed the looks of admiration that the brother and sister had gotten from onlookers both in Idlewild Airport, New York, and here in Shannon. They had clean-cut looks and they both seemed in such high good humor. They had always gotten along well together, no rivalry, no resentment ever. They had spent long hours together during their mother's illness, and since he had been away from home before, after and even during that time, they had been thrown together a lot. They always enjoyed each other's company. In the plane they had chattered together happily. He had never been close with Philomena or Catherine or Maureen like that. Nor with his brothers. There had been too much hardship in their family. The fight to exist had taken all their time. Friendship was a luxury they didn't have when they were growing up.

He had hired a car from one of the big companies that had a desk at Shannon Airport. Jack Coyne had had only one chance. One chance to be in car rental in a bigger way than he had ever dreamed, but he had lost it forever. To have cheated Patrick O'Neill was the most foolish act of his life.

"Come on, kids," Patrick called as he held the door of the car open. "Come on, climb in, I'm going to take you home." Their faces showed the excitement they felt.

Patrick looked at them with a lump in his throat. They were extraordinarily beautiful, he thought, both of them. It was not just the pride of a father who has worked his guts out so that his children would have everything he never had. Surely he was being objective as he looked at them standing close together in the early morning sun.

Grace had a head of hair that looked like an advertisement for a shampoo, her curls seemed to be shiny and bouncy and there was no way they could be kept down. Two minutes after she came from her shower, or even running out of the waves when they went to the ocean, it was the same. She had big blue eyes and a dimpled smile. Her father called her his little princess, and her brother had called her a baby doll. Her mother said she was like an angel in human form.

It was just as well for Grace O'Neill that she went to a school where the nuns did not believe in praising the girls and that she had an aunt who regarded all good looks as a personal calling from the devil leading to sin and possibly damnation.

Grace was a cheerful child, not nearly as spoiled as she could have been, the idolized baby in that big house. She had realized early in life that you got your way much more easily by smiling and thanking rather than sulking and crying. Nobody told her this; she had always known, or else she had seen it work with her brother and picked it up from him. It was unusually nice to be the center of attention, with people admiring and patting her on the head.

Kerry O'Neill was tall and blond; he looked like a Swede, not as if he came from Irish stock. His hair curled softly around his neck; on another boy it could have looked sissy, but not on Kerry. His skin was always lightly tanned, summer or winter. His eyes were a bright and unsettling blue. They were rarely still, but moved here and there almost as if they were looking for something. It didn't matter, though, because they looked back at whoever he was talking to often enough to show he hadn't lost interest. You got the notion that Kerry's restless eyes moved even when he was asleep.

His smile was wide and all-embracing. Nobody could smile like Kerry; all those white teeth seemed to crack his face in half. The smile never got to his eyes but that's because his eyes moved very fast. They hadn't time to smile. Grace had once seen a picture of the Blue Grotto in Capri, and said that it reminded her of nothing as much as Kerry's eyes.

Kerry never said much, but people didn't realize this. They usually thought he was very interesting because he agreed with them or listened or seemed to be taking part in conversations all the time. It was only with Mother that Kerry had talked a lot. When he came back from school he would sit and talk for ages in Mother's room. Mother had been in bed for so long it was hard to remember when she had been up and around.

They drove across the countryside in the early morning sunshine, pointing things out to each other. Patrick told them that this was a city, Limerick, and that Nenagh was a big town. City? Big town? They couldn't believe it. It was like seeing one of those model villages he had taken them to once, where ordinary mortals seemed like giants.

"We don't go on too much about how much bigger things are back in the States," he began carefully.

"Of course not," Kerry said. "They'd think we were boasting about home."

"And it would be bad-mannered," Grace agreed.

They couldn't believe when they saw signs for Killarney. Please could they go there. It was in the wrong direction, their father said. People in Mountfern thought Killarney was the other end of the country nearly, but one day he'd take them there. And there were signs to Galway. Yes, he had seen Galway Bay on his last visit. Then the roads became narrower, they left the main routes and headed into the midlands. Soon the signs for the town came up. "Not far now," Patrick said. His heart was beating faster at the thought of taking these golden children to the spot they had come from. Back to their home.

They wanted to know why were there no signs for Mountfern.

"It's too small for a road sign. It's only when you're on the road going past it that there are directions. It's only a little place." He hoped he had explained this sufficiently to them.

"It's only little now," Kerry said. "One day everyone will know it."

Patrick flashed him a grateful look and then said no more. They came to the first of the two signs saying Mountfern half a mile.

"Hey, have you passed it?" Kerry called out.

Patrick explained that this was one way which brought you along River Road, he wanted to come in by Bridge Street so that they could get an impression of the place.

"Will they have a band on Main Street?" Grace giggled.

"Nothing would surprise me," Patrick said as they came to the turn and approached the place that had always been a name on his father's birth certificate.

Everyone knew they were coming. From their garden the vicar and Mrs. Williams waved at the car.

Judy Byrne was parking her small car outside her house; she peered out of the window to get a good look at the handsome American and his family.

Mrs. Sheehan was looking out of the top window of the barracks. There were two or three people standing outside Conway's, who held their hands to their eyes to shield them from the light and get a good view. It was too early even by Conway's peculiar opening hours to have gathered drinkers; these must be people talking on their way back from mass.

Patrick explained that some people in the parish went to mass every day.

"Do we have to?" Grace asked anxiously.

"No way." Her father patted her reassuringly.

Daly's was opening for business, so was Leonard's. Sheila Whelan's blinds were up long ago, but normally it was a sleepy, slow-moving place.

On the bridge a group of children had gathered; they bent forward to glimpse the passengers in the car, then they hung back again, lacking in confidence. It annoyed Patrick to see the Irish children so uncertain when his own two were so sure, so easy.

Quickly he turned the wheel and maneuvered them into River Road. Loretto Quinn waved enthusiastically from the shop, young Father Hogan striding along in his soutane waved his breviary cheerfully. Then they were passing Ryan's licensed premises.

"Is that a real place where they sell liquor?" Grace asked.

"Yes, why?" Her father was interested.

"It looks like a kind of toy shop, you know, in a board game. It just needs a thatched roof and it's a typical Irish cottage."

"Ah, we'll be having the thatched cottage bit ourselves," Patrick said.

"Why are we stopping?" Kerry asked.

"Let's get out for a moment." Patrick held the doors of the car open for them.

They scampered out, stretching their legs after the drive. With an arm around each shoulder he walked them to the footbridge and pointed out the ruins of Fernscourt.

"That will be our home," he said. He was glad that they were looking at the old house which stood magical in the morning mists and sunshine, its ivy walls and odd shapes looking more picturesque than anything Hollywood could have dreamed up as a beautiful ruined castle. He was glad that they couldn't see the tears in his eyes. The effect couldn't have been more satisfying. His son and daughter looked in amazement at the sight in front of them.

Across the river from the little wooden bridge where they stood was a great path of laurel bushes. On either side cattle grazed among old rocks and boulders, some covered with moss. The ruins of a great house stood open to the skies. Ivy tumbled from the highest walls, and old portals stood open: doorways leading nowhere except into further open-roofed space. There were gorse bushes and heather dotted around the place, splashes of bright yellow and deep purple.

"You're going to build all this up, make it like it was?" Kerry was unbelieving.

He had seen the artist's impressions certainly, but nothing had prepared him for seeing the place as it was . . . a magnificent ruin.

"That's what we're going to do," Patrick said proudly.

"It's going to look like a castle," Grace breathed.

"That's the idea," Patrick said.

"And how much land, Father?" Kerry was shielding his eyes with his hand and looking around the landscape of a dozen different shades of green.

"Not as much as I'd have liked. You see a lot of people were granted their land back, you know they were tenants but they were able to buy it outright, so naturally that's theirs now and they don't want to sell. It was only the house and the immediate surrounds we got from the Land Commission. I got a couple of acres from fellows who were anxious to sell . . . but you see the problem . . . ." He was about to explain, but Kerry saw it too.

"You don't want to be seen to be buying up the land, taking it away from the peasants again, in case you are seen to be the bad guy wearing the black shirt, instead of the good cowboy."

"Right son, got it in one." Patrick was pleased mainly that Kerry was so interested.

"And will this all be gardens . . . ?" Grace gave a sweep of her hand.

"Yes, coming down to the river . . . there's going to be a dock for boats there, and footpaths."

"And where will the entrance be?" Kerry looked left and right.

"Funny, that's one thing still in dispute. The original one went off that way. There's a big overgrown path, that's the way vehicles will be coming on site. I'll take you around and show you. The Dublin architects want to keep it that way. They say it follows the original plan, even though nothing else will be like the original. The American architects say it would be better to open up that overgrown path over there and have the entrance coming from the town, from the big bridge."

Kerry said nothing for a while, just looked at each side and then straight ahead.

"Why couldn't it be here?" he asked.

"Here?"

"Yes. Just here, where we are. This is the best view you'll get of the place with the river in front, and you say it's going to be facing the river, so why not here?"

"But there isn't room. People would have to get out of their cars and coaches and haul all their bags way up there. It's only a footbridge, Kerry."

"No, make it into a proper bridge and have that part of the drive. Hey, why *don't* you do that? It would be very impressive."

His handsome face lit up thinking of it.

"It's a great idea but there isn't room. Look how sharp the turning would be. The buses would back into the unfortunate pub, go through the front window."

"Knock it down," Kerry said simply.

"I can't knock it down."

"You're going to knock Fernscourt down," Kerry said, indicating the ruins.

"Yes, but it's falling down and anyway it's mine."

"That pub's practically falling down, and you could buy it, then it would be yours to do what you wanted with it."

It was so simple when you were fifteen.

"Where would they go? Kerry, suppose we were to do it, where would the family who live there go?"

"If they're publicans then they could work for us, just moving across the river from their home, *and* they'd have a nice lump sum."

"I'll think about it," Patrick said. "But as I was going to suggest we have a drink there now, maybe we should sit on this possibility for a while, don't you think? No point in alarming people or telling them too much."

"You're so right," Kerry said. "Then they'd know we're interested and they'd raise the price to the roof and stick, knowing they had us over a barrel."

Patrick looked at his son with a mixture of dismay and pride. It wasn't hard to know where he had gotten his business sense. But did it always have to be as cold as that? Transplanting a family who had hopes and dreams of their own. He looked back at his site. The boy was quite right, the only possible place to have an entrance was here at this little footbridge. A big wide entrance with lanterns maybe, and should there be old gates or not? It was something he would discuss with Rachel when she arrived. Later on.

Kate and John had seen them coming and she had run in to change her blouse. She put on her best one, the one with the high neck, and fixed on the cameo brooch. This way she felt she looked more like the lady of the house than someone helping behind the bar. She dusted on a little face powder and added a dab of lipstick.

Carrie saw them as she was slipping out to give the hens a cake of bread that she had burned. The poor hens weren't at all particular, but Mrs. Ryan was. Very recently she had been rather sharp with Carrie about the late hours spent with Jimbo Doyle and had reminded her tartly that she was responsible for Carrie's welfare while she lived in the house. When she heard the voices and recognized Mr. O'Neill's, her heart skipped a beat. Jimbo had taken a four-day job helping a roofer in the big town. Mr. O'Neill thought he was working for him. Oh God, there would be trouble in store.

Eddie and Declan saw them coming and sighed. It meant they would have to wash their faces; they went glumly to the kitchen and took up the facecloths like robots. They had the worst grime removed by the time their mother arrived to do the very same thing for them.

The twins saw them coming and stopped dead in what they were doing, which was playing chess on the landing window seat. Never in their lives had they seen anyone like Mr. O'Neill's family as they stood in the sun on the footbridge pointing and waving and making a sort of diagram with their hands.

Dara looked at the face of the young man in the grey sweater and white flannels. His head was thrown back and he was laughing. He was the most magnificent boy she had ever seen in her life. And this wasn't in a magazine, or at the cinema. This was here on their own bridge in Mountfern. She was about to say to Michael that he was gorgeous, but she saw her brother staring at the blonde girl. She wore a short tartan pleated skirt and a lemon-colored sweater. Her curls had a tartan ribbon in them, holding them up in what wasn't really a pony tail because it wasn't all tied in but could have been one if she had managed to squeeze in the curls. Michael was looking at her as if he had been blind from birth and had suddenly been given his sight.

Judy Byrne was furious when she realized that she had not been quick enough. Mr. O'Neill had asked her about what he called her fine cottage. Had she thought of letting it and moving to some smaller place even temporarily? Judy had not seen the drift of his conversation. She had been anxious to make it clear to this handsome and charming American, the first serious bachelor to come their way for a long time, that her roots were firmly planted in Mountfern, that she was a woman of this place who would not be moved.

In fact the little house would have been ideal for the O'Neills. Every time Judy thought of it she raged again at her own blindness. It would have been central; it was just the right size. He would have paid most generously anything she had asked. But the real benefit would have been that Patrick O'Neill and his children would have been living there in her house. There were a million places Judy could have gone for the months that were involved. Sheila Whelan had a spare room. Poor Mrs. Meagher of the jewelry shop was thinking of letting a room. Oh why had she been so foolish as not to see that of course the man would want a place to live while he was building his hotel? She would have had every right to call, to be a family friend. What more natural than that she should return to her own house from time to time?

Judy worked three afternoons in the physiotherapy department of the hospital in the town. But there was plenty of work for her in Mountfern and around. She had come home when her mother was bedridden, and even after her mother's death she saw no reason to leave the small quiet country practice. Dr. White made sure she had plenty of work. He always said that she was indispensable with patients who were recovering from a stroke or who had broken an arm or a leg. It was a satisfying life in many ways. But she was lonely, and there were so few chances to meet anyone at all suitable in these parts, at her age. And now that she had met one, and he had been very charming, she had sent him right into the arms of that foolish Marian Johnson.

Marian Johnson had nearly died of delight when she realized why Patrick O'Neill was asking about the gate lodge. In the beginning she had been about to apologize for the place, saying that it was so run down there was hardly anything that could be done with it. In fact it was a perfectly serviceable house where Joe Whelan's people had once lived. That was long ago; they used to open the gates and take the messages, and lived rent free for years, but the family had all scattered. Even before Joe Whelan hightailed it for Dublin after some peroxide blonde, he had been living in Bridge Street with Sheila in the post office.

There had been vaguely unsatisfactory people in it since then, but the Johnsons had never stirred themselves to arrange a better let. Suddenly she saw unlimited possibilities.

"I was hoping to do it up so that people, nice people, could live there. I can't think who would like it, though." She smiled an arch smile, but let it fade suddenly when she got the feeling that Patrick might have seen through it. He spoke quite directly.

"I had been thinking of asking you about it myself. I was wondering, though, if it might be a little too far from town."

"Not at all," Marian cried. "Don't you have a car? Won't the girl have a bicycle, and won't the boy be off with the Jesuits or the Benedictines or wherever?"

Patrick had smiled.

"If you're sure it won't be too much trouble?" he said.

Marian Johnson said it would be no trouble at all. It would be a pleasure for her.

And indeed it was. Jimbo Doyle was in and instructions were given in crisp barks by Marian. No expense was spared, chimneys were swept, baskets of logs were cut, the best bedding from the Grange Hotel was brought to the Lodge. Some of the antiques that Patrick had admired in the house were also given a new home. Windows were stripped clean of the overhanging ivy; the little garden was dug, a space cleared for Patrick's car, and he was assured that all would be ready when he came back from America with his children. He would also need someone to look after them.

This, Marian found a bit of a quandary. No young skit of a girl would be any use, it had to be someone responsible. A local widow, perhaps, Patrick had suggested, someone who might be glad of the chance to live with a family for some months. Marian thought deeply. Not Mrs. Meagher in the jeweler's. She was too recently widowed to think of making any plans, Marian said. She was also a handsome if neurotic red-haired woman who would most certainly cause trouble of some kind. Not poor Loretto Quinn with her little huckster's shop on River Road. She could hardly cope with her own establishment. Certainly not Mrs. Rita Walsh of the Rosemarie hair salon, whose reputation was widely known.

Marian decided to consult Sheila Whelan, who of course knew exactly the person. Miss Hayes. She was sixty if she was a day; she was efficient. She could cook, she could mend, and she would stand no nonsense if the children were troublesome.

Miss Hayes was an inspired idea. Marian Johnson took all the praise and the thanks.

"And what shall I call you, Miss Hayes?" Patrick said to her on the first evening.

"Miss Hayes would do very well," she said.

"It's just that everyone is so friendly around here. I didn't want to do the wrong thing."

"Oh I'm sure you would never do that, Mr. O'Neill."

"I hope the children will settle in well here." Patrick was not a man who was ever at a loss for a word, but Miss Hayes was proving that his charm was not as irresistible as he had hoped.

"I'm sure they will, Mr. O'Neill. It would be strange children that wouldn't love a house like this, a room each, their own wireless and a bathroom for themselves and no one else." Miss Hayes shook her head in awe of the second bathroom.

Grace and Kerry giggled behind Miss Hayes's back after their first evening meal. But not too loudly; she had an air of authority about her, and also she had just fixed them a truly great meal.

Grace fell asleep almost at once. The door of her room was open and Patrick went in to kiss her forehead with the curls damp from her bath. She looked babyish, younger than her twelve years as she lay asleep there. He stood and looked at her for a long, long moment.

Kerry was not sleepy, he said.

"Do you want to drive over with me and walk in Fernscourt by night?" he asked.

Kerry shrugged. It was as if he had gone back to his old self—the Kerry who had nothing much to say to his father.

"Not really," he said.

"Sure." Patrick was easy. He wouldn't rush the boy. "Go in your own time; see it your own way."

"Yes, that's what I'll do, Father," Kerry had said. His face, in spite of his golden tan and his piercing blue eyes, looked curiously empty.

They were the talk of the town. Tommy Leonard said that he had asked Kerry how old he was. He had asked him straight out.

"You spoke to him?" Maggie Daly was over-excited by it all.

"Yeah, that's the way people ask questions," Tommy said. "With speech. Words and all."

"What did he say?" Michael rescued poor Maggie.

"Didn't you ask him yourself? Wasn't he inside in your place for ages?" Tommy Leonard was jealous of the time that the two star-like Americans had spent in Ryan's.

"I couldn't ask much. Mam asked us to show them the animals. God, imagine asking *anyone* to look at our animals let alone people like that."

Tommy Leonard was mollified. He was actually in the poor position of not knowing *what* age Kerry O'Neill actually was. He had asked, it was true, but Kerry had just smiled at him knowingly and asked him to guess.

Tommy Leonard had guessed fifteen, and Kerry had just smiled again. As an encounter it hadn't pleased Tommy, he got no glory in recalling it.

"Wasn't she beautiful?" Maggie said, in what was almost a whisper.

"She was more than beautiful," Dara said firmly. "She had classic good looks."

Dara didn't know exactly what that meant, but she had heard it said once about some actress. It seemed the highest praise there could be to have good looks that were classic. It gave them a virtue somehow, took them out of the ordinary variety.

"Imagine, she's going to be at school like the rest of us." Maggie could hardly take it in.

"I'm sure she'll hate it." Dara was sympathetic to Grace and outraged that school wouldn't live up to her hopes.

"Everyone hates school," said Jacinta White, who hadn't met Grace and Kerry personally. She had only waved to them as they passed in the car with Mr. O'Neill. Jacinta and her brother Liam were peeved not to have met the new arrivals; it left them at a disadvantage somehow.

They had planned to go fishing that day; often the six of them waded up the river with their simple fishing rods. They had all been catching fish for as long as they could remember, and they used to laugh at the fishermen who came from Dublin and far-off places with all their expensive tackle. Young Mr. Slattery had once told them that the whole principle of fishing for thousands of years had been some sort of an old hook, some sort of an old stick and a length of thread to connect the two. Only fancy folk who wouldn't know a pike from a perch, or either of them from a brown trout, went to all this ungodly fuss about rods and tackle. Sometimes young Mr. Slattery came and sat with them and told them things about the river. He always sounded as if he were making some kind of joke about it, or as if he didn't really believe what he was saying himself. He said that the Fern wasn't cold enough or fast enough for game fish. You wouldn't find any salmon leaping around it or refined sort of trout. These were classier fish that needed a load of oxygen. The Fern was a coarse fish for a coarser fisherman. It was low in oxygen, and full of slow ponderous fish like the tench that could live with no oxygen at all. Like the people of Mountfern themselves. Young Mr. Slattery puzzled the children, he was neither one thing nor the other.

Today, somehow, the fishing had lost its appeal. And they didn't play in Fernscourt anymore. It was not the same now that they knew the bulldozers were coming to take it down. They were all restless and unsettled. They wanted Grace O'Neill and her big brother Kerry to be there again. Like they had been yesterday. But nobody said it. Jacinta White said it in a sort of way.

"Will we go up to the lodge and ask them if they want to come fishing?" she suggested.

They all looked at each other doubtfully.

The mood was against it. Grace and Kerry O'Neill were the kind of people who made the running. You didn't go knocking on their door. They came to join you when they were ready.

Jack Coyne made one attempt to regain the lost business. He called to the lodge formally. He was met by Miss Hayes, a quiet woman who did dressmaking and who lived in a couple of rooms in Bridge Street.

"What has you ending up here?" he asked ungraciously.

"Did you wish to see Mr. O'Neill?"

"Yes, I wished that, please." He was mocking her now.

"Would you like to come into the sitting room? The family are at breakfast at the moment."

"Who's that, Miss Hayes?" Patrick's voice called out good-naturedly.

"It's Mr. Coyne, a car dealer." Miss Hayes was disapproving.

"Oh, Mr. Coyne, I had the pleasure of doing business with you once. Do come in and join us for coffee. Another cup if you'd be so kind please, Miss Hayes?"

Jack Coyne was distinctly wrong-footed now. He came into a sunny alcove where two smartly dressed children were having breakfast, at a table by a big window. The children stood up politely at his approach. Jack Coyne wished he had dressed more smartly for the occasion. He had thought he would find them unpacking and confused.

"I didn't want to disturb you but I was going to inquire if you wanted a car." Jack decided to come straight to the point. He nodded at the two children who sat down again, realizing that there would be no further greeting. Patrick made a great play out of pouring the coffee and was extremely anxious that Jack Coyne had the right amount of sugar and cream. Then he turned his blue eyes and his crinkly smile directly on Jack.

"A car?" he said, interested and amused, as if he had been offered a flying saucer.

"Yes, you won't want to be hiring that car-rental job outside for any longer than you have to."

"No indeed." Patrick still looked amused.

"And since I'm the local man, a businessman too, in my own small way, I thought I'd put it on the line for you, Mr. O'Neill, ask you to come down to Coyne's Motor Works and tell me what you had in mind, and I could go and look for it for you."

Patrick looked at him blankly. As if he didn't understand. "You mean *you* would go and get *me* a car from a third party? Is this what you are proposing?"

"Yes, well that's what getting a car for someone is." Jack was confused now.

"But why would you do that, Mr. Coyne?"

"Why? Well so that you would get a good deal, a proper car from someone you could trust."

"Who would that be, this person I could trust?" Patrick's eyes were innocent and blue.

Jack Coyne shuffled and stumbled over his words. "Like I'm here, I'd know the people, I'd be in the way of knowing who would give you a fair price and who would . . . well . . . who would be the kind of fellow who would see you coming as it were."

Patrick looked at him directly. "I'd have to avoid those, wouldn't you say?"

"You would too, and sometimes it's hard to tell one from another; the man who would look to your interests and serve you well, and the man who would just try to make a quick few quid out of you."

"Yes." Patrick was grave.

"And we're all in business, as I say, Mr. O'Neill, and there are those of us who might make a quick few quid always from passing trade as it were, people who had more money than sense, but when it comes down to a good working relationship . . ."

Patrick O'Neill beamed all over his face.

"I think that's very neighborly of you, Mr. Coyne, and I will take your point about the kind of sharks who would fleece the passing trade for a few quick bucks . . . It's that kind of thing that can destroy a place. One visitor leaving with one story like that could kill tourism stone dead. I agree with you so much. So thanks again for marking my card. I'll be on the look out."

Jack Coyne heard the goodbye in the tone. He stood up.

"So you might call in to Coyne's Motor Works?"

"I'll sure as anything see you around these parts, Mr. Coyne."

In the hall Jack Coyne got the feeling that the wordless Miss Hayes had heard everything, and realized he was getting the bum's rush.

"Haven't you a good enough living below in the town making clothes for people without cleaning up after this lot?" he said to her.

"Like yourself, Jack Coyne, I'm always willing to see a business opportunity," she said with a smile.

Olive Hayes had no relations left except a sister who was a nun in New Zealand. She had always dreamed of going out to spend a winter in the South Island. If she worked for Mr. O'Neill, if she let her little place behind Meagher's jewelry to this building fellow who needed a place in Mountfern, if she continued her making of curtains and any other dressmaking she could manage, then she would have the fare in a year.

Mr. O'Neill thought he would be out of the lodge and into his new castle in a year but he didn't understand about the way things were done here. It would be several years. And in that time Olive Hayes could gather a small fortune, enough to take her to New Zealand, and to give her sister's order a financial contribution which would make her a welcome visitor for as long as she wanted to stay. Indeed she thought sometimes that if the weather was as good as her sister wrote it was, and if she liked it there, she might stay altogether. But these were only half-formed plans. And nobody except Sheila Whelan in the post office had any inkling of them. She hadn't told that bossy Marian Johnson who hired her, and she certainly wouldn't tell that crook Jack Coyne. She closed the door after him and went to refill the coffee pot.

The girl was a lovely little thing; the boy looked as if he could be a great deal of trouble.

Judy Byrne called the Grange. She said it was about old Mr. Johnson's arthritis.

"You said yourself there was nothing more you could do for him," Marian said.

"Yes, I know, but in this fine weather he should be feeling a lot better. I was wondering did he want to go over the exercises I tried with him before."

"He said they weren't worth a curse. You can neither lead him nor drive him. It's always been the same."

"Oh I don't know, sometimes the right word at the right time . . . I have to be over that way, will I call in and have a chat with him?"

"No point, Judy, he's gone fishing."

"Well tell him to take care of himself and not to get damp out on that river bank."

"You're very nice to be so concerned," Marian said.

"Not at all. How are things?"

"Things are frightfully busy, what with the lodge and everything . . ."

"Oh, are you getting involved there? I thought they wanted to be left on their own."

"I wouldn't dream of interfering, but there are some things of course that simply have to be done, and poor Miss Hayes is splendid but she does have her limitations." Marian gave a little tinkle.

Judy Byrne banged down the receiver and told herself aloud yet again that she was possibly the most stupid woman on earth. It would serve her right if she were to be invited by that Marian Johnson, whose face was like a meringue, to the wedding of the century at the Grange, with a honeymoon to be spent across the river in the elegant Fernscourt, new home of the bride and groom.

The children of Mountfern could talk of nothing but the O'Neills but they didn't know how or when they would meet them again. It was solved on the day that Grace was driven by her father to Fernscourt. And left there.

Patrick was engrossed in conversations with surveyors and engineers. Grace wandered around touching the long strands of ivy and holding them up so that they trailed in different directions.

With solemn dark eyes Dara and Michael watched her. After an eternity, Dara made the first move.

"We'll ask her would she like an ice cream in Daly's," she said firmly.

"We don't have enough money," Michael protested.

"We have enough for two."

"But we'd have to buy three."

"You can suddenly decide at the last minute you don't want one."

"All right."

They walked hesitantly up to Grace, who was standing on tiptoe to examine what she thought might be a bird's nesting place.

"Would you like to come for an ice cream or something?" Michael asked gruffly.

Grace's face broke into a dazzling smile. "Can I?" she asked.

Michael was wordless again.

Dara took over. "We'd love you to come down to Daly's, and show you the rest of the town."

"I was longing to see everything, but I didn't want to . . ." Grace looked doubtful. "You're all friends already, I didn't want to get in the way."

"Nonsense." Dara was brisk. "You're just as much entitled to have an ice cream and walk around Mountfern as anyone else."

She linked Grace O'Neill's arm and walked purposefully across the foot-bridge. Michael followed happily, and Patrick O'Neill watched from a distance with a pleased smile.

Eddie Ryan was escorted home to the family business by an irate Declan Morrissey, the manager of the Classic Cinema. Eddie had drawn mustaches on Audrey Hepburn, and on Doris Day. He had drawn them not with a pencil, nor even a ballpoint pen, but with creosote which could not be removed and which meant that no new poster could be affixed on top of the mutilated ones. Declan Morrissey said he did not want the child to be disemboweled but as near to it as could be done within the law.

"You are a thorn in my flesh," Kate Ryan told her son as she marched him upstairs to where John was working with papers and notebooks scattered around him.

"John, I know that Wordsworth and the lads never had this kind of distraction, but I'm going to have to interrupt you and ask you to beat Eddie within an inch of his life."

"What has he done now?" John was weary.

"According to Declan Morrissey, he has defaced the Classic Cinema in a manner from which it will never recover."

"Didn't Declan do that himself with his rows of colored lights around it?"

"*John!*"

"I know, that has nothing to do with it. Right, Eddie, before I take my belt to you . . ."

"Ah no, Dad, please no."

"Before I take the belt, have you *any* reason or explanation? I am a reasonable man. I will listen."

There was silence.

"Pure badness, I'm afraid," Kate said.

"There's nothing else to do. If there was anything at all to do I'd do it, but there isn't." Eddie looked very sad.

Kate and John looked at each other, weakening momentarily.

"But the others don't put creosote on Morrissey's walls," Kate said.

"And have us heart-broken every day of our lives," John said.

"They've got a life of their own," Eddie said. "A life with people in it."

For some reason that he never understood the strap was not raised.

He was ordered to go and apologize to Mr. Morrissey, to take a scrubbing brush and Vim and do his best. To tell Mr. Morrissey that his parents would pay Jimbo Doyle to have a go at it if all else failed.

"A life of their own with people in it," Kate said wonderingly to John. "Imagine, that's all he wants, poor little clown."

"I suppose it's what everyone wants," John said and went back to his writing, delighted that he didn't have to beat his small and very difficult son.

Nineteen sixty-two was the summer of the bicycle.

Mr. O'Neill had done an extraordinary deal in the big town. It all happened the time he went to buy a car. Apparently he got friendly with the man who sold it to him, and had gone to have a drink with him. The man's brother had been trying to emigrate to America, but he had no one to stand for him at the other side, no one to give him a job and to be responsible for him. This was a great pity because the poor fellow had just been crossed in love. A woman he had his eye on for many years had upped and married another man entirely. So the brother had only one hope and that was to start a new life in the New World. He wasn't a man who was afraid of hard work.

It all evolved in the conversation that Mr. O'Neill could get his manager back in the States, a Mr. Gerry Power, to sponsor him in, and the thing was arranged in a matter of days. All the man had to do now was to have his medical and get his visa. Nobody could believe the speed at which it was done. How could this benefactor be thanked? Mr. O'Neill had seen a load of old bicycles. What about a job lot of those at a knockdown price. A price? Not at all, they were a gift. Thirty-odd bicycles were delivered to Jack Coyne's for nothing. Jack was to test the brakes and do any re-fitting that was necessary. The bikes were available for all who wanted them. Dara and Michael cycled around in circles on theirs; they were the first to get them. The Whites had bikes already, and so had Tommy Leonard, but Maggie didn't, so a small one was found for her. Grace and Kerry had theirs and there had been some cans of paint thrown in with the deal. The bicycles were all the colors of the rainbow.

Jack Coyne scratched his head many times as children came to choose their free bicycles and to paint them on his premises. He had a suspicion that Patrick O'Neill had in fact pulled a fast one on him. The man had not bought his car through Jack, that was all right, that was his privilege to go where he wanted to. But this business of unloading all these broken bicycles on him. In theory it looked as if Coyne's were being given the turn. But in fact it was different. There was no money anyway in fiddly jobs like that, and then added to it was the problem that Jack would have to charge half nothing to Patrick O'Neill anyway to try to show that he had mended his wicked ways. And half the kids in the town painting their bicycles on the premises.

He felt sure that Patrick O'Neill wasn't so stupid as to think that this was doing him a favor.

"Who can have bikes? Is it only people of eleven?" Patrick looked down at the small furious boy with hair sticking out in all directions.

"Who are you?" he asked.

"That doesn't matter," the child said. "I just wanted to know if it was worthwhile or if I'd be belted out of there." He jerked his head at Jack Coyne's.

"What do people say?"

"Mr. Coyne says he can't get them out of his sight quick enough. Father Hogan said we should give them to those in need first."

"But aren't we all in need?" Patrick asked him.

"That's what I said, but you couldn't argue with a priest."

"I know it." Patrick was sympathetic.

The small boy wasn't prepared to let the conversation wander into philosophical waters.

"So what are the rules, Mr. O'Neill?"

Patrick liked him, he was a little toughie.

"You know my name, why can't I know yours?"

"Because then you'd say there were too many bicycles gone to our family because of the twins," Eddie said.

"Oh it's young Mr. Ryan, I see."

"Well it's no use now." Eddie's hands were deep in his pockets.

"Are you able to ride a bike?"

"Everyone is." Eddie was scornful.

"No they're not. Come on, pick one out. If you can ride it straight up and down here for me without wobbling, you can have it."

Eddie was back like a flash with a bike and a following of half a dozen children.

Patrick watched him attempt a few false starts and then get going. He came back triumphantly.

"Well?" he cried.

"No," Patrick said.

"What do you mean no. I stayed on, didn't I?"

"Yes, but you rode on the wrong side of the road, you young fool. You'd have been killed if anyone was coming toward you."

"You didn't *say* you were counting things like that."

"Sorry, friend. Try again next week, same time, same place, new test."

Eddie grinned back at him. This was the kind of deal he understood.

Grace O'Neill said she thought that Mountfern was the most beautiful place she had ever been. She said that they were all so lucky to have grown up here, it was like a magic place. The children preened themselves when they heard this. Grace didn't boast about all the places she had been. She didn't say that New York was better than Mountfern, and she had been to all kinds of things and places they had only seen in the films. She had been up the Empire State Building, and on Broadway. She had been up the Statue of Liberty and she had been across the Brooklyn Bridge. But this was only revealed when they questioned her. Normally she said little about what had been her home up to now. Her chat was all of the future. They knew that her mother had died. They asked her was it awful. Grace said that the worst part had been knowing somehow for ages that she was never going to be really well. They had stopped making plans for the things they would do when mother got cured. She didn't know when it began but that was the worst part. The time she had died was hard to remember, there were so many people coming in and out of the house.

She had looked so sad when she talked about that, they changed the subject. Maggie Daly had asked could they see some of her American clothes and all the girls had gotten on their bicycles and cycled off to the lodge just like that. Of course Tommy Leonard and Michael Ryan and Liam White were far too grown up and male to want to do anything stupid like cycling nearly three miles to see clothes. But they felt a bit empty sitting there by the river when all the girls had gone. It wasn't that they would have gone if they had been asked. But they would like to have been asked. They would have preferred if the girls hadn't gone at all.

Kerry didn't come and join in the games. He was far too old for them. He was nearly old enough to be on the bridge with the fellows and girls who were almost grown up. But he didn't hang around there either.

Grace said he cycled a lot on his own; he had found some ruined abbey he liked. And he used to read too, and he was catching up on some work he had to do before he went to his boarding school, and he had some Latin lessons from Mr. Williams the vicar, who had said that life was very droll when you had the Protestant parson teaching the Roman Catholics Latin, even though it was never used in Mr. Williams's church and nothing else was used in Canon Moran's establishment down the road.

"O'Neill's children seem to have taken over the place like the Lords of the Soil," Fergus said to Kate.

"I'm quick to find fault, quicker than you are, and I can't see anything against them," Kate said.

"Oh, cocky little pair of swaggerers," Fergus grunted. "Sailing around on their bicycles as if they owned the place. Which they do of course. Own the place."

"Ah, come on, Fergus, at least half the place is on wheels now, that can't be bad."

"That's what the people of Hamelin said to each other about the Pied Piper. At least they're all dancing, that can't be bad."

"God, Fergus, nothing would please you about that unfortunate family. Seriously, the children smile and they're being patronizing, they don't smile and they're being standoffish. What could they do to please you?"

"Go back to America," he said.

"You're worse than Eddie when you have that puss on you. What have you so much against them?"

Kate was bright and fresh-looking in a pink blouse and a red pinafore dress. She had bought the blouse in a sale and the pinafore dress was something she had worn years ago, before Declan was born. With a smart black belt to take the maternity look off it she felt as smart as paint. Fergus looked at her, a long admiring look.

"The main thing I have against them is that they are going to take your business away."

"Oh Fergus." She was touched to the heart.

"Don't 'Oh Fergus' me, go on being nice to them, silly little overdressed vipers in your bosom." He blew his nose loudly. "Just wait until those children have taken away your children's inheritance. See how you'll feel then."

Kate was totally at a loss.

"It's not the children's fault," she began.

He put away his handkerchief. "You're quite right. They make me feel old and grubby and silly. Your children make me feel . . . I don't know, splendid, fascinating."

"Which is what you are," Kate said, and then went back to work.

Six

Everyone asked Miss Hayes what they were like at home, the Americans. Was there a ton of money spent in the place? What did they talk about? Olive Hayes was never sufficiently forthcoming. They were very nice people, she reported, thoughtful and considerate. She had never worked in a house before, it was all a very new experience for her. People thought Miss Hayes was a poor informant. Soon they didn't bother to ask her anymore. She was a woman with no stories to tell.

Olive Hayes was a woman saving her fare to New Zealand. She was going to keep her position in this small comfortable house with the American family. There would be no tales about the arrogant resentful Kerry, the impatient father who could find nothing to say to his son, but who idolized his beautiful daughter. Nor would Miss Hayes talk about Grace outside the house even though there was nothing but good to report. She was a delightful child, anxious to help, willing to learn. She made her bed and kept her room in perfect order. She always asked permission if she were to invite the other children into the house. She had a ready smile and she soldiered on bravely to keep the peace between her father and brother. Miss Hayes had never felt any yearning to marry and rear a family. But sometimes when she looked at Grace O'Neill in the kitchen, helping her to wipe dishes and tumbling out stories of how the day had been spent, she sighed and a soft look came to her long angular features. It would have been good to have had a daughter like Grace O'Neill.

Kitty Daly had thought that the summer would never end, long endless boring summers with that crowd on the bridge being so dismissive and all Maggie's friends being so loud and awful. But it all changed when Kerry O'Neill came to town. He came into Daly's Dairy from time to time. Kitty hated working in the shop during the summer and was normally so sulky and unhelpful that her parents thought it was counter-productive to have her behind the counter. They had a girl from out the country, and Charlie who hauled and dragged things in and out and did deliveries.

Kerry held out his hand the first time he called.

"Hi, I'm Kerry O'Neill," he had said, as if Kitty didn't know. As if every-one for miles around didn't know.

She shook his hand and mumbled.

"What's your name?" he asked, as if he had expected her to give it.

"Kitty. Kitty Daly."

"Oh this is your place?" He looked around the clean bright shop in admira-tion. Its cakes and bread in one section, milk, butter and bacon at another counter and the main body of groceries all together behind the main counter.

"Yes, it is." Kitty wished she could think of something else to say, but she couldn't. She gave a big shrug to let this gorgeous fellow know that she thought it was all terrible. So that he wouldn't think of her as a poor country hick. But he didn't seem to think it was dreadful.

"It's a very handsome store," he said. "You must like working in it, you must feel proud of it."

Kitty was about to change her stance completely and express great pride in the dairy.

But her mother spoke first. "Oh there'd be white blackbirds before Miss Kitty here would do a hand's turn in the shop."

A dark red stain came into Kitty's face, but Kerry seemed to understand at once.

"I'm just the same," he said, looking straight at her, though he spoke lightly. "I'm very interested in my father's hotel but he thinks I'm only fooling around. It's not just, is it?"

"No it isn't." Kitty Daly was hoarse with excitement as the bright blue eyes of Kerry O'Neill rested on her for a little longer. Then he had bought a bar of chocolate and was gone. She watched him walk easily down Bridge Street and go into Leonard's. She resisted the urge to run after him and talk more. She would see him again. He was here forever. And he liked her. He had made it obvious. Kitty saw her mother looking at her and immediately put on a face.

"I suppose you'll go getting notions about him now, that's the next cross we'll have to bear," Mrs. Daly said in tones of great weariness.

"It's a pity that older people have such sad, sick minds," said Kitty, and resolved to be very nice to Mrs. Walsh from the Rosemarie hair salon in case there was a chance she might give her a cheap hair-do.

Grace O'Neill said that she would love to catch a fish. A real fish herself, and then she would cook it and eat it. Nobody she ever knew before had done anything like this. She made life seem much more exciting than it was for the children of Mountfern. She loved everything. She thought it was wonderful that they had a river all for them, not in a park or anything, but in their own town. And she thought it was great to know everyone's names. Grace made a point of saying, "Good morning Mrs. Williams; Hi, Mr. Slattery; Good day Father Hogan." She said that in the United States you never met anyone you knew or who knew you. Reluctantly the others agreed that it was all right. Before Grace's arrival they had always thought it tiresome to be under the ever-watchful eyes of the whole town no matter what you did or where you were going. It was hard to see it as a positive asset.

But fishing. That was something the girls hadn't been involved in.

"You won't like it, the fish look terrible when you do get them out of the water," said Maggie Daly.

"They have all blood by the side of their mouths," Jacinta White said.

"And their eyes look terrified," said Maggie, maybe with fellow feeling. Her own eyes often looked big and frightened.

"And they wriggle and twitch and you'd be dying to throw them back in," Jacinta said.

"Except that the poor mouth is torn off them." Maggie was perplexed by the enormity of the decision. "So you wouldn't know what would be for the best, to kill them quickly and get it over with or let them back with half their jaw gone."

Dara hadn't joined in, which was unusual.

Then she spoke.

"I think that's a lot of sentimental rubbish. If Grace says she would like to fish then we should. After all we've lived beside the river for all our lives and we've never objected before . . ."

Grace flashed her a grateful and admiring look.

"But we never did it ourselves . . ." Maggie began.

"Because we've no guts," Dara said firmly, and with that female fishing was on. They were going to get rods and hooks. Michael was terrific, he'd show them.

"Michael won't want us hanging around with them," Jacinta said.

"I'm sure he won't mind showing us how it's done," Grace said, with a sunny confident smile.

Michael didn't mind showing Grace how it was done, and he was pleased that his twin had suddenly developed an interest in fishing. Tommy Leonard was helpful too, and Liam White. They bent over hooks and bait. Maggie Daly forced herself to look into jars of maggots, even though it made her stomach heave. Michael explained that you had to just nick the edge of the maggot with the hook so that the maggot still wriggled about in the water and the fish would believe it was a live grub and snap at it. There was other bait too: bread made into a paste, or bits of crust. Maggie wondered could they stick to this, but Michael and Tommy and Liam said you had to use maggots and worms as well.

Jacinta said she felt sick watching the hook going through the worm. But Grace and Dara looked on steadfastly. Taking a deep breath, Maggie looked on too and said nothing about the nausea rising in her, together with the feeling that this was all a silly phase. They would get over it soon, and go back to being as they were. She hoped Grace would like looking at the tombstones in the Protestant graveyard, but it was probably wiser not to suggest it too soon.

Grace wanted to know could she try out some of the rods which Michael said they had back at the pub. It was nearly teatime. There was indecision. Suddenly the twins looked at each other in the way they often did, as an idea seemed to come to them at exactly the same time.

"We'll ask can you come to tea," Dara said.

"Just what I was thinking."

"Oh no," Grace protested.

"Yes, then we can look at the rods."

Grace was firm. "Miss Hayes will have my tea ready. No, I can't call her, that would be very high-handed. But maybe I could ask Father if I can cycle back again tonight."

That was agreed, and they scattered to go back to their houses as the six o'clock bell pealing out the angelus was heard all over Mountfern.

Maggie walked along River Road with her hands in her pockets. Dara hadn't asked her to come back after tea. Michael hadn't been keen to show her any rods. Tommy Leonard and the Whites were chatting on cheerfully. They didn't notice that Maggie hung behind and was very quiet.

But next day Maggie was called by her mother.

"Come down quickly, Maggie, your friend is here."

Something about the way she said friend was unusual. Usually Mrs. Daly said that Jacinta or Dara was there, in a way that you knew she was casting her eyes up to heaven. Maggie ran down the stairs of Daly's and into the shop.

There was Grace, full of chat to everyone, asking questions about what kind of pastry this was on the cream cakes, and what kind of filling was in the eclairs.

"Would you like to taste one?" Mrs. Daly asked her.

"Heavens no, thank you Mrs. Daly, thank you so much; I was only interested, that's all. I ask too many questions, I'm afraid."

"Nice to see someone awake and not half dozy all the time." Maggie's father was full of approval.

Maggie stood there, feeling very shabby in her beige shirt and brown shorts. Grace was in a yellow and white dress with a big white collar, she had little yellow shoes. She must have a dozen pairs of shoes, Maggie thought enviously, always something to go with her outfit.

Grace took her arm. "Is it all right if we go off now?" she asked to nobody in particular but to everybody at the same time. Grace forced other people to be charming too. Mrs. Daly was nodding and smiling, Mr. Daly was wishing them good weather, Charlie looked up from the boxes he was collecting, to grin at them.

Out on Bridge Street Grace looked at Maggie anxiously. "It was all right to come, wasn't it? I wanted you to show me the tombstones you were talking about."

"Yes, but . . . ?" Maggie was bewildered. Surely Grace wouldn't want to go off with her, with just Maggie when there was so much else to do, so many other people to meet and such an amount of revolting wriggling maggots to be threaded onto those hooks.

But apparently that was what Grace did want.

"Please, Maggie," she said. "I'd love to see the names and the things people said."

Maggie was still hesitant.

"The fishing . . ." she began.

"Oh we can join them later, I met Liam on my way here. I said we'd be along in about an hour or more."

"What did he say?"

"He said 'fine' or something." Grace was unconcerned.

She left her bicycle parked at the back of Daly's, and arm in arm, they went up Bridge Street to the top of the town. Grace peeped into the Garda barracks just to see what it looked like, she said.

Sergeant Sheehan told her to come in and have a look around.

"Do you have prison cells here?" Grace asked with interest.

"Not here, child." He looked at her affectionately.

Seamus Sheehan had only sons; this was a beautiful sunny girl. The little one of the Dalys seemed dazzled by her almost.

"What do you do with criminals?"

"They go to jail in the big town. I've a room back there with a big padlock on it if you'd like to be kept in detention."

Grace giggled. "No, I was only getting to know the place."

"Quite right too." Sergeant Sheehan seemed much more cheerful today, Maggie thought, like her father was, and her mother, and like Miss Byrne the physiotherapist who made it her business to come over and ask Grace how they were settling into the lodge, and hoping it wasn't too damp for them.

Grace was fascinated with the graves and the tombstones. She said she would bring a notebook the next time so that she could write them all down.

"We won't be buried here, of course," Grace said conversationally.

"No, we'll be in the Catholic graveyard. Well *we* will, anyway," Maggie explained. "If you stay then I suppose you will too."

"Of course we'll stay, why would we not stay?" Grace sat on the edge of an old untended grave. "Hey, we should do something for this poor James Edward Gray, nobody's weeded around him for years. Of course, we're going to stay."

Maggie was helping to remove some of the bigger dandelions from James Edward Gray's resting place.

"People were wondering would you not find it all too dull for you here," she said in a small voice.

"Heavens no, it's fantastic. You want us to stay, Maggie? You don't want us to go away, do you?" Grace's beautiful face was troubled. She looked really anxious.

Maggie couldn't remember why she had felt so upset yesterday evening as she had walked home along by the Fern, and how she had wished that the O'Neills had never come here.

She looked at the worried blue eyes of Grace O'Neill, and with a great big smile that went all over her face, Maggie Daly said, "Of course we don't want you to go away; it's great that you're here." And she meant it.

She meant it not just at that moment but for a long time. Like when they joined the fishing party which was waiting for them at the footbridge.

"Sorry," Grace said casually, "I dragged Maggie off to show me the graves. You're right, they're fabulous. We're going to try and smarten up James Edward Gray a bit."

"Where's he? In the corner near the wall is it?" Dara asked.

Maggie breathed a sigh of relief. Dara wasn't a bit annoyed that Maggie had taken Grace away. People like Dara didn't get annoyed, Maggie told herself. Only mean-spirited people like herself got jealous and possessive and annoyed. Grace was telling Michael that on consideration she wondered could he bait their lines with those lumps of bread they had been talking about yesterday; she said she thought it would be easier to learn on bait made from crusts and then she could progress to maggots later.

Dara was disappointed. She had a jar of maggots ready for threading onto hooks. But Michael said Grace was right, better get used to this kind first, because it was always easier to hand.

Grace flashed Maggie Daly a smile. Things were much easier than they seemed, the smile said.

*   *   *

Kitty Daly thought that Mrs. Ryan wasn't bad for a grown-up; at least she wasn't a religious maniac like her own mother was. She was a woman you could talk to a bit.

"Do you think I could work for a bit in the bar, Mrs. Ryan?"

"No, Kitty, I'm sorry."

"Why not?"

"You're too young. That's one reason. We don't need anyone. That's another."

"I'm almost fifteen. That's not young."

"I know it's not." Kate sighed. All this terrible sulking and mulish behavior probably lay ahead with her own Dara. "But it is too young for bar work. I suppose this is a silly question, but why couldn't you work in your own shop?"

She took one look at Kitty's face and decided that it was a silly question. The girl looked distressed.

"Did you want the money for something in particular?"

"Yes."

"Well, maybe you could try to see if there is any other way of getting what you want. Like if it's clothes, could you make them?"

"It's hair, Mrs. Ryan."

"Hair?" Kitty had the Daly curls, frizz really. There was nothing startlingly bad about the child's hair. It was clean and neat, and a brownish reddish color.

"Yes, a good cut would make all the difference, and no matter what else Mrs. Walsh is she does know how to cut hair."

Kate let the comment pass. No point in drawing an argument on herself with this difficult girl.

"Could you do a deal with her? Sweep up the hair from the floor, make people cups of tea, put the towels out to dry for two weeks, say, and then she might give you a haircut free?"

Kitty considered it without much pleasure.

"It wouldn't be much fun."

"No, but if she agreed it would get you the haircut."

"Two weeks is an awfully long time."

"True. I suppose you'd have to work out whether it's worth it or not."

Kitty thought a bit. Mrs. Ryan was a lot better than most people's mothers. She didn't say things like, your hair was fine the way it was, or, at your age I didn't have the chance to go to hairdressers. She put her mind to the question properly.

"Yes, well I'll give it a go," she said ungraciously.

"Kitty."

"Yes, Mrs. Ryan?"

"Do you want a hint?"

"All right."

"If I were you, I'd tell Mrs. Walsh how much you admire her own hair, and the way she cuts other people's, and you were wondering if you could make her a proposition. I'd be over-polite if I were you, because Mrs. Walsh is a very busy person with a lot on her mind, and she'd be quick to dismiss an idea unless it was put to her nicely." Kate Ryan saw the defensive look on Kitty's face, and hastened to say, "I mean, Kitty, I couldn't care less if you shaved your head bald and painted the Irish flag on it. I think your hair is fine as it is, but I know what you mean about a good cut giving it a better shape. So you can take my hint if you like, or ignore it if you like. Now I must get along with my work."

Kitty thanked her, less grumpily than she had been going to. And in fact it was a good idea. She would ask Mrs. Walsh straight away. Imagine Mrs. Walsh going to bed with men for money. It was unbelievable, but that is what she did. Everyone knew, but no one talked about it much. Imagine men paying to go to bed with anyone as old as Mrs. Walsh.

Kerry O'Neill had no great hopes about his new school. He had gone there with his father for an unsatisfactory visit, and Father Minehan had marked out a certain amount of work that would have to be done. He had agreed that since Kerry was fifteen it would not be practical for him to learn the Irish language at this stage, but he would be expected to master enough of it to get the general sense of things Irish.

He was a forbidding-looking man, white, ascetic, with a nervous smile. He had managed to suggest more than once to Kerry's father that the school, which was a very illustrious one, had fallen on hard times due to a massive and expensive rebuilding program. There was a building fund that would cripple the community eventually; they couldn't raise the fees yet again this year, so they often had to rely on the generosity of those parents who were lucky enough to be financially secure to help in some of the extreme times of need.

Kerry had been quiet and respectful through most of the interview. At an early stage in the proceedings he realized that Father Minehan didn't respond to charm. He walked admiringly around the old buildings and asked bright questions about the original building and the time that the order had first set it up.

"It's only been here a hundred years. It's not one of our older foundations," Father Minehan had said a little testily.

"Don't forget, I'm from the United States. That seems very old to me," Kerry said with a smile.

Father Minehan softened then. Kerry had said the right thing.

Coming home in the car his father looked at Kerry.

"You handled that one well, son. Our sort of cleric, wasn't he?"

Kerry didn't join in what he considered his father's all-men-together mode. "I think he was all right, he has a job to do."

Patrick was annoyed. "What do you mean, he has a job to do?"

"Well, just that. He has to keep me in my place, arrogant young American know-it-all, trample me down a bit. He has to try to fleece you for his building fund. Irish-American: more money than sense, get him to sign a check."

Patrick gave a genuine shout of laughter.

"It didn't take you long to sum him up. Still, it's got a great reputation. It's one of the finest schools in Ireland."

Kerry turned away to look out of the window; he knew what his father would say next, and he knew the tone he would say it in. Patrick was about to say that he got the poorest of educations in grade school and had to go back when he was twenty to learn more than reading and writing. He often said this. But he never got the response he was hoping for. Kerry O'Neill never once said that it certainly hadn't made any difference, as Father had done so well. He never said anything at all.

* * *

Grace, on the other hand, was looking forward to starting school. It was different for her, she told Kerry, she knew all her friends already, she would be in the same class as Dara and Maggie and Jacinta. They had told her all about the worst things, and how to get around Sister Laura. Grace was going to have to learn Irish, and Sister Laura had suggested she become familiar with the alphabet and a small amount of vocabulary before term began.

The others had been very helpful, although the boys had taught her a really rude phrase which she might easily have said unless Dara had told her what it meant. She had gotten her navy uniform in the big town, and even the plain skirt and jumper and the pale blue shirt which looked so dull and drained the color out of the other girls, could not take from Grace O'Neill's healthy good looks. She bought a navy hair ribbon and tied up her golden curls.

She paraded with her school bag for her brother.

"How do I look?"

"Great." His mind was elsewhere.

"Thanks a lot."

"No, seriously, you do look great. You look older than you are."

"Older in this?" Grace was disbelieving.

"Yes, you look much more grown up than all the other puddings here. Don't let these fellows make any more rude remarks. You hear?"

"Oh Kerry, it wasn't fellows telling rude remarks. It was Tommy and Liam and . . ."

"Just not anymore."

Grace wished now she hadn't told him. He didn't understand how funny it had been.

"Sure, sure," she said to placate him.

"You've no mother, Grace, and Father lives in his own world. Somebody has to look after you. That's why I sound like an old bear, an old hen . . . whichever it is that does the clucking and fussing."

"I think it's a hen," she laughed, and ran toward him to give him a hug. "It's hens that fuss. It's the bears that hug. You're very good to me, Kerry."

The door opened and Patrick came in.

"Is that your new uniform? You look fantastic; a real scholar," he said admiringly.

Grace still had her arms around her brother's waist.

"Kerry's been setting me right, and giving me all kinds of good advice about going to school."

Patrick looked pleased. He often wondered what the children talked about when they were on their own. They seemed quite content.

"I just thought someone should mark her card," Kerry said with a note of insolence that Grace noticed too. She looked up at him anxiously, and let her arms drop.

"Good." Patrick was easy and relaxed. "I'm glad you're doing it. I'm afraid that I have too much faith in you pair; I think you were born knowing everything, being able to do everything. I don't mark your cards enough, I suppose."

"That's a good complaint to have, Father." Grace was hasty in her attempts to avert this scene, whatever it was.

She spoke quickly. "I hear so many people complaining about their parents who tell them this and order them to do that. You just stay as you are. Tommy Leonard says his father is at him night and day."

"Not enough to get him to keep a clean tongue in his head," Kerry said.

Suddenly Grace felt weary. "Look, fight if you want to, I'm not going to keep chatting. I think I'll go to bed."

The light had gone from her face. Both her father and brother looked stricken.

"I wasn't fighting, Gracie, really," Kerry said.

"Listen to me, honey, I couldn't fight with anyone, not tonight, now that I see you all dressed up to go to your Irish convent school. My heart is so full, Grace. I wish, I wish so much . . ."

They knew what he wished. They knew that Father wished their mother were alive. But he didn't say it. He just said that he wished things were different.

Grace had met most of the girls who would be in her class and who lived in Mountfern. But there were quite a few from out in the country. When they saw the newcomer they were dazzled. At first they giggled a bit at the beautiful girl with the golden curls tumbling down from a topknot tied with a shiny navy ribbon. And they nudged each other at her American accent.

Sister Laura made a small speech of welcome at assembly and said that she knew the girls of Mountfern convent would be, as they always were, welcoming to a stranger in their midst and help her to feel at home. Dara whispered to Grace that this was all nonsense. There never had been a stranger in their midst before. Grace was the first one. Maggie saw Grace and Dara laughing together at assembly, and tried to stop this feeling that she was being left out of things.

Sister Laura was speaking about the school year that lay ahead. She had every hope that 1962–1963 would be a year that they would all remember for the amount of hard work they put into their studies. Even those who had no formal examinations this year would, it was hoped, show a diligence that would long be remembered in the establishing of the convent in Mountfern as a legend in the houses of the order. Sister Laura said that sister houses had been achieving a reputation for scholarship which had so far evaded Mountfern. Let 1962–1963 be the year that all changed, the year they emptied their minds of silliness and let the sun of learning shine in.

They stood there in the navy uniforms. Kitty Daly splendid with the new hairstyle which had caused Kerry O'Neill to say "You look nice. Did you change something about yourself?" and sang the hymn to Our Lady to mark the beginning of the new term. Kitty had put all silliness out of her mind and was concentrating heavily on the information that Kerry did not go to his boarding school for another week. Grace would be out of the way at school. If Kitty were to feign a terrible sickness and go home, they would never suspect her of malingering, not on the very first day of term. Then she could walk up as far as the Grange, and if that old bag Miss Hayes didn't get suspicious, she should surely find a chance to run into Kerry. Sister Laura was right, start the year as you mean to go on.

Dara sang lustily as well. It had been a great summer holiday after all, in spite of all the changes at Fernscourt. She and Michael had said last night, as they sat on the window seat, that they wished they had somewhere to go, some special place still like that room they had in Fernscourt that was theirs. But wasn't it funny that none of them ever wanted to go back and play in the ruins now? They had only been once with Grace and it was like going back somewhere that belonged to another part of their life. Mr. O'Neill had urged them to continue playing there, but things had changed, there were bicycles for one thing, and the fishing for another. And it was great to have someone as lively as Grace around. Maggie was a great friend, but she was very mousy, and always afraid of what would happen, and of someone objecting or getting annoyed. Grace hadn't a fear in the world. She was magnificent.

Sister Laura sang to Our Lady, Queen of the Angels and Star of the Sea, and wondered why she felt Grace O'Neill was unsuitably dressed for school. The child wore her navy school uniform; she had no hint of make-up. She did not have pierced ears and great loops of earrings. She had no bosom apparent beneath her navy jumper. She was singing the hymn as assiduously as the others. What was it about her that made her seem not a twelve-year-old, but something much more precocious? Sister Laura liked to consider herself a fair woman. She hoped that she was not taking an unreasonable dislike to the child just because she had a beautiful face, tanned skin and golden hair.

Jacinta White nudged Maggie Daly to ask her why she wasn't singing.

"Sorry," whispered Maggie, and joined in the hymn.

Jacinta was relieved. She thought Maggie's face looked very worried, as if she had something that was upsetting her. But of course Maggie often looked like that.

Fergus Slattery called to the Grange to see old Mr. Johnson about a sale. It appeared that Patrick O'Neill had made an offer, a most generous offer for a small paddock owned by the Johnsons, and the right of way to bring horses to and fro from this field from the main road across the Johnsons' land.

"I can't see a thing wrong with it myself, but the American said to be sure, and do it through a solicitor, so here we are, Fergus. I'm sorry for bringing you all the way up here, I thought maybe your father might come, and we'd have a bit of a chat."

"He has a cold on his chest, and Miss Purcell won't let him out of the house. He says he's going to look for a writ of habeas corpus if she keeps him there much longer." Fergus spoke absent-mindedly. He was looking at the papers. "What does this fellow want the land for up here?"

"I can't tell you, that's for certain. Marian says he's doing it out of the generosity of his heart, because he knows we're a bit strapped for cash. We wanted to get a bit of a paint job done but it costs the earth these days."

"Is that field useful to you?"

"Not at all, it's only a nuisance to us. The hedges and walls are all broken, anyway, but it says somewhere there, doesn't it, that he's going to build them up?"

Fergus had been reading this. "Yes, he can build walls and low constructions for the maintenance of cattle, livestock or horses. I suppose that's what he wants, to set up a rival stables, take the one bit of business you have left."

"I don't think so." Mr. Johnson was mild. "He's signed an agreement with us about using our horses, paying a retainer even, in case he doesn't have sufficient guests for them. He's going to be the making of us, Fergus. Paying a great big rent for that falling-down Gate Lodge, too, and a year in advance because we had to do a bit of smartening it up."

"Smartening it up! From what I hear, you practically built a new house," Fergus snapped.

"What have you against him, boy?"

"It's a good question, Mr. Johnson, and a timely one. I'll look at this document now, and stop all this sounding off."

Fergus read the totally straightforward deed of sale drafted by a perfectly honest solicitor. Reluctantly he agreed that if Mr. Johnson wanted to sell, then there was nothing here that was out of the way, and that the price offered was well higher than the normal rate per acre hereabouts.

As a last, and almost petty gesture, Fergus asked whether Mr. Johnson could see *any* reason, apart from the goodness of Patrick O'Neill's heart and his wish to give them decorating money, why a businessman should suddenly make an offer for that particular field.

Mr. Johnson's mild old eyes looked surprised.

"Well of course there's a reason, Fergus. He needs a place where he can keep horses himself. And suppose he and Marian fall out, suppose Marian sets her cap at him too obviously and he isn't willing, well he'd need to have a fall-back position if he's offering his guests riding lessons, pony trekking, hunting and all. It's to cover himself."

Fergus was astonished at such clarity of vision.

"And does Marian see it like this?" he gasped.

"Now, now, now Fergus, do women ever see things the way they are? Have you known a woman who could see further than romance and yards of veil and wedding days? Let them go on like that, it doesn't do anyone any harm."

Fergus felt a chill. It was like playing God with people's future, he thought, as he arranged the signature of the deed of sale.

Olive Hayes wrote a long letter to her sister in New Zealand every month. She kept a carbon copy of it, and knew her sister probably did the same. They could refer back easily to small incidents that each had described over the years and they never forgot anything, no matter how trivial. Miss Hayes knew of the health of the elderly Reverend Mother who was always expected to die and then rallied, just when a successor had been more or less agreed for the community. Over on the other side of the earth in a convent on a cliff in South Island, Sister Bernadette knew about the O'Neill family, and how little Grace continued sunnily her life in Mountfern. Grace had even asked Miss Hayes if she would like to come to the sale of work up at the convent which was usually for the children's parents.

"You helped me make all the jam and cakes. You're more entitled than anyone," Grace had said.

Miss Hayes had been very pleased, but she wondered was she stepping out of place.

"Perhaps Miss Johnson?" she had said tentatively.

"Ugh, ugh, no thank you very much," Grace had giggled. "We don't want to be giving her ideas, Miss Hayes."

Olive had found that very endearing. She told her sister that Patrick O'Neill had gone to the States again. He traveled the whole way there as easily as some people took a train from the big town to Dublin. Miss Hayes felt that he had waited until Kerry was safely installed at his boarding school before he went. It was no trouble to look after Grace, but Kerry might have been a handful.

Miss Hayes looked back at the carbons of her previous letters and noticed with satisfaction that she had made this very same pronouncement in July when the O'Neills had arrived. Now, five letters later, she was interested to know that she had been right.

Kate Ryan decorated the Slatterys' office with holly at Christmas time. She thought how strangely unfestive it all was compared to everywhere else in Mountfern. The church had its huge crib and in the window of the presbytery there was a Christmas candle and another smaller crib, lovingly tended by Miss Barry who hadn't touched a drop since the summer.

Leonard's stationery and paper shop was all done up with the paper chains and streamers it sold. Mrs. Meagher was still in mourning for her husband, but she had sprigs of tinsel and glitter around the Christmas-wrapped brooches and earrings in the window of the shop. The cinema had two large Christmas trees with lights that flashed on and off. Declan Morrissey said it gave him a headache to look at them, and every single year he managed to fuse the lights in the cinema when he was putting up these ridiculous Christmas decorations. Daly's Dairy had very smart plaited rings of ivy and holly twisted around each other and tied with a red ribbon. They had been made by Kitty apparently, who was a changed girl according to all accounts, and had seen how to do this home-made decoration in one of those American magazines she was always reading.

In the post office there were some colored paper chains, a big silver banner saying Peace on Earth, and a collection box discreetly placed in case anyone might interpret the season of good will as a time to give a few pennies toward gifts for a children's orphanage. Dunne's pub had a big plastic Santa Claus in the window. There was hardly any point in their putting up any further decoration since they were yet again on the verge of packing up and going to Liverpool. Jimbo Doyle had put a Christmas tree for his mother in the window of their small house, and had agreed after much nagging to get proper fairy lights that worked. His mother had said that she was sick of hearing all the work Jimbo was doing in other people's houses while their own looked like a very good imitation of a rubbish heap.

In the Garda barracks, Seamus Sheehan looked in some doubt at the decorations Mary had bought on her last visit to Dublin. He wondered whether they were appropriate to the walls of a Garda Siochana station. Arty-looking cut-out robins and reindeer with little holes where you inserted mistletoe or holly. But Mrs. Sheehan had been adamant. She had read about them in a magazine which said that all the best people in Dublin had these in their homes now, and she wanted to drag a bit of style into Mountfern no matter how much they all resisted it.

Judy Byrne had planted two neat window boxes of her small house with holly bushes and miniature Christmas trees. They looked very festive and elegant at the same time, people told her. Patrick O'Neill had made a point of coming in to congratulate her on them. He had stayed for a drink at Judy's insistence because of the season. She ran next door to Foley's with a tray and came back with a large whiskey for Patrick and a small sherry for herself.

She told Patrick that she didn't keep drink in the house. She thought it was a pity for single ladies to start opening the bottle at a regular hour each evening. Single women had to be so careful. Not that she was saying a word against

Marian Johnson of course, and in a hotel poor Marian had to be sociable. Still it *was* a danger, and it could run away with you all too easily.

Across the road Mr. and Mrs. Williams had their house neatly draped in holly and ivy. The Protestant church had been decorated by their few parishioners. Dr. White and his wife had threatened to have no decorations this year if this ridiculous row about mistletoe wasn't solved. Jacinta wanted a big bunch of it on the door just as you came in; Liam wanted none of it in or near the house. Never had a battle been fought so long and bitterly. Tommy Leonard said it was better than being at the pictures listening to the two of them. Dr. White decided eventually that a small discreet sprig of mistletoe be placed over the kitchen door, that it should not be publicly referred to, and that if this row began again, both Jacinta and Liam would remember Christmas 1962 as the year they not only had no decorations but no presents and no turkey either.

Miss Purcell wasn't best pleased when she saw Kate Ryan on a chair with a sprig of holly and a pack of thumb tacks.

"It was never the way here; Mr. Slattery never requested it," said Miss Purcell, lips in a hard line and the two red spots coming up magnificently on her cheeks.

"I know, Miss Purcell." Kate was falsely apologetic. "It's quite ridiculous really, but the children went up to Coyne's wood and they picked lovely bits full of berries, so I thought the least I could do . . . you know Mr. Slattery wouldn't want to offend . . . and in the spirit of Christmas . . ."

She finished no sentence and did not explain that she had asked Michael and Dara to collect a big box and deliver it to the office for her. A Christmas card from Fergus's sister Rosemary in England and then old Mr. Slattery, Fergus and Miss Purcell in paper hats sitting around a small turkey dinner. It didn't seem nearly celebratory enough for someone as warm and funny as Fergus.

He was pleased and surprised. He had been at the district court in the town, his father had gone to talk to an old crony on the grounds of a will that might be changed, but really in the knowledge that a bottle would be opened. Fergus looked at the holly with pleasure.

"We never had that; it's lovely," he said simply.

"Not even when your mother was alive?"

"Not really. She was never strong, you know. She didn't have all that energy like you have."

To herself Kate thought that it didn't really take much energy to stick a few bits of holly on a wall behind pictures, or around a doorway for a man and a boy. But she said nothing. She didn't mention that Grace O'Neill had said the very same thing; her mother had been unwell always. They didn't have Christmas decorations, it would have been tiring for her.

"I got you a present, Kate," Fergus said. "You're a hard person to buy for; you have everything."

"I felt the same about you." She produced a big wrapped parcel.

"Isn't that great, to be the two people who have everything," Fergus said, and waited for her to open hers first. It was a day excursion ticket to Dublin, two gift vouchers—one for Switzer's and one for Brown Thomas—and a note saying: "On presentation of this paper to her employer, Mrs. Kate Ryan will be granted one day's leave from her lawful employment during the working week."

Kate stared at it in delight.

"I thought you could go to the January sales, and those vouchers are to make sure you go to Grafton Street and see nice things. You're not to be buying up household goods in Clery's, mind." He spoke gruffly to hide his pleasure in her delight.

"I'll enjoy every minute of the day." She hugged him. "Fergus, you are a darling. Thank you very much."

"Well now, let's see what you gave me." He opened the box. It was a beautiful edition of *Moore's Melodies* with huge over-flowery illustrations by Daniel Maclise.

"I remembered you said you like Thomas Moore—that day at the concert, when Michael's class was murdering some of the melodies. I thought you'd like this." She beamed at him and saw to her consternation that his eyes were far too bright. She spoke quickly until he had recovered a calm voice himself. "I got it inside in the town. You know, Gorman's bookshop, I asked them to look out for an old edition and they came up with this. John and I have been looking at it ourselves. I hope you like it."

Fergus had recovered his voice.

"I love it. Miss Purcell and my father won't know what's ahead of them this Christmas day. They're going to get a blast of the lot here . . . I might come over to your place and sing them through for you as well."

Kate said that was a promise and she was holding him to it. At some stage over Christmas Fergus Slattery was to walk up River Road with his Moore book in a plastic bag in case it rained on it, and he would sing the entire repertoire for whoever was in Ryan's Licensed Premises.

"That should empty the place for you and lose you your trade before O'Neill takes it away," Fergus said.

"Now Fergus, it's Christmas time. Stop talking about him. And wasn't John Ryan right, as he is in so many things? For all his great chat and plans there isn't a sod turned on that site yet. It's going to take longer than he thinks to get his hotel going in a place that moves as slowly as Mountfern."

Kerry came home from school on a day when Patrick had to be in Dublin for further talks with the Tourist Board. The train would need to be met. Marian Johnson was only too happy to oblige. She had heard that Patrick was trying to arrange that Brian Doyle the builder see to it, and Brian had replied with spirit that he was a building contractor, not a chauffeur. He would be quite happy to do anyone a favor, but would not be asked to do a driving job as if it were part of his terms in getting the Fernscourt contract.

Patrick had admired this viewpoint and apologized. Many another man would have had less pride and courage than Brian Doyle, and would not have jeopardized their chance of the biggest building job in these parts in years. But Brian was not one to sit back and allow anyone to assume he was what he was not. He did himself more good by his truculent attitude with Patrick than he ever knew.

Marian was pleased too, although she thought Brian Doyle was insane. She stood on the platform raking the crowd of passengers who got off, looking for Kerry.

He seemed to have gotten taller or thinner somehow at school. Very handsome in his school blazer, and carrying his sports bag as well as his suitcase. He smiled pleasantly at Marian, and looked around for Grace.

"She's busy decorating the lodge for Christmas," said Marian, who had told the child there was no room in the car. "She'll see you back at home. Your father has to be in Dublin. He said to tell you he's very sorry."

"I'm sure he is," Kerry was polite and cold.

"So I thought we might have a little lunch, you and I in the hotel . . . to get to know each other." She twinkled at him, but Kerry didn't twinkle back.

"We do know each other don't we . . . ?" he said, bewildered. "You're Miss Johnson . . . from the Grange."

"Marian," she said.

"Yes, well."

It was most unsatisfactory. Marian had wanted to lean her elbows on the table of the Grand or the Central and have a lunch with this handsome blond son of Patrick's. Now it was all falling to pieces.

Kerry looked at her carefully and long. It was as if he were deciding what to do. And then it was as if he had decided to turn on the electric light of his charm.

"Well Marian . . . if you're sure I may call you that, I'd love to have lunch with you even though we do know each other already. That would be very nice."

They went to the Central. Marian waved at the people she knew whose heads went close together to discuss what she could possibly be doing with this teenage boy. They had tomato soup, boiled bacon and cabbage followed by apple pie and ice cream. Kerry told her little about school, less about his father and nothing about their life as it used to be in America. However he did learn about what had been going on in Mountfern, and that Grace seemed to love her school, had plenty of nice little girls as friends. Grace and his father had been taking riding lessons and both were progressing very well. There had been endless delays about clearing the title for the final land purchase in Fernscourt.

Marian prattled on in what she had hoped would be their lunch of getting to know each other, and she managed to present herself to Kerry as three different ages during the space of half an hour. She was getting younger as the lunch continued. She said that she was quite demented trying to get the O'Neills to give up this ridiculous idea of having Christmas lunch on their own, as a family. They should join her and her father, and there would be four other guests, charming people whom they would like, one of them was actually the Honorable and was terribly natural and unassuming, as if she were like everyone else.

On the journey back Marian had the vague feeling that she had gotten to know Kerry O'Neill not at all, but he had gotten to know almost all there was to be known about her.

"I'll call in later when your father gets back from Dublin," she said as she dropped him at the lodge and he was thanking her courteously.

"Why will you do that?" He was perfectly polite.

"Well. Gosh. Well, to see if he got back all right and to tell him that I met you safely."

Kerry looked at her, a clear unflinching look.

"Or maybe I'll drop in tomorrow . . . or sometime," Marian said foolishly.

She saw Grace racing out of the lodge to throw her arms around Kerry.

"Where *were* you? Miss Johnson said I couldn't come. I've been looking out for you for ages. Come in and tell me all about it, I've been dying for you to get here . . ."

The door of the lodge closed behind them. Marian saw the long stern face of Olive Hayes who was washing up at the kitchen sink. Marian told herself, as she had done many times before, that she mustn't rush it. Patrick O'Neill was a man not long a widower, a busy man with a million things on his mind. He had a tight self-sufficient little family. It would be foolish to try to break into it until they were ready.

That was the silly mistake Judy Byrne was making all the time, with her little invitations to a drink, and then fluttering in and out of Foley's instead of realizing that any man likes a woman with a good Waterford glass decanter on the sideboard.

They had a tradition in Mountfern that there was only one mass on Christmas Day. It meant that one priest was then free to go around and take holy communion to the people who weren't able to leave home. The mass was at nine o'clock. And the whole parish was there.

Judy Byrne wore a mantilla to communion, which looked very well on her. Miss Purcell, who really would have preferred a seven-thirty mass but would never criticize the clergy, wore a nice blue scarf that Kate Ryan had knitted for her, because she knew Miss Purcell had a blue coat.

Sheila Whelan had had a tiring night: young Teresa Meagher had had yet another row with her mother and wanted to leave home. There were no buses on Christmas Eve. Sheila had spent a great deal of time making cups of hot chocolate and taking further bars of Kit Kat out of the shelves. She cajoled and soothed. She told Teresa that if somebody left home at Christmas it had a terrible effect because it didn't just destroy *that* Christmas, but every other Christmas afterwards for both sides. She knew this, she told Teresa, very very well. She didn't go into details about how Joe Whelan had left her at Christmas, and how the big row over the road many years ago with Rosemary Slattery had been at Christmastime also. There was something about the season and all its expectations. Sheila talked long and gently about Teresa's mother feeling sad and lonely this Christmas, the first since her husband died; she must be given some little extra understanding; no of course, not over things that were totally unfair, but just an overall understanding.

Eventually the troubled child went to sleep on the sofa. Sheila put a rug over her, and a cushion under her head. Then she crossed the road and heard the whole story again from Teresa's mother, the insolence, the selfishness . . . Again she tried to talk of a daughter who had lost her father, and eventually Mrs. Meagher's red puffy eyes began to close, so Sheila left her.

She had urged them for form's sake to dress properly and go to mass as if nothing had happened. They were all going to Christmas lunch with the Whites. Judy Byrne was going too. Sheila would have preferred to have spent the day stock-taking, or sitting and listening to Radio Eireann. They had lovely programs on Christmas Day for people at home. It would be a real treat not to have to leave the house at all.

Patrick O'Neill walked his son and daughter up the church for their first Christmas Day in Mountfern. They had given Miss Hayes a lift from the lodge, but she didn't sit with them. She said she had friends to meet, and Christmas greetings to exchange. Everyone looked at the trio. Patrick in his camel-haired overcoat, stocky and handsome, smiling at this one, at that. Kerry taller definitely, he must have grown another two inches during his first term at boarding school. He wore a belted tweed coat, the kind many a youth of his age might wear, but it looked impossibly stylish because of the way the collar was turned up. Grace had a new outfit brought back from New York. It was a soft pale pink, a dusty pink coat with big velvet cuffs and collar in a darker pink. She had a velvet beret, a sort of tam o'shanter perched on top of all those golden curls as well. People turned to each other to smile at the beautiful child. Grace saw Dara and Michael and gave a little wave; they both stared at her open-mouthed.

Her father must have given this to her this morning already. She hadn't mentioned it yesterday. Maggie Daly sat in her brown coat which used to belong to Kitty. She felt like a colorless blob. Canon Moran was blessing everyone and wishing that the spirit of the Holy Child be with them now and always, and all Maggie Daly could think of was her own awful coat. No wonder Our Lord wasn't kinder to her, if she couldn't even drag her mind to think of him on his birthday of all days. Maggie gloomily accepted that she didn't deserve golden hair and a pink coat, or to be Dara Ryan's best friend.

The children all went for a walk in Coyne's wood on Christmas afternoon. It was a lovely clear, crisp day, and they wrapped up well and set out.

Kerry O'Neill came too. He told them about his school and spoke as if he were exactly the same age as everyone else, instead of being fifteen. Grace hung on to his arm a lot, and encouraged him to tell more tales, like the night the boy in the dormitory was listening to a transistor radio on an earphone and forgot where he was, and kept singing along with the Beatles. Yeah, Yeah, Yeah . . . and all the time Father Minehan was standing at the end of the bed watching him.

Kerry O'Neill remembered everyone's names. He was interested in everything they did. Tommy Leonard did one of his great imitations of Miss Barry the priest's housekeeper when she was on a tear. Michael explained to Kerry the best parts of the river, and told him a great hint about always noting a place where the cattle went to drink from. The cows stirred up mud, and also disturbed the water plants as they came to drink, so this meant fish would find it a good area for feeding, and you should position yourself about ten or twenty yards downstream and wait for them there. Kerry took all this in gravely and agreed with Jacinta White that Christmas wasn't Christmas without mistletoe, and at the same time agreed with her brother Liam that too much palaver could go on about it, just let it be there was the best solution. He asked Maggie Daly if all their family had that nice auburn hair. Did her sisters who were away nursing in Wales have it too? And Maggie pinked up happily and said that nobody had ever called it auburn before. Kerry said he heard that Dara was a demon fisherwoman, great at threading the maggots on the hooks and had caught a huge pike that struggled and fought. He said he thought Mountfern was the greatest place in the world, and as dark fell and they all went back to their homes, there wasn't one of the children who had come to Coyne's wood that would have remembered the day six months ago when they thought it was the end of the world because somebody had bought Fernscourt.

Part Two

Seven

Old Mr. Slattery died in the spring. He died exactly as he would have liked, sitting on his fishing stool and leaning back against a tree. Many people must have passed him by that afternoon thinking he was asleep. Miss Purcell's back was like a ramrod at the funeral mass. Her little wine-colored hat was replaced by a precisely similar one in black, and her disapproving face was set in harder lines than ever.

Fergus had felt achingly sorry for her.

She had mothered and bossed and bullied the old man for years. In return she had received a courteous fearful attention from him. What would she find as a replacement? He was very swift to tell her that he wanted no change in the situation.

"Oh indeed, and then when you up and marry, Master Fergus, when I'm an old woman, what will happen to me then?"

"I don't think I'll up and marry, I'm nearly thirty, and anyway if I do, won't she be a lucky woman to get the both of us?" He didn't say that Miss Purcell was an old woman already.

Fergus had one sister, Rosemary, married and living in Manchester. She came home for the funeral but she and he were like strangers. Rosemary was ten years older, she had been headstrong, he believed, and impatient. There had been rows, he remembered, when he was only six or seven and then she had left home. It had been made up of course but only in a fashion. Not properly. Letters at Christmas and cards on birthdays. No visits, no phone calls. There had been no rows with her little brother, but somehow Fergus hadn't expected his sister to come home. She came without her husband James, and without her sons. There was little mention of her family during the preparations for the funeral. She wore smart black and smoked the moment they were outside the church. Miss Purcell, who had been with the family at the time she left, hated her and barely disguised it.

"Back for the money," she hissed at Fergus, who only laughed. There was very little money, he had read his father's will. A legacy for Miss Purcell, a couple of hundred pounds to the church for masses, a small insurance policy whose small proceeds went to his grandsons in Manchester. There was nothing for the long-gone Rosemary. She would know that too. The business and the house were for Fergus. There was a touching personal note of gratitude that the young man had come back to Mountfern to keep the business going. Fergus had blinked a bit over that, he hadn't known how much his father had appreciated it. Rosemary sat and drank a whiskey with him; the conversation was brittle. He had the feeling that this was the last time he would ever see her, and he was determined for both their sakes that he would be pleasant and allow no recriminations to come into the conversation.

"Does it seem strange to be back home again?" he asked her.

She shrugged. "It's not home to me, never was really."

He hid his irritation. "I know. I forget. Well, people were glad to see you again."

"Did you think so? I think most of them had forgotten I ever existed. Real country bumpkins most of them."

"I suppose they must seem that way to you."

"And to you?"

"Oh I'm jes' an ole country bumpkin myself . . . like to sit in me ole rockin' chair and talk about the times gone by." He smiled at her, expecting some kind of an answering laugh.

Rosemary frowned at him. "You're turning into an old man, Fergus. It's a fact. You walk in small steps as if you were wearing slippers, and a sweater . . ."

Fergus felt the smile die on his face. He had been playacting to entertain her.

"Good Lord, I must watch that," he said, deliberately taking giant steps across the room. "Is that any better?" He took her glass to refill it and strode across the room as if he were playing grandmother's footsteps. This time it worked. She laughed at him affectionately.

"You're much too smart for here, Fergus. This is a dead-end town. Quit while you can, get to Dublin, even if you haven't the guts to sell up entirely. Drop it before it's too late and you turn into a vegetable or an alcoholic, or both."

He didn't comment on the fact that it was she who had had three whiskies while he had not finished his first.

"And what would I do that would be so exciting in . . . say Manchester?" he asked, hoping he kept the sarcasm out of his voice.

"You'd meet real people, not just the butcher, the baker, the candlestick maker. You'd find someone for yourself, instead of having to be like a eunuch here."

"Is that what they say I am?" He was very angry indeed. But there must be no more screaming matches with Rosemary in this house. History must not repeat itself.

"It's what I can see you are," she said, her eyes too bright, her hair slipping from the coil at the back of her neck. "What else could you be in a place like this, making sheep's eyes at that woman from the pub who does your typing? And never doing a thing about it."

"Sorry, Rosemary, hold on a minute, I've got to get us more water," he said.

He went into the kitchen and filled the jug, which he gripped with both hands to the sink until his knuckles were thin and white. How *dare* she speak of Kate like that? He would like to have hit her across the side of her silly drunken head. But it was a matter of hours. They would talk for another short while, then tomorrow she would have breakfast and he would drive her to the train in the big town. He would offer her something from the house as a souvenir. He had been going to suggest an old Victorian sewing box that had belonged to their mother. But, God damn it, no. It was too good for her, and Rosemary didn't look like anyone who would ever sew. Just keep the peace for a few more hours. That wasn't a weak thing to do, surely; it was a strong thing. He came back in smiling.

"Sorry, I was waiting for it to run cold. Where were we? I was making sheep's eyes at Kate Ryan. Who would I be making sheep's eyes at in Manchester?"

"I didn't say you were to come to Manchester." She sounded sulky now.

"But I will someday, surely. Not to work but to visit. I'd love to see my nephews. They must have nearly left school by now. Tell me about them."

He settled himself in his chair, his smile of interest and concern masking his rage.

"They've left," she said gruffly.

"Surely not? Hugh can only be barely sixteen?"

"Headstrong, impatient, won't wait, won't get an education." She looked into the fire.

"And what does James say about it?"

"He's hardly ever there to say anything. He's not around much."

Rosemary still looked into the fire.

Fergus poured them both a last drink, and moved to less troubled waters. He suggested that Rosemary take a silver cigarette box back with her as a memento. Awkwardly she accepted it, and before she went to bed she gave him what passed for a kiss on the cheek. A sort of lunge.

"You're not the worst, Fergus, even though you're a bit of an eejit," she said, and her tones were those of love and praise, inasmuch as she could give either.

He lay awake for a long time and wondered about sheep's eyes. What way did one sheep look at another that the world regarded as foolish?

Eddie Ryan asked Mr. Williams the vicar if he could become a Protestant and be accepted into the Church of Ireland faith. Mr. Williams listened to him gravely and said it was a very big step and perhaps he should think more about it, maybe even discuss it with his priest or his parents. Mr. Williams was a kind man; never for a moment did he betray his knowledge of Eddie's latest deed, which involved breaking the little shutter in the confessional, something that had never been done since the church was built and had hardly ever been done in Christendom according to Canon Moran and Father Hogan. Eddie explained that the church was empty at the time, and he wondered what it felt like to sit where the priest did, pushing the shutters back and forth to listen to the penitents. He got a bit excited and kept whizzing them to see which one would close quickest, and that was when one came away from its moorings entirely.

Jimbo Doyle had to be summoned, and it was all very serious and high level. Canon Moran said he couldn't believe that the child would say the church was empty. Wasn't our Blessed Lord in the church in the tabernacle, watching Eddie Ryan desecrate church property and disassemble the place where the holy sacrament of penance took place?

Father Hogan kept saying, "What Cromwell left undone Eddie Ryan will finish," and pretending to panic when he saw him coming near the church.

It would be easier for him to be a Protestant.

"I have thought about it," he assured Mr. Williams. "I'm dead certain. Would I need an admission card to start coming here on Sunday?"

"Of course not, Eddie, but . . ."

"And if there's any questions, trouble like, you'll tell them I asked to join. That it's all above board. If they come hounding me?"

"Who would come hounding you, Eddie?"

"Almost everyone in the place, Mr. Williams, you wouldn't credit it. My mother said if she set eyes on me again today she wouldn't be responsible for what she'd do. Sergeant Sheehan said he has a room in the barracks with a lock on it and he's thinking of putting my name on it because it's where I'll end up. I couldn't tell you what the priests are like, because we're all meant to be . . . whatever it's called these days, you know loving all other religions . . . so it wouldn't do you any good to know what they're like down at the presbytery just now."

"Life can be very difficult." Mr. Williams was trying hard not to smile.

"You wouldn't know the half of it up here, with no flock so to speak of, and pots of money."

The impoverished Mr. Williams listened to this wryly.

"I don't have all that much, Eddie."

"I bet you have four pounds though," Eddie said.

"Well, I do, but I need it. I can't give it to you, no matter how great your need."

"No, my need isn't great. If I join your church I won't have to pay it."

"How, exactly?"

"I can say I'm a different faith, a different crowd altogether. I can't be responsible for some sum of money they say I owe in the last faith. For repairs. I'd never make four pounds. Never."

Mr. Williams was very kind. He could see that Eddie Ryan was not trying to put a touch on him; the sum was too huge to be possible even for the wildly optimistic.

"Why don't you weed a few graves for me, Eddie, tidy up the graveyard. I could pay you say, five shillings. If you did a good job, then after several five-shilling days you could return to your old faith and pay your debts, and everyone would be happier."

"I thought you were supposed to be looking for converts, and snatching people away from the true faith."

"Oh no, we don't do much snatching here, more patting people down; that's what it seems to be about these days. Will I give you a sack for the grass and the weeds?"

* * *

Dara and Grace were in the graveyard looking after James Edward Gray. They had brought cowslips and primroses and had made an unsuccessful attempt to remove some of the moss and lichen from his stone with Vim. It had looked much better before their efforts, they realized. Maggie had been a bit funny about James Edward Gray, claiming that she found him and *she* was the one to look after him. Grace and Dara had agreed and gone to look for someone else who was pretty neglected. But Maggie had come after them in tears and said they could have James Edward Gray and keep him, she didn't care. Then she had stormed off home. She had been a bit like that lately, maybe it was trouble at home.

Maggie's elder sister Kitty was a bit bossy, and she had two sisters who were nursing in Wales. They could have lost their religion or not written home, or something. Mrs. Daly was an awful one for doing the right thing and the trimmings on the Dalys' rosary at night were as long as the rosary itself. Maggie must be getting some kind of trouble from her mother. That could be the only explanation of why she was so touchy these days.

Tommy Leonard came to collect Michael.

"There's no fish. What's the point?" Michael said.

"There's often no fish. As far as I'm concerned there's nearly always no fish. What are you after, some kind of record catch?"

Tommy was indignant. He had spent half an hour explaining to his father why a boy of thirteen should be allowed to go and fish with his friend, and now Michael didn't want to come.

"It's pointless, can't see any reason to drag all that stuff miles up the bank and miles back," Michael said.

"Lovely! When did this happen, this road to Damascus? Just when I was assuring my father that there was no better, healthier way of spending the afternoon."

"I don't know," Michael said.

"Listen Michael, you are a pain, and a big pain. What *is* it? Why was fishing what we did yesterday, and suddenly today it's what we don't do? I don't mind, I just want to know."

Michael punched Tommy to show that there was no personal ill-will involved.

"You know the way it is sometimes. There seems no point in anything. Anything at all," Michael said.

"Do I know how it is? Of course I know how it is. I feel that way most of the time. But why today? Now I'll have to go on my own or go back to the shop and say to my father he was right, I am a selfish pleasure-seeking lout . . ."

"Oh all right, I'll come with you."

"What about Dara and Grace and the others? Where are they? Did they all give up fishing too, suddenly? Did everybody except me?" Tommy wondered.

"Oh, who knows where they are? The Whites have gone to Dublin with their mother for the day; Dara and Grace are giggling somewhere, you can be sure of that."

"Where's Maggie?"

"I don't know. I think she's as angry with all this giggling as we are. Come on then Tommy, if we're going to spend the day getting pneumonia for no fish, let's go and catch it."

"The sun is shining, you clown," Tommy said.

The sun had come out and Miss Hayes was planting some pansies that Kate Ryan had given her. Mrs. Ryan was very good about all kinds of flowers and Miss Hayes had heard some disparaging remarks that Judy Byrne had made about the appearance of the gate lodge of the Grange. Miss Hayes was feeling personally slighted. She had called at Ryan's merely for advice. Mrs. Ryan had given her the pansies and gotten her a lift back too from a passing customer. It was too far to walk in the sun, she had said.

Olive Hayes watered them well in, just as she had been advised. She would make a macaroni and cheese for the tea, that little Ryan girl was coming this evening. She and Grace O'Neill were very thick with each other. They never stopped talking and laughing. It would do your heart good to see them.

Grace and Dara left the graveyard hastily when they saw Eddie being instructed in the details of grave-tending.

"It's more than flesh and blood could bear, we'll have to leave," Dara said as soon as she saw her small brother.

"He's not that bad," Grace laughed.

"You don't know how bad he is, he'll probably dig up half the bodies in the graveyard. We're well out of it before he gets at it."

They scrambled to the wall where they had left their bicycles.

"We'll walk home through Coyne's wood. That way we won't get drawn into the fishing," Dara said.

"Yes, sure. Or else we could just say that we're not going fishing today." Everything was simple to Grace.

They wheeled their bikes through the woods which looked beautiful in the Easter sunshine. They heard pigeons and cuckoos, and small rabbits ran across their path as they walked.

"It's like fairyland here," Grace said happily.

"Is your father glad he came?" Dara asked.

"Oh yes, of course he is. Why?"

"He was in our pub the other night. I thought he looked kind of tired and upset."

"He gets upset over Kerry. Remember at Christmas I was telling you; and there's been something on his mind at the moment. I don't know what it is, he won't tell me. That means it's either about Kerry or about women."

"Women?" Dara's eyes were round.

"Yes, women falling in love with him. You know, I told you yucky Marian Johnson has."

"Oh yes, but you wouldn't mind that," Dara dismissed Marian.

"And I think Miss Byrne, you know, the chiropractor."

"Physio."

"Yes, whatever. And there's this woman in America." Grace looked troubled.

"Lord he *does* collect them," Dara said in mystification.

"I know, he's very old and everything, but he's very nice," Grace said defensively. "And rich of course," she added, in order to be strictly fair.

"Who's the woman in America?"

"A Mrs. Fine."

"Do you think it's serious? Isn't she married to someone else, if she's a missus?"

"No, he's dead or separated. There's no Mister Fine around."

"Do you like her?"

"She's OK. I don't want Father to marry anyone else. That's all."

"I know, but maybe he's not going to. Wouldn't she be here or he be over there if they were getting married? After all they're pretty old. They wouldn't want to be wasting time."

"He calls her a lot. He called her twice on Christmas Day."

"Oh that means nothing. Mrs. Whelan says people are always telephoning each other on Christmas Day and putting the heart across everyone else."

"I don't know." Grace was doubtful. "I had this friend in the States, Brigid Anne Moriarty. Well, she told me that her mother said Father was going to marry again, that everybody knew it, that he had a lady friend he worked with, and that they were going to get married quietly in New York."

"How did Brigid Anne know all this, and you and Kerry didn't?"

"Who would tell us? Anyway I told Kerry this on the day of mother's funeral."

"You mean Brigid Anne knew your father had a lady friend *before* your mother died?" Dara's face was horrified.

"But you see it wasn't true; obviously it wasn't. It was only a tale people told because Father was so well known among all these people, and because Mother was an invalid for so long."

Grace looked wretched as she went over this. Impulsively Dara threw her arm around her friend's shoulder.

"Don't worry about it, Grace, *please*. It's not happened. It's not going to happen. We can head off the awful Marians and awful Judys, and Mrs. Fine can't be any threat, otherwise she'd be here."

"Yes, I'm sure that's right."

"So why are you still sad?"

"Because I'm thinking about the day of the funeral and how upset Kerry was when I told him about what people were saying. But you're right. It's not going to happen: I won't think about it anymore."

They came out of the wood and cycled to the lodge. Miss Hayes said that Mr. O'Neill had been on the telephone to say he would not be back for tea. He had gone to Kerry's school. The boys had spent some of the Easter holidays there to take part in the Easter vigil and church services. They were meant to be getting holidays in a week. But Kerry was coming back tonight.

All through their macaroni and cheese they chattered excitedly about Kerry coming home. They cleared the table and washed the dishes with Miss Hayes. Dara marveled at the peace and quiet in this house, no Carrie clattering pans in the kitchen, no bar on the other side of the green door, no Leopold howling, no Declan complaining that he was going to be the baby in this family until he was an old-age-pensioner, no Eddie bringing some new doom and destruction down on them. No bustle. It must be lonely for Grace sometimes too, of course, so far from everyone.

They sat in Grace's room, and Dara tried on all her clothes. The shoes were a little too small, which was a pity since Grace had so many she could have given Dara any amount without missing them.

"Does your father ever fight with Michael?" Grace asked.

"No, no he doesn't."

Grace sighed heavily. "No, I think it's just my father and Kerry. It's something in them that doesn't mix."

"Of course Daddy gets very irate with Eddie, almost every day of our lives," Dara offered, in the hope of reassuring her friend.

"Eddie's different, as you said yourself."

"Yes," Dara agreed. "Eddie's very different, nobody could mix with him."

Dara cycled home and saw a man slipping into the Rosemarie hair salon, having looked up and down River Road nervously first. Could the unlikely rumor they had heard at school *possibly* be true? She must tell Grace tomorrow morning. She hoped Grace wouldn't be lonely as she waited for Kerry and her father to come home.

Grace wished she had never told Kerry about that stupid thing that Brigid Anne had said, about the gossip that Father had some other lady in mind to marry. Obviously it hadn't been true. It was nearly two years since Mother had died, and Father had no intention of marrying again. Father Devine had introduced him to several likely people, awful women from the parish, widows and terrible people. But Father used to laugh about them with her so Grace had no worries.

Kerry had a picture of Mother in his billfold, and also in the plastic folder at the back of his assignment book. Grace had seen him taking it out to look at it one day when he thought nobody was watching. And the picture of Mother that stood on the piano . . . Kerry was always adjusting it and making sure it stood right where it was best lit.

There was a portrait of Mother hanging in the hall. Mother had never liked it, she thought it made her look as if she had been dressed up to play the part of a fine lady. Father had laughed and told her that she *was* a fine lady. Kerry didn't like that picture, he never stopped to look at it. Once Grace asked him why he didn't like it, and he had said that Father had only dressed Mother up in jewelry and silks and paid a society painter to do the portrait, to show what a big man *he* was. It had nothing to do with Mother herself.

Kerry had said that when things were his to do what he liked with, he would take the picture outside and burn it. Then Mother would know how well he had understood her. Kerry said some very odd things from time to time.

Grace wished she knew why her father had driven all the way up to his school to collect him. Perhaps it was a sign that Father was going to be warmer to Kerry, but somehow she didn't think so.

Father Minehan was a fussy man. Anything that could be said directly and simply, he managed to dress up and obscure. Patrick had been fifteen minutes in the dean's study and still didn't know why he was being asked to take Kerry away. That very day.

"So, when all aspects are considered, and taking everything into account, very often, the greater good is achieved by the simpler option," Father Minehan said.

Patrick looked at the priest with disgust. His blue eyes were hard and unsmiling.

"Briefly, what did he do?" he asked again, but his tone was more curt.

"There are so many explanations and ways of looking at what we do and why we do it . . ." Father Minehan was beginning again.

"In two or three sentences, Father." Patrick had never been so ill-mannered to a man of the cloth. His old training made him feel a thrill of wrongdoing because he was interrupting a priest with a bark of command.

"If it were as easy as that . . ."

"It is as easy as that. I have driven for two hours to a school where I thought you were educating my son, a school to which I have given generous contributions I may add, and I hear, or think I hear that you want him to leave. Now. Why?"

Father Minehan was at a loss to answer a question so directly put. He remained silent.

"Come on, Father, I can't stay all week playing guessing games. What did he do?"

"Let's take it slowly, Mr. O'Neill."

"Let's take it at a nice brisk pace, Father Minehan. Did he bugger one of the other boys?"

"Mr. O'Neill, *please!*"

Now, for the first time, the priest was shaken into a direct response.

"He's a fifteen-year-old boy, Father, almost sixteen. Eventually, I suppose, if I ask enough questions we might get an answer. Was he drunk? Did he hit one of the masters? Did he miss mass? What in God's name prompted all these letters and phone calls that the FBI couldn't work out?"

"I'm trying to explain."

"God damn it, you are not trying to explain. Did he screw one of the maids? Did he deny the infallibility of the pope? If I drive here and take him away with me leaving behind buildings I'm goddamn paying to erect, I would like to know why."

"He took a great deal of money."

Patrick felt an ice-cold pool in the base of his stomach.

"That's not possible."

"I assure you . . ."

"How much?"

"Two hundred pounds."

"Have you any proof of this?"

"Oh yes."

"Perhaps you would be good enough to let me have it."

"Do you want your son here?"

"Not immediately. Let me hear it from you first, then we'll ask Kerry his side of things. Right?"

The old Patrick had returned on the outside. A brisk smile, the kind he used in his business deals . . . a charm not fulsome, just there. He composed his face to listen.

It was a tale of a charity football match in aid of deprived children. Patrick held his mask face with difficulty. The priest was so unctuous. He spoke of deprived children as if they were another species of life. The rugby match had attracted a lot of attention. People came from all over to attend it. There were three Irish internationals playing on each side. It wasn't often that you saw such talent gathered on one afternoon on the playing fields of an Irish school. The entrance fee had been two shillings.

The boys in the school all attended, of course, people from the neighborhood and rugby fans from all over Ireland, as well as some people from the newspapers. Father Minehan's voice lowered again, in case someone from the newspaper might be in the room with them. It was all highly unfortunate. Over fourteen hundred people attended the match, many of them being men of property and generosity who gave much more than the two-shilling entrance fee.

Over two hundred pounds had been collected at the small tables placed near the school gate. It was taken into the school in leather bags, each with the amount it contained neatly written on a label attached to it. The money was in Father Bursar's office ready to be checked into a bank account next day. It disappeared. There was a search. The search revealed among other things that some of the senior boys were not in their dormitory; they came in later over the wall. They were met by a reception committee.

Kerry O'Neill had an envelope with fifty-seven pounds of the collection still in his pocket.

"Balls," snapped Patrick. "Nobody could spend all that in a night. What did he do? Buy a couple of properties down town?"

"He has not said what he did with it," Father Minehan said simply.

"But he hasn't said he took it, surely?"

"He cannot say otherwise. He is not a fool."

Again Patrick felt ice water moving in his stomach.

Kerry had packed. They had told him that morning that he was to have everything ready; he would be leaving with his father. When he came to the dean's study he had his fawn overcoat thrown casually over his shoulders.

Patrick was annoyed by this, and by seeing the boy's luggage outside the door. It was showing they were beaten before they began.

"Can you throw any light on this, Kerry?" He was firm, not accusatory, but wasting no time in pleas or expostulations.

"I'm sorry you had to drive up here, Father." Kerry was perfectly calm.

"Tell us what you have to tell." Patrick didn't look at Father Minehan, who stood there in classic thoughtful pose with one arm across his waist, supporting the elbow of the other arm. A hand with long white fingers spread discreetly over his face.

"I'm afraid there's nothing to tell, Father."

"You deny you took this money."

"No, I can't deny that, I'm very sorry."

"You don't mean you took it?"

"Yes, I did."

There wasn't a sound from the priest.

"In the name of God why did you do that? I could have given you money. I give you a bloody allowance every month, for Christ's sake."

Kerry stood still; regret was the only emotion Patrick could see on his face. Mild regret. No shame, no sorrow.

"So what did you want it for?"

An inclination of the head toward the priest, that was all.

"Could you leave us alone, Father Minehan?"

"No, Mr. O'Neill, this is my study. I do not choose to leave it."

Patrick made a decision.

"Yes, that's your privilege. Now you asked me to take my son away. I shall do that. Thank you for the part your community has played in his education so far."

Father Minehan had been prepared for a day of recriminations and explanations, and bringing in bigger guns like the Father Superior. He couldn't believe it was over already.

"Well, I have to say . . ." he began.

"I hope you have to say very little. We will not discuss any fees that might be owing by me to you, since I think we will agree that donations already given would make the pursual of those fees a grotesque impertinence on your part . . ."

"I assure you that . . ."

"I accept all your assurances. If I am owed any balance why not add that to the already significant sum I have given to the college? And I expect full and favorable reports and references on my son's progress and achievements in this school. I have fulfilled to the letter your request to me, once I understood it. I am taking him away with me in the next five minutes. Within the next five days I expect a detailed report which I can give to the principal of the next college he will attend. *And,* Father Minehan, I shall expect the most glowing of verbal references, should any school call you to inquire about Kerry."

"Well, there will have to be—"

"You are quite right, there *will* have to be arrangements made to that effect immediately, otherwise, I will create such a stink and a scandal that the smell will remain over these college walls for three generations to come. I will talk of the blackmail in order to get subscriptions, the extortion of further money from the children by making them pay to see rugby matches in your own premises. I will speak to the newspapers about the lax security and discipline that allows children in your care to scale walls and disappear in the evenings." He lowered his voice suddenly. "But all this would be very unpleasant and I am sure quite unnecessary."

He walked with Kerry from the school to his car. He looked at the creeper on the walls and remembered the day he had driven here to start Kerry off as a pupil.

Kerry sat in silence as they drove.

Patrick waited five minutes for an apology, an explanation.

He looked at his son's arrogant profile; he remembered his dead wife's hopes. He drew into a petrol station. Beyond the pumps where there was some waste ground.

He got out and with deliberate steps went around to Kerry's side of the car and opened the door. Kerry got out, a look of polite mystification on his face. Patrick hit him.

As Kerry reeled from the blow, Patrick hit him again on the jaw and rained blows into his body. Winded, Kerry made no real effort to defend himself, except to cry out . . .

"You big ape, you bog man . . . you're nothing but a bloody Irish bog man; that's why you wanted to come back to the bogs, you never left them."

Patrick had stopped punching anyway. He indicated a gents' toilet. "Be back here in five minutes. We're going home," he said, and he got into his car, wearily watching Kerry stagger away, bruised and bloodstained, to try and repair the damage to his face and clothes.

Eight

They knew that something had happened in the O'Neill family. And whatever it was, Grace was not going to talk about it.

Tommy Leonard thought that it was because Mr. O'Neill was being bad-tempered. He had heard stories of him shouting at people about delays and messing and inefficiency. And to Tommy Leonard all fathers were bad-tempered, because his own was a demon altogether.

Jacinta and Liam White thought that it might have something to do with someone being sick. Their father had been called up to the lodge one evening. So maybe it was an illness. Dr. White wouldn't tell them; he never talked about his patients. But if it was something simple like measles or mumps he would have said, so it could be a fatal disease.

Maggie Daly had heard that they were going away, people had said that Mr. O'Neill was so fed up with not getting the hotel built straight away he was going to pull out and forget the whole thing. Maggie half hoped they would, but in another way she wanted them to stay. She didn't hate Grace; she wanted to be her friend. The best that could possibly happen was that Grace would want the three of them—Dara, Maggie and her—to be friends, to be a proper gang with nobody left out.

Kitty Daly kept asking Maggie why Grace didn't come to play anymore, and whether Kerry had come back from boarding school. She was not at all satisfied when her little sister didn't seem to know.

Dara knew that Kerry had come back from school because she had been there the evening that Mr. O'Neill had gone to collect him. But the next day she had a telephone call from Grace asking her not to say anything to anyone about anything.

"What do you mean?" Dara was totally confused. "If someone says hello, am I not to say hello back?"

"This is serious," Grace said.

"I know it is. I'm serious too. Why can't you *tell* me what I'm not to say anything about? Why aren't you here anyway?"

"Is anyone listening to you?"

"No, I mean Dad's in the pub. Mam's at work, Carrie's in the kitchen, Michael's in the yard, Eddie is probably eavesdropping somewhere. What *is* it?"

"There's been a bad row, and I can't come out for a few days. Not till we're back at school, we might even be going away."

"Where, where are you going?"

"I don't know, *please* Dara, don't tell anyone what I told you."

"You didn't tell me anything. I don't understand any of this."

"About my father and Kerry not getting on. You know?"

"Oh that. No, I won't tell anyone. I wouldn't have anyway."

"And could you try to take the drama out of it all?"

"I didn't know it was a drama . . ."

"I've got to go now." Grace hung up.

They didn't see Grace until the first day of term, a whole week. She looked very pale.

Jacinta was triumphant. "I told you it was a disease," she said proudly. "It could be TB."

"Why don't you ask her?" Maggie said.

"You don't ask people who are riddled with TB if they're riddled with it; you pretend everything is normal," Jacinta, the doctor's daughter, replied.

Maggie noticed that Dara wasn't racing up to Grace as usual. Dara was on her own.

Good, Maggie thought. Now she knows how it feels to be left out of things.

But if anyone looked left out of things it was Grace. She was like someone recovering from a bad bout of flu.

Even Sister Laura warmed to the girl.

"Did you get any time to do those Irish lessons I set you?" she asked, in a kinder tone than she usually used when checking on homework.

"Yes, Sister, I have them here." The girl produced pages of sentences:

"I am going to town. Was he going to the town? We were not going to the town." All neatly written in the slopy writing and purple ink that the nun objected to, and was annoyed with herself for the unreasonable objection.

"That's very good," she said, impressed. "You must have spent a lot of time working."

"I spent all last week. I sat in my room all day, Sister." She looked downcast.

"Well, you're an example to them all, I must say. How is your brother getting on at his school, tell me?"

It was a courtesy, a little personal remark to show that Sister Laura cared about Grace and her family. The girl's face flushed a bit.

"He liked it very much, but the place was a bit damp so they decided because he has a weak chest . . . they thought . . . they said it would be better if he went to another school. Which isn't damp. More modern. So he's going there."

"Very wise, you can't be too careful with chests," Sister Laura said.

It was an odd thing to move the boy at the beginning of the summer term, very upsetting to child and school to have changes in the middle of the academic year. And surely the place couldn't be all that damp in the summer.

Still it was no business of hers. Sister Laura put her mind to the business of keeping the children's minds on school when everything outside was tempting them out of the classroom and on to the river bank, into the woods and over the springy green fields around Mountfern.

Patrick and Kerry sat at the breakfast table in the lodge. Miss Hayes left the refilled coffee pot on the table and explained that she was about to cycle into Mountfern for the messages. She wished Kerry good luck at his new school and said she hoped it wouldn't be damp like the last place. There was nothing as bad as a chill that settled on the chest. And she was gone.

She knew of course that there had been hell to pay between father and son. Mr. O'Neill had said to her on that evening when he came back with the boy, looking as if he'd been in a fight with a crowd of thugs, that there were a few things the family wanted to discuss in confidence and they would probably go away for some days to do so in privacy. Olive Hayes had given it a little thought and said that it would be much better if *she* were to go away and let them have the house on their own. She had stocked up the larder and gone to a cousin in Galway without either giving or getting any further explanations. She knew that she had done the right thing; Mr. O'Neill had gripped her hand firmly when she returned and said that they had been greatly blessed to have found someone like her. He had also added that there would always be a place and role for her when the new hotel was built. *If* it was *ever* built. Life was full of obstacles, he had said with his engaging smile.

And so now she left them alone once more so that the father and son could say goodbye in whatever way they wanted to without having to lower their voices for fear of her overhearing them.

In fact they sat in silence for some minutes after they heard her bicycle creak out through the big iron gates of the Grange.

"I've done a lot of thinking, Kerry."

Kerry looked at him politely.

"We seem to have discovered that it wasn't for drugs, or for alcohol. It was not for anyone else . . . you do not appear to have made any friends. It was hardly for a woman, and at your age you are unlikely to have done anything for which you could be blackmailed. There was no race meeting where you could have lost it, and you aren't known in the bookies near the school, so it couldn't have been that. If you bought anything with it then that item was not delivered. You will not tell me and I have not been able to find out."

Kerry said nothing.

"Is that a summary of what has happened?"

"Yes, you left out a bit here and there." Kerry rubbed his bruised jaw.

"I wish that I hadn't beaten you. I've said that."

"I don't mind. It makes us quits."

"It *does* not make us quits. In no way does it make us anything like quits."

Patrick stood up and walked toward the window.

"It leaves me knowing that I can't control my temper; that's a weak position to be in. I am also left with the knowledge that you stole an enormous sum of money for a purpose which you cannot or will not explain, which leaves me in an even weaker position. How am I to continue in this way of life that I am trying to build for us if I cannot trust you? You may take money from Miss Hayes's purse; you may reach over the counter in Daly's and put your hand in the till. I may have to drive to this new school and hear a similar story.

"All that's happened to you is that you got beaten. Your life goes on exactly the same—new school, clean slate, reputation totally unsullied even to your little sister."

Kerry remained very still.

"In five minutes Marian is coming to drive you into the town, and you are getting the train to a school I have not seen. The principal has had a lying letter from that death's head Minehan. I've seen a copy of it. He will *not* have gone behind my back, so you start here with nothing on your record. This is your last chance, Kerry, your only chance."

"Yes, Father."

"No, I mean it. We've done a cosmetic job on it; we've papered it over. The last school was damp, you had a wheeze in your chest, medical advice . . . even Grace more or less believes it now. You've been given a new start. I'd like to embrace you and come with you to the school, and tell this new head priest, whoever he is, that I'm proud of my son and I want him to do well, like I did last time, but I don't have the stomach for it. So Marian is taking you to the train. And we agreed that in front of anyone around here we act as normal, as if we were the best of friends."

"Sure."

They heard the wheels of Marian's car.

"And maybe we can be the best of friends again someday."

"I hope so, Father."

He looked so handsome and straightforward standing there. Patrick really did believe that it was going to be all right. He had gripped Kerry's hand and put his other hand on the boy's shoulder when Marian came in.

"Yoo hoo! I'm not too early am I? I always think it's best to leave plenty of time, that way nobody's rushing too much." She glanced eagerly, like a bright fluffy bird, from one to the other. Patrick felt a sense of shame at using her like this. She was an honorable if boring and fussy woman. It was not fair to keep involving her like this when he had no intention of involving her more permanently. Marian would be useless in a crisis. She was perfect for domestic trivia. But she would have no idea what to do in any important area of life. Unlike Rachel Fine.

Patrick had telephoned her immediately after he had gotten his son cleaned up, seen by the doctor, and sedated. After he had reassured Grace with bland words, he had asked Rachel what to do. Rachel said that since he hadn't beaten it out of the boy, he was unlikely to discover it by any further force. She said that if she might draw on a metaphor taken from her own trade, the design and decor business . . . he should paper over the cracks. Pretend that everything underneath was as elegant as the surface, and make sure he created a believable surface. He had waited long enough to get back to his roots and realize his dream. Surely he wasn't going to let it all disintegrate into a public dog fight that would entertain the locals and people for miles around. Dignity had to be kept, position maintained. Give Kerry one more chance.

For a week Patrick had worked on her advice; it seemed the natural thing to do. He had almost forgotten how practical Rachel was, and how well she knew the right thing for him.

He wished Rachel were here in Mountfern.

He wished he had encouraged her to come with him.

After the first day of term Grace seemed to be all right again. Not as cheerful as last term but still more like her old self.

"Do you mind if we don't talk about it?" she asked Dara.

"That's all right." Dara was a bit huffy.

"It would be the same if there was a problem in your family, you wouldn't want to tell an outsider . . ."

Dara agreed grudgingly.

Maggie was much more understanding.

"I'm sorry I've been a bit . . . I don't know . . . recently, Maggie. I was just worried about something. Do you know the way it is?"

Maggie knew. She said so clearly. Grace was pleased.

Arm in arm with Maggie she went off to the graveyard, and they finished the tomb of James Edward Gray to everyone's satisfaction.

Mr. Williams said it was wonderful to see young people be so helpful. Not far away Eddie Ryan gloomily chopped nettles and gathered up sacks of grass and groundsel and dandelions. Grace discovered that Maggie took the same-size shoes and said she must come along to the lodge some evening and see if she wanted any that were there. Maggie never asked Grace what it was she had worried about. From time to time she wondered but still didn't ask.

Dara made a few pronouncements that if you were a true friend you could tell *everything* and any holding back meant that it wasn't friendship at all. But Dara bore her no ill-will, and organized Irish classes for Grace which worked so well that soon Grace O'Neill was getting better marks in class than the rest of them. Maggie's wish had come true, they were a gang, with Jacinta on the fringes of it.

They were all very disappointed when the summer holidays were approaching and Grace announced out of the blue that she was going to go on a trip with her father and brother. It was meant to be a familiarization tour of Ireland, she confided, but really it was a spying mission. They were going to spend a night in lots of different hotels and see what they were doing right or doing wrong. They would get ideas for their own hotel. A friend of Grace's father, who used to work with him back in the States, had suggested this would be a good thing to do. They were off as soon as term ended, just after Kerry came back from his boarding school.

Kerry had liked his new school very well, he said. No, he didn't want to ask anyone back during the holiday; it wasn't a place like that. You got to know everyone a bit, rather than a few people a lot. He was very enthusiastic about the voyage of inspection.

Once more Patrick O'Neill marveled at the wisdom of Rachel Fine. Even at three thousand miles she seemed to know what was best both for him and his troubled son. He would call her and say that she must come to Ireland this summer. After all, if John Fitzgerald Kennedy, the President of the United States, was coming to Ireland, why shouldn't Rachel Fine do the same?

It wasn't only the O'Neills who went away. Suddenly their whole gang started to disintegrate. The twins looked at each other in dismay.

Tommy Leonard was told that he was a grown man now, thirteen and a half going on fourteen, no less. He could stand in the paper shop this summer and work to build up the business that was going to be his one day. And he would like it. There would be a smile on his face, and none of his scruffy friends trick-acting in and out of the shop.

The Whites were sent to Irish College. Their father said it was pointless half learning a language, and they were both packed off to learn Irish dancing, to a place where they fined you if you were heard to speak in English and the man who ran it, An Fear Mor, was a person of great power and authority.

Maggie Daly had to work in Daly's Dairy, just like Tommy had to be in Leonard's. They both envied Dara and Michael for living in a business that didn't allow them to be behind a counter.

The twins were on their own again. They never actually admitted that they had grown apart in the last year or so. But they knew it. They missed golden-haired Grace with her plans and her excitement; they missed Tommy with his good humor, and the two Whites who argued with each other about everything and had outlandish views on almost every subject. They missed Maggie, who never dreamed anything up, but who always, after a little hanging back, would join in whatever they suggested.

The only problem was getting rid of Eddie.

Eddie wrongly thought that because Dara and Michael were now without their usual group, they would be delighted to have his company. More than once he got ready to go out with them and was bitterly disappointed when he was not allowed to go.

"I'd be better than no one," he said.

"No you wouldn't," Dara replied.

"You'd be much worse than no one, actually," Michael said.

"Why can't I come?"

"Because you're not our generation. You're a different generation to us. We are going to be thirteen in September, teenagers. You are only a very juvenile person."

"How will I ever grow up, unless I am with older people?"

Eddie was stung by the lack of avenues.

"Listen Eddie, enough is enough; it doesn't matter if you ever grow up, it couldn't matter less. You begin all nice and please this and please that, but by the time we'd have gone twenty paces with you, there'd be some row."

"No Dara, there wouldn't."

"Look at the past," Michael said mildly. "It's always happened."

"Now we must be off." And they were gone. Eddie kicked the stones around the back yard in disappointment.

"I can find you plenty to do if you like," Kate said. "And stop kicking. You're taking the top off your new shoes."

"They're not new," Eddie said mulishly. "Nothing is new, they're only Michael's shoes."

"And we'd like to have them for your brother Declan too, please, so kindly stop kicking with them or you'll have them taken away for the day, and you won't go far in your bare feet."

John had watched sympathetically. He waited till Kate had gone, and then called Eddie into the bar.

"Come here, I want to show you something."

"I don't want to do any work," Eddie said.

"Not at all, why should you, haven't you done the crates?"

"Yes."

"Well come on then. I'll show you something funny."

This was better than anything that had been offered so far. Eddie went suspiciously into the bar, his hair standing up in spikes that no amount of combing, brushing or even dampening would ever change. His father had an old, faded chocolate box out on the counter. Eddie scrambled onto a high stool to see.

"Look at this, Eddie, come on, it's funny."

"What is it? It's only an old picture."

"It's me years ago."

"Why are you wearing women's knickers?"

"Those aren't knickers; that was trousers."

"Go on."

"Yes, that was the day your Auntie Nuala went to Australia with the nuns, there was a picture taken here outside the door. That's your Aunt Nuala all dressed in black."

"She's very young-looking to be a nun."

"Ah she was too; they gave them a school education you see, and then in turn she became a nun and educated children out there."

"It seems daft to me," said Eddie, who was not a great scholar.

"There's a bit of daftness in it, certainly," his father agreed. "Wouldn't she be better up with Sister Laura in her own home town? Still, what I was going to tell you was this: look at my feet."

"You've no shoes on."

"Didn't I kick the front of my shoes out just like you were . . . No, no, not giving out to you. Shoes are your mother's province. I wanted to tell you the whole front came away, and I couldn't go with them all to see her off in the town. That was the last I ever saw of her, that day in 1930. Imagine. And I was so put out that I didn't get the trip to the town, I went for a walk up to Coyne's wood, and in my poor bare feet I spent the whole day building myself a house in a tree. I was covered in scratches and cuts, and when they all came back sobbing and crying from seeing Nuala off, they nearly murdered me, but the house was there. It's still there. I went past it the other day."

"It couldn't be."

"It is, bits of it, thirty-three years in the wood where it's very hard to find. Anyone could have a house that's easy to find. I thought having a secret one was better."

"You never told anyone?"

"No, not until now."

Eddie believed his father absolutely, but he was suspicious.

"So why are you telling me?"

"I've been having all kinds of old rheumatic aches; I don't think I'll climb into it again. I thought you might go and keep an eye on it for me."

"How would I find it?"

"Good question. When you go into Coyne's wood from this side, you go up the path; you know, the one that has all the rowan trees."

"The red ones, is it?"

"Yes, the mountain ash trees. Anyway where they end you go in to the right, you'll have to bend down a bit and then it's in there. You'll find it. Maybe you could even build it up a bit."

Eddie was looking enthusiastic at last. "It'd be better than having a place of my own," he said eventually.

"Much better."

"You won't tell Dara and Michael, and have them spoiling it? They'd come and take it over and turn me out of it."

"Not at all. Not a word."

"Right." Eddie gave a last look at the box of photographs. "Were we desperately poor in those days that they couldn't get you a new pair of shoes?"

"We'd be hard pushed to get *you* a new pair of shoes these days, so will you wear your old ones when you go up to Coyne's wood?" his father said. "And for the love of God, will you make sure you've done your jobs before you go."

They all had chores to do each day before they were free to play. Michael had to polish the brass and shine up the counter in the pub. The ashtrays would have been emptied, and the glasses washed the night before, but he had to air the place and see that there were no grease stains or dust where the customers would sit.

Dara had to feed the hens, now moved to the backyard, as their coop had become very smelly and messy in the side garden and completely spoiled the classy look of the place.

The hens clucked enthusiastically over household scraps mixed with bran. She also collected the eggs they laid in their nesting boxes; she gave Jaffa her breakfast; took Leopold for a run up as far as the Rosemarie hair salon and back; and inspected the whereabouts of Maurice the tortoise, in case he had got stuck under a stone, or in case Eddie and Declan had broken their vow and started to play with him again.

Of all these jobs, Dara hated most being seen out with Leopold. Whenever another human being approached, Leopold would cower and shiver and whine piteously, rolling his eyes as if expecting a further beating. Never had a dog been lavished with such love, never did a dog give the impression of being whipped by his masters to within an inch of his life every evening.

In the Rosemarie hair salon, Rita Walsh, who sometimes had an overnight guest leaving in the morning, didn't like the regular appearance of the Ryan girl with that awful dog racing up to her doorstep and turning around again every morning.

"Why don't you take him down toward the bridge?"

"I'm too ashamed to be seen with him, Mrs. Walsh," Dara said truthfully. "Up this way I don't ever meet anyone except you, or maybe Mr. Coyne, so I don't have to explain."

The child probably never noticed anyone leaving at an early hour. That was a relief.

Eddie and Declan had to stack boxes neatly for the distributors and collectors who picked them up when they brought new supplies. All four young Ryans had to bring in vegetables from the back field: potatoes that had to be washed at the yard sink, cabbages or cauliflowers, carrots or turnips. Then they were free for the day, lunch at one sharp.

Patrick wanted a history of Fernscourt written, and who better to ask, he had said, than the local scribe literally on the very doorstep. Of course there were people in Dublin who would do it, and do a professional job on it. Later indeed some aspects of their expertise might be used in editing and layout and even some of their hints in how to express parts of it. But there could be nobody who would do the job with such local knowledge and in such personal terms as John Ryan.

"You're never going to do it for him?" Kate was astounded.

"Why on earth not? It's a job, a writing job, there'll be something at the end of it, not just a few pages of a child's notebook scribbled on. That's what *you've* always looked for, something to show for it."

"But not this. Not glorifying him and what he's doing."

"It's not glorifying, and he's doing it whether I write the history of Fernscourt or some Ph.D. up in Dublin writes it. It's a professional job, there's a fee, whoever does it."

"I don't know." Kate was troubled.

"Well I do. My only problem is, will I do it right? Maybe he has too much faith in me; I could have sold myself too well."

Kate changed immediately.

"I don't know what you're talking about. Won't you do it as well as anyone? Better, because you're from these parts. You're the obvious one to do it."

John smiled quietly. The battle had been won. First it meant he had to do a lot of reading and research. His head was ever now in books about Georgian houses, antiquarian journals and the records of archaeological and historical societies. He became a familiar figure in the library in the big town where he went once a week, and they bent the rules in order to let him take some of the reference books back to his pub. It was different when a man was writing a book. He wasn't an ordinary borrower.

He discovered that Fernscourt was only one of many houses built at the time and all over the country. That year 1780 seemed to have been a great year altogether. He told that to Brian Doyle one day, and Brian said that it was always a feast or a famine in the building trade. You either sat on your backside for three years eating crusts or you had them screaming at you to dig the foundations for almighty jobs in three counties. It was interesting to know that the lads in 1780 had the same kind of aggravation.

Of course it was the time when Grattan's Parliament was sitting; it was the eighteen years when there was an Irish Parliament in College Green in Dublin, before it was snuffed out and the Act of Union was passed. Those parliamentarians needed big houses all over the place. But the Ferns didn't sit in Parliament, they were farmers with estates in the north of England. They had bought the land here in the 1770s for one of their sons. The house itself had been built in the same style as many others.

John Ryan was affronted to read in one journal that Fernscourt was considered a minor and rather inferior example of the art. He had shown it to Kate in disbelief.

"The wise man would forget that piece of information," Kate advised. "Patrick O'Neill is not paying for any reference to minor and inferior houses: you should pretend you didn't uncover that particular bit of lore."

"I'm meant to be doing serious research." John's face was very red.

"Of course, and you are, but that's only one person's opinion. You don't have to give some crackpot's view, do you? I mean if I met someone up in Bridge Street who said that you were no good to man or beast would I believe them?"

"What?"

"Of course I wouldn't anymore than you have to believe that fellow. Just get on to the facts, the things that can't be challenged, how many windows there were, what kind of people worked on it. Oh, Fergus said to tell you that he'll help you get documents from the land registry if you want; he says that once you translate legal documents into English instead of fusty old law you get great information out of them. I don't agree with him myself, typing them as I do all day. But Fergus would understand anything you put in front of him. He could make sense of the Dead Sea Scrolls at a glance."

"He's got a very quick mind, Fergus," said John admiringly. "You must find it a great change working with him." He smiled quietly.

Kate thought for a moment.

"Yes, he is great to work for. He's a real schoolboy though, a tall thin overgrown schoolboy, he's not a fellow you'd fall in love with like you are."

"Okay, that's all right, then," John Ryan said in mock relief.

It was a great relief to get rid of Eddie. The twins knew they were harsh to him, but Eddie wasn't like other people. He didn't understand hints. You had to be fairly brutal. They didn't have any money for ice cream, so there was no point in going to Daly's. It would only embarrass Maggie and make Mrs. Daly cast her eyes up to heaven and mouth silent prayers. Mrs. Daly's mouth was moving the whole time. Maggie said she got through dozens of memorares that she was saying for special intentions, while she was serving in the shop.

The twins knew that they mustn't be seen in Leonard's unless they were buying the paper or getting a writing pad. Grown-ups were allowed to leaf through the magazines, but there was no similar facility for children with the comics. And Tommy would hate them there.

There weren't many people on the bridge. Those who were there had organized a jumping competition. Usually you jumped from the big rock at the side. But today they were raising it and making it higher in stages. First by an old box, then by a stone on top of the box. Then by a plank on top of the stone. Dara and Michael watched for a bit. It was mainly boys that were jumping, shivering in their underpants. But there were a few girls too. Teresa Meagher in a black bathing costume much admired by all, and laughing overexcitedly as she jumped with the best.

The twins tired of it after a while. They walked across the bridge away from the town and back down the river bank on the other side. This was the road which would soon change. Instead of being a path with reeds on one side and a hedge on the other, it would be a road to the huge hotel. They didn't talk about things like that; it had been long accepted. The hedge was full of fuchsia growing wild as anything. Mam had told them that in city places this was a very rare flower, and people paid big sums of money to buy little bushes of it to put in their gardens; sometimes it didn't even grow properly. Dara stopped beside a huge tree of it.

"Isn't it like something in the South Sea Island picture book?" she said.

"Here, I'll climb it and be like a native," Michael said, leaving their picnic bag on the path.

As he went to the back of the tree to find a good starting-off place, he gave a great shout.

"Dara, look, careful, careful you don't fall."

In front of them, totally hidden by the trees and bushes, was an opening. A cave, or better still, a tunnel. They couldn't believe it. They had found their new home at last. They hardly dared go in beyond the entrance in case it was already somebody else's home. Those colorful tinkers who came by once a year and annoyed everyone old, by stealing chickens and leaving all their mess and rubbish behind them. They might be in there. Mad Marty who disappeared for months on end and then turned up again, wilder than ever. It could be his home. It was too good a place to be nobody's.

"Helloo . . ." they called as they went around the corner. It was pitch dark.

They paused and shouted again.

"Do you mind if we come in?" Dara called.

"Just for a moment," Michael added.

There was no reply. Surely if anyone was there they would have said *something*.

The twins looked at each other in delight and pealed with laughter at their over-caution and politeness.

"There's nobody here at all," Dara said.

Michael ran to Mrs. Quinn's for candles; he was back in no time and they went in together. They each held two of the half dozen candles that Loretto Quinn had parted with so willingly, as well as a box of matches. It wasn't like a cave or a tunnel in books or comics. There were no dripping rocks, just earth and stone, and it was quite high. Even grown-ups could have walked without bending.

The twins stepped forward, each with a tight feeling of anxiety about what might be ahead.

"It doesn't smell like coffins or anything," Michael said.

"We don't know what coffins smell like."

"No," Michael agreed. "But it doesn't smell frightening."

Dara wanted to show she hadn't been superior. "It doesn't look as if it's going to fall and block our way back, either," she said, more to reassure herself than her brother.

"No indeed, it's very sound."

"And it might be coming out somewhere soon?" Dara's voice was thin.

"Bound to, we must be up at the house now."

And then, around the next turn, they saw the urns and the long shallow steps at the back of Fernscourt. They saw them through the branches of thorns and brambles. Beyond those were huge big beds of nettles. That's why they had never seen the opening. Who would want to wade through feet of nettles, big high stinging ones, when there were so many other things to explore?

They realized it couldn't belong to them if they told anybody. So they told nobody at all.

But they thought about it all the time, and they brought back their belongings, slowly and little by little, so as not to create any suspicion. The old orange box, the tableware, the so-called curtains and rugs, the broken cutlery. Once more it was home. This time by candlelight. When they were older and could do what they liked they would ask Brian Doyle, if he wasn't dead, if they could make a skylight in the tunnel, because sometimes it was a bit hot and dark, and they would have liked the sunlight.

The roof looked sound enough. Surely Brian Doyle and his workers would be able to put in a window for them. There was a scaffolding: a very rough and ready kind of arrangement of wooden poles and boards keeping the ceiling up. It looked very firm and steady. The twins tested it gingerly, and then more firmly. It was rock solid. They wondered who had built it and why it was there. But they were afraid to ask anyone about it now in case it might all be taken away.

At home they tried to find out what an underground tunnel might be doing in these parts.

"Would there have been other ways into big houses in the old days?" Michael asked one suppertime. Dara frowned. It was too obvious.

Their mother had noticed nothing out of the ordinary.

"Like back doors, do you mean?" she asked absently. "Carrie, don't leave the saucepan on the table, there's a good girl. It just means it harder for you washing the cloth." Mammy was very good at scolding to Carrie; it didn't seem like scolding at all.

"I don't know. I suppose there were, and in those kinds of places people probably didn't bring in a ton and a half of mud with them. Eddie, do you have to bring half of Coyne's wood home with you every day?"

Mam obviously didn't have any idea of a tunnel. But then she hadn't been brought up here. Maybe Dad knew. Dad had been here forever.

But they'd have to be even more careful approaching him.

"You're very interested in old houses, aren't you, Dad?" Dara had a prissy kind of face on, not her normal look at all.

"Well, I suppose I am a bit," John Ryan agreed.

"Would you remember what Fernscourt looked like before it was burned down?"

"No, child, I wouldn't. I was only two when it was burned. Tommy Leonard's father would remember, and Maggie Daly's dad, but don't go asking them too much about it. They were there at the burning of it. In those days it seemed the right way to go. My own father stood looking at the flames from our front doorstep. He said to me often. But there's pictures of it of course, you'd be able to see what it was like in those."

"Yes well, but . . . ." Dara didn't want to be sidetracked by old pictures and the possibility of a history lesson.

"Would they have had secret rooms in it do you think? You wouldn't be able to see those in photographs."

"I don't *think* so. Why, did you think they might?"

Michael came in hastily. "We were just wondering, you know, taking an interest in everything around us, like you're always saying to do."

"Oh that's great," John said approvingly. "Yes, I love to see you doing that."

"So we take an interest in all kinds of things you see," Dara added. "Like, would they have had tunnels out of a house like Fernscourt, you know, underground tunnels?"

"All tunnels are underground," Michael said quickly, not to put her down, but to warn her not to be too explicit.

If John saw the way the wind was blowing he gave no sign.

"I never heard of any underground tunnels around here," he said absently, brushing the earth and dust off the thin shoulders of his son. "But as I say, the place was well gone by the time I was old enough to play in it, so there could have been. I'm sure it would be quite possible to find one if you looked hard enough."

He caught the look of alarm, and went on. "But it would be so well covered over, that sort of thing, that I don't think anyone would ever find the entrance."

There was a hint of relief in their faces.

"What would they have been for, if there were tunnels? That is from houses like Fernscourt, say?"

"Do you mean, say, possibly going from the house to the river? That is if there was a river?"

They nodded eagerly.

John Ryan paused; they waited for an explanation. He seemed to know the kind of thing they were talking about, but then his face became puzzled again.

"It's very hard to say. It would have been exciting, whatever the reason was. Of course if you found one of those things you'd have to be very careful. I mean a person would have to take great care that the roof wouldn't fall in, or that it wasn't all crumbling before they went and explored it."

"Oh there's no danger, it's quite safe," said Michael. "I mean I'd say they'd be quite safe."

"No parts where it's supported with props or anything?"

The twins looked at each other. *How* could he know?

"Like scaffolding," their father said helpfully.

"Well . . ."

"Um . . ."

"That'd be the bit to stay well away from if you ever found one," John Ryan said firmly. "It's like in old mines; those would be the parts where it would all cave in."

"I suppose you could test it by pushing and pulling at bits near the entrance if you ever found one," he went on.

They went away in case they let anything slip.

"He said it would have to be an exciting reason for it," Michael said.

"We knew that," Dara said. "But what could it have been?"

It provided hours of happy speculation for them.

Dara decided it was built by a young Miss Fern to meet her lover in a boat.

Michael decided it was built by a cousin of the Ferns who had an intent of storming Fernscourt one night and claiming it as his own. But they told no one. Without actual lies they managed to suggest they spent the time hanging around the bridge in the town. Kate was glad to think that they were making other friends.

"Am I beautiful, Carrie?" Dara asked. She was sitting on Carrie's bed, watching the preparations for the day off.

"I don't know." Carrie giggled at the question, but mainly concentrated on her own appearance in the speckled mirror over the dressing table. The table was covered with powder and hairpins and nearly finished pots of make-up that had been cast-offs of other people.

"I think I might be beautiful, if only I had curly hair," Dara persisted.

"You might be." Carrie was doubtful. "Isn't it sickening that we don't have curly hair. Your Mam has a rake of it, and she doesn't need it at all."

"Why doesn't she need it?"

"Well she's old and she's got her fellow. It's the likes of yourself and myself that need curls." Carrie looked at her reflection without pleasure.

"Why do you want to get all dressed up just for going home?" Dara asked with interest.

Carrie looked at her suspiciously. "Well, why do *you* want to be beautiful?" she countered.

"I want to be beautiful so that Kerry O'Neill will admire me," Dara said simply.

Carrie looked at her and softened. "You're grand as you are," she said. "And listen, I'll tell you a secret; I'm not going home to my people at all today, I'm going on an outing, with a fellow. With Jimbo Doyle."

"Not Jimbo Doyle," Dara screeched.

"Why not? He's very nice, Jimbo is, and he said he'd take me for a walk up to Coyne's wood on my day off." Carrie looked annoyed now, and a little uncertain.

Dara bit her lip. She had offended Carrie greatly, she must make it up somehow.

"I know he's nice, and he's a great singer. I heard him singing "The Yellow Rose of Texas" when he was building the rock garden. You could ask him to sing to you up in Coyne's wood."

"Yes, I suppose I could." Carrie was doubtful. She felt that Jimbo Doyle hadn't planned on an afternoon of singing among the quiet trees and on the springy moss of Coyne's wood.

They held their resolve to tell no one about the tunnel. No one at all.

"Not even Grace?" Michael said.

Dara paused. She thought about it.

"Not even Grace," she said.

"If we told Grace, we'd have to tell Maggie and Tommy and everyone else," Michael said.

"Yes." Dara frowned. "And that would change it. Do you think we're being a bit childish about all this?"

"Not at all," Michael reassured her. "I think we're doing the right thing."

They grinned at each other. The twins were back where they had always been. Best friends against the world.

There was a postcard from Grace from Donegal where the waves were huge and they had been swimming. They were having a great time, she said, and whenever she thought they were coming back to Mountfern, Father thought of somewhere else to visit. But they would be home soon; she missed everybody and longed to see them again. She sent cards to Tommy and Maggie too, and sent her love to Jacinta and Liam but didn't dare to write to them in case they would be punished for having communications in English rather than Irish.

Ryan's pub filled up with all the men who were working on the site. Every lunchtime there was a good crowd around the bar. Kate found herself rushing back from Slattery's office and straight in behind the bar. Sometimes she looked at John with a smile of triumph. At least some of their fears about the new hotel were proving groundless. There was a bit of business coming their way. For the moment anyway.

* * *

Judy Byrne ran into Marian Johnson in Meagher's jewelers. Mrs. Meagher had to send out the repairs and she was most apologetic that the clock wasn't ready.

"I did want it for the lodge by the time they came back," Marian was saying.

"Oh, when will that be?" Judy Byrne had come in to buy a brooch for her niece's birthday. She was looking without much pleasure at Mrs. Meagher's selection.

"Hard to say. Any day now, I imagine," Marian said airily.

"He doesn't keep in touch, then?"

Marian was furious.

"Heavens, Judy, it's their house to come and go as they please. I'm not a boarding house landlady type, you know, Judy. They've just rented our gate lodge, that's all."

"So he doesn't write. Well, I expect we'll know they're back when we see them." Judy thanked Mrs. Meagher for letting her see the brooches and said she would think about them and come back later.

Sheila Whelan knew exactly where the O'Neills were, and when they would be back. She had telegrams from America and messages that didn't go through to Brian Doyle the builder. Patrick rang her every second day.

Brian Doyle had the demolition men ready; he was surprised that O'Neill said they could go ahead and make the arrangements to take down the walls without him. He thought the man would have been on the crane that swung the great ball himself.

Brian Doyle didn't know that Patrick O'Neill and Rachel Fine had discussed this lengthily on the phone. They agreed that it would be wiser for him to stay away from the tearing down. Be there for the building up, not the pulling down.

Nine

Patrick O'Neill had discovered that few Irish hotels stayed open in the winter time. Very few of them. They said that nobody would come to Ireland in the bad weather, and it cost a fortune heating a place up and paying staff all through the lean months when there would be no business.

Patrick thought that this was short-sighted. Nobody ever came to Ireland for the weather anyway. When you thought of sunshine, you didn't immediately think of Ireland. It was the people who brought visitors to Ireland, the people and the scenery and the activities. Those things were there in the winter too, and cheaper to get to.

Charter flights in winter from the United States would be very reasonably priced. But there was no point in telling that to these hotel owners. They saw their season as beginning in May and ending in September. Some of the more adventurous opened as early as the Easter weekend.

Patrick O'Neill sighed at the waste of it all. But then he sighed a lot these days. It had been much harder than he would have believed possible to get this far in his attempts to rebuild Fernscourt. It had been a year since he had bought the place. Twelve months of delays and impediments, and only now was he able to get the ruins knocked down so that the building proper could begin.

It was the biggest test of Patrick O'Neill's character that he had ever known. A vein began to jut out on his forehead with anger and frustration. He found himself standing up, sitting down, taking long deep breaths in the middle of ruinously expensive transatlantic phone calls.

Twice he decided to abandon it, but slept on the decision, and the following morning decided that he would go ahead. Three times he was on the point of firing Brian Doyle and shouting that any builder in the goddamn Western world would be on his knees for a lifetime, begging for such a job. Three times he restrained himself. He did bawl out an architect, a mild man who said that it was always the same with Americans. They came over here like God Almighty and expected the people to change their ways for them. Patrick didn't see himself in that role; he liked to think of the O'Neills as the sons of the soil coming back, not the overlords giving orders. He apologized to the architect, who told him not to think of it again. Everyone knew that the pressure in New York drove most people mad most of the time.

He had been back to America twice. At the end of that time not one stone had been laid on another. But he kept his smile.

And he convinced the conservationists that he wasn't destroying anything valuable. That had been a stroke of luck, sighing over it in Ryan's pub one day, and then John Ryan discovering a quote from some archaeological journal to back up his claim that the house was of minor importance architecturally.

He found himself telling genial lies in two continents. Standing on the bridge with Fergus Slattery: Was he disappointed at the length of time things took? No, no, this was the pace, this was the way it had to be done. He would not have the town typecast him as a rushing, bustling Yank. And then back in the other home, in his New York headquarters talking to Gerry Power: Sure, sure, things didn't get done at the same speed. They hadn't the technology; no of course he didn't have second thoughts. No, he wasn't mad at them.

And to Rachel Fine, sipping a brandy in her red-gold apartment, which always looked so soft and restful compared with the rest of New York, he told more truth than to anyone. He told her that at times he thought he would blow up into a million pieces with frustration over it all. He could see now why his countrymen back home had achieved nothing, *nothing*. No wonder their economy was so pathetic, so shabby. He knew now why they stood toothless and laughing with their hats on back to front, because they had never bloody learned to work. They knew nothing of the actual ache that work brings, and they didn't want to know it. No goal was high enough to force them to do more than the very minimum. He could rail like this to Rachel because he knew she would never agree with him. She would smooth his forehead and tell him that Irish people rose in every walk of life . . . they had their own country . . . well almost . . . Look at her people, the Latvians . . . they had let the Soviets take over and Latvia would never rise again. All the Latvian Jews who could escape had come to America, but there would be no going back and building castles there nowadays.

Rachel would encourage him softly, remind him of all he had achieved so far, tell him that no other grandson of a cottage dweller had gone back to buy the big house and make it into a great business that would employ his own far and wide. He liked to hear that; it gave some reason to all the work and the endless delays and complications. One evening he asked Rachel why she encouraged him. She had been against it at the start, and wanted him to make his life in New York.

"Only a very foolish woman wouldn't encourage a dream. What would you be if your dream were to be taken away, or people talked you out of it? You would lose your fire and enthusiasm. You would only be a shell."

He held her closely to him. She was a wonderful woman. What a shame, what a bloody great shame that she was who she was, a divorced Jewess. Even if everyone else would let him, he could never marry her. It just wasn't possible.

But the day came, and the machinery moved in, huge cranes and a great ball that swung backward and forward, and the stone walls of Fernscourt came down. Rachel Fine had advised at long distance that the stones should be kept to form any walls or rock gardens. There must be a place to store them and surely big stones dating from the days when America was still a fledgling must be attractive and beautiful in themselves. Brian Doyle had said it was a cracked idea, but then he had been hoping to use the stones himself in other building work if they had been thrown out, so he secretly admired the Yank with the big notions and the belief that everything could be done in five minutes.

Grace linked arms with Kerry happily as they walked in the Irish country-side. This was the first real holiday they had taken together. She chattered on about the convent in Mountfern and told him tales of the girls and the tricks they played on the nuns. She begged him for stories of his school. Did he like being away at boarding school? Was he lonely? Was he glad it was holidays now? Grace wanted Kerry to be glad about everything. Like she was.

"It's a shame we can't be there," Grace said for the tenth time, as the O'Neills walked along a cliff path in Donegal. "I'd love to see it."

"Yes." Patrick was absent-minded. He looked out at the ocean. Had his father seen these hills when he was leaving Ireland, or were they too far north? He could never discover whether it had been from Galway or way down in Cork from the harbor at Cobh that those earlier O'Neills had taken a ship for the United States. None of the family knew or ever wanted to find out. John Ryan said it might have been Galway. It would have been a likelier place to have started from rather than all the way down in Cobh. Ships used to go from Galway all the time in those long-ago days.

"It wouldn't take us all that long to go back. Why didn't we leave last night?" Grace was insistent.

"Oh, I don't know, Gracie. We'll see it in a few days when we get back there. Aren't you having a good time?"

"Oh yes, but . . ." It was such a big thing, why were they missing it? She wished he would explain.

"Father doesn't want us to be there for the demolition, it would be better not to associate ourselves with destroying . . . with knocking down what's there." Kerry spoke without blame or praise, just as if he were giving directions from a map.

Patrick looked at him sharply. "Hey, what makes you say that?" He half laughed.

"Well it's true, isn't it? That's the way I'd feel."

"Yes, it *is* true in a way." Patrick was very surprised.

"We're the good guys, the ones who ride into town when all the shooting's over. Right?"

"Right in a sort of a way."

"I think it's ridiculous," Grace argued. "Everyone's delighted we're build-ing a new hotel; they love us for being there. Why all this running away and hiding for the best bit, the big machine going boom boom? I'd *love* to see that."

"So would I," Patrick said simply.

He was going to call Brian Doyle and find out how it all went. He wished that Brian had the gift of explaining things in style, with some description, a little color. Doyle would be likely to tell him about the overtime, the breakages, the need to revise this figure and that, and leave out completely any of the symbolism about the old order changing.

"I wonder what they're doing at this very moment?" he said as he led his son and daughter down a sandy path onto a magnificent beach and they ran along beside the waves like any ordinary family.

Not like a man who watched his son nervously, wondering what could have made the boy step so out of character and remain so adamant about not discussing it again. Not like a man who had arranged the demolition of a huge house and planned to build his own monument on the spot where his father and grandfather had been turned out onto the roads.

Half the town came by and watched the demolition machinery getting into action. The best view was from Ryan's pub on River Road and many of them watched with a glass in their hands.

Jack Coyne stood with a look of false cheer. He cursed that day long back when he had shortchanged Patrick O'Neill. The man had always been perfectly courteous to him since, but not one bit of business had he thrown his way. Jack Coyne's small pointed face glanced from one to another. Everyone else had benefited from the Yank. Look at the trade that John Ryan had, and it was the same in the town; there wasn't a business that hadn't been promised or already received some profit. Why on that day of all bloody days in the world had he taken the quiet American for a fool who didn't understand the rate he would get for a dollar? Why had he not seen that those blue eyes were the sharp eyes of a businessman?

Jack Coyne stood, hands in pockets, looking across the river at all the machinery which could all have been hired through him. Coyne's could have gotten the demolition people in and taken a legitimate ten per cent. He shook his head and told himself that in this life you never knew. You never bloody knew.

"Big day this," Jack Leonard said to no one in particular.

"Nearly as big as the day we burned it down," said Tom Daly, and there was an uneasy laugh. Nobody talked much about those times now, the days and nights when big houses all over the country were burned as a symbol of all they represented.

It was forty-one years since Tom Daly, Jack Leonard and a dozen more had joined hastily organized groups from the big town to go out on their mission. Old Mr. Leonard and old Mr. Daly were so respectable now, such pillars of Mountfern with their dairy and their newsagent businesses, it was quite impossible to imagine them as twenty-year-old firebrands. It was a different time, a different culture. Neither Tom Daly nor Jack Leonard had a good word to say for those young fellows who had been going up north on the border campaign blowing up electrical installations, taking pot shots at sentry posts and considering themselves national heroes. No, the 1920s had been a proper war.

John and Kate pulled pints, filled small glasses of whiskey, and even dragged a few chairs out into the sunshine. Leopold stood shivering with terror at the noise across the river and recoiled from every attempt to stroke or reassure him.

"You're such a kind woman, Kate, why don't you have that animal put to sleep?" Fergus asked as Leopold turned two anguished eyes on him and bayed to the skies.

"That animal is healthier than most people here, and much better looked after," snapped Kate. "I can't bear people who make superficial judgments about things they know nothing about."

"Don't bite the nose off the man," John laughed. "Leopold's a great actor,

Fergus, he plays to the gallery. He goes and lies outside Reidy's the butchers every day after he's had a good meal here and they give him a bone, every single day. And he howls at Loretto Quinn until she gives him half a pound of biscuits. Wherever the unfortunate cat sits he goes and wails at it, until Jaffa has to get up and let him sit there."

"He's just making up for having had a desperate childhood," Dara said. She was nearly thirteen now, tall and strong. Her thick dark hair went in slightly underneath as a result of heavy hair-grip work at night. She would have loved a perm in the Rosemarie salon, and Mrs. Walsh said she would do a light natural perm, but Dara's mother wouldn't hear of it. A perm at twelve? Who would permit such extravagance? It was all very well for her mother, who had curly hair anyway, to speak like that. Dara was full of resentment. To make matters worse Michael, who didn't need curls, had a great sort of wavy fit in his hair. *And* he had longer eyelashes. Much. It was so unfair, like almost everything.

"Tell me about Leopold's childhood." Fergus liked the leggy girl who was so like her mother in looks, and in that independent streak.

"He was found in one of Jack Coyne's trucks."

"That's a poor start," agreed Fergus.

"And someone had squeezed his throat, and hurt his hind leg," Michael finished for her.

Fergus often thought they could make a good double act on stage.

"And for ages after we got his poor back leg mended, he used to hold it out to people to shake hands with them," Dara said.

"Oh all right, you've convinced me, he had a rotten childhood, puppydom wasn't the best time of his life. Let him live, let him grow older and madder like the rest of us."

The twins giggled.

"I thought you two would be very upset to see it all come down." He indicated across the river.

"No, one time maybe . . ." Michael said.

"But not now, not now . . ."

"Not now that we're more grown up . . ."

"And have our own life. It used to be a bit of pretend life there, you see."

"Oh well, it's different now that you've grown up. I see what you mean." He could have been laughing at them, but they didn't think so. "And have you found somewhere else to live when you grow old, really old like me? Now that you won't be living across there?"

"We have our plans . . ." said Dara.

"Nothing definite of course . . ."

"That could be spelled out . . ."

Fergus hastened to agree. "No, no, much better not. Spell out as little as possible, I always say."

"There is one thing, Mr. Slattery . . ." Dara said.

"Yes . . ."

"It's sort of advice we might need . . ."

Michael flashed her a warning look.

"No, it's all right, I'm only going to speak sort of generally."

"Best way to start," Fergus agreed encouragingly.

"Yes, well, it's like this. Does every bit of land have to be owned by some-one?"

"I beg your pardon?" They had never taught him how to answer questions like this when he was up in Dublin at the Incorporated Law Society.

"I mean, is the whole of Ireland all divided up and parceled up? You own your house, we own this place, Mr. O'Neill owns Fernscourt now. Are there bits nobody owns?"

"That's a bit difficult to answer in general terms. There *are* bits, I suppose, that nobody really owns, like say the Curragh. You know, in Kildare. If you have land near it you can graze your sheep there, and it's the same with some bogs. A lot of people can cut turf there without actually owning it. Is that what you mean?"

"Not quite. You know, would all fields and ditches and boreens be owned by some one person? You couldn't say suddenly, I own this ditch because I found it."

Fergus scratched his head.

"But you couldn't really *find* a ditch, could you? It would be there all the time. You couldn't look at it one day and claim it?"

"But suppose you couldn't see it?" Dara persisted.

Michael didn't want her to say any more.

"God, Dara, you have me foxed," Fergus said. "But as your mother will tell you, I'm no good at all as a solicitor. I ask stupid questions like how in the name of the Lord could you try to own something you can't see? I only irritate clients. I'll be struck off the rolls any day and be left wandering around with straws in my hair."

Dara looked alarmed. "No, please, it's our fault. You see, it's that we have to ask these questions so that you won't actually know what we're talking about . . . No, shut up, Michael. It's all *right*. Mr. Slattery's not going to tell anyone, he's like Canon Moran."

"The image of him," Fergus said ruefully.

"No, you can't tell people's business, like he can't tell their sins," Dara insisted.

"That's a fact. They'd strike me off the rolls."

"Would they hit you?" Michael asked interested.

"I think it might mean rolls, like the rolls at school. You know, for roll call," Dara said helpfully. "But anyway, it won't happen, because you won't tell anybody what we've been discussing."

"I most certainly will not," he said solemnly, not that he had any idea of what they *had* been discussing.

"Wouldn't you think Patrick would have been here to see his day of triumph?" John Ryan said as a great cheer went up when the last bit of wall fell down.

Kate neatly scooped the froth off the top of five pints of stout with a wooden spatula.

"He knows all about it, you can be sure. He'll be on the phone to Brian Doyle in ten minutes' time."

"I was sure he'd have been here. He hates that house and all it stood for. He doesn't want me to say a good word about the Ferns, he hates the bit about them being fairly decent in the Famine. He would be delighted to see the stones going down."

"No, Patrick O'Neill is more interested in what's going up there instead,"

Kate said, putting the pints on a tray and coming around the counter to take them outside. "He's forward-looking like all the Americans."

"Would we have been better if we had gone to America, do you think?" John asked, half seriously.

"I don't know, maybe now isn't the time to debate it." Kate laughed good-naturedly as she swept out with the tray of pints to the people outside.

Rita Walsh wondered if the arrival of the hotel might mean that there would be a proper living out of hairdressing after all. It would make a nice change. She had heard a great deal about the plans for Fernscourt from Marian Johnson who now had her hair done regularly and had even sought advice about skin creams and manicures. Rita thought it unlikely that a man like Patrick O'Neill would think seriously about Marian Johnson, whose dry scalp and flyaway hair were getting so much attention these days. Yet it was hard to know. A man like that might be keen to ally himself with old money, and the quality. The Johnsons knew everyone in the hunting set.

Rita surveyed her little salon without much pleasure. American women or rich Dublin women might not find it to their liking, but it would be madness to spend good money on new equipment. Rita had a fair bit saved for the days when she would no longer be able to stand on her feet and give perms. And indeed earn money from a position that didn't at all involve standing on her feet. Both of these sources would end eventually. She kept all her savings in Sheila Whelan's discreet post office. There was no bank in Mountfern and Sheila often acted as an unofficial adviser on people's finances.

Rita decided to be swayed by the advice of the postmistress. Sheila was not one to inquire why the earnings were large sometimes, and irregular. She would answer only the questions that were asked, never raising any others.

Sheila Whelan said that her advice would be to hold on a while until the building of the hotel got under way, then when it really did look as if Fernscourt were rising from the ground and about to bring new life into the town, that was the time to buy new hairdressing equipment. And chairs and anything else that would make the Rosemarie hair salon attractive to visitors. There was no sense of irony in any of this, no hint of what might be the present attractions of the establishment. Just wait until the hotel got under way, then everyone could make their plans.

In Rachel Fine's New York apartment the small travel clock on the table beside her bed said that it was six-thirty in the morning. In Mountfern it would be lunchtime and the ruins might well be down by now. Rachel had not slept well. All night she had dreamed that there had been some terrible incident at this demolition ceremony.

That a body had risen from the ruins calling out, "I am the spirit who will not be mocked . . . you shall not build here in peace."

She had gotten up twice in the night and sat beside the window, looking out on the moonlit city to reassure herself that everything was normal. She wished this part was all over. Perhaps when this part was finished, then things might go well. He might send for her and she would come to Ireland and make herself part of the place, so that he would never send her away.

* * *

Patrick found the afternoon went very slowly. He didn't want to call until he was absolutely certain that it had actually happened. Later that evening he would talk to the States, tell Gerry Power that it had been done, and tell Rachel. Already it was a picture in his mind . . .

He could imagine it. Even before he called Brian Doyle, he could see knots of children coming onto the bank to watch. He hadn't realized that the rest of the town would come too and that they would drink pints in John and Kate Ryan's during the day, and cheer when the walls fell. He made Brian tell him every detail. At first Doyle thought he wanted proof that the job had been done properly, and had been full of huffing and shrugging, but when he realized that the man only wanted a description of the day, he became most lyrical.

Patrick couldn't believe it when he heard that the people had cheered the walls coming down.

"What did they say . . . did they call for three cheers or what?"

"Well, it was just a big cheer went up," Brian said.

"Like what? Did they say 'Hurrah,' or 'More, more,' or what?"

Brian was beginning to wish he had never mentioned the cheer. "You know, a big shout. No words, just a shout."

"There *have* to be words in a shout."

"No there don't, Mr. O'Neill. It was like, let me say a great *Waaah!* Now do you know what I mean?"

Patrick said he did. He was very pleased.

"Do you know they gave a great cheer when the last walls of Fernscourt went down?" he said when he called Gerry Power.

"Is that a fact?" Gerry was a man who was quite happy to go back to Ireland sometime in the future for St. Patrick's Day and maybe ten days there. He thought Patrick was insane to plow all his fortune into this venture.

"I wonder why they cheered," Patrick said.

"So shocked to see a proper day's work done for once, they couldn't help cheering, I guess," said Gerry.

He told Rachel that evening. "A big cheer, Brian Doyle said. Like a great *Waaahh!* sound. Oh God, I *wish* I had been there. I would have given anything to be there, to have heard it."

"I think you were quite right not to go," Rachel said. "Your instinct is always right for that sort of thing. Don't associate yourself with the knocking down, only with the building up. You've always done it here."

Rachel knew why they had let out a cheer. It was something to do, something to see on a dull morning in a one-horse town. It all meant a bit of work here and there and the promise of more work for the people who stood around, apparently, if the story was to be believed, with great double glasses of beer in their hands in the middle of the morning. No wonder they cheered.

"They cheered because the dream is coming true," she said. "Because the old house is gone and the new life is about to start."

The site had been excavated, the foundations were ready to start. Brian Doyle had already had four major rows with the architects. The Irish architects had refused to work with the American architects unless guarantees were received that there would be no more last minute interference. The Irish Tourist

Board had revised its grant, the situation on charter groups was still not clear from Aer Lingus. Two farmers whose land had not been bought up by Patrick O'Neill tried to get Fergus Slattery to claim they had been victimized. Two small tenant farmers, who had willingly sold him half an acre each a year ago, now felt they hadn't gotten enough for it, and wanted Fergus to represent them. Fergus refused to have anything to do with any of them.

"Greed. That's what this man has brought to Mountfern, inordinate greed. Those men never thought of profits on their miserable bits of land before, they were bloody glad to have it."

"I don't think you can go around preaching to them like that, Fergus," Kate Ryan said disapprovingly. "You should shrug and say that it's a pity but there isn't really a case. Pretend to be on their side, be clever."

"Like Hereford bullock O'Neill," Fergus growled.

Kate laughed. "He *has* got curls but that's no nickname for him. Yes, like him. He's great at being tactful. That's what's got him so far, I suppose."

"Or telling downright lies," Fergus said.

"He hasn't really, has he? I know you don't trust him, and neither do I. I don't trust him because I think he knows he'll ruin us if his business ever gets off the ground. I don't know why you care about him."

"Because he's hurting you . . . all of you," Fergus said.

Kate looked up, startled, and Fergus remembered his sister's drunken slurred accusation . . . he was good for nothing except making sheep's eyes at the local publican's wife. Was that so?

No, in truth, hand on heart, it wasn't just Kate, it was the whole household. That stupid dog with the terrified eyes trying to shake hands with you by raising its twisted back paw. That John Ryan scribbling his poetry in a child's exercise book and thinking that Patrick O'Neill was a great fellow. Those two small lads with a face on each of them that spelled out devilment. Those dark handsome twins, entirely self-contained, speaking half a sentence each, suntanned and energetic as wild monkeys; he used to see them scrambling in those brambled hills on the other side of the Fern . . . There was something about the whole family that touched him in a way it was hard to understand. Truthfully, it was not the handsome mother with her quick wit. No, eunuch or no eunuch, he was making no sheep's eyes at her.

Fergus made a series of promises to himself there and then. He resolved that he would go off for a long weekend to a seaside town and have a sexual adventure of great passion with a young attractive woman. That he would close the office when President Kennedy arrived and drive as many of the Ryans as wanted to come with him to Dublin to see the parade. He would speak in less eccentric tones to local farmers who were, after all, only anxious to get a bit of whatever was going. And lastly, he would watch Patrick O'Neill like a hawk. Never in his life had he known a feeling so strong and convincing as this one. That O'Neill and his family were going to destroy the Ryans.

The O'Neills were back. Everyone knew it half an hour after they had driven down Bridge Street. Judy Byrne knew because she was polishing her brass. She hated being caught doing anything so domestic. She preferred Patrick to think of her as a woman in an important medical role.

Sheila knew because she heard someone in the post office calling out that their car was parking. Sheila gathered her telegrams and messages quietly, and put them in a big anonymous-looking envelope to have them ready.

Maggie Daly knew and was delighted.

Grace and Kerry came into the shop. They were buying cream cakes and bacon and eggs for their tea. Miss Hayes hadn't expected them, so they were getting supplies. Maggie's smile nearly split her face in half when Grace raced over to hug her. Kitty, who was filling the shelves in a very bad humor, was equally delighted when Kerry came over to her without any prompting at all.

"Hi," he said, "did you miss me?"

"Were you away?" Kitty asked with spirit.

Kerry liked it. He had his elbow leaning on the shelf.

"Yes, we *were,* and I bet you knew it," he said.

"Sorry." Kitty was triumphant now. "I don't really keep up with all the comings and goings of people I hardly know. I'm much too busy."

"Then I'll have to get to know you better, so that you *will* notice when I'm not around," Kerry said, with a smile that would melt all the ice in the deep freeze.

Tommy Leonard knew they were back because he saw their car, and his father said he hoped there would be no racing out on the road and abandoning his post. Tommy fumed behind the counter, but the O'Neills came in to buy papers and postcards. They were going to send a card to all the hotels where they had stayed, to say thank you. To show them what Mountfern looked like. In a few years they would all know only too well where it was and what it looked like.

Kerry asked Tommy about the fishing, and wondered had they been swimming in the river. He said that, after all the beaches they had seen around the country, he was dying to go for a swim.

"Not until after the shop closes," Tommy's father said firmly.

Tommy wished his father wouldn't. Not in front of Kerry O'Neill, who was a grown person, and who seemed to be treating Tommy as equally grown.

"Workers of the world," Kerry said sympathetically.

"We close at six," Tommy said rapidly. "It would be lovely then."

"Tea at six," said Mr. Leonard.

"Seven then?" Kerry suggested.

"Right oh." Tommy was thrilled.

"At the bridge?"

"It's a bit crowded and noisy there." What Tommy meant was that he and his friends were considered too young for the gang on the bridge.

"The footbridge, then?"

"That's it." Tommy started patting the papers and magazines, proudly happy.

"See you then, Tommy."

Grace looked gorgeous. Very suntanned, in a blue and white striped dress.

"See you, Grace," Tommy beamed.

"My God, when I think of the time you children have today," said Tommy's father, a sour displeasure coming over his face.

The twins didn't know they were home because the twins were in the tunnel. Kate Ryan said they were out. She didn't know where. Hadn't they been down on the bridge? No? Well, they'd be back for their tea at six. Had Kerry and Grace enjoyed the tour? Were they impressed with Ireland? What did they think of the land over the river there without the ruins? It took a bit of getting used to. Wasn't it a pity they had missed it all? Kate chattered on cheerfully to the two blond children who stood in the crowded bar as easily and confidently as they stood in any other place in Mountfern. Their father was getting a drink for a group that was busy describing in detail the moment when the old ivy-covered masonry toppled down.

The twins would be very sorry to miss Grace. No, she had no idea where they were; they always came back at teatime covered in dust and dirt. Like they did every day.

Going swimming at seven o'clock, yes that was a great idea. Not right in front of the pub, if they didn't mind. People liked the idea of a quiet stroll down River Road in the evenings, not to get into the middle of a screaming mob of children splashing. A bit further along. No, not exactly opposite the Rosemarie hair salon either, that mightn't be such a great idea; just on the bend. Sure, she would send any stragglers up that way, and tell Dara and Michael.

"Aren't you marvelous the way you can talk and work, Mrs. Ryan," Grace said admiringly. Kate was pleased.

"Ah, it's a knack, like riding a bicycle. You find yourself pulling pints and washing glasses almost automatically. I don't even notice myself doing it, like those people who can knit and look at television. You'll find it yourself if you work in the bar over beyond. Or will you work in the hotel, do you think?"

"I don't know, Mrs. Ryan. Isn't that funny? We never seem to talk about what it's going to be like when it's a working hotel. Just getting it built seems to be as far as we go."

She smiled almost apologetically, and Kate realized, with a sudden stab, the power of such beauty. A man would do anything for a face like Grace O'Neill's, anything to keep those blue eyes laughing and happy.

Patrick asked the children to telephone Miss Hayes and let her know they were on their way. Brian Doyle had a litany of complaints that had to be heard. Jimbo Doyle had backed a lorry-load of tree branches into the presbytery and broken the front windows, and had to spend two days replacing them with new glass.

Father Hogan had been very droll about it, and said that the canon and himself had been very relieved that it was only Jimbo and a lorry-load of timber. They had been afraid it was something serious like Eddie Ryan about to dismantle the place on them.

Teresa Meagher had hitch-hiked to Dublin and sent a message through the post office that she was never going to come back to Mountfern as long as she lived. Mrs. Meagher was going to sell the jeweler's. Brian Doyle wondered did Mr. O'Neill want to buy it.

"What do I want with a souvenir shop like that?"

"It might be useful as property on Bridge Street. She'd be glad of a few thousand now; you'll always need an office or some kind of base in the town." Brian was a businessman.

"That's the kind of thing I'd expect from Jack Coyne, not from you, Doyle. I have no intention of buying a woman's only property when she's in a state of distress. What will she feel in six months? Conned and resentful."

"You're a smart man, all right," Brian said grudgingly.

Papers Flynn was at the back door asking to speak to the lady of the house; he had some lovely little bantam eggs for her.

Declan asked, could he bring a ladder around to the front of the house. Eddie was stuck in the chimney.

"Mother of God! What is Eddie doing in the chimney? Is he all right?" Kate was very alarmed.

"He's all right, it's just that he can't get out."

"Which chimney did he go up?" Kate's eyes were wild.

"He didn't go up any. He went down one."

"He *couldn't* have! He wouldn't fit."

"Only his arm," Declan said.

"Oh God, *what* are we going to do with him?" She ran out and was relieved to see Eddie perfectly safe but with his arm wedged in a chimney pot.

"Don't move," she shouted up at him. "I'll send someone up to you, though by rights I should leave you there for the night."

"I'll explain it all when I get down."

"Indeed you will," said Kate.

She turned to Declan. "I don't suppose you could throw any light on what possessed him to start climbing into the chimney, could you?"

"It was going to be his new career, I think." Declan sounded doubtful.

"Terrific," Kate said. She went back into the pub and looked around to see who might go and rescue him. Who would be the best person to disturb? Her eye lit on the tall figure of Kerry. She explained the problem and told him where the ladder was kept. Kerry said he had always fancied himself as a knight doing brave deeds for beautiful ladies.

Even though she thought it was far too flowery, it pleased Kate.

"It's all great fun," Grace said wistfully. "It's so quiet at home. It's like a three-ring circus here."

"You can say that again," said Kate resignedly.

Eddie's sweeping brush had fallen down the chimney. He had bent down to try to retrieve it, and in the effort his foot had slipped. He was well and truly stuck now, no way of getting his footing on the slippery roof from which three slates had already been dislodged and many more were beginning to shift.

Kerry climbed up easily and, watched by an admiring Grace and an anxious Declan, walked lithely over to the struggling boy.

"Relax friend, Superman is here," said Kerry.

"This is not as easy as it looks," Eddie said firmly.

"It doesn't even *look* easy," Kerry said. "It looks very dangerous indeed."

That was the right thing to say. Eddie didn't have to worry about his dignity anymore.

Kerry maneuvered Eddie's feet onto a sure base, then he was able to withdraw his arm from the chimney himself.

"Something very wrong with the flue," he said.

"You could be right," Kerry said.

"Should have a cowl, in my view."

"Very possibly."

Kerry had no idea what the child was talking about; possibly he was even mentally deficient. He always looked fairly sinister, and was reported to be in constant trouble.

"I'll be off now," Eddie said, sliding down the roof. "It was handy you happened to be passing."

"Yes, one of those coincidences."

Eddie slid to the drainpipes and nipped down the ladder, which he was about to take with him.

"Leave the ladder, you bonehead," Kerry shouted.

"I need it for my trade," Eddie shouted back. Then thought better of it. "But I don't mind leaving it here for a bit."

Shamefacedly he went around the side of the bar and in the back door. Nothing, not even his rescue from the jaws of death in the chimney, would excuse his walking through the pub during opening hours.

"Were you frightened, Eddie?" Declan asked.

"Oh shut up, Declan, you're a stupid pudding," Eddie said ungratefully to the agent of his rescue.

Kerry sat on the roof of Ryan's and looked over the river at the site where the new hotel would rise. How much better it would be to approach it from here, turn the footbridge into a magnificent wide bridge with big lanterns on each end. On the other side of the river he saw Dara and Michael walking along the towpath.

They were startled to see him sitting on their roof. When they got near enough to shout, they saw Grace. She ran across the footbridge to meet them, and they all stood in a little semi-circle looking up at him.

"What can you be doing up there?" Dara called.

"If I told you, you'd never believe it, so let's say I came early for Christmas," Kerry laughed.

He looked so handsome up there with the sun shining on his hair, a white open-necked shirt and a dark suntan. Dara shielded her eyes as if she were looking at an angel.

"Will we all go up there?" she asked.

"I don't mind, but your folks might object," Kerry called.

"It's six o'clock," Michael said. "Time for tea, anyway."

"Typical male, thinking of what to eat," Dara said scornfully.

She ran to the ladder and climbed easily up. Kerry reached his hand down from the rooftop to haul her up over the slates. He made room beside himself.

"It's *great* up here," Dara said excitedly. "Look at all you can see." River Road below them wound slowly to the bridge. They could see the cars inside Coyne's Motor Works. Usually you only saw the outer walls. They saw all the empty boxes and crates in the back of Loretto Quinn's, and further over they could see into the small back gardens of Mr. Slattery's house and of the other houses in his terrace, the back of the Classic Cinema and as far up Bridge Street as into Dr. White's. Companionably they pointed out places to each other. Behind them Coyne's wood stretched away up toward the Grange and down the river to the other side they could see the banks getting greener and more country-like as they were further from Mountfern and leading on toward the ruined abbey. From here Dara could see very clearly the big bushes of thorn and bramble that hid the entrance to their tunnel at the Fernscourt end. The fairy fort had remained untouched. Her eyes followed what must be the path of the tunnel—a slow incline, easy for rolling barrels or shifting crates or whatever they used to do in years gone by.

She felt Kerry looking at her and following her glance.

"Where do you go during the day?" he asked.

She wondered if he was psychic.

"Here and there, different places," she shrugged. A bit too casually, maybe.

His arm was touching hers as they sat side by side. He picked up her hand.

"Well, wherever you go, you sure get scratched," he said, looking at a great scrape from a coarse blackberry bush at the mouth of their tunnel.

"It's nothing." She was about to take her hand away.

His fingers traced the length of the scratch from the inside of her wrist up her arm.

"Looks painful," he said sympathetically.

"No, no it's okay." She found her voice was suddenly hoarse.

"You should take more care," he said.

"Why?" Her voice was quiet. He was still holding her arm and lightly tracing the long red mark.

"We're all going swimming later. You don't want to have cuts like this that will sting when we go swimming."

She looked up at him in alarm. His words were innocent, casual. She felt suddenly that he was saying something else.

It was like a lot of little electric shocks prickling all over her.

Ten

Kerry came home for a long half term.

Without the others knowing exactly why, this seemed to change things for everybody. Having him join in made things different, more grown up somehow.

Sometimes Kerry came along when they went swimming up at the bend of the river. And sometimes he didn't. They never knew if he was going to be there or not. Grace never knew either.

Sometimes he would cycle along with her, other days he would head off in a different direction. Or he would lie in his room and read.

Kerry got on much better with Father these days, Grace thought. There had never been anything like those awful days at Easter when she had to go to her room and work all day on those Irish exercises, while her father and brother had this war that involved Kerry refusing to explain something, and Father alternately wheedling or shouting threats.

Grace didn't believe that Kerry had left his first boarding school because the walls were damp. But Father had said he would greatly appreciate it if Grace did not interfere and ask questions. Kerry had only shrugged when she asked him. They had both said she should put it out of her mind, and that was what Grace had tried to do.

Sometimes it was easier than others. When the three of them were running along the beach up in Donegal and laughing. Then it was easy. Sometimes when they were there in the lodge, all three of them, Father's eyes would leave his papers and look at Kerry long and thoughtfully. Then Grace knew that whatever it was had not been forgotten.

She loved it when Kerry joined them. She was so proud of him, and he was such fun to be with. It was Kerry who said that it had to be simple to make a raft. After all, people had been doing it to explore the world or escape from desert islands for years now. It had to be only a matter of binding bits of wood all the same length together, didn't it? Suddenly they were all looking for wood —Tommy Leonard in the back of his shop, Maggie trying to break up the packing cases behind the dairy, or beg bits of wood off Charlie, who worked there. Michael found old poles in a shed in the back yard. Liam White sent a postcard from the Irish College which he said was diabolical, with awful girls giggling and terrible dances that four-year-olds would be ashamed to do at night, and nobody being able to speak any longer in any language. He had been driven mad with jealousy by Grace's letter telling him about the raft.

"You wrote to Liam?" Michael asked.

"Sure," Grace said. "Didn't you?"

Michael felt mean, somehow, that he hadn't. Grace was so nice to everyone. First she had made certain that it wouldn't cause dreadful punishments for Liam to get a letter in a language like English, and then she sat down and wrote. Michael wished he was away somewhere so that Grace would write to him. He could imagine her going in to Mrs. Whelan to get a stamp and licking it carefully to put on the envelope. He could imagine her sitting at the desk in the sitting room of the lodge, looking out the window and thinking of more things to say.

The raft looked great and Kerry had been quite right, of course it floated. They wondered why they had never made one before.

"I hope it's not dangerous," Kate said when she heard about it. "Kerry's much older than you lot. Make sure you don't do anything foolish."

The twins were annoyed. It was like a criticism of Kerry. And some days when they expected him, he never turned up.

On Wednesdays it was early-closing day, and so Tommy and Maggie could escape from their shops. Kitty came along too, unexpectedly. She was much more pleasant than usual, and admired the raft greatly.

"Can it go on long journeys?" she asked.

"Yes, to the sea, if you like," Kerry offered.

Dara didn't like Kitty coming along, with her waist and her chest. She looked around for support but didn't get any. Maggie was Kitty's sister after all;

she had to be nice to her, and Grace was literally nice to everyone. Nobody seemed to be shooing Kitty away.

"I expect you could take the raft all the way down to the old abbey, if you wanted to," Kitty said.

Kerry was interested in the abbey; it didn't sound too bad, but there'd be a lot of paddling the raft, coming back upstream from that far. Wouldn't it be easier by bicycle?

"Much," Kitty said, and they exchanged a long look.

That had been a lovely day. Kitty had drifted off and Dara was glad she hadn't sulked over her having joined them. In a way it was a compliment, older people wanting to be with them.

They climbed on and off the raft all day. Tommy had said it was a great pity that they couldn't get empty barrels, or oil drums, then it would float magnificently. But who would give them anything like that?

"They'd have them in Coyne's Motor Works," Kerry said.

"Mr. Coyne wouldn't give you the time of day," Michael said.

"I'll ask him nicely." And Kerry had raced down to Jack Coyne's yard.

Jack Coyne thought there might be a belated chance to get back in O'Neill's good graces if he were nice to the lad. He carried up two empty oil drums and even gave them a couple of lengths of rope.

It bobbed up and down like a dream then, and they all jumped on and off it. Dara's long hair got into her eyes, she envied Grace's springy curls which seemed to dry in seconds. Even Maggie's frizz looked great when it was wet. Only drippy, dopey Dara looked awful. She sniffed and pulled at the damp, straight locks in disappointment.

"Here, I know, we'll gather it up with a rubber band," Kerry said.

"It would look worse than ever then." Dara hated him looking at her, suddenly. She felt cold and ugly in her navy swim suit and all this lank wet hair. But Kerry was full of practical ideas. Just as he had insisted it was easy to make the raft, he knew what to do with Dara's hair. Unselfconsciously he got his own comb and combed the long wet strands. It felt lovely sitting there on a tree trunk while he combed. She never wanted him to stop. The others were maneuvering a complicated way of climbing on to the raft straight from the bank; nobody noticed Kerry combing Dara's hair.

He went to where his trousers were folded on the bank and found a rubber band; he tied the wet hair neatly into a pony tail, having pulled out the dark fringe first.

"Now," he said triumphantly, "now that's better. It won't get in your eyes. And it looks great too. Truly grown up."

Dara saw the admiration in his eyes and she yearned for a mirror, but of course there wasn't one.

"Look in the river," he said, reading her thoughts.

She looked and she could see the reflection of the clouds racing across the sky and she could see herself. A bit stern, she thought, and severe. But she saw the reflection of Kerry behind her and he was smiling.

"Thanks," said Dara in a shaky voice. "I think it's much better like that. Tidier, you know."

"And prettier, you know." He smiled.

Dara felt an ugly red flush like a rash starting on her neck and going down her chest. She was terrified he would notice.

"Race you into the river," she said suddenly.

He had dropped the comb and was there before her. A clean dive far out into the center of the river. Dara flopped in at the edge and swam out toward the raft.

"Your hair is smashing like that," Maggie said admiringly.

"Kerry always says that Dara looks like Pharaoh's daughter," Grace said.

"Is that good or bad?" Dara had seen a picture of Pharaoh's daughter in a book of stories from the Bible; she looked terrific.

"Oh good, of course," Grace said.

"But old, definitely ancient," Tommy added.

"Not in *her* time, she wasn't, Tommy." Michael was defensive.

Kerry was sitting on the raft.

"Don't forget what she found down by the river, Dara, a baby in a basket. I don't think they'd believe you here in Mountfern if you came home with that story."

"I don't know. Canon Moran might, he'd believe anything."

"He's about the only one who would," Maggie said seriously. "I think we'd better look away from the weeds and the rushes in case we find anything like that. It would only lead to endless trouble."

They all laughed at Maggie; Grace put her arm around her, and Kerry said that she was magnificent. Maggie was never so pleased in her life, and quite glad that Kitty had gone away. She would have felt foolish being the center of all this praise and laughter in front of Kitty.

Her mother thought her hair looked better like that, which gave Dara grave doubts about it.

"It would look great if I had pierced ears," she said without very much hope.

"Out of the question," Kate said.

"I *knew* you'd say that, no debate, no discussion, just out of the question. It's always the same."

"No, it's not. I'm a magnificent mother," Kate said.

"Huh."

"I was just telling Fergus the other day how good I was. How I didn't murder you and Grace when you wrote Maurice's name on his shell with nail polish."

"We took it off with polish remover," Dara protested.

"But it might have hurt him."

"It's a *shell*, Mammy. Next you'll be saying it hurts the potatoes to dig them up, or the cabbages, and we'll all die off like flies because you'll be afraid of hurting things."

"I am endlessly patient. Fergus agreed."

"He must be bored to death, listening to you telling this litany of how great you are." Dara was full of scorn.

"No, he was fascinated. And so was Grace when I was telling her about what it was like when I was young. She thought it was very interesting. Not like you, my Dara, who would run a mile rather than hear my views on anything."

Kate spoke lightly, but Dara felt that her mother was being serious.

And it was true, Grace *did* love to hear tales of the old days. She wasn't just pretending in order to be polite, she would sit and ask all kinds of questions.

She told Dara and Michael that their parents were far nicer than anyone else's, which was true, but it was nice to be told. Dara wondered what Grace would do if she wanted to have pierced ears. She would ask nicely and she would get what she wanted. That's what happened every time.

"Do you know, Mammy I was just sitting here thinking."

"And what were you thinking, Dara?" Kate looked at her and smiled. "You know, pet, you really do look very nice with your hair pulled away from your face like that. I think you've inherited my excellent bone structure, instead of the puddingy, sandy looks of the Ryans."

"I was just thinking that a fine-looking woman like yourself would want to be proud of her only daughter. Glad that her one girl would be a credit to her, with a smart appearance . . . and possibly to complete the look, pierced ears."

"No, Dara."

"Why?"

"Because you'd look like a gypsy, like a tramp. *No.*"

Dara looked crestfallen. She could read the tones, and this was a very definite no.

"Listen, I know it's not the same thing, but I'll get you a nice ribbon for your pony tail, you know the way Grace wears those ribbons."

"Oh Mam, Grace could wear anything in her hair and it would look great. I'd look like a jack-in-the-box with ribbon."

"You've no idea how lovely you are," said her mother. "And we will discuss your ears when you're sixteen. Not a day before then, not an hour."

"That's over three years. I can't believe it's going to be as long as that," wailed Dara. "I'll be so old then, nobody will want to look at my ears, or any part of me."

"Yes, well that's possible, but just to get value out of these days when everyone *is* looking at you, I'll get a ribbon. Would you like a striped ribbon or spots?"

Dara spent a long time curling her pony tail with pipe cleaners. It looked great next morning, tied up with an old blue ribbon she had found in Carrie's room.

Dara was first at the raft, but Kerry O'Neill didn't turn up. Dara thought the day was very long. No Maggie, no Tommy, no Whites, and mainly no Kerry. Three times Dara asked Grace where he might be. Three times Grace shrugged; you knew what Kerry was like. He turned up or he didn't.

Grace and Michael lay on the raft for ages, just talking. Dara felt very discontented, and dangled her feet in the water from the bank as she looked back up at Coyne's wood in case she would see Kerry O'Neill approaching on his bicycle.

The twins sat on the window seat and looked at the moon shining on the river.

"Can we take Grace to the tunnel, do you think?" Michael asked.

"We *said* it was going to be ours," Dara complained.

"Yes, well it is, of course."

"So why take Grace?"

"She's your best friend."

"I know. That's not the point; we'd have to take Maggie and Tommy. It would stop being special."

"We wouldn't, we could have it as a secret, the three of us."

"You can't keep secrets in threes."

"How do we know? I bet you and Grace have secrets. Things you don't tell me."

"So, if we do, what is the point?"

"The point is that if you do, then it means she *is* able to keep a secret. It would be great to bring Grace to the tunnel."

"No," said Dara.

"Okay."

"What do you mean, okay?"

"Just that. If you say no, then we don't. If you'd wanted someone to come and I'd said no it would be the same."

"No sulks, Michael?"

"No sulks, Dara."

Fergus Slattery left his invitation to Dublin too late. The O'Neills had gotten in before him. Just two hours before him. He called formally to the pub and told John that he was going to hire a station wagon to take the Ryan family to Dublin to see President Kennedy. He had friends with a solicitor's office on the very route of the cavalcade and they could sit at the window there above the crowd and see the whole thing.

John's good-natured face had a look of sorrow to refuse such generosity. But hadn't Patrick O'Neill been in that very morning with a similar suggestion? Imagine the Ryans being asked twice in the one day to go to see the President of America! Patrick was taking his own big car, Marian Johnson was taking her station wagon, and between them they were inviting the Ryans—John had decided to close the pub—and Sheila Whelan, whose nephew was going to be at the post office to deal with emergencies.

"Well, well, that's a pity," Fergus said between clenched teeth. "And what a chance to pass up. A seat on the very route itself."

But it appeared that Patrick had some American friends with three hotel rooms overlooking the route so they would miss nothing.

Fergus had a whiskey, which burned his throat. Would he even bother to go now? The whole outing had gone as sour on him as the drink. He could hardly swallow. And to think that O'Neill had the decency to ask Sheila Whelan. That was something Fergus should have thought of himself, but hadn't. Why did the man make all the right moves, *and* make them first?

Fergus walked back down River Road and back home.

"Miss Purcell," he shouted. "Miss Purcell, would you like to go to Dublin next week and see John Fitzgerald Kennedy with me?"

"Are you drunk, Mr. Fergus?"

"No, Miss Purcell, I am sober. I am, however, inviting you to watch the President of the United States visit Ireland."

"There's no need to shout, Mr. Fergus. I'll think about it." Miss Purcell was flustered—the red spots were beginning to burn brightly, like bicycle tail-lamps.

"Good, while you think about it I am going across the road to invite Father Hogan if he'd like to come too. I think the canon's a bit too frail for the journey, and anyway some cleric had better mind the shop in case there's a call for spiritual assistance."

"You're inviting Father Hogan?" Miss Purcell was now in seventh heaven. To travel to and from Dublin with the curate!

"Yes, I hope he'll have the graciousness to say thank you Fergus, I'd love to come, rather than deciding he's going to *think* about it."

"I'd love to come, Mr. Fergus, thank you very much," said Miss Purcell. "You see, I didn't really believe it was true. I didn't want to say yes too quickly."

Fergus found a strange stinging behind his eyes, and wondered was he going soft in the head, or had the whiskey in Ryan's been drugged.

Dara dreamed that Kerry could drive and that he had invited her to go to Dublin in his car, and it had broken down, and they had to stay in a wood. They built two beds out of bracken and moss and slept beside each other holding hands.

None of them would ever forget the day that John Fitzgerald Kennedy came to Ireland. He was so boyish and young, they all said. Imagine him having that huge responsibility, and being in charge of half the earth, in a manner of speaking.

Fergus met Jimbo Doyle, who said that a van had been arranged on loan from Jack Coyne for a few pals, and he was taking Carrie out of Ryan's with him. He told Fergus that he had asked her only just in time, because there was a question of Mr. O'Neill himself including her in his party as part of the household.

"Would you believe that?" Jimbo said wonderingly. "And Carrie just a maid in the house."

"She's not just a maid, she's your girlfriend. Hasn't she as much right to go and see Kennedy as anyone?" Fergus snapped.

"I know she's my girlfriend, Mr. Slattery, but she *is* the maid in their house too. I mean, that's her job." Jimbo spoke in some bewilderment.

"I'm sorry. I'm an ignorant lout."

"You are not," Jimbo said. "You're one of the most educated men for miles around these parts."

The solicitor who had invited Fergus to bring some friends with him may have been startled at the young priest and the elderly housekeeper. But then he was a city man to begin with; he probably expected country people to be eccentric.

The crowds were shouting and cheering long before the cavalcade even came in view. Two newspaper photographers perched from nearby windows and they could even see a television camera team on the corner. Father Hogan and Miss Purcell waved the Irish and American flags they had been given, and as he saw their great excitement and pleasure, a lump came in Fergus's throat, and he made himself a promise that he would try to be less selfish. All right, so he didn't walk over people like that O'Neill did, but on the other hand he didn't have the same genuine feeling for what would make people happy. Once or twice he had wondered how the Ryans were faring in the unfamiliar posh hotel. But soon the momentum had gathered and taken over, and like everyone else he was leaning out of the window waving, certain that there was a special wave and smile up at them.

Marian talked a lot about the trip to Dublin. She told everyone in the Rosemarie hair salon that Patrick O'Neill was a simply superb host.

"Has he done much entertaining in that cottage of yours?" Judy Byrne asked as she waited, thumbing through Rita Walsh's rather old magazines.

"No, they keep very much to themselves in the lodge, just family, you know." Marian sounded much more knowing than she was. She could not believe it possible that a family could live in her grounds and she would know so little of their everyday life. They were perfectly pleasant, if mildly startled when she came to call; they refused all offers of hospitality that she and her father showered on them. Marian had heard that a woman was coming across from New York, a Mrs. Fine. There had already been two phone calls to the Grange for her. It was a mystery. Patrick had made no booking; usually he was assiduous about booking well in advance and paying a full rate.

Who was Mrs. Fine?

She longed to ask if anyone in the salon knew, but she hated to reveal her hand.

She would call at Ryan's perhaps, and inquire there.

Marian didn't even need to do that. She met Grace and Dara as soon as she left Rita Walsh's door.

"Your hair looks lovely." Grace was always so enthusiastic, so willing to praise.

"Thank you, dear. Grace, who is Mrs. Fine?"

"I don't know what you mean."

"I mean is she somebody who is a family friend?"

"No, she's not a family friend."

"Is she coming over here to Ireland?"

"Not that I know of, Miss Johnson."

"It's just that there have been two calls for her, and I hadn't heard anything. Your father is usually so good about booking people in; I was wondering whether it had slipped his mind . . ."

"No, it wouldn't have slipped his mind. She can't be intended to stay in the Grange. They must have gotten it wrong back in the States."

"So who *is* she then, dear?"

"A sort of designer, I think; someone rather old who works with Father."

"And she and Mr. Fine aren't friends of yours back home?"

"No, I think it's all a work thing."

"I see." Marian was satisfied.

Grace linked arms with Dara on the way toward their raft on the bend of the river.

"I'll tell you something, because I tell you all my secrets."

"You don't have to." Dara still felt guilty about the tunnel.

"Well, I will. The woman that Marian's rabbiting on about, she's the woman I was telling you about. The one that was meant to be interested in Father. You know, the things people said."

"Oh heavens." Dara was worried for her friend.

"No, it couldn't be anything. I know that now. Father isn't interested in women and all that sort of thing. It's too late, and he's only interested in being part of things here."

"Well, that's all right then." Dara was relieved that there were no more storm clouds on the horizon.

"Kerry, Mrs. Fine's coming."

"She's not. He wouldn't dare."

"I thought I'd tell you now, so that you wouldn't make a scene."

"He can't mean to bring her *here*." Kerry looked around the lodge in dismay.

"No, not here, I mean to Mountfern."

"Is she staying in the Grange?"

"No, or Marian knows nothing about it, if she is."

"It's revolting." Kerry was walking around, agitated.

"Please don't make a scene. We've been over this a hundred times. We've said it *can't* be true. Not all this time, not at their age."

"Look at what we hear about the people going to the Rosemarie hair salon, they must be about a hundred."

"But not Father!"

"Why not? He's just the same."

"I'll ask him if you like. Let me ask him." Grace was anxious to avoid what would happen if Kerry asked.

"No, don't ask him. Don't sink to asking him. If she comes to this place then he'll have to explain her, let him explain her himself without us asking." Kerry's lip was curled in disapproval.

Papers Flynn called to Dr. White's office as if he were the most regular visitor there, coming for prescriptions and patent medicines. Mrs. White was surprised to see him at the office door; his usual approach was to the kitchen door in search of cardboard, when he would not be averse to a cup of tea.

Then she saw he had a gigantic bump on his forehead and a cut all around it.

"Oh Papers, have you been in the wars?" she asked, concerned for the gentle old man whose wits were long gone.

"I don't know what happened, Mam, but I was sitting there minding my own business in the dump near the brothers' school and I saw Miss Barry from the presbytery, who often gives me a cup of tea. Anyway she threw this bag of bottles in, and she didn't look at all to see if there was anyone there, and it's opened my head. I can't imagine what came into her."

Mrs. White sighed. It was about time for one of Miss Barry's batters. But really and truly she was getting quite dangerous, if she had nearly laid out Papers. Still she could hardly be faulted for thinking that a rubbish dump might be free of people sitting on the debris having their tea. Mountfern was a very mad place, Mrs. White often told her husband, on the frequent occasions when she was trying to encourage him to find a practice somewhere with a bit more life in it.

Jimbo Doyle put his head around the door of Leonard's paper shop.

"Tommy, do us a favor."

"What is it, Jimbo?" Tommy looked around to see if his father was watching. His father had accused Jimbo of reading every paper in the shop and buying none of them; it had been highly embarrassing.

"Look up the paper and tell me what's on in the Slieve Sunset tonight."

"What's on there? Is it turned into a cinema?"

"No, smartie, they have different kinds of talent contests. I wanted to know about the Country and Western one. If it's tonight I might have a go, get Carrie out there, have a real night."

"I'll look it up for you." Tommy was good-natured. It wouldn't cross his mind that Jimbo should be buying a paper.

"Ah there you are, Jimbo," his father cried suddenly. "Come to mend your ways and buy a paper at last, have you?"

Jimbo was very hard to insult.

"Not a chance of it Mr. Leonard, just called in to say hallo to your fine son here. We were having a bit of a chat about matters musical."

Tommy loved this; his eye had been racing down the advertisements in the local paper and found the appropriate listing.

"Yes, Dad, Jimbo and I were just talking about these talent contests. There's a very interesting one on tonight out in the Slieve Sunset, tonight at eight o'clock sharp, it says Jimbo, and it's Special Nashville Nite, spelled n-i-t-e, with fun for one 'n' all."

"Isn't it terrible to think that it was for the likes of this the republic was born," Mr. Leonard sighed. "For people who spell night, N-I-T-E. For half-wits who name their hotels half in one language and half in another and who encourage louts to get notions, togging themselves up in fancy dress as cow-boys."

Jimbo thought Mr. Leonard must be talking about some loutish element which he imagined patronized the Slieve Sunset.

"No, it's a very nice crowd you'd get out there," he explained. "They have all kinds of restrictions, and there's no bad language of any kind allowed near the tables. The bar is different, but once you get near the tables where the ladies sit, it's out you go if a curse word is heard. You'd be impressed by it, Mr. Leonard, I tell you."

"I would," said Jack Leonard. "Oh I know I would."

"I'm taking Grace into town, she wants to get a couple of things to wear. Would you like to come for the trip?" Marian asked Kerry.

She loved this motherly role with Grace and thought she could extend it to the whole family.

"No thank you, Miss Johnson, I'm off to go bicycling."

"Will you be back for lunch? Did you tell Miss Hayes?" Grace asked him.

"Oh, I've explained to her, I'll be gone all day. I'm going to look at that ruined abbey down the river. She's making me some sandwiches."

Grace knew that Kitty Daly was taking a picnic off on her bike too that day. She knew also that Kerry was keeping well out of Father's way. He was very annoyed to hear that Mrs. Fine might be coming to Mountfern.

Rachel Fine looked at the Slieve Sunset hotel in disbelief. It was quite bad enough of Patrick to say they couldn't stay in the same hotel for discretion . . . but to put her up in this dump was inexcusable. The Grange was a country house, covered in virginia creeper, the Grange had horses in stables. It had a decanter of sherry to which the guests helped themselves before dinner. It had a lady with a plummy voice called Marian Johnson who was the daughter of the house and who ran the place very well. So what was Rachel doing in this fleapit? It was such a low-grade motel, it was definitely an insult.

She pulled off her long cream gloves and sat on the bed to inspect the room. There was no chair to sit on. Hideous drapes in huge sunbursts clashing with a carpet of equally hideous, but non-toning, shades. The light switch was not even beside the bed. There was no bathroom, you could share a tub or shower room with Lord knew how many people. A handbasin with a dripping faucet, a small uneven-looking wardrobe as an excuse for a closet. Four rattling wire coat hangers inside.

Rachel's head was aching. She had flown from New York to Shannon. She had rented a car on Patrick's suggestion. He had been hard to pin down on the telephone, but it was something to do with wanting her to see a bit of the country. Big clown. She could still see the countryside if he had come to meet her.

And what was all this need for discretion, here of all places? Here nobody knew them. It could be like that one week they had spent in Mexico where they could check into any hotel as man and wife, where they could hold hands at dinner. Who in Ireland would know or care that they stayed in the same hotel? Why, there was even his daughter as chaperon.

Tired and angry, Rachel began to unpack. She smoothed out her best silk suit; she had expected to hang it over a tub of steaming, scented water when she arrived, but *that* was not on. She looked at her face in the mirror. She looked every day of forty-eight and a few more days as well. She could *kill* him. But she wouldn't. She hadn't waited this long, and put up with so much already, to blow the whole thing in a dump in a one-horse town in a second-rate country.

Patrick was locked in a never-ending argument with architects and structural engineers all morning. He had said goodbye to Kerry the previous night, glad that the boy would be gone before Rachel arrived. He hadn't even said anything about her coming. With Grace there was no problem; the child had no idea of any relationship, and anyway she was so taken up with the Ryan twins she had no time for anyone else.

It was a warm day and the architects were being excessively stubborn; the whole planning could be negated even at this stage, they insisted, if he wouldn't tell them where he had finally decided to place the entrance.

"I'll tell you any goddamn place to get the show on the road, but we can change it again later, that's the deal," Patrick said.

That was not the deal, apparently. It was very wearing. Brian Doyle had been no help either.

"There's only two places you can put the entrance, in the name of God, Mr. O'Neill," he shouted, exasperated. "Where it is, where it was always meant to be. Or where the Yank architects say, which is along that sort of overgrown towpath, which will cost you another thousand pounds just to cut back the brambles. All you've got to say is one or the other."

None of them had seen what his son had seen, that the best and indeed the only place to have an imposing entrance, was from the small piece of ground where Ryan's Licensed Premises stood at this very moment.

Patrick decided to end the meeting. Kerry had left. Rachel was arriving.

Marian was billing and cooing about dinner for the two of them that evening, when he most certainly would not be free. But most important of all, he realized, he had to talk to the Ryans. He had always despised other businessmen who pussyfooted about. He was going to ask those people straight away if there was any chance that they would consider selling. It was tempting to let other people do the dirty work, ask the questions that were almost impossible to ask. But Patrick O'Neill knew that in almost every aspect of life, if you want to do something it's best to do it yourself. If he did it quickly he might even have the conversation finished one way or another before lunch. Then he'd hightail it up to the Slieve Sunset and pray that Rachel wasn't spitting blood once she had seen the style he had relegated her to for her visit.

Miss Purcell had been in a very good humor since the trip to Dublin. She had been treated as the highest in the land with a window seat at which the young president looked up and waved directly. There had been tea and sandwiches, and Father Hogan had been a delightful companion for the day. Mr. Fergus was so odd of course, and put people off by his funny manner, but there was no doubt he had a heart of gold. She had ironed his shirts lovingly for him; she hoped he would look very well in this nice hotel he was going to, and people would admire him. She hoped he would meet a nice class of person, and have a good social life. He refused to play bridge, and he was on his own far too much. Miss Purcell didn't really want to see a wife for Mr. Fergus—that would mean too many changes—but she would like him to have more people of his own class and education to talk to in the evenings. He had taken to long walks, and heavy pints in Ryan's Licensed Premises with farm laborers.

She was glad of the thought of two weeks on her own. She could spring clean the house properly. It would be very quiet, of course, without Mr. Fergus and Kate Ryan and the clients trooping in and out. But the Lord knew the man was entitled to his two weeks off, and she went out on the doorstep to examine the skies, hoping for good weather for the young master on his holidays.

At that very moment a small car drew up and a very well-dressed woman jumped out.

"Pardon me, but seeing that you live here, can I ask you where I should go to find Mr. Patrick O'Neill who is doing major building works in these parts?"

Miss Purcell was delighted, an American lady just arrived in town. What a chance to meet her at once, just because she had gone to look at the weather.

"Of course I can tell you," she said. "You turn right at the big bridge you see here before you, then go along River Road. Park your car outside the public house called Ryan's and cross a footbridge. It's a bit of a walk but that's the site."

"That's where the old Fernscourt was . . ." the American lady said.

"The very place," Miss Purcell said. "Mr. O'Neill's building a fine new hotel there, they tell me."

"So I walk over the footbridge and it's a fair way?" The woman looked down at her very elegant high-heeled shoes. "Well, I guess I'm going to have to get used to different ways."

Miss Purcell was bursting with assistance.

"Seeing you have the car with you, you could always go back the way you came up to the main road, along a bit and then you'd see a rough sort of entrance, and a narrow path where there are lorries and tractors and the like.

They have all kinds of signs telling people to beware of this and beware of that, so you should blow your horn at them all the time to let them know you're coming."

The woman thanked her. "No, I'll risk the little walk. And if I can't make it the whole way, I'll just holler."

Miss Purcell looked after her with interest. Now, who could she be? She looked a bit . . . overdressed, a bit foreign to be any kind of lady friend. Maybe someone he had met on an aeroplane or somesuch. Time would tell. They'd soon know.

Fergus Slattery had been out in the country making a will for a dying farmer. It was the last thing he had to do before he went back to pack. The old man clutched at him and thanked him for his patience.

"But then you wouldn't be your father's son if you were any other way," he wheezed.

"Was my father patient?" Fergus had worked beside the older man for years and realized that he was certainly well read and certainly slow.

"He had all the time in the world for you. It's the hallmark of the busy man; they never look rushed."

That was true of Patrick O'Neill, Fergus thought ruefully; he seemed to have time for chats and pints and strolls along the river bank. He had time to come and talk to the angling club and show them new flies he had brought from somewhere on his travels, chatting in a leisurely way, while all the time there were huge deals being done in New York to move money here and there, to finance even huger investments for his Fernscourt project. Already the walls were in evidence—only feet above the ground, but within a few months of leveling of the ruin the new order was beginning to appear.

Fergus shook himself back into the present.

"Well, I do have all the time in the world, so now if there's any little thing here that isn't clear to you, I can read it over again with you, Danny."

"No, it seems fair enough, fair enough."

"And sure, you've all the time in the world yourself, if you want to change anything," Fergus lied into the man's eyes. "When I come back from my holidays you can ask me to come up here again, if you've anything you want to add or take away."

"When you come back from your holidays, boy, I'll be in the churchyard, and we both know that. I'll tell your father that you're doing a good job."

"If you see him, will you ask him to send me a message about what in God's name he did with the papers in the Scanlan case? They're irretrievably lost and I have someone on to me about them every month."

The old man laughed, the thought of death pushed further away.

Fergus felt better himself. He thought he might call into Ryan's for a lunchtime pint. Since he had closed his own office he was childishly light-hearted; he felt his holiday had begun. He said goodbye to the old man he would never see again, and drove off toward Ryan's.

That funny thin woman with the dutch-doll coloring hadn't lied, Rachel thought, when she saw what a fair step it was to walk toward the busy site. She looked again at her shoes and said this was madness. Even squinting into the sunlight she couldn't see Patrick among the bulldozers and the men going in and out of a prefab hut which must be the site office.

She stood for a while looking at the scene which was the heart's desire of the man she loved. It was as incomprehensible to her, now that she was four hundred yards from it, as when she had been three thousand miles away from it. Perhaps she had been foolish to come here on her own. Maybe she should have waited. But that hotel was beginning to make her flesh crawl. She had lain without closing her eyes on that uncomfortable bed in the garish room. Sleep would not come. But it had benefited her nothing to come this far. Unless, of course, he was in the habit of calling at this public house for his lunch. She went up to the front door and into Ryan's.

She had assumed it would be a simple place; it certainly didn't look much from the outside but at least they had the good sense not to change the front and destroy the whole feel of the place like so many others, notably the dreaded Slieve Sunset, had done. She had thought it might be dark, and there might be men who would resent a woman calling in for a morning drink.

What she had not expected was a totally empty saloon with a husband and wife embracing each other behind the bar. The woman was dark-haired and good-looking, with tears running down her face. The man was sandy and plump, and looked as if someone had just told him that he had won the Irish Sweepstake.

But it was far better than that. John Ryan was holding the *Irish Press* newspaper of that day, in which his first poem had been published.

It was a poem called "Sleep in Peace," and it was telling the Fern family to sleep peacefully in their graves because the old order had changed. They must rest on and never come back because everything was so changed that they wouldn't be able to walk as Lords of the Soil, as they once had. It was both gentle and savage. John had written it to put in the book that he was doing for Patrick, then his confidence had failed and he thought that perhaps Patrick wouldn't like it. Kate had urged him to show it to someone who might know. She had typed it out and posted it to the *Irish Press,* which sometimes published poetry.

There it was, in black and white in the paper. He had only turned to the page five minutes before, and had come in shouting and roaring like a bull from the garden. Leopold, genuinely frightened for once, was whimpering under a table.

Rachel Fine had never seen such intense excitement and pleasure. She felt utterly out of place, as if she had intruded into a marriage bed.

"I guess I'm a little early for bar hours," she said.

They disentangled themselves and Kate wiped her eyes.

"You must excuse us, Ma'am," said John. "But you arrived at a big moment for us. Can we ask you to share it . . . whatever you like to drink. Anything at all. This is a big celebration."

Kate was composed. "My husband has just had his first literary work published. Here it is in the newspaper. We're so pleased. It's been *so* long."

"And Kate never lost faith in me; she never thought for a minute that I wouldn't succeed." The man's face gave off rays like the sun.

Rachel looked politely at the paper. "Oh, it's about the Ferns," she cried.

"They used to own that house . . . well the house that *was* over there." John was so excited he could hardly talk.

"John, give the lady the promised drink and give me one too," Kate said.

Rachel looked from one to other. "I'm useless; I'm an orange-juice lady. I have no business being in a bar at all. I'm sorry not to be more festive on your great occasion."

"I'm often an orange-juice lady myself," Kate confided. "But I daren't say it in a public house. It's bad for business. You are most welcome to a nice glass of Club Orange if you're sure that's what you'd like."

John was staring at the paper as if it might vanish before his eyes.

"I'm Rachel Fine," Rachel said, stretching out her hand. "I work for Patrick O'Neill, I'm his designer and adviser."

Kate thrilled with sudden recognition. My God, he's got a fancy woman, she said to herself as she shook hands with the well-groomed woman and poured her a Club Orange to celebrate the success of the poem.

Rachel suggested that John go and buy up several copies of the paper, which he thought was a great idea. If Leonard's didn't have any more copies left, they could telephone somebody in the big town to keep some copies, or even the paper itself. They could get them copied too on a photocopier. He would inquire about that too when he was in Bridge Street.

"Don't be gone all day," Kate said. "There's bound to be a bit of a crowd in at lunchtime."

"I'll be back. Won't I want to show them?" Like an excited child he headed off down River Road. Kate knew he would stop first to tell Loretto Quinn, and could see her clapping her hands with pleasure for him.

"You must think we're quite mad," Kate said to Rachel. "Any other day of the year, you'd come in here and find us the most quiet respectable pub in the country. In fact I'd be up in the solicitor's office where I work in the mornings. But today is such a red-letter day, you have no idea, you really don't."

"I do, I can see only too clearly how pleased you are for him," Rachel said.

It wasn't the words, which were ordinary enough, but it was the way she said them that made Kate more expansive than usual. Normally she never told anyone what she felt about John.

"You see I wouldn't mind if he never wrote a poem that was published. I wouldn't want any fame or money or anything for me or for us out of his writing. But it's him. Often he says he's only a fool to be scribbling and writing, and maybe he's half-cracked to have such notions. Now he'll never think that again. His dream is official, as it were." She gave a little laugh at this definition of John's dream.

"That's a wonderful way of putting it," Rachel said. "His dream is official. Like Patrick's dream. I suppose now that he sees brick going on brick, he knows it's official." The two women looked across the river at the huge building site up the slope.

In a gentle voice Kate said, "Patrick will be over shortly, he nearly always comes in at lunchtime."

In a couple of sentences they had exchanged a great deal of information. And without saying very much at all they knew they were going to be great friends.

It was indeed busy at lunchtime as Kate had predicted, and with all kinds of unexpected people. Miss Barry had decided to begin what looked like a spectacular breakout by sitting on a bar stool and ordering a brandy and port. She had rarely been seen in a public house before; all her drinking had been done from surreptitious paper bags bought in off-sales in the big town.

Kate managed to get her out by saying that they had neither brandy nor port for sale in the pub, but if Miss Barry liked, she could give her a half bottle of each in a private transaction since she was sure that Miss Barry wanted them for medicinal purposes at home. This brought Miss Barry to her limited senses and she slipped away with two small brown-paper parcels toward a three-day binge and a spectacular hangover.

Fergus Slattery came in to say goodbye and said the place was like Portsmouth on pay night, with all the activity. When Kate told him about the poem, his pleasure was so genuine it touched her heart. He went straight to John and congratulated him loudly. He promised to tell everyone at the hotel he was going to that he knew the poet himself, and John Ryan's ears pinked up with the pleasure of it all.

Jimbo Doyle, who wouldn't have read a poem in a million years normally, said that all the children above with the brothers and the nuns should be made to learn it off by heart, and that it should be recited at the next concert.

In the middle of it all Patrick O'Neill came in. He didn't see Rachel, now on her third orange juice and happily settled in. He looked preoccupied and somehow annoyed to see so many people.

"Any chance of a word with yourself and John today?" he asked.

"Fire ahead," Kate said. "I may have to interrupt you, John's buying drinks for everybody, he had a poem published."

"That's good," Patrick said mechanically. "It's just that . . ."

"Oh Patrick," Kate's face was stricken. "Don't say, 'That's good,' it's much more than good. For God's sake the man has had his first poem published and you just say 'That's good.' It's magnificent, that's what it is." Her eyes had begun to blaze at the inadequacy of his remark.

Patrick realized he had been crass. "I'm sorry, I had something on my mind . . . I beg your pardon . . . where is he . . . must tell him how pleased I am."

"That's more like it."

"I am sorry, I know it sounds mean-spirited of me, I genuinely am pleased, it's just that there's something I'm anxious about . . ."

"Oh, she's here . . ." Kate cried triumphantly. "I'm sorry, I should have said it before . . . she's over there in the back rooms. Rachel, Rachel, Patrick's here."

Patrick's face was in a tight line where his mouth had been. How had it happened that Kate Ryan seemed to have guessed immediately that Rachel was more than a member of his staff, and why did she feel able to call this fact out familiarly across the pub?

He had been mad to let Rachel come here in the first place. He saw her then, surrounded by local people and laughing. But she looked wrong, she could never be part of this place. He must make that clear soon. Sweet Lord, how had it all turned into this, making things clear to people, speaking his mind?

Rachel looked up and waved at him nice and casually, as she would have done back home.

"Well Mr. O'Neill, I made it to Ireland. Isn't it a great place?" she said, and his heart softened toward her again.

Things were getting very complicated indeed.

By three o'clock the bar was empty. John and Kate were exhausted. The glasses were washed; two clean cloths, washed through after the polishing, lay across the beer and stout pumps. The place was ready for any afternoon visitor who might stray in, and for the teatime trade.

"God, if we were to have a crowd like that again we'd have to hire a young lad," John said.

"There speaks the man with the second income," Kate teased.

"Wasn't it great when Patrick read it out?" John said.

Kate had thought Patrick's mind was miles away but she didn't say that.

"I'm very, very proud of you," she said.

"Would we risk it and go up to bed for a while?" he said.

"Are you mad?"

"Ah go on, we could ask Carrie to step in here."

"And what would she think?"

"Does it matter what she thinks?"

"Don't be ridiculous, John, the children could come home."

The twins had gone for a picnic with Grace, Eddie was out with his gang of toughs, Declan could be anywhere.

"Let them, the door would be locked."

"We'll lock it tonight instead," she said.

"And what am I going to do here, mad with desire for you?"

"Why don't you look through your other poems, the ones we liked, and you could maybe give me some of them. I'll type them and you can always say I have had work published already, I enclose an example . . ."

"But there's only one example . . ."

"You don't have to tell them that," Kate said.

"God, you're a fox, Kate. Between yourself and Patrick O'Neill you could rule the world. There's a pair of you in it."

"I hope not," Kate said, shivering slightly.

"And what are you going to do if you're not going to fulfil your marital duties?" John asked sulkily.

"I'm going to have a little walk. I'm restless and over-excited . . . but *no* I do *not* see a way to cure all that. I'm not going to let us become the talk of the neighborhood by abandoning our pub and going off to bed in the middle of the afternoon." She skipped out of his way and took her cardigan off the back of a chair.

"Go on, John, get your poems down, truly now . . . I love the one about the nun looking into the river, the nun with the very sad face."

She walked out and stretched in the sunshine. She had said the truth, she *was* restless and over-excited. She was happy for John in a way she had never expected to be, but everywhere around her, like a big black cloud, she felt a sense of danger. Even when Patrick had said he wanted to talk to them she had thought it was going to be something bad, and was glad that the crowds and the circumstances had meant he couldn't bring up whatever it was. It was like a reprieve.

She felt there was something odd about Kerry. It wasn't that he never smiled—his face was one big smile, for God's sake, with those perfect white teeth. And he couldn't be more polite. It wasn't anything to do with Grace. The twins seemed to love her, and she was a warm little thing, all smiles too.

She really couldn't say that the work on Fernscourt had harmed their business. When else had they been full on a Tuesday at lunchtime? And perhaps these people would keep coming back even when the building works were over. So why then was she restless? Was it the holidays and knowing that young Fergus was off to find himself a woman? Surely not. She *wanted* Fergus to find himself a woman.

She crossed the footbridge and looked up at the site. Patrick would not be there now, he had told Rachel that he would drive out to the Slieve Sunset with her and see if they could make any improvements. Kate wondered why on earth she hadn't been allowed to go to the Grange and then remembered that Grace was at the lodge and might suspect something. Could that be it?

It would be very hard to be in love with Patrick O'Neill, hard to come first in his life. There would always be business, or the children, or travel or long-distance telephone calls. Kate sighed thinking of it all, and wished Rachel Fine luck in her uphill struggle. She remembered how warm and nice Patrick had been that day last week when they had gone to see President Kennedy arrive in Dublin. He had been so anxious to please them all with drinks and sandwiches in the big Dublin hotel. He had hardly ever stopped smiling and laughing. It would be easy to fall in love with him. She walked up the slope that the twins used to think of as their own private path at one time, now more open and exposed with a lot of the brambles and briars cut away. She hadn't been in to look at the site since the foundations were dug and already the walls were showing, so that you could see the shape it would be.

Kate felt she must know what it was going to be like, no point in being like an ostrich anymore. She was going to go right up there and look, and ask Brian Doyle which room was which, and talk about it to Patrick O'Neill, and ask Rachel Fine what kind of colors it was going to be. She quickened her step and threw back her head with confidence. *There's a time for everything, she thought. I wasn't ready to know about it before, but I'm ready now.*

She saw Brian Doyle waving at her frantically as she approached the site. He had both hands in the air and was shouting something. But she hadn't heard what it was by the time she felt the terrifying sharp pain. It was so sudden and worse than anything she had ever known, like the terror in a dream or a nightmare. And it only lasted seconds, because that was all it took for Kate Ryan to be hit sideways by the huge bulldozer, flung up in the air and crashed to the ground. It only took a few seconds to break her spine.

John knew only when the third person rushing away from the site to get help refused to look him in the eye and tell him what had happened. Roaring like a bull, he ran across the footbridge and had to be held back from the scene by three men. White-faced Brian Doyle begged him not to go near her.

"Jesus, the only thing we *do* know, John, is not to move her. For God's sake believe that. Stand back from her, don't touch her. You could make it worse."

John sat down like a child and put his big face into his hands. Strong men who had known him and had drunk pints in his pub for twenty years couldn't find the words or the gestures to touch him. They stood awkwardly around, eyes averted from the crumpled body on the ground.

Patrick O'Neill knew when there was a great hammering on the door of Rachel Fine's room in the Slieve Sunset hotel.

"No, of course Mr. O'Neill is not here," Rachel called through the door. "What on earth makes you think he is?"

"Sorry ma'am," the young girl called. "We've had a message from Brian Doyle, he said he's trying everywhere in the country to find Mr. O'Neill, there's been a terrible accident . . . a terrible accident and Mr. O'Neill's got to come at once."

Patrick was out of bed and had pulled his trousers on.

"What kind of an accident?" He shouted through the door.

"On the site of the new hotel in Mountfern."

"What happened?" Patrick had opened the door now; Rachel was cowering behind it. Patrick had pulled his shirt on at the same electrifying speed.

"Someone's been killed, I think. Some woman."

"A woman, killed on the site?" Patrick's shoes were on and he had picked up his car keys.

"Did he say what woman? What was a woman doing there? Did he say how it happened?"

"No, he said if we found you to get you over there as quick as possible."

Patrick was down the corridor by this stage and the girl was round-eyed at the thought of the American millionaire who was building the big hotel five miles away being in bed in the middle of the afternoon with a strange American woman and not being a bit ashamed of it. Weren't things going to liven up a bit here when the Yanks started coming over in force?

Mrs. Whelan in the post office knew fairly early on because Dr. White stopped his car outside her door and ran in to collect her.

"Put some kind of sign on the door, do anything but come with me, Sheila. They're going to need someone sensible at the pub to look after them."

She didn't question whether she was the right person or not, she just closed the door behind her and stepped quietly into his car.

"Have you told the canon?"

"Someone has. Father Hogan will be there in a minute, he's got his own car."

"Do you know is she bad?" Mrs. Whelan's voice was calm.

"No, all I know is that they've had the sense not to move her. I've got the ambulance coming anyway. I didn't wait to see her, we can always send it back if it's not needed." His face was set hard as he headed for the accident.

The twins were the last to know. They had been in their tunnel all afternoon. Grace had gone to the big town with Marian Johnson to get some more summer clothes. The invitation had not included Dara and Michael, pleasant but scruffy children from that pub. Anyway Marian wanted to get to know Grace, make an ally of her.

So for the first time in days they had a chance to play again in their home. They had been happy to note from the Fernscourt end of the tunnel that there seemed to be no intention of clearing the undergrowth and bramble which disguised the tunnel's mouth. The new gardens would end well over two hundred yards further on. The string had already been stretched over the part where the high hedges were going to be planted and the stone walls were to be built.

All they had to worry about now was whether the entrance would be down by the towpath.

They had torches with batteries, and an old bicycle lamp up high on a ledge. They had rescued a torn tablecloth that Mammy had said was beyond mending. There were two boxes filled with hay which were sofas and would double up as beds when they came to live here permanently. The day's play had seemed long for the first time. The kind of games they used to invent in the ruins seemed suddenly rather childish. But neither wanted to admit it to the other. Nor even to admit it in the heart. If the game was over, what was there?

In the hot tunnel, which for the first time seemed a bit close and smelly today, they played and hoped it was soon going to be evening.

They came out and pulled across the fuchsia bush as they always had done. Not twenty yards down the towpath they heard the people calling them. There must have been a search party out for them.

It was Loretto Quinn who saw them from across the river. She waved and shouted. "Where on earth have you been?" she cried.

Dara and Michael looked at each other in dismay.

"Nowhere."

"Just playing."

But by this time the children from the bridge had come toward them in a group, and then suddenly hung back as if not wanting to be the first to say the words.

"You've got to go home now," Tommy Leonard said eventually. "They've been looking for you for hours."

"We've only been just around . . ."

"Just around here and there . . ."

Tommy's face was serious. "Something very bad's happened."

The other children held back.

Loretto Quinn was there by now, she was kneeling down on the ground in front of them to be nearer to their height, but that made her much too low and then they had to bend to hear what she was saying.

"You have to be as brave as two little lions now. Do you hear me? They all need you to be brave."

"What happened?" They spoke together, faces calm, timing precise.

"Your Mammy got hit by a machine up in the site, she hurt herself very badly. They've taken her to the hospital in an ambulance."

The children crowded closer to hear. Now that someone else was telling the twins, now that a grown-up had taken the burden off them, they wanted to be part of it.

"Is she dead?" Dara asked.

"No, she's not dead," said Loretto Quinn.

"Is she going to die?" Michael asked, equally calmly.

Loretto remembered the people who had given her false hope and told her that her Barney might recover when they took his lifeless body from the River Fern all those years ago. They had meant well, but they had been no help.

"They think she might die, yes," she said. The group of children drew back suddenly and Loretto held the twins in her arms and supported them from the towpath, across the bridge in the eyes of dozens of people, and back to the pub.

Mrs. Whelan took them into the kitchen. "Your daddy's in hospital now. Do you think your place is in there with him, or is it here with me looking after the children?"

Eddie and Declan's faces were swollen from crying. They sat in unaccustomed stillness on kitchen chairs while Carrie made bread at Mrs. Whelan's suggestion.

Dara thought for a minute. "I suppose she'd want us to keep an eye on Dad in case he'd get too upset at the hospital."

"Right," said Mrs. Whelan and she sent someone in the bar for Jack Coyne who would drive them into the town.

Part Three

Eleven

The church was crowded at eleven o'clock mass on Sunday. The two priests, who were faced with getting their own lunch due to the non appearance of Miss Barry, had answered many requests to say masses for Mrs. Ryan. Young Father Hogan became impatient when a poor old tramp called Papers Flynn came with half a crown to have a mass said for the poor woman in the pub.

"No need to give an offering, Papers," Father Hogan had said gruffly. "We'll be saying mass for her anyway."

"I want my mass said for her," Papers insisted. She had been very good to him always, he said, given him a yellow blanket to wrap around him under all the newspapers he normally wore when sleeping in a ditch. She had never given him a lecture about sleeping out. It was as if she understood somehow.

The young American girl had come with five dollars.

"I guess this might not be the way to do it, but when my Mother was alive she used to give an offering for a mass. Could you write Mrs. Ryan's name in your book, Father? And could you say a mass for her?"

Tramps and children. Father Hogan had never thought it was going to be like this. Tramps, children, drunken housekeepers, kind if doddering parish priests. And trying to explain why it was God's will that a young woman, mother of a family, should be struck by a huge bulldozer as she walked unheeding on a summer's day. They never told you in the seminary that it was going to be like this. But maybe, of course, they didn't know.

It was Canon Moran who would say eleven o'clock mass; Father Hogan would go and struggle with the range. He sighed as he folded his own vestments from the earlier mass in the vestry and watched Canon Moran take tottering steps out toward the altar. He had arranged sensible altar boys like

Tommy Leonard and Liam White. With the canon you couldn't have any possible troublemakers.

The canon turned to face the congregation and in his thin reedy voice he said, "Your prayers are asked for the happy death or speedy recovery of Katherine Mary Ryan of River Road."

Fergus put a finger in his collar to loosen it. He wondered what he was doing sitting here listening to this mumbo jumbo. Happy death! Should it not be speedy death rather than lying there paralyzed, in traction, so heavily sedated because of the pain that she didn't even know her own family or where she was? What did this old fool mean? Praying for happy deaths and speedy recoveries, that's what you said about old people lingering on and on, it was a way of announcing to the parish that old Jimmy this or Michael that was on the way out. Like the old fellow he had made the will for a few days back. It wasn't for Kate Ryan, a young woman. A young woman who had been killed—or almost killed—by a machine on that man's land.

Fergus felt himself getting a hot flush of anger and loosened his collar and tie still further.

He thanked God for the wisdom of Sheila Whelan who had phoned him the night it had happened. She had simply said that she knew he would want to know, rather than come back a week or two later from his holiday and find out what had happened in his absence.

Miss Purcell had sniffed, of course, and said that Mrs. Whelan had a deal of impertinence interrupting the man on his holiday. But Miss Purcell knew nothing, and Sheila Whelan knew everything. She knew that he would have come back from the ends of the earth.

Loretto Quinn was not following the mass; she was saying the thirty days' prayer. She had promised Our Lady that she would start the prayer immediately. She knew that Our Lady would realize how important Kate Ryan was to her family, and spare her. She prayed determinedly, trying to mean the words, and never once thinking that Our Lady might also have known how important Barney Quinn had been.

Sheila Whelan wasn't following the mass either. She was trying to work out a plan in her head. The Ryans hadn't thought a day ahead of the day they were living. Someone had to think for them. They couldn't live on the way they were. They needed a woman in the house, someone who could serve in the bar, someone who could keep an eye on the children, and see to it that Carrie did what she was meant to do. She had a cousin.

She wondered would it work. The cousin had been disappointed. A man had given her an engagement ring and there were plans for the wedding. Mary Donnelly had given up her fine job teaching and drew out her savings to put a deposit on a house. The man had disappeared, with the savings.

In fact Sheila Whelan was the only member of the family to know anything. Mary Donnelly felt that Sheila, having been abandoned by her own husband, might understand. She had told her everything only six weeks ago.

Mrs. Whelan decided to ring her and suggest it anyway. No harm could come from suggesting something and for poor Mary, bruised and betrayed, anything would be better than staying where she was and enduring the pitying glances of friends and relations.

* * *

John Ryan was not at mass, he was at his wife's bedside. Kate's face was very white, her breathing was troubled and she gave little snores and half-choking sounds. Kate had never snored although she claimed that John would raise the roof unless she nudged him and pinched him to change his position in bed.

There was a tube attached to her arm and another to her bladder. She didn't look like Kate, she looked like a picture of Kate that had been given to medical students to experiment on.

Once or twice she seemed to know him.

"John," she said once.

"I'm here, love."

"I'm sorry, John."

Then nothing more for a long time.

"The children?" she asked quite clearly.

"Fine, not a worry about them, in great form."

"Who . . . who?"

"Carrie's coping very well, Loretto's in and out, Sheila Whelan came in all three days. We're fine, they're fine."

"Three days?" She seemed mystified.

"Since it happened," John said.

"My God, three days."

"Don't think about it, you're getting better, they say you're on the mend." His face was red with exertion.

Kate had slipped away into unconsciousness again.

Dara had washed Eddie's neck and Declan's ears before they went to mass. She had refused their protestations.

"Mammy says she could plant rows of potatoes in your neck, Eddie. Stand still and let me scrub it."

"Put some soap and water on the facecloth," roared Eddie.

"There's plenty on it. It's just that you're so filthy."

Declan stood waiting for his turn. "Maybe I'd do my own ears to save you the trouble," he offered.

"No," Dara said. "I'll do them."

Michael sat saying nothing. Carrie had come back from early mass and was standing unhappily wondering about the lunch.

"Are you clean, Michael?" Dara asked.

He shrugged.

"Ah, come on, Michael, it's the only thing we can do for Mammy, not to be like tinkers. That's what she'd say."

"We don't know what she'd say." He was mutinous.

"What do you mean?"

"You have half of Mountfern saying 'Your mother would say this,' and the other half saying 'She'd say that' . . . When will she be able to say something for herself, not have us all listening to other people saying it for her?"

"When she *is* able to say something I'm sure she'd prefer you to stop moping and *do* something."

"All right." Michael went at Declan's ears with such savagery that the boy roared for mercy.

"Isn't it disgusting to think that our mother has to look at such awful things as necks and ears," Michael said.

"I bet yours were just as bad and maybe still are, for all we know."

"Stay *still*, Declan. It hurts less if you don't move, you clown."

Michael thought he'd like to skip mass; he felt sure that God would under-stand that he could pray better for Mam if he were to walk up the bank a bit. He remembered a great day he had walked off for miles up the Fern and met old Mr. Slattery who was deep in conversation with a Dutchman. The Dutchman was telling him all the names they would call the fish if they were in Holland. A perch was a *baars,* and a pike was a *snoek*. Old Mr. Slattery had been delighted with that word and had said that if ever Michael went to foreign places like Amsterdam or The Hague he could talk about *snoek* with the best of them.

Michael had often thought that he and Dara might take trips to foreign parts when they lived in Fernscourt. They would travel once or twice a year. How stupid and babyish they had been. He should have known that good things never happened really. Everyone said that Mam was going to get better, and they said she'd be running in the door again like she always did in no time. But Michael didn't believe it. People were saying it the way they said that it was going to be a great summer or that they were going to beat Offaly in the match. Just a hope. Not something real. Michael wished he could tell God about this on the river bank, and explain without being all mopey and dismal-sounding that it couldn't help anyone to keep Mam sick in hospital, but it would help everyone to make her better. He was sure that God would listen better on the banks of the Fern than in the church with everyone coughing and fidgeting. But there was no way you could explain that to anyone.

Only a madman or a heretic would suggest not going to mass on a Sunday when his mother was lying with a broken back.

Mrs. Daly caught sight of Maggie leaving the house. "Where are you going, Maggie? It's too early for mass."

"I was going down to collect Dara and Michael to walk them to the church," Maggie said.

"Don't be going in there on top of them all, they'll have the house filled with people."

"No, their Dad's gone into the town, they'll have nobody," Maggie said.

"You can see them in the church. Don't be dragging up there and living in their pockets at a time like this."

"But isn't this the time they *would* like people around?" Maggie asked simply.

"Stop contradicting me at every hand's turn. Comb that mop of hair of yours, will you, Maggie, and wait till the bell rings before going to mass."

Mrs. Daly's mouth was in a thin disapproving line.

In the lodge Olive Hayes was sitting at the kitchen table writing a long letter to Sister Bernadette on the other side of the world. Miss Hayes had put a breakfast on the table but none of the O'Neills had been able to eat. There had been yet another row between Mr. O'Neill and his son. And Grace had wanted to go and stay in the Ryans' pub after the terrible accident. But her father had said no. You could have cut the atmosphere at breakfast with a knife. As Olive Hayes wrote page after page she paused now and then to think how true it was that riches did not automatically bring happiness. This very morning she had seen the O'Neills sit white-faced around their table leaving the scrambled eggs, crispy bacon and home-made bread untouched. She had seen Marian Johnson go by in a ridiculous hat that must have cost a fortune and looked like a bird's nest. Marian's face was tense and anxious.

And now Mr. O'Neill and his daughter had driven off to eleven o'clock mass but Kerry had not gone with them. He had gone to his room. That meant he would miss mass entirely this Sunday. Olive Hayes wrote on in wonder to her sister about how changed the world had become. Could either of them ever imagine a situation where a boy of sixteen would refuse to go to mass on a Sunday because of some row with his father? It was outside their comprehension.

Tommy Leonard came up River Road and called to collect the Ryans for mass.

"I thought I'd walk with you," he said to Dara. "It's the only thing I can think of that might help."

Dara was grateful.

"And Dara, I did something else. I went up to Miss Byrne and asked her did backs ever mend, and she was full of information. She said that after a bit when they know how bad the injuries are they will decide on what program to follow. It's programs, you see, one kind for one kind of a back one kind for another. She said they do marvelous things now."

Tommy's face shone with the good news. Dara managed a watery smile.

Michael looked very white, Tommy thought, as if he had been sick.

"I'd say you could have a dispensation not to go to mass," Tommy said after some reflection.

"Did you get that straight from the pope?" Michael asked with a sort of a grin.

Tommy was pleased. At least he had made both of them smile a bit. They walked down River Road, the four Ryan children and Tommy.

"Will I have to walk ahead of you or behind you?" Eddie asked.

"Of course not," Dara said.

"You're all right with us," said Michael.

Eddie's face registered great alarm. Things must be worse than he thought if he was allowed to walk with the twins and Tommy Leonard. Mam must be in a very bad way altogether.

Kitty Daly wheeled her bicycle out quietly.

If anyone asked her why she needed a bike to go the few yards to mass she would say that she was going out to her best friend's house afterward. This was a girl who lived on a farm three miles out beyond the bridge.

But nobody asked her, so Kitty looked up and down Bridge Street and set off at a great pace toward Coyne's wood. While the mass bell was ringing over Mountfern she pedaled on and got to the old stile at the same time as Kerry O'Neill.

Hand in hand they walked through the paths that had hardly changed since their grandparents and great-grandparents had been young and had visited Coyne's wood all those years ago.

Patrick O'Neill could have done without this parade. But he knew that not to have come to mass would have caused more comment still. His face was grim as he walked into the church. A year ago he would have known nobody here, now there wasn't a face that he didn't recognize nor a person who didn't know him.

He knelt beside Grace and wondered to himself how the church had survived so long with ineffectual old men like Canon Moran in charge of parishes. Possibly because there were no thrusting young men anxious to topple them as there were in ordinary business.

Or if the thrusting young men *did* feel like that then they were not in the right calling. Thrusting young men reminded him of his son, and the great wave of annoyance came over him again. As it had when he had spoken to Kerry and told him about the accident.

"We're insured aren't we?" Kerry had said.

Patrick had remained silent.

"Well we are, Father, hey?" Kerry's voice had sounded impatient.

"Yes we're insured," Patrick had said.

"And Father, the whole place is hung with notices. Christ, they can't even expect *our* insurance to pay."

Patrick hadn't trusted himself to speak. He realized that if Kerry O'Neill reacted this way he had inherited it from his father.

Patrick saw Fergus Slattery loosening his collar and tie and looking around him a bit wildly. He wondered was the lawyer coming adrift in some way. There had been that very unpleasant and unexpected scene in the hospital where Fergus had shouted at him, not caring who heard.

"Don't think you can buy your way out of this, O'Neill, as you bought everything else."

The man had been almost deranged.

Patrick had put out a hand to calm him and Fergus had flung it away.

"Your tactics won't work with me, O'Neill, you can't glad-hand me like you do everyone in the county. Kate Ryan was injured—possibly fatally injured —on your premises by a machine in your ownership by a man in your employ. Making a few grand gestures about American surgeons, friends of yours no doubt who'll say that her spine was broken always . . . that's not going to change the mind of the courts of law."

"Ah Fergus, will you stop and think? Who's talking about courts of law? We're talking about making Kate better."

"*I'm* talking about courts of law, district courts, circuit courts, the High Court, the Supreme Court. Don't worry, O'Neill, this time you're not getting away with it. This time you won't smile your way out of ruining people's lives."

They had calmed him, other people had. Patrick had walked away knowing that his presence was inflaming Fergus Slattery more every second.

Patrick wondered if Slattery was sweet on Mrs. Ryan. There was something very passionate and personal in the way he talked. But he realized that in fact it didn't matter whether Fergus Slattery was in love with Kate Ryan or not, what mattered was that he held Patrick totally responsible for the accident. And so might a lot of other people.

Marian Johnson was at eleven o'clock mass. She had tried on her three hats and examined herself with distaste in all of them. They were aging, every single one of them. She looked like a middle-aged frump.

But then she didn't want to wear a headscarf. People like Marian Johnson always wore hats, it said something about who you were to wear a hat at mass.

She had driven quickly to the church and looked in the mirror of her car without pleasure. She saw Patrick and Grace, and thank heavens there was no sign of that foreign-looking American woman who had arrived a few days ago. She had heard some very unsettling stories about Patrick being discovered in the same room as this Mrs. Fine when they were searching for him after the accident.

But that couldn't be so. Anyway she would be here at mass with him if she were a close friend of any kind.

She had hardly spoken to Patrick since Kate Ryan's accident. He was so preoccupied and either on the phone to America or over in the hospital as if it were his fault.

Heavens, everyone was saying that he hadn't a thing to blame himself for. It wasn't his fault if that woman didn't know what dangers and hazards there were there. Living right across the river from them. It was terrible for her of course, and all those children.

Marian's eye fell on them in a row: the solemn dark-eyed twins who were such friends of Grace O'Neill, and two scruffy little boys with spiky hair.

She heard Canon Moran's reed-thin voice pipe on about happy death or speedy recovery. The man must be getting senile. How could you recover from a broken spine speedily, for heaven's sake? Then she saw Dara taking the smaller scruffy boy by the hand and leading him out of the church.

With his other hand rolled into a fist and stuck into his eye, the child was roaring.

"He said happy death, Mammy's not going to have a happy death; they said she was all right. They *said* she was all right."

Kate struggled during the night. She was very agitated and wouldn't be comforted.

"Shush shush now. I'm here, there's nothing to worry about," the night nurse soothed.

"There's everything to worry about." Kate was suddenly clear and rational. "I can't stay here, I have to go home. They'll never manage."

"Of course they'll manage, they're managing fine, isn't that what your husband has been saying to you every day for a week?"

"A *week*? I don't believe it."

"Don't think about it now, try to rest."

"It can't be a week," Kate Ryan said, and her over-bright eyes closed heavily as she went back to something that was neither sleep nor complete unconsciousness. She had been there for a time that she couldn't work out. Every time things cleared people told her some different time scale.

Her breathing was heavy and jerky.

The night nurse took her pulse and marveled at the resilience of the human body. To be able to survive those injuries. To be able to lie still while people worked out just how bad those injuries were.

They were managing in a sort of a way. Often it was the well-meant curiosity and concern that was the hardest to take. People came with stories of bone setters who had made the crippled walk, with details of saints who had interceded with God in startling ways and with herbal cures which had been known in these parts for years and never once known to fail.

People came with kind worried faces saying that Kate should be kept still for six months or that she should be on her feet now before the paralysis had time to set in, or that she should have hot seaweed baths.

The support of a small community had its good side and its wearying side. Nobody could be offended, nobody could be ignored. And it didn't have the advantage of taking their minds off things. Everyone was talking about the same thing. How to get Kate Ryan cured and back in their midst.

Jack Coyne was the last person John wanted to see come into the pub.

"It's all right, don't stand up. I'm not here socializing."

"Sorry, Jack, what can I get you? It *is* a public house; I have to try and keep things normal for everyone's sake."

"No you don't, things are *not* normal. You've contacted a solicitor, I suppose."

"Ah Jack, stop will you . . ."

"Someone has to keep you straight, John. You'll need a big firm of solicitors, Fergus will be the first to tell you that. Don't just go to someone in the town, go right to Dublin. You'll have to in the end."

"It's doctors she needs and a run of luck, not lawyers for Christ's sake."

"She's the businesswoman in this family, she'd be the first to agree with me."

"Please, Jack. I know you mean well. You're not helping."

"I can give you the name of a big firm. I let one of the partners have a car last year, he came down here fishing. Jesus Mary and Joseph, John, O'Neill has to be stopped. He has to be stopped, I tell you, and you'll need the big guns on him. He can't come in here to this parish throwing his weight around, favoring one, ignoring another and in the end getting Kate into this terrible mess."

"It's not the time . . . I beg you."

"If you don't act now it'll be too late, he'll outfox you. There's a lot of people in this place standing up for you, John, don't let them down."

"Mr. Ryan?"

"What is it, Carrie?"

"Mr. Ryan, Jimbo asked me to find out kind of if you were going to be taking Mr. O'Neill to the law for all that's happened to Mrs. Ryan."

"And what on earth business is it of Jimbo's, can I ask?"

"I know, Mr. Ryan. I didn't want to ask you at all, but he said a lot of the fellows who work for Mr. O'Neill were wondering and that I was in a grand position to know, working here and all."

She looked wretched, her long lank hair falling into her eyes. John knew that if Kate were standing here she would hand Carrie a hair clip so that she wouldn't blind herself.

He looked at her helplessly without saying anything.

"I'm very sorry, Mr. Ryan." Her face was scarlet. "It's just that he said it would be easy, but I didn't know what else to do but ask. There'd be no point in my listening at doors."

"No point, Carrie." He was weary. "Tell Jimbo that you think suing

Patrick O'Neill is the last thing on my mind. There's no plans to stop him in his building, their jobs will be all right. That's what it's about."

"I suppose it is," Carrie said miserably.

"Was that Miss Johnson from the Grange leaving in such a hurry?" Mrs. Daly from the Dairy wanted to know.

"It was indeed." Rita Walsh tossed her head. She had just had words with Marian Johnson. Unpleasant words. Rita had said like any human would have said that it was a tragedy about Kate Ryan, wasn't it appalling to think she had been so badly injured only yards from her own home, in a place that used to be green fields and wild brambles.

Marian Johnson had taken this as some kind of criticism of Patrick O'Neill; she had answered hotly that the Ryan woman should have been able to read the dozen notices around the building site.

It had all been very unfortunate; the hair-do had not been a success. Every attempt to organize a parting in Marian's many-crowned head had been interrupted by further defense of the American. Rita had been foolish enough to pass some remark about Patrick being well able to look after himself and if he wasn't, hadn't he that foreign-looking woman, the one he had installed over in the Slieve Sunset, to look after him? This had caused an unexpected reaction, and Marian had left before her hair was finished.

"It's pathetic at her age," Mrs. Daly said disapprovingly. "She's well into her forties, what does she think is going to happen? A big white wedding up in the church with Canon Moran blessing the happy couple? She should have sense."

Mrs. Leonard from the stationer's was coming out from under one of the big heavy chrome hairdryers. She didn't want to miss anything that was going on.

"I was in Conway's this morning—you know, the shop part, not the pub of course." She gave a tinkle of a laugh. "They were saying in there that they hoped there'd be no bad feeling over this. An act of God is all it was."

"Well yes," Rita said unthinkingly. "But an act of God that happened because of that man's machinery and bulldozers. If he hadn't come back and filled the place up with things you'd never expect in the heart of the country . . ."

She felt Mrs. Daly's shoulders tense slightly under the pink cotton cape. She knew that for a second time that morning she was going to find herself in disagreement with a client.

"That's all very well, Rita," Mrs. Daly said, "but it doesn't do to forget what benefits that man is bringing to this place. It would be a pity if people were to go around saying things carelessly that might drive him out of it. He's in a terrible way, I hear, near to tears over the whole thing, and he's like a child about Mountfern and wanting to be part of it. The smallest thing could blow him away from here like a puff of wind. We'll have to watch what we say."

Rita looked in the mirror and her eyes met Mrs. Daly's eyes, small and round like Mrs. Daly's face, satisfied with life the way it now was since the American had come to breathe hope into the town and to give Daly's Dairy the chance of supplying a large hotel.

"I know what you mean," Rita Walsh said. "It doesn't do to give the wrong impression."

"Exactly." Mrs. Daly wriggled her plump little shoulders and waited for Rita's expert fingers to arrange the finger wave to the best advantage on her forehead.

Dr. White came into the post office with relief. Here at least nobody would expect him to know the ins and outs of Kate Ryan's injuries, the likely chance of her ever being able to walk again.

The door to the back room was open and the doctor saw the big stocky figure of the American at the telephone.

"Well, Sheila," Dr. White said mildly, "I didn't know this was going on. Is it a serious romance or are you just setting up an opposition to the Rosemarie hair salon?"

"Ah, leave poor Rita alone." Sheila Whelan didn't bother denying the reputation of Mrs. Walsh's establishment. Neither did she offer any explanation for the presence of Patrick O'Neill in her sitting room, but she had quietly closed the through door with her foot.

"Can I get you stamps, or are you eligible for the old-age pension suddenly?" she asked.

"God, I feel I could do with the pension. Be like old man Slattery used to be, take my little stool and bag and spend my days eyeball to eyeball with lovely eight-pound—ten-pound, even—pike. Dangle a few little herrings in front of them, that's what a man should do with his days on this earth."

"Never saw the sense of it myself," Sheila Whelan said. "Taking one kind of fish to attract another kind of fish, and not even eating the ones you take out of the river. Still."

"That's it. Still, let people do what they want to. I came in for one thing and one thing only, to avoid running into the canon. I saw him coming up the road, and I fled in here. I can't take another dose of the Lord's will, and the goodness of Our Blessed Lady."

Sheila Whelan smiled. "Come on out of that, you're a very saintly man."

"Yes I am, but it's not the kind of saintly that sees the hand of God and his mother in paralyzing Kate Ryan all in the cause of building a flashy hotel."

"She'd have been paralyzed whether the hotel was going to be flashy or whether they were building a library for cloistered nuns over there."

"You always stand up for him." Dr. White jerked his head toward the door.

"No, that's not so. I don't always stand up for him or always stand up for anyone, but Lord God it's not his fault, is it?"

"I suppose like the rest of the town you're terrified he'll go, and take his money with him."

Sheila was mild. "What do I see of his money? I'm hardly making a fortune from his being here. A lot more work, and certainly revenue for the Department of Posts and Telegraphs. I'm hardly benefiting myself."

"Of course not." Dr. White was ashamed.

"I know what you mean though, Martin. And it's very hard to look at it. The way people look out for themselves. But it's not a thriving place, this. I suppose you'd have to expect it."

"You're too tolerant."

"I'm not. I can't sleep at night thinking of Kate Ryan's injuries, but that doesn't mean I blame that poor man in there. He can't even make a call without a circle of people around him waiting to hear what he's at."

"And hasn't he a phone above in the lodge?"

"A lot of these are calls to the States, it's easier on him to be here. I've shown him how to get through."

"Oh well, that's all right. Business as usual then, or maybe he's onto some smart lawyers over there, fellows that will come over here and say he isn't even in the remotest way responsible for what happened."

"That is very unjust and very unlike you, Martin White."

The doctor looked at her, startled. Perhaps he had gone too far. He waited to see if she would explain why it was so unfair. But Sheila Whelan said nothing. It wasn't up to her to explain that Patrick O'Neill was on the phone to America trying to get a particular specialist to come over from America and examine Kate Ryan.

He had been on the telephone all day trying to get the right people. His phone bill would be staggering.

Patrick said he didn't care how offended anyone was, he was flying the specialist from New York and he would be here on Monday. No, he didn't care whose toes were being stepped on, in a case of life or death, in a case of paralysis he would presume that medical men and women would be large enough and sufficiently generous-spirited to realize that the patient came first. No aspersions were being cast, no offense should be taken.

He knew that the New York man would probably confirm everything that was being done here, so where was the harm, where was the insult?

The hospital, which had been horrified to hear of outsiders, succumbed as Patrick had known they would.

He couldn't bear to think they might bungle it, move her when she shouldn't be moved, or leave her in a country hospital when she should be at the remedial center in Dublin. Only when he heard an independent and expert view from a man he had chosen and paid would Patrick believe that everything possible was being done.

The whole thing had an air of unreality to it. He thanked God that he hadn't broached the matter of the entrance to them; if he had spoken of it then he would always have felt sure that Kate's accident was in some way connected.

One night John found the twins asleep on the window seat.

Before he woke them he made three mugs of hot chocolate, and they drank them together as the summer moon shone down on the river and the building site.

"You're very good the way you manage, but you'll have to get some proper sleep, not with crooked necks and cramps here on the window." His voice was gentle.

"Everything's different," Michael said.

"I know, son."

There was a long silence.

"Do you think . . ." Dara began.

"I don't know. I hope so, but I really don't know."

A little later he took their empty mugs and left them on the chest of drawers under the Sacred Heart lamp and saw the twins off to bed.

Dara had wanted to have Grace O'Neill to stay. She said it would be lovely to have someone to talk to at night.

John Ryan had hated saying no, but he felt it would be wrong in some way. He felt that until things were sorted out, O'Neill's child shouldn't really sleep under their roof.

Twelve

*K*ate stirred in the hospital.

"Mrs. Ryan, you're fine. Fine. Don't move too much."

"Nurse, is my husband here?"

"He's been here all morning, he stepped out for a smoke. Will I get him?"

"No, send him home."

"He doesn't want to go home, he wants to be here with you."

"He has no business wanting that, he's got a business to run. How will he keep it if he's here?"

Kate was fretful and worried. Sometimes it was clear to her that she had cracked her spine and broken several vertebrae, sometimes nothing was clear. There were bits when she wanted to cry and cry it all out of her and then she knew she would feel fine, she could get off this ridiculous table she was on and tear out these tubes and go home. There were other bits when she thought she would never move again. It wasn't clear to her what happened.

Sometimes she would ask. But she would drift off before the explanation.

John had peeped through the circle of glass in the door and seen that Kate was awake. He had stubbed out his cigarette and come in eagerly.

"What time is it?" she asked.

"It's midday, love, I just heard the angelus."

"Then what are you doing here?"

"What?"

"The pub opens in half an hour, John, who's going to open it?"

"Not today, love, they all know I'm here with you."

"They won't know that till they get to the door and find the place closed. John, have sense. Please. Please don't leave me to make all the decisions, even though I'm lying here with a broken back. For God's sake do something on your own initiative. Just once."

The nurse had called for assistance and the houseman came in. Kate was thrashing around and the injection was swift in coming.

John stood rooted to the spot.

Kate's face was calm again as if in a normal peaceful sleep.

"I don't know what to do," he said to the young nurse pitifully.

"I think you should go home, Mr. Ryan, she's had a very strong sedative now, she won't be able to talk for a while."

"But what would I do at home?"

"I don't know, maybe you could open the pub as she said."

John Ryan turned and went out with a heavy tread.

Sitting outside in a hired car was Paudie Doyle, the younger brother of Brian. He was eighteen and had a drivers license. Patrick O'Neill had hired him with the car and said that he was to drive the Ryan family backward and forward from the hospital to Mountfern—a hundred times a day if needs be. And to be there always at their beck and call.

He was a kind young fellow and he couldn't bear to see the look of pain on John's face.

"In about twenty-five minutes the pubs will be open, or maybe you might know someone who'd open early for you. Would that be nice? A drop of brandy maybe?"

"Thanks, Paudie. Drive me home to my own place like a good lad. I've got to open up, got a business to run, you know."

"Of course you do, I thought you'd have someone else doing that. They would you know, people are very willing to do anything to help. You know they are."

"I know," said John dully. "I just don't seem to be able to think of anything they could do."

Kate had been right of course, there were plenty of people anxious to know how she was and to give the Ryans their custom.

Grace wanted to know was it all right if she stayed to lunch.

"Certainly." John was pleased that the twins would have company. He sent her on into the kitchen behind and concentrated on serving. Patrick sat on a stool and asked about everything, and when Fergus came in, he sat on the stool beside the American.

"And what did the injection do, did she go out at once or did it take time?" Patrick asked.

"Why don't you ask him to put a bulletin up on the door as they do in Buckingham Palace?" Fergus asked suddenly.

Patrick looked at him, startled.

"There are fourteen people in this public house needing pints, half ones, glasses of whiskey, bottles of minerals opened for them. Would you not have the common sense to let the man get on with it instead of interrogating him about every twist and turn of his unfortunate wife."

"Fergus." John was shocked.

"I mean it, John, you get on with serving while you still have a pub to serve in." Fergus had a voice very near tears.

"He's right, of course." Patrick stood up. "I'll call back to ask about Kate when you're not busy, John." In four steps he was out the door.

John Ryan was very upset.

"Ah, Fergus, what did you have to go and do that for? Now I'll have to go after him. He's been so good to us, Fergus, you have no idea. He has cars for us everywhere, we'd never be able to get in and out to the hospital, and he's paying for a specialist to come from America, someone who actually treated the Kennedys coming the whole way to look at Kate. What did you have to go and insult him for? He was only being interested and asking."

"*I'm* interested but I want you to keep your business," Fergus hissed, indicating a small group at the other end of the counter needing refills. "And I could drive you in to see Kate, I could give you my car, for God's sake. He's not the only one who wants to help."

"But that's it. He *does* want to help. Don't be on at him like you were up in the hospital. It only makes things harder." John was still looking at the door wondering if he should run after Patrick.

"No, you're right." And Fergus swung off the stool to stride out also—leaving John Ryan without two customers he realized as he walked sadly along River Road and saw the figure of Patrick O'Neill walking sadly among the machinery and small walls of his building site on the other side of the river.

Kerry O'Neill had bought a get-well card in Leonard's. He had chosen it carefully. Not a funny one, and not a mournful one either, full of flowers and verses about Good Friendship and Health.

Tommy Leonard thought that Kerry was very considerate to put so much thought into it. A lot of people just bought the first thing or the cheapest thing they saw.

Kerry's father didn't share this view. He thought Kerry was cold and distant about the accident, he felt there was something a little calculating about finding a meaningless printed card and signing it ". . . from all your friends in Mountfern, and Kerry O'Neill." But then very little that Kerry did or said pleased Patrick these days. The boy seemed to be entirely wrapped up in himself. There was no room for anyone else in his life.

The chicken was boiled a long time now. Carrie looked at it anxiously—it was beginning to break up in the pot. Usually the mistress came out and made a white sauce at this stage; she used to come like a whirlwind into the kitchen. Up to the stove and pound pound pound in a small saucepan, flinging in the milk, the butter and the flour at random, it seemed. The instructions were given to Carrie like a series of short and rapid machine guns being fired. Kate Ryan used to speak firmly but kindly:

"Potatoes drained and into the dish, now. Thanks, Carrie, and plates warming, there's a good girl. Thanks, Carrie. Pass me the carving knife and fork. Right, call Michael, it's his turn to serve today." It used to go like clockwork. But today nothing was right. Carrie didn't have enough hands. The children were all sitting inside like lords and ladies waiting to be served, the master was in the pub where it seemed half the parish had come up to drink like pigs at a trough.

Carrie was flustered and confused. When she put the chicken down it started to go cold out of the pot so she put it back in again while she got out the potatoes, then the chicken seemed to have broken into fragments with all the shifting it about.

Since the mistress wasn't here to criticize her, she thought she'd risk taking the potatoes to the table in the big black pot. She ran with it because it was so heavy. She hadn't known that the young O'Neill child was sitting at the table inside. She began to run out again but the pot slipped. She banged it on the table and there was a noise, a sizzling noise. The pot had burned a huge weal into the table.

Carrie looked at it, her face as aghast as the five children's faces that looked first at the burning table and then at her.

She couldn't bear it anymore. There was nobody to advise her. Carrie ran from the room in tears.

John heard a commotion and excused himself from the bar.

In the breakfast room the children were trying to scrape the burn marks from the table. They looked up guiltily.

"Well God, that's a nice way to behave," he said, looking from one to another to see who was the culprit.

"Nobody here was responsible, Mr. Ryan." The clear voice of the little American Grace was coupled with a dimpling smile.

She was like a little blonde angel interceding for frailer folk. But he knew without her having to tell tales that poor Carrie had done it again.

In the kitchen things were worse than he had expected. The chicken looked more like chicken soup than any kind of boiled fowl. The cabbage was over-cooked and smelling badly in its saucepan. A pot of something else that might have been a milk pudding had burned dry. Wearily he took the burning saucepan from the stove and looked glumly at the scene.

There was no sign of Carrie but he thought he saw a figure in the back yard near the old pump, sobbing into her apron.

Dara was beside him. "Try to pick the best bits out of the chicken, Dara, and give everybody two potatoes. Leave the table, we'll see to it later."

"What about the cabbage?"

"Give it to the hens when it cools down."

"And the rest of the chicken, all these stringy bits?"

"It would hardly be tactful to give that to the hens, if you see what I mean."

Dara giggled. "You're very funny, Daddy," she said approvingly.

"Wouldn't I need to be?" said John Ryan.

"It's all hopeless, Father," Grace said. "There's this maid and she brought the pot of potatoes to the table and burned the table top and then she ran out and cried, and it's all just hopeless."

"What do they need?" Patrick asked.

Grace was thoughtful. "I think they just need proper help, you know, someone efficient like Miss Hayes."

"Yes, yes."

"Well, will you get them someone?"

"I think not, Grace. I think we might do more harm than good. We wouldn't know who to send in, we could pick the wrong person."

"Marian should know, she runs a hotel."

"I don't want to get Marian involved."

"She has a crush on you," Grace said.

"Don't be silly."

"You know it too. Don't you like her?"

"She's fine, but don't give me this silly talk about crushes. That's teenage stuff, not old men and old ladies."

"So we won't get them a maid? The Ryans I mean."

"No, there are times when I think you have to stand back a bit."

Grace said she wanted to help. Please, she didn't *mind* things being untidy, or whatever they were trying to keep from her because she was a guest. Couldn't she just join in like the family?

Michael and Dara found things for her to do. She took Leopold for his walk, she picked vegetables, she brought the washing in from the line.

She encouraged them to go out to play. They hadn't been allowed to visit their mother in the intensive-care ward but Grace said she was sure Mrs. Ryan wouldn't want them sitting around the house being gloomy. She'd want to think of them swimming and doing normal things. Little by little they agreed, but there was always such confusion at home it was easier not to go out at all.

"I never knew running a house was like this," Dara wailed.

"I don't know what anyone gets married for," Michael said with feeling.

"But it needn't be like this, I suppose." Grace meant if you had enough money to pay someone to do it properly.

Like Miss Hayes was being paid to keep things right in the lodge. There was always bread in the bread bin, cake in the cake tin. There were clean towels and sheets. Why were things so confused in the Ryans' household?

"We used to think that we'd live in Fernscourt once," Michael said unexpectedly. "Dara and I had a section of it all planned. And we'd have no proper mealtimes or bedtimes, or sheets or cleaning shoes . . . I think it would have worked."

He sounded very wistful.

Grace patted his hand. "It's terrible for you being the eldest," she said.

"Yes, well, joint eldest," Michael said, struggling to be fair.

"But it's harder on boys, I remember—" She stopped suddenly.

"What?" The twins spoke together.

"Nothing."

"Go on, Grace, what do you remember?" Dara was insistent.

"I don't want to remember it, I can't remember it."

"Please, Grace." Michael had a better way with him, obviously.

"Okay, the reason I didn't want to finish it was because . . . well, I remember when my mother was ill, Kerry said it was harder being a boy because you wanted to cry just as much as a girl wanted to cry but the world didn't let you cry, you had to pretend somehow that it didn't matter so much to you. Kerry said that was the hardest bit because he couldn't show Mother how much he loved her by crying with her."

The twins were silent.

Grace looked apologetic. "So now, so you see why I didn't want to finish it, I didn't want to talk about my mother who *did* die in the same breath as talking about your mother who is *not* going to die. Do you see?"

Dara gave her a great hug and Michael squeezed her hand.

Grace lost her troubled look and smiled with them both. "Let's finish these goddamned apples and then we'll go for a swim."

They peeled and cored the apples in the gloomy knowledge that somehow Carrie would make a brown unappetizing mess from all their hard work.

Mrs. Whelan was quiet and to the point, it would be doing everyone a great favor if John could see his way to providing a busy life and home for her cousin Mary Donnelly. There was no need to go into details but the girl had a bit of a crisis in her private life and the last thing she needed was to be left alone brooding. She was extremely capable, she would not want a large salary—just a change for the few weeks, months, whatever it was until Kate was home.

John was never so relieved. He had been shattered by the events of the day: Kate wrestling with her pain and shouting at him that he couldn't take the initiative, ever; Fergus and Patrick almost coming to blows and then both walking out of the pub; Carrie having retired to bed in hysterics and the kitchen looking as if a bomb had hit it. Opening time in another half an hour. He was never so relieved as to hear of this efficient Mary Donnelly who could come on the bus in two days if called for. Where would she sleep?

Mrs. Whelan had thought of that too. There was an outhouse at the back and it didn't need a great deal of work. They could get a couple of men off the site to fix it up, run an electric wire through it, a coat of paint.

There would be plenty of beds up in the Grange and Marian Johnson had offered any kind of help, a small second-hand bed would be great.

John didn't know if he could accept all this. Sheila was adamant that he should.

"When something awful happens people feel helpless, the one thing they want to do is to be of assistance. Let them help, John, it will make them feel much better if nothing else."

John held her hand gratefully. Only this morning he had been thinking, when young Paudie Doyle had said that people wanted to help, that he didn't know what to ask them. And now Mrs. Whelan was making it possible.

Once she got the green light from John, Sheila went to Brian Doyle.

"You said you wondered what you could do," she began.

And it was done in a trice. Men and materials were arranged. The old outhouse was stripped of its rubble, broken wood and boxes were carted away. Other things which most certainly were rubbish but should not be thrown out without reference to Kate were transferred into an even older outhouse which was around at one side of the pub. They were stacked neatly there waiting the verdict of the mistress on her return.

The whitewash on the walls was done three times to make sure it looked presentable.

The new house became the focal point for all the children.

Jacinta and Liam White were back from their Irish College, even more at loggerheads with each other than usual and according to themselves still unable to speak a word of Irish.

Liam said that Jacinta had been tiresome and in love with the boy who taught dancing. Jacinta said that Liam had been embarrassing and was caught smoking first and then caught being sick later as a result of the earlier smoking. They told the twins that their father had said Mrs. Ryan was most definitely not going to die, but he said that nobody knew when she'd be home. They had asked him would it be days or months or years and he still couldn't say.

"I suppose it must be months anyway; this is why we're doing the place up," Dara said gloomily.

Maggie Daly wanted a more cheerful view. "Listen, it could be tomorrow for all we know, but she'll still need someone to help her. Didn't you say yourself it's non stop?"

Dara brightened. "That's what it is, non stop. As soon as one meal's finished and washed up it's time for the next. People eat far too much, you know."

Maggie burst out laughing.

Brian Doyle who had come to supervise, gave them a shout. "If you two girls have come to be entertained by all this and to giggle would you think of putting on a kettle and getting some tea for these men here? All right?"

This reduced Maggie and Dara to further hysterics.

"Non stop, a woman's work, non bloody stop," Dara said as they headed for the kitchen.

"Dara, you'd better mind your language, your mother'd make a swipe at you if she heard you saying bloody," said Carrie, shocked.

Dara paused a moment thinking how great it would be to have Mam running around the place like she used to and able to make a swipe at anyone instead of lying on her back in the hospital.

Grace told Marian Johnson about the new room and she sent down a bed from the Grange. Fergus Slattery brought a wardrobe he said he didn't need. He drove it up in his car and carried it in himself. Maggie's mother sent Charlie with a small table, a blue cloth and a statue of Our Lady with a little blue glass that held a night light which you could put in front of the statue. The Leonards sent a rug for the floor and a brand-new unopened pad of writing paper and envelopes, in case the new lady wanted to write home. Loretto Quinn gave a chair. The Williamses said they had a roll of linoleum which they had bought by mistake and the shop wouldn't take it back; they had been hoping to hear of a place that might need it.

John looked in from time to time and said that as far as he could see it was better by far than any other room in Ryan's Licensed Premises and private house.

When Mary Donnelly got off the bus on Tuesday her new home was ready for her.

She was given a short briefing by Mrs. Whelan in the post office and then she walked purposefully down River Road carrying her small grip bag. She had left her big case with Sheila Whelan so that the family would not realize how long she was coming to stay.

She knew the most important place to head for, and went straight to the kitchen.

"I'm Mary," she said to Carrie. "It must have been an awful shock for you and nobody telling you what's expected and what's not."

Carrie looked at her gratefully. "That's just it, Miss," she said. "If only I knew what they all want . . ."

"We'll have to sort it out," Mary Donnelly said, hanging up her coat on the back of the door.

"Why didn't you come to me, Sheila? I'd have gotten a better job done, anything you wanted," Patrick said.

"I thought it was better not to deal with you directly." Her voice was bland.

"Whyever not?" But he knew. He knew exactly why.

"Better let others do it, I thought."

"I feel responsible, yes, that Kate hurt herself on my property, but I don't feel guilty about it, for Christ's sake."

"Of course not."

"And everyone else must feel the same. They do, don't they?"

"Not really. People take sides easily in a thing like this. For one reason or another."

"I thought it was that crackpot attorney that was the only one, and that he was upset because he's got the hots for her."

"Really!"

"No, sorry, I shouldn't have said that, but you know . . ."

"I don't know, and you should not have said it, and it is *not* true."

"Sheila, don't turn against me, you were the first person who welcomed me to this place, don't turn on me."

She patted his hand. "Don't be so dramatic," she said. "I'm just marking your card a little like I did at the start, and you were glad then. Maybe I've stepped over the limit."

"Do they really think it's my fault?"

"Some of them do."

"But it's so unfair," he cried out.

"Who said life was fair?"

He remembered her own personal circumstances and nodded in silence.

"You see . . ." she began.

"Yes?"

"You see, logical or illogical, this is what they think. If you had never come here, there would have been no machines and no bulldozer on that site. None of this would ever have happened."

"If I hadn't come here, everything would have been all right?" he asked quietly.

"Well, for the Ryans it would," Sheila said simply.

Dr. White didn't like the American. It had nothing to do with his importing a Yank specialist. That rather pleased White because it got up the noses of the hospital consultants, always an arrogant bunch.

But the American felt that money or business was the universal answer.

Once he had commented that Dr. White's practice would expand considerably when the hotel was built.

"I hope that your guests will have scant need of my professional services. It would spoil their holidays," Dr. White had said politely.

"Yes, but when they do get a bellyache they'll be people of substance, you can charge them properly."

"I'll charge them what I charge everyone, I won't fleece sick people just because they happen to be rich and American," Dr. White had said haughtily.

He knew Patrick called him a stuffed shirt.

The doctor was surprised to see him calling at the office.

"Can you give me something to make me sleep, knock me out for eight hours at a time?" Patrick asked.

"No. Not just like that I can't."

"What do you want, my life story?"

"Why didn't you ask that Yank doctor who treated the entire Kennedy family? He could have given you something."

"Goddammit man, he's an orthopedic surgeon." Patrick's annoyance was so great that Dr. White smiled, and the American smiled too.

"Sorry, I'm very edgy, a proof of lack of sleep."

"Tension, I suppose. Strain. Do you have a prescription already?"

"Never needed them in my life, thought they were the tool of a weak man. But if you're lame you use a walking stick. I guess I'm lame as regards sleep."

"Fine, whatever you say."

"You'll give them to me?"

"Mr. O'Neill, you are a grown-up man, you could buy and sell everyone in this town and probably will. Who am I to deny you a prescription for two weeks of non-addictive sleeping pills?"

"What do you mean, buy and sell?"

"It's an expression, Mr. O'Neill. If you meet a bright child, you say, 'That boy would buy and sell you.' It's a term of high praise."

"Why are you mocking me, Doctor?"

"I beg you not to think that. Will two weeks be sufficient? One a night, warm milk. Keep warm, don't try to go to sleep. It will come, I assure you, with these."

He signed his name with a flourish and handed Patrick the small piece of paper.

"Do you think I'm responsible for Kate Ryan's accident?"

"No, of course not."

"You don't?"

"No, how could you be? Weren't you miles away, they say, at the time?"

"But morally responsible?"

"I suppose we could argue that since no man is an island, we are all involved in everyone's life and death and success or injury. No more than that."

"I'm so sorry it happened, if you knew."

"I know. Most people do know. Aren't you moving heaven and earth to get her better?" The doctor's voice sounded kind.

"But she's not going to get better, that's what they say."

"They say it will be long."

"They say she'll never walk again. Your doctors say that, my doctor says that."

"They say long useful life."

"In a fucking wheelchair."

"Alive not dead."

"It's like talking to the priests talking to you, Dr. White."

"I hope you use better language talking to the priests."

"I hope so, I'm sure I forget sometimes."

"Listen, it was great that your man from Cape Cod or wherever said they were doing things right in the hospital. Now everyone's happy."

"Up to a point," Patrick said.

"Sure, I know, but if you see as much difficult birth, hard life and rotten death as I do you'd realize that a wheelchair isn't the end of the world."

"No," said Patrick. "It's not. Thank you, Doctor. Your bill?"

"Forget it."

"I can't do that."

"I don't see why not. I only wrote my name."

"It has a price, your years of training, remember?"

"No, it has no price if I wish it to have none. Believe me, there are things without a price on them."

"And you believe me too, Dr. White." Patrick's eyes blazed with anger. "I know there are things that have no price. If I was out for a return on my money do you think I would be building this folly here? That's what my manager back in the States calls it, O'Neill's Folly. There's no price on this that anyone could recognize. It's an act of love. Of faith. It's not the act of a businessman who wants to make a quick buck, or indeed any bucks for a very long time."

Dr. White shook his head sadly and said nothing.

"Well, go on, say it whatever it is?"

"But of *course* there's a price. The price is your wish to be home, and to be a person of importance in these parts where your grandfather came from, not just one of a few million Irish in America. That's what you want—isn't it?—much more than money. I was just saying there are some people who want nothing or very little."

"Like the Ryans," Patrick said sadly. "They wanted very little indeed, and look at what they have now."

"It will be better for you now that you've got someone to look after things," Grace said.

"She looks a bit fierce," Dara complained.

"It doesn't matter, she's going to run things, that's what it's about."

Grace was always so sunny. Dara wondered did she ever have great times of doubt and worry? Was it only Dara? Maybe if you were as beautiful as Grace was, there was no need to worry about things. Everyone loved you.

"Are things okay at your home now? You remember you asked me not to talk about that row ages ago between your father and Kerry, so I didn't, I didn't even think about it until now . . ."

Grace was full of understanding. "I know you didn't tell anyone. You're a great friend."

They were sitting in Dara's bedroom. Grace got up to walk about; she seemed restless.

"No, things are not great at home. But I don't know whether that's because of Kerry and Father, or because of Father being so worried about everything, your mother and all that."

She looked terribly young somehow. Those curls could make her look like a toddler sometimes, otherwise they made her like a film star.

"Do they fight?"

"No, that's just it, they hardly talk at all. They sort of talk through me, if I weren't there I think not a word would be said."

"It's hard to believe that with Kerry, he's so nice and such fun."

Dara was wistful for those carefree days which seemed so long ago now. Kerry was one of the few people within miles who had not come to the pub to say how sorry he was, but perhaps he had not been able to think of anything to say.

"He's definitely no fun with Father," Grace said. Then she deliberately forced herself into a good humor again. "But I think it will all blow over, you know, this Mrs. Fine. I think Kerry was very uptight that she came to Ireland. You know, in case she and Father . . . Well, I told you."

"Yes, but it's not true, is it?"

"No, not true at all." Grace was her sunny self again. "No, she's staying miles away and she doesn't see Father at all, it was all a false alarm. Kerry must realize that now, and things will be back to normal again."

Maggie Daly wished that her mother wouldn't see things in such black and white ways. Her mother had this fear now that if everyone made too much of Mrs. Ryan's accident it would look as if they were criticizing all the progress Mr. O'Neill brought to Mountfern. This was the biggest and best thing that had ever happened to their town and they must be sure that no foolish sentimentality was allowed to intrude.

Whenever Maggie said she was going up to Ryan's, her mother said that she should watch her step and not make herself into a camp follower on one side or the other. Yet when Grace asked Maggie to come to the lodge Mrs. Daly was delighted. She spent ages hunting for a nice white collar to sew on Maggie's dress and gave her a cream cake free to present to Miss Hayes with her compliments.

Mrs. Daly had not said anything about it being camp following to go to tea at the lodge.

Judy Byrne was delighted to see Patrick O'Neill at her door.

"This is a professional call, and I must ask you to keep it very much to yourself," he said.

"Certainly." Judy's eyes sparkled with interest and anticipation.

"We don't have the same medical schemes in the States as here. Can you tell me how you work? Are you attached to the hospital?"

"Only in a part-time capacity. Sometimes I do a day here and there when some of their staff are away. And I cover for people's holidays."

"But mainly you are in private practice, is that it?"

"Yes." Judy wondered where this was leading.

"But you don't have a clinic, an office here. Is your work mainly done at people's homes?"

"I do go to people's homes, or I can go to Dr. White's office if I am needed. If it's a matter of teaching people exercises or movements they can come here." She looked defensively around her small sitting room with its desk and her shelf of text books. She didn't like him dismissing it so casually.

"And who pays you?"

"I beg your pardon?"

Judy's eyes were round in disbelief.

"I am sorry. I did say it was a business call. I must learn to speak less crassly." The famous O'Neill smile was there now. Lines radiating out from his eyes, head on one side, half contrite, half mischievous. It was the little-boy look that Patrick O'Neill had been wearing for so many years he did not even realize when it was on his face. Not until he saw Judy smiling back. Then he pressed on.

"You see, I'm just a poor hick from the States, I don't understand the way things work here. The hospital is free . . . for one thing. I didn't know that."

"Well, the county hospital is free if you go through the dispensary doctor, certainly," Judy said. "If you are a person of means then of course you would go to the nuns in the nursing home, or perhaps to one of the private rooms that the consultants have for their patients in the hospital." She thought she was explaining what he wanted to know clearly but she couldn't see the drift of his conversation.

"Yes, I see that now." Patrick had endless patience.

He knew the system now. Kate was in intensive care, when she left it she would go to a ward. Unless he got her a private room. This he had arranged to do. But she would also need physiotherapy both in the hospital and when she returned home. This was the knotty problem he had come to discuss with Judy and had wrongly thought that it could be done crisply and quickly if he designated it a business call. He must learn—he would learn eventually—that in Mountfern the dividing line between business and socializing was a minefield.

"And in your own case?" he tried delicately. "Are you reimbursed by hospital, patient, or is there someone else like the doctor that one goes through?"

He thought that if he said "reimbursed" she might find it less offensive than using the word "paid."

Finally, like drawing teeth, Patrick O'Neill extracted the information he needed.

Judy Byrne was indeed a private physiotherapist. She did not make what anyone could call a living wage by her work. She had come back to live in Mountfern when her mother was elderly. Her mother had died leaving her this small attractive house, a car and a small undisclosed sum of money in the bank.

It was possible for Judy Byrne to live comfortably on the fairly limited amount of work that came her way through Dr. White, through part-time work in the hospital, and anything else that consultants recommended her for.

She was fully qualified; she would be ideally placed to give Kate Ryan the physiotherapy she would need. Her rates were, to Patrick, very reasonable, and he thought that others would think so too. But he reminded himself yet again how different were his circumstances from anyone else's in Mountfern.

If he were to book Judy Byrne to come three times a week to Kate Ryan on her return, surely it would suit everyone? Kate, Judy and himself. But perhaps it would humiliate everyone and be the worst thing to do.

"You're doing very well, Mrs. Ryan," the nurse said.

"Did they tell you it was going to be like this?" Kate asked wearily.

"Like what, Mrs. Ryan?"

"Like wiping bottoms and pulling soiled sheets out from under people?" Kate said.

"That's only a small part of it, the main part of it is people getting better."

"It's not much better if I can't decide when to go to the lavatory. It's not better if I'm going to relieve myself over anyone and everyone who comes near me."

"Tut tut, it's not like that."

"It *is* like that, Nurse, for God's sake, that's the second time this morning. If I had ten seconds' warning I'd shout for you, but it just comes out."

"It doesn't matter to anyone but you."

"I hope it will *always* matter to me; I don't want to get to a stage where I expect people to wipe up after me."

"I've told you it won't always be like this."

"But when? When will it get better? Last week you said it would be better this week. The week before you said it would be better last week."

"If you knew how well you're doing, Mrs. Ryan, you'd be pleased instead of worrying about things that honestly don't worry us. You'd be rejoicing like we are that you've made so much progress."

"That's a load of nonsense and you know it, Nurse."

"Now Mrs. Ryan, please."

"What's your name, Nurse?"

"Geraldine."

"Right, Geraldine, and you call me Kate. We're obviously going to be together for years and years, let's not have any formalities."

"It's not going to be years and years, Mrs. . . . er, Kate."

"Will I be home by Christmas? Answer me that."

"I can't. I don't know."

"It's only July and you don't know if I'll be home by Christmas. Oh God, oh God, what am I going to do?" Kate began a low moan.

"I only said I don't know. I'm only a nurse, I'm not a doctor or a surgeon."

"Stop apologizing for yourself. What do you mean *only* a nurse?"
Geraldine grinned.

"Stop laughing at me," Kate snapped.

"You're marvelous, no wonder they're all mad about you back there in Mountfern," the girl said.

"They're not mad about me, they've forgotten me."

"Well they don't sound as if they have, we get a ton of requests from people wanting to see you, but we say only the family."

"Requests. Who in the name of God would want to come and see someone who might have diarrhea all over the bed in front of them?"

"There's a Mr. Slattery telephones two or three times a day, a Mr. O'Neill telephones every day over and over, and others—Coynes, Walshes, Quinns, Dalys—and there's a foreign woman called twice to see you, she was the one who left the plant."

"I don't know anyone foreign, she can't have been for me."

"Mrs. Fine."

"No."

"Well I'll check again, she thinks she knows you—small dark American but foreign at the same time."

Something stirred. But the events of the day she had met Rachel Fine were still blurred. It was the day John had his poem published, so he had told her. And the day that Patrick O'Neill had come into the bar urgently saying he wanted a consultation with the pair of them. John had told her that too but she couldn't remember it. Was there a Mrs. Fine? It seemed familiar and the memory was good rather than bad.

"If she comes back I'll see that Mrs. Fine," Kate said.

"And what about these other men—the Slattery man and the O'Neill man?"

"No. Not yet. I'd cry with one and I might fight with the other."

"Right. That's understood. Now."

"Oh God," Kate said. "I know what 'Now' means."

Now meant more of the same. The endless round. Changing her position in the bed every four hours to avoid the bed sores that she felt sure were going to come anyway, so great was the pressure where she touched the bedclothes under her. Now meant the physiotherapy. So far she only had to lie there but they told her that soon she would be taking part herself and strengthening her own muscles.

There were the hopeless attempts to make her control her bladder and her bowels. It was useless trying to go at certain times, the body didn't work like that. It betrayed you. There was the painful business of putting in the catheter and taking it out. Lord, had she ever valued the whole business of being able to run into a bathroom and close the door behind you with no agony and pulling of flesh?

Had she ever given one minute of thought or sympathy to all the people she heard having records played for them on Hospital Requests? People having catheters and bedsores and drips all the time. Did they ever learn to accept it as normal? Would Kate ever learn?

Thirteen

On the day that Mary Donnelly arrived in Ryan's, Leopold got ready to give her one of his traditional welcomes. He cowered against the wall shivering from his large misshapen head to his long awkward-looking tail. Then he rolled his eyes, flinched and gave a whimper of terror.

"Oh for goodness sake dog, will you stop that?" Mary Donnelly said to him firmly.

Leopold looked at her doubtfully. Usually he got a different reaction: people said, "Poor dog," "Nice dog," or "What has him so frightened?" There was nothing of this in the new woman's tone.

"I saw you, dog, not half an hour ago up in the main street of this town and you had a bone the size of a hurling stick."

Leopold hung his head as if he had been discovered.

"Now I'm not against that, it's good that a butcher gives a bone to a dog instead of burning it, but all I want is you to quit putting on the poor mouth, there's no call for that."

The children stood open-mouthed as Leopold almost nodded in agreement.

"We'll get on fine once we realize that there is no point in either of us feeling sorry for ourselves," she said.

Her eyes moved around the watching group.

"What is this fine animal called?" she asked.

Eddie was the only one with enough breath to deliver the dog's name.

Mary pronounced it several times, rolling it around to see if she liked it. She decided she did.

"Leopold," she said loudly. Just hearing his name was usually enough to set Leopold baying to the moon as if he were being tortured. He began, but stopped in mid yowl.

Mary smiled. "That's better," she said. "Any other animals?"

"Jaffa and Maurice," said Eddie, an unaccustomed spokesman for the family.

"Can I see them?"

Gravely she inspected Maurice in the mudroom and Jaffa on the wall.

On her first day she toured the house, asking the role of this and that.

Everywhere she nodded with instant understanding and convinced them that she knew the place had been run magnificently before the accident. This way they didn't feel they had to keep explaining or apologizing.

When the pub closed the first night she asked John to give her a quick instruction in her pub duties.

"It's not a thing that can be done quickly," John smiled. "A pint must be poured lovingly, slowly. No, a lot of bar work is the complete reverse of speed."

"You may or may not be right," Mary said, "and in the matter of the slowly poured pint, I have to believe you because there can be no other reason why men would sit in a bar and wait interminable lengths for froth to settle. But there are other aspects of the pub business which must be swift. Can you explain the measures to me, and what people call them, naggins and noggins and jorums and the like."

"There'd be a month of explaining in that," John said.

He saw a frown of impatience cross her face. "But we can make a start on it anyway," he added hastily.

Mary Donnelly seemed to settle in immediately. She introduced herself to the local women Loretto and Rita Walsh as the cousin of Mrs. Whelan who had come to help out until Mrs. Ryan was home. Nobody felt threatened by her. She was a small woman in her thirties, with curly brown hair and freckles. She might have been attractive with a little effort, but she wore brown jumpers and skirts and brown laced shoes. Around her neck she wore a gold chain with a cross on it, and she never put on any make-up.

Because she had been a teacher she was able to make everyone listen to her without even raising her voice. The house became much more quiet with Mary Donnelly's arrival. If anyone shrieked for each other as they had been accustomed to do she would walk purposefully over to them and say, "I wonder why you had to raise your voice like that?" It was very effective.

Because she had been a teacher she knew exactly what they should all be doing at school, and prepared a small amount of holiday work for them. This was badly received, and the children appealed to their father for a judgment against it. However, Mary had presented her case so well that they found him firmly on her side.

"She says it's only a matter of half an hour a day. It will keep you well up with your books, she'll correct it like a teacher above in the school. It'll distract you a bit in the mornings not to be thinking about your mother, and best of all your mother will be delighted with you for it."

Mary Donnelly gave most of her attention to Dara. "You'll need it in this world," she said gloomily.

"Why will I need it more than anyone else?" Dara was alarmed.

"What life is there for a woman unless she equips herself and trains herself and gets on? Women have to fight in this world. Better believe it and know it now, and don't let any soft soap about love and marriage get into your soul and start to rot it."

It seemed a bit far fetched as a reason for doing fractions and parsing sentences.

At the start she hadn't wanted Mary Donnelly at all. They could manage, she had said, she was nearly thirteen. It was grown up. In some countries you could be married at that age. But everyone had insisted and it was true that Mary did make things easier.

After the homework, she gave them their jobs like Mam used to. The hen feeding, the box stacking and the pub sweeping went on, and she was just as adamant as Mam was about being home in time for lunch. Then there was the journey in to see Mam in the hospital and the instructions to bring all the news and information. And there were books provided for them to read as they sat in the waiting room while Dad was in with Mam alone.

Mary served the bar for the afternoon. She fixed all the clients with a baleful glare, filled their pints and gave their change, but would be drawn into no conversation. If any of them dared to pass her a compliment she would say that she had no time for fancy talk, which came cheaply to an Irishman. She would ask them cuttingly if they gave such praise to their wives and indeed if they ever favored their wives with an invitation out to share a drink with them. No. No indeed. And they really thought the wives would not want to join them? How very interesting. How fascinating a mind which thought that a wife *liked* being at home sweeping floors, cleaning boots, minding children, cooking, serving and washing up meals. How hysterically funny to think that men assumed women *liked* that sort of thing.

The men in Ryan's took no more notice of her than they did of Leopold cringing and whining by the wall. Mary Donnelly was obviously cracked in the head over some imagined slight or wrong that some man must have done to her in the past. But she poured a pint properly and she was a great help to poor John Ryan and his family in their time of need.

At night Mary Donnelly helped in the bar by washing glasses, joining not at all in the conversation. John gave up trying to make her feel part of the place. Without being actually rude she made it clear that she thought his clientele were the scum of humanity. She would withdraw to the kitchen and tell Carrie that she was setting up a store of trouble by painting and preening herself for the weekly dance, or else attempt to teach Declan and Eddie to darn.

"Why are you teaching the little fellows?" Carrie asked, mystified.

"Because there might be some hope for these as the young men of the next decade if we teach them to be normal and share in women's work," Mary said.

Eddie was quite good at darning as it happened and said he regarded it as a puzzle where you had to fit all the pieces in. He threatened to knock Declan's head off his neck if he ever told anyone at the brothers that they were being taught darning at home.

Mary had no time for Michael. At first Michael was very pleased about this. He considered himself well off to be away from this bossy woman. But as the days went by and she had become part of their lives it was somewhat galling to be dismissed so summarily. He was never asked to clear or serve as he used to do, his role as a shoe polisher was laughed out of the way. Mary said she would prefer to be in charge of the shoes herself so that she would know for certain that they would be done. She didn't like leaving things to a young man to do.

She said the words "young man" as others might say "village drunk" or "known criminal". Sometimes Michael felt that there was no need for him in the home—everyone else had their little jobs to do, only he stood there useless and idle.

He offered to help Dara and Carrie clean some candlesticks. They seemed to be enjoying the Brasso, it got all over their hands and they were laughing companionably. But Mary Donnelly refused him. She was courteous but firm. Thank you, but she would really prefer the job to be done properly without any trick-acting or distraction.

Moodily Michael left the kitchen. Kicking a stone all around the back yard, he was spotted by his father.

"Would you have a moment, son?"

Michael was pleased. His father had a great box of papers out on the table in the breakfast room. Since the accident he hadn't opened any of the research he was meant to be doing on the book for Mr. O'Neill.

"Michael, I have to do something about this, even if it's only tidy it up and let Patrick give it to someone else to finish. He must have his book, that's only fair."

"I suppose he'd wait a bit, with everything." Michael sounded very down.

"Oh of course he'd wait, but that's not the point. I must leave it in some kind of state that another writer—well, that a real writer—could see what I've done. Could you help me here for a minute?"

"What am I to do?"

"Suppose I were to fill this folder with what has already been written . . . not very much of it, I'm afraid. Then this one for under way, and that one we could call 'still to look at.' "

Michael separated the three piles on the table and his father called out which category the pages and the scribbled notes were to go to. In spite of his low form Michael became interested.

"Look at those drawings. Is *that* what it looked like?"

"No, that was a much grander house. It's in the style, though, so we could point out the feature that would have been the same."

"Is that what his hotel is going to look like?"

"No, no, it's going to have the middle bit the same. He's building up the old house more or less like it would have been, then there's going to be a wing back on each side from the main house, that's where the bedrooms will be."

"I wish he hadn't come here."

"Michael."

"I know. I'm sorry. It's so hard, you see."

"Ah, don't I know myself," John sighed. "Look, that's an old engraving of what the river used to look like years and years ago." He was deliberately changing the subject, trying to steer them both away from the fruitless wishing for the impossible. "Isn't it extraordinary to think that's the same river, that's our Fern, all those years ago. Lord, George the third was still the king of England then. Do you know anything about him?"

"Was he the one who was always half cracked, in and out of mental homes most of the time?" Michael asked.

"I don't think there was a question of mental homes, but he was certainly wandering in mind. Not that the Ferns of Fernscourt probably ever knew anything about that, they'd have been snug there in their grand house and no news of the royal goings-on would get to them for months and by that time it would all be changed . . ."

Michael wasn't listening to him . . . he was looking at one of the line engravings that had come from an old journal.

His father followed his gaze. It was a drawing that showed a barge delivering goods to what looked like a flat landing place behind which there was the mouth of a cave.

It was just like their tunnel even though it was a picture of some other county entirely. Michael studied it intensely, turning it around and drinking in every detail. He raked through the text to see if there was any mention of it.

John Ryan broke in on his thoughts. "Oh, I see you're getting interested in it now! That's the whole problem I find, anyway. You start reading little bits and they make you interested and you read more little bits and you travel far from what you were meant to be writing in the first place. What's that you're looking at?"

His voice was deliberately casual—he had seen the boy find a prosaic explanation for the magic tunnel.

Michael's face was red and white alternately.

"Nothing. I mean it's not anything."

"Oh, that's one of those ways they had of getting deliveries up to the grand houses without offending the eyes of the quality. You know, like a tradesman's entrance." John was light but not dismissive.

"Oh, is that all they are?" The disappointment was huge.

"Well, that's one use for them of course, those kind of tunnels, but like anything they could have a million other uses."

"Like what?"

"Well, like whatever was needed, I mean a tunnel's a tunnel isn't it? It could be used for anything—smuggling, for lovers' meeting, for secret societies, kidnappings, escapes . . . Come on, Michael, it doesn't matter what it was built for, it's what happens to it that's important."

The boy was greatly cheered. "Do you think there might be one across there?" He nodded toward the river.

"There might well be." John was mild. "Kind of thing that could be left unearthed for years and years. Even with all the big hotel coming."

"I don't mind helping you whenever you need a bit of a hand," Michael offered. "I have a bit of time on my hands these days, Mary doesn't think I can do anything."

"Ah, be tolerant of her, will you, she has a mad figario in her head about men, that's all."

"But it's very unfair. I'd do as much as anyone to make things a bit better, or keep things going . . ." His lip trembled.

"Listen to me, Michael, I'll tell you a secret. Not for anyone else—is that all right?"

"Dara?"

"Yes, if you tell it properly, but not to be talked about outside of you two. Poor Mary was all ready to get married, she had saved all her money and given up her job, she was making her wedding dress, even sewing things on it so as to look lovely on the day—"

"Mary Donnelly married? Looking lovely on her wedding day, you must be joking." Michael interrupted.

"No, shush or I won't finish it."

"All right . . ."

"So anyway this fellow was a rat, he didn't love Mary Donnelly at all, he only loved her money, and she had given him everything she saved for to put a deposit on a house . . ."

"And he ran off with it?" Michael's eyes were bright and he was rushing ahead in the story.

"It's easy known you're so young you can see anything in it except black treachery. Think of it, every week—or every month I suppose, teachers get paid by the month—she put so much away for the great day, and this boyo took the lot . . ." John Ryan's kind face was misty at the thought of it.

"Yeah, well it wasn't fair."

"It was worse than just taking her money, you see, he took everything else, he took away any pride she had, and made a fool of her in front of everyone in her place . . . Like she'd always be remembering how she had talked of her plans, saying we're doing this and we're doing that, and all the time he had no plans for anything except to separate her from her bit of money."

"Maybe he didn't always intend to steal her money, he could have loved her and then went off her," Michael said as if it were only too possible to go off Mary Donnelly.

"I don't know whether that would be better for her to believe or worse." John spoke thoughtfully.

"Anyway she's sure taking it out on the rest of us," Michael grumbled.

"But big strong men like yourself and myself can cope with it surely?"

"We've a lot to cope with these days."

"Indeed we have, son." The sigh was very deep.

"Dad? I don't ask you this in front of people, but . . ."

"Ask away."

"Will Mam ever be able to walk again? Nobody ever says."

"That's the problem, they don't ever say. Not to me either."

"But what do you *think*, Dad?"

"I think there's a possibility that she may not. And that it's going to be very hard for her, Michael. The hardest thing in the world."

* * *

Fergus invited Mary Donnelly to the pictures.

"Why?" she asked him.

The real reason was because Fergus, hearing how good she was in the Ryan household, feared that Mary Donnelly might leave unless some little diversion was planned for her.

He could hardly say that.

"Because I like you and would like to get to know you more," he said.

"How would you get to know me at the pictures?" she asked.

Fergus felt sorry he had started on this course.

"Well it's a way to go out, isn't it? Perhaps you would prefer just to go for a drive if you don't like the cinema."

"I never said I didn't like the cinema. I just wondered what way two people would get to know each other if they sat in silence watching a film."

"I suppose it would be a matter of talking about it afterward," Fergus said desperately.

Mary thought about this.

"Usually it's a matter of taking liberties during the film, that's what I've noticed," she said.

Fergus had never gotten such a shock in his life.

"I assure you nothing would be further from my mind," he began, horrified. "I am a solicitor, a grown man."

"What a pompous thing to say, Mr. Slattery, as if desire were confined only to the lower orders. It is there in men of every class and breeding."

"Yes, well," Fergus said, totally at a loss. "If there's ever anything."

"I doubt if there will be, but thank you for raising the matter," Mary said.

"How in the name of God do you get on with that one?" Fergus asked John when they had some privacy.

"She's a godsend, that's what she is. It's the one thing that keeps Kate anyway calm in there, the thought that we've got a cousin of Mrs. Whelan looking after us. It's the next best thing to having Sheila."

"But Sheila's normal, John, she's not a nutcase like this one."

"Ah, she has her ways like everyone has their ways. She's a bit off men, that's all."

"That's a bit steep, to be off half the human race, and isn't she living in a family of four men and a girl, for God's sake?"

"I think she prays for us." John was tolerant.

"I'm surprised she hasn't taken a pike to you, and the day might well come when she does." Fergus was still smarting.

"She's certainly taking no chances, she got Jimbo to fit a lock to her door. I suppose she was afraid I'd lose the run of myself and come in and savage her."

"Do you tell that to Kate?" Fergus asked wistfully.

"I do, she doesn't believe me."

"I'd love to go and see her," Fergus said.

"She'll tell you when. You know Kate, she's very proud. She hates people seeing her the way she is, with all the tubes and the bags."

"As if I'd mind."

"She minds."

"Tell her . . . well, just tell her."

"Sure, Fergus, I'll tell her."

* * *

Dara and Michael had finished their work. Mary had made them sandwiches and a flask of soup. They weren't normally given a flask. This was an honor.

"I understand that you can go off on your own."

It had been cleared with their father. The twins nodded. They were nervous. This was their first day going back to the tunnel since the day of the accident. They were almost afraid it would be bad luck to go back there again. They might come out and find the whole of Mountfern waiting to tell them more bad news.

Without saying it they both remembered that it hadn't even been much fun in the tunnel that day, even before they learned of Mam's accident.

They had almost forgotten how much earth and rubble there was around the place and how dirty it made everything. Still, in the new system that Mary Donnelly had set up they all had to steep their own clothes in a big zinc bath of detergent. Twice a week all the shorts and shirts and underwear and pajamas went in. That way extra grime wasn't really noticed.

They pushed forward and there it was, with the tables and chairs they had been arranging at the very time that Mam was having her accident overhead. It was strange and almost frightening to think about.

They went around the tunnel as they had often done before, stroking its sides and marveling at how well made it was and how long it had lasted.

"They must have been desperate in those days to keep their groceries hidden from the public if they went to all this trouble to hide them, building a whole tunnel just so the neighbors wouldn't see," Dara said in wonder.

"They didn't *have* neighbors." Michael was more authoritative. "It was so that they wouldn't have to look at them themselves."

"What was so bad about groceries?"

"I don't think it was just a few brown-paper bags like we'd get in Loretto Quinn's, it was barrels and boxes."

"Well that's even more posh, they must have been half cracked, the Ferns," Dara said.

"Apparently it's all over the country, I read it in all that research Daddy's doing. Mr. O'Neill says that the book will be on display at the hotel with Dad's name on it."

"Do you think the hotel will ever get built?" Dara asked suddenly.

"I don't know, I suppose it will. Why?"

"It doesn't seem real anymore."

"Nothing does."

The twins sat there for a long moment. Neither wanted to say anything falsely cheering.

As usual they spoke at the same time when they did speak.

"Do you think Lourdes would work . . ." Dara began.

"I wonder if there really are miracles . . ." Michael began.

They burst out laughing.

"Maybe our minds got divided," Dara said. "We didn't get a full one each but between us we have a fantastic Super mind."

"Which is why we can only work out things when there are the two of us," Michael agreed.

"So what do we think about Lourdes?" Dara said.

"There must have been some miracles there, some of them have to be real." Michael's face was full of hope.

"Yes, Sister Laura said that if it was all a fraud the enemies of the Church would have found it out." Dara was eager also.

"So maybe if we could get her there. It could work, couldn't it?"

"And it would be better than just sitting around waiting."

Dara and Michael were much revived. It was like old times, having some kind of project. Something important to do.

The twins didn't know that the village of Mountfern was already planning to send Kate to Lourdes. Money had been collected, people had been in touch with the travel agencies in Dublin and had received details from the Joe Walsh Travel Agency and the Michael Walsh Travel Agency.

The collection had begun. Sheila Whelan was approached to put the money in the post office. She thought it should be a proper fund administered through a solicitor's office.

At first Fergus didn't want anything to do with it. It was grotesque to build up people's hopes, Kate's hopes too. Why let simple people believe that there was a way that a place would mend a broken spine? Perhaps John Ryan would feel patronized, he might not like the idea that the people of Mountfern should pay for his wife to go to Lourdes instead of waiting for him to send her himself.

"If you don't start it for us then as sure as anything Patrick O'Neill will organize it," Sheila said.

"I'll open a bank deposit account tomorrow," said Fergus.

"Father, did you know that there's a collection being organized to take Dara and Michael's mother to Lourdes?" Grace asked.

"Yes, people are very generous, they're digging very deep in their pockets."

"Who's organizing it?" Kerry asked.

"I don't know, I don't think anyone is. You can give your money at the church to either of the priests, or at the post office or to Mr. Slattery, you know —the lawyer."

"Slattery. That figures," Kerry said.

"Why?" Grace asked.

Kerry smiled knowingly. His hair was longer than he usually wore it, it clustered around his neck. His father thought it made him look like a girl. Kerry said that there wasn't a barber within miles and that he might be misjudged if he went to the Rosemarie hair salon. He was tanned and relaxed looking, like a boy who had been on a holiday in a resort, Patrick thought with some annoyance. He had seen the young Ryan boy and Tommy Leonard today; both of them looked peaked and as if they had not seen a ray of sun all year.

"Well, your sister asked you a question. Why does it figure that Slattery is taking up the money? Sure he is. He's a lawyer, as Grace said."

"And he's the leader of the other side."

"Yes, but when the time comes for litigation the Ryans will have other lawyers."

"I mean the other side here in Mountfern. He's the head of the pack that wants to run us out of town. So naturally he collects money to send the injured Mrs. Ryan to Lourdes."

"He doesn't want to run us out of town. Does he?" Grace looked alarmed.

"Of course not, your brother is playing games."

"Not so, Father. He hardly welcomed us here with open arms, did he? And now we are blacker still, one of the great and good has been injured on our property. Of course he wants us out, like a lot of them do."

"Where do you get these kinds of ideas?" Patrick's tone sounded a lot milder than he felt.

"Because I'm not stupid." It was very arrogant the way Kerry said it. The direct implication was that Patrick was stupid. Very.

"Neither am I, Kerry. I'm not at all stupid no matter what you might believe."

Kerry shrugged as if it were a matter of indifference to him what his father thought or was.

"I do know all about the collection, Grace." His remarks were now addressed to his daughter. Patrick didn't trust himself to speak to Kerry.

"I think it's a great idea. I don't believe it will cure her but they do say, and I've heard all kinds of people say this, even people who would scorn the whole idea of miracles . . . They say that nobody ever comes back from Lourdes the worse for having been there, they all come back better in some way. Happier, more resigned, feeling that compared to what they saw there then they aren't too badly off."

Kerry smiled. "That's well put," he said admiringly. "Send people off there so they see what terrible things other people have, they come home resigned . . . I never heard that line."

Patrick ignored him. "I could have given Kate Ryan a check to take her to Lourdes, Gracie, but I didn't, I felt it had to come from her own people here. Not from us."

"Like Mary Donnelly?"

"Exactly. So of course I've contributed to the fund, but nothing excessive."

"You know, I misjudged you, Father." Kerry seemed genuinely admiring now. But with Kerry it was often hard to know.

There was no time to discuss it. A shadow passed the window.

"Oh Jesus," Patrick said, "it's Marian."

Marian was full of chat. She had come to invite them all to be her guests at an upcoming angling festival.

Patrick would simply love it, she said, it was tailor-made for him, he would get the entire atmosphere of one of these occasions at first hand, he would know how to describe it to those Americans who were keen fishermen. There would be an excellent buffet lunch in a tent to which they would be invited.

It would be frightfully boring for the young people of course, lots of standing around talking and drinking. But possibly they would love it too. Or it might even be that they would prefer to be with their own friends that day. They must do whichever they pleased, come with her to the lake or stay here in Mountfern and have a great time. Their decision entirely.

Covering the snuffles and giggles of his children, Patrick said graciously and firmly that he would let her know tomorrow. He hadn't yet been able to work out their plans next week.

Patrick thought that it was no mean achievement that he had managed to conduct the entire conversation extremely courteously but without allowing Marian to sit down. In what was after all her own house.

* * *

Brian Doyle telephoned Patrick to say that it was probably unimportant but there was some paint daubed on the wooden fences around some of the digging on the site. They'd have it removed but he thought Patrick should know.

"What does it say?"

"It says Yanks Go Home, but I wouldn't take a blind bit of notice of that," said Brian Doyle.

Marian Johnson was extremely put out when her offer to show Patrick the lake and introduce him to the people who ran angling in the country was so suddenly and almost curtly refused.

Patrick had been apologetic but had given no real explanation. Marian had the bad luck to run into Jack Coyne who had said that it was devoutly to be hoped that Patrick O'Neill hadn't any plans to build a monstrosity like the Slieve Sunset, because that was the place he was seen hurrying in and out of at all hours of the day and night, and that he was there at this moment with that foreign-looking woman, the one with the beautiful hair.

Marian Johnson patted her own sparse hair, newly arranged in the Rosemarie hair salon for an outing which was not now going to take place.

It was impossible to make sense of Patrick O'Neill. He had spent his entire life getting ready to come home, to mix with the best in the land. She had been ready to introduce him to people from Prosperous and Belturbet, from Boyle and Ballinasloe. She knew the families who owned the fishing rights from Lough Ree to Lough Allen, from the Erne to the Lee. She had already made sure he had met the Master socially so that he would not be considered an outsider when it came to foxhunting. And what was the thanks she got, his sneaking away to see that woman in the Slieve Sunset. But there couldn't be anything in it. Not after all his hopes of coming home and being Irish, properly Irish. He could never get involved with a foreign woman, not at this stage.

Kate didn't remember meeting Rachel Fine before. She was dark and exotic-looking, with a beautiful suit that must have cost a fortune. She wore a scarf in such an elegant way too. Usually you only saw people in photographs wearing scarves like that; when they moved it would go into a rag.

She came toward the bed. "Your husband says you have a very sketchy memory of the day."

"Very." Kate felt at a loss with this elegant woman.

"Perhaps that's good, it means you won't remember too much about the shock and the pain."

"No, I can't remember that at all. I can only remember waking up here and someone telling me it was three days before." Kate's face closed up in pain at the memory.

"I believe there are some wonderful surgeons here, Patrick tells me that his hotshot from New York was highly impressed."

Patrick. She called him Patrick. Nobody else who worked with him did. It was coming back to her. John had told her that Rachel Fine was some kind of decorator or designer, she had been staying out in the Slieve Sunset, and then she went on a tour to see about ordering Irish fabrics and things. John had been very vague.

"You're very good to come and see me. Especially as I've been a bit like a madam and saying I didn't want people to come."

"No way should you have people gaping at you if you don't feel like it."

Rachel was gentle and easy, she was no effort to talk to. She explained that she had brought glossy magazines, the kind of thing you wouldn't dream of buying for yourself or reading when you were well. Kate, who had read nothing in the weeks she lay here, was pleased. Those magazines she could just about manage, she felt.

"Why *did* you come?" she asked suddenly.

"Because . . . when I had just arrived in Mountfern you made me welcome. I was sitting in that pub waiting for Patrick to come in, I was anxious and tense and you were kind to me. I liked you."

It was a flowery speech. Kate paused for a moment. Then it came back to her the way it had before. She was Patrick O'Neill's woman!

Perhaps the woman saw the recognition in her eyes. Anyway she went on to speak of it.

"I thought you were someone I could talk to. I can't tell you how distressed I was. How unreal it seemed when you were so lively and laughing . . ." Her eyes filled with tears.

Something in Kate responded to her warmly. Here was someone who was not afraid to say it was a bloody tragedy. For the first time since it happened, she looked into the face of another human being who was prepared to admit that Kate was very very unlucky, someone to be pitied rather than jollied along. It was a huge relief.

"Thank you," Kate began, and found to her horror that she was beginning to sob. "Thank you. I *was* lively and laughing, wasn't I? I wasn't always like this. I *was* able to run and move and grab things up rather than lie here while people rub oil and powder on me like a giant baby. I used to decide what to do and where to go myself. I did, I did."

"Yes, that's the way you were." She was matter of fact.

Kate waited for the cheery sentence saying that she'd be like that again someday. But it didn't come.

"It's so unfair," Rachel said instead. "I'd be able to cope with life if it wasn't so terribly unjust. All you were doing is looking. Standing looking and thinking about what the place was going to be like, and you end up with your back broken, lying here."

Such warmth and sympathy meant that Kate didn't have to put on any act in return, she didn't have to bite her lip and be stoic like she did for John, nor pretend a jolly getting-better-every-day role as she did with the children.

She cried and cried and Rachel held her face to her and didn't mind about the tears all over her good suit, and didn't call the nurse. After a while the crying stopped as unexpectedly as it had begun. Kate looked tired.

"Can I come and see you again?" Rachel asked.

"Please. Please."

Patrick wasn't pleased.

"Why didn't you tell me you were going to see her?"

"I don't have to tell you everything."

"It was sneaky and underhanded."

"I honestly think you can't be well to say something like that. What on earth could be underhanded about going to see someone in the hospital?"

"You didn't ask me if you should go."

"I am not your servant, nor your ten-year-old child. You have told me often enough that you want us to lead separate lives here. I am trying to do that, and now that doesn't seem to please you either." Rachel's eyes flashed in an unaccustomed display of anger.

"No, but you wouldn't have mentioned it, I would never have known if Grace hadn't told me."

"Grace. Yes."

"Oh, don't take that tone, Grace was full of how much Mrs. Ryan loved you and how nice you were, she got it all from the twins. She told me in innocence, not tattling as you are trying to imply."

"This conversation is getting nowhere. Shall we talk about something else? Work perhaps. I have some samples to discuss with you for wall hangings."

"To hell with wall hangings . . . What did she say?"

"Kate Ryan? Not much really. She cried a lot. But that was between us." Rachel stood up and walked restlessly around the plastic and formica lobby of Slieve Sunset. Since the incident of their discovery in Rachel's bedroom on the day of the accident Patrick had been most anxious that all meetings should take place in the public eye and that they be known as colleagues.

"It's just that it wouldn't be a good idea to say anything," Patrick began. He looked troubled and not like his usual decisive self.

"Say anything?" Rachel was nonplussed.

"Yeah, well I know this sounds a bit odd, but the lawyers said not to say anything, anything that might admit liability."

"You can't be serious."

"I know, that's what I said, but they say you're not dealing with decent people like the Ryans, there's always a load of gangsters waiting to get on the bandwagon if they can. Urging people on to litigation."

"But what litigation? You said you'd pay?"

"Yes I did and I will, but there's a danger that people could take you for all you had if you admit too much, that's all."

"I don't understand you at all. You told me that you had made several attempts to see her. So why are *you* going? Isn't it much more likely that *you* would commit yourself or whatever?"

"No, because I'm a careful man. I guess I was just afraid you might have said something like Patrick will look after everything."

"I didn't say it because I assume she knows it, and so does everyone."

"Let's stop this, Rachel," he said wearily.

"Yes, let's." She was back in her passive role of pleasing him now. She didn't remind him that it was he who had started the conversation and refused to let it go.

He looked old and worried.

"Wouldn't it be great if Mary Donnelly would smile sometimes?" Fergus said confidentially to Sheila Whelan. "She's not a bad-looking woman, but there's a terrible ferocity about her."

"She puts that on. Underneath she's as nice as anything."

"Well, life is short. You wouldn't have the energy to dig down for it," Fergus said.

"She's doing well enough above in the pub, I think?" Mrs. Whelan's voice was anxious. "She's not putting people off by glowering at them, is she?"

"It would take more than a glower to put a thirsty man off his drink. Not at all, she's part of the furniture there now, and John is delighted with her. He says she's the most efficient person he ever had working in a bar in his life."

"She's grand if she has plenty to do."

"There's plenty in that house all right. How poor Kate ever managed *and* did my work as well I'll never know."

"You speak of her as if she were dead, Fergus. She'll be home in a matter of weeks."

"She might as well be dead for all her life can give her now."

"Lord Almighty, I hope you don't go saying that to her."

"I haven't been allowed near her to say anything." He sounded bitter.

"Well, she just wanted the family for a while."

"Oh, but I think I'll be allowed to go next week. After all, O'Neill's tart has been in so that should open the floodgates."

"That is not only unlike you, it's disgusting."

Fergus said nothing.

"We're all upset by what happened, you're not the only one to feel it. You'd be a very unwise man to talk like that. I mean it."

He had never known her so sharp.

He nodded. "Right."

"If you know how much I mean it. We need people like you of good sense, people who are right about things and know what to do. Half the people have gone mad in Mountfern since Patrick O'Neill came, and Kate's accident is only one of the big changes we'll have to see here. Fergus, let you not change too, I beg you."

"It was a cheap, vulgar thing to say. I'm glad I have a good friend like you to put me right from time to time."

"That's the only time I ever tried to put you right in my life," Sheila said simply. She patted his hand. They were indeed friends.

The traction was over. They were moving her into a chair. Everyone spoke about it as if it were a huge breakthrough, as if she were going to be able to fly.

Kate felt leaden. She'd had a low feeling since she woke but she tried to take part in all the enthusiasm around her. After all it would be ungracious and mulish not to show pleasure at a step forward.

It didn't hurt, the moving, they were able to lift her and anticipate what would give a stab of pain and what would be fine, and really there was a lot of her that didn't ache at all.

There was a little team around her, the nice young nurse Geraldine and the staff nurse, there was Sister Winston, and two of the hospital porters who seemed to be on call for everything that involved movement, from ambulance stretchers to windows that were stuck with paint. The great Mr. Brown the surgeon was there, and so were two physiotherapists.

She got her first shock when she saw the chair. It was a wheelchair.

"I didn't think . . ." Her hand was at her throat.

Sister Winston was quick. She must have been used to this reaction. "Why be in a chair that can just face one way when you can face any way in this?"

"But an ordinary chair would do . . ."

"It would *do*, certainly, but you wouldn't be able to go to the window and back to your bed or to the handbasin."

"I don't *want* to go to any of those places, I just want to sit in a chair like an ordinary person."

"This one's been prepared for you; tomorrow we can discuss an ordinary chair."

There were so many people looking and hoping for her to be well and upright in the chair, Kate could say no more.

"Of course," she said in a small voice. "I'm sorry."

The lifting was surprisingly easy, just a gradual movement. After those weeks of lying down and thinking it was normal to wake looking at the ceiling and that people always talked bending over you slightly, it was going to be hard to readjust to sitting up again.

They had eased her into the chair, her legs wrapped well in a rug. The family would be so pleased to see her sitting up, the nurses said. The porters who had brought the chair smiled their pleasure. Mr. Brown said she was making great progress, the two physiotherapists moved here and there to settle her. And that was it. She sat and tried to smile back at all the good humor around. But the smile wouldn't come.

She felt faint, and a roaring in her ears.

They saw it at once, and her head was pushed down. A glass of water, medication was discussed and waved away. It often happened. Sister Winston had seen it all before. That's why she never let the friends and relatives in until much later.

Kate Ryan's mouth was in an O of horror, her hands gripped the sides of the chair.

"I can't feel . . ." she cried. "I can't feel it."

"What can't you feel?" Geraldine was on her knees beside the chair, holding Kate's hand. "Shush now, you're grand altogether, everyone's delighted with you . . ."

"I can't feel my bottom, I have no bottom, no legs, nothing. There's only emptiness where I'm sitting in the chair."

Mr. Brown was gentle. "You've known always . . . you've known about the paralysis. The realization comes and goes. You've adapted so well in traction, now it's just a new adapting."

"It's like air, it's not real. I can't be going to live like this till I die, can I?" Kate looked around piteously at the semi-circle.

"No, no," said Geraldine soothingly.

"I couldn't stand years of this, I couldn't stand it. There's nothing *there,*" Kate cried.

The silence of sympathy broken by clucks of encouragement frightened her even more. Perhaps there weren't going to *be* years ahead. Perhaps her life might be nearly over already.

They put the family off. It seemed the wisest thing. They said there was no cause for alarm, but she needed sedation and it would be tiring for Mrs. Ryan rather than comforting to have to cope with visitors.

They didn't tell John that his wife sat for her first day in a wheelchair staring ahead of her and thinking of a life of dependency on others. Thinking of the fears she would have . . . or they all would have if she got any infection and she might not have the strength to fight it.

She thought about the children having to push an old mother around in a wheelchair; because she would be an old mother, she might as well be their grandmother for all the say she was going to have in things, for all the fun and companionship she could give them.

She thought about the bar and what would happen if Patrick's hotel took away all their business from them as she had been afraid it would. They couldn't go on living on his charity as they already were, a private room, a car at John's beck and call, and anything she said she'd like she knew he would give her.

It wasn't his fault that she had walked past those notices saying danger, and men at work. It wasn't Patrick's fault that she had walked across the line of a man with a digger who had not expected there to be another human on that part of the site.

But Kate wept as she had never wept lying flat on her bed. This was the best she could hope for. This terrible dependent sitting posture worse altogether than lying down, which everyone knew was only temporary.

And when she had learned how to propel the bloody thing with her weak arms and learned how to lift her wasted legs out of it and onto some hideous-looking lavatory bowl, they would say she was cured and send her home. Cured! Cured to go home a cripple and watch this Mary Donnelly, whoever she was, taking Kate's place.

Mary Donnelly didn't want to speak to the men from the brewery or the men from the distillery who called to the pub.

"I've had quite enough huggermugger with men since I came to this establishment," she said to John. "And in any event you are the man of the house, whatever that expression means. You should talk to them yourself."

John sighed. Every day he realized more how much of the running of the household Kate had done. Had he been properly grateful? No of course he had not. He had taken it for granted. Now there was no time to go and write his poems, there was no time to take a walk to clear his head after the smoke and noise in the bar. The days fell into a pattern.

As August became September and Mary got the children ready to go back to school, John began to think he had known no other life than the one where he was picked up at two o'clock in the afternoon and driven in to see his invalid wife in a hospital bed. Like any life, some days were better than others. Sometimes Kate was tired and impatient after long sessions trying to use the wheelchair and maneuver herself from bed to chair, with failure all the way. Some days she was elated. There were times when he was tired and depressed and picked a row, there were good afternoons where he sat and talked to her easily without either of them thinking how the situation had changed and would still be changed when he got her home.

He was glad that she seemed friendly with Rachel. He couldn't quite see what they had to talk about and giggle at, but it was undoubtedly good for her.

She didn't want too many visitors, she said, it tired her, so it was rationed to one a day apart from the family and Rachel. John was pleased that she now saw Fergus Slattery, the poor fellow seemed to be most upset about her and very black about apportioning blame and responsibility. He even kept trying to make appointments with John to talk about the case and the compensation.

"What case?" John had wanted to know. "There's no case, surely. It was a terrible accident."

Fergus had become more impatient than ever about it. And finally Kate said that John should agree to talk about it. Just to calm Fergus down.

"You don't know the way he is, John. I worked for him, remember? He's up to his eyes in the letter of the law, not what things people are really involved in. You should see the small prints, and the clauses about this and about that, and the whereases. It's a different world. Just do me a favor and go to see him in his office, tell him how good Patrick has been, tell him we're not the kind of people who sue over things, it would be flying in the face of God."

"The office? But that would be like as if I'd gone in order to take him on."

"You're not going to get much talked about in the pub, are you? The door opening every time you're getting somewhere?"

He agreed. Unwillingly. And went to Fergus on a bright September morning.

Miss Purcell had told him of a novena that was being done for Kate, and a bouquet of masses which would be offered on the first Tuesday of the month. She wondered when would poor Mrs. Ryan be able to travel to Lourdes, the fund had been generously subscribed. Eventually John got away from her and sat down in the room where his wife used to work every morning.

"Haven't you got anyone yet?" he asked kindly, knowing that Fergus Slattery had put off getting any permanent help out of loyalty to Kate and to the belief that she might work again.

"Your wife told me off about that too. I'll have to, I will. Soon."

"Right." John didn't nag him, he knew how irritating it was to be told to do something if you didn't want to. Jack Coyne was always urging him to get a new roof or a light-up sign over the pub. Things that sounded sensible, things that he might do one day, but not immediately.

"I'll speak as simply and quickly as I can, John. I know you don't want to be here in case it looks as if you're going to take Patrick O'Neill to court, so I'll try to put you in the picture as best I can."

"I know you will, Fergus." John nodded politely like an obedient child.

Fergus felt his collar a bit tight around his neck and loosened it with his finger. He seemed almost reluctant to begin now that he had the undivided attention of the man who was usually moving away to pull pints or to greet those who came in the door.

"Well, it's a matter of just spelling it out," he said.

John looked at him and waited.

"And if there's anything you don't agree with you'll say . . . of course."

"Of course," John agreed.

"Well, obviously it *wasn't* the time before, with everything being so upset and on top of us, but now we have to think in terms of practicalities. Like what happens when Kate comes home."

John was silent. He was looking around the room thoughtfully as if imagining Kate working here, moving quickly from typewriter to cupboard, from big scales where she would have weighed the long narrow envelopes of documents before they were taken to Sheila Whelan's to mail.

"John," Fergus said.

"Yes, I know, practicalities. Well, those are being thought of in most ways. Judy Byrne will come in three times a week at first to keep Kate doing the exercises. And Patrick's getting his builders to even out the floor levels so that she can come into the pub on the chair without anyone having to lift it. He's been very generous, Patrick has, generous and thoughtful." John's glance went around the lawyer's office again, slowly and deliberately.

Fergus could barely conceal his irritation.

"I don't doubt that. *No,* look at me, John, I know you've heard me giving out about the man, I don't doubt that he has been generosity itself, but can I beg you to listen? Now two years ago there was this act passed, the Civil Liability Act of 1961, and up to this there were just three kinds of person who were deemed to exist on your land: an invitee, a licensee and a trespasser. There were no other people. So if anyone got injured the decision was, which kind of person were they? If they were an invitee they got one kind of compensation, a licensee got another—a licensee would be somebody, say, who had permission to be there in some category or other—and the trespasser got another."

He saw John fidgeting.

"Please listen John, I'm making it very short and you'll see why it is important in a minute. There used to be lots of innocent trespassers, people who weren't intending trespass . . ."

"But Kate wasn't . . ."

"Listen, will you, like children or like Kate, say, who was a neighbor and friend. So the law was changed making the landowner more liable than he used to be in the old days. So Patrick or his insurance company has a legal liability to pay compensation . . ."

"But he has, I tell you, we don't want to be blackmailing him . . ."

"The law; God Almighty, the law of the land we live in says he has to pay it, he knows he has to pay it, he doesn't live in some cloud-bloody-cuckoo-land like you do."

"Why are you shouting at me, Fergus?"

"I don't know. I don't know. I think it's because I'm being so long winded and you won't wait till I get to the point."

"All right."

"So the system is you have to sue Patrick. Kate has to sue him. That's the machinery, that's the way it's done. His insurance company won't pay, can't pay until there's a case set up, until the proper requirements of the law are complied with."

"We don't want to sue him."

"He knows that, you know that, I know that, his lawyers know that. Even his insurance company knows that. Jesus, Mary and Joseph, people are suing each other day in and day out who are the best of friends."

"I don't believe you!"

"But it's the way, it's the system. You know Marian Johnson up at the Grange. When she was about eighteen she drove her father home from someplace out the country and they had an accident, he was badly injured, he sued her. The insurance company gave him compensation. He didn't sue her because he was her enemy, he sued her because that's how it's done. That's the way you unlock the money."

"It seems very hypocritical and devious to me."

Fergus was weary. "It's not really, John, it's sensible, it's the only way to keep control, otherwise insurance companies would have to be paying out huge awards and they couldn't afford it and the premiums would be enormous. This way at least they know it's a genuine case when the parties are prepared to go to court about it. It gives them a sort of authenticity, if you see what I mean."

"You're very good at explaining the law, and you obviously understand it too, which is more than a lot of lawyers . . . but Fergus, do you have any understanding at all about what it is to be a neighbor? I mean, you're here in this house in the middle of the street, nothing changes for you no matter who comes to live here. You don't depend on good will and rubbing elbows with people like we do in a pub. It doesn't make sense to go into a court of law and say things about a neighbor, things that cannot be unsaid." John was calm but he seemed very resolute.

Fergus tried again.

"There'll be very little said, and you and Patrick won't have to do any of the saying. The question is, would you like a different solicitor?"

"Not you?"

"I'm very close to you, to all of you. Perhaps it might be easier with someone from the town. It often is."

"If we want to have anyone, Fergus, then Kate and I would want to have you."

"Right."

"Do we need to do anything immediately?"

"No, not for a while, leave it with me."

"Oh and Fergus, could you explain to Patrick O'Neill about it all being friendly when it starts? You know, tell him about Marian Johnson in the Grange and her father and all. It would make it a bit less formal."

"I don't need to tell him that, he's a businessman, John, he knows."

"I'd like you to tell him all the same."

"If it comes up easily I will," Fergus said.

Fourteen

Patrick was pleased to get a message from Rachel that Kate would like to see him on Friday afternoon.

"She must be getting better." He said.

"She says she is," Rachel said doubtfully. "I think she looked a bit feverish, excited. Still, it's better than that terribly depressed way she was last week."

"What would she like? She has a radio, you say?"

"Yes, she hardly listens to it. She might like a game—Scrabble, say. She could play it with the little guys when they go in."

"That's a great idea, Rachel," he beamed. "Where in the world will I get Scrabble? I may have to go to Dublin for it, or Shannon."

"Don't be silly. I'll get it for you."

She had already got a set, and many other things. She wanted Kate to think that Patrick was thoughtful and concerned.

John sat on the edge of the bed and told Kate everything.

"He seems dead set that there's going to be a case," she said, biting at her lower lip.

"I'm just reporting everything that he said, and trying to give you the sort of tone he said it in."

"You're doing very well." She grinned ruefully. "I can practically hear him speaking."

"He's so out for our good, he wants the best for you."

"The best for me is not to have to lock horns with Patrick O'Neill in public. The best would be not having to lie here worrying myself sick what he'll think, what he'll do when we turn on him like an ungrateful dog. That's what it's going to be like, John, no matter how many fine words Fergus says about the law . . ."

She was distressed, her eyes full of tears and her face red with exertion.

John took her hand. "You're not going to spend any time lying here worrying, not even five minutes. I'll tell you what we'll do . . . and you're the one who can do it."

Soothing and shushing down her protests he explained to her that she could sort everything out if she happened by accident to arrange that Patrick O'Neill and Fergus Slattery should both turn up at the same time in her hospital bedroom.

Then it could all be said out in the open.

Fergus was told by the hospital that Friday would be a good day to come in and see Mrs. Ryan. He drove glumly to the hospital. She had been so low the last time, it had been an effort to keep up any kind of conversation at all.

He had brought the application forms of the four young women who had applied for jobs as his secretary. He knew two of them, daughters of local farmers who had done secretarial courses. He thought they would be very unlikely candidates, he wanted Kate's advice badly. Wouldn't it be great if she was in good sparkling form? Dr. White said that some days she was the old Kate, laughing and joking, and you would think she was just lying down for a rest. Other times she had been awake all night, convinced she had not very much longer to live, and was railing at the injustice of it.

Please may it be a good day. For all their sakes.

She was as flushed as a girl, he hoped it was a good sign. She was delighted that he had brought the confidential files and urged strongly in favor of Deirdre Dunne, a girl who lived about three miles away.

"Look, she's given you all kinds of detail, like how it will be no trouble to get a lift in and out. That's sensible. And I know Deirdre, her father comes into Ryan's. A tighter-mouthed man you never met. He wouldn't tell you what day it was let alone anyone else's business."

She was indeed like the old Kate, teasing him, sending him up, full of plans.

Rachel Fine had said that her room should be moved downstairs; soon builders would go in and flatten out all the steps in the downstairs so she could come into the pub and the kitchen. The parlor was going to be made into a big bed-sitting room for her, with a special bathroom beside it. There would be a rail all around it, and garden doors—you know, those French windows with glass in them down to the floor—out to the side yard, which would be made posh, and she could wheel herself out there.

Fergus took off his glasses and wiped them because they had misted up with delight that she was able to think of a life after this white hospital room, and with pity that it would be limited by wheelchairs and rails around walls.

John Ryan came in then, told him to sit where he was, no need to go, he'd been in and out a dozen times during the afternoon and would be again. Just then there was a tap, and Patrick stood there.

He looked shy in his country tweeds and his crisp shirt, and his curly hair combed just outside the door. In his arms he held a big gift-wrapped parcel and a glass bowl with fruit in it. Nothing very dramatic, just healthy-looking apples and thick-skinned oranges and two yellow pears.

Fergus wished he had brought something like that instead of the box of sweets which lay on the cabinet beside the bed.

"They tell me that I'd find you better today than any day." Patrick was lit up with pleasure. You could see it.

Kate stretched out her arms in greeting from the bed.

"Thank you for all you've done. I can never thank you enough. The room, the car for everyone to come in and out. You've been too good."

"I couldn't do enough, Kate, to tell you how sorry I am that it had to happen. And if it did have to happen why did it have to be on my land, with bulldozers working for me?"

There was no mistaking his sincerity.

"Don't I know that. I've every proof of it," Kate said.

Patrick seemed to notice for the first time that John and Fergus were in the room. He went to John first and shook him by the hand.

"My, doesn't she look well, after all she's been through."

It was just the right touch, Fergus thought miserably. He in no way minimized her agonies, yet he concentrated on the hopeful side. Then it was Fergus's turn.

"Slattery, you must be as pleased as all of us. It's a good time to meet."

"Yup." Fergus got this urge to behave like a taciturn cowboy every time he met Patrick O'Neill nowadays. The fact that he was somehow ungracious made him even more annoyed with himself.

"And I'm very glad you both happen to be here at the same time," Kate said, looking at them eagerly from her bed, her cheeks pink, her hair tied with a yellow ribbon matching the ribbon in her lacy bedjacket, both given to her by Rachel Fine.

"Why is that?" Fergus was suspicious: Kate was too bright, John was looking at the floor.

Patrick knew nothing about it, whatever it was. He smiled to know what Kate was going to say.

"Because I am determined to get out of here and live a proper life again, and I'm tired of people coming to my bed and talking about formalities. All I want to know now, and it will help me to get better, is that there will never be any animosity between us no matter what formalities there are."

"How could there be animosity?" Patrick cried.

"Kate, why don't you leave this until later? Until you're better," Fergus said levelly.

"One of the things stopping me getting better is this," she said. "Honestly it is, I swear it, at night I wake up and think my life is over, it's so unfair; and other nights I wake up and think of the things people tell me down in physiotherapy—that I should claim this and I should claim that, and it would make life more bearable, and it's all from faceless insurance companies anyway so nobody gets hurt. Then I think of Patrick living beside us and what it's going to be like, and of Grace and Kerry and the twins and how I'd hate a fight more than anything . . . So that's why I'm asking you, my friends, will it be done without animosity?"

Fergus opened his mouth and closed it again like a fish.

John said nothing, but laid his hand supportively on Kate's arm.

Patrick O'Neill smiled more broadly than ever as if he could have heard no better news than this current subject Kate wanted to discuss. "But of course we'll talk about it, from now until you feel too tired. Kate, John, I assure you I was only waiting until you felt *able* to talk about it. And obviously since you have Mr. Slattery here too I feel he would be glad it was brought up as soon as . . ."

"I assure you, Mr. O'Neill," Fergus began a trifle pompously.

"No, I know it just happened to come up, but let me say something, straight out. For weeks now I've been wanting to say to someone of you three and never finding the right moment. I *know* the law, I am so well insured it would make your head swim. The courts will decide a compensation and they will pay it.

"Kate, you can never get your spine back, but you can get *some* comforts, goddamn it. I'll see to it that you do."

"But we don't want to go to court against *you*, Patrick," John said, avoiding Fergus's eye.

"Nobody wants to go to court and maybe we mightn't even have to go inside the door," said Patrick. "It could all be settled at the last moment. That's what always happens. But that's the machinery, that's the formula . . . the same way as there's a process for getting a license for a pub or permission to hold a raffle . . . That's right, isn't it, Attorney?"

Fergus nodded, not trusting himself to speak. The man was making himself clear in a way that Fergus hadn't been able to do. John and Kate hadn't trusted him. He felt his mouth full of acid. "That's right," he said.

"So, let's get the insurance guys, hey? God, if you know how much they get me for every year. It will be a pleasure to get them to give you as much as we can squeeze from them. All I say, though, is that it's a tremendous shame that it has to be over something like this."

He was so full of generosity, no mention of the no-claim bonus he would lose, no mention of the pressure that giant insurance companies who handled his business both here and in America would put on him. Fergus felt moved by the man's warmth. But in his heart he felt sure that Patrick was right. Some settlement would be reached on the steps of a courthouse, and at this moment Patrick knew exactly how much it was.

Fergus felt an urge so strong that it was almost overpowering to take him on and fight him in every court of the land, refusing offers, settlements and recommendations until he got for Kate Ryan something that would even in a paltry way compensate for the life that Patrick O'Neill and his mechanical bulldozers had taken away from her.

Later he remembered, with his mouth in a thin line, that the cute fox O'Neill had said nothing about the private room in the hospital being a gift from Patrick to Kate or the use of a car for the Ryan family being a gift from Patrick to Kate. Oh, no. These would be included in the settlement when the time came.

He remembered how pleased Kate had been with the game of Scrabble. He wished he had thought of it, with a pain that almost tore him in two.

He felt that there was great truth in Mrs. Whelan's words that everyone had gone a little mad since O'Neill came to Mountfern. He hoped he hadn't gone madder than most. Fergus knew that he must do something practical rather than sit and rage against what had been done and couldn't be undone.

He decided to teach John Ryan to drive and get them a second-hand car somewhere so that O'Neill couldn't claim months more of transport when the day of reckoning arrived.

It was so strange going back to school without their mother to harass them and organize the huge hunt for satchels, text books and clean shirts, and shoes being taken to the mender's. This is what the end of the summer holidays meant before.

Mary Donnelly had it all in order. The Ryans' house had never worked in such a streamlined way before. There was no fuss about going back to school. All the clothes were ready mended and ironed anyway. The children had almost forgotten a time when they didn't strip and air their beds every day, and when there wasn't a weekly examination of shoes and clothes, so that the one could be brought to old Mr. Foley's odd wordless brother who stitched away silently at the soles of Mountfern in the back of Foley's bar. Clothes were all darned or mended at that weekly session too.

Kate Ryan in her hospital bed looked in amazement at neat patches and false hems to be told that Dara and Eddie were a dab hand at any kind of dressmaking now. Michael and Declan had resisted it and were responsible for shoe polishing instead.

A cupboard had been cleared in the dining room and all schoolbooks and bags were stored there. The four children had a shelf each. The summer exercises had continued, and even Eddie was able to approach an exercise book now without scribbling all over it. Mary had always shown such surprise and horror at any doodling it was easier to leave the book clean.

And when school did begin Mary seemed to regard it with a reverence that the children found disconcerting. She almost spoke of school in hushed tones. She managed to inquire about their progress and particularly about what homework they had to do with an air of such interest that they did not realize how much they were giving themselves away and putting their lives into her hands.

"Now, Dara, let me help you clear away, you've got all those geography questions to do tonight, you said. And Michael has that big long poem to learn. Eddie, you aren't too badly off—only ten sums, was it?"

They would look at each other glumly. Why had they been so specific? Now there was no escape.

The breakfast room became a study both before and after tea. There was always a dictionary, an atlas, rulers, pencils and spare paper. The wireless was turned down respectfully. Callers were discouraged and if their father ever came looking for them for anything, the children heard Mary speaking to him in low urgent tones explaining that they were doing their homework. It was said in the voice that someone might have used about the College of cardinals being in conclave to elect a pope. And after a few false starts it worked. The homework did get finished, and almost in silence. It was easier to learn the poem, Michael would decide, rather than have Mary offer to hear it to him at breakfast and expose his ignorance. Dara would find that Mary, when approached about homework that had been completed, was always cooperative and helped to get her better marks, but Mary would not even discuss work that had been left undone.

Eddie felt life was too short to have to put up with Mary mentioning that she must ask Brother Keane why the children in Eddie's class got no homework. It really was simpler to admit to the homework and do it. Then at least he would be free.

Declan at seven didn't have very much homework, but he liked the scene around the table. Mary had drawn him a map of Ireland and he spent each evening coloring in the different counties and labeling them. He had asked Mary was this the kind of thing a person could do in a circus as a trick. Mary had said that to be truthful it hadn't been done much, but there was no reason why there couldn't be a first time. And she could say hand on heart that to know the thirty-two counties of Ireland, how to spell them and where they all were would be something that would advance you in *any* career. So Declan sat happily mastering difficult spellings like Monaghan and Laoghais.

Sometimes John looked in at the industry and gave a deep sigh of relief.

By the time he got Kate home, some kind of order would reign in the house, and all the time Kate's new domain was being built. With huge financial help from Patrick O'Neill, and great advice and care from Patrick's lady friend Rachel Fine. Even Leopold was better behaved these days, John noticed, and slept outside Mary's door on a sack which he dragged out to the yard each evening. It was as if he lay there protecting her from the world.

"What does Kerry do all the time? He's never around and his school doesn't open for another week." Dara and Grace were sitting in Dara's room. Sometimes Grace came to do her homework too; Mary Donnelly looked in and out casually to make sure that the time was not being wasted around the table, but the little O'Neill girl seemed industrious enough.

"Kerry never says. I think he studies quite a bit. This is his last year, he wants to get a good Leaving Certificate."

"And will he?" Dara loved to hear news of the handsome Kerry. "Will he get a lot of Honors do you think?"

"He thinks he'll get four. Or so he says, I don't know." Grace seemed doubtful.

"Why don't you know?"

Grace wondered whether to speak and then decided she would.

"Well, I just said I think he studies a lot, I'm not sure. You see, he goes to these extra lessons."

"The Latin, with Mr. Williams?"

"No, as well as those. He goes into the town twice a week, there's a schoolmaster there and Kerry's meant to be going for math."

"Maths," corrected Dara automatically.

"Yes, well, whichever, he's not going to it. He takes the money from Father and he gets a lift with Paudie Doyle or Brian or someone, but the teacher called last week to say he was sorry that Kerry hadn't showed up for the lessons." Grace shook her head.

"Where was he?"

"That's it, I have no idea; and as it happened, I answered the telephone. Not Miss Hayes, and not Father. So I just said that I'd pass on the message and the man said he just wanted to clear things up because Father had sent him some kind of letter thanking him for his time."

"Oh dear," Dara said.

"So it looks as if Kerry wasn't going at all. But saying that he was."

The girls sat in silence to contemplate the enormity of this.

"What *could* he have been doing instead?" Dara hoped he didn't have a girlfriend or anything awful like that.

"I asked him, but he just laughed, said it was great I had headed the guy off at the pass, that was the way he said it. And you know Kerry, Dara, he didn't say any more and he will not say any more."

"Does your father know?"

"No, he doesn't know."

"And Miss Hayes, she wouldn't . . ."

"No, I have a feeling that even if she did know she wouldn't . . ."

"Well then, it's all right." Dara was always optimistic.

"I suppose so." Grace was less sure.

Tommy Leonard told Michael that the Lourdes fund for Mrs. Ryan was getting huge now. There was going to be enough for someone else to go with her. People were wondering who it would be. Would it be Mr. Ryan? Or would one of the children get to go? Imagine Lourdes, in France. Imagine being there.

"Do you really think Our Lady came there? She did, didn't she?" Michael was very anxious to have it confirmed. If Our Lady hadn't, if it had all been some kind of misunderstanding, then there would be no chance for Mam.

"I suppose she must have," Tommy said. "I mean, it would be the kind of place you'd go, France."

Michael agreed.

Tommy said that Maggie Daly was often afraid that Our Lady might come to Mountfern, like she came to Fatima. Maggie didn't look up into trees in case she saw her.

"Why doesn't she want to see her?" Michael was interested. "I mean, if she came here you'd want to *see* her."

"Maggie thinks that you'd be martyred if you saw her, it's what always happens," Tommy said.

"Poor Maggie, she's always worrying," said Michael sympathetically.

"Not like Kitty. Kitty was off on the back of a motorbike with Kerry O'Neill." Tommy loved a bit of excitement.

"Kerry's not old enough to have a motorbike, is he?"

"Oh, Kerry's old enough for anything, he took it out of Jack Coyne's yard and brought it back secretly, and he and Kitty went off miles on it."

"How do you know?"

"Maggie told me. Did she not tell you?"

"No. I wonder why," Michael said.

"Why didn't you tell me all about Kerry and the motorbike and everything?" Dara was furious with Maggie.

"I—I don't know. It was a secret," Maggie stammered.

"If it was a secret, Maggie Daly, why did you tell Tommy Leonard?"

"I don't know."

"Oh, you don't know, you don't know," Dara blazed. "You're so boring, Maggie. You don't know anything, you have nothing to say."

"I know," Maggie said wretchedly.

There were Halloween games in Ryan's kitchen. Snap apple with everyone's hands tied behind their backs and the apple hanging from a string in the middle of the room. And bobbing for apples in the sink of water, and trying to pick up the sixpence in your teeth from the floor.

Carrie loved the fun of it, and John Ryan came in from the pub occasionally.

Rachel Fine looked on; she had been seeing to Kate's new room and was in and out of the house a lot. The Whites were there, bitterly disputing whose turn it was to play, and Tommy Leonard was there.

"Where's Maggie?" Tommy asked at one point.

"I didn't ask her," said Dara. "I forgot. Like she forgets sometimes."

Dara's face was set and cross. She was very annoyed that Maggie had not told her about her sister's carrying on. And she was even more annoyed to hear about Kerry O'Neill off gallivanting on a borrowed motorbike.

"I'll run down for her," Michael said. "She'd be upset. I'll just go to Daly's now."

"I'll come with you," Grace offered.

Dara felt that she had been too mean. She would go herself for Maggie. But it was too late. Michael and Grace had run off.

They came back later without her.

"Her mother said she had a cold, she was in bed."

"Oh well then, it wouldn't have mattered anyway," Dara said airily. But in her heart she felt ashamed of herself. And she felt that Maggie didn't really have a cold.

Grace was very nice to Maggie. She insisted too that Maggie come with them on the day that Patrick O'Neill drove some of the children in on what he called an official visit to Mrs. Ryan in the hospital.

The twins were delighted to show their mother off to Liam, Jacinta, Tommy and Maggie, and Kate was touched to see the small crowd around the bed.

"There's a small fortune in the Lourdes fund, Mrs. Ryan, you'll be able to take the whole family with you," Tommy said enthusiastically.

"My goodness, isn't that generous? But if anyone's going it should be other invalids, don't you think?" Kate said.

"Mrs. Williams has a broken arm," Jacinta suggested.

"You don't go to Lourdes with a broken arm, eejit, you have to have much worse." Liam looked half fearfully at Kate.

"Oh, I think you can go with anything, really," Kate said, trying to make light of it.

"Now." Jacinta was triumphant. "And Mrs. Williams is always very nice, giving us things out of her garden. She should be one of the first to go."

"She is a Protestant of course," Tommy said doubtfully.

"Not to mention a vicar's wife," Kate said, trying to keep her face straight.

"It might convert her to the real faith, though, if she was taken there," Maggie suggested.

"Particularly if her arm was cured." Patrick O'Neill laughed.

He shooed the children out of the hospital room and told them there would be lemonade and biscuits.

"You're marvelous to bring them all in to see me," Kate said. She felt easy and relaxed talking to the big American.

"I love playing the big guy," he mocked himself.

"No, you don't, not at all. You're very fatherly to them all. My twins tell me how kind you've been up at the lodge, teaching them chess and Scrabble and spending the time playing with them, a busy man like you."

She smiled at him warmly.

"They're very easy to like, your children," he sighed.

"Well, aren't yours also?" She was genuinely surprised.

"Grace is."

"Fathers and sons always have friction. It's a known thing."

"John doesn't."

"You should hear him with Eddie."

"Kate, I know you'll forgive my saying this, but most of the Western world has some kind of friction with Eddie at some time or another. No, my case is a bit different."

He looked very strained somehow.

"Would it help to tell me about it?"

"Someday, maybe. Yes, it might help a lot. But not just now. I have a gang of people who were promised refreshments, I can't go back on that. And you'll be back home to us soon, isn't that great?" He seemed genuinely delighted.

"In a couple of weeks," Kate said. "Then it will be as before."

His eyes rested on her for a moment. "It will not be as before, Kate. But please God it will be a good life." He had so much concern in his voice that it quivered a little.

Kate swallowed and gave him a smile.

They didn't say any more because there wasn't any need.

Dara got a postcard from Kerry O'Neill from the town near his school.

"We are here for a half day, they took us to see a castle on a river. The river is brown and muddy, I think it's nothing compared to the Fern. Glad to hear your mother is coming home soon. Hope to see you all in Mountfern during the Christmas holidays. Kind wishes to all, Kerry."

Dara hugged it to her and knew every word, not only every word but how every letter of each word was formed.

"Just tell me straight out, Maggie, no dithering, did Kitty get a card from Kerry O'Neill too? Just a yes or a no would do."

"No. There was no card from Kerry for Kitty. I can tell you that."

Maggie spoke firmly. Because what she said was true. There had been no postcard for her sister. But Kitty had been looking very cheerful, and there were letters from time to time, which were not discussed. And they did have a postmark of the county where Kerry's school was. But it would be foolish to enter into that kind of speculation. Maggie never wanted to draw things on them. And she had been asked specifically about postcards, nothing else.

Maggie was glad when Dara took her arm. It would have been stupid to upset Dara over something that might not even be true. Kitty could have been getting letters from anyone.

"I hope Mrs. Ryan will like the way I run things," Mary Donnelly said doubtfully.

"Why wouldn't she?" John was unused to Mary in an insecure role.

"She's the mistress of this house, it will be hard for her coming back after five months and seeing another woman in her place."

"But hasn't she told you over and over how delighted she is with you, and all you've done for us?" John was bewildered. Mary had been a visitor several times to Kate in the hospital. They had gotten on very well.

"But her coming home, and to that grand room, it will be hard for her not being in total charge again. If you'd like me to go I'd quite understand."

"Mary, we'd die if you went." John was alarmed. "You couldn't go, not now that she's coming back at last. Please don't think of leaving. Is it that you think she'd be giving you orders? Because Kate's not like that. She'll be only too glad for things to go on the way they are. You'll be happy here. Please don't go."

"I'm very happy here, Mr. Ryan. It's very nice, it's the first place I ever thought of as home, and it's a place where people don't make your life a torture for you."

"But who would make your life a torture for you. Ever?"

"My mother did, my colleagues at the school. The other women around where I lived."

John was at a loss for words.

"Well," he said eventually, aware that it wasn't enough.

"So what I say is that Mrs. Kate Ryan, if she had to be married and evidently she had, could have done far worse for herself with the husband and three sons that she found."

John knew he would never hear such praise again.

"Thank you," he said very seriously. "I hope we will always be able to have your trust, my sons and I."

Fergus had found Mary a surprising ally when he was trying to teach John to drive. She had urged the two of them to go out as often as possible, saying that she could well keep an eye on the bar. It never occurred to her that Fergus might have any work to do himself, so she was always putting forward unlikely hours like 11 a.m. as good for a quick lesson.

As it happened the little girl Deirdre he had gotten for the office was every bit as reliable as Kate said she would be. She was always able to tell a caller that Mr. Slattery had gone out on urgent business with a client, and she would take all the details. Somehow, like her father, she gave off a look of utter secrecy. You felt that she would survive well under torture, rather than reveal the most trivial of business.

And she wasn't telling lies, she explained to Fergus. After all, Mr. Ryan was a client, and teaching him to drive was important business.

It took twenty lessons, and then John felt confident enough to drive all on his own into the hospital. This, too, was a secret and a surprise for Kate. Several times he nearly blurted it out, and Rachel Fine nearly let it slip as well.

Then together Fergus and John went to Jack Coyne and put it to him squarely: he was to supply the soundest second-hand car in the world. Not just the country, but the world.

It was to be ready and roadworthy and shining clean on the morning of Friday November 23, for that was the day it would be driven into the town by John Ryan, and he was going to pick up his wife and bring her home to Mountfern.

They all wanted to go, all the children. John said there would be no room in the car. But they wanted to see her face when she saw him driving, that was part of the fun.

Very well, they went with Paudie Doyle as usual, they drove in convoy. Fergus first with Sheila Whelan, then John in the Vauxhall, and then the four Ryan children speechless with excitement in Paudie Doyle's Austin.

There were a lot of tears in the hospital, and Geraldine the nurse said she would miss Kate more than any other patient.

People in wheelchairs came out to say goodbye, and in her own wheelchair she went to say a word to people who weren't even able to move.

She said she'd be in and out of the hospital for treatment.

All the time she thought she was going to be in Paudie Doyle's Austin.

"Where will all the children fit?" she asked Rachel.

"Hush, wait, wait."

Kate knew something was up but she could never have believed anything as splendid as the sight of her husband drawing up in the big black Vauxhall.

Both her hands went up to her mouth as she saw him at the wheel. "Glory be to God, he'll kill himself," she said, and then they all cheered.

John Ryan got out with a flourish. "Here's your coach, Katy Ryan, and your coachman come to take you home and anywhere in the world you want to go."

In a blur she saw the children's faces in front of her. The twins were struggling with what looked like a banner and Kate saw it had a welcome-home message on it. Eddie and Declan looked faintly mutinous as if they had wanted to share in the banner but had not been allowed to have any part of it.

John had learned to drive, this was their car, he kept saying it. In the confusion it was hard to take in, they had a family car now. The children were racing around it in excitement, Rachel Fine was trying to line them up so that she could take a picture.

John had learned how to drive a car! They could maybe go off for a day without having to ask Jack Coyne or Fergus or Paudie Doyle. *How* had he learned to do that? Were there any more surprises and could she cope with them?

"I'm only crying because I'm so happy," she said into Declan's tousled head. He had run to throw his arms around her when he saw the tears.

"*I* wanted to have a welcome home," he snuffled.

"But you have a welcome home for me," she protested. "Isn't all this lovely? It's the best welcome I could have."

"I wanted to put *my* name," he said, fists digging into his eyes still. "They wouldn't let me"—a hate-filled glance at the twins.

"But you can do your own when we get back, when we're back in Mountfern. Tell me, Declan, Eddie, am I really going back or is it a dream?"

Eddie took it on himself to explain the realities of the situation. "It's real enough," he said grudgingly, pleased to have been singled out to define things.

Kate put her hands out to the twins and their banner. "Let you both hold it high up there so that Rachel can get it into the picture," she said.

Her eyes told the twins that the banner was something that had touched her so much she hardly dared speak. She sat with her hands holding theirs tightly as the picture was taken.

And then they moved her to the car. She was near to hysteria as they lifted her into the front seat.

"Don't tell me you can really drive this, John Ryan," she gasped. And then out the window to the nurses: "Listen, don't give my room away, I'll be back with more injuries in half an hour."

But the pride as she sat beside her husband in their own car was shining out like a beacon.

The entourage would follow them, Fergus with Sheila as his passenger, Rachel in her own car, and the Ryan children traveling for the last time in Paudie Doyle's car.

A rug had been placed over Kate's knees, and she sat straight and proud like a queen in the front of the second-hand Vauxhall that Jack Coyne had found as the bargain of the century.

When Rachel turned aside so that nobody would see her brushing away the tears, she saw that the nice nurse and the lawyer were doing the very same thing, wiping their eyes at the sight of so much delight.

Mountfern never forgot the day that Kate Ryan came home from the hospital. Years later they could remember every detail of that evening.

It had been arranged that the bar remain open as usual, with Mary Donnelly serving. Sheila Whelan was brought in as well, in case there would be extra people there pretending to be having a drink but in reality waiting to see the return of the invalid.

There was a great cry that they were coming when the car was reported to have come in view of the Rosemarie hair salon, and Rita Walsh was out waving from the salon doorstep. Loretto Quinn ran up from her shop, and Brian Doyle ran over the bridge to be there too.

The procession went through the bar, where old men got off stools and shook hands, unable to say the words. They were relieved she was back, and stricken to see her still so pale and sitting awkwardly in a wheelchair.

Carrie was excited, in a new navy dress with a white collar, and she ran in and out of the kitchen a dozen times asking Mary when would she serve the tea. A dozen times Mary replied that she should ask Mrs. Ryan.

But Kate was beyond listening to any subtleties like this. There was so much to admire.

Why had nobody told her that the whole place had been repainted? And the steps, all those steps—one down here and one up there—had gone. That must have been huge work, leveling everything.

It *was* a big undertaking, John Ryan agreed, as if he had done it himself. All they had done was stand back and use the back doors while Patrick's men were withdrawn from work on the hotel to do a job on it.

Then there was the room. Kate couldn't believe it. Walls of light green, huge glass doors framed by green flowery curtains. The big bed was white, with a green and white cover. All around the room there was a broad white shelf like a counter, almost. The wheelchair would fit under it, and there were magazines, sewing things, books, files laid out at intervals to suggest activities for Kate. One section of the shelf was a dressing table. It had a mirror and lights around it like a film star would have in a dressing room.

The bathroom was huge. Rachel called it the dressing room. It had huge presses for Kate's clothes, on rails that could be lowered so that she could reach them and choose what to wear. There were drawers that moved in and out silently, effortlessly. Not like the drawers that stuck and had to be pushed and pulled. The bath had a seat, and a shower, the lavatory had rails. But it wasn't like the hospital bathroom, all white and clinical. It was soft green colors, with big fluffy green towels and bath salts in a big green glass jar.

In her life Kate had never seen anything so elegant. And it was hers. It wasn't something she was looking idly at in a magazine.

They crowded around, Fergus and Brian Doyle, Rachel and Loretto, John in the middle and the children on the edges pushing in and out to see her face.

And that's how they all remembered it because that was when the news came in from the bar where the wireless was on. The news that President Kennedy had been shot in Dallas.

They all went slowly toward the bar to wait for more news. The phone kept ringing, people wanted to tell other people. There was television up in the Grange and some of those with cars said they would drive there and see if they could find out any more. Anything was better than not knowing what had happened to him—the president who had waved at them all in Dublin only five months ago.

"It'd be better for him if he died, poor bastard," Brian Doyle said in the middle of a silence. "Young man like that stuck in a wheelchair for the rest of his life. He couldn't take it, he'd go off his head."

It was a long minute before anyone realized what he had said. They were all thinking of John F. Kennedy, not about Mrs. Ryan, a younger woman stuck in a wheelchair for the rest of her life.

Then Brian Doyle noticed a couple of faces crumpling up and remembered.

"But of course they can do great things now," he said desperately. Nobody helped him out.

"Great things altogether," said Brian, wishing he were dead and six feet under the clay.

Fifteen

The spring of 1964 was a wet one in Mountfern. The river flooded its banks twice, and there were even photographers sent from Dublin to take a picture of the Fern in flood. The trees hung heavy over River Road and let loose what felt like waterfalls when anyone shook them.

The children's raft broke loose from its moorings and bobbed down to the big bridge in the town, where it remained battering itself against the side.

The schools smelled of wet clothes and everyone had colds.

People still managed to go out for a drink, however, and often the wet weather meant that there was more custom than ever in Ryan's bar.

In her light room with its soft green colors Kate Ryan sat and spent the first spring in a wheelchair.

She would have gone mad, she realized, if she had not got the side garden to look out on through the big glass doors. She was the first to know when snowdrops came, when crocuses started to open and when the primroses and cowslips began in a yellow corner that she had never noticed before.

Jaffa the big orange cat looked out longingly, waiting for the days to come when the sun would shine and she could sit and sleep on the old stone walls. Sitting still in her chair, Kate Ryan scratched the cat's ears and told Jaffa that for her the day would come. She sighed a lot and wondered had it rained like this always but because she had been so busy she had never noticed it?

Little by little the people of Mountfern came to accept that this would be Kate Ryan's life. They ceased to shake their heads over the sudden accident, the one quick blow that would leave her forever paralyzed. Once people had seen the bright attractive room and the handsome dark woman in her chair, laughing and cheerful for their visit . . . then that was how she remained in their minds. They didn't tell each other any more about how swift she had been, and how light running up and down the steps of Mr. Slattery's office. They talked no longer of the way she ran down River Road like a young girl.

Rachel had found a great roll of green rush matting. She said they should cut it off in lengths and spread it out to make a path over Kate's new carpet.

Otherwise people would be afraid to visit her in the room for fear of bringing in mud with them.

Rachel came every day; she had become adept at helping to lift the two white, wasted-looking legs out of the bed and on to the wheelchair. Then she would bend while Kate pulled herself out of bed by putting her arms around Rachel's neck.

She wasn't able to do it with Carrie; the girl was too nervous and might move away. She didn't want to ask Mary Donnelly to help her. It would place too much of an emotional burden on Dara. And she didn't want John to see her like that *every* day. On the mornings when he came in and found her dressed and sitting at some part of the giant desk that went three sides of the room, he could almost believe that things were normal.

The two women had tea and a chat, as if they had been neighbors for many years, as if they had been young married women together and shared all the years of childbirth and watching toddlers. Neither of them ever felt it was odd that they had only met on one day before they were in the roles of hospital patient and visitor. It was as if they had always known the easy companionship and the undemanding shorthand of friendship.

Kate could tell of her unreasonable dislike of Mary Donnelly, Rachel of her irritation with Marian Johnson.

"He has no interest in Marian Johnson," Kate assured her friend.

"She's much more suitable for this life . . . the life he wants."

"Oh, but no, you mustn't think that. Can you imagine him loving her? Even loving her a little bit?" Kate shook her head at the idea of it.

"He can't love *me* much, either. One day I'll accept that I'm not part of his plan. Then I'll be free."

"But you'd be very lonely," Kate said.

Rachel smiled, relieved. This was the counsel she had wanted to hear.

"Will Mrs. Fine be here for long?" Dara asked.

She had gotten into the habit of sitting with her mother as soon as she came back from school, and the others agreed without ever saying it that this was Dara's time.

"I don't know, my love, I don't ask her. Do you mind if we ask her for meals now and then? It's terrible for her up in that awful hotel all the time."

Dara agreed immediately. "Oh we must ask her as much as possible, she'd start talking to herself if she had to stay in the Slieve Sunset all the time."

Kate laughed. Dara had become so grown up, she was able to talk to her much more freely than before. The months must have made a huge difference to the girl, living here in the pub without her mother, unsure of what was going to happen and if Kate would ever come home. It was a very noticeable change. Before the accident Dara had been a tomboy, dying to get away from the house, to escape any kind of involvement or conversation, sighing at grown-up conversation, and flinching away from any confidences. And now, that was all gone. She seemed older than Michael too, while once she had waited for his every move before she decided what to do herself. She was technically a woman, and Dara already felt the stirrings of . . . well if not love . . . at least hero worship. Kate had noticed how her face changed when she spoke of Kerry. That little crush must have developed since the previous summer.

Kate felt she could tell Dara things that sometimes might seem a bit petty when she told them to John. Maybe it was a conspiracy kind of thing between women . . . she hoped she didn't overdo it. Dara seemed to approve of Rachel coming to the house. Her connection with Patrick O'Neill was never mentioned; Kate was far too loyal to bring up the matter herself, but she felt that Dara instinctively had some understanding of it.

"Will Mary Donnelly be here for much longer?"

Kate tried to look concerned and kind. "I've no idea, she must suit herself." A sharp note had come into her voice.

"Why don't you like her, Mam? She's very helpful."

"I know, I know. What do you mean I don't like her? Don't be silly, Dara."

"But you don't. Why? It's not as if she's after Dad or anything. She hates men, she even hates them when they're only Michael's age."

"She's so childish to be going on with all that kind of rambling out of her," Kate snapped.

"Is that why you don't like her, because she's against men?"

"No, I'll tell you the truth, I don't like her because she's doing what I should be doing, she's standing there serving people in the bar and not talking to them when I would be talking to them pleasantly, she's going down to Loretto Quinn and beating her down over the price of this and that instead of paying her. She has the kitchen clean and tidy, better maybe than I'd keep it. She has Leopold changed beyond recognition. But she has Carrie terrified of her, and crying if she breaks a saucer. She has the sheets clean on the beds but she has a smell of boiling in the house from Monday to Saturday."

Dara looked at her mother open-mouthed.

"And mostly I don't like her because she has two good legs that start at the top and go down to her feet and she can put one of them in front of the other and walk. If she's in a hurry she can put one in front of the other quickly and she can run. She doesn't have to drag herself by her arms and strain and stretch and pull and at the end of it be just a few inches toward the edge of the bed. I suppose *that's* why I don't like her."

Dara still couldn't speak.

"Because I'm a mean old pig," Kate added as an explanation.

Dara flew into her arms, literally hurled herself at Kate.

"You're *not* a mean old pig, it's the unfairest thing in the world that you should be like this. I told Sister Laura that God must have a very cruel streak in him to let you be just in the path of that machine."

Dara sobbed into her mother's shoulder as Kate patted the dark hair and the heaving slender body.

"What did Sister Laura say about God's mean streak?" she asked gently.

Dara drew away from her for a moment and looked at her with a tear-stained face.

"She said that Almighty God had a purpose in everything, and that we couldn't see it now. In years to come we'll see it. Do you think we will?"

Kate held the hands of her daughter and spoke slowly. "I don't know. That's the truth. I don't know. If it was something that might be cured, *then* perhaps all these months and even a couple of years in a wheelchair might have a purpose."

"But . . ." Dara waited anxiously.

"But because it's *not* going to be cured, and I will never walk again, I find it hard to believe that God has a purpose. God *can't* believe that I'm a better citizen, a better Christian to him stuck in this chair. Maybe it's just that he knew I might be a desperate sinner if I was out of the chair so he keeps me in it. That could be his purpose, I suppose." She half smiled.

"But you wouldn't have any sins would you, Mam, in or out of the wheel-chair?" Dara could never imagine that grown-ups committed sin anyway, they were allowed to do everything just because they were grown up, it seemed impossible to know what was left except murder and worshipping idols which Mam wouldn't be likely to be at.

"I suppose the biggest sin I have is not accepting what God has sent me. That *is* a sin, you know, Dara. I'm going to have to confess it to Father Hogan when he comes today, and I'm going to tell him also that I don't want to go to Lourdes. That's going to be even harder."

Dara's eyes were filled with tears again. "You *must* go to Lourdes, Mam, you must, it's the only hope. That's what Michael and I say all the time. There have been miracles and you could be one of them."

"No, darling Dara, I'm not going, there's no miracle for me there. If Our Lady wants to cure my spine she can do it in Mountfern, I am not going to spend all those people's money going there, and have all their hopes disappointed. That's it. I didn't mean to tell you so suddenly, I was going to put it gently, maybe even differently. But you're such a joy to me and such a comfort, I treat you like a grown-up daughter instead of a child."

The tears had dried and Dara was as pleased as anything. "Well, I'm going to have to look after you properly if I'm a grown-up. If you get your way about Lourdes can we have your word that you'll be sensible about Mary Donnelly and be civil to her in case she packs her bags and leaves?"

Kate burst into peals of laughter. Dara's voice was such a good imitation of her own when she was being bossy. Even her face had the same look.

"I'll be so civil, it will frighten you," she laughed.

"There's no need to over-do it, Mam," Dara said disapprovingly.

John was taking a stroll with his daughter along the river bank.

"I'm glad that Rachel is here," he said. "Your mam likes her a lot. It will take her mind off things."

"Do you think her mind's on things a lot?" Dara wanted to know.

"It's so hard to know. She says she's almost forgotten her life before the wheelchair. She doesn't even dream of herself as being able to walk anymore." He sounded sad.

"Don't get all depressed, Daddy, she hates that more than anything."

"I wouldn't be depressed in front of her, Dara. But Lord, on my own or with you, can't I let the mask drop a bit?"

They walked on companionably past the people fishing, careful not to disturb them by idle chatter. They were both remembering some of the scenes when a red-faced and furious Kate would shout and cry that she wanted no sympathy, no sad faces around her. She had even thrown a jug of milk and had broken plates and saucers, flinging them at John when he was in what he considered a gentle and concerned mood. Kate had taken it as defeatist and said it made her worse.

"I can't even bloody walk, you can all do everything, so for Christ's sake stop moaning and saying, 'Poor Mam, Poor Kate'. What is the point of that? I'd prefer to be dead. Dead, dead and buried long ago than to be poor Kate, poor Mam."

She had frightened them so much they had rung for Dr. White. He came to see her, and the family waiting outside got little consolation from him as he came out.

"Nothing wrong with Mrs. Ryan except that she is paralyzed," he said bluntly. "And that she is surrounded by people who don't give her any reason or point in living. They call the doctor if she shows any bit of fire and life, and their way of supporting her is to offer her pity. Good evening."

They never forgot it. Even Declan and Eddie knew that the mood was to be optimistic. Mam wanted to believe that things were getting better all the time. That's what gave her the energy to drag herself from bed to chair, from chair to lavatory or bath stool, and to push herself to the garden or the kitchen or the pub. If she didn't believe that things were getting better all the time, she wouldn't even sit up in the mornings.

Dara linked her father as they turned to come back along the road. "What do you think *really*, Dad, about the hotel? Is it going to take away all our business? Mary Donnelly says it could be the ruination of us."

"Mary, for all that we are blessed to have her, is wrong about almost everything."

Dara looked at her father affectionately. "It would be a terrible thing to hate men, not to see them as friends."

"I think it would be a pity all right," John agreed. "I think you'd lose out on it in the long run. And on the same subject, what's a beautiful girl like you doing on a summer evening walking the river bank with her old father? Why aren't the Tommy Leonards and the Liam Whites and the others of Mountfern beating me out of the way? Tell me that."

"Because they're all eejits, Daddy, and you're not."

"That's nice to hear. But isn't there anybody who isn't an eejit? Anybody at all?"

"Not a one." Dara was airy about it. It was just a fact. "I might be hard to please, like Mary Donnelly, or just a bit slow in seeing my chances. I keep dreaming of course, that something marvelous would happen, like that beautiful Kerry O'Neill would notice me."

"Would you like that?"

"I'd *love* it, but I'd have to fight the whole town for him. Grace says he and his father don't get on."

"Nobody gets on with their father," said John, patting Dara's arm.

"Stop fishing, Daddy," she said.

"I think Declan's turning into a proper hooligan," John said to Kate.

"God, he must be really bad if you say a word against him." Kate was surprised to hear such criticism. "What has he done now?"

"He hasn't *done* anything, it's just that he has the instincts of a gangster. He goes around punching things for no reason."

"What kind of things?" Kate was alarmed.

"I don't know, the hen house for one thing, he nearly knocked it down."

"I could knock that down myself even in this thing." Kate gave a disgusted wave at her wheelchair.

"You could knock the house down in that chair, you look so terrifying when you head for us," John laughed. "No, he just seems to tear things apart automatically without even knowing he's doing it."

"He's upset."

"We're all upset," her husband said.

"No we're not, we're fine. He's just a baby. Send him in to me when he gets back. I'll play with him for a bit."

"He'll probably have you on the floor."

"It's just being the youngest . . . poor little fellow."

"I was the youngest, I'll have you remember, and look at how well I turned out."

"You did, too." She looked at him admiringly. John Ryan had lost some of his beer belly, he stood more erect and, despite new lines on his face, he looked a younger man than he had been at the beginning of the summer.

Kate found herself turning to him for a lot more than just physical assistance. He had been able to manage in some kind of fashion without her for almost half a year. There were a lot of areas where she had to look to him now for advice.

"Do you think it's going to affect them all?" She spoke in a small voice. "You know, will it change their lives altogether . . . all this?" Again she waved in exasperation at her legs and the chair.

"No, I think they'll be less affected by it than we expect. You know how adaptable children are, they get used to any old thing after a while." He spoke gently and lovingly to take the possible hint of indifference out of his words. "I think that now you're home they'll all get on with their lives. Normally—almost embarrassingly normally."

"I hope so." She closed her eyes.

"Kate, we've been through all this before. What makes you start worrying now?"

"I expect hearing that Declan's going around kicking things, and I think maybe I treat Dara as too much of a grown-up. I've taken her childhood away from her."

"No, no." He was soothing. "She's flattered that you talk to her as an equal. No, don't worry about that."

"And Eddie?"

"He's with a gang of toughies, he hasn't time to think about anything except walls to be climbed, orchards to be robbed, jam jars to be discovered in far places so that he'll collect enough to go to the pictures."

"So that leaves Michael. He's too quiet these days, isn't he?"

"He is, and I was going to say that if you don't think it's the act of a madman I was going to ask him to go off fishing for a day with me. We keep telling people the Fern is full of pike. Why don't we go and see is it true?"

She reached over and touched his hand. "Do, of course, and tell Michael I love him."

"I won't tell him anything of the sort, he'd knock me into the river."

"No, I mean say it without saying it."

"He knows, but I'll say it without saying it anyway."

"Will you come out fishing with me on Saturday?"

"*Fishing!* In this weather? We'd be frozen, and what would we catch?"

"We spend our time telling people that the Fern is alive with pike all year round. Shouldn't we see are we right?"

"God, Dad, it'd be miserable out there. Why would you never ask me a thing like that in the summer, I'd love it in the summer."

"I'd love it in the summer, too, son, but the pub wouldn't be half empty like it is this weather."

"But why, why now?"

"I wanted us to have a day out—a chat even."

"What have I done?"

"Oh Jesus God, you haven't done anything. It's great when your son thinks the only reason you're going to ask him out for a treat is to attack him, punish him."

"But you never ask me out," Michael complained with what John had to admit was some justification.

"And I don't seem to make too good a fist of it when I do. All right, if it's not fishing what would you like to do on Saturday after lunch?"

"I suppose the pictures are out?"

"You suppose correctly."

"Could we do the book?" His eyes lit up.

John genuinely didn't know what he meant.

"The book, Dad, Mr. O'Neill's book, you haven't done it for ages. I mean, take out the boxes of papers and things . . ." His voice trailed away. John was just standing there with a blank expression. "I mean, you *are* going to do it . . . to finish it?"

"What? Oh yes. Yes."

Michael looked relieved. "Well then, could we look at some of the research and I could help you like I did before?"

"Yes. Certainly."

"Is anything wrong, would you prefer to go fishing? I suppose if we wrapped up . . ."

"No. No, you're a very good fellow . . . no."

"So have you been thinking about doing the book . . . or maybe after everything . . . you sort of didn't want to?"

"I think you're a genius, that's the very thing we'll do on Saturday. We'll take the boxes upstairs out of everyone's way and you can indeed help me. What with everything that happened I never found a moment to get down to it again, and it's been there at the back of my mind . . ."

He beamed at Michael, but the boy had the feeling that there was some sort of struggle taking place. His father had been deciding there in front of him whether to go on writing the story of Fernscourt for Grace's father.

"It's not as if it would make Mam any better by not doing it," he said suddenly, and his father gripped him on the shoulder.

"That's the truth, Michael. We must never forget that."

"Well, how much purgatory did he give you?" Rachel asked when Father Hogan had left and she was allowed to come in to see Kate.

"It's not purgatory he gives me, you heathen, it's penance, it's to keep me out of purgatory."

"It's all nonsense, you're a saint already. Did you tell him about Lourdes?"

"Yes, he hated it, poor man, but he's going to help me. He said to put it a different way, say that I'd like it to go to a parish fund to send others there, get even more money, and not to dwell too much on the fact that I'm not going to take it up myself. It might hurt people or offend them."

Rachel nodded.

"You look restless. Is anything wrong?"

"Hard to hide anything from you Kate. I've been thinking, I should go back. Back to the States."

"You don't call it home, you don't say back home."

"It doesn't feel like home, not this year."

"Maybe because you are in the middle of moving . . . all these plans about the hotel, and what it will look like and what will be here. No wonder the office in New York doesn't seem real. But your flat—think of that. It's going to be like paradise compared to the Slieve Sunset."

"Yes."

"You don't have to go, you could stay here with us."

"No, I have to go. I'm only inventing work here . . . and . . ."

"But isn't he glad that you like the place so much, feel so at home here in Mountfern? I'd have thought he'd have been delighted with you."

"I thought that too."

"Whyever not? What did he say?"

"He just wondered why I was spending so long here. I stupidly said something about getting the feel of the place. He was extremely curt with me."

Kate reached for Rachel's hand. It was hardly credible that this elegant woman with the wine suit trimmed with suede, with a silk blouse which must have cost a fortune—a cream silk with a floppy bow—should be as awkward as a child when it came to the great Patrick O'Neill. No sixteen-year-old could have been more distraught.

"You'll come back here again, it's not just a job." Kate soothed her as she had soothed her daughter earlier in the day.

"But the message is loud and clear. It will never be my home."

Rachel had never been so careless of her make-up, her silk blouse or the fine wool rug that lay on Kate's lap. She cried as she had cried in Yiddish to her mother years and years ago when the children on the block had called her a little Jew girl.

Each time Kate got a letter from Rachel she wrote back that very day. That way their letters stayed in order. They weren't crossing in the mail; they could ask and reply.

Rachel must have written just as quickly.

They learned to depend on each other in a way they would never have believed possible. Rachel wrote about working for O'Neill Enterprises in New York, though finding that the heart had gone from the business since Patrick O'Neill was many miles away in an Irish village.

Kate found it a great ease to be able to tell someone how boringly well Mary Donnelly ran the house, and how irritating it was to be told a dozen times a day, perfectly accurately, that they were blessed to have found her. It was true, which made it worse! Kate said it was a sneaky relief to be able to tell Rachel that if she heard one more Mountfern person say that Mary Donnelly was a genius she would go berserk and race around the pub in her wheelchair knocking over tables and pouring drinks onto the floor.

Rachel wrote that she had to put up with the insults and veiled triumph, Gerry Power, who had said in one hundred different ways that he was sorry it didn't work out for Rachel in Ireland. In one hundred different ways she had deliberately misunderstood him and said with a broad smile that it had all worked out magnificently and he *must* go over someday himself and see the wonderful place that Patrick had bought for himself.

Kate could admit that her new-found all-girls-together relationship with Dara was becoming very rocky, and Rachel could admit that sometimes weeks went by without Patrick telephoning her, even though she stayed in to wait for his calls.

Week after week the two women wrote of their lives, month after month they told of the changes that were happening. Neither really noticed things changing, it was only by looking back over the old letters that each realized how the other's life was moving from one direction to another.

Kate wrote of John more and more as the man who made the decisions, not as the man who was trying to cope. She never said it in so many words but Rachel could read it like a thread in the letters. There was the tale about John and the rough crowd of tinkers who came into the pub. Everyone had feared a fight if he were to throw them out, and a worse one if he were to let them stay. But there had been no fight in Ryan's, the tinkers were served as pleasantly as they could have wished. It was just the number of times that John said how heartbroken he was from Sergeant Sheehan dropping in that sent the band on their way. John had leaned conspiratorially over the counter and said that a man wasn't free to breathe in this day and age without that sergeant coming and poking his nose into what people had in the boots of their cars or on the crossbars of their bicycles. The tinkers, who were practically festooned with pheasants they had taken illegally from Coyne's wood, were on their way, with grateful glances at John and vaguely dispiriting promises that they would return.

Rachel read how John Ryan now had poems published by two newspapers, to a total of seven published works, and there was the distinct possibility of an anthology. The history of Fernscourt and its surroundings was proving long and complicated, but there were no pleas to hasten it from the man who had commissioned it, so it was taking its time.

There was the story of John and the man trying to sell him an insurance policy: John had refused it and the man had turned ugly. He had said that John must be expecting to come into a big windfall from the Fernscourt insurance people. John had been icy in his dismissal, but the man had retorted that he was only saying what half of Mountfern was saying behind his back. Kate had been upset but John had shrugged and said that a village had to have something to talk about, and since they hadn't had a two-headed calf born recently, nor a cure at the may bush, nor even a visit from a politician, they had to fill in the long winter evenings somehow.

Kate read about art galleries that Rachel had visited, and a course of ten lectures that she had been attending. She heard of trips taken by train to cities in the United States which were further apart than the whole width of Ireland.

She knew that Rachel had seen a lot of movies and heard too little from Patrick, and that she was now considered a world authority on Ireland by the people in her circle.

Without Rachel having to write it, Kate knew there were a lot of empty nights.

Without Kate having to put it down on paper, Rachel knew that Kate sometimes found the imprisonment in her chair almost more than she could bear. The frustration seeped across the Atlantic in spite of herself. The days when it seemed to rain and rain and her lovely side garden with all the plants that she was meant to admire from her green room had turned into a mire of mud.

There were the times when it was obvious that Kate Ryan might in fact explode if she hadn't this safety valve, this marvelous friend she could write to and explain everything as it was.

Like how irritating Dara could be, how downright maddening her own lovely daughter had become.

Dara had lost her unruly look, Kate said in these letters, she had become graceful in a way that was very hard to describe. She had also become almost impossible again. Everything was a shrug, a sulk and a sigh.

The record player that had been a gift from Grace played high and loud in her room, then the sounds of that dreadful Radio Luxembourg and its awful music replaced the record player.

Kate wrote in a matter-of-fact way about Patrick. She told how he was working night and day, and had little time for socializing. She knew this would please Rachel on the other side of the Atlantic Ocean. It was also totally true.

Judy Byrne, who came twice a week to do the exercises that were meant to strengthen Kate's arms, and improve the muscles that would pull her from chair to bed to bath and back, often let slip how she had invited Mr. O'Neill to this concert, or that exhibit, but never had he been able to accept. Judy shook her head sadly as she pummeled Kate, and made her repeat again and again the tiresome and stressful movements, saying that there hardly seemed to be any point in having all that money and power if you were never able to enjoy yourself.

Marian Johnson had said more or less the same thing: How sad it was that Patrick O'Neill didn't get more cooperation from everyone so that he would have some leisure time, poor man. Marian would tinkle in that *unwise* little-girl laugh and say that he had been simply desolate not to have been able to go to the hunt ball, or the charity dinner or whatever social ruse she had tried yet again in vain.

Life went on as before in the lodge, Kate wrote, or so she thought. Grace was utterly charming, and the more loathsome Dara became the more sweet and endearing did Grace appear to be. She would sit for any length of time talking to Kate, asking her advice, begging to hear stories about Kate's own teenage years. Dara couldn't bear to be in the same room as her mother these days.

Kate had heard some disturbing things about Kerry. That he had been in a game of poker up in Foley's bar, that he had been playing for high stakes with men who should have known better than to play cards with the son of the man who was going to change the face of the town and make their fortunes for them. She didn't tell that to Rachel, since it was only a rumor, no point in worrying her over something that might not be at all likely.

Several times she apologized for the trivia and small-town gossip, and she said she was sure Rachel thought of her as a poor country cousin who was to be pitied for the narrowness of her life.

But as the months went on Kate apologized less. She realized that Rachel did indeed love to hear of the small town where she had felt so much at home. Rachel wrote about how she had glorified Mountfern in her memory now. She had forgotten that there was any rain, any mud or any bad temper. She had begun to think of the terrible Slieve Sunset as a place of worth. As she spent Christmas in the Catskills the notion of her ever sitting down at a table and having turkey with the Ryans seemed so remote that she wondered how she could ever have considered it as part of her lifestyle.

John realized that without the trade from the site they would be in a poor way. The foremen, the surveyors, the visiting experts of one sort or another came for drinks at all hours of the day. They didn't necessarily drink a great deal but they sat and discussed plans . . . opened out big grey bits of paper, argued over lists of supplies.

It was all much more comfortable for them than the prefab site offices that Brian Doyle had put beside the actual Fernscourt, which was rising very slowly from its foundations. It was Mary who noticed that they bought packets of chips and this was often their only lunch.

"Do you think there'd be a future in sandwiches at all?" she asked Kate.

Kate was annoyed she hadn't thought of it first. Grudgingly she agreed that there might be a small profit in providing something to eat. She arranged to make a dozen sandwiches a day—ham and salad, cheese and home-made chutney. Anything that wasn't eaten would be devoured by the family in the evening.

John was against them at first. Turning the place into some kind of café, he sniffed, not what ordinary men wanted. But when he saw Brian Doyle and the two engineers eating two rounds each the very second day, he changed his tune.

Kate and Mary smiled their first genuine smile of friendship. And Kate said that they might even think of serving soup later on if there seemed to be any demand for it.

Mary nodded her head approvingly. "You're absolutely right," she said. "I think you should get the soup going as soon as possible. Better do something before the Yank takes all the business off you with a smile."

"That's what's going to happen, isn't it?" Kate said.

"Unless we try to fight back," said Mary gruffly. "And we'll have to fight the way he does. Like a man, of all things. Like a dirty, rotten man."

In fact there seemed to be delay after delay in building the hotel. Patrick O'Neill said that if he were a superstitious man he would think that he wasn't really *meant* to build it.

First there was an earth subsidence, not too serious, but serious enough to mean a rethink. And then, expensively, a redoing of a whole wall.

There was the time that all the cattle had gotten in through a hole in a fence and done unimaginable damage to wood that had been stored in an open shed. The hole in the fence was never explained, but was said to be the work of a crowd of kids after school one day. Patrick tried to find out if it had been malicious but Brian Doyle told him that children were the devil incarnate.

There was no use looking for malice or virtue in them, they were just bestial by nature.

There was the time that no vehicle seemed able to start or move on the site, and it was discovered that those which didn't have bags of sugar poured into them had water mixed with the petrol. Jack Coyne couldn't be blamed because he was away at Shannon Airport on the day it was all discovered. But there were definitely tales that he had been telling youngsters how to immobilize cars should they ever need to know, and further tales that he had said it would be a real laugh if none of the cars up on the site could move. Nothing could be proved. Those who were most protective of Patrick were those who most wanted to ensure that he stayed. They would never confirm any of his suspicions that there was vandalism and that much of it was directed at him.

Then there was a problem about a farmer who had said he would sell his acre of land and it turned out when the title was investigated that he didn't own the land at all, it had been signed over to his son years ago. The son being a cunning man realized there was capital to be gained and the deliberations delayed the work that should have been underway long back in that particular area.

Patrick wondered whether the bad-tempered attorney Fergus Slattery had anything to do with it, but was reliably informed by Sheila Whelan that the reverse was true. Fergus had refused to act for the mean-minded son on the ground that opportunism was something best left to wily Americans, and that since a fair price had been offered, the normal man should accept a fair price.

Each time Patrick visited Kate Ryan he felt better in his heart. The frailty, the wan look seemed to be less. Or maybe he was only telling himself this.

He liked to sit in her airy green room and talk. Here he was far from the problems that seemed to beset him everywhere else. It was a peaceful room even though it was only yards from a noisy bar. It reminded him of Rachel's apartment, an oasis of calm right in the middle of the mad Manhattan noise. Then he remembered suddenly that it was the same woman who had created both places. He never discussed Rachel although he knew how friendly the two women had become; he spoke no words of his increasing despair over ever finishing his project, his life's dream. Nor of the anonymous letters he had gotten telling him that Irish businessmen could well have developed that site, or even more upsettingly that he was responsible before God and man for Mrs. Ryan being in a wheelchair.

He smiled as he talked. The crinkly lines were still there around his eyes, but Kate thought they had etched a little deeper and there were other lines too. His voice was still cheery and his laugh hearty but some of the evenings they sat and talked she wondered was he forcing his humor and begging his laugh to echo a little more.

Kate suspected that he was a man who had a lot of doubts about the way his life had taken him. She never brought the subject up.

He had accepted her paralysis when she was in the hospital. But it seemed totally out of place in Ryan's pub. He kept looking up expecting her to swing in as she used to behind the counter. It seemed to come as a repeated shock each time he heard the high slow whine the wheelchair made on its approach.

Sometimes she did serve there, if there were friends in. A ramp had been made to a corner wing of the bar where Kate could position herself.

But usually it was that appalling virago Mary Donnelly who looked at him as if he were the devil made into flesh each time he appeared. He had been told that she felt some similar distaste for all men, but he felt singled out for her particular dislike.

Leopold had a new collar. Mary had been at a carnival where they made dog collars with names on them. In a fit of generosity she had bought one with the words Leopold Ryan. The dog had been suitably grateful and seemed pleased with it. He would approach people and arch his neck pathetically, looking like a whipped hound showing off his wounds, but in fact wanting his collar admired.

"We have to have you looking well for Princess Grace," Mary whispered to him.

Dara heard her. "Why don't you like Grace?" she had asked straight out.

"I couldn't like the seed or breed of anyone who would do such harm to your poor mother."

"But it wasn't their fault . . . the accident," Dara cried.

"I don't just mean the accident. I mean the living, taking the living away from her."

"But Mam has a very good life," Dara said, not understanding. "She always says that she hates us not to think of it as a real way of living."

Mary had opened her mouth and closed it again. "That's a fact," she said unexpectedly. "She's a great deal happier than most."

In the hope that it might soothe some of Dara's outbursts Kate suggested that she invite Grace to spend the night with them. They might enjoy chatting together and it would save Grace the long journey back to the Grange.

"Oh, so I *am* allowed to have her to stay now. There was a time when it wasn't suitable."

"I never said that," Kate said.

"No, but Daddy did when you went to the hospital first. It wasn't suitable, he said, because of . . . oh, I don't know why."

Kate sighed. "That was a long time ago, Dara, all those kinds of worries are long behind us now."

"I don't think she'd really want to stay here anyway."

"Whyever not? She always seems happy when she comes to visit."

"Oh, that's just being polite." Dara was lofty.

"The offer is there, if she'd like to come." Kate kept her temper with difficulty.

"She might come, of course," Dara said as if it were all a favor to her mother.

Rachel had written that although she didn't know from personal experience, every other mother of every other thirteen- and fourteen-year-old girl in the entire world told her the same story. And the story had a happy ending. They grew out of it. Kate hoped with all of her heart that Rachel was right.

It's hard to change the habits of a lifetime, and when Deirdre Dunne came across the two young Ryan boys as part of a gang that wrote silly things on the walls of Fernscourt, she said nothing. She just walked past with her eyes ahead of her as if she were slightly wandering in her mind.

The kids, who had hidden when they saw her, breathed with relief and told each other that Deirdre Dunne was as mad as Papers Flynn and Miss Barry and would be no threat to them. Happily they carved out "Yank Go Home" and "This is Ireland not America" with big nails, scratching away.

Deirdre Dunne had grown up on a small farm where the great philosophy had been to say nothing. She had been warned not to say anything since she was a child, and even when the neighboring farmer was known to come back drunk from a market and beat his wife senseless, the same rules had held.

It would sort itself out, she was told, and indeed it had. One day the farmer fell into a ditch on the way home. It was a cold night and he had a weak chest anyway. Deirdre had seen his wife pass the ditch where he lay, and throw more brambles and briars over it in order to make sure that there was even greater delay in finding the body.

Or had she pieced together afterward that this is what the woman had been doing. But like a true Dunne, and the daughter of her taciturn father, she said nothing.

She was almost designed to work in the office of a law firm which dealt in the human everyday business of the community. Sometimes she wondered whether she stood too far back. People like Mr. Slattery and Mrs. Whelan did get involved when they saw things as a matter of right or wrong. Perhaps it was more honorable.

Fergus Slattery was very pleased with Deirdre. A pale girl with sandy hair, she was quiet as a mouse and efficient as one of those huge new computers people were always talking about. She was as discreet as he could have hoped and when a rich farmer left a totally untoward sum to Mrs. Rita Walsh of the Rosemarie hair salon you would never have known from Deirdre's impassive face that it was anything except the norm.

She had high praise for Kate's filing system and was just as adamant that he kept in touch with how it worked. It had fallen into great chaos in the months after Kate's accident and it was a measure of Deirdre's intelligence that she had brought a notebook to the hospital to Kate to ask for confirmation of new decisions she had made.

One of the files that Deirdre had to open was called Katherine Mary Ryan versus O'Neill Enterprises and the International Insurance Society.

Part Four

Sixteen

The twins were to have a fifteenth birthday party in September. The excitement was intense, there weren't many parties in Mountfern. To be honest none of them had been to a party since they were children. But Kate Ryan had insisted. By letter she and Rachel had decided that something which would concentrate and channel all Dara's energies would be a good idea. Kate didn't suggest the party herself, of course, that way Dara would reject it as some plot. The wish had to come from the twins themselves.

So Kate spoke of the party to everyone else in a sort of sighing voice, saying she supposed now that Dara and Michael were so grown up they would want a party when they were fifteen.

It didn't take long. Carrie wanted to know what they would do at the party, would there be dancing? Loretto Quinn said she'd love to be fifteen again and she thought it was the best age of all.

Grace was asked by Miss Hayes what she was going to wear to the twins' fifteenth birthday party. And Tommy Leonard's father told him that he would have thought that poor John and Kate Ryan would have had more sense than to lash out money entertaining hulking young folk who wouldn't give them a word of thanks for it.

And so Michael and Dara realized that a party was a possibility.

"Where could we be?" Dara wailed. "We can't be in the pub, or in Mam's room, and the kitchen is a mess and the breakfast room is tiny."

"There's no point in asking for a party unless there was somewhere to have it," Michael agreed.

But Kate had that planned too. The big outhouse attached to the pub looked fine from the outside. It was whitewashed and as its only entrance was from the side garden nobody knew what a mess it was inside.

If it were to be cleaned out . . .

They could always use it for something . . .

And it would be ideal for the party.

So John suggested that as a way of earning more pocket money they should all work on it. Even involve their friends if they wanted to. It involved a few days of dragging rubbish off to the dump. There were broken beds, old bits of wood with nails sticking out of them. There was a box of jam jars with spiders in them, and a load of things that had been taken from the other outhouse in the other yard to make room for Mary Donnelly.

On the afternoon that the boys had whitewashed the big room, Jacinta looked around it in admiration.

"It's fabulous looking, it's good enough to have a party in."

And that was it.

They wheedled and begged and cajoled. And pretending an unwillingness, Kate and John gave in. The music was not to be too loud. Everyone was to be well gone home by midnight, the children had to organize the food themselves. There was to be no trick-acting, overexcitement nor people jumping into the river. They agreed to everything and began the preparations.

Kate wrote to Rachel saying that she felt as guilty as anything pulling all these strings but it did seem to be working like a dream. Dara had even hugged her in excitement one day.

She wrote that the invitation list had been assembled and discarded and readjusted more often than anyone could believe; there had never been such a magnificent way of keeping them all totally content.

Grace had all the Beatles records, and Gerry and the Pacemakers and Freddie and the Dreamers, so she would bring those.

Tommy Leonard wondered about the lighting, they would need some kind of power brought out into the place.

John Ryan said he wasn't made of money, installing electrical lighting into a place that would be used once. But he would be able to get them one extension lead which meant they could plug in one lamp, and the record player as well if they had an adapter.

Maggie said you could make marvelous lights with old turnips and pumpkins like people did at Halloween.

There was endless scooping and hollowing, and Loretto Quinn provided a box of night lights that would be put inside.

Kitty Daly said it all sounded terrific, which alarmed Maggie greatly. She had hoped that Kitty would think it was childish and beneath her and not want to come. Maggie knew that Dara had set her heart on Kerry O'Neill being on his own and maybe taking an interest in Dara herself. It would be very complicated if Kitty was there too. But before Maggie had to discuss it with anyone a letter arrived in Daly's with the good news that Kitty had been accepted for nursing in Dublin. It was a good hospital and the Dalys were pleased; their elder girls had gone to Wales where there was a shortage of any kind of nurses, so Dublin seemed like a step up to the Dalys.

Dara asked Rita Walsh was there anything in the world that made hair look shiny like all these advertisements, or was it all a cod? Mrs. Walsh told her that it was all a cod really, but gave her some sample bottles of conditioner and said to comb it through and leave it on for as long as possible.

Carrie said that if Dara was really badly stuck she could use the new hair lacquer she had bought, but to go sparingly on it.

Eddie said that Dara was trying on lipstick in the bathroom and rubbing it off on bits of toilet paper. They all said that Eddie was a boring sneak to have announced this for no reason except getting Dara into trouble because Mam said she looked like a tart with that white-colored lipstick on. Eddie said he didn't care what people thought of him because he'd be grown up soon and out of this place and he would never write to anyone not even at Christmas. And when he got rich he'd send a telegram saying "Yah Boo" and Mrs. Whelan would have to take it down and have it delivered.

Eddie's mother said that he was going to end on the gallows, and that if she had her legs she would get up and catch him and paste him into the wall.

Eddie's father took him aside and said that life was all about rubbing elbows with other people and not making fights out of nothing.

"But if I do *anything*, I'm murdered," Eddie complained. "Dara can do anything she likes and people think it's grand."

"To be fair," said John, "you do things like daubing the walls of Fernscourt with white paint. Dara only puts white paint on her own mouth in the privacy of the bathroom."

That startled Eddie, who didn't know that his father was up to date on the last little activity.

"Yes, well. Yes," he said, at a loss.

"And another thing, Eddie. You don't really want the O'Neills to clear out, do you?"

"Well, you know. It's not right him coming in here and changing everything." He was a small parrot of Jack Coyne's whining tone.

"So no more of it. If you're going to write on walls and get caught for it, then for God's sake get yourself caught for writing something you mean, not something a fellow with a grudge told you to write."

"A fellow. What fellow?" Eddie was too innocent.

"Do you know why Jack Coyne does all this? He doesn't give a damn about Mountfern and whether it's changing or not. He doesn't give a damn about your mother having the accident there, for all that he claims he does."

"He says it was all that man's fault."

"That's balls, Eddie, and if you think about it you'll realize it is. Patrick O'Neill doesn't send any business to Jack Coyne because he was cheated by Jack years back, and he knows what a gangster he is. Jack can't bear that, and it makes him look a fool."

Eddie's eyes were round.

"I'm telling you this *not* so that you'll tell all those other beauties you hang around with, but just so that you'll know. When you're sent to a reformatory or whatever you should know *why* you're going."

"I wouldn't be sent to a reformatory?"

This was much more frightening than his mother's belief he would end on the gallows. What made him sure that he was in real danger of a reformatory was this plain speaking. His father was treating him as a grown-up and telling him that Mr. Coyne was a cheat. And he had said "balls." As far as Eddie was concerned that clinched it. Things must be in a bad state if his own father would use words like that to him instead of belting the ear of anyone else who might be heard to say it.

Eddie was allowed to help at the party, he was told, but under no circumstances was he to join in. And when asked to leave he must leave at once with no arguments. It seemed a poor sort of deal. But it was the only way he would be let near the place at all.

"Will I empty ashtrays?" Eddie asked helpfully.

Dara and Michael looked at each other in despair. Wouldn't you know that Eddie would manage to bring up the subject of smoking somehow.

"There will be no need for that, thank you," Dara said in a glacial voice.

"Just be generally helpful," Michael said.

"Doing what?" Eddie asked.

It was unanswerable.

He couldn't take their coats; they wouldn't have any. He couldn't pass around the bottles of orange and lemon because they would all be on a table. He wouldn't be allowed near the record player and it was probably better to keep him well away from the food too. The thought of Eddie presenting a plate of sausages or serving a trifle was not one that gave any pleasure.

"Maybe you needn't help at all," Dara said after some thought. "Maybe you would like an early night."

Michael was more sensitive; he knew that an early night was something Eddie Ryan would never like, now or anytime in the future.

Eddie's face was bitterly disappointed. "I can't go to bed on the night of the *party,"* he said, hurt disbelief all over his round freckled face.

Even in her wish to have him one hundred miles away from the scene Dara saw that this would be too harsh.

"Perhaps you could control the animals," she said.

"What animals?"

"Our animals—curb them, sort of."

"Do you mean Leopold and Jaffa?" Eddie was totally bewildered.

"Well yes, and Maurice."

"God, Dara, what could a cat and a tortoise do at the party?" Eddie asked.

"Aha, you put your finger on it. Not much, but Leopold might break the place up. Perhaps you could be in charge of Leopold."

"Like how? Not take him on a walk now, that wouldn't be fair." Eddie was cunning.

"No, but . . . um . . . put him on a lead and sort of patrol with him. They do that at parties in America, I saw it at the pictures, somebody patrols the grounds with a dog. You know, you must have seen them, they wear sunglasses and uniforms."

Dara was thinking of a security guard she had seen in a film.

It worked like a dream.

"All right, I'll borrow some sunglasses and get Leopold's lead and patrol a bit." Eddie sounded pleased with this role.

"Not inside, of course," Michael said hastily.

"Of course not." Eddie was superior. "Leopold mightn't know it was all posh now, he might think it was the old shed still and squat down."

"Yes, that's what we don't need," Dara said, feeling faint.

* * *

They spent ages on the invitations. Nothing in the Leonards' shop was right for them. Either they were teddy bears holding balloons asking people to come to a jolly party or they were heavy silver lettering saying "You are invited." One was too babyish, one was too formal.

In the end they bought plain white cards and wrote them out individually. They knew that these invitations would be kept for a long time in the different homes of Mountfern. Written invitations didn't often arrive in the mail.

There had been long debates about the food. Dara had wanted food on a plate, like a real supper. Michael said that sausages and rolls would be better, food on a plate would be messy, people might let bits of gravy fall off.

Carrie was looking out big dishes that could cook lots of sausages at the same time. Mary got one of the beer companies to give them brightly colored trays which they could use for serving the rolls. There would be sandwiches too on the ground that everyone loved tomato sandwiches at moments of high excitement, and there would be tons of chips and nuts.

The pudding was a trifle which Kate would make herself. She loved putting on the hundreds and thousands, she said, and she explained to Grace that it was because she never had jelly and cream or trifle herself when she was young that she got so excited over party food. Her parents had not been festive people, birthdays were low priority.

Grace told Mrs. Ryan that her own mother had often been too ill for any real birthday, but she did remember years back when Kerry was twelve and Grace was nine, Mother had put on paper hats and they had all had a birthday tea in the garden. The three of them.

Father had been out at work. Like he always was.

Kate patted the golden curls and wished that Dara would be eager and confiding like this.

Still, it had to be said that since the party was planned Dara was a much easier soul to live with. Kate was forgiving, it was hard being fifteen whether you had a family that loved you or not. Dara did, Kate hadn't, but at fifteen nobody was too clear about that sort of thing.

The cake was to have thirty candles, and it was a surprise. Kate had asked Marian Johnson, who knew all kinds of people, to recommend a firm that would deliver a cake already iced.

Marian had been very cooperative and even got something off the price because she knew the people who owned the firm.

Kate thought it was sad to see Marian boasting of all the connections she had and the people she knew socially. It was not at all the way to make Patrick O'Neill think more warmly of her. Patrick needed someone like Rachel. How blind and stupid he was not to realize it. How insensitive he was to write her a note every three months or so just at the exact moment when she was making a resolve to forget him and get on with her own life.

Rachel had sent the twins magnificent shirts for their birthday. Michael's was black and red, Dara's was silver and white.

Kate had encouraged Dara to buy a white pleated skirt. But not directly. She had just left a magazine about, and let enough hints fall without saying she thought it was nice. Grace as usual did the persuading. She said she thought the skirt looked fabulous and when Dara got her birthday money in advance of the day she went into the big town and bought it.

They were dressed and nervous, ages before people came. Michael was handsome in the unusual colors, Dara dazzling, Kate thought, in the shimmering silver and white. Her eyes were huge and dark, her hair shone like satin. Kate looked at them proudly.

"I hope it will be a night you'll always remember," she said, trying to keep the choking emotion out of her voice.

"I wish you were able . . ." Michael began.

"To be able to run in and out a bit," Dara finished.

Kate brushed the tear away quickly and decided to be very unsentimental. "Not at all, that's the last thing you'd wish. If I had to come in and upset the proceedings you'd hear this old chair a mile away. It will be great altogether, the place outside looks like a palace. Your father will go in from time to time to make sure you have enough of everything."

The twins nodded. That was understood. Their father would be calling in to make sure there wasn't too much of everything, that's what was really meant.

It was awkward in the beginning, because these were people they saw every day. The girls were at school together in the convent, the boys in the brothers, they knew each other from Fernscourt in the old days, some of them from the bridge, and some from the raft, Coyne's wood or just around the town. They saw each other a dozen times a week, in the cinema, on their bicycles. They were suddenly ill at ease in their finery in a room hung with hollowed-out shells holding lights.

The conversations began and died.

Apart from Grace O'Neill: she seemed not to notice any little silences any shyness, her laughter pealed, she begged for chips, and more fizzy orange. She praised the room over and over, she admired the girls' dresses, and said that she was just dying to dance. Could they get some music started? And arm in arm with Maggie, who looked nervous in a pink dress with a thousand polka dots on it, she rummaged through the records, exclaiming over them even though they were her own. In no time the party had started.

Eddie, patrolling, would stop wistfully and lift his sunglasses to watch the dancing inside what used to be the old shed. It was full of mystery and enchantment tonight, but Eddie could never pause too long. Leopold would look up thoughtfully at the sky and Eddie knew that an unmerciful baying was about to begin, so the dog had to be hastened away to the river bank until the wish to howl at the stars had passed.

Tommy Leonard told Dara that she looked beautiful.

"That's the only word for it," he said, anxious that there should be no misunderstandings. "It's not just pretty, or nice, it's beautiful."

"Thank you Tommy, you look great yourself," Dara said, pleased.

"No, it's not just a question of looking well or not looking well. This is a description of what you *are*. Beautiful."

Poor Tommy was bursting with eagerness to make it clear that this was no ordinary exchange of pleasantries. But Dara wasn't really listening. She was looking at the door.

Kerry O'Neill had sent a note saying that if he was able to make it he would very much like to attend the party.

The note had been addressed to both of them.

Grace had said that Kerry was very unpredictable. He had left school, had gotten six Honors in his Leaving Certificate, and he was about to start work in a hotel in Donegal. Father had thought the best way for Kerry to learn the business of running a hotel was to start in someone else's. Nobody knew when he would be off.

Grace hoped it wouldn't be before the party, but with Kerry she said you never knew.

Dara hadn't wanted to keep asking. It looked so babyish.

Maggie wondered if her dress clashed with her hair. Pink and polka dots would not have been her choice but this was a dress which had never fitted Kitty properly and was therefore pronounced almost new in the Daly family. Maggie had brought it to Miss Hayes over in the lodge and Miss Hayes had trimmed it with a red ribbon and assured Maggie that all girls with red in their hair wore this color now.

Maggie danced with Liam White a lot at the party. Liam said that Maggie was easier to dance with than the others because she was smaller than normal girls and there wasn't the same danger of being knocked down by her doing rock and roll. Maggie thought this was a mixed compliment, but at least it did mean she was being asked out into the center of the floor a lot.

Jacinta White asked Tommy Leonard did he intend to dance with the hostess all night, because there was a good variety of other partners around.

Michael realized that as host he must dance with everyone, but his head turned from time to time to watch Grace as she whirled with her golden curls tied in a huge black velvet bow, and her head thrown back laughing. Grace was so alive and so beautiful. He would love to have danced with her all night, but he knew he couldn't. He went over to Maggie Daly, who looked very nice. Maggie was talking to Liam by the record player.

"Will you dance?" he asked her.

"Who, me? Are you sure?" Maggie looked startled.

Michael was annoyed. He was only asking her to dance, for heaven's sake, why did she have to look as if it were some huge thing and she wasn't worthy of it?

John looked in on the pretense that they might need more mineral water from the bar. He sneaked back and reported to Kate that all seemed to be under control.

"Nobody smoking, no one with a bottle of brandy under the table, and they all have their clothes on," he said.

"My God what a terribly dull party!" Kate exclaimed jokingly, and the two of them smiled at each other in the bar. He touched her face suddenly and she held his hand to her cheek.

Brian Doyle at the counter saw it and wondered if all that sort of thing had gone by the board for the Ryans. He presumed it had. You couldn't get up on an unfortunate woman who had all those injuries, could you. It was a terrible thing to happen to them. But still, Brian brightened, they were in their forties after all, they'd probably given all that sort of thing up long ago. Brian was thirty-four with a girlfriend in the town who was going to pack her bags and move off to another town if he didn't make a move one way or another. He put the idea out of his mind and ordered another pint.

* * *

Carrie wanted to know should she serve the sausages and Mary said give them a bit more time yet.

Mary kept a weather eye out for Leopold and Eddie. She could see why the twins had resisted having their brother around, but she wanted to make sure that Eddie didn't tie Leopold to some far-off tree and forget him. The animal wasn't used to being taken on such heavy walks with the lead.

When Mary saw them pass again, she made signs and invited Eddie to join her in the kitchen.

"What's it about?" Eddie was suspicious.

"I thought you and Leopold and I might have a sausage or two ourselves before the rush starts, what do you think?"

Eddie thought it was great. Carrie served them all and brought a big bottle of tomato ketchup as well, which was more than the people outside at the party would have.

Jimbo joined them for a few moments and gave Carrie's ear a nuzzle.

"Enough of that, Jimbo," Mary said firmly.

"It's only a bit of affection," Jimbo said.

"It's roguery and trickery and what's more it's unhygienic in a place where food's being prepared," Mary said.

"All right." Jimbo was good-natured.

Eddie was given another sausage to reward him for his hard work patrolling.

"What are you patrolling?" Jimbo asked.

Eddie was at a loss. He didn't rightly know.

"What is it exactly?" he asked Mary.

"Anyone knows you have to patrol at a function," Mary said.

"Will there be patrolling across the river when the hotel starts?" Jimbo asked.

"Bound to be," said Mary.

"Maybe I should get in quick and apply for it."

Eddie smiled to himself. It *was* a real job, he had been afraid it might have been Dara and Michael making something up to keep him out of the way.

Kerry was the last to arrive. Dara was the first to see him; she tried to stop herself running to the door, but she got there very speedily all the same.

Kerry looked wonderful. He wore a pale blue shirt with dark blue stitching all over it, it was like the kind of thing a cowboy might wear. He carried two packages, one he left by the record player, one he gave straight to Dara.

"Happy birthday, Princess," he said.

"Why do you call me that?" It was what Mary Donnelly called Grace when she was speaking disparagingly.

"All beautiful girls are princesses on their birthdays, and you more than most." He smiled at her warmly.

Dara got that breathless feeling as if she had been running.

"May I open it?"

"If you like."

She was almost afraid to lose him by struggling with the wrapping paper too long, and yet it would be terrible to rip it off.

She managed to open it, and he was still standing there. It was a beautiful hair clip with a big red rose attached. If you wore it, it would look as if there was a rose in your hair. Dara looked at it in delight.

"I must put it on, I'll go to a mirror and see what I'm doing."

"Don't run away. Here, I'll put it on for you." He lifted the thick dark hair and slid the grip with its big silk rose into place. He had drawn the hair right back from her face on that one side; it gave her a faintly gypsyish look.

"Is it nice?" Dara asked eagerly.

"It's quite lovely," Kerry said.

At that moment the record player began to play a slower number, "Michelle." Without asking her or breaking the mood, Kerry's arms went straight around Dara and they were dancing.

Dara looked around her and sighed with pure pleasure. The lights from the lanterns were twinkling on the white walls, the paper garlands hung artistically around, the tables looked festive with all the bottles of fizz and plates of snacks. Outside the night air was warm and the flowers in Mammy's side garden looked romantic and like something in a calendar picture. She and Michael were fifteen, almost grown up, all their friends were here. But mainly Kerry O'Neill, who was eighteen and the most handsome man in Ireland, had come in the door, given her a magnificent rose for her hair, told her she looked beautiful, and was holding her in his arms as they danced to Paul McCartney. Dara hadn't known it was possible to be so happy.

Maggie Daly said to Michael that she thought this party was like something you'd dream about.

Michael didn't really listen, he was wondering if as host he could reasonably change the music. He wanted to put on something more lively, like the Rolling Stones. And it was particularly silly to have Grace dancing with that good-looking but basically thick fellow John Joe Conway. Grace was so nice to everyone, she shouldn't be so polite to stupid John Joe Conway, letting him hold her close like that.

The sausages were passed around, the trifle was eaten, every bit of it. The parents and a few people from the pub, plus Declan and Eddie in his dark glasses clutching Leopold for dear life, gathered for the birthday cake. Mary Donnelly, Carrie, Jimbo, and by chance Papers Flynn who was passing by, all gathered at the door for the blowing out of the candles. There were no speeches but a lot of clapping and cheering which made Leopold over-excited and Eddie had to clench his mouth closed for fear of rousing the neighborhood.

Then the grown-ups, relieved that the party was going so well, retired, and someone had taken out the bulb of the only real light so now the place was lit entirely by the lanterns on the walls.

It smelled of the end of the summer, of Nivea Cream and Blue Grass perfume, of cheese and onion potato chips, of sausages and of the September flowers in the garden.

The music was almost all slow now. It was as if the energy for jumping around to the noisier tunes before supper was no longer there.

Michael didn't mind if there were girls he hadn't danced with yet; they probably didn't want to dance with him, they all seemed happy. He stood and talked to Grace or they moved out to dance. All the time she laughed and listened to him and told him things, and many times she said, "Michael, you are wonderful," and he knew she meant it.

Liam White danced a lot with Maggie.

Tommy Leonard looked wistfully for an opportunity to dance with Dara again, but he never got one because Dara had never left Kerry O'Neill's arms from the moment he had come into the room and given her the beautiful rose for her hair.

"It's a quarter to twelve. I suppose we should start making some noises," Kate said.

"You don't know the whole principle of drinking-up time," John said.

"Jesus, Mary and Joseph, you scared me to death. Tell me they have no drink in there."

"No, I was speaking figuratively," John said.

"Don't," said Kate.

"I meant we told them twelve, so just after twelve we go in making noises, that's the way things are done."

"How right you are," Kate said. She felt a yearning to hold John close to her tonight. And she knew he felt the same.

She had always thought that people in wheelchairs didn't feel like that anymore, that the feeling just sort of disappeared when so much else had gone.

There were so many things she hadn't known.

"I hope this isn't all very babyish for you," Dara said to Kerry.

"How do you mean? It's lovely!" He looked at her fondly.

"No, this party, lemonade, no real drink, no band, it must be a bit . . ."

"I don't want real drink, we'd never get a band as good as the Beatles to come to Mountfern so we have their records instead . . . What are you worried about?"

"Nothing," she said.

"That's good," said Kerry, "because you're very beautiful when you are not worried. I don't want to see you frown again. Is that a deal?"

"It's a deal."

Tommy Leonard asked Jacinta White to dance.

Jacinta was pleased.

"It's been very successful, I suppose," Tommy said.

"Yes, it's terrific." Jacinta liked Tommy a lot.

"But the O'Neills took over a bit, didn't they?"

"Did they?" Jacinta was genuinely surprised.

"Maybe they didn't." Tommy struggled to be fair. "I just thought they did, for a bit. Like as if they were the only ones that mattered."

John Ryan came in and collected the empty bottles rather noisily.

"It can't be time yet, Daddy," Michael hissed at him.

"No, not at all, only about ten past twelve. I was just clearing a few of these away." John was pleasant.

He noted that the light bulb was laid neatly beside the record player. He put it back in its socket and the place became suddenly very bright. John continued collecting the bottles as if he were unaware how the appearance of the place had changed.

In ten minutes, without his having to call out any message or threat, the party ended.

The youngsters of Mountfern walked home by River Road or up toward the main road or in some cases with their bicycles they headed off to the small farms around Mountfern.

The river rippled and rustled in the dark, the moorhens and ducks clucked gently in their resting places as children's feet swished by. The moonlight shone on the nearly completed buildings in Fernscourt, where a new Georgian mansion had risen from the ruins, and where the two great bedroom blocks swept away behind it looking like half-folded wings. For most of them it had been the first night like that they had ever known, and they were filled with thoughts of a future where there would be many more.

The twins sat on the window seat and talked for ages about the party. They talked about how funny Liam was and rude without meaning to be, and how pretty Maggie had looked, and what a clown that big John Joe Conway was, and wasn't Eddie a scream with the dark glasses, and how nice Carrie had been and wasn't it great that Declan had been shy and hung back, and how Mam hadn't come near them and how funny Dad was at the end.

Dara didn't tell Michael about the end of the party.

Michael didn't tell Dara about how much he loved Grace. Yes, love. That wasn't too strong a word for it.

Dara ran her tongue across her lips again and tried to remember Kerry's kiss. It had been so soft.

His mouth had pressed on hers gently at first, and then a little more firmly. That was the first time, that was when they were in the darkest corner of the room, where nobody would see.

She had closed her eyes. She didn't know why but it seemed to come naturally, and he had said again that she was beautiful, so it must have been a normal thing to do.

Then when the party was over and they were all going through the side yard and filing out, he had pulled her back suddenly and behind that archway with the climbing rose, he had held her face between both his hands and kissed her again for a long long time.

"Happy birthday lovely Dara," he had said.

During all the goodbyes, he had said he would see her soon. She stopped herself from asking when.

The next day and the day after she stopped herself asking Grace had he gone away to Donegal. She knew he wouldn't go without saying goodbye. Not after that kissing.

Dara hugged herself and wanted to cry out to the night skies about it all. But she didn't; she told nobody. Not Michael. Not Grace. Not Maggie.

And certainly not Tommy Leonard, who had said he loved the party himself personally of course, but he would have thought that Dara might have found it a bit dull, what with only dancing with the same person all night.

"No," Dara had said airily. "Funny that. I didn't find it dull at all."

Rachel was responsible for the entire design and decor of Fernscourt. She knew she would come to Ireland again, since this could not be done at long distance. For a while she had hoped she could cut Patrick and his hotel from her life totally. Then she would hand over her meticulous files to her successor, or to whatever firm of interior decorators Patrick could employ.

But this was not to be.

Too much of her life had been spent too deeply enmeshed. She was not going to leave before she saw his dream castle built and built right.

Patrick would not allow himself to be convinced by the unscrupulous in any other field, but when it came to the design of this hotel he had several very blank spots. He had been going to build a phony castle with turrets and Disneyland looks because someone had suggested that this would be suitable for a conquering O'Neill. Rachel had been the one to insist that the original house be built again and the bedroom wings tucked away at an angle.

He would have had it filled with shamrocks, shillelaghs and leprechauns if her watchful eye had not been through every stage with him. Now that the building was complete, and the decorating about to start, it was time for Rachel to return.

She was stronger now, and harder. She was a more lonely woman than the Rachel who had left here eighteen months ago hoping every moment that he would beg her to stay. Now when she came back it would be with fewer illusions.

And with fewer millstones around her neck.

Like she knew she would not set foot in the Slieve Sunset.

She asked Kate to put her mind to thinking about this, and within hours of getting the letter Kate was on the phone.

"I've found you the perfect place," she said, overjoyed that her great friend was coming back to Mountfern and coming to be beside her. It had taken a little persuasion. But she had found exactly the right place for Rachel to stay.

Loretto Quinn was appalled.

"A smart American woman with all those grand clothes like Mrs. Fine. No Kate, honestly, I couldn't cope with that. I only agreed to do all this because you said there'd be a few shillings in it once the hotel was built. No, I don't want the fright and the worry of trying to please people that are way beyond me like that."

"Shush, Loretto, listen. This is the best thing you could have. Rachel will be coming back and forward all the time, she will want her own place, she might even take them permanently."

"Won't she be staying in the hotel yonder when it's finished?"

"It won't be finished for ages and the Grange is too far away. Your place would be just ideal. I only thought of it this morning when she was on the phone. I am a sort of genius so I am."

"You might be and all, Kate, but you scared me to death. There's only beds and chairs in those rooms, there's no proper furniture, only the plainest of white curtains on them that you'd see in a lunatic asylum . . ."

"Leave it just as it is, I beg you. That's Rachel's job; that's what she gets paid a fortune for, knowing what to put on this and what not to put. You and I couldn't see it in a million years. She'll give you great advice altogether. I mean it. Look at what she did for me. She'll have your bedrooms the talk of the town. Marian Johnson will be green with envy; she'll be climbing the drainpipes to get a peep at them."

The thought of Marian Johnson being envious of poor little Loretto Quinn was such a happy one that the women laughed imagining it.

"What'll she put her clothes on till it's all done up though?" Loretto was practical.

"I know, we'll get one of those coat rails they have in shops, a big long one. Jimbo could get you one from one of the bigger shops away in the town. I'll ring a few places for you."

"It wouldn't be too bare?"

"Nothing can be too bare, apparently. That's what having style is all about."

Rachel brought them all gifts. For Dara a red dress with white tassels, bright and showy and ready to transform her into the colorful girl that Kate always knew she could be. For Michael a huge book about fish and fishing all over the world, for Eddie a bicycle lamp that looked like something from outer space, for Declan a box of horrible joke items including a cushion that made a sound like a fart when you sat on it.

Rachel had remembered that John had lost weight—there was clearly nothing she had forgotten from Kate's letters—so she had brought him two smart linen jackets: one in navy, one in a daring gold-tan color. He looked bashful trying it on but delighted with the inspection in the mirror.

Kate was right, John Ryan had slimmed down and looked somehow taller. He was so pleased with the tan jacket he planned an entire outfit based on the color and said Rachel would have to come to the big town with him one day to advise him.

For Kate there were magnificent green, blue, and gold silk scarves, each one more elegant than the next. Rachel had magic in her fingers when it came to draping them and arranging them. Everyone gasped as Kate spun her wheelchair around for admiration in the blue and silver scarf. Leopold, who had been watching through the glass door, set up a howl of approval and chased his tail happily.

It was lovely to be back in this place, and better to be back on her own terms. Rachel didn't have to worry about Patrick, about what mood he would be in, or what time he got back from Dublin. She didn't have to feel alarmed when Marian Johnson put her ludicrous oar in trying to drag up remembered incidents and share jokes. No indeed, she didn't miss Patrick here, and as Kate had said, it *did* make her feel more independent. More her own woman.

She was touched at how welcome they made her and especially by the nervousness of Loretto Quinn, who was up at Ryan's apologizing for the bedrooms before Rachel had even seen them. She hastened to inspect them and put the nervous woman at her ease.

"This is magnificent, Loretto," Rachel had said. "And if you wouldn't take it amiss I'll have plenty of spare samples of fabrics and little extras and if you like we could do these rooms up for next to nothing while I'm here."

Loretto thought that she was in heaven. In days beautiful lilac-colored curtains had arrived—and by an extraordinary coincidence they were just the right size—together with the heather carpet and the cream fabric with lilac flowers for bedspread and cushions. In front of her eyes and with no fuss Loretto saw her rooms transformed. She would walk upstairs and look at her tasteful guest rooms and clasp her hands with pleasure.

There had also been some extra material in big heavy red for a bedspread for Loretto's own room, and red and white curtains. Rachel for all her glamor was as nice as anything; she had even found a very bright colorful extra piece of linoleum that was just the right size for Loretto's shop, and since it looked so smart in that nice green and red, why not paint the counter red and the shelves green? Those young lads of Kate Ryan's would only be delighted to help out. People began to praise Loretto in terms that they never had before. Wasn't she the smart little thing now to brighten up her huckster's shop in readiness for all the visitors? Who would ever have thought that she had so much sense?

When Patrick called on Loretto Quinn he couldn't believe the transformation. Her pathetic little place looked smart and cheerful. Even the woman herself looked as if she had been made over by some women's magazine for a before and after feature.

"Mrs. Fine about, is she?" he said casually.

Loretto had been given her instructions very clearly.

"She's away on business, Mr. O'Neill."

"What business?"

"Mrs. Fine didn't tell me, sir."

"When's she coming back?"

"She didn't say that either, Mr. O'Neill."

"She's being mighty secretive about her movements, I must say."

"Oh no, nothing like that, she's full of chat, Mrs. Fine, such a nice person. I was nervous of her coming here in the first place, but now I can't think why. She couldn't have been more help to me."

Patrick had suspected he saw Rachel's hand in the transformed shop.

"Yes, I'm sure that's true, Mrs. Quinn, it's just that I expected her here to give me a report on everything."

"Did she know you were coming here, Mr. O'Neill? She couldn't have surely?"

"No, well it was a last-minute thing."

"There you are." Loretto was triumphant that her new friend Mrs. Fine hadn't been at fault.

"I'll take a look at her rooms while I'm here," Patrick said grumpily.

Loretto looked embarrassed. "I don't think . . . I mean . . ."

"Oh, Mrs. Fine wouldn't mind, Rachel would like me to see that she had a nice place to stay."

"It's just that . . . you see. If I let rooms to one person I can't be responsible to let other people in. You do see that, Mr. O'Neill. I can't be letting people traipse through."

"I'm not other people, I'm not traipsing through . . ." Patrick was very annoyed now.

"But you do see. Perhaps when Mrs. Fine gets back, if *she* would like to show you her rooms, it would be different."

Patrick banged out of the shop.

The woman was right, of course, but for God's sake the last time he had been here she was like a bag lady shoveling potatoes out of dirty old bags. Now she was all dressed up, the potatoes were in big clean containers, Loretto was taking attitudes and striking poses about showing the rooms upstairs. It was too much.

* * *

Patrick didn't risk going into Ryan's Licensed Premises. He had managed to fight with everyone he met since getting back, so he decided to put off the possibility of taking John by the lapels or entering into a screaming match with Kate in her wheelchair. He parked his car out of sight of them, and walked across the footbridge. The mansion gave him scant pleasure this morning. All he could see were the faults—the ugly angle of the drive for one thing. How much better it would have been to have come straight down in one long tree-lined sweep to the river. But how could he have suggested that when, the very day he was going to propose buying their property, Kate was crippled for life on his own building site? Then he didn't like the huge forecourt, either. It was too bare, too like a parking lot. Which was what it was. Rachel had urged him to leave three trees there but he had thought they would hide the house too much and they would be just further objects to negotiate for buses and cars. He had been wrong and Rachel had been right.

Where *was* she for God's sake?

Brian Doyle was glad to see him anyway. That made a nice change, Patrick thought grimly. He took off his jacket and sat down in Brian's site office.

"Tell me why you're glad to see me, Brian, is it because I am such a good kind employer responsible for the livelihood of at least two hundred people give or take, responsible for your own inflated lifestyle and yet another new car which I see parked outside? Is that why my presence makes you glad? Or is it because I'm the first peasant within five hundred miles who bought the Big House and made it live the way we want it to live? Or is it because of my curly brown hair and twinkling blue eyes?"

Brian looked at Patrick in alarm. He supposed the man must have been drinking, it could be the only explanation.

"Would you like a cup of coffee?" he began.

"This may come as a shock to you, Brian, but I would not like a cup of coffee. I have never, since all this began, liked any cup of coffee I have had here. It has become an interesting guessing game to know whether it *is* coffee, or tea or Postum or the water that all these things have been washed up in."

"Oh well then, forget it." Brian wasn't at all offended at the insult to the coffee made on site, he took it that Mr. O'Neill was beyond coffee, and wanted a drink fast.

"Will we go down to Ryan's and talk then?" he said agreeably.

"We will *not* go down to Ryan's, we will talk here. It may have escaped your notice that it is ten-fifty in the morning, not a time for adjourning to a pub even by your standards."

"Jesus Christ, nothing would please you today."

"You may be right. Why were you glad to see me?"

"There's been a lot of messages for one thing, people wanting to get in touch with you. The phone's not stopped all morning."

"Right," Patrick grunted. "Where's Rachel?"

"Who?"

"Rachel Fine. Has it escaped your notice that she has been working with me since 1963 in the design and interior decoration of this hotel which has made you a millionaire ten times over?"

You couldn't insult Brian Doyle, which was one of his great strengths.

"Oh, Mrs. Fine? I've no idea where she is, she's been in and out, but you know what she's like, a very helpful lady—never gets in the way, does her work, leaves a note about it and is gone."

"Yes, well what note did she leave?"

"It was measurements, someone here gave her the wrong figures for the dining room, they'd got it all wrong, the shop was going to send twice too much material. Mrs. Fine headed them off. She's saving you a packet that lady, I tell you. A packet."

"I'm glad somebody's saving me a packet, with the way that other people throw it around."

"Maybe when you feel more yourself," said Brian in the tone that you'd use to talk to a drunk about to fall off a bar stool.

"I *am* myself, you idiot," said Patrick. "I just want you to *ring* these guys as you call it. *Ring* them on that phone, as you call it, and tell them I'm not here."

"Everyone calls it *ring*, it's not a word I made up," cried Brian, stung at last to some kind of response. "And you told me yourself that you always grasped the nettle, Mr. O'Neill, you always took the bull by the horns, you said that was the one sure road to success. I've been following your example, I've been doing it myself, and it does seem to work. I've been doing much better."

"You've been doing much better because I handed you the job of a lifetime on a plate and you are taking a lifetime to complete it!" Patrick was aware that his bad temper was doing him no good but he wasn't ready to stop yet.

"Now Brian, listen to me. You do what I say, and do it now. I'm getting the hell out of here before I have a heart attack and the litigation about the hotel becomes legal history and with any luck you'd never get paid the last bit."

"And when do I say you're going to be here?"

"You don't know. You haven't a goddamn clue."

Patrick grabbed his jacket and got up to head for the footbridge.

"But Mr. O'Neill, can't I show you what we've done . . ."

"I see what you've done, the front is like a tarmac in an airport."

"Shit, Mr. O'Neill, everything was in the plans . . ."

"Don't you say shit to me . . ."

"But don't you want a tour of the site as usual?"

"How can I if I'm not here?"

Patrick was half way down to the footbridge when he saw Dara Ryan running toward him excitedly.

"Hallo, Mr. O'Neill," she called, pleased to see him.

"Well Dara, good to see you." He noticed that she was becoming a striking-looking girl, tall, dark, in a white tee shirt, jeans and a red flower tucked behind her ear—or maybe it was a bit of jewelry.

"When did you get back?" she asked.

"A little while ago. Everyone I've met has fought with me so far. You're not going to have a fight are you?"

"Lord, no." She seemed eager to talk. "Did you have a good time?"

"In Dublin. No, not really, not at all in fact. Nothing but meetings and more meetings and nothing much at the end of it. Despite what you may think I actually don't enjoy fighting."

"I never thought you enjoyed fighting," Dara said. She was anxious to ask him something. He wondered what it was.

"Well, you're right." He smiled warmly at her. It was true, he didn't enjoy a fight. He had not enjoyed the scenes some weeks back after a demarcation dispute between two sets of workers. In front of fifty men he had told Brian Doyle that they had three hours in which to decide which men did what work. If it were not agreed then every single man would be paid off that afternoon. There had been something in his face that sorted out the dispute in far less than the three hours he had given them.

It was a victory but he hadn't enjoyed it.

"And what are you doing here on the footbridge? Were you lying in wait for me?" he asked.

"Not really, I was wondering when you'd be back, there's a folk concert up in the grounds of the ruined abbey, lots of quite well-known singers, and I was wondering . . ."

"I think I'm a bit old for it, Dara," he teased.

"No, I meant if Kerry was interested in going. I wasn't sure when you were both coming back so I kept an eye out."

He looked at her and sighed. "Kerry won't be back for the concert," he said.

"He's not with you?"

"No, he wasn't in Dublin, he went straight to Donegal, did he not tell you?"

"I must have gotten it wrong," said Dara Ryan. The light had gone out of her big dark eyes.

"Can we go out for a walk?" Rachel said. It was a very sunny afternoon but with a nice breeze.

"Sure, hold on a moment until I get some gum and stick my spine together, then I'll leap up and come with you," Kate said without rancor.

"I meant me going for a walk, you going for a push."

"It's boring," Kate said. "You have to shout over my shoulder, I have to crane my neck. I wish I had a pram, people can talk *to* babies, not over their heads."

"We can talk when we get there," Rachel said.

"Get where?"

"Mystery tour."

"Why not? Let me drape one of your scarves elegantly around me so that I'll knock the eyes out of anyone we meet."

They went first to Loretto Quinn's. Kate couldn't believe the changes that had been made. Normally Loretto was so indecisive she couldn't decide whether to wrap your potatoes in newspaper, put them into a paper bag or feed them straight into your shopping bag. Now it appeared that in under two weeks her entire shop had been refurbished. There was even a man redoing the sign over the door.

Two men in the shop lifted Kate's wheelchair inside so that she could see. She propelled herself around touching this and stroking that. There was so much room here now. The place looked an entirely different *class* of a shop. Much more upper-class or something. Yet her prices were the same. Kate was full of praise.

"But it's all Mrs. Fine, Kate, she's a walking saint—a bit like yourself. I don't know why she did all this for me, I really don't. I'd never in a month of Sundays have been able to think of it all myself, or if I thought of it, I'd never have been able to do it."

Loretto looked taller, Kate thought, suddenly, which was nonsense. But maybe she was standing up more straight now, and she had tidied herself up. It wouldn't do to be the old wishy-washy Loretto with pale hair falling into her eyes and a grubby pink overall. She wore a smart brown shopcoat, with a white blouse underneath. Her hair was clipped back with a smart red barrette, undoubtedly a gift from Rachel.

Kate sighed. "You're a sort of magician, you know, you've changed Loretto's life," she said to Rachel as they went back along River Road.

"It's easy to change other people's lives, it's your own that's the problem," Rachel laughed.

"Hey, is the tour over? That was very short as a mystery tour—up to Loretto's and back."

"No, no, it hasn't begun. I thought we'd go across the footbridge and look at the hotel."

It was said lightly, but they both knew it wasn't light. Kate hadn't been across the Fern for more than two years. Not since the day she had walked across the footbridge herself and been carried out of the site unconscious in an ambulance.

"Oh I don't think so, Rachel."

They were at the footbridge. Rachel came around to the front of the wheelchair and squatted down in front of Kate. Her perfectly arranged hair in its short natural looking curls that took her thirty minutes to arrange every morning hadn't been disturbed. Her make-up made her look like a young girl. Her big dark eyes were troubled and fixed on Kate.

She spoke very seriously.

"I'm not some kind of psychologist trying to get you over the shock of where you had your accident. Lord, Kate, why would I want to do that? You could live for the rest of your life without going back to the spot where your back was broken. What good on earth would it do you to see the place? Not that you *will* be able to see the place now anyway."

"So why do you want me to go over there?"

"I want to talk to you."

"Can't we talk here or go back to my green room and talk?"

Kate sounded upset but Rachel pretended not to notice.

"Please, Kate, I want to talk to you about the hotel. We might as well talk about it in Brooklyn if you don't come with me and see what I mean."

"I know what it's like, I've heard."

"Please."

"You're the one with the legs, I might as well give in graciously."

"This is giving in graciously?" Rachel laughed.

The little path that Rachel hadn't been able to walk on that summer day because of her high heels and flimsy shoes was now a tarmacadamed all-weather pathway. With little seats placed here and there, often set into rocks or under trees. It wasn't neat and orderly like a public park, it was more as if someone had decided here would be a good place to sit and talk. The ground had been turned and dug and planted, with evergreen bushes here and lawns there. The steep slopes were planted in terraces.

"I had no idea there was so much work done here," Kate breathed as they paused to look at shrubs and rock gardens.

"It cost a fine penny I can tell you, fleets of gardeners still working on it, but it's destined not to need too much maintenance once it's finished."

On and up they went toward the house.

Although she had seen it many times from her own home across the river, Kate was unprepared for the sheer size of it. This was a huge place. She looked at the big sweep up to the front door. A dozen tour buses could come in and turn here, and perhaps fifty cars park as well, but this wasn't the real car park, that was around the side. The three-story house faced across the river. It was a reproduction of a classic Georgian house, with its high windows, its fanlight over the door. Plain and clean-lined and already, Kate noticed, at least twenty well-watered plants of virginia creeper. In five years the place would look as if it had always stood there. Patrick had been given very good advice.

Kate noticed the broken urns that she had heard about, the expensive ornaments that had been dashed to the ground one night. There had been talk about it in the pub, children some said.

There had been much more than the usual run of vandalism and hooliganism around the place. Sergeant Sheehan had confided that it looked as if it were orchestrated, which seemed hard to believe. After all, who would have a grudge against Patrick O'Neill setting up a business that would bring prosperity to everyone, the Sergeant had asked.

Kate looked up at the house in wonder. It was so like those old pictures that John had unearthed in journals and lithographs of the time. It was like the sepia pictures that he had also shown her. A big house with its two bedroom wings folded away neatly behind, not spoiling the impression of the main house. She could hardly wait to see inside.

There was a ramp into the hotel at one side, where Rachel pushed the wheelchair easily.

"What made you think of this?" Kate asked in self-mockery. "Was it so as I could come to call?"

Inside there were men working still, putting in light fitments. Others were working on the huge staircase going up from the hall. Some of the men knew Kate to see and came over to welcome her. Others remembered her from the day of the accident. Everyone knew Mrs. Fine and everyone could have given their view on her relationship with the big man Mr. O'Neill, if pressed.

"The elevators are installed but they haven't been passed as safe yet, so all things considered I don't think we will . . . ."

"Too right," Kate agreed enthusiastically. "To be carried unconscious from here a second time would be overdoing it."

Brian Doyle, who was surprised to see her there in the first place, scratched his head in wonder.

Kate decided she had been very stupid. Rachel had taken her on a tour of the Thatch Bar, a huge place with seating for two hundred and a stage for the entertainment. Four thatchers had been working on it for months and the roof looked like velvet. Not at all like the real thatch around here, often neglected and full of weeds, but perfect and what was more the perfect American idea of a dream Irish cottage.

They had been around the back and seen the terrace where little stone tables had been installed. The plan was to serve drinks out here in the summer.

Then inside the house one of the paneled rooms was called the Study Bar.

Here, from a bar surrounded by old books in glass cases, further drinks would be served. Of course there would be a cocktail lounge too, just before going into the dining room.

Slowly it sank in.

"I see why you took me on the mystery tour, Rachel, dear Rachel," Kate said.

"Can you wheel me to one of those nice stone seats we passed, somewhere where no machinery can fall on us? And we can have our little talk."

In silence Rachel found them a quiet place. Looking downhill and over the footbridge they could see Ryan's Licensed Premises nestling where it always had nestled.

"I didn't realize. I really didn't realize," Kate said simply. "Nothing was hidden from me, no lies were told, but I just couldn't see."

"That's why I wanted you to come here," Rachel said.

"We might as well close down now, rather than wait until the opening."

"No, that's not what I was trying to tell you," said Rachel.

"Well what then?"

"I'm not sure yet, something different."

"What's different than closing down when you've no business?"

"No, I mean could you do something different, could you change things a bit?"

"Dancing girls maybe?" Kate was bitter-sounding now. "That's about the only thing he hasn't thought of . . . a big neon sign, Ryan's Raunchy Roadhouse . . . see the ladies in corsets flinging their legs around. Maybe Canon Moran could come and take the money at the door."

"What would make them come down a path, cross a bridge to go somewhere else?"

"Somewhere much duller."

"What would make them?"

"If I knew that, would my heart be pounding inside me?"

"Think, Kate, think what visitors want, what do you want when you go somewhere?"

"I don't ever go anywhere. I go to Mass, and what do I want then, I want it to be Father Hogan because he's quicker, I want there not to be two collections, I want not to be parked in a draft."

"Kate. I'm trying to help you."

"I *know* you are, but why ask me what do I want when I go somewhere? I swear I don't go anywhere. I've only been on three holidays in my life, the first one down here when I met John, the second our honeymoon in Killarney and the third when we went to Dublin to see President Kennedy. How do I know what I'd want or what anyone would want?"

Rachel gave up trying to draw things out of her. She leaned over. She counted on the well-manicured fingers of her hands.

"Listen, one, they might want fishing gear, you could specialize in bait and hooks."

"*Bait?*" screamed Kate. "*Bait* in a public house where people are supposed to be drinking, a nice smelly jar of worms and a glass of Guinness!"

"No, I meant around the side. Two, they might want stationery to write home, postcards. You could sell those."

"How could I tell Jack Leonard I was going to sell writing pads and envelopes? Have sense, Rachel, you've been here long enough to know that we wouldn't *do* that sort of thing to each other."

"What else do people need?" Rachel went on remorselessly. "Three, they'll need their hair fixed, and I can tell you that Rita Walsh is getting ready for that in the Rosemarie hair salon. She has offered me a free permanent in return for a little advice about how to make the place right."

"And did you help her?"

"Sure I did, I got her a bit of this and that, suggested she rent a few new dryers—hers would frighten you just to look at them. Then I told her the truth, that Patrick had been planning a beauty salon in the hotel itself and I had said give the Rosemarie a year to see if it can cater for the guests. Rita has no time for her other activities these nights, she's too busy getting the place right before the grand opening."

Kate was impressed. "That's Rita and Loretto fixed up, and I suppose Jack Coyne might get a bit of business now. Is the feud over?"

"Not really, but Patrick must see that it is handier to have someone across the road in case the guests want to rent a car. He'll have to watch him like a hawk, and all accounts direct to the hotel, not to the client."

"So that only leaves the poor Ryans, and we won't sell bait or stationery. What had you planned for us?"

Rachel took Kate's hand. "Please, Kate, don't be like that with me."

"It's unforgivable, you're quite right. Here, lean over and give me a kiss, I'm afraid to lean over at you in case I upset the wheelchair and roll down into the river."

They held on to each other for a long minute.

"Right. Seriously, I've gotten over it now, that rotten spiteful temper of mine. Please help me, Rachel."

"I was wondering would you consider doing traditional Irish teas, and selling souvenirs. Potato cakes maybe, toasted brack, Irish soda bread."

"We couldn't. Not in a pub. Rachel, you don't understand pubs and drinking people. They would go stark staring mad if there was a hint of a leprechaun for sale or a cup of tea being served."

"Not in the pub. Beside it."

"Where we had the twins' party?" Kate asked in disbelief.

"It wouldn't be a big job," Rachel was saying thoughtfully.

"It would be way beyond us even if we'd consider it, which we would not in a million years."

"No, it wouldn't be expensive, a couple of the men could come from here, they're paid by the week anyway and sometimes there just isn't any work *for* them, and Patrick is never anxious to pay people to stand about, he prefers to have something for them to do—"

"And I know," Kate broke in, "there's going to be a few extra pieces of linoleum and carpet and end rolls of tablecloths and starts of rolls for curtains, and you'll furnish the whole place for us and we'll think we did it ourselves. And one day when Dara is dressed as an Irish colleen and the boys are all doing step dancing between tables of soda bread, we'll say to each other, *'Whatever* was it like in the old days?' "

Rachel looked at her and saw the tears were pouring down Kate's face. "I'm so sorry, Kate. Oh God, I'm sorry."

* * *

Kate sat alone in her room for a long time. She told herself that she hadn't learned much since her accident, she was still impatient and quick to judge what was right and what was wrong. But at least she had learned something about thinking before you speak. She wouldn't burden John with all she had discovered today, no more blurting out everything. She would definitely think before she spoke. In the old days she used to say it was the hallmark of a knave and a con man, someone who would have weighed up the pros and cons before venturing an opinion. But that was the old days.

She tried out some of her notions.

You need to test market ideas, she had read somewhere.

"Dara do you think we should run a guest house? You know, have people to stay and charge them. For staying like?"

"I know what a guest house is, Mammy," Dara said.

"Well, should we?"

"Here? There's hardly room enough for us in this house, let alone other people. Where would they sleep?"

"I suppose we could build rooms for them?"

"But why? Why on earth would we do that?"

"I don't know. I just thought we might. Everyone else seems to be— Loretto, and I believe Rita Walsh is thinking of it too."

"What would we want to get into it for with all that competition?"

"We have a license, they don't. We could have a bar trade. Maybe keep commercial travelers."

"Are you feeling all right, Mammy?"

"Perfectly. Why do you ask?"

"Only a very unwell person would think up such an idea. And *now* of all times, where's all this business going to come from suddenly? Nobs across the river by the busload, ordinary people on this side, and now you want a guest house full of drunks."

"I didn't say that."

"Yes you did, you said there'd be a whole lot of commercial travelers who'd want to get blind drunk at night and stay in rooms that we'd have to build on for them."

"I never heard of anything so mad," Kate said, exasperated.

"That's what I thought, Mam, that's why I asked you were you feeling all right. If there were all these drunken commercial travelers roaming the land looking for places to stay we'd have heard of them surely?"

"Loretto, where do you buy your eggs?"

"From about four farmers' wives, I spread it around a bit to give them all a turn, and then I have four families who come and deal with me as a result."

"Are they very dear?"

Loretto was puzzled. "No of course they're not, they're whatever the cost, you know."

Kate felt that Loretto should really be able to explain things a bit more clearly. "I meant it must be hard on you having to depend on farmers' wives."

"It's not a bit hard, aren't they dying to sell the eggs and make a few shillings? What made you think of that?"

"I was thinking of how much handier it would be if you had someone near you with a lot of hens, someone you could rely on."

"Oh, I'd hate that," Loretto said airily. "I'd have to pay them whatever they said, it wouldn't be the same at all. I like the women coming in and chatting. Everyone likes that, that's the way they buy eggs above in Bridge Street too."

"I see." So there was no point in thinking of a small poultry farm.

Loretto's face suddenly took on a new expression.

"Oh, Kate, I'm very thoughtless, I forgot you had a few hens. Did *you* want to sell me the odd half-dozen or anything?"

"No, we've only five hens and we eat all they produce and more. No, I was just thinking about the economy, that's all. I do sometimes, but it's always a mistake."

"Sheila, did you ever wonder why nobody ever started a launderette in this place?"

Mrs. Whelan said the thought had never crossed her mind.

"It has to be something that nobody thought of, that's all. You can rent the machines, you know, you don't have to have any great outlay. Then all you do is watch the people coming and filling them up with coins."

"It wouldn't ever take off here, of course," Mrs. Whelan said simply.

"I don't know, the place is getting bigger, what with the hotel and everything, it's going to be a much bigger place than we thought."

"It is and it isn't, Kate. But the hotel will have its own laundry, you won't see the guests taking a pillow case of dirty washing down to Bridge Street . . ."

"Or . . ."

"Or to wherever someone would put it." Mrs. Whelan seemed anxious for Kate to divulge no mad little hopes.

"A laundermat or whatever they're called would need a place where there'd be young people living on their own, there isn't even a bank here employing a dozen youngsters. No, nobody would be seen going to a laundermat. Can you see Miss Purcell taking Fergus Slattery's smalls to a public washing place? The humiliation of it!"

"You don't think it would work?"

"No, Kate, I think it would be foolish."

"I see."

"Times will get better."

"Times are fine now. It's later I worry about."

"You'll manage, you always have."

"I don't know, I really don't."

"Fergus, it's Kate Ryan."

"Well now." The warmth and delight in his voice were obvious.

"I wanted to talk to you about a worry. Would you be able to come out here at lunchtime?"

"I'll come right away." He took a file from the cabinet. Deirdre paused in her work to notice that it was Kate Ryan's compensation file.

"Is she going to talk about it?" she asked.

"I think so," Fergus said.

Mary Donnelly looked at him suspiciously.

"She's been a bit flushed and feverish. You won't upset her?"

"I never upset any woman, Mary," said Fergus. "That has been my weakness and sorrow in life."

"Don't make a mock out of something very serious." Mary banged into the kitchen but she was back in twenty seconds.

"I forgot, Mrs. Ryan, you said you'd look after the bar for an hour . . ."

"I forgot too," Kate said agreeably. "Still, I can do it. No one comes in this early, we'll have the place to ourselves. You go on about your business, Mary."

Fergus marveled at the easy graceful way Kate maneuvered the wheelchair into the bar. Up the ramp behind the counter.

He went to his accustomed place on a high stool.

"Would you like a drink since you're in the right place for it?" She smiled.

"No, even mad country solicitors don't start this early." He looked at her. Mary was right, her eyes were very bright, her color high.

"What is it?" He was gentle.

"I hate saying this to you of all people, because I always shut you up about it, but I'm worried. I think that we're going to be in big trouble when Fernscourt opens."

"You're in big trouble already." He looked at the wheelchair.

"No, we are not going to go over that again. I can't fight a man on the grounds that I went in despite all those notices and got hurt. I'm talking about something else, about the trade. I think he and the hotel are going to take all our trade."

Fergus was silent.

"So I just wanted your advice. I was thinking of all kinds of things we might do. I mean I could do anything. *Anything.*"

"Oh Kate."

"Don't 'Oh Kate' me . . . I can and will do anything to keep this place in the black, I really will. It's just that I got a bit frightened. I seem to be the last person in Mountfern to realize how changed everything is going to be."

"But I tell you."

"No, don't go on about how terrible he is and how he should have stayed in America, that's useless. It's practical advice I want. Look at everyone else: Loretto is all smartened up, and have you seen Rita Walsh's place, it's like something in Grafton Street."

Fergus smiled bitterly. "I've looked at everyone all right. Oh, they were all able to jump at the smell of money. Simple country town, how are you? This lot have their eye to the main chance, they'd be a fair match for the shysters on Broadway or the Bowery or the Bronx, wherever it was your man made his money."

"Don't make people out to be grasping, they're not, they're just . . ."

"No, not all of them are, I give you that. There are a few who have their loyalty. Not a lot, but a few."

"But what loyalty?" Kate was puzzled. "Who are they being loyal to if they don't want to make a bit of money out of all the changes?"

"To you for one," Fergus said simply.

"Oh, don't be ridiculous." She was really annoyed now. "What has it to do with me? I don't want to be the cause of any fighting. I was talking about the changes and how we should all be ready for them. Yes, us too. I've been thinking about nothing else. How it's going to change our lives. How everything's going to be different."

"It will be different all right." Fergus was grim. "You were up there yourself, Jimbo told me that Rachel brought you up for a gander at the place. How many bars did you see? Not counting the ones they'll have in the function rooms whenever there's a do on. I counted them. I counted four, didn't you? That's a fair amount of drinks for a guy to get through before dinner, if he wants a hightail or a screwball."

"Highball, screwdriver," she corrected him automatically, as she would Michael.

"I know, I wondered if *you* did."

Her eyes flashed at him angrily. "All right, Mr. Know-it-all, if you know so much can you tell me what to do?"

"Yes, certainly I can." He took the file from its big brown envelope and laid it on the bar.

She flinched away from it. "*No*, that is *not* what I want. I don't want his charity, I don't want it all to be in court. That's not what I want at all, a future based on money I got from him by a trick of law. I want to earn a living, be his equal that way." She was both troubled and annoyed.

So was Fergus. "Stop being a Christian martyr, Kate, it's too late for all that."

"I will *not* have this place divided over my accident, I will not have them taking sides, I don't want the whole of Mountfern getting upset about this and fighting over it . . ."

"If I have to tell you this once more I will lose what marbles I have left, and I assure you they are not many. It is *not* his charity it is his insurance, and the whole of Mountfern is not fighting about you. Can you get that into your thick skull?"

"Fergus!"

"I mean it. I really have lost patience with you. You pay insurance here, if a man falls off this stool and breaks his head, it's your insurance that pays for it, Einstein, not you and John. That's why you pay the bloody thing."

She laughed and relented. "I suppose you're right. I'll talk to John about it tonight. We must stop behaving like ostriches."

He looked a little mollified.

She reached across and took both his hands in hers. "You are a good true friend to us, I mean that."

As they sat holding hands the pub door opened silently and in the way nuns have of moving without appearing to take steps Sister Laura rolled silently into the bar.

Kate cursed the greater freedoms that allowed nuns to enter public houses instead of denouncing them.

Fergus wondered was there a law of timing like a law of gravity. Something that almost made people arrive in places at the wrong time.

"I hope I haven't come at a wrong time, Mrs. Ryan."

Sister Laura had a great devotion to St. Francis of Assisi which was unfortunate because Leopold sensed an animal lover and opened his great jaws, closed his sad eyes and gave a treble wail drowning any possible explanation that Mrs. Ryan and Mr. Slattery might have been about to make about their untoward conduct.

"There's no doubt about it, Sister, but your lot are everywhere now," Fergus said admiringly. "I'll be off."

"Well, if you're sure you've finished." Sister Laura's eyes were innocent.

"It's very hard ever to be finished in a pub, Sister, but of course your lifestyle hasn't as yet led you to explore that side of the human condition."

He waved from the door. "Kate, I'll come up with some ideas and when you've talked to John I'll come and discuss them."

"Thanks." Kate waved back.

"Very nice young man," Sister Laura said, sitting down as if she had been used to going into pubs all her life. "Does the most marvelous work for the community for minimal cost. Of course it's really time he got married and settled down. Bachelors don't seem to fit into today's world like they did in previous generations. Steady him down, don't you think?"

"Well yes . . ." Kate was at a great disadvantage now. Anything she said would be bound to be taken the wrong way.

"I won't stay long, Mrs. Ryan, it would turn away trade seeing a nun in here. What I wanted to say was that we've had a letter from a convent in France and there are a lot of families there who are very anxious to make contact with Irish Catholic families and have Irish Catholic girls come out there."

Kate sighed. "You know, that was something I had really hoped for Dara, to do an exchange with a French girl, but we didn't have the money this year when I was working it out. The cost of having a girl here would not be great, I know, but we'd have to entertain her, take her places. That would cost money."

"No, this is au pair. You know, doing a little light domestic duties and speaking English to the children."

"When would that be, Sister?" Kate was interested.

"It was summer they were really thinking about. Two families in particular. We have the highest references. It's in the Loire country where the châteaux are. It would be a great opportunity."

"I'll have to talk to Dara's father, Sister Laura. There are a lot of things to take into account. The fare, and that. And if she'll go! She's very thick with the Americans, she may not want to go off to France in the middle of her summer."

"She'll learn no French and very little else from an American girl." Sister Laura had fairly trenchant views about everything. "I'll be off anyway and if you do decide, let me know."

"I will indeed, Sister. Thank you for your interest."

"She's a nice bright girl that Dara," Sister Laura said. "She's a very bright girl. She lost a lot of ground the year you had your accident, poor child, she was grieving for you a lot."

"I don't know how she managed at all," Kate said.

"Of course she's probably like a lighting devil nowadays, they all *are* at home." Sister Laura spoke in a matter-of-fact way that made Kate giggle.

"I don't seem to be able to do much right, that's true," she admitted.

"I think you'd find her a lot more appreciative after a spell in France, they learn to be grateful for home comforts."

The nun had bright laughing eyes. Kate wondered what life would have been like for Sister Laura if she hadn't entered the convent. Would she have been an all-wise all-knowing mother of a fifteen-year-old? Very possibly.

* * *

"John?"

"Hold on a minute, I'll come in to you." He came in and perched on the edge of the long table that went around the walls. He looked at the pages of notes and files strewn around Kate but didn't ask her what they were.

"Wasn't that a great idea, that long table? In a million years I'd never have thought of anything so useful." He patted the furniture admiringly.

"Is there nobody in the bar?" Kate didn't want business neglected.

"Divil a one." He was hamming at her. It annoyed her suddenly, there would be enough call for all that stage Irishry later.

"Well listen, if you have a minute I want to tell you . . . well to ask you really. To discuss . . ." She shuffled all the papers with her writing on them together.

"Yes?" He was mild and encouraging. Could he really be so blind to his surroundings, and to the fact that his business was going to the wall?

"We'll have to change a lot, I was thinking."

"I know. I know."

She didn't want to hear a soothing voice, she wanted some fire, she wanted him to take the initiative.

"I think we've been fools sitting here believing that it's all going to be sunshine and laughter when the place beyond opens . . ." She paused for a moment, half expecting him to say something in defense of Patrick, but he said nothing.

"I think we'll have to start up something else, it would be mad to think they'll leave all the bars they have over in that place to drink in ours."

"Particularly on a bad day," John agreed. "And our own crowd will want to be where there's all the activity. So we'd better offer them something else apart from drink."

Kate looked at him surprised. "What would you think about a café, you know, traditional sort of teas? I know it's not what you're used to, what you expected things would be like."

John didn't look at all taken aback by the idea, she realized. He must have come to the same conclusion himself.

"Nothing's what we were used to," he said, touching the wheelchair. "Nothing was what we expected things to be like. But we've survived, and we'll go on surviving."

Seventeen

Fergus Slattery told Kate that the case was on the court agenda for next September. That it would now have to be heard, no further delays would be tolerated. Fergus hoped that the case would coincide with the hotel opening. He would love the thought of the great O'Neill missing his party because he was in court hearing a huge award for compensation being given against him. The thought of it made Fergus almost dizzy with delight. He felt his life had become grey and tired; only the thought of Kate's compensation gave it any fire at all.

Sometimes Deirdre saw Fergus finger the slim pile of documents as he took out a letter or added one to the pile. It was moving very slowly, and even when Counsel had been briefed and it should have gone much further ahead, all kinds of things intervened. There was the delay caused by the courthouse in the big town being declared unfit for use, and so cases were adjourned. Then there was a backlog occasioned by that delay. Then the insurance company changed by merging with another insurance company and all the documents had to be reissued.

Fergus had never failed to refer briskly and efficiently to the delays and adjournments, he was always up to date on the last letter that had been sent backward and forward and you would believe that he had no other case on his files.

Patrick was invariably polite and equally informed; he made it his business to be equally up to date in case he might be accused of not caring what happened.

He had offered on more than one occasion to pay some money on account. It had always been coldly refused. Barely within the bounds of civility, Fergus would hint that by paying any sum now Patrick would be getting himself in well as a philanthropist with the courts later when the assessment came.

"Any sum I paid now would be without prejudice and would be to alleviate hardship."

"They don't live in hardship, they don't need handouts and American food parcels to alleviate poverty," Fergus had snapped.

"Do you dislike all Americans, or is it only me?" Patrick had asked one day, exasperated.

"I'm interested to note you describe yourself as American, O'Neill. Anytime I've heard you speak you always call yourself an Irishman . . ."

It was never announced that the Ryan compensation case had been listed for hearing, but still everybody knew. Kate and John realized to their alarm that people had begun to take sides. There were those who wished the Ryans to take O'Neill and all belonging to him for as much as they could win in the Irish Sweepstakes. There were, it seemed, as many who said that the whole thing was flying in the face of all the generosity that Patrick O'Neill had shown to this parish. That they hoped the compensation would be insignificant and that somehow by this he would know that nobody in Mountfern or anywhere in the environs wished him anything but good.

"We'll have to pretend we don't know what they're saying, after all they never say it in front of us," John said.

"But that's very hard, why don't we tell people that we have no fight with him, and try to explain all that business about insurance companies and how it's all a formula?"

"We can't start explaining our business like that, you'd be the last to want us to air it all."

"But it's so unfair," wailed Kate. "Why should we spend our lives pretending that things are fine."

"A lot of people do," John said mildly.

"Not the *whole* time," she stormed.

"A fair bit of the time." He spoke so quietly she stopped in her tracks. She picked up his hand and laid it to her face.

Perhaps John was pretending things were fine for a fair bit of the time. And she had never noticed.

Michael couldn't see any difficulty ahead about the court case. Several times Jack Coyne had said that the twins shouldn't be too friendly with Grace O'Neill since one day they were all going to have to face each other across the bar of the court. But that was nonsense. Everyone knew that it was all a matter of what insurance the companies would pay, nothing to do with Mr. O'Neill himself who had been so good to them all.

When Michael talked to Grace they never felt there was any problem between their families. That's what made it so galling to hear the fellows at school talking about the big battle ahead. And even more infuriating to have those two eejits of younger brothers joining in all the silly antics and writing "Go home O'Neill" on the walls.

In the summery feeling of his first love Michael Ryan was able to brush all these annoyances aside. It was only Grace he thought of.

The lodge was three miles away. He could cycle two and a half miles and she could cycle half a mile and they could meet in that nice clump of trees on the hill which looked down on Mountfern. But it took so long, and then there were the explanations of where he had been. And Grace had to explain.

And all he wanted was to lie with her and stroke her and read her the poems he made up about her, about her eyes and her feet and her soft skin. And recently her beautiful breasts. Oh God, how he yearned for it to be like it had been just after the party, but there was *nowhere* they could see each other now without causing the most immense fuss.

Perhaps Mam understood more than he thought because occasionally she would ruffle his hair and say that it wouldn't be long now before the hotel was open and Grace would be living across the river from them all. But Mam said it with a shiver too, as if it were going to be somehow very frightening when the hotel opened. Michael was counting every day until his Grace could move from the lodge, which seemed a million miles away.

She had told him she loved him, she told him she had never dreamed it could be so lovely lying beside him as he stroked her from head to toe, and she trusted him and let him linger where he wanted to, she said she liked it too, and she knew he would never force her to do anything she didn't want to. Which of course he wouldn't. Never in a million years.

Kerry was learning a lot about the hotel business in Donegal; old Mr. Hill who had been running a family hotel for years there was a good teacher. He was getting a sizable fee to have O'Neill's son in his place for a type of apprentice- ship, and he was determined to earn it.

The boy would learn the business from every angle. He would work in the kitchens and at the reception desk, he would groom the ponies for the day's trekking, he would stand by the trolley as the beef was being carved. Dennis Hill said that he could give a better training than the Shannon Hotel School if he was asked to.

"Why don't you?" Kerry asked him one day. "You could easily set up a sort of training course here."

"And build up a whole breed of rivals to myself?" Mr. Hill shook his head.

"Well what about us, aren't we rivals?"

"Not at all, boy, aren't you down in the midlands there where no one in their right mind would want to spend a holiday, a big turf bog of a place miles from the sea. You're no rivals to anyone there."

His eyes were laughing. Dennis Hill was no fool, he knew that O'Neill's Fernscourt would be no threat to him as it was so far away; he also knew that if he did a good job on this handsome troublesome playboy then O'Neill would send business his way for a long time.

Hills of Donegal was a famous hotel already, its name easily remembered, its clientele faithful, its food vastly superior to almost anything Ireland offered. Dennis Hill had a large family; he kept his hotel open at a loss all winter so that they could practice for the very busy summer season.

He had never taken a foolish step.

Sometimes he looked at Kerry O'Neill's striking face and cold eyes and wondered what would become of the boy. At the first sign of any trouble here Kerry would be packed off from the Hills of Donegal household back to his father, who seemed a grand fellow all set to make an outstanding success of his venture if reports could be believed.

Dara got postcards from Kerry, but they were inside envelopes so that anyone and everyone couldn't read what he wrote. There were things you wouldn't want anyone to read, like how he wanted to kiss her lovely lips again, and he wanted to smell her beautiful hair and hold her in his arms. And there were things you would want everyone to read, like how much he missed Mountfern and was looking forward to being back.

She wished he realized that he didn't *have* to write on a postcard, he could have gotten a notepad and written pages and pages to her. Dara wrote pages and pages back.

Tommy Leonard said when she bought the notepad that she must be going to get like St. Paul and write epistles that nobody read.

"What do you mean, that nobody reads, aren't we demented with St. Paul?" Dara said.

"Yes we are, but the Corinthians and the Ephesians and whoever didn't take a blind bit of notice of him."

"They did too. He converted the lot of them."

"No he did not. Most of them went on their own way."

Tommy's father came over and asked through gritted teeth would it be possible for his son and young Miss Ryan to continue this interesting screaming match about the New Testament outside working hours.

Kitty Daly came home from Dublin for a weekend. She looked very much more grown up, they all thought. Her skirt was very short and she had a lot of make-up. Instead of taming her wild frizzy hair she let it all hang in a long curtain down her back. They nudged each other at mass when she went up to holy communion.

"I'd say she's up to no good in Dublin," whispered Dara, who always feared that Kitty had her eye on Kerry O'Neill.

"She can't be up to that much if she's going to communion," said Michael, which settled it.

Mrs. Meagher told Kate Ryan in great confidence that her bold strap of a daughter Teresa was pregnant at last. It had only been a matter of time. Mrs. Meagher wept. It was bound to happen. What in the name of the Lord was she to do? Kate soothed her, sent for more tea and spoke in low tones. Teresa could stay in Dublin, that was one thing, or she could have the child and they could bring it up in Mountfern together, that would be another. It would be a nine-day wonder and then Mountfern would let them settle down, mother and daughter living together, and then a new life to look after. It might be the making of them. Mrs. Meagher didn't think so.

There was no question, apparently, of the father being forced to marry Teresa; the girl was vague to the point of confusion about who the father might be. Mrs. Meagher wept again.

Kate said that they were living in 1966, not the dark ages, surely she wouldn't want to *force* some child to marry another child over this?

Mrs. Meagher said if there was any chance of it that is exactly what she would like.

"Wait for a little while," Kate begged. "Don't go around telling everyone, just wait, something will turn up to make it seem clear to you."

She was so calm, so confident sitting there in her chair, unruffled, and unshocked. Mrs. Meagher really *did* feel better and was glad she had come to see her.

She would have been interested to know that five minutes after she left Kate Ryan had reached out of the wheelchair, and caught Carrie's arm in a hard grip.

"Listen to me, Carrie, listen to me good. Get some kind of organization into your life with Jimbo, do you hear? Fix a day whenever you like, and don't get yourself thrown aside."

"What do you mean?" Carrie was frightened.

"I don't care if you have a baby, I'd like a baby for God's sake, I'd love to be playing with it, looking after it. I'm never going to have any more of my own, but it's going to be no good to *you*. It may well be 1966 but as far as Mountfern is concerned it's centuries ago and you'd be an outcast."

"B-but there'd be no question of that . . ." Carrie began to stammer.

"Of course there would, Carrie. I'm not a fool. And you do like him, don't you? So put it to him straight. Say you'd like to get married. Give yourself some kind of a chance."

"But he wouldn't think I'm good enough. You know he's doing great as a singer, he'd want someone with a bit more class."

"Then for Christ's sake develop a bit more class."

"Why are you shouting at me, Mrs. Ryan?"

"I don't know, Carrie, I really don't."

"Will Kerry be home for a weekend soon?" Dara asked Grace.

She got the usual reply. "Oh, you know Kerry."

It was a very unsatisfactory reply indeed. Because she didn't really know Kerry. She would love to get to know him much, much better. She wished he would say in these cards if he was ever coming back home.

Brother Keane said that the boys were to write a letter to Mr. O'Neill that would try to put into words how grateful they were for the new playing field. It would have taken years and years to have gotten what they now had through the generosity of this good man. Their own sons would have barely been playing on a good field like this if it hadn't been for Mr. O'Neill.

Tommy Leonard was the best at English; he was chosen to write the letter. Every boy in the school was to sign it. It would then be framed in carpentry class and presented to Mr. O'Neill at a public ceremony.

Tommy's first three efforts were refused. Brother Keane said to him in a voice like thunder that it was hard to believe Tommy could be so insensitive as to begin by saying "Despite the fact that you did not think this school good enough for your own son . . ." Really and truly, Brother Keane thought, all this jazz and the like had young boys half cracked these days.

Brian Doyle liked Rachel Fine. She had a very good way with people, he noticed, she spoke in a very low voice so that they strained to hear rather than shouting over them. Sometimes he felt she wanted to criticize something here and there but never did. Once or twice he actually asked her did she like something or if she could suggest an alternative. Very reluctantly she would give her views. Like the dock. Brian was going to paint it brightly. Rachel wondered would it be better in natural woods. It looked much better without the garish paint, but Rachel never claimed any of the credit, she joined in the general admiration and praise of Brian Doyle.

He wondered why O'Neill hadn't married her yet.

* * *

"Kerry's coming back this weekend," Michael said.

"Never!" Dara felt something like a lump of coal in her throat.

"Yes, he called last night, he's got a couple of days off. Grace's father was very surprised."

"When does he arrive?"

"I think he's going by Dublin so it won't be till Saturday."

"He never said."

"Does he write much to you?"

"The odd card." Dara was deliberately casual.

"It may have been a last-minute thing." Michael was reassuring. "He probably didn't tell any of the other girls either."

"What other girls?"

"Oh, can't you be sure that Kerry would have girls everywhere?"

Michael looked at Dara's face and was sorry that he had said that.

Maggie Daly's mother had sent her in to inspect Loretto Quinn's and see was it true that the place had smartened up beyond all recognition since the Jewish lady had gone to live upstairs. The Dalys had heard disturbing rumors that it would nearly be a rival for their own place. Loretto of all people! God help her, she used to look like a poor tinker.

Loretto was kind to Maggie and spent ages helping her choose between one kind of sweet and another while poor Maggie did her best to spy on the lay of the land.

"Wouldn't you have these sweets for nothing in your own place?" Loretto asked innocently.

"Yes, but I'm not meant to be eating too many of them." Maggie knew she was hopeless at this kind of subterfuge.

Mrs. Fine came down the stairs just then; she had armfuls of materials with her.

"Heavens, haven't you the most beautiful auburn hair!" she said, standing in admiration.

"Who me?" Maggie looked around in case someone else had come into the shop.

"It's gorgeous, isn't it Loretto?"

Privately Loretto thought all the Dalys had terrible heads of frizz, but maybe Mrs. Fine was just being kind.

"Lovely altogether," she agreed.

"It's Maggie, isn't that right?"

Maggie was delighted. "That's it, Mrs. Fine."

"Listen Maggie, I have something here that will look lovely with that hair." She put down her materials and found a length of ribbon. It was in a copper satin.

"Shall I fix it in your hair for you, would you like that?"

Maggie was thrilled. This woman looked like something out of a magazine herself. She was very old of course, but her style was the talk of the place and here she was playing with ribbons in Maggie's hair.

"I'd love it," she said.

Rachel took a strand of the hair and half plaited it in with the ribbon. She swept back some of the rest of the hair. Then she took a compact out of her handbag and showed Maggie the mirror.

"Look, aren't you lovely!" she said.

It was true. Maggie *did* look much nicer. Her face split into a huge smile.

"You must keep it, you're like a little Pre-Raphaelite," Mrs. Fine said.

Neither Loretto nor Maggie knew what it meant but it sounded good. Loretto's eyes held genuine admiration and Maggie could see it. She went home to abuse from her mother because she couldn't remember how or in what ways Loretto's shop had improved.

Liam White told her she wasn't looking as scraggy as usual, and Michael Ryan stopped on his bicycle for a chat.

"You look a bit different today," he said in approval.

Mary Donnelly said that if they were going to make any kind of a fist of this café they were going to run in the hopes of getting a bit of custom, they should have a plan.

"We'll have to get into the minds of Americans, that's a hard thing to do," Kate said.

"Aren't you best friends with an American woman, for heaven's sake?" Mary said as if she expected Rachel to help them every bit of the way.

And in many ways Rachel did. She told them of places that sold cheap but very authentically Irish pottery and even ordered it for them so that she could get a proper discount for them. She told them that American visitors would love to feel they were somewhere that was *really* Irish.

"Do you mean leprechauns and begorras?"

"No," said Rachel, but she didn't say it with a great deal of conviction.

"Do you mean a hint of leprechauns and begorras?" Kate suggested again.

"That's exactly what I mean, a hint of it."

"Jesus, Mary and Joseph," Kate said. "It's worse than I thought."

Eddie had another breakage. This time it was the side mirror of Judy Byrne's car. It had been parked outside Ryan's while Judy was inside doing the exercises with Kate. Eddie had been seeing how far it would turn around. Not as pliable as he had thought.

It was there in his hand when Judy came out.

"I'll fix it."

"You won't," said Judy. "You'll pay for it."

Mary suggested a source of money to him. "Your mam will pay you piece work for hemming the green napkins for the café."

"Me hem table napkins? You must be mad," Eddie stormed.

"Look at it this way: there aren't many jobs open to you, and you've done the Protestant graveyard already, so what else is there? You've a fine hand with a needle, I'm always telling you that."

"Just as long as you don't tell anyone else . . ." Eddie warned.

"Do a dozen a night, up in your room if you don't want anyone to see you, or you can come out to my house if you like, and sit there with Leopold and the wireless."

It wasn't the life Eddie Ryan had planned for himself. Sitting in a converted outhouse hemming green linen serviettes with a mad dog and Radio Eireann for company. Mary's wireless didn't seem to get Radio Luxembourg.

Still, it paid for Miss Byrne's old mirror, and Mam was very nice to him and sometimes said that he was an old dote despite everything.

* * *

Dara and Michael waited for Grace to collect them on Saturday to go to the pictures. They met Tommy and the Whites just outside—it was going to be very crowded. Declan Morrissey rubbed his hands happily. If he had his way he'd show musicals all the year round. This was the third or fourth time he had *Seven Brides for Seven Brothers* and it was always the same, you got the old and the young alike to come to it.

Michael was pleased to see the queue, it meant that they might all get separated. Then he and Grace could go to the back somewhere. There couldn't be any touching Grace if the others were all there.

Maggie was late. "Sorry," she apologized, even though it didn't matter, they were still in the line waiting to get in.

"Sorry, Kitty called from Dublin, she wanted me to think up some story about why she's not coming home for the weekend."

"She picked a poor one to invent a story for her," Tommy Leonard said affectionately.

"I know, I get so flustered," Maggie said.

"Why can't she tell them herself?" Dara said.

"She didn't want to talk to Mam, because Mam would worm it out of her, so she called when Mam was at benediction."

"Worm what?" Dara said.

"She's meeting Kerry in Dublin, that's why she's not coming home," said Maggie excitedly, and looked around at the faces of her friends.

Kerry arrived on Sunday evening. He called into Ryan's at a slack time. Kate was behind the counter in her wheelchair.

"What can I serve you?" Her smile was pleasant.

"I don't drink alcohol at all, Mrs. Ryan."

"Very sensible of you, but then that's a little hypocritical of me. If everyone was to feel like you do where would our business be, I wonder?"

"Your business is going okay, isn't it?" He looked pointedly around the almost empty pub.

"Usually a little more lively than this." Kate felt annoyed somehow that this young fellow hadn't come in when they were doing a really good business. She wondered why she was trying to impress him.

"I just came to find out if I could take your lovely daughter for a walk by the river on this beautiful evening," he asked.

"My lovely daughter has homework to do." Kate smiled.

"I'm sure she'll be able to do it later." Kerry smiled.

"At just fifteen she's a little young to let walks with young men get between her and her studies." Kate was still smiling a smile she didn't feel.

"Oh now, Mrs. Ryan, she's not *just* fifteen. I had the pleasure of being at her fifteenth birthday, a long long time ago. Way back last September, if I remember rightly."

"You remember rightly, Kerry."

"So you are saying she can't come out with me. Is this what I hear?"

"No it is not what you hear, you must go and ask her herself."

"Oh well, that's all right then. May I go into the house?"

"No, I'll call her."

Dara had seen him coming from the window seat. She had combed her hair and rubbed a little lipstick on and off again.

"Hi," she said.

"Lovely to see you again," he said warmly. "I was trying to persuade your mother here to let us go for a walk."

Dora looked at him levelly. "I'd love to, Kerry, but I have all this homework to do," she said.

He was surprised. "Can't you leave it till later?" He was sure he would convince her.

"No, at this stage there's so much to be done. I wish I'd worked harder earlier in the year but you know how it is, I'm afraid I've left it all to the end."

"You're not graduating this year." There was an edge to his voice.

"You've obviously never met Sister Laura, she thinks this is the most important year in our lives. We have exams nearly every week."

Kerry was furious. "Another time then," he said, and walked out.

Kate looked at her stricken daughter.

Round One to Dara, she thought with a mixture of pride and anxiety.

Miss Hayes had never known a prayer to St. Anthony to fail, but this time it had. Nowhere could she find the two silver salvers that had stood on the sideboard.

Marian had admired them often and said that they were magnificent silver. She had been startled to discover that Mrs. Fine had bought them for Patrick at an auction, at his request.

Mrs. Fine often bought old Irish silverware, and had said that the O'Neills should have the pleasure of looking at it before it went to the hotel eventually.

Every two weeks Olive Hayes cleaned the little collection. Mrs. Fine had visited once and praised her highly for the wonderful way it had been cared for. Now Miss Hayes was worried—what could have happened to them? It was unlikely that they had been robbed. There had been no break-in, and anyway there was always someone in the house.

Marian Johnson did drop in from time to time but she would never . . . of course not. And those little Ryan twins and Maggie Daly from the dairy. No, it was out of the question.

She would have to think again—was it possible that she had placed them somewhere else? Or perhaps Mr. O'Neill had already taken them to the hotel, or to have them valued.

Olive Hayes was very troubled.

Americans would want entertainment. Kate knew that.

But what kind? It couldn't be amateurish in their café when it was professional and well organized across the river.

What would they expect in an Irish café? If it was to be truly authentic then of course there wouldn't be singing and dancing, nobody would be doing anything except getting stuck into their tea and scones. But this plan was for something that wasn't quite authentic but looked as if it might be.

What a pity that none of them played the harp, and that they didn't have a big tuneful harp handy in one of their outhouses.

* * *

Carrie asked Jimbo would they get married sometime.

"Sure, we'll get married sometime," Jimbo said.

Carrie felt vaguely dissatisfied with this reply.

Jack Coyne asked Loretto did the great O'Neill spend the night above in the rooms with your woman.

Loretto said certainly he did not.

Jack said Loretto was right to keep her mouth shut. He would do the same in her place. Loretto was annoyed about that, since she was not being diplomatic. It was the truth. Patrick O'Neill came to call sometimes but he never stayed the night.

Dennis Hill telephoned to know whether Kerry's father had recovered from his illness.

Olive Hayes told him that there had been no illness.

"There has to have been an illness, why else did he go home?" Mr. Hill wanted to know.

Miss Hayes decided to rescue the situation. "There was a bit of trouble all right, it wasn't exactly an illness," she said.

Mr. Hill never pried. He had just been calling out of courtesy, he said. When would they expect Kerry back?

"I'll ask him to call you himself," said Miss Hayes.

She told Kerry that he should call Donegal. She told him that Mr. Hill was now under the impression that what he had thought was an illness was in fact a little trouble.

Kerry smiled a great charming smile at her. "You are a great ally, Miss Hayes," he said.

"I wouldn't rely on it, Kerry," she said.

"I get the picture," Kerry said.

Dara and Maggie were on the footbridge, when Kerry came along.

"Maggie, could you do something for me? Please." His eyes were a piercing blue. They looked straight at little Maggie.

"Sure," she said good-naturedly.

"Could you go up to the hotel and see if my father is around? I want to go up and talk to Brian Doyle about something, but my father thinks I've gone back to Donegal so I want to make sure he isn't there. Can you look and see if his car is there? Do you mind?"

"Not at all, but am I the right one . . . ? I often get things wrong."

"No, you're perfect, you look so innocent no one would know you were my spy."

Maggie scampered up the path by the laurel bushes.

"Well," Kerry said to Dara.

"Well what?"

"Well what was all this drama, you had homework to do? I came straight out and put myself on the line and asked your mother . . . and you turn me down. What was all that about?" He looked very angry. Dara's heart began to pound. It had been a very risky thing. She had wondered afterwards had she been mad.

"No reason," she said, shrugging.

"Don't do that, it's so silly, it makes you so cheap, so common. I came to see you. I thought you liked me. Why are you playing silly games?" His handsome face looked hurt.

"Well . . ." She didn't know what to say.

"Because if you don't want to see me, that's fine, just say it straight out. But if you do, let's go up to Coyne's wood."

"When?"

"What's wrong with now?"

"You can't mean now. You've just sent Maggie on a message."

"That was so that I could talk to you. My father's in Shannon today."

"You told her a lie . . . !"

"It was so that I could ask you what was wrong."

"And you met Kitty in Dublin too!"

"Silly little Maggie, getting everything wrong. I *saw* Kitty in Dublin and she clung and clung. Kitty the clam I call her."

"We can't go off and leave Maggie to come back and find us not here."

"Yes we can if you want to."

It was the longest moment of Dara's life.

"No, I'll wait for Maggie. You sent her on a fool's errand," she said.

If Kate Ryan had been watching she would have said, "Round Two, Dara."

"John, will you read me some poetry?"

"Aren't you too tired, love?"

Kate sat in her green room, her eyes too bright, her face drawn.

"No, I have that feeling I'm not going to sleep."

"Let me get you into bed first then I'll go and find something you might like. I haven't written anything for so long."

"How could you?" She touched his hand in sympathy. "But tonight I want you to read me other people's poetry, not just your own, and no, I won't go to bed yet."

"Other people's poetry?" He was disappointed.

She was deliberately light and joky. "Yes, isn't it very presumptuous of them, but other people did write poetry, like Yeats, or Oscar Wilde or James Clarence Mangan."

"Will I read you the *Lays of Ancient Rome?* I love that . . ."

"No, something Irish."

"Or *Hiawatha* . . . I've never read the whole of *Hiawatha* aloud. *That* will send you off to sleep all right."

"No." She gripped the sides of the wheelchair in impatience.

"All right, all right . . ." He went to the bookshelves and ran his finger along the backs of books for what seemed a long time. Eventually he took out a book and began:

> "Oh my dark Rosaleen
> "Do not sigh do not weep . . ."

"Stand up over there so that I can see you," Kate said. "Now start again."

He read the poem with gestures, putting a lot of emphasis into it and giving the repetition a fine sonorous sound.

"That was very good," Kate said approvingly.

John's face was empty. "That wasn't me reading poetry to you, that was an audition, wasn't it?"

"Yes," Kate said in a small voice.

"Well?"

"It was very good. Could you bear it?"

"Of course, if we *have* to."

"We have to."

Rachel was adamant about not letting him stay the night. If Patrick wanted to preserve the fiction that he and Rachel were just good friends, then preserve it. She did not even countenance making love in her rooms. She was a respectable woman staying in Loretto's, she didn't want any reputation, thank you very much. And Patrick always had to leave early.

Once or twice they had managed it in Coyne's wood, and in the back of the car and in a far distant corner of the river bank on a rug. It had been exciting and uncomfortable at the same time.

"I may have to go back to New York for a week, come with me," Patrick said suddenly one May evening, in Loretto's.

"What for?"

"Well, we could make love properly for one thing without risk of half the town discovering us or getting curvature of the spine." He was grinning at her in the way she loved and hadn't seen a lot recently.

"No, I have a lot to do here."

"You've nothing to do here, stop fooling yourself."

A flash of anger. "Shall I list the things I have to do here . . ."

"No, don't be tedious, Rachel, we both know why you're here, we both think it's a great idea, so what? Just quit pretending it's a real career and you can't be taken from it to come to New York for a week."

Never had she been so angry. Never.

They both knew why she was here, it was so obvious was it?

She knew she must keep calm. Nothing must be thrown away for the very unimportant luxury of losing her temper.

"What had you in mind for us in New York?" she asked levelly.

"I don't know." He put on a teasing smile. "Maybe we could get ourselves to a justice of the peace and get hitched, that way I wouldn't have to be thrown out of here like a college boy at ten o'clock at night."

"Would you like to get married?" Her voice was calm.

"No, what man *likes* to get married? Hell, of course I don't want to get married, Rachel, I'm too old, you're too old, we're fine as we are. Hey?"

No response.

"Hey? Rachel, you're not sulking now, are you? We're fine as we are. Why complicate it? Why think I love you more if you tie me down by some bit of paper?"

She looked at him levelly.

"Well, say something, woman, for God's sake, have I done the one unforgivable sin saying this? You did ask me would I *like* the idea of being married. I'm telling you. Straight up."

"Sure," she said.

"What does that mean?"

"Not much, I guess."

"So what did I say that was so terrible?"

"I suppose what was terrible was that you thought a piece of paper would only tie *you* down, you never thought that it might also tie down whoever you married. It's a bargain you know, marriage, not just one person being lassooed by another. It's a sharing thing."

"You didn't do very well during your attempt at it," he lashed out.

"You weren't exactly faithful during *your* attempt at it," she said straight back.

He was silent.

Rachel sat still in her chair. Her cream linen suit and her little sprig of purple heather worn at the lapel matched the room perfectly.

She didn't look at Patrick, she looked across at the sun setting over Fernscourt. Her face was not sad, she was calm and entirely in command. She was thinking that this was the end of the road. She had traveled so far, so many years and so many thousands of miles and it would end now, in recriminations like so many relationships.

"It's got nothing to do with you. With you as a person," Patrick began.

Rachel said nothing, she didn't even listen, it was as if she had always known it was coming, this conversation, the goodbye.

"In fact I want your company and to be with you more than anybody. You know that."

She looked across and saw men still working in the fading light. They were getting overtime now to finish the job in time.

"Shit Rachel, why did you have to go and suggest we get married? Why couldn't you let things go on the way they were?"

Almost reluctantly Rachel lifted her eyes from the men who were finishing the stone wall around the forecourt, and brought her glance to Patrick.

"I did not bring up marriage, Patrick, *you* did. You said we would find a justice of the peace in New York and get hitched. Please be fair."

He was wrongfooted over this. "Yeah sure, but you said . . ."

"Forget what I said. Don't let it end in a war of words—you said, I said. What does it matter? And as you said it has nothing to do with me as a person."

She stood up, straightening her skirt. "I'll show you out now."

"Well . . ."

"Good night, Patrick. I'll be going to Connemara in the next day or two, probably tomorrow. We'll consider we said goodbye now. Right?"

He put his hands on her shoulders. "Listen . . ."

"Yes?" Her eyes were large and dark, they looked into his very directly, they didn't dart about anxiously trying to read his face.

"Listen Rachel, I'm not worth it."

She smiled patiently as she might have smiled at a child.

He was struggling for words.

"Even if I were, if I could . . . even if I did feel . . . there would be so many complications, there'd be all hell to pay. You have no idea how much trouble and everything . . ."

He looked at her, pleading, begging her to understand that their marriage would be opposed by Church and society even if he could bring himself to propose.

Rachel Fine had some dignity left. She chose not to understand what he was saying.

"Patrick, you've a lot of work to do tomorrow and so have I." She kissed his cheek.

"But . . ."

She had closed the door behind him.

She leaned against the door as she had seen so many heroines do in movies. But no heroine had ever behaved as stupidly, she thought, no woman who ever leaned against a door like that had been such a downright idiot as Rachel Fine letting her man go like that.

Possibly to the arms of Marian Johnson. And even, when the hotel was built and he was lonely, possibly he might marry Marian Johnson. Church and society wouldn't oppose that, they'd be delighted with it, and the divorced Jewess could be moved from the scene. She didn't cry, she felt too empty to cry. She didn't go to the window to see him driving off.

She just stood motionless for a long time.

John Ryan sighed. Sometimes he wished he could discuss things with someone. Mary Donnelly was out, she hated Patrick O'Neill with a passion. He couldn't speak to Fergus because young Slattery seemed to hold the O'Neills personally responsible for Kate's accident and could only think of the day when the huge compensation would be paid over.

Dr. White was not a good ally. He seemed to think that John was a bit of an old misery. On more than one occasion the doctor had told him straight out that Kate's condition could be made much more bearable if her immediate family surrounded her with hope and optimism.

No point in talking to his son, the boy was like a moonstruck calf pining over the little American girl.

He felt unwilling to bring his worries to Dara. She was still a child and it made him seem weak to tell his own daughter that he couldn't communicate with her mother.

As he went ahead with the preparations for Ryan's Café, John's heart was heavy.

One afternoon when Mary was minding the bar, when Kate was busy hemming green table napkins for the café, when the children were at school and the menagerie reasonably peaceful—Leopold snoring in the garden, the cat purring like an engine on the windowsill—John sat down to write a poem.

This time he didn't write about the land or the people who had once walked this land. This time he wrote about the cage he found himself in; the cage which he couldn't escape from because he himself had built the bars. They were bars of concern and love and good manners. They were rules he had made so that he would not hurt anyone else. He wrote how by forcing yourself to take one course of action and adopt one set of attitudes you can also be untrue to yourself and deny your real worth.

It was the cry of a strong man who found himself trapped and couldn't see an escape. He looked into Kate's room—she had fallen asleep over her sewing. Gently he took the needle and green linen from her hands and arranged the cushion behind her back in the chair. He left the poem beside her and went for a long walk. He walked up to Coyne's wood and beat at the undergrowth with a stick for a while. Then he found himself climbing that big mossy hill toward the Grange.

He went in and asked for a pint of beer.

Marian's place was slipping, he noticed, the bar was not clean and it was late afternoon, there were still ashtrays full and glasses uncollected. The stocks hadn't been checked, you could see some bottles had nearly run out and others had marks of liquid down their sides.

It had been years since he had come here and it used to be much smarter in the old days.

The youth serving had neither manner nor charm. He gave the wrong change and didn't apologize when it was pointed out.

Who would stay in the Grange when there was a luxury place like Fernscourt opening three miles away? John gave a little shiver. He had heard too of the way that Patrick had interviewed the staff, how he had told them that American guests liked to be made much of, to have their names remembered. They liked people to say "You're welcome" when they said "Thank you." Patrick had searched Ireland for the right manager and, not being satisfied with any of the applicants, had gone to another hotel and offered Jim Costello twice his salary to leave at once and come to manage Fernscourt. Costello, an attractive go-getting young man, had given the matter five minutes' thought, which had raised his salary even higher, and then left the hotel after serving three weeks' notice and finding a successor for himself. Costello was the right man for Patrick O'Neill. A man who would not burn his bridges, he had left his old employers on good terms and he could always go back if Patrick and he had a falling out; on the other hand he had impressed his new boss with his quick thinking and decision. He was a man of great charm; he had drunk many a pint in Ryan's and delighted everyone with his easy ways.

Patrick O'Neill and Jim Costello wouldn't have employed a surly youth like this boy behind Marian Johnson's bar. John pondered on just how much the old order was changing.

He left, thanking the boy and getting no response, and walked down the hill. There was a scurry at one stage when he passed the big clump of trees, as if he had disturbed a courting couple. He smiled to himself, thinking how stony and uncomfortable the ground must be.

For half a moment he wondered whether it was Michael and Grace he saw disappearing into the bushes. But he dismissed the notion. For heaven's sake, it was the middle of the afternoon.

What would they be doing up here? And anyway they were *far* too young for that sort of thing.

Mary Donnelly was glaring at an inoffensive couple of farmers who took no notice of her whatsoever.

"This is a great pub, Mary," John said as he came in.

The farmers looked up, amused.

"If you can't say it who can?" one of them laughed.

"Have you been drinking?" Mary asked suspiciously.

"You're right, Mary. God, it would need to be a sharp man to fox you. I was up having a pint in the Grange, as it happens."

"And it wasn't to your liking?"

"It was not. There was no warm service with a smile like you get when you come in this door. Oh boy no. There was only glares and surly shrugs. What human would want a pint in a place like that? People want to be made welcome in a place, that's what running a pub or a hotel is about, it's not just about pouring alcohol down their throats."

The farmers looked at each other and grinned conspiratorially.

Mary flushed a dark red. "If you're saying that I . . ."

"I'm saying that it's lovely to be back in a friendly atmosphere," he said firmly. "That's all, and if we're going to keep any custom from going over to O'Neill's Thatch Bar we'll have to let them know that they're welcome here, and really welcome too."

He banged out of the bar and into the house.

Mary was open-mouthed. That was the first time John had ever admitted publicly that there was a threat from O'Neill, and imagine admitting it in front of two customers. He must be really upset.

Kate was sitting by the open french window, wearing her gardening gloves and tidying up one of those high urns that Rachel Fine had cleverly positioned, one on each side of the door. These were Kate's alone, she grew herbs and heathers in them, they were easy to reach and made her feel she was really gardening.

"I've been thinking," John said.

He pulled off her gloves and held her hands.

"So have I. When I read your poem and realized what it's like for you, not wanting to upset me, and not knowing how to talk to me, I felt I could have put the power into my body and run after you. I woke up and read it and I could feel such energy surging through me, I was sure I'd have the strength to stand."

Her eyes were wild with trying to explain, she was like a child straining to have more movement than she had.

"Gently, Kate. Gently," he soothed her.

She would not be calmed. She thought as she had so often thought about that summer's day when he had wanted to make love and she said no, it was ridiculous in the middle of the afternoon, and that she had felt restless. Restless indeed! If she had stayed with him as he had wanted she would never have wandered into Fernscourt and into this life in a chair.

"You *do* have great strength," he told her. "Aren't you the strongest woman in this county? I mean it."

"But tell me that you *know* I'd be nothing without you. The children will grow up and go away, and the pub may win or lose but the only thing I want is for us to be together. Insofar as we can ever be together because of this bloody chair." She hit the arms of the wheelchair in frustration.

"But you're only saying what I know. I know you love me." He was smiling a huge smile of pleasure.

"I can give you nothing. Nothing a wife can give."

"Stop, stop."

"I've been so selfish, I never sort of helped you or anything."

She was talking about some of her earlier attempts to give John pleasure. They had both been embarrassed and Kate had cried at not being able to do it properly. John had been embarrassed at something so obviously selfish that could not be shared. They had attempted it less and less.

"I'm all right, look at what you have to bear, for God's sake. It doesn't seem all that important to me that we can't make love as we used to."

"But I was thinking we could." Kate's eyes were definitely excited, her color was high.

"How do you mean?"

"Draw the curtains," she said.

He closed the glass doors and pulled the soft green and white curtains.

"Come here," she whispered.

"Wait till I lock the door. It would be the one time we'd have Leopold, Mary, Carrie, the children and half the bar arriving in on top of us."

She laughed like a teenager.

"Get me out of this bloody chair, John Ryan, and love me."

He lifted her onto the bed. Her dress opened easily; she had all her clothes made front-fastening so that she could dress herself with the minimum of fuss.

"But we c-can't . . ." he stammered.

"Why not? It's my body. It won't hurt, I won't feel much but I can feel above the belt, if you know what I mean. That's nice."

"But can I . . . inside you . . . wouldn't that be bad for you?"

"Why would it? It's just paralyzed, it isn't out of bounds." She was high with excitement and was stroking him encouragingly.

"Kate, I don't want to do anything that might damage you . . ."

"It won't. I checked."

"You checked? When did you check?"

"This afternoon. I called Dr. White."

"My God! What did he say?"

"He said fire ahead, and that he was delighted, he thought we'd never get around to it."

Fergus Slattery called and was told that Mr. and Mrs. Ryan were in Mrs. Ryan's room and weren't to be disturbed.

"Nothing wrong?" Fergus inquired.

"John is like a lighting devil today, perhaps they're having a row," Mary Donnelly said. "There isn't a man in this house that will speak straight to you, I'm afraid."

She was still smarting from Michael's cross-questioning. He had been highly alarmed to find that his mother and father were closeted together, and felt sure that the only reason could be that Dad had actually seen him with Grace. The thought was too mortifying even to entertain for a moment.

What could Dad be telling Mam, and how soon would he be called in and *what* would he say? And why couldn't that awful Mary stop snarling at him and tell him what *kind* of a peculiar humor had his father been in when he came home?

Michael, white with anxiety, had gone to throw stones from the footbridge, and pray. If God arranged it so that Dad hadn't seen, then he would . . . what would he do? He couldn't offer to give up being with Grace because that was what he wanted most in the world. Suppose he offered God a rosary. Not enough. God was known to be particularly against Immodest Touches, and whatever he and Grace were up to it would certainly come into that category. Perhaps if he gave God a promise that he would go to confession soon, and fixed a firm date. Perhaps that might do.

"Was it important, your message?" Mary remembered belatedly John's startling instructions that she was to be high on charm.

"You could always write it down, Mr. Slattery, and I'd see that they got it."

"No, I'll phone them later," he said.

"They've taken the phone off the hook," Mary explained.

"God, it must be a terrible row altogether," Fergus said.

Rachel looked into the window of Meagher's. As always she was looking out for the kind of thing that Kate might be able to display in a glass cabinet when they got the café going.

Meagher's window was not the most inspiring of places, and the woman who ran it seemed to know little or nothing about the odd selection of stock she carried. People had told Rachel that it was the late Mr. Frank Meagher who was the one who knew something about the business. The window held the usual collection of musical boxes, travel clocks and some really appalling candlesticks, and there in a box with tissue paper were the two silver salvers that Rachel had bought for Fernscourt. Salvers that had been on Patrick's sideboard on the only occasion when Rachel had visited the lodge. She had been there once when she knew both children would be far away.

Rachel stared unbelievingly at the two pieces of silver. They were worth everything else in the window three times over. Patrick surely could not have sold them. Surely, surely not. Rachel went in and bought a brooch shaped like an L which she would give to Loretto. She spoke to Mrs. Meagher, a sad-faced, worried-looking woman about the silver salvers, and with shaking hand managed to pay for the brooch. She needed to be in the open air quickly.

In the Lodge Olive Hayes had come to a decision. She was going to mention the salvers to Mr. O'Neill.

The only question was the matter of approach. Should she ask whether he had in fact taken them elsewhere for safekeeping? Or should she say that she had not been able to find them?

There was nobody she could discuss it with. If only her sister Bernadette were not at the other end of the earth.

She could have talked about it with Sheila Whelan of course. Even if it had been Marian, Sheila would not have told the whole town.

She could even have approached Mrs. Ryan in the pub. She would never have thought of it as a slight on her own twins.

Sergeant Sheehan was the kind of man she could speak to quietly, but it wouldn't have been fair. Once she spoke to him it would have to be official.

No, it would have to be Mr. O'Neill himself, without the luxury of asking advice from others.

Patrick came in, his face weary.

She decided to give him a while to settle down.

But he had read her face. "What is it, Miss Hayes?"

"How did you know there was anything, sir?"

"I haven't worked with people since I was fourteen years of age without learning something. What is it?"

"It's the silver salvers, sir, for the hotel, that used to be on the sideboard."

"It's all right, Miss Hayes." He looked very weary.

"I only noticed today they aren't there."

"It was a misunderstanding. They'll be back."

"Oh, that's all right then." She moved away, about to go back to her kitchen.

Patrick realized that she was not going to launch into a line of questions or explanations.

"Miss Hayes."

"Sir?"

"I value you more than you'll ever know."

Her face became brick red with pleasure. "Thank you very much indeed, Mr. O'Neill. It's a pleasure working here. You are all very appreciative people."

"I meant what I said about coming to the hotel with us. I think we'll need you."

"Oh, we'll discuss that nearer the time, Mr. O'Neill."

"How sensible you are. I'm afraid those nuns in your sister's place will snap you into the convent and you'll never be heard of again."

She went away smiling. But she looked back at him before she got to the kitchen and saw that the smile had fallen away and under the genial affable face that he presented to the world Patrick O'Neill was angrier than she had ever seen anyone in her life.

Brian Doyle had handed him a note. It was all sealed with sticky paper.

"Mrs. Fine said you were to open this on your own over a desk or something. It's got something very fine in it that might fall out." Brian was uncaring, but keen to deliver the message exactly as Rachel had instructed.

"All right."

He had opened it in his car. Alone.

Patrick,

I am writing this because there is no way you and I could discuss it usefully.

In Meagher's the jewelry store on Bridge Street you will find the two silver salvers. Mrs. Meagher bought them from Kerry three days ago for a fraction of their worth. Mrs. Meagher is not to be blamed for trying to cheat him, she is also selling them at an equally impossible price.

I have no idea, nor do I want to know what happened. For all I know you may be party to this, but I think not and I wanted to forewarn you. Naturally I said nothing at all to Mrs. Meagher that would indicate I knew anything about the pieces.

For your own information Mrs. Meagher is a gossipy, unstable person who is unhappy here in Mountfern and has been considering leaving. Her problem is that she has little capital and even less get up and go.

I leave it with you. Obviously I will be happy to do anything to help but I feel this is something you will want to handle on your own.

I told Brian Doyle a rigmarole about this letter needing to be opened carefully, I thought that way you would be sure to read it on your own. I feared if I said it was very urgent and private he would have had every kettle on the building site at work on it. But perhaps I misjudge him.

Love always,
Rachel

"Mrs. Meagher, how are you this fine day?"

"Dragging the divil by the tail as usual, Mr. O'Neill. How is it that you are always so cheerful?"

"It's in my nature, I expect." Patrick smiled broadly.

He pulled up the small rickety chair close to the counter. "About those salvers that my son brought in, the ones that are in the window."

"He said he had full authority . . ."

"Oh yes, no problem like that at all . . ."

"And if you want them back, Mr. O'Neill . . . I did think that maybe it wasn't a good enough price but your lad seemed very pleased . . ."

"Not at all, nothing like that . . . no no." Patrick's voice was soothing.

"So I hope I didn't do anything out of turn . . ."

"You know the way children are, Mrs. Meagher, you do your best and then you wonder *what* was the right thing to do . . ."

Mrs. Meagher sat down on the other side of the counter and leaned across to Patrick.

"Mr. O'Neill, you don't know the truth you're saying . . ."

Patrick O'Neill drove himself slowly back to the lodge to wait for his son. In his briefcase he carried the two silver salvers.

"I'll give them a little polish, will I?" Olive Hayes had suggested.

"That would be lovely, Miss Hayes."

The evening shadows lengthened, he sat alone looking in front of him. He had telephoned Loretto Quinn's. No, there was no sign of Rachel and she had not said where she would be.

He had telephoned Ryan's and she was not there. The ridiculous harridan who looked after the bar for them said that Mrs. Ryan was not to be disturbed.

There was no sign of his daughter either.

The key turned in the lock.

Kerry came in.

He was surprised to find his father sitting alone and with no work in front of him.

Surprised but not alarmed.

"This is all very peaceful," Kerry said slightly mockingly.

"I'd like to go out, Kerry." Patrick's voice was very calm.

Kerry decided to be flip. "Well then you *must* go out, Father, don't let me stop you," he said.

"We'll go right away."

Something in his tone made Kerry follow his father's look, and on the sideboard he saw the two gleaming silver salvers.

His face did not change. "I see," he said.

"Good." Patrick looked dangerously quiet.

They left the house without words.

Miss Hayes watched them from the kitchen window. They walked toward the woods.

"Why did you do it?" Patrick asked his son.

"I needed the money."

"You are a fool as well as a thief. Do you have any idea how much they were worth?"

"A great deal more than that woman gave me, but that wasn't the point."

"What was the point?"

"The point was that I needed that amount and she could give it to me, so it couldn't matter less what the real value of those trays was. They only represented to me a way to get what I needed."

"So if you are going to steal from my house and make us a public exhibition in my town, my place, it doesn't even matter that you get a fraction of what these items were worth."

"No. Their worth is not important."

Patrick's hand went into a fist without his having any control over it.

Kerry saw. "Don't forget all you spent on that orthodontal work, Father. I mean, if you're talking about value for money, why smash it all up? It cost you a fortune to get me all this bridge work."

The spasm of white anger passed; it was replaced with something much deeper. Something, Patrick felt, that was going to be with him for a long time.

"Do you hate me, Kerry?"

"Of course I don't, Father."

"Then why?"

"I told you, I needed money. Why do you have to be so Italian about everything? Love, hate—life isn't like that."

"What is it like then? Tell me, I'd love to know what life *is* like."

Kerry leaned against a tree. He looked impossibly beautiful in the evening light. He looked like a painting of a young hero, not a cheat and liar who had stolen from his own father and showed not an ounce of remorse.

"Life is about excitement, Father, it's not about the past and the old days and the old order and righting wrongs that were done centuries ago—if they were done at all."

"Excitement?" Patrick said.

"Yes, that's about the best I can do to explain." Kerry seemed bored.

"Is there not sufficient *excitement,* as you call it, in Donegal? Why did you have to come to that center of excitement—Mountfern—and humiliate me in my own place?"

"You are not humiliated, Father, I'm sure you got out of it."

"You're goddamn right I did. I bought Meagher's shop."

"Hey," Kerry laughed. He gave a natural, amused little laugh. The boy was not even remotely touched by what he had done.

"I told Mrs. Meagher that there had been a misunderstanding, she told me that children were all the same. I listened to her woes, one of them being that she couldn't find a buyer. We need a place in Bridge Street. She's leaving almost at once. She will say nothing about your misunderstanding. I will say nothing about some of her circumstances."

"Like her daughter being a teeny bit pregnant." He laughed again.

"We don't have you to thank for that, do we?"

"Teresa Meagher, Father. Please. You must think I'm hard up!"

"Why did you need the money?"

"My business, Father."

"No, Kerry. My business now."

"Are you going to beat me again?"

"No, of course not."

"There's no of course about it, you want to."

"No, I want you to tell me. Tell me why."

"You're such a man of the world, you have this sixth sense, you tell me, Father. You always say you have a feel for things."

"Cards?" Patrick said.

Kerry paused. "Yes," he said.

"Was that it at school all that time ago?"

"Sort of. Betting, big talk."

"Aren't you a fool."

"No, sometimes I win."

"I'm sure you do. At the start of every game in the sucker's build-up."

Now it was Kerry's turn to look scornful. "How would you know, Father? You're much too cagey, too cautious to play a hand of cards."

"I did once. For long enough to know I hadn't the time to invest in it."

"Very praiseworthy," Kerry mocked.

"No. Very practical. That's what it was. If I wanted to play cards I'd have learned how to do it, not get taken by every half-assed two-bit man around, like what seems to be happening to you."

"I was unlucky one night, that's all."

"Unlucky? Do you even know the odds?"

"It all depends, Father."

"It does not depend. There are odds on filling a straight, there are odds, you fool, on getting a house if you have two pairs. Actual odds—you don't know them and you expect to steal my silver to pay for your idiocy."

"Yes, I can see that from where you stand, it's hard."

"No it's not hard. It's easy."

"How do you mean?"

"You get taught, taught to play properly. If that's what you want."

"It's not like that. You can't enroll in night classes."

"You can if you want to."

"How on earth?"

"Brian Doyle's brother is a card player, deals in a club somewhere out the Galway Road. One of the best, they tell me."

"He can't be great if he's dealing cards in a club near Galway."

"He liked the liquor as well. That's what slowed him down. Go to him next time you're home, bring him a bottle of Powers, say you'd like to learn a few fancy deals, waterfalls, that kind of thing. He'll straighten you out."

Kerry's mouth was open.

"He doesn't deal from the bottom, he doesn't have marked cards. He'd be the first to tell you of people who have no fingers to play with if they do that sort of thing."

"This is Ireland, Father, not Chicago in Prohibition."

"This is card playing all over the world, Kerry."

"Do you mean that I should go to this guy? You'll set it up?"

"I won't set it up, you set it up. You heard of him, turn up there. Meanwhile get your ass back to Dennis Hill. I suppose you told him some lie."

"I had to. They were pushing me a bit for the money, these guys."

"Are they in the hotel?"

"God no, the hotel's as dead as a dodo. They're over the border, in Derry."

"That should be excitement enough for you."

"They're good people, it's just that someone else was pushing them."

Kerry got a feeling that his father wasn't interested.

"How did you find out, Father? About Meagher's?"

"My business."

"And you don't seem to have . . . well, too many hard feelings."

"I don't have any feelings. That's what is so strange. I have no feelings at all. Maybe you always felt that toward me so you know what it's like. But it's new to me. When I got up this morning I suppose if anyone asked me how I felt about you, I'd have said I loved you. When I saw those salvers in Meagher's and had to negotiate with that stupid woman, and saw you leaning against the tree there . . . I might have said I hated you. But now. Nothing. Nothing at all." Patrick seemed mildly regretful.

Kerry knew that his father was speaking from the heart.

"What happens to me now, Father?"

"As I said, you go back to Dennis. After the opening you and I talk again, it could be you want to go to the Shannon school. You could go abroad to a hotel in France, Germany, Switzerland. We'll have visitors from there too, and that seems to be the way of the future.

"Of course you might want to go to university. I don't know, Kerry, let's not look too far into the future."

"And this . . . this business?"

"It's over now, isn't it? I mean there's nothing else gone in the house, I won't go into the church and see our candlesticks on the altar?"

"No, Father."

"Well that's it. Twice. Anyone's allowed two mistakes. The third time is it."

"How do you mean, it's it?"

"It's goodbye, it's notice in the paper time, I am not responsible for the debts of . . . That sort of thing."

Kerry was silent.

Patrick rattled his car keys. "I don't expect you to stop playing cards—that would be childish of me—and anyway if you're going to talk to Francis Doyle, you may get quite good and make a nice living. I don't expect you to stay clear of debt. If you do get into debt again come to me, come back and we'll discuss it. Within reason, and in return for work or whatever, I will try to help you, and you must come home here for the holidays and stand by my side at the opening and all of that. But if you steal from me or from anyone else, then it's over, it's as if you were never my son."

No emotion in his voice. No pleas ho hate. No wishing for love.

For the first time in his life Kerry felt a chill of fear.

Rachel and Patrick missed each other by minutes. She went to walk along the towpath in the evening light. He went into Ryan's for a drink. There was always company there, he thought, always a welcome.

It was odd that the only people who should make him feel really welcome were the very people whose business would suffer most by his coming to Mountfern in the first place. He looked at John and Kate Ryan and how they seemed to sparkle so well at each other. As if they were still very much in love. After all these years. After that terrible accident.

He wished that Rachel were at home. He had seen that there were no lights, and there was no car outside Loretto's.

He would have liked more than anything else to talk to her tonight and to have slept with her, to have laid his head on her breast while she stroked his hair and soothed away his worries. She knew him so well, and he had hurt her so badly.

Rachel walked alone on the towpath past bushes and brambles and briars. She couldn't understand why they hadn't been cut back to give the guests a better walk to the town. But there had been some story about a fairy ring which it would have been bad luck to cut down.

She met Maggie Daly walking along.

"All on your own?" she asked. A foolish question, she thought, just as she said it.

"Just like you, Mrs. Fine," the child said with no hint of insolence. She was only stating a fact.

"Where's everyone?" Rachel persisted.

"I think Grace went for a cycle ride with Michael, and Tommy's been playing football with John Joe Conway and Liam White, and Jacinta's gone to get a new coat, and Dara's . . . I don't know where Dara is. So I came for a walk on my own."

"I don't know whether it's a great idea or not. I do that sometimes."

"What else is there to do?" Maggie asked simply.

"What would you like to do? Now, this minute."

"I think I'd like a gorgeous new dress in just the right color that would make everyone notice me and people say, 'Would you look at Maggie Daly?' That's what I'd like."

"Well come on home with me and we'll look through some books and magazines and we'll see what might suit you."

Maggie hesitated for a moment. Her mother had been a bit disparaging about Mrs. Fine, something to do with her not being baptized, and leading an immoral life. But her mother didn't know where she was, and wouldn't it be lovely to have Mrs. Fine give her ideas like she had with that beautiful ribbon that everyone had admired?

"I'd love that," she said, and they went across the footbridge, away from the sound of Ryan's and up to Rachel's rooms.

Mary Donnelly was glad the row had blown over. In fact it must have ended in some kind of reconciliation. They kept smiling at each other that evening in the bar. At one stage she even saw them holding hands.

It was probably about that business of John going to be reciting poetry in the bar. He had been dead against it at the time, but tonight he had books of old Irish poems out on the table and was busy marking some of them as if he were a boy back at school. And talking about boys back at school, Michael had recovered his good temper and even apologized to her for being short with her earlier. A misunderstanding, he had said humbly.

She saw John take his wife's hand and bring it to his lips when he thought nobody was looking. The way they smiled at each other gave her a lump in her throat. For the first time for a long while she thought of the man who had let her down and wondered what it would have been like to have him take her hand like that. Then she put the thought out of her mind and concentrated on being charming, which frightened the farmers more than anything she had done so far.

Eighteen

"Wasn't it odd that the Meaghers left so quickly?" Loretto said.

"Oh I don't know, they got a chance of a place in Dublin, a small lock-up shop, and Patrick paid them a good price for the shop in Bridge Street. It was all for the best to go quickly. She's never been the same since poor Frank died."

Kate had congratulated herself several times on the amazing foresight she had had in telling Mrs. Meagher to hang on for a bit, something was bound to happen. And hadn't she been right! Imagine Patrick O'Neill wanting a small place in the center of town. It had solved the Meaghers' problems at a stroke.

Loretto was still musing. "She'll have the divil of trouble with that strap of Teresa in Dublin. If she was able to run wild in Mountfern, imagine what she'll get up to in Dublin."

Kate didn't agree. "She may have done all her running wild, she could be about to settle down for a bit now, have a quiet period for a change."

Loretto looked at her in wonder. "Isn't that extraordinary, Kate. Her mother said almost the very same thing to me herself."

"Would Dara be insulted if I offered her some material to have a dress made?" Rachel asked Kate.

"Insulted? She'd grab it out of your hands. But you can't be giving them things. You're too generous as it is."

"No truly, I have lovely bits of material, really nice pieces of fabric. They're samples, some of them are for drapes or wall hangings—furnishing fabrics. But they're quite elegant enough for a skirt or a dress."

"Well wouldn't she love it!"

Kate was never without something in her hands these days—if it wasn't the table napkins it was tray cloths. They were sitting companionably in the green room. The summer was almost with them, and the weather was warm enough for the two glass doors to be left wide open.

Carrie served tea on a trolley, another gift from Rachel; she said she had ordered some for the hotel. Kate hoped she was telling the truth; sometimes she thought that Rachel disguised her generosity by pretending it was some cast-off from the hotel.

"Am I imagining it or is Carrie thickening around the waist?" Kate whispered.

"You *are* imagining it." Rachel pealed with laughter. "My goodness, what a suspicious mind you have. Perhaps Carrie and Jimbo just sit and talk when they're out together."

"Not very likely," Kate said dismissively. "But you're right, I mustn't start fancying things."

"Is anything worrying you? Anything apart from Carrie?"

"No." It was not very convincing.

"I don't mean to pry," said Rachel.

"I'd tell you if it was sensible." Kate sounded as if she were ashamed of herself.

"Worries are rarely sensible." Rachel smiled.

"I'll tell you. I worry a bit about Dara and Kerry. I get this feeling that Kerry is a bit . . . well, a bit dangerous."

"I worry about Kerry too," Rachel said unexpectedly. "And I think Kerry is very dangerous."

The two women sat, heads close together, sewing forgotten, and sighed over the impossible situation. The more that Dara was warned against him the more attractive he would be to her. And if Kate were to put difficulties in his way about meeting her daughter, he would enjoy the challenge and come home more often still from his Donegal posting to move heaven and earth in pursuit of Dara.

Jacinta White told Dara that Mrs. Fine was the mistress of Mr. O'Neill. They had been lovers for years in America. Jacinta knew this on the highest authority. She said that Liam didn't believe it because he didn't really understand mistresses and lovers. But it was true.

Dara, who thought it was indeed true from the days when Grace had told her of their fears that Mrs. Fine might become their stepmother, denied it utterly.

"You're full of drama, Jacinta," she said, defending her own friend Grace from having a wicked father and defending her mother from having a wicked friend.

"And you're full of airs, Dara, and you haven't a hope with Kerry O'Neill." Jacinta flounced off in a bad humor.

"What's wrong with Jacinta, why won't she come with us anymore?" Grace's eyes were big and innocent.

"Oh, Jacinta's an eejit, she's always taking notions over one thing or another." Dara gave no explanations.

"She's very jealous of you, of course," Grace said.

"Of me?" Dara sounded like Maggie now.

"Yes, she likes Tommy and Tommy has time for nobody but you."

"Oh that's not true. Is it?" Dara was pleased.

"Michael tells me that Tommy writes your name all the time on his notebooks at school. Michael says he writes mine, but he says Dara is interleaved with all those celtic letters—you know, on the front of notebooks."

"Heavens." Dara wasn't quite sure what to say. It was nice to be someone fêted on the cover of exercise books, as Grace herself was. But it was not Tommy Leonard that she wanted writing her name.

"I wish I was really really beautiful like you are, Grace," Dara said suddenly.

Grace stared at her in amazement. "But you are *much* more beautiful than I am." She seemed to be burningly sincere. "I've only got a round chocolate-box face, I look like that silly boy blowing bubbles in the picture up in the Grange. I have no looks, you are the one with the gorgeous face . . . Dara you *must* know that. Kerry was saying . . ."

"What was he saying?" Dara was eager.

"He was saying that," Grace said.

"How did he say it, I mean what was it exactly . . . ?"

"Just that." Grace couldn't see any need to dawdle on what Kerry, who was only her brother, said. "And you look terrific when you have a suntan, Dara, you look great. I look as if I have a skin disease if I stay out in the sun."

There was going to be no more about what Kerry had said and when he had said it. Dara hadn't much pride, but she had too much pride to ask again.

He was home the next weekend.

"Fair and square. Permission and everything." He grinned at his father, and to Grace's pleasure Father smiled back.

Things were definitely better these days.

"How do we spend Saturday?" Kerry asked his sister when Father had gone off to the hotel. Patrick O'Neill didn't work office hours, he worked a great deal too many hours for Brian Doyle's taste.

"Oh good, are you going to be around?"

"Well yes. I think so."

"Michael and I are going fishing. I've gotten rather good at it lately." Grace giggled a bit. "We cycle off for miles and find really quiet places." She looked down and up again and caught Kerry's eye.

He wasn't smiling.

"You *are* sensible aren't you, Grace?"

She pretended not to understand.

"Oh very. Anyway the places we go, the river isn't dangerous. It's narrow and shallow, usually."

"That's not what I mean."

"Oh."

"Father's not going to look after you, as long as he has his folly . . ."

"Why do you call it that? You used to love Fernscourt."

"Someone has to. You're very young, Grace, it would be terrible if you made a silly mistake."

"No, Kerry, I wouldn't."

"But it's different for boys. Does Michael respect you, or does he take advantage of you?"

"We just kiss a bit. That's all." Grace looked down again.

"That had better be all, and don't go to far-away places to kiss. Listen to me, Grace, I know what I'm talking about. Michael's only a kid but he could make you do something . . . something foolish."

"No, it's not like that . . ." She wished the conversation would end.

Just then there was a ring at the door. Miss Hayes didn't go immediately so Grace seized the opportunity.

It was Rachel Fine.

Kerry looked annoyed.

"I'm sorry, but Father has gone up to Fernscourt," he said, barely politely, when Grace had ushered Mrs. Fine into the room.

"I'm very sure he has." Rachel smiled pleasantly. "He was always an early worker, and all days of the week. No, I didn't come to see your father, Kerry. I came to visit with Miss Hayes."

Kerry smiled at her as if this were the way things should be. Rachel Fine was welcome in the lodge if she had only come to talk to the help.

Olive Hayes had spoken once or twice before to Mrs. Fine—a very pleasant woman, she had always thought. A Jewess they said, and a lady friend of Mr. O'Neill, but there had never been any impropriety in this house and not in Loretto Quinn's either. She was surprised to see her come into the kitchen.

"Patrick has told me how well you run this household for him, Miss Hayes, and perhaps I am speaking out of turn when I ask you if you have enough free time to make a few simple summer dresses."

"For you, Mrs. Fine? I'd not be able to make anything good enough for you."

Rachel smiled easily. "No, I won't ask you to take on my complicated figure, Miss Hayes, you would have nightmares trying to get anything to hang straight on me. I meant for some of the girls, for Dara Ryan, Maggie Daly . . ."

"Make dresses for them . . ."

"Yes, I've been told that you're the dressmaking genius of Mountfern . . ."

Rachel took out two lengths of silky material—one copper-colored, one in a clear aquamarine. They were beautiful fabrics.

Miss Hayes ran her hand lovingly under the folds. "Oh, these are too good altogether for children, Mrs. Fine."

"Suppliers send me samples, Miss Hayes. There's two and a half yards there in each of them, they're no use to me and I was thinking that if you could make a dress each for the girls—"

She broke off. Grace was standing at the kitchen door.

"Aren't they *gorgeous*," she said in admiration.

Rachel was pleasant. "I have all these pieces, Grace, and I was asking Miss Hayes if I could persuade her to make dresses for Dara and Maggie. Miss Hayes is very gifted. She made a wedding dress last year that was the talk of the town, Loretto told me."

Olive Hayes looked very pleased.

"I didn't know that." Grace was interested.

"Oh, I do a bit now and then in the afternoons." Miss Hayes was as pleased as punch.

"So if you and I could come to an agreement about a fee, do you think . . ."

"It would be a pleasure, Mrs. Fine."

Grace fingered the copper silk weave. "Who's this for?"

"It's for Maggie, it's the exact color of her hair."

"Is it?"

"Yes, it will look quite lovely on her. This is for Dara."

"Do they know, or is it a surprise?" Grace had heard nothing about it.

"They know that I was coming to see Miss Hayes, and they've seen the fabric."

"Heavens," Grace said.

"I've plenty more, Grace, if you . . ."

"I didn't mean to ask."

"No, and I'm sure Miss Hayes . . ."

"I'd love to make something for Grace, but she has such expensive clothes already, I didn't like to . . ."

None of them were finishing their sentences but there was already an easy friendship between the three.

Kerry could see this when he came out to see what was happening. And his handsome face frowned slightly.

Sister Laura didn't know that there was such an interest in clothes, but she did realize that there wasn't sufficient interest in work. And she was disappointed that she couldn't drum up any greater enthusiasm about these exchanges with little French girls. All the families would have to find was the fare, and Lord knew they were well able to find money for other things like drink and television sets.

Sister Laura wished that she'd had such opportunities when she was young. Nobody ever went anywhere then. She had always wanted to see the great cathedral of Notre Dame in Paris, and go to Chartres. Girls had so many chances today. And an easy life too! No school on Saturdays now. Sister Laura's lips were pursed about that. It was better far when they had lessons right up to lunchtime, and this new way made the weekend far too long, they got up to all kinds of mischief.

Dr. White had urged Sister Laura to take more exercise and get more fresh air. Dutifully she took a Saturday constitutional through Coyne's wood, down to River Road, along up Bridge Street and back to the convent by the Protestant church and graveyard.

In Coyne's wood she found Dara Ryan sitting on a stile watching eagerly to see who came through the trees. The child seemed disappointed—even dismayed—to see her teacher.

Down by the river bank she saw Grace O'Neill—holding hands, no less—with Dara's twin brother. They were much too young to be at that class of thing. Sister Laura barked a greeting at them that made them drop hands hastily.

When she called into Daly's for a cream cake—which Dr. White had told her should form no further part of her diet—Sister Laura was met by a saga of complaints about little Maggie who, according to her mother, had taken up with the foreign woman and was spending all her waking hours admiring herself in the mirror. Across the road from Daly's was Dr. White's. Sister Laura quickened her step and lowered her eyes in case she might catch the doctor's observant eye and he would read the cream cake written in her guilty face. Instead she saw Jacinta swinging on the gate and for once anxious for a chat.

Jacinta said that it was great to see nuns being normal now, and eating cream buns. Everything had gotten much better since the Vatican Council.

Sister Laura realized she had a mustache of cream on her face and pounded up Bridge Street in a very bad temper, thinking that fifteen-year-old girls in 1966 were a severe cross to have to bear.

She was glad she had not been called to the Married State. It was quite enough to have to deal with them in the classroom.

Kerry came through the wood and smiled easily.

"Well this *is* a lovely thing to discover in the woods on a summer day."

"Hello Kerry."

"Is that all you have to say to me?" He slid his arms around her but she wriggled out of them.

"What is it? Don't you like me?"

"I like you well enough."

"So what's with all the hard-to-get nonsense, then?"

"I'm not being hard to get, it's just that I haven't seen you for a while, I thought it would be nice to talk, you know, rather than . . . straight away."

"Sure, let's talk." He sat down on the ground and stroked her foot. "Could we talk about your ankles, for one thing? They're very beautiful . . ."

"Oh, please." Dara was at a total loss.

"Why don't you like me to admire you?" He looked genuinely bewildered.

"Because . . . because it's like as if you're not admiring me as a person, it's only an ankle or a mouth or whatever." She looked troubled.

"Oh Dara, that's not so, if you must know I like you as a person. You are totally special. I've told you that so many times."

"No you haven't, we haven't talked much at all, you and I."

"You're right!" he said, grinning broadly. "We haven't talked nearly enough. I think about you so much, that's what makes me think we did talk much more than we have. Will you come and walk with me, we'll walk through here and down to the river, and honestly"—he held both his hands up in the air — "no touching, promise."

Dara felt very silly, but it did look like a sort of a victory.

"That would be nice," she said and leaped from the stile.

Kerry got up lithely from his sitting position without putting his hands on the ground.

"That was clever," Dara admired.

"Oh come on, anyone can do that," Kerry challenged.

"Maybe, but you had your legs crossed."

"Go on, try it."

Dara sat down on the mossy ground and crossed her legs. "Let me see, what did you do?" She automatically kept trying to put her hands on the ground.

Kerry stood looking at her, laughing.

"It's not nearly as easy as you make it look." Dara was cross.

"Here, I'll sit down beside you and show you."

But when Kerry sat down beside her they were very close.

He looked at her flushed face.

He bent a little closer to her.

Dara bit her lip with indecision.

"It's very easy," Kerry said. He put his head slightly to one side and smiled at her.

"I don't think I'm going to be able to do it . . ." Dara said.

"Oh, I think you are," Kerry said. His face was closer still but he made no move to hold her.

She moved toward him. Their lips brushed lightly.

Kerry pulled back slightly. "No hands," he said triumphantly, showing both hands as he had done before.

But it didn't matter now. Their lips were together and nobody was working out technical details like that.

Kate was impatient that evening.

"Dara, where on earth were you? You look as if you rolled around on the ground, you're so full of leaves and dirt."

It was so precisely what Dara had been doing that she got a shock, but she realized her mother was on a different track.

"Really and truly you twins are like tinkers. When you see how neat and clean Grace looks, and even Maggie has smartened herself up a lot. I don't know what we're all working our fingers to the bone earning money to dress you pair for, we might as well buy the clothes and just rub them in the ground."

"I'm sorry," Dara said automatically.

"No, you're not. Where were you anyway?"

This was the question she had been trying to avoid.

"Oh, Michael will explain, I'd better go and have a wash," she said, and ran off.

Minutes later Michael burst into her room. "That was beautiful," he said furiously. "Why did you have to do that?"

Dara giggled. "I'm sorry, I couldn't think of anything else. What did you say?"

"I said we were down playing on the towpath. Where all the brambles were. You should have warned me."

Dara was sitting on her bed hugging her knees.

"I think that if we're going to spend this summer with the O'Neill family in different parts of the forest we should think up a story and stick to it," she said.

"Were you with Kerry?" he asked.

"Of course." She looked triumphant.

"Gosh, Dara. What were you doing?"

"Never mind!"

"You'd better be careful. Kerry's very old, and experienced."

"I know."

"You're awfully silly when you put on that face. You think you sound grown-up and clever, but in fact you sound silly. Like Jacinta when she's having one of her awful moods."

"You should hear what *you* sound like sometimes—Grace says, Grace thinks, Grace always believes, Grace was wondering . . . Like a record stuck and going on over and over."

"I don't," Michael said. "Do I?" he asked anxiously after a minute.

"A bit. Listen, let's not have a fight about it. Mam's on the warpath. The main thing is to keep the peace."

"Sure." Michael was distracted. "Does everyone else notice, about my mentioning Grace I mean?"

"No."

"Grace always says that I believe people too easily, I get taken in," Michael said.

Miss Purcell had a problem. Old Mr. Slattery had once said there was no problem that could not be solved by walking along by the river. Canon Moran said that God often spoke to the heart in peaceful riverside surroundings more clearly than he spoke in the midst of rush and bustle.

Miss Purcell took a riverside walk to try to work out her worry. Should she leave Fergus Slattery and go to work at the presbytery? To leave your post was an act of desertion. That was true. To work for the priests of God was a high calling. That too was true.

To forget the Slattery family who had been good to her for many years would be base ingratitude. To replace Miss Barry would mean that Miss Barry would definitely have to go for treatment to the county home. Would that be a good or a bad thing?

Miss Purcell walked on long and purposefully, hoping to hear some voice that would make things seem clear.

What she did hear among the reeds and rushes was some giggling and laughing. She craned her neck to see what was going on and stepped up to her ankles in water.

She saw two fleeing figures, children she thought. One of them was almost definitely that little O'Neill girl, she couldn't identify the boy. When she came back bad-tempered, with soaking feet and no decision made, she met Fergus in the hall.

"Really, Miss Purcell, if you go paddling the point is to take off your shoes and stockings," he said in a mock-reproving voice.

Miss Purcell was in no mood for light hearted banter. "I don't know what this place is coming to," she said. "I saw that young O'Neill girl and she's only a child, up to no good at all, keeping company up in the reeds. She can only be fourteen or fifteen. It's disgraceful." Two red spots burned in Miss Purcell's face.

"Oh a chip off the old block, her father's the greatest whoremaster for a hundred miles," Fergus said casually.

"Mr. *Slattery,* please." Miss Purcell had never listened to this kind of conversation before and she didn't intend to now. Unwittingly Fergus had made the decision that no voice had made for her on the river bank. Miss Purcell would spend the autumn of her life with the Clergy. Where she wouldn't hear words or sentiments like that.

Kerry had a long weekend, he didn't have to go back until Monday night he told Dara. He would be able to see her on Sunday *and* on Monday.

"Don't come to the pub . . . I'll go out and meet you," Dara said.

"I'm trying to be respectable," Kerry said. "Do the right thing, ask your parents' permission and everything. Is that not the way to go?"

"Of course it's not," Dara said. "They'd never give their permission for what we do."

Kerry smiled. "They wouldn't know."

"They'd guess. I'll say I'm going up to the lodge."

"Whatever you say."

"And where will I meet you?"

"I'll come and find you in the wood."

He did. But only late in the evening. Dara had been waiting, she was upset and annoyed.

"We didn't make a time," Kerry said. "We didn't fix a date and a place, you wouldn't let me come and pick you up. So what's all the drama?"

"There's no drama," Dara said.

"Good, I hate girls that make a fuss over nothing," Kerry said.

Dara heard two warnings in that.

One warning. There had been and probably still were plenty of other girls. And also the warning that fussy girls mightn't last long in the picture.

Dara gave a watery smile.

"Sure, anyway it was nice here. I love this wood, I always have."

"It's beautiful in the evening," Kerry said. "I think it's one of the loveliest places ever. Imagine Jack Coyne having a wood called after him. I wish we had an O'Neill's wood."

"It's not really Jack's wood, there have always been Coynes in this part." Dara didn't want to give the ferret-faced man from the motor works any part of the mossy, flower-filled place.

Kerry seemed restless. Edgy almost.

"What did you do today?"

He looked at her in surprise. Dara swallowed. It hadn't been such a terrible question, had it?

"I beg your pardon?" he asked.

"I was just wondering what kind of things you did." She bit her lip and wished she had let the silence be. It was so hard to talk to him today; yesterday he had been like an angel.

"If you must know I went to a bar way out on the Galway road."

"A bar. But you don't drink?"

"No, Miss Curiosity 1966, you are right. I do not drink. But I do play cards and that's what they were doing there."

"Cards in a pub on a Sunday?"

"In a back room. Brian Doyle's brother works there—well, sort of deals cards there. It was great."

"Did you play for money?"

He paused. As if he were debating something.

"No. Not this time."

"Will you another time?"

"Yes, no point in it otherwise."

"Why didn't you put money on the cards today then?"

"Francis said not to, just to watch, watch him dealing. It was great."

"Could I come with you next time?"

"No way. I'm even a bit young for this place, they'd think you were a baby in a cradle."

"I'm pretty grown up."

"You are very pretty, and very grown up," Kerry said, slipping an arm around Dara. "So I won't let them set eyes on you."

Dara smiled happily. She wriggled out of his arm for a moment as Sheila Whelan walked past, greeting them both briefly.

"I hope she won't tell," Dara said.

"What can she tell?" Kerry sounded bored.

She changed the subject. "Did you have woods like this back in America?"

"Not like this. We had trees of course on our property . . . but it was different from this."

"Did you walk under the trees?"

"Yes. With my mother, when she was well."

Even Grace hardly talked about their mother. Dara held her breath a little.

"What was it like?" she asked tentatively.

"It was good. We used to walk in the evenings, and watch the fireflies. You don't have them here?"

"Fireflies?" asked Dara.

"I've never seen any. I wonder why that is."

"What are they like?"

"Like little points of light, like a million tiny stars."

"They must be lovely," Dara breathed.

"It was lovely then, but it all changed. Anyway, it's silly wanting fireflies when we have so much else here."

"What have we here?"

"We have some very beautiful girls for one thing."

"Oh, lots of them is it?" Dara pretended a sense of outrage and started to run off down the slope.

"Yes thousands, but you're the most beautiful. By far." He ran after her and caught her easily.

Because Dara wasn't running very fast.

Dara Ryan is too young for Kerry O'Neill, Sheila Whelan thought to herself. Far too young. She shouldn't be up in Coyne's wood alone with him at this time of the evening.

But Sheila had never told anyone anything about anyone else's business. And even though it was a fifteen-year-old girl, she felt this sense that she must not interfere.

She wondered, if she had a daughter of her own, what would she like a good friend to do? It was impossible to know.

Fergus Slattery had a distressing case to cope with. The parents of a fifteen-year-old boy came to him saying that their son had been named as the father of a girl's baby. It was a matter of a paternity order.

They were stern unblinking people who did not believe such a thing to be possible.

"It couldn't be done, a child of fifteen to father another child," the farmer said in bewilderment.

"It could be done all right," Fergus said. Even though he was twice the boy's age and had fathered nobody he knew it could indeed be done.

"The girl's a dirty tramp who lay with half the country," said the farmer's wife.

Fergus had already spoken to the terrified schoolboy.

"We'll get nowhere talking like that. Your son is too young to marry, it's a simple case of finance. We have to work out what can be fairly paid."

"You're not saying that our child is responsible for this girl's bastard?"

"I'm saying that we'll save ourselves a heap of trouble if we try to bring it down to pounds, shillings and pence, and keep all the recriminations for your own kitchen around the fire, or even better not have them at all."

"God knows what you can be thinking about Mr. Slattery, you mustn't be of this world at all."

"I'm probably not of this world," Fergus agreed. His face was grim, what he had been thinking of was Michael Ryan. Suppose by some horrendous ill chance Michael were to father a child of Grace O'Neill's. What in God's earth would happen then?

He wondered should he warn Kate Ryan or was it the action of a mad maiden aunt?

Dr. White called to see Kate as a matter of course and courtesy rather than because he could do anything for her.

He never referred again to her inquiry about whether sexual intercourse would be wise or indeed possible. He was a dour man without great charm but Kate liked him. She trusted him because he never gave her false hopes, and he had always been able to interpret the more flowery pronouncements of consultant doctors at the hospitals, and the specialists she had seen.

"Nothing wrong with you these days except a broken back," Martin White said in a manner that some would have found offensively direct.

"No, not a thing. That and being the mother of teenagers. It's a hard old station, isn't it?"

"Ah, don't talk to me. We have Jacinta around the house day and night now, a fit of the sulks. Some awful slight or row or something, she has us demented."

"Oh dear. Who with?" Kate hadn't heard any of this.

"Your lot I think, and that little one of the Dalys' and Tommy Leonard. Never mind, it'll pass, that's what we keep telling ourselves. The only thing is will *we* survive it?"

"Oh, I hope Dara and Michael weren't out of turn with her . . ."

"You wouldn't know what it was all about. Jealousy I think, mainly. Jacinta complains that Dara and Michael have fallen in love with the O'Neill children and are wandering around starry-eyed hand in hand, and the old gang as they knew it isn't the same. Fat lot of time we had for that sort of thing or indeed talking about it, at their age."

"I thought they all played together still." Kate's voice was tinny.

"God, Kate, they may well do. Jacinta would remind you of one of those circular saws when she gets started, I don't listen half the time."

Kate allowed him to change the subject.

At supper the children's father spoke sternly.

"There's going to be an end to all this rambling off on your own from now on, you're all to be where we can keep an eye on you."

"That would mean being in the bar," Eddie was quick to protest.

"Shut up, Eddie, not you for once."

"Why not?" Eddie was outraged.

"I meant not only you, I meant all of you. Dara, Michael, are you listening to me?"

They exchanged glances.

"Where *do* you go anyway?" their father persisted.

"Here and there," Michael said.

"Mainly the lodge," Dara lied.

"That's odd, your mother had a message from Miss Hayes above in the lodge asking if you could favor her with your presence for a fitting for this dress she's making you. She hasn't seen hair nor hide of you up there all weekend, apparently."

"She must have been in a different part," Dara mumbled.

"Yes, it's a huge place all right, four rooms I believe, you'd easily lose a battalion up there."

John's face was not amused. He hadn't liked what Kate had reported to him. The thought of anyone making free with Dara made him feel bile rise in his throat. The fact that Dara was so obviously lying made it quite sure that Dr. White's information had been correct.

"Where do you want us to be?"

"Where I can call you, by the footbridge, or down by the real bridge at the end of the town."

"We're not old enough for the bridge," Eddie said.

"Get on with your tea, Eddie," John Ryan said wearily.

"Why's nobody interested where *I'm* going to be?" Eddie wanted to know.

"Do you think he suspected?" Michael asked Grace that evening. They stood on the footbridge while Michael explained the new edict.

"No of course not."

"I want to be with you, on your own. We're not doing anything *really* wrong."

"We can still be together," Grace was soothing.

"It's not together with awful people about."

"They're not awful people, they're our friends."

"People like John Joe Conway." Michael was mutinous.

"Don't be ridiculous, Michael, you're always imagining that he has some interest in me."

"Everyone's interested in you, Grace, we know that, it's just that John Joe is so coarse, I couldn't bear him looking at you, touching you . . ."

"He doesn't touch me."

"Looking at you even."

"That's crazy to talk like that."

"I am crazy about you." He put out his hand toward her.

"Watch it," Grace said, "we're in full view of the pub."

"This is going to be great for the rest of the summer," said Michael.

Olive Hayes asked Mrs. Fine to be present for the fittings.

The dresses were all at the same stage—the aquamarine for Dara, a soft rosy pink for Grace and the unusual burnished copper for Maggie.

"Don't you have another friend, isn't it Dr. White's daughter who goes about with you? I could get her some material too," Rachel offered.

"Jacinta. Oh, she'd love that," Maggie said.

"She doesn't deserve it," Dara said sternly, remembering Jacinta's view of Mrs. Fine as a mistress.

"Come on, Dara. Don't be mean. We're all having a dress, why not Jacinta?" Grace was always generous.

Rachel looked at the beautiful blonde daughter of frail Kathleen O'Neill and Patrick. She had always felt the child was withdrawn and hostile toward her until recently. Now Grace was looking at her delightedly as if she were her closest friend.

"Could *you* suggest it to her, Mrs. Fine? We had a sort of falling out with Jacinta. Could you tell her about the dresses? It would mend things again."

"Oh *please,* Mrs. Fine," Maggie asked.

"What do *you* think, Dara? I'd need to have everyone's point of view."

"I think Jacinta's being silly. But Grace is right, and if *you* said it she couldn't snarl and take offense."

"All right." Rachel was pleasant about it. "I'll stop by the house, I have an excuse anyway." It was true. Rachel wanted to ask Dr. White if it would be too tiring for Kate to go on a shopping trip to Dublin with her. She felt her friend needed a break away from the pub and the worry about the new café.

"This needs to be lifted a little here, do you think, Mrs. Fine?"

Miss Hayes didn't want to take any initiatives. She held the fabric in place where she was going to put the little dart that would shape it.

The others looked at Maggie Daly's small thin shoulders and her little pointed breasts seen to their best advantage.

"You look great, Maggie," Dara said spontaneously. "You look totally different to usual."

Maggie saw only the compliment, she didn't want to believe it. "You're only saying that," she said.

"Why would I say it? Doesn't she?"

Grace was looking at her wordlessly. "Honestly Maggie, it's extraordinary, you look like a painting."

Maggie clasped her hands together and pulled them apart in delighted embarrassment. It was as if she were clapping.

"I'll never be able to thank you enough, Mrs. Fine, imagine there being this bit of curtain just the right color."

"I know, isn't it extraordinary!" Rachel marveled, thinking of the hours she had spent in the material departments of Brown Thomas and Switzer's looking for the exact shade.

"You're terrific, Mrs. Fine," Grace said, delighted that Maggie was getting the Cinderella treatment.

Rachel looked at the beautiful daughter of the man she loved and knew she must not say anything that would threaten this new friendship.

"It makes a very nice change for me to see three good-looking girls getting dressed up than to see yards and yards of wall coverings, and to work out why half the bedroom carpets are one shade and half are different when they were all meant to have come from the same batch. This is the fun part here, I assure you."

She mustn't give them any hint about how it was the only part. This and her conversations with Kate Ryan.

Why else was she in this town? She felt that she and Patrick were miles apart. Further than they had ever been, even when they were on different sides of the ocean.

Jacinta White didn't want a dress.

"I don't have to follow everyone else, be a copycat," she said.

"I think you're right. Anyway you look good in those pants."

Jacinta looked down at her jeans and boots in surprise. "What?" she said suspiciously.

"I was never able to wear anything like that—slacks, trousers, pants, whatever you call it. My bottom was too big. I always wanted to, though."

Jacinta would not be won so easily.

"Oh, I haven't much time for clothes," she said loftily.

"Sensible of you. Anyway, it's always there if you want it."

"Thank you, but I haven't time for fittings and choosing and all that sort of stuff."

Rachel saw the aching loneliness of a fifteen-year-old who had fallen out of the pack. She knew that any more persuasion would result in further refusals.

"Maggie and Grace were saying that they wanted you to have a dress too. But don't be dragged in if you don't want to." Rachel prepared to leave.

"I bet Dara didn't want me to have a dress. Dara's a pain in the neck, she thinks Tommy Leonard is her little slave. It would sicken you."

"I think Dara did want you to share in all these remnants, actually, and I definitely heard that she fancied Kerry O'Neill rather than Tommy Leonard."

"Well, she's out of her mind fancying Kerry O'Neill, he's far too old for her, and he has girlfriends all over the place. You don't have any material that would make jeans, do you?"

It was very ungracious.

"No, but what I do have that might be nice is a bit of leather fringe. We could put some on your shirt and some on your boots."

"On the boots?"

"Yes, isn't there a man up in Foley's who does shoe repairs? If we asked him nicely he could stitch some of this fringe onto the top of the boots."

"And you would give it to me, would you?"

"With pleasure," Rachel smiled.

Fringes on her shirts and her boots, that would make Tommy Leonard sit up and wipe the smile out of Dara's eye, Jacinta thought.

"I'll come along with you now and get it," she said in case Mrs. Fine might change her mind.

Patrick was in Meagher's with Brian Doyle organizing the changes.

The place was going to be a small office and travel agency.

He would employ just one person, who would arrange tours for the guests and do any other business that Mountfern might need.

He saw Rachel coming down Bridge Street with that sulky child Jacinta, the daughter of the gloomy doctor fellow.

Patrick was about to go over to them but he stopped himself.

In front of this child they would have to behave as near-strangers. They would have to play a role.

Was it worth it? There were so many of these non-conversations all day. What was the point of another? He stopped just on the door way of the shop and turned back in again. Rachel saw him, and her heart felt cold. He had actually gotten to the stage of avoiding her now.

"Kerry?"

"Yes Mr. Hill?"

"A word if I may?"

"Of course."

"My own sons don't listen to my advice, you probably don't listen to your father. That's the way things are, always have been possibly."

Kerry held his head politely on one side, waiting for the old man to come to the point. He was working in the bar this week, and liking it. The summer business was beginning to build up and Kerry was an easy conversationalist, people got on well with him.

Dennis Hill looked at him without speaking for a few seconds.

"That crowd who were in last night, McCann, Burns, those . . ."

"Yes Mr. Hill?"

"They're not the class for this hotel. Too rough. They don't fit."

"Are they barred?"

"Of course they're not barred. They were never here before, they came to see you. They're from Derry."

Kerry's eyes narrowed slightly. The old man noticed more than he thought.

"Yes, I did meet them outside the hotel, I thought it was good to ask them to come in and swell the crowd. But if you think they're not the right kind of guests, I won't encourage them to come back here. Is that what you'd like me to do?" The insolence was well hidden, you'd have to dig deep to find it. But it was there.

"No, I don't mind if they come in or not, we're well able to move people on if they're difficult, don't worry about that. It's you I'm thinking about."

"Me?"

"You. They're a rough crowd. I don't mean their accents or the way they dress. I mean what they do."

"What do they do?"

"A good question. A very good question. Nothing you could describe too well, or put down in the space on your passport where it wants to know your occupation."

"I think they're in business."

"Yes, that's what I think too. Mainly criminal business."

"Oh Mr. Hill . . ."

"Some of it's just on the right side of things, but only some of it and only just."

"So?"

"So. I'm warning you about them. You need take no notice, you might appreciate having your card marked. You might just wish that I'd clear off and shut up."

"No, Mr. Hill, I appreciate your advice."

"Which means to hell with your advice. All right Kerry, I've done my duty. Now about your holidays. Would you like to take off now before we get really busy in July and August?"

Kerry got the feeling that the old man was sending him away from his new friends. He was about to make an excuse and then he thought of Mountfern in the sunshine, and the sparkling river and the beautiful little Dara waiting like a fruit to be plucked.

"That's very nice of you, Mr. Hill, and I'll think about what you said."

"I'm sure you will Kerry," Dennis Hill sighed.

Kerry went out with Tony McCann and Charlie Burns that night to play cards. He was luckier than he had been before. Or was the advice of Francis Doyle, Brian's pisspot brother, really working? Anyway he would be going back to Mountfern with a billfold full of pound notes and fivers.

Patrick told John and Kate that young people's lives were like a holiday camp nowadays. There was his Kerry being offered three weeks' holiday from Hill's hotel. Kerry was buying a car no less, imagine it. Not nineteen years of age, and he had everything he wanted.

"Isn't that why you killed yourself working, so that your children *could* have everything they wanted?" Kate asked him.

"I suppose so." Patrick was doubtful.

"Well it certainly was," John said. "What else would any of us do anything for, if we didn't have the next lot coming after us to provide for?"

"What would you do if you hadn't a family and children?" Patrick asked with interest.

"I think I'd put a pack on my back and wander off around the world talking to people about this and that, as it took my fancy."

"Like Papers Flynn," Kate scoffed.

"I'd go further afield than Papers, but that's what I'd do." John was adamant.

"You would not!" Kate flashed. "Even if he had none of us trailing out of him, he'd still stand here looking at his river."

She wanted to find out Kerry's plans for his holiday at home. She didn't like the sound of the car, she felt it might be used to spirit Dara to places well beyond the jurisdiction.

"Won't Kerry find it very quiet for him here? Playing with youngsters?" Her eyes were innocent. But she swore that Patrick saw what she was getting at.

"I'll keep an eye on him as much as I can," he promised.

"Perhaps he'll go off to other parts of the country. Specially if he gets a car?" Kate was hopeful.

"No, I've a feeling that he sees a lot of attraction here. Still, as I said, we'll make sure that he doesn't get too carried away."

He had said nothing, and he had said everything.

Kate gave a little shiver of fear.

"I wish there could be another party," Maggie said.

"Why don't you ask your family if you could have one? There's plenty of room in your house," Dara said.

Maggie rolled her eyes. "Us have a party! It's on our knees saying the thirty days prayer tacked on to the rosary and ending up with a trip to devotions. That's my mother's idea of a good evening."

The others giggled. Maggie seemed to have much more confidence these days. She apologized less, she was even joining in the swimming from the bridge. Maggie used to be shy to be seen down in the middle of town in her bathing suit; nowadays she would sit and laugh with the others, not self-conscious anymore.

The old raft they had made way back, which had floated down to the bridge, became their center of activities. They used it to dive from. Sometimes they piled boxes up on it to make a higher diving platform. Tommy Leonard could dive from the bridge itself. He was like a swallow, Dara said admiringly, he just seemed to swoop down. The rest of them bent their legs or belly flopped.

Only Tommy, John Joe Conway and Jacinta were any good diving from the bridge, they were the undoubted champions.

Gradually Jacinta had come back into things. She couldn't stay away anymore, the fun had moved to the bridge at the end of the street where she lived. This was the summer they were old enough for the bridge, there was no way Jacinta would stay out of things.

And being so athletic was an advantage. It was no use when you were at the pictures or being watched parading up and down Bridge Street, but it was marvelous when you were the only girl who could dive from the wall of the bridge and when Tommy Leonard admired you.

"Do you mind if I buy a car from Jack Coyne? I know you and he don't get on," Kerry said.

"How have you enough money to buy a car?"

"We said there would be no discussion about money, ever again."

"No, we said there would be no discussion about stealing unless it happened again."

"Well it hasn't."

There was a silence.

"I won it up north."

Patrick nodded. "Very well. Now about Coyne, he's a mean, dishonest little shit, but Rachel warned me against alienating locals, however unlikable. Go ahead. Watch out that it's a real car, mind. Make sure he doesn't sell you a lemon."

"No, he'll be so anxious to get into your good books he'll give me a fantastic bargain." Kerry grinned.

Patrick smiled too. This was good thinking. That is exactly what Jack Coyne would do. How sensible his son was to capitalize on it.

"You might find that the pattern has changed a bit this summer," he said.

"Changed in what way?"

"Not so much wandering off on your own, it looks like, everyone swimming by the bridge."

"Well, I'll have a car, that should change the pattern a bit more."

"You might find a bit of resistance along the way. Dara Ryan's mother for one." Patrick spoke lightly.

Kerry was sunny. "That's no problem, there are plenty of other girls to take for drives. And anyway I like swimming too."

He smiled at his father as if there weren't a problem in the world.

Loretto Quinn told Rachel that Jack Coyne was like the cat that got the cream. The young O'Neill boy had said he would like to buy a second-hand car from him. Jack Coyne had sped off to the town in high excitement. He said he was going to find a little honey of a little car for the boy. Loretto hadn't known him as pleased for years.

"He calls in here a lot. Is he an admirer do you think?" Rachel asked.

Loretto pealed with laughter. "Jack Coyne an admirer? Lord, all that man ever admired was a roll of fivers. But it's very flattering of you to think I might have a caller, Mrs. Fine."

"You're a fine woman, Loretto. Why wouldn't you have callers and admirers?"

"Ah, Mrs. Fine, you've improved me but not that much. Not in a place like this. Anyway I wouldn't want them, I'm happy as I am. Much happier since you came."

Rachel was pleased. Even if she had to resign herself that her coming to Mountfern had not achieved its aim, at least she could console herself that she had done a lot to help the women and girls of the place. Rachel was reading about the women's liberation that seemed to be sweeping the States at the moment. Not much of it had found its way to Mountfern. But she was definitely helping to improve the quality of life for a few of the female citizens of the place anyway.

Maggie Daly hung up her new dress all by itself on the back of her door. She didn't want to put it in the wardrobe in case it got crushed. And anyway she couldn't see it in the wardrobe.

She wondered what Kitty would say about it. Kitty was coming home for a weekend.

Kerry's car was red and had an open roof. It wasn't quite a sports car but it was almost.

He took Grace for a lap of honor up and down Bridge Street, turning neatly in front of the Classic Cinema, which nearly gave Declan Morrissey a heart attack as he thought the boy was through the cinema doors. Grace's hair, blown by the wind, stood like a halo around her head. Michael fixed a smile on his face and wished with such intensity that it hurt him physically that he was old enough to drive, that he had the money to buy a *white* sports car and that he and Grace could drive around Mountfern like that.

Dara fixed a smile on her face as she sat beside Maggie on the wall of the bridge.

She wished with an intensity that hurt her that she could be sitting where Grace was and that Kerry and she would do one more tour of the town and then drive off for miles in the beautiful car. She wished that her hair curled under and that she had her ears pierced. Then she would be truly happy.

Father Hogan and Canon Moran were taking a walk when they saw the red car. They were about to cluck at each other and say that Mr. O'Neill really spoiled his children and gave a bad example when the car stopped.

"Do you want to test it out? I only have it an hour." Kerry sounded excited.

"Test it out?"

"I'll take you for a test ride."

The priests looked at each other in amazement. Nobody had ever offered them anything so racy.

"Us?" Canon Moran croaked in disbelief.

"Yes Canon, one at a time, it only seats two."

"It's very nice of you, Kerry . . . but my old bones."

There was naked longing on Father Hogan's face.

"What about you, Father, you'll risk it won't you?"

"Aren't you very good to be bothering with the clergy . . ." Grace had gotten out and was holding the door open, Father Hogan had gathered up the skirts of his soutane and settled himself in.

"But of course I bother with the clergy, Father Hogan, aren't they the most important people in town?" Kerry smiled and slipped through the gears to roar off with Father Hogan in the passenger seat.

It was a warm evening, warm enough to come back to the bridge and swim again after tea.

At seven o'clock they gathered there again.

Jacinta did some spectacular dives. This was the first time Kerry had seen them, he was full of praise. Jacinta was gruff and red with delight. She looked at Tommy Leonard to see whether he had noticed. But Tommy's eyes were wide. Maggie was approaching in her new dress. She looked quite different to the Maggie they all knew.

"I didn't know we were going to wear them now, I thought we'd wait till there was something special," Dara grumbled.

"What will there be special?" Maggie asked.

"You look like a picture," Michael said.

"That's exactly what I told her," Grace said eagerly.

"Hey, you're even more dazzling than your big sister," Kerry said.

Dara felt plain and foolish.

Mam had been watching her like a hawk—where are you going, what are you doing, will you be with Michael? It was maddening. Just as she was coming out Mam had told her not to be dressing up like as if she was going to a ball, so she wore her striped tee shirt and the plain blue skirt.

She felt like a deck chair in the outfit, canvas and stripes. Who would look at her? And here was Maggie with her hair all brushed and shimmering and reminding Kerry of Kitty up in Dublin.

The light went out of the evening for Dara. Hands in the pockets of her dull plain skirt, she turned away. The others were so busy admiring Maggie they hardly noticed.

Dara began to walk toward River Road. There was nothing here for her, every moment she stayed just pointed out how dull she was. She couldn't do dives like Jacinta, she wasn't lovely like Grace was or Maggie was turning out to be. She was boring old wooden Dara.

She had turned into River Road and was nearly at Jack Coyne's when she realized Maggie was running after her.

"Why won't you stay?"

"What do you care?"

"We were having fun, weren't we?" Maggie asked anxiously.

"Oh Maggie, can't you ever make up your mind about anything?" Dara snapped.

Maggie looked at her, dismayed.

"You're so weak. You don't even know whether we were having fun or not. You ask me were we? I don't know about you. I wasn't, so I came home. But at least I know. You never know."

"What don't I know?"

"See!" Dara was triumphant. "You don't know if you'd like an ice cream, you don't know if you'd like a trip in Kerry's car, you don't know if you want to swim or to wear a bathing cap. You don't know *anything*."

"What did I do, Dara?" wailed poor Maggie after Dara's back.

Dara didn't even turn around, she just shouted over her shoulder. "You did nothing. You never do anything. That's just the point."

Maggie stood stricken on the river bank, Dara stormed home and threw herself on her bed to cry.

Mary came up and knocked on the door. "Your mother would like you to go to her room and talk to her."

"Tell her I'm in bed."

"Dara. Please. Your mother sent me up specially."

"I'm in bed, I'm not going down."

"She can't come up."

There was a silence.

"So please, Dara, will you come down?"

The door opened and Dara's tear-stained face appeared. "That's the most cruel blackmail I ever heard. Reminding me that Mam can't ever get up the stairs. How mean and unfair." She stormed past Mary and nearly took the hinges off the door of her mother's green room.

Mary sighed. It went against her principles to say that boys were easier around the house than girls at this age. But maybe it was because women were so much more sensitive.

"Yes?" Dara stood inside the door she had just banged.

"I was wondering if you could help me."

"Do what?"

"To think of a name for our café. We will have to get it painted for one thing and then if we call it something we can start painting that on trays and perhaps even embroidering it on aprons."

Dara looked at Kate as if her mother had gone mad.

"I don't care *what* you call it," she said.

"You'll be looking at it for a long time."

"Not necessarily," Dara said.

"Well, even if you're going to leave home, you might want to have a say in what the café is called."

"No, Mam, honestly I don't. I'm not being rude, I don't mind what name you choose." She made as if to go.

"Ryan's Ridiculous Café, maybe?" Kate tried. "Ryan's Rubbishy Café, Ryan's Wreck of a Café. Ryan's Roadhouse." She pretended to be considering each of them. Dara couldn't raise a smile even.

"Could you sit down do you think?"

"No Mam, if you don't mind . . . I'd prefer to go to bed."

"It's not eight o'clock, you're the one who told me not two hours ago that it was inhuman to ask people to be home by ten o'clock. Do you remember?"

"Yes."

"Is there anything I can do? Anything at all."

"No. No there isn't, really. Thanks all the same."

"Dara?"

"Yes."

"I asked you to come down because I love you, no other reason, I love you with all my heart and I don't want you to be unhappy. I know it's not much use just to have *me* loving you, but it might be a help sometime, so just remember it will you?" Kate smiled at her and continued, "No, of course you don't need to sit here anymore. I got lonely too sitting by myself and I thought it might work if you came and sat with me, we might get less lonely. But it didn't work. Off you go to bed. Good night now, love."

"You'll think of a name."

"Yes I will, or you will or someone will."

"Why does it have to have a name at all?"

"I'm not sure," Kate said. "Rachel thinks it would stick in people's minds more. You know the way they like things to be defined—Emerald Isle, Land of Shamrocks. I suppose we're the same with other places, we think of Spain and we think of castanets."

"You *could* call it Shamrock Café," Dara said.

"Ryan's Shamrock Café," Kate said slowly. "That might do."

"Good night Mam."

"Good night my love."

Dara longed to rush back and throw herself into her mother's arms, but it would have meant too many tears and trying to explain what she was crying about. So she resisted it and went back upstairs to the window seat, where she sat and watched the sun set over the River Fern, and saw Michael walk disconsolately home at five minutes to ten.

Grace flashed by in Kerry's little red car.

"Were you swimming and all till now?" Dara asked Michael.

"Jacinta said you went off in a sulk. Did you?" he asked.

"Of course not," Dara lied. "What did everyone do?"

"If you'd stayed you'd have found out," he said and went into the boys' room and closed the door.

Dara felt more alone than she had ever felt.

She thought about Mam saying that she loved her. It was a nice thing to say but Mam was right, it wasn't much use at the moment.

The next evening they had all made separate resolutions.

Dara was not going to sulk. She wore a red shirt over her black bathing suit, and the silk rose that Kerry had given her on her fifteenth birthday all those months ago behind her ear. She smiled at everyone.

Maggie had decided not to wear her good new dress. It had been overdoing it, they had all gotten annoyed with her somehow. She wore an old Viyella dress that used to belong to Kitty once, it was faded and shrunk now. It made Maggie look about ten.

Jacinta's father had told her that he was prescribing himself headache remedies because of the continuous whine tone in her voice, so she had resolved to speak more cheerfully.

Michael had decided that it was not the end of the world if John Joe Conway said "Fine girl you are" every time he looked at Grace. And that it only made *him* look the stupid one if he reacted all the time.

Tommy Leonard had decided that Dara *did* like him, she wasn't sighing at him, she was sighing at everything around her.

Liam White thought that he might ask Maggie Daly to the pictures. She was so small he could even get her in for half price as an under twelve.

Grace made a vow to be much nicer to Michael. It was awful for him, his parents had turned into policemen and insisted that they all move in packs.

Someone must have seen them. She shuddered to think what her own father would say if anything was reported to him. But then he was so busy and out so much he wouldn't notice.

They sat swinging their legs on the bridge, the four girls, Dara, Maggie, Grace and Jacinta. The boys perched on their bikes and chatted to them.

Half a dozen others came and went, John Joe Conway with his loutish laugh saying there was nothing to look at since the girls were all covered up.

There was no sign of Kerry.

Then they saw him walking down Bridge Street, the evening sun hitting his golden hair. He looked like a young god as he walked, in his open-necked blue shirt the exact color of his eyes, and his white trousers gleaming. He looked like a cowboy in a Western, the good guy who had come in to save the town. Tonight he did not have the red car—he had left his bike slung casually against the railing of Slattery's house.

He was coming to join the gang on the bridge. The evening could begin.

They had never seen Kerry swim in this part of the river. Up beyond the footbridge yes, long ago. But here was more public somehow. Up in the old place with the raft it had never mattered whether you could swim or not, it was wallowing and flapping about in the water from the bank to the raft and back.

But here it was altogether more showy.

They watched as Kerry kicked off his canvas shoes and slipped off his trousers. He was wearing his swimming trunks underneath. He stood in the golden rays of the evening sun, blinking. Then he threw off his blue shirt, and laughed at them.

"It only gets worse thinking about it," he said as if he were totally unaware that all their eyes were on him. Lean and tanned, golden and confident, he stood on the parapet of the bridge and did one long clean dive into the River Fern.

Tommy Leonard thought gloomily that that was that. There went his only chance of being good at something. Kerry O'Neill turned out to be much better at diving than Tommy. Wouldn't you know?

Dara looked at Kerry in wonder. He was perched on the raft, the drops of water clinging to his tanned shoulders and arms making him look shimmering. He was so very very handsome and he was smiling straight up at her.

"Come on, Dara, let's see you do it."

Without thinking, Dara peeled off her red shirt, took the silk rose carefully from her hair and scrambled up on the wall of the bridge.

"Careful, Dara," Michael said.

"Move more to the middle," Tommy Leonard warned.

Dara dived in. She seemed surprised at herself when she surfaced, shaking the water from her face.

"Great stuff," Kerry said, moving over on the raft to make room for her.

"Very good, keep your legs straight though," Jacinta called.

"Is it very high?" Grace shouted.

"Not bad, don't stop and consider it." Dara laughed.

In her smart stripy bathing suit Grace turned to Michael for advice. "What do you think?"

"Why don't we go down the side? We can dive from the raft," he said.

But Grace wanted to do the high dive.

Once up there it looked very far.

"Stop thinking about it!" Dara called.

This was good advice. In a splash Grace was beside them in the water. She looked back up at the bridge.

"I never thought I could dive that far," she said in wonder.

And so it was that they all managed it. It was the only summer when they were all able to jump or dive from the bridge itself. They all remembered summers years ago when some people went from the high bridge, but there was never a summer surely where everyone was able to do it.

Little Maggie Daly realized that. It looked like a million miles.

"Try a jump first," Liam White encouraged. "Once you've done the jump it's easy to do the dive."

"Is it deep enough?" Maggie asked fearfully.

"It's over twenty feet," Liam laughed. "That's enough water for you, Maggie."

Quivering with determination that she would not be left out, Maggie clambered up onto the wall.

"Hey Maggie, it's too high for you," Kerry called.

"Come down the side," Grace shouted.

Maggie took no notice. She leaped out as far as she could and appeared from the huge splash she had made still quivering. She climbed onto the raft beside Dara and Kerry.

"It's not that cold," Kerry said soothingly.

Maggie was shivering not from cold but from fright.

Now they had all done it, even Maggie, and in the evening light, pleased with themselves, they climbed back up again. Dara straightened her legs, Tommy Leonard did a back flip which Kerry said was terrific and insisted on getting Tommy to teach him.

Suddenly Tommy felt important again.

Grace told Michael that she thought he dived better than either Tommy or Kerry because he had more style and less showing off.

Jacinta said they could get a much better angle if only they could have a proper springboard attached to the bridge.

Maggie climbed up again. This time she was going to try a dive. Just as she was poised to go her foot slipped.

Maggie Daly fell at an awkward angle, not into the deep water that flowed under the bridge. But to the side where her head hit the corner of the raft with a sickening crack.

For years afterward they remembered that sound. It was so sharp. It was like the crack of a rifle shot, or of a big twig snapping on the mossy earth up in Coyne's wood.

And they looked unbelievingly as Maggie lay splayed half in the water and half over the raft.

At a very awkward angle indeed.

It wasn't the blood coming from the corner of her eye that was so frightening. It was the way Maggie lay.

As if her neck was broken.

They didn't have to go for Jacinta and Liam's father. Dr. White heard the screams himself.

He was coming out of the presbytery where he had been talking seriously about Miss Barry's limited life expectancy if she were allowed to continue in her present ways.

His heart lurched when the sound of panic and crisis reached him. He started to run. As he ran he knew the thought that was going through his head like a refrain was unworthy. Please God let it not be Liam or Jacinta, Please God not Liam or Jacinta. Please God.

Charlie who worked in Daly's was coming out of Conway's pub when he heard the commotion.

Charlie was a man who frightened easily. He ran back into Conway's and ordered himself a brandy.

"That's not like you, Charlie," Mr. Conway said.

"There's been an accident on the bridge," Charlie said.

Mr. Conway lifted the flap and ran out from behind the bar.

"Mother of God may it not be John Joe," he cried, and ran down Bridge Street to see if he could find his big bostoon of a son John Joe, whom he had given three blows in the ear earlier on.

He saw John Joe running up toward him and his face flooded with relief.

John Joe was crying, fighting for words.

"It's Maggie Daly," he cried. "They think she's dead. She can't be dead, can she?"

Mr. Daly was given a sedative. Dr. White was able to get him on to a bed and to roll up his sleeve while it was injected into his arm.

Mrs. Daly was different. Her face was white and still. But she was calm to the point of being unnatural.

"It was the will of Our Lord," she said in a matter-of-fact way. "He wanted Maggie this evening. Tonight she is with our Blessed Lord and his Holy Mother. She is in a better place by far than Mountfern."

Martin White looked at her angrily. How could a mother be so philosophical? What kind of God would want Maggie by dashing her to her death from a bridge at fifteen years of age with the complete understanding and acquiescence of her mother? A vein started to throb in his forehead.

"It's all right, Martin." Sheila Whelan was gentle at his side. "Everyone has to mourn in their own way."

"This is grotesque," he whispered.

"No, isn't it great that she has this kind of faith?"

"It's not faith, it's hysteria. Her child is dead, she hasn't shed a tear."

"You're always very good to people here in this place, don't start making judgments on them. Not now."

It was a timely warning. Martin White looked gratefully at Sheila Whelan. He spoke now in his normal voice.

"I'll leave you with Mrs. Daly, Sheila, and I'll try to sort out the children. They're almost all in shock."

He left the Daly's house, walking through the little knot of people who had already gathered around the door to sympathize.

The children were in Fergus Slattery's house.

Miss Purcell had made cups of tea and opened a tin of biscuits.

Dr. White had told them to get out of their wet things and put on their clothes.

He had asked Fergus and Miss Purcell to get them rugs and blankets. Fergus had turned on two electric fires. One at each end of the room.

He had been coming out of his house when he heard the screams. He was at the bridge in moments, at the same time as the doctor. His eyes had met Martin White's, and the doctor had shaken his head.

"Get them into your house, Fergus, and let someone tell Seamus Sheehan to come down."

Fergus shepherded the children into his house and sent them off to various rooms to change.

Then he went to telephone the Ryans. John wasn't there. Kate said it was his only social engagement in the year, a meeting of the county Historical Association. As a published poet and a man finishing a book about Fernscourt, he was now highly regarded there.

Fergus cut across her pleasantries. "I have your twins here in the house with me. They're fine, they're both here."

She caught the tension in his voice at once. And knew something terrible had happened.

"What is it? Tell me immediately," she said.

He did. Without frills. She would hear within minutes. He wanted her to know that what could be done was being done, and that he would look after Dara and Michael.

"God, why does it have to be the night that John is out, the one night in the whole year? Will I come up there? Eddie could push me."

"No, there are too many people up at the bridge. There's nothing you can do. The children are all right here. I know it's hard, but stay where you are."

She saw the reason in this.

"I'll call Patrick," she said firmly. "Otherwise he's bound to get a garbled version too, above in the lodge. Are his two there?"

"They're here," Fergus said grimly.

He looked at Grace and Michael clinging to each other wrapped in a blanket, Grace unable to stop shivering and refusing to be parted from Michael even to the point where she could remove her wet bathing suit under her dress.

Kerry was sitting on a chair, his handsome face drawn with shock. Tucked into his side, almost under his arm, was Dara Ryan, white and still disbelieving what had happened. Kerry absently stroked Dara's dark hair, which had a curiously inappropriate artificial rose stuck in the side.

Fergus didn't like to see the young Ryans so firmly enmeshed with the O'Neills. But this wasn't a time for such thoughts. He tried to put the haunting little face of Maggie Daly—those huge worried eyes and all that massive hair— way out of his mind. What could have possessed a frail nervy little thing like that to jump from a high bridge? And why didn't some of the others stop her? Looking around the stricken group in his house Fergus realized that this is what they must all be thinking too.

The night seemed to go on forever.

John Joe Conway's father excused himself from the bar and went into his workshop at the back. There would be need of a small coffin.

John Joe followed him out and railed at him. Why did his father always have to think of business, and making money, when someone was dead, for

God's sake? John Joe kept saying the word over and over because he couldn't believe it.

His father was short on explanations and excuses.

"What would you like us to do with Maggie? Leave her lying there looking at the sky? The only thing we *can* do for the dead is to give them a decent burial. If this is ever going to be your place John Joe, you'll have to learn that."

"I don't want to run a business, I don't want to be grown up," John Joe said.

His father gave him a long look. "I know son, it's not the greatest thing in the world being grown up and being in business. But look at the alternative."

For the first time in their lives John Joe Conway and his father looked at each other with something like understanding.

Rachel was in her room reading when she heard the commotion from the bridge. At first she thought it was just horseplay and high spirits. Then she became worried. She closed her book and came downstairs. Loretto was standing fearfully on the doorstep, her hand at her mouth.

"There's been an accident," she said to Rachel. "Jack Coyne's just run up to see what happened. I couldn't go myself."

"Of course not." Rachel knew the story of how Barney Quinn had been taken from the river in his new truck that he was so proud of. She put her arm around Loretto's shoulder.

"Come back in. Can you make us a cup of tea? Jack will come and tell us soon. We can't help by peering out here."

Gratefully Loretto went back into the kitchen.

They were barely sitting at the table when Jack Coyne rushed in. He had tears in his eyes, something the women had never expected to see.

"Poor stupid little girl," he said over and over before he could even manage to give them her name.

"Poor stupid little thing, she hadn't begun to live and now she's lying under the bridge with a broken neck."

Even though Jacinta and Liam's mother had come down to collect them, they wanted to stay with the others. They wanted to stay in the unreal world of Mr. Slattery's, where there were cups of tea and people pressed biscuits on them, where the night began to fall outside and the electric bars of the two fires began to glow red in the room where nobody turned on the light.

Fergus was in and out, reassuring without fussing them. Comforting them by the very fact that he didn't say it was all right, he said it was terrible.

Marian Johnson arrived to know whether she could take the O'Neill children back to the lodge. Fergus looked into the room and raised his eyebrows in a question. The children had heard her voice in the hall. Kerry shook his head. Grace said nothing, just huddled closer to Michael.

"I'm sorry, Marian, they think they should stay here for the moment. I'll get them home later, or their father will."

Marian was disappointed not to be able to participate.

"One feels so helpless," she said to Fergus. "I just wish there was something I could do to help."

He felt a wave of affection for Marian. She was ridiculous and snobby at times of course, but she was lonely, and what was so vile about regarding Patrick

O'Neill as possible husband material? Marian was a decent honorable person for all her nonsenses. Fergus added to his list of things he disliked about Patrick O'Neill the way he made a fool of this woman. Leading her on to believe there was some interest, when everyone knew he had installed his mistress in rooms above Loretto Quinn's huckster's shop.

Sergeant Sheehan had seen a few sad things in the course of his work. And many accidents that were the result of thoughtlessness. He had no daughters, only sons, he would always have liked a little girl. He thought fondly that a daughter would have hung on his every word in a way that his wife did not. A daughter would not have been ambitious for him and wanted his promotion and preferment, and even for him to meet people of importance and be recognized by them. He knew it was a sentimental notion. People with daughters had just as many problems with them as he had with his sons.

Look at poor Mrs. Meagher and that Teresa for example. And Dr. White's little girl could be a bit of a madam, they said.

But poor Maggie Daly. Nobody had ever anything to say against her. Even her own disagreeable mother could only complain that the child was not constantly in the church at prayer.

Seamus Sheehan's hands were gentle as he lifted the broken body off the raft and laid it on the stretcher.

He and Martin White had been up to their waists in water pulling the raft toward them. The doctor had pronounced life extinct.

Seamus Sheehan had closed Maggie Daly's huge frightened eyes tenderly and arranged her thin body with the arms straight by her sides. He was watched by a crowd of about fifty people.

The child looked incongruous and unsuitable for death in her skimpy blue bathing suit. Young Grace O'Neill had lifted a shabby print dress in a faded color and given it to him.

"That's what she was wearing."

"You're meant to be back up in Mr. Slattery's house."

"I couldn't bear her to be without her clothes. You know Maggie," the child said.

Then Michael Ryan had come running to take Grace away.

Sergeant Sheehan thought the shabby dress was even less suitable. But he laid it over her, before they drew the sheet over her head.

Quietly and with great dignity in front of the shocked and silent crowd Dr. White and Sergeant Sheehan carried Maggie Daly back up to the stretcher. The ambulance had come from the town very quickly. But now that there would be no need to speed back the men stood waiting while Maggie's own people lifted her body from the river. She would be taken to the hospital; the post-mortem formalities would have to go ahead. The date for the inquest would be fixed and then the body would be released to come home to Mountfern, to lie surrounded by candles in her own house, and then the church and then the graveyard.

A great sense of heaviness came over Sergeant Sheehan. He wished he could stand in the water and cry all alone.

The sun was becoming a red ball of fire, and mocking them with its beauty and its sense of peace in the light it shed over the small town.

* * *

Fergus realized that when the O'Neills went home everyone else would.

Patrick's big car drew up outside his door and he came in with his quick light step.

Grace had somehow managed to disentangle herself from Michael, and was in her father's arms.

Then Fergus saw him put a hand on Kerry's shoulder.

"I've come to take you home," he said firmly. "None of us are going to help Maggie by sitting here in the dark. Maggie is at peace now."

It was a good thing to say somehow. Fergus wished he had said something like that himself. It seemed to break the stranglehold.

The children began to move normally, not like puppets. They even got ready to go back to their homes.

Tommy Leonard said he'd walk up River Road with the Ryans.

Liam pulled Jacinta and said to come on, their mother would be annoyed and would come looking for them again.

"I can't believe it," Dara said. "It's not something you can believe, I keep looking around for Maggie, I feel she should be here, coming with us. She should be running to the door ahead of us."

Dara had put into words what they all felt.

Their group was never together without Maggie, and running to the door is exactly what she would have been doing, hurrying people up, apologizing to Mr. Slattery for having stayed so long, asking anxiously where they were going to meet next morning in case there was some change, and they were all going to meet without her.

There was a charged silence when Dara spoke. It was almost too true in its realizing the way they were all thinking.

Suddenly something in Jacinta snapped. "Well, if it hadn't been for you, Dara, she'd never have done it," she said. Taking no heed of the horrified looks she went on. "Stop being all upset now that it's too late. You were horrible to her yesterday and had her crying and running after you, and even today you were just showing off and didn't throw a word to her.

"Maggie would never have done a dive like that unless she was trying to show that she was as good as the rest of us. Show Dara, please Dara. That's all Maggie ever wanted to do. It wasn't much, and now she's dead, she is dead from trying to please Dara . . ."

Jacinta began a laugh which veered from tears to laughing, and the sound got higher and higher.

Patrick O'Neill let go his daughter and strode over to Jacinta. The one quick crack across the face was all it took. Jacinta was silent.

"I want to go home," she said eventually.

"Take her home, Liam. I suppose your father will dislike me more than ever now but try to tell him it had to be done, will you?"

Patrick took his children out of the door, down the stone steps and into the car. Fergus saw him lift Kerry's bicycle and fling it into the boot as lightly as if it had been a toy.

Tommy Leonard and Michael took one of Dara's arms each.

"She was hysterical," Fergus said. "It takes people different ways. She didn't mean a word of it. None of it is true."

The little procession went silently to the door.

"It was a terrible accident, that's what it was. An accident," he called after them into the night. And it stirred something in his mind, something about people telling *him* it was a terrible accident three years ago when Kate Ryan had gone into the town in an ambulance.

As expected the hospital released Maggie Daly's body within twenty-four hours.

Mr. Conway had been in there to see to things.

Mrs. Daly wanted her laid out in the house.

Dr. White protested. This was a child, it would be too distressing for everyone. A child didn't have the tradition that a lot of the older people might know and want. Better to close the coffin and leave it overnight in the church.

Mrs. Daly had said with that ominous calm that she thanked the doctor for all his services so far, but his words were useless. Friends and neighbors would come to pray for Maggie's soul by her body in the way it had been done for centuries.

Martin White went in a rage to the presbytery.

"Canon Moran, you have a duty, a duty I tell you to stop that madwoman talking about sins on Maggie Daly's soul. There are no sins, for God's sake. What kind of a mockery is this, getting people into a hysteria, coming and droning prayers for nonexistent sins?"

"Calm yourself, Dr. White, I beg you." The old canon's faded eyes looked at him kindly. "You're not going to tell me that prayers to God and his Blessed Mother could ever be wasted, could ever go unheard?"

"Oh, forget it, Canon," Dr. White said and banged the presbytery door behind him.

"He's under great strain, poor man," the canon said forgivingly to young Father Hogan, who was making a poor attempt at scrambling some eggs for the two of them.

Martin White had to admit that the American had done the right thing to his daughter. He had heard an account of the scene both from Fergus Slattery and from young Liam.

Jacinta was unwilling to speak about the incident.

Her father came and sat by her bed.

"We all lose our tempers, you know," he began.

Nothing.

"I lost mine with the canon now, it's an easy thing to do. You must have inherited it from me."

Silence.

"The only thing to do is to apologize for it as soon as possible. That neutralizes it a bit, like an acid and an alkali. You know?"

"*You* never apologize," Jacinta said. It was true. He rarely did.

"Say something to Dara. She's very upset."

"We're all upset," Jacinta said.

"What *is* all this?" Dr. White looked old and tired suddenly.

Jacinta bit her lip as she looked at him. "You wouldn't understand, Daddy," she began.

"I might," he sighed. "I just might if you told me."

"It's just I got cross with Dara, she's got everything, she's gorgeous-looking and they're all mad about her, Kerry and Grace, and her brother Michael's lovely to her not like Liam, and Maggie sort of worshiped her, and Tommy Leonard can't stop talking about her." Jacinta's face was red and her shoulders were heaving.

"Of course I shouldn't have said it but it's not all that terrible, people often say things in a hurry and don't mean the half of it."

She looked at him to see if he had any glimmer of understanding. To her surprise he was patting her hand.

"I know," he said. "It's very hard."

"Oh Daddy, I'm sorry," she wept.

He held her while she cried and he patted her as if she were a baby.

Then when the storm had died down he said gently, "I'll go and bring the car around, you get up out of this bed now and get dressed. I'll take you over to Ryan's, and you can tell Dara you didn't mean it. That it's not true."

"Do I have to?"

"Yes, you have to.

"Dara has been sitting there all day, apparently, and not taking in what's going on all around her. She's in a very bad way."

"It's not due to me surely . . ."

"No, it's not all due to you. This time yesterday your little friend died. Died, Jacinta, that's a terrible thing to have seen. No wonder you are all upset. What we have to do is try to make it a bit easier on everyone, not harder."

"Very well." Jacinta swung her feet out of bed.

She stood in her pajamas choosing which garments to wear. She looked for a moment at the shirt with the leather tassels on it. But she rejected it, it was too festive for these times.

Kate was surprised to see Dr. White and Jacinta. She had heard various versions of the incident. But in view of everything else that had happened it seemed almost minor. Surely Dara would understand when the shock lessened that Jacinta had only been grumbling and complaining the way she always did.

"I'm afraid Dara's up in her room," she said.

Dara had come down for meals and said nothing. She had eaten nothing either. She said that the food literally would not go down.

Kate had decided to leave her for one day.

John had been up to see her several times, maddened with his grief not to have been in Mountfern when it happened. Shocked still at the news that was waiting when he came back happily from his meeting and the beer and sandwiches that had followed it.

But Dara hadn't talked to him. He told Kate that she sat there white-faced, twisting this false rose on a wire stem and a clip back and forth in her hands. Sometimes tears came down her face. Strange tears without any sobs, they looked as if they were painted on.

"Can Jacinta go up and see her?" Dr. White asked tentatively.

"She doesn't seem to want to talk to anyone. It's terrible times for all of them, all of you." Kate gave Jacinta a slight pat on her arm as some kind of token that she wasn't siding against her.

Jacinta understood. "I said something a bit stupid yesterday. I wanted to tell her I didn't mean it."

"Well then, why don't you go up and tell her? I'm sure she'll be relieved," Kate said.

She poured a whiskey for Martin White without asking him whether he wanted one or not, and he took it without asking himself the same question. They sat and waited for their daughters to make their peace.

"Dara?"
"Yes."
"Can I come in?"
Jacinta stood at the door.
Dara looked up listlessly.
"I'm sorry for what I said."
"What?"
"It had nothing to do with you. She just fell. She would have fallen anyway."
"I know."
"But I'm sorry I said it."
"That's all right."
Jacinta and Dara had never had the arm-in-arm friendship of any of the other girls. There would be no embracing, no tears, no emotional reconciliation.
"It's like a nightmare, isn't it?" Jacinta said.
"I wonder did she know," Dara said.
"Did she know what?"
"That she was going to die."
"She couldn't have. It was so quick."
"But they say people do . . ."
"No, Dara, she couldn't have, it was too short. Try to think of a jump or a dive, it's over in a second, it would have been for her too."
"Yes."
"Will you . . . will you be all right?"
"Who, me?" Dara sounded like Maggie without realizing it. "Yes, I'll be all right."

Jacinta came back into the bar.
"That didn't take long," Dr. White said.
"She doesn't feel like talking. She said it was all right."
"I'm sure it's all forgotten now," Kate said. She didn't really feel that at all, but she had to say something to try to console this wretched child in front of her.
"She looks very lonely there, as if she could do with some company," Jacinta said.
"I know. But what company? Even if I could get up the stairs I'm not what she wants. And she can't talk to her father, or even Michael." Kate looked anxious.
Dr. White stood up. "Come on, Jacinta, we've done what we came to do, no point in wearing everyone out."
"Will they have her in an open coffin?"
"Apparently." Martin White was grim.
"The children shouldn't go."
"Of course they shouldn't, it's not the goddamn middle ages, but that

madwoman will probably go out to the highways and byways finding children to terrify them."

"I wouldn't be afraid of seeing Maggie lying in a coffin," Jacinta said suddenly. "In fact I'd prefer to. Anything would be better than seeing her all broken on the raft."

Martin White and Kate Ryan exchanged surprised glances. They hadn't thought of it like that.

They brought Maggie's body back that evening. Twenty-six hours after she had died Barry Conway's hearse drove down Bridge Street and parked almost opposite his own premises.

The front parlor in Daly's had been made ready. Candlesticks burned and holy water fonts hung on the wall.

Her father looked a broken man, her sisters from Wales looked unfamiliar and startled. Kitty, who had been going to come home from Dublin for the weekend, sat white-faced in a corner. Charlie brought more and more chairs into the parlor.

They were not going to sit there all night, it was not a wake in the old sense of the word. But between nine o'clock and midnight almost every single man and woman in Mountfern would call to tell the family how sorry they were about what had happened.

They would look at the face, and say a prayer. Then they would leave their mass card, a silver or black-edged card stating that the holy sacrifice of the mass had been offered for the repose of the soul of Maggie Daly. Most of them wrote Margaret Daly. Maggie seemed the wrong kind of name for a dead person.

"I'm not going to go," Kate stormed to John.

"Of course you're not to go," he soothed.

"No, I mean even if I had my own two good legs I wouldn't go."

"Easy, Kate, easy."

"The children? Do you think Jacinta was right? Would it be better for them to see her . . . ?"

"I think it might." He was quiet but firm. "Don't forget they have already seen her dead. This has to be better."

"Will you tell Dara?"

"Yes." His heart was heavy. "I'll go up now."

"If you like, Dara, I'll walk along to Daly's with you. Is that what you want to do, or would you prefer to remember her the way she was, laughing and running around?"

"Will her eyes be open, Daddy?"

"No, pet, they'll be closed."

"I couldn't bear to see her eyes, but I would like to say goodbye to Maggie in some way."

"You tell me when you want to go, I'll come with you."

"Michael?" It was the first time she had mentioned him all day.

"He says he would like to say goodbye to her also. You always say the same you two, it never changes." His smile was gentle.

"It must be the only thing that doesn't. Everything else has changed. For the worse."

"Call me when you want to go, Dara."

"Is Michael ready now?"

"Yes, he is, love."

"Can we go right away?"

They walked in complete silence by the river.

They didn't even look into Loretto Quinn's. They might have seen Rachel sitting by her window. And Loretto sitting downstairs with all the memories of the night that Barney died clear in her mind. They didn't look into Coyne's Motor Works. They might have seen Jack Coyne doing something he hadn't done for a long time. He was sitting at his table with his mug of tea in front of him as usual.

But Jack Coyne was not reading the newspaper, which is what he usually did at night, hunting bargains through the small ads. Jack was reading aloud to himself a verse of poetry.

He had been trying to remember it all day and in desperation had gone up to the brothers. Brother Keane had lent him an anthology.

And he had found it under Yeats.

> Come away, O human child!
> To the waters and the wild.
> With a faery, hand in hand,
> For the world's more full of weeping than you can understand.

He didn't read any more of the poem. He didn't even know what it was about, but it seemed to sum up what had happened in Mountfern.

Tommy Leonard stood at the door.

He knew that sooner or later Dara would come to Daly's.

He moved over to join the three Ryans. "I wanted to wait so that we could go together."

"Thank you," Dara said simply.

John Ryan almost felt he should let them go in on their own.

Just as they got to the door of Daly's Dairy, Dara paused. The others stopped, thinking she didn't want to go in.

"We should ask Jacinta and Liam to come as well," she said.

Michael ran up to Whites'; in minutes he was back with the two White children behind him.

"Grace's father didn't want her to come," Dara explained. "He doesn't understand that this is the best thing we can do."

Just then a car drew up. Grace got out and she walked slowly, almost hesitantly over to the others.

"Father didn't want me to come, but Mrs. Fine saw you all walking down the road so she called him, and he drove me here at once."

Nobody asked where Kerry was. It was as if they had forgotten him.

Unaware of the sympathetic looks they were getting from the adults, the six children walked into the house. They went to the front room where the candles flickered and they heard the rise and fall of prayers.

Maggie looked like a wax doll. Her face was a clear almost transparent white. Because she had been injured so badly by the fall her hair was arranged to cover the sides of her face. The great cut over her eye wasn't visible.

She was dressed in a white gown with long sleeves, and had a rosary threaded through her hands.

She didn't look what they thought of as dead, she looked odd. Too still, and as if she were acting a part.

Mrs. Daly sat by the coffin. "Thank you for coming to pray for Maggie," she said.

The children knelt down. They hadn't intended to, but that was what Mrs. Daly seemed to expect.

They said a decade of the rosary together, then they stood and looked again, a last look.

It was as if they had forgotten the presence of her family and the other adults in the room. They talked to each other in low voices.

"It doesn't look *too* frightening," Tommy said.

"She doesn't have that worried look she sometimes has," Grace said.

"She won't have to worry about things anymore," said Michael.

"It can't be possible that she won't get up," Jacinta said.

"She was very nice, you know, very, very nice," said Liam White.

"I'm terribly terribly sorry, Maggie," said Dara.

Eddie Ryan arrived at the door of Daly's.

Sheila Whelan exchanged glances with Martin White and Judy Byrne who were standing in the corridor.

She was about to discourage him.

"It's all right," said Eddie. "I know nobody would want me here."

"It's not that . . ." Sheila began.

"I'm too young to see anyone dead. But I brought some flowers."

Sheila looked at the wilting collection in his hands. Some of them were wallflowers taken from Judy Byrne's windowboxes, some were the purple wild valerian that grew in the cracks of walls. There was a selection of cowslips and some dandelions.

There was little life or bloom in any of them since they had been squeezed in a hot hand.

They were almost entirely weeds. To Eddie Ryan they were flowers.

Sheila took them gently from the boy's hand. "Thank you very much, Eddie. I'll see that these are put in a special place. Mrs. Daly will be very grateful that you had such a kind thought."

"They might need a bit of water if they're to go on the coffin," Eddie said anxiously.

And Mrs. Whelan said she'd see to it, never fear.

Everyone said that it would break your heart next day to see the children at mass. They sat so still near the front of the church. The nuns were all there from the convent, and all the brothers too. The men had come from the building site; many of them knew the Dalys in one way or another.

Rachel asked Kate if it would be out of place for her to attend the service. She didn't want to do anything that would be out of place.

"You'll be expected to be there," Kate assured her. "Weren't you one of her great friends?"

The small coffin covered in summer flowers stood at the steps of the altar. Father Hogan had asked Sister Laura if she could assemble some of the better singers in the school to act as a choir.

She found a dozen of the older girls whom she hoped would not cry. Girls who were two classes ahead of Maggie. She arranged they should sing "Ave Maria" and "Panis Angelicus," and at the end of the mass they would have "The Lord's My Shepherd."

There was no time for a rehearsal, Sister Laura said to them, it had to be right first time. She put all her sorrow and loss into conducting the hastily formed choir. It meant that she didn't have to think of why the Lord saw fit to take Maggie Daly so soon in such a strange way.

Rachel had been to one Catholic service in her life. A big Italian-American wedding where the church had been filled with mink coats and expensively decorated by a florist. She had particularly remembered the incense, it was a heady thing and went up your nose, making you slightly light-headed.

She got the same feeling in the church in Mountfern. Tommy Leonard and Michael Ryan were serving the mass; this meant they were attending the priests as assistants of some sort, Rachel noticed. They wore choirboy surplices, both of them were pale and they swung the thurible with the incense around the coffin that held the body of their friend. Rachel didn't see Patrick in the church, though she knew he was somewhere there. She hadn't told him she was coming nor asked his advice. This was nothing to do with Patrick or her wish to fit into his community. This was all to do with the death of Maggie Daly, her friend.

As the pure high voices of the girls from Mountfern Convent sang the words of the Twenty-third Psalm, the tears came down Rachel's face. It seemed curiously inappropriate to hear the children singing the words about "He leadeth me the quiet waters by." It was odd to be able to think of quiet waters as a kind of heaven when the child had ended her life in the water not two hundred yards from this church.

Rachel remembered the excitement on Maggie's face over the dress. The look of disbelief when she saw herself in the mirror that day up at the lodge, the way she had clapped her hands with pleasure.

Rachel thought about Maggie's anxious look and her unsureness: "Are you sure I'm not staying too long, Mrs. Fine?"

"Is it really all right if I keep this ribbon all for myself?"

"I used to want all my hair to fall off and start again until I met you, Mrs. Fine, now I think it's grand, I'm delighted with it."

"Tell me what it was like for you growing up, was it all Jews and Jewesses where you lived or were there ordinary people there too?"

And on that last day: "I did wear the dress once, Mrs. Fine, but it wasn't really the right time to wear it. You know me, I'd get it wrong. But next time I'll make sure that it gets a proper showing."

Rachel heard that Sheila Whelan had suggested Maggie should be buried in her new dress, it had meant so much to her.

Mrs. Daly had not even considered it. The child would not go to Eternal Life in the trappings and vanities of this life. She would wear a white shroud.

The dress still hung on the back of Maggie's door.

Rachel felt an overwhelming urge to ask for it back, but she knew it would be misunderstood.

She couldn't bear to think of Kitty Daly wearing it someday. Or it being given away and worn by some other girl in some other town who had no idea how much it had meant in the short frightened life of a girl who was being buried before her sixteenth birthday.

Uncaring of the careful make-up and the streaks that must be all over her face, Rachel let the tears fall. She looked across the church and saw Kate Ryan, still in her wheelchair. There were tears falling on her face also.

They followed the small coffin to the grave. In the background the river sounds went on, familiar and almost unheard now by everyone who lived by its side. The June sunshine came down on the graveyard and marble headstones shimmered and shone as if they were lovely exciting things instead of the record of death.

The children stood almost huddled together for comfort. Kerry was a few paces behind.

As the last holy water was shaken and the last prayers said, the grave diggers began to fill the great dark hole in the ground, a space that looked far too big for Maggie.

The children waited motionless until the very last sod was in place. They gathered up the flowers and wreaths and laid them on top. Only then would they leave.

As they walked through the other headstones—the celtic crosses, the plain iron cross shapes, the marble slabs—they remembered all the times they had spent examining the words on the tombstones in the churchyard. Fingering the inscription to William James Fern who died young at Majuba Hill in the Transvaal. He had been young all right but not as young as Maggie. And the tombstone of James Edward Gray which had been so neglected and they had tried to smarten it up for him. They decided that they would go again and do something to James Edward Gray's resting place.

Maggie would have liked that.

"I suppose you think it's barbaric that people will come in here to spend hours drinking on account of the funeral," Kate said to Rachel.

"No, I think it's very comforting somehow," Rachel said. "I'm becoming more and more assimilated you know. Not looking from the outside in anymore."

"I've always said they gave your mother the wrong baby in that hospital, you're more Irish than we are." Kate said it as a high compliment.

"It was the last thing I expected when I came here," Rachel said. "I used to hope that he would find it a disappointment, and decide to go back, back home to New York. I never thought for one moment that I would feel it was home myself."

Kate looked at her in concern. Despite her praise for Mountfern there was a very lonely note in Rachel's voice. As if she had been abandoned.

"You do know how much you mean to everybody here."

Rachel smiled. "Yes, I feel very much at home, very peaceful here. More so than Patrick does in ways. He expected so much, and I expected so little. That must be it."

"What kind of things do you expect now?" Kate spoke gently.

"I've no long-term plans anymore, no strategies, hardly any hope. I just go along one day at a time."

* * *

Dara walked up to Coyne's wood with Leopold.

Mary Donnelly said you should never underestimate Leopold. There were times when no human being could give you the company and solidarity you needed and Leopold often rose to those times.

More to please her than from any great hopes of companionship Dara took Leopold to the wood.

To her surprise he was very well behaved, pausing considerately to inquire her intentions at every turn rather than racing off wildly on one direction or sitting down whimpering and refusing to follow.

Dara thought that secretly Mary must have been training Leopold. He actually *looked* much better too, as if somebody had been brushing him. Dara had never thought you could make any impression on that coat but in fact it looked quite shiny and his eyes were bright rather than alternately dulled with despair or rolling in a madness.

She sat on a tree trunk and Leopold went sniffing and snuffling but keeping a courteous eye on Dara in case she decided to move. She didn't move. She sat there with a long daisy, and threaded the heads of other daisies on its stem to make a flowery bracelet.

She hadn't wanted to spend any more time with the others. Tommy Leonard had been nice, he said it was bad at a time like this to go off on your own, you needed others around you whether you felt like it or not. Michael said he was going to go up the river and fish on his own. He hoped Dara didn't think that was rude. She squeezed his arm. She understood completely, as people always said they seemed to feel the same about everything.

She didn't expect Kerry. This was a part of the wood she had never been with him. It was a place off the main path, a big bank of fuchsia hedge surrounded it. Kerry came in softly through the trees.

"If you like to be on your own I'll go away," he said.

He was still in the dark grey suit he had worn at the funeral. He had opened the collar of his shirt and his black tie was loose around his neck. She had never seen him more handsome.

"No, no I'm glad to see you." She spoke simply.

She sat playing with the daisies, her hair falling over her face as she bent in concentration. She wore a plain white tee shirt and a denim skirt, changed from the good navy dress with the white collar she had worn at the funeral. She looked very young and lost.

Kerry squatted down beside her. He picked a daisy and started to make a collection of daisy heads on one stem too. For a while they said nothing.

Leopold realized that this was somehow important. He stopped his burrowing and sniffing. He sat politely with his head on one side as if waiting for the conversation to begin.

"I wish I could do something to help you," Kerry said.

"I'm all right. It's just so terrible for Maggie."

"It's like being asleep," Kerry said.

"And she wouldn't be in purgatory or anything. You know, waiting to get into heaven."

"Oh Dara, of *course* she wouldn't!" Kerry laughed tenderly at the very idea.

"Well why were we all praying that she'd be forgiven her sins and soon see God? She can't be there yet can she?"

"Where?"

"Heaven. She'd not have gone straight to heaven unless she died coming out of confession."

Kerry was confused. "Dara sweetheart, it's like being asleep, I tell you. I saw my mother when she was dead, it was a big sleep. Grace said she saw Maggie's face last night, her eyes were closed. That's all it is."

"And are you sure that she's not in the fires of purgatory?"

He reached out and held her close to him. "I'm very sure. I know definitely."

Dara sobbed into his chest. "Oh, I'm so glad, I couldn't bear Maggie to be all by herself in purgatory, she'd be terrified."

Sister Laura said that there would be a lot of delayed shock about the accident. The girls were taking it too calmly. They went up and tended a grave in the Protestant churchyard, they planted a tree near the footbridge. They had asked Mrs. Daly without success if they could have her copper-colored dress. They didn't know what they wanted to do with it but they wanted it anyway.

Sister Laura couldn't understand why Dara, Grace and Jacinta did not want to come up to the school to join in a special novena for the repose of Maggie Daly's soul.

"It's reposed already," Dara had said, and the others had gone along with it.

Sister Laura was confused. Dara really meant this, as if she had been given a special message that Maggie was sleeping the sleep of the just. And the others all agreed with her.

Grace and Michael went fishing a lot. Or that's what they said they were doing. Michael left early and came back late.

Nobody expected any games or swimming to continue on the bridge. Tommy Leonard had to work in the shop almost all the time, Jacinta and Liam had a horrible cousin from Dublin staying with them and they had to entertain her. They were rightly too embarrassed to bring her anywhere near their friends so it was a matter of cycling energetically to the old ruined abbey by day and going to the pictures at night.

Dara was all alone.

This is what she wanted to be.

She wanted to walk by herself, she wanted to think.

Sometimes Kerry O'Neill came to find her, and when he did they walked, often without saying a word for a half hour or more. Then he might take her face in his hands and kiss her gently. Or he would lay his arm comfortingly around her shoulders as they walked.

"It will pass one day," he said. "One day you'll realize that it's a different sort of memory." He looked very thoughtful.

"Did you feel that about your mother?"

"Yes. One day it didn't hurt as much thinking about her. I didn't believe people when they told me. I thought they were just being nice."

"What did it feel like, after the day you changed?"

"I felt she was at peace and I must leave her there and not keep thinking of her all the time, and regretting, and wishing and getting angry . . ."

"Ah, but you loved your mother, you were good to her. Grace told me you used to sit by her bed and read to her."

"That was hardly much consolation." His face looked bitter.

The silence fell again, easy and companionable.

Dara didn't ask him why he thought his mother needed consolation. He didn't ask Dara why she sounded so guilty about her friend.

"Do you dream about Maggie?" Dara asked Grace.

"No, I haven't." Grace seemed apologetic. "I do think about her but I haven't dreamed of her at all."

She looked at Dara anxiously. Dara's face was very white.

"I do," Dara said simply. "Every night."

"Were you nice to your father?" Dara asked Fergus Slattery unexpectedly.

"No, I expect I was fairly unpleasant to him. I am to most people. Why do you ask?"

"I was wondering do you wish he was back here so that you could explain things to him?"

"No, Dara, he was old. His life was lived. It's different with Maggie, everyone wishes she were back so that they could explain things to her. And anyway you have nothing to explain, you were all very nice to her, she had a load of grand friends even if her mother was a bit of a trial." He was trying to be light without being flippant.

"No, I don't think her friends were good to her," Dara said. "I think she was lonely and frightened all her life, and I didn't know it until now when it's too late."

"Kerry, why do you like me? Seriously. I'm not joking." Dara's big dark eyes were troubled.

"Because I like to be with you. You are beautiful and loving, you are bright and intelligent, and funny. And that's enough for a start, isn't it?"

"I'm not old enough for you," Dara said.

"What's age got to do with it?"

"I don't know enough, I'm only a schoolgirl when all's said and done. You should have someone much brighter, who knows things."

"You know enough things for me."

"It's very mysterious." Dara shook her head. "If I were rich I'd say you were after my money, and you *know* I'm not going to sleep with you . . . So I can't see why." She spoke in a very matter of fact tone.

"You might sleep with me someday," Kerry said.

"I don't think so."

"We can but hope," he said lightly. "But in the meantime we have to try to take you out of this melancholy. Maggie wouldn't have wanted you to be like this."

"I'm sick of people telling me what she would or wouldn't have wanted," Dara snapped. "Her mother was telling me that Maggie's in heaven looking down on us all and very heartsore about the kind of films that Declan Morrissey is getting in the Classic Cinema."

"Gently, Dara," he said, reaching for her hand.

"I'm not mad or depressed, I just feel very confused," she said.

He held her close and the confusion seemed to go further away. After that, he held her close all the time.

They didn't laugh and race away from each other as they once had. They didn't swim and splash and shout in the river. They lay together on the mossy ground of Coyne's wood and clung to each other.

The sunlight came flickering through the trees above and Kerry O'Neill peeled off the little blue shirt that Dara wore. He opened her simple cotton brassiere and took it gently away from her. He lay his head on her breasts and heard her heart beating.

At no stage did she stop him.

They lay like that and he stroked her so that it felt both exciting and peaceful at the same time.

At no time did she feel it was wrong.

Only when he made a move to take off his own clothes did Dara stir.

"I don't want to," she said.

He sat up coldly. "As you say."

"Don't be cross. Don't change."

"Don't be a tease then, don't promise and then go back on it."

"I didn't mean to," she said piteously.

"But you liked it. You like my holding you."

"I don't know what to say."

"Well, tell me when you do." He had leaped to his feet and was walking angrily through the trees.

"I think Dara spends all her days with Kerry in Coyne's wood," Kate said to John.

"Don't they all go out together? I thought they were never out of each other's sight," John said.

"No. The Whites have this cousin, poor Tommy's stuck in the shop, Grace and Michael are off fishing."

"How do you know all this?"

"When Rachel took me up to Bridge Street today I was in Leonard's. I was talking to Tommy. He looks very badly still."

"Why do you think she's with Kerry?"

"She looks flushed and nervy but she doesn't have the look of a child who sat alone all day in a wood."

"What will we do?" He was anxious.

"I don't know. What *can* we do? I mean even if she is with him, we can't upset her anymore by hounding her," Kate said resignedly.

"I don't suppose he . . ." John didn't finish the sentence.

"And I don't think if he wanted to that she would really . . ." Kate didn't finish the sentence either.

Olive Hayes was sitting at the kitchen table writing to Bernadette. The young Ryan girl knocked at the door.

"I'm afraid Grace has gone off out. I thought she was meeting you and your brother," Miss Hayes said.

"Oh yes, they're all down at the river," Dara said, covering up for Grace and Michael. "I was just passing and I thought I'd call in just in case Kerry was here."

"No, child, he went off in that car of his. Off to a place way out on the Galway road."

"Oh I see." Dara looked disappointed.

"Do you want a drink of milk or tea or anything before you go back down to the others?" Miss Hayes thought the child looked disturbed. It must have been harrowing for them all to have watched a violent death.

"The others?" Dara said vaguely.

"Down on the river. You said they were all on the bank . . ."

"Oh yes, I forgot. The others." Her voice sounded dull.

"Are you all right, Dara?"

"Fine, Miss Hayes. I'll be off now."

Olive looked out of the window. The child didn't take the road down toward the river. She headed out to the main road.

Dara had never hitch-hiked before. She would have to be very careful not to stop anyone she knew.

A big and unfamiliar van came into view. It wasn't anyone from Mountfern so she held out her hand.

It was a traveler looking for a bit of chat, even from a schoolgirl. He had a van of chips and peanuts.

"Do you know this place . . . it's a kind of roadhouse?" Dara told him about the pub where Kerry said he had been playing cards.

The man knew it well, he'd be stopping there himself. A few other places on the way before they got there. Funny sort of a place for a girl to be going on her own.

Dara told him a story about looking for her brother. The commercial traveler thought this was perfectly reasonable. He chattered on, hardly noticing that the grave dark-eyed girl spoke little in return.

He talked about Mountfern.

"That place is going to get a rare shake-up, used to be the sleepiest town in the midlands," he said.

He seemed to expect a reply. "Is that right?" Dara asked.

"Well, seeing as how it's where you came from you'd know better than I would. I bet you're looking forward to the new hotel?"

"Yes, in a way." She was looking out the window.

"It'll bring a fortune to the town, you might get a job in it yourself when you grow a bit older." He was a good-natured man, he would like to think that this attractive girl could stay in her own place rather than be forced to emigrate.

"Of course there's always going to be some who'll lose by it. You're not connected with the Grange there where I picked you up?"

"No, no, I was just visiting someone in the lodge."

"Well the Grange will feel the pinch, I tell you. Who'd stay there when there's the new place? And who'd have a drink in Ryan's, come to think of it?"

"Why not?" She turned to look at him.

"Your man, the American's going to have a real bar, not a fancy lounge with uppity prices, but a normal bar across the bridge there from them, it will take all their trade. Very hard on them. Poor man's wife in a wheelchair already after an accident and now this on top of it all."

Dara turned away and looked out the window.

"Tell me, did you know that unfortunate child who was killed there last week, wasn't it the saddest thing . . . ?"

His voice trailed away as he saw the glint of tears on the girl's face. "Of course you must have known the girl. I'm sorry," he said, mad with himself.

Dara just kept looking out at the road taking them toward Galway.

"Will I wait and see that you meet your brother all right?"

"No thanks, I'm fine now. Really I am."

"You must take no notice of me, Mikey the big mouth, that's what they call me."

"No, you were very kind to give me a lift."

"The little girl who died is in heaven of course."

"Of course," Dara said in an odd flat voice.

There didn't seem to be a back room when she went in first. Just a shabby-looking bar with a loud jukebox. There were cigarette butts on the floor and bits of litter everywhere.

It must be through the door that said toilets on a hand-scrawled sign.

She pushed through the door and saw ahead of her another one, she touched it and it opened a little. Kerry sat at a table with a drunk. Kerry was shuffling cards in a way that they seemed to make an arc. His face was clenched in concentration.

She stood looking at him for what felt like a long time before he looked up and saw her.

His face didn't change, he looked neither annoyed nor surprised.

"Hi," he said and continued with the shuffle.

"Not that way, Kerry, get your thumb in there properly." Francis Doyle's voice was slurred.

Dara sat down and watched. The drunken man helped himself to more whiskey from time to time. Neither of them even acknowledged her being there.

"I felt lonely so I thought I'd come out here," she said eventually.

"Sure." Kerry was pleasant but abstracted.

"To find you," she said.

"And you did," he said.

Francis Doyle took no more notice of her than if she had been a fly that had buzzed into this close, overpowering room. She felt slightly light-headed as if she might faint.

"Are you going to talk to me?" she asked Kerry.

"Not now, no."

"When?"

"When I've learned the waterfall," he said.

Dara's mind went blank as she sat in the airless room. She was unaware of her surroundings or how long she sat there. Then she felt Kerry touching her shoulder.

"I'll drive you home now," he said in a light casual way as if it were the most normal thing in the world to find her in this strange place miles and miles from home.

He held open the door of the little red car. They drove back to Mountfern, fast through the twisty roads. Dara didn't speak. But she felt more at ease. She settled herself low in the car and once or twice she closed her eyes. On a hill a few miles from Mountfern the car stopped. Kerry looked at her.

"What are we going to do with you, Dara?" He said it with a mixture of affection and irritation.

She turned to him. "I don't know. I felt so empty. The only thing that made any sense was to be with you."

"But you don't *want* to be with me. You made that clear in the woods."

"I don't want to sleep with you."

"We were wide awake."

"You know what I mean."

"I know you keep pushing me away. Why should I think you want to be with me?" He looked puzzled.

Dara took Kerry's hand and held it to her lips. "I've never loved anyone before. You see this is the first time and it's very confusing. It's all mixed up with everything else that's happened, and I feel strange and frightened."

She looked terribly young. He took her hand and kissed it gently the way she had his. He said nothing.

"You mightn't even love me at all," she continued. "So I had nothing to lose by going to find you. I'm not playing any sort of game."

"I don't know if I love anyone," Kerry said. "But if I do the nearest I'd come to it would be you. Come here to me."

He took her in his arms and she stretched across the little red car to reach him.

He had ten more days' holiday.

Dara still looked pale and anxious. But she went to sit in the woods each day. Some days he came there, some he did not. She never knew whether he would be there or not.

Each time he held her close to him, he seemed to be more demanding and urgent. Dara felt her resistance changing in degree. What she had fought off a week previously seemed acceptable now.

"When is Kerry going back to Donegal?" Kate asked Rachel.

"Patrick says he still has a few days."

"I wish he'd go now."

"Don't worry so much, Kate."

"I can't help it. She looks totally feverish and her mind is a thousand miles away when she's here, or to be more precise three miles away up at the lodge."

"I asked her to come for a drive with me, but she said no." Rachel had done her best.

"I know you did, you're very good. I suppose we can just hang on until he goes."

"Do you have friends in Donegal?" Dara asked.

"Not really. It's mainly work, you know . . . I play cards sometimes, with a couple of guys I met, Tony McCann, Charlie Burns, they live in Derry across the border."

"Don't they have red buses and red letter boxes there?"

"You've never been to the north?"

"No, how would I go to the north, Kerry?"

"They have red everything, and red, white and blue flags."

"Well it's part of England."

"It's part of the United Kingdom."

"Same thing."

"Don't you care about it not being part of Ireland?"

"Not very much. It will be eventually, I suppose."

"McCann cares, and his friends care. They feel very strongly about it." Kerry's voice sounded as if he were quoting rather than talking.

"That's all big talk because you're an American," Dara said.

"What do you know about it?"

"Nothing," she giggled.

"Will you miss me when I go back?" he asked.

"Very much. Do you have to go back?"

"Maybe I could stay . . . perhaps I could think of an excuse to stay . . ." he said teasingly.

"Really?"

"If I stay will you be nice to me?" He had reached his arms out for her.

"I'm always nice to you. How would you get off work?"

"I can get anything I want," Kerry said.

"When's Kerry going back?" Kate asked with an innocent air.

"I don't think he is," Dara said, eyes dancing.

"That's right, Grace said he was hoping to get some more time," said Michael.

"Doesn't he have to work in Hill's?" Kate's voice was crisp.

"Oh, Kerry could talk his way out of anything," Michael said.

Dara frowned: she didn't want Kerry presented as too much of a playboy. "He'll be able to arrange more time, there's going to be no problem," she said.

She looked excited and eager.

Kate's mouth was a hard narrow line.

"Would you like me to take Dara off on a trip somewhere?" Fergus asked Kate next day.

"Dara?"

"It would keep her out of Kerry O'Neill's clutches. At least you'd know she was safe with me. Everyone's safe with me," Fergus added gloomily.

Kate didn't give the usual good-humored riposte. She said nothing for a moment.

Then she said, "No, I think it's time for Dara to go on a trip much further afield."

"Where do you mean?"

"I don't know. I'll talk to John about it. We have to stop pretending it isn't happening."

"Of course we don't know if anything *is* happening." Fergus began to backtrack.

"We have an educated guess," Kate said grimly.

They sat in the side yard. The whitewashed walls of the big outhouse which had been where the twins had their party now had clematis and honeysuckle growing up and winding around. The front of that building out on River Road looked well too, bright-colored windowboxes getting ready for the day it would open as Ryan's Shamrock Café.

John and Kate often sat for a while in the side yard. After a night in a room that smelled of cigarette smoke and porter it was like a cool waterfall to sit here where the flowers took over. The night-scented stock and the jasmine were everywhere.

"What will we do with Dara?" Kate's voice was heavy and sad.

"I've been thinking," John said slowly.

"I knew you would." She looked at him hopefully.

"Do you remember what Sister Laura wanted us to do in the first place? Why don't we send her to France?"

Nineteen

$\mathcal{M}$adame Vartin looked like the Mother of Sorrows. She had a long white face and a thin mouth that trembled as if on the verge of tears constantly. She had pale blue eyes swimming in sadness. Monsieur Vartin was quite different— he was small and round and laughed like a machine gun firing in continuous rattles and blasts. Neither of them spoke a word of English. Mademoiselle Stephanie, who was a cousin of Madame Vartin, spoke enough to explain Dara's duties to her.

She was to prepare breakfast for the three small Vartin children, she was to take them for a walk and teach them five phrases in English each day. Then she was to play with them till their lunch; after that she was free to study. At dinner she was to help serve at table and to clear afterward.

She got pocket money which worked out at about £3 a week and there was nothing to spend it on as they were miles from anywhere in the middle of the country. The children were horrible and Monsieur was inclined to touch her a lot, pressing up against her when he passed by. Madame's eyes brimmed with such sadness Dara felt almost afraid to talk to her at all. If it had not been for Stephanie, Dara felt she would have gone mad. It was hard to know what Stephanie did in the house. She was often to be seen folding linen or gathering flowers. She made curtains for one of the rooms, a job that took her almost all the summer. Sometimes she took the small car and drove off in the afternoons, sometimes she picked fruit. Dara couldn't make it out at all.

"Avez-vous un vrai job, Mademoiselle Stephanie?" she asked one day. Stephanie laughed at her and quite unexpectedly gave Dara a kiss on each cheek.

"Je t'adore, mon petit chou," she said, still pealing with laughter.

Dara was confused. Why did Stephanie adore her? Why didn't she say whether she had a job or not? Why did she use the familiar *tu* form? Ever since she had arrived she had known that she must be formal and call everyone except the children *vous*. It was a mystery. For a couple of days Stephanie would keep repeating *un vrai job* and shake her head with laughter each time.

Dara could hardly believe how quickly she had managed to find herself transported to France. She, Dara Ryan, who had never even been to London or Belfast had been through Paris in a car and had seen the Arc de Triomphe and the Eiffel Tower. Then she had been driven by Mademoiselle Stephanie to this far-away falling down house in the French countryside.

Mademoiselle Stephanie, blonde and curvy, said she liked the opportunity to practice her English; one day she would visit Ireland and meet all the great and famous people in Ireland. Dara wondered fearfully if Sister Laura had exaggerated the attractions of Mountfern or the connections of the Ryan household.

But mainly she wondered why she was here. It had been so sudden, the explanations all quite unsatisfactory.

Mam had been no help. She had been all excited and said it was wonderful, that Dad had found the money, and what a great, wonderful chance for Dara. Michael had said it was a pity they didn't take boy au pairs, Grace said it was the most exciting thing she had heard of in her life. Tommy Leonard had said he would write to her every few days in case she was lonely. Mary Donnelly told her that of all men, Frenchmen were known to be the lowest.

Kerry had said nothing.

She had rushed to tell him in Coyne's wood and he had shrugged.

"Well if you *want* to go, that's great."

"I don't want to go and leave you."

"Why don't you do what you want to do, Dara?"

It was a frightening echo of the way she had spoken to Maggie. She remembered the way she had spoken to Maggie the night before the accident.

"You don't ever know what you want." She had shouted that as an accusation, and Kerry was saying the same thing to her. She looked at him aghast.

He relented a little. "Have a lovely summer," he said, and kissed her on the nose.

"Will you write to me?" she asked.

"I'll send you a card."

"Will you?"

"I said I would." He sounded impatient.

"Will you stay here now that I'm going back or do you think you should go back to Donegal?"

"Who knows, little Dara? Who knows?" He had kissed her again on the nose.

She had gone to the lodge twice in the hope of seeing him. But he had been out both times.

Grace thought he might have gone to some place he liked miles out on the

Galway road. Miss Hayes said that she hoped he had not. It was a place with a bad name, full of drunks and layabouts.

"No it's not, it's just shabby and dirty," Dara had said and they looked at her with surprise.

She longed to ask Grace to write and tell her about Kerry. She longed to tell Grace how much she yearned to hear of him. But it would be useless, Grace had no idea how much Dara envied her the easy access, the nearness and the closeness to Kerry.

She nearly asked Michael, but she couldn't do that either.

"I'll miss you a lot," Michael said the night before she left.

"No you won't, you have Grace."

"That's different, I'll still miss you, Dara," he said, surprised. "You're my twin, for heaven's sake."

"So I am," she said emptily.

"Is anything wrong?"

"Everything's all changed."

"We're just getting older."

"Maggie didn't," she said.

And suddenly here she was in the French countryside taking children for walks down strange kinds of country roads that had no character in them at all. The fields didn't have proper walls, they went on for miles and miles without any fences even. The farmhouse was terribly shabby on the outside, but very rich and full of huge furniture on the inside.

There was Maria, an Italian maid who had great tufts of long black hair at her armpits and who seemed almost as miserable as Madame. Only Madame, Maria and Dara went to mass on Sundays, which seemed to make nonsense of the nuns saying they were Catholic families looking for equally good Catholics to come and stay. Monsieur had been to the church five times he told her, for his christening, his first communion, his wedding, and the christening of two of his three children; the third managed without him. At least that's what Dara thought he was saying; he seemed to be counting out the occasions proudly on the fingers of one hand for her. She shuddered to think what Canon Moran, or anyone at school would think if she told them, and for some reason she didn't quite understand, she felt that she wouldn't tell them.

Madame's visit to Lourdes involved a lot of preparation. An open suitcase sat on the landing and there was a lot of folding and refolding of clothes, and placing and replacing of missals and small prayer books. There was never a smile or an eagerness, just a more determined business than ever. Dara wondered what the woman could be going so far to pray for.

"Desirez-vous un miracle, Madame Vartin?" she asked boldly on the morning of the departure.

The thin dark woman stopped and looked at her as if she had never seen Dara before.

"Un miracle!" she repeated. *"Un miracle. Tiens!"*

And suddenly and totally unexpectedly, she took Dara by the shoulders and kissed her on each cheek. There were tears in her eyes.

Dara felt terrible. Perhaps Madame Vartin was very sick. How stupid to ask her if she was seeking a miracle! Dara wished she could have bitten back the words, but strangely Madame's softness remained, and when she was being waved off by the entire family at the door she had a special pat for Dara. It was impossible to understand the French.

Dara went for her usual walk in the orchard to find apples that would stave off hunger until the impossibly late meal that evening. She decided to write a long letter to her mother and went upstairs to get her writing paper.

There was summer lightning out over the strange unwalled fields of France. She ate the green apples, and she wrote about Madame going to Lourdes and her own tactless remarks. Dara had gotten into the habit of writing to her mother just like she talked. She knew that the letters were not read out at home, but that her mother gave edited extracts.

"I wonder why she's so sad," Dara wrote. "I mean she doesn't have any awful things to put up with like you do, not being able to walk, and getting stuck behind the counter listening to old bores drinking and chattering on for hours. I can't understand why Monsieur married her really, he must have known she would be a misery. She looks like a disaster area even in their wedding picture. But I think you'd need to live here for a lifetime to know what any of them are at."

Next morning she knocked on Mademoiselle Stephanie's door to ask for a stamp. They gave their letters to the mailman when he arrived with the incoming mail.

Mademoiselle Stephanie was still in bed, which was odd. Beside her was Monsieur Vartin, which was so unexpected that the letter fell from Dara's hand.

"I'm terribly sorry . . ." she began.

Mademoiselle Stephanie didn't seem in the slightest put out. She indicated the middle drawer of the desk for the stamps, and asked Dara to remember to give the mailman some other letters which were on the hall table.

Now that Dara had gone to France it was a little more difficult for Michael to meet Grace without calling attention to himself. Eddie and Declan were particularly revolting this summer; they made kissing sounds when he said he was going fishing with Grace. Admittedly Dad and Mam shushed them up, but it was very annoying.

Grace didn't seem to care, which was a relief. She came into the pub as regularly as when Dara had been around. She asked to see Dara's letters but Mam said that letters were only for the people they were sent to. If Grace wrote to Dara then she would get letters back, and so would Michael.

Dara felt tears of homesickness fall down her face. Madame Vartin found her reading her letter, and put her bony thin arm around the girl's shoulder. She said soothing things in French and Dara said cheerful things between noseblows, things like she wasn't really lonely, and she was just being silly.

Then she looked at Madame Vartin's long sad face and she became more weepy than ever.

She had tried to tell Madame Vartin about Maggie. It was so hard to explain, she had looked up words in the dictionary but even then it was too complicated. Sometimes she had to abandon the story in the middle. And anyway she was more sorry for Madame Vartin than she was for herself. It became almost unbearable when she saw Monsieur give Madame a little peck on the cheek as if nothing untoward had ever gone on in her absence.

Dara sighed. Perhaps men were by nature faithless. Sister Laura had more or less implied it, said that it came from nature where a male animal was used to servicing several female animals. Mary Donnelly never said anything else. Dara thought sadly of the world of men. Starting with Kerry.

There had been letters from everyone, even a card from nice Fergus Slattery. Pages from the Whites, and almost daily something from Tommy Leonard. But from Kerry nothing at all.

He couldn't have found somebody else already. He *couldn't* have. Why say all those things, and want to be so close to her if he could forget her so quickly?

But then Dara thought gloomily of Mrs. Whelan's husband who had gone away, of Kerry's father who wouldn't make up his mind between Mrs. Fine, Miss Johnson and quite possibly Miss Byrne the physio-therapist. And Brain Doyle had a girlfriend in the town that he hardly paid any attention to.

And those men who called on Rita Walsh in the Rosemarie hair salon. Dara knew now they hadn't come to fix hair dryers or to see to the hot water. No, now that she was a sophisticated woman who knew about the world. Now she realized only too well why they went there, and why they looked so secretive when they came out and scuttled off home.

Dara thought about all the men she knew and only her father and brother seemed blameless to her. Her father wouldn't look at another woman and Michael had put Grace on such a pedestal that he probably just kissed her chastely. She couldn't imagine Michael doing what Kerry had. She thought about Kerry for a bit and supposed she'd better tell in confession about all that stroking and kissing. Though how to describe it was a mystery.

It would be lovely to know enough French to confess to a French priest. By the looks of things you'd get away with murder here.

"How's Dara getting on minding the children by the Loire?" Fergus asked.

"It's the poor French children I worry about," Kate laughed. "I got a letter from her this morning and she said that she has taught them all to say *pogue mahone*. They think it's Irish for good morning."

Fergus laughed. "Knowing the French I'd say they'd be pleased to think their children were being taught anything as racy as kiss my arse. A very lavatorial sense of humor, I always found."

"Don't be lofty, you always found. When did you always find? On your five-day trip to Paris ten years ago was it?"

"How many days did *you* spend in Paris, brain box?" he asked.

"No days. And now I'll never go."

"Remember we wanted you to go to Lourdes."

"Yes, but it would have been the wrong thing, Fergus. Lourdes doesn't mend broken spines. Nothing does. People would have been so disappointed and I would have felt I would have failed them somehow if they saw me in a wheelchair for the rest of my life."

"I think it's a load of rubbish," said Fergus.

"You can't mean that." Kate was shocked. "Why would Our Lord let people believe it and go there in millions if it wasn't true?"

"Have you ever considered that Our Lord mightn't be there?"

"No I have not, and neither have you. This is being said to shock me, like a schoolboy. Of course you believe in God."

"Well if I do I don't like him much," Fergus said. "He's taken away my housekeeper weeping and wondering where her duty lies. She came to a tearful conclusion, Canon Moran and Father Hogan's need is greater than mine."

"I'm delighted," Kate said. "Best thing for her, for them and for you."

"Why for me?"

"You'll have to live like the real world lives now, instead of having everything done for you, being a peter pan with occasional flashes of bold atheism now and then. It will be the making of you."

"What will I do?" shouted Fergus.

"Find a wife," Kate said.

"No, seriously what will I do now? Miss Purcell's going."

"I'll get you someone to come in and clean the house. That's all you need."

"But the cooking, the washing."

"I'll teach you to cook. I'm teaching Grace O'Neill so I might as well have two pupils, and until you find someone who takes in washing properly you can bring it here."

Kate wrote to Dara about the lessons. She said they were priceless. She said that Grace hadn't known you could get rashers of bacon cut for you, she thought they started life in plastic wrappings. She said that Michael put half the dough in his hair and on the kitchen walls, and that Fergus was in grave danger of becoming a kitchen bore. He kept saying there was nothing to it, and when were they getting on to something a bit more elaborate?

The entire Vartin family had taken to saying *pogue mahone* as a greeting each day, and Dara wished mightily that she could be around the first time one of them actually said it to anyone who understood Irish.

As an act of solidarity she decided to tell Madame Vartin what it meant. It was the only gift she could give her, a little superior knowledge. Laboriously she translated it: *Va baiser ma fesse.*

Madame's face was quite stunned when she heard it, and Dara wondered had she gone too far? But no. Madame Vartin thought this was a nugget of information and hugged it to herself with glee.

"*Pogue mahone,* Stephanie," she would say to her rival each morning, and she and Dara exchanged winks of delight when nobody was looking.

Rachel told Patrick that he might need to organize activities for the bad weather. She chose a particularly wet and gloomy day to tell him this so that he could see what she meant.

"Fishermen would be out on a day like this, and golfers never let a little rain get between them and their game," Patrick said.

"Their wives?" said Rachel.

"They can get their hair fixed, their nails done."

"Not every day they can't."

"What do you think then?"

"Some activities, maybe cooking classes even. How to make traditional Irish fare."

"Not a bad idea," Patrick said. "Who would we get to do it?"

"Let's think nearer the time. There could even be people around here?"

"Hey," said Patrick suddenly. "Kate Ryan's done well teaching Grace, and

Grace says she's very funny and has long stories about the ingredients and everything. Do you think she could do it?"

"I don't know where you get your ideas, Patrick," Rachel said in admiration.

Jim Costello, the young manager, had not yet met Kerry, son of the house. Jim had been away finding staff and interviewing applicants when Kerry had come home.

He had not been in Mountfern for the tragedy. He knew the Dalys, of course, and remembered the little girl with the long hair and big eyes as a friend of Grace O'Neill's. He called to the dairy to sympathize on his return.

He was surprised to see an older girl there. "I don't think we've met," he said and offered his hand.

"Mountfern is really looking up now that I'm off nursing in Dublin," Kitty Daly said, eyeing him up with unconcealed pleasure. "You *and* Kerry O'Neill. I must say it's the place to be."

"I haven't met him yet, I hear he's a matinee idol," Jim said.

"He's all of that. He's like something from another world," Kitty said.

"Ah well, no chance for the rest of us then." Jim was courteous, admiring and yet distant. He had come to offer his sympathies, it would be crass to let it turn into flirting. And anyway Jim Costello was much too cautious a young man to become too involved with anyone in a small town. His career was of much greater importance than any dalliance with a local girl, even one as pretty as this tall willowy girl with the beautiful crinkly hair.

As he left he said again that he was so sorry about her sister.

"It's impossible to believe it happened," Kitty said bleakly. "This is the first time I've been home since, and three times I've gone upstairs to call her. And I keep expecting all those friends of hers to come traipsing in looking for her."

"I didn't mean to upset you."

"No, it's nice to talk a bit. My dad won't talk about her at all and my mam has more conversations with her in heaven than she ever had when poor Maggie was on earth." She smiled gratefully as Jim Costello went out the door.

"Let's write to Dara," Grace said.

"You always say that when you want to wriggle out of my arms," Michael complained.

"Not true. Anyway I'm much better about remembering your poor sister stuck with all those awful screaming children than you are."

"How can she be learning any French if she keeps writing to us and reading our letters?" Michael grumbled, annoyed to be distracted from his long embraces with the lovely Grace.

But Grace was sitting up and had gotten out the notepad. "Come on, Michael. Stop fooling around . . . I'll start. What will I tell her?"

"Don't tell her about Declan Morrissey getting drunk and asking Mary Donnelly why she was never married. I want to tell her that."

"That's not fair, that's the best part. I can remember nearly all the speech."

"No, I thought of it, you say something boring about clothes or something first."

"I don't write about clothes. Hey, I'll tell her Kerry's coming back for a weekend."

"He'll probably have told her that himself."

"I don't imagine Kerry writes, he's bad at letters."

"Well, to Dara he would surely?" Michael thought that it would be very bad of Kerry to be so neglectful.

"Yes, maybe." Grace was doubtful.

"And I'll write about Kitty Daly being back."

"I don't know." Grace was still more doubtful.

"Grace, for heaven's sake, you're the one who said let's write; now you don't want to say anything."

Eddie Ryan went into Leonard's. Tommy looked left and right. His father was busy talking to Mr. Williams. Swiftly Tommy handed Eddie three aniseed balls from a jar.

"Thanks," Eddie said briefly.

"Don't eat them here," Tommy hissed.

Tommy paid Eddie protection money of a sort. He fed him a small amount of sweets that would not be missed from giant jars in order to buy some peace and quiet from Eddie's gang. Eddie swaggered in most days and the arrangement was sweets of Tommy's choice, otherwise they all came in together and Tommy's father got into a temper, ordered them out and told Tommy that the young Ryan boy was an out and out hooligan. Tommy didn't want any guilt to attach to Dara by association.

He wished that she would write. All he had so far was a picture postcard of some château on the Loire with a list of complaints about the food, and the price of ice cream and the price of stamps.

"Any news of Dara?" he asked Eddie.

"You ask me that every time," Eddie said.

"And you usually have a smart answer rather than saying yes or no," Tommy snapped.

"There was a letter this morning, Mam read bits of it at breakfast. What would be in the bits she doesn't read, do you think?"

"Maybe about how great it is to escape from you, Eddie."

"If you're going to be like everyone else then we will drop our deal?" Eddie said with menace.

The thought of Eddie's gang jostling and pushing and creating havoc in the newsagent's shop made Tommy Leonard feel faint.

"We'll go on the way we are," he said.

"I thought that's what you'd like," Eddie Ryan said cheerfully.

Tommy watched him go out of the shop and head for the shop that used to be Meagher's until Mr. O'Neill had bought it. It was a sort of travel agency and tours office. Surely Eddie wasn't going to terrorize them and be paid off in excursions by coach to the Ring of Kerry?

Tommy found the days very long, and on his half day he found the hours very long. Twice he had headed off up the street to look for Maggie to come and talk to him. He didn't dare tell anyone that in case they thought he was going mad or that he hadn't cared about her death.

Tommy woke a lot with his heart beating thinking of Maggie's fall.

Jacinta and Liam had discovered that the cousin wasn't too bad after all. Her name was Amanda, which was a bit rich for Mountfern, and she loved horses. She had been very disappointed that they didn't ride, being in the country and everything. In desperation they asked their father if they could ask Miss Johnson to teach them.

Marian had two tame ponies she said, they were practically geriatric she admitted; nobody could come to any harm on them. She bit her lip when she had said that. The raw grief of the children in Mountfern was still in everyone's minds.

"Why don't they have the ponies and play with them up in the paddock?" she said to Dr. White. "There'll be no fees, no lessons, it will take their minds off things."

"You're a decent woman, Marian," Martin White said, and meant it. He used to think that she was a bit uppity and gave herself airs, but he didn't like her being publicly humiliated by O'Neill either. And it would stop his children from driving him into the asylum on the hill where he had sent so many patients over the years.

Grace saw the activity in the paddock behind the Grange. "Would we be in the way if we joined in?" she asked.

Liam and Jacinta were delighted to see Grace again, at first they were ashamed of Amanda, but Amanda turned out to get on famously with Grace. Like everyone else.

When Marian saw that Patrick's daughter was interested she brought further and better horses, and a regular little riding school began.

"Come on, Michael. Get a hat, that's all. She insists we wear hard hats."

"Don't be mad, where would I get something like that? It's like asking me to get a top hat or a bowler."

"Please, Michael."

"No. I can borrow yours if I'm going to have a go, which I may not, I haven't decided yet." Michael was very disappointed at the turn things were taking.

He had seen a summer ahead of them where he and Grace would sit and talk and fish and hold each other and kiss. He would wander with her, telling her the secrets of his heart as he was starting to do already. He would tell her his plans and hopes for when they were older, and how he would study hard—at accountancy perhaps, he had heard her father say that a man who was trained as an accountant was trained for everything. He would tell her how they would travel together. But Grace wanted to play childish games and walk round in circles sitting on an aged pony.

"Grace, we don't have all that much time together, why are you wasting it?"

"It's not wasting it, we'll know how to ride horses," she said unanswerably. "Your way we just sit and talk and whatever."

"But remember, before, they sort of split us up, didn't want us going off on our own. Do you remember, that's why we all went to the bridge." He gave a shiver.

"I remember." Grace patted his hand soothingly. "But then isn't this all to the good? If they know we're all together with Jacinta and Liam and Amanda, they'll be pleased. They won't start breaking things up?" She looked at him with her big clear eyes as if it were the most obvious thing in the world and he was the only one not to see it.

"Don't you want to be with me?" he asked nakedly.

"Oh, Michael, of course I do, but we have all the time in the world to be together. Can't you enjoy this? It's new, it's fun."

Jim Costello took about five minutes to sum up Kerry O'Neill as trouble. And he spent a further five minutes working out how he was going to cope with him. This job at Fernscourt was the prize; it was up to him to make sure that nothing ruined it for him. If he made a success of Fernscourt, then in five to seven years there wasn't a bank in the country that wouldn't advance him money for his own hotel. And in the meantime he would meet exactly the kind of tourists and have just the right way to entertain them as he could have dreamed. His last hotel had been a trifle stuffy, still concentrated on the business-lunch trade which was only a status thing. Jim Costello knew that you made nothing by serving unimaginative and underpriced set luncheons to the local solicitors and bank managers and insurance brokers, but in a small place, that was what kept the image of a hotel high. Here in Fernscourt it was different.

He liked Patrick O'Neill and admired him. But the son. Jim Costello had been in the hotel business all his life. Since he could remember he had been in his father's small hotel, then in the Shannon training school and in France and Switzerland; he was twenty-four and he knew how to spot trouble. The man at the bar who was going to be troublesome, the customer who might not pay his bill. The respectable woman who was using a hotel foyer as a pick-up place. One of Jim's strengths was that he always saw it in time, just *before* the incident happened, and managed to head it off.

With Kerry he spotted it the very first time he met him. When he sauntered into the hotel with Tony McCann from Derry.

There was something about Tony McCann that seemed like a challenge. He greeted Jim as if he expected to be thrown out.

Kerry on the other hand was full of charm. "My father tells me there's nothing you don't know about the hotel business," he began.

"Let's hope he still says that when his hotel is open," Jim laughed back easily.

"Bit of a backwater this—for a hotshot like you," said Tony McCann.

"I don't think so, it's a friendly place and we hope to be so busy that I won't have much time for the bright lights myself."

Tony McCann looked at Jim Costello without much pleasure. "One of these ambitious fellows, all work and up a ladder, I suppose."

"That's me, the fellows at school used to hate me too—study study, creep, teacher's pet. Are you in the hotel business too, Mr. McCann?"

"No."

"You're in what?"

"This and that."

Kerry stepped in smoothly. "Tony's a friend of mine up in the far north, just brought him in to see the ancestral home rise again."

"Are you pleased with it?" Jim spoke directly to Kerry.

He shrugged. "It's my father's dream, I guess he's really got what he wanted. It's looking good."

"But you'll be coming back . . ."

"Relax, Jim, there's going to be no fatted calf killed for me, not for a long time. No, you're safe here for a few years yet."

Jim flushed with annoyance. He had to decide now how to handle Kerry. Did he remain poker-faced and remote, loyal entirely to his employer? This way he would build a wall of resentment between him and the boy, who was only a few years younger. Or did he make Kerry an ally of sorts? Wouldn't that be easier? He decided to go the friendship way.

"I'd say there's plenty to keep us both occupied if you *do* come back. Your father has some very grand plans."

"Do you think they'll work out?"

"Not all of them by any means, but enough of them will and I'd say he's a man who would learn by mistakes. Am I right?"

Kerry seemed amused to be consulted. "Yes, that's true in most areas. He's extraordinarily practical, but I'm not sure about this one. He wants so much for it to succeed it could blind him."

"As I said, let's hope it will and the problem won't arise." Jim had decided how to play it: friendly but not servile, discreet but not what the Americans called tight-assed. He would always repeat pleasantly to Patrick any conversation he had with the son. With Kerry you'd need to cover your back.

He hoped McCann would clear off out of the place too. He was pleased to see Kerry's car drive off to the big town with McCann and then come back without him. The fellow had obviously gone back north. What on earth had brought him down for such a flying visit? There was something watchful about him as if he hadn't believed Kerry O'Neill came from this kind of set-up and had come down to check.

He reminded Jim of a very tough Guard he had once known who came on Saturdays for a steak and a few whiskies to thank him for being lenient about closing time during the week. That Guard had a swagger when he came in to collect. Tony McCann had the same kind of swagger, as if he had come to Mountfern to collect.

It wasn't easy to find Kate alone. Patrick made three tries. Finally he hit a morning when Mary seemed occupied with deliveries in the yard, when John had driven to the town and the guard seemed to be relaxed.

Kate was sitting by her big french window, studying the typing manual from which she intended to teach Dara. He had tapped lightly on the door, and she hadn't looked up when he came in.

"I'd have thought you knew all about typing," he said.

Kate looked up surprised. "It's you Patrick, sit down won't you? I didn't know you were in the place at all."

She smiled at him encouragingly but she got little response. He sighed deeply.

"Did you come in to draw big heavy breaths at me?" Kate asked.

"No. I'm just low, that's all."

"What has you low?" She was sympathetic but not totally sure that he was serious.

"I *am* low, Kate. I feel everything's gone wrong. So many terrible things have happened. That child, that poor child dead and buried."

"Ah, sure, Patrick, that has us all low. There's neither rhyme nor reason in it."

"It was never meant to be like this. Pointless tragedy, and confusion everywhere."

Kate looked at him. It seemed out of character, this type of talk. She waited to hear what it was about.

"You see, I got everything I wanted—the land, the permission to build—and God knows how, I've actually built the thing."

"So what's wrong?"

He went on with his catalog of what was right first. "The children like the place. That's not saying it as it is, they love it. This is a real bonus, I thought they would be pleading for brighter lights, but no. That's largely due to your children, by the way."

"I know, my twins have formed a welcome-the-O'Neill-family movement, haven't they?" Kate was polite and almost hid her anxiety about just how warmly they were welcoming them.

"No, don't worry about that, Kate. Grace and Michael are a couple of kids still, and you got Dara well away out of Kerry's clutches."

So he had realized! She laughed guiltily.

But he had moved on. "I worry now all the time. About the way it all happened, it's as if it weren't the right thing to do somehow . . ."

"Coming back?"

"Yes, or coming back in this way. Nothing's gone right since . . ."

"That's not like you—not the Patrick we know."

"Shit, Kate, can't you quit acting like someone's li'l old grandmother? Every time I look at you in that bloody chair, I think to myself that if I'd stayed where I was, you'd be on your two feet. When I see all the signs being put up on the road, when I have to meet the people from the tourist board and talk about projections and over views and market share, I wonder what the hell it's all about. Why I'm not out on the freeway in New Jersey buying up a couple more neighborhood bars. What am I *doing* changing every single thing I touch here, getting the priests and the parson to tidy up their graveyards? Christ, that wasn't what I wanted to do. I wanted to be welcomed here, but nobody remembered anyone belonging to me—"

"Oh, stop all this self-pity, for God's sake," Kate interrupted. "You knew that on day one, nobody remembered the O'Neills from a hole in the ground, so stop saying it's come as a surprise to you now. Four long years ago you knew that. You wanted a life here where you came from, and you've got it. Stop bellyaching about changing things and being remembered . . ." Her face was flushed with anger at him.

He reached over and took her hand. "I suppose you don't believe me, but it's looking at you that gives me the worst feeling of regret. Honestly and truthfully if I could turn it all back I'd never have come if it meant doing this to you."

"You *didn't* do it to me, you big loud-mouthed clown. I did it. I walked under the bloody bulldozer. You had signs, I didn't see them. How many times do I have to say to you and to Fergus, to everyone. I'm *not* looking at you every day and saying 'Why oh why didn't he stay in New Jersey, and I'd be able to walk?' "

Her eyes blazed and she had flung his hand away.

"If I say I wish you had stayed in New Jersey—and I do, believe me, I do say it many times a day—it's not because of that . . . not because of my being in this chair . . . oh no."

"Then what . . . ?" Patrick was alarmed.

"I wish you had stayed in your precious America because if you had then there would have been a living for us here, for John who never really wanted it in the first place but who worked so hard at it for us, for his wife and children, and a living for the children themselves if they want to stay here. It's been in John's family for years, it's not easy to see it go up in smoke because of some Yank looking for his roots."

Patrick's mouth was open.

"I mean it, I knew I shouldn't have started but since I have I won't suddenly clam up like you do, I'm not cunning and watching what I say. *That's* the reason I wish you hadn't come here, not because I had an accident. I have to think of this whole bloody business as an accident otherwise I'd go insane."

Patrick was shocked. "But we've been over this a dozen times, all of us. You're not going to lose business, you're going to gain it. You'll have the customers from the hotel . . . We've been through this."

"Yes, we'll have them buying musical shillelaghs and leprechauns, that's what we'll have. They won't come in to drink here, neither will anyone with an ounce of sense in their head when they can have your Thatch Bar."

"You never said . . ."

"Why *should* I say anything to you? You never say anything real. You always work out where the advantage lies and then you speak. I was damned if I was going to tell you how I felt, specially since we didn't put in any objections in the beginning. Like Fergus said we should."

"Please, please let me assure you, let me promise . . ."

"I don't want any charity, I just want us to be able to make our own way as we always did. Surely you'd understand that."

"I understand that better than anyone would. Jesus Christ, I know about dignity and having your place somewhere. I was raised by a man who was a wino, a bum, we had no place anywhere, I wanted to be called Mr. O'Neill, I wanted to make my own way more than anything in the goddamn world . . ."

"You never said that about your father before . . ."

"Why *should* I tell you, or tell anyone? It's my business, and it's a part of my life I don't boast about."

"Oh no, you wouldn't mention anything unless there was some purpose . . ."

"What do you mean? What are you saying?"

"Nothing much, just showing how bad-tempered I can be, I expect." Kate seemed to have run out of steam suddenly.

"There's enough for us both here, Kate."

"I hope you're right."

"Do I really only say things that are for my own gain?"

"I never said that," Kate insisted. "I said you didn't speak without thinking —like the rest of us do."

"I suppose you're right, but you've got to cover your back in my world," Patrick said. His tone changed.

"I came to say something to you, something quite serious."

"What is it?" There was alarm in her eyes.

"No, serious, as opposed to trivial," he reassured her. "I wanted to warn you about the case."

Her eyes narrowed. "Fergus said it wasn't proper to talk about it at all, that we must remember not to speak of it even to the children because of . . . well, because of Michael and Grace I suppose."

"Yes, my lawyers said the same thing. Talk about covering their backs . . ."

"So?"

"So, I wanted to say this, just between the two of us. You've had a terrible injury, nothing will make you walk again. You must get something, the *only* thing, that can make life a bit better. You must get as much money as you can."

Kate looked at him, startled.

"This is just us. For three days I've been trying to get you alone, and then we nearly messed it up by having a fight. You only have one chance, Kate."

"Why are you telling me this?"

"So that you will get what is fair."

"Still, it's not right of you to talk to me about it. Fergus said that if you did then I was to . . ."

"Fergus said, Fergus said, don't talk to me about Attorney Slattery, he makes me sick, that fellow with his calf's face—"

"You will *not* say that about Fergus." Kate flashed again.

"Sorry, sorry. Peace, peace." Patrick spread out his hands. "Look, I'm just trying so hard and I seem to fall every step of the way . . ."

"But Fergus said that if you came and offered . . ."

"And for once he was right, the attorney Slattery. If I *was* such a bastard as to come and offer you a deal then of course you should not talk to me. But I'm not, Kate, I'm offering you a warning: They will try to make you accept a low offer out of court. If it goes to court they'll try to trip you up, try to make you take less, try to prove to the jury, who are ordinary people without great wealth, that you live a fine life and that since your little pub would never have been a gold mine, and since you're a woman who should be damn grateful to have a roof over your wheelchair, then the least compensation should have you on your poor broken knees with gratitude."

"Why . . . ?" she began.

"Why? Because I know you, I know your pride which is a great strength but also a weakness. The 'I'm fine thank you' air you wear around you like a cape . . . nobody is to dare offer a word of sympathy to Kate Ryan or if they do they'll bear the consequences."

"I cope the way that suits me," Kate said.

"You cope brilliantly, and it's not just to suit *you*, it's to help your husband and your family and everyone. Nobody feels you're a cripple, but in three weeks' time if it goes to court you have to drop it, you have to lose this brave way of going on. You've *got* to tell them what it's really like, otherwise you'll get nothing."

"You mean, lie? Act?"

"I do *not* mean lie and act, you stupid woman, I mean tell them the plans you had for this place and how you can't damn well see them happening now. The life you had with your husband, how you wanted another child and that's over."

"Why do you want me to stand up and spin these self-pitying tales, make a public exhibition of myself, tell a tissue of lies just to get money in the bank? How little you understand anything."

"Jesus Christ, how little *you* understand anything. I didn't break your back, if I did I could pay for it. Sometimes I wish I *had* broken it, gone out with a cleaver and broken it. That way I could have gone to jail." His face was working and he was close to tears.

She looked at him wordlessly.

"What kind of pride is this that means you are denying your family what is rightfully theirs?"

"You sound just like Fergus," she said.

Patrick stood up. He shrugged helplessly.

"I'll leave you, Kate, before we start again." He smiled and his face was transformed as it always was. He looked at her sitting so still in the chair.

"It's no wonder half the town is in love with you," he said. "I could fall in love with you myself."

"Oho, it's a well-known thing that, to say you could fall in love with the unattainable. That's very Irish, Patrick, you've inherited a lot of your forefathers' little ways of going on. That's the kind of thing all those mountainy old bachelors would say."

"I'm a mountainy old bachelor too—by nature, I guess."

"That will certainly disappoint the gossips here."

His eyes were cold. "What do they say, the gossips?"

"That you intend to ask Rachel to marry you someday."

He was startled. For Kate who was Rachel's close confidante to speak like this.

"Well," he said.

"However it's not something Rachel and I talk about," she said.

"You don't, like hell."

"You mustn't flatter yourself too much. We *used* to talk about you certainly, but not nowadays."

There was an unsettling truth in the way she spoke. There was a little silence.

"I don't handle things very well sometimes," he said eventually.

"There are some things that it isn't a matter of handling, or coping with or sorting out like business deals."

"I know."

They sat companionably for a few moments.

Kate was a much more still person than she had been before. There was a time when Kate Ryan could not have allowed a silence of longer than two seconds.

Patrick was not a man much given to sitting and musing either. But here he sat and looked ahead of him into the flower-filled garden where the big orange cat sunned herself and the soft cluck of the hens in the distance was soothing. There was no sign of the terrible dog, perhaps someone had been dispatched to take it on a far-distant walk so that its baying could upset another parish.

"I must go now," he said.

"You were very good to come and see me. Thank you for what you said. No matter what happens I'll remember that and appreciate it."

He leaned over lightly and kissed her on the forehead. He had never done that before.

"And you promise me you'll remember what I said? It doesn't make you weak, it makes you strong."

"I'll remember," she said.

And he left.

Kate sat still for a long while. She could understand why Rachel was so enmeshed with this man. He was alive and aware and reacting all the time.

It must have been a heady thing for Rachel to realize how essential she was to him and how much he needed her.

No wonder she felt bereft now that he most likely didn't need her anymore. Kate's fists beat on her useless legs. The only point in living was to be needed, to be an inspiration, to be the power in something. Nobody understood that, nobody.

Fergus, with all his childish spite against the O'Neills didn't have the glimmerings of an understanding. He didn't know *why* she was a person who needed compensation. It didn't have all that much to do with paralysis. It had to do with having no role.

John Ryan in a million years would not understand. He would say she was being hysterical, and that of course she was important, more than important . . . but essential to all of them.

But Kate Ryan knew she wasn't essential anymore. They didn't need her like they had once needed her. John was stronger and more his own man, he made decisions with certainty, he coped with the pub as she had once wished and prayed that he would. He still found time to write his poems. He was not as gullible as she had once thought him to be. He was firm with the children, he drove a car, their own car, around Mountfern. He was a slimmer, fitter man than the man of three years ago, more confident in every way.

But he didn't lean on Kate as he once had. He didn't need her at every turn of the day.

That was why she needed some goddamn compensation. Not that money was any good, but the reason she should get anything was because her husband didn't depend on her anymore.

And the only man who had the faintest understanding of this was the man who was *meant* to be their great enemy. Patrick O'Neill.

"I can't like that young Costello," Fergus said to Kate.

"You can't like anyone with hand, act or part in Fernscourt."

"Wrong. There's a lot of decent people working for him. Don't make me out to be unreasonable."

"Lord, you're the most reasonable man in the world usually; this is your only blind spot. What has poor Jim Costello done now?"

"I heard him talking to Canon Moran, meant to be a sort of private chat. But I could see what he was getting at."

"You listened to his confession!"

"No, it was in the open air out in the church grounds. You know, beside the garden that O'Neill's workmen built up for them. He was telling the poor doddery old canon how great it would be if the bishop came to the opening."

"Well the bishop *is* coming to the opening, surely?"

"Yes, but Jim wanted him to speak at the blessing bit and he was explaining this awful insincere way to the canon that Mr. O'Neill wouldn't like to suggest it, and Mr. O'Neill wanted it to be the canon who spoke, but wouldn't it be great if the bishop were to say a few words too. You know, a lot of devious bullshit."

"And you're the one always giving out about Patrick's language!"

"The poor old canon thinks he's the one now who thought of asking the bishop, he's back up at the presbytery trying to word the letter."

Kate changed the subject. Fergus was getting moody.

"And how is your Miss Purcell up there with the clergy?"

"As happy as anything."

"Well it leaves you a bit freer, anyway. Whatever you want to do you don't have to take her future into consideration."

"I don't want to do much, Kate. I just want things to stay the same."

To his surprise she leaned across from the wheelchair and patted his hand. "I know. I know just what you mean," she said.

"Are you going to the hotel opening, Mary?" Fergus was civil.

"It's very kind of you to be so interested but the answer is no. Some one person should be here to keep the door open in case in the Republic of Ireland there happens to be one or two souls who are *not* going to the opening and think they might be served a drink in a wayside pub."

Mary's face was flushed with anger and loyalty to her stance about the rightness of everything the Ryans did and the wrongness of the O'Neills.

Fergus blinked wearily. He had brought this attack upon himself and there were many ways that he supported her entirely. But she was a trying woman.

He had only broached the subject of the opening to her on instructions from Sheila Whelan.

"Say the odd kind word to Mary when you're passing," Sheila had asked.

"Have you a suit of chain mail for me to put on when I'm talking to her?"

Fergus had been bitten too often to feel easy about saying anything to Mary Donnelly.

"She's a great woman when you get to know her. She has all the qualities of a good wife—loyalty, determination, everything." Sheila sighed.

"Are you trying to make a match for her by any chance?"

"Oh, I think it would be a brave soul who would attempt to make a match for Mary these days."

"Or for me?" Fergus teased.

"Oh, we're dying to marry *you* off, Fergus," Sheila said.

"Who's we?"

"Kate and myself, we'd love to settle you down. But I'm only giving you a big head. Listen, when you see that cousin of mine, Mary, will you tell her she's to go to the opening of the hotel. It's only a false kind of loyalty to the Ryans saying she is going to boycott. Use your charms."

"My charms haven't much of a track record," Fergus had said gloomily.

And indeed he felt he was right, Mary Donnelly showed no reaction to his charming manner except to reject the notion of going near the new hotel. She sniffed and said that the Ryans were going not to show offense, and because they had a standard of manners much higher and more generous than the O'Neill family.

Fergus sighed again. Talking to Mary was like trying to climb up a waterfall.

"Can I talk to Kate? I have to get her to see Kevin Kennedy, that's the barrister. I want to fix up a proper consultation but Kate's always too busy making potato cakes, or hemming serviettes or some other nonsense. If the woman could only understand that she must give her whole heart and mind to Kevin Kennedy and the court case, then she won't *have* to hem all those table napkins."

"Will you be able to get her a great compensation do you think?" Mary looked eager and excited. "I'd love more than anything for her to take a fortune off that man. I'd really love it."

"That's not the way it's going to be, he'll pay nothing, it's the insurance company. I don't know, I really don't. These cases are like throwing a dice. It could be any figure that comes up."

"There must be some system."

"There is a sort of system, but it depends what way it's presented. It's very practical you know, very matter of fact. What were her earnings, what could be said to have been lost in terms of money? There's something built in for pain and suffering, and then there's a category called mental distress. But it all depends on judges and juries in the end, and they're often cautious men, careful with other people's money even if it's insurance companies. Oh God, I wish I knew."

"You sound very worried." Mary's face looked quite pleasant when she wasn't making some strong point, she had a softness about her that wasn't in her normal style.

"I am worried, Mary, I'm worried that Kate and John are turning down their only chance of getting what they deserve and are owed. They don't seem to grasp that this is the one and only time they'll ever get any stake together for any kind of life."

"And show that bastard what the courts of Ireland think of him."

"Yes, but with respect, Mary, mightn't we do better if we played down that side of it?"

"I know what you mean, I'm as bright as the next man. I'll sing low on the revenge bit—is that what you mean?"

"That's what I mean."

"I'll feel it in my heart though," Mary said.

"So will I," said Fergus.

"Oh bring him along, certainly," Kate said when Fergus suggested a consultation with Kevin Kennedy.

"He's quite important, Kate, you won't just play along and joke and make eejity remarks about it being half your own fault?"

"I never make eejity remarks. Remember when I was your right-hand woman in the office, don't say I make eejity remarks."

"I remember. I remember well," Fergus sighed.

"So, I'll be polite and use long words. But isn't he on our side, is he not our lawyer, why do I have to be impressing him and putting on an act for our own counsel? Isn't it the judge and the jury I have to do the tragic queen act for?"

"It's no act, Kate. You are badly injured in the name of Jesus, will you stop being the bravest girl in the school about this and start thinking of your future and your family's future?"

"You're cross with me."

"I'm furious with you. You think it's not quite nice somehow to let anyone know how much your life was changed that day, how much your chances lessened. One day, one day when it's too late you'll wish you'd listened, you will be very sorry then. In three or four years' time when the pub might need a new roof, or when Dara might wonder why there was no money to send her to university or the kids might want to go on a school trip to Rome or John, God forbid, might get a virus pneumonia and be off work for four months and you'd have to pay someone to come in and run the pub . . . Won't it be a great consolation to yourself to say that way back in 1966 when you had your chance, your one chance to explain your case, you were too refined, too well-brought-up or some kind of bullshit to get the compensation you and your family deserved? Fine warm comfort these high and mighty principles will be to you and your family then."

His eyes blazed with rage on her behalf.

Kate changed immediately. She sat upright in her chair and reached for a notebook.

"You are perfectly right as always," she said without a trace of irony. "Tell me what kind of things will we cover with Mr. Kennedy when he comes."

Kevin Kennedy wore an expensive suit but it was crumpled, and his shoes needed a good shine. Kate looked at him and decided that he was a bachelor whose housekeeper was lazy and indifferent. He had a big mane of greying hair, a rather theatrical bow tie and nicotine-stained fingers which groped restlessly for more cigarettes still. Kate judged him to be about fifty, and realized after a very short time that he was much sharper than he gave the impression of being. He seemed to shamble through explanations and accounts but yet he remembered everything that had been said and came back to points which she had been sure he had forgotten.

He was very good at drawing her out. Kate found herself responding easily to his questions about the limitations to her life caused by the accident. She agreed that their earnings were considerably diminished since she could no longer work for Fergus in the mornings and since they had to pay out a salary to Mary Donnelly. Kate told how her concentration had lessened, she found it very hard to read a book to its end, whereas once she always had her nose in some book from the library.

Fergus was startled to hear this, she had never said it to him. But that was often Kevin's gift, he managed to make people tell things. Very often when he was on the other side of a case cross-examining, his gentle persuasive voice made people tell things they wished to keep secret. But here in Kate's green room Kevin Kennedy was slowly drawing the picture he would need.

Fergus sighed with admiration as Kevin talked to the Ryan couple about how their life had changed, the pain, the huge incapacity, the lack of being able to act as a real mother to the children the way other mothers could, like going up to the school or joining in any outings and activities.

"And of course your normal married life, the life between the two of you that you would have expected to have?" Kevin Kennedy was gentle.

Fergus felt a hot flush coming up his neck.

Long ago, long before Kate's accident, he had put the thought of her sex life with John Ryan far from his mind. He knew it must exist but he never wanted to think about it, and yet it used to come back to him, the notion of the two of them entwined. He assumed that since the accident it had been out of the question. To his embarrassment John was beginning to stammer.

"Well, I wouldn't say that it was exactly over . . . you know, sort of . . ."

Fergus felt the bile rise in his throat. Surely John could never be so gross and unfeeling as to expect Kate . . . No, it wasn't possible. He felt unsteady for a moment.

"I'll slip out and get something from the bar . . ." he said.

"Thanks, Fergus." Kate was cool. "I asked Mary to get a tray ready, perhaps you could bring it to us . . ."

He went out, loosening his collar.

"Kate said she thought sandwiches and a bottle of the good Jameson," Mary suggested. "I have it here ready and all, I didn't want to go and disturb you."

"That's good of you."

"Are you all right, Fergus?" She looked genuinely concerned.

"Yes, I'm just tired. Give me a large one while I'm waiting."

"What are you waiting for?" Mary obediently poured him a double and waved away the pound note he offered.

"I don't know really, just giving them a chance to talk, I suppose," he said, wondering how long would Kevin Kennedy spend on lack of conjugal rights, and compensation for same. Wildly he wondered whether John was saying that really it wasn't fair to blame Patrick O'Neill in this area because he and Kate were able to have a very satisfactory coupling despite everything.

Fergus felt his hands shaking and he gripped the glass tightly with both of them.

"It must be very hard, this kind of thing, when you're a friend of the family as well." Mary was sympathetic.

"Have a drink, Mary."

"No thanks, Fergus, I don't think . . ."

"Have a bloody drink."

"Very well, keep your hair on. I'll have a vodka and tonic, thank you very much."

"Not at all. Good luck."

Mary raised her glass solemnly. "Good luck, really and truly good luck. They're relying on you."

"No they're not, they think they're grand, they think it's lovely to be financially ruined and crippled."

"Shush now."

"I won't shush. And anyway nobody would rely on me, it's Kevin they should rely on."

"Oh him?" Mary sniffed. "From Dublin, and a man."

"Yes, I suppose those are points against him. I wonder has it crossed your mind that I too am a man, Mary. Perhaps you should take that into consideration when you and I are having these little social drinks."

"I know you're a man, Fergus," Mary said.

"I'm glad someone does, I've almost forgotten myself."

"But you're not a real man, not like ordinary men." Mary was full of beaming approval. "Here, will you take this tray in that you came out for or they'll think you fell into bad company."

"You're not the worst, Mary," Fergus said, picking up the tray and carrying it back into the room.

They seemed to have exhausted sexual dysfunction or the possibility of suing for removal of conjugal rights. They were on to the topic of what they could expect to be awarded.

The tray was left beside Kate on the big round table which Rachel had found and covered with a floor-length green cloth. Nowhere else in Ryan's pub had the elegance of this room.

They looked like four ordinary people having a drink, Fergus thought as Kate poured generous measures and added a splash of water from their only cut-glass crystal jug. No sign of their business together.

Sheila Whelan came back quietly by bus.

It should only be two hours and three quarters, but the bus visited every townland on the way. It took mountainy routes and it went almost full circles into the countryside to pick up and drop farmers from crossroads that were off the beaten track. There was plenty of time to sit and think.

Think about Joe with his gaunt face and his sad tales clutching her from the hospital bed.

It hadn't turned out as he had hoped, he told her. He wanted to come home to Mountfern. To die.

"There's no question of dying, Joe," she had soothed him, her words automatic, her expression effortlessly kind. Even to the man who had left her all those years ago, hurling abuse to justify himself as he went.

His life had not indeed turned out as he hoped. There were children, four—two sons and two daughters—children that Sheila was not able to bear, and he had scorned the idea of adopting and raising another man's sons.

The woman he had left everything for was a restless woman. The children had been reared wild, left to run wild. None of them would settle in anything, school or work. The eldest boy had gone to England a few hours ahead of the Guards, it turned out.

Joe had got to thinking about Mountfern in recent weeks. He thought of all the people he knew there, Jack Leonard and Tom Daly. He hadn't heard that Tom Daly's little girl had met with such a terrible accident. Sheila told him about Maggie, but his mind wandered away in the middle of the story. She stopped after a while when she saw he wasn't concentrating. It was too sad a tale anyway.

He remembered Jack Coyne and that nice dour Dr. White. Was old man Slattery around? No, well the son was a grand young fellow. And of course the canon. It would be good to wander down River Road to Ryan's like in the old days. He had heard of the new hotel across the river, there was a lot of talk about it in the papers. He hadn't known of Kate Ryan's accident but he was sure that they'd got great compensation.

And since there were no real ties with Dublin, no—for all that he had a home—it was a house really—and she would understand that he wanted to go home at the end. She'd probably be pleased for him. When all was said and done. So could he come back to Mountfern? Could he come home?

Sheila had talked to the nurse who recognized instantly that Sheila Whelan was someone to whom the truth was told. She heard that Joe had weeks and possibly only days to live. She had confirmed what she suspected—that he would never leave his hospital bed.

She told him he could come home.

She begged him not to worry what people would say and what people would think. Nowadays, she said, people were much too busy with their own business to worry about the middle-aged postmistress and her husband. She said that Dr. White would be able to continue any treatment.

Joe's eyes had filled with tears at her goodness. He had never meant to hurt her in the past, he had never wanted to be cruel.

She said she understood. She sat and held his hand until he fell asleep. Three days she was there helping him make his plans, telling him where they would put his bed.

He said it would be good in a way for her to have a man around the house again, and that was the only time she had cried. The tears had come down her face and she wept at the useless lives most people led and how little anyone understood about anyone else.

She asked the nurse to make sure that nobody was kept away because of her visits but the nurse shook her head and said that poor Mr. Whelan's wife wasn't in the best of health and wasn't able to come and see him. Sheila read this to mean that the woman who had borne Joe Whelan's four children suffered from her nerves or drink or both. She discovered that there were neighbors who would supervise the funeral, kind people in the small Dublin street who had known nothing of any previous existence in Mountfern.

When he fell into his coma and she was assured that he would not know anyone around him again, she left as quietly as she had come and took the bus back to Mountfern. She did not feel saintly or unselfish; she felt a weary tiredness. And for the first time in her life she felt something like anger. Anger about people who stood by and let things happen. At herself for wasting all those years thinking that Joe knew what he was doing and that there was some sort of plan. She might have been better not to have been so dignified and discreet. She could have gone after him and fought for him. And got him back.

Or she could have gotten a court order and got maintenance from him if she hadn't valued her good name so highly and been too proud to ask for it. That way she would have strong shoes to wear instead of making do with patched soles and avoiding puddles. She would have had the money to go to Rome when the diocese was making the pilgrimage. She could have given Mary Donnelly something better than she had, some holiday or some outfit to get her over the worst days of the pain, the days when you need some distractions.

Instead she was coming back on the bus to Mountfern where nobody except Kate Ryan would know whether Joe Whelan was alive or dead. She would ask Canon Moran to say a mass for his soul, but she would just say that it was for a friend. It wasn't that the canon would ever tell anyone but she had been so silent and secretive about this, she would keep it that way to the end.

But for the rest of her life she was not going to sit and take a back seat. She was going to take part in things, not just observe them.

Twenty

Patrick finished the steak and kidney pie. "That was quite excellent, Miss Hayes."

"It's a pleasure to serve you, Mr. O'Neill."

He sat by himself at the table. Grace was having supper at the Ryans'. It was a night of a cookery lesson, she had explained. He knew it was just another chance to see young Michael but he pretended to take the cookery classes very seriously. Kerry was miles away in Donegal. When Olive Hayes had gone back to her kitchen he sat quite alone. As he sat many an evening.

It would be different when the hotel opened, he told himself. There would not be this stark realization that he found himself reading through his meals, and sitting idly after them, fiddling with the television, if he didn't get out more work. He had discouraged Marian from suggesting outings, and now she had ceased trying to interest him in little trumped-up schemes. He wished he could ask Rachel here.

He stood and stretched . . . the evening seemed to stretch as well.

He had put off so long and so firmly any thought about what would happen to Rachel when the hotel opened that he found himself doing it again automatically. But tonight somehow he felt able to think about it.

She *could* take instruction. And if she did, then there would be no problem about her previous marriage, since it wasn't a Catholic marriage. Hell, it wasn't even a Christian marriage.

And she *could* fit in here, there were ways where she seemed to have adapted better than he had.

Rachel got on so well with Kate Ryan, with Sheila Whelan, with Loretto Quinn. Brian Doyle said that she was the only person connected with the entire enterprise who might be considered sane. Mary Donnelly, that madwoman running a one-woman band for the annihilation of men, said that Rachel was one in a million.

Why did he hesitate to ask her even to something simple like supper in his own house?

He knew why, it was out of guilt.

He still felt that this woman was part of his past. He had gone willingly and excitedly to her arms while the children had stayed in a big white house in New Jersey with their always-ailing mother.

And Rachel wasn't Irish, or part of the great scheme. That's why he kept her at such a long arm's length.

Dara's postcard arrived at Hill's Hotel for Kerry. It sounded very casual with an attempt to be sardonic:

> I heard there was a bank strike at home, I didn't know there was a postal strike as well!! But then how does everyone else manage to write to me, I wonder? It's a puzzlement, as they say in *The King and I.*
> France is magnifique.
> I'll be back in Mountfern on the last Thursday in August.
>
> Love Dara.

Kerry read it and smiled. He would have taken a hotel postcard and written straight back, but he had a lot on his mind. He had lost a great deal on three consecutive nights.

It was time to call Father.

But if he won tonight, it would all be sorted out. No need to tell Father about anything.

Tony McCann was apologetic. If it were up to him there wouldn't be a problem in the world, Kerry knew that, didn't he? If it were only McCann himself or Charlie it would have been a no-problem area. But *these* fellows . . . McCann's voice trailed away a little. For the first time Kerry began to feel a little afraid.

"Do you not have any idea where he is, Miss Hayes?"

"No, Kerry, he doesn't tell me where he goes. He just said that he would be back late."

"Whatever time he comes in, do you hear me, whatever time, can you get him to call me?"

"I'll leave a note, certainly. I don't want to intrude but is there anything wrong?"

"No no—heavens no." His voice was falsely bright.

"It's just that you sound so urgent somehow. I wouldn't want Mr. O'Neill to be alarmed."

"No no, it's nothing." He sounded impatient.

"I'll leave him a note then in case I'm gone to bed. I'll say you'd like him to ring back but it's not urgent."

Kerry spoke very slowly and deliberately. "Tell him it *is* urgent but there hasn't been an accident or anything. It's very urgent."

"Very well, Kerry, whatever you say."

Patrick came in at eleven-thirty.

He had spent a very pleasant evening with Rachel. He called at Loretto's and asked whether she would like a drive. He wanted to look at the ruined abbey in case it would be a place they could take the guests on the barge that he was going to operate from the new landing stage.

"You're going to have night boat trips?" Rachel was surprised.

"No, but maybe it's not a bad idea. They could go through the trees and along the river, the only light . . . the fireflies in the darkness."

"They don't have them here," Rachel said.

"Fireflies? Of course they do."

"No. Didn't you notice?"

"Anyway, will you come with me in the car and let's see if this abbey is worth our time?"

"It's been around since the fourteenth century, I think it might be worth a glance all right. Let me get sensible shoes."

They had walked easily and companionably like the old days. Three times he was about to tell her that he wanted them to be more open and seen to be close friends. Three times he stopped himself.

After all he wasn't yet ready to offer her anything much, and he would clear it with his children before changing things even slightly. He left things as they were.

Next morning up at the hotel Jim Costello came to Patrick, there was an urgent call from his son in Donegal.

"Would you like a bit of peace and quiet to take it?"

"No thanks, Jim, it won't be long."

Jim had sensed the tetchiness in Kerry O'Neill's voice. He moved away.

"Did she not leave you my message?"

"That's some greeting, Kerry. Yes, Miss Hayes did leave a message but it was late when I got in."

"What time?"

"Eleven-thirty." Patrick took a deep breath. "I went for a walk with Rachel Fine up around the old ruined abbey . . . she thinks that we could . . ."

"I'll hear Mrs. Fine's thoughts another time, Father. I'm in a bit of trouble. Financially."

Patrick's voice was ice cold. "Yes, Kerry?"

"And I would be grateful if you would bail me out."

A silence.

"Are you still there, Father?"

"Yes. I'm still here."

"What did you say?"

"Nothing yet."

"Will you?"

"I don't think so."

"You *said* you would."

"No, I said I would discuss it, we are discussing it. How much?"

"A thousand pounds."

Patrick was shocked. Literally shocked. "You can't be serious."

"I am."

"Well find it then."

"We made a deal."

"We made no deal, I said I'd discuss it. I will not hand out a year's wages to an insolent young punk who calls and demands it as if it were his right."

"Father, this is serious."

"You bet your fucking life it's serious," Patrick said.

"I thought you were going to—"

"I thought my father was going to do a lot of things for me too, like getting me enough to eat and shoes to wear. But it didn't happen. Learn the hard way, Kerry."

"Aren't you going to discuss it?"

"Yes I will discuss it. When you come back." Patrick's anger was ebbing a little.

"I could come back today."

"No you could not. You can stay there and do the work you are meant to be doing. I will discuss it in a few weeks' time, when you're back here for the opening. Meanwhile get out of it the best you can, and if you steal from Hill like you stole from me, I'll see you go to jail."

There was a silence.

"Life isn't easy, Kerry, it's a matter of finding ways around things; and if one thing doesn't work, try something else. You'll discover that."

"Yes, I probably will," Kerry said slowly.

Rachel Fine sat in her sitting room and watched the evening fall on Fernscourt.

She felt very tired. The game was too arduous. She blew cold, he ran after her—she showed some response, he ran away. It was so immature, so unsatisfying. Somehow tonight, for the very first time, Rachel was prepared to stop the struggle, the never-ending spiral of hope, the belief that things were going well.

He was a man who hadn't enough room in his heart for a full-time loving relationship. He never had time for it with his wife Kathleen either. Whether she had been frail or not he would still have wandered, and it was not without importance to note that he had wandered to a business colleague rather than find a sheerly social relationship.

She sighed, thinking of the years behind and the years ahead. The music on her record player was low so as not to disturb Loretto below. Chopin, soothing and familiar. Perhaps even at this late stage of her life she might even take up the piano again. When she was back in New York.

Would she be back in New York?

Yes, sooner or later. Why not make it sooner, go at her own time? See the opening just because she had worked so hard for it. Give him one ultimatum so that he would never say he didn't know, and then go. But she had to be prepared to go, not to give herself nine lives like a cat, otherwise what was the point of giving ultimatums?

There was a soft knock on her door. Loretto would never have let him upstairs, and yet who else could it be?

She walked wearily over to the door and opened it.

There stood Kerry O'Neill, the boy she had always hoped would be her stepson one day.

He leaned against the jamb of the door. "Hi Rachel."

"Hello Kerry."

She made no move to ask him in.

"How are you?"

"Fine, and you?" They still stood there.

"Reasonably fine, I'd be better with a drink, to be very frank."

"Well you know me, Kerry, a non-drinking lady. But I'm sure if you were to go to Ryan's . . ."

"I don't want to go to Ryan's," he said sharply.

She shrugged.

"Surely my father keeps something to drink here."

"Your father lives in the lodge, Kerry. I live here."

"So you never see him?"

"At work."

"I want to talk to you, not him."

"I told you I don't have anything to drink."

"I know. It doesn't matter, I have." He waved a bottle of whiskey. "Now can I come in?"

Mary thought she had seen the blond figure of young Kerry O'Neill slip quietly across the footbridge earlier, but since he hadn't come into the pub and there was nowhere else he could be heading, she must have been mistaken.

Rachel stood back and let Kerry come into her sitting room. He stood looking at it with his cool objective eye.

"Lovely," he said at last.

"Thank you."

"I mean it, you have wonderful ways, Rachel. Anyone else would have ruined this place and filled it with clutter."

He sat in the chair by the window where Patrick always sat and looked across in the darkening evening at Fernscourt.

"I can provide a glass and water," Rachel said.

"Great, this is far too elegant a place for a man to sit drinking from a bottle."

He was so engaging, just like his father. His compliments were not so frequent and lavish that they sounded automatic. Instead, they made people feel very touched and grateful to be praised.

She brought a tray to the little low table—Irish crystal glasses and a jug. A pretty china bowl with ice in it, a tray of cheese biscuits and for herself an orange drink. She sat down opposite him. She had not invited him, but since he was here she would be gracious. Being a hostess was second nature to Rachel Fine, she had waited on Kerry's father for many years in the same elegant way.

"Your health," she said politely, raising her glass of orange.

"And yours." His eyes were bright, he raised the very large goblet of neat Irish whiskey and looked at the patterns of the glass admiringly.

Rachel was very good at not being the first to speak. She had learned that first from her mother, who said that the men in the family were the ones to be considered, and then from many many nights waiting to assess Patrick's mood before she spoke. She knew how to leave a perfectly agreeable silence that would encourage the other person to begin.

Kerry smiled as if he could see into her mind. It was a knowing smile full of confidence.

"And how long are you going to be with us?" he asked genially.

Rachel was shocked by the insolence of his tone. So shocked that it made her speak sharply.

"I was just going to ask *you* the same question. Are you with us for long or do you have to get back to Donegal?"

Kerry smiled even more broadly; he sensed a fight and he welcomed it.

"Oh, *I'm* here for the duration, Rachel, this is my home."

She controlled herself with difficulty. "Well of course, and has your father decided what part you will play in the hotel?" Polite interest, but letting him know that everyone realized it was Patrick who called the shots.

"I'm sure you're much more aware of what my father has decided or has not decided than anyone."

She smiled coldly but made no reply. From years of training herself not to over-react, not to fly off the handle, Rachel had perfected a calm and measured response even to situations that were outside the bounds of any manners or fairness.

"My involvement is always in ideas for design, and sometimes it's an uphill job." She forced a little laugh that she did not feel. "I can tell you the designer is the one who always ends up taking the blame—it's too stark, it's too cold, it's not Irish enough—my, but you need extraordinary patience in this job. Lucky I have it!" Again her tinkle was very false and again she felt that Kerry recognized this.

"Perhaps you've been too patient."

"How do you mean?"

"You know, hanging around too long, hoping that when this is over—when that is over—the world will settle down as *you* would like it, as *you* design it."

She wondered how much more of this she could take, this pretense of deliberately misunderstanding his discourtesy.

"At least the day of the opening is in sight," she said. "We'll see then if it works."

"And what will you do then? Go back to Brooklyn?"

"I live in Manhattan."

"Sure, but you *do* live in New York, will you go directly back there? After the hotel opens?"

His question echoed so much her own bitter thoughts and decisions of earlier that evening that it brought a heavy, weary feeling to Rachel. It was as if she suddenly decided to give up the bright sunny response.

"I don't know," she said simply. "I'm not sure."

"Rachel!" He was teasing. "Not sure? Of course you are, you've every step planned out, haven't you?"

"No. Not every step."

"Most of them then. You've been part of my father's life for a very long time. A lot of people didn't rate your chances very highly."

"I don't know how you could know any of this. You were a child."

"Sure I was a child, I didn't know really, not for certain, not until my mother's last illness. That's when I knew."

Rachel looked at him impassively.

Kerry poured another large goblet of whiskey, his hand trembling slightly.

"Those nights when she was alone in the house, and he was with you—in Manhattan, as you remind me. Out until the early hours of the morning. Sometimes I stood on the landing and watched him come in, go into the bathroom and rinse his mouth, freshen himself up before he came up to her bedroom. She was always awake, always waiting for him to come back from you. From your apartment in Manhattan."

Rachel looked at his white and angry face.

"He sat in a chair drinking whiskey, that's why he used a mouth rinse, it was not to hide traces of me. He sat talking about her illness, about you all. That's what I gave him in those months, just a chair, a whiskey, and an ear for his troubles."

"He had plenty of ears at home if he had come there."

"Sure he had, but you were so young, your mother was so frail, he couldn't . . ."

Kerry's eyes blazed at her suddenly.

"Don't you dare to talk of my mother, don't bring her in casually like that . . . don't speak of her."

"Kerry, this is absurd. *You* mentioned your mother, you mentioned something that has upset you in the past, I was merely telling you what it was really like . . ."

"I don't want your version of what things were really like. If it were a true version it would be fairly sordid."

"You are unfair to your father and to everyone if you persist in believing all this . . ."

"Oh, it was all hand-holding and platonic. Don't be pathetic, Rachel."

"I am *not* pathetic, I am telling you what is true. During the time of Kathleen's last—"

"I told you not to mention her name."

Her eyes filled with sudden unexpected tears. She turned her head away in a vain attempt to hide them.

Kerry put his glass down on the table. "I'm sorry."

She didn't trust herself to speak.

"I mean it. I am sorry. I guess I'm upset. I shouldn't take it out on you."

She stood up wordlessly as if to say that his visit was over. But Kerry decided that it was not over yet.

"Please, I said I spoke out of turn. Please?"

He had such a persuasive way, she noticed almost dispassionately. Kerry believed that if you were charming enough in sufficient doses it would open every door. And he had usually been right.

"I didn't intend to come here and harangue you, I intended—"

"What did you intend?"

"I guess I wanted to know what was happening. Is that so bad? Things are fairly unsettled. Father has me up at the other end of the country, he's so unapproachable, he tells me none of his plans, I hear from this side one set of things, from another side a different . . . It sure is a rumor factory here, isn't it?" He grinned companionably, the shouting put well behind.

"And what do they say on all these different sides?"

"Oh, some say that my father is the object of a hate campaign, vandalism, slogans, mysterious happenings; others say that since the prophet Elijah there hasn't been such a welcome appearance. Then they say that the hotel will be open on time and that it hasn't a chance of opening; that Father's going to marry Marian Johnson and she's going to change her hairstyle and get some new clothes, or that he's going to marry you and you're going to keep all your nice clothes the way they are but change your religion . . . And I hear that he has hundreds of bookings from the States and that he has no bookings . . . So do you see why I came to have a talk in case you could set me straight on some of these issues, anyway?"

She looked at him, and realized that he was making it all up, there was no way that people in Mountfern would confide such things to the son of Patrick O'Neill. But he was right in his summing up of the different viewpoints.

Kerry patted the chair beside him. "Come on, Rachel, sit down and talk to me. I won't get nasty again. Promise."

She sat down, knowing it was a very dangerous thing to do.

"There, that's better. And now have a drink. Come *on* Rachel, if you're going to be an honorary Irish person you'll have to learn to drink."

It was easy and comforting to sit there with him instead of sitting on her own.

He had admitted his temper and his feelings. It was only natural that a boy should love his mother and want to keep his memories of her almost frozen in the viewpoint of the troubled teenager that he was at the time.

Rachel sipped the drink that he mixed for her, a whiskey and dry ginger. It tasted sweet and warming, not like the wine she sometimes sipped at functions, which was bitter and alien. Here in the sunset looking across the river with the handsome boy admitting his petulant temper and smiling at her like a conspirator it was easy to sit and talk and drink the sweet, fizzy, harmless liquor.

Kerry talked of the hotel in Donegal, how lonely he was up there and how the place seemed so remote. He often went to Derry across the border, it was exciting somehow to be in a place that was ruled by another country, to see other flags flying. Most of the people in Derry were basically Irish, he explained to Rachel, and they felt much more at home in the republic. He had met a few guys who were easy to get along with there. Rough guys, not the kind who would be welcomed with open arms in the front doors of Fernscourt, he said scathingly. Still, they were alive all through, which was more than you could say for many of the people you met in this country, north or south. Rachel took this to mean that they were able to play cards with him or point him to some kind of game down town.

And Rachel found herself telling Kerry more than she intended to about some of the problems in getting deliveries in time and how she always tried to shield Patrick from the more troublesome side of things, partly because he had so much to think about he really could not be expected to give time to wondering why some weavers in Connemara had not been able to come up with the consignment they had promised months back. And partly because any complaining or even mild criticism always seemed like a condemnation of his decision to come back to this land and build his dream castle.

Together they sighed amicably about the difficulties of dealing with the great Patrick O'Neill. There was none of the usual fencing between them and no hint of the flash of anger and the instructions not to speak his dead mother's name.

Rachel told of how Maurice, the Ryans' missing tortoise, had been discovered in the hen house where apparently he had been living for months in total contentment. And Kerry told how he had discovered that Jimbo Doyle really was making it big on the ballad-singing circuit; he was even booked for an appearance in Donegal, which had to be the Vegas of Ireland.

The sun sank behind the big house and the trees. The river took on its black rippling look where it seemed like a dark ribbon instead of a living, flowing thing.

Somewhere, possibly from down near the bridge, they heard the sound of a fiddle playing, an air that sounded sad and plaintive, but all Irish airs seemed sad to Rachel and Kerry. The boy reached across and patted her hand. There were tears in Rachel's eyes again but this time she wasn't hiding them, they fell down her face.

"I could have fit in here, I could have stayed and been part of it," she wept.

"But now you think you'll go back?" His voice was soft, like honey.

"I decided today I'll have to go back. He thinks he doesn't need me, he thinks he can manage on his own . . ." She let a sob come through her voice.

"I know, I know."

"You can't know."

"Well I do, he doesn't need me either. He never did."

Rachel looked at him, tear-stained. He was so different tonight, vulnerable, understanding.

"I think he finds it hard to express himself to you . . ." she began, trying as usual to build bridges.

"I'm only his son, his flesh and blood. It shouldn't be so very hard to express himself."

"He does care for you . . . I know."

"And I know how fond of you he is too. I didn't always want to see it, I can tell you, but . . ."

He looked so straightforward. Rachel felt fuzzy and a little confused, but she could see that Kerry was being genuine toward her and she wanted to reassure him that he was important to his father.

And now Kerry was admitting that she, Rachel, was a part of Patrick too. She was certainly a little heady.

She placed her hand on Kerry's knee. He lifted it to admire her rings.

"These are very beautiful," he said softly. "Did you choose these yourself or were they a gift?"

She saw no guile in the words. It was a question. She held her hand away and admired the topaz and the emerald.

"Your father bought me the topaz a long long time ago. The emerald I bought myself. I have a little garnet too, but I don't wear them all at once."

"No, no." He was holding her hand and admiring the way the light caught the stones.

"It means fidelity, a topaz," she said dreamily. "I remember that very well."

"Is it your birthstone?" Kerry asked interestedly.

He was so relaxed and easy to talk to tonight, Rachel wondered why she had ever thought him prickly and difficult.

"No, I'm Gemini—that's the emerald." She turned her hand in his to examine the green stone.

"I got the emerald because of that and also because it means 'success in love.' I guess I wasn't so lucky there."

Kerry said nothing, he fingered the tie tack he always wore these days. Even when he wasn't wearing a formal shirt and tie he seemed to have this pin on his lapel somehow.

"My, that's a topaz also," Rachel realized for the first time.

"Yes. Topaz, that's right." His voice seemed strained.

"And was *that* a gift or did you buy it, like I bought my emerald?" She was being giggly now.

"It was both, in a way. I paid for it to be made into a tie tack, but it was a gift, from my mother. Father gave her a topaz for fidelity also, you see. He never asked where it was when she died, I don't know if he realizes this is where it ended up."

Rachel felt a sudden lurch in her stomach. "I think I'm going to be sick," she said, staggering to her feet.

Loretto Quinn was serving Jack Coyne next morning when Kerry appeared in the shop. He was in his stocking feet, walking lightly, and his clothes were crushed and rumpled.

"Hi Loretto. Well hi Jack, how are things?"

"Things are reasonable." Jack wasn't able to reply as quickly as usual, he was so startled to see O'Neill's son come in casually through the back of the shop, meaning that he must have been upstairs.

Upstairs with O'Neill's woman.

"So they are with me, pretty reasonable. Loretto, can I have some oranges please, perhaps half a dozen . . . Sorry Jack, am I cutting in ahead of you?"

"No, please." Jack could hardly wait to see what else the young Kerry O'Neill was ordering.

Kerry said he'd take eggs, bread, four slices of that really great bacon—how could anyone in America *think* they had tasted bacon until they came to Ireland? And he'd better take a packet of those aspirin tablets too.

He smiled at them both, punched Jack playfully, and said that the little red sports car was a dream on wheels and he thought he'd either have to buy it so that it would be his own or possibly play Jack a game of poker for it.

Then light and cheerful he ran back up the stairs, leaving Loretto and Jack open-mouthed below.

Rachel woke painfully. Her head was pounding and she had a sense of unreality. What *could* have happened to make her feel so ill? Bits of it came back to her. The whiskey, the long chat with Kerry.

Then with such a shock that she sat bolt upright she remembered vomiting.

Her hand flew to her throat and she looked around her wildly. The bed was rumpled. Kerry's jacket was thrown on her chair. His shoes were lying on the floor where they had been kicked off. The other side of the bed had a little table and on the table was Kerry's watch, his cigarette case and his lighter.

With disbelief Rachel tried to take it in. She felt too frail to contemplate what could have happened. She wanted to lie down and pull the sheets and blankets over her poor hurt head. But she couldn't lie down. Not yet. Not until she knew.

As if on cue Kerry came into the room. He was wearing his shirt open, he was smiling.

"Hi there."

"What . . . what?"

"It's orange juice," he said delightedly, misunderstanding her. "I squeezed six oranges so you'll love it. And if you feel strong enough I'm going to do you some eggs."

"Not eggs," Rachel said.

"Oh yes eggs, Rachel, they're known to be good for you. I got some bacon but I wasn't sure. I didn't know . . ."

"No bacon." She struggled with the words.

"Sure sure. Well coffee anyway, after the juice."

He sat on the bed familiarly, too close to her she thought in alarm, and pulled back.

She realized she was in her slip and that her brassiere was open. She realized that Kerry O'Neill was looking at her affectionately. The room seemed to swim and tilt a little.

"Kerry, how did . . . how did . . ."

"I got them in Loretto's," he said sunnily. "Oh, and I got you some aspirin too. Sip the juice first, then I'll fix you some aspirin with the coffee."

"You told Loretto . . . ?"

"She's really improved that little store, hasn't she? Jack Coyne was in there, he's an okay guy, I think. Father always says he's a gangster but these things are relative. To some people Father is something of a gangster. But enough about him, let's talk about you and me . . ."

Rachel gave a jump.

". . . and what we're going to have for breakfast if it's too non kosher to fry a little bacon." He smiled at her warmly and Rachel Fine with her drawn, lined face, her aching head and upset stomach looked up at him piteously. And knew she was somehow in his power.

It was the last Thursday in August and Dara Ryan had returned to Mountfern.

She felt quite different to the Dara who had left two months earlier. Older, wiser, more a woman of the world, she thought. After all she had lived in a household which had things going on under its roof that Dara would not have believed possible. She was going to look with new eyes on the clientele, male and nocturnal of the Rosemarie hair salon. She hoped she had become more sophisticated-looking. A girl she was talking to on the train told her that she could easily be eighteen, she looked *much* older than almost sixteen.

Dad thought she looked older, which was great. He held her at arm's length when he came to meet her at the station in the town. Grace and Michael had wanted to come too he said, but he had to refuse them, he needed the car for supplies.

Dara looked around and indeed the back of their old black car was filled with boxes. Things for the café, Dad said, every day now there was more stuff being brought in. They were ready to open it for business anytime now.

"And what kind of form is Mam in? She doesn't get depressed too much now, does she?"

Dara kept looking lovingly at her father; she knew that in a changing world he would remain constant. It was hard to imagine Dad in bed with anyone, including Mam before the accident, but Dara knew that he wouldn't ever cheat on Mam like that appalling Monsieur Vartin.

"Your mother is a marvel," he said simply. "I don't know where and how she gets the ideas and the energy. She's an example to us who have the legs. She's so delighted that you're coming home. For ages now she's been saying only eight days more, only six days more . . ."

Dara was pleased. "Isn't that nice, I was just the same, I hope we won't start to fight and ruin it."

"Of course you will." John was philosophic. "But not immediately. We'll have a few days of a honeymoon period first."

They drove down Bridge Street. Liam White was waving, and John slowed to a stop.

"You look different, did you have an illness?" he asked.

"Jesus, Mary and Joseph, Liam, that's lovely," said Dara.

"No, you look foreign. Maybe it's the air, or the food."

"I think she looks great altogether." Dara's father was partisan and proud of his dark, handsome daughter.

"Oh, you look fine," Liam said, as if that had never been in doubt. "The question is, will it last?"

"Where's Jacinta?"

"Off somewhere with Tommy, she's the only one able to get him out of the shop. His father is afraid of Jacinta."

"Aren't we all?" Dara said with some feeling.

Dara looked over at Daly's shop. It still looked the same. People came in to buy cakes and butter and groceries. Life went on. Dara swallowed hard. Everyone else had had two months to get used to Daly's Dairy without Maggie. Dara would too one day. Charlie was cleaning the windows, he waved his wet cleaning rag at her. The shop that used to be Meagher's seemed to have been all done up.

"What does Mountfern need a travel agency for?" she asked.

"Oh, there's amazing needs created in this place nowadays," her father said almost ruefully.

Dara's eyes raked the town for Kerry.

Perhaps he was back. Could he be running the travel agency? Would she ask Dad was he around? No, she was only minutes from home. And she had sent him a card giving the exact date of her return. There was bound to be some message from him when she got there.

The sign was up for Ryan's Shamrock Café. Nobody had told her it would look so big. There was a new door now in the front of the building that used to be the outhouse, the place where they had their party almost a year ago.

The old windows had been repainted and new glass fitted. On each windowsill brightly colored boxes of geraniums stood nodding in the sun.

Dara gasped. "I never knew it was like this . . . like . . ."

"Like nothing on earth," her father finished cheerfully. "Still, it might keep a roof over our heads. Now here's your mother waiting for you."

Kate sat in the door of the new café. She was all dressed up, one of Rachel's scarves draped around her, which was what designated the outfit as for an occasion. She stretched her arms out in welcome as Dara scampered from the car.

Dara's heart gave a little jump.

Mam's smile was wide and warm, but she had big circles under her eyes and she was very pale.

Mam didn't look at all well.

* * *

There was huge excitement at Dara's return.

Grace and Michael came rushing in. Grace hugged her and said that she had become very French.

Michael said she had begun to lisp and speak broken English.

"What ees zat you say?" Dara punched him until he admitted it was all jealousy on his part.

Eddie wanted to know why she hadn't tried snails. He'd told all his friends that Dara was eating snails for her breakfast, dinner and tea and now he'd look like an eejit.

Declan asked could *he* go to France next summer, he wouldn't mind looking after children, it would be nice to have something younger than himself that he could boss around and give orders to.

Carrie asked if they ate everything raw—Jimbo told her he had heard that.

Mary Donnelly said she was pleased to hear that Frenchmen were not always making free with their attentions, as had often been reported.

Grace and Michael giggled at this and Kate and Dara exchanged glances. Mary had not been told about the discovery of Monsieur Vartin and Mademoiselle Stephanie.

It was marvelous to be back at home with everyone speaking English and everyone speaking at once.

But it was awful not to be able to ask about Kerry. Nobody had mentioned his name.

After supper Dara linked Grace out into the garden. They were meant to be doing a tour of the café.

"And what news of your big brother?" Dara tried to be light and joky.

"Oh, didn't he write to you? I *told* him you were coming home today. He was on the phone looking for Father."

"How was he?"

"He was mainly sounding off about Miss Hayes. I had to keep the telephone very close to my ear in case she'd hear, he'd called the night before for Father, and a . . . oh, I don't know, she hadn't given the right message. But I did tell him you'd be back today."

"Thanks, Grace." Dara was bleak.

"Was it great, France?" Grace was eager. "Did you go out at all to any parties or dances?"

"No, nothing like that."

"What was the best part?"

"We had a picnic . . . they call it peek neek, honestly. They had huge loaves of French bread and cheese and peaches and wine . . . And we went to this place on a river, not the Loire itself but a smaller river like the Fern, and we went swimming, all of us. Even Madame. And we stayed there till quite late and it got dark, and they all seemed very happy . . ."

Grace looked at her, trying to see why this had been the high spot.

Dara went on. "They seemed so safe, sort of. As if they'd always be together, and I understood all the conversation, which I usually didn't. I think it might have been the wine . . . And suddenly there were all these little pinpoints of light everywhere. Fireflies they were."

"Oh, yes, fireflies are lovely," Grace said.

"I told them we didn't have any here, and Monsieur said I must look again when I got home. That was the best time, I think."

Grace seemed pleased that Dara had a happy if unfathomable memory. She hugged her friend. "It's great to have you home again," she said.

And Dara felt a great ache.

It would have been great to come home if there had been a note from Kerry saying when he'd be back in Mountfern. If Maggie had been running up River Road after supper, hands clasped and eager to hear every detail. If Tommy had come in making jokes about the French.

And if Mam's face hadn't this tired look, and if she'd been able to eat her supper instead of moving the cold chicken and ham from one side of the plate to the other.

Loretto Quinn had to tell someone so she picked Sheila Whelan.

"It could be totally innocent," Sheila said.

"It has to be," Loretto said. "Mother of God, you don't think that they'd have been sleeping together as man and wife would you?"

Sheila sighed a "no".

"But what was he doing back in town, let alone above in her room?" Loretto's open face was puzzled. "Rachel told me herself that he wouldn't be coming back until the opening. And young Dara Ryan said that Mr. O'Neill said he was still above in Donegal."

"It's a mystery all right," Sheila said. She had a feeling that something was very wrong here. If Kerry really had been sneaking into Mountfern and to Rachel for any purpose under the sun, not to mention the interpretation which would be put on it, then why had he advertised it so publicly?

People didn't die without orange juice and eggs. He could have waited until Jack Coyne had left the shop, he would have heard his voice before he came in. Kate Ryan had always been worried about Kerry, she had said there was something very strange about him, he didn't react like ordinary people.

Maybe Kate had been right.

Tommy Leonard was disappointed that he had missed Dara coming back. He had gone out with Jacinta to find good angles where Mountfern could be photographed.

Mr. O'Neill was having a photographer next week who would take glossy pictures of the place and they would be turned into postcards. Some would be sold in the hotel, some in Leonard's. Privately Tommy thought that if the visitors could buy them at the information desk in the hotel they would be most unlikely to want to trek the whole way to Leonard's to buy the same thing. But his father had been very respectful and over-thanked Mr. O'Neill.

Jack Coyne came in to buy a paper. He ignored Tommy and went instead to the older man. Jack lowered his voice so Tommy made an effort to hear. It seemed to be about Kerry O'Neill having breakfast with Loretto Quinn. Or was it Mrs. Fine? In either case hadn't they little to talk about!

Tommy's thoughts went back to Dara. He wished he hadn't gone out with Jacinta, he felt sure no good would come of it. Liam White said that Dara had changed totally, gotten a smaller waist, a bigger chest and a sort of bold flashy look about her as if she had seen it all and done it all. Tommy knew that this couldn't be true, but he did wish that he had been able to see her himself and make these observations about her chest and her waist instead of hearing it all from Liam.

He stood there, legs aching, wishing that his father had not been so infected by Mr. O'Neill's diligence that he now kept the shop open until nine o'clock in the evening.

Fergus went for a stroll which took him, as his strolls nearly always did, to the door of Ryan's.

"Can I have a look at the Parisienne?" he asked John.

"She's within, chattering to her mother, saying 'oui' instead of yes half the time. The boys are giving her a desperate teasing over it. Take your pint and go in to see them."

"Ah no, I'll let them talk. I'll see her plenty in the next few days." Fergus knew how much Kate had been looking forward to the daughter's return.

"Wasn't it a great chance for her, Fergus?" John was very pleased with the way it had all turned out. "We didn't know what we were sending the child to, really, it was just that . . ." He let the sentence trail away.

"Well, didn't it all work out very well when you consider . . ." Fergus Slattery didn't finish his sentence either.

He thought that this particular conversation was better left untold in this house. He hoped that the handsome young Dara Ryan had her head well turned by Frenchmen and that she would forget O'Neill's dangerous-looking son.

It was so good to have Dara home. Kate wondered how she had survived without her daughter. With Dara there was no need to pretend, with Dara there was a feeling of hope all around her. Kate knew that Dara could hear the true plans and the true worries about the Shamrock Café.

"It's not what we had planned, like, for our lives," Dara had complained.

"A lot of things weren't what we had planned," Kate said, touching the sides of the wheelchair.

Dara had noticed how much Kate hated the chair. Since the very first day she had been in it, it represented the prison bars to her. She could not make herself see it as a liberation, a way of getting about. Instead she regarded the chair as a hated object and put all her anger toward it, as if it were the cause of all her incapacity. She wanted it out of her sight when she was in bed, no matter that she might need it in the night. She disguised it by draping rugs and scarves over it.

Dara seemed to understand. Once she had written a notice on it: "I'm only a chair for God's sake, Mrs. Ryan." Kate had pealed with laughter when she woke and saw it.

They could talk easily now, the trip to France had been an inspired idea.

Dara gave her mind eagerly to the problems of survival when the new regime arrived.

"There's only one thing I don't like, Mam."

"Tell it then."

"I don't like you going up to the hotel to give cookery lessons."

"Aha," Kate said.

"What do you mean, aha?"

"I have a little plan about that, I can't tell you yet, but let's say it's not going to be a problem."

"Tell me, I tell *you* everything."

"I'll only go for a very very short time."

"What's the point in it, then?"

"This is the point, once I've gotten myself established, then Dr. White will tell me, and indeed tell Patrick, that the strain is too much, and I can't do it anymore, so . . . so I'll have to continue the lessons here. Do you understand?"

"Mam!"

Impulsively Kate opened her arms and Dara rushed to her.

"It's so good to have you home, child. I missed you so much. What do people do if they don't have a daughter? Tell me that."

"Oh Mam, it's great to be back. They were nice in their way and they went to endless trouble over things but they'd have you starved half the time and they were riddled with sin."

Kate laughed until she nearly cried; her pale face looked more colorful now.

Dara felt happier but she still resolved to ask Mrs. Fine if Mam had been having any bad turns. She would ask her tomorrow. She half listened to Mam as she wondered whether Kerry might be home for the weekend. Grace was useless for any information. But of course he would come home this weekend. Now that he knew both from her postcard and from Grace on the phone that Dara was back.

Kate looked at Dara's face, lightly tanned from the hot French sunshine. She knew how Rachel would admire her, and indeed make further representations about getting Dara's ears pierced for her and giving her little gold studs.

It was odd that Rachel wasn't here. She hadn't been in all day.

Rachel Fine stayed in her room all day.

She crouched like an animal in the forest that is afraid to move because it doesn't know if it has been too badly injured. She heard the noises of Mountfern on a late summer morning. The carts that went by, the delivery vans, the sounds of hammering from across the river. She heard voices too in and out of Loretto's shop and children calling to each other as they chased along River Road.

Kerry had gone as light-heartedly as she had ever seen him. He had kissed her affectionately on the nose; he had been teasing and flirtatious. As he would have been after a night in bed with any woman.

They hadn't been together in that way. But she had no way of proving it.

A hundred times she told herself that no one would believe she could have opened her body to Kerry O'Neill, who was a boy, who had been a child when she first met and loved his father.

It would have been like an act of incest.

"So I'll head for the hills of Donegal now before anyone knows I've been here. And thanks, Rachel, thanks for everything," he had said.

What was he thanking her for?

"But people do know, they'll think . . . You said you spoke to Loretto, to Jack Coyne . . ." she croaked.

"That's not what I mean. They don't count. I don't want to meet my father, I'm going to have to tell him about some money I owe, sooner or later. No point in getting him steamed up before I ask him."

Rachel looked at Kerry and fought back waves of dizziness and nausea.

And when he was gone she felt a coldness through her bones that made a mockery of the sunny summer day outside.

She didn't answer when Loretto called up to know if she should bring up a parcel of materials that had just been delivered. So Loretto, more confused than ever, just left the parcel on the stairs and shook her head from side to side.

Rachel didn't go to see Dara, newly returned. She didn't call to collect mail at the post office, nor did she touch the parcel on the stairs.

When Brian Doyle sent round to know had some fabrics arrived, because young Costello was behaving like a pregnant cat over them, Loretto said there was no point in trying to get any answer from upstairs.

Brian said that he had always known it would happen, most people in the place had now gone clinically insane and the place for them all was the asylum on the hill.

He had been told that Kerry O'Neill was in Donegal and yet he had nearly been killed by the little bastard reversing his car at top speed this morning.

He had been told that Rachel Fine was waiting night and day for some swatches of material and now they had arrived she had apparently gone to ground like a broody hen.

O'Neill was like a lighting devil, and that leggy young Ryan child from the pub had snapped the head off him when he had addressed a civil word to her.

It was time to ring the asylum and tell them to come down with the straitjackets and take the people of Mountfern away.

As soon as he got to Fernscourt, Patrick was called to the phone in Brian Doyle's hut.

"Dennis Hill here, Patrick. I just rang to know if everything's all right?"

"That's good of you Dennis. It's crawling along, crawling, but we might have hot water to make them a cup of coffee at the opening. You will come, I hope?"

"I meant about your little girl."

"Grace?" Patrick was alarmed.

"Is she recovering?"

"Recovering?"

"The accident. The accident on the bridge."

"Grace didn't have an accident." Patrick's heart was beating very fast. Could something have happened to Grace this morning that he didn't know about? He shouted to Costello. "Was there any accident on the bridge this morning, did anything happen? Answer me!"

Costello was quick. "Nothing at all," he said crisply.

"And Grace, is she all right?"

"I saw her cycling by not five minutes ago with Michael Ryan."

"Thanks, Costello."

Patrick's breathing had changed its pace now.

"Sorry, Dennis. I was away from the phone for a moment. What did you hear?"

Mr. Hill's voice was cold. "I heard what your son told me yesterday, he had a call saying his sister had an accident in a fall from a bridge, she had been playing jumping and diving games with other children. He said that he had to go to Mountfern at once. Naturally I gave him permission."

"There was no accident," Patrick said dully.

"And I am delighted to hear it," Dennis Hill said courteously. There was a pause.

Mr. Hill spoke again: "He's a difficult lad, your son."

"Come to the point. Did he steal anything?"

"No, nothing like that!" Mr. Hill was surprised.

"Well you'd better check before you fire him. You *are* going to fire him, aren't you?"

Another pause.

"Yes, yes I think it's better to send him back to you. There's something there that attracts him."

"Well I'm damned if I know what it is." Patrick's voice was weary.

"Could be a girl. He's a handsome fellow."

"The only one he spends any time with is an under-age schoolgirl. But that would figure. He's never done anything that you'd hope he would."

"They don't, you know, children. I've got sons here in the business, and sons-in-law. They think I'm an old fool, they want me to clear out of it. That's the thanks you get for building up a business and handing it to them on a plate."

"Thanks Dennis."

"What for? I'm letting your boy go, that's not much to thank me for."

"I mean for letting me know about your sons. It's less lonely somehow."

"You'll survive. The girl's good, isn't she?"

"Ah yes, the best."

"I've got one good fellow in my brood, wants nothing to do with the hotel, works out on a headland on a small farm. Best of the lot of them, it's a pleasure to sit and talk to him for hours. You'll find that with the girl."

"When I see Kerry should I tell him to call you?"

"Why prolong it all? Speeches, lies, excuses. Tell him to pick up his things when he wants to."

As Patrick replaced the receiver, he hoped he wouldn't see Kerry for a while. Like a day anyway. He might lose control completely. A boy who could use the circumstances of Maggie Daly's death, graft them on to his own sister. And all as an excuse to go to some gambling game or other. He might very possibly kill him.

Kerry looked across the Fern. His father's car wasn't outside the hotel. That meant he must be at home. He would set out for the lodge. Easier to talk to him there anyway. He would go by River Road—he would meet too many people on Bridge Street. This way he only had to pass Coyne's, Ryan's and the Rosemarie hair salon. Jack Coyne he had already met; Kerry smiled to think how the story would be reported. Jack would find a dozen excuses to talk to people that he would not normally have any business with.

He wondered if Rachel would offer any version of events. Probably not. He would hear soon.

He turned on the car radio and they were playing "Pretty Flamingo." He turned the volume up high, pulled down the visor to keep the sun out of his eyes, and took a corner very fast.

The car that he pushed off the road was his father's. The sound of Manfred Mann was silenced by the screeching of brakes.

Kerry stopped the car and let out a sigh of relief. It had been close and it had of course been his fault. He ran his hand through his hair as he watched his father climb out of the car that was half in the ditch. His father walked toward him slowly and flung open the door.

"Get out of that fucking car," he said in a voice that Kerry had never heard before. It was as if he were being held back by two strong men. Kerry could almost see them straining to pull him back.

While all the time his father wanted to tear him limb from limb.

He got out. "I'm sorry. I was over too far . . ."

His father said nothing.

"And going a little fast, I guess."

Silence.

"Still, no real harm's done. Can we get it out, do you think, or should we walk back for Jack Coyne?"

"What are you doing here?"

"I was coming to see you. I wanted to talk to you urgently and then I was going to head for Donegal. I said I'd be back at lunchtime."

"You don't have to be back by lunch or at all."

"But I said to Mr. Hill that I'd do my best to get back today, he trusts me, and I think I should—"

"Hill doesn't trust you as far as he can throw you, Kerry, he's just fired you."

"He wouldn't do that."

"He has done that. Just that."

Kerry thought for a moment.

"He suddenly made up his mind and called you to tell you, rather than tell me. That's unlikely."

He was cool still, not blustering or defending himself with excuses and lies.

"You probably find it unlikely because you forget that some people have generous human impulses. Dennis Hill didn't like thinking of a girl falling off a bridge in a terrible accident, and her brother having to hotfoot it to her bedside. He called to learn how she was."

"I see." Kerry's face was impassive.

"No you don't see. You'll never understand that it would turn anyone's stomach, what you did."

"I had to say something. I wanted to get away."

"What a great thing to choose."

"I needed to be out of there, I needed to be here."

"Why?"

"I wanted to sort something out and see you."

"You're looking at me, Kerry. Say what you have to say, and say it quickly."

"Father, the money?"

"The money you called about yesterday, that ridiculous sum . . . You are not getting one penny of that from me."

"I wanted to come and tell you personally the kind of people they are."

"I don't care if they are cousins of the pope, they're still not going to find me coughing up their winnings at poker."

"I'm not saying they're respectable people we don't want to offend. They're the opposite, they're very tough."

"Good, then you've met it at last. People who are not going to give in to your every wish."

"You wouldn't say good, Father, if you knew . . . Tony said that they're getting very annoyed with me."

Patrick looked at his son.

"You are a spoiled selfish brat. It is my fault, it is not your mother's fault. I didn't see what was happening to you, I saw every other goddamn thing but I didn't see you for what you were. I was too busy. God forgive me."

"I'm sure he will forgive you, Father, God always forgives people who talk nicely to him and turn up at mass, no matter what they've been up to."

"Don't give me that."

"And people who put stained-glass windows into churches, and new buildings into Catholic schools, God loves them mightily."

Kerry's eyes were flashing. He would not be stopped.

"You can get away with it, Father, you always have, you can cut corners, you can break promises, you can give every slut in town a topaz, but as long as the Easter donations are generous God turns a blind eye."

Patrick moved at him, his arm up as if to strike.

Kerry went on. "And God understands a bit of battering too, if it's done in the right cause. Go ahead. Go on, I don't care. I don't give a damn."

Patrick withdrew.

"You'll care when you're working in a real job for the first time in your life to pay these punks, you'll care then when three-quarters of your wages will go to pay off a debt that not one of these farmers here could sleep a wink if he owed in a lifetime."

"You don't think for a *moment* that they'll wait to be paid at fifteen pounds a week. That would take more than a year. They want it now. On Monday at the very latest."

"Give up, you'll never get it. If you play for it you'll just end up paying twice as much. Work for a year, two years, regard it as your apprenticeship. They'll wait."

"They can't wait, they're not ordinary people. They're in an . . . organization."

"Cut that shit, they've organized themselves to smell a sucker and to rob a bank or a post office or two. Those fellows have no cause but themselves."

"You don't understand . . ."

"I know that for a fact, Hill warned me about them a while back. There may be some fellows in a movement in Derry since the border campaign ended, but not your gang. They're in it for themselves."

"Hill's an old fool, he knows nothing."

"I said you would stop by Hill's for your things, and he knows you're not to be trusted so there's no point in trying to make up any shortfall by dipping into the till before you leave."

Kerry looked at him sharply. Things had gone very far if his father had warned an outsider against him.

"Can I stay at the lodge when I come back?" he asked.

"Yes."

"Have you told Grace."

"That she is meant to be lying like her friend Maggie under the bridge, but that in her case there's some hope she'll survive? No."

"What *will* you say?"

"As little as possible. To you and about you."

"That will be hard if we're living in the same house."

"I'm moving into the hotel shortly, so is Grace. You can have the lodge until Christmas. We've paid for it until then."

"Miss Hayes?"

"She'll be going to her sister in New Zealand in a couple of weeks."

"And my room in the hotel?"

"Will not exist, Kerry."

"I'm not going to make a speech or plead, Father, this isn't about the future of the hotel or anything. It's about now. Could you give me just this amount? Then I'll never ask you again."

"No."

"Please. I've never said please before, maybe I should have. But I'm begging you."

"No. If I do it now, then next month it will be fifteen hundred pounds. Go to them, tell them they have to wait a year or whatever it takes for you to make it."

Kerry's eyes narrowed.

"It's on your head then, Father. If you won't give it to me I'll have to get it elsewhere."

"That won't be easy, you're running out of credibility."

"I think I know where I can get it," Kerry said and he almost smiled.

He got back into his car and drove away toward the main road. Patrick walked to Jack Coyne's and got three lads to come up and move his car. He didn't tell them how it had ended up in the ditch but he did not like the way Jack Coyne was looking at him.

There was something knowing and triumphant about the way the small ratlike man kept glancing at him.

"Have you been talking to Kerry?" Carrie asked Dara in a conspiratorial whisper.

"No, he's not home yet, but he might be back at the weekend. I keep hoping," Dara said.

"But he *is* here. I saw him."

"You never did!"

"Yes, last night. I said that's funny, Kerry home on a Thursday in the middle of the week. And then again this morning, he drove past here at a hundred miles an hour."

"Had he anyone with him?" Dara was almost afraid to hear the answer.

"No, not at all. Why should he have anyone with him, isn't he your fellow?"

Carrie saw things over-simply, Dara thought.

Dara sat on the window seat looking out at the moonlight. She couldn't believe that Kerry had been in Mountfern without even coming in to say hello.

Grace could never have told her a lie. There could be no awful thing that they were keeping hidden from her, like that he was going out with Kitty Daly. No, Michael would never be a party to that.

Michael came to sit beside her.

"There's nothing you're keeping secret from me, is there?" she asked.

"How did you guess?"

"Oh God." Dara's hand went to her throat.

"You see, Grace will soon be living across there," he began.

"What is it?"

"I was wondering, I was wondering if I could . . . if we could show her the tunnel."

"Is that all?"

"Well, I know it's quite a big thing to ask."

Dara didn't seem to listen.

"Was Kerry home today?" she asked. "Did he stay at the lodge last night? That's all I want to know. It's not very much to ask."

"Of course he wasn't. If he was, he'd have talked to me. He talks to me quite a lot, as it happens."

"He wasn't back then?"

"No. How many times do I have to say it?"

"Carrie must be going mad, that's all," Dara said.

"And what do you say about . . . ?"

Michael let his voice trail away. Dara was sitting happily on the window seat, her leg tucked underneath her, all the anxiety gone from her face. She didn't want to talk about tunnels or to talk about anything, she wanted to think about Kerry O'Neill.

Kerry said his goodbye's briefly in Hill's hotel. The staff were sorry to see him leave; some of the students who had been working as chambermaids for the summer were particularly sorry. He had been so sunny, so handsome, like summer lightning around the place.

He told McCann that he could get the money and have it on Saturday afternoon.

McCann had said he would come with him to get it.

That was not what Kerry wanted.

"Look you've been in Mountfern, you know the set-up, it's a one-horse place. We're the kings of the castle there, if I say I'll get it I will, and then I'll get it to you."

"No point in your driving all over the country," McCann said laconically. "I'll come with you. Then I'll get the bus back."

It was a dispiriting drive. The back of the car was filled with Kerry's stuff, they couldn't give a lift to any of the girls they saw on the road even if they had wanted to. Which Kerry didn't.

They listened to music the whole way down. Tony McCann liked "These Boots Are Made for Walking". He said it was a great song, and sang it tunelessly with Nancy Sinatra.

Kerry said he liked "Pretty Flamingo", he didn't know why but it reminded him of Dara Ryan, who was only a kid but very attractive.

"Is she pink and does she stand on one leg?" McCann had wanted to know with a laugh.

Several times Kerry O'Neill wondered why he found McCann such good company.

In Mountfern he told McCann there were three pubs he could drink in, and that he would be an hour at the most. Then he'd come with the money.

McCann had said that a check would be fine. His friends knew that Kerry wouldn't be foolish enough to give them a check that didn't work. That would be more stupid than not giving them anything at all.

Kerry had nodded fervently.

He settled McCann in Foley's, realizing that between taciturn old Mr. Foley and the silent McCann little chat would be exchanged.

Then he drove down Bridge Street, looking neither right nor left of him. He realized that when he was back here full time it would be like living in one of those fish tanks that old Hill had in his hotel where people could look at the lobsters from every side. He averted his eyes from Fergus Slattery and turned right into River Road.

Loretto's eyes were like dinner plates as he walked past her and up the stairs to Rachel Fine.

Her face was as white as a sheet. She was sitting at a table with papers on it. A coffee cup sat beside her, full but cold.

She looked up in alarm as he came in softly.

"We have to talk, Rachel, you and I," he said.

And he pulled up a chair beside her.

Friday afternoon. Could she really have been home only twenty-four hours? Dara felt she had been back for weeks.

She had gone to look for Jacinta and been told she was at her riding lesson with Marian Johnson.

Some time or other Dara would have to go into Daly's. It had better be now.

Mrs. Daly smiled at her warmly and wanted to know all about France.

"Did you get to Lourdes at all while you were there?"

"No, Mrs. Daly, but the lady I was staying with did. I asked her to say a prayer for Maggie. I wrote the name down for her on the back of a holy picture."

Mrs. Daly was pleased. She patted Dara's hand.

"You're a good child in spite of everything," she said.

Dara repeated this to Tommy Leonard in a cross voice. "In spite of what? What did she mean?" she asked.

Tommy couldn't take his eyes off Dara. She looked utterly lovely, he thought.

"In spite of being good-looking, she means. Mrs. Daly hates good-looking people, she likes them with faces like ironing boards."

Dara giggled. "I don't suppose you can come off with me for a bit?"

"I can't. I used up all my time off going to hunt out sites and vantage points with Jacinta yesterday. You look just great, you know."

"Thanks, Tommy. Well, if you've spent your free time with Jacinta I can but go in search of fun and games elsewhere. Sit out on the street and wait till King Kerry turns up for the weekend."

"Oh, King Kerry as you call him is here already." Tommy was pained to have to acknowledge it but at least it was good that Dara didn't seem to be tied up with him the moment she came back.

"He can't be!"

"Well then, he has a double. I saw him with a fellow from a horror movie going into Foley's, maybe they've taken to drinking in there."

"Kerry doesn't drink," Dara said.

"He could have started," Tommy suggested.

"Today was it?"

"Oh, don't go up looking for them in Foley's, Dara, for heaven's sake."

"I've no intention of going looking for them anywhere," Dara flounced. "Kerry will come and look for me when he's ready."

Dara waited on the footbridge. She knew he would have to come and find her.

She saw the shadows getting a little longer. She leaned over and looked at her reflection in the water. She looked all right, she thought. Not a beauty, but all right.

Where *was* he?

She didn't hear the car stopping and his light step behind her. She felt his arms around her waist and as she looked into the river she saw him reflected there. He kissed her.

"In front of the pub, with them all looking out the window?" she protested.

"Right, let's go somewhere with no windows. Get in." He opened the door of the little red car.

Dara walked toward it slowly. Was she being very cheap, very easy-to-get by going with him right away? He hadn't written. Not once. Not even a card.

He hadn't gotten in touch when he got back. But for seeing her now, he might never have stopped.

He looked up at her from the car. "You're so beautiful, Dara. I hope those Frenchmen didn't get what you wouldn't give me."

He was talking out loud. Anyone could have heard him if they had been near the pub window.

She scrambled into the car at once.

"I'm only getting in to keep you quiet," she said.

"Aren't I clever?" Kerry smiled at her and the car sped off up River Road and toward the stile in Coyne's wood.

In the wood he stood and looked at her.

"I can't take you in, I don't know what it is. In two months you've changed. I missed you," he said, head on one side, smiling to charm her.

"No of course you didn't, you never thought of me at all. You never wrote, not once. You didn't even come to see me when I got back even though I sent you a card to tell you."

"I wanted to but I couldn't, I just wasn't able to," he said.

Dara looked hard at him. He was so handsome. But of course he was making excuses.

"They tied your hands?" she asked.

"No, of course I should have written but I'm hopeless. No, I meant to be there to welcome you, but I had problems. A lot of things to sort out." His face was troubled.

"What were they?"

"Okay, I'll tell you. I was trying to get free from Donegal so that I could be here all the time. Here with you. It took a bit of organizing."

"And have you organized it?" She sounded doubtful. She expected him to say it hadn't worked out.

"Yes," he said surprisingly.

"By good timing, by the most spectacular good timing in the world, I'm free, just as you come back."

"You're leaving Hill's Hotel?"

"Yes, ma'am." He did a mock salute.

"How did you do it?"

"Not easy, a lot of aggravation I assure you. I'm still tidying up loose ends. I've got all my things in the car, see?"

"You mean you've just left *now?*"

"Just now. You're the first person I came to see." He reached out for her.

He looked as if he didn't want to talk about it anymore. Dara moved to what she thought were safer waters.

"I'm very pleased you're going to be around. Even if you *are* faithless and forgetful, I like you."

"Why am I faithless and forgetful? I raced here to find you. Let me hold you."

"Not for a moment."

"Why? What is it?"

"I'm much older now and I understand more. I don't want to hold you and have you . . . um . . . touch me . . . and then for me to say no and you to get all upset."

"Well it's very simple, you don't say no, and nobody gets upset."

Dara looked at him with her big dark eyes. "That's not what I want, and even though I like being with you, and like it a lot, when all is said and done it *is* my body, isn't it? And I can do what I like with it. Or not do what I like with it."

He stood smiling at her, and admiring. "Well, well, well," he said.

"I thought I'd rather say it now. Sort of before anything got started so that you wouldn't storm off."

"Very wise." He nodded his head sagely, making fun of her.

"So, it's a bargain, then. You don't get all upset if I say I don't want to go any further."

"Sure, and you don't get all upset, as you say, if I don't turn up all the time like a little lap dog. I'm going to be living here now and it will have its ups and downs. Give me some time and space to sort it out. Don't go asking a lot of questions all the time."

"It's a deal," she said. "And I promise not to keep asking questions, if you'll tell me one thing. Is it true that you still don't love anyone but if you did love anyone it would probably be me?"

"Where did you hear that?" He smiled.

"You told me once. When we sat in your car. After I had come to look for you in that roadhouse."

"It was true then and it's true now," he said. "If the situation changes in either direction, you will be the first to know."

The weekend would be their last one before term began.

Grace said she hoped that she would be living in the hotel by the time school started.

"Kerry never said." Dara was puzzled.

"Kerry's not coming to the hotel yet. I mean I'm sure he will later." Grace seemed flustered.

"Why on earth isn't he going to the hotel? What happened?" Dara was astounded.

"Nothing, nothing at all."

"I'm your best friend, for heaven's sake. I tell you everything, Grace, why don't you tell me?"

"I haven't even told Michael. I think there was some kind of row, I think Father didn't want him to leave the hotel in Donegal, but he insisted; he said he had to come back to Mountfern."

He had to come back to Mountfern. Dara hugged this to herself with delight. He had indeed gotten into trouble over it but he had braved it all because he wanted to be back in Mountfern. With Dara.

Twenty-One

$\mathcal{B}$y Sunday Kate was concerned about Rachel.

She hadn't called on Thursday to welcome Dara home. She hadn't been in on Friday, nor Saturday.

Sunday morning Loretto called to the pub to buy two bottles of stout.

"Going to have a bit of a spree?" Kate asked as she wrapped them in brown paper.

"No, I'm having Jack Coyne to his Sunday dinner, he was very helpful to me over a lot of heavy lifting and putting up shelves. I thought I'd cook him a meal for once."

"Terrific. Where did Rachel go, by the way?"

"Rachel?" Loretto looked shifty.

"Yes, she must have told me but I've forgotten. She hasn't been in here for days, was it to Connemara this time or Dublin?"

"I don't . . . um . . . know." Loretto wanted to leave. She had no intention of telling Kate what had been going on.

Later that evening Kate looked across the footbridge and saw a figure walking on the other side, along the towpath that led down from the bridge.

It was Rachel Fine, wearing a headscarf and sunglasses.

It wasn't cold enough for a headscarf.

It wasn't bright enough for sunglasses.

It was almost as if she didn't want to be seen.

On Monday morning Dara knew she would see Kerry. He had told her that the weekend would involve a massive reconciliation job with his father, so he wouldn't be around.

Dara did herself up to the nines. She was dying to see him again. She knew too that he didn't want her telling too many people that they met. That suited her very well, she was anxious to keep her own parents as much in the dark as possible.

"You're looking very flash, Dara."

"Sophisticated is the word," Dara said. She was alarmed if Jack Coyne thought she was flash. She must have gone too far with the lipstick.

"Like a dog's dinner, anyway." He was admiring.

"Considering what Leo's dinners look like, that's not much of a compliment."

"Leopold's not a dog, he's a freak," Jack Coyne said. "You should have let me drown him instead of having him there turning away custom."

"Oh, don't be ridiculous. People love him."

"Well, that's debatable. Any sign of Kerry O'Neill, by the way?"

"No, why do you ask *me?*" Dara was suspicious.

"I thought you might have heard from him. Specially seeing you're all dolled up."

"Lord no." She was overly casual. "Kerry O'Neill isn't my type, nor me his, I'm certain."

"Well, they say his tastes run to the maturer lady all right, but you'd never know."

"Maturer?"

"Much maturer. Old even, some would say. Still if you *do* see him tell him I have that poker game in mind. He mentioned one the last time he was here a few days ago."

"Then he *was* here the other night."

"He was certainly here at breakfast time in the morning getting aspirins and orange juice for his lady love upstairs."

"His what?"

"No, I'm saying nothing, but I'm surprised Loretto hasn't passed it on to your mother. Still, what with herself being your mother's friend and everything I suppose it's a bit complicated. Forget I said anything, will you."

He was gone, leaving Dara fuming on River Road. She bent down and pulled up a handful of dried grass from the riverbank to wipe off her lipstick.

Jack Coyne was always a pain and she knew that Mam and Dad didn't like Eddie and Declan hanging around his yard. But surely not even Jack Coyne could make up something like that about Kerry and Mrs. Fine unless he had some reason.

Mrs. Fine. She was older than Mam, surely. It was disgusting.

"Oh, Patrick, this *is* a surprise!" Marian Johnson patted her hair with pleasure.

"Hardly a surprise," Patrick growled. "It is my office."

"No, I heard you were going to Dublin."

"No." Patrick was unforthcoming. "What can I do for you?"

"Nothing really, I just came down to have a look around the place, to see the coach house and stables."

"They're outside, Marian," Patrick said dryly. "They often are in houses like this."

He realized he had been overly sharp.

"Come on, I'll take you on a tour," he said good-naturedly. "Not that there's anything to see of course, we're only playing at ponies and horses here, the guests will all be taken up to the Grange."

"I know." She patted his arm gratefully. "I don't know what we'd do without you. You've changed the whole face of Mountfern."

"That's not what I set out to do," he sighed.

"All for the better, of course. You've improved the place out of all recognition. I mean, look at poor little Loretto's place across the river there . . ." Marian waved a dismissive arm at the bright shop frontage of Quinn's grocery and greengrocery. "That used to be a real huckster's shop, and now it's grand enough for Kerry O'Neill to be seen coming and going at all hours of the day and night." She smiled what she hoped was a mischievous smile.

Patrick looked at her almost pityingly. "I know, Marian. I know. Don't wear yourself out trying to think up ways of telling me what half the town has told me already."

"I don't know *what* you mean." She flushed angrily.

As Dara passed Loretto Quinn's she saw Mrs. Fine standing at the upper window. She was looking out over the river. She hadn't seen Dara.

For a moment Dara hesitated. Jack Coyne had been very definite. Then she shook herself. It was ludicrous. Mrs. Fine looked a hundred.

On a sudden impulse Dara decided to go up and tell her that Mam was upset. It might do some good and it couldn't do any harm.

Loretto was out the back somewhere, so Dara ran straight upstairs.

"Mrs. Fine?" She tapped lightly on the door and went in.

Rachel Fine turned around from the window. However badly she looked from down below she looked worse now. Dara could hardly hide her shock.

"Sorry, Dara I wasn't expecting you. You look very nice."

"Thanks Mrs. Fine . . . um . . . Are you all right and everything?"

"I've had a bit of a cold, I think. Flu perhaps."

"Oh, I see. Mam was wondering where you were."

There was a silence.

"Well, I'll be off then, I suppose," Dara said awkwardly.

"You enjoyed France? It . . . . it must have made you grow up a lot."

"Yes, I got lonely a bit of course, I didn't really expect that. I missed everyone here. All the time."

Another silence.

"Mam's very fond of you, Mrs. Fine, she wouldn't be afraid you'd give her an old cold."

To Dara's fright, big tears came into Rachel Fine's eyes.

Rachel went to her bedroom and sat in front of the dressing table mirror. She looked old and tense, she looked lined and pathetic. Methodically she removed her make-up, cleansed her skin, applied a gel that was meant to restore the cells and carefully put on her make-up again.

As she did the feathery strokes around her eyes, Rachel Fine began to wonder was she going mad. First avoiding her friend for days and then making herself up like a call girl to go and see a kind woman in a wheelchair who wouldn't notice if she arrived dressed in a pillow case.

Kate was a little prickly at first.

"I must say it's nice to see you. Dara will be glad to know you called."

"I've seen Dara. She told me you were wondering why I hadn't been in."

"I didn't send her with that message." Kate's eyes flashed.

"I know," Rachel said wearily.

The first silence they had ever known fell between them. Eventually Rachel spoke.

"It's no use, Kate, I'm empty, drained, there's no me to talk to. I'll go away, you've nothing to say to me, nobody has."

Kate's eyes blazed with anger. "I have nothing to say to you! Don't give me that. Take offense if you bloody want to, sulk, imagine yourself wronged, insulted in some way, but don't give me that about my having nothing to say, I have a million things to say, to ask, to tell, to share. I'm not the one who slides past the door, I'm not the one doing the avoiding. I can't avoid anybody for God's sake. I don't have that little luxury anymore."

"I didn't think you'd be upset."

"No of course not, what right has a vegetable to be upset? Poor old Kate, she's lucky she had anyone come and visit her at all."

"Kate, you know . . ."

"I know nothing. I'm scared sick about this café I've talked them all into doing. I don't want to make John into some kind of clown doing party pieces for Americans, the next thing we'll have his cap on the floor and ask them to throw dimes into it. I don't want the boys to be serving cakes and potato bread in case their friends call them sissies. I don't want Michael to be besotted by Grace with her honeyed words and smiles. I don't want that bloody Kerry O'Neill raising his little finger and taking the clothes off my daughter, my beautiful Dara, and then throwing her aside . . . So now tell me about the wonderful trouble-free family life I have."

"What's the worst bit?" Rachel asked suddenly.

"I think it's Kerry. He's playing her like a fish on a line. He'll have her as soon as he wants to, he's the kind that gets everything he wants, and doesn't care about who he hurts on the way."

"You're right."

"I'm so frightened, and I wanted to talk to you, and now you've turned against me too. I'm sorry to be such a fool." Kate groped around ineffectually for her handkerchief and cried salt tears down her newly powdered face.

Rachel's eyes were full of tears. "I couldn't come near you because I didn't want you to know how stupid I've been. I've done something so stupid you wouldn't believe it, I was too ashamed . . ."

"You don't have to tell . . ."

"It's Kerry . . . I've done something so stupid . . . so terribly stupid . . ."

Hand in hand the two women sat in the darkening evening, and Kate patted the beautifully ringed hands of Rachel Fine, who told how she had put herself in Kerry's power.

Tony McCann did not have a bank account. But he had been in and out of this particular branch so often to get change, to cash checks made out to him by other people, that he always regarded it as his bank. He had missed it during the strike.

He handed over the check for a thousand pounds.

"In the money, I see?" the cashier had said to him pleasantly.

"If it were all mine I'd be hundreds of miles from here on a beach sipping rum and Coca Cola," said Tony McCann.

The cashier sighed and thought about it for a moment. "How do you want the money?"

"Ten-pound notes, a hundred of them," McCann said. He looked idly around the bank as she went away to verify the check. How did people work here five days a week for forty years? Surely they must all have been tempted to take a carrier bag of wads of fivers and run. It was remarkable that so few of them did when you came to think of it.

"Mr. McCann?" It was a man now, a senior man in a suit, with a pinched-looking face.

"Yes?"

"There seems to be a problem about the check."

"That's not possible."

"I'm afraid so. It has been cancelled and reported stolen."

"It's me. McCann."

"Yes?" Kerry O'Neill's voice was anxious suddenly.

"The check doesn't work."

"I don't believe you."

"You'd better believe me."

"The bitch. The stupid bitch."

"You'll sort it out then?"

"I'll sort it out."

"Mr. O'Neill?"

Brian Doyle was hesitant. Patrick O'Neill was like a devil these days, even the most mild request was met by a bout of bad temper.

"Doyle?" He was curt.

"Mrs. Fine wants to have a word with you."

Once Brian had called Rachel by her first name, and that had not found favor either with his boss.

"Good, then I'm sure she will," Patrick said.

"On the telephone," Brian explained, as if he were talking to a child.

It had been as much as Patrick could do to stay sane when faced with the Irish telephone system. He had been assured that it was a European thing, not just Irish, but that didn't make it any easier to bear. He said he would make a mental note not to open a chain of hotels on the continent of Europe, and people had smiled at him indulgently. The eager American, hustle bustle. He knew what they said.

But if Rachel was on the telephone for him that meant he had to leave his office and walk across to Brian Doyle's headquarters, that was where the only phone link so far had managed to be installed.

Patrick moved quickly. He would not let Doyle see how annoyed he was to be summoned by Rachel, whom they all knew to be his fancy woman, to walk across the courtyard, through the Thatch Bar and over to those excrescences that Doyle called his headquarters.

"Yes?" He said curtly, watching Brian pretend to busy himself elsewhere in the cramped space.

"Can we talk?"

"Here?" He couldn't believe it.

"No. Anywhere. It's important."

"Why didn't you come up here in the first place instead of having me walk half way around the country to tell me you were coming?"

"I don't want to come there."

"I don't have time to go over to Loretto's."

"No, I don't want you to come here either."

"Is this a game of hide and seek, by any chance?"

"Please."

"Where then?"

"Coyne's wood. At the far end up by the old ruined church on the small back road that leads to the Grange. There's a gate."

"Jesus," Patrick said.

"I'll leave now, I'll wait. You get away when you can."

He held the receiver in his hand for a while and out of the window of Doyle's headquarters, through the clutter of the ledge, he saw across the Fern in the distance a figure come out of the door of Loretto Quinn's shop and get into a small green car.

"Thanks, Brian," he said as he replaced the receiver.

"Lovely day for a bit of a spin out into the country," Brian said.

Patrick gave him a look that told Brian that the wise man addressed no words at all to the great O'Neill these days.

Canon Moran was picking flowers near the stile up in Coyne's wood. That was all Patrick needed.

The old man looked up with pleasure as the American approached. This was a bonus for him, he liked a good chat.

Patrick looked at him thoughtfully. It was a good life being a country priest in Ireland. Canon Moran had all the respect and none of the work in the parish. He had baptized and married and buried people from the place for as long as anyone could remember. There was no way he would be sent away nor his honors stripped from him.

He could wander in a second childhood, collecting summer flowers.

"You know what you were asking me, about marriage to those who had never been baptized?"

Patrick tried to keep the maddened irritation out of his face.

"Yes, Canon Moran. It was just something I wondered about in the abstract. Like I sometimes wonder about the angels. You know, thrones and dominations and seraphim. I wonder why they'd have a VIP system in heaven."

Canon Moran had often wondered about angels too, and particularly about guardian angels. He couldn't ever see on what basis the poor angels were given mortals to look after. Some angels must have had a very easy time and others a desperate job altogether.

Patrick wondered was he going to spend the entire morning debating guardian angels with an almost senile cleric who held an armful of daisies and heathers and some prickly yellow gorse. Still it was better than discussing marriages to infidels. He looked around wildly for any trace of Rachel.

The canon's old eyes may have been sharper than Patrick thought.

"Well, I won't hold you up, you're a busy man, Mr. O'Neill, a busy man, a good man, and a generous man. It's very heartening to know that men like you with all your worldy wealth still keep the laws of God."

Patrick was rarely at a loss. But now he had no idea what to say.

Canon Moran filled the gap for him. "And if ever you should need any further talk—just in the abstract of course—about the marriage of unbaptized persons who convert to the Catholic faith, then I know just the man in Archbishop's House. We were in the seminary together. He didn't end up in a quiet place like Mountfern, he's a big expert in canon law and there's nothing he doesn't understand about previous marriages contracted outside the Church or any other church which would be recognized as solemnizing a Christian marriage according to their own lights . . ."

"Yes, yes."

"They would be entirely null and void and wouldn't need to be taken into consideration," Canon Moran finished triumphantly.

"Well yes, that's good. I'll remember that if I need to think about it," Patrick said.

"It would be good if you needed to think about it, Mr. O'Neill. Life can be lonely at times, and we're all very pleased here that you've come back to the land of your fathers. We wouldn't want you to feel . . . well to feel a bit alone back there in that big place."

For a second time Patrick was without words. He was touched by the old man; he felt a lump in his throat.

Again Canon Moran filled the pause. "So I expect you'll want to be off for a bit to wander down there by the trees with all the climbing roses on them. They look so beautiful at this time of year, someone should make them into a calendar, I always think."

The old man walked back toward the road and Patrick went slowly down to the trees where the roses did indeed wind around the big heavy trunks and the branches, and where Rachel sat on a fallen tree.

"How's Jimbo's singing career these days?" Kate asked Carrie.

"He's doing very well, he's going to cut a record," Carrie said proudly.

"Is that a single or an LP?" Kate was well up in records from hearing the children talk.

"It's going to be an EP, ma'am. You know, the middle kind of one." Carrie's face was shining.

"And does he like all this traveling around? I hear he was as far afield as Donegal."

"Oh he likes it all right, Mrs. Ryan, it's grand for him. But I don't like it all that much, to tell you the truth."

Kate was sympathetic. "And does he not suggest you go along with him?"

"He's always suggesting it, but how can I?"

"It's hard all right."

"Well it is. You see he's never suggesting I go along as Mrs. Jimbo Doyle, if you know what I mean. Just as Carrie." She looked very glum.

"Suppose he got work around here, wouldn't that keep him at home?"

"But that's the point, there's plenty of work around here, with the hotel he could be working seven days a week. But he has his heart set on being a star, you see, so the work is only interfering with it."

"But if he got singing work, I mean. When the hotel opened."

Carrie's face lit up. "Wouldn't that be the makings of us. But Mr. O'Neill thinks of Jimbo as a handyman, he wouldn't employ him as a singer."

"I could have a word, maybe."

"Oh ma'am, and if you were to say it to Mrs. Fine, maybe Mr. O'Neill would listen to her, too."

"We'll see what we can do." Kate promised, and Carrie went out to the kitchen and made a big dinner for Leopold in order to have somebody to celebrate with.

"Wouldn't it be great if poor Jimbo got a chance to do a turn over in Fernscourt when it opens?" Kate said to John.

"Less of the poor Jimbo, there was a bit about him in the papers on Sunday. He's doing fine."

"Well then, it shouldn't be hard to get him taken on now and then in the Thatch Bar."

"I wouldn't say he'd have time for that," John said.

"What do you mean?" Kate couldn't follow the reasoning.

"We'll offer him a job singing in Ryan's Shamrock Café. If he's good then let him sing here, not have him across the river."

Kate got a sudden cold feeling. There was a time when she was the one who would have thought up that plan.

"That's a better idea altogether," she said dully.

"Of course it is." He patted her hand.

"Dara will you give me a hand with these table napkins?"

"*No*, Mammy, *no, no, no.*"

"That's lovely, I must say."

"I'll do anything but that, I hate hemming bloody napkins."

"Do you think I like it?"

"Well, you've got nothing—" She stopped.

"Nothing better to do. How right you are. Sit in a wheelchair, give her some napkins to hem, stop her hands from becoming paralyzed as well as everything else . . .."

"Oh Mam, really . . ."

"What do you mean, really? Really nothing. That's what you were saying, wasn't it?"

"It's not like you to be so sorry for yourself."

"It's not like you to be such a selfish little madam."

A pause. "I'm sorry, and that *wasn't* what I was going to say . . ."

"What were you going to say?"

"I stopped but I'll have to say it now because the way you finished it is worse."

"Well what was it . . ."

"I was going to say you've got nothing more important to do like I have, I want to . . . well, I want to be around a bit . . ."

Kate looked at her blankly.

"Sort of outside, you know, not in here putting hems on squares."

"I'd like to be outside a bit too."

"I know, Mammy, I know, but you've sort of had your life. *Oh God*, I don't mean that. It's so easy to say the wrong thing. I mean, you've had this bit, the bit of hunting and deciding and doing things that matter."

"Yes."

"You don't understand."

"I do. I've had the bit that matters. You haven't. Off you go, find the bit that matters."

"Sometimes there's no pleasing you, Mam, do you know that? You get annoyed if we don't tell you what's going on, you get more annoyed if we do tell you. It's not just that you have all this . . ." Dara waved at the chair. They never used words like cripple or paralyzed or invalid in the house. Sometimes, not often they spoke of the "accident."

Kate looked thoughtful, not annoyed, and not so sad, either.

"I will do a bit of hemming, Mam, but not now, I want to be around, if you could know what I mean at all."

Kate seemed to have recovered her humor.

"No, I do see what you mean. You must be around. But Dara, he may not be back for fun and games this time, he may have other things on his mind."

"Oh, him?" Dara flushed and flounced a bit. "I wasn't thinking of him."

"Of course not, and even if you were why should you listen to me about him? It's just that I think he's here for a purpose this time."

"God, you're very dramatic at times." Dara was gone, mascara and lipstick in the pocket of her white jacket ready to put on when well out of sight of Ryan's Licensed Premises.

Patrick sat down on the fallen tree beside Rachel.

For a moment neither of them said anything. The wood smelled fresh and flowery. Canon Moran had tottered away; there was nothing to disturb them. Butterflies went in and out of the trees, and sometimes a bird rustled in some kind of activity. It was a peaceful place.

"We should have spent more time here," Patrick said.

She smiled at him. Perhaps this might be a bit easier than she had feared. He had sounded so forbidding on the phone.

She twisted her hands together. "It's so difficult to tell you this."

He moved his cuff slightly so that he could see his watch. "But I am going to hear it. Right, Rachel?" he said.

He had the smile she had known for so many years. It was the smile when someone was going to waste his time. But he owed them. So he would listen.

It was to that smile that she would have to tell her tale.

"Give me a large brandy will you, John."

"Things must be bad over there if you're at the large brandies before lunch," John Ryan said mildly, putting the glass in front of Brian Doyle.

"I'll be hiding it in a tea flask, I tell you."

"Any one thing, or things in general?"

"Who knows? Nothing would please him. He went off to meet your one up in Coyne's wood as if they were a pair of kids. That didn't last long, he's back inside there now with a face on him that would stop a clock."

"It can't have gone well, the outing," John agreed. "Did Rachel come back with him or what?"

"Did she come back with him? Indeed she did not. Those two are like the things you see—you know, kind of statues of a man and a woman. When one comes out the other goes in, one means sun, one means rain. I saw them once somewhere. Blackpool I think it was."

John laughed. "Are they as bad as that?"

"Oh, God, John, the older people are the worse it hits them, this love carry-on. I think I'm too old for it myself and I'm years younger than O'Neill."

"You'd better hurry up and marry that girl of yours in the town before someone else does," John advised him.

"I don't want to be tied down. Men are miserable when they're tied down; they're meant to roam free, wild like nature intended."

"It's easy known Mary Donnelly's over in the post office today," John said.

"She is too, I went in to send off some forms for O'Neill that had been lying on his desk for a month and he wouldn't look at, but today he took the face off me about them, and there was the hatchet face standing behind the grille, snapping and barking at poor Fergus Slattery because there was too much sealing wax or something on his parcels. God, wouldn't a man want to be free, not tied to a woman who'd yap the arse off him."

John was mild. "I don't know, look at the people around here who are not tied to women—Jack Coyne, Fergus Slattery, Papers Flynn, O'Neill himself . . . You can't say that makes a flight of free birds, now can you?"

"Go on out of that. You've one of the few happy marriages around, and look at the thanks you got for that. I'll have the other half of that brandy now, if you don't mind."

"It's just as well you weren't laying into the booze like this when the structure was going up," John commented. "Nobody would dare go into the place at all for fear of it coming down on top of them."

"You could do yourself a favor, Eddie," Jack Coyne said.

"What's that, Mr. Coyne?" Eddie was suspicious now. He saw in his mind the shadow of Sergeant Sheehan at every turn.

"You know where they're digging out the road for the new entrance up on the road beyond. Where all the vehicles are parked?"

"Yes, I know it."

"I was just thinking that if someone was to let the brakes off a couple of those vehicles, well there'd be an unholy mess when they started to move them again in the morning, there'd be people skating into each other and falling over . . . It would be great sport altogether."

Eddie looked at Jack Coyne and remembered what his father had said about him. "There's been enough accidents up in that place," he said in a voice more courageous than he felt.

This was unanswerable. Jack was taken aback, but he rallied.

"It wouldn't have anything to do with anything like that, and wouldn't that make you of all people anxious to make sure that O'Neill doesn't get away with everything and ride roughshod over the whole place?"

"I'm out of it now, Mr. Coyne."

Eddie spoke in a cloak and dagger voice.

"You are like hell," Jack said. "Wait till I tell your father, not to mention Sergeant Sheehan, what you've been up to with cans of distemper."

"They'd want to know who gave us the distemper, Mr. Coyne."

"I suppose O'Neill's paying you more than I am. That's what it always is in the end."

"You never paid us anything, Mr. Coyne." Eddie was stung.

"So you're looking for something now, you mean little jerk."

Eddie walked away in what he was sure was exactly the way the good sheriff would turn his back on the bad guys in town.

"Don't turn on the light."

Rachel turned on the light and saw him lounging in her chair.

"Why did you do that?" Kerry asked. "I wanted us to sit and have another nice talk in the dark summer evening. Maybe you could have another drink and become amorous again. Hey, that would be good."

"If you don't leave I will," she said.

"You're not surprised to see me."

"I got your message. I knew you'd be here sooner or later."

"It's sooner because there was some little misunderstanding about that check you gave me."

"I changed my mind. I cancelled it."

"That was a very foolish thing to do."

"Are you going?" she asked him.

"No, and neither are you. This is Mountfern, Rachel; this is not an apartment; it's a couple of rooms over a downtown store. It's where you have to stay because you aren't good enough to stay in the Grange, and because you'll never stay in Fernscourt."

She moved toward the door.

"Wait," he ordered. "Just see how hopeless it is for you, Rachel. Write this check out again, with a note saying that it was all a mistake. *Do it*. Tell them that you apologize for the embarrassment caused to Mr. McCann."

"*Mr.* McCann." Rachel gave a great shout of mirthless laughter. "That guy's never been called Mr. in his life, and never will be. You don't frighten me, Kerry. I'm going for Patrick."

"You're going for my father."

"Of course I am. If his son is behaving like this and harassing me then he will want to be told."

"Rachel, Rachel." Kerry was languid. "You live in a world of romantic movies and women's magazines. You see yourself as the lady who has been slighted and insulted. Grow up. Look at the reality. You're a has-been, you're a passed-over, middle-aged woman . . ."

"You're not hurting me."

"I'm glad, because that's not my intention. I just want you to see how ridiculous you are. Once people can see how absurd they are, they are better off for it."

He walked over to her, a notepad and a pen in his hands. "Write it Rachel. It makes sense."

"Like hell will I write it."

"I'll tell my father what fun and games we had."

"You can, I've already told him."

Kerry's face didn't change. Not a muscle moved.

"He knows nothing happened between us."

"Does he?"

Kerry looked down at the check. He looked back at Rachel.

Something about his smile alarmed her.

"So could *you* explain why you wrote the check in the first place?" he asked.

He knew by her face that he had hit home. That was the one bit of her unsatisfactory conversation with Patrick in Coyne's wood that had been worse than all the rest put together. He had listened impassively from his seat on the fallen tree. The drink, the dizziness, the passing out, the tears, the hangover, the arrogant behavior of Kerry going down to the shop in the morning . . . all those things were capable of some kind of explanation. But why had she given in so readily to the demand for money? Unless she had hoped somehow to pay him off.

It had seemed a long day to Dara since she set out that morning all dressed up and had the upsetting meeting with Jack Coyne.

People were behaving strangely in Mountfern today. Jacinta said that there was some terrible row between Mrs. Fine, who was Mr. O'Neill's mistress and Mr. O'Neill, and he had ordered her back to America because of something unmentionable she had done.

Dara asked what it had been but Jacinta said her lips were sealed.

Liam White said he thought Mrs. Fine had gotten drunk and made a pass at Kerry.

Tommy Leonard said there was some scandal about Kerry, he had had breakfast in the wrong place. But he, Tommy, knew nothing about it and wasn't going to start speculating.

Mary Donnelly admired Dara's dress and said that now that she was so grown up why didn't she find herself some nice new friends instead of just staying all the time in the same little circle.

"It isn't a circle, it's just whoever is here," Dara cried out in confusion.

Nobody had ever talked about circles before in Mountfern.

She came home confused and somehow let down. She sat with her mother for a little. Even Mam looked odd, she thought.

Kate looked with love at her beautiful daughter. Please may something happen that would take this dangerous Kerry O'Neill away from their place.

His deliberate cruelty to Rachel, his blackmail, the cynical way he treated everyone around him made Kate shiver.

"Are you all right, Mam?" Dara had noticed the way her body had trembled suddenly all over.

"I'm fine. Can you pass me that light wool stole . . . the new one Rachel brought me?" Kate settled it around her shoulders.

Dara had a look as if she were going to say something and had thought better of it.

"What is it?"

"Well, I don't suppose it's possible that Mrs. Fine could fancy Kerry. I know it sounds ridiculous, but do you think it could by any chance be true?"

When Dara saw the look of shock and embarrassment followed by anger come to her mother's face, she knew that there must indeed be something in what awful horrible Jack Coyne had said. She wished with all her heart that she had never asked.

It was about the most revolting thing she had ever heard in her life, and the worst thing was that her mother had known about it already.

"What are you going to wear?" Fergus asked Kate.

"To the hotel opening?"

"No, Kate, to your court case."

"I thought you said it would be settled before we *got* to court."

"I did, and that's what Kevin thinks too, but we have to be prepared to go into court. All of us."

"I didn't think about it."

"Well *do* think about it."

"Do you want me to paint my cheeks white and draw circles under my eyes?"

"No, but I don't want you dripping in all Rachel Fine's silks and scarves and jewelry, either."

"Fergus, I'm weary of this. It's a sum. It's a sum no matter what I wear. It's going to be ten thousand pounds at most and two thousand pounds at least. Isn't that what we all agreed?"

"That's what you and John and I and Kevin Kennedy and about three others agreed. It's not what those hotshots across the river and their big faceless insurance companies agreed. It's not what a jury of pudding-faced farmers and shopkeepers agreed. Not yet."

"What do you want me to wear? I'll wear it." She sounded tired.

"It will be over soon." Fergus sounded tired too.

Dara's bedroom door was open, she was standing by a picture of Our Lady Queen of the May.

"What are you thinking about?" Michael asked.

"Should we pray for a lot of money next week or would that be wrong?" Dara asked.

"I don't know."

"I was just wondering what you thought. You say so little these days, I thought you might have *some* opinion." Dara was annoyed.

Michael was even more annoyed. "I say very little, I have no opinions, *you* are the one who says nothing, you've this awful shrug, this awful way of just putting anyone down."

"Ha ha." Dara was bitter. "I've often heard of people accusing others of the very fault they have themselves. *You* haven't a word to throw to a dog these days, yes even Leopold doesn't bother to come and snuffle at you anymore, you might as well snuffle at a block of wood."

"I only have to come into a room for you to leave it," Michael cried. "Look at you now, standing up already, off again. I don't care. I don't care one tuppenny damn, just don't go around saying that it's *me* that's being difficult, you're the one like a bag of weasels."

"I'm standing because I haven't sat down yet, you great clown. I only asked you a civil question, a reasonable question, like should we be saying the thirty days prayer or not. It's the kind of thing we used to talk about once. When you talked, that was."

Dara's lip was trembling a little. Michael saw it.

"I don't think prayers work," he said. "I'm not sure but I don't think they do."

"I'm not sure either, but suppose they did, would it be wrong?" She looked very near tears.

"Why the sudden interest in money?" Michael asked. "We never needed it before."

"I know, I just thought it might help to make things better, stop everyone from being so worried. Stop all the terrible things happening."

Awkwardly he put his arm around her shoulder. "It's not as bad as that."

"Sometimes it is."

"I know, for me too."

"Oh you! Everything's fine for you." She sounded envious.

"Not all the time. I'll tell you sometime."

"We never talk these days," she said.

"Remember when we got into such tempers because we couldn't sleep in the same room anymore!" Michael said.

"I still think you got the better room."

"Yeah, but I got Eddie and Declan."

She smiled at him. This was better, more like old times.

"Let's go out," she said. "It's the last day of freedom. We'll go to the tunnel."

"It's such a sunny day . . ." Michael began.

"Oh come on, it was always a sunny day when we went to the tunnel." She looked eager.

With great misgivings Michael agreed. They walked along River Road past Loretto Quinn's at the very moment that Rachel came out, in her cream linen suit with its cream and brown blouse.

She stopped when she saw them. Uneasily.

Dara stopped too.

Rachel spoke first.

"Can I give you a ride?" she asked.

"No thanks, we're just going for a walk," Michael answered.

Dara said nothing.

"Well, if you're sure . . . ?"

Michael looked at Dara, waiting for her to answer. There were no words so he had to speak again.

"Honestly, thanks. It's our last day of the holidays."

"Yes, the last day of the holidays," Rachel repeated. "You will never forget this holiday . . ." Her eyes went toward the big bridge. "Nobody knew it was going to turn out like this."

She got into her green car and drove away.

"Why were you like that?" Michael asked.

"Like what?"

"You know."

"I can't tell you. Not yet."

"All right." He looked disappointed, Dara noticed. Perhaps she would tell him in the tunnel.

Miss Hayes had gone to Dublin. There were a lot of things she had to do. There was the matter of her passport, and her traveler's checks. There were formalities about her ticket with a travel agency, a meeting with some distant cousins, and she wanted to buy material to make a few nice suitable garments for the journey. Mrs. Fine had been very helpful about the need for pure cotton, and avoiding synthetic fabrics. Mr. O'Neill got her a lift to the town, and she would take the day excursion train from there.

Kerry came to the lodge to see Grace. He looked disheveled and scruffy.

"I wish you wouldn't behave like this, Kerry, like someone on the run. I know you and Father had some big row again, and nobody even told me. Grace isn't supposed to know anything upsetting . . . but he hasn't thrown you out, it's you who are making the big drama out of it."

"It's sort of complicated. I just have to straighten things out and then it will all be fine. I don't want to be at home, not until things are settled."

"Can you tell me about it?"

"No, Gracie. Not yet."

"Kerry, where are you staying?"

"I'll tell you eventually, honestly."

"You're so jumpy, you said you wanted to talk to me about something. What is it?"

"Gracie, you believe that everything's marvelous. Everyone's good and all things are going to end happily ever after."

"I don't believe that, but I only concentrate on things that make me happy. You concentrate on things that make you miserable, like fighting with Father and only seeing the old fussy side of Miss Hayes. She'd be so pleased to do all your clothes for you . . ." Grace shook her head in wonder that Kerry couldn't see the easy route to everything.

"I have to go out, there's someone I have to meet, then I'll come back, and you and I will talk about plans and the future and you can lecture me to your heart's content."

They were barely into the tunnel when Dara felt at peace. She had been happy here with Michael like they had been happy when they played in the ruins of Fernscourt.

"You know, there are plenty of these tunnels, we used to think this was the only one in the world," she said.

"For us it was," Michael said.

They walked along the narrow passage to their special room. Dara chattered away more easily than she had done for a long time.

"It looks different," she said.

"Of course we haven't been here for ages," said Michael.

They lit the candles in the old rusty candelabra they had found on a dump and polished.

The place was full of shadows and shapes, as it always was.

But Dara saw that there were bunches of grasses tied in a way that they never had them before. She saw there were cushions that they used to keep on the floor as seats all piled up on the broken couch. She knew instantly that this was not the way they had left it.

She knew that Michael had brought Grace to the tunnel. Her heart turned over at the betrayal.

She decided not to make an issue out of it. There had been too much drama. But she wouldn't tell him about Mrs. Fine and the terrible story that she knew was true. She couldn't trust him anymore.

So they talked lightly of other things. They talked about school tomorrow. And they talked a little about Mam's case next Thursday. When they would both be in their classrooms trying to concentrate on their work.

Dara fought down the feeling that her twin brother had been disloyal. She tried not to think of him in this tunnel with Grace. She thought he looked a bit edgy and worried, as if he had seen something that was upsetting him, but since he didn't say what it was, she didn't ask him.

Papers Flynn said to Sergeant Sheehan that it was going to be a cold winter; he had heard that as a fact.

"The winter is months away," Sergeant Sheehan said, wondering what this was leading up to.

"There's a very nice kind of a shed behind the presbytery, a place where no wind would come whistling through at all, if a person was to want a bit of shelter."

"The very thing for a bit of shelter," the sergeant agreed. "Unless of course you'd be lifted out of it by some housekeeper that isn't herself a person of the cloth at all."

"That would be a hard thing if it were to happen. I just mentioned it in case anyone would think of making it their headquarters," Papers explained.

The sergeant nodded sagely.

Papers was getting old. There was a time when he would take his chances in anyone's shed. His main priority in life was to avoid being organized. But now he found battles hard to fight. This was his way of asking Sergeant Sheehan to square it with Miss Purcell and the clergy that he could live there when the cold weather came.

Patrick said that he didn't mind if the rest of the hotel wasn't finished for another decade, he wanted his own suite completed and ready to move into this week.

"That wasn't on the schedule," Brian Doyle was unwise enough to say.

"Your schedule, Doyle, should be published and bound and sold, it would be the comic best-seller of the year."

It was totally impossible to insult Brian. "That might well be right but we'll have to take men off other work to sort it out for you. It's not just getting it ready, it's making it so that we don't have to traipse through it all the time."

"That would be very acceptable," Patrick said with heavy irony. "Not to have this army of craftsmen you employ traipsing through my quarters. Yes, that would be a great bonus."

"When do you want to sleep here?" Brian was practical.

"Tomorrow night."

He wanted to be resident in the hotel before the compensation case began. He wanted to be well out of his son's way. It was becoming increasingly obvious he should be in his own place. At once.

He walked around the unfinished set of rooms that were to be his new home. Three bedrooms, two bathrooms, a sitting room, a study and a small kitchen.

The main rooms faced the Fern and were on the first floor of the house. He hadn't wanted a kitchen but Rachel had insisted. He wouldn't always want hotel food. There might be times when Grace would want to cook for the family. It was good to have a place where they could close the door and leave the hotel to get on with itself.

His study was the biggest room. Two walls were lined with shelves. Rachel said they could get antique furniture later, visit auctions in big country houses maybe, but for now he should have space for his papers and his books.

Had she ever seen herself with him there, he wondered. There was no hint ever in her suggestions, that she might join him in this life style. No room for her clothes was ever taken into consideration. Instead she had urged him to fit out rooms for both Kerry and Grace from the outset so that they would always consider it their home.

Grace had been busy throughout, deciding where she wanted her closet, her bureau. Kerry's room, though it existed, had not been furnished or discussed, it was now an official dressing room.

Brian accompanied Patrick on his tour of inspection.

"Tomorrow night," he repeated in the tone that he would use to soothe a dangerous drunk or someone who was both soft in the head and violent.

"Good." Patrick deliberately misunderstood the tone, and averted his eyes from the open floorboards, the electric wires and cables still loose from the wall.

The windows were smeared with squiggles to show that there was glass in them, and there were heaps of wood shavings where the carpentry was still in progress. Furniture in crates stood in the corridors.

Patrick smiled at it beatifically.

"As long as I have my own little place here, Doyle, I'll be fine," he said.

"I often think, Mr. O'Neill, God forgive me, that if you'd come home and built yourself a nice bungalow on this site you'd have saved yourself and everyone else a lot of trouble."

"How unselfish you are, Doyle. Imagine thinking that you could have passed over the entirely disproportionate wealth I have made available to you, not to mention all the extra you made on the side."

He clasped Brian warmly by the hand and patted him on the back at the same time.

"Tomorrow around six o'clock I'll move in. Come and have a drink with me here to celebrate."

"I will, Mr. O'Neill, I look forward to that. I was always a great fan of *Alice in Wonderland* myself."

Rachel's choking feeling in her throat returned as soon as she got into her car and drove away from the twins. Dara had been filled with scorn and hate.

And no wonder. A girl of barely sixteen, in love for the first time with a handsome boy who probably filled her head with lies and false assurances. And then the town is saying everywhere in whispers that he has slept with her mother's friend.

No wonder those dark eyes blazed with contempt and hurt.

Rachel remembered those days in June when she had gotten very close to the girls. She had loved the elder-sister role. That was all part of a Celtic mist of fantasy now.

But it wasn't time for self-pity yet; she must get into the hotel, get her business done, and be on the road as soon as possible.

If she were to have any tatters of dignity left over the whole incident, then she must keep calm and workmanlike until she was well out of sight of the cast of interested spectators.

She parked her car and walked purposefully up the hotel steps in search of Jim Costello.

They had run into a problem over some of the Irish-linen panels. It was proving difficult to get exactly the same shade of dye in each batch. Young Jim Costello had understood the matter at once. It was a question of deciding whether to attempt to get them all the same or to have deliberately different toning shades.

Together they had walked the public rooms, climbing ladders and dropping swathes of material.

Jim wanted this hotel opening to stagger his rivals and quite possibly his future employers or backers. Rachel knew that he was as eager and keen as anyone to get it right.

Eventually they agreed that it would be gradings of color. They had to do this in case some wall panels were to fade in the sunlight and could never be replaced exactly.

It would mean another visit to the small linen mills.

The workmen saluted her on her way out to the car. They had respect for her since she never threw her weight around and had a quick smile, but didn't stop to bore them with woman's kind of chat.

Leaning against her small green car was Kerry.

"What are you doing?"

"Waiting for you."

"You've waited in vain. I'm just leaving. Excuse me . . ."

She tried to get past him. He did not move.

She turned around and walked purposefully back up the steps. Kerry ran after her; it was as if he knew that she was heading straight for his father.

"I'm giving you one last chance," he said.

She didn't stop. He was beside her now.

"Look at this house, Rachel, this is your one chance to have it all, it's what you gave your whole damn life for, isn't it? Don't throw it away. Write that check out. This minute. Or I tell him everything."

"Come with me and we'll tell him together." She was heading for the staircase.

"I have to have the money. McCann's people are very angry with you and with me because of you. These guys don't play around."

He stood in front of her barring her way up the stairs.

"Will you get out of my way?" She raised her voice so significantly that the workmen all stopped whatever they were doing and nudged each other. A barney between O'Neill's woman and his son in full view of everyone was worth watching.

At that very moment Patrick O'Neill appeared on the landing at the top of the stairway. He took in the scene in a second and saw the gawping faces looking at the unexpected floorshow.

He did the one thing guaranteed to end the excitement and to wound more seriously than any other action he could have taken. He looked at them both dismissively and walked past them without addressing a word to either of them.

Most of the journey to the weavers was on a good straight road, which was just as well. Rachel drove with minimum concentration. Her eyes blurred over sometimes, and she had to blink hard to clear her vision.

For no reason at all she thought of a little old man who was in the garden of the Hadassah nursing home, a psychiatric home for elderly Jewish clientele. It was the home where Rachel's mother had died. The old man sat in the garden looking almost unbearably sad. Once Rachel felt compelled to ask him what was upsetting him so much.

"I'm not mad, you see," he had said to her resignedly. "I'm as sane as you or any other visitor. My nephew put me in here because he wants to steal all my inventions and pass them over as his own. But it *sounds* like such a mad thing to say, that it only gives everybody further proof that I am indeed mad."

She had been struck at the time by the logic of the old man's argument. But she had only shaken her head sadly and marveled at how sane the very far from sane could sound.

Today, driving across Ireland in the late summer sun, pausing sometimes for a flock of sheep, a herd of cattle, or on one occasion for a great group of young laughing nuns who were going on some kind of outing, Rachel Fine remembered the old man and wished she had been more sympathetic to him.

Grace was startled to see Kerry looking so wild when he came back to the Lodge.

"I've just seen myself reflected in the window and you are quite right, I do look a wreck. Listen, I'm going to clean up. Grace, can you put all these newfound cooking skills to work and fix me some eggs. Then we'll talk."

She heard him singing in the bathroom, and her face brightened as she went happily to the bright sunny kitchen of the lodge.

She would be sorry to leave this little house in the middle of all the trees. She would miss the pleasant company of Miss Hayes, and her bedroom where the small brown rabbits often hopped up on her windowsill and snuffled their noses against the pane.

Still, it would be exciting in the hotel.

Jim Costello had told her that there was nothing as heady as a successful hotel, the place buzzed with activity and you got the feeling that it was alive twenty-four hours a day. She smiled at the memory.

He had added that every hotel needed a really beautiful woman to be at the center of it, and now Fernscourt was going to have that as well as everything else.

Kerry came out, his hair damp, wearing clean white trousers and a white sweater.

"That's more like it," he grinned at her. "Now tell me what you've been doing."

Grace felt that it was he who should do the telling. She had been doing nothing, she said.

"Nothing? Every day, all day, off on a bicycle with young Ryan. Don't tell me you've been doing nothing." His eyes were very bright.

"Well, you know, we've been fishing and talking and just fooling around." She giggled apologetically.

His face looked hard somehow. "What kind of fooling around?"

"Oh heavens, you know. Nothing too serious."

"It had better not be serious, it had damn well better not be."

"What do you mean?" She was frightened.

"Don't make yourself cheap; you're not to throw yourself away on some kid from a pub who's wet behind the ears but who knows like any animal what he wants and will do all he can to take it."

Grace jumped up, eyes blazing. "Michael is *not* an animal. I will not have you speak of him like that."

"I will until I know he has done you no harm, that he hasn't forced you to do anything you shouldn't have done."

"I've done plenty of things I shouldn't have done, like you have as well," Grace cried with spirit. "Anything I do with Michael I do because I want to."

"You must not want to; he must not make you *want* to. You're so young, you're my sister, you shouldn't put out for any country hick."

"It's not like that."

"It had better not be."

"And what about you, you and Dara, why is nobody saying anything to you about all this?"

"That's different." He was dismissive.

"But why is it different?"

"I'm a man; it's different for men."

"Dara isn't a man."

The phone rang sharply into the silence between them.

"That's Michael," Grace said in relief. But it wasn't; it was a man with a Northern Ireland accent to speak to Kerry.

Kate sent Declan away when she heard that the doctor had arrived.

Martin White smiled at the youngest Ryan, who hadn't yet turned into a hooligan like his brother Eddie.

"Will you miss them when they go back tomorrow, or will it be a bit of peace for you?" he asked.

"I suppose I'll feel they can get up to less trouble inside the walls of the convent and the brothers' than roaming wild around this place," Kate sighed.

"I know, my two have gone cracked on this riding nonsense, hard hats and crops and boots, and God knows what else, you're lucky you were spared that. You're pale, any pains and aches?"

"I've an upset stomach, I seem a bit nauseous somehow, but I think that's only tasting all this food we're going to be offering in the café . . . if there's anyone to offer it to."

"Do you need to take this on?"

"It's take this on or go under."

"The compensation maybe?" he suggested tentatively.

"It won't keep a family, Martin. Oh Lord God how I'm dreading Thursday, the palms of my hands start to sweat at the thought."

Dr. White said that he would give Kate a mild tranquilizer on the day of the case.

"Will it make me dopey and stupid-sounding?" Kate wanted to know.

"Nothing could do that." Dr. White was amused.

"Maybe I don't need any tranquilizer. I'm slow enough already." She seemed very down.

"It will take the sharp edge off the anxiety, that's all. It won't affect your powers to say yes or no to a million pounds."

"I'm not the one saying yes or no. It'll be John—John and Fergus."

He looked at her sharply. In the last few weeks she had seemed less alive to him. It was hard to pinpoint exactly what it was.

"I know I don't have a degree in psychiatry, but is there anything wrong, Kate? Anything you want to talk about?"

She gave him a brittle smile. "Anything wrong apart from being paralyzed, in a wheelchair for life, possibly losing all our trade to a bar across the river? No, not much."

Dr. White was often accused of having a poor bedside manner. He was unsparing of his time and energy to help a patient but he was never at hand with the coaxing and condolences that a lot of the parish felt they needed from time to time.

He stood up and prepared to leave. He didn't even acknowledge what Kate had said.

"See you on Thursday," he said briefly and was almost out the door when Kate called out.

"Martin. I'm sorry."

"Why should *you* be sorry?" He had his hand on the door.

"I mean for being a smart aleck. You were being kind. There *is* something wrong. But it's very hard to say it."

Dr. Martin White stood sympathetically waiting for her to find the words. He would have stood there all day and all night if necessary and Kate knew it.

"I'm not in charge anymore. I'm not a person who decides things . . ." She fumbled with a lace-edged handkerchief. The doctor looked at her, trying to get her to say more.

"It's just that there's no *me* nowadays, as if I'd lost my personality or something."

He was blank in his lack of comprehension. "I don't know what to say to you except that you must be half cracked. Aren't you a legend for miles around, and as for being in charge, wouldn't you buy and sell the rest of us? They say it was you that thought up that café idea. Bound to be a gold mine."

Kate knew when there was no more to be gained. She thanked the doctor, said that it must be just an attack of nerves over the court case, and told herself again that it was a strange irony that the only one in the whole place who understood what she felt was Patrick O'Neill. She had a very strange dream about Patrick that kept coming back to her because it was so vivid.

She dreamed that she was in Coyne's wood with him and he had taken out a huge shovel and started to dig a great hole.

It was a grave, he said, like one of the mass famine graves and it was for all the people in Mountfern. They should have died over a hundred years back at the time of the Famine, but they had gone on living by mistake. That was why he had come back, to finish the job properly.

In the dream she asked him if anyone would be saved, and he had said only Kate herself could go free. She wasn't from this place to begin with, and so if she ran now, she could go back to where she came from. She had tried to run and had woken in terror with none of the usual joy that a dreamer would feel waking from a dream like that. Because asleep or awake, Kate Ryan would never run through the wood, and she kept seeing Patrick's face smiling sympathetically at her. He seemed to be across a room as he smiled. A courtroom.

Michael and Dara walked quickly across the bridge.

They told each other they had better hurry to Leonard's to buy exercise books and pencils for tomorrow. They ran past the presbytery and up Bridge Street. They weren't really hurrying to buy their stationery, they wanted to be over the bridge before the thoughts started to come, as they always did.

And because in their different ways they wanted to think about the tunnel.

Dara thought that if Michael had taken Grace there, then she too could have used it. It made her furious to think that this was why she had lost Kerry O'Neill, because she wouldn't trust him, she wouldn't love him properly. And she had wanted to so very much. Why hadn't she told Michael ages ago that she would take Kerry to the tunnel?

There it would all have been safe and it would have been like a home.

Grace and Michael obviously thought so, she told herself bitterly, remembering the sofa piled with cushions.

Michael had thought they would never leave the tunnel. Everywhere he could see signs of Grace and he being there together. It was astonishing that Dara hadn't noticed. But what was alarming him much more was what he had seen. The cushions on the sofa like that—he and Grace hadn't put them there, and there was a rug that didn't belong to them. There were matches and some orange peel.

Somebody else had been in the tunnel.

He could not believe that Grace would have told anyone else. And it wasn't possible to believe that she might have been there with anyone else.

Jim Costello spoke briefly to Brian Doyle.

He said he knew O'Neill's demand to have the rooms ready was ridiculous, but for God's sake let Doyle not forget who was paying their salaries.

"He's more nervous about the bloody court case than he is about sinking his whole fortune in the hotel," Jim said wonderingly.

"Wouldn't you think he'd have more sense?" Brian had little time for finer feelings.

"In a way I can see what he means. The whole place is waiting eagerly to know what will happen. If Kate Ryan doesn't get enough, the mood will turn against him fast. It won't be easy for him to carry on here."

"Ah, that's only a small problem compared to the troubles he has with his family life . . ."

Jim hadn't gotten where he was by being a gossip. "I don't know much about that, I only see the work side of him."

"You do in your arse. You know like the rest of us know that his son had a go at his woman, and if the place doesn't go up in fireworks over that, then it never will."

"At least his daughter is no trouble to him," Jim said primly.

Brian knew everything. "I saw you had your eye peeled in that direction. Sound man," he said approvingly.

"She's only a child, but are we going to see your fiancée Peggy at the opening?"

"Probably," Brian muttered without any great enthusiasm.

"Good, make sure she's on the invitation list, they're posting them next week."

"Isn't it a miracle that it's going to open at last?" Brian looked around him in surprise.

"Take that look off your face, Brian, people will think you're surprised it's staying up. That's not good for business."

Kerry was listening carefully to the voice at the other end of the phone.

The lady had told the bank that after all she had made a mistake, the check had not been stolen.

Kerry let out a great sigh of relief. Rachel must have seen that it was pointless.

He had never felt so relieved in his whole life. But the voice on the phone told Kerry that his problems were far from over. They were only starting. There would be no criminal proceedings since the check was no longer deemed stolen. But it was still stopped. It could not be cashed.

Kerry still had to find his thousand pounds.

"It's impossible," he said in a thin unnatural voice.

There was a silence.

Then he was given a proposition. He could do something for them instead. Repay his debt that way.

His whole body strained and his knuckles were white as he waited to hear what they wanted him to do.

It would involve storing some merchandise out of sight in a very safe place. A place that nobody knew about.

Kerry could feel his muscles relaxing. He knew the exact place.

Michael went to the lodge that evening.

Miss Hayes had come back on the excursion train from Dublin, she was showing her materials to Grace.

"I'd make you a dress for the opening, but you'll want something smarter from the shops," Miss Hayes said.

"Why can't you wait till the opening?"

"The ship sails before."

Michael seemed impatient and not anxious to join in the conversation. Grace eventually seemed to understand and went outside with him.

"Did you tell anybody? About the tunnel—did you tell anyone else?" His eyes looked wild.

"Why? What's wrong?"

"I went there today with Dara. She didn't notice we'd been there, but it's all changed, someone else has been there, maybe even sleeping there."

Suddenly it clicked in Grace's mind. Of course that was where Kerry had been spending the nights.

Michael had made her swear she would tell nobody, but she had told Kerry the last time he was home from Donegal. She hadn't thought it mattered. Not Kerry.

Looking at Michael's face she realized it did matter.

"No," Grace said. "Of course I didn't, you told me not to tell anyone, didn't you?"

Dara walked in Coyne's wood. She didn't expect to see him, and she didn't want to see him.

But he was there, as some part of her knew he would be. Because she didn't feel very surprised.

He looked happy and relaxed, not strained as he had been before.

Dara said nothing. She stood there in her yellow and white candy-striped dress with the big artificial yellow rose pinned to it. Mademoiselle Stephanie had given her that when she was leaving France, that and a wink of complicity.

Tomorrow she would go back to school, and this strange summer would be over. There was no birthday party planned for the twins this year. Their party room was a café now, and the date was almost coinciding with their mother's compensation case.

She looked at him levelly.

He put his head on one side and smiled.

Dara would not smile back.

"What is it? Tell me."

"You know. The whole town knows."

"I don't." He was innocent and bewildered.

"Mrs. Fine."

"She's pathetic," he said with scorn. "She is quite pathetic. You know that she fancied my father for years, he got tired of her and now she made . . . Well, it's too much to talk about really."

"No it isn't."

"Well, she made some silly advances toward me, she got all drunk and slobbery, and crying, and saying she loved it here in Mountfern and these are her type of people and why couldn't she stay . . ."

It sounded familiar and likely from Mrs. Fine's conversations with Dara's mother. From what she had overheard and picked up in the past.

"And then she became silly. Well, it's gross, and I had to untangle myself, and put her to bed. I went back the next morning to see that she hadn't done herself in or anything, and I got her breakfast and because I did these uncharacteristically nice things the whole place says I'm sleeping with her."

Dara looked at him. Willing it to be true.

"I mean, Dara, look at me. Am I the kind of guy who would go for a woman of that age, a little tubby Brooklyn Jewess? It's ludicrous."

He was so handsome, he was not the guy to go for a woman old enough to be his mother.

"Are you going to say anything to me or will you stand there all day just repeating accusations?"

"I don't know."

He looked hurt and bewildered.

Dara spoke. "When I was in France I saw these fireflies. I didn't know what they were, they were like little teeny weeny fires in the evening. I asked Madame what they were called. She said *'mouche á feu.'* They used to make me pronounce words so that I'd get it right. I kept saying it, *'Mouche á feu, voici la mouche á feu.'* Firefly, firefly. And I thought of you. I thought of you every time."

He took her in his arms, and she laid her head against his chest. She could hear his heart beating.

Dara spoke almost dreamily. "I found out why we don't have them in Ireland, I asked, and now I know. They're sort of exotic fireflies, and Ireland is too cold and wet and windy for them. They wouldn't survive here. They wouldn't survive at all."

Grimly and with far less pleasure than he thought that he would feel, Patrick O'Neill moved into his hotel. He decided to do it without ceremony, without any marking of the occasion. He would reserve all the festivity for the grand opening.

He moved his own things in and slept a night in the place he had created. He did not sleep well.

All kinds of unwelcome thoughts came to him, dreams, and half dreams. He got up eventually and walked in the moonlight, as he had walked years and years ago it now seemed, when the place was a ruin.

The moon hadn't changed much nor had the river that it shone down on. But everything else had.

Twenty-Two

$\mathcal{O}$live Hayes left Mountfern exactly the way she wanted to, in dignity and with style but with no razzamatazz.

For four years she had lived quietly in this family, kept their confidences and made no judgments about them. Now she would no longer be part of their lives.

Kerry barely acknowledged her departure.

She had known this would be the case. She was no longer of any use to him. There had been a time when he had been charming, but charm was a currency, no need to spend any of it on Miss Hayes.

She felt a great sense of peace and achievement, and no last-minute regrets about leaving. It was what she had always planned.

Mr. O'Neill's generosity made it possible to come back if things did not work out. She was letting her little house in the town to a young couple with a baby. They paid a small rent and would continue to put that into Sheila Whelan's post office for her.

When Olive Hayes called quietly and decorously to say goodbye to the people in the pub, she had a quick moment with Kate. Unlike most of the place who would have wished her luck in the compensation case, Miss Hayes had a different wish.

"I spent a lot of time, Mrs. Ryan, wondering what to say about this and perhaps I am just an interfering old busybody, but perhaps, being confined to the house, you mightn't realize that Kerry O'Neill is a very dangerous young man."

"Oh Miss Hayes, don't I know it," Kate sighed. "I know only too well how unstable he is. I did my best by sending her to France, but I can't banish the child from her own town forever."

"With respect, it's not that he's unstable, he is very aware of what he is doing and what he wants. He is totally self-centered. Perhaps with the help of God your daughter will see through him."

"Get out there fast to those nuns and start them praying." Kate smiled wanly.

Olive Hayes took her seriously. "When I heard that he would be living in the lodge on his own, I did ask Bernadette to get some prayers said for a special intention."

Kate held her hand for a long moment before Olive Hayes left Mountfern.

It was, as Michael expected, not nearly as easy to see Grace once she was in the hotel. The excitement of the new life, the attention and the fuss kept her busy all the hours that she had free from school.

They had arranged to wave to each other at certain times at night and make mirror flashes across the river.

Michael had worked out "I love you" in Morse code, but Grace said it was endless, and you'd be exhausted working out all the short-long short-longs of it just for one sentence.

Tommy Leonard seemed to understand. "Wasn't it easier before girls?" he said to Michael.

"Like when there was just Adam in the garden of Eden?" Michael laughed.

"No, you know what I mean."

"But you don't have any problems with Jacinta; she's there all the time, living on the other side of the street and everything." Michael was envious.

"It isn't Jacinta I want, you thick oaf."

Grace told Michael that her father was giving her a new dress for the opening. She was to go to Dublin to buy it. She was going to ask for the day off from school. Could Michael come with her and help her choose?

School had reopened and the notion of giving Michael a day off to go shopping with a girl in Dublin was about as acceptable to the authorities as suggesting a trip on a flying saucer.

"Come on, Mike, think of something."

"But it's not just Brother Keane, he'd have to explain to Mom and to Dad and if I went without saying anything to them, Eddie would hear and tell, or Tommy Leonard would. Lord, Grace, we can't just waltz off to Dublin as if we were adults."

"We are adults—in lots of ways." Grace pouted at him.

"Yes, well." Michael reddened, thinking of their last visit to the tunnel. He felt it was official to go there now, now that Dara had given permission. So he was more adventurous in his approach to Grace as a celebration of this.

"Don't be such a mother's boy," she taunted.

That hurt. Especially since it was really his mother he feared most. He had the feeling that she worried about his friendship with Grace. And that she would be astounded to think he would even suggest the shopping trip.

That morning Kate had spoken for the first time to Dara and Michael about the upcoming court case.

She had said that she wanted them to give her all the support they could. What she needed was to know that they wouldn't go around blabbing or being silly about it. That they would be the model of good behavior for just these few days, since the eyes of Mountfern would be on the whole family for a short time. Some people wished them to get a fortune; some wished them not to get anything significant in case it would prejudice the hotel in any way. But the truth of the matter was that there would be a respectable sum of money which would be placed in a bank for the children's education.

It was all upsetting having to go to court, but what would make it worthwhile was the knowledge that the Ryan children were working hard and would deserve any benefit that might come to them.

She had been quite solemn, and for the first time for a very long while she had sounded sad.

She had said that in many ways her own life was over, and that this was not something to feel bitter about; people's lives ended in different ways. But it would all have a meaning if her children were to be strong and to have a bit of class when faced with the wagging tongues and overexcitement of a small parish.

Michael and Dara had promised that they would not let her down.

Going to Dublin midweek on a train, telling Brother Keane a pack of lies—that would be letting her down.

Michael said he couldn't go and help Grace choose a dress.

Grace said that was all right, then, she might ask Jim Costello was he going to drive to Dublin anytime soon, she could get a ride in his car. Michael wasn't to give it another thought.

The District Court sat every week in the town, and cases that were of a higher jurisdiction or that were appealed were heard when the Circuit Court came four times a year for a period of three weeks each time.

At one stage there was a judge who had been interested in fishing who had driven out to the Fern each evening after the summer sessions and sat on his little stool looking for all the world like an old tramp. He and Fergus Slattery's father had struck up a friendship without either ever knowing the other was involved in the law, so great was their interest in the fish that swam the Fern and the methods of taking them out of the river.

Nowadays, with better roads and better train services, the barristers and judges didn't spend long in the town. They rarely came as far as Mountfern.

Kate and John Ryan were surprised to see Kevin Kennedy come into the pub the night before the case.

"Fergus didn't say you were coming," Kate said, flustered.

She moved the wheelchair in her quick agile way back over the ramp, and they beckoned him into her big green room. How right it had been to make this room into a proper sitting place for her. Seeing that she was going to sit for the rest of her days it made it much more bearable to sit in pleasant surroundings and not to apologize for wherever you were.

John got Mary to take over his place pulling pints. Most of the clientele would know who Kevin Kennedy was anyway and what it was about.

"Good luck and get them a fortune," said one man as Kevin squeezed his way past the counter.

"Luck is exactly what it's about," he said, turning around, "it has not a thing to do with what people deserve, or they would get a king's ransom."

His serious voice startled the drinkers. They had expected some sort of joky answer.

"Fergus doesn't even know I'm here . . ." he began when they were in the room.

"Well, don't you think maybe . . ." John began.

"No, no, I'm on my way to him, it's just that we've had an offer. A firm offer. Six thousand pounds. A yes or a no. That's what they say."

"Yes," said Kate.

"We must ask Fergus," said John.

"What do *you* think?" Kate asked John.

"I don't know what to think. We could go into court and fight all day and come out with less but the fact they offer it at all twenty-four hours before the case means they think it might go further against them."

Kevin Kennedy looked from one to another.

There weren't many consultations on his cases, usually it was a matter of working straight from the brief, from the case to advice. But when he had met the people involved in their houses, he had often felt his city prejudices against country people were confirmed. They were so often inarticulate, and often grasping. This time it was different. There was a gentle pace of life that he liked in Mountfern; there was a graciousness about this couple and their handsome dark-eyed children whom he had seen briefly.

There was a sense of repressed energy about the crippled Kate Ryan that gave her more life than most women who were able to walk and run. She was quick, opinionated and impatient, and she had had a long hard lesson in having to learn that she must lean on others. He liked the husband too. All very genial and easygoing on the outside, but he had a logical reasoning mind. Fergus Slattery had said the man was a poet too, in a small way.

He felt involved with these people in a way he hadn't felt involved for a long time. He had been through every case reported: the factory worker who only this year had been awarded £3,000. The sum had been based on his earnings, and how much more he could have expected. He had been twenty-eight, he had lost an eye. Everyone had accepted that £3,000 was fair; he had been earning £14 a week.

There was an agricultural laborer in his mid forties. His injuries were terrible even to read about. He got £7,000. His case had included the plea that he would never be able to marry and have a family. The award was considered high. There was that woman who had spent four months in the special hospital in England. Her barristers had proved such mental anguish, the compensation was £7,000.

They were looking at him, as if he should know. And he didn't know. He couldn't tell them either what was fair or what would happen.

"It's very tempting to say that we'll take it," Kate said. "It's so tempting that I have to think it's the wrong decision."

John had his hand on hers as he spoke. "It would be such an easy way to finish it off. To say we'll take it and put it in the bank for the children to go to university maybe, or for rainy days which may well come this way." He nodded his head across in the direction of Fernscourt, and Kevin Kennedy remembered the danger to their small business from the new hotel.

"So you'd like to refuse it . . . ?"

"I think we shouldn't accept it too readily," John said. "I know that sounds like sitting on the fence . . . I'm not a gambling man, and I'm not in the world of doing deals or bargaining, but I have this feeling you shouldn't accept the first offer. Am I right?"

Kevin was about to say there was no need to accept anything now as there would undoubtedly be time to do so tomorrow, but Kate spoke first.

"I'm sure you know how much more than just a mere solicitor Fergus has been to us. It's as if his own spine were broken." She spoke clearly and without any sense of drama. She just wanted to be sure he understood how important the tall gangling country lawyer was in their lives.

"Yes, of course, of course," he murmured.

"So I suppose you will bring him in on this, won't you, and ask him what he thinks we should do. I don't think John and I should really make any decision without Fergus being here."

"Of course. I just wanted to get a gut reaction. Sometimes a surplus of lawyers can confuse people rather than help."

"Did you get a gut reaction?" Kate asked.

"Yes. You'd take anything, Mrs. Ryan, anything not to have to face a court. It's your back, it's your legs, we should listen to you. Your husband is aware of all this, but he's thinking about what you'll both feel years from now, and trying to take that into account. I'm with Mr. Ryan, but then, it didn't happen to me."

Fergus said, as they knew he would say, that it was not enough.

Kevin Kennedy said that it was about what they could hope for from the jury.

Dr. White said that was a lot of money, he had many patients with broken bodies after car accidents and they hadn't got a third of that.

Fergus said that they were dealing with multimillionaires here, big foreign international companies with coffers of money which they guarded like misers and wouldn't give out to the people that were struck down and obviously deserving it.

John said that he knew he was a cautious man but wouldn't six thousand pounds go a very long way, and buy them everything they ever needed? And since no money would buy Kate the chance of walking again, then maybe they should take this now and be done with it. But, then . . .

Kate sat very still as they talked.

They leaned over to make a point; they interrupted each other. Four men all wanting the best for her, and coming at it in their different ways. She felt curiously detached from it. As if up in the air looking down at them, the doctor, the solicitor, the barrister and the publican.

They talked themselves out at around the same time, and they all looked at her.

"It's up to you in the end, Kate. Whatever you say, that's what we'll do."

She looked slowly around the little group.

"Fight," she said. "I think we owe it to the children to do this for them. Let's fight to the finish."

Kevin Kennedy said that he was going to spend the night in Mountfern. He had heard there was a delightful old-world place called the Grange. Everyone exchanged glances. What was wrong with it? He wanted to know. Nothing, it was just that Patrick O'Neill stayed there.

"He's moved," Kate said. "He went into the hotel."

This surprised the others, but then Kate always knew everything ahead of most people.

"That's fine then." Kevin Kennedy was businesslike. "I'll give them a call. If our friend Mr. O'Neill has moved out, that's all right, then."

* * *

It was a sunny morning.

"I don't know whether that makes it better or worse," Kate said.

John had slept on the divan bed in her room. Not that either of them slept very much. He had gotten up to make tea twice. He pulled back the curtains over the glass doors to reveal Leopold sitting mournfully outside.

"If that animal lets as much as the smallest yowl out of him, I'll kill him with my own bare hands," Kate said.

Leopold seemed to sense the danger. He raised his front paw hopefully, as if someone might shake hands with him through the closed door.

She looked sleepy and anxious.

John stood beside her bed. "Could you get another hour if I closed off the light again, and left you in peace?"

"No, no. I'm too jumpy."

"So am I. I can neither stand, sit, nor lie."

"What are you going to do?" She saw him pulling on a jumper over the shirt he had worn the previous day. He obviously wasn't going to get washed and ready for the court at this early hour.

"I don't know. I feel trapped in here, somehow."

Something in her face made him realize how trapped Kate must feel all the time.

"Not that I'm going to go out or anything," he said hastily.

"Take me out too."

"It's only halfpast six in the morning."

"Come on, we'll go for a walk."

He dressed her, and she slid into her chair. Quietly they let themselves out the front door of the pub—they didn't go through the backyard for fear of waking Mary Donnelly.

The river was glorious in the September early morning. Leopold trotted with them, delighted with the chance of an early-morning outing but staying at a respectful distance.

Up past the Rosemarie hair salon, its pink curtains drawn firmly.

"Do you think she's still at it?" John asked.

Kate laughed. "Not at all, she's far too busy getting ready for American hairstyles, she even has books on how to do it so that they'd like it."

"Oh, she always knew how to do it so that they'd like it," John said. "They tell me of course, I wouldn't know from any personal experience."

And as they came back again to the footbridge and the day was about to begin for everyone else, they stopped and looked over at Fernscourt.

They could see Patrick O'Neill in his shirt sleeves at one of the windows on the first floor.

"It's a hard day for him too," Kate said.

They looked across the river to the dock, up the path with its rockeries and shrubs leading to the great sweep where the drive came in. They looked at the steps up to the big house, the bedroom wings fanning back on either side, the workmen beginning to arrive in twos and threes.

And they saw Patrick standing still at his window.

He must have seen them too.

But because it was the day that it was, nobody waved at anyone else.

* * *

Rachel was coming to get Kate dressed.

They had been such friends for so long that nobody saw anything remotely odd about this merging of both sides of the case.

They had several differences of opinion about what she should wear with the simple gray-and-white dress which had been ironed by Carrie, and then done again by Dara, and finally given a going over by Mary.

Rachel said no lady could be seen without gloves. Kate said only the gentry wore gloves around here.

Rachel said a little eye shadow made Kate look much more attractive. Kate said that a country jury would think eye shadow meant she was the whore of Babylon.

"Stop making people into yokels, Kate, this is the sixties; they all move with the times here like everywhere else."

Kate said she wasn't going to risk it. She had promised Fergus she would look demure.

They were ready far too early.

Rachel tried to distract her with tales that didn't have any bearing on what was about to happen.

That was harder to do than she had imagined. Almost all her conversation was related to Patrick or to his hotel.

"Grace is going to Dublin for the day," she said, thinking this might be a fairly neutral road to go down.

"Don't I know!" Kate exclaimed. "My poor Michael is distraught over it all. I told him that it was very vain of Grace to go miles and miles to buy *another* new dress when she has trunks of them, but that was the wrong thing to say. No criticism of the lady."

"Princess Grace," Rachel said.

"She *is* a bit of a madam, isn't she? But I'm prejudiced. Anyone who could lead Michael Ryan any kind of dance should be in the darkest hob of hell in my view."

"Perhaps she'll not get anywhere with the young hotel manager." Rachel smiled at the wonderful partisan nature of Kate's reactions.

"I'd prefer if she tired of Michael, really, and did it soon, so that both the twins could get over these glittering young O'Neills sooner rather than later."

"Yes, we'd all be better if we had gotten over the O'Neills early in life," Rachel said bitterly.

Rachel looked very sad, and for the first time since Kate had known her she thought that her friend looked old. The life had gone out from her face. And when that vivacity wasn't there for all to see, there were lines instead, lines that looked quite deep.

She took Rachel's hand in hers and stroked it silently for a moment. She hardly trusted herself to speak in case she said the wrong thing or that she started to cry.

"Stop it, quite enough self-pity," Rachel said. "It's your day of woe today, not mine. Do you feel all right?"

"Yes, Dr. White gave me something to calm me down. I feel fine."

"Have you been to the lavatory?"

"Yes, *and* I've hardly had food or drink pass my lips so I should be all right."

They talked to each other through the mirror, each seeing the reflection of

629

the other. It wasn't quite the same as talking face to face. You could be more indiscreet.

"Kate?"

"Yes?"

"He wants you to get a lot, you know that. He was delighted you refused the offer. He says . . ."

"No . . . please, no."

"You're my friend, you'll always be my friend, even when I'm an old lady in a home in Flatbush."

"Of course I will."

"When he's married to somebody with ten saints' names who had the good fortune to come from this one-horse town . . ."

"Rachel . . ."

"What loyalty do I owe him? He says you shouldn't take any less . . ."

The chair spun around. Kate's eyes were blazing.

"No, do you hear me, *no*. You must stop. If there's going to be any dignity, anything saved from this circus and farce that I'm heading off to, then the only way is to do it honestly . . ."

"I wasn't going to . . ."

"Yes you were, you were going to tell me what his side are prepared to go to. I can't know that, don't you see that? I must never know what they're willing to give."

"It's just because you're my friend. I wanted the best for you," Rachel cried, still bewildered by the intensity of it all.

Kate's voice lowered. "I *know* you mean well, but can't you see, if I have any hope at all of living what passes as a normal life with this man as my neighbor across the river, with my son head over heels with his daughter . . . with us depending on him for our custom from his hotel . . . then how would I feel if I had seen his hand?"

"He's on your side, that's all I was saying."

"I know, I know. Now please, can I beg you to say no more than that. Now, Rachel Fine, can you kiss me goodbye and good luck?"

Rachel bent to kiss her in the chair. She put her arms around Kate and laid her cheek against Kate's thin cheek.

"May you always have the best of all possible things and even things that are impossible," she said in a shaky voice.

"Haven't I you as a great good friend? That's worth a lot to me," Kate said as she maneuvered her chair to the door.

John and Dr. White were waiting for her in the pub, Fergus and Kevin Kennedy would be already at the courthouse.

Rachel stood in the green room after Kate had gone. She didn't know if this was praying or not, but she went to the mournful picture of the Madonna, one she had chosen herself because there were a lot of green and blue hues in it and it went with the room.

She stood in front of it and looked into the big sad eyes of the picture.

"Please don't let them cheat her, don't let them talk her into a cheap deal. Go on, please. It's not much to ask. There are thousands of good things and bad things happening all over the place today. Let this be a good one for Kate Ryan. Please."

* * *

The morning was hot and heavy. Dara's mind would not stay on parsing. "Come on, Dara, wake up. Subordinate adverbial clause modifying what?"

"What, Sister?"

"What is it modifying?"

"I'm not sure, Sister Laura."

"You might be a lot surer if you looked at the book instead of outside the window, it isn't written in letters of fire on the Dublin Road. The clause, for your information, reads . . . Come *on* Dara, this is very simple if you just concentrate."

"I know, Sister." The girl's face looked wretched.

Sister Laura knew all about the case that was coming to court today.

"There's no better way of taming the language than this. You'll know forever how sentences are constructed." The nun's round face was eager to help the white-faced child.

"Who else knows . . . ?" Sister Laura decided to take the attention away from Dara Ryan.

"Sister! Sister!" A few of them waved their hands.

Sister Laura looked around the classroom to choose, and her eye fell on the empty seat where Grace O'Neill normally sat. The child had gone to Dublin for the day. Her father had asked permission.

"Grace will say she has to see the doctor. That's not true, she's going to buy a dress. But it's not as frivolous as it seems, Sister Laura. I want her to be out of Mountfern on the day of the compensation case, so I asked the young manager to invent an excuse to take her. It would be more diplomatic. More sensitive."

He had been right, of course. He was a very good man. Not just because he had given them the money for the school hall or all that extra material for curtains that the Jewish lady had delivered. But he really was kind and out for people's good. Sister Laura couldn't bear it when she heard people speaking badly of him. It was only envy, envy of a man who had done so well and come home to spend his money where his father had been nobody. She knew that if the compensation had been up to him, he'd have given the Ryans all they ever needed. But of course it would have been very hard to live with for them, knowing that it was his charity.

Sister Laura's eyes turned to the holy picture which hung in the classroom, Our Lady of the Wayside. She looked into the sad eyes of Our Lady and made a quick prayer that she would ask her Son to give proper compensation to the Ryans. Then she said that she would parse the sentence herself and would like the entire class to give their undivided attention.

Brother Keane had warned them not to trifle with him today; he had a toothache. Nothing that was bad enough to mean he had to leave his charges and go into the town to the dentist, but certainly something that was bad enough to remind him of its existence every waking moment. He felt it was only fair to the boys to apprise them of this fact.

Michael wondered again and again where Grace and Jim Costello would be now. There had been no difficulty in her getting off school and she had said they were going to set out early.

Michael had cycled across the Grange early to wish her a good trip; she had come down the stairs all dressed up in a yellow flowery dress he had never seen before. She looked as fresh as a daisy.

"You look terrific," he had said. "You don't need a new frock at all. Wouldn't that be lovely for the hotel opening?"

It had been the wrong thing to say. Still, she had been pleased he had cycled all that way to see her. She kissed him without his suggesting it. Just put both her arms around his neck and stood on tiptoe to kiss him, and at that moment Jim Costello's car had pulled up.

"I know we swore we wouldn't talk about the case," she whispered to Michael.

"I know." He swallowed.

"But whatever happens we'll still be as we are. And I hope your Mom gets a lot, I really do."

Something in the way she said it made him feel put out. But perhaps it was the fact of that awful Jim Costello with his sickening smile sitting waiting for her. That must have been what it was.

The classroom was airless. A dying wasp beat uselessly against the window. Even if it got out, it wouldn't last another hour. Michael wondered if he should finish it off now with his ruler.

Brother Keane was looking at him. Did he imagine it or was there some sympathy in the teacher's swollen face?

Today they were doing an exercise which the class hated more than anything. Brother Keane would ask them to speak on any topic for one minute. There were to be no ems or ahs. There was to be no fooling around or imitating the speaker. The brothers hoped it would make the boys more articulate and able to express themselves. The boys hated it, and though never short of a word in the playground, they were struck dumb when asked to speak in front of the class.

"Michael Ryan. Give us the benefit of your knowledge and experience of the pike, a fish which abounds in our River Fern."

There was a snort around the room. Either this was a trick question of Brother Keane's or else he was going soft. The pike was dead easy to talk about; they'd all been fishing for pike since they were old enough to be allowed near the water.

"What would you want to know about it, Brother?" Michael's face was anxious. "There's so many ways to start."

"Well, kindly choose one, and don't hold up the class anymore." Brother Keane's hand was on his face.

"Well, like any fish the pike needs oxygen, not for its lungs because they don't have human lungs or animal lungs even; they don't have any lungs to speak of. Not lungs as we'd know them."

"Could you tell us what they do have instead of what they don't, please. Start again."

"Pike have to take in water through their mouths, and in that water there's a bit of oxygen like there is in the air. And they let it out the gills. But that's what all fish do. So what's different about the pike? The pike has a bad reputation like a wolf has in the animal kingdom. They say he preys on the other fish and lies in wait for them in the reeds on the river bank. But in a way that's all to the good because a pike is carrying out a function; he's making the river bed a cleaner better place. It's his nature to go for what he can. It's only ignorance, really, to condemn the pike; we'd all be pike if we could, and the world might be a better place if there were more pike in it ready to go out and scavenge for themselves."

The boy's face was red and angry. Nobody had said a word against the pike. Not ever, to Brother Keane's knowledge.

Out in the yard earlier, Brother Keane had heard voices raised about the court case which was being decided at this very moment.

The boy was said to be very friendly with the daughter of the house, and it was probably a question of divided loyalties.

Brother Keane liked Michael Ryan. Compared to his younger brother, Eddie, he was like the Archangel Gabriel.

"That's very informative and well explained," he said, to the mystification of the class. "Now Tommy Leonard, may we have your discourse please on the benefits of the Rural Electrification Scheme."

"Ah, God, Brother, that's much harder than pike," said Tommy Leonard, who had been discovering that life was very far from fair.

Mrs. Daly asked Rita Walsh when there would be any news from the court house.

But Marian Johnson answered first, she said that it could be anytime from eleven in the morning on. It might be settled outside without their having to go in. She knew this from the highest authority. A Mr. Kennedy, who was representing the Ryans, had stayed in the Grange last night. A very pleasant man, from Dublin. He was going to spend a second night there no matter what the outcome. He said it was too far to drive back to Dublin, and the Grange was exactly the kind of place he had always wanted to stay in but never come across.

Marian patted her hair reflectively and Rita Walsh sensed another reason to bring Miss Johnson and her thin flyaway hair back on a regular basis to the Rosemarie hair salon.

Canon Moran and Father Hogan had been asked by several parishioners to pray for a special intention. And indeed to offer Mass for that intention. Nowhere had the intention been defined.

The priests agreed that it must have to do with the court case, and that one side definitely wanted the Ryans to get a great deal of money and the others wanted them to get very little in case it would somehow offend O'Neill.

"It's a poser, isn't it?" Young Father Hogan had said.

"Not at all, we will just pray that justice will be done in the courts today. That covers it all," said Canon Moran, who had lived a very long time and understood almost everything.

"I'd better leave you and stop hiding here in this nice quiet place." Sheila Whelan had drained the teapot.

"It *is* a nice quiet place. You were very good to settle me here." Mary Donnelly spoke gruffly in her gratitude.

"Wasn't it lucky they got you, just when they needed someone? They'd never have survived without you."

Mary hardly remembered that summer and its shock and sadness now. She rarely thought of the man who had let her down so badly. Even when she was condemning men in general, the face of this one did not come easily to mind.

Sergeant Sheehan passed by as the women came out into the sunshine.

"Starting early, Sheila," he said jokily.

"Lord, I've been discovered," she laughed.

She looked thoughtful when he had gone.

"What is it?" Mary noticed her face.

"I don't know, I was tempted to talk to him there about something, but I can see I'm getting as bad as the rest of them."

"What was it?"

"Probably nothing, but I saw a lot of activity over on the towpath. You know, beyond the bridge on the other side of the river. Lights in the middle of the night over there, and banging about."

"What on earth were *you* doing on the towpath in the middle of the night?"

Sheila had been walking because she couldn't sleep.

She had heard that Joe had died. The nurse had let her know quietly, as she had asked.

She would go to no funeral in Dublin, nor would she tell anyone but Kate Ryan of his death.

Still, it had been impossible to close her own eyes, knowing that Joe Whelan was lying in the mortuary of that Dublin hospital where they had all been so kind to him, and where presumably his woman would recover enough to go and pay her respects, and three of his four children would be with her. The fourth mightn't dare come back from England in case he faced charges.

It had been too hard to try to sleep, so she had walked instead.

"Oh, you know me, Mary, I'm as odd as two left shoes."

"Maybe you imagined it," Mary said.

"Maybe I did," said Sheila.

Fergus felt his hands shaking when he started to shave, so he had put down the razor immediately. He didn't need to come to the court spattered with blood. He wondered what would make them steadier. He thought absently of a small brandy and port; his father used to take that concoction sometimes when he had what was called a chill.

But Fergus rejected it. Warming and steadying it might be, but very soon he might need one every day before shaving, even before getting out of bed.

By the time he was ready to leave the house, his hands had calmed down. He'd done a magnificent job on his face, he thought, not a nick anywhere, and he tied a firm knot on his dark gray tie.

He knew that Kevin Kennedy would barely comb his hair, and yet here was he—the poor country solicitor, an unimportant figure—titivating himself like a peacock. Like a medieval champion going to battle wearing his lady's favors.

God, let him be right, urging them to go on. Kevin Kennedy had said to him a dozen times that it was impossible to know with country juries, but then Kevin was a city man who always feared the country and was never at ease when milk didn't come from bottles and when land didn't mean small manicured gardens.

Fergus gave a wan wave across the street to Sheila Whelan before he climbed into his car and drove to the town. He knew she was the one person in Mountfern who would have the tact not to wish him luck as if it was all a bet on the two-thirty.

Please God let them get twelve thousand pounds. A sum that would see them right for the next fifteen years, until the 1980s. Let them get that. Let Kate know no more anxiety and fear.

Kate sat in the car looking out calmly left and right as they drove the straight road into the town. The September countryside was beautiful this year, it had been a good summer but not too dry. They passed through villages as small as Mountfern, but places with somehow more importance because they were on the main road. Of course, that would all change soon. Already there were new signposts; they wouldn't be a little Midlands outpost for much longer.

"I should come out driving with you more," she said to John, who frowned furiously at the road. "You went to all that trouble to learn to drive for me, and I hardly ever get into the car with you. From now on we're going to have grand drives together, the two of us."

Martin White said gruffly that he hoped they'd be able to afford a better car than this one when the day's work was finished.

"I never thought of getting a new car, did you, John?" Kate was startled at the very idea.

"Lord, not at all, isn't this one fine for us and whatever we want to do in it?"

"Well, what will you do with the money?" Martin White had known them long enough and well enough to ask that question.

"The future, the children . . ."

"Shore the place up a bit . . ."

"Try to keep the business we have . . ."

"And maybe attract a few of the nobs that come to the place across the river."

Suddenly they both laughed.

"We're like the twins," Kate said, wiping her eyes.

They were driving up to the steps of the courthouse.

It was a big ugly building. Neither John nor Kate had ever been in it. Dr. White said he had, a few times, and it was the most disappointing place you ever saw. From outside it was all pillars and steps and looked very imposing. But inside you wouldn't give it the time of day.

The Garda station was attached to one end, and the library to the other, so most people had some kind of knowledge of bits of the building anyway.

It was right slap in the middle of the town, otherwise, they might have been able to pull it down and build something more suitable. Nobody would regret its passing; it was no national monument. It came from a time when justice was administered by the English anyway, so nobody would have any sentimental attachment to it.

But to take down the courthouse would mean dismantling the town. It would also mean losing the only landmark. "I'll meet you on the courthouse steps' was as good a way of making sure you'd find someone in the crowded narrow streets as any other. The bus stop was opposite the courthouse. There were always a few people gathered on its steps, most of them having nothing at all to do with the business of law and justice.

But today they recognized a few people who had to do with their own case. Mike Coyne, a cousin of Jack who worked on the local newspaper. Two of the hospital staff who would have been called as witnesses. And parked right at the bus stop where he was certain to be moved on was Fergus.

Fergus stood beside his car like a soldier on point duty. He could hardly believe it when John Ryan drove Kate and Dr. White into his sight's and all three of them were laughing aloud, as if they hadn't a care or a worry in the world.

People stood around in little clusters. Kate's wheelchair was taken without fuss from the back of the car and moved up to where she was sitting. Gracefully and without making any big production out of it, she slid from one seat to the other. She looked at ease in her chair.

She had been told that there were seventeen steps up to the courthouse door, and there were two choices: either two strong men lifted the chair with her in it—Dr. White and John would do that—or else she could go in a back way through damp long corridors.

She said she preferred the back way. It would be too nerve racking for those carrying and those watching. And she said that somebody should write a letter to the local paper on the lack of facilities for wheelchairs.

They headed toward the back door.

But they didn't get there. Down the steps at a fast pace came two men, the Dublin solicitor and a local man; more men followed—one was in robes, a barrister—and behind him Kevin Kennedy, also in robes.

Fergus felt his heart turn over and realized there had been a last-minute offer.

"Wait for a moment," he called in a strangled voice to the little procession with the wheelchair.

"Is anything wrong?" Kate asked, turning around.

John narrowed his eyes. "It's Mr. Kennedy, he seems to want to talk to us."

"Oh, Jesus, let them not have an adjournment," said Dr. White, who had often made it known that he had little respect for lawyers.

Far far away, it seemed, Patrick O'Neill stood by himself at the other side of the wide steps.

Kate thought it was strange for him to be alone, she had so many people with her. Then who would have come? Grace was at school, Rachel was back in Ryan's pub, and Kerry? Who knew where he would be?

Patrick looked nervous and very much alone. She longed to call out to him. She wished she could send him a message saying his own words back to him, telling him that they would always be friends. It was as he had told her, a formality that was necessary to maintain their friendship.

But she couldn't speak. And anyway they were coming toward her, her side. Kevin Kennedy, and Fergus. Their faces were impassive. Neither of them spoke; they each looked at the other.

"You say it, Fergus," Kevin Kennedy said, standing back a little to give the stage to Fergus Slattery.

"They have made a suggestion." Fergus felt his voice was very thin.

"Yes, Fergus, and what do you think?" John asked.

"What do they say?" Kate was calm.

"They say eight thousand pounds," Fergus said in a voice that came from a million miles away.

"Eight thousand pounds." John said the words.

"Two thousand pounds more than they said yesterday," Kevin Kennedy said, as a further explanation.

"My goodness," said Kate.

There was a silence.

Behind Fergus and Kevin, the other side stood in a little group. Patrick was still at a distance from them. He was not joining in.

Kevin Kennedy spoke then. "As your counsel, I can only give you my opinion, you do not have to take it. You do understand that, Kate?"

He hadn't called her Mrs. Ryan. Nobody noticed.

"Yes indeed, and what do you say?"

"I say that you should have a quiet moment with your husband, and ask each other do you believe that you can live with this as fair and reasonable compensation, and if you can, then I will accept it for you."

There was a pause. Nobody moved.

"And if you think that you will always wonder and worry about what you would have gotten if you fought on, then we will fight on."

Almost imperceptibly Fergus, Kevin, and Martin moved away, and John and Kate were left looking at each other.

John bent down and looked into her eyes. They didn't say anything; neither of them said a word, nor did they nod a head. Then after the long look John stood up.

"We'd like to take it," he said simply, his hand in his wife's cold hand.

Fergus let out his breath like a whistle. "You're doing the right thing, I'm sure of it. I'm sure of it," he said happily.

Kevin Kennedy was smiling too. And Martin White.

The little circle was almost unwilling to break up, but Fergus was the one to do it.

"Come on, Kevin, let's go and tell them," he said like a schoolboy.

Kate held John's hand to her cheek. She didn't need to say anything and neither did he. Dr. White was the only one to speak.

"Look, they're coming over," he said, and there, moving first with halting steps, came Patrick O'Neill. But as he got near them he broke into a run.

In the small dark public house behind the courthouse they went to drink a toast. They drank to insurance companies and to justice being done. Kevin had to go back into court as he was in other cases, cases that had not been settled so amicably on the steps.

He shook their hands and said he hoped to meet them again socially, as he was going to spend the rest of the week in the Grange. In fact, it was so infinitely better than the Grand, the Commerical, or the Central. It was fortunate for him that through this case he had discovered the ideal place to come when he was on circuit. He was delighted that everybody was satisfied. That's what barristers actually wanted, despite their reputation as loving the sound of their own voices.

And Fergus told himself that £8,000 was almost what he had wanted for them, so near that it made no difference. It was worth so much not to have poor Kate go through all that ordeal she had been dreading.

And Dr. White was quite forthcoming for him, and told stories of cases way back where he had been called as an expert witness.

John noted that this pub would not survive if it hadn't been lucky enough to be so well positioned right behind the courts, the library, the county council offices, and the barracks. It had shabby scored tables, and torn dirty linoleum, but it was in the right place. He found his mind straying and hoping that Ryan's Licensed Premises was really in the right place, that it would really get all this extra business that had been promised. He didn't want to worry Kate with it, not now, not for a long time until she had gotten over the trauma of all this.

He looked at her sitting there with them all. Nobody who came in would know she was in a wheelchair; she looked a handsome lively woman, her head thrown back; laughing at some silly tale the doctor was telling. They were all half hysterical with relief that it was over.

Patrick was in high good form too. He resisted the urge to keep buying drinks for everyone and waited instead while the doctor went to the counter or Slattery threw a ten-pound note on the tray of the boy in the dirty apron who was serving them. They were all so happy, so relieved that it was over. He knew he had to go along with the good will and the delight. Because it could do nothing but harm and destruction if he were to let them know that Kate Ryan hadn't gotten half enough for her compensation. The insurance companies were prepared to go to £12,000 outside the court, and even to £14,000 as soon as the case began.

At £8,000 they thought they had gotten away very lightly indeed. But Patrick knew that if this were ever known it would destroy everything he had tried so hard to build.

And of course it wasn't known. It wasn't the kind of thing that the insurance companies would ever reveal. Instead it was reported with excitement in Mountfern. It was quite possibly the exact sum of money that pleased everyone. It was large enough to seem like a sum you look at in the bank and consider yourself a family of substance, which the Ryans would never have been able to do under any other circumstances. But it was not so large it sounded like a punishment. As the news filtered through Mountfern, heads nodded with satisfaction. Even the Dalys, who had always said that anyone could be hit at any time by a bulldozer and that it was a scandal to go suing that good man who was such a benefactor, could find no reason to condemn the settlement. Even Jack Coyne, who said O'Neill should be hounded to the ends of the earth to prove he couldn't go around throwing his weight and machinery into the citizens of this place, had to stop his tirade.

By anyone's standards, including Jack Coyne's, £8,000 was a lot of money.

Sheila Whelan was one of the first to visit Kate.

"You must be so glad it's all over," she said. As always, she had said exactly the right thing and struck the note that Kate wanted to hear. There were no congratulations offered, nor curious questions on how the huge sum of money was going to be spent. Kate was grateful to sit and talk to her.

"There'll be a procession through shortly, I'll leave you alone," Sheila said. "You'll want to talk to everyone else."

"No, I will not. I feel like issuing a bulletin and sticking it up outside over the fuchsias there, saying Mrs. Ryan would like to thank all the inquirers . . ."

"Sit out in the pub, I'd advise, then you won't have to have heart-to-hearts with people, and if anyone you really want to talk to comes, you can come back in here." There was a look of strain around the postmistress's eyes.

"Did anything happen?" Kate asked.

"Not now, I'll tell you all about it again."

"Is it bad?"

"No, it's all over now."

"Oh Sheila." They sat in silence. The sympathy was so great, there were no words for it. A man who walked out and who only wanted to come back when he was on his deathbed. Such things couldn't be mourned in formal ways. They had to remain unsaid.

Sheila had been right; the procession did go on all day. Rita Walsh was in, delighted at the news, overjoyed that it was all over, wondering should they invest it in something that a gentleman friend of hers had told her about. It was like a syndicate and you all put in so much and there was hardly any risk, and people had been known to double their investment in a year. Rita could get the details. Kate told her that she herself would like nothing better but unfortunately John was an old stick-in-the-mud. Rita sympathized over the dullness of husbands in general and said that the offer of advice was always there if Kate needed it. A woman has to look to herself, Rita advised sagely. Kate couldn't meet John's eye as he pretended not to be listening; she was terrified they would break out laughing.

Canon Moran and Father Hogan came in together. They said they were out taking a little constitutional and good news of the happy outcome had reached them. They wanted to say how very pleased they were that God's justice had been done, and it was a wonderful example of how patience and resignation to the will of the Lord was often rewarded, even on this earth.

At least, Canon Moran did all the speaking. Father Hogan looked in disbelief at the trays of currant bread and scones that he saw on the counter. The rehearsals for the Shamrock Café were well under way. There were tables and chairs already in position, and any day now it would be ready to go. John had decided on no big opening ceremony, just let it creep on people.

Father Hogan's pink round face was alight with excitement. "We'll be able to come by here regularly on our constitutional, Canon," he said, as Kate was murmuring that out of their very generous compensation she and John were most anxious to make a small contribution to the needs of the parish. It had been a highly satisfactory visit for the clergy.

Dara heard on the way out of the convent. Jacinta White told her.

"Eight *thousand* pounds. You'll be the quality now." Jacinta sniffed.

"Don't make jokes like that." Dara could hardly take in the amount.

"It's not really a joke, you'll be as good as anyone already."

"We were always as good as anyone."

Jimbo Doyle rang Carrie to tell her.

"I know already, they're all here celebrating," she said.

"Will I come and bring my guitar?" asked Jimbo.

"I don't think they're celebrating *that* much," Carrie said firmly.

Miss Purcell, who was now happily installed in the presbytery looking after the canon and Father Hogan, dropped a note into her old employer, Fergus

Slattery. She said that she was delighted that he had been able to get so much money for Mrs. Ryan and her family, and that his late father would have been proud of him. Miss Purcell added primly that money wasn't everything, but she was sure that the Ryans would use what they got wisely, and perhaps Fergus could tell them about the damp that was seeping through at the Sacred Heart Altar since good people to whom much had been given were often anxious to give some of it back to God at the earliest opportunity.

Michael and Tommy were walking out of the schoolyard when they heard. Tommy was still complaining about the unfairness of teachers. Brother Keane had now in fact succumbed and been taken to the town to visit the dentist by a delivery man who thought he had been bringing boxes of notebooks, pens and other stationery supplies to the brothers, not taking one of the brothers with a swollen face off to a dentist.

One of the younger lads came running up.

"Your Ma got a fortune," he shouted.

Michael felt his stomach constrict.

"Eight thousand pounds," shouted the young fellow, delighted to be the one who brought the news.

"That's all right," Tommy said. "That's about what they said would be fair —in our house."

Patrick had told the Ryans that he would come in later for a drink, he had a few things to attend to in the hotel first. He had clasped their hands warmly, and any reserve that might have been between them was now gone.

Back in his office, he sat with a curiously empty feeling at his desk. For once there were no interruptions; most times he had never been able to have a full five minutes without some crisis. But today nobody came near him. Brian Doyle had said that he heard it was a fair settlement and Patrick had agreed.

The sour taste in his mouth just wouldn't go. Last night he had wanted to offer £12,000 and had been told very sharply that it wasn't up to him to offer anything.

"Let me add to it, secretly," he had asked.

They wouldn't hear of it. A claim had to be settled and be seen to be settled. It was not fair on other insurers if Patrick was going to play Father Christmas with awards.

If the Ryans were known to have received something way above what they would expect and were about to accept, then would not all other claimants have similar expectations?

There was nothing to stop Patrick O'Neill making any ex gratia payments himself, out of his own funds. But it must not come with the name of the insurance company.

But Patrick knew that if it came from him, it would be charity.

He sat at his desk and wished that his daughter was back from Dublin and that she would walk in the grounds with him talking to him as she once had, before she had become coquettish and head-turning.

He wished that Kerry was different. That was it, just different. Like another person. He could see hardly any way now that he and his son would have any warmth and understanding between them. A gambler, a liar, a callous boy caring nothing for anyone. And quite possibly Kerry had been with Rachel. The thought of his son in an intimate embrace with Rachel was a thought he had tried to keep far from his mind.

Rachel lying back on the bed, confused with unaccustomed drink, laughing maybe, in a silly way. Her thick hair spread out on the pillow, and Kerry, his own son, leaning over her. It was *not* believable. He hit his desk with his fist. He would not believe it.

He had always been able to cope before, or if there was something that he couldn't deal with he had put it out of his mind. He had decided not to think about Kathleen's illness when he was not with her, and so never in his long drives to work or in his business day had he let it come into his mind. After he had beaten and fired his first dishonest manager, he had allowed no thoughts of the man, no regrets to come back to him at any stage. Kerry's expulsion from school, his stealing the silver, these he had managed to banish. But the image of his son and Rachel was too horrifying to get rid of.

Everything was turning out like a nightmare, just a few short weeks before the day he had dreamed about since he was a boy. The day he would open his own huge palace on the spot where the landlords had once driven his grandfather to an emigrant ship.

Fergus Slattery sat alone in his office too. Deirdre Dunne with her usual discreet face, pursed lips and habit of looking left and right before she delivered any utterance had said that it was an excellent result and he must be very satisfied.

Now, as he sat by himself and tried to give time to the other files that were on his desk, Fergus let his mind go back over it all.

He still wished that O'Neill had never come to Mountfern. There was nothing the man could do which made Fergus glad that he had invested the savings of a life's work and investment into changing the face of the village his grandfather left.

Why couldn't he have just come back for holidays, like these people he was hoping to find to fill his hotel? He could have worn a shirt with shamrocks on it, bought a fake shillelagh, had his picture taken beside the tinkers with their donkeys, or at a cottage where he might conceivably have roots.

But O'Neill had to do it his way, no matter who got hurt. And to Fergus's mind a lot of people had. Not just Kate Ryan.

People had changed and become greedy. Everyone seemed to be doing things for the wrong reason. Look at his own poor Miss Purcell, for instance, talking about having to do up the Sacred Heart Altar in the church and get rid of all the damp to smarten the place up for the visitors. If it was important to spend all that money getting rid of damp around the small side altar, and Fergus didn't think it was one of life's essentials, then it should be done for God surely, or for the people who were going to pray in the church, Mountfern people, so they wouldn't have to see weeping walls and fungus around the statue of the Sacred Heart and drips coming down to endanger the altar lamp. The visitors in Fernscourt might not even be Catholics, and if they were they would probably go off to mass at the old abbey fourteen miles away and take in a bit of history as well. And the vicar was busy getting his graveyard weeded and cleared up before the visitors came. This *had* to be the wrong approach too, Fergus thought. If old Protestant graves and tombstones were to be honored, then why wait till some Americans, possibly of Episcopalian stock, came to see them?

But Fergus wasn't going to get anyone to agree with him. Kate had often warned him against becoming an old eccentric before his time. He was thirty-one. Could his time have come now, by any chance?

Loretto Quinn heard the news from Rita Walsh. She was dying to run up and say a few words of congratulation to Kate but she couldn't leave the shop. At that moment Jack Coyne came in.

"Would you mind the place for me, just ten minutes? I'll be back by then."

"God, what am I, a messenger boy?"

The man who owned Coyne's Motor Works and thought of himself as a substantial businessman did not like being thought suitable to fill in behind the counter in what he would always think of as a huckster's shop.

Loretto was struggling out of her shop coat, one of the smart coats that Rachel had gotten her months back. Rachel had said it was always a good idea to have something to wear to show you were working and to take it off when work was over. Loretto had agreed eagerly, and also it happened that everyone said how smart she looked in the shop coats, anyway, so it had been a great suggestion.

Jack Coyne grumbled but agreed to hold the fort for ten minutes.

"One minute later now and I'll leave and pull the door after me."

Loretto was gone, flying up to Ryan's to add her good wishes.

"Who's minding the shop?" Mary Donnelly wanted to know. Mary was beaming like a sunrise and couldn't do enough for people.

"Jack Coyne said he'd keep an eye on it," Loretto said.

"He has his eye on you," Mary said in a doomed voice.

"Never in a million years. He hasn't said a word." Loretto tossed her head. She *had* wondered why Jack Coyne came so often to call. And perhaps in his narrow mean face there were the traces of interest.

"Oh, certainly he has," Mary said. "Wouldn't it be a nice tidy little business to add to his own?"

"Yes. Well." Loretto seemed a bit put out. And yet again Kate and John Ryan exchanged glances across their pub.

Happy to be on the same wave length and happy that the ordeal was over and their future was secure.

Jim Costello was glad the court case was out of the way because now his boss could give undivided attention to the hotel opening. It had all been full of problems, and there was a pressing need for Patrick to call everything to order. Jim suggested a meeting with an agenda.

Patrick was scornful. This was ninnies' work—agendas, and "it was agreed" and "it was decided"—that was the stuff for nobodies. He hadn't made his fortune by sitting on his butt attending meetings.

"There are areas which have to be sorted out in the presence of other people," Jim said—rather prissily Patrick thought.

"Like what and like which people?"

"Like line authority and what position you want your son to hold in the hotel, and that must be discussed in his presence. That's one thing.

"Like what penalty clauses you have arranged with Brian Doyle about what he calls the last little finishing touches and I regard as work still left undone.

Like whether Mrs. Fine is or is not in charge of the decor and the arrangements for the presentation on the opening day."

Patrick felt stopped in his tracks. These were three punches he hadn't expected to be hit with. He took the easiest one first.

"There's never any problem with Rachel," he said. "Give her complete charge. She's had years of knowing how to get along with people, she doesn't get their noses out of joint like I do. What's the fuss anyway? Who's objecting?"

"No, that's not the point. Mrs. Fine says that you don't want her to make the arrangements for the opening. She says that she won't be here for it, and you want the public-relations people from Dublin to make the arrangements. They've been on the phone twice wanting to know. Mrs. Fine just smiles at me and says she won't be here, *you* just say 'Rachel will sort it out.' I'm sorry, Mr. O'Neill, I know it sounds like whining and running to you with every little problem. But can you see how hard it is to decide what is and what is not my responsibility? They're all quite major things and rather sensitive areas."

Patrick looked at him. Costello was unflinching; he didn't sound like a moaner. The man had right on his side.

"I see your point. First tell Doyle that I'll kick his ass from here to Galway tomorrow morning and then from Galway right across to Dublin unless he has all those shithouses, or whatever they are, moved tonight. Do you hear me? Tonight."

"The things he calls offices or store rooms."

"I don't care if he calls them the *Cathedral*, they're shithouses and they are not to be here tomorrow morning. But he is, and eight A.M."

"Yes. Will I arrange . . . ?"

"Just tell him I'll see him here at eight A.M. And Costello?"

"Mr. O'Neill?"

"If you see my son tell him to fuck off. If he wants to show up properly attired on the day of the opening then I shall of course be pleased to see him. Not otherwise."

Jim Costello's eyes flashed. "No, I'm afraid I can't give any message like that for you. That is family business. I will *not* be put in the position of delivering one kind of ultimatum and then delivering back the news of another kind of shrug. I'm sorry, but no."

Patrick looked at him with admiration. "I was right to pick you. Alright, I'll deal with Kerry, but your side of it is clear. He has no position in this hotel."

"And the other . . . ?"

"I'm going to find Rachel myself. Do you have any idea where she might be?"

Jim shook his head and seemed about to say it wasn't any of his business. But Patrick forestalled him with a laugh.

"Hey, relax. If you're not going to do my dirty work for me with my son, then I don't suppose I have any hope of getting you to patch up a lovers' quarrel for me, do I?"

He punched his manager genially on the arm and went out the door of his hotel to stand on his steps and glare at the offending prefab huts that Brian Doyle would be asked to remove the next instant. He noted that Jim Costello had had the good sense not to acknowledge even by a glance that Patrick had just let slip to him that the dispute with Rachel Fine was a lovers' tiff. Jim Costello had been a very good choice indeed.

* * *

Where was Rachel?

Kate had expected her at any moment, but she knew now that she need not doubt her friend. Rachel would be here at some time, it didn't matter when. She would be so glad to share the good news, and to know that a whole day and even more did not have to be spent arguing in open court.

She would be delighted too that Patrick was so pleased and thought it was a fair sum.

Kate looked at the door more than once. She was anxious to go back into her cool green room and talk to Rachel alone.

Rachel walked alone along the riverbank. She walked from the dock upriver, on a path that was overgrown still but not as covered with briars and brambles as the stretch from Fernscourt downriver to the bridge.

It was quiet here and she would meet nobody. She walked, a small woman in her flat-heeled stylish brogues. Rachel had hardly walked without high heels since she was seventeen years of age, but in Mountfern she had learned to change so many of her ways that changing her footwear seemed minor. She had her hands in the pockets of her suede jacket, her Hermés scarf tied jauntily around her neck.

To anyone watching, she looked an elegant woman enjoying a stroll by the river. Over the years she had learned to keep her feelings well away from the public view. Her face was in a pleasant half smile. But her thoughts were very different from the gentle expression on her face.

Patrick O'Neill had said that Kate would get at least £12,000 and the insurance company was quite prepared to pay £14,000 without any great quibble. How had it come out at so little in comparison to that? And why had Patrick said or done nothing to show that he thought it had not been adequate?

From what she had heard, and Rachel had heard plenty of accounts, there had been roistering and celebrating, and banging each other on the back, and everyone was now everyone else's best friend.

She felt sick to the bottom of her stomach that he could be so hypocritical. And even more sick that she had not had the guts and courage to shout down her friend and tell her what the bottom line had been.

If, a few short hours ago, Rachel Fine had been brave enough to resist this girl-guide mentality of having to fight fair that Kate had been babbling about, the Ryan family could have had £14,000 in their bank account. Enough to make them secure forever. No matter what happened to their business as a result of the building of Fernscourt.

Rachel turned and looked back at the hotel. She knew very surely that she would not now wait for the opening, she would go back to New York as soon as she could manage it without upsetting innocent people.

She would go back home.

There were a lot of people in the bar when she came in. She went straight to Kate and kissed her on each cheek.

Kate's eyes were full of tears. "Isn't it wonderful? It's like a dream," she said.

Rachel swallowed.

"Have you been talking to Patrick?" Kate asked.

"No. No, not since."

"He's delighted, he thinks it's fair."

"I'm sure he is." Rachel was pulling away.

"Oh, do you have to go, really? I wanted to talk to you more than anyone."

Rachel had rarely been so moved. She couldn't say anything.

"And Rachel, I wanted to thank you for trying to do what you did. But it wouldn't have been fair, you do see that, don't you? It couldn't have worked. As it is, it all worked out just as we wanted. That's what he said they were going to give, and that's what we took." Kate's eyes shone. Her face was tired but her eyes were dancing with light.

"He said that?" There was no incredulity in Rachel's voice, just a flat tone.

"Well, yes, we asked him, you see, afterward. In the pub."

"Yes of course. Kate, I'll be back, later or tomorrow, and we'll talk for all the hours that are in the day, but this is something I can't put off."

"All right, I won't hold you, and thank you again for all the support. I'm going to sleep well tonight, for the first time for a long while."

Rachel laid her hand against Kate's face in a way she had never done before. It was as if she were trying to say something through the palm of her hand that she couldn't say in any other way.

Then she hurried out of Ryan's and walked down River Road. She didn't cross the footbridge to Fernscourt, nor did she stop at Loretto Quinn's. Rachel Fine walked the whole way to the bridge and turned left. Then she walked up the steps and knocked at the door of the ivy-covered house where Fergus Slattery lived and had his office.

It was short and it was clear.

Rachel found herself giving no complicated explanations, she did not stop to go into her motives, nor did she twist her hands and her handkerchief as she had when she was trying to explain to Patrick that she had gotten drunk with his son but had not made love with him.

Fergus was a different kind of listener. There was no stony impassive face, he reacted angrily and loudly to every sentence.

She gave him all the details of the various meetings, the strategy, the decision to offer six but to expect a strenuous refusal, the decision to go to ten the moment that eight had been refused and to settle at anything up to fourteen even as the case was about to begin. Then it was over and they sat in silence for a full minute.

"I suppose you wonder why I'm telling you all this."

"No, it's very natural that you should tell me, you're Kate's friend, you are hurt on her behalf." He was gentle.

"But I'm also Patrick's friend. You must know that."

"Yes, of course I know that."

"It's not just because it's over, and because Patrick doesn't want me here anymore . . ." She saw him raise his eyebrows in surprise, and went on hurriedly. "No, it has nothing to do with that, surprisingly."

"Of course," he said, but she wondered whether he believed her.

"It's because it's not fair. Patrick has always been fair. And recently some madness has entered into him, and he's not being fair at all."

She looked very troubled. He saw what a very beautiful woman she was in this afternoon light, huge dark eyes moving restlessly about her.

"You do know that nothing can be done now?" Fergus said. "We have taken their offer and accepted it willingly. I thought it was enough, and so did Kennedy. But more important than that, Kate and John were perfectly satisfied."

"I know." Rachel's voice was small.

"And everyone in this place thinks it was enough, so they have their pride, and people don't say it was too much, so the Ryans won't become objects of hate and envy."

She looked at the tall gangling young man with the white face and the hair that would never sit in any order or style. Rachel could see that he had always loved Kate Ryan in a hopeless, ineffectual sort of way. His face was stricken to think how poorly he must have represented her on this, the only occasion he had ever had a chance to ride out to battle for her. Perhaps he was trying to justify the small award by saying that it was what the village would tolerate.

"She could have had so much more if she only would have listened to me this morning. I tried to tell her but she wouldn't hear."

"No, that's Kate for you," he sighed.

"But we were friends. It couldn't have been unethical between friends."

"What do you want me to do, Rachel?"

She looked at him, surprised.

"No, I mean it. What should I do now? My own instinct is to put it out of my mind, pretend we never had this conversation. Do you think I should do anything different?"

"Are you mad at me?"

"Most certainly not." He leaned across his desk and took her hand to reassure her on this. "You have always been a great friend to Kate, I have to say that sometimes I thought she spent too much time with you, seeing that you were so close to O'Neill, and that O'Neill is in many ways her adversary."

"He *is* her adversary, even though he doesn't intend to be," Rachel said. "He will close their business, and eight thousand pounds is not enough to compensate them for that." She was agitated and distressed.

Fergus let a little silence fall between them.

"Fergus, would *you* have listened if I had told you, instead of trying to tell Kate?"

Again a little silence, but eventually he spoke.

"Truthfully, yes. I think I would have listened. It would be unethical and if anyone heard me saying this, I would be in danger of being struck off the rolls, but I would have listened."

Rachel warmed to his honesty. "I don't think it's unethical to help a friend."

"The Incorporated Law Society might not see it that way." He smiled ruefully. "They mightn't be so understanding about how fond I am of Kate."

"You sort of love her, don't you?"

"Yes, that's it, sort of." He spoke without embarrassment, but he looked out the window onto Bridge Street not at Rachel as he spoke.

"She has everything, you know, life and common sense, and a quick lively mind which I don't, and . . . oh, a lot of things. But you're right, it's only a sort of love, not real love. I don't want to take her away from John, I don't want to go to bed with her. I suppose in ways I avoid getting involved with people, and this type of feeling I have for Kate does as a substitute. Very silly, really."

"I had to tell you, Fergus. It's up to you what you do now that you know. If you want to go along with this charade that it was the greatest award since Lord knows when, then do. I won't be here. I'm going home."

"Isn't this your home?"

"I thought it was, but it's not."

"We'll miss you. I wish you were not going away."

Eddie Ryan avoided Jack Coyne very deliberately. But Eddie couldn't avoid trouble. He had been so used to playing around Coyne's Motor Works that vehicles of every sort fascinated him now.

Mr. Williams had an old battered station wagon. He left it outside the graveyard where he was busy tending the graves. Eddie couldn't see anyone around. The grass in the graveyard was high. Mr. Williams was bent low.

Eddie looked left and right and slipped into the driving seat. He would drive the car to the end of the road where there was a farmhouse with two gates. He could drive in one and out the other, and back to where the car was now.

He had reckoned without the herd of cows which were coming out one entrance on their way back to the fields after milking. They seemed to be coming in the windows, and his grasp of driving was not as sound as he would like to have thought.

The cows were delighted with a break in the normal milking routine and were prepared to stand chewing the cud and dribbling until the last day dawned. At that moment a tractor came around the corner. Eddie knew the explanations of what he was doing in the vicar's station wagon would be difficult, not to say impossible. He left the car rapidly and slipped past the staring cows. He heard the tractor hit the car, and kept running until he got to Bridge Street.

His face was innocent when the story got to Ryan's pub, the tale of poor Mr. Williams's car, and poor Brigid Kenny's cows, and Brigid Kenny's poor son on the tractor, who was somehow held to blame for it all.

To his shock and outrage he heard Mrs. Whelan from the post office coming in and telling his father and mother that Brigid Kenny had seen young Eddie running away from the farm. Mrs. Whelan, of all people. She had always been so nice.

Eddie's father was furious.

Eddie was asked to come out to the backyard.

That could only mean one thing.

Kate was furious too. The danger, the stupidity, the downright disregard for human life.

"You'd think that in this house of all houses there would be some attention paid to what can happen when people get hit by vehicles," she stormed at him as Eddie had slunk back into the house with his hands, legs and bottom aching from the hiding he had been given in the backyard. He looked miserable and wretched, and a tiny grain of sympathy stirred in her.

"Why are you so awful?" she asked him, interested genuinely. And he could detect the change in her tone.

"I don't feel awful inside," he said, his tears not far away. Tears that had not come during the beating.

"What do you feel inside?"

"I feel it's all very boring," he said truthfully. "I'd love to be somewhere else, somewhere that I'd be important, and that people would talk about me."

"They're talking about you tonight."

She tried not to let her voice sound as if he had been forgiven in any way. Terrible things lay ahead, like the apology to Mr. Williams, like asking Jack Coyne to give an estimate on how much it would cost to repair the damage to the station wagon, like trying to explain to Brigid Kenny (a sour woman at the best of times) and to her son (who was slow by any standards, even among the Kenny family), what exactly Eddie Ryan had been doing on their property running amok.

"I suppose I'd like to be important to someone," Eddie said simply.

Kate looked at him, and to his amazement she had tears in her eyes. "You're very important to me."

"Only to be giving out to and telling people you're sorry about me." He wasn't complaining, that's just the way he saw things.

"Why do you think that?"

"Well, when I asked was I getting anything to wear at the opening, they all laughed. Nobody even thought I'd be *at* that opening. That's not being very important."

He was totally unprepared for her to lean forward from her wheelchair and take him in her arms.

"I know what you mean, Eddie. It's hard not being important enough to go to Dublin to get an outfit. I'd like to go too. I'd love to go in and out of the shops, in Grafton Street, and down Wicklow Street. Not to buy there, it would be too dear. Then I'd go to George's Street, and I'd buy something there, and a bit of other shopping—oh, stuff that would bore you, household things. And maybe into a bookshop, get a present for your dad, and then give myself plenty of time and walk down the quays with all my parcels and get the train home. And your father would meet us in the town and drive us home, and I'd try on whatever I'd gotten, and turn around on my own two good legs and show it off, and you'd all say what you thought, and people would take notice of me, and I'd be important again."

She was still holding him to her as she spoke. When she released him and held him away from her, she saw that the boy was biting his lip.

"I never knew, Mam . . . I never knew," he said.

"It's all right, Eddie," she said. "We'll survive."

"If I had the money, Mam, I'd take you to Dublin for the day," he said.

"I know you would."

She was silent now, so Eddie crept away.

Things were very odd at the moment; there were no two ways about it. Mrs. Whelan shopping him, Dad belting the life out of him, and Mam throwing her arms around him and saying she'd love to have two proper legs again.

And there were more peculiar things happening at every turn. Mr. Coyne, who was a hundred if he was a day, had brought a bunch of flowers to Mrs. Quinn, who was nearly a hundred, and the two of them were carrying on like something out of a musical. And Kerry O'Neill had told him to fuck off when he had asked him what was he doing with a boat going up and down between the bridge and the dock. Marty Leonard, who was Tommy's younger brother, said that Tommy had four pictures of Dara stuck up in his room and he kissed each one good night before he went to bed. And Father Hogan had asked him what were the opening hours going to be in the Shamrock Café and was there any chance that he could buy some of the potato cakes to eat walking along the road.

Eddie thought that everyone in Mountfern was going mad.

Dara found that her mother seemed withdrawn and somehow wistful these days. She sat and looked out into her garden where the summer flowers were coming to an end.

"Will I bring you the trowel and fork?" Dara asked.

"No. Let's leave it for a while. Who sees it?"

"You do, we do."

"That's what I mean."

"Well, we were always the ones who saw it, it hasn't been on Telefís Eireann or anything," Dara replied with some spirit.

"Are you happy with your linen dress for the opening?" Kate asked suddenly.

"Happy isn't the right word, it looks what it is, a boring linen dress that gets a huge balloony bottom in it if you sit down. It's a nice blue color, and Mrs. Fine gave me that necklace. I suppose it's all right, and for all that will be looking at me over there, it's fine. Why?"

"You can have a new dress if you like," Kate said.

"What kind of dress, Mam?"

"Whatever you like."

This had never been said in the history of their lives together. Dara's mouth was open. There had been a long lecture on thinking that they were millionaires because of the compensation. They had been warned against false expectations and a change of lifestyle. Now out of the blue she was being offered any kind of dress she liked.

"Do you mean something from a shop in Dublin?" she said in disbelief.

"Certainly."

"But why, Mam? We're meant to be saving the money for the day we might need to expand the Shamrock Café. And the fees for university."

"It's my money, it's mine, I got it by breaking *my* back. If I say you can have a new dress you can have one. Do you hear me?"

Kate's eyes were full of tears. Dara rushed to her and threw her arms around the woman in the chair.

"Mam, I'm sorry, of course I want a dress, I just didn't want you to be spending all your money on me. That's all."

She could feel Kate's body heaving.

"I'd *love* a dress. I'll go to Dublin on the excursion train on Saturday. I'd *love* it."

"And Michael, he can go and get a jacket. Will you go with him and see he doesn't buy an old rag or anything?"

"I will, Mam."

"You're going to be dressed like the finest in the land. I'll get you both off school mid-week one day. If Princess Grace can go to Dublin for her clothes, so can the Ryans take time off from their studies to do the same thing."

Sergeant Sheehan was tired. It had been a day when nothing that could have been straightforward was straightforward, everything had more turns in it than a corkscrew. Even the relatively simple business of organizing extra guards for the hotel opening had turned out to be a minefield of petty politics. Was there nobody who would talk straight left in the town? His face creased into a smile when he saw Sheila coming out of the church.

"What were you praying for? Let me guess. You were praying not to have to walk into one more person asking you eejity questions like I do."

She looked at him affectionately. She had known Seamus and Mary Sheehan for years, she had been with Mary sometimes to see their unfortunate son in the home over on the hill. Seamus was usually too upset to go with his wife, and it was a long lonely journey for the woman to go on her own.

"No, Seamus, I wasn't praying at all."

"Well, God, you've enough to do. I hope that mad Miss Purcell hasn't roped you in to clean the church and take the damp out of the Sacred Heart Altar."

Sheila laughed. "Oh, I get roped in like everyone, but I was in there for a different purpose entirely, and you were the very man I was hoping to meet as a result of it. In fact, I was going to come over to the barracks."

"Anything wrong?"

"I'm not sure. I think something may be very wrong. Will you come in and I'll tell you about it?"

"What'll you be doing in Dublin?"

"Shut up, Eddie," said Dara. "You know it's meant to be a secret, we don't want half the place to know we're going. Mam's saying it's a special favor and not saying that we're going on the train. Sister Laura and Brother Keane only think we're going into the town with Daddy."

"But what'll you be *doing,* will you be going to George's Street?"

"God, he's heard of George's Street, is there any end to his sophistication?" mocked Dara.

"I just want to know."

"You're not coming with us, you're not." Michael was vehement. "You'd ruin every single minute of the day, not just for us but for everyone on the train, and everyone in Dublin as well."

"I couldn't ruin the day for them *all,*" Eddie protested.

"You could, they'd be the worse off for your being there. Go *away,* Eddie." Dara was impatient.

"I just thought maybe you'd take Mam," he said.

"What?" They looked at him in amazement. Eddie had never suggested anything remotely unselfish in his life.

"Yeah, she might like an outing, and get something to wear herself."

"She doesn't need anything to wear. Mrs. Fine gets her things," Dara said.

"She might like to get her own."

"She'd hate all the fuss and the noise and how could she manage in the chair?"

"You could push it down the quays. Down to O'Connell Bridge," Eddie said.

"Is this some trick?" Dara asked.

"What's behind it?" Michael wanted to know.

"I was just being nice," Eddie said.

They didn't believe him, but they did tell their father.

* * *

John Ryan thought it was well worth putting to Kate. He came into her room to suggest it.

"How about if the children were to take you with them tomorrow?"

She was flustered and pleased. But no, she couldn't think of it; it would be too much of a drag. It would slow the twins down too much, it would spoil their day.

"Nonsense, I've talked to them, they think it's a terrific idea; they'd love you to go. And if they want to wander off and leave you for a bit, they can, and come back to you, can't they? It'd be just like here or going into town, or the time we went to the abbey on the lake, people came and went from you and you had a grand time."

"I did." She smiled happily. "Thank you for thinking of it, John." Her voice was small and full of emotion.

"Oh, I didn't think of it," he said airily. "Credit where it's due. It was Eddie, apparently, gangster Eddie who thought you'd like the trip."

He grinned at her, expecting her to think it as unlikely and funny as he had. He was surprised to see some of the pleasure go out of her face. Kate had thought that this was all John's idea to give her a treat. But it hadn't been his idea at all.

Fergus had known that he had to face the Ryans fairly soon. He would never tell them about his conversation with Rachel, and he knew that no matter how bitter and resentful on their behalf she might feel, she too would keep her counsel to herself.

But he had to go soon, otherwise, it would grow to become a huge secret and it would get out of all proportion.

He had hated having to go there knowing what he did, but after the first time it was easy. Nobody else knew that O'Neill's side had gotten away so lightly. Fergus believed that O'Neill must accept a great deal of the blame in this regard. It was not, he thought, just his natural and long-standing dislike of the man; it was just the way things had to be.

To try to take some of the fire from Rachel's anger he had pretended to think O'Neill might have been an innocent party. He knew that this is what she had wanted to believe. But in his heart there was nothing that would take away his belief that O'Neill was a villain and would remain one until the end, whatever the end might be.

Fergus was astounded that he had defined his feelings for Kate Ryan so openly to O'Neill's woman. He had hardly defined them to himself before this. But the very act of articulating that he half loved Kate, and that it was not the kind of emotion that would destroy him or make him destroy anyone else, was a liberating thing.

When he sat in Ryan's and joked about the potato cakes for the café, and planned outrageous stage Irish jokes to be played on the visitors to the hotel when they arrived, Fergus felt a kind of freedom. It was as if some burden had been lifted. As if he knew that he could leave this place if he wanted to, he wasn't tied by any cords. He knew he would stay here forever. But now it would be because he wanted to, not because of anything unsettling that would never be said.

* * *

Grace was in Fernscourt examining her room without much pleasure. Not long ago it had been great fun here. Mrs. Fine was pointing out where the light was best to put her bureau, Father had taken her in his arms and hugged her on almost every occasion, saying how wonderful it was that the dream was coming true, and Jim Costello had been around smiling and admiring.

It was all very different now. Father was distant and distracted, there was no sign of Mrs. Fine, and Jim had been so prissy. Yes, that was the only word for it.

"Grace, I'm going to have to ask you not to throw yourself at me, the situation is quite impractical."

Impractical. How *dare* he come on like this, using words like impractical, and suggesting that she had thrown herself at him. She had merely told him she was a big girl now and ready for anything.

Jim Costello had told her that she was the most beautiful girl he had ever seen in his whole life. *That* bit, at least, was something. But he had said that it would be playing with dynamite to get involved with her at this stage, under the eyes of her father and brother.

And then he had gone and more or less said this aloud in front of them. Grace hadn't known where to put herself.

She wished she hadn't been so harsh to Michael about the trip to Dublin. It had turned out that Father had wanted her out of Mountfern on the day of the court case, and Father might have been able to arrange for Michael and Dara to have gone too.

Grace sat on her bed and felt that it had all been handled very badly. She was even having second thoughts about the very expensive dress she had bought.

Mrs. Fine would have chosen something better for her.

Dara and Michael sat on the window seat. It was nearly like old times.

"What are you reading?" Michael asked.

"It's a letter from Madame Vartin. It's quite hard to read, she's awfully squiggly writing."

Michael grinned. "And an awful squiggly habit of writing in French."

"Oh, I can read the French easily enough," Dara said loftily, if not very truthfully.

"What's she writing about then? Here, let's see." Michael reached for the letter.

"No, there might be things in it you shouldn't read."

"From Madame Vartin? You said she was a religious maniac."

"Yes, but she might be writing about sex."

"Oh, I know all about sex," Michael said.

"Do you?" Dara was eager and begging. "Do you really know all about it? Is it great?"

"Well not *all*, not . . . well not everything. But it's pretty great as far as it goes."

"I often wondered did you . . ."

"Sort of, not completely . . ."

"How nearly . . . ?"

"Give us the letter."

The confidences were over, Dara realized. She read a paragraph from the letter.

"This is the bit I don't understand, it's got something to do with Monsieur leaving his job—or being sacked I think. I hope. Anyway she says he is too young to make a retreat. What in the name of God would he make a retreat for anyway? He's full of mortal sin all the time and glories in it."

"Where does it say about him going on a retreat?" Michael read the paragraph and began to laugh. "Fine use of money it was sending *you* off to France, even I know that, and we're all desperate up in the brothers'. It's retiring, you eejit, *"Faire sa retraite* means *retire."*

"He'll be jumping on Mademoiselle Stephanie all day," Dara said gloomily, and then brightened up. "Oh, no, he won't, she's getting married, isn't that great?"

"They all sound cracked to me," Michael said.

"There's Grace going down the towpath," Dara said suddenly.

Michael jumped up on the seat to look. True, Grace was walking purposefully along toward the bridge. She wore her blue jeans and those funny little red lace-up shoes she had, and a blue and red stripy shirt, and there were red ribbons in her hair.

She looked as pretty as a picture.

Michael was pale and unhappy. Dara decided she would break their code of not offering advice.

"Do you know what I would do if I were you?"

"No," said Michael gruffly.

"I'd ask Grace straight out. I'd say, 'Is anything wrong, things seem to have changed?' At least that way you'd know."

"She'll just smile and say nothing's changed," Michael grumbled.

"She might actually tell you if there is something wrong."

"I don't want to hear it if there is," Michael said. He feared that Grace was greatly smitten by the handsome young hotel manager, and because Jim Costello had the sense to play hard to get Grace fancied him all the more.

"Do girls like being asked direct questions like that?" he asked doubtfully.

"I do," Dara said. "If anyone asked me a direct question like that, I'd respect them, and that's the truth."

"Dara, I was just passing," Tommy Leonard said.

"Oh Tommy, how could you be just passing? The brothers' is at the other side of the town to the convent."

"I know, I heard they built them that way on purpose, so that we couldn't all get at each other."

Dara giggled. "Not at all, it never crossed their minds."

"Listen, I hear you're one of the few people in the world who likes direct questions rather than beating around the bush . . ."

In her head Dara heard a warning bell. She didn't want to lose Tommy Leonard as a friend.

"I used to be like that, it's true, but I've gone off it again," she said hastily. "I hate direct questions now, and I snap the head off anyone who would ask me one."

"Phew, I'm glad we sorted that one out," said Tommy Leonard in a mixture of disappointment and relief.

* * *

Grace told Michael that she couldn't imagine what he was talking about. Of *course* she loved being with him. But there was so much school work to do, and she had a little table fixed up for herself in one of the residents' lounges where she could work in the evenings. And she couldn't be going out all the time. And sometimes when she did get through with homework there were things about the hotel she had to learn. After all, she would be living there and working there always.

"But not immediately," Michael cried. "We're going to go to the university, aren't we? And get degrees and travel, before we come back to work in Mountfern."

"Oh, yes, of *course* we are," Grace said.

But she didn't sound convinced.

"Then why are you learning about the reception desk now from Jim Costello?" Poor Michael let it all slip out.

Grace gave him a long look.

"I'm sure you wouldn't want me to be discourteous to anyone on my father's staff," she said, and Michael heard a ring of the boss's daughter in her voice that he had never heard before.

Since the day Kerry had told her about Mrs. Fine and the awful scenes, Dara felt as if a huge boulder had been lifted out of her rib cage. She had known always, of course, that Kerry couldn't possibly . . . not of his own free choice . . . but people had been so definite.

And of course, that was the interpretation that would be put to it. As Kerry had said, he had been uncharacteristically nice, and look at the thanks he had gotten for it. If he had fled, which is what you'd expect him to do from a drunk boring woman who was telling him her life story and looking for consolation of every sort . . . then things would have been better by far.

She didn't get to see him often. He had told her that because of this very bad row with his father he was doing a very ordinary menial kind of a job, he was keeping quiet about it, and in a few weeks it would all be over and they could see each other as much as they liked. He had made her promise to cut school one day and he would drive her to Galway. They would walk along the beach in Salthill in the autumn sunshine, they would buy bag after bag of lovely crisp chips, they would eat those ice-cream cones with big bars of milk chocolate stuck in the middle of them. And best, they could wander around hand in hand and kiss each other in the main streets of Galway if they wanted to.

"I know a place we could go, Kerry," she said suddenly. "It's a tunnel. It used to be a secret place for Michael and me when we were younger but nobody uses it now." She looked at him eagerly.

To her shock his face changed completely.

"No," he said sharply. "No tunnel, that's out of the question."

He stood up. It reminded her of that time he had walked away before when she had refused his embraces. The sense of loss was sharp in her memory. She looked at him longingly.

"Will you promise without any whys. Just for me?"

"Yes, I promise," Dara said, feeling slightly ashamed of herself as she did so.

* * *

Martin White wasn't surprised to hear that Kate Ryan wanted him to call. She said it was for a check-up before she committed herself to the big journey to Dublin.

"It's about more than that isn't it?" the doctor said.

"How did you know?"

"I thought it was possible one day there not long ago."

"I couldn't be . . ." Kate looked horrified.

"Why couldn't you? You know the way it's done, and I'm delighted you're able to do it." Martin beamed uncharacteristically.

"But not with me like this."

"Of course it could, and will."

She leaned forward and clutched his hand. "I'm very strong, you'll admit that, and a lot of my strength came from you giving me things straight. Be straight now. Will it be dangerous?"

Martin took her thin hand in both of his. "Not only will it not be dangerous, it will be wonderful. I couldn't be more pleased for you."

"Do you think you'll go to jail?" Declan asked Eddie when they were both in bed.

"No. Not this time."

"Will you next time?"

"I might. Why?"

"Then I could have your bed."

"You'd be just as bad as I am if you were brave enough."

"I am brave."

"No you're not, you think there's a ghost in the press."

"I don't really think there is, I think there might be."

"There is, a big one, but *I'm* not afraid of it. Good night."

Eddie turned over and went to sleep knowing that Declan would be awake for hours looking at the door of the big cupboard in the corner of the bedroom, fearful over what might come out of it.

The river had never looked so lovely as that night. There was a flutter of birds in the trees, and they heard the cry of a fox in the still night. For two city people to recognize a fox at a distance wasn't bad. Rachel was wearing her flat shoes as if she had known they were going to walk, and he helped her over the fallen branch of a tree or through the complicated little gates that the local people called stiles.

They had driven there separately. Rachel insisted. They had parked both cars on the river bank. Behind them Coyne's wood rose dark and mysterious and further over were the hills around the Grange.

The sound of their footsteps was soft and rustling in the leaves. They came to an old wall, a good vantage point to look up at Fernscourt. Until now they had talked not at all, yet there was no air of expectancy. No tension or waiting for one of them to bring up the subject.

It came up very naturally. Patrick laid his hand over hers.

"I wish it had been different," he said.

"Oh, so do I," she sighed. But not with accusation; more like people sighed when it was no longer spring or when the heat went out of the day.

"It isn't anything to do with the not being Irish bit . . . believe me."

"I do believe you. You see, you've always had a different feeling about being an American than the other people I've met in my life. They all loved being American, *and* being whatever else they were, but to you being American meant losing being Irish, so you had to come back and recapture it."

She walked apparently contentedly beside him, and they came to the foot-bridge opposite Ryan's.

She led the way across into Fernscourt. He had been hesitant in case on this, her last night, she might not want to go into the place that had taken all his money, his time and his heart. They walked to a seat which she had arranged a long time ago when the garden plans were being discussed.

They sat and looked across the Fern at the lights in Ryan's pub where there were still a dozen or so in the bar. And at Loretto Quinn's where the rooms were being held in case Rachel might change her mind. In the soft dark night dogs were barking, they could hear an owl hooting far away, and the moths flew around them gently. There was the permanent sound of the river, but they had grown so used to it, they didn't hear it anymore.

"I'll be very lonely here."

"No, no, you'll have far too much to do," she said. "Your days will be filled from morning to night. I'll think of you sometimes at this time, and I'm sure you will be in your office there or with Jim Costello as the host. You won't be sitting idly here watching the stars over Mountfern."

"And what will you do in New York?" He was gentle too, and wistful.

"I don't know yet. I'll work hard, I can come to anyone with great references now . . ." She waved her hand at the hotel behind them. "I've kept a portfolio of all my work. I must have known I'd need it."

"Do you think we will be friends, you and I?"

"Sometime, not for a while."

"Nobody has shared as much of me as you have. I'm not good at giving bits of myself." He looked at the ground.

She wanted to shout at him and say she was the most betrayed woman in the land. She had worked ceaselessly for his dream and to keep his relationship with his family good. She had bought presents for his children's birthdays for as long as she could remember; she had advised and cajoled and succeeded in keeping some kind of family love alive between them all. What was her reward? She was assumed to have slept with the son and then to have paid him to keep quiet about it.

"And because we *are* being so civilized, can I say just one thing . . . and you won't get up and walk away?" she said.

"Certainly." He was ultra formal.

"And you won't put on that formal mask with me."

"Very well, say it, Rachel." He smiled at her, that familiar smile with the starry lines going out from the sides of his eyes.

There was a catch in her voice which she hadn't intended. She had forgotten how much she loved his smile.

"About that night that Kerry came to my rooms."

"Yes." He sighed as if he had known it would be this.

"He came for a purpose, a very specific purpose."

"Yes, so he said," Patrick agreed.

"Don't be absurd, Patrick, don't be utterly ridiculous. There is really something lacking in you if you could believe that he could have wanted to . . . to be with me in that way."

Her voice sounded confident and dismissive. This was not the woman who had wrung her hands in Coyne's wood and explained and contradicted and apologized. Rachel was firm and decisive now, she was dismissive of Kerry and all his tales.

"For what purpose?"

"He came to warn me off, to send me home. And he has achieved that purpose."

Her eyes were angry but her voice was calm.

"What was he saying . . . ?"

"He was mainly saying that if I had any hopes of replacing his mother, I should forget them, that I was not worthy to mention her name, that our affair was sordid and disgusting and that her memory would never be . . . sullied, I think, by the insult of your marrying me. It was very bitter. Very violent."

"I think this is all very exaggerated. Kerry has no feelings for me . . . Whether I marry or not, it hardly concerns him."

"You may be right in that he has no feelings for you, but he has very strong feelings about his mother."

"He doesn't give any sign of them to me."

"How would he, to you? To you of all people. He doesn't tell you that he had Kathleen's topaz made into a tie tack, that he has her picture in a watch chain, in his billfold, and in a plastic folder just loose in his pocket."

Patrick started to speak, but Rachel went on. "And I don't say this just because he told you a pack of lies about me; in itself, that's not the worst thing."

"What *is* the worst thing?"

"The worst thing is that you believed him. That he was able to make you believe him. That Kerry—with his record of deceit, gambling, theft, lies, and utter selfishness—was able to make you, an intelligent loving sensitive man, believe him rather than me . . . the woman who has loved you, worked with you, and for you all these years. That's the worst thing, how he was able to convince you so easily . . ."

"And is that the reason you're going?"

"That and one or two other things. I think you've changed. I think the effort of making this place changed you a lot."

"How has it changed me?"

"You were always so honest. Back in New York when there was a fight you fought fair. If another guy won the contract, you shook his hand, you said it was only money, only work, you wished him well. If a guy lost, you shook his hand too. You were honest."

"I haven't cheated anyone here." Patrick was bewildered.

"You cheated Kate Ryan."

"I had to, Rachel. What else could I say? 'You were robbed, madam, but please accept my personal check for the balance'?"

"You celebrated with them that justice was done. Justice was *not* done."

"Do you really believe I am at fault over this?"

"Yes," Rachel said simply.

He picked up her hand and stroked it. "We have grown apart, you and I. There was a time when we could have talked it out all night and you would have agreed that I did the only possible thing in giving them their dignity if I couldn't give them an adequate settlement."

"Even if we had been able to talk it out all night, if we still had that kind of life, I don't think I would have agreed."

"But you would have understood why I did what I did," he sighed.

"Yes, I'd have understood."

Together they sat and looked across at Ryan's, where the lights had gone out finally and stragglers walked or bicycled home along River Road.

"Won't you stay for the opening? Please, Rachel."

"No, no, you can call me when it's all over and tell me how it went."

"It will be good to talk to you on the telephone, anyway. There are so many day-to-day things I'll want to tell you about."

"No, Patrick. No calls. Only on the day of the opening."

"No calls?"

"If we're going to live our own lives, it's childish to keep calling each other."

"But as friends, even?" He was begging her.

"No, we're not friends yet. We will be some time."

There was a long silence.

"I feel very empty. I let you down, didn't I?"

"Let's be the only couple in the history of the world who said good-bye without any recriminations," she said, standing up to go.

She bent down and kissed him on the forehead.

He put his arms around her waist and held her to him.

Gently she released herself and walked away. Down the path to the foot-bridge and across the Fern.

Patrick sat in the grounds of his hotel and watched Rachel walk without turning back all along the river bank, past the old wall and the funny stiles.

He heard her car start and drive away toward the town.

Twenty-Three

The weather forecast had said sunny with scattered showers.

"I hope they'll be scattered over the rest of Ireland and not all concentrated in this direction," Miss Purcell said sternly.

The canon had a chest cold that would not go away. Dr. White had said that a man the canon's age was to expect chest colds and not to stay in a draft.

Miss Purcell would have liked more concern and a preciser prescription. The canon would have to be in a considerable draft during the blessing ceremony. She had been very insistent about woolen underwear, and the wearing of a scarf while not actually involved in the religious offices.

Father Hogan was reassuring. Most of the time Canon Moran would stay well away from drafts. The huge marquee built by the dock was meant to be utterly windproof. And then there would be plenty of activities inside the house proper. Miss Purcell was to have no further worries.

Father Hogan also described at great length what he heard was going to be served to eat. There was an amount of salmon being delivered to the hotel that would frighten you, and there would be plates of it all afternoon if people wanted it; they could come back for helping after helping. There would be potato salad, and all other kinds of salads, and buttered brown scones.

Father Hogan said that there had been considerable discussion about whether or not to have a hot lunch, but the salmon faction had prevailed. There would be soup first, of course, served in cups so that it would be easy for people to manage it. There were two huge tureens of soup on their own little heaters, and you could come back for second cups or even a third cup here too.

By the time Father Hogan had begun to weigh up the merits of the fresh fruit salad and lashing of cream as opposed to the hot apple tart with ice cream, Miss Purcell began to wonder if the young priest could possibly be becoming *too* interested in food. She had let out his soutane once already, and it needed a further easing at the seams.

But she dismissed the thought as unworthy. And almost blasphemous. What was better than to see a healthy young priest enjoy his food? She thought back on the days that Fergus Slattery wouldn't notice what she served, so long as there was a bottle of tomato ketchup on the table.

Papers Flynn stirred in the outhouse where he had slept well all night. There was something happening today. What was it? He remembered that it was the hotel opening.

A barge had been brought from a Dublin canal, and painted in bright colors. There were going to be tours up and down the river to the old abbey near the lake. It would be great sport to watch it. Papers would find himself a good vantage point on the bank to see the comings and goings.

He was pleased to think of a day filled with such activity. He had all the details from Carrie. Papers had called there about his usual business and Mrs. Ryan had invited him into the kitchen for a plate of dinner.

Mrs. Ryan was a lady he liked a lot. She never asked him to clean himself up. She wouldn't give him any old guff about finding himself a roof over his head. Mrs. Ryan knew that Papers didn't want to be tied down. She gave him useful things like a pair of big burlap bags with strong handles on them: she thought they might come in handy for transporting his belongings, and they were the very thing.

Mrs. Ryan had taken Papers aside and said that he may have heard that recently they had been given a very substantial sum of money as compensation for her accident. Papers had heard it, certainly. Up in Matt Foley's at the top of the town they had said that the Ryans were going to spend it all on a carpeted lounge bar with music playing in the background. In Conway's pub they had said that the lot had gone into a building society and there wasn't going to be a penny of it spent ever. It was to be their nest egg, their insurance policy for years to come. He had traveled on further to Paddy Dunne's pub, where the story was that the money had been set aside to send Mrs. Ryan to a hospital outside Boston where they were able to do miracles with what other places had said were incurables. It cost five thousand pounds before they would look at you, and there would be the fare and everything, but she'd be walking again by the springtime. Paddy Dunne had read an article about the place in a Sunday paper.

Papers would never dream of asking Mrs. Ryan which, if any, of these stories were true. He was surprised when she suddenly volunteered the information.

"We've been very lucky, Papers, and I was wondering if you'd join us in celebrating our good fortune."

"Well, now, ma'am." Papers was cautious.

"'I mean, I wouldn't normally dream of *offering* anyone money, but seeing as how we got so much ourselves. It's mainly in a savings account and it's going to be used for the children's education, in case any of them are bright enough to be able to use it. But we kept a few pounds aside for ourselves, and for people we know."

She handed him three pound notes folded over.

"It's not a great deal but I don't know whether you'd like a cap, I was going to get you a cap, but John said that a man should choose his own cap for himself."

"He's right there," Papers agreed sagely.

"Or it might not be a cap at all that you'd like, so will you get yourself something, and regard it as sharing part of our good fortune?"

Papers had been very pleased indeed to have had his wishes considered and discussed so carefully without anyone making mention of the county home, which usually came up when people had his welfare at heart.

In an uncharacteristic burst of speech he had told Mrs. Ryan that he might buy himself a little spirit stove that he had seen in a shop. He had been debating if it was worth the investment, but it would give him more freedom, he'd be able to go farther afield if he had his own way of being able to make a cup of tea.

He had thanked Mrs. Ryan very formally and assured her that he would report progress on the spirit stove. If he bought it, he promised that he would be very careful with it. And ended his speech by saying that she was a great woman to be celebrating good fortune when there were many in the land who would say that it was no good fortune to have the two legs struck from under you, but was glad that Mrs. Ryan was able to rise above that.

He had been surprised to see tears in her eyes. And she had said that oddly she didn't worry about her legs being useless, she had gotten over that part of it, she just felt that she herself had lost her personality and was useless as a person. Papers hadn't understood that and he told her it was a bit deep for him. She cheered up then and agreed and told him to have a good plate of stew before he left, and to come and watch any of the activities on the day of the opening from Ryan's bar.

"You know you're invited like everyone else in the place to the Thatch Bar in the evening, he wants the whole of Mountfern to come."

"Well . . ." Papers was doubtful.

"He's not issuing personal invitations, just wants everyone to turn up for a drink and to wish the place luck. Of course, there are some who would prefer to inspect it at their own time rather than being herded together. Some people of the more independent kind, private people will take up his invitation at a later date."

Papers had been relieved to hear that, he thought at first that he might be expected to go, but Mrs. Ryan had set his mind at rest on that point. Papers could join the private sort of people, the people of independent mind who didn't want to go as part of the herd.

Rita Walsh woke with a start. Why had she set her alarm clock for seven o'clock? Then she remembered.

It was the day of the opening. She had two young girls from the convent coming at eight o'clock to start shampooing. The schools had the day off and Rita had picked two of the more reliable Sixth Years to help her. She had trained them in the art of washing hair without drowning the client.

All the towels and capes were clean and ready in little heaps in the salon.

She would get milk and biscuits from Loretto; she had tea and coffee there already, and in honor of the occasion she had bought a dozen nice blue-and-white teacups.

There would be a steady procession all morning. And since everyone would want to be finished and out by twelve-thirty, she had decided to open very early and accommodate everyone.

It was only regulars today. Mrs. Daly, Miss Johnson, Miss Bryne the physiotherapist, Dr. White's wife. Loretto Quinn was coming in to have her hair combed out, she had the set yesterday. She also had the ring. She told Rita Walsh that in your life you found one Barney. It would be too good to be true to imagine you'd find another. But Jack Coyne was a man often very much misunderstood, and he had told Loretto that it was lonely to be in business in a big way and have no company in the evening when he came in after a long day's work. Loretto had understood this too.

Rita had been very pleased for Loretto and agreed that it was often easy to get the wrong end of the stick with Jack until you knew him. She had done Loretto's hair free as a celebration and said she must come in for a lot of back-combing and lacquer since this was a special day, the day that people would hear about their engagement. Loretto must look her best.

Jack Coyne was going to the opening under sufferance. One of the terms of their very unromantic and highly practical contract had been that Jack would end his vendetta with Mr. O'Neill and that Loretto would smarten herself up and learn to drive. The new Mrs. Jack Coyne must be not only a successful shopkeeper in her right but a well-turned-out woman driver.

John Ryan woke at seven. He had slept badly. Twice during the night he had gotten up to get a drink of water, his throat felt dry and he couldn't seem to get comfortable in the bed.

If Kate had been lying beside him in the old days, she would have woken too, and gone to make them a cup of tea. They might have sat during the dark night and talked about the hotel that was finally going to open, and all the fears that they shared, as well as the totally different fears that one had and the other had not. It would have looked less shadowy, that big house across the river, and less full of terror.

But Kate had not been in the room for over three years. Sometimes John slept on the divan in her green room below. He was always aware of how much she hated it when she needed to use the lavatory, whether she dragged herself into the chair and wheeled herself to the bathroom, or used the bedpan. Either way it distressed her so much that he often felt he was more of a hindrance to her than a companion. It was more sensible for him to sleep upstairs, though it was lonely.

And sometimes he felt it was selfish, particularly after they had made love. But then, making love itself was a selfish activity these days. There was no trace of the pleasure and excitement for Kate that had delighted him before.

John looked across at Fernscourt as the morning light fell on the great marquee. Normally he never let his mind go down this particular train of thought, but today he didn't pull himself up. He stood holding the bedroom curtain in his hand and looked at the dock, the brightly painted barge, and the first signs of activity in the big cultivated grounds, and wondered what things would have been like if Patrick O'Neill's grandfather had been thrown out of a cottage in Cork or Galway or Clare, instead of in this small bend on the road in the midlands.

How different everything would have been then.

Grace O'Neill woke with a jump because there was a noise in her bedroom. But it was only her new dress and its heavy coat hanger falling from the door of her closet where she had hung it last night. She wanted to see it first thing so that she could make an instant judgment. Now it was in a crumbled ball on the floor.

She leaped out of bed to rescue it and held it up against the light. It *was* beautiful. She had been silly to think it was baby-dollish; it would look classy and striking.

Grace hoped that Michael would be cheerful today. She hated to see that hangdog look about him, as if someone had taken away his favorite toy.

She went to the window and leaned out. The huge marquee blocked the view across the river. She could not see Ryan's pub properly.

She felt sorry for Michael having to share a room with that terrible Eddie. Declan was harmless enough, but Eddie was too much.

Michael had explained that there was a partition. He had begged for one, and Jimbo had been instructed to build a plywood wall dividing the room.

She compared it to Jim Costello's room. Well, it was more a suite really. He had a study, a bathroom and kitchenette, with a big bedroom that faced the river. She had seen it when he was taking her on a grand tour.

Jim had explained that the big sofa turned into a bed at night. By day the room looked expensive and impersonal. As if it were a genuine hotel bedroom, and Jim was just passing through. There were no photographs or personal things around his room.

Grace liked to think of the frank admiring looks he gave her, and the promise that when the day was over and there was time to think, he would be able to sit down and talk to her properly.

* * *

Loretto Quinn woke and examined her hair to see how much of the set remained. Rita was going to brush it up for her and lacquer it like a board later in the morning.

There were several things she wanted to do before she opened the shop. She wanted to finish her letter to Mrs. Fine, telling her that there had been a dozen requests to rent the rooms, and that Loretto was going to give them to a young chef who said that he never lived on the premises, it always led to a hassle, and he had wanted something nearby. He had been very impressed with the little kitchen and said that the cooker was a very good make and one of the most expensive on the market.

Loretto wanted to thank Rachel for that as well; she had never appreciated it at the time. She wanted Rachel's advice on what she should wear for her wedding next spring. Would a lemon-colored suit be nice, or would it take the color from her?

Loretto also wanted to leave a note in to Fergus Slattery. Jack Coyne had said to her that the country had never been the same since the Married Women's Property Act. It was a joke, but she was going to ask Fergus just to make it clear to her in words she would understand that if she and Jack had a bust-up in the years to come, that Jack couldn't take her little shop from her. And Loretto had to iron her dress, and once she had sorted through the potatoes and shaken the earth off them, she would paint her nails pink, as people would be admiring the ring.

And she had to decide about the picture of Barney that hung over the mantelpiece in her kitchen.

She took it down and looked at his face. It wasn't a very big picture, nor a very good one. His hair was sticking out in a spiky way that wasn't really like the way Barney was. The years in between made it hard to remember exactly the way he was.

As she looked at the picture, Loretto noticed that the big old frame was coming apart; it was old and cracked. It would be dangerous to leave it hanging in that position in case it fell on anyone. Loretto's decision was made for her. She couldn't put the picture up again the way it was.

She took out the photograph of Barney Quinn and put it in a smaller frame, a stand-up type which you could put on a shelf. In front of the potted plant. But in time it could be moved over beside the plant or toward the back of the shelf.

Eddie Ryan woke and looked out the window.

He had promised his mother that he would do nothing today that would bring any disgrace on the family.

"It's an important day, and I'm in a bit of a fuss and bother about it already, so it would be the living end, Eddie, if you were to be a worry to me, if I had to be looking around asking people where is that boy and what's he up to now."

"Maybe I'd better stay in bed all day," Eddie had said quite seriously. It seemed to be the only way he could guarantee being no trouble at all.

"No, I'd be afraid you'd fall out of the window or hang yourself or something. I wouldn't be able to take my eyes off the house while we're over there," Kate had grumbled.

Mam had bought him a great jacket that day in Dublin; it was full of pockets and zippers and wasn't at all the kind of thing he thought Mam would buy. He'd been sure it would be something like a blazer or a suit jacket when he was unwrapping it.

"How did you know this is what I'd want?" His eyes were shining.

"I guessed," Mam had said.

She told him it was in the nature of a bribe, a promise of peace on the day of the opening.

Declan stirred and rubbed his eyes. "Is it morning?" he asked. Declan sometimes behaved as if he were retarded.

"No," said Eddie. "It's the middle of the night, and all those ghosts you're so afraid of have been at it again. They've bitten the head off Jaffa. Oh, God, it's lying on the ground all covered with dried blood."

Declan let out a screech that could be heard on the Dublin road, and leaped out to see if this was true.

Carrie, who had been getting sick in the bathroom for the fourth morning running and was beginning to work out that there might be a very unsettling reason for this, got such a fright at Declan's screams that she knocked over the entire contents of a tray that was perched dangerously on a white chest of drawers. The tray held—or had held—talcum powder, Dettol, dried-up calamine lotion, milk of magnesia, a glass eyedropper, and a bottle shaped like a crinoline lady full of blue bath salts.

The recriminations were lengthy. The court of inquiry into why all those particular things were on a tray was endless. Kate said that it was a great thing for a woman in a wheelchair to be told that the bathroom she could never go up the stairs to see had now turned into some kind of boxroom or rubbish dump, filled with old chests of drawers and trays and the Lord knew what else.

Dara was accused of having weighted it down too much with the crinoline lady. Dara, woken from sleep with what she considered monstrously unfair charges, said that the crinoline lady was, if anyone would care to remember, a gift from Marian Johnson to say thank you when Dara had gone to help in the Grange at a function. Dara had thought she was being paid, which was the only reason she had gone, and had been outraged by the blue crinoline.

Mam had said then to put it up in the bathroom somewhere out of people's sight, and now she, Dara, was being blamed for it.

Eddie said he would stick a compass in Declan's heart if he told anyone why he had cried out, and that this was no joking matter.

Poor Declan tried to say that he had been having a nightmare; he had dreamed that a ghost had bitten off the head of the cat, and that the side yard was awash with blood.

John said that it was too much for a human to bear. One of his sons was a hardened criminal, the other a certifiable lunatic.

Jack Coyne woke with a feeling of wellbeing that surprised him. What was he feeling so good about?

He remembered that despite all the trials and tribulations, a few of them aided and abetted by Jack himself, Fernscourt was going to open today.

Well, he was going to the festivities of course, no point in making any lone point over something that was happening, anyway, and passing up a free dinner.

Anyway, there would be lots of fellows there from the Tourist Board and from Aer Lingus and the American airlines. And there would be journalists and local councillors, two bishops no less, a rake of priests, four TDs at the last count, not to mention the high and the mighty for miles around. If he couldn't get a bit of business out of today he'd be in a poor way.

Then he remembered Loretto and how she had agreed to everything. It had been well worth getting her those flowers back a bit, and saying that he would be happy to go dancing of a weekend. Women really and truly liked those kinds of things. It was the way they were. And Loretto had been very practical, too, and agreeable to some of his suggestions. She had been adamant about maintaining her own little shop rather than considering its possible sale as a site for some other business once the hotel got going. She had been equally firm about not learning anything whatsoever about maintenance work. She didn't want to spend her life in greasy overalls lying under some lorry. She had agreed to learn how to drive, however, which would be very useful for car delivery or collection or going for spare parts.

She had a nice smile, Loretto had. He had never noticed her at all until recently, thought she was a streelish little one in a shabby boxeen of a shop.

It was extraordinary how she had livened up when O'Neill's foreign woman came to live there. And would anyone be able to explain what had happened to send *her* packing so suddenly?

Fergus Slattery heard the telephone ring at seven-fifteen. That had to be some crisis.

He dragged himself unwillingly from a dream where he was advising the Rolling Stones about their grammar, and telling them that the song "I Can't Get No Satisfaction" actually and literally meant that they *could* get satisfaction, which was fine if this is what they wanted to say.

The Rolling Stones had been delighted with Fergus and had asked him to get on the payroll. He wouldn't have to leave Mountfern but could advise by phone or letter on anything that needed revision. They promised to come and see him when next they were passing that way, and Fergus had told them they'd get a great bed and breakfast in Ryan's. Dara had been so grateful to him and had apologized for ever thinking he should be put down like an old horse.

Loath to leave such entertainment, he went in his bare feet to the phone.

"It's Rosemary."

"*Who?*"

"I know we haven't seen each other a great deal over the past while, Fergus, but I *am* your only sister."

"My God, Rosemary, is anything wrong? It's the middle of the night. Did something happen?"

"Of course something happened. I'm hardly ringing you for a chat out of the blue."

"What is it? The boys . . . was there an accident . . . ?"

"The boys are fine wherever they are. They don't bother to let me know."

He waited.

"It's James. He had me out of the house, changed the locks. He can't do this to me. He can't throw me out of my own home." She was near to tears.

"When did this happen?"

"The locks were changed last night, I stayed in a guest house. I was waiting until I could ring you to know what to do."

A wave of pity came over him for this tall shruggy woman, with no warmth and no charm. He remembered her visit at the time of their father's funeral, her lack of any kindness, her cruel taunting remarks.

And now, at this ungodly hour of the morning, she had finally been locked out of the family home in Manchester.

"Wait until nine-thirty, Rosemary," he said.

"What will you do then?"

"I will do nothing, but you'll go to a solicitor—a solicitor in Manchester, mind, not in Mountfern. And you'll tell him what happened, and the circumstances leading up to it, and he will tell you what to do."

"I don't know any solicitors in Manchester, for heaven's sake. If I did have any legal contacts, do you think I'd be ringing you?"

"No, I know that. I know that very clearly."

"So what's the point in saying find a solicitor, find a solicitor? I could have looked one up in a phone book myself."

"I think that's probably the best thing to do." He kept his tone even.

"Are you serious?"

"Yes, Rosemary. It sounds distant and may even sound harsh, but I can't give you any advice whatsoever. You must see that."

There was a silence.

"I'm sorry about it all. Do you think it can be sorted out, the difficulties with James?"

"Difficulties." She gave a snort of laughter and said the word again, mimicking his accent. "Difficulties! No, I don't think they can be sorted out, as you say." Her tone was scornful.

"Well, then, the best I can wish you is that you are able to work out adequate provisions and a settlement, and that it is done with as little hurt and animosity as possible."

"Jesus, but you're a pompous bore, Fergus."

He had been going to say that if she wanted a holiday she could come to the house where she had grown up in Mountfern. He would not say this now.

He thought of the night that he had been going to give her the old Victorian sewing table belonging to his mother, and had changed his mind over some insult that she had slung at him. Perhaps her whole life was a series of such non-happenings.

"I hope I'm not as bad as you make me out, but I'm sure, like all of us, I must have my faults." He put on a mad simper as he said this. He tried to look at himself in the hall mirror, but the light was bad and he could only see his tousled hair and his crumpled pajamas.

He did a little dance while holding the phone and leering at his reflection. It pleased him to know that Rosemary could have no idea of his manner.

There was no more to say now, so Rosemary had rung off. Fergus was well into his capering dance now so he continued it, round and round the hall, pretending to hold up a ball gown and curtsying at himself every time he came to the mirror.

As he passed the hall door in a spectacular twirl, he saw two eyes looking at him through the letter box.

Fergus stopped in his tracks. "Who's that?" he asked fearfully.

"I'm sorry, Fergus." A thin voice came apologetically through the slit in the door.

He threw open the hall door, and there was Loretto Quinn, a letter in her hand.

"I was just about to put this through the door, but I heard these swishing sounds so I looked in, in case something was wrong."

Loretto had never looked so alarmed in all the years he had known her.

"But you were pleased to see that everything was as normal." Fergus beamed at Loretto as he took the letter. "I always have a little dance like this to start the day. They advised us years ago in the Four Courts, they said there was nothing like it for settling the mind into a good legal way of thinking."

Loretto's mouth was still open as Fergus bowed to her theatrically and closed the door.

Jim Costello woke with a toothache.

He gave himself five minutes to decide whether he could bear it for the day or whether it would incapacitate him for the day. He decided it would render him speechless.

He rang Dr. White and asked the name of the dentist in the town. Then he rang the dentist.

The dentist was sorry, but he had limited surgery hours today; he was actually going to the official celebrations at the opening of a big new hotel.

"I'm the manager of that bloody hotel, and there won't *be* an opening unless you do something with my tooth," Jim said, maddened with pain and the man's slow obstinate voice at the other end of the phone.

"Well well well."

"Can you do it, or can you not?" As he spoke, Jim Costello realized how like Patrick O'Neill he was becoming in his speech. It sat better on a middle-aged American tycoon than on a young Irish hotelier.

He changed his approach.

"As you can see, I am utterly relying on you. Just a temporary dressing, anything. You've been highly recommended in these parts."

"I don't really . . ."

Jim played his final card. "And if you knew the whole story about the problems we've been having and all the celebrities who are expected today . . . Well, you'll meet them yourself. If it ever gets going at all."

That did it. The man said Jim was to get into a car and drive like the clappers, he'd open his office early for him. A chance to hear the inside story about Fernscourt was too much to pass by.

Mary Donnelly woke and spoke to Leopold, who had been waiting patiently for her to stir.

Leopold was a more intelligent dog than many people gave him credit for. He knew the way to stay in Mary's good books was by not waking her or snuffling around for anything interesting and certainly not by offering any of his paws in the form of a handshake. Mary was of the opinion that there was far too much insincerity and over-greeting going on in the world. She liked silent ruminative thoughtful encounters. Leopold had adapted to her ways.

He was surprised that she seemed to be making a speech to him; it was not her usual way of greeting the day. He held his head on one side and tried to understand what she was telling him.

It had nothing to do with a walk. But there was no abuse in it, either. He couldn't fathom it at all.

"Leopold, this is a black day for this house. But apparently none of us are allowed to mention it. The new way of going on is to pretend a problem doesn't exist. That way we can all go on drinking and slapping each other on the back.

"Listen to me well, Leopold. This is the beginning of the end. You and I could be walking the roads of Ireland with packs on our backs. There's going to be nothing in the profits of this establishment to put a dinner on the table for either of us once this hotel gets going. But to be fair, Leopold, they never put your dinner on the table. More the floor."

The dog looked at her trustingly.

"Don't mind me, Leopold," she said, scratching his ear. "I am totally mad. Not a little mad. Totally and completely mad."

Brian Doyle woke with a thick head. They had been celebrating until a late hour. O'Neill had said that as far as could be seen to the naked eye, the structure seemed sound, and more or less approximated to the plans that had been given to Brian Doyle. He had bought Brian several drinks on the strength of this. Then, back in the town, Brian had decided to finalize the arrangements for taking Peggy, his girlfriend of many years, to the opening. He would call for her at noon, his brother Paudie would drive them so that they need not worry if there were a few drinks taken during the day.

He had been neglectful of Peggy, particularly during these last weeks. He had wanted to explain to her that this was all over. He had not been prepared to meet her mother, a battle axe if ever there was one. The mother had said that Peggy would be going to no opening or closing of any hotel whether built by Brian Doyle or built by the Emperor of China.

Peggy had, according to her mother, belatedly come to her senses over Brian Doyle, she realized that having her name up with him for so many years had brought her nothing but heartbreak and humiliation and, what was more distressing still, had cut her off from any other avenue and future. So that was all in the past now, thanks to the good Lord who had opened her eyes, and she had instructed her mother to pass the burden of the message on to Brian if he ever made an appearance in the next year or so.

This was the heavy artillery.

Brian sat in Peggy's mother's kitchen letting the words wash over him and trying to work out where Peggy might be.

"Don't start it all up again," said the woman in front of him, who had not ceased to speak since he entered the house. "You're a bachelor, Brian, stay one. For God's sake, will you go back out to that hotel and pat it and stroke it and be with it morning noon and night? That's what you want."

"I can't go to bed with the hotel," Brian said eventually.

"And as sure as your name is Brian Doyle, you can't go to bed with my daughter either. Sweet talk or no sweet talk. Ring or no ring."

It hadn't crossed Brian's mind that a ring should form part of the proceedings. There was plenty of time for that.

He had left the house disconsolately and on the street run into Seamus Sheehan, the sergeant from Mountfern.

Since Seamus was off duty they went to a pub and Brian explained that he was not a knave or a philanderer at heart, it was just that he was too young to settle down.

Sergeant Sheehan said that basically all men were too young to settle down, his long life in the Guards had taught him that. He cross-questioned Brian about the tunnel behind the bedroom wing, and whether there was any entrance in it under the brambles and briars.

Brian said that he couldn't bear to think of any more entrances or exits to that hotel than there were already. There had been an unmerciful carry-on about where the drive was going to be at the start; most people thought that it was never going to get off the ground at all.

But Sergeant Sheehan went on and on. Any entrances to old shafts or tunnels or anything they had come across?

Brian Doyle had said that when it was a question of a fairy fort, some of the men he had working for him were as superstitious as old shawlies who would go and tie things to a May tree. They had just avoided going anywhere near it and in the end the best thing had been to build a trellis and drape these creepers over it. Made a kind of wall of sorts.

No, he had no idea if there was anything in it. He didn't give much thought to the fairy world himself, there was too much happening in the so-called real world. If they were there, which seemed highly unlikely, then leave them to get on with it; that was Brian's philosophy. Oh, the sergeant meant non-fairies? No, he could not imagine that anyone with a marble left in their head would want to be burrowing around under all those blackberries and old thorns. But then Brian was always the last to be told anything. The whole Pioneer Total Abstinence Association could be having their annual general meeting in those bushes before anyone would think of telling the poor builder.

But wasn't it a bloody miracle that the place was finished and none of them were in jail or up in the asylum on the hill?

Too late Brian Doyle remembered the youngest Sheehan boy was in that very asylum. He looked glumly into his pint. There were some things you could never backtrack your way out of, and it was wiser not to try.

Sergeant Seamus Sheehan woke and made his wife a cup of tea.

"This is your big day," she said sleepily. "Is the weather good for it?"

He opened the curtains a little and peered out.

"It's bright," he said. "It'll be sunny with scattered showers, they said."

"Ah, well, that's grand, and they'll have a tent set up so you won't notice the showers."

She was pleased that her husband would be on show and a man of importance today. There were very senior men from Phoenix Park, the Garda headquarters, coming to the reception, and there were local guards from around coming in to help with the traffic and because there would be VIPs coming to the reception. Seamus would have more responsibility than he ever had before.

Seamus Sheehan was glad he hadn't told his wife about the plan to close in on the tunnel that morning. He had been in the town last night setting it all up with the force there.

He had been praised for the excellent surveillance he had kept, and the superintendent said that he was a model of what an efficient rural sergeant could do by knowing the people of his place and being able to spot anything untoward.

McCann, Byrne and Red Molloy were no mean prize to get in one net.

The plan was to take them early *and* have it wrapped up before the guests started arriving.

Whatever they were up to, that crowd, it must have something to do with the opening. A possible kidnapping.

Guaranteed, of course, to get the worst publicity for Ireland if it took place when a load of American journalists were actually on the spot feeding their faces with salmon and brown bread. They would get them into different cars and take them by different routes to the Garda station in the big town.

Charlie Byrne was the thicko, he'd certainly tell them what was going on.

Sergeant Sheehan was glad that it would all be over well before his wife had put on the new suit that was hanging up outside the wardrobe so that it wouldn't get crushed, together with the frilly white blouse and a handbag so new that it was still in the paper bag from the shop and had tissue paper inside it to make it keep its shape.

Kate felt that the day had started poorly. All that shouting and the upset in the bathroom.

But these were as nothing compared to the fact that Carrie was now almost certainly pregnant. That was the first thing to be coped with.

She called the girl into her room and asked her to close the door.

"Have a plain marietta biscuit, Carrie, take one there from the tin on the windowsill."

Carrie's eyes were huge. "I was just going to have a drink of bitter lemon or something, ma'am . . ."

"No, the biscuit is best. I remember myself."

Carrie's eyes were full of tears. "It must be definite, ma'am," she said. "I'm very sorry."

"Why are you saying you're sorry to *me*?"

"Well, you've been very nice to me. I don't want to go bringing disgrace on you. That's the last thing I'd want."

"You won't do that. It's all a matter of what way we look at it."

"What do you mean?"

"Mrs. Fine used to say to me that life was all about how you looked at things. If you saw the sunny side, then things were sunny . . . You know, the Americans have some book about it."

Carrie looked at her, bewildered.

"So what I mean is this, there's going to be no tears, no apologies, no shame. No saying to Jimbo that you're sorry. It's not *your* fault, any more than it is his."

"But he could say I'd been with anyone. Jimbo's going to be a known singer. There's going to be people here today who will have heard of him." Carrie was full of awe.

"Yes, but he's your Jimbo. He's not going to walk out on you?"

"If I gave in to him, let him have his way, what's to stop him thinking I let other fellows have their way?"

Kate's face was very impatient.

"Loretto Quinn and Jack Coyne are going to announce their engagement today. I wouldn't be surprised if Brian Doyle might even stir himself to propose to that long-suffering Peggy. What more natural than you and Jimbo too?"

"But ma'am, he mightn't want to . . ."

Kate wasn't listening. "Yes, a big occasion like this, a very good place, we could even get a bit in the newspapers about it: Singer to wed, it's a good time of year to think of an Easter wedding."

"Easter?"

"Yes, well that's for Loretto and Jack. But you and Jimbo might find that to fit in with his career you might suddenly get married straight away, before Christmas."

"Oh, ma'am, wouldn't it be great if he'd agree?"

"Of course he'll agree. He'll be delighted," said Kate with much more confidence than she felt.

Sheila Whelan woke with a heavy heart.

Patrick O'Neill had been in last night, anxious to talk.

"You're about the only one I can really sit down and talk to." He looked tired and lonely.

"Haven't you half the country to talk to?" She smiled.

"Not really." He gave a heavy sigh.

"You'll miss Rachel tomorrow?" Sheila was one of the few people who could speak like this without causing him offense.

"I'll miss her, that's for sure. She put so goddamn much into it, I wanted her to see the opening, even if afterward . . . well . . ." His voice trailed away.

"Probably better for her to go at once if she was going to go at all," Sheila said.

"Yes, women see it that way. I'm going to call her tomorrow night. At midnight our time it will only be early evening in New York. She agreed that we would talk on the telephone tomorrow."

He looked boyish and eager. Not the great O'Neill opening the most talked-of hotel in Ireland, who kept his lady friend in doubt about his intentions all the time she was here. Sheila Whelan thought that men were impossible to understand and that perhaps the less time and effort spent trying to understand them the better.

"What are you doing tonight? Getting a good sleep for tomorrow, I hope. You'll have a long day."

"I can't sleep at all these nights. I walk the grounds a lot. I had a few drinks with Doyle. I don't know which of us is more surprised that he hasn't ended up in one jail for fraud and I haven't ended up in another for attempted murder!"

"Go on, you'd be lost without Brian to give out about. You'll miss him, I promise you."

"Sheila, you're very discreet—" Patrick began.

"Not any longer," she interrupted him.

"What on earth do you mean?"

"Just that. I'm *not* discreet anymore. If I see something I don't like, then these days I say it. It's hard to get used to. I keep hoping I'm doing the right thing."

She had told him no more despite his concern.

Sheila knew that if anyone was going to be hurt by what she had done it would be Patrick. She had discovered that Kerry O'Neill was taking boxes and packages into a disused tunnel which led to Fernscourt.

He was involved with a gang of hoodlums, probably thought they were freedom fighters instead of bank robbers, which was what they were. Sheila knew that on the morning of the hotel opening the tunnel would be closed off, the gang taken into custody, and as a courtesy to Patrick O'Neill and to all the employment he was bringing to the area, his son would not be questioned until the following day.

There was a belief that Kerry O'Neill, though most certainly some kind of an accomplice, was not involved in the criminal side of things. Or not yet. Sergeant Sheehan said that it was all being done to pay his gambling debts.

She thought of Seamus Sheehan's son in the home, of Patrick's son running with bank robbers, of her own husband's son, who couldn't come back from England for his father's funeral.

Many times Sheila had wished that she had given birth to a boy. A child of her own who would grow up under her eyes. This morning as she dressed for the day and all it would bring, Sheila felt glad that she had no son. She was better off today only worrying about herself.

Dara's hopes of a long leisurely time to get ready had been dashed. First there was all the work clearing up the bathroom, then Mam wanted to be helped.

Mam looked very pale and even unwell. There was a light sweat on her forehead and she had that distraught look she sometimes got.

"It's going to be fine," Dara said soothingly.

"What is?"

"The opening. The day!"

"Oh, yes. Yes, of course."

Dara looked at her, concerned. Mam hadn't been at all well of late. Look at the way she had felt after the trip to Dublin. Don't say it was going to be the same now. Dara held up the navy-and-white outfit. It had been chosen by Rachel Fine, of course. Hadn't everything? It was smart, but Dara would have dressed Mam in something less severe. It had a lot of small buttons down the back which would need to be fastened.

Mam smelled of good soap and talcum powder. More gifts from Mrs. Fine. Perhaps as the years went by Mrs. Fine's gifts would wear out, and her influence would die away. Mam had said very firmly and very briefly that she would not be coming back again to Mountfern.

Dara sat by the dressing-table part of the green room. She looked long at Mam's face to see any signs of illness.

"Would you tell me if there was anything wrong, if you felt badly?" she asked her mother.

"Yes and no. Yes, if we could do anything about it."

"Then there *is* something wrong!"

"No, I feel jittery today, that's all, a bit like going to the compensation case. You know the feeling."

Dara knew the feeling; she *had* the feeling. She wasn't at all sure that Kerry would like her dress. She had spent such hours choosing it in Dublin, and spent so much money on it. It looked a simple red silk. In the hand it looked only like a crumpled scarf, but when Dara put it on, she looked great! Or she hoped she did. But you'd know with Kerry.

She had fastened the tiny buttons, and Mam looked very well, smart and stylish. The dress had a full skirt. Mam never wore clothes that let you see her legs properly, even though they looked perfectly all right.

Dara felt the overpowering sympathy that she sometimes did for her mother, who could not stand up and who knew that she would never be able to stand again.

"Dara, one little thing about today."

Dara sighed. It was going to be about not smearing on too much make-up, not disappearing with Kerry, about being understanding to Michael, or keeping an eye on Declan, or trying to stop Eddie from alienating the whole parish.

"Yes, Mam," she said dutifully.

"If I were your age, and I were as lovely as you . . . I would not want to listen to someone saying what I'm going to say now, but it's only very short, and then we don't have to talk about it again today. All right?"

Dara nodded. What alternative had she?

Kate took her hand. "I just want you to know how sad I am that Rachel isn't here today. She worked on every stone of this place as much as any of Brian Doyle's men, as much as Patrick ever did. And at this moment she's in New York City, probably crying her eyes out and thinking of it all."

Dara had taken her hand away and was moving restively.

"And the reason that she's not here is Kerry. She did nothing wrong, nothing bad, nothing that she couldn't stand up in the pulpit and talk about. She got a little drunk, and she's not used to drink, that's all."

"Mam, please . . ."

"I said it's short. Kerry drove her out, Dara, for these reasons: he didn't want her to marry his father. He has always been much more fond of his mother than of Patrick; he thought that Rachel should not replace her.

"Then he got into great debt at a card game and he asked Rachel for money . . . It's very complicated, but he didn't get it finally, so he let everyone think that he and Rachel were together. You've heard that, I know. I just wanted to set it straight in your mind."

"Oh, Mam, I heard the real story from Kerry," Dara said.

"You heard a story from Kerry. I doubt if it was the real one."

Kate's eyes were far away. "You're a grown girl, Dara, you are sixteen— although I think that's young, I'll still think you're young when you're twenty-six . . . I am not poisoning you, I'm warning you. That's all. Of course you'll be with Kerry today, and he will be charming and lovely and make you feel good. But I felt you had to know that he is dangerous."

Michael wondered for the fiftieth time was his jacket a bit sissyish. It had looked fine in Dublin. But hadn't everything? Tommy had said it was great; you'd expect Michael to break into a waltz as soon as he put it on. Grace had been noncommittal. She had been slightly annoyed that he had found the time and possibility of going to Dublin with Dara when he hadn't gone with her.

For no reason Michael kept remembering Maggie talking about the hotel opening. She said there would be television personalities coming to it and that maybe they would all be introduced to them on account of knowing the O'Neills so well. They had laughed at Maggie for her enthusiasm. And she was dead for over three months when the hotel did open.

Something had gone out of their summer, something more than Maggie. They stopped being a group somehow. They hardly saw Jacinta and Liam now, and as he had feared Grace was a million miles further away now that she was just across the river.

Tommy Leonard wished that he had a new jacket like Michael's. He wished that he didn't have skin that looked as if it had been treated with Harpic lavatory cleaner and he wished that he had smooth blond hair that looked good whatever way it fell, instead of spiky awful hair not unlike Eddie Ryan's.

He had heard there was going to be dancing in the Thatch Bar. His mind went back a year to when the Ryans had that great party in the outhouse that was now the café. He remembered not being quick enough or interesting enough to keep Dara's attention when Kerry came into the room. He wondered could anyone ever be quick or interesting enough. It wasn't *only* looks. Dara wasn't so shallow that she would go for appearances only. But Kerry was so sharp and clever. He knew when to say nothing and when to smile. He seemed to know what people were thinking, and say it first.

Suppose Kerry was to get a job somewhere else. Would that make everything all right? Or would the whole place still be watching out for him, looking up the road, almost waiting for him to come back?

Whatever Tommy wore, Kerry would wear the opposite, and he was sure Kerry would look just right today. If Tommy wore his best suit, you could be sure that Kerry would be in some pale blue sweater and jeans, and if Tommy wore his corduroys and Aran sweater, Kerry would be in a formal suit and tie. Wouldn't it be wonderful to see what he was picking out to wear?

Kerry was up very early.

Everything had been neatly stored in the tunnel. They knew to keep well away, today of all days.

It all had been simple. Just provide a depot, they said, the tunnel was a fine idea. Better than a warehouse, a lock-up shed.

The boxes had been stacked. There were crates of drink, and big boxes with cartons of cigarettes.

Kerry understood about the weapons. He wasn't so clear about the drink and cigarettes. McCann had been laconic. These things are sold, they make money, money is needed for supplies.

From time to time he wondered what kind of movement they were in. At times he even suspected basely that they might well be in no movement except a gang of their own. But it didn't concern him now. He had stored their goods; he had wiped out his debt.

The day was starting. He felt that tingle of excitement he knew when something new was about to start. Kerry felt good. There was nothing he couldn't do. Look at what he had done already.

He had shipped Rachel Fine back where she belonged.

He had paid his poker debt.

He would sort out the situation with his father. Father wanted a son around here, for Christ's sake. He wouldn't make a lot of waves.

There would be speeches, and no doubt Father would say something about how sad it was that his wife Kathleen hadn't lived to see this day.

Kerry knew his mother would not have wanted to live here in this town. But if she were to see what was happening, she would be proud of him. That her son had not forgotten her. He fingered his tie tack. That he had not let anyone else take her place.

Papers Flynn liked Kerry O'Neill.

He never understood that Kerry could be laughing at him. Kerry often complimented him on his clothes and said that he thought it was a great idea to tie so much string around the waist—it could be the in thing if the fashion writers got a hold of it.

Papers didn't rightly know what Kerry was saying half the time. But the boy always seemed to be smiling, which was good. And of course Kerry sometimes slept rough too. Papers knew that he slept in that tunnel.

He had been in to investigate it for himself a few times. In theory it should have been a great place to stay, but Papers thought it was a bit closed in, he preferred somewhere less restricting.

Papers never asked himself why someone with Kerry O'Neill's wealth slept out. There didn't have to be a reason. He would greet him nowadays as a fellow knight of the road.

On the morning of the opening he was pleased to see Kerry on the river bank.

"All spruced up and ready for the great occasion, I see," Kerry said to him.

Papers grinned, pleased. "It's going to be a nice day for it," he said, looking at the sky.

"Well, Papers, just so long as it won't interfere with your enjoyment of the salmon." Kerry laughed.

Papers felt he was being invited to more than a drink in the Thatch Bar. He didn't know how to cope. He decided to change the subject and trade information instead.

"If you've still got your place in the tunnel, you'd want to keep an eye on it," he said confidingly. "I saw Sergeant Sheehan and Mrs. Whelan looking at it last night, and the sergeant was there again this morning."

Kerry's heart turned into a lump of lead. It was one thing losing a thousand pounds at a poker game. It was another thing altogether losing the contents of those boxes in the tunnel.

If they were discovered and seized Kerry's chances with the crowd he had been dealing with were very poor indeed.

He left Papers abruptly and walked to a point between Loretto Quinn's and Jack Coyne's establishments, where he could see the towpath properly. Sergeant Sheehan was walking back toward the bridge.

The staff could hardly believe that Mr. Costello was not there to direct everything in his quick light voice that brooked no argument. Instead there was a series of conflicting orders. Nobody could say whose job it was to set out the glasses and whether they should get their final polish before they left the hotel for the marquee or when they were in place on the tables.

The drink which had been kept in cold rooms . . . should it be moved out early or left to the last minute? The temporary staff hired for the day, who was in charge of their arrangements?

Please God let it be true that it was only a quick visit to the dentist, they told each other. Otherwise there was going to be the most appalling confusion and nobody liked to think of Mr. O'Neill's face, and the humiliation in front of all the people who were going to be arriving.

If Jim Costello were here the staff wouldn't be making ten trips back and forth when two would do. Jim would have a timetable, a schedule, and a calm manner that would snuff out any crisis before it had time to develop.

If Jim Costello had been here he would have seen the red, sweating face of Kerry O'Neill as the boy plowed back and forth through all those brambles and briars around the fairy fort. As he got the last lot through, there was a groan and the sound of falling earth. The pit posts had collapsed, barring the way behind him.

Kerry laughed aloud with relief. His laugh could be free while he was underground. When he came to the surface he controlled it. From now it was simple.

Kerry was in his shirt sleeves, struggling with boxes and crates. To the staff who had been hired for the day he was just one more worker bringing just one more load to join the general store of food and drink.

To the regular staff he was O'Neill's troublesome son who had decided to do a bit of work for a change because Mr. Costello had been struck with the toothache.

Nobody found it the slightest bit odd to see boxes being stored in the huge glass conservatory at the back of the main house. After all, this was a gala, there were probably going to be drinks in every room, not only the official bars, the marquee and the Thatch Bar.

There were more boxes than Kerry would have believed possible. His heart pounded with the fear of discovery, and his arms and back ached with having to carry the weight of so many loads.

The conservatory had been an inspired idea. It was one of the few rooms that would not be in use, and the chance of them being accidentally investigated by an eager barman would be unlikely.

It had been decided that there was too much glass in this room, too many panes, and too many plants to make it a suitable place for a party. Jim Costello had been at enough functions to know that it was not wise to mix euphoria, free liquor, and plates of glass.

Kerry's carefully stacked boxes would be safe here. Until they could be collected tomorrow. One phone call saying what he had done. And then he was clear.

"I can either take the tooth out now, which will guarantee you have no pain, or I can give you a temporary filling and we'll try to save the tooth later."

Jim Costello did not need a moment's thought. "Give me a mirror," he asked.

He looked. The missing tooth would show—only a little, but it would be seen.

"I'll have the filling, if you will," he said. He lay back in the chair.

He knew there was nothing to be gained by fussing and looking at his watch; the man was going to take his own time doing the job no matter how agitated the patient was. Better relax and realize that the world can, if necessary, go on without you.

* * *

Grace was surprised to see Kerry.

"You look terrible," she said.

"Can I use your bathroom?"

"Yes, but what happened?"

"I want to clean up. I have to go back to the lodge and get changed, and I don't want anyone to see me like this and ask questions. God, how I hate questions."

"Sorry," Grace said sulkily.

In a few minutes he looked more presentable. Now no one would comment.

"Well, are you looking forward to the day?" he asked.

"Yes and no. Michael is still very down. I hate people not to be good-tempered."

"What's wrong with him?"

"Oh, he's being silly, he'll get over it. When can we go back into the tunnel?"

Kerry laughed suddenly. "Anytime you like," he said, then he stopped. "Hey wait, don't go back there; there's been a subsidence. It's dangerous now, some of those old posts have given way."

"They couldn't have—"

"They have," he said curtly. "And anyway, no fooling around, you hear. You're not to be just anyone's. You're Grace O'Neill, you're very important."

She hugged him. "Oh, Kerry, it's nice that you're all cheerful again. Maybe today . . . maybe Father . . ."

"Yes, it could happen. Why not?" Kerry left her room and ran lightly down the stairs, through the hall filled with sprays and blooms and people from the florist's. As he was going down the steps of the hotel to his car, he saw Jim Costello coming up.

"Your big day," Kerry said pleasantly.

"Yes, great beginning with a butcher in a dentist's chair," Jim said ruefully.

"I heard. Is it okay?"

"Look at it this way. I don't think he loosened too many of the others, and I've wiped away most of the blood."

Kerry laughed. He used to think Costello an arrogant little guy. But he did have a sense of humor. And a great sense of command. Kerry stood and watched while he managed to restore order to the huge hall in moments.

Jim Costello looked back at Kerry too. The fellow seemed high or excited. He laughed too readily, like people do when they are in the middle of something dangerous.

Kate had sought the moment to tell John their news. She had not been able to find it.

She had thought that last night when the bar closed, they might sit in the garden and she would tell him then.

But the bar just wouldn't close. The sense of excitement about the opening was everywhere.

Mary Donnelly had worked like an automaton. She said it might be the last good night's business they ever had. Keep serving, keep pouring, keep clanging the till.

There was no danger of a raid. Sergeant Sheehan wouldn't be so discourteous. And even if some of his superiors would be here for the official opening of Fernscourt, none of them would arrive the night before, so a little after-hours drinking would not be anything to come down on too heavily.

There was no time last night. They were both too tired. She had been going to tell him this morning, until all the drama in the bathroom and Carrie's predicament had intervened. It almost seemed like a surfeit of pregnancy to tell John about hers!

Perhaps this evening, in the peace and quiet. Perhaps that would be a good time.

She settled herself in her finery, and waited for him to come and wheel her across the footbridge and to the party.

The music was marvelous. *Tales from the Vienna Woods,* a selection from *The Gondoliers* and some rousing Sousa marches. Jim Costello had known the right band to hire, and the right repertoire for it to play.

On all sides of Mountfern they smiled when it struck up. The gala opening was under way.

For ages Dara sat on the window seat looking at the crowds gathering.

She could see cars coming down the big drive that led from the main road to Fernscourt. Local people walked up River Road and were crossing by the footbridge.

She saw Dad wheel the chair across, and a little lump came in her throat. Mam would so much have liked to have walked. Poor Mam, missing Mrs. Fine in spite of everything.

Dara had not been upset by her mother's remarks. That was what Mrs. Fine *would* have said, after all. All that about Kerry being dangerous.

She stood up and smoothed the red dress. It did look very, very good. And nobody had said anything about the make-up, which meant that she didn't have quite enough on. She would put on more lipstick and go across. Kerry would be waiting for her.

Mary Sheehan couldn't understand it. Her husband had said that he had to do one simple job, which would put him in great standing with the lads and the superiors today. He had brought guards in early from the big town, saying that there was a cache of stolen goods in some hole or tunnel over on the towpath.

The guards arrived early in order to have it all cleared by the time any festivities began. They had gone in and found nothing but children's playing things.

Seamus Sheehan had looked in disbelief at the clay and the splintered wood. This hadn't been heaped like that last night. The tunnel had stretched farther. Surely it had?

But then he hadn't followed it. He hadn't needed to. The boxes and crates had been here in this room. This room now with nothing but children's tables, chairs, and a broken sofa.

Sergeant Sheehan stared in front of him as he sat stupefied in his chair. It was no use that Sheila Whelan backed him up. What did people from the big town make of Sheila except to think she was the local postmistress? They weren't to know that she was the soundest person in the place.

He had been a fool not to have gone in straight after McCann had left last night. He had thought it would be better to do the thing by the light of the day.

He had been wrong.

One of the men from the tourist board stood near Patrick and told him who the people were. This was the Protestant bishop arriving now, a very big gesture; people would talk of this for a long time. There were TDs from all political parties and one cabinet minister. There were other hoteliers there, and the man from the tourist board said that their faces were forty shades of green. They muttered from one vista to the next about the size of the grant O'Neill must have gotten, the money he must have sunk in it, the hopelessness of trying to compete with anything like this, the folly of believing that there could ever be a return on such expenditure.

Patrick loved it. Every moment of it.

And he loved it when Mr. Williams, the vicar, introduced him to the Walters and the Harrises. People of substance, who had estates near Mountfern. Mr. Walters said his father used to come here a lot in the old days, and Colonel Harris said that he had old pictures of the place in its previous existence. It was wonderful to see it rise again.

They spoke as if a mere half century of being a ruin had been a slight inconvenience and that it had been no trouble for Patrick to get the place started again.

Patrick gave several grateful looks at Jim Costello. The man was a wonder. He managed to be everywhere and yet unobtrusive. Small, handsome, and efficient, courteous and determined. What he would give to have had a son like that!

His own son was behaving well for once. His face looked flushed and excited. He was the center of attention as he moved easily among the crowd.

But while Costello moved about seeing that people were all right, that no one was alone or feeling outside things, Kerry moved like a glorious light that has no purpose except to be looked at and admired.

The twins crossed the footbridge together, as they had done so many times.

In the days when their lives were full of fantasy and imagination they could not have dreamed up anything as splendid as this.

"You look terrific, Dara."

"Thanks, Michael. So do you. Very very smart."

Dara wanted to hold his hand for some reason, to reassure him. They walked up through the laurels. The marquee for lunch was by the dock and the barge. But the drinks and welcoming party were around the steps and the main hall.

They came into the crowded forecourt and Dara saw him. There stood Kerry in his new white jacket that he had told her about, his pink-and-white shirt. He looked like a hero, not a man. She saw him laughing and bending a little to listen, then he threw back his head and laughed again.

He was with Kitty Daly, who looked stunning. Her long hair hung loose like a huge halo around her, almost like a cape over her magnificent dress.

Kitty was wearing the copper-colored dress that had been made for Maggie. On Maggie it had been a big flowing dress. On Kitty, who was tall and leggy, the copper dress was a mini-dress.

She looked at Kerry O'Neill with all the confidence of a beauty who doesn't need to wonder if other people are looking at her.

She would expect them to be looking. And liking what they saw.

"Are you all right?" Jim Costello spoke to Dara Ryan, who was holding on to one of the huge urns near the steps.

"Yes. Yes, why?"

"I thought you looked dizzy for a moment."

"No. No, I'm fine. Thank you very much."

Jim looked at her appreciatively. "You look very well, I must say, Dara, really very smart."

"Thanks, Mr. Costello."

He wondered why her voice was so dead. She really did look well in that red silk. Unlike Grace, who looked like a meringue in all that pink linen and broderie anglaise.

But Dara Ryan had no life in her eyes; she had hardly heard the compliment.

Michael came back with two glasses of orange. They had sugar around the edge and a slice of real orange cut so that it was fixed to the glass.

"Have this," he said.

Dara took it silently.

"She can't know; she wasn't here for the dress and everything."

"I know, I remembered that."

"She must have just found it at home." He was trying to take the pain out of Dara's eyes.

"Yes. Yes, that must have been it."

"And I'm sure he doesn't like her *really,* it's only with all that hair and everything . . ." His voice trailed away.

Papers Flynn and Mary Donnelly raised their glasses to each other as they sat in the warm autumn sunshine outside Ryan's pub.

Mary produced soda bread and slices of ham.

"Much better fare here than we'd get across there," she said.

"It's that, all right." Papers ate happily.

"I never go for salmon all that much," Mary said.

"Full of bones, it would have your throat in ribbons," said Papers, who had never tasted salmon in his life.

Eddie saw Leopold crossing the footbridge.

He remembered his mother's advice: do nothing, nothing at all, without careful thought. He stood there and tried to think carefully. What would a normal person do? Would they ignore Leopold? Or would they take him home? Would they offer him a plate of salmon? The more he thought, the more Eddie realized that careful thinking helped him not at all.

He watched the dog go around the hotel and out toward the back.

The action moved down toward the marquee. Luncheon was being served. The band had started to play lunchtime numbers like songs from *The Student Prince* and *The Merry Widow.*

Dara watched as Kerry's arm guided Kitty toward the huge lunch tent. He had never even looked for her.

She stood high on the steps of Fernscourt and watched them. Why had he not looked for her? Why had he said he loved her only short days ago; why did he hold her and say she was precious and beautiful beyond all imagining, if he was going to be with Kitty Daly? Did he know all the time that Kitty was coming, that she had turned out to be so beautiful?

Dara didn't believe that he could have held her in his arms and thought of Kitty. It was impossible. Kerry was so good, so true, and he wanted the best for her. For everyone.

Suddenly it made sense to her. He did want the best. And up to now she had been the best in Mountfern. She had been young and not bad-looking, and she had loved him. But now there was a better best. There was Kitty, and he had to have her. The way he had to have that jacket which had cost a fortune. And he had to have the car. And money for gambling.

With a shock she realized that he might have had to get Rachel Fine out of Mountfern. He hadn't liked her and she might have married his father and become a person of importance. She shook her head. All this and seeing Maggie's dress. It made her feel dizzy, as if she were going to fall.

She sat down on the steps, and to her astonishment Leopold came and laid his head on her lap.

"What in the name of God are you doing here, Leopold?" she asked him, and he looked up at her from an awkward angle, trying to explain that he thought there might have been a bit of fun and he had come because everyone else was there.

Eddie appeared at that moment, looking anxiously around from behind an urn.

"Can I take it that you'll be responsible for him now, could we say that I handed him over to you?" Eddie said.

"Wouldn't you know that you'd have to let us down by bringing Leopold?" Dara said.

"I didn't, he came across all by himself."

"Yeah, carrying his invitation in his teeth."

"What'll we do, Dara?"

"We'll take him home. Come on," she said.

"But it's not over. There's lots more to go." He was disappointed.

"Wouldn't it be safer to go, Eddie, before you do anything dreadful that'll be remembered for years, like the confession box?"

Eddie was philosophical. "I suppose it would be best," he said.

They made a funny little threesome, Eddie with his spiky hair, Dara in her magnificent red silk dress, and Leopold, happy now that he had seen all there was to see.

Kerry O'Neill was coming out to look for Dara, and he saw them reach the footbridge. She had probably been sent to take that awful brother and awful dog home. She would be back later. He would see her then.

Michael found Grace with Tommy and Jacinta and Liam.

"She didn't know," he said. "That it was a special dress for Maggie."

They agreed. Grudgingly. Kitty couldn't have known.

"It looks quite different on her, anyway," Grace said. Grace was very disappointed with her own outfit. She wished that Mrs. Fine was still here; she was great at advising people. Mrs. Fine had been so nice to them that time, that short time at the beginning of the summer.

Marian Johnson could look wonderful, Mrs. Fine had said, if she wore tailored clothes. She needed well-cut almost mannish garments, not the soft fly-away things she usually wore.

Today Marian looked very smart in a dark blue and white suit and a blouse with a cameo brooch like Mrs. Whelan wore. She was with a very shabby big untidy man that people said was a barrister. Grace heard them say that he was Marian's escort. Imagine having escorts at that age.

She went over to her father who was standing momentarily alone.

"Do you miss Mrs. Fine, Father?" she asked unexpectedly.

Patrick put his arm around his daughter. "It's funny you should say that. I was thinking of her this very moment. She's going to call tonight. Or I'm to call her. Anyway, when it's over, we'll talk."

"So you're still good friends with her?" Grace looked pleased.

"No, sadly not. But tonight is special; she and I will talk tonight and then not again for a long while."

Jim Costello toured ceaselessly. He found smears on some glasses. They were dealt with effortlessly, not by any shouts and roars but by a quick quiet word with someone and the use of the phrase "this minute, please" on almost every occasion.

He ensured that the rooms where valuable antiques were kept had people watching them, and he checked that the revelers had not got into the conservatory. He frowned slightly at the boxes which had been stored there. He looked at the top one. Whiskey.

It was probably some fail-safe idea of O'Neill's. He was determined that nobody in the county would go dry. He must have ordered a few more crates put in this morning.

At least they were out of the way; nobody would think they were meant to come and carouse in here.

"Where's Dara?" Grace asked Michael.

"I don't know. I've been looking for her."

Michael was afraid that Dara might be crying somewhere.

"Do you think she's upset about Kitty being with Kerry?" Grace asked.

"I don't know. Do you think he really likes Kitty, or what?"

"I expect he just wants to have fun with everybody," Grace said.

"Isn't that what everyone wants?"

Michael saw Grace look around as Jim Costello passed by. A feeling of sadness came over him. Having fun with everybody. Yes, that probably was what everybody wanted. It was what the O'Neills wanted anyway.

Everyone was in the marquee now listening to the speeches. The band was silent and respectful as the dignitaries spoke. All of them praised the courage and foresight of Patrick O'Neill, to come back to this spot and build his monument. They said that faith like his was needed more and more. They looked forward to the day when Americans who came to stay in his hotel would themselves come to build in Ireland and put stone on stone in friendship as their ancestors had done. There was hardly anyone in the main house to see the curtains move in the breeze that came in the open window. And there was nobody there to see when the curtains flapped against the ashtray and knocked it over. The cigarette smoldered on the carpet for a long time before the breeze fanned it into a flame and the flame caught the curtains. The long blue drapes that Rachel Fine had worked on so long to get the right texture, the right shade, and the right look for Fernscourt.

The kitchen staff were far away from it, Jim Costello was hearing himself praised in the marquee, the staff who would serve in the Thatch Bar were busy setting up the place for the onslaught they would have descending on them as soon as the speeches were finished. There wasn't a man in Mountfern who wouldn't prefer a pint to the glasses of champagne which were on offer in the big tent.

There was nobody to see the way the singeing became a flame and the way a breeze carried the flame to the top of the curtains. The residents' lounge burned discreetly and thoroughly behind the closed doors.

By the time the door burned down, the blaze was out of control.

"Did you see Dara?" Kerry asked Tommy Leonard. "I've been looking for her all day."

"Yeah, I can see you have." Tommy's eyes were fixed pointedly on Kitty Daly's arm, which Kerry still held.

"Well, if you see her tell her I've been trying to find her."

"Certainly," Tommy said. "I'll tell her your sight was taken from your eyes and you're going around with a white stick bumping into things, desperate to find her."

Sergeant Sheehan saw the fire first.

In years to come he would always remember that. The disappointments of the morning, the shame and the laughter were as nothing when compared to being the hero who discovered the fire and arranged the fire-fighting force.

He wasted no time, when he saw the smoke. He yanked Jim Costello from the marquee and together they ran toward it.

Then to the kitchen with shouts about telephoning for further help. By this stage the carefully placed fire extinguishers would be useless. A hose was in place within minutes, and the sergeant got Jimbo Doyle, who had the loudest voice in the county, to give the alarm through the main house in case there was anyone in any of the bathrooms or in any other part of the building.

The Thatch Bar was emptied of its staff, who were marshaled into a line of water carriers.

Chauffeurs of cars, three bus drivers, and five taxi men from the big town were roped in.

A serious fire-fighting effort had begun before they saw any need to alert the people in the marquee. There was no danger to life, and even if the fire could not be contained, there was very easy emergency escape for everyone across the footbridge and over the River Fern.

Sergeant Sheehan had been the first to see the fire. The first in Fernscourt, that is.

Papers Flynn had seen the smoke much earlier.

A lifetime of never getting involved leaves its mark. Papers never brought up any subject first; he was a person who responded rather than initiated. You only got into trouble by paying attention to anyone else's business.

He sat in the sun outside Ryan's and saw the smoke coming out of a side window. Papers looked at it silently for a long time.

Mary Donnelly had gone into the house with Mrs. Ryan's daughter. That boy who was always in trouble had come back, too, and the nice dog. Papers had always admired Leopold and thought him a fine animal.

He wondered should he say anything about the smoke, but the habits of a lifetime held him back.

Eddie came out and joined him on the seat.

"I could go back if I wanted to," Eddie said.

"Oh, you could, right enough."

"I wasn't sent away or anything."

"No, no, you wouldn't be."

"Well, I usually would be, but not this time."

Papers nodded in agreement.

"I'll have to make that clear to Mam. I came back of my own free will. I wouldn't want Mam sitting in the chair there thinking maybe I'd been ordered to leave."

The mention of Mrs. Ryan in her wheelchair galvanized Papers. Suppose there was a fire and Mrs. Ryan wasn't able to get out?

"Would you think that's smoke over there?" he said to Eddie.

Eddie squinted at it. "It is, it is all right."

He ran back into the pub. Mary and Dara were just coming out.

"I'm going back, Eddie, it's up to you, but maybe you'd prefer to stay here," Dara said. She looked very serious but not as if she were fighting or giving out to him.

"There's smoke," Eddie shouted.

Dara took no notice of him.

"Mary has pointed out rightly that Mam and Dad paid a fortune for this dress, and I must go back and get value out of it for them. Even if I don't feel like it."

It was as if she were talking to herself.

"I think the hotel's on fire," Eddie said.

This time he managed to get their attention.

And by now the figures of Sergeant Sheehan and Jim Costello could be seen, running as fast as they could. Eddie was right; the hotel was very definitely on fire.

Patrick's speech was almost over. He had thanked everybody who should have been thanked, but it wasn't tedious. The officials who had helped him all felt included in his generous tribute to the authorities, and the people of Mountfern felt individually acknowledged as he looked around the crowd and his eyes seemed to rest on them. Each and every person knew how much they meant to him, he said. He explained that a homecoming would be nothing if it weren't for the people. Buildings were symbols but the people were the heart of it all.

He said his family meant a great deal to him, but in a sense he had found a greater and wider family of friends.

He was about to end by wishing that this new family of friends should join him in the Thatch Bar when the cry went up. It was a terrible sound, the cry that told them that Fernscourt was on fire and it was going to burn to the ground unless something was done quickly.

They started to move the people from the marquee.

"Over the bridge" was the cry but nobody wanted to go. They stood in groups watching with horrified fascination as the flames leaped from the windows of the residents' lounge and appeared, too, in the narrow windows of the piano bar. The line of people passing the buckets was slow. The hose seemed a trickle.

Men ran up, throwing off their coats, to join the firefighting. Orders were given and countermanded. The guards arranged for buckets to come from the river; everyone told everyone else that the fire brigade was coming.

"Ring them again, someone, and tell them to send everything they've got," Martin White said.

Then he moved over to Kate Ryan's side. "Back home with you now. That's an order."

"The children," she said.

"They'll follow. Come on, Kate. I'm taking you home." John had moved the chair on and wheeled it rapidly toward the bridge.

Mrs. Daly blocked their way. "We should get people to pray," she said. "That's what we have to do now. It's about time we realized it."

"You've realized it for years, Mrs. Daly," John said. "Now, could I get past you there? I'm a bit anxious to move Kate across so that I can go back and fight the fire."

She stood aside, hands still clasped.

"God, she's worse than I thought," John muttered as he wheeled Kate swiftly across the bridge.

"She might be right," Kate said grimly as they came to the pub.

Dara thought they looked very formal somehow, like a picture. A man standing, a woman sitting, both staring at something. Something impossible to believe.

Kate put her hand up on her shoulder to cover John's hand which was resting there.

"How in the name of God did it start?" Kate asked.

"It'll be all right," he soothed. "Look, it's less than before, it's much less. They've got it under control."

Dara came to stand beside them.

"Where's Eddie?" Kate asked.

"He's here, and there's Declan coming across the bridge now."

Eddie came up to his mother. "I was over here when it happened, talking to Dara and Mary and Papers. I had nothing to do with it, Mam," he began.

Kate drew him close to her. "Of course you didn't Eddie, darling Eddie," she said into his hair.

Eddie pulled away and looked at her. Nobody had ever called him darling Eddie in his life.

"In fact I was the first to spot it," he said.

"Of course you were." She held his hand very tight and her eyes were full of tears.

Michael caught up with Declan on the bridge.

"Come on, Mam will want to make sure we're all safe," he said.

"Now we're all here, I'm going back across," John said.

"You're going in that door behind the counter," said Mary.

"I can't sell a drink while the place is burning down across the way, I have to help."

"Aren't there plenty of big strong men huffing and puffing and playing fire engines over there? People want to buy drinks to calm their nerves. You're a publican, it's your duty to sell them."

The Ryan family smiled, all together. The same smile. John went back into his pub.

Patrick O'Neill had been quick to organize as well.

No standing dumbstruck at the awful and unexpected happening. Like Jim Costello, he was quick to see the frail and the feeble and get them organized.

"Colonel Harris, I wonder if I can ask you to help the canon out that way. That's very good of you. Liam, it would be a great help if you could get a chair for Mrs. Daly; she wants to do a bit of praying but I think she should do it sitting down. Jimbo, get the drivers to get back into their cars and move them way down the drive."

And all the time, with his dream burning before his very eyes, he kept assuring people it was under control, and that the brigades were coming, and there would be order restored in no time.

Carrie stood with a tear-stained face in a straw hat which had gotten very crushed by people trampling on it, but she had put it back on for some kind of comfort.

"Don't worry now, Carrie," he said. "We'll all be in the Thatch Bar this evening laughing over this."

It was then he saw that part of the roof on the Thatch Bar had caught.

Kerry worked with the rest on the fire line. Beside him Tommy Leonard and Jack Coyne passed buckets.

The hose was taken to deal with the straw roof on the bar. So they were relying on the human chain to keep the first fire under control.

"Well at least it's only a hotel," Jack Coyne said, panting. "Think what it would be like if it was an army barracks or something, with all those guns and explosives in it. Everyone here would be blown sky high."

"Jesus Christ," said Kerry, dropping his bucket.

"Kerry?" The people near him looked at him in alarm.

"Oh my God!" Kerry shouted. "Get back. Costello, get them back, get everyone away from it, get them away from it. Get back."

They thought he was hysterical. They pushed him out of the way in their efforts to fight the fire.

They would pause to wipe their foreheads and look to the main road, hoping for the comforting sound of many fire engines.

But it was a long way from the town.

Jim Costello didn't like Kerry's manner.

"Will somebody get O'Neill's son away from here?" he called in his cool voice, the voice that was used to being obeyed.

But Kerry had run onto the steps.

"There's guns," he shouted, "guns and gelignite! The whole place is going to blow up."

"Don't mind him."

"It's under control, we're winning, we've beaten it."

All around him were the soothing sounds of people who thought it was a brainstorm.

"I beg you, Costello." Kerry was grabbing wildly at Jim's coat. "They're in the conservatory."

Jim remembered the boxes. The boxes and crates.

"They're whiskey, you madman," he said.

"The top ones are. The others are ammunition."

At the pub they couldn't understand it. Why everyone had started to run down to the river.

At first people protested, what was it about, they were winning, the fire was beaten. When they heard what it was about they ran too, helping others, and looking over their shoulders in the panic of disbelief.

Grace had been looking for Michael when the cry went up that everyone was to abandon the firefighting. There was something in the hotel that was about to explode.

She looked around wildly for Michael but there was no sign of him.

"Get Grace back over the river," Patrick shouted to Jim Costello as he rounded others toward the footbridge.

"Come on, Grace." Jim ran with her for a few yards, then he left her at the laurels. "Go *on!*" he shouted as she paused.

"I don't want to be on my own . . ."

"You're not on your own, stupid. Look, there are all your friends up by the pub."

"Did Michael go without me?" Grace's lip trembled.

"Go on, please, Grace. That's my job, to get you over the river. Please, just go."

"And you?"

"I'll see you later on. I'll come and look for you."

"Promise?"

"I promise," he shouted over his shoulder and ran back to the crowd trying to hold Kerry O'Neill back from the flames.

The boy's face was wild.

"I put it there, I have to take it out."

Jim Costello felt Patrick O'Neill standing beside him.

"What's in it, Kerry?" Patrick asked.

"I don't know. Guns, ammunition of some kind."

"Of what kind?"

"I don't know, I tell you."

"Was it set to explode?" Jim looked at Patrick with new respect.

"No, Father, it wasn't meant to be here, it was McCann's friends."

"What were they trying to do with it?"

"I was storing it for them in the tunnel until they collected it."

Seamus Sheehan was beside them, and Dr. White.

The sergeant spoke. "Is it gelignite?"

"I don't *know*, I tell you. How do I know what gelignite looks like?"

"Were there detonators with it?" The sergeant was quiet.

No tempers, no lack of control, and here they were, five men standing beside a possible inferno.

"What do they look like?" Kerry was piteous now.

"Were there separate containers, boxes?"

"Yes. Yes, I think so."

"And you've put them all together. In there?" The sergeant indicated the burning building.

"Yes, I didn't look, I didn't have the time."

"We'd better not risk it," said Sergeant Sheehan, and they turned to leave.

"I'll go down the driveway to tell the fire brigade." Jim Costello was a quick thinker.

"Get any drivers, anyone in the buses far away down the drive," Patrick called.

He looked at neither his son nor the doctor, neither his hotel manager nor the local sergeant as he began to walk away toward the footbridge.

"Father . . . Father, they're in the conservatory, the fire hasn't gotten there yet, we could get them out," Kerry cried.

Seamus Sheehan shook his head. "It's too hot, they could go any minute, flames or no flames."

Kerry broke away and ran toward the house.

The sergeant made a move to run after him. Jim Costello was already half way down the drive toward the main garages of the hotel.

"Don't die saving him, Sheehan," called Martin White. "Let him go, he put the stuff there, let him go up with it."

They heard the sound of the fire engines about five seconds before the explosion.

It wasn't as huge as they had thought it would be. But it was huge enough to blow the back out of Fernscourt, and the fire now raged so that they knew it would never stop even if the fire engines dared come near it.

Nobody knew if there would be another explosion. To go anywhere nearer than they were would be suicide. And as it was they weren't sure what had happened to Kerry.

It seemed like slow motion as they watched it from the bridge. Hands to their mouths, stifling cries, and the sound of Mrs. Daly's prayers as a low drone in the background.

Then they saw the figure of Patrick O'Neill walk slowly up the steps of Fernscourt.

It could only have been seconds, but time stood still before he came out dragging Kerry with him.

Kerry was walking, his face was in his hands.

The crowd saw Martin White take off his jacket and put it around Kerry's shoulders. They couldn't see what had happened when the doctor took

Kerry's hands away from his face but they did see Patrick and Sergeant Sheehan turn away in pain from Kerry O'Neill's burns.

They had to let some of it burn itself out. It looked stark and terrifying, the Thatch Bar naked apart from a scattering of scratchy burned straw.

Patrick had been handed a brandy of a size that nobody had ever drunk and survived. He stood in the very spot where the entrance to his hotel might have been.

If things had been different.

If Kate Ryan had not had her accident that day.

If things had all been quite different.

The son who had been sharp enough to see where the entrance to their hotel should be had not been sharp enough for anything else. He was heading into the hospital in the big town in the back of an ambulance.

All around him Patrick heard the consolations and the encouragements. It would rise again.

The insurance would pay for everything, wasn't it a miracle that nobody had gotten killed or seriously injured?

They clutched at his arm, he even felt himself being hugged by people too full of emotion to trust themselves to speak.

All around him, he saw people finding each other, exclaiming they thought the other was lost.

He saw Jimbo wiping big tears out of Carrie's eyes with a green table napkin that said "Ryan's Shamrock Café."

He saw the lawyer Slattery who had always hated him and the O'Neills taking off his coat to put it around the shivering Grace. The coat looked enormous on her and it hid her silly pink and white dress.

Slattery had gotten her a cup of coffee and was speaking to her soothingly.

Sheila Whelan was of course beside Patrick. Knowing that he wanted to say something rather than platitudes.

"My God, Sheila, look at the misery I brought to people," he said. "Look at the sheer waste and misery."

"You didn't bring it, Patrick. It came all on its own."

"Jesus, who brought it if I didn't bring it?"

"You could say I did. I told Seamus Sheehan about the tunnel."

"What in the name of God took him in with that gang?" Patrick asked.

"Seamus heard it was because he owed them money." Sheila spoke gently.

"Yes. I wouldn't give it to him." Patrick's heart lurched and he looked at his ruined hotel. "I expect he had to get it somewhere. My God, if I had known the price we'd have to pay."

"You'd have had to call a halt somewhere," she consoled him. "You couldn't have gone on paying for everything all his life, that would have been worse than your father paying for nothing all of his."

"Oh God, how am I going to tell Rachel?"

The sun shone down as mockery on the smoldering ruins of Ireland's finest hotel. Its light played on the remains of what had been described as the dream of international cooperation come true.

In groups they stood and ran it over in their minds, the causes and the possible outcomes.

As usual, because it was Mountfern there were as many theories as there were people speaking.

The electricity was faulty, the chimneys had never been right. It was a cigarette, it was an attempt to assassinate some of the VIPs. It was a bottled-gas cooker, it was a bonfire to get rid of the rubbish.

They said that he would rebuild it right away, it would open in the spring. That he would take over the Grange and put his guests there, that he would walk out tonight and never come back. And then the roof went in.

It went with a series of cracks and groans as the timber fell and knocked down further stonework, and the shower of slates fell on top.

There was something very final about the way it fell.

The people of Mountfern raised a great roar as it went in. It was a startling sound. A roar went up from all the throats at the same time.

It was neither a shout of triumph nor a great wail of regret.

It was just a roar.

Patrick's eyes suddenly filled with tears. He didn't understand these people at all.

He saw Jack Leonard and Tom Daly, who had cheered when they had burned this house down in 1922; they had cheered as the ruins fell, Brian Doyle had told him. Today they cheered again.

How had he thought that this was his place and these were his people? He didn't even begin to understand why they had made that sound.

The twins stood together. Very close.

They weren't exactly touching but you could hardly have put a piece of paper between them. Tommy Leonard envied them their closeness. He had nobody like that. Nobody who would always be there no matter what.

For as long as he could remember they had been like that. Not so much this summer perhaps, but way way back. When they were both his best friends. Before he started to love Dara. He was right beside them but he couldn't think of anything to say that wouldn't sound appalling. He really was getting more and more like Eddie Ryan, he thought to himself grimly. It was an awful fate.

If he had been Kerry O'Neill he would have known the right thing to say. The word or the gesture that would have been what they needed.

He said, "At least we have each other. Everything else has changed and gone, but we'll always be together in one way or another, won't we?"

Dara's eyes filled with tears.

"I don't mean love or anything, but as great friends. Won't we?"

Tommy looked from one to the other, anxious that there should be no misunderstanding. Anxious that he wasn't being seen to presume.

Dara laid her hand against his face. She didn't even try to wipe away her tears.

"I don't know what I'd do without you, Tommy Leonard," she said.

Although he could hardly believe it, Tommy knew, when he went over it again in his mind, that Dara meant it.

Mary served, and Sheila had gone behind the bar to help her.

Carrie, face aglow with Jimbo's delight and pride, ran back and forth with sandwiches and soda bread that they would never be serving now to American visitors.

Brian Doyle said he was glad that Peggy had gotten on her high horse and not come to the opening in the end, because a) she was highly strung and b) she might get very put out by all these weddings in the air—Jimbo Doyle's and Jack Coyne's, two of nature's bachelors.

Brian said that it would be like a sacrilege to discuss who'd get the job of building the place up again, but he wanted it known that it was a heartbreak and an agony from day one and he wouldn't wish it on his worst enemy.

Kate sat with John in the side yard.

There were no words between them.

She had told him the news in the most natural way.

John had sat with his head in his hands, bemoaning all that had happened.

"I'm weary, Kate, weary and sad. There has been nothing but destruction and death since that place was begun. There's never any hope, no beginnings."

"I'll tell you something about new life and new hope, that you'll hardly believe," Kate said.

They sat together in the yard that was filled with flowers. He held her very close, he pressed her to him.

He would take such care of her, he would make sure that it would all be all right.

A new life. Another person. Another Ryan.

They called Patrick to the phone. Again. He had taken so many calls that Jim Costello had eventually monitored them, standing in Kate's green room and dealing with whoever called.

But this time he called Patrick. It was long distance. From New York.

"Rachel, Rachel." His voice choked and he couldn't speak.

But at last he found the words. The words to tell her about the end of the dream. Then he put down the receiver and walked through the glass doors into the yard filled with flowers where Kate and John Ryan sat in a world of their own.

They looked up at him as he stood there, a big man always filling their place, dominating their lives.

"I came to tell you. I'll be going home," he said.

Silver Wedding

For Gordon Snell,
my dear love and my best friend

❖{ Contents }❖

CHAPTER ONE

Anna

Anna knew that he was doing his best to be interested. She could read his face so well. This was the same look she saw on his face when older actors would come up and join them in the club and tell old tales about people long gone. Joe tried to be interested then, too, it was a welcoming, courteous, earnest look. Hoping that it passed as genuine interest, hoping that the conversation wouldn't last too long.

"I'm sorry, I'm going on a bit," she apologized. She pulled a funny face at him as she sat at the other end of the bed dressed only in one of his shirts, the Sunday papers and a breakfast tray between them.

Joe smiled back, a real smile this time.

"No, it's nice that you're so worked up about it, it's good to care about families."

He meant it, she knew, in his heart he thought it was a Good Thing to care about families, like rescuing kittens from trees and beautiful sunsets and big collie dogs. In principle Joe was in favor of caring about families. But he didn't care at all about his own. He wouldn't have known how many years his parents were married. He probably didn't know how long he had been married himself. Something like a silver anniversary would not trouble Joe Ashe.

Anna looked at him with the familiar feeling of tenderness and fear. Tender and protective—he looked so lovely lying there against the big pillows, his fair hair falling over his face, his thin brown shoulders so relaxed and easy. Fearful in case she would lose him, in case he would move on gently, effortlessly, out of her life, as he had moved into it.

Joe Ashe never fought with people, he told Anna with his big boyish smile, life was much too short for fights. And it was true.

When he was passed over for a part, when he got a bad review, there was the shrug: "Well, so it could have been different but let's not make a production out of it."

Like his marriage to Janet. It was over, so why go on pretending? He just packed a small bag and left.

Anna feared that one day in this very room he would pack a small bag and leave again. She would rail and plead as Janet had done and it would be no use. Janet had even come around and offered Anna money to go away. She wept about how happy she had been with Joe. She showed pictures of the two small sons. It would all be fine again if only Anna would go away.

"But he didn't leave you to come to me, he had been in a flat by himself for a year before he even met me," Anna had explained.

"Yes, and all that time I thought he would come back."

Anna hated to remember Janet's tearstained face, and how she had made tea for her, and hated even more to think that her own face would be stained with tears like this one day, and as unexpectedly as it had all happened to Janet. She gave a little shiver as she looked at the handsome easy boy in her bed. Because even if he was twenty-eight years of age, he was still a boy. A gentle cruel boy.

"What are you thinking?" he asked.

She didn't tell him. She never told him how much she thought about him and dreaded the day he would leave.

"I was thinking it's about time they did another film version of *Romeo and Juliet*. You're so handsome it would be unfair to the world not to get a chance to look at you," she said laughingly.

He reached out and put the breakfast tray on the floor. The Sunday papers slid after it.

"Come here to me," said Joe. "My mind was running on the same lines entirely, entirely at all, 'at all' as you Irish say."

"What a superb imitation," Anna said dryly, but snuggling up to him all the same. "It's no wonder that you're the best actor in the whole wide world and renowned all over the globe for your great command of accents."

She lay in his arms and didn't tell him about how worried she was about this silver wedding. She had seen from his face that she had already been going on about it far too long.

In a million years Joe would not understand what it meant in their family. Mother and Father's twenty-fifth anniversary. They celebrated everything in the Doyle household. There were albums of memories, boxes chronicling past celebrations. On the wall of the sitting room at home there was a gallery of Major Celebrations. The wedding day itself, the three christenings. There was Grannie O'Hagan's sixtieth birthday, there was Grandpa Doyle's visit to London with all of them standing beside a sentry outside Buckingham Palace, a solemn young sentry in a busby who seemed to realize the importance of Grandpa Doyle's visit.

There were the three first communions, and the three confirmations; there was a small sporting section, Brendan's school team the year he had been on the Seniors. There was an even smaller academic section, one graduation portrait of Anna herself, very studied and posed, holding her diploma as if it were a ton weight.

Mother and Father always joked about the wall and said it was the most valuable collection in the world. What did they want with Old Masters and famous paintings, hadn't they gotten something much more valuable, a living wall telling the world what their life was all about?

Anna had winced whenever they said that to people who came in. She winced now, lying in Joe's arms.

"Are you shuddering at me or is that passion?" he asked.

"Unbridled passion," she said, wondering, Was it normal to lie beside the most attractive man in London and think not of him but of the sitting-room wall back in the family home?

The family home would have to be decorated for the silver wedding. There would be a lot of cardboard bells and silver ribbon. There would be flowers sprayed with a silver paint. They would have a tape of "The Anniversary Waltz" on the player. There would be windowsills full of cards, there might indeed be so many that it would call for an arrangement of streamers with the cards attached as they had for Christmas. The cake would have traditional decorations, the invitations would have silver edges. Inviting people to what? That was what was buzzing around Anna's head. As a family this was something they should organize for their parents. Anna and her sister, Helen, and her brother, Brendan.

But it really meant Anna.

She would have to do it all.

Anna turned toward Joe and kissed him. She would not think about the anniversary anymore now. She would think about it tomorrow, when she was being paid to stand in a bookshop.

She wouldn't think of it at this moment when there were far better things to think about.

"That's more like it. I thought you'd gone to sleep on me," Joe Ashe said, and held her very close to him.

Anna Doyle worked in Books for People, a small bookshop much patronized by authors and publishers and all kinds of media. They never tired of saying that this was a bookshop with character, not like the big chains which were utterly without soul. Secretly Anna did not altogether agree.

Too many times during her working day she had to refuse people who came in with perfectly normal requests for the latest best-seller, for a train timetable, for a book on freezer cookery. Always she had to direct them to a different shop. Anna felt that a bookshop worthy of the name should in fact stock such things instead of relying for its custom on a heavy psychology section, a detailed travel list, and poetry, sociology, and contemporary satire.

It wasn't as if they were even proper specialists. She had intended to leave a year ago, but that was just when she met Joe. And when Joe had come to stay, it happened to coincide with Joe not having any work.

Joe did a little here and there, and he was never broke. There was always enough to buy Anna a lovely Indian scarf, or a beautiful paper flower, or find the most glorious wild mushrooms in a Soho delicatessen.

There was never any money for paying the rent or for the television, or the phone or the electricity. It would have been foolish of Anna to have left a steady job without having a better one lined up for herself. She stayed in Books for People, even though she hated the name, believing that most of the buyers of books *were* people anyway. The others who worked there were all perfectly pleasant, she never saw any of them outside work but there were occasional book signings, poetry evenings, and even a wine and cheese evening in aid of a small nearby theater. That was when she had met Joe Ashe.

Anna was at work early on Monday morning. If she wanted time to think or to write letters, then to be in before the others was the only hope. There were only four of them who worked there; they each had a key. She switched off the burglar alarm, picked up the carton of milk and the mail from the mat. It was all circulars and handbills. The postman had not arrived yet. As Anna put on the electric kettle to make coffee, she caught sight of herself in the small mirror that was stuck to the wall. Her eyes looked large and anxious, she thought. Anna stroked her face thoughtfully. She looked pale and there were definitely shadows under the big brown eyes. Her hair was tied up with a bright pink ribbon matching exactly her pink T-shirt. She must put on a little makeup, she thought, or she would frighten the others.

She wished she had gone ahead and gotten her hair cut that time. It had been so strange, she had made an appointment in a posh place where some of the Royal Family went to have their hair done. One of the girls who worked there as a stylist came into the bookshop and they had started talking. The girl said she would give Anna a discount. But the night she met Joe at the benefit evening for the theater, he had told her that her thick dark hair was beautiful the way it was.

He had asked her, as he so often did still, "What are you thinking?" And in those very early times she told him the truth. That she was thinking about having her hair cut the following day.

"Don't even consider it," Joe had said, and then suggested that they go to have a Greek meal and discuss this thing properly.

They had sat together in the warm spring night and he had told her about his acting and she had told him about her family. How she lived in a flat because she had thought she was becoming too dependent on her family, too drawn into everything they did. She went home, of course, on Sundays and one other evening in the week. Joe had looked at her, enthralled. He had never known a life where adults kept going back to the nest.

In days she was visiting his flat, days later he was visiting hers because it was more comfortable. He told Anna briefly and matter-of-factly about Janet and the two little boys. Anna told Joe about the college lecturer she had loved rather unwisely during her final years, resulting in a third-class degree and in a great sense of loss.

Joe was surprised that she had told him about the college lecturer. There was no hassle about shared property, shared children. He had only told her about Janet because he was still married to her. Anna had wanted to tell everything, Joe hadn't really wanted to hear.

It was only logical that he should come to live with her. He didn't suggest it, and for a while she wondered what she would say if she were invited to take up residence in his flat. It would be so hard to tell Mother and Father. But after one long lovely weekend, she decided to ask Joe if he would move in properly to her small ground-floor flat in Shepherd's Bush.

"Well, I will, if that's what you'd like," Joe had said, pleased but not surprised, willing but not overly grateful. He had gone back to his own place, done a deal about the rent, and with two tote bags and a leather jacket over his arm he had come to live with Anna Doyle.

Anna Doyle, who had to keep his arrival very secret indeed from her mother and father, who lived in Pinner and in a world where daughters did not let married men come to spend an evening, let alone a lifetime.

He had been with her since that April Monday a year ago. And now it was May 1985, and by a series of complicated maneuvers Anna had managed to keep the worlds of Pinner and Shepherd's Bush satisfactorily apart while flitting from one to the other with an ever-increasing sense of guilt.

Joe's mother was fifty-six but looked years younger. She worked at the food counter of a bar where lots of actors gathered, and they saw her maybe two or three times a week. She was vague and friendly, giving them a wave as if they were just good customers. She hadn't known for about six months that they lived together. Joe simply hadn't bothered to tell her. When she heard, she said, "That's nice, dear," to Anna in exactly the same tone as she would have spoken to a total stranger who had asked for a slice of the veal and ham pie.

Anna had wanted her to come around to the flat.

"What for?" Joe had asked in honest surprise.

Next time she was in the pub, Anna went to the counter and asked Joe's mother herself.

"Would you like to come around and see us in the flat?"

"What for?" she had asked with interest.

Anna was determined. "I don't know, a drink maybe."

"Lord, dear, I never drink, seen enough of it in this place to turn you right against it, I tell you."

"Well, just to see your son," Anna went on.

"I see him in here, don't I? He's a grown-up now, love, he doesn't want to be looking at his old mum, day in day out."

Anna had watched them since with a fascination that was half horror and half envy. They were just two people who lived in the same city and who made easy casual conversation when they met.

They never talked of other members of the family. Nothing about Joe's sister, who had been in a rehabilitation center on account of drugs; or the eldest brother, who was a mercenary soldier of some sort in Africa; or the youngest brother, who worked in television as a cameraman.

She never asked about her grandchildren. Joe had told Anna that Janet did take them to see her sometimes, and occasionally he had taken the boys to a park nearby where his mother lived, and she had come along for a little while. He never took them to her home.

"I think she has a bloke there, a young fellow, she doesn't want a lot of grandchildren trailing around after her." To Joe it was simple and clear.

To Anna it was like something from another planet.

In Pinner, if there were grandchildren, they would have been the central pivot of the home, as the children had been for nearly a quarter of a century. Anna sighed again as she thought of the celebrations that lay ahead and how she would have to face up to them, as she had to face up to so many things on her own.

It was no use sitting in an empty bookshop with a coffee and a grievance that Joe wasn't as other men, supportive and willing to share these kinds of things with her. She had known there would be nothing like that from the first evening together.

What she had to do now was work out how the silver wedding could be organized in October in a way that wouldn't drive everyone mad.

Helen would be no use, that was for certain. She would send an illuminated card signed by all the sisters, she would invite Mother and Father to a special folk Mass with the community, she would get the day off and come out to Pinner in her drab gray sweater and skirt, her hair dull and lifeless and the big cross on a chain around her neck constantly in her hand. Helen didn't even look like a nun, she looked like someone a bit dopey and badly dressed retreating behind the big crucifix. And in many ways that's what she was. Helen would turn up, all right, if everything was organized, and in her canvas bag she would take back any uneaten food because one nun loved gingerbread and another had a weakness for anything with salmon in it.

With a sense of despair Anna could see months ahead into the future, with her younger sister Helen a member of a religious community in South London, picking her way through the food like a scavenger and filling a tin of biscuits with foil-wrapped tidbits.

But at least Helen would be there. Would Brendan come at all? That was the real worry, and the one she had been trying to avoid thinking about. If Brendan Doyle did not get the train and boat and then the train again and make it to Pinner for his parents' twenty-fifth wedding anniversary, they might as well call the whole thing off now. The disgrace would never be disguised, the emptiness would never be forgotten.

An incomplete family picture on the wall.

They would probably lie and say that he was in Ireland and couldn't be spared from the farm, the harvest, or the shearing or whatever people did on farms in October.

But Anna knew with sickening clarity that it would be a paper-thin excuse. The best man and the maid of honor would know there had been a coldness, and the neighbors would know, and the priests would know.

And the shine would be taken off the silver.

How to get him back, that was the problem. Or was it? What to get him back for? Perhaps that was a bigger problem.

Brendan had always been so quiet when he was a schoolboy. Who would have known that he felt this strange longing to go away from the family to such a remote place? Anna had been so shocked the day he told them. Utterly straightforward and with no care about what it would do to the rest of the family.

"I'm not going back to school in September, it's no use trying to persuade me. I'll never get any exams, and I don't need them. I'm going to Vincent. In Ireland. I'll go as soon as I can leave."

They had railed and beseeched. With no success. This is what he was going to do.

"But why are you doing this to us?" Mother had cried.

"I'm not doing anything to you." Brendan had been mild. "I'm doing it for me, it's not going to cost you any money. It's the farm where Father grew up, I thought you'd be pleased."

"Don't think he'll turn the farm over to you automatically," Father had spluttered. "That old recluse could just as well leave it to the missions. You could easily find you've put in all that hard work for nothing."

"Father, I'm not thinking of inheritances and wills and people dying, I'm thinking of how I'd like to spend my days. I was happy there, and Vincent could do with another pair of hands."

"Well, if he does, isn't it a wonder that he never married and provided himself with a few pairs of hands of his own around the place without asking strangers in to him?"

"Hardly a stranger, Father," Brendan had said. "I am his own flesh and blood, his brother's child."

It had been a nightmare.

And the communication since had been minimal, cards at Christmas and on birthdays. Perhaps anniversaries. Anna couldn't remember. Anniversaries. How was she going to assemble the cast for this one?

The maid of honor, as they always called her, was Maureen Barry. She was Mother's best friend. They had been at school together back in Ireland. Maureen had never married; she was the same age as Mother, forty-six, though she looked younger. She had two dress shops in Dublin—she refused to call them boutiques. Perhaps Anna could talk to Maureen and see what would be best. But a warning bell went off loudly in her head. Mother was a great one for not letting things go outside the family.

There had always been secrets from Maureen.

Like the time that Father had lost his job. It couldn't be told.

Like the time that Helen ran away when she was fourteen. That was never breathed to Maureen. Mother had said that nothing mattered in the end, everything could be sorted out just so long as family matters weren't aired abroad, and neighbors and friends weren't told all of the Doyle business. It seemed to be a very effective and soothing cure when things went wrong, so the family had always stuck to it.

You would think that Anna should phone Maureen Barry now and ask her as Mother's oldest friend what was best to do about Brendan and about the anniversary in general.

But Mother would curl up and die if she thought there was the remotest possibility of any member of the family revealing a secret outside it. And the coldness with Brendan was a big secret.

There were no family members who could be asked to act as intermediaries.

So what kind of party? The day was a Saturday, it could be a lunch. There were a lot of hotels around Pinner, Harrow, Northwood, and restaurants and places used to doing functions like this. Perhaps a hotel would be best.

It would be formal, for one thing. The banqueting manager would advise about toasts and cakes and photographs.

There wouldn't have to be weeks of intensive cleaning of the family home and manicuring the front garden.

But a lifetime as the eldest of the Doyles had taught Anna that a hotel would not be right. There were all those dismissive remarks about hotels in the past, destructive and critical remarks about this family, which couldn't be bothered having the thing in their own home, or the other family, which would be quite glad to invite you to a common hotel, an impersonal place, but wouldn't let you over their own doorstep, thank you very much.

It would have to be home, the invitation would have to say in silver lettering that the guest was being invited to Salthill, 26 Rosemary Drive, Pinner. Salthill had been a seaside resort over in the West of Ireland where Mother and Maureen Barry used to go when they were young, it had been lovely, they said.

Father had never been there, he said there was little time for long family holidays when he was a boy making his way in Ireland.

Wearily Anna made the list; it would be this size if there wasn't an Irish contingent, and that size if there were. It could be this size if there was to be a sit-down meal, that size if it were a buffet. This size if it were just drinks and snacks, that size if it were a proper meal.

And who would pay for it?

Very often the children did, she knew that.

But Helen had taken a vow of poverty and had nothing. Brendan, even if he did come, which wasn't likely, was working for an agricultural worker's wages. Anna had very little money to spend on such a party.

She had very little money indeed. By dint of hard saving, no lunches, and a few wise buys at Oxfam, she had saved £132. It was in the building society hoping to become £200, and then, when Joe had £200, they were going to Greece together. Joe had £11 at the moment, so he had a longer way to go. But he was sure to get a part soon. His agent had said there were a lot of things coming up. He'd be working any day now.

Anna hoped that he would, she really and truly did.

If he got something good, something where they recognized him properly, something steady, then everything else could fall into place. Not just the Greek holiday but everything. He could arrange a settlement for his sons, give Janet something that would make her feel independent, begin the divorce proceedings. Then Anna could risk leaving Books for People and go to a bigger shop; she would easily get promotion in a large bookshop, a graduate, experienced in the trade already. They would love her.

The time had gone by in thought, and soon the keys were turning in the door and the others arriving. Soon the door was open to the public. Planning was over yet again.

At lunchtime Anna made up her mind that she would go out to Pinner that evening and ask her parents straight out how they would like to celebrate the day. It seemed less celebratory than telling them that it was all in hand. But to try to do that was nonsense, really, and she could still get it wrong. She would ask them straight out.

She rang them to say she would be coming over. Her mother was pleased.

"That's good, Anna, we haven't seen you for ages and ages. I was just saying to Daddy I hope Anna's all right and there's nothing wrong."

Anna gritted her teeth.

"Why would there be anything wrong?"

"Well, it's just been so long, and we don't know what you do."

"Mother, it's been eight days. I was with you last weekend."

"Yes, but we don't know how you are getting on. . . ."

"I ring you almost every day, you *know* how I'm getting on and what I do, get up in Shepherd's Bush and get the tube in here, and then I go home again. That is what I do, Mother, like a great many million people in London do." Her voice rose in rage at her mother's attitude.

The reply was surprisingly mild. "Why are you shouting at me, Anna, my dear child? I only said I was delighted you were coming over this evening, your father will be overjoyed. Will we have a little steak and mushrooms? That's what we'll have as a celebration to welcome you back. Yes, I'll run down to the butcher's this afternoon, and get it. . . . That's simply great you're going to come back. I can't wait to tell your father, I'll give him a ring at work now and tell him."

"Don't . . . Mother, just . . . well, I mean . . ."

"Of course I'll tell him, give him pleasure, something to look forward to."

When she hung up, Anna stood motionless, hand on the receiver, and thought about the one time she had brought Joe to lunch at Salthill, 26 Rosemary Drive. She had invited him as "a friend" and had spent the entire journey making him promise not to reveal that he was (a) living with her and (b) married to someone else.

"Which is the more dangerous one to let slip?" Joe had asked, grinning.

"They're both equally dangerous," she had said with such seriousness that he had leaned over and kissed her on the nose in the train in front of everyone.

It had been all right as a visit, Anna had thought. Mother and Father had inquired politely about Joe's acting career and whether he knew famous actors and actresses.

In the kitchen Mother had asked if he was Anna's boyfriend.

"Just a friend," Anna had insisted.

On the way home she asked Joe what he had made of them.

"Very nice but very tense people," he had said.

Tense? Mother and Father. She had never thought of them as tense. But in a way it was true.

And Joe didn't know what they were like when there was no outsider there, Mother wondering why Helen hadn't been there on two occasions during the week when they had telephoned her convent. Father striding around the garden snapping the heads off flowers and saying that boy was so restless and idle that he could only end up with the job of village idiot sucking straws on a small farm, it was hard to know why he had to go back to the one village in Ireland where they were known, and live with the one man in Ireland who could be guaranteed to give the worst impression of the Doyles and all their activities, his own brother, Brendan's Uncle Vincent. Just to inherit that miserable farm.

Joe had seen none of this side of things and yet he still thought her parents tense.

She had pursued it. Why? How did it show itself?

But Joe didn't want to be drawn.

"It's like this," he had said to her, smiling to take any hurt out of his words. "Some people just live that kind of life where this can be said and that can't be said, and people think what can be told and what can't. It's a way of going on where everything is a pretense, an act. . . . Now that doesn't bother me if people want to live like that. It's not my way, but people make up a lot of rules and live by them. . . ."

"We're not like that!" She was stung.

"I'm not criticizing you, my love. I'm just telling you what I see. . . . I see Hare Krishnas shaving their heads and dancing and waving bells. I see you and your family acting things out just like they do. I don't let the Hare Krishnas get up my nose, I won't let your old man and old lady either. Right?" He had grinned at her winningly.

She had grinned back with a hollow empty feeling inside her and resolved not to go on about home anymore.

The day came to an end. One of the nicer publishing reps was there as the shop closed. He asked her to come and have a drink.

"I'm going to darkest Pinner," Anna said. "I'd better set out now."

"I'm driving that way, why don't we have a drink en route?" he said.

"Nobody's driving to Pinner." She laughed.

"Oh, how do you know I don't have a mistress out that way, or am hoping to acquire one?" he teased.

"We wouldn't discuss such things in Rosemary Drive," Anna said, mock primly.

"Come on, get in, the car's on a double yellow line." He laughed.

He was Ken Green, she had talked to him a lot at the bookshop. They had both started work the same day, it had been a common bond.

He was going to leave his company and join a bigger one, so was she; neither of them had done it.

"Do you think we're just cowards?" she asked him as he negotiated the rush-hour traffic.

"No, there are always reasons. What's holding you back, these moral folk in Rosemary Drive?"

"How do you know they're moral folk?" she said, surprised.

"You just told me there'd be no talk of mistresses in your house," Ken said.

"Too true, they'd be very disappointed to know that I was one myself," Anna said.

"So would I." Ken seemed serious.

"Oh, stop that." She laughed at him. "It's always easy to pay compliments to someone you know is tied up, much safer. If I told you I was free and on the rampage, you'd run a hundred miles from me instead of offering me a drink."

"Absolutely wrong. I especially left your bookshop for last. I was thinking all day how nice it would be to see you. Don't you accuse me of being faint-hearted."

She patted his knee companionably. "No. I misjudged you." She sighed deeply. It was easy to talk to Ken, she didn't have to watch what she said. Like she would when she got to Salthill in Rosemary Drive. Like she would when she got back to Joe later on.

"Was that a sigh of pleasure?" he asked.

With Joe or with Mother or Father she would have said yes.

"Weariness. I get tired of all the lies," she said. "Very tired."

"But you're a big girl now. Surely you don't have to tell lies about your life and the way you live it."

Anna nodded her head glumly. "I do, truly I do."

"Maybe you only think you do."

"No, I do. Like the telephone. I've told them at home that my phone has been taken out, so that they won't ring me. That's because there's a message on the answering machine saying, 'This is Joe Ashe's number.' He has to have it, you see, because he's an actor and they can't be out of touch."

"Of course," Ken said.

"So naturally I don't want my mother ringing and hearing a man's voice. And I don't want my father asking what's this young man doing in *my* flat."

"True, he might well ask that, and why he didn't have a machine of his own and number of his own," Ken said sternly.

"So I have to be careful about not mentioning things like paying the phone bill. I have to remember I'm not meant to *be* on the phone. That's just one of the nine million lies."

"Well, is it all right at the other end of the line? I mean, you don't have to lie to this actor chap?" Ken seemed anxious to know.

"Lie? No, not at all, what would I have to lie about?"

"I don't know, you said all the lies you had to tell everywhere. I thought maybe he was a jealous macho fellow, you couldn't tell him you went for a drink with me. That's if we ever get anywhere near a drink." Ken looked ruefully at the taillights.

"Oh, no, you don't understand. Joe would be glad to think I went for a drink with a friend. It's just . . ." Her voice trailed away. What was it just? It was just that there was an endless, utterly endless need to pretend. Pretend she was having a good time in the odd place where they went. Pretend she understood this casual relationship with his mother, his wife, his children. Pretend she liked these fringe theaters where he played small parts. Pretend she enjoyed lovemaking every time. Pretend she didn't care about this heavy family business ahead of her.

"I don't lie to Joe," she said, as if she were speaking to herself. "I just act a bit."

There was a silence in the car.

"Well, he *is* an actor, I suppose," Ken said, trying to revive the conversation a little.

That wasn't it. The actor didn't act at all, he never pretended to please anyone else. It was the actor's girlfriend who did all the acting. How odd that she had never thought of it that way before.

They sat and talked easily when they eventually found a pub.

"Do you want to ring your people to say you've been delayed?" Ken suggested.

She looked at him, surprised that he should be so thoughtful.

"Well, if they've bought steak and everything . . ." he said.

Mother was touched. "That was nice of you, dear. Father was beginning to look out for you. He said he'd walk down to the station."

"No, I'm getting a lift."

"Is it that Joe? Joe Ashe, the actor?"

"No, no, Mother, Ken Green, a friend from work."

"I don't think I got enough steak. . . ."

"He's not coming to supper, he's just driving me there."

"Well, ask him in, won't you? We love to meet your friends. Your father and I often wish you brought friends back here more often. That all of you did over the years." Her voice sounded wistful, as if she were looking at her wall of pictures and not getting a proper charge from them.

"I'll ask him in for a moment then," Anna said.

"Could you bear it?" she asked Ken.

"I'd like it. I can be a beard."

"What on earth is that?"

"Don't you read your gossip magazines? It's someone who distracts attention from your real love. If they get to meet upright fellows like me, they won't get the wind of evil, sensual actor lovers who have their answering machines tied to your phone."

"Oh, shut up!" She laughed. It was easy laughter, not forced.

They had another drink. She told Ken Green about the anniversary. She told him briefly that her sister was a nun, her brother had dropped out and gone to work on the farm of her father's eldest brother, Vincent, a small run-down place on Ireland's west coast. Feeling a little lighter and easier already, she told him that this was why she was having supper with her parents. For the first time in a long while she was going to come right out in the open, ask them what they wanted, tell them the limitations. Explain the problems.

"Don't go too heavily on the limitations and problems, if they're like you say. Dwell more on the celebratory side," he advised.

"Did your parents have a silver wedding?"

"Two years ago," Ken said.

"Was it great?" she asked.

"Not really."

"Oh."

"When I know you better, I'll tell you all about it," he said.

"I thought we knew each other well now." Anna was disappointed.

"No. I need more than one drink to tell the details of my whole life."

Anna felt unreasonably annoyed that she had told him all about Joe Ashe and about how he had to be kept a secret at home.

"I think I talk too much," she said contritely.

"No, you're just a nicer person. I'm rather buttoned up," Ken said. "Come on, drink that back and we'll head for the Saltmines."

"The what?"

"Isn't that what you said your house was called?"

Anna laughed and hit him with her handbag. He made her feel normal again. The way she had felt a long time ago when it was great to be part of the Doyle family, instead of walking through a mine field, which is what it was like these days.

Mother was waiting on the step.

"I came out in case you had any difficulty parking," she explained.

"Thanks, but it seemed to be quite clear . . . we were lucky." Ken spoke easily.

"We haven't heard much about you, so this is a nice surprise." Her mother's eyes were bright, too bright.

"Yes, it's a surprise for me too. I don't know Anna very well, we just talk when I go to the bookshop. I invited her for a drink this evening, and as it was one of her evenings for coming to Pinner, it seemed like a good chance of a drive and a chat."

Ken Green was a salesman, Anna remembered. He earned his living selling books, getting bigger orders than booksellers wanted to give, forcing them to do window displays, encouraging them to take large cardboard presentation packs. Naturally he would be able to sell himself as well.

Her father liked him too.

Ken managed to ask the right questions, not the wrong ones. He asked easily what line of business Mr. Doyle was in. Her father's usual mulish, defensive look came on his face. His voice took on the familiar pitch he had when he spoke of work and rationalization.

Most people shuffled and sort of sympathized, mixed with coaxing Desmond Doyle along when he began the tale of woe, the company that had been going along very nicely thank you until in the cause of rationalization a lot of jobs, perfectly sound secure jobs, went. Desmond Doyle's job had gotten changed, he told Ken Green. Changed utterly. It wasn't the same breed of men in business these days.

Anna felt weary. It was always the same, Father's version of the story. The truth was that Father had been sacked over what Mother called a personality conflict. But it was a secret. A great secret nobody was to know. At school it was never to be mentioned. Anna's first great habits of secrecy must have begun then, she realized. Perhaps that was when the secrecy all began. Because a year later Father was employed again by the same firm. And that was never explained either.

Ken Green didn't mutter agreement about the world in general and the ways of businessmen in particular.

"How did you manage to survive the rationalization? Were you in some essential job?"

Anna's hand flew to her mouth. No one had been as direct as this before in this household. Anna's mother looked with alarmed glances from one face to another. There was a short pause.

"I didn't survive it, as it happens," Desmond Doyle said. "I was out for a year. But they brought me back, when there was a change of personnel along the line, when some personality differences had been ironed out."

Anna's hand remained at her mouth. This was the first time that Father had *ever* acknowledged that he had been a year unemployed. She was almost afraid to see how her mother had taken it.

Ken was nodding in agreement. "That often happens. It's something like putting all the pieces into a paper bag and shaking a few of them back on to the board. Though the pieces aren't always put back in the right holes?" He smiled encouragingly.

Anna looked at Ken Green as if she had never seen him before. What was he doing, sitting in this room, interrogating her father about forbidden subjects? Was there the remotest possibility that Mother and Father would think she had discussed private business with him?

Mercifully Father hadn't taken it at all badly; he was busy explaining to Ken that people had indeed been relocated into the wrong positions. He himself, who should have been Operations Manager, was in fact Special Projects. Special Projects meant as little or as much as anyone wanted it to mean. It was a non-job.

"Still, that leaves it up to you to make what you will of it, that's the thing with non-jobs. I have one, Anna has one, and we try in our different ways to make something of them."

"I do *not* have a non-job!" Anna cried.

"It could be called that, couldn't it? There's no real ceiling, no proper ranking or way of getting recognition. You make it a good job because you're interested in publishing, you read the catalogs, you understand why books appear and who buys them. You could stand filing your nails like that colleague of yours with the purple hair."

Anna's mother giggled nervously.

"Of course you're right. When you're young, Ken, people have chances to make something of their job, but not when they're old. . . ."

"So you were all right, then." Ken was bland.

"Come now, don't be flattering me. . . ."

"I wasn't." Ken's face showed that nothing was further from his intentions. "But you can't be more than forty-six, can you, forty-six or forty-seven?"

Anna fumed at her own stupidity, inviting this lout home.

"That's right, forty-seven next birthday," Father was saying.

"Well, that's never old, is it? Not *old* like fifty-eight or sixty-two."

"Deirdre, can we make that steak stretch to four pieces? This young fellow's doing me good, he has to stay for supper."

Anna's face burned. If he said yes, she would never forgive him.

"No, thank you, Mr. Doyle. No, I mean it, Mrs. Doyle. I'm sure it would be lovely but not tonight. Thanks again. I'll just finish my drink and let you get on with your evening."

"But it would be no trouble and we'd like to—"

"Not tonight. Anna wants to talk to you, I know."

"Well, I'm sure if it's anything . . ." Anna's mother looked wildly from her daughter to this personable young man with the dark hair and dark brown eyes. Surely Anna couldn't have come home with some announcement about him. Was the message written in her face . . . ?

Ken put her out of her misery. "No, it has nothing to do with me. It's a family thing. She wants to talk about your silver wedding anniversary and how you're going to celebrate it."

Desmond Doyle was disappointed that Ken was definitely leaving. "Oh, that's not for months," he said.

"Anyway, whenever it is, the main thing is that you discuss it and do what you both want, and I know that's what Anna came home to talk to you about, so I'll leave you to it."

He was gone. There had been handshakes all around and a quick grip of Anna's arm with his other hand.

They watched him pull out into the road, and he tooted his horn very gently, just an acknowledgment.

The three Doyles stood almost wordlessly on the doorstep of Salthill, 26 Rosemary Drive.

Anna faced them. "I just told him casually that we were going to make plans, I don't know why he made such a big thing out of it."

She got the feeling that neither of her parents was listening to her.

"That wasn't the only reason I came back. I came, anyway, to see you both."

Still a silence.

"And I know you won't believe it, but I just said that to him because . . . well, because I had to say something."

"He's a very pleasant young man," Desmond Doyle said.

"Good-looking, too. Smartly turned out," Deirdre Doyle added.

A wave of resentment washed over Anna. They were already comparing him favorably with Joe Ashe, Joe whom she loved with her body and soul.

"Yes," she said in a dull voice.

"You haven't talked much about him before," her mother said.

"I know, Mother, so you told him two seconds after you met him."

"Don't be insolent to your mother," Desmond Doyle said automatically.

"I'm twenty-three years of age, for chrissake. I'm not insolent like a child," Anna stormed.

"I can't think what you're so upset about," her mother said. "We have a lovely supper for you, we ask a civil question, pass a remark about how nice your friend is, and get our heads bitten off."

"I'm sorry." This was the old Anna.

"Well, that's all right, you're tired after a long day. Maybe the little drinks on top of all that driving didn't agree with you."

Anna clenched her fists silently.

They had walked back into the house and stood, an uneasy threesome, in the sitting room. They were beside the wall of family pictures.

"So what do you think we should do, eat now?" Mother looked from one to the other helplessly.

"Your mother went down to the shops especially when she heard you were coming tonight," Father said.

For a mad moment she wished that Ken Green hadn't left after all, that he was here to drive a wedge through this woolly mass of conversation, this circular kind of talk that went nowhere. It just rose and fell, causing guilt, creating tension, and then was finally patted down.

If Ken were still here, he might have said, "Let's leave the meal for half an hour and talk about what you would really like to do for your anniversary." Yes, those had been his very words. He hadn't said anything about what should be done or what might be expected, or what was the right way to go about it. He had said as he was leaving that Anna would want to talk to her parents about what they would both like for this day.

Like. That was a breakthrough in this family.

On an impulse she used exactly the words she thought Ken Green would say.

Startled, they sat down and looked at her expectantly.

"It's your day, it's not ours. What would *you* like best?"

"Well, really . . ." her mother began, at a loss. "Well, it's not up to us."

"If you all want to mark it, that would be very gratifying, of course . . ." her father said.

Anna looked at them in disbelief. Did they really think that it wasn't up to them? Could they possibly live in a wonderland where they thought that life was a matter of all their children deciding to mark the occasion together? Did they not realize that in this family everything was acting . . . and that one by one the actors were slipping off the stage—Helen to her convent, Brendan to his remote rocky farm in the West of Ireland. Only Anna, who lived two rail journeys away, was even remotely around.

A great wave of despair came over her. She knew she must not lose her temper, that the whole visit would have been useless if it ended in a row. She could hear Joe asking her mildly why on earth she took such long, wearying journeys if it only ended up making them all tense and unhappy.

Joe had life worked out all right.

She felt an ache, a physical ache to be with him and to sit on the floor by his chair while he stroked her hair.

She hadn't known it was possible to love somebody so intensely, and as she looked at the troubled man and woman sitting obediently on the sofa in front of her, she wondered if they had ever known any fraction of this kind of love. You never could think of your parents expressing love, it was gross beyond imagining to think of them coupling and loving like real people did . . . like she and Joe did. But Anna knew that everyone felt that about parents.

"Listen," she said, "I have to make a phone call. I want you to stop worrying about dinner for a moment, and just talk to each other about what you'd really like, then I'll start organizing it. Right?" Her eyes felt suspiciously bright. Maybe the little drinks *hadn't* agreed with her.

She went to the phone. She would find an excuse to talk to Joe, nothing heavy; just to hear his voice would make her feel fine again. She would tell him that she'd be home a little earlier than she thought, would she get Chinese take-out or a pizza or just some ice cream? She wouldn't tell him now or later how bleakly depressing her old home was, how sad and low her parents made her feel, how frustrated and furious. Joe Ashe wanted to hear none of this.

She dialed her own number.

The phone was answered immediately; he must have been in the bedroom. It was a girl's voice.

Anna held the phone away from her ear like people often do in movies to show disbelief and confusion. She was aware she was doing this.

"Hello?" the girl said again.

"What number is that?" Anna asked.

"Hang on, the phone's on the floor, I can't read it. Wait a sec." The girl sounded good-natured. And young.

Anna stood there paralyzed. In the flat in Shepherd's Bush, the phone was indeed on the floor. To answer it you had to lean out of bed.

She didn't want the girl to struggle anymore; she knew the number.

"Is Joe there?" she asked. "Joe Ashe?"

"No, sorry, he went out for cigarettes, he'll be back in a few minutes."

Why hadn't he put the answering machine on? Anna asked herself. *Why* had he not automatically turned the switch, like he did always when leaving the flat? In case his agent rang. In case the call that would mean recognition came. Now the call that meant discovery had come instead.

She leaned against the wall of the house where she had grown up. She needed something to give her support.

The girl didn't like silences. "Are you still there? Do you want to ring him back or is he to ring you or what?"

"Um . . . I'm not sure." Anna fought for time.

If she got off the phone now, he would never know that she had found out. Things would be the same as they were; nothing would have changed. Suppose she said wrong number, or it doesn't matter, or I'll call again. The girl would shrug, hang up, and maybe might not even mention to Joe that someone had called and rung off. Anna would never ask, she wouldn't disturb what they had.

But what had they? They had a man who would bring a girl to her bed, to *her* bed, as soon as she was out of the house. Why try to preserve that? Because she loved him, and if she didn't preserve it, there would be a big screaming emptiness and she would miss him so much that she would die.

Suppose she said she'd hold on, and then confronted him? Would he be contrite? Would he explain that it was a fellow actress and they were just learning their lines?

Or would he say it was over? And then the emptiness and ache would begin.

The girl was anxious not to lose the call in case it might be a job for Joe.

"Hang on, I'll write down your name if you like, won't be a jiff, just let me get up, should be up anyway. . . . Let's see, there's some kind of a desk over here by the window. No, it's a dressing table . . . but there's an eyebrow pencil or something. Right, what's the name?"

Anna felt the bitter bile in her throat. In her bed, lying under the beautiful expensive bedspread she had bought last Christmas, was a naked girl who was now going to carry the phone across to the simple table where Anna's makeup stood.

"Does the phone stretch all right?" Anna heard herself asking.

The girl laughed. "Yes, it does, actually."

"Good. Well, put it down for a moment on the chair, the pink chair, and reach up onto the mantelpiece, good, and you'll find a spiral-backed pad with a pencil attached by a string."

"Hey?" The girl was surprised but not uneasy.

Anna continued. "Good, put back the eye pencil, it's kohl anyway, it wouldn't write well. Now just put down for Joe: 'Anna rang. Anna Doyle. No message.'"

"Sure he can't ring you back?" A hint of anxiety had crept into the voice of yet another woman who was going to spend weeks, months, even years of her life trying to please Joe Ashe, say the right thing, not risk losing him.

"No, no, I'm with my parents at the moment. In fact, I'll be staying here the night. Could you tell him that?"

"Does he know where to find you?"

"Yes, but there's no need to ring me. I'll catch up on him another time."

When she had hung up, she stood holding on to the table for support. She remembered telling them that the hall was the very worst place to have a telephone. It was cold, it was too public, it was uncomfortable. Now she blessed them for having taken no notice of her.

She stood for a few moments, but her thoughts would not be gathered, they ran and scurried like mice around in her head. Finally, when she thought she had at least recovered the power of speech, she went back into the room where her mother and father sat. They who had never known the kind of love she knew or the kind of hurt. She said that if it wouldn't put them out, she'd like to stay the night, then they'd have all the time in the world to discuss the plans.

"You don't have to ask can you stay the night in your own home," her mother said, pleased and fussing. "I'll put a hot-water bottle in the bed just in case, the rooms are all there for you, not that any of you ever come and stay in them."

"Well, I'd love to tonight." Anna's smile was nailed firmly on her face.

They had gotten to the actual numbers that should be invited when Joe rang. She went to the phone calmly.

"She's gone," he said.

"Has she?" Her voice was detached.

"Yes. It wasn't important."

"No. No."

"No need for you to stay over and make a big scene and meaning-of-life confrontation."

"Oh, no, none of that."

He was nonplussed.

"So what are you going to do?" he asked.

"Stay here, as I told your friend."

"But not forever?"

"Of course not, just tonight."

"Then tomorrow night after work . . . you'll be home?"

"Yes, indeed, and you'll be packed."

"Anna, don't be so dramatic."

"Absolutely not, calmness itself. Stay there tonight, of course. No, for heaven's sake there's no need to go immediately. Just tomorrow evening. Right?"

"Stop this, Anna, I love you, you love me, I'm not lying to you."

"And neither am I to you, Joe, about tomorrow night. Truly."

She hung up.

When he called back ten minutes later, she answered the phone herself.

"Please don't be tiresome, Joe. That's a great word of yours . . . tiresome. You hate when people press you on things and ask you about things that concern them, tiresome you call it. Maybe I'm learning from you."

"We have to talk. . . ."

"Tomorrow after work. After *my* work, that is, you don't have any work, do you? We can talk then for a bit like about where I'm to send your mail, and there won't be any answering machine messages, so you'd better set something else up."

"But . . ."

"I won't come to the phone again, you'll have to talk to my father, and you always said he was a nice bloke with nothing to say. . . ."

She went back to the discussion. She saw that her mother and father were wondering about the phone calls.

"Sorry for the interruptions, I've been having a row with Joe Ashe, my boyfriend. It's very antisocial to bring it into this house, if he rings again I won't talk to him."

"Is it serious, the row?" her mother asked hopefully.

"Yes, Mother, you'll be glad to know it's fairly serious as rows go. Possibly final. Now let's see what people should have to eat."

And as she told them about a very nice woman called Philippa who ran a catering business, Anna Doyle's mind was far away. Her mind was back in the days when things had been new and exciting and when her life was filled to every corner by the presence of Joe.

It would be hard to fill up all those parts again.

She said that they could ask for sample menus and decide what they wanted. They would write to everyone in very good time, individual letters, personal letters with the invitation, that would mean it was special.

"It is special, isn't it? Twenty-five years married?" She looked from one to the other, hoping for reassurance. The cozy, claustrophobic sense of family that the Doyles had managed to create around them. To her surprise and regret it didn't seem to be there tonight. Mother and Father looked uncertain about whether a quarter of a century of marriage had been a good thing. This was the one time in her life that Anna needed some sense that things were permanent, that even if her own world was shifting, the rest of civilization was on fairly solid ground.

But maybe she was only reading her own situation into it all, like those poets who believed in the pathetic fallacy, who thought that nature changed to suit their moods, and that skies were gray when *they* were gray.

"We'll make it a marvelous occasion," she told her father and mother. "It's going to be even better than your wedding day, because we're all here to help celebrate it."

She was rewarded with two smiles and she realized it would at least be a project for the great, yawning, frighteningly empty summer that lay ahead of her.

CHAPTER TWO

Brendan

Brendan Doyle went to the calendar to look up the date that Christy Moore was coming to sing in the town twenty miles away. It was sometime next week, and he thought he'd go in to hear him.

He had written it down on the big kitchen calendar the day he had heard it advertised on the radio. To his surprise, he realized that today was his birthday. It came as a shock to think it was already eleven o'clock in the morning and he hadn't realized that it was his birthday. In the olden days he would have known it was his birthday weeks in advance.

"Only three weeks to Brendan's birthday," his mother would chirrup to anyone who might listen.

He had hated it when he was very young, all the fuss about birthdays. The celebrations. The girls had loved it of course, wearing smart frocks. There were never any outsiders there; Brendan couldn't remember having a real party, one with other children and crackers and games, just the family all dressed up and crackers and Jell-O with whipped cream and nuts and cherries on it. There would be presents from all the others, wrapped properly, with little tags, and birthday cards as well, which would all be arranged on the mantelpiece. Then there would be a photograph of the birthday boy all on his own, maybe wearing a paper hat. And then one with the rest of the family. These would be kept in the album, and brought out triumphantly when any guests arrived. The first of the birthdays, Brendan, wasn't he getting so big? And then this was Helen's birthday, and then Anna's. Look. And people looked and praised Mother. She was marvelous, they said, marvelous to do all that for them, go to so much trouble.

His mother never knew how he hated it. How he had hated the singing, and seeing her clapping her hands and running for the camera during the "For He's a Jolly Good Fellow."

He wished they could just sit down and get on with it instead of all these antics and actions. As if they were all onstage.

And all the secrecy too. Don't tell Auntie Maureen about the new sofa. Why? We don't want her to think that it's new. Why don't we want her to think that? We just don't want them saying we put a lot of store by it, that's all. But it's gorgeous, isn't it? Yes, but we don't want them to say that we think it's something special; when Auntie Maureen asks about it just say, "Oh, the sofa, it's all right," as if you weren't impressed. *You* know.

Brendan didn't know, he had never known. They always seemed to be hiding something from somebody. From the neighbors, from people at school, from people in the parish, from Maureen Barry, Mother's great friend, from Frank Quigley, who worked with Father, who was meant to be the greatest friend of the family. And especially from everyone back in Ireland. Don't tell this to Grannie O'Hagan, and never let a word of that be said in front of Grandpa Doyle.

It was quite simple to live by Mother's and Father's rules if you understood that nothing was to be said outside the family.

Brendan thought that there was very little of importance said within the family either.

He remembered his birthday the year that Father had lost his job. There had been *huge* secrecy at that stage of their lives. Father used to leave the house in the mornings at the usual time and come back again as if things were normal. What was it all for? Brendan had wondered then, and wondered still.

And here in Vincent's farm, the small farm on the side of a hill where his father had grown up, he felt even more remote from the man than he had when he lived in Rosemary Drive pretending that he was bright at school, pretending that he was going to get A's and go to university. When all the time he knew he was going to come back here to this stony place where nothing was expected and nothing claimed to be what it was not.

He had never been *Uncle* Vincent; even though he was the oldest of Father's brothers, he was Vincent from the start. A tall, stooped man, much lined and weather-beaten. He never spoke until he had something to speak about. There was no small talk in the small house on the side of the hill, the house where Father had grown up one of six children. They must have been very poor then. Father didn't speak of it or those times. Vincent didn't speak of any times. Although a television antenna waved from almost every small farm in the countryside hereabouts, Vincent Doyle saw no need of one. And the radio he had was small and crackly. He listened to the six-thirty news every evening, and the farm report that went before it. He sometimes came across some kind of documentary on the Irish in Australia, or some account of the armies of Napoleon coming to the West of Ireland. Brendan never knew how he tracked these features down. He didn't buy a daily newspaper or any guide to look up what was on. And he wasn't a regular enough listener to know what was being broadcast when.

He wasn't a hermit, a recluse, or an eccentric. Vincent always wore suits. He had never come to terms with a world of jackets and trousers. He bought a new suit every three years, and the current one was moved down a grade, so that one day it would have been the good suit for going to Mass and the day after a new purchase it would have been relegated to a different league. It could be worn when he went to tend the sheep, and even when lifting them in and out of his trailer.

Brendan Doyle had loved this place that strange summer when they had come for the visit. Everyone had been very tense all the way over on the boat and train, and there were so many things to remember. Remember not to talk about sitting up all night on the way to Holyhead. Remember not to talk about the crowds sitting on their luggage, or people would know they had gone steerage. Remember not to say that they had waited for ages on a cold platform. There were to be no complaints, it was all to have been fun. That was the message that Mother kept repeating over and over during the endless journey. Father had said almost the opposite, he had told them not to go blowing and boasting to their Uncle Vincent about all the comforts they had in London. Brendan remembered asking a direct question; he had felt slightly sick before he asked it, as if he knew it wasn't the thing to say.

"Well—which are we? Are we rich like we're pretending to Grannie O'Hagan, or are we poor like we're pretending to Uncle Vincent and Grandpa Doyle?"

There had been a great pause.

Horrified, his parents had looked at each other.

"Pretend!" they had cried almost with one voice. There was no pretending, they protested. They had been advising the children not to gabble off things that would irritate their elders or bore them. That was all.

And Brendan remembered the first time he saw the farm. They had spent three days with Grannie O'Hagan in Dublin and then a long, tiring train journey. Mother and Father seemed upset by the way things had gone in Dublin. At least the children had behaved properly, there had been no unnecessary blabbering. Brendan remembered looking out the window at the small fields of Ireland. Helen had been in disgrace for some horseplay at the station, the main evil of it was that it had been done in the presence of Grannie O'Hagan. Anna was very quiet and stuck in a book. Mother and Father talked in low voices over and over.

Nothing had prepared him for the sight of the small stone house and the yard with the bits of broken machinery in it. At the door stood his grandfather, old and stooped, and wearing shabby old clothes, a torn jacket and no collar on his shirt. Beside him was Uncle Vincent, a taller and younger version but wearing a suit that looked as if it were respectable.

"You're welcome to your own place," Grandpa Doyle had said. "This is the land you children came from, it's a grand thing to have you back from all those red buses and crowds of people to walk your own soil again."

Grandpa Doyle had been to London once on a visit. Brendan knew that because of the pictures, the one on the wall taken outside Buckingham Palace, and the many in the albums. He couldn't really remember the visit. Now, as he looked at these two men standing in front of the house, he felt an odd sense of having come home. Like those children's stories he used to read when an adventure was coming to an end and they were coming out of the forest. He was afraid to speak in case it would ruin it.

They had stayed a week there that time. Grandpa Doyle had been frail and hadn't walked very much farther than his front door. But Vincent had taken them all over the place. Sometimes in the old car with its rickety trailer; the trailer had not changed since that first visit. Sometimes Vincent couldn't be bothered to untackle it from the car even though there might be no need to transport a sheep, and it rattled along comfortingly behind them.

Vincent used to go off to see his sheep twice a day. Sheep had a bad habit of falling over on their backs and lying there, legs heaving in the air; you have to right them, put them the right way up.

Anna had asked was it only Uncle Vincent's sheep that did this or was it all sheep. She didn't want to speak about it when she got back to London in case it was just a habit of the Doyles' sheep. Vincent had given her a funny look but had said quite agreeably that no harm could come from admitting that sheep fell over, it was a fairly common occurrence in the breed, even in England.

Then Vincent would stop and mend walls; sheep were forever crashing through the little stone walls and dislodging bits of them, he explained. Yes, he confirmed to Anna before she had to ask, this, too, was a general failing in them as a species.

In the town he brought them into a bar with high stools and bought them lemonade. None of them had ever been in a public house before. Helen asked for a pint of stout but didn't get it. Vincent hadn't minded. It was the barman who had said she was too young.

Even way back then, Brendan had noticed that Vincent had never bothered to explain to people who they were; he didn't fuss and introduce them as his brother's children, explain that they were over here for a week's visit, that in real life they lived in a lovely, leafy suburb of North London called Pinner, and that they played tennis on summer weekends. Mother and Father would have managed to tell all that to almost anyone. Vincent just went on the way he always did, talking little, replying slowly and effortlessly when he was asked a question.

Brendan got the feeling that he'd prefer *not* to be asked too many questions. Sometimes, even on that holiday, he and Vincent had walked miles together with hardly a word exchanged. It was extraordinarily restful.

He hated it when the week was over.

"Maybe we'll come back again," he had said to Vincent as they left.

"Maybe." Vincent hadn't sounded sure.

"Why do you think we might not?" They were leaning on a gate to the small vegetable garden. There were a few rows of potatoes there and easy things like cabbage and carrots and parsnips. Things that wouldn't kill you looking after them, Vincent had explained.

"Ah, there was a lot of talk about you all coming back here, but I think it came to nothing. Not after they saw the place."

Brendan's heart skipped.

"Coming back . . . for more than a holiday, you mean?"

"Wasn't that what it was all about?"

"Was it?"

He had seen his uncle's eyes looking at him kindly.

"Don't worry yourself, Brendan boy, just live your life the best you can, and then one day you can go off and be where people won't be getting at you."

"When would that day be?"

"You'll know when it arrives," Vincent had said without taking his eyes away from the few rows of potatoes.

And indeed Brendan *had* known when the day arrived.

Things changed when they went back home to London after that visit. For one thing Father got his job back, and they didn't have to pretend anymore that he had a job when he didn't. And there had been all kinds of terrible rows with Helen. She kept saying that she didn't want to be left in the house alone. She would interrogate them all each day about what time they were going out and coming back, and even if there seemed to be five minutes of unaccounted-for time, she would arrange to go and meet Brendan when school finished.

He had tried to ask her what it was all about, but she had shrugged and said she just hated being by herself.

Not that there was ever much fear of that on Rosemary Drive. Brendan would have loved some time on his own instead of all the chitchat at mealtimes, and getting the table ready and discussing what they ate and what they would eat at the next meal. He couldn't understand why Helen didn't welcome any chance of peace with open arms.

Perhaps that was why she had gone to be a nun in the end. For peace. Or was it because she still felt the need to be with people, and she thought the numbers were dropping at Rosemary Drive, with Anna moving out to her flat and Brendan a permanent resident in Ireland?

It was strange to have lived for so long with this family, and lived so closely during weeks, months, years of endless conversation and still to know them so little.

Brendan had decided to go back to that stone cottage on the day that his school ran a careers exhibition. There were stands and stalls giving information about careers in computing, in retailing, in the telephone service, in London Transport, in banking, in the armed forces. He wandered disconsolately from one to another.

Grandpa Doyle had died since that family visit when he welcomed them to the soil they came from. They had not gone home for the funeral. It wasn't really *home,* Mother had said, and Grandpa would have been the first to have agreed. Uncle Vincent wouldn't expect it, and there were no neighbors who would think it peculiar and talk poorly of them for not going. There had been a special Mass said for the repose of his soul in their parish church, and everyone they knew from the parish sympathized.

The headmaster said that a decision about how to spend the years of one's life was a very major decision; it wasn't like choosing what movie to go to or what football team to support. And suddenly, like a vision, Brendan realized that he had to get away from this, he had to escape the constant discussions and whether this was the right decision or the wrong one, and how he must tell people he was a management trainee rather than a store clerk or whatever new set of pretenses would appear. He knew with the greatest clarity that he had ever possessed that he would go back to Vincent's place and work there.

Salthill, 26 Rosemary Drive, was not a house that you walked out of without explanations. But Brendan realized that these would be the very last explanations he would ever have to give. He would regard it as an ordeal by fire and water, he would grit his teeth and get through it.

It had been worse than he ever could have imagined. Anna and Helen had wept and pleaded and begged him not to go away. His mother had wept, too, and asked what she had done to deserve this; his father had wanted to know whether Vincent had put him up to this.

"Vincent doesn't even know," Brendan had said.

Nothing would dissuade him. Brendan hadn't known that he possessed such strength. For four days the battle went on.

His mother would come and sit on his bed with cups of hot chocolate. "All boys go through a period like this, a time of wanting to be on their own, to be away from the family apron strings. I've suggested to your father that you go on a little holiday over at Vincent's; maybe that will get it all out of your system."

Brendan had refused. It would have been dishonest. Because once he went he would not come back.

His father made overtures, too. "Listen, boy, perhaps I was a bit harsh the other night saying you were only going to try to inherit that heap of old stones, I didn't mean that to sound so blunt. But you know the way it will look. You can see how people will look at it."

Brendan couldn't, not then, not now.

But he would never forget the look on Vincent's face when he'd come up the road.

He had walked all the way from town. Vincent was standing with the old dog, Shep, at the kitchen door. He shaded his eyes from the evening light as Brendan got nearer, and he could make out the shape in the sunset.

"Well, now," he said.

Brendan had said nothing. He had carried a small tote bag with him, all his possessions for a new life.

"It's yourself," Vincent had said. "Come on in."

At no time that evening did he ask why Brendan had come or how long he was staying. He never inquired whether they knew his whereabouts back in London or if the visit had official approval.

Vincent's view was that all this would emerge as time went by, and slowly over the weeks and months it did.

Days came and went. There was never a harsh word between the two Doyles, uncle and nephew. In fact, there were very few words at all. When Brendan thought he might go to a dance nearby, Vincent said he thought that would be a great thing altogether. He had never been great shakes at the dancing himself but he heard that it was great exercise. He went to the tin on the dresser where the money was and handed Brendan forty pounds to buy some new clothes.

From time to time Brendan helped himself from the can. He had asked in the beginning, but Vincent had put a stop to that, saying the money was there for the both of them and to take what he needed.

Things had been getting expensive, and from time to time Brendan went and did an evening's work in a bar for an extra few pounds to add to the till. If Vincent knew about it, he never acknowledged it, either to protest or to praise.

Brendan grinned to himself, thinking how differently things would have been run back in Rosemary Drive.

He didn't miss them; he wondered if he ever could have loved them, even a little bit. And if he hadn't loved them, did that make him unnatural? Everything he read had love in it, and all the films were about love, and anything you heard of in the papers seemed to be done for love or because someone loved and that love wasn't returned. Maybe he was an odd man out, not loving.

Vincent must have been like that, too, that's why he never wrote letters or talked to people intensely. That's why he liked this life here in the hills and among the stony roads and peaceful skies.

It was a bit unnatural, Brendan told himself, to become twenty-two all by yourself, without acknowledging it to another soul. If he told Vincent, his uncle would look at him thoughtfully and say, "Is that a fact?" He would offer no congratulations nor suggest a celebratory pint.

Vincent was out walking the land. He would be back in by lunch. They would have that bacon cold, and plenty of tomatoes. They would eat hot potatoes with it because a dinner in the middle of the day without a few big, floury potatoes would be no use to anyone. They never ate mutton or lamb. It wasn't out of a sense of delicacy to the sheep that were their living; it was that they had no big freezer like some of their neighbors, who would kill a sheep each season. And they couldn't bear to pay the prices in the butcher's shop for animals that they had sold for a greatly smaller sum than would warrant such a cost by the time they got to the butcher's cold store.

Johnny Riordan, the mailman, drove up in his little van.

"There's a bunch of letters for you, Brendan, it must be your birthday," he said cheerfully.

"Yes, it is." Brendan had grown as taciturn as his uncle.

"Good man, will you buy us a pint later?"

"I might do that."

The card from his father was one with a funny cat on it. Quite unsuitable from an estranged father. The word *Father* was written neatly. No love, no best wishes. Well, that was all right. He sent an automatic card to Father with just "Brendan" on it each year, too.

Mother's was more flowery, and said she could hardly believe she had such a grown-up son, and wondered whether he had any girlfriends and if they would ever see him married.

Helen's card was full of peace and blessings. She wrote a note about the sisters and the hostel they were going to open and the funds that were needed and how two of the sisters were going to play the guitar for money at Piccadilly station and how the community was very divided about this and whether it was the right way to go. Helen always wrote about a cast of thousands, assuming he knew all these people and remembered their names and cared about their doings. At the end she wrote, "Please take Anna's letter seriously."

He had opened them in the right order. He opened Anna's slowly. Perhaps it was going to tell him some bad news; Father had cancer or Mother was going to have an operation. His face curled into a look of scorn when he saw all the business about the anniversary. Nothing had changed, simply nothing, they had gotten trapped in a time warp, stuck in a world of tinsel-covered cards, meaningless rituals. He felt even more annoyed about the whole thing because of Sister Helen's pious instruction to take Anna's letter seriously. Talk about passing the buck.

He felt edgy and restless, as he always did when drawn into family affairs. He got up and went outside. He would walk up the hills a bit. There was a wall he wanted to look at. It might need a bit more work than just rearranging the stones like they did so often.

He came across Vincent with a sheep that had gotten stuck in the gate. The animal was frightened and kicking and pulling so that it was almost impossible to release her.

"You came at a good time," Vincent said, and together they eased the anxious sheep out. She bleated frantically and looked at them with her silly face.

"What's wrong with her, is she hurt?" Brendan asked.

"No. Not a scratch on her."

"Then what's all that caterwauling out of her?"

Vincent looked for a long time at the distressed sheep. "That's the one that lay on its lamb. Crushed the little thing to death," he said.

"Stupid sheep," Brendan said. "Sits on her own perfectly good lamb, then gets stuck in a gate, that's what gives sheep a bad name."

The ewe looked at him trustingly and gave a great baaa into the air.

"She doesn't know I'm insulting her," Brendan said.

"Devil a bit she'd care. She's looking for the lamb."

"Doesn't she know she suffocated it?"

"Not at all. How would she know that?" Vincent said.

Companionably the two men walked back toward the house to make their lunch.

Vincent's eyes fell on the envelopes and cards.

"Well, now, it's your birthday," he said. "Imagine that."

"Yes." Brendan sounded grumpy.

His uncle looked at him for a while.

"It's good of them to remember you, it would be scant remembering you'd get if you had to rely on me."

"I don't worry about remembering . . . not that sort." He was still bad-tempered as he washed the potatoes at the sink and put them into the big saucepan of water.

"Should I put them up on the mantelpiece for you?"

Vincent had never said anything like that.

"No, no. I wouldn't like that."

"All right." His uncle collected them neatly and left them in a little pile. He saw Anna's long typed letter but made no comment. During the meal he waited for the boy to speak.

"Anna has this notion I should go over to England and play games for some silver wedding celebrations. *Silver!*" He scoffed at the word.

"That's how many?" Vincent asked.

"Twenty-five glorious years."

"Are they married that long? Lord, Lord."

"You weren't at the wedding yourself?"

"God, Brendan, what would take me to a wedding, I ask you?"

"They want me to go over. I'm not going near it."

"Well, we all do what we want to do."

Brendan thought about that for a long time.

"I suppose we do in the end," he said.

They lit their cigarettes to smoke while they drank their big mugs of tea.

"And they don't want me there, I'd only be an embarrassment. Mother would have to be explaining me to people, and why I didn't do this or look like that, and Father would be quizzing me, asking me questions."

"Well, you said you weren't going, so what's the worry about it?"

"It's not till October," Brendan said.

"October, is that a fact?" Vincent looked puzzled.

"I know, isn't it just like them to be setting it all up now?"

They left it for a while, but his face was troubled, and his uncle knew he would speak of it again.

"In a way, of course, once in a few years isn't much to go over. In a way of looking at it, it mightn't be much to give them."

"It's your own decision, lad."

"You wouldn't point me one way or the other, I suppose?"

"Indeed I would not."

"It might be too expensive for us to afford the fare." Brendan looked up at the biscuit tin, Maybe this was an out.

"There's always the money for the fare, you know that."

He did know it. He had just been hoping that they could use it as an excuse. Even to themselves.

"And I would only be one of a crowd. If I were to go, it would be better to go on my own sometime."

"Whatever you say."

Outside they heard a bleating. The sheep with the foolish face, the one that had suffocated her lamb, was still looking for it. She had come toward the house, hoping that it might have strayed in there. Vincent and Brendan looked out the kitchen window. The sheep still called out.

"She'd have been a hopeless mother to it even if it had lived," Brendan said.

"She doesn't know that, she's just living by some kind of instinct. She'd like to see it for a bit. To know that it's all right, sort of."

It was one of the longest speeches his uncle had ever made. He looked at his uncle and reached out to touch him. He put his arm gently around the older man's shoulder, feeling moved to the heart by his kindness and generosity of spirit.

"I'll go off into the town now, Vincent," he said, taking his arm away. "I'll write a couple of letters maybe and maybe work pulling a few pints tonight."

"There's enough in the biscuit tin," Vincent said gently.

"There is, I know. I know."

He went out into the yard and passed the lonely ewe still calling for her lost lamb and started up the old car to drive to town. He would go back for their silver anniversary. It was only a little time out of this life. The life he wanted. He could give a little time to show them he was all right and that he was part of the family.

CHAPTER THREE

Helen

The old man looked at Helen hopefully. He saw a girl in her twenties in a gray sweater and skirt. Her hair was tied back in a black ribbon but it looked as if any moment it might all escape and fall wild and curly around her shoulders. She had dark blue restless eyes and freckles on her nose. She carried a black plastic shopping bag, which she was swinging backward and forward.

"Miss," said the old drunk, "can you do me a favor?"

Helen stopped at once, as he had known she would. There were passersby who went on passing by and those who stopped. Years of observation had taught him to tell one sort from the other.

"Of course, what can I do?" she asked him.

He almost stepped back. Her smile was too ready, too willing. Usually people muttered that they didn't have change or that they were in a hurry. Even if they did seem about to help a wino, they didn't show such eagerness.

"I don't want any money," he said.

"Of course not," Helen said, as if it were the last thing that a man with a coat tied with string and an empty ginger wine bottle in his hand would want.

"I just want you to go in there and get me another bottle. The bastards say they won't serve me. They say I'm not to come into the shop. Now, if I were to give you two pounds, then you could go in and get it for me."

From his grizzled face, with its wild hair above and its stubble below, his small, sharp eyes shone with the brilliance of the plan.

Helen bit her lower lip and looked at him hard.

He was from Ireland, of course, they all were, or else Scotland. The Welsh drunks seemed to stay in their valleys, and the English didn't get drunk in such numbers or so publicly. It was a mystery.

"I think you've had enough."

"How would you know whether I've had enough or not? That's not what we were debating. That, as it happens, was not the point at issue."

Helen was moved, he spoke so well, he had such phrases . . . *the point at issue.* How could a man who spoke like that have let himself go so far and turn into an outcast?

Immediately she felt guilty about the thought. That was the way Grandmother O'Hagan would talk. And Helen would immediately disagree with her. Here she was at twenty-one thinking almost the same thing.

"It's not good for you," she said, and added spiritedly, "I said I'd do you a favor, it's not a favor giving you more alcohol, it's a downright disservice."

The drunk liked such niceties and definitions, he was ready to parry with her.

"But there is no question of your *giving* me alcohol, my dear lady," he said triumphantly. "That was never part of our agreement. You are to act as my agent in purchasing the alcohol." He beamed at his victory.

"No, it's only going to kill you."

"I can easily get it elsewhere. I have two pounds and I will get it elsewhere. What we are now discussing is your word given and then broken. You said you would do me a favor, now you say you will not."

Helen stormed into the small store.

"A bottle of hard cider," she asked, eyes flashing.

"What kind?"

"I don't know. Any kind. That one." She pointed to a fancy bottle. Outside, the drunk knocked on the window and shook his head of shaggy hair, trying to point to a different brand.

"You're not buying it for that wino?" asked the young man.

"No, it's for myself," Helen said guiltily and obviously falsely. The drunk man was pointing feverishly at some brand.

"Listen, don't give it to him, lady . . . I beg you."

"Are you going to sell me this bottle of cider or are you not?" Helen could be authoritative in short bursts.

"Two pounds eighty," the man said. Helen slapped the money, *her* money, down on the counter, and in an equally bad temper the bottle was shoved into a plastic bag for her.

"Now," Helen said, "did I or did I not do what you asked me?"

"You did not, that's only rat's piss, that stuff, fancy bottles for the carriage trade. I'm not drinking that."

"Well, don't then." There were tears starting in her eyes.

"And what's more, I'm not spending my good money on it."

"Have it as a present." She was weary.

"Oh, high and mighty, Lady Muck," he said. He had a good quarter of it drunk from the neck by this stage. He was still holding it in its plastic bag.

Helen didn't like the look on his face, the man was working himself up into some kind of temper or even a fit. She looked at him, alarmed, and saw a huge amount of the despised cider vanishing down his throat.

"The urine of rodents," he shouted. "Bottled by these creeps of shopkeepers and dignified with the name of alcohol."

He banged on the window again loudly. "Come out, you cheat and rogue, come out here and justify this garbage."

There were fruit and vegetable boxes piled neatly with apples and oranges, with potatoes loose and mushrooms in baskets. The man with the nearly empty cider bottle began to turn them over onto the street systematically.

The staff ran from the shop; two of them held him, another went for the law.

"Thank you very much," said the boy who had served Helen. "That was a very nice day's work."

"You wouldn't bloody listen to me," shouted the man, who had foam flecks at the side of his mouth by now.

"Her sort don't listen to anyone, mate," said the irate shopkeeper, who was trying to immobilize him.

Helen moved from the scene awkwardly. She walked away almost sideways, as if she were trying not to turn her back on the chaos and distress she had created. But then, this happened so often.

It was always happening, Helen found, everywhere she went.

Back in the convent she wouldn't say anything to Sister Brigid about it. It would be so easily misunderstood. The sisters wouldn't grasp that it would all have happened anyway. The man might have gotten even more violent and upset if nobody had bought him the drink. He might have broken the window or hurt someone. But Helen wouldn't tell the upsetting tale. Brigid would be bound to look at her sadly and wonder why trouble seemed to follow Helen Doyle wherever she went.

It might even put further away the day when they would allow Helen to take her vows and become a member of the community rather than just a hanger-on. How much did she have to prove? Why did Sister Brigid keep putting off the time when Helen should be considered seriously as one of their community? She worked as hard as any of them; she had been with them for three years, and still, there was this feeling that it was somehow a passing whim.

Even the most minor and accidental events made them see Helen as unstable in some way. It was terribly unfair and she wouldn't add to the long list by telling them about the confusion she was walking away from. Somehow it would be seen as her fault.

Instead she would think about the silver wedding celebrations and what she could do best to help.

Well, obviously she hadn't any money or anything, so there could be nothing expected from her on that score. And as well as the vow of poverty that she had taken—or to be more honest, was trying to take—she was a bit unworldly these days, she had left the mainstream of everyday life. And even if she did go out to work each day, as all the sisters did, she didn't see the side of life that Mother and Anna would be concentrating on, the more material end of things. And she wouldn't be any good rounding up neighbors and friends. Perhaps she could see whether they might have a special Mass or liturgy. But Helen was doubtful whether the old priest in the parish church where the Doyles went was going to be well up on the modern liturgy of renewal.

Better leave it to Anna, who had plenty of time for all that sort of thing. Anna got so touchy when Helen did things to help; it was often better to do nothing, to say in a calm voice, Yes, Anna, No, Anna. Three bags full, Anna. This is what Brigid would suggest. Brigid was very big on the calm voice. Or on Helen's developing it. It often sounded like blandness and even hypocrisy to Helen, but Brigid said that it was what the world in general seemed to want. And there were times when Helen thought gloomily that she might be right.

Certainly Mother always wanted things underplayed and understated, and in most cases not mentioned at all. Mother would like not calm so much as silence. Perhaps Mother might be pleased if Helen had been born deaf and mute.

By this stage she had arrived at St. Martin's, the house where the sisters lived. Brigid never called it the convent, even though that is what it was. Brigid called it just St. Martin's, or home. She didn't criticize Helen Doyle for using a more formal and official word to describe the redbrick house where eleven women lived and went about their daily business as social workers in various London agencies.

Nessa was working with young mothers, most of them under sixteen, and trying to teach them some kind of mothering skills. Nessa had had a child herself a long time ago; she had brought the baby up on her own, but the child had died when it was three. Helen couldn't remember whether it was a boy or a girl. The other sisters didn't talk about it much. But it did give Nessa the edge when it came to looking after children. Brigid usually worked in the day center for vagrants. Serving them lunches, trying to organize baths and delousing. Sister Maureen worked with the group that was rehabilitating ex-prisoners. The days were gone when these kinds of nuns just polished the big tables in the parlor in the hopes of a visit from a bishop. They went out to do God's work and found plenty of opportunity to do it in the streets of London.

Helen had moved from one area to another since she had come to join St. Martin's. She would like to have worked with Sister Brigid running the day center. What she really would have liked was if Brigid would let her run it on her own and just call in from time to time to see how things were getting along. This way Helen felt she would be really useful and special, and that once seen in a position of calm control over the well-being of so many people, she would have no difficulty in proving her readiness to be a full member of the community.

She realized that obedience was very much part of it, and like poverty and chastity, this was no problem to her, Helen believed. She didn't want to be laying down the law and making rules; she would obey any rule. She didn't want money for jewels or yachts, she laughed at the very notion of such things. And chastity. Yes, she was very sure she wanted that, in a highly positive way. Her one experience of the reverse side of that coin was quite enough to reassure her on this particular score.

She had worked in the kitchen, done her turn as a skivvy. She was never sure why Brigid hadn't liked her using that term. *Skivvy.* She had not been able to understand that people used that word quite respectably nowadays, as a sort of a joke. Debs said they were skivvying for a while before going skiing, it meant minding someone's house. Australians over here for a year often got jobs in bars, in restaurants, or as skivvies. It wasn't an insulting term.

Helen sighed, thinking of all the gulfs in understanding there were everywhere. She let herself in the door of St. Martin's. It was Sister Joan's month for running the house, as Brigid liked it called. Joan called out from the kitchen as she heard her come in.

"Just in time, Helen, I'll take the stuff from you now. You couldn't have timed it better, as it happened."

With a lurch Helen remembered the reason she had taken the large black plastic bag that had been swinging emptily beside her on her journey home. She had meant to come by the market and buy cheaply what the sellers hadn't gotten rid of during the day. She had forgotten it once, and that was why she had been heading toward the grocery store where she had assisted her compatriot in destroying his liver even faster than he was already doing. She had been given three pounds to buy the vegetables. She had spent it on hard cider for an alcoholic.

"Sit down, Helen. It's not the end of the world," said Joan, who didn't know the details of the story but recognized the substance and knew there would be no vegetables for the casserole.

"Sit down, Helen, stop crying. I'll put on a cup of tea for you just as soon as I've scrubbed some of those potatoes. We'll have baked potatoes with a little bit of cheese. It will be just as nice."

Nessa was tired; it had been a particularly bad day.

An eighteen-year-old mother had sat whimpering in a corner while her fate was being discussed by social workers and a woman police officer. Her baby would live, thanks to Nessa, but what kind of life?

The mother had not turned up at the center for two days running, and Nessa became worried. The door to the block of flats always swung open, and as Nessa went in, she almost fell over Simon crawling along the filthy corridor. Beer cans and bottles were strewn everywhere, the place smelled of urine, there were dangers every few feet, broken bicycles, crates with sharp corners. Simon was crawling earnestly toward the open door. In a minute he would have been on the street where no car or motorcycle would have expected a child to crawl. He would have been dead.

As it was, he was alive, the sores from his stinking diapers being treated. Antitetanus injections were being given against the germs he must have encountered, and his bruised eye was pronounced mercifully intact.

His mother hadn't beaten him, of this Nessa was sure, but she was too feebleminded to look after him. He would be in care when he came out of hospital. A lifetime of care lay ahead of him. But care with a capital *C*.

Nessa was not in the mood for Helen's tears and explanations. She cut her very short.

"So you forgot the vegetables again. So what, Helen? Let's have a little peace. That's what would be really nice."

Helen broke off in mid-sentence. "I was only taking it all on myself. I didn't want you to blame Sister Joan."

"Oh, for God's sake, Helen, who in their right mind would blame Sister Joan or any sister? Cut it out, will you?"

It was the sharpest remark that had ever been made in St. Martin's House, a place of peace and consideration.

Sister Joan and Sister Maureen looked shocked at Nessa, with her white, tired face, going up the stairs.

Helen looked at all three of them and burst into tears again.

Sister Brigid never seemed to be aware of any little atmosphere. It was one of her characteristics. Sometimes Helen thought it was a weakness, a rare insensitivity in an otherwise remarkable character. Other times she wondered whether it might in fact be a blessing and something that Sister Brigid cultivated purposely.

There was no mention made of Helen's red eyes and blotchy face as they sat, heads bent, waiting for Sister Brigid to say the simple blessing over their food. Nobody acknowledged that Nessa looked white and drawn, though they were solicitous about passing her things and smiling at her a little more often than they smiled at the rest of the table. Eleven women, including Brigid, the quiet Mother Superior, who never used that title. She had been very stern with Helen for calling her Reverend Mother.

"But isn't that what you are?" Helen had been startled.

"We are sisters here, it's a community, this is our home, it's not an institution with ranks and rules and pecking orders."

It had been hard to grasp at first, but after three years Helen felt that she had surely earned her place. Biting her lip, she looked at the ten women chattering around the simple meal, made more simple still by the fact that she had forgotten the vegetables.

They talked easily about the work they had done during the day, the practicalities, the funny things, the optimisms, the chance of more help here, of fighting the cuts there. Brigid had said that they must not bring their problems to the supper table or even home to the house, otherwise St. Martin's would be weighed down by the collective grief and anxiety of these workers in the sad end of society. They would become so depressed if they were to dwell every night on the amount of misery and pain they had seen in their different worlds that it would be counterproductive. People needed escape, time out, retreat. They didn't have the luxury of going *on* retreat like the nuns of a previous generation, but neither did they have the demands and responsibilities that many trained social workers who were married women or men had. There were no children needing time, love, and attention; there were no social demands nor the intensity of one-to-one relationships. Brigid told them often that small communities of nuns like theirs were ideally situated to serve the many and apparently increasing needs around them in London. The only thing they had to fear was too great an introspection or a depth of worry which might render their help less effective because it was becoming self-important.

Helen looked around at their faces. Apart from Nessa, who was still looking frail, the others were like women who had few cares. You would not know from listening to them that some of them had spent the day in magistrates' courts, in police stations, in welfare centers, or in squatters' houses and run-down housing projects, or, like herself, in a clothing center.

She was pleased that they laughed when she told them about the bag lady who had come in to get a coat that morning. Helen's job was to arrange the sorting, the dry-cleaning, and the mending of clothes that came into the bureau. A generous dry-cleaning firm let them use the big machine free at off-peak hours if they ensured that paying customers didn't realize they were sharing them with hand-me-downs for tramps.

The woman had been very insistent. "Nothing in green. I've always found green an unlucky color, Sister. No, red's a bit flashy. In my day only a certain kind of woman wore red. A nice mauve, a lilac shade. No? Well, safer to settle for a brown, then. Not what you'd call cheerful for spring. But still." A heavy sigh. Helen Doyle was a good mimic, she caught the woman perfectly; all the others could see her as clearly as if they had been there.

"You should be on the stage, Helen," said Joan admiringly.

"Maybe she will one day," said Maureen innocently.

Helen's face clouded. "But how can I? I'll be here. Why don't any of you believe I'm going to stay? I've joined as much as you'll let me." The lip was trembling. Dangerously.

Sister Brigid intervened. "What did she look like in the brown coat, Helen?" she asked firmly. The warning was plain.

With an effort Helen pulled herself back to the story. The woman had asked for a scarf, too, something toning she said, as if she had been in the accessories department of a fashion store.

"I found her a hat in the end, a yellow hat with a brown feather in it, and I gave her a yellow brooch I was wearing myself. I said it sort of brought the whole color scheme together. She nodded like the Queen Mother and was very gracious about it, then she picked up her four bags of rubbish and went back to the Embankment."

"Good, Helen." Sister Brigid was approving. "If you can make it seem like a fashion store with a bit of choice, then you're doing it exactly right, that woman would never have taken what she thought was charity. Well done."

The others all smiled, too, and Nessa's smile was particularly broad.

"There's no one like Helen for these old misfits," Nessa said, as if to make up for her earlier outburst. "You always get onto the wavelength so well."

"It's probably that I'm there already," Helen said. "You know, about taking one to know one and all that."

"You'd never be a bag lady, Helen," Brigid said affectionately. "You'd lose the bags." The laughter around the supper table at St. Martin's was warm and good-natured.

Helen felt very much at peace and very much at home.

She thought she heard Nessa get up in the middle of the night and go downstairs. It was an old house full of creaks and sounds. They could each recognize the others' steps and coughs. Like a family.

Helen was about to get up and follow her down to the kitchen for cocoa and a chat. But she hesitated. Brigid had often said that when people were upset, the last thing they needed was someone to arrive in on top of them offering tea and sympathy. Helen had listened without agreeing. It was what she always wanted. There hadn't been any of it at home. Daddy too tired, Mother too anxious, Anna too busy, Brendan too withdrawn. It was why she had found this other family. They always had time to sympathize. It was what their work was all about. Listening.

Surely she should go down now and listen to Nessa, and maybe tell her all about the drunk today and how upsetting it had been. But maybe not. As Helen was deciding, she heard Sister Brigid's light step go down the stairs.

She crept to the landing to hear what they were talking about.

Strangely it was all about the garden and what they should plant. Shrubs would be nice to sit and look out on, Brigid said.

"When do you ever sit down?" Nessa spoke in a tone that was both scolding and admiring.

"I do sit down, lots of times. It's like that thing we got to charge the batteries for the radio, it puts new energy into me, into all of us."

"You never seem tired, Brigid."

"I feel it, I tell you. I'm getting old anyway. I'll be forty soon."

Nessa laughed aloud. "Don't be ridiculous, you're only thirty-four."

"Well, forty is the next milestone; I don't mind, it's just that I don't have as much energy as I used to. Who'll do the garden, Nessa? I'm too full of aches and pains. You can't be spared from the children."

"After today I think I could be spared only too easily. I don't have any judgment . . ."

"Shush, shush . . . Who will we ask to do it? It's hard work, you know, trying to make that little patch look like something restful and peaceful."

"Helen maybe?" Nessa sounded doubtful.

Helen, on the landing, felt a dull red come up her neck and to her face.

"Oh, she'd do it certainly, and she'd be full of imagination." Sister Brigid sounded doubtful, too. "The only thing is . . ."

Nessa came in immediately. "The only thing is she'd lose interest halfway through after we'd bought all the plants, and they'd die. Is that what you mean?"

Helen felt a wave of fury come over her.

"No, it's just that I don't like her to think that we're shunting her to do something that isn't really . . . our work, you know."

"But it's *all* our work, isn't it?" Nessa sounded surprised.

"Yes, you know that, I know that, Helen doesn't. Anyway, we'll see. Come on, Nessa, if us old ones are to be of any use to this community, we'd better get a few hours of sleep a night." She was laughing. Sister Brigid had a lovely warm laugh that included you and wrapped you up.

"Thank you, Brigid."

"I did nothing, said nothing."

"It's the way you do it, say it." Nessa was obviously feeling better now.

Helen slipped back into her room and stood for a long time with her back to the door.

So they thought she wouldn't finish things? She'd show them, by heavens she would show them.

She'd dig that garden single-handedly, she'd build a magic garden where they could all sit and think and be at peace and they would realize that Sister Helen, more than any of them, knew that anything done for the community was as important as any other thing. Then they would have to let her take her vows. And she would be completely part of their world. And safe. Safe from everything else.

Like everything Helen had touched, the building of the garden had its highs and lows. Helen found three boys who said they were anxious to help the sisters in their great work building a refuge and they'd be happy to join in with a bit of the heavy work. They brought spades and shovels and Sister Joan said it was beyond the mind's understanding how much tea they wanted, how they couldn't have this butter on their bread, or margarine, it had to be a particular spread. And they wondered if there was a little something going on at lunchtime. Sister Joan said nervously that the nuns all had their meal in the evening, but fearing that the volunteer work force would abandon everything, she ran out and bought provisions.

After three days Sister Brigid thanked them and said that there could be no further imposition on their kindness.

The lads had begun to enjoy the good food and overpowering gratitude of the nuns and didn't really want to leave at all.

They left the place in a possibly greater mess; earth had been turned over certainly, but no pattern or plan had emerged.

But Helen soldiered on, she dug until she had blisters, she spent her scant time off in bookshops reading the sections of gardening books that concentrated on "Starting Out."

She learned the differences between one kind of soil and another.

She told the sisters amazing things each evening about the sexuality of growing things.

"They never told us a word about this at school," she said indignantly. "It's the kind of thing you should know, about everything being male and female even in the garden, for heaven's sake, and going mad to propagate."

"Let's hope it all does propagate after your hard work," Brigid said. "You really are great, Helen, I don't know where you find the energy."

Helen flushed with pleasure. And she was able to remember those words of praise, too, a little later when the problem of bedding the plants came up. The nice woman who said she really admired the sisters even though she wasn't a Roman Catholic herself and disagreed with the Pope about everything, brought them some lovely plants as a gift. Red-faced with exertion from planting them, Helen assured the others that evening they were very, very lucky. It would have cost a fortune if they had to buy all these, nobody knew how expensive things were in garden centers.

She had barely finished talking when the news came that the plants had all been dug up from a park and a nearby hotel. The repercussions were endless. The explanations from every side seemed unsatisfactory. Helen said she had to protect her sources and wouldn't give them the name of the benefactor. But in mid-conversation she mentioned to the young policewoman that Mrs. Harris couldn't possibly have taken them deliberately, she wasn't that kind of person, and that was enough for the two constables to identify exactly whom she was talking about. Mrs. Harris had been in trouble before. A latter-day Robin Hood was how she was known down at the station, taking clothes from one wash line, ironing them, and presenting them as gifts to another home.

Only Helen could have gotten herself involved with Mrs. Harris. The other nuns sighed. Only Helen could have gotten them all involved, was Brigid's view, but she didn't say anything at the time.

Helen realized that the garden couldn't be considered her full-time work. And even when she had reassured the community that she was taking on no further assistance from gargantuan eaters of meals or compulsive plant thiefs she felt she should take on more than just a horticultural role. She was determined to play her part as fully as possible. She said she would do half the skivvy work, leaving Sister Joan or Sister Maureen free for a half day to do something else.

It worked. Or it sort of worked.

They all got used to the fact that Helen might not have scrubbed the table or taken in their washing when it started to rain. They knew that she would never know when they were running out of soap or cornflakes. That she wouldn't really rinse out and hang up the dishcloths to dry. But she was there, eager and willing to help.

And she did answer the phone and more or less coped when people came to call.

Which is why she was there when Renata Quigley came to see the sister in charge.

Renata. Tall and dark, somewhere in her mid-thirties. Married for fifteen years to Frank Quigley.

What on earth could she want, and how had she tracked Helen down to St.

Martin's? Helen felt her heart race and she could almost hear it thumping in her ears. At the same time there was a sense of ice-cold water in the base of her stomach.

She hadn't seen Renata since the wedding, but she had seen pictures of her, of course, in magazines and in the trade papers Daddy had brought home. Mrs. Frank Quigley, the former Miss Renata Palazzo, exchanging a joke or enjoying herself at the races or presenting a prize to the apprentice of the year or walking among the high and mighty at some charity function.

She was very much more beautiful than Helen had thought, she had skin that Mother would have called sallow but looked olivelike and beautiful with her huge dark eyes and her dark shiny hair with its expensive cut. She wore her scarf very artistically caught in a brooch and draped as if it were part of her green and gold dress. She carried a small leather handbag in green and gold squares.

Her face was troubled, and her long, thin hands with their dark red nails were twisting around the little patchwork bag.

"Can I please speak to the sister in charge?" she asked Helen.

Helen looked at her, openmouthed. Renata Quigley didn't recognize her. Suddenly the memory of an old movie came back to her, and some beautiful actress looking straight at the camera and saying, "Nobody looks at the face of a nun." It was the kind of thing that would drive Sister Brigid mad. Helen had never forgotten it. Until this moment she had never realized how true it was. There was Renata Quigley on her doorstep looking straight into her eyes, and she didn't recognize Helen, the daughter of Deirdre and Desmond Doyle, her husband's friends.

Helen, who had caused so much trouble that time.

But perhaps she had never known. With another shock Helen realized that Renata might have been told nothing at the time.

While all this was going through her mind, Helen stood at the door, a girl in a gray sweater and skirt, with a cross around her neck, her hair tied back with a black ribbon, her face perhaps covered in grime from the garden where she had been when she heard the doorbell.

Perhaps she didn't even look like a nun.

It was obvious that Renata didn't connect her with the child she had known in Rosemary Drive, Pinner, when she had come to call.

"I'm sorry, there's nobody here but me," Helen said, recovering slightly.

"Are you one of the community?" Renata looked doubtful.

"Yes. Well, yes. I'm here at St. Martin's, part of the house, one of the sisters." It was straining the truth but Helen was not going to let Renata Quigley go until she knew why she had come here in the first place.

"It's a little complicated, Sister," Renata said nervously.

Helen's smile nearly split her face in half.

"Well, come on in and sit down and tell me, that's what we're here for," she said.

And she stood back and held the door open while Frank Quigley's wife walked into St. Martin's. Into Helen's home.

That face, that dark, lean face with the high cheekbones. Helen Doyle knew it so well. She remembered well her mother saying with some satisfaction that it would run to fat all the same in the end, mark her words, all the middle-aged Italian women you saw with several chins, they, too, had been lean girls with long, perfectly formed faces. It was in their diets, in their life-styles, in the amount of olive oil they managed to put away.

When she was a child, Helen had been irritated with her mother for all this kind of niggling. What did it matter? Why was Mother so anxious to criticize, to find fault?

But later, later Helen was to look at pictures of the face and wish that her own were like it, that she had hollows and soft golden skin instead of round cheeks and freckles. She would have killed to get that dark heavy hair she saw in the photographs, and wear those loop earrings, which made Helen look like a tinker running away from an encampment but made Renata Palazzo Quigley look as glamorous as an exotic princess from a far land.

"I came here because I heard that there is a Sister Brigid . . . I thought perhaps . . ." She faltered.

"I suppose you could say I'm Sister Brigid's deputy," Helen said. In ways it could be true. She *was* in charge of the house when they were all out; that could be considered being a deputy. "I'll be glad to do what I can."

Helen fought back the other thoughts in her mind. She simply closed a door on Renata's picture in a silver frame on a small table with a long white cloth reaching to the floor. She closed another door on Frank Quigley, her father's friend, with tears in his eyes. She tried to think only of this moment. A woman had come to St. Martin's for help in some way, and Sister Brigid was out. Helen was in charge.

"It's just that you're very young . . ." Renata was doubtful.

Helen was reassuring. She had her hand on the kettle and paused to look at Renata.

"No, no, I'm much more experienced than you think."

She felt a little light-headed. Could she really be saying these words to Frank Quigley's wife?

It had been impossible in Rosemary Drive that time when Father had lost his job. Helen thought back on it, and it flashed in front of her as if she were watching a video on that machine that she had gotten for St. Martin's once because the company had *assured* her it was free for a month and there would be no obligation. It had all been very difficult, the business about the video, like everything.

But nothing was as frightening as the time her father had left Palazzo. There was a council of war every night and Mother had warned them that they must tell nobody.

"But why?" Helen had begged. She couldn't bear her sister and brother to accept that this was the way things should be from now on. "Why does it have to be a secret? It's not Daddy's fault that they changed the place. He can get another job. Daddy can get *any* job."

She remembered still how Mother had snapped at her. "Your father doesn't want *any* job, he wants his job at Palazzo back. And he will have it back soon, so in the meantime nothing is to be said. Do you hear me, Helen? Outside this house not one word is to be said. Everyone is to think that your father is going to work as usual in Palazzo."

"But how will he earn money?" Helen had asked.

It was a reasonable question. To this day she didn't regret it, as she sometimes regretted the things she had said, the offers she had made, the questions she had asked.

Anna had said nothing, for an easy life she had explained.

Brendan had said nothing because nothing was what Brendan always said.

But Helen couldn't say nothing.

She was sixteen years old, grown-up, in her last year at school. She would not stay on and get A's like Anna. Even though she felt she was twice as bright as Anna in many ways. No, Helen was going to see the world, try her hand at this and that, get on-the-job experience.

She was so full of life, at sixteen some people thought she was years younger, a big schoolgirl. Other people thought she was years older, a lively student going on twenty.

Frank Quigley had no idea how old she was the afternoon she went to see him in his office.

The dragon woman, Miss Clarke, had protected him as she always had. Helen wondered if she could possibly be there still. It was years ago. Surely she had given up hoping that Mr. Quigley was going to look into her eyes and say that she was beautiful without her glasses.

Helen had left her school blazer downstairs with the doorman and had opened the top buttons of her school shirt in order to look more grown-up. The dragon woman had eventually let her in. There were very few who could withstand Helen when she was in full flow. Explanation came hard upon explanation, and all the time she was moving toward his office. Before the dragon realized it, Helen was in.

She was flushed and excited.

Frank Quigley had looked up, surprised.

"Well, well, Helen Doyle. You're not meant to be here, I'm sure."

"I know." She laughed easily.

"You should be at school, not bursting into people's offices."

"I do a lot of things I shouldn't do."

She had sat on the corner of his desk swinging her legs, shoulders hunched up. He looked at her with interest. Helen knew she had been right to come here; the silence of Rosemary Drive was no way to handle things. There had to be confrontation.

"What can I do for you?" He had a mock gallantry. He was quite handsome in a way, dark with curly hair. Old, of course, as old as her father, even. But different.

"I suppose you could take me to lunch," she said. It was the kind of thing people said in films and on television. It worked for them, perhaps it would for her too. She gave him a smile much braver and more confident than she felt inside.

"Lunch?" He laughed in a short bark. "Lord, Helen, I don't know what kind of life-style you think we live down here—" He broke off, looking at her disappointed face.

"Aw, hell, I've not had lunch out for years."

"I never had," Helen said simply.

That did it.

They went to an Italian restaurant which was almost dark like night and there were candles on the table.

Every time Helen tried to bring up the subject of her father he skirted around it. She knew that in those television series about big business they always came to the point at the coffee stage.

There was no coffee. There was a Sambuca. A licorice-tasting liqueur. With a little coffee bean in it and the waiter set it alight. Helen had never seen anything so marvelous.

"It's like a grown-up's birthday cake," she said delightedly.

"You're fairly grown-up for seventeen," Frank said. "Or is it older?"

This was to her advantage. If he thought she was older than sixteen, he would listen better. Take her more seriously.

"Almost eighteen," she lied.

"You've been around, despite the schoolgirl getup," he said.

"I've been around," Helen said.

The more traveled he thought she was, the more he would listen when the time came to talk.

The time didn't come to talk.

He had been affectionate and admiring and had patted her cheek and even held her face up to the candlelight to see if there was any telltale ring of red wine around her mouth before she went back to school.

"I'm not going back to school," Helen said very definitely. She looked Frank Quigley straight in the eye. "You know that, and I know that."

"I certainly hoped it," he said, and his voice sounded a bit throaty. Something about the way he stroked her cheek and lifted her hair made it difficult to talk about her father's job. Helen had felt it would somehow be wrong to bring the subject up when he was being so attentive. She was relieved when he suggested they go back to his place so that they could talk properly.

"Do you mean the office?" She was doubtful. The dragon woman would keep interrupting.

"I don't mean the office," he said very steadily, looking at her. "You know that and I know that."

"I certainly hoped it," she said, echoing his words.

The apartment building was very luxurious. Mother had always said she could not understand why Frank Quigley hadn't bought himself a proper house now that he was a married man. But then he probably had expectations of the big white house with the wrought-iron gates and the large well-kept gardens. The house of the Palazzos.

But Mother couldn't have known how splendid the flat was. *Flat* wasn't the word for it, really. It was on two floors, there was a lovely staircase leading up to a floor which had a big balcony with chairs and a table outside, the balcony ran along the whole length of the place, past the sitting room and the bedroom.

They went out the sitting-room door to look at the view from the balcony. And Helen's heart lurched with a sudden realization as they left the balcony to return indoors through the bedroom.

Her hand went to her throat in an automatic gesture of fright. "Your wife . . . ?" she said.

Long, long afterward, when she played it back in her mind, she thought of all the things she could have said, should have said, might have said. How had it been that the only thing which *did* come to her to say was something that could obviously be taken to mean that she was willing and enthusiastic, but just afraid of discovery?

"Renata isn't here, Helen," Frank Quigley said softly. "You know that and I know that, just as we both knew you weren't going back to school."

She had heard that it wasn't healthy to try to blot something out of your memory, to try to pretend that it had never happened. Helen didn't care whether it was healthy or not; for a long time she tried to forget that afternoon.

The moment of no return, the look of bewilderment and anger when she had shied away from him first.

The urgency, and the pain, the sheer hurt and stabbing and fear that he was so out of control that he might do literally anything and kill her. The way he rolled away and groaned, not like that first groan but with shame and then with fury.

"You told me, you said you'd been around," he said with his head in his hands as he sat on one side of the bed, white, naked, and ridiculous-looking.

She lay on the other beside the silver-framed photograph of the lean, olive-faced Renata. Silent and disapproving-looking beside her marriage bed. As if she had always known what might happen there one day.

Helen had lain there and looked at the picture of Our Lady, it was the one you saw everywhere called Madonna of the Wayside. At least Our Lady hadn't had to go through all this to get Our Lord. It had been done miraculously. Helen looked at the picture because that meant she didn't have to look at her father's friend Frank Quigley, who was crying into his hands. And it meant she didn't have to look at the white sheets which were stained with blood and she didn't have to think about how badly he had injured her and if she would have to go to a doctor. Or if she might be pregnant.

She didn't know how long it was before she made a move to the bathroom and cleaned herself up. She didn't seem to have been very badly injured; the bleeding had stopped.

She dressed herself carefully and dusted herself with Renata's talcum powder, which wasn't in a tin like ordinary powder; it was in a big glass bowl with a pink swansdown puff.

When she came out, Frank was dressed. And white-faced.

"The bed . . . ?" she began.

"Forget the bloody bed."

"I could—"

"You've done enough," he snapped.

Helen's eyes filled with tears. "I've done enough? What did I do, I came to talk to you about my father and why he'd been sacked, it was you, you who did all this. . . ." With her hand she waved in the direction of the bed.

His face was contrite. "Your father. You did this to try to get Desmond back his piffling little job. Jesus Christ, you'd whore around to get your father a penny-farthing nothing place in a supermarket."

"It is not a nothing job." Helen's face burned with anger. "He was a very important person there, and now, now he's been sacked and Mother says we are not to tell anyone, neighbors, relatives, anyone, and he goes off each morning pretending he's going to work. . . ."

Frank looked at her in disbelief.

"Yes, he does, and I just wanted to have lunch with you and tell you straight out how bad it was and you'd understand because you were Dad's friend way back at school in the brothers when you used to climb over stone walls . . . he told me . . . and you're doing so well there and married to the boss's daughter and everything . . . And *that's* all I wanted, I didn't whore around, I've never slept with anyone in my life and I didn't mean to sleep with you, I wasn't to know you'd fall in love with me and all this would happen, and now you say it's all my fault." She burst into tears.

He put his arms around her and held her close to him.

"Christ, you're only a child, what have I done? Christ Almighty, what did I do?"

She sobbed against his jacket for a bit.

He held her away from him and his eyes were full of tears.

"I'll never be able to make amends. Literally there's nothing I can do to tell you how sorry I am. I'd never . . . never if I hadn't thought . . . I was so sure that . . . but that doesn't matter now. What matters is you."

Helen wondered if he had always loved her, or was it only now? People could fall in love so easily.

"We'll have to forget this," she said. She knew that a woman had to take the lead in such matters. Men would dither and give in to temptation. Anyway, there was no temptation for Helen. If this was what it was like, then the rest of the world could have it, as far as she was concerned.

"It happened, it can't be forgotten. I'll do anything to make it up to you."

"Yes, but we can't keep on seeing each other, it wouldn't be fair." She looked over at the picture of Renata.

She thought he looked puzzled. "No, of course," he said.

"And we won't tell anyone, either of us." She was girlishly eager about this.

"Lord, no, nobody at all," he said, looking highly relieved.

"And my father?" She spoke without guile, she spoke as Helen always spoke, eager to get over the meaning and burden of what she wanted to say, heedless of timing or other people's feelings.

She saw a look of pain cross Frank Quigley's face.

"Your father will get a job. He told me that he didn't need one, that he was looking, that he had plenty of offers." Frank's voice was cold. "He will be reinstated in Palazzo. Not overnight, I have to talk to Carlo, these things have to be done tactfully. They can take a little time."

Helen nodded vigorously.

"And you, Helen. Will you be all right, will you forgive me?"

"Of course. It was a misunderstanding." Her voice sounded eager, as if she, too, wanted to be let off a hook.

"That's what it was, Helen, and Helen, listen to me, please. The only thing I can tell you is that it won't always be like this . . . it will be lovely and happy . . ." He was straining to try to tell her that this gross happening would not be the pattern for the rest of the lovemaking in her life.

He might as well have been talking to the wall.

"Are you sure I couldn't do anything about the sheets, like a Laundromat or anything?"

"No."

"But what will you say?"

"Please, Helen, please." His face was pained.

"Will I go now, Frank?"

He looked unable to cope.

"I'll drive you . . ." His voice trailed away. His face showed that he didn't know where he was to drive her.

"No, it's all right, I can get the bus. I know where I am, I'll just get the bus home and say . . . say I don't feel well." Helen gave a little giggle. "It's true in a way. But listen, Frank, I don't have the bus fare, could I ask you . . ."

She couldn't understand why Frank Quigley had tears pouring down his face when he handed her the coins and closed her hand over them.

"Will you be all right?" He was begging to be reassured. He was not ready for what she told him.

"Frank." Helen gave a little laugh. "I'm not a child, for heaven's sake, I was sixteen last week. I'm a grown-up. I'll find my way home on the bus."

She left then because she couldn't bear the look on his face.

Of course, he had to stay away from the house in case he wasn't able to control himself when he saw her. That's what she told herself.

She never remembered him coming to Rosemary Drive again after that. There had always been some excuse: he was on a conference, he was abroad, he and Renata were going to see some of her relations in Italy. He was terribly sorry, it was such bad timing. Mother said he was getting above himself; still, wasn't it great that they never had to go to him cap in hand to ask him to reinstate his old friend in Palazzo's? At least that idea had come straight from Mr. Palazzo himself, who had realized that this was no way to treat valued managerial staff.

Helen never knew whether her father realized that it was Frank. It was hard to talk to her father, he had built a little shell around himself almost for fear of being hurt, like Mother's shell for fear of letting themselves down somehow.

She had found those last school terms endless; the world had changed since that strange afternoon. She was always frightened of being misunderstood. She had started to scream one day when the singing master at school asked her to come into the storeroom and help him carry down the sheet music to the school hall. The man hadn't touched her, but she had this sudden claustrophobic fear that he would think she was encouraging him somehow and that he would begin this hurtful business and then blame her. As things turned out, he *did* blame her very much indeed and had said that she was a neurotic, hysterical fool, a troublemaker, and if she were the last female on earth, he wouldn't touch her with a ten-foot pole.

The principal of the school seemed to agree with him and asked Helen sharply why she had begun to scream if she agreed that there had been no question of an attack or even an advance.

Helen had said glumly that she didn't know. She had felt that she was in some kind of situation she couldn't handle and that unless she *did* scream, something else would happen and it would all be too late and too complicated.

"Has anything of this sort happened to you before?" The principal was not entirely sympathetic. Helen Doyle had always been a difficult pupil, gushy, anxious to please, always creating waves of trouble around her.

Helen had said no, unconvincingly.

The principal had sighed. "Well, you can be certain that it will keep happening to you, Helen. It's your personality. This sort of thing will turn up in your life over and over again, situations that you can't handle. That is, unless you pull yourself together and take control of your own actions."

She sounded so final it was as if she were passing a life sentence.

Helen had been dazed at the unfairness of it all.

It was then that she decided to be a nun.

And now, years later, she was almost a nun. Well, she would be a nun if Sister Brigid had not been so adamant about telling her that she was only using the convent as a crutch, that she was using it as a place to hide and that those days were over in religious life.

Helen felt safe in St. Martin's. And even as she made a mug of coffee and sat down to join the beautiful Renata Palazzo Quigley, whose face had looked at her from a silver frame on that frightening day . . . she felt safe. Safe from the memories and the fear of that time.

"Tell me what you want and I'll see if there's anything we can do," she said with the big smile that made everyone love Helen when they first met her.

"It's very simple," Renata said. "We want a baby."

It was very simple. And very sad. Helen hugged her mug of coffee to her and listened. Frank was too old at forty-six. Too old. How ridiculous, but adoption societies wouldn't consider him. Also, he had a poor medical history, some heart trouble, nothing very serious, because of stress at work, and all businessmen had this in today's world. Natural mothers and fathers were allowed to bring a child into the world into any kind of appalling conditions, tenements, places of vice, nobody stopped them and said that they couldn't have any children. But for adoption everything had to be perfect.

Renata had heard that sometimes, if she were only to meet the right person, there must be occasions where a child could be given to a good loving home, to a father and mother who would love the little boy or girl as their own. There surely were cases when this happened.

There was a look of longing in her eyes.

Helen patted the hand of the woman who had once looked at her from the silver frame.

She had told Renata that they would meet again in a week, when she would have made some inquiries. She thought it wiser not to consult Sister Brigid for the moment. Sister Brigid, being an authority figure, had to keep so well within the limits of the law . . . Better just let Helen inquire a little. All right? All right.

She told nobody. They said she looked feverish and excited, and Helen entertained the community with tales of how she made her garden grow.

"Anyone call?" Brigid asked.

"No. Not anyone really, you know, usual callers." Helen avoided her eye. It was the first time she had told a direct lie at St. Martin's. It didn't feel good, but it was for the best in the end.

If she could do this one thing, if she could do what she hoped she might be able to do, then even at the age of twenty-one her whole life would have been worth living.

It was Nessa's turn to do the kitchen for half a day. Nessa was the one woman at St. Martin's who found Helen almost impossible to get along with. Normally when they worked together, Helen stayed out of Nessa's way. But this time she positively hung around her neck.

"What happens when the children are born to really hopeless mothers, Nessa? Don't you wish you could give them to proper homes from the start?"

"What I wish isn't important, I don't rule the world." Nessa was short, she was scrubbing the kitchen floor, and Helen kept standing in her way.

"But wouldn't a child be much better off?"

"Mind, Helen, please. I've just washed there."

"And you always have to register the births, no matter what kind of mother?"

"What do you mean?"

"I mean, do you have to go to the town hall or the registry office or whatever and sort of say who the child is?"

"No, I don't always."

"Oh, why not?"

"Because I'm usually not the one who does it, it depends. It depends. Helen, do you think that if you're not going to do any work, you could move out of the kitchen so that I could clean it?"

"And no babies end up without being registered?"

"How could they?"

"I don't know." Helen was disappointed. She had thought there might be long twilight times when nobody knew who or what the baby was. She hadn't understood how the welfare system at least checked its citizens in and out of the world.

"And foundlings, babies in phone booths, in churches, where do they end up?"

Nessa looked up in alarm. "God, Helen, don't tell me you found one?"

"No, worse luck," Helen said. "But if I did, would I have to register it?"

"No, Helen, of course not, if *you* found a baby, you could keep the baby and dress him or her up when you remembered, and feed the child when it occurred to you, or when there was nothing else marginally more interesting to do."

"Why are you so horrible to me, Nessa?" Helen asked.

"Because I am basically pretty horrible."

"You can't be, you're a nun. And you're not horrible to the others."

"Ah, that's true. The real thing about being horrible is that it's selective."

"And why did you select me?" Helen didn't seem put out or hurt, she was interested. Actually interested.

Nessa was full of guilt.

"Oh, for heaven's sake, I'm just short-tempered, I hate doing this bloody floor, and you're so young and carefree and get everything you want. I'm sorry, Helen, forgive me, I'm always asking you to forgive me. Really I am."

"I know." Helen was thoughtful. "People often are. I seem to bring out the worst in them somehow."

Sister Nessa looked after her uneasily as Helen wandered back into the garden. There was something more than usual on her scattered brain and it was weighing very heavily.

Helen rang Renata Quigley. Same address, same apartment, same bed presumably. She said that she was still inquiring but that it wasn't as easy as people thought.

"I never thought it was easy." Renata sighed. "But somehow it does make all the going out to functions and to this celebration and that celebration a little easier if I think that somebody as kind as you, Sister, is looking out for me."

With a thrill of shock that went right through her body Helen Doyle realized that she would meet Frank and Renata Quigley at her parents' silver wedding party.

Frank Quigley had been the best man back in those days when he and Father were about equal.

Before everything had changed.

The garden was finished and more or less ran itself. Sister Joan loved being in the clothing center, and she was quick with a needle, so that she could do an alteration on the spot, move the buttons on a jacket for an old man, praise him, admire him, say that the fit made all the difference in the world. Let him think it was custom-tailored.

There was no real work for Helen, no real place.

Once more she asked Brigid about taking her vows.

"It's very harsh to keep me on the outside. Seriously, I have been here for so long, you *can't* say it's a passing fancy anymore now, can you?" She begged and implored.

"You're running, Helen," Brigid said. "I told you that from the word *go*. This is not like a convent in the films, a place in a forest where people went to find peace, it's a working house. You have to have found peace already to bring it here."

"But I've found it now," Helen implored.

"No, you're afraid of engaging with real people, that's why you're with us."

"You're all more real than anyone else. Honestly, I've never met any group I like so much."

"That's not the whole story. We shelter you from something. We can't go on doing that, it's not our role. If it's men, if it's sex, if it's the cut and thrust of the business world . . . we all have had to face it and cope with it. You're still hiding from something."

"I suppose it is sex a bit."

"Well, you don't have to keep indulging in it." Brigid laughed. "Go back out into the world, Helen, I beg you, for a couple of years. Stay in touch with us and then, if you still feel this is your home, come back and we'll look at it all again. I really do think you should go. For your own good."

"Are you asking me to leave? Truly?"

"I'm suggesting it, but do you see what I mean about this not being like the real world? If this was a real place, I'd be telling you to go or promoting you. It's too protective here for you, I feel it in my bones."

"Let me stay for a little while. Please."

"Stay until after your parents' twenty-fifth wedding anniversary," Brigid said unexpectedly. "That seems to be preying on your mind, for some reason. And then after that we'll see."

Helen went away from Sister Brigid's little workroom, more wretched than she had been for a long time.

She looked so sad that Sister Nessa asked if she wanted to come and help with the young mothers. This was the first time the invitation had ever been made.

Helen went along, for once silent and without prattle.

"Don't be disapproving or anything, will you, Helen?" Nessa asked nervously. "We're not meant to be passing judgment, just helping them cope."

"Sure," Helen said.

She sat as listlessly as any of the girls who were on low-dose antidepressants or who lived in fear of a pimp who had wanted them to have an abortion. Nessa looked at her from time to time with concern. But Helen was quiet and obedient. She did everything she was asked to do. She was useful, too, in a way. She went out to the flats of those who had not turned up. Nessa had always been nervous since the incident of little Simon, who had crawled out of his flat almost into the mainstream of rush-hour traffic.

In the late afternoon Nessa asked Helen to go and find Yvonne, who was eight months pregnant with her second child. Her eldest—a beautiful girl with Jamaican eyes like her father, long gone, and a Scottish accent like her mother, who had given birth to her at sixteen—was waiting at the door.

"Mommy's gonna do wee-wee," she said helpfully.

"That's great," Helen said, and brought the toddler back into the house.

From the bathroom came the groans and the cries of Yvonne.

Suddenly Helen found courage.

"You're better in your bedroom," she said suddenly to the chubby child, and moved a chest of drawers to make sure the child couldn't get out.

Then she went to cope with what she thought was a miscarriage in the bathroom.

But in the middle of the blood, the screams, and the definite smell of rum all around the place, Helen heard a small cry.

The baby was alive.

Yvonne remembered nothing of it all. She had been so drunk that the day passed in a terrible blur.

They told her she had lost the child, that she had flushed it down the toilet.

The ambulance men had been tender and gentle as they lifted her on to the stretcher, they had looked around the place and even down the toilet bowl in confusion.

"They told us she was near to her time, she couldn't have gotten rid of a full-term fetus, surely."

But Helen, the cool-eyed girl who said she was a voluntary welfare worker at the mother and child center, and that she lived with the sisters at St. Martin's, assured them that she had not been able to get into the flat and had heard continuous flushing of the chain and then found the place covered in blood.

The small, round three-year-old seemed to back her up, saying that her mother had been a long time wee-weeing and that Helen had been a long time at the door.

Nessa, ashen-faced and trying not to let herself believe that this would never have happened if she had sent anyone else but Helen, agreed that Helen had been gone ages and ages and could get no reply. Helen had made a call to Nessa, saying that there were problems but that she knew she would get in if she could persuade the child to open the door. She had called from a nearby shop where she had stopped to buy a bottle of milk for herself because she felt faint thinking of what might be inside.

That night, with Yvonne in her hospital bed, with Yvonne's three-year-old lodged temporarily in a local orphanage until the care order could be signed, Helen told Brigid she felt restless and she would like to go out for a walk.

"You *are* restless tonight," Brigid said absently. "You've been out to the garden half a dozen times."

"I wanted to make sure it was all right," Helen said.

Carefully she picked up the little bundle, the boy who would inherit the Palazzo millions, and took him in her arms. She had him wrapped carefully in a towel and in one of her own nighties. She had a soft blue rug, which used to lie folded on the back of her chair, wrapped well around him.

She slipped out the back gate of St. Martin's and walked until her legs were tired. Then, in a shop where nobody would recognize her and mention to one of the sisters that they had seen one of the community carrying a baby, she found a phone and telephoned Renata.

"I have it," she said triumphantly into the phone.

"Who is this, you have what?"

"Renata, it's Sister Helen from St. Martin's. I have your baby."

"No, no, it's not possible."

"Yes, but I must give him to you now, tonight, this minute."

"It's a little boy, you got us a little boy?"

"Yes. He's very, very young, he's only one day old."

Renata's voice was a screech. "But no, one day. He will die, I cannot know what to do for a child of one day . . . ."

"I don't know either, but I bought him a bottle of milk and he seems to be taking it off my finger," Helen said simply.

"Where are you?"

"I'm in London, of course, about two miles from the convent. Renata, have you any money?"

"What kind of money?" She sounded worried.

"Enough to pay for a taxi."

"Yes, yes."

"So will I come to your flat? And give him to you? No one must know."

"Yes, I don't know, perhaps I should wait till . . . I don't know what to do."

"I went to great trouble to get him for you." Helen sounded tired.

"Oh, I know, Sister, I'm so foolish, it's just that it's so quick and he is so very little."

"I'm sure you'll learn. You can always ring someone and ask them. Will I get a taxi now? It might cost a lot."

"Yes, come now."

"And Frank's not there, is he?"

"Frank, how did you know my husband is Frank?"

"You told me," Helen said, biting her lip.

"I suppose I must have. I don't know what to say."

The taxi driver said that this wasn't where he wanted to go. He was on his way home. South London is what he wanted. Not miles out to Wembley.

He saw the tears beginning to form.

"Get in before I change my mind," he said. "Anyway, at least you've had it. Let's look on the bright side, I could have ended up delivering it."

"That's true," Helen said, and the taxi driver looked at her anxiously, wondering if he would get his fare when he got to Wembley.

She recited the address of the apartment house as if by rote and asked the driver to wait. The lady of the house would be down in a moment and would pay him.

He told the other cabdrivers afterward that he had spotted her as trouble the very moment he saw her, the moment that her eyes had filled with tears when he said perfectly normally that in the evenings he wanted to go south of the river rather than up to this neck of the woods in Wembley. Anyway, he said, it all seemed to have happened at once; the lady came down and was carrying a purse with money. Classy, she was, and foreign. She took one look at the baby and she started to scream.

"He's got blood on him, he's not properly formed, no, no, I didn't want this! This is a baby that still is not ready to be a baby. No, no."

She backed away from the girl in the gray skirt and sweater with her hand up to her mouth and at that moment a fellow in a Rover came along and leapt out. He took one look at what was happening and shook the foreign woman till her head nearly fell off, then he took the child and seemed to recognize the girl in the gray. He kept saying, "Oh, my God," too, as if she were something from outer space.

Then there was a bundle of notes stuffed in the taxi driver's window, four times the fare out to bloody Wembley. So he had to go, and he never knew what it was all about and how it ended.

It ended badly. As everything Helen Doyle had ever touched seemed to end.

She had refused to go into the flat, crying, too, now, louder than Renata, but neither of the women cried as much as the bewildered, hungry baby that had been born in a bathroom that morning.

Sister Brigid was eventually summoned, to make some sense out of the whole scene. She came with Nessa, white-faced but calm.

Nessa saw to the baby, and Brigid listened to the hysterical explanations.

The Italian woman was saying that she had intended only to inquire if any mother wanted to give her baby privately for adoption; she hadn't asked anyone to take one for her.

The tall Irish businessman was pleading for Helen, saying that she had done it for the best, as she had always done everything for the best, but the world was never able to perceive it that way. He sounded tender toward her and yet terrified of her as well.

He knew her parents, he explained. Desmond Doyle had been one of his oldest friends.

"She is the daughter of those Doyles?" Shock was being piled on shock for Renata.

"Yes, she can't have known it was us."

There was something in the way the man spoke. There was something that sounded a warning. Brigid looked from one stricken face to another to try to read the signals.

Helen was opening her mouth. "But I *did* know, I *did* know, it's only because it *was* Frank that I'd do this, I'd never have taken a baby and told all those lies. If it hadn't been Frank, I'd not have risked the baby's life. I felt I owed it to him, after all, after everything. . . ."

Brigid had worked with people for all her adult life. Mainly people who were in some kind of distress. She didn't know what was going to be said now, but she felt it was crucial that whatever it was, Helen should not say it. Helen was in mid-flight; through the tears and the gulps the story was coming out.

"I never meant it to be like this, but they could have given it such a good life, so much money, and Frank's too old to adopt a child, and she said he had been having heart attacks—"

"You told her that?" Frank snapped at his wife.

"I thought she was a nun miles away. How did I know she was bloody Doyle's daughter?"

Helen was oblivious. "I wanted to make amends, to make up for everything. To try to put things right. After all, my life worked out all right and I got everything I wanted, but Frank didn't, he had no children and he had heart attacks, he was punished . . . I wanted to try to even it out."

Renata was looking from one to another now in confusion. Out in the other room Sister Nessa had quieted the baby, and Helen was gathering her breath again.

"You work with Mr. Doyle still?" Brigid asked quickly.

"Yes, and he helped my father when he was sacked, he asked Mr. Palazzo to give him back his job . . ."

Brigid saw an avenue of escape. She stood up as she spoke.

"So Helen with her usual impetuous nature decided to thank you for this by getting you a child when it was not going to be easy through the proper channels. Isn't that right?"

Frank Quigley looked into the gray eyes of Sister Brigid, competent, unemotional, strong. Irish perhaps a generation ago, but now with a London accent. She reminded him of bright men he met in business.

"That's it. Exactly, Sister."

Helen hadn't stopped crying. Brigid felt she might not have stopped speaking either. With what seemed like a deliberate effort she put her arm around the girl's shoulder.

"Let's take you home, Helen, back to St. Martin's. That's the best thing now."

"Will I drive you?" Frank asked.

"No, but if you could get us a taxi, Mr. Quigley."

At this moment Nessa came in; the baby was asleep. They would take him to the hospital, the one they knew, and where they were known. He would be looked after.

"It seems a pity in a way, Sister." Frank looked at Sister Brigid, and she looked back. The glance was a long one.

It was a pity in many ways. They could give the boy everything, including more love than he would ever know from Yvonne.

"Yes, but if we do this, everything breaks down. Every single thing."

He felt she was tempted.

"Not everything, just a few forms to fill out. The mother thinks he is dead."

"Please," Renata said. "Please, Sister."

"I'm not God, I'm not even Solomon," said Brigid.

They knew it was hard for her, and they drew together, the handsome couple. Helen watched them with a look of pain in her face.

The doorman had been asked to hail a taxi, and the unlikely foursome walked to the lift, Helen tearful and supported by Sister Brigid, red-haired Sister Nessa carrying the tiny baby wrapped in its blue rug.

Renata stretched out her hand to touch Helen's arm.

"Thank you, Sister Helen, I know you meant kindly for me," she said.

"Sister Helen has a great big heart," Brigid said.

"Thank you," Frank said at the door. He did not look at Helen, he looked instead admiringly into the gray eyes of Brigid.

"There are countries where it is all legal. If you like, someday you can ask me and I will tell you what I know," she said.

"Good-bye, Frank," Helen said.

"Thank you, Helen. Sister Brigid is right, you have a great big heart." He touched her cheek.

In the taxi they were silent, until Helen said, "You called me Sister Helen, does this mean I can stay?"

"It means we won't ask you to go yet. But maybe now that you have faced some things you haven't faced before, it mightn't be as necessary to hide as it once was. Perhaps you will be able to make your life somewhere else. Travel the world, even."

This time Helen didn't think that Sister Brigid was asking her to leave. She felt better than she had felt for a long time.

She looked at Sister Nessa, holding the tiny boy close to her breast.

"Isn't it sad that you can't keep the baby, Nessa?" Helen said with a rush of generous spirit. "To make up for the one you had that died. It could be a kind of substitute, couldn't it? A consolation."

She didn't even notice the two women glance at each other and then look out the windows on each side of the taxi.

CHAPTER FOUR

Desmond

*O*f course the corner shop was more expensive than the supermarket, but then it *was* on the corner, that's what you were paying for. And the fact that it stayed open so late at night.

Desmond liked stopping in there. There was a mad, magical feel about the place and the way Suresh Patel was able to pack in so many goods on his shelves

. . . and in such a way that they didn't all come tumbling down. Desmond often said that Mr. Patel must have a secret. Over in the big supermarket chain, Palazzo Foods, where Desmond worked, the principle was totally different. You had to give maximum space so that the customer could walk around and choose and, best of all, be persuaded by something that had not been on the original shopping list. Mr. Patel's business was at the other end of the market. They came in because they had run out of sugar or they hadn't bought anything for supper and the shop they intended to go to had been closed. They came for the evening paper and a tin of beans sometimes. Mr. Patel said that you'd be surprised how many people must be going home to a lonely evening. He often felt better off standing in his shop talking to whoever came and went.

Desmond's wife, Deirdre, said she had nothing against Mr. Patel personally, he was extremely polite and respectful always, but everything was that little bit dearer there. The place was a hodgepodge, a bit like those hucksters' shops you didn't go into years ago at home in case things mightn't be quite . . . well, fresh.

And she never knew why Desmond would stop and buy an earlier edition of the paper in the corner shop when he could have gotten one nearer work and had the pleasure of reading it on the way home.

Desmond found it hard to explain. There was something solid about the little place. It didn't depend on the fluctuations of faraway suppliers and huge multinationals. If Mr. Patel noticed a customer asking for something, he gave it a lot of thought. Like the time Desmond had asked for red-currant jelly.

"Is it a jam or a condiment?" Mr. Patel had asked with interest.

"I think it can be either." Desmond had been equally interested in the definition. Between them they decided that once it had been bought, it would be placed on a shelf with the mustards, the chutneys, and the little green jars of mint sauce.

"Soon I will know exactly the tastes and temperaments of a fine British suburb. I will know enough to write a book, Mr. Doyle."

"I think you know that already, Mr. Patel."

"I am only starting, Mr. Doyle, but it is all so interesting. You know the saying they have in your country about all human life is here . . . that's what I feel."

"All human life is in my job, too, but I don't welcome it as much as you do." Desmond smiled ruefully.

"Ah, that's because your job is so much more important than mine."

Deirdre Doyle would have agreed with him. Mr. Patel was right to look with respect at a man like Desmond, who, though well under fifty, was Special Projects Manager at Palazzo. Palazzo was a name like Sainsbury's or Waitrose. Well, not quite like them, but in certain areas it was just as well thought of, and back home in Ireland, where nobody knew any of the others anyway, a Palazzo sounded much grander.

The Patels didn't live in Rosemary Drive, naturally they lived somewhere else, somewhere more suitable for Indian and Pakistani people, Deirdre said, when anyone brought the subject up.

Desmond knew that in fact Suresh Patel, his wife, his two children, and his brother lived in the tiny storerooms behind the small shop. Mrs. Patel could speak no English and the brother was fat and looked as if he had some illness.

He used to sit there and smile perfectly pleasantly, but he spoke little and did not seem to be any help in the running of the corner shop.

For some reason that he never totally understood, Desmond never mentioned that the Patel family lived there. That their two children, immaculate in school uniform and wearing blazers and spectacles, came out each morning from this tiny place. Desmond felt that somehow it demeaned the Patels to be thought to live in such a small place, and somewhere in his subconscious he felt that Deirdre might think it demeaned the neighborhood to have Pakistanis actually living there rather than just trading.

The shop was busy in the early morning, people buying papers, bars of chocolate, orange drinks, and plastic-wrapped sandwiches. The stuff that kept the commuters more or less alive on their journeys to work. The oil that ran the machinery of British industry.

Not that Desmond felt too cheerful about his own part in British industry. He was on his way to work at the big headquarters of Palazzo Foods, the supermarket chain which was now ninth largest in Britain. Desmond had begun to work for it back in 1959, when it was simply called Prince. That was the year he and Frank Quigley had left Mayo and come to London by train, boat, and train to make their fortune. They arrived during the heat wave that went on month after month; they thought they had come to paradise.

As Desmond took his regular morning journey down Rosemary Drive into Wood Road and on to the bus stop at the corner, he often looked back on those days when things were simpler and when he and Frank worked behind the counters in the two Prince Stores. One day they might be slicing bacon, another day dressing windows. Every day they met the customers and they knew everyone who worked in the shop.

It was Frank who had seen that this was a company where they could rise and rise; it was no stopgap job. Prince Foods was breaking new ground, it was getting bigger, soon it would expand and Frank would be a manager in one branch and Desmond in another if they played their cards right. Frank played his cards magnificently. Desmond had always been slower to see the opportunities. But he saw how everything was changing and saw sadly that the higher he rose—dragged, pulled, and cajoled by his friend Frank—the farther he got from the people, which was what he had liked about it all in the first place.

Desmond Doyle had been a thin, wiry young man then, with a thick shock of fair brown hair. His children had often teased him about the old photograph, saying that he looked like a proper teddy boy, but their mother wouldn't allow that at all. That was the way all young men of style looked then, she would say firmly. He looked different now, combing his hair in a way in which it might look as if it were covering his head and wearing shirts that had a neck size far wider than he wore that first summer when he had only been able to buy two shirts as his entire wardrobe and there was always one hanging on the back of a chair drying.

He supposed that many people looked back on the old days as good days even though they had been practically penniless days. He certainly did.

He could never understand why people liked the Palazzo Building so much. It was a perfect example of Art Deco, they said, a thirties masterpiece. Desmond always thought it looked like one of those big brutalist buildings you saw in documentaries about Eastern Europe. It was a square, menacing-looking place, he thought. It was strange that there was a preservation order on it and articles in magazines talking about its perfect proportions.

Frank had been instrumental in getting that building for Palazzo; it was then the disused headquarters of an automobile company that had gone bankrupt. Nobody else had seen its potential, but Frank Quigley, who knew everything, said that they had to have storage space for stock, they had to have a depot and maintenance center for their vans, and they had to have some kind of central offices. Why not combine them all behind this splendid facade?

A facade is what it was. Wonderful stairways and reception rooms on the ground floor. But upstairs a warren of prefabricated and jerry-built offices and partitions. Accounts had been modernized and gone on-line in computers, so that was housed in a modern extension at the back. But there was a strange limbo land on the third floor, a place where there were names on doors and people often bursting in saying, "Oh, sorry." There were vague storage areas where paneling that hadn't worked or plastic display units that hadn't fitted were left pending decisions.

There in the heart of this hidden chaos, the unacceptable face of Palazzo, lay Desmond Doyle's workplace. The Special Projects Department. Officially it was the nerve center of new ideas, plans, concepts, and illuminations that would wipe the competition off the map. In reality it was the place where Desmond worked and drew his month's salary and kept his managerial title because he was the boyhood friend of Frank Quigley. Because they went back a long way and because they had set out on the same day over a quarter of a century ago.

Frank Quigley, the quiet but powerful Managing Director, the man who had seen the way to jump and jumped with the Italians when it came to takeover time. The man who had married the boss's daughter. It was thanks to Frank that Desmond walked up to the third floor of Palazzo and opened the door of his office with a heavy heart.

The Special Projects Department was coming under scrutiny. There had been definite rumors that a big investigation was upcoming. Desmond Doyle felt the familiar knot of sour bile in his stomach and the panic beginning to grip his chest. What did it mean this time? An accusation that the section wasn't pulling its weight, a demand for exact quantifying of how much the last in-store presentations had realized, and the projected figures likely from the children's promotional exercises.

The antacid tablets seemed to do no good anymore, he was eating them like sweets. He was weary of the confrontations and the need to seem bright. Once that business of looking bright and being on top of things had been the be-all and end-all of his day. Not anymore. At an age which the rest of the world persisted in thinking of as young, Desmond Doyle felt like an old, old man. Forty-six going on ninety. That's what he would have answered truthfully if anyone had asked him caringly about his age.

His office, blessedly free from the photographs that covered the walls in his home, had a pale print of a Connemara countryside. It looked somehow more mauve, blue, and elegant than he remembered it, but Deirdre said it was the very spirit of the West of Ireland and he should hang it there so that it could be a conversation piece. He could talk about it to visitors, tell them this was the place he came from. Those were his roots.

Poor Deirdre, thinking that was the kind of conversation that took place in his boxlike cubicle of an office. He was lucky to have walls that were not that rough glass or Perspex; he was lucky to have a desk, a telephone, and two filing cabinets. The luxury of chats about roots based on overpastelized views of County Mayo was not anything he had known. Or would ever know.

He no longer felt that the words stuck with cardboard lettering on his door were important . . . there had been no Special Projects in the old days, it was only a made-up word. There had been real jobs like Stores Development Manager, Operations Manager, or Merchandising Manager. These were what the business was about. Special Projects meant nothing to Desmond Doyle because he knew that in his case it was nothing. In other countries it was a real job; he knew that from reading the retail magazines. In Palazzo Foods it meant only a pat on the back.

Desmond remembered way back reading an advertisement which said, "A title on the door means a Bigelow on the floor." A Bigelow was some kind of carpet. It was a lovely, innocent advertisement trying to drive young executives mad for status. He had told Deirdre about it once, but she had missed the point. Why shouldn't he have a carpet too? she had asked. Perhaps they could get an irregular carpet themselves and fit it over the weekend, then it would look important and nobody would have to go to war over it and risk a confrontation they might lose. Wearily at that time, he had settled for a small rug, which he kept under his desk so that nobody could see it but assured Deirdre that it gave the place class and superiority.

Desmond wouldn't lose his job in Palazzo even if the whole Special Projects Department was deemed to be useless, a criminal waste of time. It was hardly a department, anyway; he had that young pup who was meant to be a trainee and the very occasional services of Marigold, a big Australian girl with a mouthful of teeth and a mane of hair who was on what she called OE, Overseas Experience, and had worked in a funeral parlor, as a dentist's receptionist, and in the office of an amusement park, all to get an idea of what the world was like before she went home and married a millionaire from Perth, which was her goal.

She was a handsome, friendly girl who would sit on Desmond's desk companionably, asking if he had any correspondence or memos to type. She thought typing was the golden key to unlocking the world. "Tell your girls to learn to type, Dizzy," Marigold told him often. She never accepted that one of his girls had a B.A. and worked in a bookshop and the other was a sort of worker nun. Neither of them would take Marigold's golden key to the world.

If Special Projects was dissolved, Marigold would be sympathetic. She would tell Dizzy that Quigley was a sod and what's more, he always tried to pinch her rear. She'd offer to buy him a beer and tell him he was too good for Palazzo and should look around for something better. The young pup of a trainee would hardly notice; he would go and pick his nose in some other part of the store. The pup's father was an important supplier; he would be kept on no matter what happened.

As would Desmond himself. He had been let go once. Never again. Frank Quigley would see to that. His job or a form of it was his for life. He had almost fourteen years more with Palazzo. The company had a policy of retirement at sixty. In fact, it was less than fourteen years, it was now only thirteen and a bit. They would find something for him to do in that time.

Desmond Doyle would not find himself explaining his existence and justifying his role to his old friend Frank. No, if there was anything unpleasant like that ahead, you could be sure that Frank would have pressing business in the farthest part of the land or a meeting that was so important it could not be rearranged. Desmond would have to talk to Carlo Palazzo himself, the father-in-law, but in no way a godfather figure.

Carlo was a man who thought about his family and his soft leather jackets; he had always wanted to be in the fashion business, and now with the profit he was making from Palazzo he could have his showrooms and his life's dream. Carlo Palazzo, a mild-looking Italian whose accent seemed to become more pronounced with every year he spent in North London, made none of the day-to-day decisions about his supermarket empire. He left the running of all that to the bright Mr. Quigley, whom he was sharp enough to have spotted many years ago as the type of hungry young Irishman who could run it. And who could marry Carlo's daughter, too.

There were no children yet, and Desmond knew that this was a great sadness, but he kept hoping. Even though it seemed increasingly unlikely with every year that went by, fifteen years of marriage and Renata now well into her thirties.

Carlo was an optimist about his grandchildren. But he was a practical man about his profits, and if it were he who would conduct the investigation, Desmond sighed, there would be no emotional confidences today, only harsh facts and even harsher questions. What has Special Projects added to the sum of Palazzo's profit in the last six months? Just list the achievements, please, Desmond. Yes?

Desmond drew his pad nearer to him to get the sorry list together. It wasn't that he had no ideas—he was bursting with ideas—but somehow they got lost in this welter of departments and other pressures and needs.

Like the time he suggested they have a bakery on their own premises. That had been a long time ago and very much ahead of its time. Desmond had not been adventurous enough, he had suggested only that they make brown bread and scones. But his reasoning had been so sound it had been taken over on a larger scale than he had ever dreamed. He had said that the smell of freshly baked bread was very attractive when a customer came in the door; it was the living guarantee that it was absolutely made that day. The fact that they could see it being baked in hygienic conditions spoke volumes for the general hygiene of the rest of the store as well.

But somehow it had left him; it was never the Desmond Doyle idea, or the Special Projects suggestion, it had become part of Merchandising, and then a separate section called Bakery started and there were articles and photographs in all the papers about the unusual loaves and bread shapes and the yeast breads they made. Palazzo bread had become a legend.

Desmond didn't waste too many tears over it; an idea was only an idea, and once you gave it to other people, then it was no longer yours. In terms of seeing it through, it didn't really matter whether you got credit for it or not, it was out of your hands. But if you *had* gotten credit, of course, if you had the reputation of being Mr. Ideas in the company, then life would have a different color to it during the working day. There would be a bigger office, a proper name on the door, and even one of those carpets. Mr. Palazzo would ask him to call him Carlo and invite Desmond and Deirdre to their big summer parties in the large white house that had a swimming pool and a big barbecue. And he would beg Deirdre to try on a soft blue leather jacket that had just come in from Milan and exclaim that it looked so good on her, she must have it. As a gift, as a token of the esteem in which they held her husband. The ideas man in Palazzo.

The list was looking scrappy. Marigold came in saying she had a raging hangover, which had not been improved in the cafeteria, where she had gone to get some cold orange juice to dilute the miniature of vodka. In the cafeteria, Marigold had heard that Mr. Carlo was on the warpath. There had been a less than lovely session with his accountants, and he wasn't going to get enough pocket money to play with those dishcloth rags of leather jackets. So he was about to reorganize everyone. Stupid little wop greaseball, Marigold said. If he was back in Australia, he'd be man enough to get the hell out into whatever turned him on, like these pathetic frocks and coats, rather than pretend he knew how to run a business, which everyone knew was run by that gangster Frank Quigley.

Desmond was touched by the partisan nature of Marigold's response.

"Sit down there now and stop exciting yourself. You'll only make your head worse," he said sympathetically.

Marigold looked at him, her eyes pink and puffy but full of concern.

"Jesus, Dizzy, you're too good for this shower," she said.

"Shush, shush. I'm going past the freezer, shall I get you some ice for that? A cure's no good without ice."

"No wonder you'll never run the bloody place, you're a human being," said Marigold with her head in her hands.

Marigold had only been with Palazzo six months; she said it was nearly time for her to move on already. She had been thinking of a hotel next, or a job as receptionist in a Knightsbridge hairdressing salon where you might see members of the Royal Family coming in.

Greatly revived by her chilled vodka and orange, which she had tried to persuade Desmond to share without any success, she put her mind to dredging up some details of work done in the section during the period she had worked there.

"Jesus, we must have done *something*, Dizzy!" she said, her face frowning with concentration. "I mean, you were never coming in here every day and looking at that picture of the pale blue outback in Ireland all day, were you?"

"I wasn't . . . I don't think I was. There always seemed to be things to do, but they were other people's things, you see." Desmond sounded apologetic. "So they don't count as being from here. It's not going to look very impressive."

"Where will they send you? If they wind it up?"

"This is one of the smallest offices. They might leave me here, reporting to someone else, you know. Same place, same job, different line of responsibility."

"They'd never give you the heave-ho?"

He reassured her. "No, no, Marigold, don't worry about that. No."

She smiled at him roguishly. "You mean, you know where the bodies are buried?"

"In a way," he said.

He spoke so softly and sadly Marigold let it go.

"I'll go out and see what I can gather from the letters I typed for you anyway," she said.

*　*　*

It was more or less as Desmond had thought it would be. Carlo sat in the small office, not even remotely impressed by the efforts Marigold made in calling him Mr. Doyle and talking about people on the telephone and saying he was in conference. Marigold had even been in to borrow two china cups and saucers for the coffee rather than use the two scarlet mugs with *D* and *?* on them that were usually brought into play.

Carlo Palazzo spoke about the need to redeploy, to continue to expand, to experiment, never to stand still. He spoke about the competition. He talked about inflation, recession, about industrial unrest, and about the difficulty of parking cars. In short, he brought in almost every common topic of gloom to support his reluctant decision that the department *as such* should be fused with other departments, and its work, important and useful of course as it was, might best be served by being redeployed.

When he came around to using the word *redeployed* for the second time, Desmond felt that it was like going to the movies and recognizing the part where you had come in.

He felt a great weariness. A realization that this would happen again and again in the next thirteen and a half years. Until possibly the decision might be that he should work in the parking lots, that would be the best redeploying.

Desmond's head felt heavy, and he wondered how best to explain it to Deirdre that evening. He knew there would be no diminution of salary, he knew there would be no public announcement. Only the title would have gone. He was down to essentials now.

"And do you think I should continue in whatever new deployment is agreed from this room, this office?" he asked.

Carlo Palazzo spread out his big hands. If it were up to him, then, of course.

"But it's not, Mr. Palazzo?"

It wasn't, it appeared; it was reorganization and taking down some partitions and having an open flow, and a lot more light, and a change in some of the inventory-taking.

Desmond waited patiently. He knew that it would be told, and no amount of hurrying tactics would work.

He let his eyes wander to the picture with its unlikely blue skies and its soft grassy slopes. Mayo had never been like that. There had been very big white skies and stony walls and small brown fields. The picture was chocolate-box stuff.

Carlo Palazzo was coming to the point.

The point was definitely upcoming, Desmond thought to himself. He felt the familiar acid taste coming from his stomach to his mouth. Please let there be some kind of office. Something which need never have to be explained. Some part of the building where there would be a person, a person like Marigold who would answer the telephone to Deirdre. Someone who would say, "Hold on and I'll put you through," when his wife rang and asked, as she always did, to speak to Mr. Doyle, Special Projects Manager, please. With an upward inflection on the *please*.

Please let there be some word *manager* somewhere along the line, and let Deirdre not have to spend the rest of her life phoning a business that would not know who he was, let alone where he was.

"So we thought it best if your work was to be in a roving capacity," Carlo Palazzo said.

"Not roving, Mr. Palazzo," said Desmond Doyle. "Please, not roving."

The Italian looked at him with concern.

"I assure you, Desmond, that the work will be just as important, more important in many ways, and as you know, there is no question of changing the salary structure; that will remain, with the usual emoluments."

"Any kind of base. Anything at all." Desmond felt the sweat on his forehead. God Almighty, he was beginning to beg. Why could he not have talked it all the way through with Frank Quigley?

He and Frank, who had played on the stony hills of Mayo together, who had never seen a West of Ireland sky like the one in the picture, they knew the same language. Why had the barriers of years meant that he couldn't say to Frank straight out that he must have an office even if it was a doorway leading nowhere? It wasn't much after all these years to give Deirdre the belief that her husband was of managerial stuff in a large and important retailing organization.

There was a time when he and Frank had been able to talk about anything, anything at all. Like how Frank's father drank away a fortune of compensation in three weeks buying large measures for the whole town. Like how much Desmond wanted to escape from the farm and the silent brothers and sisters who seemed happy to stalk the barren land after the scrawny, difficult sheep.

They had told each other of their first conquests with girls when they had come here, two ignorant young paddies in the fifties; they had shared everything from the day they had gone to work for Prince Stores. But then a hunger had taken Frank over, and it must have been about that time that the close friendship died.

And Frank had gone forever up, forever and ever, he ran everything now. But the Palazzos had bought out Prince Stores and made it their own. It was known that Carlo Palazzo had never made a decision larger than what sauce he would have on his pasta without consulting Frank Quigley. So it was Frank who was dooming his old pal Desmond to be on a roving basis.

Did Frank not remember Deirdre? Did he not know how hard this was going to be for him?

Frank came so rarely to Rosemary Drive these days. But still, every time they met each other it was as if the old days were still the same. They banged each other on the shoulders and laughed, and since Desmond never made anything of being on such a low rung of a ladder they had joined so long ago, Frank equally never made any reference to his own high position. Only at the marriage to Renata Palazzo had the real gulf between them become apparent.

Nobody else from Desmond's level was at the wedding; everyone was many degrees above.

Deirdre had hated that wedding. She had been looking forward to it for months and even believed that she and Renata Palazzo would somehow become great friends. It had always been so unlikely that Desmond had never taken her seriously. Renata was years younger than they were, she was from a different world. Deirdre persisted in thinking of her as an Italian immigrant of her own age who would be shy and needing some kind of sisterly advice.

Desmond would never forget how Deirdre's smile had faded at the wedding when the bright yellow dress and coat made in matching man-made fiber came up against the pure silks and the furs of the other women. She who had left the house so cheerily that morning had been sinking into the background even during the church service when an Italian opera singer was getting through "Panis Angelicus" for the newlyweds. By the time they had arrived at the marquee and joined the line of guests waiting to be received, she was tugging at her dress and his arm.

It had been a black day for her, and her hurt had darkened the day for Desmond, too.

But none of it had been Frank Quigley's fault. Frank's smile never lessened, not ever in the years since then.

You could always go to Frank. You didn't have to say things in so many words. You could use code.

Where in the name of God was Frank today, this new black day when Carlo Palazzo was telling Desmond Doyle that he would have no office, no door, no telephone on a desk possibly?

Should he ask whether he could shortcut the whole thing for them by putting on one of the beige coats that the men who swept the shops put on, and getting down to work immediately with his bucket and pail and cleaning cloth, wiping the vegetable racks just after the doors closed? Would it perhaps be easier than waiting for half a dozen further slides? But then anger filled him, too; he wasn't a stupid man, he wasn't a fool who could be passed over like this. He could feel his face working in a way that was beyond his control. To his horror he saw something like pity in the older man's face.

"Desmond, my friend, please," Carlo began uncertainly.

"I'm all right." Desmond stood up behind his small desk. He would have strode across to the window so that the telltale tears in his eyes could subside. But his office wasn't one for striding, he would have had to squeeze past the filing cabinet and possibly knock over the small table or ask Mr. Palazzo to move his chair. It was too confined a place for grand gestures. Of course, come next week there would be no place for any gestures at all.

"I know that you are all right. I just don't want you to understand me wrongly. Sometimes, even after all these years in this country, I can't make myself clear . . . you know."

"No, you make yourself very clear, Mr. Palazzo, clearer than I do, and English is meant to be my native tongue."

"But perhaps I have offended you in something I said. Can I try to say it again? You are so valued here, you have been here so long and your experience is so necessary . . . it is just that circumstances change and there is an ebb and flow. Everything is being . . . what word will I use . . . ?"

"Redeployed," said Desmond flatly.

"Redeployed." Carlo Palazzo seized it and ran with it, not knowing he had already used it twice. His smile was broad. As if this word somehow rescued things.

He saw from Desmond's face that it didn't.

"Tell me, Desmond, what would you like best? No, it's not an insulting remark, not a trick question . . . I ask you what would you like best in work, what way would be the best way for things to work out for you today? Suppose it were possible for you to stay here, would that be your dream, your wish?"

The man was asking seriously, it wasn't a game of going forward and back. Carlo wanted to know.

"I don't suppose it would be my dream, no. Not to stay in this room as Special Projects Manager."

"So." Carlo looked for some silver lining desperately. "So why, then, is it so bad to leave it? What other place would have been your dream?"

Desmond leaned on the corner of the filing cabinet. Marigold had decorated the place a little with a few borrowed plants she must have grabbed from the carpeted offices. Desmond hoped she hadn't actually taken any of Carlo's own greenery. He smiled a little to himself at the thought, and his boss smiled back, looking up eagerly from the chair in front of the desk.

Carlo had a big, kind face. He didn't look shifty, he was the kind of Italian who always played the kind uncle or indeed the loving grandfather in a film.

It was Carlo's dream to be a grandfather many times over, to have a lot of little grandsons with half-Irish and half-Italian names running in and out of that huge white house. Children to leave his share of Palazzo to. Did Desmond dream of grandchildren, too? He didn't know. What a dull man he must be not to know his own dream when he was asked it by this big straightforward man.

"It's so long since I allowed myself to have a dream, I suppose I've forgotten what it was," he said truthfully.

"I never forgot mine, I wanted to go to Milano to work in fashion," said Carlo. "I want to have the finest craftsmen and stitchers and designers all together and to have my own factory with the name Carlo Palazzo."

"You have your own name over your work," Desmond said.

"Yes, but it is not what I wanted, not what I had hoped, I only have a little time in what I would have loved. My father he told me I must go into the food business, with my brothers, with my uncles, not playing with clothes like a ladies' dressmaker, he said."

"Fathers don't understand," Desmond said simply.

"Your father . . . did he not understand perhaps?"

"No, my father neither understood nor didn't understand, if you know what I mean. He was always an old man. When I was ten, he was old, and it wasn't just that I *thought* it, he looks it in every picture. He only understood sheep and hillsides and silence. But he never stopped me, he said I was right to go."

"Then how do you mean fathers never understand?"

"I didn't understand. I did all this for my son. I wanted him to have as good an education as possible, I didn't understand when he left."

"Where did he go?"

It had never been admitted outside Rosemary Drive. Never beyond the walls.

"He ran away, he ran back to the sheep and the stones and the silence."

"Well, you let him go." Carlo didn't seem shocked that Desmond's son had run off uneducated to the back of beyond.

"But not with a good grace." Desmond sighed.

Carlo was still puzzled. "So did you want a life of high education?"

For some reason the small, eager face of Suresh Patel flashed into Desmond's mind, his dark eyes feverish with the wish to heap degrees and diplomas on his family.

"No, not a high education. Just a place, I suppose, a place that was mine."

Carlo looked around the featureless office, which he probably remembered as being even more featureless over the previous months without its injection of borrowed plants.

"This place? It feels so important?"

Desmond had somehow come to the end of the road.

"To be honest, Mr. Palazzo, I don't know. I'm not a man of very strong opinions. I never was. I have ideas, that's why I suppose Frank and you thought I'd be good here. But they are personal ideas, not corporate ones, and I'm inclined to get a bit lost whenever there's redeployment and the like. But I'll manage. I'll manage. I've always managed before."

He didn't sound frightened now or self-pitying. Just resigned and practical. Carlo Palazzo was relieved that the mood, whatever it had been, had passed.

"It's not going to happen overnight, it will be in two to three weeks, and in many ways it will give you more freedom, more time to think about what you really want."

"Maybe it will."

"And there *will* be a title of manager, it hasn't been quite worked out yet, but when Frank gets back, I'm sure . . ."

"Oh, I'm sure he will," Desmond agreed readily.

"So . . ." Once more Carlo spread his hands out.

This time he was rewarded with a half-smile, and Desmond stretched his own hand out as if to shake on something that had been agreed between two men of like mind.

Carlo paused as if something had struck him.

"Your wife? She is well?"

"Oh, yes, Deirdre's fine, thank you, Mr. Palazzo, blooming."

"Perhaps she might care to come some evening to have . . . to have a meal in our house with us, the family, you know, Frank and Renata and everything. . . . You were all such friends in the old days . . . before any of this . . . that's true, yes."

"That is very kind of you, Mr. Palazzo." Desmond Doyle spoke in the voice of a man who knew that no such invitation would be issued.

"That will be good, we will enjoy that." Carlo Palazzo spoke in exactly the same voice.

Marigold held the door open for the great chief Mr. Palazzo. He looked at her with a vague and pleasant smile.

"Thank you, thank you . . . um."

"I'm Marigold," she said, trying to iron out her Australian accent. "I'm lucky enough to work for Mr. Doyle. There have been several important calls, Mr. Doyle. I told them that you were in conference."

Desmond nodded gravely and waited until the footsteps were gone for Marigold to hiss at him, "Well, what happened?"

"Oh, Marigold," he said wearily.

"Don't 'Oh, Marigold' me, didn't I make you look good? Didn't you hear me? Bet he thinks a lot more of you now. Saying I was lucky to be working for you."

"I expect he thinks you're sleeping with me," Desmond said.

"I wouldn't half mind."

"You're possibly the nicest girl in the world."

"What about your wife?" Marigold asked.

"Oh, I don't think she'd like you to sleep with me, not at all."

"I mean, isn't she the nicest girl in the world, or wasn't she once or what?"

"She's very nice, very nice indeed." He spoke objectively.

"So no chance for me then." Marigold was trying to jolly him along.

"Palazzo's not the worst. That's a great Irish expression for you, to say a man is not the worst, it's grudging praise."

"He didn't give you the bum's rush then?" Marigold's face lit up.

"No, he gave me the bum's rush all right."

"Aw, shit. When? Where?"

"Soon, a week or two, when Frank gets back."

"Frank's not away," Marigold said furiously.

"No, but you know, we say he's away."

"And where are they sending you?"

"Here and there, roving apparently."

"Is there any good in it, any good at all?" Her eyes were tender, her big handsome face concerned, and she bit her lip at the unfairness of it all.

He couldn't bear her sympathy.

"Oh, it's all right, Marigold, there's plenty of good in it. I don't see this as anything we should fight them on the beaches for, do you . . . ?"

He looked around the office and made a theatrical gesture with his arms.

"But roving?" She seemed upset; he had to reassure her.

"It's more interesting than sitting here and seeing nothing at the end of it. I'll roam up and see you from time to time, you'd brighten my day."

"Did they say why?"

"Redeployment of resources."

"Redeployment of balls," Marigold said.

"Maybe, but what's the point?"

"You didn't *do* anything. They shouldn't take your job away."

"That could be it. Perhaps I really *didn't* do anything."

"No, you know what I mean, you're a manager, for God's sake, you've been here years."

"There's still going to be a manager's title, of whatever sort. . . . We don't know yet, we'll know later. . . ."

"Later, like when Frank gets back."

"Shush, shush."

"I thought you two were meant to be such friends."

"We were, we are. Now please, Marigold, don't *you* start."

She saw, sharp and quick, Marigold, and impulsively she said it.

"You mean you're going to have all this out with your wife tonight, is that it?"

"In a way, yes."

"Well, consider me a bit of a dry run."

"No. Thank you, I know you mean well."

She saw the tears in his eyes.

"I mean very well, and I'll tell you this: If your wife doesn't understand that you're one of the best . . ."

"She does, she does."

"Then I'll have to go around to your house and tell her she's got one beaut guy and I'll knock her head off if she doesn't know it."

"No, Deirdre will understand. I'll have had time to think about it, explain it properly, and put it in perspective."

"If I were you, I wouldn't spend any time rehearsing. Ring her up, take her out to lunch, go on, find a nice place with tablecloths and buy a bottle of grog, tell her about it straight, there's no perspective."

"Everyone does things they want to in the end, Marigold," he said firmly.

"And some people, Dizzy, do nothing at all," she said.

He looked stricken.

Impulsively she flung her arms around him. He felt her sobbing in his arms.

"I'm such a loudmouth," she was saying.

"Hush, hush." Her hair smelled lovely, like apple blossom.

"I was trying to cheer you up, and look at what I ended up saying."

Her voice was becoming more normal. Gently he released her and held her from him, looking admiringly at the lovely Australian, the same age perhaps as his own Anna or a little older. The daughter of some man out on the other side of the world who had no idea of the kind of jobs this girl was doing and how she entered into them with all her heart. He said nothing, just looked at her until she sniffed herself to some kind of calm.

"Great if the old greaseball had come back and found us in a clinch, would have confirmed everything he suspected."

"He'd have been jealous," said Desmond gallantly.

"He would in a pig's eye, Dizzy," she said.

"I'm going out, I think," Desmond said.

"I'll tell them you're practicing roving if they ask," she said, almost grinning.

"Don't tell them anything," he said.

That was what he always said.

He phoned Frank from a call box near one of the entrance gates.

"I'm not sure if Mr. Quigley's available. Can I say who wants him?"

Long pause. Obviously a consultation.

"No, I'm very sorry, Mr. Doyle, Mr. Quigley's away on business. Was this not told to you? I believe Mr. Palazzo's secretary was to let you know. . . ."

"Sure, I just wondered if he was back." Desmond was mild.

"No, no." The voice was firm, as if speaking to a toddler who hadn't quite understood.

"If he calls in, tell him that . . . Tell him . . ."

"Yes, Mr. Doyle?"

"Tell him nothing. Say Desmond Doyle rang to say nothing, like he's been saying all his life."

"I don't think I quite—"

"You heard me. But I'll say it again." Desmond said the words again and felt some satisfaction at the sound of them. He wondered if perhaps he was going mad.

It was the middle of the morning and there was a strange sense of freedom about walking out through the big Palazzo gates. Like a child being sent home from school with some kind of sickness.

He remembered at the brothers years ago how he and Frank had played hooky for the day. Nobody knew that term over here, *skived* is what they called it. They had told the head brother that they had inhaled a bag of chemicals in the schoolyard and that their eyes were red and they were choking. They managed to persuade him that the cure would be fresh air.

Desmond could still recall thirty-five years later that freedom, as they ran and skipped over the hills, liberated in every way from the small classroom.

One of the things they had found lacking then was any way of finding people to play with. Everyone else was sitting resentfully in the classroom. They had felt the lack of a gang and had gone home earlier than they would have thought likely.

It was somehow the same today. There was nobody that Desmond could ask to come and play. Nobody to buy a bottle of grog for, as Marigold had suggested. Even if he were to take the train to Baker Street and go to Anna's bookshop, she might not be free. And she would be alarmed, it was so out of character. His only son, who had been lucky enough to recognize some kind of freedom and run for it, was far, far away. His other daughter, away in her convent, would not understand the need that he had to talk, the great urgency to define himself somehow.

It was a poor toting up of twenty-six years in this land that he could think of no other person in the whole of London that he could telephone and ask to meet him. Desmond Doyle had never thought of himself as a jet-setter but he had thought of Deirdre and himself as people with friends, people who had a circle. *Of course* they were. They were going to have a silver wedding anniversary shortly and their problem was not looking for people, it was trying to cut down on numbers.

What did he mean that he had no friends? They had dozens of friends. But that was it. *They* had friends. He and Deirdre had friends, and the problem had nothing to do with redeployment or managerial titles, the trouble was a promise made and a promise broken.

He had sworn to her that night so many years ago that he would rise in the business, he would be a name for the O'Hagan family in Ireland to take seriously. He had said that Deirdre would never go out to work. Her mother had never gone out to work, and none of Deirdre's friends who married back in 1960 would have expected to go and look for a job. Ireland had changed since then, had become more like England. Mrs. O'Hagan's nose, which seemed to turn up very easily, would not turn today if a young woman went on for further education or took any kind of work to help build a family home.

But those were black days long ago, and the O'Hagan scorn had been hard to bear. And Desmond knew that his promise was given under no duress. He had held Deirdre's small hand, and on the night they were about to tell her parents the news, he had begged her to trust him. He remembered his words.

"I always wanted to be in buying and selling. I know it's not the thing to tell your family, but even when the tinkers came to town, I loved it, there was an excitement about it, about the way they put out their scarves and bright glittering combs on the ground. I knew what it was about."

Deirdre had smiled at him confidently, knowing he would never bring up anything as alien as tinkers in the O'Hagan household.

"I want *you*," he had said, "I want it more than anything in the world, and when a man has a dream, there's nothing he cannot conquer. I'll conquer the retail business in England. They'll be glad they didn't lose you to a doctor or a lawyer. The day will come when they'll be so glad they settled for a merchant prince."

And Deirdre had looked at him trustingly, as she had always looked ever since.

He supposed that she was still his dream, but why had she not come to his mind when Mr. Palazzo had asked him?

Desmond found himself walking the well-trodden path toward home. His feet had taken him on automatic pilot to the bus stop. At this time of day there were no crowds, no lines, how pleasant to be able to travel like this instead of during incessant rush hours.

Suppose he *did* ring Deirdre. He knew she was at home, she was working over that infernal silver silver wedding list again. Surely she would appreciate his honesty and directness.

She loved him in a sort of way, didn't she? Like he loved her. And he did love her. She had changed, of course, like everyone changed, but it would be ludicrous to expect her to be the fluffy, blond, desirable young Deirdre O'Hagan who had filled his thoughts and his heart so urgently. Why wasn't she the dream? She was connected with the dream in a way. The dream was to make good his promise. But he couldn't have told that to Carlo Palazzo in a million years, not even if he had been able to articulate it, which he hadn't. Not until this moment when the bus was approaching.

Desmond hesitated. Should he let the bus go, find a telephone, and invite his own wife out to lunch and tell her his own real thoughts? In the hope that they could somehow share them the way they had shared every little heartbeat during that time when they stood strong against the might of the O'Hagans about their marriage.

"Are you getting on or are you not?" the conductor asked him, not unreasonably. Desmond had been standing holding the rail. He remembered Marigold saying to him, "Some people, Dizzy, do nothing at all." But he was nearly on the bus.

"I'm getting on," he said. And his face was so mild and inoffensive that the tired young bus conductor, who also wanted a different and a better life, abused him no further.

He sorted it out for Deirdre as he walked toward Rosemary Drive, little phrases, little reasoning steps. There would be more scope in a roving managerial position, he would get to know the workings of the company at firsthand rather than being tucked away in his own little aerie. He would explain that Frank had been called away; he would mention that the exact wording was not firmed up but the magic word *manager* would be included. He would not mention the Palazzo invitation to supper, because he knew it would not materialize.

He felt no bitterness toward Frank for avoiding the confrontation. Nor, indeed, for initiating the move. Frank was probably right; the functions of Special Projects had indeed been taken over.

Frank might even be giving him a chance to find a better niche. He wished he could summon up more enthusiasm for this niche, whatever it might be.

It would confuse Deirdre to see him arriving home unexpectedly for lunch. She would fuss and say over and over that he should have warned her. The importance of his news would be lost in a welter of worries about there being nothing on hand.

Desmond decided that he would go into the corner shop, and tell Mr. Patel that yet again he had provided a service. They sold pizzas there, not very good ones, wrapped in rather too much plastic and with the wrong ratio of base and topping. Still, that might do. Or he might get a can of soup and some crusty

French bread. He didn't remember whether Mr. Patel sold chicken pieces; that might be nice.

There were no customers in the shop, but more unusually there was no-body sitting at the cash register. On the few occasions when Suresh Patel did not sit there himself as if at a throne, still able to advise and direct his tiny empire, there was always another occupant. His silent wife, wordless in English but able to ring up the prices she read on the little labels. Sometimes it was the young, owlish son or the pert little daughter. Mr. Patel's brother didn't seem capable of manning the family business.

Desmond moved past the central aisle and saw with that lurching feeling of recognition that a raid was in progress.

There was that slow-motion sense of things not being real. Desmond felt as he looked at the two boys in their leather jackets beating the fat brother of Suresh Patel that this was like an action replay when watching a football match.

Desmond felt the old bile, but this time it was a sharper feeling. He thought he was going to choke.

He took two steps backward. He would run out and raise the alarm, he would run around the corner to the street where there would be more people passing by. *And,* if he was honest, where there would be less chance of the two muggers catching him calling for help.

But before he could go any farther, he heard the voice of Suresh Patel calling to the boys with the bars.

"I beg of you, I beg of you, he is simple in the head, he does not know anything about any safe. There *is* no safe. There is money in the night deposit. Please do not hit my brother again."

Desmond saw with another shock that he could feel physically in his own stomach that Mr. Patel's arm hung at an odd angle. As if it had already been beaten. And already broken.

Even if Marigold had not said to him sadly that there were some people who never did anything at all, he would have done what he did. Desmond Doyle, the man so mild that he had to be moved from an office lest he take root, so meek that he made a young Australian beauty cry over his future, knew suddenly what he had to do.

He lifted the stack of trays which had held the bread delivered that morn-ing, and he brought it suddenly down on the neck of the first leather jacket. The boy, who could hardly have been as old as his own son, Brendan, fell with a thud to the floor. The other one looked at him wild-eyed. Desmond pushed him, jabbing him with the trays, and maneuvered him toward the back rooms, the living quarters of the whole family.

"Is your wife in there?" he shouted.

"No, Mr. Doyle." Suresh Patel looked up from the floor as people look up in films when rescuers arrive.

The brother who didn't know where the safe was smiled as if his heart were going to burst.

On and on Desmond pushed and prodded, his strength flooding to him. Behind him he heard voices come into the shop. Real customers.

"Get the police immediately, and an ambulance," called Desmond Doyle. "There's been a raid. Go quickly, any private house will let you phone."

They ran, the two young men delighted to be on the safe end of a heroics job, and Desmond pushed a cabinet up against the door to the room where he had cornered the bewildered boy in the leather jacket.

"Can he get out that way?" he asked.

"No. We have had bars on the window and everything. You know, in case something like this . . ."

"Are you all right?" Desmond knelt on the floor.

"Yes. Yes. Did you kill him?" He nodded toward the boy on the floor, who was regaining consciousness and starting to groan.

Desmond had taken his iron bar away from him and stood prepared to deal another blow, but the boy was not able to move.

"No, he's not dead. But he'll go to jail. By God, he'll go to jail!" said Desmond.

"Perhaps not, but it doesn't matter." The shopkeeper tried to get himself to his feet. He looked weak and frightened.

"What matters then?" Desmond wanted to know.

"Well, I have to know who will run this shop for me—you see my brother, how he is, you know how my wife cannot speak, I must not ask the children to desist from school, they will miss their places and their examinations. . . ."

Far away Desmond heard a siren. The two heroes were bursting back in, saying the law was on the way.

"Don't worry about that," Desmond said gently to the man on the floor. "That will all be organized."

"But how, how?"

"Have you any relations, cousins, in businesses like this?"

"Yes, but they cannot leave their own places. Each place, it has to make its own way."

"Yes I know, but when we get you to hospital, will you be able to give me their names? I can get in touch with them."

"It is no use, Mr. Doyle, they will not have the time . . . they must work each in their own way."

His face was troubled and his big dark eyes filled with tears. "We are finished now. It's very simple to see," he said.

"No, Mr. Patel. I will run the shop for you. You must just tell them that you trust me and that it's not any kind of trick."

"You cannot do that, Mr. Doyle, you have a big position in Palazzo Foods; you only say this to make me feel good."

"No, it is the truth. I will look after your shop until you come back from hospital. We will have to close it today, of course, put up a sign, but by tomorrow lunchtime I will have it working again."

"I cannot thank you . . ."

Desmond's eyes also filled with tears. He saw that the man trusted him utterly. Suresh Patel saw Desmond Doyle as a great manager who could do what he willed.

The ambulance men were gentle. They said he had very likely broken a rib as well as an arm.

"It might be some time, Mr. Doyle," said Suresh Patel from the stretcher.

"There's all the time in the world."

"Let me tell you where the safe is."

"Not now, later, I'll come to see you in hospital."

"But your wife, your family, they will not let you do this."

"They will understand."

"And afterward?"

"Afterward will be different. Don't think about it."

The policemen were getting younger, they looked younger than the villains. One of them was definitely younger than Desmond's son, Brendan.

"Who is in charge here?" the young policeman asked with a voice that had not yet gained the confidence it would have in a few short years.

"I am," said Desmond. "I'm Desmond Doyle of 26 Rosemary Drive and I'm going to look after these premises until Mr. Patel comes back from hospital."

CHAPTER FIVE

Father Hurley

*N*obody except his sister called Father James Hurley Jimbo; it would have been unthinkable. A man in his sixties with silver hair and a handsome head, he had the bearing of a bishop, and a lot of people thought he looked much more bishoplike than many of those who held the office. Tall and straight, he would have worn the robes well, and even better the cardinal's red. But Rome didn't go on appearances, and Father Hurley's name had never been brought to any corridors of power.

It was impossible to find anyone who would speak a word against him. His parishioners in several County Dublin districts had loved him. He was able, it seemed, to move just fast enough with the changes that came to the Church after the Vatican Council, but not too fast. He could murmur calming things that soothed the most conservative, and yet he seemed to go far along the road that allowed the laity to have a say. He wasn't exactly all things to all of his flock, but he certainly avoided irritating them.

And in a Dublin where anticlericalism among the younger liberals was becoming rife, this was no mean feat.

He was not a television priest, he had never been seen on the screen debating any issue. He was not the kind of man who would officiate at the marriage of known atheists having a church wedding just for the show, but neither was he the old-fashioned curate who went to Cheltenham in March with a pocket full of fivers, or cheered on the dogs at a dog race as they followed the hare. Father

Hurley was a traveled, educated, soft-spoken man. People often said that he looked like an academic. This was high praise. And he was amused that it was sometimes regarded as even higher praise when he was described as looking not like a priest but more like a vicar!

James Hurley seemed to have moved quietly from parish to parish without either upward or downward movement. There did not seem to be the sense of advancement that such a well-spoken, thoughtful man might have been led to expect, but it was rumored that he never sought any promotion. You couldn't say he was unworldly—not Father Hurley, who liked fine wines and was known to enjoy pheasant and to relish lobster.

But he always seemed totally contented with his lot, even when they had sent him to a working-class parish where he was in charge of fourteen youth clubs and eleven football teams instead of the drawing rooms and the visits to private nursing homes of his previous position.

He had been at school at one of the better Catholic schools in England, not that he ever talked about it. His family had been wealthy people, and it was rumored that he had been brought up on a big estate in the country. But none of this ever came from the man himself. He would laugh easily and say that nobody in Ireland should try to shake his family tree for fear of what might fall down. He had a sister who lived in the country with her husband, a country solicitor of substance, and their only son. Father Hurley did speak of this boy, his nephew, with great affection. Gregory was the only part of Father Hurley's private life about which he ever volunteered information.

Otherwise he was just a very good and interested listener to other people's stories. Which is why people thought he was such a good conversationalist. He talked only about them.

In the various presbyteries where Father Hurley's life had taken him there were pictures of his mother and father, now dead, in old-fashioned oval frames. There was a family picture taken at Gregory's first communion, and another one of Gregory's confirmation. A handsome boy with his hand lightly laid on his parchment scroll and his eyes smiling through the camera as if he knew much more than any other graduate who was posing for stiff formal photographs that day but took it all very casually.

For the people who told Father Hurley their own life stories, their worries and their tittle-tattle, Gregory was an ideal conversation piece. They could ask for him, and hear an enthusiastic response, enough to look polite, then they could return to their own tales again. They didn't notice that after a certain date the stories about Gregory never originated with Father Hurley and that his replies were vaguer and less informed than they had been once. He was far too diplomatic to let that be seen. That was another thing people said, he would have been very good at the Department of Foreign Affairs, or a consul or an ambassador even.

When James Hurley was a boy his mother had died, and he had always thought of Laura as being a combination of mother, sister, and best friend. Laura was five years older than he was, she had been seventeen when left in charge of a big crumbling house, a small crumbling brother, and a remote and withdrawn father who didn't give any of himself to his children any more than he had given of himself to his wife or the estate he had inherited.

Father James Hurley knew all that now, but then he had lived in a childlike fear of offending his stern, cold father still further. Laura could have gone away to a university, he always thought, if it had not been for her little brother. Instead she stayed at home and took a secretarial course in the nearby town.

She worked in the local grocery, which was eventually taken over by a bigger firm. Then she worked in the local bakery, which merged with three nearby bakeries, and her secretarial job there was over. She worked as the doctor's receptionist and during her time there he was taken off the medical register for professional misconduct. Laura used to tell her little brother, Jimbo, that she seemed to have a fairly unlucky effect and a dead hand on those she went to work for. Her little brother, Jimbo, used to suggest she come to work in his school in the hope that she would close it down.

She encouraged him in his vocation, she took long walks in the country roads with him, and together they sat on mossy banks and on the stile between the fields and talked about the love of God the way others might have talked about sports or the movies.

Laura Hurley had knelt with tears in her eyes to receive her brother's first blessing after he had said his first Mass.

Their father had died by this time, remote and uninvolved to the end. James had become a priest; he might have become a soldier or a jockey, it would have been on the same level of interest for his father.

While away at the seminary, James had often worried about Laura. She lived in the gate house of what had been their home. The big house was not really big in terms of the landed estates thereabouts, but it had been substantial. But Laura felt no sense of having come down in the world, living in the cottage where once people lived rent-free if they opened and closed the gates after the Hurley family. Laura had always said cheerfully that it was much easier to keep a small place than a big one, and since their father had gone first to a nursing home and then to his eternal reward, she was alone, so it didn't make sense to run the big house. When it was sold, there were so many debts that had gathered from James being a student, from Father being a patient in a private nursing home, that the place had been thoroughly mortgaged. There was little in the bank, there was no dowry for Miss Laura Hurley, faithful sister and dutiful daughter.

Laura never thought like that. She was happy, she walked her two big collie dogs, read her books in the evening by her small fire, and went to work by day for the local solicitors. She said laughingly that she hadn't managed to close them down as she had done to every other business she worked for, but she had managed to change them utterly.

Like changing the confirmed bachelor status of young Mr. Black. The Mr. Black who had once been the most eligible man in the county. At the age of forty he looked at Laura Hurley, aged thirty-four, and a lot of his iron-hard resolve about staying single, uninvolved, and free began to chip away.

Then the letter arrived: "Dearest Jimbo, you'll never believe it but Alan Black and I are going to get married. We would very much like it if you could perform the ceremony for us. Since we're not in the first flush of youth, to put it mildly, we won't make an exhibition of ourselves here with everyone coming to stare. We would like to come to Dublin and be married in your parish if that's possible. Dearest Jimbo, I never knew I could feel so happy. And so safe and as if things were meant to turn out like this. I don't deserve it, I really don't."

Father Hurley always remembered that letter from his sister; he could see it, the words almost tumbling over each other on the small cream writing paper.

He remembered the way his eyes had watered with a feeling of pleasure that things really did seem to have some point if this kind woman had found someone generous and good to share her life with her. He couldn't remember Alan Black except that he had been very handsome and rather dashing-looking in the past.

Father James Hurley felt that at twenty-nine he was a man of the world. And in a strange way he felt protective of his older sister as he joined her hand with Alan Black's at the wedding ceremony. He hoped this man with the dark eyes and dark hair just graying at the temples would be good to Laura and understand her generosity and how she had never sought anything for herself.

Several times he found himself looking at them and with a hope that was more than a wish. It was a silent prayer; he willed his sister to have a good relationship with this tall, handsome man. Laura's face was open and honest, but even on this, her wedding day, nobody could call her beautiful, her hair was pulled back and tied with a large cream-colored ribbon which matched the color of her suit. The ribbon was large enough to be considered a hat or head covering for church. She had a dusting of face powder and a smile that warmed the small congregation to the heart. But she was not a beautiful woman. Young Father Hurley hoped that the attentions of the handsome solicitor would not wander.

Years later he marveled at his own callow approach and wondered how he ever could have thought himself any use in advising men and women in their lives on their road to God. In a changing world there never was and never had been anything more strong and constant than the love Alan Black had shown to his bride. From the day that they had come to see him, back suntanned and laughing from their honeymoon in Spain, he should have realized that his own judgments based on appearances and vanity were superficial. Why should Alan Black, a bright, intelligent man, not be able to see the great worth, goodness, and love in Laura Hurley? After all, James Hurley had always seen it himself, why should he think it would pass Mr. Black, the solicitor, by?

And as the years went on, he used to go to stay with them. They had done up the little gate house and built on extra rooms. There was a new study out at one side of the house, filled with books from ceiling to floor. They lit a fire there in the evenings, and often the three of them sat in big chairs reading. It was the most peaceful, happy place he had ever been.

Sometimes Laura would look up from the chair where she lay curled up and smile at him.

"Isn't this the life, Jimbo?" she'd say.

Other days when he visited she might walk with him through the fields and over the stiles and hedges and ditches they had once owned.

"Did we ever think it would turn out so well, Jimbo?" she said often, ruffling the hair of her young brother, who would never be the great Father Hurley to her.

And then they told him they were building a similar long, low room at the other side of the house. It was going to be a nursery playroom. They would never call it the nursery, they said, they would call it the child's room whatever his or her name was. *Nursery* was only a baby word. The name was Gregory. Father James held the baby in his arm for the baptism. A beautiful child with the long, dark eyelashes of his father. Gregory Black.

He was their only child; Laura said they would like to have had a brother or sister for him, but it was not to be. They made sure he had plenty of other children to play with. He turned out to be the dream child that every doting uncle hopes for.

Gregory would run from the window seat of his own big, low room when he saw the car approaching.

"It's Uncle Jim," he would shout, and the old collie dogs would bark and leap and Laura would rush from the kitchen.

When Alan got back from work, the smile was broad and the delight obvious. They loved to see him come for a couple of days mid-week. They loved the way he got on so well with their son.

Gregory wanted to be a priest, of course, when he was around ten. It was a far better life than working in his father's office, he told them all seriously. As a priest you had to do nothing at all, and people paid you money for saying Masses that you'd be saying anyway, and you could get up on a pulpit and tell them all what to do or else they'd go to hell. Sensing a delighted if half-shocked audience, Gregory went on eagerly. It was the best job in the world. And you could refuse to forgive anyone in confession if you didn't like them and then they'd go to hell, it would be great.

They came to Dublin to see him, too, and James Hurley never tired of talking about this warm, bright boy. Gregory wanted to know everything, to meet everyone. He could charm crabby old parish priests and difficult women parishioners who were always quick to fancy slights.

"I think you would be good as a priest actually," his uncle said to him laughingly one day when Gregory was fifteen. "An awful lot of it is public relations and getting along with people. You're very good at that."

"It makes sense," Gregory said.

Father Hurley looked at him sharply. Yes, of course, it made sense to present an amiable face toward people rather than a pompous one; of course, it was the wise thing to do to take the path that would not bring the wrath of authority around your ears. But fancy knowing that at fifteen. They were growing up a lot faster these days.

When Gregory got his place in UCD, he was studying law; that made sense too, he said. He had to study something, and law was as good a training as anything else. Meanwhile it kept his father, grandfather, and uncle happy to think another Black was going to come into the business.

"And is that what you are going to do?" Father Hurley was surprised. Gregory seemed to him to be too bright, too lively to settle in the small town. There wouldn't be enough to hold his sharp eyes, which moved restlessly from face to face, from scene to scene.

"I haven't really thought it out, Uncle Jim. It's what my mother and father would like, certainly, and since I don't know yet, it makes sense to let them assume that it's what I'll do."

Again there was a slight chill in the words. The boy had not said he was lying to his family; he had said that since nothing in this world was definite, why cross your bridges before you came to them? Father James Hurley told himself that once or twice when he was saying his evening office and when the memory of Gregory's words troubled him. He began to think that he was becoming a foolish fusspot. It was ridiculous to read danger into the practical plans of a modern young man.

Gregory graduated well and was photographed on his own and with his father, mother, and uncle.

His father was now white-haired, still a handsome man. He was sixty-three now, forty-two years older than his boy. Alan Black had always said that it didn't matter whether you were eighteen years older than your son or forty-eight years older, you were still a different generation. But that in his case it had been everything and more than he had hoped, the boy had never wanted a motor-bike, hadn't taken drugs or brought hordes of undesirables back to the home. He had been a model son.

His mother, Laura, looked well on his graduation day. She didn't twitter like other mothers did about having produced a son who could write "Bachelor of Civil Law" after his name and who would shortly be admitted to the Incorporated Law Society as a solicitor as well. Laura wore a bright pink scarf at the neck of her smart navy suit. She had spent what she considered a great deal of money on a haircut, and her gray hair looked elegant and well shaped. She did not look fifty-six years of age, but she did look the picture of happiness. As the crowds milled around the university campus, she grasped her brother by the arm.

"I almost feel that I've been too lucky, Jimbo," she said, her face serious. "Why should God have given me all this happiness when He doesn't give it to everyone else?"

Father Hurley, who certainly did not look his fifty-one years, either, begged her to believe that God's love was there for everyone, it was a matter of how they received it. Laura had always been an angel to everyone, it was just and good that she should be given happiness in this life as well as in the next.

He meant it, every single word. His eye fell on a woman with a tired face and a son in a wheelchair. They had come to watch a daughter graduate. There was no man with them.

Perhaps she, too, had been an angel, Father James Hurley thought. But it was too complicated to work out why God hadn't dealt her a better hand in this life. He would not think about it now.

They had lunch in one of the best hotels. People at several tables seemed to know Father Hurley. He introduced his family with pride, the well-dressed sister and brother-in-law. The bright, handsome young man.

A Mrs. O'Hagan and a Mrs. Barry, two ladies treating themselves to a little outing, seemed very pleased to meet the nephew of whom they had heard so much. Father Hurley wished they wouldn't go on about how often and how glowingly he had mentioned the young man. It made him feel somehow that he had no other topic of conversation.

Gregory was able to take it utterly in his stride. As they sat down at their own table, he grinned conspiratorially at his uncle.

"Talk about me being good at public relations, you're the genius, just feed them a little bit of harmless family information from time to time and they think they know all about you. You're cute as a fox, Uncle Jim."

It was a rescue from being thought to be the gossipy overfond uncle, certainly, but it did seem to classify him as something else. Something a bit shallow.

Gregory Black decided that he would practice law in Dublin for a few years in order to get experience. Make all his mistakes on strangers rather than his father's clients, he said. Even his old grandfather, now in his late eighties and long retired from the firm, thought this was a good idea, and his uncle, who had no children of his own. His parents accepted it with a good grace.

"It would be ridiculous to keep him down in a backwater after he's been so long on his own in Dublin," Laura told her brother. "And anyway, he says he'll come down and see us a lot."

"Does he just think that or will he really?" Father Hurley asked.

"Oh, he will. The only thing that made it difficult for him when he was a student was all the train and bus travel. Now that he'll have a car, it will be different."

"A car of his own?"

"Yes, it's Alan's promise. If he got a good degree, a car of his own!" She was bursting with pride.

And Gregory's gratitude was enormous. He embraced them all with pleasure. His father, gruff with delight, said that of course, in time Gregory would change this model and trade it in for another smarter kind. But for the moment . . . perhaps . . .

Gregory said he would drive it until it was worn-out. Father James Hurley felt his heart fill up with relief and pleasure that this dark, eager young man should know how much love and need encircled him and respond to it so well.

His parents went back happily to the country, his uncle went happily back to the presbytery, and the boy was free to do what he wanted with his life, with a brand-new car to help him on the way.

And Gregory did indeed visit home. He drove smartly in the entrance of the gate house and fondled the ears of the collie dogs, children, and even grandchildren of the original collies that his mother had loved so much. He would talk to his father about the law and to his mother about his social life in Dublin.

He seemed to have lots of friends—men and women, Laura told her brother eagerly—and they went to each other's houses and even cooked meals for each other. Sometimes she baked a steak and kidney pie for him to take up to his flat. She always gave him bread and slices of good country ham, and bacon, and pounds of butter. Once or twice James Hurley wondered what she thought they sold in shops around the area where so many single people lived, where his nephew lived, but he didn't ever say anything. His sister loved the feeling that she was still looking after the big, handsome son she had produced. Why disturb that good, warm feeling? To use his nephew's own words, "It wouldn't make sense."

He hardly ever coincided with Gregory back home because the priest was never free on weekends, Saturdays were busy with confessions and house calls, Sundays with the parish Masses, the sick calls, and the evening benediction. But when he did get back himself mid-week for an overnight now and then, he was pleased to see that the pleasure of the visits totally outweighed what might be considered the selfish attitudes of their only son.

Laura talked delightedly of how Gregory had this big red laundry bag she had made him, and often he just ran into the kitchen and stuffed all the contents into her washing machine.

She said this proudly as if it had taken some effort. She mentioned not at all that it was she who took them out and hung them up to dry, she who ironed and folded the shirts and had all his laundry clean and packed on the backseat of his car for his return journey.

Alan talked about how Gregory loved coming to have Saturday dinner with them in the golfing club, how he appreciated the good wines and nice food that were served there.

Father Hurley wondered why Gregory hadn't on some occasions at least put his mother and father into the car they had bought him and driven them to one of the hotels nearby to treat them to dinner.

But as usual it made no sense to bring up something so negative. And he remembered with some guilt that he had never thought of treating his sister in the old days. He had a vow of poverty perhaps on his side, but there were things he hadn't thought of then. Maybe it was the same in all young men.

And Gregory was great company. He could talk a lot without saying anything, something that could be a compliment or an insult. In Gregory's case it was something to be admired, praised, and enjoyed.

Sometimes Gregory went swimming with his uncle out in Sandycove at the Forty-Foot, the men's swimming place. Sometimes he called in to have a drink in the presbytery, where he would raise the nice crystal Waterford glass to the evening light and admire the golden whiskey reflecting in the midst of all the little twinkling shapes of glass.

"Great thing, this ascetic life," Gregory would say, laughing.

You couldn't take offense at him, and it would only be a very churlish person who would notice that he never brought a bottle of whiskey with him to add to the store, ascetic or not.

Father Hurley was totally unprepared for a visit from Gregory in the middle of the night.

"I'm in a bit of trouble, Jim," he said right away.

No "Uncle," no "sorry for getting you out of bed at three A.M."

Father Hurley managed to shoo the elderly parish priest and the equally elderly housekeeper back to their respective quarters. "It's an emergency, I'll deal with it," he said soothingly. By the time he got into the sitting room, he saw that Gregory had helped himself to a large drink. The boy's eyes were too bright, he had sweat on his brow, and he looked as if he already had had plenty to drink.

"What happened?"

"A bloody bicycle swerved out at me, no proper light, no reflecting clothes, nothing. Bloody fools, they should be prosecuted, they should have special lanes for them like they do on the Continent."

"What happened?" The priest repeated the words.

"I don't know." Gregory looked very young.

"Well, is he all right, was he hurt?"

"I didn't stop."

Father Hurley stood up. His legs weren't steady enough to hold him. He sat down again.

"But was he injured, did he fall? Mother of God, Gregory, you didn't leave him there on the side of the road?"

"I had to, Uncle Jim. I was over the speed limit. Way over it."

"Where is he, where did it happen?"

Gregory told him, a stretch of dark road on the outskirts of Dublin.

"What took you up there?" the priest asked. It was irrelevant, but he didn't feel he yet had the strength to stand up and go to the phone to let the police and the ambulance know there had been an accident.

"I thought it was safer to come back that way, less chance of being stopped. You know, breathalyzed." Gregory looked up, like the way he had looked up when he had forgotten to take one of the dogs for a walk or hadn't closed a gate in a far field.

But this time a bicyclist lay on the road in the dark.

"Please tell me, Gregory. Tell me what you think happened."

"I don't know. Jesus, I don't know. I felt the bike." He stopped. His face was blank.

"And then . . ."

"I don't know, Uncle Jim. I'm frightened."

"So am I," said James Hurley.

He picked up the phone.

"Don't, don't!" screamed his nephew. "For God's sake, you'll ruin me."

James Hurley had dialed the police.

"Shut up, Gregory," he said. "I'm not giving them your name, I'm sending them to the accident. Then I'll go myself."

"You can't . . . you can't . . ."

"Good evening, Sergeant, it's Father Hurley from the presbytery here. I've had a message, a very urgent one. There's been an accident . . ." He gave the road and the area. He thought the time was in the last half hour or so. He looked over at Gregory; the boy nodded miserably.

"Yes, it seems it was a hit-and-run."

The words had a disgusting finality about them. This time Gregory didn't even lift his head.

"No, Sergeant, I can't tell you any more. I'm sorry, it was reported to me in the nature of confession. That's all I can say. I'm going out there now to see what happened to the unfortunate— No, it was just confessed to me. I know nothing about any car or who the person was."

Father Hurley went for his coat. He caught a sight of his nephew's face and the relief that flooded it.

Gregory looked up at him gratefully.

"I never thought of that, but of course it makes sense. You *can't* really tell, because of the seal of confession."

"It wasn't confession. I could tell but I'm not going to."

"You couldn't break the sacred—"

"Shut your face!"

This was a different uncle from the one he had ever seen before.

He took a small bag with him in case he would have to administer the last sacrament to a seriously injured victim on the side of a dark road outside Dublin.

"What will I do?"

"You will walk home. And you will go to bed."

"And the car?"

"I will deal with the car. Get home and out of my sight."

The bicyclist had been a young woman. She was, according to the student card in her wallet, a Ms. Jane Morrissey. She was nineteen. She was dead.

The police said that it was always the same no matter how often they saw it, a dead body on the side of the road when some bastard had not stopped; it was terrible. One of them took off his hat and wiped his forehead, the other lit a cigarette. They exchanged glances over the priest, a pleasant, soft-spoken man in his fifties. He prayed over the dead girl and he sobbed as if he were a child.

He did it all for Laura, he told himself afterward on sleepless nights, because he couldn't drop off and be in a deep, dreamless, unconscious state for seven and eight hours a night anymore. He had changed it to confession because if it hadn't been, then he would have had to report his sister's only boy as a hit-and-run driver. Even within the sacrament of confession he should still have urged the boy to confess and admit.

In real life things weren't like an old black-and-white movie with Montgomery Clift playing the tortured priest in an agony of indecision. Today a priest would insist that if a penitent wanted absolution, he must face up to the responsibility of his actions, he must make his restitution.

But James Hurley had thought of Laura.

This was a way to save her. It was a way to tell that weak son of hers that he was regarding the matter as one between sinner and confessor. There wasn't a leg to stand on in civil or canon law.

He lied to the police sergeant. He said it had been a hysterical call from someone trying to confess, that he had no idea who the driver was. He lied to the parish priest about the caller in the night; he said it was a man looking for alms.

He lied to his sister when she asked him why he couldn't come down soon and see them again. He said there was a lot going on in the parish. The truth was that he couldn't look them in the eyes. He couldn't listen while they told him some new tale of Gregory's excellence.

He had driven Gregory's car to a service station on the other side of Dublin in a place where nobody had known him. He had lied to the garage owner, said that he had driven the parish priest's car and hit a gate. The garageman loved to hear that a priest could do wrong too. He knocked out the dent and gave it a thorough going-over.

"The parish priest will think you kept it in great condition now," he said, glad to be in on some kind of a game.

"How much do I owe you?"

"Ah, go on, Father, there's nothing in it, say a few Masses for me, and my old mother, she's not been well."

"I don't say Masses in exchange for repairs." The priest had turned white with fury. "In God's name, man, will you tell me how much it cost?"

Frightened, the garage owner stumbled out an amount.

Father Hurley recovered and put his hand on the man's arm. "Please forgive me, I'm desperately sorry for losing control and shouting at you like that. I've been under a bit of strain, but that's no excuse. Can you know how sorry I am?"

Relief flooded the man's face. "Sure, Father, there's nothing like giving a car a bit of a tip against an old gate for putting the heart across you, and especially in the case of a respectable clergyman like yourself. Think nothing of it, it wasn't even as if there were any harm done."

Father Hurley remembered the white face of Jane Morrissey, nineteen, student of sociology, with the side of her head covered in rapidly drying blood. He felt faint for a moment.

He knew his life would never be the same again. He knew he had entered a different kind of world now, a world of lies.

He had placed the keys of the car in an envelope and left them in the mailbox of Gregory's flat. He had parked the car in the car port and walked back to the presbytery.

He read in the evening papers about the accident and listened to the appeal for witnesses on Radio Eireann.

He played a game of checkers with the old parish priest with his mind a million miles away.

"You're a good man, James," said the old priest. "You don't let me win like the others do. You're a very good man."

Father Hurley's eyes filled with tears. "No, I'm not, Canon, I'm a very weak man. A foolish, vain, and weak man."

"Ah, we're all foolish, weak, and vain," said the parish priest. "But given all that, there's goodness in some of us as well, and there certainly is in you."

But those frightening days were long over now, and still sleep didn't come. He had established an uneasy and formal relationship again with his nephew.

Gregory had phoned at once to thank him for the car.

Father James Hurley had said calmly into the phone, "I'm afraid he isn't here."

"But that *is* you speaking, Uncle Jim." Gregory was puzzled.

"I've told so many lies, Gregory, what's one more?" His voice sounded tired.

"*Please*. Please, Uncle Jim, don't talk like that. Is there anyone there listening to you, you know?"

"I've no idea."

"Can I come and see you?"

"No."

"Tomorrow?"

"No. Stay away from me, Gregory. Far, far away."

"But I can't do that, not forever. I don't want to, for one thing, and what about Mother and Father, for another? It would look . . . well, you know how it would look."

"I don't think they'd guess in a million years. I think you're safe. They would believe better of you. To them it will be just a small paragraph in the papers, another sad thing that happened in Dublin."

"No, I mean about us . . . if we're not going to be speaking."

"I suppose we'll speak again. Give me time. Give me time."

Gregory couldn't get through to him, not for weeks. If he turned up at the presbytery, his uncle apologized but said he was rushing out on a sick call. If he telephoned, it was the same.

Eventually he chose the one place where he knew he could get the undivided attention of the man who was running away from him.

In the confession box the little partition slid back. Father Hurley's handsome head could be seen leaning on his hand, not looking straight at the penitent but looking forward and slightly down. In a listening position.

"Yes, my child?" he began comfortingly.

"Bless me, Father, for I have sinned," Gregory said, beginning the ritual. His voice was too familiar not to be recognized. The priest looked up suddenly in alarm.

"Good God, have you decided to make a mockery of the sacraments as well?" he whispered in a low voice.

"You won't listen to me anywhere else, so I have to come here to tell you how sorry I am."

"It's not me you have to tell."

"But it is. I've told God already through another priest. I have decided to give a certain amount each month out of my salary to a charity to try to make up for it, even though I know it won't. I've given up drink. God, Uncle Jim, what more can I do? Please tell me. I can't bring her back to life. I couldn't have even then."

"Gregory, Gregory." There were tears in Father Hurley's eyes.

"But what is the use, Uncle Jim? What good will be served if you don't speak to me, and you don't come back home because you don't want to speak about me? I mean, if I had been killed that night, too, it would all have been different. You'd have been locked in with my mother and father. So shouldn't we be glad I'm alive, anyway, even if that poor girl was killed in an accident?"

"By a hit-and-run drunken driver."

"I know, I've accepted it."

"But not the punishment for it."

"But what *good* would it do? Really and truly. It would break Mother's heart and disgrace Father, and humiliate you, and suppose it all came out now, weeks later, it would look so much worse. We can't relive that whole night. I would if I could . . ."

"Very well."

"What?"

"Just very well. We will be friends."

"Ah, I knew you'd find it in your heart."

"Good. Well, you were right, I've found it in my heart. Now can you allow someone else in to make their peace with God?"

"Thank you, Uncle Jim. And, Uncle Jim . . ."

The priest said nothing.

"Will you come and have lunch in my flat sometime? Maybe Saturday. No liquor but a couple of my friends. Please?"

"Yes."

"Thank you again."

He went to the boy's flat. He met two young men and a girl. They were pleasant, easygoing company. They drank wine with their lunch and argued genially about whether the Church still ruled everything in Ireland. Father Hurley was practiced in this kind of conversation; most of his friends' children took this line. He was bland and unfailingly courteous, he saw the point of view on this hand, on the other hand, and on yet further hands. He had a soothing murmur, an ability to appear to lose a point in order to let the opposition concede a point too.

He watched Gregory carefully. Only mineral water went into his glass. Perhaps the boy was shaken and was trying to start a new life. Perhaps James

Hurley really should find it in his heart to try to forgive the boy even if he couldn't forgive himself. He smiled at his nephew and got a warm smile back.

They all helped to clear the table out to the small, smart kitchen.

"Hey, Greg, what's this bottle of vodka doing here if you've given it up?" asked one of his friends.

"Oh, that's from the days before; take it with you." Gregory spoke easily.

Father Hurley wondered whether his own soul had become somehow poisoned, because he had a suspicion that his nephew's eyes were somehow too bright for a boy on plain water; perhaps he had been topping it up with vodka out in the kitchen. The other drink was kept on a sideboard.

But if this was the way he was going to think all the time, then there was no point in having any relationship with his nephew at all. He put it firmly from his mind. Into that store of other things he was simply refusing to think about these days.

He went to see Laura and Alan during the week. They were delighted to hear about the presence of the girl at the Saturday lunch party; they thought she might be a current girlfriend.

"She didn't seem to be relating to him especially." Father Hurley felt like an old lady gossiping at a tea party.

"She's been around for a while," Laura said happily. "I think this may be the one all right."

It had been a strange visit. Everything his sister and his brother-in-law said seemed to grate on him.

They told him he was lucky to have certainties. Sometimes in the law there were gray areas.

He smiled grimly. As if there were no gray areas in his line of work!

They said how lucky they were with Gregory. The son of a friend of theirs had joined Sinn Fein, first as a legal adviser, then as an active campaigner, and then as a fully fledged member of the Provisional IRA.

"At least he had some ideals, however misplaced and mad," Father Hurley said.

"Jimbo, you must be mad, there're no ideals in that lot," Laura cried.

And as always he smiled self-deprecatingly. There was no way he was going to explain to them that he thought any cause was better than the weak-minded cause of saving your own skin, which their son had done. With his connivance.

He looked uneasy and unhappy; Alan Black, in his diplomatic way, changed the subject.

"Tell us, are you officiating at any nice society weddings these days? We love to feel near the high and mighty of the land through you, Jim."

No, Father Hurley told them. Young people always had some friend of their own to marry them nowadays; they didn't go for old family friends of the parents. No, not a posh wedding coming up. A silver wedding, though, he said brightly, and in England no less.

They were interested, as they always were, in everything he did. He explained he had married this couple way back in 1960—it didn't seem like a quarter of a century ago but apparently that was what it was! The daughters and son of this couple wanted him to attend. They had said it would be meaningless if he didn't have some kind of ceremony for them all.

Laura and Alan thought that it was only right that this couple, whoever they were, would want Father Hurley again.

"I didn't know them very well," he said, almost as if talking to himself. "I know Deirdre's mother, Mrs. O'Hagan, slightly, and I knew Mrs. Barry, the mother of the maid of honor, Maureen Barry. But I didn't know the young man at all."

"You never mentioned them." Laura was drawing him out.

"Well, no, I suppose I marry a lot of people. Some I never see again. I always get a Christmas card from Deirdre, mind you. I used not to remember exactly who they were, Desmond and Deirdre Doyle and family . . ." He sighed heavily.

"Did you not like them?" Laura asked. "It doesn't matter telling us, we don't know them, we won't ever meet them."

"No, they were perfectly nice. I *did* like them, as it happened. I suppose I didn't think they were well suited, that they'd stay together . . ." He gave a little laugh to lighten the mood. "But there you go, I was wrong. They've been together now for twenty-five years and it doesn't seem a day too much."

"They must like each other." Laura was thoughtful. "Otherwise they wouldn't want you around and have a big do and everything. Will there be a renewing of vows?"

"I don't know. It was their daughter who wrote to me."

He relapsed into silence, but silence in the big book-lined room of Alan and Laura Black was never anything to worry about.

He thought about that wedding, the year that Gregory was born. He remembered how Deirdre O'Hagan had come into his sacristy saying that she had heard from her mother that he was going on a six-month temporary assignment to London. It was partly a study assignment and partly in case he might want to join the Irish chaplaincy scheme in Britain. There were so few English vocations, and so many of the Catholic flock were Irish or second-generation Irish who preferred a priest from their own tribe.

Deirdre O'Hagan had seemed distressed and tense. She wanted to know if he could organize a marriage for her in the next month or so.

It had all the hallmarks of a shotgun marriage, but she would not be drawn into any conversation about the reasons for the speed.

He had asked mildly that she should consider having the ceremony in Dublin, but she had been adamant. Her fiancé's people were from the West.

But surely Dublin was nearer to the West of Ireland than London was.

Deirdre O'Hagan—whom he had remembered as the pretty, giggling university student daughter of Kevin and Eileen O'Hagan, who were supportive and well-off parishioners—seemed to have developed a will of steel. She was marrying in London and said it would be a kindness to her family to involve a curate whom they knew and liked, but of course if he wasn't able to, she would make other arrangements.

Father Hurley had tried at the time, he thought looking back on it, to involve the girl in some questioning of the suddenness of her decision. He had said that one shouldn't go into matrimony too hastily and for all the wrong reasons.

He had obviously sounded stuffy and inquisitive, for he remembered her voice—clear as a bell and cold, very cold.

"Well, Father, if one was to take your own attitude to matrimony, one would never marry at all and one would suddenly find that the whole human race had died out."

Despite this poor start, the wedding had been perfectly pleasant. The boy's people were simple, small farmers from the West, they didn't field a very large contingent. The O'Hagans were there in force. A nice man, Kevin, quiet and thoughtful. He had died some years back, but Eileen was still going strong.

The maid of honor had been that handsome young woman Maureen Barry, who ran the smart dress shops nowadays. He had seen her only the other day when he had said the requiem Mass for her mother. He wondered if she would go across to London for this ceremony. He wondered if he would. He sighed again.

"You're not in good form, Jimbo." Laura was concerned.

"I'd love to be an old settled priest, you know, totally certain about everything, no doubts at all."

"You'd be unbearable if you were," she said affectionately.

Alan looked up from his book. "I know what you mean. It would be easier if there was just one law and you had to administer it, abide by it. It's all this awful business of trying to judge each case on its merits that confuses things."

James Hurley looked at his brother-in-law sharply, but the solicitor had no hidden meaning, no insight about his son and the trouble he had caused. He was thinking in terms of the district court and a justice being lenient here and strict there, according to what he knew of the person before him.

"You'd end up like the Nazis if you couldn't make your own decisions," Laura consoled him.

"Sometimes they're not right, though." His face was still troubled.

"You'd never do anything unless you thought it was right at the time."

"And afterward? What happens afterward?"

Laura and Alan exchanged glances. Jim was never like this.

Alan spoke eventually. "Well, at least it's not like a hanging judge in the old days. You didn't actually sentence anyone to death." It was meant to be reassuring. It didn't really work.

"No. No, not to death."

"Shall we take the dogs for a walk?" Laura said.

They walked, the brother and sister, sprightly and strong, through the fields that they had walked since they were children.

"If I could help?" she said tentatively.

"No, Laura, I'm a weak man to be letting you see my black side."

"You're my younger brother, for all that you're a grand important priest."

"I'm not grand and important. I never got a parish, I never wanted one. I don't want to take charge."

"Why should you, then? People don't have to."

"There are some things they have to take charge of."

She knew he would talk no more about it, and his brow seemed to clear as they walked home in the fading light.

He knew after that afternoon that if the whole terrible business was to have any value whatsoever, he must cease these self-indulgent moods. What was the point of saving them worry on one score only to cause it on another? So, they had been spared from knowing that their son had killed a bicyclist while drunk and had failed to stop; that had been peace of mind. Why take that peace away from them again by letting them think that he was cracking up and heading for serious nervous trouble?

In the months that followed, he hardened his heart to the doubts and he fought the sense of betrayal when he sat with the only family he ever had or would ever know. He began to laugh easily at his nephew's jokes and managed not to wince at some of Gregory's more insensitive remarks. The priest told himself over and over that to expect a fallible human being to be perfect was to go against the revealed word of God.

He took pleasure in the simple joy that Gregory Black's parents got from their son. He reminded himself that in all his years of parish work he had never come across a family where there was such peace and genuine accord. Perhaps the price for this might never have to be paid in their lifetime.

He forced his smile not to falter when he saw Gregory helping himself liberally to the gins before dinner, the wines with, and the whiskeys after. The non-drinking resolution had not lasted very long. Neither had the girlfriend.

"She's too determined, Uncle Jim." He had laughed as he drove Father Hurley across the country rather too fast for the priest's liking. "You know everything is an absolute with her. No gray area."

"It's admirable in its way," Father Hurley said.

"It's intolerable. Nobody can be that sure, that definite."

"Did you love her, do you think?"

"I could have, I suppose, but not with all this black and white, honesty or dishonesty, you're either a saint or a devil. That's not the way it is in the real world."

Father Hurley looked at the handsome profile of his sister's son. The boy had forgotten the girl he had killed. The ambiguity and hypocrisy of that night literally had been put out of his mind. He was driving his uncle because Father Hurley's car was out of action, and Gregory had wanted to come down midweek, wanted to talk to his father about a loan. There was something coming up, he had heard a piece of information, the kind of chance that comes only once in a lifetime. Something he really shouldn't know, but if he invested now. Boy!

Father Hurley felt sick that he should be allowed to receive this confidence. But then, what was he except another gray-area person? Someone prepared to lie when it made sense. It was a strange visit. Gregory's father seemed apologetic about not being able to raise the money that Gregory needed and a little mystified that he wasn't being told exactly what it was needed for.

Gregory's smile didn't falter, but he said he would drive out to be on his own for a while near the lake.

Laura said after he had left that it was very sensible of him to go and work out his annoyance while sitting looking at the lake. She said that she wished Alan had just given him the damn money, it would all be his after their time, why couldn't he have it now?

By ten-thirty he hadn't come back.

Father Hurley knew he was in the pub, the roadhouse out on the lake drive. He said he'd fancy a walk himself, it was a nice night. It was a three-mile walk. He found his nephew in the bar being refused a drink.

"Come on, I'll drive you home," he said in what he hoped didn't sound a tone likely to anger his very drunk young nephew.

When they got to the car, Gregory pushed him away.

"I'm perfectly able to drive." His voice was steely.

James Hurley had a choice once the boy was behind the wheel—go with him or let him go on his own.

He opened the passenger door.

The corners were legion and the surfaces were not good.

"I beg you, take it slowly, you don't know what's coming around the corner, there's no way we can see the lights."

"Don't beg me," Gregory said, his eyes on the road. "I hate people who whine and beg."

"Then I ask you . . ."

They were on top of the donkey and cart before they saw it. The frightened animal ahead reared and was emptying the two old men and their belongings onto the road.

"Jesus Christ."

Helpless, they watched as the donkey, roaring in pain, dragged the cart over the body of one old man and started to slip down the bank toward the lake.

Father Hurley was running toward the cart where two children were screaming.

"You're all right. We're here, we're here," he called.

Behind him, he felt the breath of his nephew.

"You were driving, Uncle Jim. In the name of Christ, I beg you."

The priest didn't stop. He had caught the first little tinker child in his arms and pulled her to safety, then the second, and with all the strength in his body he pulled at the braying donkey too.

"Listen, I beseech you. Think about it, it makes sense. They'll hit me with everything, but they can't put a finger on you."

It was as if Father Hurley hadn't heard him; he had children and cart up to the road where the two dazed old men sat. One was holding his head in his hands and blood was coming through his fingers.

In the moonlight Gregory's face was white with terror.

"They're tinkers, Uncle Jim. They're not meant to be out here without any signs or warning or lights . . . nobody could blame you . . . they heard you saying you were driving me home."

Father James Hurley knelt beside the old man and forced him to take his hands away so that he could see the wound.

"It's all right my friend, it's all right. When somebody comes, we'll get you to the hospital, it'll only be a stitch or two."

"What are you going to do, Uncle Jim?"

"Oh, Gregory."

The priest looked up with tears in his eyes at the only son of the two people who would realize tonight that perhaps life wasn't meant to be all that good on this earth and that some people had been too lucky.

CHAPTER SIX

Maureen

✦❧❀❧✦

The one thing Maureen's mother would have insisted on had she been alive was that the funeral be done right. Maureen knew exactly what that meant. It meant that there be sufficient notice in the paper for everyone to attend, that there be a judicious invitation back to the house, not everyone but the right people. Both on the day she was brought to the church and on the following day after the burial itself.

Maureen arranged it meticulously, a last homage to the mother who had given her everything and had made her what she was.

She wore a magnificently cut black coat and asked a hairdresser to come to the house so that she would look immaculately groomed in front of all the people who turned up at the church. Maureen did not consider this vanity, she considered that she was carrying out to the letter her mother's last wishes: that Sophie Barry go to her rest mourned publicly by her exquisite and devoted daughter, Maureen, successful businesswoman, person of standing in Dublin.

Her mother would have approved, too, of the drinks and canapés served in the big drawing room and the way that Maureen moved among the guests pale but calm, introducing here and thanking there, and always being able to re-member if it was a wreath, a Mass card, or a letter of sympathy that had to be acknowledged.

She had nodded in total agreement to all who told her that her mother was a wonderful woman, because this was only the truth. She nodded that it was better that her mother hadn't had a long illness, she deplored the fact that sixty-eight was too young to die, she was pleased that so many people told her that her mother had been so proud of her only daughter.

"She never talked about anything else."

"She had a scrapbook of all your achievements."

"She said that you were more than a daughter, you were her friend."

Soothing words, gentle touches, graceful gestures. Just as Mother would have liked it. Nobody got drunk and became boisterous but there was the kind of buzz about the whole proceedings that Mother would have thought the mark of a successful gathering. Several times Maureen had found herself planning to talk to her mother about it afterward.

But then people often said that this was the case. Particularly when you had been close. And there were few mothers and daughters as close as Sophie Barry and her only child, Maureen.

Possibly it was because Sophie was a widow and Maureen had been left fatherless for so many years. Possibly because they looked so alike, people read more into their togetherness than there was. Sophie had only become gray late in her fifties, and when she did, it was a steel-dark gray, as shiny and glamorous as had been the raven-black hair. She had been a size twelve up to the last day and said that she would die rather than wear one of those tentlike creations that so many women seem to sink into after a certain age.

Sophie's good looks and harsh standards did not always endear her to the more easygoing in her circle. But she had what she wanted from them, their total admiration all of her days.

And Maureen would make sure that it would continue in terms of whatever needed to be done now. The house would not be sold with unseemly haste, the mortuary cards would be simple and black-edged, with some tasteful prayer that could be sent as a memento to Protestant friends, too. Not something dripping with indulgence-gaining imprecations, no photograph. Mother would say that's what maids did. Maureen would know better than to insult her memory.

Friends had offered to help her go through her mother's things. It can be upsetting, they said, it's often easier if an outsider comes to help. Everything can be divided into categories much less emotionally. But Maureen smiled and thanked them, assuring them that this was something she would like to do herself. She didn't particularly want to go through things alone, but Mother would never have let a stranger look at her private papers in a million years.

Father Hurley, who had known them for years, offered to help. He said it was often a lonely business and he would be happy even to sit with her as company. He had meant well, and Mother had always liked him, she said he was a credit to the Church, nicely spoken, very cultured, knew everyone who was anyone; high praise from Mother. But still, Mother would not have let him become involved in her private papers. A gentle, moving sermon, yes, exactly the right kind of priest for this parish, but he couldn't be involved in anything personal. That would be for Maureen alone.

Walter would want to help, of course, but it was out of the question. Walter had been kept at arm's length during the whole proceedings. Maureen had no intention of marrying him or of being seen to rely on him. Why, then, should he be allowed to be present at all the funeral ceremonies as her right-hand man? This would be giving a false impression to all those old biddies, friends of her mother, women who had nothing left to talk about in their own lives and speculated instead about each other's children. Maureen, unmarried at forty-six, must have given them many good years of chat and supposition, she thought with a grim pleasure.

Kind, courteous Walter, who was thought to be suitable for her because he, too, was unmarried, of a good family, and had a good practice at the bar. Maureen knew that if she wanted to, she could marry Walter. He didn't love her, and she felt nothing even remotely like love for him. But Walter was the kind of man who wouldn't have expected love at this stage in life. Once when he was a younger man, perhaps an unsuitable dalliance or two, maybe even a real affair that didn't work out.

Walter had his male bonding in the law library, he had a busy social life. People always wanted an extra man.

Mother had liked Walter but Mother was far too intelligent to push her toward him. Anyway, Mother would have been the last to use the argument about insuring against a lonely old age. Look at her own years as a woman without a man. Her life had been very full.

Once Maureen had made it clear that she had no thoughts about Walter as a life partner, her mother had never pushed the notion again. There had been no talk of including Walter in a bridge party, a theater outing, or the party made up to go to the Aga Khan Cup at the horse show.

Walter was kind, courteous, and could indeed, after several glasses of good claret, be a little emotional. Sometimes he talked of lonely roads and sacrificing all else on the altar of one's career. But Maureen would laugh at him affectionately and ask him to consider what on earth she and he had sacrificed. They had lovely apartments, good cars, hosts of friends, and the freedom to go where they liked. In Maureen's case, to London and New York buying clothes, in Walter's to the West of Ireland fishing.

In a Dublin which more and more would have accepted such a state, they were not lovers. It had been suggested one evening and rejected, with charm and elegance on each side, and broached once more in case the first refusal had been only a matter of form. But they remained two attractive single people whose eyes often met resignedly over a table, as yet again a hostess had brought them together as an inspired idea for a dinner party.

It was ironic that of all the men who had wandered into Maureen's life, the only one that Mother would have considered suitable was the one who came too late, who came along when Maureen knew she didn't want to change her ways. If she had met Walter, a young, earnest barrister in his twenties when she had been struggling to establish the shops, she might well have settled for him. So many of her friends had settled for men whom they could not possibly have loved in any real sense. These were not great loves, the wedding ceremonies that Maureen had attended all through the 1960s, they were alliances, refuges, compromises, arrangements. Deirdre O'Hagan, who defied everyone and married her first love in that long summer when they had all been in London, that might have been real love. Maureen was never sure. Even though she had been Deirdre's maid of honor, and they had slept in the same room the night before the wedding, she had not been certain that Deirdre ached for Desmond Doyle and cried out to be with him. As she herself had cried out to be with Frank Quigley.

It was a strange friendship, hers with Deirdre. Their mothers wanted them to be friends so desperately that they gave in at the age of fourteen and agreed to go to the same tennis parties, and later the same hops and rugby-club social evenings on Saturday nights.

By the time they got to UCD they were in fact friends of a sort. And they each knew that their salvation lay with the other. If Maureen said she was going anywhere with Deirdre, then Mother would relax. It was the same in the O'Hagan household; Deirdre could always use Sophie Barry's daughter, Maureen, as an excuse.

That was why they had been able to go off to London together that summer. The summer they should have been at home working for their degrees. The summer they met Desmond Doyle and Frank Quigley on the boat to Holyhead.

Maureen wondered what Frank Quigley would say if he knew that Mother had died. She didn't know how he talked these days, whether his accent had changed, if he spoke as a lot of Irishmen living twenty-five years in London spoke, with two distinct strands in their voices and telltale words of both cultures coming in at the wrong place.

She had read about him; who hadn't read about Frank Quigley? He was profiled always among the Irish who had done well in Britain. Sometimes she saw pictures of him with that sullen-looking young Italian he had married to advance himself still further in the hierarchy of Palazzo.

Of course, Frank might be so suave nowadays that he would write an elegant note of sympathy on a gilt-edged card. He might be so down-to-earth and still such a rough diamond that he would say she should have died a quarter of a century earlier.

One thing Maureen knew was that Frank Quigley would not have forgotten her mother, any more than he would have forgotten Maureen.

This was not arrogance on her part, believing that her first love would remember her with the same intensity as she remembered him, when she allowed him into her mind at all. She knew it was true. Still, it was irrelevant; he might hear about it from Desmond and Deirdre, but it was hard to say whether they all remained friends still.

Admittedly Desmond still worked in Palazzo, but despite Mrs. O'Hagan's great reports of her son-in-law's managerial promotions from time to time, Maureen had the feeling that Desmond had stuck somehow low on a scale and that all the patronage and friendship from his old friend Frank couldn't pull him any higher.

The day of sorting through Mother's things could not be put off forever. Maureen decided to go on the Sunday following the funeral. It would not take long if she put her mind to it and did not allow herself to become emotionally upset by everything she touched.

Already she had wept over her mother's glasses in their spectacle case, which had been given to her in the hospital. Somehow it seemed sadder than anything else to see the sign of Mother's frail, fading eyesight handed to her in a useless little case. Maureen, usually so decisive, hadn't known what to do with them. They were still there, zipped into a side compartment of her handbag. Mother would not have been so softhearted. She would have been cool and practical, as she had been about everything.

They had only fought once, a long time ago, and it had not been about Frank Quigley or about any man. Mother hadn't thought that the clothing business looked all right or sounded respectable enough.

Maureen had blazed her anger. What the hell did it matter how things looked or sounded? It was how they were, what they were about that was important. Mother had smiled a cool, infuriating smile. Maureen had stormed out. Up to the North of Ireland first, where she got a thorough grounding in retail dress sense from two sisters who ran a smart clothes shop and were pleased and flattered to see the dark, handsome young university graduate from Dublin come up to learn all they could teach her. Then she went to London.

It was then that she realized how she had never been really close to Deirdre;

they had met rarely while she was there. Deirdre had been tied up with two babies at that stage, and Maureen had been going to trade fairs and exhibitions and learning what to look for. Maureen told Deirdre nothing of her coldness with her mother for fear that it would go straight back to the O'Hagan household, and presumably Deirdre had secrets, worries, and problems that she didn't tell Maureen either.

And anyway, the coldness didn't last. It had never been an out-and-out hostility, there were always postcards and short letters and brief phone calls. So that Mother could tell Eileen O'Hagan how well Maureen was doing here, there, and everywhere. So that appearances could be kept up. Appearances had been very important to Mother. Maureen determined that she would honor this to the very end, far beyond the grave.

Maureen Barry lived in one of the earlier apartment houses that had been built in Dublin. She lived ten minutes by foot and two minutes by car from the big house where she was born and where her mother had lived all her life. It had been Mother's home, and Father had married in. For the short married life that they had. He had died abroad when Maureen was six, forty years ago this year.

It would be the anniversary of his death shortly, in three weeks; how strange to think that she would attend the Mass they always had said for the repose of his soul totally on her own. Normally she and Mother went together, for as long as she could remember. Always at eight o'clock in the morning. Mother had said that it was discourteous to involve others in your own personal mourning and memorials. But Mother had always told people afterward that they had been to the Mass.

The living arrangements were yet one more way in which the relationship between the two women was widely praised. Many another mother would have clung to her daughter and kept her in the family home as long as possible, not noticing or caring about the normal wish of the young to leave the nest. Many a less dutiful daughter might have wanted to go away to another city. To London perhaps or even Paris. Maureen was successful in the fashion world. To have two shops with her own name on them by the time she was forty was no mean achievement. And such smart shops, too. She moved from one to the other with ease; each had a good manager who was allowed freedom to run the day-to-day business. It had left Maureen free to buy, to choose, to decide to lunch with the fashionable women whose taste she monitored and even formed. She went to London four times a year and to New York once every spring. She had a standing that her mother would never have believed possible in those bad days, the bad time when they had not seen eye to eye. It hadn't lasted long, and every relationship was allowed to have some valley periods, Maureen told herself. Anyway, she didn't want to think about those days now, not so soon after Mother's death.

It had indeed been so sensible to live apart but near. They saw each other almost every day. Never in all the years since she moved into her apartment did Maureen open her front door and find her mother unannounced on her step. Mother wouldn't dream of calling on a young woman who might be entertaining someone and wished to do so privately.

It was different about Maureen going back to her old home. No such strictures applied there. Maureen was welcome to call at any time, but Mother managed to let her know that at the end of a bridge party was a particularly suitable time to drop in for a sherry, because everyone could have the chance to admire both the elegant daughter and the evidence of her consideration and devotion to her mother.

On the Sunday she walked to the house where she would never again see her mother walking lightly down the hall to open the door, viewed through the multicolored stained glass of the hall door panels. It felt strange to go to the empty house, because by now there would be no kind friends and relatives staying around as support. Mother's great friend Mrs. O'Hagan, Deirdre's mother, had been very pressing and begged Maureen to come and see them, to drop in for supper, to use the O'Hagan house just like she had her old home.

It had been kind, but not the right thing. Maureen wasn't a little girl; she was a middle-aged woman, for heaven's sake. It was not appropriate for Mrs. O'Hagan to invite her up to the house as she had done thirty years ago, when she and Mother had decided that Deirdre and Maureen should be friends.

Mother had always set a lot of store on what Eileen O'Hagan thought about this and that. Eileen and Kevin were her greatest friends. They had always invited Mother to join them at the theater or the races. They had never to Maureen's recollection tried to find a suitable second husband for her. Or perhaps they had. She would not have known.

As she walked through the sunny streets toward her old home Maureen wondered what life would have been like if Mother had married again. Would a stepfather have encouraged her or fought her when she wanted to take up her career in what she had called the fashion industry and her mother had said was common drapery and glorified salesgirl work?

Would Mother have been coquettish with men years ago? After all, Maureen herself did not feel old and past sexual encounters at the age of forty-six, so why should she assume that her mother had? But it was something that never came into their lives.

They talked a lot about Maureen's young men, and how they had all somehow failed to measure up. But they had never talked about any man for Mother.

She let herself into the house and shivered slightly because there was no little fire lit in what Mother had always called the morning room. Maureen plugged in the electric heater and looked around.

Two weeks ago on a Sunday she had come here to find Mother looking white and anxious. She had this pain, possibly indigestion but . . . Maureen had acted quickly, she helped her mother gently to the car and drove calmly to hospital. No point in disturbing the doctor, calling him away from his Sunday breakfast, she had said to Mother, let's go to the emergency room. They were there the whole time in a hospital, they would set her mind at rest.

Mother, looking more and more anxious, agreed with her, and even at this stage Maureen had noticed with sinking heart that her mother's careful speech sounded slurred, her words running together.

They were seen at once, and within an hour Maureen was waiting outside the intensive care unit to be told the news that her mother was having a massive stroke. One that she might very well not recover from.

Mother recovered, but not her faculties of speech; her eyes, bright and burning, seemed to beg for an end to this indignity.

She could press once for yes and twice for no on Maureen's arm. Maureen had spoken to her alone.

"Are you afraid, Mother?"

No.

"You do believe that you'll get better, don't you?"

No.

"I want you to believe that. You must. No, sorry. Of course, you can't answer that. I mean, don't you want to get better?"

No.

"But surely for me, Mother, for all your friends, *we* want you to get better. God, how do I say something that you can answer? Do you know that I love you? Very, very much?"

Yes, and a lessening of the strain in the eyes.

"And do you know that you are the best mother that anyone could have?"

Yes.

Then she had been tired, and not long after that she had slipped into unconsciousness.

They had been right—the friends who had stood in this room, Mother's morning room that got the early light—when they had nodded and said Sophie Barry could not have lived the dependent life of an invalid. It was better that she had been taken quickly away from pain and indignity.

Could it really only have been two weeks since that Sunday morning? It felt like ten years in so many ways.

Maureen unfolded the black plastic sacks. She knew that a great deal of Mother's things could indeed be thrown away, there was no one to gasp and wonder over old mementos of cavalry balls years ago, or programs of long-forgotten concerts signed with some illegible squiggle. No grandchildren to ooh and aah over worlds gone by. And Maureen in her own busy life would not look at them; a lot of things would go.

She sat at the small writing desk: an antique. She might take it for the hallway of her own flat. It was such an impractical thing, dating from a time when ladies penned only little notes or invitation cards. It had nothing to do with today's world. Mrs. O'Hagan had been surprised that Maureen was going to remain in her flat. She was sure that Sophie would have wanted her own home to continue in the family. But Maureen was adamant. She lived a life too full to involve cleaning a house with as many nooks and crannies as this. Her own space was custom-made for her, wall-long closets for her clothes, a study with proper filing cabinets as a mini-office, a big room where she could enter-tain, its kitchen in full view of the dining table so that she could talk to her guests as she served them their dinner.

No, it would be a backward move to come home to this house. Mother knew that, too.

First she went through the finances. She was surprised how disorganized Mother had become lately. It was sad to see little notes Mother had written to herself: a reminder here, a query there. It would have been so easy for Maureen to have set up an uncomplicated system like her own; five minutes would have done it, a letter to the bank asking them to pay so much each month to electricity, gas, insurance fund. It would have cut out all these final demands and letters of bewilderment. Mother must have appeared much more in control than she was.

Then there was an endless correspondence with a stockbroker. Like every-one of her generation, Mother had believed that wealth was measured in stocks and shares. Only the broker's letters were to be found: Mother had kept no copies of her own side of the correspondence. It was a sorry tale of confusion and disappointment.

Maureen felt weary and sad as she finished the series of responses to what had obviously been querulous demands for information and explanations why shares that everyone knew were excellent seemed to have vanished into nothingness. Briskly Maureen wrote a letter to the broker, explaining that her mother had died and asking him to send her details of the nature of the portfolio as it stood now. She wished that she had involved herself more, but with Mother there was such a dignity, there was a boundary you didn't cross.

Maureen kept all the letters she had written in her slim briefcase; she would photocopy them later, back at her own apartment. Mr. White, who had been Mother's solicitor, had already congratulated her on her efficiency; he wished that many more young women could be as organized, but then, of course, she hadn't built herself a big business without having a good financial brain and a sense of administration. He had shown her Mother's will, a simple document leaving everything to her beloved daughter, Mary Catherine (Maureen) Barry, with gratitude for all her years of devoted love and care. The will had been made in 1962. Just after the reconciliation. After Mother had accepted that Maureen was not going to abandon her idea of how she would live her life. Since the day that Sophie Barry had written down her gratitude for the devoted love and care, twenty-three more years of it had been given. Surely she never would have believed that for over two decades Maureen would remain single and remain her close friend.

It was taking more time than she had thought, and she felt a strange sense of loss, different entirely from the grieving at the funeral. It was as if she had lost her idea of Mother as someone almost perfect. This nest of confusion stuffed into the drawers of a lovely writing desk spoke of a peevish old woman, confused and irritable. Not the calm, beautiful Sophie Barry, who until two weeks ago had sat like a queen in her throne room in this, her morning room, with its tasteful furnishings. Maureen didn't like discovering this side of her mother.

She had made herself a cup of coffee to give her more energy for the task and reached out resolutely for the next big, bulky envelope. She remembered the way Mother used to say, "Maureen my child, if a thing is worth doing, it's worth doing properly." That used to apply to anything from cleansing her face twice a day with Mother's special cream and then splashing it with rosewater to going back and having six more tennis lessons so that she would look that much better at the summer parties. Well, if Mother could see her now, something Maureen doubted, she would certainly agree that the devoted daughter was doing the job properly.

She was totally unprepared for the papers she found in the envelope marked SOLICITOR. She thought it might be some more fussy dealings about shares or pensions, but these were letters from a completely different solicitor, and they were dated forty years ago. There were a series of legal documents, all signed in 1945. And they showed that Maureen's father, Bernard James Barry, had not died of a virus when he was in Northern Rhodesia just after the war. Sophie Barry's husband had deserted her forty years ago. He had left his wife and child and gone to live with another woman in Bulawayo, in what was then Southern Rhodesia.

Maureen realized that, for all she knew, she might have a father still alive, a man of seventy years, living in Bulawayo, Zimbabwe. That she might even have stepbrothers and sisters, men and women not much younger than herself. The woman described as his common-law wife was called Flora Jones and had come from Birmingham in England. Wildly, Maureen thought that Mother would have said that Flora was a maid's name.

She wasn't in the habit of pouring herself a stiff drink in the middle of a Sunday morning. Maureen Barry, disciplined in this as in everything else, realized the perils of drinking alone. She had seen too many of her friends lapse into it, at the end of a long, hard day with no one to relax with. She had learned this from Mother, as she had learned everything. Mother said that widows could slip into tippling if they didn't exercise some control. Widows, what did Mother mean, acting out a lie for forty years? What kind of closeness was it that meant she couldn't tell her only daughter the biggest event of her life? What manner of woman could perpetuate a myth about a man who had to be buried abroad?

With another ripple of shock running through her like the continuous waves after an earthquake, Maureen realized that her mother, who had been a sane woman, had gone out every May and had a Mass said for the repose of the soul of Bernard James Barry, a man who must have been alive for some, if not all, of the time that she was doing this.

There was whiskey in a decanter. Maureen smelled it; it reminded her of when she had a toothache years and years ago and Mother would put a whiskey-flavored piece of cotton on the gum to numb the pain. Mother had loved her so much.

Maureen poured out a large measure of neat whiskey, drank it, and burst into tears.

It was a measure of the lonely life she led, she realized, that she had no one to tell. There was no bosom pal to ring up, no house where she could run around and share this staggering news. Like her mother, she had kept aloof from intimacies. There was no man she had let close enough to her thoughts to confide in. Her work colleagues knew nothing of her private life. Her mother's friends . . . oh, yes . . . they would be interested. My, my, would she get a hearing at O'Hagans' if she were to turn up with the news.

Flora. Flora Jones. It was like a name from a musical comedy. And now presenting Miss Flora Jones, the Carmen Miranda of our town. There had been letters about divorce, and copies of letters from Mother's solicitor repeating over and over that not only was there no divorce in Ireland, and that his client was a staunch Roman Catholic, but that this was not the matter at issue, the question at issue apparently had been money. Maureen leafed, still unbelieving, through the documents . . . kept meticulously in order—this was a younger, firmer Mother, more in control forty years ago, wounded and enraged and determined that she was going to get the last penny from the man who had betrayed her. A sum had been paid over. A sum which in today's money would have been considered staggering. The solicitor of Bernard James Barry in Bulawayo wrote to the solicitor of Mrs. Sophie Barry in Dublin that his client was willing to realize most of his assets in order to provide for his wife and eldest daughter. His client, Mr. Barry, had now, as was already known to Mrs. Barry, a second daughter by Miss Flora Jones, a daughter whose birth he was most anxious to legitimize.

Mother's letter of reply to that had been extraordinary; it was written exactly as Mother spoke. Maureen could hear her voice as she read the words.

She could literally hear Mother's voice, slow, measured, articulate, a younger, stronger voice than of late.

". . . while you will understand that there can never be any question of a divorce since it is against the rules of the Church to which we both belong, I cannot legislate for you and your actions in a foreign land. I am writing this letter without the approval of the solicitors but I think you will understand its general drift. I have accepted your settlement for Maureen and myself. I shall pursue you in no court, nor under any jurisdiction. You shall be totally free from me if and only if you never return to Ireland. I shall announce your death. Today is April 15. If you return this letter to me with your promise that you will never come back to Ireland again, then I will say that you died abroad of a virus on May 15.

"If this promise is ever broken, or if you try to get in touch with Maureen in any way even after she is legally an adult, I can assure you that you will be made to regret it to the end of your days. . . ."

It was the way Mother spoke to a tradesman who had offended her in some way or to a handyman who had not done a job to her satisfaction.

He had accepted her terms, the man in Bulawayo, the man Maureen had thought was dead for forty years. He had returned the letter, as ordered to do. Attached to it by a small pearl-topped pin was a postcard. A brown sepia picture of mountains and savanna.

The words on the postcard said, "I died of a virus on May 15, 1945."

Maureen put her head down on her mother's desk and cried as if her heart would break into little pieces.

She didn't feel the time passing. And when she looked at the clock, the way the hands were placed seemed meaningless. It said a quarter past two or ten past three. It was bright, so it must be daytime.

She had come to the house at ten o'clock; she must have been in this semi-trance for over two hours.

She walked around feeling the blood beginning to flow again in her veins. If anyone had looked in the window of the morning room, they would have seen a tall, dark young woman, looking considerably less than her forty-six years, apparently hugging herself around the waist of her smart navy and pink wool dress.

In fact, Maureen was holding in each hand the elbow of the opposite arm, in a physical attempt to hold herself together after this shock.

She felt a rage against her mother, not just because this man had been ordered summarily out of her life and threatened not to contact his own flesh and blood. But she felt a burning anger that if her mother had kept this secret so successfully for so long, why on earth had she not destroyed the evidence?

If Maureen had never found these papers, she would never have known. She would have been happier, more safe and sure in the world she had built for herself.

Why had her mother been so casual and cruel? She must have known that Maureen would find the evidence someday.

But of course, Mother knew that Maureen would not betray her. Maureen would keep up appearances to the end.

Like hell she would.

It came to her suddenly that she could do anything she liked about this whole farce. She had entered into no melodramatic promises about mythical deaths. She had entered into no promise not to contact him for fear of some awful punishment.

By God, she was going to find him, or Flora, or her half sister.

Please, please may they be alive. Please may she find her father from this welter of documents, the latest being from 1950, confirming a final transfer of assets.

Please, God, may he still be alive. Seventy wasn't that old.

She began to work with the kind of controlled, furious energy that she had not known since the night before her first big high-fashion sale when they were up almost all night in the stockrooms marking clothes down, and recataloging and estimating the takings of the following day.

This time she approached her mother's belongings with different categories in mind. She found two boxes, which she filled with early photographs and memorabilia of herself when a child.

If she did find this man, if he was a man with any heart, he would want to know what she looked like at her first communion, in her field hockey outfit, dressed for her first dance.

Items which would have been carefully cut up and destroyed were now filed in boxes and labeled KEEPSAKES.

She sorted and arranged and tidied until she was ready to drop. Then she tied up the bags which were real rubbish, folded the clothes and other items which were to go to the Vincent de Paul Society, and ordered a taxi to take back the boxes of keepsakes to her own flat.

There wasn't a drawer now that hadn't been emptied and dusted out. Much of the ordinary kitchen equipment would go to Mrs. O'Neill, who had come to clean for Mother over the years. Jimmy Hayes, who did the garden, could have the lawn mower and any of the gardening tools he wanted. Maureen also wrote him a letter asking him to take for his own use any plants that he particularly liked and to have them removed quickly. She had decided now that the house would go on the market as soon as possible.

She laid her hand on the small writing desk, the one she had been going to take for the entrance hall of her own apartment. She patted it and said, "No." She didn't want it now. She wanted nothing from here.

The taxi driver helped her in with the boxes. Because he was curious, she told him that she had been clearing away her mother's effects. He was very sympathetic.

"Isn't it a pity now that you didn't have anyone to help you do a job like that?" he said.

That's what people often said to her in different ways, like wasn't it a wonder that a fine girl like herself had never married and settled down?

"Oh, my father would have done everything, but he was away, far away," she said.

She had mentioned her father. She didn't care about the surprised look that the taxi driver gave her, or how odd it was to have a father far away when a mother had died.

She felt that by mentioning him she was making him be alive.

She had a long, long bath and felt better but ravenously hungry. She telephoned Walter.

"I'm being very selfish and literally using you, so feel free to say no, but are there any nice restaurants open on a Sunday night? I'd love to go out for a meal."

Walter said nothing could suit him better, he had been doing a particularly tedious kind of opinion where there seemed to be no solution or a thousand solutions, and one was as hard as the other. He would love to escape from it.

Together they sat and ordered good food and wine by candlelight.

"You look a little feverish," Walter said with concern.

"I've a lot on my mind."

"I know, it must have been very distressing today," he said.

Her eyes seemed to dance at him across the table. She had never looked more beautiful, he thought.

"I know it's not the time, but then there never is any really good time, but perhaps you might think of . . ."

"Yes?"

"Well, should we go on holiday together, somewhere we would both like? You once said you would like to visit Austria."

"There's no fishing in Austria, Walter." She smiled at him.

"There are probably no fashion trade fairs, either, but we could manage for two weeks, couldn't we?"

"No, Walter, we'd drive each other mad."

"We could leave each other alone."

"Can't we do that better living apart?" She gave him a very bright smile.

"There's something on your mind." He looked hurt and troubled.

"Yes, there is, and I can't tell you now. But please remember tonight and that I wanted to tell you something. I will soon."

"When?"

"I don't know. Soon."

"Is it another man? I know that sounds very corny, but you have that kind of look about you."

"No, it's not another man. Not in that sense. I'll tell you, I've never lied to you, and when I do tell, you'll realize."

"Now I can't wait," he said.

"I know, neither can I. I wish people worked on Sundays, why does the world close down on Sundays?"

"You and I work on Sundays," Walter complained.

"Yes, but offices all over the world don't, damn them."

He knew it wasn't worth asking any more, he would hear nothing. He leaned over and patted her hand.

"I suppose I must love you to let you get away with all of this performance."

"Oh, will you go to hell, Walter. Of course, you don't love me, not even in the slightest, but you're a great friend, and I'm sure, though I don't intend to find out, that you're a smashing lay as well."

The waiter's arrival just at that moment, in time to hear Maureen's extravagant compliment, prevented Walter from saying anything in reply.

She slept a little but not much. She was out of her bed, showered and dressed, by 6:00 A.M. The time difference would be three hours. She would start telephoning International Inquiries and giving the out-of-date numbers, hoping that it would not be too long a haul. She had almost weakened enough to ask Walter if there were international directories of solicitors worldwide that she could study down at the Four Courts, but no, she must give him no details, no hints; later she would tell him. He deserved that. She hadn't decided what she would tell everyone else when she found her father—if she found him.

It was not as difficult as she had feared. It was probably twenty times as expensive in terms of telephone calls, but she didn't care.

The firm no longer existed in Bulawayo, helpful operators got her listings of other solicitors, and finally she found that the original company had moved to South Africa. She found herself talking to people in cities she had never even thought about, even if she had acknowledged their names . . . Bloemfontein, Ladysmith, Kimberley, Queenstown.

She found one of the names that had signed one of the letters in Pretoria. Maureen Barry was crisp.

She explained that her mother had died and that it was her last wish that she, Maureen, should contact her late father. To whom should she now make the inquiries?

It wasn't a file that would have been kept open for forty years, the man told her.

"But you haven't thrown it away. Lawyers don't throw anything away."

"Can't you inquire at your end?"

"I have. They know nothing, the firm has changed, they say, and it's true that all the documents were handed back to my mother at her request. I have to try at your end."

He sounded like a nice man despite his accent and the way he said *rilly* instead of *really* and tried to work out what was the best way to go in the *ind* instead of the *end*.

"I fully realize that this is professional work. To research on my behalf, I am totally prepared to pay a professional fee for your time and expertise," Maureen said. "Would you like me to approach you through solicitors here to put it on a more formal basis?"

"No, it seems to me that you are a person who could be dealt with in her own right."

She could hear him smiling from across the world, a man whom she'd never met in a country she would never visit (nor would any of her friends) on account of its policies. Mother had been heard to say once she felt very sorry for those whites having to give up all their privileges and nice homes. But it hadn't gone down well. Mother hadn't been a fool; she wouldn't go that route again.

He said he would call her shortly.

"I wonder if you have any idea how shortly I hope it's going to be."

"I think so," he said in his curious clipped accent. "If I had just lost one parent and had the hope of finding another, I would know that there was a lot of urgency involved."

She didn't know how she got through Tuesday and Wednesday. He phoned her, the man from Pretoria, on Thursday at 8:00 A.M. with an address of a solicitor's firm in London.

"Is he dead or alive?" she asked, her hand at her throat, waiting for the reply.

"They didn't tell me. Truly they didn't tell me." He sounded regretful.

"But these people will know?" she begged.

"These people will be able to get a message to whoever is concerned."

"Did they hint?"

"Yes. They hinted."

"What?"

"That he was alive. That you would be talking to the principal involved."

"I'll never be able to thank you," she said.

"You don't know yet whether you have anything to thank me for or not."

"But I'll tell you. I'll ring you back."

"Write to me, you've spent enough on telephone calls. Or better, come out and see me."

"I don't think I'll do that. Would you be of any use to me? What class of an age of a person are you at all?"

"Stop putting on that accent. I am sixty-three, a widower, with a beautiful home in Pretoria."

"God bless you," she said.

"I hope he's alive and good to you," said the stranger from South Africa.

She had to wait an hour and a half before she could talk to the man in the London firm of solicitors.

"I don't know why you're talking to me," he said in a slightly peeved tone.

"I don't know either," Maureen confessed. "But the original agreement was that my father and I should not get in touch during my mother's lifetime. I know it sounds like something from Hans Christian Andersen, but this is the way it happened. Can you listen for two minutes, only two? I can explain it quickly, I'm used to business conversations."

The English solicitor understood. He said he would be in touch.

Maureen began to have far greater faith in the speed of the law than she ever had before. Walter would tell her about delays and adjournments; she knew herself the endless palaver about contracts with suppliers. But suddenly, in the middle of the most important event of her whole life, she had talked with two law firms which seemed to understand her urgency. To sense her impatience and respond to it. On Thursday night she checked the answering machine in her flat, but there was nothing except a kindly invitation from Mother's friend Mrs. O'Hagan to drop in any evening for a sherry just as you did with your own poor mother. And there was a message from Walter, who was going to the West of Ireland over the weekend. There would be lots of lovely walks and gorgeous food, he said, as well as fishing. And there needn't even *be* any fishing if Maureen would care to join him.

She smiled. He was a good friend.

There were two clicks where people had hung up without leaving a message. She felt restless and then annoyed with herself. How could she expect these people to act so swiftly? And suppose her father *was* alive and in England, which was the way it looked now . . . perhaps he didn't want to get in touch, or he did and Flora didn't want him to, or his daughter. She suddenly realized that there might have been other children.

She paced the apartment, walking the length of her long living room, arms hugging each other. She couldn't remember when she had last been like this, unable to settle down to anything.

When it rang, the phone made her jump and the voice was hesitant.

"Maureen Barry. Is that Maureen Barry?"

"Yes." She spoke half words, half breath.

"Maureen, it's Bernie," the voice said. And there was a silence, as if he were waiting desperately to know what she would say.

She was able to say nothing. No words would come out.

"Maureen, they told me you had been trying to get in touch. If that's not so . . ." He was almost ready to ring off.

"Are you my father?" she whispered.

"I'm an old man now, but I was your father," he said.

"Then you still are." She forced a lightness into her voice. It had been the right thing to do; she heard him laugh a little.

"I rang before," he said, "but it was one of those machines. You sounded so formal, I had to ring off without saying anything."

"I know, people should be hanged for that," she said. Again it was right, he was relaxing.

"But I rang again just to hear your voice and think: This is Maureen speaking, actually the sound of her voice."

"And did you like the sound of it?"

"Not as much as now when it's a real conversation. Is it a real conversation?"

"Yes, yes, it is."

There was a silence, but it wasn't a heavy one; it was as if they were both settling into the strange ritual of talking to each other.

"Would you like to meet me?" she asked.

"There's nothing I would like more. But would you be able to come to England to find me? I'm a bit feeble now, I couldn't come to Ireland to see you."

"That's no problem. I'll come as soon as you like."

"It won't be the Bernie you used to know."

She understood he wanted her to call him Bernie, not Father. Mother had always referred to him as poor Bernard.

"I never knew you anyway, Bernie, and you only knew me for a short time. It will be no shock to either of us. I'm freewheeling down to fifty, a middle-aged woman."

"Stop, stop."

"No, it's true. I'm not actually gray, because I have such a regular relationship with a hairdresser . . ." She felt she was burbling on.

"And Sophie . . . she told you . . . before she . . ." He was hesitant.

"She died two weeks ago, Bernie . . . it was a stroke. It was quick and she wouldn't have recovered, it was all for the best. . . ."

"And you . . . ?"

"I'm fine. But what about seeing you, where will I come, and Flora, and your family?"

"Flora is dead. She died shortly after we left Rhodesia."

"I'm sorry."

"Yes, she was a wonderful woman."

"And children?" Maureen felt this was an extraordinary conversation. It sounded so normal, so run-of-the-mill, yet she was talking to her own father, a man she had thought was forty years dead until four days ago.

"There's just Catherine. She's in the States."

Maureen was pleased somehow.

"What's she doing there? Is she working, is she married?"

"No, she's neither. She's gone with this rock musician, she's been with him eight years now. She sort of goes along wherever he is, to make a sort of home for him. She says it's all she ever wanted. She's happy."

"She's lucky then," Maureen said almost without thinking.

"Yes, she is, isn't she? Because she's not hurting anyone. People say she's a loser, but I don't think that. I think she's winning if she has what she wants without hurting anyone else."

"When can I come and see you, Bernie?" she asked.

"Oh, the sooner the better, the soonest the very best," he said.

"Where are you?"

"Would you believe Ascot?" he said.

"I'll come tomorrow," she said.

Before she left, she went through her mail quickly. Hardly anything to do with work came to her apartment; all business mail was addressed to her main shop. There were a couple of bills, circulars, and a letter that looked like an invitation. It was from Anna Doyle, the eldest of Deirdre O'Hagan's children, a formal invitation to a silver wedding for their parents and a note saying that she apologized for the ludicrously early notice, but she wanted to make sure that the key figures were able to come. Perhaps Maureen could let them know.

Maureen looked at it almost without seeing it. A silver wedding seemed such a small milestone compared with what she was about to embark on herself. She wouldn't think now about whether she would go or not.

It was a very comfortable nursing home. Bernard James Barry had left the Colonies in style, Maureen realized. She had hired a car at Heathrow and driven to the address he had given her.

She had taken the precaution of telephoning the home herself to inquire whether her arrival would not put too much strain on her father, who said he had bad rheumatoid arthritis and was recovering from a mild heart attack.

She had been told that he was in the best of health and was already eager for her to arrive.

He was dressed in a blazer with some colorful crest, he had a carefully tied cravat, he looked the perfect gentleman, lightly tanned, a lot of thick gray hair, a cane and a slow walk, but in every way the kind of man her mother would love to have entertained back in Dublin. He had a smile that would break your heart.

"I have the Egon Ronay guide, Maureen," he said after she had kissed him. "I thought we should go out and have a proper lunch to celebrate."

"You're a man after my own heart, Bernie," she said.

And he *was* a man after her own heart. There were no apologies, no excuses. In life there were only just so many chances for happiness, he didn't regret his daughter Catherine taking hers, he didn't blame Sophie for seeking happiness through status, it was just that he couldn't stick with it himself.

He had known all about Maureen, he had never lost contact, not until Kevin O'Hagan died. He had written to Kevin at his club and asked him for news of his little girl. He showed Maureen a scrapbook he had made, cuttings from the newspapers about Maureen's shops, photographs cut from society magazines about Maureen at this dance or that reception. Photos, too, of Maureen with Deirdre O'Hagan, including one showing her in her maid of honor outfit.

"Would you believe they're having a silver wedding this year?" Maureen winced at the picture of the very inelegant 1960 wedding outfits. How could they have known so little then; had she only developed a clothes sense much later?

Mr. O'Hagan had written regularly, it was only when his letter was returned from the club with a note that Maureen's father had heard of his friend's death. He had been instructed to leave no evidence of the correspondence in his house; part of the deal had been that Bernard Barry be mourned as a dead man.

They talked easily, old friends with a lot in common, it seemed.

"Did you have any great love that you didn't follow?" he asked as he sipped his brandy. At seventy he felt entitled to a little luxury like this, he said.

"Not really, not a great love." She was uncertain.

"But something that could have been a great love."

"I thought so at the time, but I was wrong. It would never have worked. It would have held us both back, we were too different, it would have been unthinkable in many ways." Maureen knew that her voice sounded like her mother's as she said this.

She found it easy to tell this man about Frank Quigley, about how she had loved him so much when she was twenty she thought that her whole body and soul would explode. She found it not at all difficult to use such words, although she had never even articulated them before.

She told how she had done everything but sleep with Frank that summer, and the reason she held back was not the usual fear of pregnancy that had held every other girl back, but simply that she knew that she must not get more involved than she already was, as he would never fit into her life.

"And was this something you believed or was it something Sophie told you?" His voice was gentle, without accusation.

"Oh, I believed it, I believed it utterly. I thought there were two types of people, us and them. And Frank was definitely them. So was Desmond Doyle, but somehow Deirdre O'Hagan managed to get away with it. I remember at the wedding we were all pretending Desmond's people came from some estate in the West instead of a cabin on the side of a hill."

"She didn't get away with it entirely," Maureen's father said.

"You mean, Mr. O'Hagan wrote to you about that?"

"Yes, a bit. I suppose I was someone he could talk to who wasn't involved, who never would be."

Maureen told how Frank Quigley had come to Dublin uninvited, for her graduation. How he had stood at the back of the hall and made whooping sounds and shouted as she went to receive her parchment.

He had called to the house afterward. It had been terrible.

"Did Sophie order him away?"

"No, you know Mother—well, maybe you don't—but she wouldn't do that, she killed him with kindness, she was charm itself . . . 'Oh, and tell me, Frank, would my late husband and I have met your people when we were in Westport?' You know the kind of thing."

"I do." He looked sad.

"And Frank somehow behaved worse and worse. Everything she did seemed to make him more Bolshie and thick and badly behaved. He took out his comb during supper and combed his hair, you know, looking at himself in that bit of mirror in the sideboard. Oh, and he stirred his coffee as if he were going to go through the bottom of the cup. I could have killed him, and I could have killed myself for caring."

"And what did your mother say?"

"Oh, something like 'Have you enough sugar, Frank? Or perhaps you would have preferred tea?' You know, terribly polite, not a hint that anything was out of place unless you knew."

"And afterward?"

"Afterward she just laughed. She said he was very nice and laughed."

There was a silence.

"But I went along with it," Maureen said earnestly. "I can't say she threw him out, she didn't, she never denied him the house, she even inquired about him from time to time with that little laugh. It was as if somehow by mistake we had invited poor Jimmy Hayes, who did the garden, in for supper. And I went along with it because I agreed with her. I went along with her way of thinking."

"And did you regret it?"

"Not at first. He was so foul-mouthed and called me all the snobby bitches under the sky, he almost proved Mother's point, my point. He said he'd show me, that he would be received in the highest houses in the land, and that one day my crabby old mother and I would regret that we hadn't welcomed him to our crummy house. That's the way he spoke."

"Out of hurt." Her father was sympathetic.

"Yes, yes, of course. And of course, he *did* become a merchant prince and Deirdre O'Hagan married his equally ignorant and unacceptable best friend . . . so he was right. His day did come."

"And is he happy?"

"I don't know, I think not. But maybe he's like a lark in the spring. I don't know."

"You're lovely, Maureen," her father said suddenly.

"No, I'm not, I'm very stupid, was very stupid for too long. It wouldn't have hurt anybody to use your phrase, it wouldn't have hurt anybody at all for me to say to Mother when I was twenty-one that I was off with Frank Quigley, pedigree or no pedigree."

"Maybe you didn't want to hurt her. After all, I had abandoned her, and you didn't want it to happen to her twice."

"Ah, but I didn't know you'd abandoned her. I thought you'd gotten an awful virus and died."

"I'm sorry." He looked contrite.

"I'm delighted, you old devil," she said. "Nothing has given me as much happiness in my whole life."

"Come on out of that! An old man ready for a wheelchair!"

"Will you come and live with me in Dublin?" she asked.

"No, no, my dearest Maureen, I won't."

"You don't need to be in a home, you're as fit as a fiddle. I can see that you're well looked after. Not in Mother's house, we'll get something together. Some place bigger than my flat."

"No, I promised Sophie."

"But she's dead now. You kept your promise while she was alive."

His eyes were sad.

"No, there is a kind of honor about a thing like this, they'd reassess her, you know, they'd go over everything she said, it would be degrading her afterward. You know what I mean."

"I do, but you're being too honorable in a sense. She didn't give you the chance to stay in contact with your own daughter, she didn't give me that chance, she didn't play really fair with us. I thought you were dead until a few days ago."

"But at least she told you in the end," said Bernard Barry, his face happy.

"What?"

"Well, at least she told you that she wanted you to find me. I heard that from the solicitors. When she knew she was dying, she wanted you to have the chance to meet me again."

Maureen bit her lip. Yes, that was what she had said at the outset, when she was making those early inquiries to Bulawayo.

She looked closely at her father's face.

"I must say I was touched and pleased at that. I thought she was implacable. Kevin O'Hagan told me that there was an anniversary Mass for me every year."

"I know," Maureen agreed. "It's coming up again shortly."

"So she did something she needn't have done, I owe it to her not to go back and disturb her memory. Anyway, child, I don't know anyone there anymore, not since Kevin died, and I'd only be an object of curiosity to them all. No, I'll stay here. I like it, and you'll come and see me from time to time, and your sister Catherine and her young man will come. I'll be in clover."

Her eyes filled with tears. She would never tell him that Mother hadn't sent her to find him, she would let him think something good as he sat at sunset thinking he was in clover.

"I'll find lots of excuses to come and see you then. Maybe I'll open a shop in Ascot here or in Windsor. I mean it."

"Of course you do, and won't you be coming over for Kevin's daughter's silver wedding? Won't that be another excuse?"

"I mightn't go to that. Frank Quigley was the best man, you know. It's meant to be a kind of a reunion of everyone who was there, dredging up all the past memories and everything."

"Isn't that all the more reason to go?" asked Bernie Barry, the man with the tan and the twinkle in his eye who fell in love on a business trip forty years ago and had the courage to follow his star.

CHAPTER SEVEN

Frank

He never knew why everyone made such a fuss about traveling. Frank loved to get into his car and head off a hundred miles or more along highways and past signposts. He felt free and as if there were a sense of adventure about it all. Even if it was only a catering exhibition that he had been to a dozen times before, he enjoyed it. And why wouldn't he? As he often reminded himself, not everyone else on the highways had a Rover, this year's model, with fitted stereo and radio filling the sleek, comfortable world with music. Or whenever he wanted it, with *Italian for Businessmen*. Nobody in Palazzo Foods knew that Frank Quigley could understand every single word of Italian spoken in his presence. He never let a flicker of the eye acknowledge that he had understood what might be being said. Even when it was about him. Particularly when it was about him.

Sometimes Frank thought that his father-in-law, Carlo Palazzo, might have a suspicion, but if he had, he kept it to himself. And he would have admired Frank all the more for it. He had let Frank know a long time ago that they had been watching him and grooming him, and that he would never have gotten to first base with the boss's daughter unless Carlo Palazzo and his brother had wanted it that way.

Frank had known this already; it came as no surprise that a wealthy girl like Renata would be heavily protected by her father and uncle from fortune hunters. He knew that he was suitable because he didn't need to marry the Palazzo princess to rise in the company. He didn't even need Palazzo. Frank Quigley would have been able to walk into any business in Britain. He had no initials after his name, he had never finished his formal schooling. He didn't need any of it. He had the flair and the ability to work long, hard days and nights. They had known all that fifteen years ago when they let him take Renata out to dinner. They knew he would lay no untoward hand on the dark, shy heiress to the Palazzo fortunes until they were wed. And the Palazzos knew that if ever he were to be the teeniest little bit unfaithful to his wife, it would be something anonymous and discreet and far from home. There would be no hint of scandal.

Frank sighed about the unwritten rules. He had sailed a little near the wind on one or two occasions but nothing he couldn't handle. Until now. Now the situation was very different, and he needed every moment alone that he could seize in order to work out what to do. If it were business, if it were only business . . . ah, then he would know exactly what to do. But Joy East was not business. Not when she was in her yellow T-shirt and nothing else, walking confidently around her house, proud and sure of herself. And sure of him as he lay there admiringly, afternoon after long sunny afternoon, smiling at her mane of streaked brown-and-gold hair, her perfect teeth, her long, tanned legs.

Joy East, the designer who had gotten Palazzo into the smart magazines, who had raised their image from the tatty to the stylish, as Frank Quigley had raised their sales and their progress from the mass of small so-called supermarkets to the very front rank. Joy East, who had told him the first night they had looked at each other with non-professional eyes that they would be the ideal match. Neither wanted to change life-styles, neither was in any position to force the other to do so. Joy wanted her independence and freedom, Frank wanted to remain in his marriage with the boss's daughter. Who better to suit each other than two people with everything to lose by being silly and everything to gain by enjoying each other's company discreetly? She had told him this partly in words, partly by her look, and partly by the way she had leaned across the restaurant table and kissed him full on the lips.

"I checked first," she had said, laughing. "There's nobody in the place except tourists."

It had been exciting then, and it had continued to be exciting. Frank had rarely met women like Joy. The finer and indeed the main points of the women's movement had passed him by; this new independence seemed to him very exotic. Joy East was proud of her single state; she had almost married, she told him, a very lucky escape when she was twenty-three, but she had called it off days before the wedding. Her father had been furious and they still had to pay a huge whack of the wedding reception cost, and the cake, and the limousines. Not to mention all the talk and the fuss. Everyone would have preferred her to get married just to save all the embarrassment. And the man? Oh, lucky escape for him, too, Joy thought, laughing and thinking about him not at all.

She lived in a small house on the corner of a road which had been not at all fashionable when she found it but which day by day was seeing the moving vans of ever smarter neighbors. Her white-walled garden was private and had vines on the walls. Her long, comfortable living room could fit sixty comfortably at one of her parties. Joy gave wonderful parties and often said that it was terribly easy to flatter and please people by asking them for two hours of drinks and canapés at your house.

And they loved her in Palazzo for doing it. So generous of Miss East, the board always said, above and beyond what Miss East needed to do for them. It bought her further goodwill. Their admiration was unstinting. Joy East could invite clients, press people, foreign contacts, and local dignitaries into her house with such ease. She hired caterers and then contracted cleaners afterward. Joy told Frank that it was no trouble; in fact, it was positively useful. She had her house cleaned once a month professionally, she had a freezer full of hors d'oeuvres. She always cleared away her ornaments and valuables before any gathering. You never knew if strangers might be light-fingered, much better to leave out forty big blue glass bowls as ashtrays. They had cost one pound each in some warehouse. She had another forty in a cardboard box in the garage on a high shelf over the small sports car.

Frank Quigley, the handsome Managing Director of Palazzo, and Joy East, the Design Consultant who had been in charge of Palazzo's image, from its Art Deco building to its smart carrier bags, had been having an affair for three years and they both could say with certainty that nobody knew about it. They were not fooling themselves like so many other lovers in the world who believed that they were invisible. They knew that nobody else had the slightest suspicion. Because they had been very careful and they had lived by a set of rules.

They never telephoned each other except on legitimate business for the company. And Joy made no telephone calls to the Quigley apartment about anything at all. Once the affair had gotten under way, Renata was never brought to Joy East's house, whatever the social occasion. Frank Quigley felt that it would be undignified for his wife to be entertained in a house where he himself had been entertained so many afternoons a week in a very different sense of the word. Frank would not let his wife lay her fur coat across the wide bed where he and Joy had spent so many hours. Even though he swore to himself that Renata would never learn of the relationship, he still felt that he owed it to her not to betray her by pretending to be an equal guest in a house which was in reality so much his home. He didn't think about any other kind of betrayal, because Frank had always believed that his strongest quality was an ability to compartmentalize his life. He had always been able to do this. He never thought of his violent, drunken father and his weak, forgiving mother . . . not since he had left them to live in London. But when he had returned to visit them and his brothers and sisters, who had never left the small town in the West of Ireland, he brought no tales and even no thoughts of his London life back with him. He had managed to come back if not exactly shabby then at least unkempt. None of them would have guessed at his life-style in the business world and the social life of retailing. He had bought Renata a shapeless tweed coat for her one duty visit there and had told her they should play down the comfort they enjoyed back in Wembley. Renata had understood very quickly; she had gone almost wordlessly to help in the kitchen with the women while Frank had talked to his brothers and offered a little investment here and buying into something there . . . all of them polite ways of giving money without being seen to do so. During the four days he had spent in the place where he had grown up, his leather briefcase and handmade shoes were locked in the trunk of the hired car with Renata's silk scarves and jewelry box.

Frank had said that you diminished everything by trailing one life and one set of memories with you. Better far to live whatever life you were living at the moment to the full with no connecting links.

So a wife could not be brought unawares to the house of a mistress.

Similarly, when the Quigleys entertained, as they always did at Christmas, Miss East would be said to be out of town. They met on common ground, all right, like at his father-in-law's, but the conversation was always about work. Frank was literally able to divorce himself from the other side of their life together and talk guiltlessly about plans and projects. He got none of the sense of illicit excitement that he knew others felt about an extramarital affair. He knew that Joy felt the same. She must have felt the same. After all, it was she who had laid down the ground rules.

Joy had been direct in saying they would have no sense of overresponsibility to each other. She was not going to suffer the agonies of the typical Other Woman, she had assured him. There would be no image of poor Joy sitting alone with a sandwich on Christmas Day listening to "Jingle Bells" on the radio. No, she'd been thirty when she'd met him, and she had lived ten years more or less alone. She had a hundred places to go for Christmas and would spend no time feeling abandoned. They would take the time they could have without destroying either their careers or their plans for the future. She was free as the air to go where she pleased without consulting him. If a trip to the States came up, she would take it, and he could find other ways of filling those afternoon hours until she returned.

It had been idyllic . . . yes, a real afternoon idyll over three years. In summertime they often sat and drank cold white wine and peeled each other pears and peaches in the warm walled garden. In winter, they sat on the thick rich carpet beside the fire and watched pictures in the flames. At no time did they ever say what a pity that they couldn't get away together for a week, for a holiday, or for a lifetime. Renata's name was never mentioned between them. Nor was David, the name of the man in the advertising agency who had great hopes about the lovely Joy East and sent her large bouquets of flowers. Sometimes she went out with him on weekends, but so great was the sense of independence between Frank and Joy that Frank never asked whether they slept together or if David's attentions were in any way a threat to his own position. He assumed that David had been kept at arm's length with a convincing story about work and not wishing to get involved.

Frank had listened to the stories of colleagues, men who had had, as they put it, a little fun, played around a bit, thought they had a good thing going. Always and in every case there had been some disastrous turnabout of events. And it was invariably obvious and predictable to the outsider but never to the man involved. Frank examined his own relationship with Joy as minutely as he would have examined a contract or a proposition put to him in his office. If there were any flaws, then he couldn't see them. Not until the Christmas party at Palazzo last year, which was when the trouble had begun. And even then it had been small and insignificant. At first.

It was all very clearly etched on his mind. Supermarkets found it hard to have Christmas parties like other firms did, since they were literally serving the public at all hours. But Frank was ever mindful of the importance of some kind of ceremony and group loyalty, particularly at a festive time.

Frank had persuaded Carlo to have the party on the Sunday before Christmas each year. It would be a lunchtime party, with Carlo as Santa Claus for the kiddies. Wives and children all came, there were small gifts for everyone and paper hats, and because it was a family day out, the usual office party nonsense didn't happen, with young secretaries being sick behind the filing cabinets and older managers making fools of themselves doing a striptease.

Renata had always loved it and was very good with the children, organizing games, and decorating with paper streamers. Every year for as long as he could remember, Frank's father-in-law had looked fondly at his daughter and said that she was so wonderful with the bambinos, wasn't it a pity that there were no bambinos of their own. Every year Frank had shrugged and said that the ways of the Lord were strange.

"It's not for lack of loving," he would say regularly, and Carlo would nod gravely and suggest that perhaps Frank should eat more steaks; a lot of red meat never did a man any harm. Every year, with patience and a smile fixed easily on his face. It was a small price to pay, it was not intended as humiliation, it wasn't received as such. Frank took it as an old man's affectionate and perhaps tact-lessly expressed regret. It was one of the few areas where he humored Carlo Palazzo. In business they spoke as equals, always.

But last Christmas the party had been different. Joy East was usually in charge of decorating the big warehouse where they had the festivities. Not the actual work of pinning crepe up on the walls and laying out the trestles with the sausage rolls and mince pies, of course, but with organizing a color scheme, providing huge paper ornaments or giant sunflowers, as she had done one year. Arranging for someone to make mighty bells out of silver paper. Seeing to it that a big green baize-covered table full of gifts be arranged for Santa Claus Carlo and that the photographer from the local and sometimes even national papers be present. Together Frank and Joy had organized a huge Christmas calendar that would have the name of every employee on it. It cost practically nothing to print, and yet everyone who worked in Palazzo took it home proudly to keep for the next year. It sometimes changed their mind if they were thinking of leaving. It was hard to leave a place where you were so highly thought of as family that they put your name among the names of board members and senior managers on the calendar.

Last Christmas Joy said she was going to be away in the time before the party. There was this packaging fair she really had to go to. It was important; she needed new ideas.

"But that's on every year at this time and you don't go," Frank had com-plained.

"Are you telling me what I can do and can't do?" Her voice had been steely.

"Of course not. It's just that it's become such a tradition . . . your ideas for the Christmas party . . . always. Long before you and I . . . always."

"And you thought that it would always be so . . . long after you and I?"

"What is this, Joy? If you're trying to say something, say it." He had been brusque to cover his shock.

"Oh, I'm never trying to say anything, I assure you. I really assure you of that. Either I say it or I don't say it. There's no question of trying to say anything."

He had looked at her sharply; her voice had sounded slurred when she was repeating the word *assure*. It was unthinkable that Joy East had been drinking, drinking in the middle of the day. He put the suspicion out of his mind.

"That's good then," he had said with false joviality, "because I'm the same. If I want to say something, I say it. We're two of a kind, Joy."

She had smiled at him oddly, he thought.

When she returned from the packaging fair, they met as had been arranged at her house. One of the many things that made it all so safe was that Joy really did work from home in a small, bright studio filled with light, and Frank did have legitimate reason to call on her. But even better, her house was very near the offices of the firm of accountants they used as tax advisers. Frank had even more legitimate reason to visit them regularly. If his car was ever seen in the area, he was well covered.

Joy said she hadn't done much at the packaging fair. It was Mickey Mouse stuff.

"Then why did you go?" Frank had asked, irritated.

He had been responsible for finding other people to take over Joy's work in preparing the hall for the party, and nobody had anything like her flair.

"For a change, for a rest, for some time off," she had said, considering her words.

"Jesus, I never think a trade fair is a rest," he had said.

"It is if you hardly leave your room in the hotel."

"And what did you do in your room in the hotel that was so important?" His voice was cold.

"I never said it was important, now did I?"

"No."

"It wasn't at all important what I did in my room. I read the catalogs, I had room service, I had a lot of nice cold white wine. Oh, and I had a nice Scotsman, head of a stationery firm. But nothing at all important."

Frank's face had gone white, but he was still in control. "Is this meant to hurt me?" he asked.

"But how could it? We're two of a kind, you've often said it. You have your life with your wife, I have my life with the odd ship that passes in the night. Nothing hurtful there."

They were lying in her bed. Frank reached out for a cigarette from the slim case on the bedside table.

"I usually prefer you not to smoke here. It does sort of linger in the curtains," Joy said.

"I usually don't need to smoke here, but the things you're saying sort of linger in my mind and make me anxious," he said, lighting up.

"Ah, it is all a game, isn't it?" Joy said perfectly amicably. "I thought about this a long time while I was away. What you and I have is not love, not one of those great passions that make people do foolish things . . . it's just a game. Like tennis, one person serves, the other returns it."

"It's much more than a game . . ." he began.

"Or like chess." Joy was dreamy now. "One person makes a crafty move, and then the other responds to it with something even craftier."

"You know very well what we have. There's no point in finding fancy words for it. We love each other . . . but we have set limits to this love, you and I. And we admire each other and we're happy together."

"It's a game," she repeated.

"Well, people who go out to play a game of golf or squash or chess together are friends, Joy. For God's sake, you don't decide to spend a day with someone you don't like. Use this example if it gives you pleasure, keep saying *game, game, game.* But it doesn't mean anything. It doesn't change anything. We're just the same, you and I."

"Oh, you *are* playing it well." She laughed admiringly. "Trying to diffuse it all, asking no questions about whether there really was a Scotsman or not. I think you'd be a very dangerous adversary in a game."

He put out his cigarette and reached for her again. He held her close to him and spoke into her long, shiny hair with its stripes of gold among the brown and its smell of lemony shampoo.

"Well, so would you . . . a terrifying adversary. Isn't it just as well that we're the best of friends and the best of lovers and not enemies at all?"

But he had spoken more cheerfully than he felt, and her body had not been responsive to him. She had a half-smile that was disturbing and had nothing at all to do with any pleasure which she might or might not have been feeling.

At the party Joy was dressed in a dazzling navy and white dress. The gleaming white collar was cut low into her cleavage, revealing a lot of breast and an expensive lace-trimmed brassiere. Her hair seemed to shine like gold and copper. She looked ten years younger than thirty-three, she looked like a young beautiful girl on the prowl. Frank watched her with alarm as she moved through the crowds of Palazzo employees. This time there was no doubt about it; she had been drinking. And well before she arrived at the party.

Frank felt a cold knot of nervousness in his stomach. Joy sober he could cope with easily, but she was an unknown quantity drunk. His father's terrible and unpredictable rages flashed before him suddenly. He remembered the time that the entire dinner had been thrown into the fire in a fit of temper . . . nearly forty years ago but as clear as yesterday. And what had always stuck in Frank's mind was that his father had not intended to do it; he had wanted to eat his dinner, as he told them over and over all night. It had given Frank a fear of drunks; he drank very little himself and he scanned his managers and sales force for signs of the bottle. It was the feeling that you couldn't rely on someone who was so dangerous. They would probably be all right, but you couldn't be sure. He looked at Joy East's flashing smile and low neckline as she cruised around the room, ever refilling her glass at the trestle tables, and he felt not at all sure that the day would end all right.

Her first target was Carlo, struggling offstage into his Santa outfit.

"Wonderful, Mr. Palazzo," she said. "Wonderful, you go out and knock them dead, tell them what Santa will put in their pay envelopes if they're good little girls and boys and work like good little ants."

Carlo looked puzzled. Frank acted quickly to draw her away.

"Joy, where are the tubs for the children? Please?" His voice was urgent.

She came up close to him and he saw that her eyes were not focusing properly.

"Where are the tubs?" she asked. "The tubs are being presided over by your wife. The saintly Renata. Santa Renata." Her face broke into a big smile. "That would be a nice song . . . Santa Renata . . ." She sang it to the tune of "Santa Lucia" and seemed pleased with it, so she sang it a little louder. Frank moved slightly away. He had to get her out. Soon.

At that very moment Renata appeared to explain that the pink wrapping paper was on the gifts for girls and the blue for boys. One year her father had given the girls horrible monsters and spiders and the boys comb-and-mirror sets. This time they were taking no chances.

"That's right, Renata, take no chances," Joy said.

Renata looked at her, startled. Never had she seen Joy East looking like this.

"You look . . . very smart . . . very elegant," Renata said.

"Thank you, Renata, *grazie, grazie mille,*" Joy said, bowing flamboyantly.

"I have not seen you wear clothes like this and look so full of life before." Renata spoke quietly but with a little awe in her voice. She fingered the edge of her expensive but very muted woolen jacket. It had probably cost four times as much as the striking garment that Joy was wearing, but Renata looked like a bird of little plumage, dark hair, sallow skin, and designer suit in lilac and pink colors with a braid of lilac-colored suede at the edge of the jacket, nothing to catch the eye. Nothing at all.

Joy looked at Renata steadily.

"I'll tell you why I look so different. I have a man. A man in my life. That's what makes all the difference."

Joy smiled around her, delighted with the attention from Nico Palazzo, who was Carlo's brother, and from Desmond Doyle and a group of senior management who were all in the circle. Renata smiled, too, but uncertainly. She didn't know quite what response she was meant to make, and her eyes raked the group as if to find Frank, who would know what to say.

Frank stood with the feeling that the ice in his stomach had broken and he was now awash with icy water. There was nothing he could do. It was the sense of powerlessness that made him feel almost faint.

"Was I telling you about this man, Frank?" Joy asked roguishly. "You see me only as a career woman . . . but there's room for love and passion as well."

"I'm sure there is."

Frank spoke as if he were patting down a mad dog. Even if he had no connection with Joy, they would have expected him to be like this. Soothing, distant, and eventually making his escape. They must all see now what condition she was in; they must have noticed. Was it only because he knew her so intimately, had traced every feature of her face and body for three years with his hands, that he realized she was out of control? Everyone around seemed to be treating it all as normal Christmas high spirits. If he could stop her just now, before she said anything else, then all might not be lost.

Joy was aware she had an audience and was enjoying it. She put on a little-girl voice that he had never heard her use before. She looked very silly, he thought quite dispassionately. In her sober state she would be the first to criticize any other woman with an assumed, lisping voice.

"But it's forbidden in this company to love anyone except Palazzo. Isn't that right? We all love Palazzo, we must have no other love."

They laughed, even Nico laughed, they were taking it as good-natured banter.

"Oh, yes, first love the company, then other loves," Nico said.

"It's infidelity to love anyone else better," Desmond Doyle said, laughing.

Frank flashed him a grateful look; poor Desmond, his old pal from those long-ago days in Ireland, was helping him inadvertently, he was taking the heat off. Maybe he could be encouraged to say more.

"Well, you've never been unfaithful, Desmond," Frank said, loosening his collar. "You're certainly a long and loyal Palazzo man." He felt sick to his stomach after he said it, remembering suddenly the time that Desmond had been allowed to go after the rationalization and how he had to fight hard to get him reinstated. But Desmond didn't seem to see the irony. Desmond was about to answer with something cheerful when the voice of Joy East cut in again.

"No one should be married except to the company. When you join Palazzo, you must marry the place, marry Palazzo. Very hard to do. Very hard. Except for you, Frank. You managed it all right, didn't you? You really *did* marry a Palazzo!"

Even Nico, who was very slow, must have realized by now that something was wrong. Frank had to move quickly. But he must not appear to be rattled. He must take it indulgently as anyone would take the public idiocy of a normally exemplary colleague.

"Yes, you're right, and I'm glad you reminded me, because my father-in-law will be down on us all like a ton of bricks if we don't get the presents going soon. Renata, should we get the children to line up now . . . or does somebody make an announcement? Or what?"

In other years Joy East had arranged everything like clockwork. Renata had a look of relief all over her face. She had thought that there had been an insult, a jibe, but obviously since Frank didn't see one, she had been wrong.

"I think we should tell Papa that the time has come," she said, and moved away toward her father.

"I think we should tell Papa that the time has come," Joy said to nobody in particular.

Desmond Doyle and Nico Palazzo exchanged puzzled looks.

"Joy, you must be tired after all that busy time at the packaging conference," Frank Quigley said loudly. "If you like, I can run you home now before it all gets too exhausting here."

He saw the relief on a few faces around him. Mr. Quigley was always the one to cope with the situation, any situation.

His smile was hard and distant as he looked at Joy. It said in very definite terms that this was her one chance to get out of what she had walked them into. There wouldn't be any other chances. His smile said that he was not afraid.

Joy looked at him for a few seconds.

"All right," she said. "Let's say I'm tired after the packaging conference, tired and very, very emotional, and that I need to be taken home."

"Let's say that then," Frank said easily. "Tell Renata to save me a nice boy present from Santa Claus," he called out. "I'll be right back to collect it."

They looked at him in admiration as he led Miss East, who was behaving most oddly, out of the big hall and toward the parking lot.

There was complete silence in the car, not one word spoken between them. At her door she handed him her small handbag and he took out the key. On the low glass table was a bottle of vodka with one third of it gone and some orange juice. A heap of unopened Christmas cards and a small, smart suitcase, as if she were going on or had come back from a journey. With a shock he realized that she must not have unpacked her case after her trip to that conference.

"Coffee?" he asked. It was the first word spoken.

"No thanks."

"Mineral water?"

"If you insist."

"I don't insist. I couldn't care less what you drink, but I wouldn't give a dog any more alcohol than you've had already."

His voice was icy cold.

Joy looked up at him from the chair where she had sat down immediately.

"You hate drink because your father was such a drunk," she said.

"You're telling me what I told you. Have you any further insights or shall I go back to the party?"

"You'd like to hit me, but you can't, because you saw your father beating your mother," she said, a crooked smile on her face.

"Very good, Joy, well done." His hand was clenched, and he would have liked to have struck something, a chair, even a wall to get rid of the tension he felt.

"I said nothing that wasn't true. Nothing at all."

"No, indeed, and you said it beautifully. I'm going now."

"You are not going, Frank. You are going to sit down and listen to me."

"Now that's where you're wrong. Since I did have a drunk for a father, I am only too used to listening to drunks. It's a useless exercise. They don't remember anything the next day. Try telephoning the time. Tell it all to them, they love a good sob story from people with enough drink in them to float a navy."

"You have to listen, Frank, you have to know."

"Another time, a time when you can pronounce my name without stumbling over it."

"About the conference. I wasn't there."

"So you said, you told me. A Scotsman . . . well, well. Don't tell me it's preying on your mind?"

"I wasn't anywhere near it. I didn't leave London."

Her voice was odd; she seemed to have sobered up a bit.

"So?" He was still poised to go.

"I went to a nursing home." She paused. "To have an abortion."

He put his car keys in his pocket and came back into the room.

"I'm sorry," he said, "Very sorry."

"You needn't be." She didn't look at him.

"But why, how . . . ?"

"The pill didn't suit me. I changed the type several times, but still . . ."

"You should have told me." He was gentle now. Forgiving.

"No, it was my decision."

"I know, I know. But still . . ."

"And so I went to this place . . . very nice place, actually, it's a real nursing home for other things, too, not just terminations, as they call them." Her voice shook a little.

He laid his hand over hers, the coldness was forgotten. "And was it very bad, was it awful?" His eyes were full of concern.

"No." Her face was bright, and she smiled at him, a smile only a little lopsided. "No, it wasn't awful at all. Because when I went in there and went to my room, I sat and thought for a while, and I thought, Why am I doing this? Why am I getting rid of a human being? I would *like* another human being around me. I would like a son or a daughter. So I changed my mind. I told them I had decided not to go through with the termination. And I went to a hotel instead, for a couple of days, then I came back here."

He looked at her, stricken.

"This can't be true."

"Oh, yes, it's true. So now you see why you couldn't just toddle off back to the party. You had to know. It was only fair that you should know. And know everything."

If he lived to be an old man, something that his doctor said was highly unlikely, Frank Quigley would never forget that moment. The day he learned he was going to be a father, but not the father of Renata's child, not the father who would be congratulated and embraced by the Palazzo tribe. A father who would be ostracized and cut off from the life he had built for himself for a quarter of a century. He would never forget her face as she told him, knowing that for the first time in their very equal relationship she held all the cards. Knowing that drunk and upset and having broken all their rules, she was still the one in charge. Because of biology, which said that the women bore the children, she was winning, and that was the only reason. Frank Quigley would not have been beaten by anything except the human reproductive system.

He had played it just right, of course, at the time. He had telephoned back to base and said that Joy needed a bit of attention. He had sat down and talked to her, but his mind was in overdrive. His words were soothing and supportive; his real thoughts were taking a journey into the future.

He allowed his real reactions only a moment's indulgence while he relished the thought that he had fathered a child. If Carlo knew, there would be a lot less of the chat about eating more red meat. If Carlo knew. Carlo must never know. And Renata would be hurt beyond repair. Not only at the infidelity, the knowledge that an affair had been going on under her very nose for years, but at the fact that this woman had produced a child, the one thing that Renata had failed to do.

As he stroked Joy's fevered forehead and assured her of loyalty and his great pleasure at the news and the way that things had turned out, Frank was working out logically and coldly what he must do next, what avenues were open to him.

As he urged cups of weak tea and thinly sliced bread and butter on the weeping Joy, he listed the possibilities that lay ahead and the disadvantages of each one. When he found the one that had the least dangerous mine field attached to it, that was where he would head.

Joy could have the child, and he would acknowledge that it was his. He would say that he did not intend to leave his marriage but felt in fairness that the son or daughter should grow up knowing the care of a father. He considered this for seconds, only to dismiss it.

In a more liberated society this would work. But not with the Palazzos. Not for one minute.

Suppose Joy were to say that she was having the child and that the identity of the father was to remain unknown, undiscussed? Again not something beyond the imaginings in the 1980s for a liberated woman. But again this was the world of Palazzo. It would be frowned upon, it would be speculated about, and worst of all, if Joy were ever to hit the bottle again, it would all be revealed.

Suppose he were to deny paternity. Literally say that Joy was lying? He wondered why he had even considered this route. Joy was a woman he had intended to spend a great amount of time with; he didn't love her only for the good sex they had, he loved her mind and her reactions to things. Frank asked himself why this possibility had crossed his mind. He had never thought of stabbing Carlo in the back and taking over the company. He had not decided to woo and win Renata only for her money and position. He was not that kind of bastard. So why even entertain the idea of turning his back on the woman who had been his lover for three years, the woman who was going to bear his child? He looked at her, slack-jawed and awkward in the chair. He realized with a shudder how much he feared drink and the effects of it. He knew that whatever happened now, he would never be able to trust Joy or trust himself to her again.

Suppose he were to persuade her to have the termination, for everyone's sake? There were still two weeks in which it would be safe. Perhaps he could persuade her.

But if he couldn't, then he risked a hysterical response. And if she were to go ahead and have the child, knowing that he wanted it aborted, then things would be about as bad as they could ever be.

Suppose he were to ask her to go away, to start a new life with a set of glowing references. Joy move away from London? Joy start life afresh with a small baby just to please Frank? It was unthinkable.

Suppose he were to ask her to give the child to him. Suppose that he and Renata were to adopt this baby. The child would inherit the Palazzo millions. Everyone would be pleased. Frank and Renata had done the rounds of the adoption societies; at forty-six he was too old to be an adoptive father. Not a real father as it turned out, but then nature was never known to be a great supporter of bureaucracy.

But Joy had deliberately decided to have the child because she wanted another human being around her. She would not consider it. Or not now, at any rate. Don't dismiss it utterly. She might, later on in the pregnancy. It was unlikely yet not impossible.

And then it would be adopting his own child. That would be very satisfying. In honesty he would have to tell Renata, but they need not tell her family.

Frank stroked the forehead, administered the cups of tea, and thought his own thoughts as he consoled Joy East with murmurs and sounds that would never constitute any kind of promise or contract in the unlikely event of their being recalled.

The weeks had passed somehow. The bad behavior at the Christmas party was hardly commented upon, Frank was as usual congratulated for having as usual averted any little silliness. Joy was back at work, head held high in the new year, plans and ideas tripping out of her. There were no recurrences of drinking. Also, there were no lazy afternoons by her fireside.

They met for lunch early in the new year. Frank had said in front of several of the managers that the place was lacking in anything new. What it needed in these days after Christmas was some pizzazz. He would take Joy East out to lunch and have a brainstorming session, he said. Women always loved a business lunch, and he wouldn't mind one himself. They went to the best restaurant, where they were bound to be seen.

She sipped her diet tonic water, and he drained his tomato juice.

"An expense-account lunch is wasted on us." Joy smiled at him.

"As you told me that time, I'm a drunk's son. I'm afraid of drink," he said.

"Did I say that? I don't really remember all the things I said that day. Is that why you don't come to me in the afternoons?"

"No, it's not that," he said.

"Well, why not? I mean, there's no need for any precautions now, it would be like bolting the stable after the horse had fled . . . we should get value . . ." Her smile was warm and welcoming. Like the old Joy.

"It might be bad for you. They say it's not good at this stage of the pregnancy," he said.

She smiled, pleased that he was caring. "But you could come and talk to me anyway, couldn't you? I've waited a lot of afternoons."

That was true, she had kept her word about not contacting him. Ever.

"We do have to talk," he said.

"So why are we trying to talk in a restaurant where everyone sees us? Those women over there, they're in-laws of Nico Palazzo. They haven't had their eyes off us since we came in."

"We will be seen in public for the rest of our lives. This is exactly where we must discuss how our lives will continue. If we go to your house, we slip into the old ways, we're back in the days when we only had ourselves to consider." His voice was calm. But she seemed to sense his anxiety.

"You mean, you wanted a get-away car and witnesses if I'm going to tell you anything unpalatable. Is that it?"

"Don't be silly, Joy."

"No, I'm not being silly, you're trying to get out of it, aren't you? You're actually scared to death."

"That's not so, and stop smiling that smile that isn't a real smile. It's a paper-thin smile you put on for customers and contacts. It's not genuine."

"And what was ever genuine about *your* smile, Frank? Did you not know your smile never reached your eyes, never? It stopped always around the mouth."

"Why are we talking like this?" he asked.

"Because you are full of fear, I can smell it," she said.

"What's turned you against me, did I say anything?" He spread his hand out in wonder.

"You don't need to make those Italian gestures at me, I'm not a Palazzo. What did you say? I'll tell you what you said. You said we should sit down in a public place and make decisions about the rest of our lives. You forget that I know you, Frank, you forget that you and I know when you meet an adversary, the first rule is to meet him on common ground, not your territory or his. You're doing that. We both know that if there's a danger of a row, the rule is: Make sure the meeting is held in a public place. It stops people from making scenes."

"Are you feeling all right, Joy? Seriously?"

"It won't necessarily work, you know, drunk or sober. At home or out I could make a scene if I wanted to." She looked mulish.

"Of course you could, what *is* this? We're friends, you and I, where's the hostility?"

"We are not friends, we are fencing with each other, we are playing games, looking for the advantage . . ."

"Well, then, if that's all we are, what on earth are we having a child together for?"

"We're not having a child together," Joy East said. *"I am having a child."*

There was a look of triumph on her face like he had seen only when she had beaten a rival, won an award, or somehow gotten her way against all the odds.

It was then he knew that she intended him to dangle there, forever watching his step, forever in her power. It was her child and her decision, but only for as long as it suited her. She was never going to promise him either secrecy or involvement. Her plan was that he should never know. That he would be forever tied to her.

Frank Quigley had come across schemes like this before, the supplier who had bought up the market but hadn't told you. He would want you to advertise the produce and then suddenly could raise the price because you were committed. Frank had dealt with that one in his time. Someone had tried it on him, but only once. Frank had smiled and said there was no way he was going to pay more than the agreed price for the product. But wouldn't they look foolish, the man had said, having spent all that money advertising it and then having to admit they didn't have it? No, not at all. Frank had smiled back with easy charm.

They would just take out another advertisement apologizing that the suppliers had proved unreliable. Everyone would think well of Palazzo for its honesty, the suppliers would be ruined. It had been so simple. But then it had only involved fruit, it hadn't involved a child.

He had brought into play every available ounce of charm that he possessed, and limp as a wet rag at the end of the lunch, he congratulated himself that they were at least speaking normally on the surface.

They talked about the company. Twice he made her laugh, real laughter, head thrown back and pealing with mirth. The two women who she had said were Nico's in-laws looked over with interest. But there was nothing for them to take home with them as gossip, this was the most innocent lunch in the history of the world. Otherwise it would not have been here and in full view of everyone.

He had told her about his Christmas, and then she told him about hers. She had gone to stay with friends in Sussex. In a big family home where she had been before, full of children, she said.

"Did you tell them?" he asked. He felt the conversation must not be allowed to wander too far from what they were both thinking about lest he be labeled callous.

"Tell them what?" she asked.

"About the baby?"

"Whose baby?"

"Your baby. Our baby if you like, but basically, as you said, your baby."

Joy gave a little purr of satisfaction. It was almost as if she were saying, "That's better. That's more like it."

"No," she said. "I'm not telling anyone until I've decided what to do."

And then there was no more. They spoke as they always had about plans and schemes and the inadvisability of letting Nico know anything at all that was taking place. The wisdom of Palazzo's buying the new site in that area which was meant to be coming up—Joy was afraid it was coming up too fast. The big houses were changing hands for a lot of money and then even more money needed to be spent on them to make them smart. That kind of people would shop in fancy delicatessens or even go into Harrods, she felt, Palazzo's would be wiser to aim for somewhere less ambitious, somewhere where you could get a huge parking lot. That's the way things were going now.

"We could even try to make a feature out of the parking lot," Joy had said excitedly. "You know how gloomy they look at best, and how they look like places you're going to be murdered in at worst. Perhaps it could all be brightly painted and there could be a covered terrace around it, a type of cloister effect, we could rent space to market stalls, give the place more life . . ."

She had been talking in terms of staying on, Frank had noted.

Joy East, if she were planning anything at all, planned to take three months' maternity leave and return to work once her child was born. Frank was not going to be informed about his role. That was the way she was going to play the game.

He had left that lunch white with fury, far angrier and even more determined to regain control than he had been before Christmas. He would not be left suspended like this.

If she would not reveal her intentions like any normal person, then he was not going to respond normally.

Two could play a game of cat and mouse.

Long before Joy mentioned her pregnancy to anyone else, Frank had made his contingency plan.

Based entirely on Joy's own projections about the need not to go too far upmarket for their customers, Frank Quigley commissioned surveys.

He had explained to the young men and women in the market-research bureau that they wanted confirmation of their belief that they should expand into less well-off areas. The survey was to be done nationwide but on a very small sample. It was the kind of survey which if Frank had seen cold he would have dismissed on the ground that its findings could not possibly be conclusive. But this time he wanted to let the board see from an outside agency that the way forward was to expand and to leave North London far behind. To open up on a trial basis in the Midlands, in the North of England even. The key to it would be design and image. Palazzo was to be presented as stylish and desirable. Joy East was the one to create that image.

It would be promotion, it would be a seat on the board for Joy. He would see her once a month at board meetings, true, but he would not see her every day.

And she would not see his father-in-law every day.

And she would not be in danger of meeting his wife.

He had few weapons, he had to outwit her by cunning.

She had to think that the promotion, the move, and the change were against his wishes.

The survey, which Carlo Palazzo fondly believed he had commissioned himself, was complete by March, when Joy East broke her news with maximum drama. She announced it under the heading of Any Other Business at the weekly management meeting.

Her eyes had been suspiciously bright. Frank knew what was coming.

"Well, I suppose this *is* other business in a way. I bring it up in case you should hear it elsewhere and wonder why I had said nothing of it to my colleagues. I will be seeking three months' maternity leave in July. . . . Obviously I'll work around it to make sure that any promotions are well covered, but I felt you should know that it was upcoming." She smiled around sweetly, meeting the eyes of the fifteen men in the room.

Carlo was at a total loss. "Well, heavens, good Lord, I did not even know you were thinking of getting married . . . my congratulations."

"Oh, no, nothing as settled as that, I'm afraid." A tinkly laugh. "Just a child. We don't want too much of a shock to the system like getting married as well."

Nico's jaw dropped, the others shuffled their praise and pleasure, but looking sideways at Carlo and Frank to try to gauge the mood of the meeting.

Frank Quigley looked pleasantly surprised and admiringly amused.

"This is very exciting news, Joy," he said evenly. "Everyone is delighted for you. I don't know what we'll do without you for three months, but will you be able to come back to us after that?"

The inquiry was warm and courteous; nobody could have seen the way their eyes locked hard across the table.

"Oh, yes, indeed. I've been busy making arrangements. These things aren't done lightly, you know."

"No, indeed," he said soothingly.

By this stage Carlo had recovered enough control to be able to murmur a few pleasantries, but he called Frank to his office.

"What are we going to do?" he asked.

"Carlo, it's 1985, it's not the Middle Ages. She can have thirty children if she wants to. You're not shocked, are you?"

"Yes, of course I am. Who is the father, do you think? Is it anybody at Palazzo?"

Frank felt he was acting a part in a play. "Why should it be? Joy has a full life of her own outside here."

"But why, why on earth?"

"Perhaps she felt she is in her thirties, she is alone, she might just *want* to."

"It's a very inconsiderate thing to do," Carlo grumbled. "And inconvenient, too. Look at the way it will upset our plans for the north."

Frank spoke very carefully. "When were you hoping to get that operational, not until the new year? Its planning stages will only be coming on stream in autumn when she comes back to work . . ."

"Yes, but . . ."

"But doesn't it suit you down to the ground, not that you should *say* that to her, of course? You were already worried that she might not want the move. Now that she's having a child, it might be just what she'd need: new environment, fresh start, more space and room up there, away from London . . ."

"Yes . . ." Carlo was doubtful. "I think this has thrown a big wrench in the works."

"Then if that's where you want her, you should make it sound very, very attractive for her. Put it to her in a way that it seems just the right step for her to take . . ."

"Perhaps *you* should explain it to her."

"No, Carlo." For the second time Frank felt that he was actually acting out a part onstage. "No, because you see, in a way I don't want to lose her from the London side of things, even though I think in my heart you're right. It's best for the company that she should go up north and get Palazzo into a different league, a national league."

"That's what I thought," Carlo said, believing it.

"So I'm the wrong one to persuade her."

"Suppose she thinks I am banishing her away?"

"She can't think that, Carlo. Haven't you all the documentation and surveys and inquiries to prove you were thinking of it ages back?"

Carlo nodded. He had, of course.

Frank let the breath out slowly between his teeth. Nowhere in that whole paperwork did Frank Quigley's name appear; in fact, in the files there were several letters dissenting slightly and wondering whether Miss East would be better kept in London. He couldn't be faulted now.

Frank did not have long to wait. Joy burst into his office, eyes blazing and clutching a piece of paper in her hand.

"Is this your doing?" she asked.

"I have no idea what you're talking about." He was bland, unruffled.

"Like hell you don't. You're sending me away. By God, you're not going to get away with this, Frank. I'm not going to be shunted out of your sight when things get too hot to handle."

"Sit down," he said.

"Don't tell me what to do."

He walked past her and called out to his secretary in the next room. "Diana, can we have a big pot of coffee? Miss East and I are about to have a row and we need fuel."

"Don't think I'm bowled over by that kind of witticism," Joy said.

"It wasn't a witticism, it was the plain, unvarnished truth. Now what *is* this about? Is this Carlo's plan to put you on the board and give you responsibility for the expansion?"

"Carlo's plan, don't give me Carlo's plan. It's your plan to get rid of me."

His eyes were cold. "Don't let's add paranoia to everything else."

"To what else, what else are you talking about?"

His voice was low and hard. "I'll tell you what else. You and I loved each other, I still love you. We agreed to make love, you were the one looking after contraception. When it no longer worked for you to look after it, it would have been fair to tell me and let me be in charge of that side. Yes, Joy, that would have been the fair thing. It was not fair to allow me to let you conceive a child by accident."

"I would have thought you'd be glad to prove you were able to," she snapped.

"No. You would have thought wrong. Then to continue your unfairness, you will not let me know what your plans are for the child we conceived. I have agreed that it's your responsibility if that's what you want. You said you would let me know. You have not let me know. You have played some kind of game with me throughout. I don't know any more than I knew at Christmastime."

She was silent.

"And now you come screaming in here with some cock-and-bull story that I'm banishing you off to the provinces, whereas the truth is that I did everything in my power to get you to stay here. You can believe this or not as you wish, but that is the case."

There was a knock on the door, and Diana came in with the coffee. She laid it on the desk between them.

"Is the row over?" she asked.

"No, it's just getting to the peak." Frank smiled.

"I don't believe you," Joy said when Diana had left. "Carlo never had a thought of his own."

Frank went to a file and showed her a letter. In black and white it said that it might be a waste of Joy East's capabilities to have her tied up away from the nerve center of the business. He told her that there were more. He could find them if she needed proof.

"Then it's Carlo, he can't bear the shameless unmarried mother bit . . . it's he who's sending me away."

"Joy, I warned you about the danger of paranoia. If you look through these files, that survey was commissioned back in January. Months before you made your announcement."

"That bloody survey. Who are they anyway? They seem like a Mickey Mouse outfit to me," she grumbled.

Frank had a moment's regret. She was so sharp, no complaint, and bright; her thinking was exactly on the same line as his own. What a pity that it had to end in this acrimony and game-playing.

"Well, however they are, Carlo believes everything they say, and they may have a point, you know. You said a lot of it yourself already, long ago, before all this."

"I know." She had to admit that this was true.

"So what will you do?"

"I'll make up my own mind without any patronizing pats on the head from you," she said.

"As you wish, Joy, but may I remind you, this is *my* office and it was *you* who came to see me. It's not unreasonable that I should ask, since you seem determined to involve me."

"When I've decided what I'm going to do, I'll let you know," she said.

"You said that before."

"But that was only about *my* child. This is about *your* company. You have a right to know."

He sat for a long time staring ahead of him after she left, her cup of coffee undrunk. He thought she had looked frightened and a little uncertain. But perhaps he was only imagining it.

She was a clever woman, and she knew that she could make him sweat it out, not knowing what she was going to say next and where she was going to say it.

He thought about it again that evening in their apartment. Renata sat on one side of their big marble fireplace looking into the flames, and he sat on the other. There were often long, companionable silences between them. But that night he said nothing at all.

Renata eventually spoke.

"Is it boring sometimes being with me in the evenings?" There was no complaint in her voice. She was asking as she might have asked the time or whether they should turn on the news on television.

"No, it's not boring," Frank said truthfully. "It's restful, actually."

"That is good," Renata said, pleased. "You are a very good husband to me, and sometimes I wish I had more fire and light and sparkle."

"Oh, Jesus, I get enough of that at work. It's like a Guy Fawkes bonfire. No, you're fine the way you are."

And he nodded to himself, as if agreeing with what he had just said. He didn't want to change her for a different model, a brighter, shinier brand.

The weeks passed with no further word from Joy; the plans for the expansion continued. Carlo said that Joy East was certainly giving it a lot of attention; whether she intended to go or not was anyone's guess.

"Don't force her," Frank advised. "She'll go, but not before she's ready."

He hoped he had read it right. Because she was succeeding in unsettling him.

He got an ornate invitation to a silver wedding celebration for Desmond and Deirdre Doyle. He looked at it grimly. In ten years, possibly, he and Renata might be sending out something similar. But he wondered if it was likely.

He wondered also what Desmond had to celebrate, a wedding that everyone had assumed was shotgun even though it turned out not to have been the case. A lifetime of being snubbed by the awful O'Hagan family back in Dublin. A life's work getting nowhere fast in Palazzo. Difficult children. The eldest shacked up with some out-of-work actor, apparently, the boy hightailing it back to Mayo, of all places, and Helen. A nun, a very odd, disturbed girl. Frank didn't like to think about Helen Doyle, who had appeared twice in his life, both times trailing disaster behind her and around her.

No, the Doyles had little to celebrate, which was probably why they were having this party.

An unlikely outing it was going to be.

But not as unlikely as the outing that Renata told him about when he came home from work.

"Joy East has invited us to dinner, just you and me and her, she says."

"Did she say why?"

"I did ask her, and she said she would like to have a talk with us."

"Is it at her house?"

"No, she said that you always say when something has to be said it should be said on neutral ground." Renata sounded puzzled.

Frank's stomach churned with fear.

"I don't know what she means by that," he managed to say.

"Well, she said she's booking a table in this restaurant . . . and that she checked with Diana that you are free, so she rang me to see if I were free."

"Yes. Well."

"Do you not want to go?" Renata sounded disappointed.

"She's been very odd lately. This pregnancy has unhinged her a bit, I think, that and the move . . . not that she's said yes or no to that, by the way. Can we get out of it, do you think?"

"Not without being very rude. But I thought you liked her?" Renata looked confused.

"I do, I did, it's not that. She's a bit unbalanced. Leave it with me."

"She said to ring her tonight." Renata seemed withdrawn.

"Yeah, I will. I have to go out again anyway. I'll ring her while I'm out."

He got into his car and drove to Joy's house. He rang the doorbell and knocked, but there was no reply.

He went to a public telephone and called her. She answered immediately.

"Why didn't you let me in?"

"I didn't want to."

"You *told* me to call."

"I told you to telephone, it's a different thing."

"Joy, don't do this, don't have a scene in front of Renata, it's not fair on her, she's done nothing to deserve it, nothing. It's cruel."

"Are you begging, do I hear you begging?"

"You can hear what you goddamn like, but just think, what harm has she ever done you?"

"Does this mean yes or no to my invitation?" Joy asked in a cool voice.

"Listen to me . . ."

"No, I am not going to listen anymore. Yes or no?" There was a threat in the question.

"Yes."

"I thought so," said Joy East, and hung up.

It was the same restaurant where they had had lunch last January. When Joy's stomach had been flat and when Nico's in-laws had seen them laughing. Now it was different.

Joy, still on mineral water to Frank's enormous relief, was gracious and anxious that they should be well seated and choose wisely from the menu. She did most of the talking, as Frank was edgy and Renata very reserved.

"You know the way in films they say: 'You must be wondering why I asked you to come here tonight . . .' " She tinkled.

"You said you had something to talk about." Renata was polite.

"I do. I have come to some decisions finally after a lot of thought, and I think it's fair that I should tell you about them. Frank because of work . . . and Renata, you because of Frank."

He felt the floodgates begin to open. God damn her to the pit of hell. It wasn't even a woman scorned, it wasn't that kind of fury. He would have played straight with her. Or sort of straight anyway.

"Yes?" Renata's voice was anxious. Frank hadn't trusted himself to speak.

"Well, about this baby . . ." She looked from one to the other. And waited. It seemed like an age, but it was probably three seconds.

Joy continued: "I think it is going to change my life much more than I imagined. For a month or two I wondered if I'd done the right thing. Perhaps even at this late stage, I should give the child away, give it to some couple who would have a loving, secure home. I might not turn out to be such a great mother figure, all on my own."

She waited for one of them to deny this politely. Neither of them did.

"But then I thought no. I went into this knowing what it was about, so I must go through with it." She smiled happily.

"Yes, but what has this to do with us exactly?" Renata asked. Her face was fearful.

"It has this to do with you. If I were going to give the child to anyone, I would most certainly have offered you the chance. You would be such good parents, this I know. But since I'm not, and since you might have harbored some hopes . . ."

"Never . . . I never thought of it." Renata gasped.

"Hadn't you? I'm sure *you* did, Frank. After all, you haven't been able to get any joy out of the adoption societies, Carlo tells me."

"My father has no right to speak of such things," Renata said, her face a dark red.

"No, perhaps not. But he does, of course. Anyway, it was to make these matters clear that I asked you here, and to tell you that I will be going north soon, much sooner than anyone expected. I've sold my house here and bought a really lovely old Georgian farmhouse in need of repair, but magnificently proportioned, small and beautiful, and a perfect place for a child to grow up. If he or she is only going to have me around, then the poor love had better have a pony and somewhere to play as well!" Her smile was all-embracing.

Renata took a deep breath. "And will the child's father be involved at all?"

"Not at all. The father is someone I met casually at a packaging conference, a ship that passed in the night."

Renata's hand flew to her mouth in an involuntary gesture.

"Is that so shocking?" Joy asked. "I wanted to have a child, and he was as good a person as anyone else."

"I know, I mean, it was just that I thought . . ." Her voice trailed away, and she looked at Frank, whose face was stony.

"What did you just think, Renata?" Joy was like honey now.

"I know this is silly." Renata looked from one to the other. "I suppose I was afraid that the child might have been . . . Frank's child. And that this is why you even contemplated offering it to us . . . please, I don't know what I am doing talking like this . . . please." There were tears in her eyes.

Frank was frozen. He *still* didn't know which way Joy would jump. He couldn't put out his hand to comfort his wife.

Joy spoke deliberately and slowly: "Oh, Renata, surely you couldn't have thought that. Frank and I? We're too alike to be a number, to be the Grand Affair of the century. Oh, no. And anyway, Frank a father, that's not very likely, that wouldn't have been in the cards, would it?"

"What . . . what do you mean . . . ?"

"Oh, Carlo told me about his problems . . . I'm afraid your father is very indiscreet sometimes, but only when he knows it won't go further. Please don't say back to him that I ever mentioned it. But he was always so sad that Frank did not give him the grandson . . ."

Frank spoke for the first time in a long while. He thought he had managed to take the shake out of his voice.

"And your child? Shall you tell him it was a one-night stand in a hotel room?"

"No, no, of course not, something much more romantic and sad. An untraceable, wonderful person, long dead. A poet maybe. Something sad and beautiful."

Somehow they finished the meal; somehow they found other things to talk about. The hurt went a little from Renata's eyes, and the lines of tension from Frank's face. And the serenity and bloom of pregnancy settled ever more on Joy East. She paid the bill confidently with her credit card, and when Renata went to the ladies' room, she sat and looked calmly across the table at Frank.

"Well, you won," he said.

"No, you won."

"How did I win, tell me? You frightened me to death and now you're denying me any part in the child's life. How is that winning?"

"You got what you wanted. You got me out."

"You're not starting that again?"

"I don't need to. I investigated the market-research bureau. They told me you hired them, they even had the date, it was just after we had lunch in this restaurant. As usual, it turned out the way you wanted it to. I'm out of your hair. The coast is clear for the next project. I do wonder who she'll be. But I'll never know. Any more than you'll know what it's like to play with a two-year-old, your two-year-old. Because you're not capable of fathering one. That's both your alibi and my excuse for cutting you out."

"You never told me why. Why all this hate?"

"It's not hate, it's determination. And why? I suppose because you have cold, cold eyes, Frank. I didn't see that until lately."

Renata was coming back across the room. They stood up; it was time to go.

"You'll be back for the meetings . . . and everything?" Frank said.

"Not all of them. I think if this operation is to be a success, we mustn't let anyone involved think that we keep running to London all the time. Major decisions should be made in the place itself. Otherwise they'll just think they're a little outpost instead of important on their own terms."

She was right, of course, as she had been so often.

He held the door of the taxi open for her. She said she was too big to fit into her little sports car anymore.

For a brief moment their eyes met.

"We both won," she said softly. "You could put it like that."

"Or neither of us won," he said sadly. "That's another way of putting it."

And he put his arm around his wife's shoulder as they went to where the Rover was parked.

Nothing would ever be the same between them after tonight. But the world had only cracked a little for them. It hadn't blown apart as it might have. And in a way that was winning.

CHAPTER EIGHT

Deirdre

The article said that anyone could be truly beautiful if she would give twenty minutes a day. Deirdre settled herself with a happy little wriggle into her chair and pulled the packet of biscuits toward her. Of course she could give twenty minutes a day. Who couldn't? Lord, weren't we all up and awake for sixteen hours, for heaven's sake? Twenty minutes was nothing.

She repeated the words *truly beautiful*. She could hear them being said about her when the day came. Doesn't Deirdre look truly beautiful? Who would think she was married for twenty-five years? Imagine that she's the mother of three grown children.

She sighed with pleasure and began to read. Let's see, what would she have to do? It would be her own little secret, investing this amount of time. The reward would be sensational.

First it said you must assess yourself and list your good points and weak areas. Deirdre took the little silver pen with a tassel on it from her handbag. This was fun, great fun. What a pity she had to do it on her own. Her eldest daughter, Anna, would say that she was fine as she was, no need to list figure flaws and dry patches in her skin. Her second daughter, Helen, would say it was ludicrous to be a victim and to think that looks were important; with all the suffering in the world women couldn't afford to take time analyzing their blemishes and deciding whether their eyes were deep-set or too close together.

Her son, Brendan, far away from her now, living in Ireland on a remote hillside in his father's part of the country . . . what would Brendan say? She found it almost impossible to imagine how Brendan would react anymore. She had wept night after night when he had first left home with few explanations and fewer apologies. Only when he had asked her straight out on the telephone . . . when he had cut across her tears to ask, "If you had your choice, if you had the power to choose my life, what would you have me do that would be so good and so important for us all?" she hadn't been able to answer him. Because to say that she wished things were different was no answer. You couldn't wish a circle to be square or black to be white.

But according to this beauty article, there were things you could wish to be different and make them different. Like the shape of your face, a little judicious use of the blusher and the lightener could do wonders. Deirdre looked at the diagrams happily, she *would* learn to do it right. There was nothing worse than people who attempted it and got it wrong, they looked like Coco the Clown.

That was something that she could imagine Maureen Barry saying in the old days. She and Maureen used to have so much fun at one time. Deirdre's mother had been bosom pals with Mrs. Barry, and so the girls had carte blanche to do anything they liked as long as they were with each other. Deirdre thought back on those holidays in Salthill years ago. She had called the house in Rosemary Drive "Salthill" as a reminder, but she saw the name on the gate so often that it didn't really suggest the sea and sunshine and total freedom of their teens.

Maureen had been so entertaining those times, there was nothing that they felt they couldn't tell each other. Not until the summer they came to London, the summer that everything changed for both of them.

Deirdre wondered about the girls they had been to university with in Dublin. Did they often wonder what had happened to blond Deirdre O'Hagan? They would all know, of course, that she married young; maybe she would even put an announcement of her silver wedding in the *Irish Times*. Rub their noses in it, the uppity ones who had gone on to be barristers or to marry barristers. The types who thought that Dublin was the center of the universe and had only heard of Harrods as a place to shop and Chelsea as a place to live. Pinner? They used to say Pinner? as if it were Kiltimagh or somewhere like that. Oh, in *north* London. I see. It was their ignorance that they weren't traveled. But still, she would put in an announcement. Or maybe it was something that the children should do . . . a little message wishing them well on the twenty-fifth anniversary. She would check the papers and see how people did things these days.

What a pity there wasn't still that closeness with Maureen Barry. If only the years could be rolled back, she could pick up the phone and ask her. Straight out. And talk to her, too, about face-shaping, and how to shadow the jawline. But she would never ask Maureen anything like that these days. Things had changed completely as the years went by.

There were no friends around here who could share the fun of all this self-improvement. No, indeed, her neighbors would think it frivolous and silly. A lot of the women went out to work, they either knew such things, anyway, or else they hadn't time for it. Anyway, Deirdre would never dream of letting them into her business, letting them know that this was a big thing in her life, that it was her one chance to prove that a quarter of a century had added up to something. Deirdre intended to impress her neighbors rather than let them share in the fun. They weren't really important, not like people back in Dublin, but still, it was good to let them see that the Doyles were people of importance, of worth.

What would Desmond say if he saw her studying this article so intently? Would he say something flowery like that she was truly beautiful already? Or might he just say, That's nice, in the curious, flat way he often said things were nice without engaging in them at all? Or might he sit down and say to her that there was really no need for all this fuss and preparation? Desmond often told her not to fuss. She hated that, she didn't fuss, she just saw to it that things were done right. If somebody hadn't lit a fire under Desmond all these years, where would they be now? she would like to know.

Deirdre would not share her beauty secrets with her husband. Long, long ago in that strange summer when it all began, Desmond would lie on a narrow bed and admire her as she brushed her long, fair curls, he would say that he never knew that peaches and cream was anything except a line in a song until he saw Deirdre's lovely face. He would reach over for her and ask if he could help her rub more of that nice cold cream in, maybe down her throat a little, maybe around her neck and arms. Maybe . . . maybe. It was so hard to remember Desmond being like that. But the article in the magazine said that she could recapture all that fresh glow, it was only a matter of proper skin care.

Deirdre would follow every single step, all those upward and circular movements when massaging in the throat cream, all that avoiding the delicate tissue around the eyes. She was going to look right on this day if it killed her. She was going to show them that they had been wrong to pity her twenty-five years ago when she had married Desmond Doyle, a counterman in a grocery shop, a boy from a poor family in the back of beyond in Mayo. A family that nobody had ever heard of.

This day would be her silvery revenge.

They had all said yes, every single person who had been expected to come. There were some, of course, who had been asked but knew that they were not meant to come. Like Desmond's odd brother, Vincent, the man who never left his mountains and his sheep in that lonely place where Brendan had chosen to spend his life. There had been a message from her son that his uncle very much regretted but it was a bad time to get away. That was the way it should have been done. Deirdre had nodded, pleased at the correct response.

And of course, the Palazzos, who ran the huge company where Desmond had worked for so long. Unfortunately they couldn't come, a sweet letter from Carlo and Maria, signed personally, wishing them all kinds of happiness and full of regrets that it would coincide with their annual visit to Italy. There would be a gift and flowers. But it was right that they didn't come. They were too high up, they would cramp everyone else's style. And Deirdre's mother, who felt able to talk to everyone, might discuss with them too closely Desmond's career in the company. She might discover that Desmond had never risen high and had at one stage been let go. This would be at odds with the glowing picture Deirdre always painted.

Frank Quigley and his wife, Renata Palazzo, said they would love to come. Deirdre thought grimly that Frank, for all his vast success and his unfair advancement up the ladder even before he married the heiress to the Palazzo fortunes, was still a good man to have at a function. He always seemed to know the right thing to say, and said it. She remembered back to their wedding day,

Frank had been the best man then, he had been well able to handle anything that had turned up. Including Deirdre's mother and father, with their faces like early Christian martyrs throughout the ceremony and the so-called festivities.

And Father Hurley was coming; he said it would be a marvelous chance to visit a couple whose marriage had worked out so well. Deirdre knew she could rely on kind Father Hurley to say the right thing all evening.

And of course, the Irish contingent would arrive. The date had been long fixed in their minds. There had been a possibility that her brother, Gerard, might not be able to make it, but Deirdre had telephoned with such surprise and hurt and bewilderment that somehow his plans had changed. She had told him straight out on the telephone that there was no point in *having* a silver wedding if the family couldn't be there.

"Will Desmond's family be there?" Gerard had asked.

"That's not the point," Deirdre had said.

Mother was coming, of course, and Barbara; they were going to make a long weekend out of it all, come on the Thursday, do a few shows, take in a lot of shopping. Barbara's husband, Jack, would combine it with a business trip, of course. That's what he was always able to do.

And when they arrived, they would have drinks on the lawn in Rosemary Drive in the late afternoon. Then they would all go to a special Mass where the priest would refer to blessings of the sacrament of matrimony in general and specific reference to Desmond and Deirdre in particular. Father Hurley would be called on as the priest who had married them to say a few words. . . . Then, after photographs outside the church and everything, they would gather back at Rosemary Drive, and champagne would be opened.

There had been no champagne back in 1960, but Deirdre would not let her brow furrow about that. If she were to be truly beautiful, she must keep worry lines away from her face.

She told herself that there really was no need to have worry lines. Everything would go perfectly.

And even if . . . no, no, smooth out the temples, don't screw up the eyes.

The beauty plan had suggested you do a countdown and a chart. Nothing pleased Deirdre more, she loved making out plans and schedules like this. Anyway, she already had her own countdown to the silver wedding in terms of things to be organized.

Desmond had shaken his head sadly, but men didn't understand the way things were done. Or maybe, Deirdre thought crossly, *some* men did, and those were the ones who got on. Men like Desmond who had never risen in Palazzo, who were leaving and going into partnership in a corner shop. Those men didn't understand.

And because Deirdre was so plugged into her countdown, she knew she had exactly one hundred ten days to go when the telephone rang and it was her mother at the other end of the line.

Mother rang only every second weekend, on Sunday evenings. Deirdre had instituted that practice years ago; they rang each other on alternate Sundays. Sometimes she felt that Mother had little to say, but that couldn't be possible. Mother wasn't good at writing letters, so these conversations were Deirdre's lifeline. She remembered everything that was said, and even kept a little spiral notebook by the phone to jot down names of Mother's bridge friends, or of the party that Barbara and Jack had been to, or the concert that Gerard had taken

Mother to. Sometimes Mrs. O'Hagan would exclaim that Deirdre had the most extraordinary memory for little things. But Deirdre thought it was only natural that you should want to recall important moments in your family's life. She was always mildly put out that Mother hardly ever remembered any of her friends and never inquired about Palazzo or about any of the outings that Deirdre had described.

It was unexpected to hear from Mother in the middle of the week, in the middle of the day.

"Is anything wrong?" Deirdre said at once.

"No, Deirdre. Lord above, you sound just like your grandmother." Kevin's mother always began every greeting by asking if anything was wrong.

"I meant it's not your usual time to call."

Mother softened. "No, I know, I know. But I'm in London and I thought I'd try and see could I catch you at home."

"You're in *London!*" Deirdre cried, her hand flying to her throat. She looked around the living room, untidy and covered with Desmond's papers, plans and projections, notes that he had been discussing with the Patels, the family who ran the shop that he insisted was far more his life's dream than the great Palazzo company. Deirdre herself was dressed in a faded apron, the place was a mess. She looked out the window fearfully, as if her mother were about to come straight in the door.

"Yes, I just got in from the airport. The underground is marvelous, isn't it? Just whizzes you in, door-to-door almost."

"What are you doing in London?" Deirdre's voice was almost a whisper. Had Mother come three months too early for the silver wedding? Was there a crisis?

"Oh, just passing through . . . you see, the tour leaves from London."

"The tour? What tour?"

"Deirdre, I told you all about it . . . didn't I? I must have. I've told everyone else."

"You mentioned no tour to me." Deirdre was mutinous.

"Oh, I must have. Maybe I wasn't talking to you."

"We talk every Sunday night of our lives. I was talking to you four days ago."

"Deirdre, is anything wrong, dear? You sound so strange. Like as if you're fighting with me or something."

"I didn't know of any tour. Where are you going?"

"Down to Italy first, and then by ship. We pick up the ship in Ancona and head off from there . . ."

"Where do you head off to?"

"Oh, a variety of places . . . Corfu, Athens, Rhodes, Cyprus, and some-place in Turkey."

"A cruise, Mother, you're going on a cruise!"

"I think that's a very grand name for it."

"It sounds like a very grand outing."

"Yes, well, let's hope it won't be too hot out in all those places. I think it's probably not the right time of year to head off . . ."

"Then why are you?"

"Because it came up. Anyway, enough of this. Are we going to meet?"

"Meet? You're going to come here? Now?"

Mother laughed. "Well, thanks a lot, Deirdre, that sounds like a great welcome, but actually I hadn't intended on going out to darkest Pinner . . . I thought you might come in and join me for a spot of lunch or coffee or whatever."

Deirdre hated Anna calling it "darkest Pinner." It was such an insult, as if the place were off the beaten track. And here was her own mother, who was from Dublin, for heaven's sake, who didn't know where anywhere was and whether it was on or off any track, saying the same thing.

"Where are you staying?" she asked, trying not to let the irritation show.

Mother was in a central hotel, very central, she said; it had only taken her two minutes to leave the Piccadilly line and be in her foyer. Simply remarkable. It would be easy for Deirdre to find, too.

"I know how to get there." Deirdre was white-faced.

"So shall we say the bar here at one-thirty? Will that give you time . . . ?"

Deirdre left a note to Desmond on the table. These days she never knew whether he was going to come back or not during the day. His arrangements with Palazzo seemed to be fluid. Frank Quigley had said there would be proper arrangements made; for a manager like Desmond, setting up on his own, it wasn't a question of severance pay, redundancy, compensation, golden handshakes. . . . It was all defined as proper arrangements. Deirdre hoped it would be finalized by the time of the silver wedding.

Grimly Deirdre went upstairs and put on her best suit. Her hair was limp and greasy-looking. She had planned to wash it later in the day, now there wasn't time. Her good handbag was being mended, the catch had worked loose. There was a grubby-looking bandage on her wrist where she had burned herself on the oven. She didn't like to open it all up and apply a fresh one; they had told her that it should be done at the hospital.

In low spirits and filled with a vague apprehension, Deirdre Doyle set out to meet her mother. She felt drab and unattractive. She looked what she was, she decided, catching a reflection of herself in the window of the train that took her into Baker Street. She looked like the middle-aged housewife from the suburbs, married to a not very successful man, no job to exercise her mind, not enough money to dress herself properly. Suffering badly from the empty-nest syndrome. Perhaps more than most: one daughter trying to be accepted in a convent where they wouldn't let her take her vows; another daughter who sometimes didn't come to see her parents more than once in a fortnight; and her son, her beloved son, gone, fled to live at the other side of another country.

She was sure that she and Mother would fight. There had been something in the tone of the phone call that she hadn't liked. Mother had been impatient with her and patting her down as if *she* were the difficult one.

It was extremely irritating, but Deirdre would not lose her temper. Years of being reasonable and refusing to raise her voice had meant that there were few arguments in Rosemary Drive.

Deirdre had always prided herself on that. It was something to show for all those years and all that had happened.

Mother was sitting in a corner of the big oak-paneled bar as if she were a regular. She looked very good; she wore a fawn linen jacket and skirt with a cream-colored blouse beneath. Her hair had been freshly done; in fact, she must have spent the hour that her daughter used to struggle in to central London sitting peacefully in a hairdressing salon. She looked relaxed and at her ease. She was reading a newspaper, and unless she was putting on an elaborate act, she seemed to be reading it without the aid of glasses.

A woman of sixty-seven and she looked somehow younger and fresher than her own daughter.

Eileen O'Hagan's eyes looked up just at that moment, and she smiled broadly. Deirdre felt her movements somehow stiffen as she walked across to meet her mother. They kissed, and Mother, who was already on friendly terms with the waiter, called him over.

"Just a glass of wine and soda," Deirdre said.

"Nothing stronger to celebrate your old mother coming to town?"

"You can't be this lady's mother. Seesters, yes . . ." the waiter said on cue. But it had a ring that was altogether too truthful for Deirdre.

"Just wine and soda," she snapped.

"Let me look at you . . ." her mother said.

"Don't, Mother, I look bad. I wish you'd told me. . . ."

"But if I had, then you'd have gone to an immense amount of fuss and worn yourself out . . ." her mother said.

"Then you admit you didn't tell me, that it didn't just slip your mind."

"It was out of kindness, Deirdre. You were always one to go to such efforts, that's why I didn't tell you."

Deirdre felt the tears sting in her eyes. She fought to keep the hurt tone out of her voice.

"Well, all I can say is that it's a pity. Desmond would have loved to have had you to the house, and the girls will be very sorry they've missed their grannie."

"Nonsense, Deirdre, Anna's at work. Helen's at prayer, Desmond is up to his eyes. Why create a great fuss?"

There it was again, that hated word, *fuss*. Deirdre clenched her fists and saw her mother glance at her whitened knuckles. This was very bad; she had vowed that there would be no argument. She must keep to that.

"Right, well, here we are anyway," Deirdre said in a voice that sounded to her own ears curiously tinny. "And, Mother, you do look remarkably well."

Her mother brightened up. "This suit has been a godsend, you know I bought it three years ago in Maureen's shop. Maureen always had great taste. I used to wonder why some of her clothes were so expensive, but her mother always said you paid for the cut and that they never really went out of fashion. . . ."

Mother patted the skirt of her outfit with pleasure.

"It should be just the thing for a cruise." Deirdre tried to sound enthusiastic.

"Well, yes, I didn't think there was any point in getting all those floral silks . . . leisurewear, cruisewear they actually call them nowadays. Better to bring something suitable, something familiar, and I have a few cotton dresses for sight-seeing." She looked animated and excited.

"And what possessed you to take off on something like this?" Even as she spoke, Deirdre knew that hers sounded like the voice of an older woman remonstrating with a difficult daughter rather than the enthusiasm that there should have been for a self-sufficient parent capable of enjoying herself on her own.

"As I told you, it came up, and I have a friend who was also free at this time, so it seemed only sensible . . ."

"Oh, good, someone's going with you." Deirdre was pleased. Two old ladies on board ship would at least have each other to talk to at the time and be able to share the memory afterward. She tried to remember which one of her mother's bridge cronies would be likely to accompany her.

"Yes, and I thought I'd seize the chance of letting you meet each other, not for lunch, we'll have that on our own, but Tony said he'd pop down and say hello . . . Ah, there he is . . . what timing!"

And as Deirdre felt the base of her stomach fill with lead, she realized that her mother was waving at a florid-looking man with a blazer and a red face who was coming across the room, rubbing his hands delightedly. Mother was going on a cruise with a man.

"This is nice," Tony said, crushing Deirdre's hot hand in his own and telling the waiter that he'd like a large G and T, Cork and Schweppes, ice and slice.

The waiter was puzzled. Mother said affectionately that Irish gin drinkers were fanatically partisan and only drank the home brew as far as gin was concerned.

"But we're very democratic, we drink the English tonic," Tony said, beaming around him. "Well, Deirdre, what do you think of all this caper?"

"I've only just heard about it this moment," she said, hardly able to find the words.

"It should be a great old jaunt altogether," he said. "No decisions about whether to go and see places, they come to see you instead. Perfect for the lazy man. And lazy woman." He actually patted Mother's hand.

"Were you afraid to tell me this, too, in case I'd fuss?" Deirdre asked, and could have bitten off her tongue.

Tony weighed in before Mother could answer.

"Oh, there you are, Eileen. She's as jealous as the others. Barbara nearly went mad when she heard that her mother was taking me instead of her, and Gerard said that in all decency your mother should take her son instead of a toy boy like myself." He threw back his head and laughed heartily, and Mother laughed with him.

Deirdre thought, he knows Barbara and Gerard. Why had neither of them said anything about this to her? How dare they keep quiet about something as big as this? And was he serious about Mother taking him? Mother could not possibly be paying for this loud, vulgar man. Or was this a joke, too?

Mother seemed to read her face. "Don't worry about a thing, Deirdre, my love, it's only his way of going on. Tony's not after the deeds of the house."

"Fat chance I'd have if I *were* after them," he boomed. "Your mother will live forever. I'll croak one of these days. I hope not on the cruise, though a burial at sea would be something to remember, wouldn't it?"

Deirdre felt a genuine sense of nausea. This man, who must be almost the same age as her mother, was a serious part of her life. And until this minute nobody had been able to tell her.

She forced the smile back onto her face and saw her mother's approving glance. She found her mouth dry and bitter as she searched for some suitable words.

But Tony was not a man who would allow silences. He had had her glass refilled, he had commandeered a dish of olives and a bowl of chips on the ground that one had to have all the trappings. He had assured her that he would take great care of her mother on the cruise, squeezed her hand hard again, and said he would leave the key at reception. The key. The man wasn't even pretending that they had separate rooms. Deirdre felt a sense of unreality wash over her, and she hardly noticed that he had kissed her mother good-bye on the cheek.

Mother had booked a nearby restaurant. It was small and French and expensive. The napkins were thick, the silver was heavy, and the flowers on the table were real and plentiful.

In her twenty-five years living in London, Deirdre had never eaten in a place like this, and here was her mother, her mother from a small country, a small city compared with this one, ordering as if she were used to it.

She was glad that Mother was making decisions. Not only could she not understand the menu, but she would not have been able to order, so confused and upset did she feel.

"Why didn't you tell me anything about . . . er . . . Tony?" she asked eventually.

"Well, there wasn't all that much to tell until we decided to go on this cruise together, and then, as soon as we set off on that, I *did* tell you." Mother spread out her hands as if it were the simplest thing in the world.

"And Gerard and Barbara . . . do they . . . did they . . . ?"

"Well, they know Tony's a friend of mine, and naturally I told them our holiday plans."

"And were they . . . did they . . . ?"

"Gerard drove us to the airport this morning. Tony's right, he's green with envy, he keeps saying it's just what he needs. He works too hard, he *should* take time off, and he can well afford it. Maybe this is the spur."

"But did he say . . . what did he think . . . ?"

"He didn't say that he'd take a holiday, and you know Gerard, he probably is thinking about it."

Could Mother really misunderstand her or was this deliberate? Deirdre was not going to be brushed aside.

"What about Barbara and Jack? What do they think of you going away with a man?"

"Dearest Deirdre, I'm not going away with a man in that sense. I am going away on a holiday certainly, and I am going with Tony, and yes, indeed, he is a man. What do you mean, what do they think? They don't think at all, I am perfectly sure."

"But Jack's family . . ."

As long as Deirdre could remember, Jack's family had been spoken of with some kind of awe. His father was a high court judge, his uncle was an ambassador. Barbara had done what the O'Hagan family had wanted by marrying such style, instead of what she, Deirdre, the eldest, had done—marrying a nobody and doing it in a great hurry.

But Mother looked totally bewildered.

"Jack's family?" she repeated, as if Deirdre had somehow begun to speak in a foreign language. "What on earth connection could they have with anything?"

"You know . . ."

"I don't think they ever met Tony. No, I'm sure they didn't. Why do you ask?"

Deirdre looked hard at her mother. Mother knew bloody well why she asked. She asked because the high and mighty Jack's family were always mentioned. They had been mentioned since Deirdre's young sister, Barbara, had started going out with a son of the well-connected tribe. Deirdre remembered the huge wedding given for Barbara, with the marquee, the witty speeches, the politicians, and the photographers. It had been very different from her own wedding day. And now suddenly Jack's almighty clan didn't seem important anymore.

Feeling a flush darken her cheek, she spoke directly to her mother.

"And do you and . . . Tony . . . have any further plans . . . like after the cruise, do you think you might get married or anything?"

"Do try to keep the surprise out of your voice," her mother said. "Stranger things have happened, you know. But the answer is no. No plans like that."

"Oh?"

"And anyway, enough about me and my trip. Tell me about all your doings." Mother smiled in anticipation.

Deirdre looked dour. "None of them are anything nearly as interesting as your plans."

"Come, come, Desmond's setting up on his own, *and* you're going to have this whole silver wedding shindig . . ."

It was such a Tony word, *shindig*. Mother hadn't spoken like that before.

"Where did you meet him?" Deirdre asked abruptly.

"Desmond?" Now Mother was being playful. "When you brought him home, of course, and told us about the wedding. But you know that."

"I didn't mean Desmond, and you know that." Deirdre was cross. "I meant Tony. How did you become involved with him?"

"We met at the golf club."

"Tony's a member of the golf club?" The surprise and disbelief were clear in her voice.

"Yes, he plays off twelve," Mother said proudly.

"But how did he become a member?" Years ago someone flashy like Tony could not have been proposed, it would have been as simple as that. Had her Desmond known how to play golf, which he did not, he would not have been acceptable. How could someone like Tony get in?

"I've no idea. I suppose the way we all became members." Mother was vague.

"And do all your other friends know him? Did Mrs. Barry know him, for example?" Deirdre had chosen Maureen Barry's mother, the great social barometer of their Dublin. Surely Tony had not been welcomed in her set?

"Sophie? Yes, of course, poor Sophie met him from time to time. Sophie Barry didn't play golf, remember, so she wouldn't have known him in that context."

"Don't tell me Tony plays bridge?"

"No, he's frightfully dismissive of old pussycats, as he calls us, spending hour after cheery hour, day after day, dealing cards."

Mother laughed merrily, and suddenly her life seemed much more fun than Deirdre's own. Desperate not to let her mother change the subject again, Deirdre tried once more.

"And, Mother, please, what does Gerard think? What does he say? No, not about taking holidays himself. What does he say about you and Tony?"

"I've no idea."

"You must know."

"No, I mean, how would I know? I only know what he says to me, I've no idea what he says to anyone else. He has a rather nice girlfriend at the moment, he may talk about it with her, but I imagine not." Mother looked supremely unconcerned.

"But he must . . . surely . . ."

"Listen, Deirdre. Everyone has their own life to lead, Gerard is probably much more worried about his career at the bar, should he become a section council, should he stop playing the field with these little bimbos and settle down? He probably worries about his health, he's nearly forty, he may think a lot about cholesterol and polyunsaturated fats. He might wonder whether to sell his flat and buy a house. What time on earth is there for him to spend thinking about his mother? I ask you!"

"But if you're doing something . . . if you're getting into something . . ."

"I'm sure he thinks I'm old enough to look after myself."

"We all have to look after each other," Deirdre said a trifle unctuously.

"That's where you are totally wrong. We all have to make very sure we don't interfere in people's lives. That's the great sin."

The unfairness of it stung Deirdre like the lash of a whip. How *dare* Mother come out with this preachy nonsense about not interfering in people's lives. For a quarter of a century Deirdre had been trying to live up to some kind of image, some expectations for her. She was the daughter for whom there had been such hopes. The eldest of the family, very bright at university, an honor student, she might have gone into the Department of External Affairs, as it was called then; she might have been on the way to being an ambassador or marrying one. She might have done the bar, as her brother had done. She might have made the brilliant match that her sister, Barbara, had done.

Instead she had fallen in love one long hot summer and trapped herself into a strange prison. Where since nothing was good enough for the O'Hagans and their hopes back home, then everything must be made to look as if it were.

Deirdre had lived her entire life on this premise, to please the mother who was now sitting opposite her, justifying her pitiable relationship with a common, flashy man by saying that the main rule of living was not to interfere! It was not possible.

Deirdre spoke very slowly. "I know what you're saying, but I think it's important too not to be entirely self-centered and to take the wishes of others into account as well. I mean, did I or did I not spend all my teenage years hearing about people who were suitable and people who were not suitable?"

"Not from me you didn't."

"But you were always wanting to know what people's fathers did and where they lived?"

"Out of interest." Mother was airy about it. "It's always nice to know who people are in case you knew them years ago or something. That's all it was about."

"No, it wasn't, Mother. You and Mrs. Barry—"

"Oh, Deirdre, Sophie Barry had nothing in her whole life except some kind of nonsensical pecking order. Nobody who knew her took any notice of it."

"Maureen did."

"Well, more fool Maureen, and anyway, I don't think you're right, Maureen lived her own life, made her own way despite all poor Sophie's rubbishing on about being in trade."

"You mean to tell me that you and Daddy were perfectly happy that I married Desmond? Don't try to tell me that. I won't believe it."

There were tears in Deirdre's eyes, tears of rage, hurt, and confusion. Suddenly the screen was falling away, the mask was being dropped, she knew she was on dangerous ground here. The polite pretense of years was being swept away.

The woman in the fawn linen suit and the cream blouse looked at her with concern. She began to speak and then stopped.

"Now, you can't deny it!" Deirdre was triumphant.

"Child, you're talking about a lifetime ago," her mother said.

"But what I say is true, you did care, you did care that Desmond wasn't top drawer enough for us."

"What do you mean for us? We weren't marrying him, you were, he was your choice, the words *top drawer* weren't even mentioned."

"Not aloud maybe."

"Not at all. I assure you, your father and I thought you were too young, of course we did, you hadn't taken your degree, we were afraid you would never get any qualification. In that I suppose we wished you would wait, that was all."

Deirdre took a deep breath. "You knew we couldn't wait."

"I knew you wouldn't wait, that's all I knew. You were very determined. I wasn't going to oppose you."

"You knew why."

"I knew you loved him or thought you did. Now that you've stayed with him and are dead set on having all this palaver in the autumn, then you were probably right, you did love him, and he loved you."

To Mother it seemed too simple: If you lived together for twenty-five years and were prepared to acknowledge it, you loved each other. Deirdre was thoughtful.

"Well, isn't that what happened?" Mother was waiting for a yes or a no or an 'I told you so.'

"More or less, but no thanks to anyone at home." Deirdre was still mulish.

"I don't know what exactly it is you're trying to say, Deirdre. Of all my children I thought you were the most contented. You went for what you wanted, you got it. Nobody forced you to do anything, you had your freedom, you went to university, you could have worked for a living, but you never did. Sophie and I used to say that you got everything on a plate. Now it seems there's some grievance."

Mother was interested but not distressed; she was concerned but not unduly curious. She tossed a salad expertly and waited for an explanation.

"Why did you let me marry Desmond if you thought I was too young?"

"I only thought, let's cause the least grief possible in the world. That's what I always think. Your father did think you might be pregnant, but I knew you weren't."

"How did you know that?" Deirdre's voice was a whisper.

"Because nobody, not even in the far back year of 1960, would have got married to someone just for that reason if she didn't want to. And you weren't. Anna wasn't born until months and months later, quite wiped poor Sophie's eye, I think. I have a feeling she had the same thoughts as your father."

"Yes."

"So, Deirdre, what's the federal case, as they say? What am I supposed to have done? We gave our permission. Was that bad? No. We came to the wedding, that's what you wanted. You said you didn't want a huge, showy number and you wanted it in England, we went along with that. We took Barbara and Gerard out of school for the ceremony.

"The house is there for you and Desmond to come over and see us, but you never do. You came once, and you were so touchy we didn't know what to say to you, everything upset you. We came to see you a few times, and we're all heading over to see you again for your silver wedding, something, it may be said, that isn't at all what we're used to, and somehow still, in spite of all this, I am the worst in the world, and by implication your father was, and your sister and brother are."

Eileen O'Hagan mopped up the dressing of her salad with a piece of French bread and looked at her daughter for an explanation.

Deirdre looked at her wordlessly.

The waiter came and took away their plates and discussed at length an apple tart and a burnt cream. Deirdre's mother went into the option with animation; it gave Deirdre a chance to gather her thoughts.

"I ordered one of each. I hate to be directive, but I thought it best."

"That's fine, Mother."

"And what were we talking about before? Oh, I know, Daddy and I were supposed to have hated Desmond or something, isn't that it?"

"Not exactly."

"Well, not just not exactly, not at all. We both thought he was very nice, bullied within an inch of his life by you, of course, but then you'd be bound to be bossy, you get it from me." Eileen O'Hagan was pleased to have passed on such sterling qualities.

"What did you say about him to each other?" Deirdre's voice was small.

"Daddy and I? Hardly anything. He was providing for you all right, that was what we worried about, I suppose, in those days, so it was good that this side of it wasn't a problem. I think we were upset that you didn't have a career."

"I had three children in rapid succession." Deirdre was defensive.

"Yes, but afterward. Anyway, I suppose we thought that maybe it was a bit hierarchical in that setup with the Italians, the Palladians—"

"The Palazzos, Mother."

"Yes, well, that's about the only negative thought we ever had about Desmond, so you can stop doing your outraged lioness bit about him."

Mother laughed affectionately.

Deirdre looked at her as if she were someone never seen before.

"And Mrs. Barry, was she not questioning you about us?"

"No, sweetheart. To be very honest, there wasn't all that much interest at all. Nobody had. You know that yourself about Dublin, out of sight out of people's minds and immediate conversation and interest."

"But not for you, surely you couldn't have forgotten me, your eldest daughter." Her lip was trembling.

"Of course, I don't forget you, silly thing, but not all the little bitty things that you think were never off our lips, this promotion, that remark that the Palladians passed about Desmond, the time that Anna was at the same reception as Princess Di."

"It was Princess Michael of Kent."

"Well, you know what I mean, Deirdre, it's not some kind of score card, you know, points for this, minus points for that."

There was a silence. A long silence.

"I'm not criticizing you, you do know that?"

"Yes, Mother."

"And even if Kevin and I hadn't liked Desmond, which was not the case—whatever we were allowed to get to know of him we liked very much—but suppose we hadn't . . . what would have been the point of saying it or letting it be thought? We weren't going to live your lives for you."

"I see."

"When I was married to Kevin, my parents were delighted, they crowed and brayed and made me very, very uneasy."

"You should have been pleased."

"No, I was suspicious. I thought that they wanted me off their hands, and I also thought they equated money with some kind of happiness or success. Your father didn't give me much of either."

"I don't believe you!" Deirdre's mouth was wide open.

"Why shouldn't I tell you this? You and I are middle-aged women, we're talking about life and love. Your father was what they call now a chauvinist pig; in those days we called it a man's man and were meant to be grateful that he wasn't chasing the ladies. He stayed at his clubs every evening until late, you remember that growing up, don't you? I bet Desmond was at home to get to know his children."

"He wasn't a member of any clubs." Deirdre sounded wistful.

"And weren't you the better for it? Anyway, I always thought I would neither encourage nor discourage any of my children, let them choose for themselves and go along with it."

"Barbara's wedding . . ." Deirdre began.

"Nearly put us in the poorhouse. What a bloody shower, Jack's family. They gave us a wedding list of their guests from their side of the family as long as your arm . . . we decided to do it the way the young couple wanted it. Though Barbara has often said to me she wished they had had less of a send-off, nothing ever lived up to it."

"Barbara said that?"

"She says it every time she has a glass of sherry, it's hardly breaking a confidence to tell you. She says it in the golf club, and she tried to say it the night she was in the audience at the *Late Late Show*, but apparently they didn't get a mike to her."

For the first time Deirdre laughed a genuine laugh, and the waiter was so pleased he came running with a plate of bonbons and a refill of coffee.

"And I know you think I should be happy with my six grandchildren, your three and Barbara's three. But I never see yours. They grew up without us, and when we did meet them, they were like white mice they were so afraid of us. And I was sick to death of Barbara's three when they were at the poisonous stage, we were unpaid, unthanked baby-sitters, and now that they're nice and interesting I don't see hide nor hair of them. And I don't think that Gerard is going to give us any news in that direction, but that's his business. I don't want to send him out to mate just so that I can have more people to call me Grannie."

She looked lively and eager, she did not look like someone who wanted more people to call her Grannie, let alone someone who had grown-ups who did.

"And suppose you and . . . er, Tony . . . get on well on this cruise, why don't you think there might be a chance of . . . well, something more permanent?"

Deirdre somehow felt that if he were accepted by Mother's cronies at home and by her sister and brother, he couldn't be quite as common and unsuitable as she had thought at first.

"No, that's not on the cards."

"As you said earlier, it's not such a barbarous idea."

"Well, it is really, Deirdre. Or his wife would think so anyway."

"He's married. Mother, I don't believe it."

"Oh, but you must, I assure you."

"Does anyone know, is his wife sort of around, are people aware of her?" Deirdre's voice was very concerned.

Her mother was silent for the first time. She looked at Deirdre with a strange expression. It was hard to read her look. It was partly sad and partly as if she had known that things would be like this. There was a little frisson of impatience in the disappointment.

She didn't answer Deirdre's question, she never answered it. She called for the bill, and they walked together back to her hotel.

She said she had a little more shopping to do, and she sent her love to Anna and to Helen. There was no point in sending love to Brendan, they both knew that he was only rarely in touch. No rapport of weekly phone chats had been established between Deirdre and her son on Sunday nights as there were between Deirdre and her mother.

Eileen O'Hagan said she wished Desmond well and thought that he was quite right to have left the Palladians or the Palazzos or whatever they were called. A man had to do what a man had to do. And so had a woman.

She said she would send a postcard from somewhere that looked nice and exotic.

She said since Deirdre hadn't offered that she would be sure to give Deirdre's warm wishes to Tony and tell him that Deirdre had said bon voyage.

And as she left her daughter, who would get the tube back to the station where the Metropolitan line would take her back to Pinner and the table full of preparations for a party one hundred ten days away, Eileen O'Hagan reached out her hand and stroked Deirdre's cheek.

"I'm sorry," she said.

"What for, Mother? Why are you sorry? You gave me a lovely lunch. It was really good to see you." And Deirdre meant it.

"No, I'm sorry that I didn't give you more."

"You gave me everything, I was only being silly, you said yourself that I was the most contented of your children. I never knew that."

Her mother opened her mouth as if to speak but closed it again, and when

Deirdre turned to wave, she saw that Eileen O'Hagan's lips were moving. She thought she was just mouthing good-bye.

She was too far away to hear her mother saying, "I'm sorry that I gave you no notion of happiness. Only how to pretend you are happy and that's no gift at all. It's a burden for your back."

Deirdre waved again just before she went down the steps to the tube station, and she hoped her mother would stop mouthing at her. After all, here in Piccadilly Circus the whole world could be passing by, and there could be anyone, just anyone, who might see them. Someone from Pinner or someone from Dublin. The world was getting smaller, and you should always behave as if you were under some kind of observation, because when it came down to it, that's what we all were most of the time. Under observation.

CHAPTER NINE

Silver Wedding

❧✿❧

They had set the electric teamaker for seven o'clock.

Desmond had grumbled that it was too early, they would both be worn out by the time the thing began. But Deirdre said it was better far to be ahead of themselves instead of running after themselves all day. Be up and organized before the caterers came.

"They're not coming until three o'clock," Desmond had said.

"Everything has to be cleared away for them."

"God Almighty, Deirdre, we're not going to spend eight hours clearing the kitchen worktops. And isn't it all done already anyway?"

She took no notice of him, she poured him out a cup of tea.

For years, since they had moved into separate beds, in fact, they had this morning ritual of the electric teamaker on the table between them. It somehow soothed them into the day, took the little edges off the slight sense of morning disappointment that they each seemed to feel.

"Happy anniversary," he said, and reached out for her hand.

"And to you," she said, smiling. "Will we give our presents now or later?"

"Whatever you like."

"Maybe later." She sipped her tea and ticked off in her mind all the things to be done. She had an appointment at the hairdresser and a manicure as a special treat. Her new outfit was hanging on the wardrobe under its cellophane wrapping. She hoped it was a good choice, the woman in the shop had been very pushy, kept calling her Madam and speaking to her as if she weren't there. Madam would look very well in pale colors, Madam doesn't want to grow old before her time. Madam could do with a little detail on the shoulder if Madam really insists that she won't wear shoulder pads.

Deirdre would like to have worn pads, almost everyone did nowadays, like the women in *Dynasty* and *Dallas,* but she remembered that time years ago when she had bought a very upholstered-looking jacket and Maureen Barry had laughed at it and called it Deirdre's Marshal Bulganin outfit. She daren't risk that again. Or risk even the memory of it.

She knew that whatever Maureen wore today it would be stunning, it would take all the attention away from her, away from Deirdre, whose party it was. The woman in the shop said she couldn't believe that Madam was really celebrating a silver wedding, but that was in the shop. The woman was anxious to flatter her and make a sale.

The woman hadn't seen Maureen.

She would take the limelight today, as she had taken it twenty-five years ago. When the bride had looked pink and frightened and flustered, and the maid of honor had looked dark and cool and elegant in a plain pink linen dress and a big pink flower in her hair. And Frank Quigley had never taken his eyes off her. From one end of the day to the other.

Would it be the same today? Would the great Frank Quigley remember his passion for Maureen Barry with regret as the one thing he didn't win in his life? If she knew Frank, he would probably have turned it into a success rather than a failure. Look at the bigger and better prize he had won. Married to the entire Palazzo fortune. He wouldn't have had that if Maureen had accepted him all those years ago.

But she wouldn't think destructive thoughts. Not today. Today was her day more than her wedding day had ever been. She had worked hard for it, put in long hours, long years. Deirdre Doyle would have today.

Desmond looked at his face in the bathroom mirror. It looked back at him, younger, he thought, than it had done a while ago. Or maybe he just imagined that because he felt better. He didn't have that constant pain in the base of his stomach that he used to have going in to Palazzo. He enjoyed leaving the house now. Mornings were so much easier.

He had suggested that he and Suresh Patel start a newspaper delivery service in the area. People would like to have a paper to read in their homes if it arrived before seven. And it was a great success. It was run by the owlish boy, who kept the accounts meticulously and also delivered the papers before heading off to school. He dropped the *Daily Mail* into Rosemary Drive for Desmond, too, and it meant that he could read it and leave it for Deirdre.

He was annoyed with her that she had not wanted Suresh Patel and his wife to come to the silver wedding.

"It's only for people who were at the ceremony," she had complained.

"John and Jean West weren't there," he had countered.

"Don't be silly, Desmond, they're our next-door neighbors."

"Well, Suresh is my partner, isn't he?"

"Only very recently, and anyway, he won't know anyone."

"Half of them won't know anyone."

"Be reasonable, can't you, his wife doesn't even speak English. What am I to say to people, 'This is Mrs. Patel, Desmond's partner's wife, who can only nod and smile'?"

He had left it. But it rankled. He felt sure that if Suresh Patel was having some ceremony in his house, the Doyles would have been invited. But it wasn't worth a major row; if he had won, then he would have had to look after the Patels all evening. And there were so many other things to concentrate on. Like his son who was coming back . . . of his own free will to be there for the celebrations. Perhaps now that he too had been able to escape from a world that had frightened him they might have more in common. Perhaps the old prickliness would have softened, if not gone altogether.

And he would be glad to see Father Hurley again; he was a kind man. Even in those bad far-off days when priests were meant to be disapproving of sin and anticipating the sacrament of matrimony and everything. There had been no condemnation when he had gone and asked Father Hurley if he could arrange to marry them as quickly as possible. Even quicker.

"Are you sure?" Father Hurley had asked.

"Oh, yes, the tests were positive," Desmond had said, fighting the panic.

"No, I meant, are you both sure this is what you want to do? It's for life."

It had been an odd question at that time. Desmond had paid little heed to it. The only important thing had been could the priest get them married in three weeks, so that their child would not be impossibly premature. The child that was never born. The child that miscarried on Christmas Eve.

He wondered if Father Hurley had ever thought about it, whether the priest, who had after all baptized Anna, realized that she was born a full fourteen months after the shotgun wedding. And that a sister or brother had been lost before that.

Desmond sighed. Father Hurley probably had enough to think about in an Ireland which was rapidly catching up with the rest of the world in terms of godlessness. He would be unlikely to spend time speculating about what had happened in marriages made a quarter of a century ago.

Anna woke around seven in her flat in Shepherd's Bush, she went straight to the window to see what kind of day it was. Good, a bright, crisp autumn day. London was lovely in autumn. The parks were at their best. She had been walking last night with her friend Judy, and they had seen possibly a dozen different shades of gold and orange on the trees. Judy said that in America, up in New England, they had special tours and holidays for leaf peekers, for people who came to peek at the leaves changing color. You could organize that in London, too.

Anna was going to work for the morning. She would only be in the way in Rosemary Drive, things would be up to high do there, the fewer people there were about the better. She would go there around three, the same time as the caterers, just to keep Mother out of their hair and from driving them up the walls. She had begged Helen not to turn up until five, the official time that the celebrations began. The thought of letting her sister, Helen, loose on any house where professional caterers were preparing a meal was enough to frighten anyone.

Helen was in very poor form at the moment, there had been some problem yet again in the convent. Apparently the rest of the community didn't want

Helen to take her vows and be a permanent member of the house. This was what Anna was reading between the lines. Helen, of course, was reading nothing of the sort, seeing only a series of petty irritations, confusions, and obstacles.

Anna sighed. If she was in a religious community, which was possibly the last place on earth she would want to end up, then the very, very last person on earth she would like with her was Helen. There was something very unsettling about Helen's very presence. On the few occasions she had come to see Anna in the bookshop it had been a matter of trying to hold on to big piles of books in displays—no other customer knocked them over, but Helen would. As she had actually swept the credit-card machine off the cash desk, breaking the glass on a display cabinet. As her coat always caught somebody's cup of coffee. Not a restful presence anywhere. She hoped that Helen wouldn't say the wrong thing too often this evening.

What could she say that would be terrible? Well, something about Brendan, along the lines of wasn't it great we forced him to come back . . . Which wasn't the case, but Father would think it was. Or about Father having left Palazzo and working with a terribly nice Paki. Helen was the only person Anna knew who actually used words like *Paki* and *Eyetie*. Yes, she could refer to Renata Quigley as an Eyetie.

Anna padded off in bare feet to make herself a cup of instant coffee. Another pleasure and advantage of not living anymore with Joe Ashe. It had to be real, the coffee, it had to be freshly ground in a machine that would split your head apart. She would not like to live forever on her own, but she was daily finding more and more positive things about not living with Joe Ashe.

He had left as good-naturedly and easily as he had arrived. He had kissed her on the cheek and said that she was being very heavy over nothing. He had said he'd miss her, and he had taken quite a few of her records and a very expensive rug she had bought for their bed. She had watched him fold it and had said nothing.

"You did give me this as a present, I think." He had smiled lightly.

"Sure, Joe," she had said. She would not be heavy over a bedspread. Only about another woman in her bed.

Judy had been very good over the breakup.

"I'm always here, ring me if you feel a bit bleak. I'll listen. Don't ring him out of loneliness, only ring him if you could take him back."

Friends were great, Anna thought, real pure gold. Friends understood when you got infatuated with people, and didn't mind you going mad for a while; they were still there when the infatuation was over. As it nearly was. Very, very nearly.

And she wasn't going to embark on anything again for a long while. Ken Green understood that; he had said that he wanted the smell of Joe Ashe's rather sickly aftershave well gone from the place before he came around in earnest. Ken was very droll. He got on very well with her father, too, which was odd, and persuaded Dad and Mr. Patel to take a small selection of his paperbacks to display with the magazines, just in case there was a market, he had said . . . and of course, there had been. Father and Mr. Patel were going to expand. There was an opening for a bookshop in the area. Ken had even suggested that Anna might think of opening one herself, in conjunction with them.

"Too near home," she had said.

"Maybe you're right." Ken was agreeable but not in the way Joe Ashe agreed with people. Joe agreed for an easy life, Ken because he had thought it out. She half wished she had asked him to the silver wedding do, but it was far too public a commitment, Mother's friends would whisper, and Grandmother O'Hagan would be bound to want to know everything even though there was nothing to know.

Brendan had arrived in London early, off the boat train in Euston. It coincided with the morning rush hour. He stood watching for a quarter of an hour while the commuter population of that part of London buzzed and scuttled and darted up ramps and down stairs, down to taxi lines, in to grab a quick breakfast standing at a counter, leaping onto escalators. They looked so self-important, he thought, as if whatever petty job they were racing to were important, as if they were people of substance. And this is what his father and mother would like him to be doing, racing down from Rosemary Drive to catch a train to Baker Street, and another tube to somewhere like here. It was a preposterous way to live, and all to be able to *say* to someone that this was success.

Brendan knew he must not spoil his gesture in coming to the celebration by voicing these thoughts.

And he also remembered that Vincent had warned him to buy some proper clothes to wear for the occasion.

"You'll always be able to use a good suit, lad," his uncle had said.

"Aw, no, Vincent, not a suit, I'd never wear a suit, for God's sake."

"Well, that's what we wore in my day. But then a jacket and trousers?"

"A parka maybe?" Brendan had brightened.

"Not a parka, you idiot, not for a big party in their house, a smart dark jacket, navy maybe, and light blue trousers. Sure you'll have them hanging on to you at the next dance you go to here."

His uncle had given him folding money. It was a sacred trust to buy something smart to wear. He had written to Anna, telling her how much he had to spend. He had hoped she wouldn't make fun of him, but he had wronged her even to suspect she might do such a thing.

Her letter was enthusiastic and grateful. She told him that Marks or C and A or any High Street store would have a bewildering selection and that she was touched and pleased that he was going to so much trouble. She wrote that she herself was going to wear a dress and jacket in navy and white with awful bits of lace trimming on both, because she thought it would please Mother; it looked what Mother called dressy and Anna called yucky, but it was Mother's day. Anna wrote how she had told Helen that since Vatican Two nobody expected nuns to arrive in places dressed in sackcloth and ashes, but of course, Helen would suit herself, as always.

Maureen Barry came out of Selfridge's and thought she saw Desmond and Deirdre's son, Brendan, walking down Oxford Street with a huge Marks and Spencer's bag as if he had bought half the shop.

But she decided that this was ridiculous. There were twelve million people in London, why should she see a member of the family she was thinking about?

And for all she knew, the boy might still be in the West of Ireland, there had been some kind of coldness. Her mother had told her that not long before she died. She said that Eileen O'Hagan had said that there had been some great cover-up, but the facts were that the son of Deirdre and Desmond had run away, and run of all places back to the very townland his father managed to escape from. The same place that Frank had run from. Maureen told herself to be reasonable. Even if the boy was in London, he would surely be out in Pinner, helping to set up tables for the function. She must stop being fanciful and thinking she had this town down to size as she did Dublin. Only that morning at the hotel she had thought she saw Deirdre's mother, in the distance across the dining room; in fact, it had been so like her she was nearly going across to say hello, but the woman had been joined by a flashy-looking man wearing a blazer with a big crest of some sort. Perhaps it was the sign that she needed glasses. She smiled, remembering how they had all told each other years ago when coming to work in London that they should get false teeth and eyeglasses on the National Health, it had seemed a scream to need either.

It was good to be back in London again, Maureen thought, she had a spring in her step and three credit cards in her wallet. She was merely going on a recce, as the film people called it, a little prowl examining the style in other people's boutiques and in the big fashion stores. And if she wanted to, she could stop and buy herself any treat she wanted. She walked in a cloud of the expensive perfume she had just bought in Selfridge's, she had bought her father a jaunty cravat there, too. He would look well in that, and he would like the fact that she had thought him a cravat man.

Helen Doyle sat in the kitchen of St. Martin's with both her hands around the mug of coffee as if to get some warmth from it. It was not a cold morning, but not even the bright shafts of sunlight coming in the window seemed to warm her. Across the table sat Sister Brigid, the others had gone. They must have known that the confrontation was coming, they had either gone back to their rooms or gone about their business.

A yellow cat with a broken paw looked trustingly up at Helen. She had found it and made a sort of splint which helped it to walk. The others said she should take it to the cats' home, but this would be curtains for the yellow cat, Helen said. It wouldn't eat much, they could mind it surely.

It was just one more sign of Helen around the house, and another chore. It would be impossible to expect Helen to feed or clean up after the cat *all* the time. The cat began a very loud purring and arched its back to be stroked. Tenderly Sister Brigid lifted it up and carried it out to the garden. She came back and sat beside Helen. She looked straight into the troubled eyes and spoke.

"You have so much love and goodness to give," she began. "But this is not the place."

She saw the lip, the lower lip that Helen had been biting nervously, begin to tremble. And the big eyes fill with tears.

"You're sending me away," Helen began.

"We could sit here all morning, Helen, you could call it one thing, I could call it another. I could say that you must find yourself and what you are looking for in some other surroundings, you will say that I am throwing you out, turning you away from St. Martin's."

"What did I do this time?" Helen looked piteous. "Was it the cat?"

"Of course, it wasn't the cat, Helen, there's no one thing, one incident. Please know that . . . could you *try* to understand that it's not a punishment, not an exam where you pass or fail? It's a choice and this house is our life, we chose it and we have to choose how it will be shared."

"You don't want me, you've all decided at a meeting, is that it?"

"No, it's not it, there was no court passing sentence on you. When you came here in the first place, it was on the understanding that—"

Helen interrupted hotly. "In the old days nuns couldn't pick and choose who they had with them, if you didn't like another member of the community, that was hard luck, you had to offer it up, it was part of the sacrifice—"

"Nobody dislikes you . . ." Sister Brigid began.

"But even if they did, in the old days it wouldn't have been a matter of a popularity contest like it is now."

"If there were a popularity contest, there are many ways you'd come out on top. And anyway, when we look back on the old days, they were bad old days, in the very old days girls could be thrown into convents literally if they were wild or disappointed in love or something. That was a fine way to build a community." Brigid was firm.

"That didn't happen to me, nobody forced me; in fact, they tried to keep me back with them."

"That's why I'm speaking to you today." Brigid was gentle. "Today no false optimism about when you will take your vows. Because you won't, Helen, not here with us. It would be unfair for me as head of this house to let you go to a family celebration in the belief that you were well on the way toward being a nun in our order. One day you will thank me from the bottom of your heart. Today I wanted you to look at your family with different eyes, look at the other options. . . ."

"You mean I'm out today. I can't come back here tonight!" Helen was stricken.

"Don't be so dramatic. . . ."

"But when? If you're giving me notice, when do you want my room?" Helen was hurt and bitter.

"I thought that if you could think for a while, don't do any more work, just think, take stock of yourself, and what you might want to do . . ."

"When?" Helen repeated.

"Christmas seems a good time." Brigid was firm. "Say two or three months. You should know by Christmas."

Frank and Renata Quigley planned the day ahead.

"Will I dress up or down?" Renata asked.

"Up as high as you can go." He smiled.

"But that wouldn't be considered . . . I don't know . . . showing off a bit?" Renata was doubtful.

"Oh, you couldn't please Desmond's wife. If you're too casual, you didn't make the effort, if you do make the effort, you're overdressed. . . ."

"So?"

"So let her have something she'll be glad to have in the photographs. The woman's a monster for snapping this and that. Every time someone farts it's recorded in that place."

"Frank, really!"

"No, you don't know what they're like. Seriously, though, their place is coming down with framed photographs. I remember a wall full of them at least."

"That's nice in a way."

"Yes, it would be if there was anything to remember. Anything to celebrate."

"But you were friends, why do you talk like this?"

"I was friends with Desmond, never with Deirdre, anyway. She resented me being free, she was afraid—rightly, I think—that poor old Desmond would feel tied down by comparison. Still, we'll dress ourselves up to the nines and dazzle their eyes out."

She smiled back at him. Frank was so cheerful these days, since they had come to so many decisions. There was the expansion of the business. It was going ahead up north, and it did not mean, as Renata had feared, that Frank would be away a lot. No, he hardly ever traveled there, her father and uncle did, and of course, Mrs. East had been very much part of it. Even with the baby boy, she seemed to thrive on work. Some women were able to do everything, Renata thought sadly.

Still, things were good nowadays, and this morning she was going to get injections and vaccinations, shots needed for the journey. Frank would go to work, as he did almost every Saturday; he said it was so quiet in the big Palazzo building that he could dictate peacefully and get more done in an hour than he normally did in a week of ordinary days. She reminded him to get a haircut. He was looking a bit shaggy around the neck.

Frank didn't need to be reminded, he would go to Larry and have hot towels as well as a trim. He would wear his best suit and the new shirt. If Maureen Barry was going to look at him, she would admire what she saw. That was why he had asked his wife to dress up, too. When Renata had the full works, she looked very good. Maureen Barry would not be able to say that the man she rejected had to marry a colorless mouse with money.

Father Hurley had a great place to stay when he came to London; he always described it as a cross between a luxury hotel and a gentlemen's club. It was, in fact, a religious house, a simple place now where they rented most of their high-ceilinged rooms as office space. Once these had been parlors with polished tables holding copies of *Missionary Annals.* It was an oasis to come back to after a day in such a big, noisy city. Father Hurley found the morning a little overtiring, it was good to know that he could come back to this house and have a rest.

His friend Daniel Hayes was principal, a soft-spoken man who seemed to understand a great deal without having to have things explained in words. He had known last night when he asked after Father Hurley's nephew that this was not an avenue to travel any farther. Diplomatically and with the polished ease of years Father Hayes slipped to another topic. Father Hayes also seemed to know that his old friend James Hurley was somehow uneasy about the silver wedding he was going to attend.

"I can tell you, Daniel, you don't know them from a hole in the ground, a nice young pair, she a real product of upper-class Dublin . . . though we didn't know the phrase then. He was a bit of a rough diamond from the West of Ireland without a penny to bless himself. Anyway, the usual story, and she was well and truly pregnant, and I knew the family—*her* family, that is—and could I marry them in a flash?"

"And you did?" Father Hayes prompted.

"Well, I did, of course, what else did we do in those days? Cover the shame, hide the sin, get the thing regularized as soon as possible. . . ."

"And did it not work out . . . they are still together?"

"I know, Daniel, it's just that there's something odd there. Firstly they didn't have a child."

"What?"

"Oh, they did later, three of them. But not at the time. They sort of played at being married, pretended it . . . as if they were taking parts in a play. . . . Right, Desmond will play the husband and Deirdre will play the wife."

"I expect a lot of people do that."

"Yes, I expect they do, and there're ways in which we're playing at being priests. But do you know what I mean? As if the whole thing didn't ring true. Like Deirdre sending me a picture of them all on a picnic or somewhere, blinking into the light, as if she had to prove it to people."

"Prove what?"

"Lord, I don't know, that they were a normal family or something."

"They might be just very unhappy," Daniel Hayes said. "A lot of people are, seriously. They go into these marriages with such ridiculous expectations. I never thought that all the celibacy bit seemed too much of a hardship to me. . . ."

"Me neither," Father Hurley agreed. His face was sad.

"Of course, when it does work, it must be the greatest thing in the world, a friendship so real and true you'd trust the other with your life. . . . We never had that, James."

"No, indeed." Father Hurley still seemed down.

"But your sister had it, didn't she? I remember your telling me that you thought she had a totally good relationship, that they seemed to know each what the other was about to say and then smiled when they said it."

"True, but their life hasn't been easy—"

Father Hayes interrupted him. "Of course not, but it's only that kind of relationship we're talking about. . . . It would surely buoy them up when things were bleak. You don't see anything like that in this wedding you're going to in Pinner."

Father Hurley had been successfully diverted. "No, it's going to be a lot of empty phrases, like it was a quarter of a century ago."

"Ah, that's what we're here for, James." His friend laughed. "If the priests can't put a bit of conviction into meaningless, comforting phrases, then I ask you . . . who can?"

The caterers arrived at three o'clock. It had all been arranged weeks ago. But Philippa of Philippa's Catering knew a fusser when she saw one, and Mrs. Doyle had all the characteristics of someone who could raise a class-A fuss. There were to be canapés and drinks for an hour or so; then the party would proceed to a Roman Catholic church, where there would be a Mass, and the Doyles would say aloud that they renewed their marriage vows. Then, pink and triumphant, they would return to Rosemary Drive, it would now be heading for seven, there would be more drinks, and the guests would be asked to help themselves to a cold buffet—salmon and cold chicken in a curry mayonnaise. There would be warm herb bread with it. Philippa, having seen the size of the house and the smallness of the oven, had advised against hot food, she had convinced Mrs. Doyle that people would most certainly think it was a *real* meal even if it was cold and there were no potatoes.

As Philippa unloaded crates from her van and set up her center of operations in the Doyles' small kitchen, she hoped that someone might have been detailed to distract this woman with the freshly done hair and the obviously new manicure who held her hands awkwardly as if the varnish would chip.

Mercifully a daughter arrived, a sensible-looking girl, dark and intelligent. She was carrying her own outfit on a hanger. Through the kitchen window Philippa had seen her thanking a man who had driven her. The girl had leaned back into the car and kissed him. Philippa liked to see something like that, it made a change in the highly tense homes she often found herself working in.

Still, if it weren't for the weddings, the bar mitzvahs, the silver weddings, the retirement parties, where would her business be? She thought that Mrs. Doyle and her husband must both be barking mad to go back into a church and say publicly that they were still married. As if it weren't obvious. As if anyone else would have either of them! However, question it not, just keep unpacking, get the table decoration started, and maybe send in a tray of tea to the bedroom so that the mother and daughter could be kept up there.

"You look absolutely beautiful, Mother," Anna said. "You haven't a line on your face, did you know that? You're like a young girl."

Deirdre was pleased. "Oh, stop it now, you're going too far."

"I mean it. And isn't your hair great! Very elegant in all those swoops."

Deirdre looked at her daughter's short, dark, shiny head of hair.

"Of course, if *you* went to the hairdresser a bit . . . just now and then for a nice set . . . you'd look very much better. I know it's smart nowadays to wash your hair every day in the shower. . . ." Deirdre was trying to be helpful.

"I know, Mother. . . . Oh, look, isn't this marvelous, a pot of tea . . . brought to us on a tray! *This* is the life, isn't it?"

Deirdre frowned. "I wish your father was back, he's going to be running late. I don't know what he had to go down to Patel's for. . . ."

"It's not Patel's, it's the Rosemary Central Stores, Mother, *and* Dad is the joint owner, *and* Saturday is very busy, so obviously he's going to help Suresh *and* he'll be back in plenty of time. You know Dad."

"What time's Brendan coming?"

"He should be here anytime. He was looking around a bit, he said he didn't want to come too early and be in the way."

"Lord, wouldn't you think he'd come . . ."

"And of course, he'll be here tomorrow and the next day and the next."

"And why he couldn't stay in his own home . . ."

"Mother, Brendan's back now, isn't that what we all hoped? He's staying with me because it's easier, handier. He's going to be here every day seeing you."

"His father could easily have moved all those boxes and files from his room."

"It's not *his* room anymore, no more than *my* room is mine, it'd be pointless having them waiting for us, much better letting them be offices and for filing and everything."

"Helen's room is still there, and she's off in a convent."

"It's always wise to give Helen somewhere to lay her head, you never know when she'll need it." Anna sounded resigned.

"Will I change now, do you think?"

"Why don't you wait a little bit longer, Mother? We'll get hot and sweaty if we get into our finery too soon."

"I hope it's going to be all right."

"It's going to be magnificent. Everyone you want is coming to it . . . we don't have to raise a finger . . . they'll all be as impressed as hell."

"Not that we're trying to impress anyone," Deirdre said firmly to her daughter.

"No, indeed, what would be the point?" Anna asked, wondering if her mother could be serious. What was this about if it wasn't to wipe eyes around the place, show Grandmother O'Hagan what style they lived in, let Maureen Barry know that life in Pinner was full of sociability, point out to Frank Quigley that though Desmond hadn't married the boss's daughter, he had still done well for himself. Show Father Hurley what a good, strong Catholic way of life went on in what he probably thought of as Heathen England. Let the neighbors see what a team they could field, thirty people, and caterers, and speeches and a good non-vintage champagne for the toasts. What was all that if it wasn't intended to impress?

When they heard the commotion downstairs of someone beating on the side door and voices being raised, they knew Helen had arrived. She didn't want to come in the front door to inconvenience people, so she had been trying to push open the side door, and because boxes of wine were against it, she had been having difficulties. She was handed a cup of tea very briskly by Philippa of Philippa's Caterers and pointed upstairs.

Helen came into the room. They knew by the droop of her shoulders that something was wrong. Anna hoped that they might get away without discussing it.

"Doesn't Mother look terrific, Helen?" she cried.

"Great," Helen said dutifully and absently.

"And Brendan's going to be here any moment."

"Is he staying here?" Helen asked.

"No, we . . . er . . . thought it would be . . . more suitable if he stayed at my place. He's there now changing, I left the key for him under a plant pot. More suitable, more central, closer to things."

"What things?" asked Helen.

"Any things." Anna gritted her teeth.

"So he's not sleeping here tonight?"

"No, he wouldn't even consider . . ." Deirdre was beginning.

"Anyway, his room is an office for Dad now, so . . ."

"Is my room an office for Dad?" Helen asked.

"No, of course not. Why do you ask?"

"I thought I might sleep here tonight," Helen said. "If it's no trouble, that is."

Anna held her breath. She didn't trust herself to speak. So Helen had decided to leave her convent. And she chose now to tell everyone. *Now,* one hour before Mother's and Father's silver wedding party. Anna fixed her eyes on the two dressing gowns that hung on the back of the door. Father's had a long cord. Perhaps Anna could take this and strangle Helen, or would that in the long run mean further disruption? It was hard to know.

She was saved from having to work it out because Brendan had arrived. He ran lightly up the stairs, and his mother and sisters ran to meet him. He looked tanned and well, they thought, and handsome, too, in a smart navy jacket, a sparklingly white shirt, and a tie with a discreet design on it.

"I got silver colors in the tie, I thought it would be suitable," he said.

Deirdre Doyle looked at her only son with pride. There would be no need to apologize for Brendan today nor explain him away. Whatever kind of life he was leading in that backwoods, at least he had dressed up today, when it mattered. And he was going to be pleasant to people, not hanging back and muttering. She would not have dared to hope for this much.

Desmond came back in plenty of time to wash and change, and at five minutes before the official starting time Philippa was able to pronounce that they all looked magnificent and that everything was under control.

More and more in her business she felt it was a matter of calming down the hostess and family just as much as preparing a good menu and serving it well.

They stood in their sitting room. The doors to the garden were open, they were ready. With as little comment as possible Anna had found an outfit to suit Helen among their mother's clothes. It was a simple green skirt and a long cream-colored overblouse. It was simple enough to have been the nunnish kind of clothes she wore . . . if she wanted it to be. But also it was perfectly adequate as lay clothes, too, if that was the route she chose.

Any moment now the guests would arrive. The Doyles had refused a drink from Philippa, saying that they would need to keep their heads clear.

Philippa noticed that there were no private moments between them. They didn't squeeze each other's hands and say: "Fancy, a silver wedding!" They didn't seem excited in themselves over the event, only that it was being marked.

The first to arrive was Grandmother O'Hagan. Deirdre's eyes raked the taxi to see if she would be followed by Tony. But mercifully Mother had decided to come unaccompanied. And just as she was being ushered in, Frank and Renata's car pulled up. The florist's van arrived with a huge floral arrangement from Carlo and Maria with many, many regrets and warmest wishes on a wonderful family occasion. It had been arranged the previous day by Frank Quigley's secretary, who had also left a message with Carlo Palazzo's office noting that it had been done.

And when the Wests next door had peered out and seen the place filling up, they arrived, and they were followed by Father Hurley, who had been driven there by his friend Father Hayes.

"Won't Father Hayes come in, too, and have a drink?" Deirdre Doyle had said. You couldn't have too many priests at something like this.

Father Hayes was tempted just to a sherry, he said it was wonderful in this world where so many people took marriage so lightly to find a couple whose love had survived for so long.

"Well, yes." Deirdre had been pleased by the compliment, if somewhat startled by the way it was expressed.

At that moment Maureen Barry arrived.

She must have left her taxi at the corner of Rosemary Drive, she walked easily through the gate and up the little path to the door. The guests were both in and outside the house, it was one of those warm autumn evenings that made it not totally ridiculous to be in the open air.

Maureen seemed to expect all eyes to be on her, yet there was nothing vain or coquettish about the way she came in.

She wore a lemon-colored silk suit, with a lemon and black scarf. She was slim and tall, and her black hair shone as if it were an advertisement for shampoo. Her smile was bright and confident, as she turned with excitement from one to another.

She said all the right things and few of the things that were in her mind. Yes, that was Brendan she had seen this morning struggling with a big green Marks and Spencer's bag. Obviously the outfit he was wearing now. Perfectly adequate, but think what a big, handsome boy could look like if he had been dressed by a tailor.

Yes, amazingly it *had* been Deirdre's mother that she had seen that morning at breakfast with the rather over-obvious-looking man. Was it possible that the great and esteemed Eileen O'Hagan was having a relationship? How her father would enjoy hearing of that, when she went to Ascot to see him tomorrow.

She kissed her friend Deirdre and exclaimed with pleasure over the wonderful dress. In her heart she wondered how Deirdre could have fallen for the obvious-looking lilac, the matronly garment with the self-color embroidery at the shoulder. It was a pastel Mother of the Bride outfit. Deirdre deserved better, she could have looked so good. *And* the dress had probably cost a fortune as well.

The Doyle girls didn't look smart either. Helen seemed to be wearing a blouse and skirt, perhaps that was the nearest that the order could come to letting her wear home clothes. Anna, who was quite striking if she had just left herself alone, was wearing a very tarty-looking navy and white outfit: everywhere there could be a white frill there was one, at the neck, on the hem, at the wrists. It was like a child's party frock.

And Frank.

"How well you look, Frank, it must be years and years," she said.

"But it's impossible that for you time has stood still," he said, mocking her tones by imitating her, very slightly.

Her eyes hardened.

"Renata, this is Maureen Barry, she and I played maid of honor and best man at the great occasion twenty-five years ago. Maureen, this is Renata, my wife."

"I'm delighted to meet you."

The two women took in each other's clothes at a glance.

Maureen saw a girl with a nondescript face and well-cut designer garments, carefully made up and wearing discreet jewelry. If that gold chain was what she thought it was, Renata Quigley was wearing the price of several houses in Rosemary Drive around her neck.

"Frank tells me you are a very successful businesswoman, and you have high-fashion shops." Renata spoke as if she had learned a little speech. Her accent was attractive.

"He's building me up a bit too much, Renata, two small outlets, but I am thinking of opening up over here. Not in London, more out Berkshire way."

"I was sorry to hear that your mother died," Frank said. He lowered his voice suitably.

"Yes, it was sad, she was very lively and opinionated always, she could have had many more years. Like Mrs. O'Hagan over there." Maureen nodded in the direction of Deirdre's mother, who was holding forth in a corner.

Renata had moved slightly away to talk to Desmond and Father Hurley.

"Of course she hated me," Frank said, not letting his eyes leave Maureen's.

"Who? I beg your pardon?"

"Your mother. She hated me. You know that, Maureen." His eyes were hard now. As hers had been.

"No, I think you're quite wrong, she never hated you. She spoke very well of you always, she said you were very nice, that one time she met you. I remember her standing in the morning room at home and saying, 'He's a very nice boy, Maureen.' " As Maureen spoke, she re-created her mother's little laugh, the unkind dismissal, the sense of amused wonder.

It was the most cruel thing she could have done.

But he was asking for it, arrogant, handsome, and powerful, playing with people's lives and planning what they would buy and where they would buy it.

"You didn't marry?" he asked. "There wasn't anyone you could marry?"

"Not anyone I did marry, no."

"But you were tempted, perhaps a little here and there . . ." His eyes still held hers. They hadn't faltered under her sarcasm, her reproducing her mother's deadly voice.

"Oh, Frank, of course, I've been tempted here and there, like all business-people are. That has nothing to do with being married. I'm quite sure you have found the same in your life. I'd be *very* surprised if you didn't. But to marry and settle down, there has to be a reason for that."

"Love maybe, or attraction even?"

"Not enough, I think. Something more prosaic like—" She looked around and her glance fell on Deirdre. "Like being pregnant maybe, or else—" She looked around the room again and stopped when she was looking at Renata.

But she wasn't quick enough. Frank said it first.

"Like money?" he said blandly.

"Exactly," she said.

"Not very good reasons, either of them."

"Well, certainly not the pregnancy one. Even more especially when it turns out not to have been a real one."

"Did you ever find out what happened?" Frank asked.

Maureen shrugged. "Lord, I wasn't even told that there was any question of it in the first place, so I wouldn't be told that the danger had passed or whatever."

"I think she had a miscarriage," Frank said.

"Did Desmond tell you that?" She was surprised.

"Not a bit of it, but it was their first Christmas in London, and I was in a bit of a bad way, a bit letdown and feeling very lost. I asked could I spend Christmas with them. The excuse was Deirdre wasn't well. She looked bad, too. I think that's what it was."

He sounded much more human, her eyes had softened, and she felt his had, too.

"What bad luck to tie themselves into all this, for nothing, over a false alarm," she said.

"They may like it, the children could be some consolation," Frank argued.

They were talking like friends now, old friends who hadn't seen each other for a while.

Philippa was relieved when the party began to decamp toward the church. She had no idea and didn't even want to imagine what went on there, but she knew it was some kind of important landmark for them. Not just to serve food and drink but go back to the same kind of church where the whole thing had begun. She shrugged cheerfully as she organized the collection of glasses, the airing of the room. At least this bizarre kind of two-tier arrangement gave them a chance to clear up the hors d'oeuvres part of things and let them lay out the salads without interruption.

The church was at a nice easy walking distance; that was why it had been thought a feasible plan. If they had all to get lifts and taxis and sort out who went with whom, it would have taken forever.

They all knelt in a little group, the thirty people who formed the silver wedding party.

It was a perfectly normal Mass, many of them congratulated themselves that they didn't need to go tomorrow since a Saturday-evening attendance was sufficient in these liberated days.

Some like Anna who didn't go anyway did not see the great incidental advantage.

Brendan always found Mass a social event back home with Vincent. He didn't think his uncle believed in any kind of God, but he went to Mass on a Sunday as regularly as he would go to get gasoline or to the markets to buy sheep. It was part of the life they lived.

Helen prayed hard at the Mass so that God would tell her what was right. If Sister Brigid said that she was running away, what was it from and which was the right direction if the convent was the wrong one? If she could have some kind of sign. It wasn't much to ask.

Father Hurley asked himself why he felt that this was all some kind of charade, almost a television version of renewal of vows. Any moment now someone would say, "Cut. Can we take that again from the top?" He didn't feel this about any other aspect of his ministry. There was just something he didn't like about a public reiteration of something that was said and meant a long time ago. Yet the faithful were always being asked to renew their baptismal vows, so why did he feel uneasy in this instance?

Frank looked at Maureen in the church and thought what a fine-looking woman she was, full of spirit, so like Joy East in many ways. He thought briefly of Joy and of his son, who was called Alexander. The son he would never get to know.

It had been thought inappropriate to take pictures at the church. It wasn't as if it were a real wedding, they would look a little ancient to be photographed, Deirdre tittered, hoping that someone would disagree with her.

Maureen did, strongly.

"Come on now, Deirdre, I still have to take the plunge, and when I do, I'll want banks of photographers outside," she said.

"And after all, people get married at *any* age, any age at all," Deirdre's mother said, which caused Deirdre's heart to lurch a little.

"And with the way the Church is going, maybe even the clergy will get married, Mother, and Father Hurley will be coming down the aisle in a morning suit," Helen said.

They laughed at that, particularly Father Hurley, who was rueful and said that even if he was forty years younger, he wouldn't be able to take on such an undertaking.

And soon they were back in Salthill, 26 Rosemary Drive. The neighbors who had not been invited waved and called out greetings, the lights were on, and soon the supper was under way.

"There's a lot of conversation, like at a real party," Deirdre said to Desmond almost in disbelief.

Her face was flushed and anxious, her hair had fallen from its hard lacquered layers and seemed softer somehow. There were beads of perspiration on her forehead and upper lip.

He felt strangely touched by her anxiety.

"Well, it *is* a real party," he said, and he touched her face gently with his hand.

It was an unfamiliar gesture, but she didn't draw back, she smiled at him.

"I suppose it is," she agreed.

"And your mother is getting on well with everyone," he said encouragingly.

"Yes, yes, she is."

"Brendan's looking in fine shape, isn't he? He said he'd be very interested in coming down to the Rosemary Central Stores tomorrow morning to see how it operates."

She was surprised. "He's going to come the whole way across from Shepherd's Bush early in the morning when he could have stayed here in his own room?" She was still peeved that he wouldn't stay.

"It's not his own room, Deirdre, it's the office."

"There'd have been room for him," she said.

"Yes, and he will stay sometime. But as a visitor."

"As part of the family," she corrected him.

"As a visiting part of the family," he corrected her back.

It was gentle. But the Desmond Doyle of a few months back would not have done it. He would have been too anxious, too willing to play the parlor game of lies, backing up whatever story Deirdre told her mother and Maureen Barry about his mythical prowess at Palazzo, trying all the while to engineer these conversations out of the hearing of Frank or Renata, who would know them to be untrue.

How restful it was at last for Desmond Doyle to have his own position, his own place. To be for the first time his own person, not Palazzo's person. It gave him by a grim irony the kind of confidence which his wife had always wanted to see in him, but which would have forever escaped him in Palazzo land.

"Mother is actually talking normally to Dad," Brendan whispered to Anna at the other side of the room. "Does this happen often?"

"Never saw it happen before," she said. "I don't want to take away from your sense of well-being, but I do think that you have captured a very rare sighting, make the most of it."

And indeed, as they looked, the little tableau broke up. One of the caterers was speaking to Mother, there was a slight problem in the kitchen.

"It's bound to be Helen," Anna said sadly. And it was.

Helen was all for putting candles on the gateau, she had bought twenty-five of them and had rooted through the bottom of the cupboard to find old cake tins holding the plastic candle holders. She could find only fourteen. She could not think why.

"Probably because that would be the age at which normal people wouldn't really want any more," Anna said crisply. "All right, Mother, go back to the guests. I'll cope with it."

"It's not a question of coping with it." Helen was hurt and angry now. "I was just making a little gesture so that we could be festive."

Philippa of Philippa's Caterers said that the written agreement had been a gateau, with toasted almonds to be applied at the last moment to the cream topping, the toasted almonds to read: "Desmond and Deirdre October 1960."

"I think it *is* better like that, Helen, don't you?" Anna spoke as she might have spoken to a dog that was foaming at the mouth or a four-year-old who was severely retarded. Ken Green said he spent a lot of his life speaking to people like this; it got you a reputation for being very patient, slightly thick, and a person who could be relied on in any crisis. Anna remembered that Ken always said that the more enraged he was, the more slowly he spoke.

"Don't you think we should leave the caterers to it, Helen?" Anna said, enunciating every word very clearly and slowly.

"Oh, piss off, Anna, you're a pain in the arse," Helen said.

Anna decided that they were definitely coming to the end of Helen's term of life in a religious order.

Helen had flounced out into the garden.

"Shall I go after her?" asked Philippa, the caterer.

"No, she's probably safer out there, there's no one she can insult beyond reprieve, and not too much she can break." Anna thought that Ken would be proud of her and wondered why she was thinking of him so much anyway.

Helen sat and hugged her knees in the garden where she had sat, misunderstood and thinking herself unloved, all the years of her childhood. She heard footsteps behind her. Anna no doubt asking her to come in and not to make a scene, Mother telling her not to sit on damp stone, Grandmother O'Hagan about to ask when she was ever going to be professed. She looked up. It was Frank Quigley.

A terror seized her throat, and she felt a momentary light-headedness. It was of course impossible that he was going to touch her, molest her in her parents' home.

But he looked so menacing in the dark.

"I heard from your father that you're thinking of leaving St. Martin's," he said.

"Yes. They want me to go, they threw me out."

"I'm sure that's not true."

"Sister Brigid says the others don't want me." She realized as she spoke that she sounded like a child of five years of age with her thumb in her mouth.

"Sister Brigid is far too fond of you to think that, let alone say it."

"How do you know? You saw her only that night, that awful night." Helen's eyes had become as big as dinner plates. The memory of the time she had tried to steal a baby for Frank and Renata Quigley, the night that had turned out so badly, and when the real descent had begun in St. Martin's.

"No, Helen, I've met Sister Brigid many times since then," Frank said. "We didn't speak of you much, we had other things to talk about. . . . She was giving me advice. She gave me very good helpful advice, I have you to thank for that."

"I meant well that night, I really thought it would have suited everyone."

"It might have, you know, but we couldn't do it that way, always running, always hiding, always pretending. That's not the way to live."

"That's the way I've always lived." Helen sounded rebellious and defensive.

"No, no, it isn't."

"In this house we always pretended, we still are tonight."

"Shush," he said soothingly.

"How did you learn to be so upright and not to have to act like the rest of us?"

"I'm not upright. You of all people should know that." Frank spoke seriously. "I have done things I am ashamed of, one of them with you. I am very, very ashamed of that."

For the first time since that day in his apartment Helen Doyle looked Frank Quigley in the eyes. For the first time for many years in any encounter she said absolutely nothing.

"I was always hoping that you would meet somebody nice and somebody young and tender, someone who would put that strange sad day into some kind of perspective for you. Show you that while it was important in one way, in many others it was not important at all."

Still, Helen said nothing.

"So I supposed I was sorry when you went into St. Martin's, because I always thought then that what happened might appear magnified."

"I never thought about it again," Helen said. She looked at him as she told him the lie, her eyes confident and her head held high.

He knew she was lying, but it was important that she didn't realize.

"That is so much the right way to be, and it certainly puts me in my place."

He smiled at her. Ruefully, admiringly. He got it just right. And he could see she was beginning to feel better.

"So what will you do when you do leave, if you're going to?"

"I'll leave. I don't know yet. Maybe I need time to think."

"Is this the place to do your thinking?" He looked uncertainly up at Salthill, 26 Rosemary Drive.

"Maybe not."

"Maybe you should go away, right away from London. You're good with children, Brigid tells me, very good."

"Yes, I like them. Certainly. They don't get as upset as adults."

"Could you mind one? For a year or two while you're thinking?"

"Do you know one?"

They seemed to talk as equals, her fear of him fell away.

"I do, his name is Alexander. I don't know him, but I know his mother. However, she and I had a fight, and she doesn't like me; if I suggested you, she would say no. If she were to advertise and, say, if you were to apply . . ."

"Wouldn't it be too much of a coincidence?"

"No, we can do it through Carlo. She asks Carlo about a nanny. Carlo says the daughter of one of his ex-managers, she knew your father."

"Is it Miss East?"

"Yes."

"What did you fight about?"

"This and that."

"Is Alexander nice?"

"I don't know, Helen."

"But you'd like to know?" She seemed to have grown up in minutes.

"I'd love to know."

"Fine," said Helen Doyle. "I have to do my thinking somewhere, it might as well be with Alexander East."

The cake was produced and cut. And when everybody had a slice of rich gateau on a plate, Desmond tapped on a glass and said that Frank Quigley, who had done the honors so well a quarter of a century ago, was going to say a few words.

Frank stood forward, he said that it was a great happiness and a great honor to be asked to speak. He made it seem both. Those who listened felt for a moment that he was lucky to have been invited.

He said that he remembered the day when Deirdre, looking roughly the same as she did tonight, had made this commitment; she was young and beautiful, she had her life ahead of her, there were many decisions to make, many paths to choose. She had chosen Desmond Doyle. Smoothly he brought them from the marriage through the early days of Palazzo, to the joys of children, to their luck in each and all of these children, a daughter rising high in the book trade—Palazzo had tried to poach her, but with no success. Another daughter giving her entire life to looking after people, and a son with a love of the land. These were three rich rewards for Deirdre and Desmond to look at and see their hopes realized.

He himself had not been so fortunate in the early days, he hadn't met anyone he loved until later on in life. His gaze passed gently over Maureen, standing cool and admiring in her lemon silk dress. But then he, too, had known the happiness of married life, though unfortunately, unlike Desmond, he had not been given the joy of fathering three fine children. But his heart was happy tonight and in no sense tinged with the envy that it might have held over the years. At the weekend he and Renata were going to Brazil, where a legal adoption had been arranged and where they were going to take home with them and give a home to a girl called Paulette. She was eight months old. Nuns had arranged the papers. She would be very much younger than his friend Desmond's children, but he hoped that the friendship would be there always, as his had been. A lifelong friendship, he said. Some things never change.

It had been masterly, there were a few tears brushed away, and the champagne glasses were raised.

Everyone was touched by Frank. Every person in the room.

Even Maureen Barry.

"My God, you are one performer," she said to him admiringly.

"Thank you, Maureen." He was gallant and suave.

"No, I mean it. You always were. You didn't have to try so hard, just to prove my mother wrong, to prove me wrong."

"But your mother loved me, she said I was a very nice young man." He put on her mother's voice. It was a good imitation.

"I'm glad about the child," she said.

"Yes, so are we."

"And will I see you all when I open my shop in England?"

"It will be a time before Paulette will be old enough for your clothes."

"Oddly enough, I'm having a children's boutique, too."

"Well then." His smile was warm. But not warm enough.

Maureen thought she would discuss it with her father. The old rascal was full of advice. She wasn't going to let drop a prize like this again.

Father Hurley said he wanted to use the phone, but there appeared to be a line. Anna was speaking to someone.

"Sure, come around," she was saying. "Listen to me, Ken Green, this is 1985, we are all free to make our own choices. My choice is that if you choose to be here, that would be great." There was a pause.

"And I love you, too," she said, hanging up, surprised with herself.

Deirdre's mother was on the phone next.

"Yes, Tony, perfectly satisfactory, no opportunity. No, no, not reneging on anything, but you know the whole art of life is knowing the right time to say things. Yes, yes. Nothing changed. Absolutely. Me, too. Lots."

Father Hurley picked up the telephone to tell Father Hayes that he was getting a mini-cab back, he would be sharing it with several others, a large car had been ordered.

Yes, he said, it had been delightful, he just felt he mustn't take up the phone, other people might be telephoning people to say they loved them.

No, he said testily to Father Hayes. He wasn't even remotely drunk, he had just been sitting listening to a woman and her granddaughter talking on the telephone. That was all.

The move to go was general now. But there was a sense of something not quite completed.

Deirdre found the camera. She had new film in it all ready for the occasion, she ran into the kitchen where Philippa's team were busy putting plastic wrap over the leftovers and storing them in the fridge. There would even be things for the freezer.

Deirdre explained how the camera worked, and Philippa listened patiently. It was a characteristic of this kind of woman that she thought her camera was complicated.

They gathered around the couple in a semicircle. They smiled. The camera flashed and flashed again.

Among the pictures in the roll of twenty-four there would be one which was bound to look good when enlarged, would look just right. There would be the picture of The Silver Wedding on the wall, for everyone to see. Everyone who came to Rosemary Drive from now on.

ABOUT THE AUTHOR

MAEVE BINCHY was born and educated in Dublin. She is the author of the bestselling novels *Light a Penny Candle, Echoes, Circle of Friends, The Copper Beech,* and *The Glass Lake.* She has also written three volumes of short stories, two plays and a teleplay. She has been writing for *The Irish Times* since 1969 and lives with her husband, Gordon Snell, in London and Dublin.